VARIATION WEST

Variation West

BY

Ardyth Kennelly

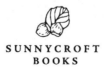

SUNNYCROFT
BOOKS

———

PORTLAND, ORE.

Excerpts and "Captain Carpenter" from *Selected Poems* by John Crowe Ransom, copyright © 1924 by Alfred A. Knopf, a division of Random House LLC and renewed 1952 by John Crowe Ransom. Used by permission of Alfred A. Knopf, an imprint of the Knopf Doubleday Publishing Group, a division of Random House LLC. All rights reserved. Any third party use of this material, outside of this publication, is prohibited. Interested parties must apply directly to Random House LLC for permission.

Cover image (top): *Mountain Meadows*, by S. H. Redmond; lithograph by Britton, Rey & Co., published by the Pacific Art Company, 1877. Library of Congress Reproduction Number LC-DIG-pga-00322.

Book design by Alissa Beddow

Publisher's Cataloging-in-Publication Data
provided by Five Rainbows Services

Kennelly, Ardyth.
    Variation west / Ardyth Kennelly.
    pages cm
    ISBN: 978-0-9904320-0-5 (pbk.)
    ISBN: 978-0-9904320-1-2 (e-book)
    1. Mormons—Fiction. 2. Frontier and pioneer life—Fiction. 3. Mountain Meadows Massacre, Utah, 1857—Fiction. 4. Beauty, Personal—Fiction. 5. Utah—Fiction. I. Title.
PS3611.E65 V37 2014
813`6—dc23

                                        2014946794

SUNNYCROFT BOOKS
4110 SE Hawthorne Blvd. #749
Portland, Oregon 97214
www.sunnycroftbooks.com

Variation east
  Magnetic's least
Variation west
  Magnetic's best!

—RHYME USED BY OLD-TIME FLIERS

Contents

Publisher's Note

ix

PART ONE

Of Brides and Other Distances

1

PART TWO

The Habit of These Groves

353

PART THREE

All on the Meadow Green

565

Publisher's Note

Variation West, the last and greatest novel by Ardyth Kennelly (1912–2005), was written between 1977 and 1994, with some revisions being made by the author in subsequent years.

Times had changed since her first book, *The Peaceable Kingdom*, was snapped up by Houghton Mifflin in 1949 and her four other novels were published in the following decade. Now, in 2014, Sunnycroft Books is delighted to be able to bring Ardyth Kennelly's new work to her fans.

That the manuscript survived and came to be published is due to the dedication of the author's beloved sister, Marion Kennelly Brownell (1915–2011), and to the steadfast support also of Marion's children—Michael Massee, Timothy J. Pettibone, and Ardyth L. Morehouse. I am deeply grateful to them for their permission and help to publish this book.

In editing the manuscript, I made only occasional, minor changes in wording, spelling, and punctuation. Nothing has been cut; the book appears here essentially as the author wrote it.

For references and biographical and historical notes on the text, please visit sunnycroftbooks.com.

Nancy Trotic
Sunnycroft Books
November 2014

PART ONE

Of Brides and Other Distances

Chapter One

✳

LIKE HAPPINESS, BURDICK'S INSTITUTION FOR THE CARE OF THE SICK WAS A secondary product, got hold of by Tot and Serapta Burdick, spinster sisters, in a roundabout way on account of the path their brother Murdock started down when he and his drinking friend Francis went to the auction at Camp Floyd and came home loaded down with cots, Army blankets and a pile of monstrously large kettles and pans he not only had no *use* for but no place to *store* except in the spare room at his sisters' house. Because of this (though for other reasons too), his wife Alice became quite intemperate in her harangue against him. All that pile of useless stuff!

Useful enough, though, Murdock knew, if she would listen to reason and he could sit down and talk with her man to man about God's idea of matrimony, which, set forth by the Prophet Joseph Smith before they killed him, was not just the condition of being husband and *wife*, though that had its virtues too, but more like prevailing as a shepherd and his *flock*. Murdock tried to explain this to Alice during their honeymoon nine years before, but she went into such paroxysms of fainting, hysteria and lunacy that he was deprived of ardor ever to bring the subject up again.

Could he have done so, however, and met with the understanding that would have privileged him to move between two, three or four households instead of just one measly cottage, think how practical these pallets, covers and big cooking utensils would be! The tenderness! You dear old sweetheart, you angel husband. (Instead of always being ripped up one side and down the other.) He often thought that what he should have done, while he was over there in England on his mission for the Church of Jesus Christ of Latter-day Saints, where he met Alice, was try to find out more about the true nature of the English before throwing in with one of them.

ONE DAY, HOWEVER, AS AMAZINGLY as a metabolic insect, Alice went through a radical transformation. Informed of it at the dinner table as they were eating their bread pudding, Murdock was thankful it wasn't his mutton chop! for he might have choked to death. "Murdock," Alice said in a tone so generally indicative of strife that he was not prepared for what followed, "I have been thinking it over, and if you are still of a mind to go into the Gospel Dispensation of the Meridian of Consummate Time, which I presume you are, *being a man*," this came out coldly indeed, "why, you have my consent to do so."

Of all the names Polygamy went by (so as not to exasperate the Gentile population and even some of the wives of the members' own bosoms any more than necessary)— such as Pluralism, Plural or Celestial Wedlock, the Principle, the Doctrine, the New Covenant and the Gospel Dispensation of the Meridian of Consummate Time—the latter was thought to be the least like waving a red flag in front of a bull. But as it was hard to remember and did not make instant or any other kind of sense, it was not much used.

Yet here to Murdock's astonishment was Alice reeling it off to him, though it had never passed *his* lips since the night he tried to inculcate her with it and had the luck to come through in one piece. Had she remembered it all this while? Heard of it recently again? Perhaps in Relief Society (no male knew what went on there). Seen it written? One time she was invited to the Lion House for a meeting of the Past Presidents of the Quilting Affiliation and through a half-open door glimpsed the great Mormon poetess Eliza R. Snow soaking her feet in a bucket. Could *that* have anything to do with her change of heart?

But he soon stopped thinking of the whys and wherefores of what he was never to understand any more than why milk clabbers or a worm turns into a butterfly, to confront the utter miracle of what this change would mean to his life. Fair young wives waiting supper! all their distinctions! different types of bedsteads! warm particularities! and somewhere down the line *collateral branches*! like the highest officials in Salt Lake City! Or did his ears deceive him?

No, they did not. It was true.

"But don't think for a moment you are going to be allowed to run wild," Alice said. "One wife and one only besides myself. I hope you've got that straight!" Her disgust at what she thought he might be thinking was plain to see. "And don't imagine you can come dragging home a pauper. The woman stands on her own bottom or she does not get in the door."

"Absolutely, my love. Goes without saying."

"Bank book. Property."

"Of course. None other need apply."

FOR THE NEXT FEW DAYS, in his joy that the rank, powers and pre-eminence of true manhood were about to descend upon him, Murdock almost skipped back and forth to the Land Office. But then realization set in. In these western approaches, where eligible females were so scarce that even a lady's shift blowing on the line had been known to get proposed to, in what direction was he supposed to look to find a beautiful (or even a homely) young girl? Let alone with money! *He* didn't know, his co-worker Francis didn't know and neither did Francis's cousin.

Plainly there was nothing for it but to go to the mercy-seat, Alice herself, for further instructions. Leaving out the incendiary word *beautiful* and even avoiding *homely* for fear of bringing in the bugaboo of looks, and mumbling and blowing his nose in his handkerchief when he came to the phrase *young lady*, he managed in quite a clever way, so he thought, to put the question to her. But without the intervention of any reasoning process, she knew at once what he was up to. "Who said anything about a girl?" she said with a cruel smile. "I said *woman*."

All right, woman. But well off? As finding one of those was about as likely as finding himself sitting center stage in Brigham's throne-like chair in the Tabernacle on a Sunday afternoon, it didn't take long for Murdock's joy to peter out. The Gospel Dispensation of the Meridian of Consummate Time was never going to dispense anything to *him*, he told Francis. And Alice knew it! She knew very well that her "consent" was but, as the old song said, "a vain illusive show that melts whene'er the sunbeams glow." So why did she act like she was granting such a favor?

"I'm sure I don't know," Francis said with a shrug. But he *did* know that a henpecked man had only himself to blame. What were his muscles for?

But Murdock was not naturally disposed to warfare. Besides, much of Alice's ample dowry was still under lock and key over in England, where the laws were different. And wasn't it better to live becalmed than in contentious storm? Philosophizing thus, Murdock rendered himself comfortable to reason but did not feel happier. And when the dowdy old petitioner came in and stood in front of the counter, his looks could have almost killed, although it was a good half hour to closing. "Yes, madam?" he said witheringly, with a glance over his shoulder at the clock.

"Oh, gracious," she said. "Here I am late and you're shutting up shop!" She did so want to know, though, she hurried on, if the legal disposition of her house and land was all in order, with her name upon it, Phoebe Griffin, as well as her late husband's name, Ermin Griffin, because—Not that she had any doubts about the workings of the *Land Office* with a gentleman such as *himself* in charge. *Her* worry was that Ermin, the state the man was in the whole last year of his life, had come in and maybe just wreaked havoc.

Mollified by the sweetness of her voice and enlivened a little with curiosity as to what state her late husband had really been in that last year of his life, Murdock bustled about, soon laid hands on the documents and formal entry she wanted and spread them on the counter in front of her. "No havoc here," he said. "Looks like everything's in order."

"I can't tell you how thankful I am," she said with a heartfelt sigh, taking the papers up to gaze on as though at hieroglyphics and fiery signs, then pushing them back at him to gather up and put on a shelf to file away later, adding, "for you letting me in and all."

"My helper has already went home," he said (pointing a moral by another glance at the clock), which indeed Francis had, it being his turn to sneak out early.

"Well, God is watching out for *me*," she said. "For I'm sure no one else could of found what I needed quick like you could. Or been so nice about it. But I won't keep you. And next time I won't come straggling in so late. But I'll tell you why I done so. I couldn't leave till my neighbor Mrs. Vigor got home from Sewing Circle to watch after Alton. She's the one got me to come down here in the first place, not only on account of what Ermin might of been up to them last months, but also in case a Gentile happened to be in charge here now. It could happen, they've wiggled in everywheres else. But say!" she said in sudden embarrassment. "Here I am talking about the Gentiles and how do I know but what—? For after all, a handsome, decent, lovely-mannered young man such as yourself might well be—"

"I was born in it," he said. "Been on a mission."

"I knew it. The minute I opened that door there! 'Latter-day Saint' is wrote all over you!"

"Wrote all over anyone with their ashpan dragging," he said, under her admiring gaze attempting a little levity. "As they used to say. That was before my time, but Grandpa said that back in Independence and Far West and those places, when the countryside was against us and nobody knew who was a *spy*, why, the way to tell for sure, if somebody's *ashpan* was dragging, they belonged."

"I remember that," she said, chuckling a little but at the same time looking sad at the thought of those rough old days. "But *yours* surely ain't dragging, so don't you say so!" She waggled a finger at him. "And anyone's that *is*, here in this Promised Land of milk and honey our leader led us to, should ask if they haven't bit off more than they can chew. These pluralists. A man can just do so much. I mean, in the line of providing. You can't get blood out of a turnip."

"You're against the Principle?"

"Good gracious, no," she said. "Who would I be to be going against a revelation of the Prophet? No, what's foolish is men grabbing here and there like travelers for pleasure that's going to get back in their tourist-car. Never a thought for the morrow. Although there's wives a-working now, taking in washing, sewing or Lord knows what, that wouldn't of *thought* of such a thing in my day. Like I was saying to Mrs. Vigor the other day. Poor little things jump in and try to help and the first wife won't even use the word *wife* when speaking of 'em. 'Concubine,' she'll say, or 'conk' or 'extra'—'fifth wheel'—anything to keep from saying 'wife.' Did you ever notice that?"

"Well, just having the one—" he said uncomfortably, "and not likely to have another—I'm not too up on all of that." Sometimes at his sisters' house, looking at what he bought at Camp Floyd and thinking how it could be if the cots were set in a row along a moonlit colonnade on a hot summer night with a lady love in each, naked to infinite temptations (lovely officers' cots of steel and brass), he would nearly cry. He felt like that now.

"Why is that?" she said. "A strong young fellow like you? Don't *you* hold with the revelation?"

He frowned and began to close up, shutting a drawer, slamming a cabinet door and screwing a cap tighter on a large bottle of ink before he set it on the windowsill.

"Oh, dear," she said. "Now I've made you cross."

"No, you haven't," he said. "I hold with it all right. It's just—"

"What *I* say," she said, "is, what's the good of *having* a Prophet, Seer and Revelator and a Restored Religion like we got if a person *don't* do as they're told?"

"There's them as *acts* like they're living the word but in their hearts they're not," he said.

"Would that be someone close to home?" she said.

He nodded.

"Well, did you ever. That was Ermin and me all over. *I* accepted, *he* didn't, and I believe that's considered kind of a wonder."

"What is?"

"Why, the wife consenting while the man makes excuses."

"Ermin made excuses? I guess we're both talking about the same thing," he said. "The Principle?"

"For a reason I'm ashamed to say," she said, "for he had his good sides too. But Ermin was a miser. Dyed in the wool. Just like in the stories. Thank goodness I had my own little inheritance so I didn't have to go to him for every spool of thread. His motto year after year was, 'It costs too much.' Then along come—I might as well say it—polygamy. 'It's a order, Ermin.' 'I can't afford it,' he says. 'Can't afford laying up treasures in heaven for following God's *orders*?' I say. I told him, 'What are we supposed to do, get up in the Celestial and be the lowest of the low because you won't do what you ought to?' 'I don't for a reason,' he says. 'It's too expensive.' I wish you could of saw him of a Sunday morning looking out the window when the Wellses went past or some of them other big families, Kimballs, Cannons or the Garns, to Tabernacle or the meeting house. The man turned pale as death. 'The wood and coal alone!' he'd say. 'The food and drink. The castor oil. The shoes!' And he'd stand there and just *shake*."

"Well, it's true it takes a few red Indians—"

"Which should not of bothered him a bit!" she said. "For Ermin *had* a few red Indians. And more than a few. Letting *loose* was his problem. Until one day—And if he'd of come home and told me he bought a mother-of-pearl organ I couldn't of been more surprised! For what did he say but that he'd *do* it. Go Plural. Cost or no cost. After all them years! Went off in the morning like always. Come home for supper a different man. Saul into Paul was nothing in comparison."

"For heaven's sake," Murdock said, thinking of how Alice too had changed from morn till night. Mysteriousness like an epidemic was going around. "My wife Alice—"

"I want to hear," she said. But giving him no chance to go on, she continued, "Ermin was a contractor and builder, did I mention that? Accidents could happen and one might of, a beam falling down, a keg of nails, a hammer, I just don't know. He didn't seem *dazed*. It was the strangest thing. Do you believe—I don't myself—in spells? He bought some

wood off a Gentile a day or two before this, rowan-wood, and while I do not know for
sure he got the best of the bargain, why, knowing Ermin he could have—Hasn't some
woods—got powers? Not that I'm saying—But here he was this night at the supper table
telling me he'll toe the line while that morning at breakfast—"

"It sure sounds strange to me. Like it did when Alice—But if you don't mind my
asking, what did he *do* after that? Start to marrying right and left?"

"Started building."

"Building?"

"Chambers. Rooms. Onto our very house," she said. "Along in a line like a string of
railway cars hooked onto a engine. Till he got to the end of the foot breadth of our land.
Each room was for a separate bride—"

"How many did he finally marry?"

"Why, not a one! By the time the rooms was finished, he was dead."

Murdock thought this over. "Well, if he'd lived he might not of found it such easy
sledding. Filling *up* them rooms. I don't know if you know it or not, Missus, but this
town's been picked clean."

"No wonder the neighbors was laughing—which I'm sure they was. Him sixty-seven
years old and going into the marriage business wholesale. You should of saw him. Like
one possessed. Rain, snow, darkness, his bowels, nothing stopped him. Putting up them
chambers was all he could think of. 'Ermin,' I says one Sunday when he's shaving. 'Are
you really *looking* in that looking glass? Because if you are, you must be starting to think
that the time to of launched all this was when you had hair on your head and teeth in
your mouth and something else somewheres else, not mentioning any names. Although
as far as *that* part is concerned,' I says, and I been sorry for it ever since, for it wasn't but
a month till he would get that sharp piece of chicken bone stuck in his craw and be dead
three days later, 'the world don't need no more human offspring like Alton.' 'Oh,' he says.
'And who's to blame for *him*, I'd like to know?' 'Well, not me, it didn't come from my
side,' I says. '*I* never had an uncle that went crazy and laid out in the front yard on his
back looking up at the sky, spitting and then dodging!' Ermin's Uncle Roscoe done that."

"That's a new one on me," Murdock said, laughing.

"It was a new one on *me* when first I heard of it," she said. She laughed too, to be
sociable, then looked sad. "Poor Ermin, all that hard labor, to come to nothing. And all
them rooms—I'm asking you—how easy is it going to be to *sell* a house you can walk
through like a string of excursion cars hooked onto an engine?"

"He should of courted and married first and built afterwards. Though as I say, I
wonder where he thought he was going to *get* the brides to fill 'em?"

"I wonder too," she said, dabbing at her eyes with a handkerchief she had extracted
from somewhere. "And you're right, he should of thought ahead. Especially as to what
God was going to say about him waiting too long and dying in arrears."

"I wish my wife was here to hear this," Murdock said sadly.

"And what am I left with?" she said, as though he had not spoken. "A house like a train that won't never leave the station. Who will want to buy it? Of course I *could* take in boarders, I've thought of that. Except I'd have to buy a lot of stuff. Beds, you know, bedding, kitchen stuff—"

He stood there like one made bright by lightning. "Mrs. Griffin," he said. "Did you ever hear the saying 'Providence don't fire no blank ca'tridges'? *Well—*"

Chapter Two

*

ON THEIR WAY DOWN TO HIS SISTERS' HOUSE TO VIEW THE BARGAINS FROM CAMP Floyd that would make anyone who had the good sense to start a boarding house now that the country was opening up a mint of money, Murdock told Mrs. Griffin it was almost as if they had been brought together for a purpose. And one thing he wanted her to know, and anyone that knew him would testify, his nature was not to try to gouge the other fellow but be fair, and temper the wind to the shorn lamb. He didn't have to tell her that, she said, a little out of breath from the pace he set, going more than halfway was wrote all over him.

But what his aspect showed most when they left his sisters' was his resentful realization that nobody ever tempered the winds to *him*. She had not bought a thing. "I am not a young woman anymore," she said, "and the sight of them big pots and pans strikes fear to my soul." She wasn't sure about the folding cots either, and wouldn't let him set one up for her. Maybe some other time, she said. But she did want to thank him. For now she was sure a boarding house was out of the question. Thanks to him, she had made her decision. She was going to sell. And who—for a nice percentage—could take on that chore for her better than anyone else? Why, because of his experience in the Land Office, him, of course. Yes, they had been brought together for a purpose, herself and as outstanding a young man as it had ever been her good fortune to meet, no doubt about that. And what better time for him to see her house than the present? As Orson Pratt once said, "Plant the hereafter in the now," which was a pretty smart saying.

There was a fire in the stove when they got there, lamps were lit in two of the rooms, the woman who had been looking after things made a beeline out a side door as they came in the front. "That there was my neighbor, Sister Vigor," Mrs. Griffin said, removing her shawl. "I'd of liked to make you acquainted, but her eyetooth fell out the other day and she don't like to be seen by strangers. But like I told her, she'll have to get used to the gap, for I don't know how she'll fill it up. Sit down, sir, make yourself to home. Will you drink some cocoa? Or would you rather have a drop of the creature?"

He knew what that was, but like a good Mormon chose to look blank.

"Spirituous liquor," she said. "If I'm not mistaken, it's a Irish Catholic expression."

"That don't surprise me," he said, letting himself down into a platform rocker.

"Do you know what I heard one time? That in the olden days *the whole entire world was Catholic*. Can you imagine such a thing?"

"Well, I know it was wrapped in darkness," Murdock said, "for a long time. But as to its being—" He broke off with a nervous start.

"Don't mind him," she said, following with her own his gaze into the next room where what appeared to be a large coal heaver sat on the floor in the corner with his legs stretched out in front of him. "That's just Alton, Ermin's and my only child. You know I mentioned him. Body of a man, mind of a babe in arms. Time was I rued the day he came down from heaven, but now I'm thankful, at least I'm not all alone."

"That's good, not to be alone."

"Perfect health, he has," she said with a note of pride. "Digest tin cans if he had to!" She came and stood close. "Now, what'll it be? Cups or glasses?"

"If this bottle could talk!" she said when she had brought one in, opened it with some effort, for it was sealed, and filled to brimming two capacious egg-cups in the shape of chickens. Handing him one and taking the other for herself, she said she really didn't have any wine or whiskey glasses, nothing but one-handled pewter mugs, so actually what she should have asked him was, cups or cups? She laughed as at a joke and took a sip and he did likewise, momentarily losing his breath, for the liquor was very strong. The reason she said If this bottle could talk! she continued, was because she found it out in Ermin's workshop after he had died and was buried. And as Ermin never drank, all she could think of was that he had got it to fortify his poor self with on the wedding nights he thought he was going to have. "What else could it of been for?" she said. "Dutch courage."

Murdock looked somewhat embarrassedly into his egg-cup, then took another sip. On that night of nights, the one extra wedding night Alice had said he could have, *he* wouldn't need Dutch courage, Murdock was sure of that.

"Poor Ermin. I can imagine it was on his mind. Strange bed. Strange pardner. He was a great one for habit. And I should of bolstered him up more, and not said what I did about—" She glanced at the door of the room on the floor of which her son sat. "But in a way, reminding him should of been a comfort, don't you think? That when the time finally came, if *begetting* turned out to be a obstacle, why, the world wouldn't be that much the loser."

Thoughtfully Murdock sipped again. "You know what I'd like to know? Where your man thought he was going to *get* all these ladies! For the town's picked clean."

"That's what you said," she said gently. "He got five rooms hooked onto the house before we run out of ground. You want to see the layout before it gets too dark?" She drained her cup and set it on the organ. "We'll have the rest when we get back."

"Five brides," Murdock said wonderingly as he got to his feet and took out after her through what appeared to be the back parlor of the house. "And I'm supposed to have just one."

"This way," she said, opening a door that still looked wet with varnish, though it was dry. "This here's the first, they're all alike."

He smelled sawdust, white-lime, damp, had a sense of high shadowy ceilings, bare walls, doors, tall narrow windows…"Say, they're quite a size," he said. Empty, echoing, but yet to Murdock, unaccustomedly warmed with ardent spirits, rooms as full of flowering limbs as a springtime orchard, and lustrous eyes, and in the wash of some kind of evening light diaphanous bosoms, and a star rising up in the soft air. I my beloved's am and she is mine whether she's got a dime or a pot to piddle in or a inch of property! and poop on you, old Alice. Francis's song went through his mind, the one he had sung on the way home from the Camp Floyd auction,

I walked up to her
And down she did fall,
For she longed to be a-playing
With my long peggin' awl…

On the way home, he planned what to say to Alice about how time slipped past like a thief in the night and how in a twinkling you could wake up dead with your spirit's purpose still before you, and never another chance. Why, just today he had heard of a man—! So strong in him at that moment was his yearning to be a shepherd with a *flock* to cleave to and keep on cleaving till he was blue in the face that the rudder of his central impulse throbbed with pain till he could hardly walk.

Alice was in the kitchen. Supper was ready, and spoiled, and she was not pleased. And would have been even less so had she been in the bedroom when he came home, because under the circumstances he might not have behaved like a gentleman. He probably would have, though, moving in too close would have given the game away about his having had three big egg-cups full of spirituous liquor and brought down no telling what upon his head. Supper, such as it was, got rid of the spirituous smell and also (that and her sulkiness) his magnetic condition to the extent that even in bed with her later, he kept as far over on his side as he could and lay on his back thinking of Ermin's weak-minded relative that spit and dodged.

He talked up to the ceiling. What he talked about in solemn, measured tones was his obligations as a man on earth and how you either took care of them obligations in a manly way or came out the little end of the horn. Take Ermin Griffin. *They* had to get it second-hand, having been but children at the time of the martyrdom. But Ermin Griffin got orders first-hand from the Prophet's own lips! having known him. The Principle, the Doctrine, the Gospel Dispensation of the Meridian of Consummate Time! And Ermin believed it, ascribed to it, but did he carry it out? No. *Intended* to, yes. But thirty years was just stretching it too thin. With only one wife, he died of a chicken bone stuck in his throat and won't get hardly nothing in the Celestial Kingdom. For wise men die, likewise the fool and the brutish person perish, and leave their wealth to others…

Alice spoke to the ceiling too. What was he talking about? Who in the world was Ermin Griffin? And where did *he* come from all of a sudden? "Don't tell me, I don't want to know. And don't think you can muddy the waters, Murdock, for I won't allow it."

"Muddy the waters?"

"As to maturity. And no one poor. Remember that."

"I wouldn't dream—" She come up to me ... And down she did fall ...

"Property. A bank book. Bottom. Or the answer is no."

For she longed to be a-playing ... O tra la la!

"I well understand. But where can a man hope to find—?"

Suddenly and resplendently he knew.

Chapter Three

✳

PHOEBE GRIFFIN HAD MATURITY. HER HAIR WAS GRAY, EVEN HER BACKWARD SON Alton's reddish hair was beginning to turn. And what was "property" if not a house on Sixth East and Seventh South with a great long concourse of new rooms snaking off down the block to the fence? As to a bank book, Murdock would bet the woman had hundreds of dollars, maybe even a thousand, in the bank. So when it came to *bottom*—

"Sometimes things are not just what they seem," Alice said severely.

But in Phoebe's case they were, and even better. Alice herself had to agree to that when she met the small green eyes in puffy eyelids and the front like a pan of bread dough running over and realized this was just the helpmeet the depraved nature of man in its conflict with the promptings of the spirit needed. And after she herself inspected the peculiarly long but quite handsome Griffin dwelling and walked past the Deseret Banking Institution where the Griffin money was drawing interest, she not only gave her consent but went so far as to offer to make the wedding cake. But Phoebe preferred to do that herself, and it was not a success. So in that and every way Phoebe was the perfect choice, and Alice permitted the bridal pair a full week's honeymoon.

BEING A LADY IN EVERY sense of the word, when Murdock came home after the week was over to spend the night, as he was supposed to do on alternate nights from then on, Alice did not ask how he had got along. And he being a gentleman did not say, not to her or anyone else except his co-worker Francis, and then only after looking all around the Land Office and even outside the window on the ledge. Then he burst out, "Holy Nauvoo!" Evening and every morning—wore down to the nubbin was what he was. But no man in his right mind would complain! Phoebe was—She had—And while he wasn't living the Principle to *enjoy* himself (the last thought in his mind), why, if a man through no fault of his own—look at the bite marks on his neck here, son—he wouldn't have to pay in the beyond? Monday, Alice. Tuesday, Phoebe. That meant nights, though technically the *daylight* hours from the time he left one wife to go to the other belonged to that other wife, the one whose night it was going to be. Even the time while he was at work was technically that wife's. But charmed like a bird by weaving serpentry, sometimes during the afternoon hours belonging to Alice, Francis would hold the fort at the Land Office and Murdock would go running back to the house he had just left that morning. "What, you again?" Phoebe would say. Alton would be present but Phoebe would give

14

him something such as the egg beater to play with, and Alton would sit on the floor with his legs spread out and play with it while the couple reeled off into the bedroom. If he had opened the door, it wouldn't have mattered. Transports or sleeping were all the same to his tiny mind.

IT WAS ALL THE SAME to Alton the day he saw his mother apparently lifeless under the ironing board she had dragged down with her when she collapsed with a blood vessel bursting in her brain. She would have lain there through the night had not Mrs. Vigor decided to forget the past and go over there and borrow an onion, also return Ermin's shoe stretcher. Had she thought there was a chance that what had been going on the past few weeks to the scandal of the neighborhood was still going on and that she might encounter it, she'd have never gone near. But she had kept watch, and *that* part of the business seemed to be tapering off. The bridegroom's coattails didn't seem to be seen so often at off hours (the way they had been) flying around the corner of Phoebe's house, the window blind had stopped coming down in the side bedroom at *two in the afternoon*. Mrs. Vigor therefore took a chance, rapped lightly, then opened the door and stepped in. "Yoo-hoo, it's me," she called. Down the hall that led from the kitchen, she could see the half-open bedroom door. "Anyone home?" Anyone in that room in there acting the fool? She tiptoed forward, and in the surprise of falling over both ironing board and Phoebe nearly broke one of her own blood vessels. A few inches away from poor Phoebe's hand the flatiron was still warm, the crocheted lace on the nightgown tangled around the ironing board still felt damp. That shows some people's luck.

And other people's forbearance, as Mrs. Vigor told Murdock's sisters Tot and Serapta when they brought their canary and came to stay and nurse their new sister-in-law. Mrs. Vigor could have stayed away and held a grudge and the woman might have died untended there on the floor. But if our Heavenly Father could forget the rudeness of Edam and the nastiness of Tyre, she could surely wipe from her recollection certain actions that if anyone had told her a year ago—well, silence was golden. But she did offer as her opinion to the Burdick sisters that just as there was a lawful limit to how *young* a girl could take on the…duties of wifehood, there ought to be a lawful limit to how *old*. Because it just seemed like an old bride when moored by head and stern—She would say no more. Only that God who giveth the sun for a light by day and the ordinances of the moon by night, when He strikes a person down has got a very good reason!

Tot and Serapta agreed that that was possibly so, but they had little time to scratch their heads and think about it. There were plenty of other directions in which to send their thoughts. *What* had they got themselves into? Serapta said of the burdens they were taking on. But Tot said, well, at least it took them out of their rut. They slept on two of Murdock's Camp Floyd cots, one in the corner of Phoebe's room and the other in the dining room. Handsome cots indeed they were seen to be when once set up, grapes and leaves of iron and brass entwined on either end, so plainly for officers and worth their price that at last Murdock received the compliments he knew he had coming all along. Also for the superior Army blankets and a large pot or two that also came in handy. Alton liked the grapes and leaves so much the sisters had a cot brought and set up for him in the first of what were to be called by them from then on "the Brides' Rooms."

The room where Phoebe lay didn't belong in the category, because it was the bedroom in which the Griffins had slept for many years. But as Phoebe was now Murdock's bride and because that was where she wound up as good as dead, *it* could be called a "Bride's Room" too. Unfortunate soul, her doctor, Dr. Jefferson Morgan, said. She could lie like that and outlive them all. Alice couldn't take care of her, not with her back the way it was, Murdock told his sisters, and if they would just step into the breach—He didn't say what they could expect for sure except to say they wouldn't be sorry.

They were sorry, a little, when all their possessions and Murdock's Camp Floyd stuff too was hauled over from the old family dwelling and Murdock and Alice sold *their* house and moved into it. The girls wondered about their dressmaking business? but Murdock had a sign made telling where the Misses Burdick could now be located, and some of their old customers did seek them out. Not many, and as the months wore on, their already indifferent sewing deteriorated, and nothing got finished on time, even those few customers fell away.

And what about when poor Phoebe passed on, if that day should ever come? Where would they go?

"Therefore I say unto you," Murdock said, as always quoting as if he was making it up as he went along, "take no thought for your life, what you shall eat or what you shall drink. Behold the fowls of the air; for they sow not, neither do they reap, yet your Heavenly Father feedeth them. Are you not much better than they?"

Well, they hoped so, the sisters said to one another, and this house of Phoebe's wasn't bad as houses went, but they were in for a lot of hard work. And if they weren't dispossessed they were very close to it, Alice having got Mama's house away from them as slick as a weasel.

But they did feel sorry for Phoebe, and as time went on grew fond of her as one will of some architectural feature like a nice fireplace or window seat. She never moved of her own accord or did more than flutter her eyelids, but as they cared for her they took her into their confidence and told her what they really thought of Alice who had pulled such a stunt, and other matters too. Alice had her eye on Mama's house with the stained-glass transoms since the day she arrived in Salt Lake City, they said. She was cold, grasping, and had hog-tied Murdock to where he could hardly call his soul his own, "and you, Phoebe, are worth a hundred of her," they told her. Did she hear them talking to hear themselves think? Was she comforted? No word ever came to them from that undiscovered country to which all that had been Phoebe had gone, leaving her mortal coil, still going through the motions of living, behind.

She stayed a feature of the house, one needing a good deal of attention, for a long time. "You watch," they told her, holding her lolling head off the pillow so they could comb her hair, "Murdock will make a lovely husband yet, even if the block teachers come here three times to his once!"

Sometimes when they got her son Alton washed and combed and fed, they would walk him in and stand him at the foot of her bed to show her he was well cared for and "as happy as a maggot in dead Earnest," a saying they thought might have amused Phoebe had she been herself, she had seemed like such a jolly person on her and Murdock's wedding day. Any news that came their way they told her. And when they opened up another of the Brides' Rooms and outfitted it with the fourth of Murdock's Camp Floyd cots, they told her that, and also why.

Chapter Four

∗

THE REASON WAS RATHER INTERESTING AND WOULD BE THE START OF THEIR Institution for the Care of the Sick, though they didn't know that *then*.

What happened was a friend of their brother's, or not really a friend, more just a Gentile acquaintance passing through, had wined, dined and tried to get Murdock to spend some of the money he now had on a partnership in a mine—Murdock was going to do it, too, but made the mistake of telling Alice—a mistake the man ought to be glad of, because when Murdock went by the Salt Lake House on Alice's orders to tell him the deal was off, he found him alone with a broken leg done up in wood and rawhide splints! The doctor had just left, the man was crying softly (the laudanum not having worn off) and saying he was in hell.

"No, you're not. You're in Salt Lake City," Murdock said.

"I'll die out here without a soul to care."

"You won't die. There's lots of people care."

"Who?"

"Why, me, my wife, I got a stepson, two sisters—" The minute he mentioned his sisters, Murdock knew where to take his friend.

"So we got another patient, Phoebe," they told her as they made her bed, "nice, gentlemanly, and him being a Gentile we run out and get him the Tribune. And really when you read it, it's a better paper than the Deseret News."

THEIR NEXT SUFFERER, RELATED TO MRS. Vigor, was a woman with dropsical lumbago.

It was like when word gets around that a certain household will take injured lambs and birds that have fallen out of their nest.

"Murdock's *cots* are coming in very handy!"

A boy with inflammation of the bowels and no mother was brought in.

"Ermin's *rooms* are coming in very handy!"

Then a case of yellow jaundice…

"Murdock's *kinfolk* are coming in very handy!" the sisters told each other jocularly.

Which was certainly true, with Phoebe having to be turned every half hour to keep from getting open sores. It did look like Murdock would help, however, once in a while. Or at least (when he dropped by) design to go in and visit the poor thing. What would it hurt him to take her hand? Phoebe was as much his wife as Alice!

18

HAD IT BEEN REAL? THE brief friendship of her ardent and luxuriant thighs? Murdock could hardly believe it. The fix she was in, like some kind of awful lesson, made him wake up as never before. And access as her husband to her bank account made him sit up and take notice too. Money is not child's play, holdings are serious business. Things like pretty girls fall into second place. He had the lever now. All he had to do was find the point to place it to get purchase. Should he quit his job at the Land Office for an enterprise of his own? Keep a horse and carriage? Sell the family home so as to have still more cash in hand and move to Phoebe's?

Move to Phoebe's? Alice went up like tinder. Live with a living corpse from morn till night? That idiot Alton? Those *sisters*? Invite the Embroidery Club to a dwelling like a string of railway carriages? The place was bad enough anyway! but now, filled with bad air, open to infection—

Murdock offered a different suggestion. "When poor Phoebe dies we'll get *rid* of both her place and this place, buy a farm and all of us live there. What do you think of that?"

What Alice thought of that was beyond words. "Hush!" she hissed when he opened his mouth to add a few details. She wanted to think.

"Tot and Serapta—Alton—could have their own place—say behind the barn," he ventured.

"Will you be still!" Her tone was so sharp he did not dare go on. But when she spoke again, the edge was gone. "It might not be," she mused, "such a bad idea."

"Oh, it wouldn't be," he said eagerly. "Fifty or sixty acres."

"You're a fool," she said. "I mean a *pest-house* might not be such a bad idea. A real one. The town has grown so in the last few years. The railroad—strangers coming in— All those silly rooms could earn their keep, and your silly—your sisters too! And in the meantime the *value* of the property will keep going up."

"Well, I don't know," he said.

"You're not supposed to know," she said. "*I* know. It could be called—no mention of pest-house, that sounds catching like smallpox or diphtheria, and we don't want that— Burdick's Infirmary? Hospital? No, wait—"

The day the painted sign went up over the front door—BURDICK'S INSTITUTION FOR THE CARE OF THE SICK—was a proud day for Tot and Serapta Burdick. And would you believe the medical doctor at the Salt Lake House sent a patient there before noon?

THE DOCTOR WAS DR. JEFFERSON Morgan, a surgical practitioner and didn't he show it! And Mr. Harland the patient, wasn't *he* bad off with that arm of his! So much so that the next day but one the doctor told the girls to put their thinking caps on, he needed a surgery. In less than an hour the doctor had one. What had been the Griffins' back parlor became the dining room, the dining room became the kitchen, the kitchen with its galvanized sink and long counter became just what the doctor ordered, an operating room. Tot was holding the lamp and shooing away flies, Serapta was shakily dripping chloroform onto a wadded towel and Doctor Morgan was cutting off the man's arm like you'd take off a turkey leg. He sutured with sinew, packed the cut with eagle down and while bandaging up the stump said, "Miss Burdick, I wonder"—he was talking to Tot—"if you'd get that component limb out of sight? Looks like the bugger here might be waking up."

"Certainly, Doctor Morgan."

A proud day! but it is amazing how heavy a human arm can be when not attached to the body. Tot buried it, wrapped in old calico, in the yard and when Mr. Harland got better and made ready to leave for the Montana gold fields, she took him out in the back yard and showed him its resting place. He thought of digging it up and taking it with him so as not to be lacking a part of himself on the day of Resurrection. But then he decided not to and keep a note on his person instead as to where it could be found when wanted.

Hᴇ ʜᴀᴅ ᴏᴘᴇʀᴀᴛᴇᴅ ɪɴ ᴡᴏʀsᴇ places, the doctor said, than the former kitchen. Nice and light in the daytime, room to move around. He often used it. So did the allopathic doctor, then later others. But the first few years it was just Doctor Morgan, a real railroad surgeon with the experience one time of even cutting a person's head off! and pickling it. The head was Blue Dick Lopez's, and he pickled it for the ranger who killed the bandit and needed proof to collect the reward. This happened far away in New Mexico. The doctor had been everywhere. *Even to Europe.* He was the genuine article, and for him to say Burdick's Institution wasn't bad was like getting a blue ribbon at the Fair.

Chapter Five

*

At first Tot and Serapta did all the work themselves. They couldn't have hired a flea. But as things picked up, they hired Mrs. Dooley to come and do the cooking. Garnet came next, related in a way to Mrs. Dooley in that she was Mrs. Dooley's brother-in-law's third wife's oldest girl. Garnet became the maid of all work. Then came Paulina. And then one day when Mrs. Dooley was sitting outside on the back steps shelling peas for noon dinner, a young Indian came around the corner of the house and made her jump nearly out of her skin. The reason she jumped was the way he looked, not because he was an Indian. She wasn't scared of *Indians*. All they were, was one of the lost tribes of Israel, the Lamanites who the Book of Mormon said would someday in the fullness of time be as "white and delightsome" as you or me. But this one certainly wasn't delightsome *yet*. He walked drawn down on one side and his stiff hair hung down over one eye—an eye not there, it seemed, under a thick gray scar from eyebrow to chin. Hungry, of course. That's what he came for, begging. Mrs. Dooley went in and got him some cold biscuits from breakfast spread with bacon grease, a piece of cold fried liver and some gingerbread. Garnet and Paulina had to see him too, so they came out but stood where they could run back in quickly if they had to. Tot emerged then to see where everybody had got to, and she sat down on the step below Mrs. Dooley, ate a handful of peas and remarked what a pitiful sight.

"Shh," said Mrs. Dooley. "He talks as good as we do."

Tot spoke up politely. "This lady says you speak American."

Wolfing down the food like a starving mastiff, their visitor did not answer. But when everything was gone, including a much larger piece of gingerbread that Paulina ran in at Tot's bidding and got and brought out and handed to him as to a wild hyena in a cage, quickly snatching back her hand, he did come out with some lingo that turned into American, and what he said was he wanted to work. This was so unusual that they could only stare at one another. Tot and Paulina both had the same idea at the same time, that here was no ordinary Indian but one of the three wandering Nephites in disguise, a Nephite being in Mormon legend like the Wandering Jew or Flying Dutchman, a living man hundreds of years old who can't give up the ghost but must roam the world performing peculiar deeds and testing our humanity until Christ comes back to earth. A kindness to a Nephite is a kindness to yourself in heaven. Later they realized, after familiarity with him doing chores about the place bred contempt—for he didn't just vanish but stayed around as man of all work—that far from being above nature, he was just a common Paiute the way he said he was. Not exactly common, however. For how many Indian braves do you see far from their tribe, running in a drove by theirself? as Garnet said. Not very many. Doing menial labor?

Loudhawk was the exception. Captured as a child by wicked Goshutes, he was taken north to Fort Lemhi on the Salmon River, sold as a slave to the Cheyennes and did not escape from them till he was grown. Back home again, he found himself neither Paiute nor Cheyenne but as strange to his whole tribe—and even his sick mother and the blue quamash—as a snake with legs. Everything had changed. The Mormonee had come into the land with spells and charms, pants, straw hats and hoes. Even great Chief Kanosh wore the pants, the hat, talked the talk, but would not touch the hoe. Chief Kanosh wanted a rifle and got a rifle. His warriors the same, and bullets too. To Loudhawk other strangers were called the Mericats. Mericats and Mormonee did not like each other though speaking both the same tongue, Mericat. So it was said at the Council Fire, where no room was made for Loudhawk. He must prove himself, he was told. Not in the old ways. Now he must go far away to Jondy Lee and get the pants, the hat and hoe, and learn to say in Mericat I want a job, I want to earn some money. He did all this and everything went as it should. With some of his wealth he bought a pony and started home, and on the way by means of an enchantment plucked a redbird off a bush (as though it had been a rose) for the daughter of Chief Kanosh. But she was gone when he rode in with it, wed in the canyonlands, and his mother was dead. He had proved himself. Chief Kanosh took his wealth. And now at the Council Fire Loudhawk had a place. He also had a voice but somehow did not raise it, even though the treaty puzzled him. The treaty said: Your people and my people shall band together against the Mericat. But Mormonee and Mericat were one tribe. Both "moving people." How do you tell one from the other? "Who's on the Lord's side, who?" the Indians heard the Mormonees sing as they rode painted and in their feathers like Indians themselves onto the cliffs to join them in battle. That's how you tell, the Mormonees were on the Lord's side. And the Mericats lay below in the Mountain Meadow…

If Doctor Morgan was not thinking of something else, he would sometimes stand and look at Loudhawk, or put out a hand and stop him in his tracks. His injuries and scars were the attraction. "Real close quarters somewhere, eh, old son?" Loudhawk would not talk just to be talking but once said he woke in blood as stiff as the Cold Moon's frost and said that many others did not wake. The doctor used to squint at him. "Open you up, think we would find lead?" Murmuring a little to himself, the doctor would study him the way a sculptor might a piece of marble. Bugger might straighten up if a fellow would—Of course it all depended on the trauma. And if the ligamentary fold—The face, of course, that was beyond repair, that cicatrized right side. Pity. Might have saved the sight in that eye. Once Loudhawk sidled in with a basket of linen strips warm from Paulina's iron and the doctor looked up from the maggoty edge of a wound he was cutting away. "Hold up there," he called, and the Indian waited.

A bandage went on, then the patient's awful lips opened for more laudanum and the doctor went over wiping his hands on a towel and said, "All right, old lad, you're next on the agenda!" But he was only joking. He'd only thought of a motion he wanted Loudhawk to make. And when he made it, the doctor, tipping his head to one side, said ye-e-s, by doing it that way the tissue supporting the heart and holding it in position would not have to be touched. Loudhawk drew back with a fearful frown, then hurried off. The doctor smiled and shrugged. Tot and Serapta smiled too, Tot thinking as she wiped the cold sweat off their patient's brow that the doctor could take the tissue supporting *her* heart and touch it all he pleased and she wouldn't care. He was so wonderful!

Chapter Six

*

Even his medical diploma, which she had a chance to see the day a patient knocked the bottle of double chloride of gold off his bedside table and Tot had to (she wouldn't let anybody else) go to the doctor's office in the Salt Lake House to fetch another, was a beautiful sight. The doctor had been busy when she got there. Behind a sheet hung up as a partition, he was giving a static-electric muscle-stimulating treatment to a patient with large bare feet. "But make yourself at home," he said, "we'll soon be done." That was how Tot had a chance to study the gold-framed diploma on the wall with its beautiful garlands of roses and green leaves and fancy colored letters saying that All the Merits of a Physician, Surgeon and Accoucher, guided by a Sound and Profound Knowledge of Moral Principles, belonged to Jefferson Morgan, to Whom Confidence and Reliance is Due in the Highest Degree!

One thing that did not look at all nice in the office was an ugly earthenware chamber pot sitting right out in plain sight. But Tot was glad for the embarrassment, because now she knew what she and Serapta could give the doctor for Christmas.

"A new chamber pot," Serapta said happily. "What a good idea! Gold edges, a painted garland—"

Tot said, "No, no, *no*." How would it look for two unmarried ladies to be giving a single man such a thing as that! No, what she had in mind was a lovely little wood cabinet with a *door* on the front to keep the article *in*. "We'll burn his initials in the front in a wreath of peonies." Serapta always joined in with her sister, so she said, "Oh, that's a *much* better idea. The only question is, will he know what the cabinet's *for*?"

"If he doesn't," Tot said, "Sister Dooley's husband will have to tell him."

The cabinet was a great success. The doctor said it could stand in a palace and be right at home. His gifts in return were a great success too, once the scraps of paper he handed round during the serving of the Christmas pudding, to Serapta, Mr. and Mrs. Dooley, Garnet, Paulina, Loudhawk (the doctor gave the Indian his in the corner of the kitchen where he ate), the new girl Hindle Lee, even two patients who felt well enough to come to the table, and Tot, proved to contain a nice little pinch of coarse gold dust! When Tot realized her present was the same as everybody else's, her face, as her sister saw with sympathy, fell. For Tot was in love and loved in vain, and if that wasn't picturesque and sad Serapta didn't know what was.

The Burdick girls were up on the picturesque and sad. Indeed, play-going and novel-reading had made romance such a principle of their lives that their neighbor Mrs. Vigor (for one) almost gave up on their fulfilling *woman's destiny*. So incapable did they seem to her of serious connected thought along those lines that sometimes she thought they didn't even know what woman's destiny *was*. Or anyway not the Salt Lake kind. But of course they did, how could they help knowing? It wasn't Romeo and Juliet. It was old man Richards traipsing past to Sunday school with wives and children stretching halfway down the block. It was *marriage*. Which in their case—Mrs. Vigor would speak frankly. They seldom went to Sunday school, a little bird whispered to her that they did not knock people over rushing to pay their tithing, but worst of all male patients, with their terrible externalities, were nursed by them! And also in the line of duty they mixed with Gentiles. These were drawbacks injurious to their interests and towards ever making their dreams come true. Though keeping their tithing paid up would have been one of the best ways to do *that*.

BUT DREAMS CAME TRUE ALL the time for nothing. And wonders happened, too! just from divine favor. Consider, for instance, who was brought in last Wednesday afternoon with what turned out to be typhoid fever. Lisheen Fielding! the actress. Straight from back stage at the Salt Lake Theater, where she was about to go on as Miss Hendershott, leading lady Florabel's girlhood chum, in *Florabel's Lover*. Tot and Serapta had been at the Monday night's performance, so they knew for a fact she was one of the set of actors, and they had the program to prove it. Beautiful Miss Hendershott, played by Lisheen Fielding, the program said. Of course they recognized the blonde-mustached young man who escorted her and her suitcase into the Institution, rushed back outside, ran down the walk, jumped in the livery stable carriage and drove off like his pants were on fire. He was none other than Miss Hendershott's handsome, stalwart sailor sweetheart, Jack Wilson, played by Lester Whiteside.

Actors do look different, though, in real life. Smaller, for one thing, which is strange considering that up on the stage where they're farther away they look bigger, while down on the ground where they're nearer they look smaller. What is the explanation for that? And somehow their eyes—go out—the way the stars do in daylight. Miss Hendershott's— Lisheen's—eyes certainly had gone out. But she was very sick. And stayed that way throughout the rest of August and into September, till finally the night came the doctor said the crisis looked near to him when either the girl would live or throw in the towel. And sure enough, right after midnight, as the first autumn rain began to streak the black window panes, her fever broke and she lived.

And woke, as you might say, as if for the first time, not only to her whereabouts but to her situation. And rotten *that* was, her lips a mass of fever blisters, nostrils covered with sores, and not a handful of hair remaining to do anything with. But worse must be faced. In the note Lester Whiteside at least had the decency to come and leave for her while she was still delirious (before the de Fermian Theatrical Company moved to Cheyenne and points east), he said Miss de Fermian told him to say that her father said he would send the wages due Lisheen at a later date. Something else due Lisheen at a later date—and due Lester Whiteside too, who had not only *played* her sweetheart but *been* it—was a child, and that prospect was daunting. But at thirty years of age, which Lisheen was if she was a day, and married and separated too, one knows more things by natural reason than one used to. So Lisheen decided to use her wisdom and wait around till her looks came back, writing letters in the meanwhile far and wide, to Lester and other acquaintances along her pathway, though not to her husband, who had been a brute.

The blisters healed, the scabs fell off, tendrils sprouted around her face, she was pretty again. But now, enceinte as she was, stuck fast in wintertide without warm clothes, that hardly cheered her. Stay! Tot and Serapta begged, as if the woman could do anything else. Doctor Morgan said they wanted to see the thespian fruit of the two actors' loins (for Lisheen had confided to him who the father was) the way Catherine the Great wanted to see a midget baby spring forth from the forced coupling of her two smallest dwarves. Amongst themselves the kitchen staff said wasn't it just like those two silly women? begging the actress to stay, while if they'd held off awhile *she'd* of been begging *them*, and a bargain could of been struck, board and room for some percentage of work, perhaps. But no. Stay, high and mighty Miss Lisheen Fielding who trod the boards, be waited on, do Burdick's Institution the honor! And didn't she act like she was doing that every day that passed.

But in a way she was. She *had* acted on the Salt Lake Theater stage, after all; her name was still on a billboard to prove it. She *could* hit a very high-pitched note. Her every move until she grew too clumsy made manifest the toe dancer. She took a pencil once and drew a picture of a coal wagon going by and it looked just like it, horse and all. And when she said she won the thirty-sixth prize, a ten-dollar gold piece, in the worldwide Castoria contest where you had to write an eight-line poem with the word *Castoria* in it, for an entry which she called "A Happy Family," which went:

> *Pulled from the breast, squeezed from the bottle,*
> *Stomachs will sour and milk will curdle,*
> *Baby's hallelujah all that night,*
> *Household bumping heads in awful fright.*
> *Don't deny, 'twas thus with Victoria,*
> *Night was hideous without* CASTORIA,
> *When colic left for peaceful slumber,*
> *All said their prayers and slept like thunder!*

Lisheen had the document to prove it, where she'd been notified.

Hindle Lee admired her as only a thirteen-year-old can admire a paragon of all virtues. But twice Hindle's age and more, Tot and Serapta did the same. They bowed down to her, had her daintily fed, protected her sleep and saw that she was not disturbed at work.

"*Work?*" Garnet said disgustedly. "Why, she don't even know how to make her own baby clothes!"

Chapter Seven

＊

BUT LISHEEN WAS WORKING. AT A LITTLE TABLE IN FRONT OF HER WINDOW, SHE had resumed the writing of her life's story. It was called *Experiences of an Actress*, and Tot and Serapta, permitted to read the first chapter, thought it would bring her fame and fortune. When that day came, how proud they would be that they had harbored her!

HER STORY BEGAN WITH EMPLOYMENT at age seventeen in the Mitigated Affliction Department of Hardman's Emporium in Philadelphia, Pennsylvania. A week later the floorwalker's insane wife ran her out of the store with the sharp point of an unopened parasol. Life brought many cruel surprises…

It was still bringing them. Sometimes they were so upsetting Lisheen didn't write for days or even weeks. Sometimes the surprises almost killed her. Like Lester Whiteside's letter. When Hindle went in to do up her room, she thought she was dead, laid out on her bed like a princess on her bier. But she wasn't. In a few days she was sitting at her table again, pen in hand. And whereas previously she had rather ignored the help, now she was glad to seek out one or the other of them for a little information. The information she wanted had to do with polygamy. That it would trice up the tack of her *Experiences* was not something she just thought of. All down through Idaho she had made soft-voiced attempts to talk about the custom's heresies and schisms to such indigenes as came her way, hoping to elicit usable responses. But to small avail. And in Salt Lake City, where she expected the scandal of magnates, Mr. de Fermian (owner and manager of the de Fermian Theatrical Company, with which she traveled) said no one was to pry or poke around. "Curiosity killed a cat," he said, "and here at the very center of Mormondom's gyrations it won't do *you* any good." See no evil, mum's the word and turn a deaf ear. "We'll take 'em and be gone," Mr. de Fermian said.

And in a matter of days the company *was* gone, leaving Lisheen at Burdick's Institution, too sick with typhoid to care about anything, let alone polygamy. She didn't even care about her hair coming out. After the crisis passed, though, and she started to get better, she made rapid progress till at last when she got up in the morning she was, as Tot said proudly, "up for all day." Up for what, however? Then was when she called for the little table at which she sat for many hours, rustling papers. One could peek in the door and see her writing. At first she wrote letters to a Mr. Templeton of Cincinnati, a Mr. Willy O'Brien of St. Louis, perfidious Lester and others. (Would Mr. Templeton answer? Perhaps he was dead, he was rather old, maybe he was still mad at her for what she did to him.) (Would Willy O'Brien answer?) (Somebody had to! and send her some money, or she'd be stuck here forever.) Then she got her journal out, the basis for her *Experiences*, and here the theatrical company was, here *she* was again trundling in the stage wagon towards Salt Lake, thinking of love and fame. At breakfast by herself in the Popular Dining Room in Silver City, she asked the waitress, "If I may make so bold, Miss, are you a Mormon?"

"We don't say Mormon, we say Latter-day Saint."

"Oh, excuse me. Well, are you—?"

"Who wants to know?"

"I understand it's a lovely religion."

"Of course it's a lovely religion, why wouldn't it be?"

"No reason. But some people think polygamy—"

"Well, they shouldn't *think*." The girl shut up then tighter than a bull's hind end in fly time, as Mr. de Fermian would have vulgarly expressed it. He was a very coarse, vulgar man, always playing Dukes and Lords. But he was right about the practice in Zion (as the Mormons called Salt Lake City and vicinity) of keeping things secret.

Lisheen took up her journal where she left off, wrote about performing Miss Hendershott, about coming down with typhoid fever, about how *that* wasn't enough, she had to have been ruined by Lester Whiteside, too. But here "the Vine o'er hills of ruin climbs…" and somehow she would find a way through her troubles. Then she turned to the *Experiences* again. "We arrived in a dust storm. The place didn't look much like the one spot on earth Jesus's feet are supposed to touch when the Heavens open and He descends again, as the Latter-day Saints believe…"

"As lazy as she is," Mrs. Dooley said when Garnet reported that she never saw the woman do a tap of work, "and old as she is, she's going to have a hard time delivering that baby or I miss my guess." Out of the kindness of her heart, therefore, when Lisheen came to the kitchen door to ask for a cup of tea to take to her room, as she did every afternoon at four, Mrs. Dooley for once invited her to come in and sit at the table, as she had something to say to her. What she had to say was that hard work was better for anyone in the family way than laying around. Take her own case, she had five as easy as falling off a log, big babies too, and never missed a lick all through 'em! She washed, baked bread, scrubbed floors and what should she be doing but treading the sewing machine right when the water broke! and here it was near eleven o'clock at night. And Frankie breeched too, he was her fourth in line, and take a *lazy* woman under them same circumstances, she would be dead!

Lisheen agreed absolutely and told Mrs. Dooley she herself *loved* to work, it was all that made life worthwhile. And she fell to it that very moment. "I'm delighted to have this opportunity to talk to you," she said. "Usually when I come to get my tea I feel you are busy and so I don't try to take up your time. But you are a member of the Church of Jesus Christ of Latter-day Saints, are you not? Isn't that the preferred title? Well, would you mind telling me—?"

But Mrs. Dooley would mind and did, so much that Lisheen could get nothing out of her whatsoever. "Why is that?" she looked up from her table to ask Hindle the next morning when she came in from the kitchen to do her room, Paulina having started with a nosebleed. "Why are they so secretive?"

When Hindle found out who Lisheen was talking about, she said, "What was it you wanted to know?"

Lisheen said, nothing world-shaking. Just a few things in regard to polygamy, human jealousy and such as that.

"I heard a man say to Doctor Morgan once—he was out here from Washington and a lamp exploded and burned his hand—that people around here try to act important and with big deep secrets because they *got* nothing and *are* nothing," Hindle said.

"And what did Doctor Morgan say about that?"

"Oh, he just laughed. But maybe it's really true. Nobody *looks* like nothing around here. Even Amelia! and she's President Young's favorite wife. You never see no pretty colors, or nothing with shine—well, there's a carriage or two about the streets that looks elegant—If it wasn't for *secrets*, the *marrying business* and the *purpose*, why, the Gentiles living here and coming in wouldn't pay no more attention to the Mormons around here than Mormons pay to the Indians—"

"What do you mean, the *purpose*? Not that I want to be inquisitive."

"The purpose of the marrying! See, that's to get the spirits earthly tabernacles so they can start their progression so that when the Millennium comes, we'll have more people on our side than they got on theirs."

"Oh." Lisheen thought this over. "I mentioned jealousy to what's her name in the kitchen and she acted like I'd blasphemed God. But human nature is human nature everywhere, and if Turkish polygamists succumb to jealousy, why shouldn't the same thing happen with American polygamists?" Dreamily then Lisheen spoke of where pashas lived and ladies in thin pants and certain gentlemen with parts sheared off, and jewels came heaped in baskets and scimitars flashed up at the drop of a turban, and Hindle listened transfixed. "What I mean to say, passion and jealousy, they're *universals*. There's hidden graves in Constantinople, and I bet you that in this very town there are bricked-up walls with skeletons behind them!"

Hindle's eyes widened and she caught her breath.

"Skeletons," Lisheen said. "I'll bet you. But you were saying even the favorite wife of President Young doesn't look like anything. But that's in public. How do you know *what* she wears when he's with her by himself? her hair all tumbling down, and what she does? There must be some reason she's the favorite."

"Well, if you'd see her—"

"I presume you attend church services?"

"Well, see, I'm baptized but—" Hindle had to go back, not easy to the young, who purpose history as the one-hoss shay that got *them* to their present destination, then fell apart. The town that Mama came from Hindle couldn't remember the name of. "But she was a widow when she married Papa. Her first husband died on the plains, on their way out here. I don't know if Papa had thirteen wives at the time that her and him got married or if he got some of them after and also if all Papa's boys had been born, Mrs. Bearpark says there's about twenty, and all the girls, I don't know the exact number—"

"Oh, my heavens, listen." Lisheen's pupils had grown large. "Your father sounds like *just the person*—If he would confide some of his thoughts to me—"

"I don't know how you'd get him to do that," Hindle said. "First because he don't live around here and my sister Lucitie and me ain't seen him, oh, for years, and secondly he ain't even living where he *lives*, which is down in Iron County."

"You mean to say he's dead?"

"I mean he's on the run. The federal men is after him, that's what Mrs. Bearpark told Lucitie and me. Quite a while ago there was something called a massacre, see, and they're blaming the Mormons, especially Papa. Why, we don't know. He wouldn't have hurt nobody, Mrs. Bearpark says she's sure, nor nobody else would either down there in the south. She says it was the Indians. But the federal men won't listen—"

"Mr. de Fermian was *talking* about a massacre," Lisheen said eagerly. "On the train he was reading a book that said—It happened a long time ago, didn't it? A massacre at a place called Mountain Meadow. Could that have been the one your father—?"

"Goodness knows."

"The man was—let's see—The book said they'd tried for years to catch him, but every time they got close he'd vanish. Was it Lee?"

"If it was John Doyle Lee, then that would be my father all right," Hindle said.

Lisheen jumped up and hugged her. "Oh, my dear girl. Tell me *everything*! It shall go in *here*." She ran back and laid her hand on the stack of papers on her little table. "We shall be rich and renowned together!"

But Hindle's "everything" took about five minutes to tell. In fact, not that. She had seen her father only a few times in her life, all before the age of five, her thirteen stepmothers never, a half-brother named Heber Alma once. What could a storyteller do with that? "But thank you just the same, my dear," Lisheen said, "you shall not be forgotten in the tallying up." When Hindle went out, Lisheen felt so discouraged she lay down and took a nap.

But another way to decorate a chapter was with Indians, and Lisheen had an aborigine handy in the Sioux or whatever the creature might be, skulking about. As up until then she had seemed not to be aware of his existence, when she began paying actual attention to him Loudhawk was like a bird whose tail someone is trying to put salt on. Bit by bit, however, he fluttered to her hand. Besides, she had a necklace that she broke and gave him the blue beads from, a few at a time. Thus when his leisure served, passersby in the hall might see him through Lisheen's doorway sitting on the floor in proper Indian fashion, talking indigenously while she sat at her table writing away. It was a sight the sisters were proud to see, that when their star boarder needed a native they had one handy. But yet they found the situation fraught with danger as well. For didn't the poem say a man's a man for a' that? And wasn't Loudhawk—well, a man? And without the grounding in principles of civilization, men weren't predictable. Not that since he came to work for them he had been *unpredictable*.

Chapter Eight

*

THE UNPREDICTABLE ONE (SAID IN THE MOST RESPECTFUL WAY) WAS THE DOCTOR. But in his case, not knowing what to look for next was part of the way he charmed. The *bunch* of flowers pinned to his coat instead of just one flower. The Latin he would lapse into. He would make snow ice cream for everyone, flavored with jalapeño. And once when a lawyer made (down at the hotel) a rude remark about Mrs. Robert E. Lee, he slapped him across the face with his glove! and the lawyer, instead of fighting a duel, begged pardon. And one time... Yes, but was it very charming to find out that he not only drank strong liquor but took morphia? Serapta brought that up only to try to console Tot when Tot felt blue. Serapta was not guessing, Doctor had told them himself, spur-of-the-moment as the man could be, all equality, fraternity one minute, cold to the point of bewilderment the next, divine right in the morning, a high-hatted king that night. Tot would say it wasn't morphia but tincture of opium and Doctor probably took hardly any. But suppose he did, she would say. When you thought of his aggravations? The people in his life that had acted mean?

His very father? so jealous and possessive of being the only doctor in the family that the son was to be put to keeping store! like where his mother's folks' money came from. But Doctor wouldn't be ordered around like that. Not him. He broke with them, father and mother too, she proving false, and educated his own self. Went to Medical College, moldy bread, ice in the bedroom pitcher, three hours' sleep a night and pay for your own corpse! So Doctor had to steal one. It was just touch and go until the very end, but wouldn't you think—? That beautiful diploma? That they'd have been proud? Not *them* parents. Never give an inch.

Traveling west, then? Telluride? That woman's operation? Billiard table, pistol at your head. "She dies, you're a goner, Doc." She must of died—later, with that fistula? so he always thought, and bore it heavy that he skipped too soon to find out for a fact. And one time... Once a señorita... the knife they rassled off her was as long as your arm. Trials like that by fire take their toll. Like heading for Leadville, him and Reddy Marie, big old Concord coach went over a cliff, ton of silver bars stacked inside got loose, and hurling to and fro as they bounced down went to work and walloped them nearly to death. But that was nothing to the walloping his feelings took when a girl named Maryland—ah, me! How many times had not, as he expressed it, "gorgeous tragedy in scepter'd pall come sweeping by"?

33

The strands of hair now combed up from the side over his baldness were longer than his foot, the sisters saw and sympathized. Felt for him when a gap came in his smile. How that would hurt the man that they heard say (as if to himself one time) that when he knew that he was born of man and woman he was astonished. "For, you see," he said, "I thought I was a damn sight more." That man wouldn't take to old age kindly. (How old was he? Forty? Maybe fifty?) Wouldn't take to sickness kindly, or enfeeblement. Losses kindly. *One* in particular that Mrs. Dooley said *struck only the men* ("impudence," she named it in a whisper), and when that happened they'd hang theirself as soon as look at you. Not all, of course, but some. Though why a man should take it to heart like that she didn't know, when you considered how tiny a part them particular ornaments was of their whole body, and how little what they did amounted to, except in the case of fathering George Washington or, say, our own dear Prophet. If impudence, though, had actually struck the doctor, none of the ladies had any way of knowing.

THE OPPOSITE OF THAT, OF course, was too atrocious to be put in words, and for a long while after inheriting Alton, Phoebe's unfortunate son, the sisters waited for a nasty shock. His mother's work, however, Phoebe had done well, and Alton conformed so to propriety along those lines that Mrs. Dooley, when she first arrived to cook at the Institution, made the remark she'd like a nickel for every licking that poor thing must of got as he was growing up. Licking? Oh, no, surely! Yes, indeed. Whipping. To teach him not to touch himself! Think of the nasty stunts he could perform if somebody hadn't learned him beforehand within an inch of his life. Oh, poor thing. The Burdick girls wrung their hands. Had Phoebe and her husband really licked their big child with his baby mind? Not to be mean and cruel but so when he grew to manhood in Zion he'd not be taken out and maybe shot. During the Reformation, Crazy Bob unbuttoned his pants in front of some ladies coming home from a quilting bee and lived about five minutes or maybe ten.

As to the Indian, Mrs. Vigor said when Loudhawk had been hired and she first saw him, didn't it seem strange that savages in the wilds knew what to do just like people that was "white and delightsome"? a favorite expression of hers from the Book of Mormon. And when she heard that battle wounds had caused him to be drawn down like that on one side and no right eye, she said, "Let's hope the arrows done their job *elsewhere* too while they was at it, dears. Because although they preach in the Tabernacle that God Himself has 'body, parts and passions'—which if He has and man is made in His image, why, 'parts' should be as polite as a person's eye—But if you ever *seen* one—!"

The maidens had, and more than once. They couldn't help it in the line of duty (two or three times), but they really didn't feel as if they'd seen much. Kind of a morbid outgrowth of baggy droop. But then one day the doctor and his driver came dragging in a great long Sydney Duck dressed in a red flannel shirt, with a mob cap on and a knife stuck in his belt. They thought at first his *name* was Sydney Duck, but Sydney was where he came from, in Australia, and the inflamed vermiform appendix in his caecum was about to bust, the doctor said. Ever anxious to remove this lobe, the doctor fought Mr. O'Heron, wild with fever, like a great fish he was trying to land. Finally it took all of them to get the man on the table, and the doctor even had to give him a slight clout to the temple with a stick of stove wood to keep him there. While the sisters rushed around then making ready for the operation, the man was stripped and covered by a sheet. But the driver had no more than stepped aside and Doctor turned away to his instrument case than Sydney Duck was up and off the table and the girls saw what they thought at first was a naked poniard putting forth as in the process of growth—so murderous, so menacing—they stifled screams—*The whole armor of God!*

After that, the rules and regulations changed at Burdick's. Garnet and Paulina could not run in and out of a sickroom with a man in it except together, or with Tot or Serapta. Because no matter how polite the man might be, or deathly sick or dying—like the homesteader whose horse had caught a hind shoe on a front shoe and tossed him and the fence tools in his arms over its head onto some jagged rocks, rupturing his stomach on both sides—they now knew what was lurking subtle as a beast. The sisters had bitten into the apple, so to speak. But as familiarity slid their awful awareness into that portion of the mental field the processes of which were outside the range of a person's nervous attention, the teamwork rule went by the board, and when Tot took Hindle out of the kitchen to help do up the rooms, she worked by herself.

"Another nosebleed?" Lisheen said when Hindle appeared with bucket and broom. She meant, was that why she was seeing Hindle and not Paulina?

Hindle explained, Tot had switched them around, Paulina now had her job in the kitchen and was she mad! But as Garnet said, it was Paulina's own fault, flirting and carrying on around Doctor till finally retribution struck. Tot would only put up with so much! especially where *he* was concerned. Hindle, not Garnet with her priority not only by reason of superior age (sixteen to Hindle's fourteen) but precedence in service, was called into the surgery to help with an operation! If that didn't prove Hindle was just a wolf in sheep's clothing, Garnet didn't know what would! For of course Garnet should have had the job.

No one really looked for a change. Who could suppose a repugnance to chloroform would suddenly build up in Serapta, administrator of it for years, to the point where she must stagger out into the fresh air and fall to her knees in a splash of vomit, and Hindle be pulled in from the corridor and told to take her place? It didn't surprise the doctor. (But of course nothing did.) "You take chloride of formyl," he said, "and you take the human organism, and once in a while you will see that cumulative deleterious effect. You will see it with eggs, you will see it with anything—peaches—all of a sudden they round on you and you're fighting for very life. Or take in India, your cobra—roaming the house for years, wouldn't hurt a flea—all of a sudden BING." He looked Hindle up and down. "So if this grim young woman can follow orders…"

Grim? Hindle's hand shook a little at first, even people's eyeballs taste the sweetness, the icy chill slices off their nose, but drop by drop…

"That's good! Now give me room here, ladies—" Room to chip out from the patient's fractured skull a vent-hole for her insulted brain. He called it that, "insulted," talking along companionably as he worked, as quilters do around a quilting frame, and his assistant Tot put a happy word in now and then. And more than a word about poor Mrs. Lappsley, all as true as gospel from the woman's own cousin.

"I'm sorry, Hindle," Lisheen said, looking up from the fire like a reader drawn unwillingly from her book. "I guess I missed the first part. What did you say?"

"I said—they called me in, Doctor did himself. I was in the hallway. And here this lady—Serapta always done it but now she can't. It poisons her because the cu-mu-lative— The chloroform. She always give it, see, but now she can't. So here's this lady laying on the table that Doctor's going to operate on—her name is Mrs. Lappsley—"

"That you say died."

"I didn't say died! Goodness gracious, no."

"Well, didn't you mention—something about a grave?"

"I said her *husband* when he died last fall, she had his grave dug twelve foot deep instead of six! Tot knew all about it. She was telling Doctor while he was operating."

"*Twelve* feet deep?"

"Well, maybe not exactly but close to it. And the reason she done it, she was the first wife and she had the right."

"Yes, but even so, why would anyone *exercise* such a right?"

"Mr. Lappsley's two other wives was so mad they couldn't see straight. On account of the Resurrection. So they went to the bishop—"

"What did the Resurrection have to do with it?"

"Well, because a grave as deep as that, imagine what hard work it would be to *climb out of.*"

"What did the bishop say?"

"Well, the grave was already dug. And the weather was scorching. And Tot said Mrs. Vigor told her Mr. Lappsley wasn't in too good standing with the church anyway. He paid his tithing all right, but Mrs. Vigor said he was one to argue, and once at Conference somebody told her he didn't sustain, so Mrs. Vigor said *she* thought the bishop didn't care *how* deep a hole the poor thing would have to climb out of! But he paid Mrs. Lappsley back all right, Mr. Lappsley did."

"How did he do that if he was dead and twelve feet in the ground?"

"Well, I'll tell you. She had this big enlarged picture of him in this big heavy frame hanging over her bed and what should happen in the middle of the night but the nail give way and down it come and cracked her skull. That's why the doctor was operating on her in the first place."

"Hush a minute." Lisheen scribbled quickly, then looked up as though about to speak, changed her mind and didn't, then burst out, "I don't want to hurt your feelings or anything, but this—" She pushed her paper away. "This crazy idiotic—How could people in their right minds follow such teachings? Polygamy is the most stupid, boring— Nobody will want to read about it! Nobody would even want to *write* about it except another simpleton as stupid and dumb as everybody else is around here!"

Hindle dusted what she had already, a lump slowly rising in her throat.

"I don't mean—Present company excepted," Lisheen said apologetically, her hand over her eyes.

"Mormons ain't got the patent on being dumb," Hindle said.

"Don't be mad. Really, I didn't mean it. It's just—oh, Hindle, I never was so *stuck*. Lester knew a poem that went 'O wind, if winter comes can spring be far behind?' But I'll never live to see the spring—" Her bulk preventing when she leaned forward to twitch the curtain back, she got to her feet and went around the table. "Why am I looking out?" she said, her nose against the glass. "An alleyway. A coal shed. Dirty snow…As dark at two in the afternoon as if it was night!"

Hindle, blinking back tears, plumped the pillows up and stood them against the headboard. "Is there anything else you want before I go?"

"Why—only for you to forgive me," Lisheen said as she turned back to the room. "And tell me—Let's see—You were mentioning—? Tot." She cast about for something more to say. "Is she going to get the doctor, do you think?"

Because of her hurt feelings, Hindle tried her best to hold aloof but couldn't. "Nobody knows," she said. "He likes her. They laugh and talk, but Mrs. Dooley says she thinks Tot could get the King of *Spain* quicker'n she could get *him*."

"Is Paulina still carrying on around him the way Garnet was telling me?"

"No, because where she is now she don't get a chance."

"Is she still mad at you for getting to do the rooms now and give the chloroform?"

Hindle laughed. "Not anymore. Though she would be if we had to trade back."

"Why? What's in the kitchen now that she likes so much? Food? The fire?"

"Boys, Mrs. Dooley says. Paulina didn't realize how many comes to the door. Delivering coal and such as that. Menfolk too, but they're nearly always married. Of course that's what Zion's Watchman Johnson is. Garnet said she heard Paulina say with her own lips that she wouldn't even *spit* on a married man. But now she's fell for Zion's Watchman Johnson when he comes in every week to deliver his Swedish paper and try to get news—see, Mrs. Dooley was born in Sweden though her husband, he's Irish, that's why she takes it—the paper, I mean—and now Paulina don't flirt with the boys at the back door anymore. The paper's called Zion's Watchman, and Mrs. Dooley told Paulina she wouldn't be any wiser if she could read Swedish because all it has in it is about Jesus coming back and the Millennium. But Mrs. Dooley takes it because Zion's Watchman is

Swedish, and she told me once she was proud to have Brother Johnson sit in her kitchen and drink a cup of cocoa like he does every week. Because he was even wrote up once in the Salt Lake Tribune!"

"For what?"

"Because when he was on his mission, he was nearly ready to be cooked and ate by cannibals. Or anyway that's what he says when he gets up and bears his testimony. Only at the last minute he converted them. Also his sugar beet for three years running has took first prize at the Fair. But one of his wives grew it, I am sorry to say."

"Why are you sorry to say?" Lisheen said, laughing.

"Because we're back to polygamy. And you said you don't want to hear no more about *that*."

Lisheen, still laughing, picked up her pencil again. "How many wives did you say this Zion's Watchman Johnson's got?"

"I didn't say because I don't know for sure. But one of them's well off, with property, one of them runs a farm and I don't know what the others does. But Brother Johnson don't do nothing, only be dressed up and put out his paper."

"Handsome, is he?"

"Prettier'n a mallart, Garnet says. But Paulina's discouraged. He sits at the table and him and Mrs. Dooley talks their Swedish and he don't even know Paulina's alive!"

Lisheen said theatrically, "Ah, woe! The tumultuary disorders of our passions!"

Chapter Nine

*

TOT'S WERE TUMULTUARY, NO DOUBT OF THAT, DISORDERED TOO, FOR NO SOONER had she sent Paulina to the kitchen (a dungeon not being handy) for flirting with the doctor than she wished she hadn't. It was an act not worthy of her. She thought of Paulina's vulnerable youth, of young creatures that can't help skipping in the fields, of the plants that can't help their colored floral organs, of how nature is always inveigling! Still, the doctor didn't back Paulina in that corner, she backed herself there! And she was so silly, so globular. But the girl couldn't help it, and Tot, thinking of how the poor thing had cried at being demoted to the kitchen, was sorry and decided to repair the damage. But the person in charge can't give an order and then five minutes later take it back! So she waited several weeks, then did not say she had been wrong but only that a new girl had been hired (a granddaughter of Mrs. Lappsley with the fractured skull) to help Mrs. Dooley in the kitchen. That meant Paulina could have her old job back. She should have been jumping for joy, but what did she do? burst out crying! begged, pleaded, promised to do anything if Tot would just let her stay in the kitchen! so that was human nature for you.

Anyway, the new girl got Paulina's old job while Paulina stayed in the kitchen dreaming about Zion's Watchman Johnson, the sight of him once a week almost like a dream too. And that should be a lesson to Tot, Serapta said, not to upset herself when Doctor chaffed the girls. He was like the Prophet's sundial in Nauvoo that said I Only Tell the Sunny Hours. Remember that sundial? Doctor only chaffed when he was taking the tincture. Or drinking. Brandy, whiskey, you really couldn't tell just what, there were so many different smells, cigar smoke, iodine, ether, bay rum and that horse smell he'd bring in with him from petting his blooded team. Doctor's sunny hours usually came after dark when he was making his rounds. He'd bow from the waist, sing a snatch or two of song and scatter compliments to left and right. Unhappy Lisheen heard from him that a woman was never so beautiful as in the gravid state, from *gravidus*, he explained, meaning heavy with young.

That rankled for days. Men lied to women, did nothing but lie. Ask anyone. "Am I beautiful slopping around with swollen feet in ugly carpet slippers and this old wrapper belonging to Mrs. Dooley? Look at me! My face, my stomach. This—*watermelon*!" An honest person would say no. Then go back to last year. "Am I the beautiful Miss Hendershott—nineteen-inch waist, size four shoes—oh, God—oh, God—" Lisheen took to crying, took to being nervous. One day when the clock—while her eyes were on it—suddenly stopped, she nearly jumped out of her skin. For of course that was a portent that meant her life was as good as over. Stylishness, adventuring and love, the stage, experiences! all that was now a thing of the past. She sat and wrote no more at her little table, did not expect to see the last snow melt that lay in sunless places, for not only the clock but all patent things (going of themselves everywhere) had stopped dead "never to go again."

News came in with Hindle and with Garnet. The old lady with the fractured skull was sitting up, walking, going home, had no memory whatsoever of the twelve-foot-deep grave or the hated husband in it. Doctor Morgan might build a watering-place over the hot springs out beyond the city limits. And just yesterday Zion's Watchman Johnson allowed Paulina to sew a button on his coat! Her hand shook like a leaf. But these were not (to Lisheen) *tidings*. She scarcely listened, wreathed as she was in gloom. "Look quick! there goes Amelia! the only one of Brigham's wives with her own carriage." Or, "Right outside! the first—some kind of bird!" Or, "The flue burnt out this morning in number six. Did you hear the roar?" Nothing mattered. Then Garnet brought a letter in. Lisheen snatched it, looked, threw it down with a shudder. Another portent! *It came from her own self.*

Garnet picked it up and smoothed the envelope, spelled out beside the name Willy O'Brien *d-e-c-e-a-s-e-d*. Lisheen made a grab. "Why, that can't be! He's *younger* than me, he's a *pugilist*, he *fights*, he's *healthy*." "No, he ain't, he's dead," Garnet said gently. "Or else it's a mistake. That's what it probably is!"

But Lisheen said no, it wasn't a mistake, nothing was a mistake except her imagining she was ever going to get out of this place alive!

She had talked of dying often, threatened to, foretold it, promised not to see the crocuses come up. But she didn't really mean it, in her heart she thought she was the exception that proves the rule. But now Willy was dead, her letter had come back and *there's no exception* hit her like a brick. She sat by the fire staring at it for hours. Didn't blow the lamp out, when night came tried to sleep in the dim light, died, was buried, moldering in the—talk about twelve feet deep! Talk about clawing your way up to the Resurrection! Done for, done for, she woke up dripping with sweat like one brought back from drowning. You lie there under a mountain and it's *forever*.

But forever is a funny thing, is only time inconstant, only life that bears within it (like an engine does its means of generating power) steadfast change. The hardest heart, the thickest ice, the stiffest monument, all will melt into the distant sky, break into rain, to tears, to clouds of sand. And that change—count on it—will change again! And so the spring came round in mint condition and almost instantly began to tarnish. And Mr. Templeton wrote from Cincinnati *You have got your nerve I must say, dear. When I think of what you did to me. I must be a fool for punishment. Thought I had burnt your letter but yesterday here I find it in my dresser drawer. I should have my head examined to do this after all that happened, but if I sent you a ticket—? Money enough—?*

It might have been that she was due, or maybe the shock, the joy. An hour later pain shot through her hold, and by suppertime she had had her baby.

Chapter Ten

✳

LISHEEN'S HAD IT! HAD A LITTLE GIRL. DIDN'T LOOK LIKE ANYONE EXPECTED. The snow had marked her, Lisheen didn't know what else, all the dumplings of the winter. And the white Mormons from the northern approaches going by with their white-bristled, blue-lit faces. Or it was the typhoid. Tot said wait till summer. Mrs. Dooley said she had a sister fair like that, or maybe not *that* fair. Mrs. Dooley's sister couldn't hold a candle, Garnet said. Lisheen nursed her, when her milk dried up she'd go back east to Mr. Templeton, leaving the baby at the Institution till she saw how things were going, then she'd come back for her. ("Are you crazy?" Mrs. Vigor asked Tot.) Unless it took too long, then she'd dry the milk up herself, how long was a person supposed to wait?

Hindle and the new girl Deseret argued about the baby's eyes. Deseret thought they'd always stay that color, Hindle thought they'd change like a kitten's from when it's blind to when it can see, skim-milk color to maybe blue. But she backed down when the baby seemed to bleach and whiten more each day, hair included. There was no mistaking. The little thing was purely an albino. Or albiness, as Doctor Morgan said. Nothing to marvel at, seen in every race and kind, frogs, the axolotl, Africans, Indians in Arizona (incidence was large) and Mexico, even the giraffe, white peacocks, not to mention the birds and beasts that look their natural way in summer and autumn but match the white terrain when winter comes. A product of Nature's irregular fancy, Doctor said.

Irregular fancy! like a baby the stage character Miss Hendershott might come forth with, pierced through with stagelight, shining with what was going to happen in the last act. With every day that passed, the new mother Lisheen grew more like the Miss Hendershott she had played. She wrapped the carpet slippers in the ugly wrapper she had huddled in and told Hindle to throw them in the Great Salt Lake, buttoned herself with a buttonhook into the tight-fitting golden-brown dress piped with rose that she was wearing when Lester Whiteside brought her to Burdick's in the first place, wedged her feet into her tiny shoes with a shoehorn, borrowed Serapta's kid curlers and was herself again, that is to say an actress in all her oblong glory, impatiently nursing a theatrical property someone had handed her, to which she had given the name Mavis. She often laid the little thing by, sang no lullabies, moved about averse to being quiet, packed up her writings, left her suitcase open and studied her image in the glass like an honors-man his manual of instruction.

Doctor might say women were most beautiful when gravid, but Lisheen in that state got about as much attention as the wall, while with wasp-waisted Miss Hendershott he was a perfect beau. Swamped by discouragement, Tot watched his antics. And also their brother Murdock's! Both sisters deplored what they saw in him, married to Alice and the widower of poor Phoebe, for whom when she finally died he never shed a tear. With all his business enterprises, had not Tot or Serapta gone up to his office the first week of every month with the profits from the Institution, they would hardly ever have seen him. But then one day he dropped in, met Lisheen and began acting weak-minded. Serapta said hopefully she wouldn't be one bit surprised but that he would try to get around Alice some way and *marry* Lisheen. Why else would he come day after day and try to convert her? while Lisheen, with her eye on the clock, the weather, the mirror and the state of her milk, just laughed and teased him. Alice would *never* consent, Tot told him. Well, then Murdock must go and see the Prophet, Seer and Revelator himself, President Brigham Young, he said.

BUT SEEING BRIGHAM WAS NOT so easy these days unless for something to do with the railroads, Pacific or Utah Central, or the banks, or Congress, or in regard to venturing into some sure business. The consequential kind, old son! or else like everyone else see him only on Sunday in his royal chair on the rostrum of the Tabernacle, with his high priests raying out to either side. Hear him like everybody else only on Sunday, when by some strange arcanum of religious intrigue he leaves the after-image not of a pale old man with puffy eyelids and water-filled hands and feet, but as tightly drawn as when he was young and had but two wives. After evening prayers now in the Lion House, he does not go across the swept street to Amelia's place *on the surface*, but as some great earth-monster tunnels underground. Or else he's out of town, he's circuiting on a royal progress. Ah, but never mind, a Twelve will deal with you. Under the Great Seal you can state your case—love's pain, women, whatever it may be—and that high official (remunerated) will decide the issue, find a judgment and put your mind at rest.

Tot knew why Serapta wanted their brother Murdock to marry Lisheen. Because with each day that passed, her sister was getting fonder of the cotton-candy baby Mavis, and Tot knew where *that* would end! with the same bitter tears Serapta used to shed when Mama wouldn't let her keep the dog she dragged home, a baby cat, or when the canary died or her wax doll melted in the sun. Even if Murdock married Lisheen and the actress became one of the family, that wouldn't help Serapta's case of wanting what didn't belong to her! Tot knew well the folly of *that* when every day seeing Doctor stop and talk to Lisheen stung her like a swarm of holy wasps.

BUT SCORPIONS WOULD BE MORE like it when they brought *her* in, Mrs. Maybelle Clarendon from the Salt Lake House, with a cracked shoulder blade, and Doctor showered *her* with attentions. Glance in there, you'd see him laughing and talking, chair drawn up to her bed…One time he even asked for a supper tray so as to *eat* with her! people almost fell over backwards. Mrs. Clarendon was married, had a living husband. Looked like nothing. Forty years old if she was a day. But she was rich! and right there was your answer. Of course he and she did have common memories of the past, as Doctor told Tot when making rounds, memories of Holmes and Silver City and the Growler Mountains, and wild old Baboquivaris, his and her trails had crossed again and again, though they never happened to meet in those days. But should that account—? And what was the woman *doing* anyway in all those places? Somewhere along the line Mrs. Clarendon, or whatever her name was then, married wealth, married a Cornishman who had found a silver mine. Then the Cornishman died and she was a wealthy widow. Then she met Jim Clarendon, former dragoon. He had never found a mine or anything else of value and was at the time they met very discouraged although a seventh son, Tot and the others found out as time went on. But when Maybelle married Jim, that changed his luck. After that he couldn't stub his *toe* without discovering gold or telluride or silver till *he* was wealthy too, as rich in his own right as his wife Maybelle was in hers. So she could truly say, and did say often without being shy about it, that why he stuck with her was love.

People didn't think so before he made his own fortune, she being older and rich and no great beauty. But that it *was* love gave her a lot of satisfaction. Of course, she said to the different ones at Burdick's Institution attending her, he would roam off to himself, like this here present prospecting trip into the High Uintas. But never without asking would she come too. And time was nothing could have stopped her. But now, you know, the easy life, it lays in wait for you. Open fire crackling when you wake in the Salt Lake House (snowflakes fluttering down outside the window), breakfast in bed, your hip bath…Doggone bath. Feet flew out from under—Jim would give her heck. That Jim! Would you bet he'd make a strike up there! He liked to say that the day he met her was the luckiest day of his life. That was just his blarney…How she prattled on to Doctor Morgan! and how he did bend an ear! Such politeness, sitting by her bed. It even annoyed Lisheen. Tot saw Lisheen pass Mrs. Clarendon's door one day and glance in with a scowl so mean and jealous she wished the doctor could see it! for that should cure him of believing her so charming! That a mean look on a cruel and obstinate face can act on some men more powerfully than beauty, Tot of course in her innocence had no idea.

Truth to tell, so wrapped up was the doctor in Mrs. Clarendon that Lisheen's smiles or frowns meant nothing to him one way or the other, which was why Tot glimpsed the actress looking so blackly in at Mrs. Clarendon's door. The short, plain, brown-haired woman's magic power, of course, had to be her money. Lisheen thought so. They all did. Not just money, her diamonds and fine things, but money's *deportment*, the carrying of herself that said so purely, head up and neck arched, God knew what He was doing dealing with *me* just like He knows what He's doing dealing with *you*. That goaded. But yet when the day came that Mrs. Clarendon was leaving to go back to the hotel, Tot felt as abandoned as at a play when the curtain comes down for the last time. Tot and Serapta always sat in the theater awhile, sometimes till everybody else had gone, and held off common life as long as they could, and Tot had the feeling of doing that when they lost their star patient. And not just the woman herself but her devoted husband Jim, who when he came down from the mountains well pleased with his prospecting trip and while his wife was still with them made the Institution his second headquarters. He brought flowers, the girls ran out of fruit jars to put them in. Bonbons, they went to everyone. Sometimes, banished temporarily from his wife's room, Jim would wander through the halls passing the time of day with whomever he met till he could rush back to her side. It was ridiculous, him so much better-looking than his wife, and younger too. *They* were ridiculous, Lisheen said. And when she heard that Mrs. Clarendon said they might come back someday and build a mansion in Salt Lake City, of all the places in the world, she laughed in scorn. *She* wouldn't build a doghouse in this town! the actress said.

The first time he burst in, Mr. James Clarendon, bonafide millionaire, still in the hobnail boots and flannel shirt he wore prospecting but fresh from the barber and smelling of bay rum, nobody *didn't* look that had the chance. Hindle, carrying Mavis to Serapta's room (to be spoiled more than she was already) while Lisheen took a nap, was one of the first to see him, and Hindle had no doubts who it was.

"Well," he said, "and what do my eyes behold?"

"Oh, this here is Mavis," Hindle said, in her shyness shifting her burden from right to left.

"Well, now!" he said, then made the remark he always made when confronted with someone's infant. "Now that's a *baby*."

Smiling proudly, Hindle held her up so he could see her better.

"Well, I should say." And now he looked closer he saw indeed a "different" child, "different" as his Irish mother would say, using the word to mean not as to resemblance of something else but betokening (she would cross herself as she said it) a mischievous identity to steer clear of. Jim in his worldliness seldom met with anything eliciting that superstitious sign, but now as he stood looking at the babe with her white little dandelion head and milky eyes and a cold chill went running down his back that said *they're walking on your grave*, his fingers itched to make the sign. The strange expression Hindle saw on his face, that she would forget, remember and think of in years to come as foreseeing the future, passed quickly. Did she really see him look like that? Or reading backwards towards the point of starting, did it just seem as if she *might* have?

After Mrs. Clarendon left the hospital, she and her husband stayed a few more days at the Salt Lake House, then left for New York, points east, Paris, France, and Italy, wherever their fancy led. Before their departure, a man from the Tribune came to talk to Jim about his interests and other such repetitions and trivialities. But from a rich man, these (like the quadrivium) are of the nature of instruments for more advanced studies, a body of rules for practice, and are so received. So Jim Clarendon held forth on the tariff, Chinamen with queues, why God never put (and never will) silver in limestone, the Colt revolver, why the little old cayuse is the best horse in the world, and why—

"Excuse me, sir. But would you mind making a remark or two about the power of money?"

"Power of *money*?" Jim said almost with indignation. "Yes, I'll make a remark, I'll put a bug in your ear. And that is that there's but one power on earth that counts a damn, and you know what it is? Why, that there is *the power over yourself.*"

The paper summed Jim up: a regular fellow. And called his wife "the beautiful" Mrs. Clarendon.

Chapter Eleven

✳

LISHEEN MUST HAVE PLANNED OUT WHAT SHE WAS GOING TO DO WHILE MR. AND Mrs. Clarendon were still in town. But would she give her poor little albino child Mavis the chance to be adopted by a millionaire? Not her! raven mother as she was. Had she gone straight into Mrs. Clarendon's room and put the proposition to her, Hindle was sure she would have taken Lisheen up on it! "But you know what *I* think?" she said. "That selfish thing couldn't of stood the thought of somebody else getting all them advantages, even her *own child*!"

"Oh, now, Hindle." Her sister Lucitie folded the ironed pillowcase on the board, laid it on a pile nearby and took another dampened one out of the basket. But instead of unrolling it, she put it back. "Say," she said, straightening up and making a wry face, "what do you say we go outside where it's cool for a while?"

"Can you do that?"

"I can if Mrs. Birdwood ain't come down from her nap."

A quick reconnaissance discovering no Salt Lake House proprietor about (and with the cook's approval, providing they didn't attract the stable boys' attention), the two sisters were soon lifting their skirts and sitting on their petticoats on the rough boards of the back outside stairway of the hotel.

"No, I tell you Lisheen couldn't of stood it, the thought of what it would mean," Hindle said, taking up where they had left off. "Well, just imagine."

"Imagine what?"

"Being adopted by a millionaire. Having everything!"

"But just because Mrs. Clarendon was *offered* the baby doesn't mean she'd have taken her. They're pretty particular, you know. And ain't the child some kind of a freak? Didn't you tell me that Doctor Morgan said so?"

"Not 'freak' exactly, he used some other expression. Sport. I think he said sport."

"*Sport?*" Lucitie said skeptically, remembering the plaid-suited drunkard Mr. Birdwood kicked off the front porch of the hotel and sailed his derby after for trying to pay his bill with pyrite. "Sport means—" She shook her head.

"It's when nature—Like for instance," Hindle said, "when a human baby or a calf or something gets born without no coloring. Nothing *wrong* with them only they're pure white instead of with natural colors—"

"And you mean to say that's the situation with this baby?"

47

"Pure white. Not their blood, of course, that's just red like anybody else's, so that reflects, see, under their skin—like sort of a baby pig."

Lucitie stated it positively. "Offered or not, them millionaires would no more of adopted a child like that than flew to the moon."

"Oh, I don't know," Hindle said. "They might have. Rich people like things other people ain't got, that there are just a few of in the world. But all I'm saying—and Garnet says it too—at least Lisheen could of made an *attempt* with Mrs. Clarendon before she left. But she didn't, not a word, and a week later here she stands and throws the *foundling home* in everybody's face! Her grip is packed, the livery stable carriage out in front is waiting to take her to the station, she's got her coat and hat on and here she's changed her mind!"

"About leaving?"

"About going away without telling Tot and Serapta what she's really going to do. See, *they* thought she was just going to leave the baby for a while, while she went back east and broke the news to Mr. Templeton, her old friend that sent her her fare. Then she was supposed to come back and get her. But at the very last minute she says she really don't want Mavis, she ain't cut out to be a mother and they should put her in a foundling home."

"Why, that's terrible."

"It *is* terrible, when the poor little soul might of been adopted by a millionaire!"

"No, I mean—"

"You should of heard her. 'She'll be happier than with me,' Lisheen says, looking towards Serapta, who's hugging Mavis like protecting her from tigers. 'Cause a foundling home,' she says, 'they bring 'em up so a child's more *self-reliant*.' Then she says something about this here climate being more *salubrious*, which Doctor told us later means more healthy. And then before any of us could say a word—we was all just standing there with our mouths open—why, she turns and runs down the walk, steps up in the carriage and off she goes."

"*I'd* of run—and she'd of had that baby put in her lap to take with her so fast she wouldn't of knew what hit her!"

"Oh, no, you wouldn't. And you *sure* wouldn't if you was Serapta!" Hindle said. "*Tot* wasn't jumping up and down with joy," she added. "In fact she looked like she could of tore Lisheen to pieces. But Serapta—! Well, it just seems like from the day that Mavis was born, Serapta had dibs on her. And last month when Lisheen started weaning her, she had Garnet and me put Mavis's crib in Serapta's room so if she cried in the night—"

"Well, that casts a different light on things," Lucitie said. "Maybe a little bargain was kind of struck between them two, Serapta and the actress."

"Oh, I don't think so."

"Why else would Lisheen do it like that? She could of just left town and never wrote no more, or if she did write, broached the subject of the foundling home in her letter. But you was all out there, wasn't you, saying good-bye, so you was *witnesses*. Maybe Lisheen thought that made it more legal or something."

"Doctor said that woman will be acting on her deathbed."

"Is Serapta going to *adopt* the baby?"

"Why should she? We all heard Lisheen as good as give the baby away. No, Serapta will just keep her and spoil her within a inch of her life forever."

"But what if Lisheen changes her mind?"

"She won't, but if she did she'd just about have to kill Serapta to get Mavis away from her."

Lucitie thought this over. "Maybe Lisheen acted like more of a mother than you realized."

"I don't know how you figure that. Here was a millionaire without no children under the same roof that she could of at least *asked*, but she made no effort whatsoever."

"Maybe she decided that all that a millionaire could give wouldn't be *nothing* in comparison with love and devotion."

Hindle looked disgusted.

"Because them things, money can't buy."

"Well, it's water over the dam now."

"A *father* in the picture would be nice," Lucitie said after a moment's reflection.

"Oh, I guess. Serapta could put up a sign saying one is needed."

"Doctor Morgan—"

Hindle laughed. "*He'll* never be no one's father!"

"Don't be too sure. There's two girls working right here in this hotel and one of them, she does the wing his rooms are in, you know, and on account of him, would you believe, she nearly got put in *jail*?"

"On account of Doctor Morgan?"

"Actual jail. For stealing *flowers* for him. To put in his room. Because it smells so terrible in there, cigar smoke, medicine vapors—She took it on herself. He didn't know, of course."

"And wouldn't of paid no attention if he did."

"Oh, I think he would have if he'd of got the flowers. Winifred run in the side entrance with old Apostle Burris right behind her, her apron's full of roses, and here comes Mrs. Birdwood—The roses was from Apostle Burris's yard! Winifred thought no one was home on account of the shutters being shut—"

"Some girl that works here is stealing flowers from an *Apostle*?"

"Well, she wasn't raised here in Salt Lake. And it was real early in the morning. Besides, the Apostle's hardly ever home, the yard's his *wife's*, one of them, I don't know which one. But poor Winifred! He was home all right. Up, too, looking out the window. So the Apostle run out and chased her back down here and she run in and him right after her and when Mrs. Birdwood barred the way, somehow he took it into his head that *she* was behind it. Mrs. Birdwood! that owns the hotel! Sending a chambermaid to steal flowers for the dining room! Mrs. Birdwood was *so mad*. So Winifred had to stand there and confess, tell who the flowers was *for* and everything."

"I can imagine *that*. This Winifred saying they was for Doctor Morgan, and Apostle Burris going off like a Fourth of July firecracker when he heard the name! They hate the doctor so."

"Well, I can tell you that's nearly what happened. But why do they feel like that? The church? Like the doctor's such a terrible man?"

"Oh, for a lot of reasons, I guess. He's a Gentile and makes fun and says the church is just Freemasons dressed up with a little—let's see—Mohammedism, and things like that. And he chums around with people from Washington, D.C. And smokes and drinks, and Garnet says takes morphia—"

"It's really not respectful for him to make fun," Lucitie said. "Tempe heard him say that we're all dumbheads—"

"Oh, he says worse than that." Hindle laughed. "But anyway, how did it turn out? the flower stealing?"

"Well, Mrs. Birdwood thought of *damages*, and it's a good thing she did, because the minute Apostle Burris heard her say the word he changed his tune. Otherwise Winifred might of really went to jail. So Mrs. Birdwood laid down the money and he took it—the cost of the flowers—Of course Winifred's got to pay it back ten cents a week for three weeks. Then he made her promise—Winifred, that is—never to steal no more and read the Book of Mormon and the Pearl of Great Price and not let herself be sullied and all like that, and then he just went home."

"Well, speaking of dumbheads," Hindle's sigh was deep for the picturesque manifold of life, "you said that there was *two* girls. That's sweet on Doctor."

"Who the other is, is Agnes Green that works in the dining room. Tempe says—she waits on tables too—if he come in and every chair was taken, why, Agnes would pull one right from under someone! Let them fall on the floor and break their back. Tempe says that Agnes says she feels her heart a-fluttering like a bird when he comes in—"

"Don't it seem like just the strangest thing?"

"Don't what?"

"Well, them girls—The doctor. He's so *old*."

"Guess what, Hindle. I *know* how old he is."

"How would you know that?"

"Because it was Mr. Birdwood's birthday last September and while we was putting the candles on the cake, Mrs. Birdwood mentioned to the cook that Mr. Birdwood and Doctor was lacking but a week of being the same age! And that was—guess what—"

"Eighty?"

"Forty-seven."

"Well, even *that's* an awful lot of candles."

"Say, I was going to ask," Hindle said after a moment, as if aroused from a dream. "What kind of looking girl is this here Winifred that stole the flowers?"

"Crowded teeth."

"And the one that waits on tables?"

"Her one redeeming feature is her eyes."

Hindle stood up and brushed off her petticoat, letting her bunched-up skirt fall over it. "Well," she said, "I'm not a-going home and breaking the news to *Tot* about no two girls here at the hotel."

"Would she be mad?"

"I'll tell you how she'd take it. Doctor was telling us once about these kings. They all been dead now thousands of years. But when they was alive, if a runner come running in and brought some news they didn't like, why, what they'd do, they'd kill the runner so fast he'd never know what hit him."

"So in other words—"

In a dumb show, Hindle quickly beheaded herself.

READERS OF THE HOLY BOOK know well that jealousy is not condoned in it. In fact, it's number two of the Deadly Sins. Yet someone who's jealous and not ashamed of it is *God Himself*, the Father, it says so in black and white. "I thy God am a jealous God," He says, and Heaven's high jurisdiction being who God *is*, He naturally does not come *under* it. But the funny part is, He's jealous of *us*! Of all the beautiful creatures living on the earth, it's just humanity's love God seems to want. Love, attention, wants our life's blood really, and that is pretty flattering to a bunch of basically no-goods. But let the average person ask the same—especially dark-complected with brown eyes—merely his sweetheart's heart and soul and mind—and people start to back out of the way. Even the less hot-blooded, cooler blondes, when too demanding, get lots of elbow room. It's like they've got a screw loose, makes one leery.

Tot's mother (jealousy itself) would not permit jealousy in her children. Because, she said, this here's the way it works. You're jealous so you fight, *our home gets loud*. And when our home gets loud, our breadwinner *don't come home*. And when he don't come home, our *home gets bare*. And when our home gets bare of joys and pleasures such as a load of coal and refined sugar, kerosene for the lamps and other comforts, why, what rears up is *jealousy again*, and there's your vicious circle come right round. So do not never let it get a toehold.

Tot tried hard when young and also when she was grown. But try though she would, the sin would rear up from time to time, and then indeed, as Mama said, a battle would ensue. Not loud, Tot fought it with herself, and in spite of still being as one-track-minded about Doctor Morgan as God was about mankind, won her battles using common sense. Could Doctor help it? No. *He* didn't attract on purpose, any more than lignite could help pulling straws into itself. For what were all these silly girls but straws? she told herself. Silly Paulina! Foolish Lisheen! Self-centered Mrs. Clarendon! Tot even saw Garnet brush close to him one day and saw his hand go out to touch her arm. Pulling in straws. Not his fault at all. Tot's fault was paying attention, and she wasn't going to do it anymore, she told her jealous image in the glass that day, taking cognizance as she stood there (thanks to the faculty of discerning primary truths she had fortunately been born with) of the fact that although a long nose, short neck or big feet might be beyond remedy, a sweet facial *expression* can make all the difference. Lookie here, for instance. Here I am—jealous, ugly. And here I am—*not* jealous! See how smooth, how much smarter a person's forehead looks. She bent in close and, smiling at herself, vowed to keep free forever of the green-eyed monster.

Chapter Twelve

✴

BUT THEN THEY CARRIED THE GIRL IN, DOCTOR AND HIS DRIVER. STRAIGHT OUT of bed she looked like in her nightgown, coat half on, her feet bare—little square feet—long loose hair—and Tot's fine resolutions glimmered out. Never had such solicitude been lavished on a human being. Doctor personally helped get her to bed. He personally took the heated brick wrapped in a shawl that Hindle brought and placed it under the covers. And when a little later two women rushed in, the patient's mother and sister as it would appear, he bowed and scraped as though they were royalty!

They *did* look something like that, the visitors. Came in a carriage, the older woman holding a tiny dog like a fur piece up against her throat, a Spanish dog with diamonds in his collar. But all turned out deception to the bodily eye and to the mental eye as well, for they were not mother and sister or even related to the girl they hung above, wringing their kid-gloved hands. They were not related to each other either, their diamonds were glass, their auburn vitrified, their carriage on the verge of turning into a pumpkin. And where they came from in their dimpled flounces and furbelows was not from marble halls but (as would come out later in the Salt Lake Tribune) two small adobe houses built a foot apart in hard-baked yards out nearly to the Salt Flats. Empty houses by the time the curiosity seekers went out there, even the blinds removed, see right through the bare windows from front to back, all the fine furnishings carted back to Dinwoodey's Furniture Store that lent them in the first place to advance the Kingdom (not by choice but due to counseling).

THE SALT LAKE TRIBUNE, BEING the Gentile paper with the moral standards of a tailless monkey in its story of what happened, put in such expressions as "naked Frailties," "carnal pleasure," "violation of the marriage bed" and "vicious indulgence of the animal passions," without one thought of how such language might corrupt the pure of heart. The Deseret News, on the other hand, in *its* account of the project beat around the bush to such an extent that the pure of heart as well as the nasty of heart could read and you couldn't prove it by either one. Zion's Watchman, the region's little trade paper (the trade being Christ's Second Coming and the Millennium), although its editor was sure such fellow Saints as had taken part in the scheme had done so for good reason and that the Gentiles' wickedness ought to be shown up, put *its* head in the sand with regard to the whole affair. Zion's Watchman Johnson, the editor, said he personally would as soon hold the Whore of Babylon on his lap as set in type words of such formal vice.

Ramona did not come from Babylon originally, she was born in Cleveland, Ohio. But if the doctor didn't know from the jump-off, and his driver too, what the girl *was*, then Garnet for one said she would be surprised. She did admit, however, that Ramona's refined features and the neat dark-blue coat with brass buttons they hung in the clothes-press the night she was brought in made her think "lady" when another word would have suited her better. And the same went for Ramona's daily visitors. Even smelling as suspiciously nice as they did, and the elder (her name was Mrs. Bohannon) with hair the color of a sunset, their gracious manners and the straight-backed way they sat on a chair would fool the smartest person.

Good, though, or bad was not the initial question. The question was, was Ramona going to make it? Her belly felt like hydraulic cement, her pulse was small and wiry, her fever diffused till you could feel it clear out in the hall. She would not take nourishment. Tot sent Mrs. Dooley in from the kitchen after a day or two to take a look and see what *she* would recommend. Tot meant in the line of food, but the cook said, after standing and asking a few questions, that maybe a strangulated bowel such as the doctor tagged it was pretty far from being the actual case. She was reminded, Mrs. Dooley said, of a girl back home one time that got in trouble. Somebody tried to help her, bungled the job and there she laid with fever half the summer, her heart but barely beating. Up and down, and up, then down again her fever went, and then she died.

"If Doctor says it's a strangulated bowel—" Tot began with annoyance.

"*He* might of been the one that tried to help her out! In fact I bet that's what happened. That's why he's so anxious. Tried to help and she ends up dying on him."

"Mrs. Dooley, I will pretend for your sake that you didn't say that."

"All I'm saying—"

"I can't believe my ears. Don't you know if Doctor knew you said such a thing, he could sue you and I don't know what all."

When a change took place decisive of recovery, as it did a day or two later, in the girl's condition Tot did not exactly *gloat* over Mrs. Dooley, but she came close to it. "I think you will grant," she said, "that when a fine physician diagnoses a case and prescribes a certain medicine and when that medicine *works*, that that proves he diagnosed it right?"

Mrs. Dooley looked up and, still remembering how the girl back home got better once or twice, then got worse and died, kept on stirring her cornstarch pudding and did not speak.

RAMONA RELISHED THE PUDDING. SOON she was sitting up, getting up and moving about the room wearing a house gown, walking in the hall. To Tot's relief she seemed not nearly as pretty when she was up and around as lying flat on her back, where she looked like a beautiful picture. Another thing, she was blonde, and in Salt Lake's flaxen throng a blonde did not stand out very far, and singing talents were quite prevalent. Ramona's talent along that line was a curious combination of singing and speaking such as some use who camouflage the lack of voice. But when she wanted to show it she could sing all right, from middle C to way up in the sky!

Is this Mr. Riley that keeps the hotel?
Is this Mr. Riley, can anyone tell?
Is this Mr. Riley they speak of so highly?
Upon my word, Riley,
You're doin' damn well!

Pretty soon she was dancing, which she couldn't help, pale though she was and skinnier than pump water. She'd lift her skirts, step out…Come on, I'll teach you. Don't you want to learn? This here I'm doing, it's a dance, it's called the Varsovienne. Well, *I* never could learn it. Yes, you could. Me neither. Oh, come on now, yes, you could. Look, it's easy. And it wasn't hard when a person put their mind to it. Hindle caught on quickly, Garnet learned and then one afternoon nothing would do but the *doctor* happening by must be instructed too, first with Hindle (feeling shy and strange to be as close as that to the thud of his heart), sashaying then with Garnet, then he bowed to the teacher and took her in his arms and off they went to the girls' singing and clapping, not loud, softly, and then they didn't clap but only sang, standing and watching the handy way the pair of them stepped. Tot didn't see it, not the dance itself. As she came through the door, they had made an end in a smiling whirl—Ramona's draperies still were fluttering—and Doctor was giving her a companionable hug!

Oh, instantly the venom tooth of the serpent…

But can it cause—? A *wish* cause—? Just of air? The girl got sick again. Struck down by thoughts? Not mine, oh, Lord, Tot prayed to the Most Jealous One of All, her vengefulness a heavy weight on her chest. Oh, please! Let her be singing—let her be dancing again! even with him! And then remembering from nowhere how she once with Murdock's slingshot killed—not meaning to, not for the world, she was a child then—killed—it died—an innocent—a bird—she said if God would please—she herself would nurse Ramona back to health! Stay up day and night and nurse her back—But Tot had no more than rolled up her sleeves to her task than here they came, Ramona's friends, Mrs. Bohannon and Opal. Ramona, wake up, we got to roust you out. Roust her out? The girl is burning with fever, can't you see? We got to take her—got to shake the dust—But look outside! that rain a-coming down, look at the trees a-bending in the wind. Can't you see it'll be the death of her? Not like if she stays! We got this threat, this Black Hand threat, you might say, got to go. Got to dress you, honey, hock up now. She can lay down in the Pullman car…

THE ROTTEN TRIBUNE PRINTED THE story first, and what a lie, the church officials said. The truth came out in the Deseret News, what it called truth but some called stretching it. Take this information: "The rod of Brother B. Y. Hampton, collector of licenses and pillar of our Church's firmament, has budded and brought forth buds, the buds have blossomed and the blossoms turned to almonds!" Meaning what, old socks? meaning that Brother B. Y. Hampton didn't just sit back like a lot of other people, not mentioning any names. *He* thought of a way to bring the Gentiles to heel, the ones sent out from Washington, D.C. to take over the federal offices in the territory and sit in judgment on good brothers doing their best. Such as polygamists, to take just one example. Such as Night Riders busting people's heads (that richly deserved it) with a slab of board. Such as fellows scattering around some night-soil. These were arrested whenever possible and treated like criminals by the federal men. They languished in jail. But clever Brother B. Y. Hampton knew how to turn the tables. It came to him like the vision on Cumorah to the Prophet Joseph! but he left that part of it out when he laid the scheme before the church's General Authorities. It took some mulling over in another room. The General Authorities didn't like just any lay person having visions. Then they filed out and said *we can't condone it!* while at the same time twinkling and shrugging as if to say *but you go ahead on your own, and if we don't know about it, how can we stop you?*

So Brother B. Y. Hampton went ahead. His first job was to raise the money. And them that say it come from the public treasury is bald-faced liars! for good people dug down deep for it. And even before it was all collected, Brother Hampton rented two adobes out there west of town, though some might say he seized 'em (that's what their owner said, but only in a whisper to his bedmate). Next, the furnishings. Some business firms will not act in conjunction (even when counseled), will they? and that is just too bad for them. You watch. But Dinwoodey's Furniture Store, having the sense they was born with, sent out a wagonload of goods to furnish the houses free gratis. (And Dinwoodey's will flourish through the ages.) And now we go to work and bore some peepholes, never spot 'em in a thousand years. Then bring in the whited sepulchres, the concupiscibles, in other words the girls who will work here for wages, not by the piece. They'll be paid a bounty, too, in gold. Get the so-called Governor, dearie mine, by the federal ballocks and you are set for life.

How they ply their trade we leave to them. The Madam is Mrs. Bohannon, she's the best, right from Virginia City. She calls them to the sitting room, this here's important, girls, drop what you're doing, set the iron back, wrap a towel around your wet head, listen. We got a job to do. And the first step, them that can write, write this, it goes to the different bigwigs around town:

Dear Sir if you find it convenient I would be most pleased to have you call to see me this afternoon or at about dusk this evening what I want is to see you on particular business boy will wait for answer—

That is all. Yours truly. Sign your name. Your little bogus dainty names: Francine, Pearl, Opal, Ramona, Florabel, Lovaine…

And did they come a-running like hungry hogs, all the high-and-mighty new Gentile appointees! Did they slaver! Did they act profuse! It took no time at all till Brother Hampton and his privileged helpers at the peepholes had a list of Gentile sexual crimes as long as your arm, interpretative adultery, unnatural intercourse and sodomitical acts that ought to put the doers behind bars for a hundred years, or maybe even get them shot at sunrise. And if him that pulled it off was a little proud and needed a bigger hat size, who could blame him? There was talk that Brother Hampton might be made an Apostle if there was an opening before the Resurrection.

But then the day arrived when the cases came up in the District Court and the so-called U.S. Attorney wouldn't touch them. Not with a ten-foot pole! Not when the law of these United States had been perverted and used in such a way! his honor said. If you conspire to *bring about* a crime instead of to *stop* it, he ruled, why, *you* are the mug that needs to get arrested. Cases dismissed! And so they all trooped out, deep-dyed criminals laughing fit to kill, exempt from fines or punishment! while an innocent man—Brother B. Y. Hampton—paid through the nose by being arrested, tried and sent to jail for a year to think about his smartness.

"WELL, POOR SIMP!" THE DOCTOR said, summing up these events in the hotel tap-room with his friends, including the Tribune reporter. "To think that if he could prove with his homemade bordellos that Gentile officials sent out by Washington have male appendages they will use if they get the chance in this vicinity of ours, where according to last year's census men outnumber women by three thousand—women posted like a garrison by sentries—that this will demonstrate their unfitness for holding office and show why they shouldn't have judicial authority over Mormon louts who only commit *decent* crimes like mayhem and murder! Don't it make you want to puke?"

At least the Tribune quoted Doctor as saying that, and the following night someone threw a slop-jar full of filth in through his open window. Down the street the U.S. District Attorney got the same attention and said he was appalled that *intelligent Saints* could pull a stunt like that, a phrase that made the doctor laugh, because, he told his friends a few nights later, "intelligent Saints" was an oxymoron, a contradiction in terms, like saying a "dry downpour." Then, again in the hotel tap-room, he went on to ask, is mankind a single stock with an almost infinite number of sub-varieties? Or are a limited number of fundamentally distinct types now linked together?

The population of the Saints, he said, seemed a race distinct from other species, set apart not, as they liked to think, by sanctity but by the vigorous pulse, strong calves and undimmed eye one sees in cases where the medullary rays of the cerebral substance are few and far between. In other words, where you see strong bodies and weak minds. The percentage is said to be one out of ten, *but* in crowded places of squalid and unetched character, and also out in the country where manure-heels flourish but the best elements of the population have been drained away to other localities, the number may be twenty-five out of a hundred.

Now! he said, I submit the following: A Mormon missionary whose scholastic instruction you could put in your eye sets forth from here without purse or scrip. He goes to the British Isles and Switzerland, Scandinavia and Germany. And when he gets there, who does he mix with? Dukes, the educated, the prosperous? His poverty, poor fellow, forces him to seek listeners from amongst a parcel of rabble. He begins and ends down at the bottom. And as the feebleminded nestle where he goes, to the tune of twenty-five to the hundred, and their capacity for being magnetized, measured by the ratio of the magnetization to the magnetizing force, is equal to what they haven't got, which is gray matter, why, who steps forth and offers to be saved?

"You note I use the expression 'feebleminded,'" the Tribune said the doctor said. (For the reporter was in the tap-room again that night.) "I do not say idiots, imbeciles or cretins. I do not speak of water on the brain. I do not talk about the fellows with the tiny heads. I say feebleminded, which is really a compliment. People think the mentally handicapped are essentially different from the normal. No. From the lowest to the highest degree of intelligence there is but one unbroken line. Along it stands, disposed according to rule—you observe the beehive motif around here—that aristocrat of mental defectives, the feebleminded moron. He can learn," the doctor said, "to dig, cultivate land, nail up a hutch, hitch up a horse, clean up a house, play ball, get married, have offspring and baptize by immersion. He can be taught his letters, to do small sums and talk back and forth about the weather with people he meets. Hot enough for you? Think it's going to snow? and so forth. And he can bow his head, shut his eyes and pray."

"A few have in the defective brain," the doctor went on, "a spot concentrated of high sagacity mysterious as parhelic suns. These can multiply in their heads four or six place numbers more quickly than you can do it with pencil and paper. Sometimes they get rich. *Without* the spot, however, which most of them naturally do not have, and due to the fact they relish what is wearisome by continuance, these people are wonderfully fitted for tedious, repetitious jobs such as teaching school, training as soldiers, making soldiers out of recruits, and going to church three times on Sunday. The charge upon their shield is tedium. They also serve who only stand and wait around to be elected to quorums or bring you your soup with their thumb in it."

"Whether," he said, "there's any connection between looking in this mountain fastness here, this Vatican of a town, like a gangly Missourian with a narrow chest and long, light-colored, dried-up-looking hair and little sunken pale blue eyes and the mental insufficiency it takes to get along in a theocracy that permeates and controls every circumstance of human life, no one has studied in a scientific way. Between the freckled blonde and the accommodation to a combination of iron military rule and Jesuitical penetration and perseverance…"

Doctor's craggy disquisition went intact (almost) from the tap-room to the newspaper and, on an off day, out it bloomed beneath a headline reading PROMINENT PHYSICIAN BELIEVES MORE MORMONS MORONIC. Under it some smaller lines proclaimed:

CONNECTION BETWEEN COMPLEXION AND COMA?
BLOCKHEADISM AND THE BLUE EYED!

They took the Tribune at Burdick's Institution. Mrs. Dooley wondered, was the doctor crazy? He must be, for if ever there was smartness on this earth, it was in this place and amongst this people. Look at the ditches alone! Look at the Tabernacle organ! Look at speaking in tongues and people raring up to translate! And as for blondes being Missourian, well, that just showed his ignorance, because they come from Sweden too, and all kinds of countries. And besides, all the angels and archangels are blonde with blue eyes, like we're *all* going to be when we get to heaven. *That is in the gospel.*

In love or not, Tot felt she must speak firmly to Doctor. He really shouldn't say belittling things about the church and them that can't help the way they're born. Because even dumb people can act just as nice as can be, like perfect gentlemen. Like, take Alton—

"Alton is an imbecile," Doctor said. "I wasn't talking about imbeciles. There is a scale along which—"

"I just think that when a person can't defend theirself, why, one has little to do to make fun."

Chapter Thirteen

*

"What did *you* think of it," Doctor inquired, "eh?"

Hindle looked puzzled. Then, "Oh, you mean the piece in the Tribune? Serapta read it to me and Garnet, or at least she *tried* to. Them was awfully hard words."

"Like what, for instance?"

"Well, let's see—"

"Jesuitical?"

"That wasn't in the paper."

"Yes, it was."

"Jesuitical?"

"You don't know what it means."

"No," she said.

"Come on, get in and I'll tell you." He opened the carriage door. "We're going to some warm springs in the country."

"Well, I don't know. Today's my afternoon off. I usually—what I do is go see my sister at the hotel. She's one of the laundresses—"

"The drive will do you good. And you like words. I know because one time I heard you say 'inamorata.'"

She looked at him, surprised. "I learnt that from Lisheen. It was in a recitation."

"Well, I'll contribute 'Jesuitical.' That's the adjective. The noun," he said as she got in, his driver flicked the reins and the team started up the road, hot and dusty despite the mountain water gurgling along on either side, "is 'Jesuit.' Three hundred years ago or along in there a secret society was formed to uphold the Catholic church against reforms and propagate the faith among the heathen—"

"Garnet's aunt was a Catholic," Hindle cleared her throat and contributed.

He nodded absently. "But pretty soon these buggers got so big, powerful and mean and got to perpetrating such rotten stunts on unbelievers that even their very *name* made people nervous. So that's why 'Jesuitical' to this day means hidebound, revengeful and either you do as I say or it will just be too bad for *you*."

"That takes in a lot," she said. "I'll remember it." Silently she formed the word with her lips, then added aloud, "Doctor Morgan, you know where you said that here in Salt Lake City if a person's got—They're probably dumb? Blue eyes?" She paused. "Well, mine are blue." She did not look at him.

"I know. And very pretty, too," he said.

It appeared from his remarks to Tom, his driver, when they got where they were going and looked around, that Doctor had in mind to build a resort or hospital over what he said were extinct geysers bubbling up to form on the surface pools as hot as water for tea and with medicinal features of different kinds. These pools steamed and bubbled, and Hindle's uneasiness became alarm. The ground feeling so hot proved that hell was really down there, burning. It must be! imps of Satan shoveling in the coal. Doctor took the water's temperature, 142 degrees, and told Tom that nine hundred thousand gallons a day would have to be piped through a cooling tank of some kind. The surroundings would be hard to make look nice. But the water would heal what ailed you, the doctor said on the way back to town. It beat the spas in Germany. Might be better than a gold mine.

He had been to Germany, he said. In Hamburg while he was there, a university student committed suicide by jumping into the lion's cage at the zoo and letting himself be torn to pieces. He relayed this cheerfully and then called out, "The sorrows of Werther with a vengeance, eh?" to Tom, who answered over his shoulder, "What's that, Doc?"

Austria. France. But good old America…"Look," he said after a pause, picking up what Hindle had been thinking was a mining specimen on the seat between them, a large, ugly rock of some kind that had given a lurch now and then as they rolled over the nearly non-existent road. "Sulphuret of silver."

"I thought that's what it was," she said. "I mean—some kind of a specimen."

"Want to hold it?"

"Well—"

It felt like a ball, pebbly, heavy, crusted over with blackish burnt-looking stuff, or maybe more like a large pear turned to stone.

"What do you think it is?"

"You just said. Sulphuret of silver."

"What else?"

"Well—" She fingered the two deep indentations, felt the—why, nose holes! a mouth! flat, blackish—

His hand was there to take it.

"Oh!" She shuddered.

"Don't fear that I will say it, for I won't." He held it up and looked at it. "Alas, poor son of a gun! Though of course it *could* have been a woman—a girl—a sight for sore eyes two thousand years ago."

She tried to imagine the world—if there really was one that long ago—but it was practically impossible. Like imagining two thousand years up *ahead* along the track of time, the sun really shining then, supper on the table, the stars coming out—

When they got back to town it was nearly dusk, soft rain was falling on the bigger leaves and looser blossoms than the warm day started out with. Warmer than usual for that time of year.

NEXT MORNING THE RAIN WAS really coming down, gritty with ice, the weather cold enough for fires in stoves and no Loudhawk to be found to build them. Where could he be? Every once in a while he ran off for a day or two, no one knew where. Serapta and Hindle got the fires going. Now in Serapta's room while they prepared Mavis's bath, Hindle stood holding her and looking out.

Tot came to the door. "Serapta, dear, I'd like to speak to you!"

"Hindle, you can rock her if you want, there in the chair."

But Hindle stayed where she was, watching the rain, too busy with her thoughts to change position. She was thinking of love and who she loved, Jim Clarendon, that's who, thousands of miles away, married, didn't even know her name, but ever since she saw him that first time, he was the only one she would ever want to have get down on his knees and propose to her. And not on account of him being a millionaire, either, though knowing *that* lit him up like an actor in the footlights, his eyes flashing like a signal mirror, the smooth of his hair like a dove's wings. She wouldn't care if he was as poor as Loudhawk. And in fact they said Mrs. Clarendon hadn't cared either but had married him and then he got rich himself, even richer than she was. And he stayed with her, so that proved he wasn't the kind to marry someone for their money! But what *did* he marry her for? an old woman like her, forty by now if she was a day! and maybe twenty-five or thirty when he met her. Of course she was congenial to everyone and passed out bonbons. And not stuck up…

But yet that morning as Hindle stood holding the baby and looking dreamily out at the weather, she buried congenial Mrs. Clarendon in the Atlantic. First came the croupy chest cold on her way to Europe (that was where the Tribune said the Clarendons were going when they left Salt Lake), then the "ceasing upon the midnight with no pain," to quote from a beautiful recitation that Lisheen said she had made up herself, then overboard the poor soul had to go. Such a pity. But she was old, had lived her life. They can provide coffins on a big liner and extra American flags to wrap them in. You don't get carried to the nearest shore. Over the side you go right then and there. The coffin disappears into the deep, losing its flag eventually, which billows off. Sea monsters swim up, moving their different arms. Awful toothed prodigies go past. Jim in black broadcloth, standing at the rail, buries his face in his hands, his shoulders heave, for Mrs. Clarendon was a good wife to him.

But the first ship his ship meets sailing west the sailors row him out to and he climbs aboard…And now he's walking in at the front door the way he did that first time, hobnail boots, a flannel shirt but shaven, shorn and smelling of bay rum. You used to have a young lady here, he says, by the name of Hindle. Is she still employed? Oh, indeed, they say, and call her, Hindle, come, someone's here to see you. She nearly faints when she sees who it is, the last person she ever expected to see on this earth. Why, Mr. Clarendon!

Hindle's dream did not (no more than Rome) take shape in one day, she was always adding to it. And for fits of abstract musing, nothing could beat inducing anesthesia, letting the drops fall on the wadded cheesecloth. It was not her habit, from her station up by the patient's head, to watch the feats of surgery going on but rather to keep an eye on the sleeping face of the patient, its sleep to be enhanced by one more drop, or not a drop, a particle of mist, or not enhanced, for too much chloroforming and the organic body is dead to the world. Too little, a mad yelp and maybe a foot half sawed off is planted in the doctor's face. A moth would turn the balance. But if you watch your step like walking a ridge pole and carefully, carefully…

Drop by drop…

Today the drops are dropping on Loudhawk, on his strange scarred face.

IT LOOKED AS HE WENT by with water or an armful of wood as if the right eye was missing, but that was because the bullet had plowed along his cheekbone and eyelid and cut through the muscles so the lid fell down. Now Hindle could see, when she brushed aside the blue-black horsetail of hair and pressed the cotton wad over his sharp nose and long upper lip, that under the eyelid the orb was still there. "Breathe deep, real deep," she said, dropping the formic ether as bemused as if the Indian had been one of the four beasts of heaven, each with six wings and shining eyes, for she had never been that close to him before. Doctor had wanted to operate on him for a long time, but Loudhawk declined the offer. However, even an aboriginal will grasp at life, and when they found him doubled up in agony in the root cellar and Doctor said his one chance was the knife, Loudhawk let himself be helped up the ladder and into surgery.

Well into the operation, Doctor said that once there was an author over in England by the name of Mr. Horace Walpole, and the reason he thought of him now was because he wrote a book called *The Three Princes of Serendipity*. What this book was about was three princes running around making happy and unexpected discoveries by accident. These discoveries the princes in the story called serendipities. "And I, dear ladies," he said to his assistants Tot and Hindle, "think I have made one myself this very minute."

"You don't say, Doctor," Tot said admiringly.

"Rock, it feels like, stuck in this here—tissue of the bugger's intestinum caecum," he said, "which if it don't bust and pus start spurting out in about a minute—"

"Oh, no, Doctor. You will get it out before that happens."

"Right together, damn things—" He always muttered to himself when operating, shot his cuffs and muttered, and when the worst was past would start to hum, sing a little, perhaps whistle. But today the tune was long in coming. Even the mutter stopped for long minutes while the clock ticked—Then it was out! a thing like a worm, heavy with pus, angry—How he did it was a mystery to her, Tot said, a thing just ready to pop like that and be so clever as not to pop it! But that was just half the story. Now for the serendipity part, Loudhawk's bullet. It had to be that, the doctor said, from his old war. Didn't the bugger say he was in a war? Wasn't he shot one time?

Hindle began to be alarmed, Loudhawk looked so dark, so wooden, his breathing was so faint. She put the chloroform bottle down.

"Got it!"

But Doctor hadn't. It slipped away. "Keep him under, Hindle. Just where you got him."

"But, Doctor—" Should she fan him? Get a cold wet cloth?

"Keep him under."

Hindle let fall a tiny drop and waited. What could she think of? What? My wedding dress. White satin edged with swansdown. My bridegroom... Mrs. Bearpark used to say that in Kentucky the word they used was honey*month*, not honey*moon*, because the honeymoon was supposed to last till the moon came round to where it was on the wedding day. You should be traveling to some fine place as you got used to each other, Mrs. Bearpark said. Then you come home and the bridegroom picks you up and carries you over the doorstep. I wonder why that is? She seemed to wake from a dream to hear Tot say, "Doctor, did you ever hear of such a thing as this? I heard of a woman one time that sewing machine needle run in her thumb and broke off and got lost and twenty years later *it come out through her foot*. The reason I think of it, would it be possible that a *bullet* like you're looking for in poor Loudhawk here—"

"What?" Doctor said crossly.

"—could do that?"

"Do what? Damn it!" It had slipped away again.

Tot told him.

He did not answer.

Drop by drop... She thought Loudhawk was dead. He was a baby once. The thought came suddenly, made her feel regretful.

Minutes later, "Hindle."

"Yes, sir. Doctor."

"Steady as she goes. We'll find it, won't we? This young lady here has got the makings—" But whatever he was going to say he never said, for he interrupted himself with, "The devilishness of the inanimate! Now wait a minute—just a little minute here— If you young creatures," his smile broke by degrees, "will hold your breath a minute, I think we can—Yes, we can and do!" He looked at Hindle only to whirl and say, "Miss Tot, may I present?" making as if to toss the bloody projectile. He was just fooling, though, it was a feint to see her dodge back screaming but half laughing.

"STAY WITH HIM, HINDLE. DON'T want him throwing up his heels if we can help it."

They couldn't prevent it, but later on when Doctor looked in, the Indian quietly slumbered. Hindle, still wrapped in her dream, was by now the mother of children running around green lawns, the owner of a mansion, had a winter garden, she had a school diploma, it was framed. She played the pianoforte, a great square one, carved, with painted pictures on the sides highlighted with gold. And when she played she took off all her rings and bracelets and laid them on a tray...

"What's the good word, Loudhawk?" the doctor said, bending over his patient. When he raised up he said, "Hindle?"

"Yes, sir."

"I presume you walk out?"

"Walk out?"

"I ask because I shouldn't if I were you," he said, "within the moment. That chloroform on your breath," he put his face playfully close to hers, "you'd have your sweetheart walking along beside you unconscious."

"Oh," she said dreamily, "I didn't know what you meant."

Again he bent back over the sleeper. "Loudhawk, come on back. The sleeping zephyrs wake and so must we."

An eyelid fluttered, lifted, dropped again over an eye like dusty brown glass.

"The sleeping zephyrs—Here, we saved it for you, son. Here's your bullet, Loudhawk, from your war, your famous victory, wherever that might have been."

The eyelid fluttered again, the eye glinted.

"How is he feeling, poor thing?" Tot said from the doorway.

"Like run through with a javelin in Gath."

"Oh, Doctor," Tot said, "what would this world do without you?"

IT ALMOST GOT A CHANCE to find out. He certainly looked like death warmed over when they carried him in, his driver Tom and a man from the hotel. Tot stood with a shawl over her nightgown holding the lamp, and if it had been *her* head busted in like that and *her* blood streaming, she couldn't have exhibited greater trouble. "Oh, dear Doctor Morgan!"

"Where shall we put him, ma'am?"

"A doctor's been sent for," Tom said.

"A *doctor's* been sent for? Oh! I see." It was hard for Tot to see, though. As if there was but one doctor in the universe.

"They laid for him," the man said. "Had it all planned."

"I seen the sonsabitches," Tom said, "flying in every direction."

"He yelled and we run out—"

"And there he was a-laying in the road."

Serapta caught the last remark as she hurried in and, seeing Tom, thought he was bringing the doctor in dead drunk, though such a thing had never happened before. Then she saw the blood, the wounds. "Oh, heavenly days, what's this?"

What it was, was the doctor bashed and battered by his enemies. Probably come and rapped on his window, Tom surmised, knowing how quick he would get up and dress to go and help somebody hurt or choking or on their deathbed, anyone in need. And outside in the dark these snakes in the grass was waiting—

"Yes, I know, but why, Tom? Why?"

THAT ONE WAS EASY, ANSWERED by the Deseret News next day and later in the week by Zion's Watchman, which said about the same thing only in Swedish. Because Dr. Jefferson Morgan was one of the blackest-hearted villains ever to step foot in Zion, that was why. In his medical office and also no doubt in his infamous private quarters at the Salt Lake House, he performed evil and injurious operations on women, operations forbidden by statute and injurious to the public welfare. He frequented disreputable houses. He defamed with slander the one true church on earth and disseminated false and malicious statements regarding the mental accountability of its members. He took morphia in large quantities, which was a well-known fact. He drank and gambled. But that was not the worst of it. He was also scheming to take possession of the Warm Springs and build a health resort and hospital out there to profit by what rightfully belonged to the Church of Jesus Christ of Latter-day Saints, whose members had settled the country in the first place and ought to own it lock, stock and barrel.

The Salt Lake Tribune told a different story! Dr. Morgan, it said, eminent local surgeon and humanitarian who went to excess in his humane principles, had formed the idea of building (in partnership with a recently discharged Army doctor from Camp Douglas) a health resort in the vicinity of the Warm Springs to the north of the city, on unoccupied land situated a considerable distance from any habitation. No obstacle being found to prevent the two doctors going ahead, they had had constructed on the property a small workshop which was to be used to erect subsequent buildings. No sooner was this workshop built, however, than a squad from the Salt Lake Police Department, acting under orders from the Marshal, tore it down. Dr. Morgan and his partner then sued the city. The city council recommended that the city file a counter-suit claiming the men were trespassers on the city's land surrounding the city's spring. When the case came to court, the Federal Justice, a widowed Gentile from Virginia—said to be intending to embrace the church of a certain Apostle's daughter (prerequisite to embraces of a different kind)—handed down a verdict against the two doctors. Their lives then being threatened, Dr. Morgan's partner packed up and left town. "Dr. Morgan, however, stating that 'there is no terror, Cassius, in your threats,' plans to hold his ground and build his spa," the Tribune said.

Now he lay at death's door with a fractured skull. That diagnosis had been the allo-pathic physician's. He took his coat off and rolled up his sleeves, ready to bore a hole in Doctor's brain pan to relieve the pressure. Tot threw herself across his body. "No!" But two days went by, two nights, of unnatural heavy sleep and slow, stertorous breathing, and by the third day Tot was about ready to send for Dr. Huber and let him bore his hole. But as she stood looking down at her beloved, all of a sudden he woke up and smiled.

Three or four days later, with two black eyes beginning to turn sea-green and a large bruise over his right eyebrow, a cut lip and a few other marks upon him, he was able to get up and go back to the hotel. "'The mind I sway by, and the heart I bear, shall never sag with doubt, nor shake with fear,'" he told his reporter friend.

Another cowardly assault, however, a few more declarations of hostile intent, another slop-jar full of filth hurled in through his window, and the brave man tossed in the sponge. Doctor left town in the middle of the night, driving his own carriage.

He did not leave alone.

Tot had been jealous of Paulina, Lisheen, Mrs. Clarendon, Ramona, and even at one time her own sister.

Everybody but the right one!

Chapter Fourteen

✳

TEN YEARS LATER WHEN HINDLE MORGAN SET OUT FOR HOME WITH HER TWO little girls, she was a twenty-four-year-old widow in mourning weeds, new ones, or almost. Doctor (she called him Doctor to the last) had met his end in the call of duty some two months before while riding to a sickbed in a rancher's wagon. One of its wheels had hit a bunch of salt grass. It lurched and threw him out. That scared the mules into a plunge that caused a rear wheel to roll over him, crushing his skull and killing him instantly. He never knew a thing about it, the rancher said, it happened so fast. Hindle hoped it was true, that he never knew.

They were living in Prescott, Arizona, when it happened. But that was as temporary as every other place they lived had been, as far south as Mexico. Hindle was still destitute of book learning. The way Doctor kept telling her she was smart and should be educated, she somehow imagined that if she went away with him he would be educating her himself in the years to come, giving her long words to spell, having her commit famous recitations to memory, teaching her decimals and geography. And such might well have been his intention. But if so he soon forgot about it, and in any case kept her so busy taking care of him and helping in the "store," as he called his practice—and moving—that even before Eula and Esther were born somewhat surprisingly in the last four years of their marriage, she would not have had the time.

Sometimes she would like a town, she liked Virginia City, Montana, but after a while he would think he had exhausted every possibility of making a strike in the surrounding country (for between doctoring and conducting research in the various local drinking palaces, he had become a prospector again) and would want to move on. Once in Orient they bought a small place and in Sutro were fixing to build, but signs like these of settling down, as he had seemed to do in the Salt Lake years, proved deceptive, and more than once Hindle wondered if those Night Riders or whoever they were had not done worse to Doctor's skull when they fractured it than anyone knew. She was sure some people at home thought *her* brain was affected. Oh, dear sister, Lucitie wrote in a letter Hindle got six months after she left with him, I wonder if you have not made a most grievous mistake you only fourteen and him as old as the hills and gray-haired wasn't there no one else you could of loved?

TO BE SURE THERE WAS, enshrined in memory, perfected in dream. Partly the old dream, partly new. Jim Clarendon still came back to Burdick's Institution, still inquired after Hindle Lee. But now she was gone. Gone where? he said, staggering back, his hand upon his heart. God knows, they told him as he turned away to hide his tears. Hindle before this scene was like the dead that they say comes and tries to speak and touch the living but can't be heard or felt. The dream would ebb away there. But the night she and Doctor went to Page's Opera House for the lantern slides on Egypt and the Holy Land and she heard about anchorites going off by themselves into the desert for twenty years and coming back wise men "with wisdom to accomplish any end," she knew how the dream should turn out. Like the anchorites, *she* would come back from her wanderings full of wisdom. And the ends she would accomplish were, Doctor would leave her for someone else who would take care of him, and when Jim Clarendon came to the Institution, this time they would know where she was and tell him, and he would go there, but when she stepped out to see who was asking for her she would be so beautiful he would think he had made a mistake and turn to go, in love on the instant with this new girl but not wanting to forsake the one named Hindle that he had loved so long, but she would call out softly and he would turn in amazement …

"The Holy Land and that old Utah Valley," Doctor said as they strolled back to their hotel after the lecture, "as like as two peas, aren't they? Mountains, plains, a salt sea dead as a mackerel, a Jordan River—no wonder it attracted the lunatic lost tribe of Urim and Thummim!" That was what he always called the Mormons. "I was in the Holy Land myself one time, you know, my love. Rode on a camel. I'm sure I must have told you."

"Those anchorites he told about that got so wise—"

"Wise!" he laughed. "Well, I guess they are. They never work. But some of them *do* pick up an odd thing or two, I have to admit, charming, and stunts like that—"

"Charming?"

"You've heard of snake charming. Well, these buggers charm *people*. Look at somebody hard and down he goes. Prolonged suspension of consciousness and inertness to stimulus. And don't I wish I had one of the filthy old beggars with me tomorrow!" At the tooth-pulling bee, he meant, when a tablespoon of tincture of opium on top of whiskey did not always bring about enough "inertness" in a rambunctious cowboy to keep him from jumping up and punching or choking his tormentor. As Doctor would be rendered nearly as insensible by drink and so forth as his patients during these affairs (the "bees" often imposed as a kind of moral duty on a dentist or medical man passing through cattle country), he would sustain the siege. But settled in practice, he said he would as soon perform an orchotomy on a Sydney Duck as pull a tooth.

However, he could be inveigled, and one day when a swollen-faced young stranger rode in from the claim he and his brother were working in the canyons and begged relief from toothache, Doctor extracted a bicuspid and for good measure a large true molar. Unfortunately, due to the young man's jerking his head to one side at an auspicious moment, his superior maxillary also got broken, and with a surreptitious glance Doctor measured the distance to the shelf where a pistol lay hidden behind some medical books. But some men are gentlemen, some are wild hyenas, and this patient was a gentleman. As well as he could through a muzzle of sticking plaster, he apologized for jerking his head, paid a gold nugget and, in vacuo with laudanum, took his leave. A veritable parfit gentle knight, Doctor said.

Doctor was out prospecting the day the young man's wild hyena brother came in to kill him. "He'll never bust nobody *else*'s jaw, I can promise you that," the boy said, "to lay and suffer worse'n Christ on the cross for nineteen days before the end! Nineteen *days*."

"Oh, do you mean to say your brother *died*?" Hindle began to cry. The baby, Eula, her firstborn, then seven months old, smiled. Bouncing and straining in her mother's arms, she crooned at the stranger and would have gone to him. Was it her that saved the day? Was it because the boy rightly saw Hindle's tears as falling not out of fright but pity? Whatever the reason, he stood uncertainly awhile, then put his gun back in its holster and walked out, at which moment Hindle, galvanized, shifted Eula to her other side, hurried and found the gold nugget and ran out after him. "Wait, please wait!" He was on his horse. "You got to take this! It's from your and your brother's mine. What your poor brother paid. I promise it won't bring you no bad luck."

He shook his head. "Save it for him," he said, looking at Eula with the idea she was a boy. "Buy him a forty-four for later on to plug his pa with." He didn't look mean, though saying a mean thing like that, but with an expression half like he was going to smile and half cry was the picture of a parfit gentle knight himself, as his brother had been, or whatever Doctor had said. And before he rode out of sight he turned and waved. Back inside the house Hindle shook like a leaf (and then the baby *did* cry), but though scared at what could have happened if Doctor had been home, she never was as scared as she might have been if she hadn't had the experience of being in the process of taking (a few years before this) Heffernan's hat and coat just as the Vigilantes came in Doctor's treatment room, rushed the man out in his shirtsleeves, and hung him, and hadn't ridden in a stagecoach one time with Whiskey Bill Pizanthia. Heffernan and Bill were real murderers. She remembered their eyes, and there was no comparison. In short, she had a way to judge! and from the curricula of her years of errantry with Doctor had more of an education than she gave herself credit for.

Not that it always showed. The apothecary could not believe, he said, that anyone with a brain in their head would stand there and not take twenty dollars for Doc's old instruments and that old battered skull. And if she wanted Doc's diploma so bad, have sense enough at least, her next-door neighbor said, to take it out of the frame and leave the frame behind! But no, that gold frame had to go too on her long trip home. A trip that if she took it by herself, all them miles a-winding to Salt Lake City with two young ones, driving that old bay, why, all he could say, the farmer said, delivering her the eggs for the last time, was, she was very foolish. Why not go and catch the train in Yuma?

She had a good reason for what she was going to do. The train would go too fast, but she didn't say so. Or that for miles and days she just wanted to think. Or that—but this she did not know herself—some dim tenet in the vast profound of ancestry was at work making her want to travel up through *Papa's* country, his country when he was a living man.

A WAKE IS WHEN YOU sit up with the dead, but her wake for her father she had held before he was even dead, on his one night left on earth, a night she watched through lonesomely for no good reason except it seemed like something a daughter should do. And she was at the window looking out when the darkness grayed and daylight opened like a stage-lit scene she imagined him walking onto, courtesy of kings, a punctual spot, a punctual relation of all the circumstances. Now there is a hole that's shaped like him in the air a moment, then it knits. But in the world a blank space that was left for special instructions would never be filled in. And Hindle went about that day like one on a new factory job who has no idea what the machinery's doing all around her. The dead cooling one degree an hour! The mystery of why they stiffen as if in fright, go stiff as a board and stay that way a day, then soften like they realize death's not so bad after all, nothing to be afraid of, they can relax. Why do they do that? When Doctor came home that night, she asked him if he didn't say one time that a corpse cools one degree an hour?

He nodded absently and handed her the paper. "Might as well read it, know the worst, I guess. As the old saying goes."

"There wasn't no reprieve?"

"Who expected one? Not him, I bet. Not with those crooks working in Salt Lake to see he played it to the bitter end, the old Mosaic performance of the scapegoat."

She read awhile and then looked up to say, "It says here it was snowing on the mountain."

"I know, I read it." He'd stirred up a toddy, took a sip.

"Well, don't that change things? What I mean to say, a person dead that's cooling where it's cold, and one that's cooling on a real warm day, they wouldn't both of them cool off the same. Would they? Anyway, it says my father took off his hat and coat—"

"I see what you're getting at. No, it's the same, my dear. One degree an hour. Thermolytic action." He took another sip.

"And the rest would happen too? It says the boys—that must mean his own boys, which would be my—" She broke off, then said, "They was there from Panguitch to take him home."

"The rest of what?"

"Why, of what *happens*. Post-mortem—what you said—"

"Rigidity?"

"And then when they go soft. And all I want to know is, from the Mountain Meadow to where they'll bury him in Panguitch is—they don't say how far—but what way would you think he'll be when he gets there?"

"Well," he said, "let's see. Over a hundred miles? I'd say—Of course you understand that certain conditions—" He took another sip. "Why do you want to know that, honeybunch?"

She didn't know, only it seemed important to go through the different stages of his transientness, like doing some last thing for him like a daughter should.

UNTIL THE OFFICERS CAPTURED HIM some three years before the final outcome, and the papers made so much of it and of his trials, the fact that John D. Lee was Doctor's natural father-in-law had not been known to him, and when Hindle drew aside the veil he was greatly surprised, not so much that her father was who he turned out to be as that she *had* a particular father and hadn't "jest grew," like Topsy in *Uncle Tom's Cabin*, or the spirit rising up from Aladdin's lamp. When he thought of Hindle, which he did about as often as he thought of his left elbow, she seemed to have been put—a stray from the lost lunatic tribe of Urim and Thummim—in his path by fate to solace his years when "dim Eclipse disastrous twilight sheds." Thus did he view the situation of their being together. Her having a father he passed by as altogether trivial. But as the notoriety of the man gradually built up, Doctor permitted himself to be drawn away enough from serious occupations to seek a little information about this strenuous connection.

Hindle being only five, however, when she last saw her father some eighteen years before this, she couldn't remember much. "He brought us a sack of flour." Perhaps from his own mill, she wasn't sure. "Molasses candy." Now it came to her for the first time that the candy had to have been *made* by someone and she wondered which wife, which daughter. Did they know where it was going? "He'd always have a riddle to spring on us." Sometimes he had sprung it on them before, because with so many children—more than fifty, the paper said—he didn't always remember who had already heard it. Then she and Lucitie would know the answer and feel like they had put one over on *him*. But even knowing his tongue-twisters beforehand didn't give them any advantage, because he could say them so much faster. Still, they would try to beat him, and fall on the floor laughing. Then Mama would say they had better stop or next thing they knew they'd be crying. If it was bedtime he would hear their prayers, and then if they'd shut their eyes he would sing a song—

"How many times did you see him?"

"In my life? Six times, maybe seven. One of the songs he'd sing was—let me see now—'Oh, My Pretty Quadroon.'" Another time, driving through the empty land at dusk towards Durango, she thought of another. She didn't know the verse, but the chorus went,

O'Brien? McFadden? or Bates?
Now what is your name?
And what is your game?
And oh what was your name in the States?

Doctor chuckled. "There's Eastern tenderfoot written all over *that* for sure!"

"Why do you say that?" she said defensively.

"Why, because in my day, in these parts a good excuse for shooting a man would be for him to ask a question. 'What is your name?' 'What is your *game*?'" He laughed again. "Bang! right through the brisket! And the bartender would testify the fellow had it coming."

"My father wouldn't step foot in a saloon."

"I well believe it. Your father's a tenderfoot, that has been his downfall. Thirty years in the West and it never penetrated. Like coolie labor."

"What do you mean by that?"

"I mean coolie labor and Mormons, they're just alike. Stick together, talk their own lingo. The coolies smoke their poppy juice in dim, dark caves. All the Mormons need to do for it to work the same is read their scriptures. Six of one and half a dozen of the other. They bow down, they're natural slaves, the both of them. Is that the *West*? Girl, the West's not *in* a man not free."

"What do you mean, bow down?" She knew, though, and smarted for her kinfolk and for herself too.

"But getting back to your song. Not only wouldn't a true Westerner *ask* you your name, he'd be downright disappointed if you *told* him. Because one of the privileges out here used to be to size up a stranger and *give* him a name! 'Skillet'—'Boston'—'Ichabod Crane'—whatever seemed the most appropriate. Unless of course he was dead by then from asking foolish questions!"

FOOLISH QUESTIONS! RIDDLE ME THIS, my child. Riddlemeree! How many shoestrings does it take to fatten a lamppost? Theophilus Thiscus the great thistle sifter in sifting thistles thrust three thousand thistles through the thick of his thumb! She watched the words come out, put her baby hand to his mouth and—snap! he had her fingers and she laughed hysterically, and he bit down but it didn't hurt, it felt like plush.

Because of years since the commission of the crime, and also considering his age, we the undersigned think the death sentence of John D. Lee should be commuted. Different circumstances prevailing then, such as a war about to take place between the U. S. Army and the rightful settlers of the Territory of Utah, when the ill-fated wagon train came through accompanied by numerous armed horsemen, our defensive forces identified them as mounted troops infiltrating the region...

Five hundred friends and neighbors of the man under sentence of death signed the petition to the Governor, but it did no good. Neither did the Gentile newspapers beginning to try to mitigate the hard features of his case. If John D. Lee deserved to die, they said, then so did fifty other Mormon militiamen who took part in the massacre but were walking around scot-free. And while he was in prison and during his trials, the pieces they printed about him showed his touches of human nature, such as how he knew all his children's names, and the dates of his fourteen wedding anniversaries. Some of these would no longer be celebrated, as after the church threw him to the wolves, more than half his wives left him flat. Those who did not—Rachel near Beaver, Caroline and family in Panguitch, Lavina in Skutumpah, Polly in Skutumpah, and Emma and family who hid out with him at Lonely Dell in the Colorado River valley—were written up as true blue.

His lineaments as the months of his capture, imprisonment and trials went on became in the papers more and more heroic, so that by the time of his being shot at sunrise on the Mountain Meadow, the scene of the old massacre, it was as if he'd "fought at Thebes and Ilium," Doctor said, bemused. The newspaper account he brought home was almost epical, an epic treatment of the condemned man's last hours, from midnight when his military escort took him from the town of Beaver to the place where, without a coat, in first light in the falling snow, he faced the firing squad and said, "Center my heart, boys. Don't mangle my body." The reason for that request, the Fairplay Flume said, was the wish to have his earthly habitation in good shape for the Resurrection, and with perfect bull's-eyes the three young sharpshooters obliged. Fifty-one was the number of children known to be left fatherless by his death, the oldest aged forty-four, a bearded grandfather, and the youngest a dimpled lass of three, though there may have been more.

Hindle read the account once and then, after the house was quiet and Doctor had gone to bed, began as though duty-bound to read it through again. Not having slept the night before, however, it was hard to keep awake, harder to keep bringing this progenitor into relation to herself, and by the time she got drowsily to the statistic of the fifty-one children, amongst whom she did not know if she and Lucitie had even been counted, John Doyle Lee's semblance as author of her being vapored into tiny specks. But then, remembering as in a dream what Doctor said one time about the male sex being constituted so if the layout was right a man could fire off two million four hundred thousand three hundred and seventy-nine pregnancies in a single lifetime, Papa went back together. Because when you got up into the millions like that, then fifty-one was almost laughable. Anyway (the paper drifted from her hand onto the floor) the thing that counts is him a-starting *you*. Don't you know it? Giving *you* a chance at baggy old life, at the old world's riddle. Now say it fast, old socks, three long slim slick sycamore saplings! She heard him, saw him, sat up cold and lonesome (while the shrill child doubled over laughing). Three long slim slick—Oh, Papa, you sleep tight now in the Celestial, and—don't let the bedbugs bite.

Chapter Fifteen

*

"My own Sancho Panza," Doctor used to say, "what would I do without you?" He called her different strange names like that, having been to Europe in his young days, Figaro, Leporello—people didn't know what he was talking about half the time. "What would I do without you?" And so she learned to handle the buckboard, harness up, care for the team and the stock he was sometimes paid with, how to start a fire and be, as he used to express it, his "fac-totum pole." The thought of driving to Salt Lake by herself seemed of little moment. He always said that in the West a *good* woman could go anywhere as safe as houses, while if she was something else it was fair field and no favors. Hindle was a good woman with a good woman's reputation, for several reasons besides moral excellence, one being that she started out somewhat plain and had throughout the years with Doctor of toil, wind and weather grown more so, her plainness become almost ill-favored by the austere and almost merciless expression she sometimes assumed in the presence of menfolk after Doctor told her nobody could tell in the early stages which fellows might be crawling with Treponema pallidum, Spirochaeta pallida!

He set this forth in detail, showing her in his medical books how horrible the germs, too small to be seen with the naked eye, looked when drawn as big as a Java sparrow. "Take this cowboy the Indians call 'Pretty Shadow' because on horseback he's such a sight for sore eyes. Or at the dance this regular Prince Charming. Or here's this banker in his broadcloth and diamond stickpin. To see them a woman might think, why, here's a prize! But what they are is walking ptomaine. It goes by stages. Ulcer. Then the suppuration of the mucous membrane. Skin eruptions, little knobs and pustules, desquamation, nasti-ness—might be mistook for Lepra cutanea or Elephantiasis Graecorum. But then the devil comes upon the scene and goes to work and cures it! The reason I say the devil is because it's all just an illusion. The cure's no cure. All the disease has done is go lie doggo, hibernate, which it may do for years. In fact if the fellow that's got it dies or gets killed at a fairly early age, he might suppose that the cure really 'took,' which it never did. But if he lives, watch out! The day will come when it will bust forth again meaner'n a wild pig! savaging the eyes, the brain, the parts, the liver, the periosteum—"

"You're talking about this germ," Hindle said. It did look very mean in the picture, like a porcupine about to shoot its quills in every direction.

"I'm talking morbid principles and pure destruction. I'm talking death and dying choked on pus. The Trappists say 'Memento mori,' remember death. *I* say—when Pretty

Shadow passes by, or Mister Fine Prince Charming wants to waltz, or the banker smiles and lifts his hat—'Memento Treponema pallidum, Spirochaeta pallida!" (In other words, I'm talking *stay with me*. I'm talking *do not leave me for anyone else, ever*. I'm saying *my old heart would break, Cordelia*.)

His lesson sank in, menfolk were to Hindle coffins, 'scutcheons, death's-heads and crossbones, and for a long time after he died she went muffled when in their company, in aloofness like an Indian woman in a blanket.

THERE WAS A TIME WHEN Doctor talked of going home to Salt Lake and suing to get his Warm Springs spa back. He thought he had a chance with the new people who must have come in up there in the meanwhile. So much had changed! Nebraska Territory, Dakota Territory, these had disappeared and in their place stood Idaho, Wyoming and Arizona. Old roads faded out, new ones went north and south and every which way. As well to pathless places though! as towns, so maps were requisite, and Doctor had one drawn for him by a freighter. The freighter was in bed at the time in the boarding house across the street, sick but getting better. He made a splendid map, shading it, using two colors of ink, lettering it floridly. Had they made the trip back up to Salt Lake that Doctor talked of, it would have come in handy, but they never did.

Hindle had forgotten they had it till she was packing up to leave and found it on a shelf, unrolled it and was struck by how pretty it was. Took hours and hours of the freighter's life, the *last* of what the poor man had left. She remembered him dying of kidney failure soon after he finished it (or dying of the Chenopodium Bonus Henricus and mercurous chloride Doctor sent her over with, to be taken morning and night), remembered how pitifully much he was like a horse or mule in a state of terror. They don't plunge and rear when they get *really* afraid, say of thunder and lightning and the wind howling. What they do is plant their feet, hang down their heads and stand like statues made of stone till the worst is over. And that was the freighter at the last.

Did Doctor thank him for the map? Hindle hoped he did, for it was a fine job, at least as to looks and (because he had traveled all over the country) as to accuracy too, she trusted. What a deep-reaching thing a map was, everything spread out like you were a bird flying over and could see the whole land at once. Even its history if you knew it, if anything had ever happened in a lot of the open country Hindle was passing through. Nothing seemed to have (happened), at least to the naked eye, even in the towns she was ready for because of their printed names and the unmentioned ones appearing like strangers out of nowhere, except that a wide place in the road called Amity had quite a sizable, new-looking graveyard on the side of a hill, so they might have had an epidemic.

"Look, I am here," she told herself, keeping track every day and hour, recognizing St. George when she came to it not only because of pinpointing it so long but because of its being the start of Papa's meridian, the papers said one of his families lived there.

Disposed to be friendly, thinking it would be nice to meet a half-brother or half-sister, she looked for a woman to ask if she knew anything about the Lees. But only one woman was to be seen, sweeping with a broom the hard bare ground around her tiny dwelling as if it had been a floor. When Hindle drew rein, though the woman saw her she darted into the house and shut the door. Sighing, Hindle drove on down the road till she came to a large but ramshackle old dwelling with a sign saying General Store flapping in the breeze. She stopped, reached back to pull a shawl up over her napping daughters, then got down out of the buggy and went in.

"Well, sis, and what can we do for you?" a man said, coming forward from the shadows behind the counter.

She asked for what she wanted, but though his eyes were fixed upon her, she had the feeling he hardly heard her.

"You don't live around here," he said.

"No," she said. "I come from Prescott."

"How's that? You going somewheres?"

Thinking of what Doctor said about real Westerners and of how bang! right through the brisket! might be some people's answer to the man's question, she cleared her throat and said, "Yes, sir. Salt Lake City."

"Don't say," he said. He looked her up and down. "Member, are you?"

"Of the church? Well, I—was born in it. Quite a while ago."

"Oh, not too long," he said. "From the looks of you. Married woman, are you? Living the Principle?"

"No," she said, startled. "My husband—passed on last month—in an unfortunate—"

"You don't look to *me* like a widow."

"Well—I am—" They stood silent a moment, then she ventured again to ask for what she wanted.

If he heard her, he made no sign. "Maybe," he said, rubbing his chin, "you got some proof?"

"Of what?" she said.

"Anyone can say they belong to the church!" he said.

"I don't know why they'd want to do that if they didn't."

"In this neck of the woods? Different reasons. You got a Temple recommend?"

"Well, no," she said, starting to feel somewhat strained. "Because we was gone so long—and never took our endowments—like I suppose people—sooner or later—"

"Maybe that was meant to be," he said, then added, "Tithing receipt?"

Like a traveler without papers at a hostile border, she began to look about with some apprehension.

"Most everyone gets their Patriarchal Blessing," he prodded her.

"Well—we had a trunk burn up in Alamogordo," she said.

"Their receipt when they get baptized?"

"My sister's got ours. We wasn't really settled like we'd like to of been."

He stared at her. "Of course you heard tell of what happened around here a couple of months back?"

"Why, no," she said. "What happened?"

"Damnedest—Shoulder to shoulder. Soldiers, newspaper writers—There was a public execution out onto the Meadow."

"Oh?" she said, keeping her voice steady.

"You mean to say you never heard of it? Why, it was wrote up clear over the *ocean*! Where was you in the meanwhile? Trapped in a cave? Them newspaper writers swarmed in here like rats. We never let 'em stay in none of the houses, they camped in the open country. Which the soldiers would of anyway. But I—tell—*you*. It was something. Stayed around more'n a week. Who'd of ever thought? *He* never, I'm sure of that, piling up his worldly goods. But that man done more harm to our total numbers in twenty years than Satan could of done in a hundred!"

"Who was that?" she said nervously.

"Why, John Doyle Lee, that's who. The one I'm telling you about. The puke they stood up and shot. A Judas if there ever was one. But shot for the wrong crime, the so-called massacre. That wasn't no massacre. Well, technically maybe it was, because the Indians done it. But otherwise—No, what he owed retribution for was drawing attention, blabbing to the Gentiles, raising a stink. It would of all been laid to rest a long time ago if it wasn't for him. Would you believe there was a *woman* amongst them newspaper writers? Come into my place here. *I* wouldn't sell her nothing. Regular morphodite. They come from all over 'cause they had the soldiers to protect them, but the minute them army mules was loaded, off they flew. Good business, though," he added as if to himself, jingling some coins in his pockets. "They got no bargains in St. George." For the first time he smiled. "You in a big hurry to get up north?"

"Quite a big hurry," she said. "It's been a while since I seen my sister Lucitie and we never know—what might of—"

"Lucitie? Married into the Eldridges?"

"Not that I ever heard. But we haven't been in real close touch. Where she worked was at the Salt Lake House, so that's where I'll go first—"

"I know that place first-hand. Et my wedding supper there one time. Real good, too. Listen. You got young ones?"

"Yes, two. They're in the wagon taking a nap." She looked around at the door, then back at him. "And I better—We got to get going."

"Sure you're not a-heading for a sweetheart?"

"No," she said, near to tears. "Just heading home."

"Don't get upset, sis. I only meant—You ain't too hard to look at."

"Do you carry raisins?" she said. "And I need darning needles. And a pound of—"

"This here is country," he said, "that a woman traipsing around alone—I wouldn't be too cocky if I was you. Out here in the desolation—" He broke off, sizing her up again. "You could scream your head off and who would hear you? Mountain lion, maybe. Wolf." He laughed.

"Sir—" she said.

"I'd like to ask you something if you will be so kind as to answer. Are you for the Principle or ain't you? You say you wasn't living it."

"We wasn't, the circumstances being such—"

"Well, listen," he said. "You got time to make up for past foolishness. In the world to come do you want to be a handmaiden at everyone's beck and call? Or is a queen in a crown more to your liking? Give it a little thought." He scratched his head as though to show he was thinking, too. "Did I mention? I'm coming up to town myself. For Conference in October. They'll be yelling to come along," he glanced down the large bare room at a partly opened door through which Hindle caught a glimpse of several women and children moving about and lowered his voice, "but let 'em yell. I'll have other business—better things to do. You know what I mean. Where can you and me meet up for a little conference of our own?"

She gave him a blank look.

"You'll be with your sister," he prompted her.

"Well, I will if I find her—if she's still where she was. But as I say—"

"No matter. I'll run her to ground. And I'll find *you*," he said. "I guess you know why. Because this here's one of them rare occasions when the two halves of a whole that was tore asunder when the morning stars sung together is inching together again." Briskly he assembled what she had asked for and figured what she owed. As she gave him the money he bent forward and, speaking in a whisper, said quickly, "You wasn't no stranger to *me* coming in that door there. And I bet I wasn't no stranger to you. I bet you looked at me and remembered the start of time when we was clapped together so tight it was like we was *welded*. So now, sis, tell me, what's your earthly name?"

"My earthly name?"

"Got to have something to go by."

"Violet. May," she said. "Thurston."

"Pleased to meet you, Violet May. As to me—Bishop Dugger. Verlie. So now listen, darling. Get a-going. Keep the pace. Don't be asking questions, people's leery. Don't be gawking, that don't set too well. Nothing to see but what you been a-seeing. Mountains, desert. And when you lay out at night, one eye open ain't a bad idea. For you could holler your head off and no one would hear…"

That night and for several nights thereafter she made sure the six-chambered revolver was close at hand when she went to bed. And kept watch in the daytime, all the closer after looking up and seeing a tiny doll of a man high above her riding along the edges of the cliffs, looking down. One minute plain to be seen, next minute gone. The thought of the man in the store haunted her, his skinned-looking hands, stiff hair with comb marks showing, pebble-colored eyes, his coated tongue that flicked out now and then at spittle like frog's spawn in stagnant pools gathered at the corners of his thick, dry, freckled lips. *Lascivious* written all over him.

The first time Hindle heard that word (or its approximation) bandied was by a chambermaid named Midge in the Hotel Enterprise in Virginia City doing up the room while Hindle brushed her coat and skirt, and Doctor was out seeing the town. As it was Sunday, and religion and church apt subjects for small talk, Midge told Hindle she was born a Mormon but apostatized because at the very moment her little brother Glen was being born dead, her father was marrying a lady that could play the violin. So when her mother pulled through and was on her feet again, Midge left. If *Ma* didn't have the sense she was born with, Midge said, *she* did. And from then on, being a person that didn't like to just sit around, she had run into enough eventualities and chances to size things up, so at least she wasn't a dummy. She had learned to draw conclusions! she said, and one was that while Gentiles were smarter, a Mormon gentleman could jump off a four-story building and be ready and willing to obey love's commands. And for very good reasons. Because while Gentiles frittered away their substance with business like tea, coffee, whiskey, smoking, chewing, eating ham and bacon, and also gambling and roughhousing (till some of their finest specimens was old before their time, teeth knocked out, bleary-eyed or outright corpses), the Mormon contingent saved up like the steam-engine saves up steam till wanted to pound heavy machinery into the ground. They're a steam-engine walking around in pants.

"In all sincerity do I say this," Midge confided. "I had a lady friend by the name of Beulah. Married a Latter-day Saint with two other wives. And wouldn't you think *that* would of done some siphoning off? like a intermittent geyser in hiatus? that my friend needn't fear he'd be laying for *her*? But such was not the case, I'm sorry to say. For two solid weeks wherever they was, Beulah said, the man's eye never dimmed nor his force beyond the reach of cunning slacken till Beulah's solid parts just turned to gristle." In the Bible, Midge said, which ever since New Year's she read a chapter out of every day, she ran across this word that *said it all* for such as him: lasvicious.

When Doctor came back, Hindle told him about passing the time of day with Midge and asked if he had ever heard the word lasvicious? No, he said, because there was no such word. *Lascivious*, however, meaning inclined to lust, lewd, voluptuous, inciting to wantonness, from the Latin *lascivia*, was good Middle English.

AND THERE WAS THE TINY horseman again looking down out of the sky. Or did she just think she saw something that wasn't there?

Passing through the settlements where Papa's different family circles revolved, or at least had done so in the past, Hindle wished she could meet someone who had known him. The newspapers with their many pieces about him through the years when he was in hiding, then tried and sentenced to be shot, stirred within her feelings such as become a daughter, even one as overlooked by the author of her being as his farrow by the wild bush-boar. But she also felt, as the pieces said for her to, that a life so clouded should be open to public observation and point a moral. To many readers, however, the publicity and highlighting of western Mormondom, attracting not only newspaper riff-raff but a company of U.S. Army mounted infantry still camped along Kanab Creek, had turned the region into a nest of hornets in a savage sulk.

So Hindle didn't plan on scouting out either the blood of ancestry or any of the five hundred of Papa's friends who signed a petition to the Governor asking clemency. Where these friends could *be* in country so sparsely settled she could not imagine, and the few scowling and preoccupied natives she did see seemed not to be "friends" with anyone, including their own mother. When she went through Santa Clara, all red sand and red earth, every door was shut, and, glimpsing her shadow in Gunlock, even a rock-snake in the dust slithered away fast.

For the comfort of seeing Salt Lake City's latitude and longitude, she took out the freighter's map and looked at it, the beautifully curlicued letters *Mt. M.* between Gunlock and Pinto as they caught her eye reminding her that the Mountain Meadow lay about a day's journey off to her left. As she knew from her reading, once the Old Spanish Trail passed so close by it that for two or three miles a traveler's horse could reach over and nibble its grass. But after the massacre, that part of the road had been obliterated and a new stretch spliced into the ancient track some twenty miles to the east, cutting off the field from any but low clandestine traffic. Then came the judge's eccentric notion to sentence John D. Lee to die whilst standing upon the mass grave to which fate or their folly had led a hundred and twenty travelers from Arkansas and Missouri some twenty years before. His execution opening the Meadow up again, at least for a few days, to the public, repugnant strangers streamed in from all quarters and lying reports streamed out. One story was that though efforts had been made to eradicate the burial place by blending it in with its surroundings, some invisible influence kept it clearly visible, a kind of awful fairy-ring for all to see. And while *danced on by fairies* may account for most such places' being a different color from their surrounding grass, this one's distinction was said to have been brought about by the *ghosts of dead men* struggling there against the grudges of their woe. But who knows? In another twenty years...

Some of the repugnant strangers talked of starting a collection for a monument. "On this spot in the year of our Lord 1857..." But others said, in Mormon Country as well throw your money down a sink-hole! Don't you remember? Years ago some dragoons passing through on their way to California wore themselves out carrying boulders and piling them up in a pyramid shape over the burial site. And what good did it do? The minute their backs were turned, down the marker came. Faster than you could say Brigham Young.

As Hindle folded the map and tucked it away, she looked over in the Meadow's direction. *She* wouldn't in particular, but others (such as go out of their way to visit publicly known places) might want to walk over the fraught ground someday. With no means of approach, however, the Meadow might as well not exist. And someday when all the Easterners came west, the Westerners turned into fence posts and every Melchizedek priest like Papa had fifty-two children, it probably wouldn't exist. Sunk under the stores and sidewalks of another Salt Lake City, its thatch, bluebells, blood, spent bullets, bunchgrass, Ragged Robin and salts of carbonate and phosphate of lime would just be folds and bends and gritty dirt. "Oh, Papa," she said, "you was such a ninny!" Saying that, she remembered her rebuke to herself one day for spilling the India ink—"Oh, you ninny!"—and how Doctor, hearing her, had looked up and said "Derived from *innocent*."

Chapter Sixteen

✷

In Parowan, green and fresh in the hot windy desert, she saw a woman hanging out clothes and the unusual sight of a boy coming out a doorway with books on his arm. When neither returned her nod, she thought *go ahead, be that way, see if I care*. But she did care. And when a few miles out of the village someone smiled at her (the first smile to come her way since the man in the store's ugly grimace), actually not a person but a beautiful shepherd dog standing in the road wagging his tail, it was like a salute with cheers. "Well, say," she said, drawing rein. "And who might you be?" Wild with joy at what he had wrought, he ran back and forth and in circles, wiggling and jumping and all but using the faculty of speech to get her to go with him up a narrow, poorly marked road through a tract overgrown with brushwood. At first she said no but then, for the pleasure of turning aside briefly from her course and to see what might befall, she did follow him till they came to a small house set amongst some gnarled orchard trees and a few aspens diffusing a tremulous shimmer to the air. "Well, here we are," she said. "Now what?"

A spare old woman came out of the house. "What are you doing here?" she said in a sharp tone. The vicinity being what it was, Hindle had an excuse ready, flimsy but agreeable to reason. "I'll tell you," she said. "The way the dog was acting down on the road, and with some animals being so smart and everything, I thought maybe someone had sent him to bring *help* or something. You know you hear of things like that—"

The old woman's face softened. "You do hear of such things," she said. "And in fact we once *had* a dog like that. I say 'we,' but he belonged to my boy Tom. And while Sport, that was the dog's name, Sport, never had occasion to *do* nothing in the smartness line, he very well could of. This one, though—" Her look brought him bounding in ecstasy to her side. "Shep here," she said, patting him, "all *he* does is—get lonesome."

Hindle started to smile but for some reason found herself biting her lip and blinking back tears instead. "Well, he ain't got a patent on that," she said.

There was a moment's silence. Then, "No," the old woman said gently, "he sure ain't."

And each at that moment gained for herself the acquaintance of the other.

Oh, what a case of coincidence! as Horace Greeley would say. For the old woman knew some of the same Salt Lake people Hindle knew. She more than knew them. She was their *blood relation*. She was Tot, Serapta and Murdock's *mother's sister*. She was their *aunt*. Aunt *Ruth*. And here Hindle had worked for Tot and Serapta and their

83

brother Murdock for two years before she ran away and got married. Aunt Ruth when she heard this fairly gasped, for she in her day had run away and got married too! She went on to say more, that who she ran away with was her sister's *husband*, Tot, Serapta and Murdock's *father*. Joe Burdick. She paused at this, then said that a funny thing about getting old was how secrets left to your conscience didn't seem to belong there anymore, or anywhere.

"Burdick," Hindle said, a little discomfited. "That was the name all right, Burdick's Institution for the Care of the Sick."

"Why didn't they just call it Burdick's *Hospital*?" Aunt Ruth said. "But anything to make things more complicated. That sounds like Opal."

"Opal?"

"My older sister. The one I'm telling you—married to Joe. Had Tot, Serapta and Murdock—"

"Your nieces and nephew."

"—while when *my* turn come—I shouldn't put it that way, it sounds flip—but what I mean to say is, when me and Joe, when our turn come—*we* just had Tom," Aunt Ruth said.

"The boy that—owned Sport—"

"Sport outlived him."

"Oh, don't tell me that."

"Well, let's see. Tom died. Then two years later the dog died. Then three years after that *Joe* never woke up. Ice cold, so I must of been sleeping by him dead half the night and never knowed it." You get so you're braced all the time, she went on, for whatever may be. Now she was alone. Shep wasn't even hers. He belonged to the folks with the cobblestone chimbley, maybe Hindle noticed as she come through the village? Sometimes they'd come looking for him, sometimes not. One of these days she thought maybe she'd try and make a dicker for him, but she hadn't yet.

Anyway, come in.

First they had cold buttermilk and bread and butter, then later a nice supper of fried potatoes and fried eggs. Then nothing would do but the travelers must stay the night. And thus it was that to the sound of their mother's and Aunt Ruth's voices, the children went to sleep on a quilt on the floor before it got dark. And had they woken in the night, even up until two and three in the morning or at early milking time, they'd have still heard the loquaciousness. It was like Robinson Crusoe and his man Friday on their island! had Friday been able to talk the language. Hindle did talk it. She used the word "apostatize" for what her mother did after she and Papa broke up. It was fine with her, she said, as Mama said herself, if the elements melted with fervent heat, if the heavens got rolled up like a scroll, if the elect rose in the air and left her out, she didn't mind a bit. They didn't mind either—Hindle, aged four at the time, and Lucitie, aged six—that being the way of children. Renouncement without legal dispensation.

Too bad, Aunt Ruth said, but that's the way it happened sometimes. Rifts so bitter as to poison even faith. If she wasn't mistaken, her sister Opal was never the Latter-day Saint *after* their big division that she was *before*. And she had it on good authority, Aunt Ruth said, that by the time Tot, Serapta and Murdock were grown they were the next thing to Gentiles, though someone was saying Murdock went on the church's usual two-year mission and came home with an English bride.

"He did," Hindle said, pleased to be able to contribute this. "Alice. I only met her the once when she come to the Institution on what looked like an inspection tour. You could see they owned the place all right, her and Murdock, and he would come for the money. But the ones that really ran it were Tot and Serapta."

"A hospital," Aunt Ruth mused. "That seems quite peculiar."

"How do you mean?" Hindle said.

"For us, you know. We never—"

"Well, what I heard—it came about by accident. Tot and Serapta was taking in sewing, Murdock was working in the Land Office, and Alice just kept house, she supposedly had a dowry. Then Murdock married Phoebe with this big long house her dead husband had built when he was going into polygamy. And pretty soon, because Phoebe was quite a lot older than Murdock, what should happen but she's took with a paralytic stroke and later died. So Murdock was left with Phoebe's house, which become the Institution, and she had money in the bank, I guess, so Murdock quit his job—"

"Did Opal get in on any of that good fortune?"

"I don't know," Hindle said. "She was dead by the time I worked there."

Aunt Ruth clicked her tongue and shook her head. "And without one word of forgiveness, from what I know. Though I must say I can't blame her. If it'd been the other way around—But at least she knows by now—" She glanced upwards, then down again. "God said He would 'punish the wicked for their iniquity and cause the arrogancy of the proud to cease and lay low the naughtiness of the terrible.' And He done so. Wherever she is, I hope she knows that. He never missed a lick."

"I've heard *that* before."

"Little did I think," Aunt Ruth said, carefully pleating, then smoothing out a corner of her apron, "when I went to live with them—him and her, Opal and Joe, me being still a girl at home when the folks passed on and nowheres else to go—what fate might have in store. Not in store all in one *minute*, of course. Tot was walking and talking, Serapta just needed her didies at night, and Opal was fixing to have Murdock. But during the wait she showed signs of losing the baby, so she stayed in bed most of the time and I kept house and cooked. Joe was easy to do for, and I don't put it past me, maybe I showed off, cooking and doing the work the best I could. And also when either of us had the time, Joe was learning me to half-sole. Shoes, you know. We was just like a couple of—well, relations. And then all of a sudden one evening we was laughing, I was looking at him and he was looking at me and all of a sudden—But I tell you this truthfully, we didn't so much as touch each other's *hand* till Opal was safely delivered and all was well. Not like amongst the Gentiles. Well, just to show you. When Murdock was born, this was in Salt Lake so there was a butcher shop, and I carried him down there and weighed him, hollering his head off, and he weighed six and three-quarters pounds. But by the time Joe went to the bishop to ask advice about getting into the Doctrine and marrying me, Murdock weighed seventeen pounds, so you see there was no big *rush*."

"No," Hindle said. "It wouldn't seem like it if he weighed that much!"

"But then come what both Joe and me dreaded like it was Judgment. For that's what it was, in a way. And that was to go to Opal and ask *her* if it was all right with her if Joe married me. Well, to put it in a nutshell, it wasn't. I truly and honestly thought she was going to kill us."

Hindle caught her breath in sympathy. "Of course she didn't—"

"No, of course not. Listen, I said we run away but we really didn't. Instead, with my stuff flying around me I left the house and moved in with some folks over on Second West that we knew in Independence, Missouri. But Joe, the bishop's strict orders to *him* was to stay with Opal till reason would prevail. Which of course it never did, so finally Joe went over the bishop's head and had a word with Apostle Cannon. Then we took our endowments and was man and wife. Opal had the best of it, in heaven she would be ahead of me in every way, bigger mansion, nicer street, more servants—but would she listen? Anyway—we rented a little house. I hadn't no more than measured for curtains, though, than Joe come home with the news that he'd been 'called' to come down here to help build up the Kingdom—"

"To Iron County?"

"Right where I am now is where we landed," Aunt Ruth said. "He asked Opal to come, would of built her a house, her and the children. But he'd just as well have asked a wild hyeenie. And right here on this spot where this house is now but in a tent with brush piled up around it and the snow coming down, I had my baby. Tom." Her face grew soft as she said his name. "But that ended it. What I mean to say, him taking so long, I guess, two days and nights, done detriment enough to stop me ever having any more."

"That's a long labor. Was your baby all right? Because sometimes—"

"All *right*?" Aunt Ruth said. "Tom was the loveliest babe, the loveliest child and grew to be the loveliest man ever to walk the earth. Well, when I tell you—! The year he was nineteen he was gave the part of the *Prophet Joseph Smith* in the July Twenty-fourth celebrations. I was running around in such circles that next thing I know they've got the smelling salts under my nose! At that time the Prophet hadn't only been martyred about eighteen years, so there was folks that knew him *as a boy* and they said Tom looked so much like him at that age they couldn't believe it! So you see—! And smart? Learn anything! surveying, angling the stars—One time he took a actual *crick* in its bed and run it a different way. But handsome and smart meant nothing in comparison to his goodness. He was, without a doubt—" She broke off, reflecting, as she slowly rocked.

The clock whirred, struck, and above its ticking Hindle heard a scratching sound she thought at first might be the dog come back—Aunt Ruth had sent him home after supper—and jumped up, but it was just the wind scraping the window with a tree branch. When she sat back down, as the old woman was still silent but had stopped rocking, Hindle cleared her throat and said, "Don't it seem like that's what always happens? That it's the lovely and good that—" She was going to say "gets it in the neck?" but changed that to "gets taken first?"

"If he only *had* been taken!" Aunt Ruth said fiercely. "How many times I wished it. How many times I prayed to God, oh, God in heaven, *please*. But God done like He always does—took His own sweet time."

Deciding they must be talking about something like pulmonary consumption, "It's just so awful when they waste away," Hindle ventured. "Can't even turn theirself over in bed, their bones a-sticking out and white as their pillow—"

"If such had been the case I wouldn't of minded," Aunt Ruth said. "What I mean to say, in comparison. But it wasn't." She paused and started to rock again slowly. And when she spoke it was slowly too, as though rendering to reason what she now must say needed great deliberation. "That old Mountain Meadow! Maybe there's places in this world as hateful, miserable and evil, but I don't know where they would be. *They* don't know either, I bet, them poor souls evermore detained up there. And your pa! with all the iniquities of the children of Israel and all their transgressions and all their sins, put onto *him*. But he wasn't their scapegoat for nothing, don't ever think."

"I guess he wasn't."

"It was parceled out pretty even amongst them. The harshness. The greed," she said. "Don't forget greed, Joe told me Tom said when they got up there and took a look around. 'Avenge the *Prophet*?' he said, catching on right away. 'Avenge our *destitution* would be more like it! with white-tops full of valuables, and guns and ammunition, and blooded stock, and riding carriages with lanterns on the sides—'"

"Richest outfit ever to cross the plains, the papers said," Hindle said.

"But also bear in mind how men love *war*," Aunt Ruth said. "Dick Kimball, when he come a-riding up that morning, I wish you could of seen him. 'Orders from headquarters.' You'd think it was Bunker Hill. Saluted, mind you. Back stiffer'n a board. I was out feeding the chickens. 'What *is* all this?' I say as Joe and Tom is rushing around loading up rifles and blankets and my *coffee pot*! 'What are you doing with that?' I say. And a kettle and loaf of stale bread, for the fresh batch hadn't rose yet. 'Oh, it's just maneuvers at the Mountain Meadow,' they say. 'Bivouac tonight, then home tomorrow.' But it wasn't tomorrow or the next day or the next. And all I'm doing is waiting. Then here comes this wagon. And I take one look at Tom laying in it and I think he's dead. But Joe rides up on

Bess and leading Prince and he says Tom's only hurt, his head's been battered but he'll be all right, they've laid on hands and prayed and he'll get better. '*Battered?*' 'Prince throwed Tom and bolted, his foot got tangled and before they could stop him—' 'You will rot in hell!' I says. Laid on hands! When I laid on my own, his head felt like a piece of cracked china that no glue from Flanders could ever fix. Eggshell thin, you see. He was *so smart*. I bet if you held his skull up to the sun you could of saw right through it! while most people's is thicker'n a churn. But he was paying. Everything must be paid for in the end. Smartness, beauty—His eyes was full of blood, his face looked terrible, the only good thing was, he was asleep. Day, night, made no difference to him. I know I made a spectacle of myself, yelling, crying and determined to *know* till Joe finally says it's not no use, the men took a oath up there never to tell or have their heart tore living from their body! So I said 'Listen, that would be a *pleasure* to what I'm going to do to you if you don't tell me—!' But he turned away. He knew my hands was tied 'cause that's the way I am. Like they was tied when in days to come Tom was choking me, shutting off my wind, and the boning knife right there in the drawer. I could of reached it. But I couldn't of no more used it than flew to the moon! Anyway Joe come in and saved the day."

"Them injuries to the head," Hindle said, shocked and mystified, "can just raise Cain."

"He was the loveliest babe, child and man ever to walk the earth."

"I'm sure he was."

"His path ahead was lovely," Aunt Ruth said. "A flowery mead. From his earliest days. Blessed by Apostle George Albert Smith! who happened to be down here counting the wells. Baptized by immersion in Tonaquint Creek. Deacon, Aaronic priesthood, never a hitch. Melchizedek priesthood, all as smooth as silk. Every earmark of a boy who would go far. I had that said to me time and again. What could stop him? Good-looking, good head on his shoulders, *good*. But that was just the trouble. *Too* good! He wouldn't do what they told him to. 'None of that in mine,' he said to his dad, and jumped on Prince. 'You can't desert!' Joe said, and grabbed the reins. 'They shoot deserters in wartime! How far do you think you'd get?' But Tom didn't care and Joe was beside himself, talking, trying to think, then not thinking, his gun's up to his shoulder not taking aim, he pulled the trigger to stop him! The bullet grazed Prince, he spooked, and Tom went flying, his foot caught in the stirrup, he got dragged, his head a-bumping and banging on the rocks—"

"Well, no wonder then," Hindle said. "No wonder."

"The only sight I seen for weeks was him unconscious. I made Joe's life a misery, but I couldn't help it. That oath, never to tell! I wouldn't have it. Little by little I kept a-boring in till I pieced it all together. And the more I heard, the more I hated Joe. Hated them all. For everything, but most especially for how nothing was done for Tom, hurt like he was, except to lay him in under a bush till the battle was over. 'Battle,'" she said mockingly. "Oh, yes. A pack of wolves amidst a bleating fold. You know how long the whole thing took? Fifteen minutes! A hundred and twenty humans melted down like wax, bleeding bodies stretched for half a mile. After it was over Joe run back to Tom. Laid his head on his chest, his heart was beating. And they trundle him home. That is to say—"

"Oh, Aunt Ruth."

"—they trundle *someone* home. Not Tom no more. I've often thought—You know you hear of changelings? In the Old Country? A child gets took, another's put in his place? Of course that's babies and children, while Tom was a grown young man. But remember, he was *laying there alone* under a bush on that meadow, no one around."

"You say he was unconscious when they brought him home?"

"Till nearly Thanksgiving. Oh, how glad we was when he come to! We jumped for joy. Only it wasn't *Tom's* eyes that opened. *Tom* was a Missing Person from that day forward. Like Charley Ross. And then the spells come on."

"What kind of spells?"

"Well, like the falling sickness. All his limbs would spasm and he'd choke on spit. But the awful part was how he got so *mean*! Meaner and meaner till we was scared of him. Scared of our own boy. I said to Joe, 'When you and them others opened up Hell that day and let the demons out, one of 'em got into Tom like climbing in through a window! And never left,' I said. Joe hid the guns, but like I told him, 'Tom don't want no gun, he wants to grab aholt with his bare hands and rend someone to pieces!' He was like Samson, see, when Samson was blind and wild and pulling the temple down stone from stone! eyeballs a-bulging and strength that swelled like the tide! And then one day—But no use," she said, "dwelling on *that*. Let us just say he died, aged twenty-two. And no one could of had a nicer funeral. It had been cold and wet but turned off nice. And now—" She paused. "He lays in a spot that anyone would like. And on his gravestone it says— But what it *ought* to say, maybe for history's sake if nothing else, is how he really died two different times, and how both times it was his father that killed him. The first time because he couldn't help it, and the last time," carefully she pleated and smoothed out a corner of her apron, "because he could."

HINDLE AND THE CHILDREN'S GOOD-BYE the next morning was tearful, even Shep when he bounded up, wagging his tail and jumping around, had tears in his eyes. Aunt Ruth didn't cry, that was one of the pleasures age had taken from her, she said, tears. Another was no sooner to think of something than to do it, without further thought. Like this morning getting breakfast, the thought come to her to write a letter to the folks in Salt Lake for Hindle to deliver. Dear Tot and Serapta—telling them—mentioning— Wishing it had turned out different. But then she pondered. Maybe not a letter. Maybe just a message by word of mouth? "You'll probably go to see them right away?"

"Probably," Hindle said. But she didn't mean it. How could she face Tot? When Doctor left town he did so because of his enemies and not in order to start life over with *her*. That that was what happened wasn't anyone's fault. But how could she explain?

"Give them my love, be sure."

"Oh, yes, I will."

"You won't waste time in Panguitch? It's clear out of your way."

"Well, I thought, you know? Pay my respects—"

"I'd be surprised if the grave's even marked."

"I'll ask someone—"

"And of course they'll tell you, being so fond of strangers," Aunt Ruth said ironically. "What if they think you're a newspaper writer?"

Hindle laughed.

"Don't laugh. It's like a deadly feud by now. When John was stood up in front of that firing—" she changed this to the softer *when he breathed his last*—"why, some of his boys turned up to claim the body and take it to Panguitch for decent burial. They're a short-tempered bunch, there's redheads amongst 'em, and when they looked back and seen the newspaper writers—there for the execution—following lickety-split, they was fuming. Not till they got to the canyonlands, though, did they start their fancy shooting at hats, canteens and satchels till them writers thought they was goners for sure! Oh, I tell you. Some of them Lee boys is wilder than deer. But they're dwindling. Thanks to the last twenty years, they been cold-shouldered right out of the country."

"I wouldn't of minded having a brother," Hindle said. "And the thought of a actual *father*—"

As though disclaiming responsibility, Aunt Ruth shrugged. "You know in the Bible— or maybe in Hiawatha—where it speaks of 'sleeping with one's fathers'? I think it means *father*, and that sounds fine to me too."

Hindle smiled at that. But traveling on, the more fatherless somehow for having missed the chance to stand at Papa's grave, she felt sad and delinquent, like whoever it was in the poem Doctor used to recite sometimes while shaving, who "hurled his father's entrails on the desert world…"

SEVERAL EVENINGS LATER, AT THE approach of an unexpected visitor to her camp outside the small settlement of Scipio, she thought of her half-brothers' fancy shooting and wished they didn't live so far away. Although until the tiny rider—plunging, slipping and sliding down the cliff's steep slope, then heading straight for her—actually drew rein and dismounted at her fire, she hoped against hope he would swerve and lope on by. But no. And who should it be but Bishop Dugger, the storekeeper from St. George. Not exactly someone she rejoiced to see! He had been watching her, he said, for quite some time due to the fact that he and his boys pastured cattle and ran sheep all along the grazing grounds on these hills and he would get to a coign of vantage and look down and there her outfit would be, moving along.

"So that was you," she said without warmth. She said when she'd glance up sometimes and see someone, she would get rather scared. It seemed like it was a scout or someone up there, watching.

Well, he did watch, Bishop Dugger said. But now tomorrow morning he was going to have to head off home, this was as far up the line as he could go, and so he thought he had better ride down and bid her good-bye till they met again at Conference time in the city.

So he was heading home now, was he? Hindle said, happy and relieved that this should be so. Well, good luck.

He wasn't in *that* big of a hurry, he said. He thought he'd just lay here by her fire if that was all right with her, and snooze till about daylight. After they visited a bit, of course.

"Oh," she said nervously, wishing she hadn't thrown on more wood when she should have covered the coals and gone to bed.

He had taken his hat off, which must have been too small or else the heat of the day had expanded his head the same way that feet expanded, for there was an indentation an inch or so wide around his corpse-white forehead.

"Been hot, ain't it?" he said, pushing back his lank hair.

"Could I offer you some supper? We had ours quite some while ago, but I can rustle you up something."

"Don't go to no big trouble, my dear."

After he had eaten she said good night, walked away and was going to climb up into the wagon bed where the children lay asleep. But as he was at her heels piously continuing their conversation about indifferent matters, she changed her mind in regard to putting herself into such a confined space and instead reached in and pulled out a blanket.

"What you going to do with that?" he said.

"Cover up with it," she said. "On the ground here by the wagon. And over *there* you're welcome to the fire. Like you said."

He looked her up and down. "Lay it over you or roll up snug?"

"Good night," she said shortly.

"Don't roll up just yet," he said. "I wanted to tell you—"

"I'm kind of done in," she said, pretending to yawn. "And I imagine that after a long day and riding down the side of that cliff, you must be too."

"Then you imagine wrong, Violet May," he said, "for I ain't been tired in my life. And when I'm getting acquainted with someone, I'm one of these likes to pour information into their *ears*, almost like siphoning something into 'em somewheres else." He paused. "In a manner of speaking. Brings 'em closer quicker."

Chapter Seventeen

*

YOU'LL NEVER BRING *ME* CLOSER, SHE THOUGHT, QUICKER, SLOWER OR ANY OTHER way. But when he sat down on the ground, she too (from apprehension but also for politeness' sake and so as not to seem to act in antagonism) took a seat on the wagon step. And after humming a snatch of song, coughing up some phlegm and giving himself a shake almost like a dog, he did apprise her of more than a few meetings and events of his history, such as when the black diphtheria struck in Independence, Missouri. "There was a scourge from God," he said. "Up, alive and kicking at breakfast, deader'n a door-nail by bedtime. Talk about wailing and gnashing of teeth and watching in the sky for Jesus! They quit a-having funerals and buried at night. And I had this little sister took it, and she died—"

"Oh, dear," she said.

"—and me and Pa, we had to bury her. The grave was ready, we'd dug it that afternoon, and after supper we went to the graveyard. But just as we lifted the coffin out of the cart, the wind blew the lantern out, and we didn't have no matches. Was it dark! We groped around, though, till we felt the open hole and slid the coffin over to the edge. Then we started to let it down—but the harness reins we was using and the sheet somebody had the smart idea to wring out in formaldehyde and wrap around the coffin got tangled up and skewed, so it stuck and wouldn't go down. So that meant somebody had to jump in the grave and straighten 'er. Well, it wasn't Pa. All of a sudden his lumbago's so bad he can't do nothing. So in *I* jump, and even though I know it's just my little sister down there with me, it's a dead person, and so deep and dark and clammy my blood is running cold. I was thirteen years old. But I climbed out twenty-one and *proud*, I'm telling you. And from then on 'Honor thy father' didn't mean no more to me than 'Honor thy backhouse.'"

"Gracious," she said.

"Oh, I tell you, honey. I done more things in my life than you could shake a stick at."

"It sounds like it."

Once he sucked the poison out of a woman bit on the thigh by a flying viper and saved her life.

Once he was frying up a pan of mountain oysters and the grease caught on fire and started a stampede.

And one time when the brethren was forcing a vote—

"I don't like to interrupt," she said. "But it's getting late and I really—"

"Oh, now, sis. At least let the moon swing free."

She started to get up but sat back down again. But when his story about forcing the vote concluded and he went to find some wood, she got to her feet, and when he came back said firmly she had to say goodnight.

"Well, too bad," he said indifferently, going to the fire. A moment later he called over his shoulder, "I hope I don't have to suck no poison out of *you*."

"I hope so too," she said. She lay uneasily but then in her blanket gradually warmed, stretched out and (though not intending to) had nearly fallen asleep when he squatted down on his heels cowboy style beside her and touched her shoulder. "Oh!" she cried, sitting up in alarm.

"Why, it's just me," he said. "The last man in the world to *impose*. Why, don't you know I could sleep right next to you, you and me rolled up in the same blanket like a pair of Pawnees at Bear Dance time and not a thing in the world would happen?"

"I'm sure that's true, Bishop Dugger, but just the same—"

"Why, you're shaking," he said, "you foolish gal, when all I come over here for was to mention—Bear Dance time is when the couples of the tribe that has been meaning to, *gets married*. All on the same day. I bet you didn't know that, did you?"

"No, I didn't. But—"

"Another thing I bet you didn't know—what they do on their wedding night. And before you get up on your high horse I'm going to tell you. They undress, roll up together in the bridegroom's blanket, and *go to sleep*. That's their custom, why I do not know. Much as all these couples might want to *covenant* with each other, they can't do so until the *following* night. It's some kind of Indian custom." He coughed delicately. "And over there by the fire just now I was idly thinking, what if that was you and me?"

"Well, it's not," she said. "So if you will please—"

"Wouldn't be easy, would it? My own case, I'd be one big throbbing pain from head to foot like Elohim throwing back the Virgin's covers. 'Slide over, darlin.' Does She smile? Has She fainted? What to expect! We never know. A marble angel? or you a-grabbing and clawing and I think it's a kiss but what you've went and done, you've *bit* me till the blood runs! and that ain't all that does so, if you will pardon me for expressing a natural fact of woman's nature in so many words—"

Hindle's blanket being all the bedroom and door to lock she had, she had wrapped it tightly around her. Now, sitting up, she struggled to free herself.

"Here, here, sis, you didn't let me finish," he said, laying a hand on her chest and forcing her gently but with formidable strength back down onto the ground.

"I got to get up."

"Oh, no you don't. Because—What I was going to say—" Now, with his hand pressed against her shrouded chest, he went from squatting to sitting on the ground with his long legs stretched out in front of him, and went on, "A man that can't control his appetites and his passions is not only not fit for the thrones, kingdoms, principalities, powers, dominions and heights and depths of *Heaven*, he ain't even fit to enter the Tithing Office in *Salt Lake City*! I think we agree on that?"

"Will you please—!"

"And while there's nothing I hate worse than a bragger, I do have to say in all modesty that I *am* fit, I *can* control my appetites and passions, and that that, as a matter of fact, is the article I deal in. The way other people—"

"Bishop—!"

"—do other things, whether from an *inborn push*, or if they have *chose* it, like a wife. But everyone's got something they take pride in. They'll climb. They'll lift. Why, not but a year or two ago a stonemason working on the Temple hoisted a block of granite onto his back that *killed* him. Of his own accord. Nobody told him to, nobody asked him. His eyeballs popped out of their sockets, he busted blood vessels till he was streaming like a fountain, and why? Man's *pride*. In whatever accomplishment—Hitting a tomato can on a post. Enduring the elements. Whatever it may be. And I don't say I don't pride myself on nothing *else*. But when the necessity arises—like say tonight, you and me, out here alone—And ain't it a night, though? Look at them stars! I been thinking of just this ever since you come in the store. All the days I was riding herd along the tops of them hills I'd be looking down, I'd see you, your little fire burning in the dark, and I'd think— how you and me would spend this night together and no Indian sweethearts that ever was, wrapped in the same blanket at Bear Dance time, could beat us at *withstanding*."

"Withstanding?"

"Now why a tribe would have such a custom, not to complete their marriage till the *second* night? As I say, I do not know," he said. "But in the case of why you and me can't complete nothing without our ordinances and endowments, and some of the order, forms and ceremonies that restrains us from conversing familiarly with the heathen, I *do* know. But the date is set. *Was* set at the world's beginning when the morning stars danced and sang. Our day. Our *night*. Bulwarks down, ramparts pierced. Nothing but," he coughed his refined little cough, "getting together."

"Good night, Bishop Dugger." She sounded brisk, but a peculiar liquefying weakness was going through her, a limpness, a dreamy sluggishness.

"Alas," he said regretfully. "Our old human nature ramping and rearing, trampling and champing, must pull in its horns tonight."

"I would certainly think so."

He half rose, then sat back down. "Terrible shame, wasn't it? What happened to Parley P. Pratt?"

She nodded, to head off his telling her what that might have been.

"Of course it was a long time ago. And I personally never knew the man, but I have heard it said he was the best Apostle we ever had. Even beat Brigham when *he* was an

Apostle. And you know why? Because Parley's head was so stuffed with knowledge it was *solid*, like a big lump of solid gold."

"Oh," she said.

"Like one time he was speaking to the Aaronic priesthood about man's bodily parts and passions. And afterwards there was a discussion. In regard to doing activities young men should not be doing. And then was when Parley reached far back into the ages for a example my uncle, or rather my half-uncle, that was there that night later told my cousin he would never forget. About this young fellow by the name of Cyrus who was so good he nearly took wings and flew. Well, as everyone knows, anybody *that* good gets the Devil's attention. So the Devil plots and plans and pretty soon he's got poor Cyrus chained stark naked onto a bed of flowers! To test him. A beautiful lady comes along. Undressed. Hair a-hanging past her hips. And she starts in on Cyrus. Pathetic. There he is spread-eagled on this bed that the *smell* of the flowers alone has already nearly suffocated him, and she is doing whatever she wants. He can't protect himself. Shall the Devil triumph through the air? Her hot breath breathes on Cyrus. Her soft nervous substance melts. When a rush of desire leaps up like a gusher, a geyser a-throwing a column of vigor straight up with power to rupture not only the man's equinoctial but his ecliptic, he really thinks he's a gone goose. But he saves himself, how do you think? *By biting off his own tongue!*"

"His tongue?" she said weakly.

"Of course times is different now. I myself wouldn't want to pull a stunt like that. But nevertheless—!" He gazed up at the stars. "I'm a lot like Cyrus. I can withstand. That's the article I deal in, bearing, resisting, not giving in. If you was to say to me this very instant, 'Verlie, I beg of you—'"

To her horror, for he was as ugly as a stiff and scurvy old buffalo hide, Hindle wanted to say almost those very words.

"I'd say to you, 'Little woman—'"

"I'm not—your—"

"'Sweetheart,' I'd say," he said, finding the edge of her blanket and opening it wide, then quickly reaching for his own blanket and spreading it down beside him while she lay like a snake bewitched by a snake-charmer's flute. "'My own,' I'd say." He loosened his belt, unbuttoned down the front his sour-smelling hunting shirt of linsey-woolsey, unfastened his cuffs, turned them back and lay down beside her, not touching but she could feel his heat radiating out and sense the tight bundles of thigh and arm muscles, the hardness of his bones and foul peg-teeth.

"Well, little gal, so here we are! But as I was saying—good conduct's wrote all over you, nobody has to wonder. I wouldn't be here otherwise, attracted as I am to virtue like a bee to honey. And you the same for the same reason, to me. So this here's our Bear Dance wedding night. You there, me here, one blanket, no monkeying around. But in Salt Lake in October—! Brother Brigham himself officiating—! That's my hope. He ain't been too well lately, so they say. Last time he wintered down here he had these watery bags under his eyes and his handshake felt squishy. One of the Apostles would be my next choice. And then you brides always want a wedding photograph, but that wakes up too many sleeping dogs. And don't try asking during a weak moment. 'No, my little frau,' I'll say. 'Frau' means wife in German. Did you know that? By the way, now's as good a time as any to mention that you won't be Frau Number One, for Jane has held that position since Far West days. She's the one that was shooting the wildcat when the gun kicked and split her lip. Then there's Catherine and Julia. Catherine's smart, Julia ain't. But would you believe it, the *smart* children went to Julia while Catherine's young ones can't hardly pound sand in a rat hole! Don't that seem peculiar? Have you got any special marks about you?"

"Marks?"

"Such as my wife Eula born with a deep hole in the middle of her back you could sink your fist into, almost. Not that it holds her up in any way, and if they wasn't told no one would know. *I* sure didn't, you could of knocked me over with a feather. Here we are, went through the rigmarole, she gets undressed and here's this hole in her back she turns around and shows me. But as I was saying—who will take care of your children?"

"My children?"

"For a week or so before you and me start back down to St. George. We won't want nobody disturbing us *then*." He turned over and faced her, raising up on his elbow. "You understand what I'm talking about? I'll save up. Jane could come to me, Catherine could pull some of her sly stunts. Julia and Eula, they'll act like it's a chore, but then I'll devil 'em. I'll go so far and no farther. I'll test my heritage. I love to see a woman beg."

"I'd never beg," Hindle said dazedly, her heart beating thick and muffled, her legs trembling and weak with an almost irresistible desire to fall open like a watermelon cut in half. "Never."

"Listen," he said. "I never knowed there was such a thing as womanly—I'll come right out and say it—craving. I just had the one wife at the time, Jane, no children, but we had Thirza along with us, she was Jane's cousin, seventeen or eighteen years of age at the time, heavyset girl, she still is. So anyway we was on our way out here and we come to somewheres in Nebraska country, where the Loup River branches out and goes three ways, and it had been storming, the water was at flood, we'd had cholera in the train— and there was these Loup Indians, naked braves, I never seen nakeder humans in my life. Around here they're decent, the Paiutes at least cover their nakedness, we wouldn't allow it no other way. But there we had no jurisdiction. Some said they was Poncas, but I never heard of such a tribe. I'm sure they was Loups, friendly, for God was watching over us. And I won't try to explain how it happened, but due to different circumstances connected with swimming the animals and floating the wagons over and so forth, why, what should happen but at the Fork where these naked Loups was guiding us, *some* of the gals and women—Thirza was one—had to get on *behind*'em, on their horses, cling onto their naked heathen bodies as tight as they could and be swum across. And then was when I realized—"

"What?"

"It was quite a shock. Jane had went up ahead to help a woman that the fright of crossing the river had started her young one to coming, leaving me and Thirza alone in the wagon. And then was when I realized—! She was like a—I said to quit it, I had never covenanted with her yet and didn't aim to till we got where we could make it legal in the eyes of God. 'What's got *into* you?' I says. 'I never seen you *act* like this!' 'I guess it's because of getting so scared crossing that river and then the relief. I don't know,' she says. 'Well, *I* know,' I says. 'It was the nakedness of that stinking Loup you was rubbing up against!' 'Oh, no,' she says. 'Oh, yes,' I says. 'Pressing your haw against that naked back, winding your arms around him.' 'Oh, no,' she says, but she's breathing like she run a mile. 'Put your face down to me, Verlie,' she pants—"

"Bishop Dugger, really—"

"But to continue, there is no greater sin than for a man to overshadow a woman in a husband's capacity if he ain't her husband. People throws up their hands and says Blood Atonement! like it was some terrible thing. They've got it outlawed now. But I say this, make the punishment fit the crime, and any man or woman that disobeys counsel, or any man and any woman that ain't got the right to do so, that lays and covenants till they're weaker'n a cat *ought* to have their blood spilt to save their immortal soul. If you and me—tonight out here—was to do what our bodies is a-aching like toothache to do, why, that would be a sin as bad as murder."

"Do you think so?" Hindle spoke thickly, as if drugged.

"But never fear, sweetheart. Some men lifts whatever's heavy that they come across. Some men shoots tomata cans off a post. But *my* pride is, to lay like I'm laying by you—" He broke off, then spoke murmuringly. "My love. All them days a-riding the plateaus looking down, thinking about this night, us laying here so sweet, *withstanding temptation*—"

"But why?" she said, pulling herself limply and weakly onto him and beginning to kiss his hot, scaly, salty face and thick, rubbery lips. "Why?"

"Because everyone has something that they do."

SHE WOKE WHEN IT WAS just starting to get light. Had it been a dream? But no, there he lay beside her soundly sleeping, sour-smelling, stubble on his face, his mouth half open. She shuddered, sick with conscience. Did she really—? while he lay testing his strength. She was scrambling to her feet when he clutched her skirt, pulled her back down hard.

"Don't start nothing this morning," he said. "I don't know as I could hold out, if you was to tackle me again." He spoke gloatingly, and she saw that his eyes were not dark as she had thought they were, but yellow as a coyote's or a snake-bird's. Revulsion rose in her, again she shuddered and pulled away.

"I don't know as I could." He grabbed her hand and now he squeezed it till her fingers interlaced with his turned white. "If you was to tackle me again and do the things you done to me last night. I don't know if I could—keep on—withstanding. Listen," he said, "Violet May—"

"I got to get up," she said. "The children—I got to get going."

"Me too," he said, letting her hand drop. "The best of friends must part. But right now I'll take a vow."

"Don't do that," she said. All she wanted was for him to be gone, and to get to a running stream and wash herself, her hair, her clothes, everything. The blanket he touched. She would throw away that white cup with the raised blue edge, the iron spoon and fork, the scalloped pie-tin she served his supper on.

"Oh, yes," he said. "A vow. That no matter what any of 'em *do* to me between now and October—and that Thirza can pull some stunts that might not land her in *hell* but may let loose a fiery blast or two in her face if she ain't careful—why, all my power and all my strength and vigor, and the potency of my life, is going to be saved up like a bank account with your name on it."

"Don't save up nothing for me."

"Why not?" he said. "It won't be no hardship. I'm in trim."

WHEN RIP VAN WINKLE CAME back, stumbling over his long white beard, his easy-going English village had altered to an up-and-coming American city. Hindle found changes, too. Intractably Mormon Salt Lake City had become not Gentile, there were too many safeguards in place for that, but perforated like honeycombed lava with the heathen's flues and working-holes, though it looked much the same. The same wide streets. The ditches. The mountains. The sky to the west reflecting the cut-glass lake instead of the other way around. The Temple had not yet got up over the top of the twenty-foot-high wall around Temple Square, but the great turtle back of the Tabernacle could be seen. The Zion's Cooperative Mercantile Institution's two front windows now displayed gutta-percha mannequins who might almost have been fashionably dressed lady-centaurs, their rumps stuck out so far behind. And the Constitution Building across the street had shot up like a weed to five stories! Brigham's offices and dwelling still marched along South Temple, his Tithing Office (for it was certainly no one else's) on the corner, his gabled house with the lion couchant on the stoop, the verandaed mansion on the corner with its widow's walk, the innocent cottage in the middle with the armed guards outside, his Favorite's "palace" just up the street. On every thoroughfare Mormon buildings, trees, bushes and grass stood four-square to all the winds that blew.

But Gentiles like thistle-down on circling eddies had fluttered down too upon the righteous fields. On some kind of an agreed basis, under somewhat mysterious conditions upon which a general "overlooking" had been established, they ran a bank, a school, churches, chapels, a livery stable, restaurants and shops. Some of the Gentiles were even Jews. There was a Gentile theater. And up a winding staircase in a building on Commercial Street, profligates could go for degrading pleasures. There were law offices, a sail maker and smoke shop.

The Salt Lake House had always been (and been allowed to be, for practical purposes) non-denominational, its proprietors Mr. and Mrs. Birdwood (he a fallen-away tithe-paying Mormon, she a fallen-away tithe-paying Catholic) hospitable to the extended, international or universal Public except in cases where that Public happened to be brown, black, red or yellow. The place looked bigger to Hindle, as though built onto, had pots of flowers on the porch, washed windows, and as she went around to the back she wondered if maybe somebody else had taken it over.

Chapter Eighteen

*

AND WHAT ABOUT LUCITIE? SO MUCH COULD HAPPEN IN TEN YEARS! BUT THERE Hindle's sister stood looking as she always had, not ironing this time but with a broom and dustpan in her hand, for she had been promoted to hotel-housemaid. It took a while for Hindle to realize what a miracle that really was. Miracle? Does not the term unduly magnify the fact that a simple young woman was just where she had last been seen? No, it does not. For Lucitie had been to England in the meanwhile, and returned. Yes! Thousands of miles away! and might never have found her way back to Utah in a thousand years. But it may be we don't have the say over our lives we think we have. It may be something's got it all laid out. Lucitie always thought so, looking back and thinking how foolishly she had fallen in love with a Gentile staying at the hotel, a bookkeeper employed by Englebrecht's Wholesale Liquors, married as it turned out, and might have ruined her. Luckily, he didn't, except with regard to her heart. But a broken heart would heal, her friend and fellow worker Charlotte Bearpark told her. Which a reputation never would if she had got in deeper than she intended. Lucitie *had* got in deeper but for some unknown reason got off scot-free. She felt, however, of such low estate about it all that when the Honorable Mrs. Machell-Smith offered her the job in England, she took it. Charlotte said she might get to see the Queen, and even Mrs. Birdwood said it was an opportunity not to be missed.

Englishmen in general though! it was really funny how a couple would come clear from England to go hunting in the wilds of Utah for two weeks for grizzlies, mountain lions, pronghorns and such as that. The husband went hunting. The wife, the Honorable Mrs. Machell-Smith (that was how her husband signed *her* name on the register, why, nobody knew), had had enough of the sport for the time being, having slain eight thousand pounds of bison on the plains before they arrived in Salt Lake, and chose to stay put in the hotel. There she read leather-bound books from a portable bookcase, wrote letters she sealed with dark green sealing wax, ate five meals a day mostly from a tray but once in a while in the dining room, where she sat at a corner table by herself in a full-rigged hat and kid gloves, the hand part of which was tucked in around her wrists, and was waited on night and day by her elderly maid Miss Gabriel.

Miss Gabriel told one and all she didn't want to come to America. She was sure something would happen. After it did and she died quite suddenly of ague and running off of the bowels (an expression that would never have crossed *her* lips), though administered to by three doctors and promised two pounds more a year by the Honorable Mrs. Machell-Smith if she would stop acting ridiculous and get up, Charlotte and Lucitie said that proved you should never go against a hunch. The Honorable Mrs. Machell-Smith was very much put out, because it was all just stubbornness, Miss Gabriel had to win an argument or die in the attempt, and now she *had* died, just to prove she was right that something would happen.

It would be the greatest hardship, the Honorable Mrs. Machell-Smith told Lucitie (whose constant presence she had arranged with Mrs. Birdwood to have at hand from the minute her maid defected by getting sick though knowing full well how it would upset her), to fulfill Miss Gabriel's last request that she be sent home to England for burial. Miss Gabriel should have known *that* from her days with them in India. *She* knew that sailors were so superstitious they wouldn't handle anything coffin-shaped. To transport a corpse you had to pretend it was a boxed-up Aeolian harp or archeological specimen, and there was always the chance that the deception would be discovered anyway and the body thrown overboard. Lord Byron handled a similar situation, so the Honorable Mrs. Machell-Smith was told by her grandmother, when his illegitimate daughter by that awful girl, whatever her name was, died in Italy by having the child's body cut in half and shipped home to be buried at Harrow in *two* packages so the sailors wouldn't know. Imagine how Miss Gabriel would carry on about that happening to her! But why should she be sent back to England? What did it matter where she lay? She had been simply unbearable for days, scorched a dress and petticoat, mislaid the key to the jewel case and lately had combed out *handfuls* of her mistress's hair. Deliberately, of course!

Lucitie dressed one's hair much more carefully. The Honorable Mrs. Machell-Smith was quite surprised at the coiffure she arranged for her, and Miss Gabriel was scarcely cold before she offered Lucitie the chance to go to England with her and Mr. Machell-Smith as soon as he returned with his wild western animals.

He returned and they went. Never again need Lucitie see the windowsill she crept over to lie with her faithless lover, the table he sat at in the dining room, the part of the porch railing he used to perch on smelling of eau de cologne and with that nice part in his dark hair. The *moon*, alas, she still had to look at out of the tiny attic window in St. George's Terrace, Gloucester road, London, and the still tinier window up under the eaves in Heathcote, the name of the Honorable Mrs. Machell-Smith's country estate in Yorkshire. But Lucitie could have borne the moon (for if you go expressly to look at it, does it not become tinsel?) and maybe in years to come might have married one of the gardeners (who at first she took for some kind of an idiot but later realized it was because he came from Yorkshire), though she didn't like to see a strong man tug at the lock of hair growing out of the fore-part of the head and keep his eyes on the ground when spoken to by his boss. She didn't like to see a *lot* of things in England.

The Honorable Mrs. Machell-Smith, for instance, showing off her American maid to her friends the way Madame Pompadour in *The Secret of the Casque*, which Lucitie and Charlotte had borrowed from Mrs. Birdwood, showed off her little black footman Zaire. It was as if she had come home with a scalp-hung wild Indian. Then, the lady never would eat a bite with the hired help. Not on the train, not on the ship, not at the Heathcote Christmas party, never. Mrs. Birdwood was as good as she was, owning the Salt Lake House as she did and her best chum being Mrs. O'Naughton the millionairess, but Mrs. Birdwood would sit at the breakfast table with the workers and eat breakfast and think nothing of it. Of course she herself had been a waitress in her very early days and Mrs. O'Naughton a dance-hall girl (so it was said). But that didn't signify, the two ladies were rich now. When someone wouldn't eat with you, that was an insult!

But so was everything in England when Lucitie got down to cases, and she didn't like it. Why, hadn't the English and the Americans fought the Revolutionary War, and hadn't the Americans wiped up the ground with the English? So where did the Honorable Mrs. Machell-Smith get off at, ordering an American to do this and that when it ought to be the other way around, the American ordering *her*! What good was Paul Revere's ride, Washington crossing the Delaware, the boy standing on the burning deck, the battle of Bunker Hill, the Liberty Bell that cracked just because it was rung so hard with joy because the British were whipped! if an American was going to let a Briton walk all over them? This patriot's passion in her surprised Lucitie. So did her consciousness of what was worthy of her American self, for she had never thought of such matters before. But now she did, became proud-hearted and self-respectful, so much so that the Honorable Mrs. Machell-Smith fired her. Lucitie was sorry for that, she'd have liked the satisfaction of quitting, but she thought she had better wait till they got back to London, not step forth into the wilds of Yorkshire.

She knew what she was going to do, work and save her money and go back to Salt Lake City, Territory of Utah, U.S.A., as fast as she possibly could. But oh, dear, work at what? And where? There was no work to be had at all. Just to get home she would even have gone back into service with some of our former foes, whether we licked them in battle or not. But without a letter of recommendation from the Honorable Mrs. Machell-Smith, and being a haughty American to boot (which she had never been before in her life), there was small chance of that. After several days of wandering amongst the poverty-struck in mean streets and alleys, dirt, filth, rats, the blind and crippled, drunk, dangerous and disease-ridden, she began to get scared. What was she to do? But Mr. Birdwood had a saying. "When things are bad they are hard to mend, but when they get *damn bad* they just cut loose and mend themselves!" And how true that turned out to be! She would tell Mr. Birdwood that if she ever saw him again. For what should happen but she turned a corner and there were two young men standing on the street both with open books in their hands. One was preaching. He was preaching the Gospel of the Church of Jesus Christ of Latter-day Saints!

Oh, how beautiful his western Rocky Mountain pronunciation sounded. How fresh and highly colored he and his fellow Mormon looked alongside England's washed-out poor. Lucitie was of course staunchly church at once. The missionaries said it sometimes happened that a person would be born in the faith, then fall away as she had done. They said the only thing that mattered was to come back into the fold again. All would be forgiven, not a thing held against her. She wouldn't even have to be baptized again. And by borrowing from the Perpetual Emigration Fund, which she could pay back at her own convenience, she would be in the next shipload of Saints leaving Liverpool for America.

The ship was an ocean-steamer. The passage across the Atlantic in midwinter (anything but inviting) took thirteen days. Another two weeks and the Great Pacific Railway had knit together the utmost limits of our vast country. Lucitie was back in her birthplace safe, sound and more than two hundred dollars in debt. She did not mind that a bit, there is no place like home, though often when the emigrating Saints talked about the Zion they were straining towards she thought oh, you poor things, it's just a *place*, hot in summer, cold in winter, the dust blows, sometimes the roads is nothing but mud, the teams mire down, the Temple ain't only up to the first row of windows, the best houses belong to the Gentiles that has struck it rich in the mines, you are going to be *very* disappointed.

But she kept still, having the feeling that Elder Tennant, who had chartered the ship and seemed to be in charge of everything, wouldn't appreciate discouragement. As there hadn't been enough Saints to occupy the whole ship, and as the lower deck was filled with Irish emigrants of the most unmitigated type, a *lot* went on that the Elder didn't appreciate. The missionaries didn't either. There were three sets of these going home after missions in Geneva and elsewhere. One thing they *did* appreciate was the young and heedless girls, especially the ones without family who got seasick and had to be looked after. A notably pretty one by the name of Kate Williamson had the honor of being nursed by Elder Tennant himself, said to be one of the thirty-eight General Authorities, though if he really *was* a General Authority, what would he be doing here? The commonest people could rub elbows with him in the fire-galley, where he would come and instruct someone to cook an egg and toast a piece of bread on a fork, then he would carry it to where the girl lay. After she got so she could sit up, a young man was with her one day combing the tangles out of her hair when Elder Tennant came with his offering. How angry he was, his eyes shot sparks, and someone took Albert Alfonce (for that was the young man's name) by the arm and rushed him away before he could even explain that fixing hair was what he did, his line of work.

He was a hairdresser! Albert told Lucitie about being hustled off and wondered if he shouldn't seek out the silly old fool and explain, but Lucitie said she didn't think some-body in authority like that would care to be so accosted. Anyway, that bold thing must have told him herself by now. Albert didn't think Miss Williamson was bold, he thought she was nice, and he thought Lucitie would think so too if she knew her. Somehow, in the fire-galley preparing their wretched supplies and elsewhere about their daily chores, Albert and Lucitie had become first acquaintances, then friends, and by the time they boarded the Great Pacific Railway cars to travel fifteen hundred miles to Utah, almost boon companions. Lucitie wished they might have been even more than that, a courting couple, for the minute she laid eyes on him she knew Albert was the one for her.

For one thing, he was not a hairy person. He did not have large hands. His neck went *in* under his ears like a slim stalk, rather than jutting straight down at the sides like a big wide pillar. He had long eyelashes, his waistcoat would button around an ordinary stovepipe, his foot looked elegant. However, at twenty-three he was Lucitie's junior by some three years and consequently looked on her as a sister. Still, that would change, she hoped. (Some wealthy people came and stayed at the hotel one time, Mr. and Mrs. James Clarendon, and the wife was *years* older than the husband.) Before they docked in New York, the two friends had confided everything to each other. Every little thing that ever happened.

Lucitie had never heard of anything like it, but it seemed that many years before—in fact in the previous *century*, if anybody could imagine such a thing—when Albert's great-grandfather was a young Frenchman living in Paris, France, there was a great uprising there of the poor against the rich. As there were millions of poor and only a small percentage of rich, such as the King, Queen, Dauphin (which meant the Crown Prince), Princesses, people with royal titles and those who just had money, the poor soon won the day, as they always can if they have sense enough to band together, which they seldom do. So then they tried to get rid of the rich, root and branch forever, by chopping off their heads. They did this with a big instrument called a guillotine, consisting of a heavy knife blade sliding between two grooved posts. It would come down, wham! and the rich person's head would drop in a basket. The executioner would then take the head and hold it up by the hair for all to see. Sometimes the eyes would twitch or the lips give a quiver, and then the bystanders would wonder if the head still knew what was going on, at least for a moment or two. This is my head, where is my body, oh…God.

Those must have been terrible days. Of course the poor didn't capture *all* the rich in their palaces and mansions. They are never all caught. Many of them got away. They went to Austria, Germany, Italy, England and even Ireland. That made the poor furious, for in the foreign lands the rich would spend all their time figuring out how to come back and domineer over everybody and glom onto everything the way they had done before. Knowing that's what they were working towards again made the poor take their spite out on even people who had *worked* for the rich, as though building their palaces and carriages, gilding their clocks, dressing their hair, making their clothes, setting their jewels and changing their money had made the artisans as much of a threat as their masters! So *their* heads came off too, to teach them not to labor frivolously but to toil only to benefit mankind in general. Which would be all right except that mankind in general can't buy diamond shoe-buckles, Dresden china milk pails, or summer houses in the form of an elephant, or have any use for a wig three feet high stiffened with alabaster powder and starch and trimmed with gardens and fountains and even a little gold coach with six tiny horses.

Albert's great-grandfather Henri (who had made just such a wig at one time for none other than Madame), when the Marquis de Beaurepaire and his family were escaping and begged him to go with them—for what would they do without a barber, hairdresser and wig-maker like Henri Alfonce?—agreed to do so. But the Marquis' trunkful of money having got lost after they arrived in London, Monsieur Henri Alfonce had to say farewell and go off on his own. He fended so well that in no great while he had his own hairdressing establishment, a French wife, daughter of an exiled maker of sable carriage-robes lined with satin, and a son named Pierre who grew up to be a hairdresser like (and in partnership with) his father Henri. When Pierre married an English girl and had a son, he was named Francois. Francois became a hairdresser too.

So three generations were working at Alfonce & Son: Henri, Pierre and Francois. But with Francois the whole ancestral line ground to a halt, because Francois didn't want to get married. Even to please his grandfather Henri on his deathbed, Francois said non, and Henri died an unhappy man. But Francois had enough of women and their hair à la Sappho, à la Venus, à la Caracalla and d'Egyptienne by day. To contend with them by night as well would have been more than he could bear.

"But Francois," they told him. (Albert told astonished Lucitie all this.) "If you don't get married and have a son, Alfonce and Son after three steps in the line of descent will die out, strangers will come in, all our family effort and struggle will have been in vain."

"Too bad," Francois said, giving a little French shrug, for although his mother was English, he had spent so much time with his father and grandfather in the shop (where more could be charged for French than English goods and services) that he might have just crossed over from Dieppe.

"You must marry, you must have a son!" Pierre the father said.

At last Francois the son gave in and married. But nothing came of it, no fourth generation, either son or daughter. So Pierre sent Francois to France and other places on the Continent, to buy hair but really to assist if possible the natural ripening of his gender by the operation of heat and motion. The stories he came home with! In Paris he met an ancient hairdresser who told him about buying hair during the Revolution. In the late afternoon, if the guillotine had been busy that morning, the friseurs would gather to buy hair from the jailers, the old man told Francois. Blond, brunette, red, black, salt and pepper, white, take your pick. It was the best quality. Sometimes it was neatly cropped and tied in hanks (a healthy young countess's would weigh anywhere from three-fourths to one and a half pounds), but sometimes it was still on the heads in the blood-soaked baskets, you had to shear it yourself. The old man told Francois there were still frizettes and cache-peignes made from hair from those very heads being worn today!

The sights Francois saw he told about for months, such as the child of seven with a full head of gray hair! He also saw England's own fattest nobleman and the largest goose liver in the world. He laid in a stock of eyebrows made out of pieces of mouse-skin, and plumpers of cork for mouths that had fallen in, realizing a profit for the shop on both items, though his father had thrown up his hands in dismay when he saw them. The transformations he bought went quickly too. Unpacking them, he told his father Pierre about the priests he met on the boat coming home who informed him that if anyone wearing a wig knelt before the altar, God's blessing wouldn't be able to penetrate through the wig, so the wearer would not be blessed. Pierre could hardly believe *that*, he said.

And Francois for his part could hardly believe the news *he* was met with, that he was about to become a father. But such was the case, though he had been gone more than a year, and not long after *Albert*, Lucitie's traveling companion, indeed put in an appearance. When Lucitie heard that part of Albert's story, that at last here he was, born, she got an expression on her face like the shepherds must have had when they saw the Star. Henri, Pierre, Francois. And now Albert, the much-desired fourth generation. Great-grandfather Henri was dead by then, but he would have been so proud. And prouder still when, trained by his grandfather Pierre, Albert became a hairdresser too. Why didn't his father Francois train him? Lucitie asked. Because Francois died when Albert was four years old. Albert also lost his mother and the illusion that Francois was his father, because he wasn't. On her deathbed his mother told him his *father* was really his *grandfather* Pierre, and made him promise never to tell Pierre that she had told him.

Grandfather (really father) Pierre and young Albert did not work in the shop alone. There were several employees. One of these was an ugly, dirty, but still young woman named Jeanne who did nothing from morning till night but make miles of braid. She had several stiff hairs growing out of her chin which she tried to keep plucked, for stiff hairs on a woman's chin mean she is a witch, one of the apprentices said. But they quickly grew back and disclosed her real nature. Not to the one who most needed to know, however! and that was Pierre. The old man would not hear a word against Jeanne, and soon, completely under the witch's spell, he married her. Then she revealed herself to be the mother of a large family. They all came to live in the rooms above Alfonce & Son. One by one Jeanne fired the old employees. Her children would learn the business, she said. Perhaps something had happened to Pierre's brain, his face sagged peculiarly on one side and the coils he twisted up no longer looked the same. Once this witch came to him with a solution of permanganate of potash for a blonde client's hair and Pierre dabbed it on. Of course the customer ran shrieking from the shop and never returned.

The witch's children would not do any of the menial tasks. Her large sons wore Albert's clothing without permission, handing them back under protest split at the seams and dirty. Finally Albert told Pierre he must choose. "Me or them." He even broke his promise to his mother and said, "I am not what the world thinks I am, your grandson. *I am your son! the fruit of your loins.*" But Pierre didn't seem to remember, or if he did he didn't care. He chose *them.* So Albert at twenty years old had been cast out like Adam and Eve from the Garden. What a disturbance of the equilibrium. First he went to the flat of a client who had always been kind to him and appreciated his work. It was a beautiful flat. The client was a beautiful lady, or at any rate gave that appearance. Lady, however, was the wrong word. Albert had not been there two hours sitting by the fire and telling her his troubles when she…

But what she had done he could not bring over his lips to say. Lucitie would have to imagine what happened next, if an innocent girl like her could even think of such behavior. Albert spoke to the client as a brother would, for it was raining outside and he had not finished his tea and buttered scones. But would she listen? No. For merely behaving like a gentleman, she ordered him out and told him never to come back. And then was when he heard on the street the American missionaries preaching about the American prophet who restored the True Gospel to this earth, and came gradually to realize that if he would join the church and go to Salt Lake City, he need never worry or be out of work or homeless or alone or undecided in his life again. God would take care of him. God and the one church on earth, with whom He kept in constant touch through its Prophet, Seer and Revelator Brigham Young. Albert, like Lucitie, also owed the Perpetual Emigration Fund for his passage to America. As they were now close friends, Lucitie told him more about the town he was going to than she did the others. And he was a little dismayed, for somehow he got the idea the streets were paved with Comstock gold, that Brother Brigham lived in a palace not unlike St. James's and that all his wives looked like beautiful princesses in full court regalia. Lucitie consoled him with the horse cars, the Irish Catholic millionaires spending money like water, the two theaters, a huge lake of ocean water (in which your head might bob under if you weren't careful but you yourself could not sink), linden trees and cool summer nights.

She also reminded him how lucky they were to have a Great Pacific Railway train to climb aboard when they got to New York that would carry them a distance in two weeks that used to take three months or longer. And in all likelihood they would be *alive* when they got where they were going, while even twenty years before maybe a person would be (alive) and maybe they wouldn't. Take a couple that started west with her own mother, Lucitie said. Nine days into the journey, the man died of cholera. (Later the same would happen to Mama's first husband, but that was another story.) The menfolk came to take the dead man out of the wagon, but the wife wouldn't let loose of him. So they tried to get some kind of control, and in the excitement the horses, poorly harnessed by the wife, took fright and ran away. This threw *her* out and killed her, the husband's corpse fell out too, and when everything calmed down a coffin big enough for both of them was nailed up and a double grave dug. By the time the funeral was over with, it was close to supper-time. So the outfit didn't roll out till next morning.

"What do you mean by 'roll out'?" Albert said. And then with a sigh, "Will I ever learn to speak American?"

Kate Williamson, the girl Elder Tennant had been so kind to on the ship, was two cars down from them, and once more Albert, in the hopes that when they got to Salt Lake and he had a shop Kate would be a paying customer, offered to dress her hair. Kate jumped at the chance, told her seatmate to go and sit somewhere else, and Albert slid in beside her. "What's that?" she said of the shabby leather satchel he was opening on his lap.

"My gibecière," he said.

"You don't say." She laughed. "But all those things!"

"Why did you think I offered to comb your hair that day Elder Tennant—? On the ship?"

"Because I was seasick?" But the look on her face said, because I'm the prettiest girl on this journey?

He shook his head. "Because as I told you before, this is what I do."

"Hairdressing."

He selected a silver-mounted tortoise-shell comb from amongst the combs and curling tongs of various sizes and, turning sideways, began to separate the glossy curls. From the seat she had taken down the aisle, Lucitie watched the procedure, not able to catch what they were saying but hearing Kate squeal with laughter every now and then. She seemed to always be squealing and grating. She wouldn't squeal if she knew that the satchel she was now fingering had belonged to the first of the line of Alfonces, Henri, as Albert had told her, and that those implements had curled, combed and frizzed hair on heads that were later cut off by the guillotine!

"Good afternoon, Elder Tennant. And how are you, Elder Hyde? And Elder Pugmire? How do you find yourselves, gentlemen?"

Hearing the obsequious voice of the convert named Brother Larkin, who it was said hoped to open an undertaking establishment in Salt Lake City, Lucitie turned to see the three notables making their way up the aisle. Here and there they stopped or were detained for a gracious word or exchange of compliments, once even "laying on hands" for a gray-faced man with such a bad headache, the wife who pushed him forward said, that he had vomited twice since dinnertime. "Thank you and bless you," she called fervently after the benefactors as they moved on and behind them the sufferer vomited a third time, this time into the lunch basket.

"Good afternoon. How do you find yourself?" Elder Tennant, who had shown such fatherly kindness to young Sister Williamson on the ship, was still showing it on the train, so Lucitie had heard at the cooking-range, instructing the girl personally in the Book of Mormon and Pearl of Great Price in his private compartment up front and providing meals enough to keep her pretty well out of the car with the kitchen in it. Other heads than Lucitie's had turned, compliant smiles lit travel-weary faces as the distinguished visitors made their way to where Kate sat sideways talking and squealing and having her hair arranged by Albert Alfonce, who perched beside her with his fitted case on his lap and a brown silk–covered hairpin between his teeth.

"Mademoiselle!" Elder Tennant said in a mocking tone with a low bow from the waist.

"Why, David—uh, Elder Tennant—what are you doing way back here?"

"How do you do?" Albert took the hairpin out of his lips and poked it into a rosette of hair. "There," he said.

"He's a hairdresser, Dav—ah, sir," Kate said, suddenly feeling a need to interpret the scene.

"Nobody told me *that*, Elder Pugmire," Elder Tennant turned and said sharply to one of his attendants.

"Oh, yes, sir!" Secure in her prettiness, Kate took it on herself to explain. "Don't you remember? On the ship? Brother Alfonce? He combed my hair and I was seasick and you told him—"

"A *hairdresser*, Elder Hyde?"

The man the angry official addressed grew still redder. "I assure you—" he began, but was cut off.

"How did this happen, Elder Pugmire?" Elder Tennant demanded.

Albert went on coolly piling up ringlets as he and three generations before him had done at Alfonce & Son's Hairdressing Emporium or in palatial boudoirs and tiring rooms, where often enough titled gentlemen stood at their elbows watching their ladies blossom.

"I think you know the rules, Elder Pugmire. You too, Elder Hyde."

"Rules, Elder Tennant?"

"Artisans first. Mechanics. Dairymen. Useful occupations. *Then* and only then a luxury trade or two."

"Yes, sir, but—"

"How did he get past Conway, that's what I want to know? You know the grading. You have heard President Young say that the meanest artisan contributes more to the accommodation of life than the most profound scholar!"

"I don't like mean people!" Kate said with a little toss of her head that made Albert's comb slip.

"Hold still!" he said abstractedly.

"The accommodation of life," Elder Tennant repeated. Turning on his heel, he started back up the aisle, his chastened attendants hurrying to keep up.

"Artisans *first*," he was saying as he strode past Lucitie. "Mechanics. Useful occupations. Landsmen! When we want bead-stringers, we will let you know. Lace makers and hairdressers. We will pass the word. Now you send Conway to me, where's he gone?"

What Albert had done with Kate's hair was to fluff it out on either temple and pin
it up in curls on top of her head with the long, carefully twisted marteau cascading down
the back, and as she made her way towards the car known as Headquarters, where she
had been getting special instruction from Elder Tennant in the ordering of events by
divine providence, and progressive revelation, different ladies asked her sweetly was she
in a wind-storm? did she just get out of bed? had she lost her comb? left-handed compliments that told Kate that in Albert Alfonce she had found a treasure.

Chapter Nineteen

*

As Albert had nowhere else particularly to go when they arrived at their destination, Lucitie suggested he come with her to the Salt Lake House, and they started out walking, carrying their belongings. He couldn't believe the town had been settled more than thirty years before, it still looked so raw and stirred up with dust, there was such a smell of fresh sawdust and drying plaster, so little shade, so many piles of things lying about, a movable frontier to all the habitable world! Lucitie thought it looked better than ever, the mountains higher, the sky bluer, and here was the Salt Lake House just as she had left it almost a year before, smelling the same too, of the soup du jour, dried apple pie, cigar smoke, cedar oil furniture polish, brown soap, ingrain carpets. She did not look in the direction of what had been her deceiver's room when he stayed there, never thought of it, and when she did think of it, of herself and him, and the moonlight, she wondered how she could ever have thought he was handsome!

By the proprietors and staff at the Salt Lake House Albert was welcomed with open arms, as Lucitie knew he would be, and his story soon told. Or it would have been had not Lucitie requested him to put in the part about the poor people rising up against the rich, in France, the terrible machine to lop off heads, and the hanks of hair for sale at the end of the day. The Birdwoods and Charlotte and the others had never heard of such a thing, though Mr. Birdwood had considerable knowledge of a military whiz named Napoleon from that general time and place. They all admired the watch Albert was going to sell to start his own Alfonce's Hairdressing Emporium, a beautiful gold one with a wreath of roses etched in the top and on the face under the gold numerals a matching wreath enameled in full color, and thought Lucitie had been very wise when she and Albert first met at the Mormon Emigration Agent's Office in London to advise him in a whisper while they were sitting together waiting to be called not to mention the watch, for then it must have gone to buy his passage and he would have had nothing to start his business with.

A week later, when he went to the Emigration Fund Office to pay the first installment on his debt, he was handed a letter instructing him to visit his Stake President at once for counseling. As he did not know who his Stake President might be or even that he had one, the brother in charge of the emigration office at that hour told him, and he soon found himself in the Consolidated Wagon and Machinery Company's small, dark and dusty office, where he was not asked to be seated. Had he sat, he would have disappeared from the sight of Elder Tennant, who occupied the swivel chair in front of the immensely high roll-top desk. But it was not Elder Tennant after all, as Albert could see after his eyes adjusted to the gloom, only a man who looked uncannily like him, as many in the metropolis seemed to do. "Oh, yes," the man said. "You."

"This letter says—"

"I know." He knew just what to do with his visitor, too, "counsel" him to remove himself to the Uintas and the desert there as quickly as possible—a desert most interestingly formed upon the barren bed of practically an ocean that used to cover all this land, he said, and of which the Great Salt Lake was just the small residue left—and with six other families help develop the town of Vernal. Was not that a great opportunity? Before Albert could answer, the Stake President was called away, departing by a back door. And soon after, a young man stuck his head in through the same door and said he was to say the visitor was free to go. Albert did not hurry, he was too amazed. And he still had the look of a mouse caught in a chamber pot when he got back to the Salt Lake House. Vernal! The Uintas! The barren bed of an ancient ocean! Six families! What could an English hairdresser do in a place like that?

"What the other poor things will have to do," Lucitie said indignantly. "Make dobies, dig ditches, build barns, carry boulders and herd cows!" His hands would be ruined! His lovely complexion—

"Well, a hairdressing establishment up *there* would be like trying to make harness out of hair-ribbons!" Mrs. Birdwood said when she heard. She too was indignant, for Albert had already demonstrated his quite remarkable skill on her hair and also her friend Mrs. O'Naughton's. "When are you supposed to leave?"

"As soon as possible," he said. "But I'm not going. Why should I? I came to America to be free."

"Oh, but you have to go," the other hotel maid Charlotte said sadly.

"Why?"

Several Mormons employed about the temporal hotel, including the stableman Mr. Lindfors, explained. Because in disobeying counsel, you disobey God. Because when the chips are down, obedience is the only test that matters. All the rest is just rabbit tracks. Because obedience is the main virtue a Saint got to have. Because if he ain't obedient, whatever *else* he is don't mean squat. Because when you submit to counsel, the Lord will overrule everything for your good. Because when you don't obey, people will think you're apostatizing and they won't sustain you.

"I don't want to be sustained. I only want not to go to some terrible place and be a pioneer. Salt Lake City, if you don't mind my saying so, is terrible enough."

"It's nobody but that old Elder, jealous over that silly girl!" Lucitie said.

"What silly girl?" Charlotte said.

"I will *not* go!"

AND ALBERT DID NOT. He apostatized. He was cut off from the church and cursed in his basket and his stores, his parts and powers of procreation. But he paid on his passage for the next three years and finally paid it out. More immediately, though, through the good offices of Mr. Birdwood, he sold his watch to a guest at the Salt Lake House, an official of the Emma Mine, and started Alfonce's Barber and Hairdressing Emporium. Twenty years before it would not have been possible, Mrs. Birdwood said, there was hardly anybody around but Latter-day Saints. But the railroad and mines opening up had changed all that, and Albert, once he got going, should have right nice clientele. Mr. Birdwood being of English descent himself and for some unknown reason very much taken with the Alfonce family background, particularly the part about the poor people chopping off the heads of the rich (though he and his wife as hotel owners fell more in the line with the latter than the former), did everything he could to help the newcomer settle in a good location. Of course they gave Lucitie her old job back, and she too began paying off her debt. But so put out was she by what Apostle Tennant (he was now an Apostle) had tried to do to Albert that she immediately backslid to the same point of obscure irreligion she was at before being re-converted in England.

It was at this time that Hindle, mother now of two small girls and the widow of Dr. Jefferson Morgan, arrived back in town, came looking for Lucitie at the Salt Lake House, found her going about her tasks, took it for granted she had been there all the time and nearly fainted when she heard her sister had in the meanwhile crossed and re-crossed the vast Atlantic Ocean! and here she thought *she* was such a traveler!

Until Hindle told her, Lucitie didn't know about Papa's sad end. But he was such a stranger she couldn't cry, not at the time she heard. She did cry a little later, after she went to bed, but that was as much for herself as him, that now she was a twenty-six-year-old orphan. But her tears soon dried when she thought of Albert. She had *him*. Only of course she didn't. Friendship was a good start, though, someone in whom to confide as they had done with each other. One night on the swaying train, the wheels clicking on the track and no light but the moonlight coming in the window, she even told him about her father being a wanted man for the past many years and why he was. That is, why they *said* he was. She was sure Papa could have explained everything if they gave him a chance.

Hindle told her that they did give him a chance, but according to the papers everything he said made things worse. Now Lucitie heard the news that he wasn't wanted anymore but dead, and hoped Albert wouldn't look down on her because of the circumstances or think him fallen away from ancestral excellence and herself low down on the social scale. Hindle said if it was her, she would say no more about it. And Lucitie took her advice, till one evening out for a walk with Albert she told him the truth. He had heard the first part, about Papa being wanted and in hiding, and now he must hear the last. In March, three hundred miles down the line, on the very spot where the massacre she told him about had taken place so long ago, they stood Papa up before a firing squad and—and—

"Like the Emperor Maximilian," Albert said quickly.

For his tact and kindness Lucitie wished she could squeeze his arm. She told him what Charlotte's mother Sister Bearpark had said, that had Lucitie and Hindle been big enough at the time of the murders to look around, they would have seen religious maniacs *everywhere*, not just Papa. The fanaticism was due to hard times and worry, Sister Bearpark said, people would never be like that again. Even Brother Brigham was a religious maniac at that particular time, thinking about nothing but the Blood of the Lamb, while now they said his mind was all on business, banks, property and the Salt Lake and Los Angeles Railway. "And Papa was in the midst, the very midst," Lucitie said.

"Best to forget it," Albert said, "the way I have in my own case. As you know, *my* father wasn't even my father, he was my grandfather. And look how he acted! Am I responsible for that? No. Are *you* responsible for what *your* father did? No. There's a verse to that effect in the Bible, if I'm not mistaken."

He might have been. But he was not mistaken in renting the place of business Mr. Birdwood recommended. It was right on the street running up from the railway station, people new in town would have to go right past it, while at the same time it was close to Main Street. Albert couldn't wait for Lucitie to see it, and when she did she gasped and clutched her chest, because what should it be but their old house! She was *born* there! Their cat Tyler was buried out in back. She could show Albert the exact spot! And talking of her poor father, he and a couple of his boys, who would be her half-brothers, had built it! "We always lived here till Mr. Blatchford come and married Mama when I was fourteen and a half and spoiled everything!" While Albert walked around thinking how his shop was going to be in the front part, where Mr. Birdwood said a candy maker and later a mantua maker had done well (one or the other had left a counter and a bell that jangled when you opened the door), and how snugly he could live in back, Lucitie stood still in a whirligig of memory, a revolution of time and events that brought tears to her eyes.

Alfonce's Barber and Hairdressing Emporium was open for business when Hindle came back to town. Nearly the first thing Lucitie told her was about Albert, about the old home, about how she and Charlotte had gone down there at night after work and helped him, scrubbed and cleaned, washed windows, polished the stove, cooked up food. On Lucitie's afternoon off she would go down and do what she could, also evenings after work when she got off early enough. Charlotte would go too when she could, which Lucitie didn't appreciate, but that was the beauty of having a hairdresser sweetheart, Mrs. Birdwood said. They were so *used* to women, they didn't pay any attention, while turn loose a sheepherder or prospector and oh, my.

But the trouble was, Albert wasn't her sweetheart, Lucitie said, he hadn't even kissed her on the cheek! "His trade, that's why," Mrs. Birdwood said soothingly. "Too much of a good thing. Like chocolate dippers."

"So what shall I do?"

"You're doing it. Helping him. Making him depend on you. Depend on you like a ship's boom depends on its crotch. It won't be long till you have him where you want him. And *then*," she went on like a science-master about to demonstrate Kepler's law of planetary motions, "you take away the crotch!"

Lucitie's face slowly reddened.

"Oh, you silly goose. A crotch for a ship's boom—that's kind of a pole with a forked top, like a great big sling-shot. I was born in Portsmouth, remember."

"I never knew there was such a thing."

"Well, there is."

And Lucitie, when she made her great journey, must have seen them herself amidst sea-works, not knowing what she was looking at. Well, she would be more and more of a crotch to him. And already he said once that if he ever went back to England, he hoped she would come too. They would bowl on the green, work together, fish along the river, save money, go to Margate. He spoke in the spirit of good-fellowship, Lucitie might have been a boy. The word "marriage" dropped into the conversation at that point would have been like a discharge of fierce lightning between clouds down onto a wild mustang.

DOCTOR KNEW THAT TOT BURDICK (who with her sister Serapta ran Burdick's Institution for the Care of the Sick) loved him better than a miser loves his gold, Hindle was sure, but he never spoke of it. He did say it was hard to write that letter! and that he never expected an answer. But Tot did write, her answer was a long while catching up. The surprise and combustion of that morning, her letter said, when the boy brought the news and Dr. Orem came to take over Doctor's patients, was one that none of them at Burdick's would ever forget if they lived to be a hundred. And she might as well tell him that at first she did not wish him luck. But now she could see things in a different light, and, well, he was *alive* at least, that was the main thing. She made no mention of Hindle. If Tot ever wrote again they did not know it, for in Santa Fe Doctor decided on a name change—Fairbrass instead of Morgan—that cut them off from the past. Hindle liked the sound of Fairbrass, it sounded like a band concert down in Liberty Park, and Fairbrass being his mother's maiden name, Doctor said, he had a right to it. But didn't he think—? Because of his doctor's diploma and everything? He laughed at that, a doctor's diploma wasn't "la balle de Flandres," he said, the only one in the world! Soon he had another one just like it, except for the name, on aged vellum (the man who made it was a regular Rembrandt) and a new painted shingle even better than the old one.

At first he thought his enemies were everywhere! Texas, the New Mexican Territory, California, like the Black Hand Society of Sicily that once they started after a man never gave up till they got him. He grew a beard, traded one coat for another, traded rigs, horses, went under his new name. But as time went on and nobody shot or stabbed or tipped the garrote on him, he knew he had made it through, and need not shun windows or friendly strangers and could negotiate a corner without trying to see around it like a snail.

Tʜᴇ Sᴛᴀᴛᴇ Sᴛʀᴇᴇᴛ ʀᴏᴀᴅ ᴡᴀs perfect when Hindle drove in, not dusty, not muddy, packed down, broad and straight as a string. Not a road or street she had been on in all these years could equal it, ditch-banks to either side, clear water running—Twenty giddy remarks she wanted to make, but the children were napping. Instead she slapped the reins and, elated to thoughtlessness, sang under her breath, *O Zion, Dear Zion, Land of the Free.* But it had been a long time and she forgot the words except how it ended, *All my fond hopes are centered in thee.* And that's what they are, she thought. Centered in thee. The mountains always standing there! The double houses! More double houses on one block here than in whole *towns* anywhere else! The old green gates! Brigham had a surplus of green paint and so the Lord told him to tell the people to paint their gates green. That's what the Gentiles said, always making fun, small pleasures for small minds. Grape-vines! trailing and climbing plants, their shade. Ash and linden—"Then said the trees unto the vine: Come thou"—how did it go?—"come thou and be our king!" She said the verse to herself that, ages ago, Lucitie learned to recite in Sunday school. Oh, her dear sister! Now that she was so close and would see her, she missed her fiercely, and being home felt oddly homesick. What Doctor used to say might not have been far wrong, that "we require heaven and we have it not," and that homesickness for any time or person is just "requiring heaven." He didn't *believe* in such a place, just that we require it.

From where she was, Burdick's Institution for the Care of the Sick was not very far, a turn right at the crossroad up ahead, four blocks east and—Wouldn't it be strange if when she was going by—? Ashamed to think it, it was so silly, she went ahead and thought it anyhow, how she would be going by and here's this carriage standing at the gate, and under the sign the front door suddenly opens, someone appears and, putting on his hat as he runs down the steps, hurries to the sidewalk—"Why, Mr. Clarendon!" She pulls on the reins—"Hindle! Oh, my God. Can it really be you? I was just in there asking—" Her response would be calm and ladylike. "What a pleasant surprise." She would only drive past for a look, circle the block, it wouldn't take long and Lucitie wasn't *waiting.* What would she say if Serapta was in the yard? If Tot should be at the window and sent Garnet out to hail her? If Tot should say she would *never* forgive her? "But Tot, he wanted me, I don't know why. Yes, I do. Because he used to say that those who think must govern those who toil, and he was *thinking,* see, and I was *toiling.* Really, when I look back that's the way it was."

But where was she? This wasn't the old corner! Where was Phoebe Griffin's long funny house with the rooms strung out like railway cars? She must have turned too early, went past too far. Something was wrong. The hospital—the sign—? *These* lots were all in garden, peas and kale, dried and neglected-looking. How could anyone forget an old location that meant so—? There stood the house next door, Mrs. Vigor's, with the cupola like somebody with a hat on sitting on the roof. What is this *garden*? What had happened here? "I've been away."

"Well, I should think you *have*," Mrs. Vigor said, contemptuousness and reproach in her remark, as if to say the horse is missing now, no use coming around to lock up the stable.

"What happened to the hospital?"

"What happened? Why, girl, it burned down in hellfire so hot it nearly boiled the water in the *ditches*, that's what happened. Lit up everything for blocks around, maybe clear to Sandy for all I know, wind a-howling and blowing, lightning, thunder, I thought the great day of His wrath is come and who shall be able to stand? It fairly roared, I run outside and what do my eyes see? Why, Satan, girl, lit all up by flames, running along the Institution roof, leaping from room to room, I *seen* him and have so bore my testimony, seen the smoke come up out of the pit, billowing and rising till the sun it become 'as black as sackcloth of hair, and the moon as blood'! I thought for sure the great day of His wrath—"

"Why, Mrs. Vigor, what a terrible thing to happen. I just can't believe it. Did anybody—die?"

"Can you ask the question?" the other said derisively. "Did they *die*?" She paused, looked up into the sky, then down. "According to the Tribune, the answer is no. Nobody died."

"No?" Hindle said, startled and relieved.

"But that's *them*, they print whatever they want, the truth ain't worth squat to that old Gentile Tribune. *Alton* died, he was poor Phoebe's son, from the smoke in his lungs two days later over at Murdock's house. That's where they all went after the fire. *Tot* died—"

"Oh, that's terrible!"

"It is. That's what I'm telling you. Not right then, but three months later. But that's what caused it. Like a cup with a crack in it will last just so long, then fall to pieces. Happened at the show, right uptown there at the Salt Lake Theater. Her and Serapta had took that pink-eyed child—"

"Mavis—?"

"Mavis. The one the actress left, spoiled beyond all reason. Anyway, they went, and Tot—set right there in her seat and passed away. Head fell forward—But yet in the Tribune the morning after the fire, the headline said no lives was lost. A lie I guess if ever I did see one. That poor thing passed away as surely 'by the flames, and by the smoke, and also by the brimstone—'" She paused. "There was an ugly Indian over there."

"Could that have been Loudhawk?"

"Whatever his name was, he was some kind of hero. But there's that old Tribune again. Nothing but lies. Couldn't speak the truth if they was to hang."

"And everybody went to Murdock's?"

"Did you know the girls?" Mrs. Vigor asked abruptly.

"Tot and Serapta, you mean? Why, gracious, I used to *work* there."

"Well, it never made a bit of sense from the beginning." The old woman's disapproving glance went to the vacant lots with their stagnant vegetation. "And less so now. Some Gentiles own the property, and what they mean to do with it is beyond *me*. Attract snakes, I guess. Rabbits. And one night I looked out and seen—" She shook her head, unable to name it. "I tell you, I would no more sell to a Gentile—Like I said that night before the rain commenced to pouring, 'Lord,' I said, when it seemed like *my* house might catch too, 'Redeemer, Lord, keep the flames from blowing in this direction and I promise you no Gentile's never going to step foot on *this* place!' You know God hates selling to Gentiles worse than anything."

"I can't believe it's gone like it never existed," Hindle said as if out of sleep.

"You say you used to work there. Which one was you?"

"I was—I was Hindle."

That's who I *was*. Who am I now? she thought as she drove away. Doctor used to say that, like a snake sluffs off its skin, our whole entire body, inside and out, gets cast off every seven years. Except our brain's and teeth's constituents (put in to last), everything else keeps changing, though we stay our *self*. Like Company B is always Company B, although the soldiers in it come and go. And that is us, a constant duplicate (over and over) of who we started out as, till the worms replace our tiny particles with dust.

Chapter Twenty

*

THEY HAD HAD SOME FURNITURE, THERE WAS CORD WOOD IN THE YARD AND also the calf that Doctor got for curing the blacksmith's son of the nervous debility caused by the indiscretions of youth. An allopath just setting up practice in Prescott bought the heating stove, roll-top desk, bowl, pitcher, slop-pail and spittoon from the office, and a young contractor going through made an offer for some of the rest of the equipment. She was about to accept it when, standing there handling the stuff, he began laughing at Doctor's turnbuckle device for pulling teeth, the hump-shaped forceps he used to use when he was a young man to extract arrowheads, his stomach syringe for pumping out poisons, and the stranger's amusement so assailed her she decided not to let *anything* go.

"I'd take it all, ma'am," the contractor said.

"Sorry."

So at great inconvenience to herself, she hung onto and shipped to Salt Lake City not only those items but the old worn wooden stethoscope, Doctor's drug-grinder, pill-making machine, leather satchel that held his static-electricity muscle-awakeners, slackeners and nerve-soothers, the Colt Peacemaker he had in his pocket when he fell out of the wagon, his scoop shovel to dig out snowdrifts, the compass someone gave him on his twenty-eighth birthday and his row of books. An unopened wooden packing case from Binns and Bellhouse, Chicago, full of sacks of roots, herbs, leaves, barks, and minerals, was shipped too. And she sent a box of tinctures in mostly opened bottles, which the druggist said was the foolishest thing *he* ever saw done, though she sealed the stoppers with wax. What did she think she was going to do with the ipecac, paregoric, belladonna, quinine, ergot and carbonate of iron anyway? Besides hold the bottles up to the light when she got where she was going and find them empty? "They won't be empty," she said haughtily. But she thought to herself they might be, thought as she was packing and leaving that they *would* be, of course. The tinctures would evaporate, the elements fall to powder, instruments be lost, and what he "doctored" with—whatever it was the doctors "doctored" with (beyond their medicine and tools)—that she'd been close to, she would never be close to again. Manitou, he called it in a joking way, the science and art, the province, the philosopher's elixir! like it was a trick to fool the public. "But yet, you know," he said, "*sometimes it breathes life into a stone*."

119

IN HIS DISPENSARY ONE TINCTURE that never did dry up, because it never had a chance, was what he said was Paracelsus's favorite remedy, ruby-colored laudanum, a name he told Hindle one time came from the Latin verb *laudare*, to praise. *He* praised it surely! and took and gave it far and wide, but only to men. The reason for that was because being a moral, not a physical, essence, it was suitable only for the masculine sex, he said, obscuring the subject further by explaining that the laws that regulate the combination of a man's elementary substances and the phenomena that accompany *his* exposure to diverse physical conditions are not binding when it comes to women. "Why is that?" "If I knew, I'd be a lot smarter than I am." "But what kind of laws are you talking about?" "The law that woman will turn yellow under prolonged ingestion, while a man won't. That a woman will grow long white hairs on her tongue, while a man won't. That a man will never get so down in the dumps from the ultimate effects of living as to claw his cheeks till they run with blood. And then you take the Five Predictables—But in cases where there's *insanity* in the family—" He made a whistling sound. "Don't look at me," she had told him. "*I* ain't going to test no laws. And another thing, if that's what you're hinting at, there's no insanity in my family."

It seemed to her he had been saying things like that ever since the news came out in the Alamogordo Gazette about her father being caught at last, "the notorious High Priest," as the paper called him, and she told Doctor she was one of the "High Priest's" daughters. Quite according to established usage, but then as more articles came out about the prisoner's progress through life, his humor and certain opinions he held, such as that God was as married man Himself—several times over—that the original Garden of Eden was located about a mile and a half south of Independence, Missouri, and that if you take a mountain lion with a baby cub and milk her and put the milk in a glass jar, the jar will break, Doctor began casting aspersions about craziness, about how a person where there was insanity in the family should protect their head from the hot sun, not laugh too hard and different warnings like that. "If you mean *my* family, why don't you come right out and say so?" Hindle had said sharply. "Sweetheart, insanity and folly are two different things!" he said. "So what are you talking about? That Papa's insane?" This was when the trial was going on. "They all are." "Me too, you mean." "You're ready to chew nails now, aren't you? Look, I'll apologize." He did so by saying, "Circumstances individuate actions. Haven't I always said so? Unless it all boils down to seminium." At least his *tone* sounded like he was apologizing, so she forgave him, but would not allow him the satisfaction of asking him to tell her in plain English what he had just said.

SHE WOULD ADVERTISE IN THE Salt Lake Tribune. "Pharmacopeia for Sale." No, dispensary. "Full dispensary. Medical instruments. Bay horse, rig, trunk, hand-carved frame." But there was time enough to do that after she settled in. Lucitie thought she should get rid of the stuff beforehand. Why stumble over boxes and packing cases she was just going to get rid of anyway? At no great profit either, Lucitie would bet. What a shame *she* had not been there to help her leave Prescott. And it wouldn't have hurt any if she had been along when Hindle went house hunting, either. At least Lucitie would have seen to it that she had a pump in the kitchen and wasn't sharing the back yard with a grouchy old bachelor.

"He paints signs and things like that, Mr. Palmstedt says. Goes to bed with the chickens and never bothers anyone. He comes from the Old Country."

"But don't he have to use that path there around by your dining room window? Next thing you know he'll be peeking in. And where is he to get his water but from your pump?" Lucitie paused, then added, "Which Old Country?"

"Denmark, I think."

"Well, at least that's better than if he was from somewheres like *Spain*." Lucitie looked worriedly through the kitchen window at the small barn some distance out back that the sign painter used as both home and place of business. "Just don't encourage him, is all I say," she said, turning back into the room. "Had I been with you when you looked for a place to rent down here on Seventh South, I'd have put my foot down. Where's the children to play? And I'd make it plain from the very beginning, this belongs to *me*, that belongs to *you*." No sooner had Hindle and Lucitie been reunited than *elder sister* and *younger sister* might have been stamped on the two in intaglio with a punch, so quickly did childhood's hierarchy assert itself, though Lucitie was not by nature overbearing and had but small advantage of years.

"Mr. Palmstedt says we'll be lucky to even see the man. Well, and speak of the devil," Hindle said, glancing through the open door at the man coming up the steps, "here's Mr. Palmstedt with my screen door now." Actually her landlord did not have Hindle's screen door but said she would get it before the week was out, that was what he stopped by to tell her. She introduced him to Lucitie and he said you could certainly see the family resemblance. He also put Lucitie's mind at ease about Stig Fogelmarck, the sign painter in the barn. Good Mormon, paid his rent, kept to himself, no bad habits. Hindle couldn't have a better neighbor. From worrying about the sign painter, Lucitie went to worrying about the landlord. If he wasn't the sort to knock on a person's door and barge in any time he felt like it, she said after he had gone, she would miss her guess! In fact, a man that would get up from the table the first time he ever sat at it and pour his own *self* a second cup of coffee probably wouldn't even knock in the *first* place, just open the door and walk in! And how would Hindle like *that*, though he wasn't bad-looking in kind of a Scandinavian way and not too old. Because the *next* step, he'd be taking off his shoes and laying down for a nap!

"Oh, no," Hindle said, "he's busy with his houses. And he's got some kind of a business. Tailor shop, I think. And a wife he's scared of."

"That man? Scared of a wife? Don't make me laugh!" Lucitie said.

"Well, he is. Because evening before last when he was here to fix the step and was sitting at the table—"

"Oh, so this *wasn't* the first time—"

"Me and the girls was just finishing supper," Hindle said, feeling guilty. "He said Fern would kill him if she saw what he was up to!"

"To even make a *remark* like that, don't you see what's on his mind?"

"He was drinking coffee. That's all he meant. Apparently she's strong on the doctrine and believes in the Word of Wisdom, and if she saw him drinking coffee she'd be mad. While in the case of his *other* two wives—"

"Just what I would have expected," Lucitie said disgustedly, "go out of your way to rent from a polygamist. Have you met the ladies?"

"Not yet," Hindle said. "Though he did have one in the rig the other day."

"No doubt his latest. *And* youngest. *And* prettiest."

Latest and prettiest Fern was indeed, as Hindle found out over the next few weeks. But not the youngest, for she was in her forties, all of a decade older than Hindle's landlord, landlording for the first time in his life because Fern, a widow when they married the previous year, owned the cottage Hindle was renting, the sign painter's barn, the small double house the other two wives, Pearl and Rosina, shared in another neighborhood and the nice house her husband had made his headquarters almost from the day of their marriage.

But Fern's better *house* was not the problem that Pearl and Rosina, who were sisters, went to the bishop about. *That*, Fern could not help, they told him. The nice house was in her family, the one she had lived in with her dead husband, not Lennart's contribution. But third wife Fern *could* help something else, and that was taking unfair advantage by giving Lennart presents when it wasn't even his birthday, let alone Christmas! such as a gold toothpick and a stereopticon, by cooking what you might call Sunday meals on weekdays—"And she's got a great big music box," Rosina put in. Also, she must be doing something else to cause him to stay with her *three* nights during the week while Pearl got only Monday and Tuesday, and Rosina only Wednesday and Thursday.

"And if this is to go on forever, it is just not fair," Rosina said.

"Fair," the bishop said like a natural exclamation of lament. "Fair."

"Well, she's his rich third wife and we're his poor first and second, and we don't even get the benefit of Lennart not needing to pay rent no more for where we live," Pearl said.

"And she thinks she's so smart flitting around in her ribbons and lace," Rosina added.

"Sometimes we come closer to blasphemy than we realize," the bishop said. "But ignorance don't prevent us from going to hell. So now you ladies ponder that while I put the matter into Higher Hands than mine."

This activity having to be taken care of in the next room with the door closed, he absented himself but was back before the two complainers could decide whether the man's eyes being close together like that kept him from being handsome or whether it was the way he showed only his lower teeth when he talked or laughed, such an unfortunate habit. "Well, sisters, here's your answer." He read it off a paper like a teletype that had just arrived. "Wives, submit yourselves unto your own husband as unto the Lord. For the husband is the head of the wife even as Christ is the head of the church: and he is the savior of the body. Therefore as the church is subject unto Christ, so let the wives be to their own husband in everything. There," he said, baring his row of lower teeth, "that should put the thing in perspective." They wished they could have told him not to do it, though with eyes that close together he *still* would not have been very good-looking.

Well, so they had paid their call. And it was not in vain, they came away reconciled, especially after it dawned on Pearl during the walk home "that all we're really talking about is one measly extra night *every three weeks*! Do you realize that?" When she finally got it through Rosina's head how that could be, "because there's two of us and one of her and seven days in the week and four weeks to the month," Rosina was sorry they had even *bothered* the bishop, though it didn't hurt to mention the *bribery* that had been going on, what else would you call it? Still, since marrying Fern, Lennart's disposition had improved, the burden of his starched shirts was off them and onto her—by her own request—and the woman did try to be friendly. By the time they got inside Pearl's side of the double house and put the kettle on, they decided not only not to keep on giving Fern the cold shoulder but to try to revive their friendship's original exultancies and kindness by sending her some of Rosina's head cheese and the edging for a pair of pillowcases which Pearl would crochet.

The head cheese accomplished what they hoped, but by the time the edging got done Fern was not speaking to either of them or ever expected to again, for she had traced the hint for more tithing and Lennart's having to pay a proxy for several days' more work per annum on the ditches than he had ever been assessed before to their buttinsky visit to the bishop. Pearl felt bad about it, Fern had promised her the black taffeta she had worn while in mourning for her husband, but Rosina said she was happy never to have to see that swan's neck and cow-pile hairdo ever in her life again.

THE AUGUST AFTERNOON HINDLE WENT uptown to shop—but mostly to subscribe to the Salt Lake Tribune, her years with Doctor having addicted her to a daily paper—out of idle curiosity she went roundabout to pass what she thought was Fern's house. It wasn't, as she found out later, but even if it had been, her landlord Mr. Palmstedt's third wife would scarcely have come out from behind her drawn blinds and closed door *that* sweltering day to risk her fair complexion to a dull overcast that, in stillness acoustical enough to hear a pin drop, brought out freckles worse than full sunlight. And not the well-complexioned only kept within, but everyone who could, including dogs and cats. Hindle saw not a living soul till she came to Main Street, where the pedestrians, the few not awning-shaded, seemed more shimmering surface dimensions than bodily form, as if a magic lantern cast their length and breadth. The heat did that, misshaped the light, filled day as full of vague uneasiness as night, *presageful*—easy enough to say after the fact, but Hindle swore she had felt it at the time. Many said the same that day in Salt Lake City, that they had sensed a *waiting between acts*, as if something was going to happen, some force like gravity going to give way, or banks of circulation go under.

In the cool, dark Tribune building under the softly turning fan, she waited for someone to come and take her subscription but also, as at an ancient drama, for the pillars to start to crack, or the ceiling to shower some preliminary plaster. Lightning? Thunder? The angel Michael? who the cook at Burdick's Institution had said years ago was going to be the first one down from the sky on the Judgment Day, one foot on the Wasatch mountains, the other on the Great Salt Lake. If the clerk in the green eyeshade and arm-garters who suddenly popped up behind the Tribune counter had said the end had started and Michael was already outside, Hindle wouldn't have been surprised, so raveled out the end the man seemed, too breathless nearly to ask her what she wanted. Why, to take the paper, she said, and he nodded but abandoned his place to run down the room through swinging doors into another great chamber, from which she heard a noise that sounded (or was it that *should* have sounded?) not like newspaper men at work, or their machinery, but like the heaping up of Jordan's waters behind a dam that was about to burst.

IT BURST BEFORE SHE GOT home. She heard the boys running through the streets crying *Extra! Death of the Seer and Revelator!* while the stars of heaven fell onto Salt Lake City, the sky departed as a scroll when it is rolled together, Timpanogos and Antelope Island were jarred out of their places. Of course Hindle ran after a newsboy and bought a paper, even though she had finally paid for a subscription and would, the agitated eyeshaded man who finally returned to the counter had told her, have a paper thrown onto her porch the very next morning. The front page was cross-barred with twenty headlines. *LEADER DIES. BRIGHAM YOUNG EXPIRES. TOXOPHORE THOUGHT CAUSE OF SUDDEN SEIZURE.* Toxo—? Anything with "tox" in front of it meant poison! Had someone poisoned *Brigham Young*? Quickly she read, "Nature is a blind and fatal Agent. Last evening, within a few hours of standing in the back yard of the Beehive House talking to Apostle Burley P. Richards and gormandizing on the ripe fruit of the *Amygdalus persica* tree, the great and illustrious leader of the Church of Jesus Christ of Latter Day Saints, President Brigham Young, fell into the convulsive fit from which he never recovered." Some missionary must have brought him some kind of unusual tree from the South Sea Islands, she thought, and wouldn't *he* catch it! But no, here was the word "peaches," and here was the information that under certain conditions the *common peach* is as capable as a rattlesnake of introducing into the torrent of man's circulation an organic radical that can deprive him of life! Only one physician of the five attendant at the great man's deathbed had so far been contacted, and he said it looked like there was a connection. Their Prophet, their Moses who had led them into Canaan, *had* stood in his back yard and sampled a few peaches, no one knew how many, and he *had* passed away, a strong, healthy man of only seventy-seven with a steady heart, good lungs and not an ache nor a pain…Fortuitously, an English toxicologist from Madagascar who happened to be passing through town had made himself available to the newspaper as consultant and gave as his opinion that "any substance on earth can poison if the humors are out of balance, be it what it may, rhubarb, wild rye, potatoes, finnan haddie or, as one may see in the present circumstance, peaches." The ossiculum, the stone of the peach, he further stated, if cracked, smelled of bitter almond, which anyone might test, always a sign of an arsenical component…

"A fine thing to say at the height of the peach season!" Lennart Palmstedt said when he read Hindle's Tribune. Unable to content himself at Pearl's, Rosina's or Fern's abodes that first leaderless evening of his life (though First Counselor John Taylor would assume command tomorrow after he stayed up all night praying by himself), Lennart had called for consolation on several people, his partner in the tailoring shop, the greengrocer and even on his renter the sign painter Stig Fogelmarck, who so far had never asked him in and did not then, proclaiming through a window that the news had broken him down and he had gone to bed. Now Mr. Palmstedt was at Hindle's lamplit table reading her Tribune, and just as he expected, it was full of Gentile lies. Lies and slander, making the President out as some kind of a pig, gobbling up peaches till they were running out of his ears. And this here so-called "expert"! Humors! Poison! The poisonest thing in town that *he* knew of was this rotten newspaper!

"Would you like some coffee?" Hindle said.

"And that's another thing," her landlord said severely, shaking his head and waving her away. "It's possible—" But he broke off, for fear of sounding somewhat stuck on himself. But it *was* possible. That Lennart Palmstedt might be an object of such moment to the Creator and Ruler of the universe that when *he* didn't hew to the Word of Wisdom (for had he not drunk coffee with his new renter?), *all Zion had to pay.* He hoped sincerely that it wasn't so. But who knew?

When at past nine o'clock the following night a knock came at the door, Hindle heard it with annoyance, though it was late for her landlord and his way was to give a rap or two, then walk right in like a relation. Being one in fact, Lucitie would not even have knocked ordinarily, but in a mood of play and wanting to surprise her sister (who had never since her return seen her in the company of Albert Alfonce, the hairdresser from England), on this night she did so. Hindle started back when she opened the door and saw the two standing there. "Well!" she said, "for gracious sakes! Come in—"

"This here is Albert, Albert Alfonce," Lucitie said, her wide pupils not growing smaller in the lamplight. "Guess where we been?"

"To the park?"

"To the *Tabernacle*! And if ever you seen a sight, it's up there tonight. Did you go already?"

"No. The children—But I read in the paper—"

"Reading won't do, you got to go in person!" Lucitie said excitedly. "It's just like I told Albert when Mrs. Birdwood let me off at five o'clock so I could go down and tell him Mrs. Birdwood's friend Mrs. O'Naughton wants him to come and fix her hair at eight o'clock tomorrow morning—she's to sit with the Gentile dignitaries—'How many times in *your* lifetime, Albert, will you get a chance to see Brigham Young laying in state?' I said. 'Once and once only!' And it's the same with you, Hindle. And you and me got a kind of an obligation, Brigham being the one that married Mama and Papa, which you know Mama said he did."

"Maybe I'll go tomorrow," Hindle said.

"Do you know how hot it's going to be *tomorrow*? Mr. Birdwood says just terrible! So why don't you go tonight? It's cooled off lovely, hasn't it?" Lucitie turned to her companion, then back. "Albert said when we got out and started walking down here—and I tell you, you really got to push your way through the crowds—that for the first time since he come to Salt Lake it really seems like a city, not just a village with big wide empty roads. But that wasn't what I was going to tell you—Oh, I know. When we come out, Albert said that he thought his hair had been rinsed in tea."

"Come out from where?"

"From the Tabernacle! From viewing him."

"Beard, too," the hairdresser said. "Lord Bury's was done that way. Gives a lovely cast to white hair. Oolong, or wulung, as the Chinese call it."

"Are you talking about Brigham?"

"Who would ever think of such a thing?" Lucitie said proudly. "Albert also would of parted his hair on the other side. But he looks lovely anyway, and his apron's gorgeous. You shouldn't miss out on this, Hindle, you really shouldn't. That's why we come down, to give you a chance, in case you hadn't got away to go."

"But look how late it is!"

"You'll never know it when you get on Main Street! Will she, Albert? Lit up as bright as day, and such a stir—"

"At *this* hour?" Hindle said.

"That don't make no difference. They're keeping open up there till every living soul that wants to pass by and view him is going to get their wish. Them there doors was opened at nine this morning and ain't been hardly a minute since that time the aisle ain't just been packed. First you stand in line—"

"I bet a nickel they'll be shut and locked," Hindle said.

"How about a dollar? No, they won't. Going all night and into tomorrow morning and into the afternoon till the funeral starts!"

"A real long line?"

"Not very," Lucitie said.

"Ten miles long," Albert contributed.

"Oh, now, Albert! No, it wasn't," Lucitie said.

"How long did it take you to get past?"

"Well, let's see—"

"Hours," Albert said exhaustedly. He had taken a seat by the open door and was fanning himself with his hat.

"You just won't notice the time at all, it goes so fast, looking at—around you, don't you know. You'll just *kick* yourself if you don't go!"

"Oh, I don't think so," Hindle said. But after a while, tempted more than a little by the pomp and parade that never again, according to her sister, would be seen on earth, she tidied up, put her bonnet on and, catching up her shawl, set forth into the balmy night to see for herself.

See and be confounded! by the sights uptown, crowds thronging the streets, rigs, wagons, and all so strangely quiet, babies, horses, wheels, muffled in decorum like a drum wrapped up to deaden sound. And there along the great wall of Salt Lake, twenty feet high, she found not only where the line started, feeding into the South Temple gate, but also where it doubled around back onto itself, a line somnambulant as a python rocksnake. It moved and didn't move, turned a corner, then stalled, as peristaltically from time to time a wave-like contraction would run down its length when someone in the line leaned with their back against the wall, or when inside the Tabernacle a viewer froze in his track by the bier and had to be pushed onward. The north rampart was the dank, dark stretch and seemed the longest. Off to the north and east, wrapped in darkness, the city burial ground lay along the hillside, but Brigham would be buried in the private graveyard in a corner of his own property under a stone that said—what did the paper say it was going to say?—*He was a Man of Marvelous Equipment.* Someone in the line repeated that news. Another said, "They couldn't buffalo *him.*" Being able to look towards the crush around the Tithing Office and down Main Street made the east wall, a city block long, seem shorter than the other three sides. Then one more turn, some going up and down dispersedly, in through the gate, winding in an irregular course past what appeared to be a quarry and at last, near midnight, arrival at the Tabernacle's consecrated portal. A man three places up stumbled when crossing the threshold into the nave but caught himself. Between him and Hindle, two women in black-curtained leghorn hats whispered to each other in agitation. "I didn't say I *would,* I said I *might.*" "Some people faint on purpose." "Well, not me, if that is what you're hinting." "To get attention."

After the brightness outside, of the stars, full moon, resplendence of corner lights, lanterns on carriages and lamps in shops and houses, the big dark Tabernacle seemed more like the vaulted night than night itself. Cooler than it, though, with the double doors all around the place (bastioned by firm spruce gentlemen) standing open to the mountain breezes. "Straight ahead. Keep going. Please keep moving." And there it loomed like a flower-laden ship in front of tall, stiff shadows, shadows that played soft passages of organ music. The dead lights flickered, roses smelled, and if ever (deathwards going) there was a time to think what is it all *for*? why, it was there and then. And Hindle tried to think along those lines.

But is it not sometimes at such a moment that the human mind turns impertinent? Gives up the grand for jackanapes reflections? Out of nowhere to Hindle's inner eye came an unchaste vision of Bishop Dugger! the storekeeper of St. George who rode down off the cliffs that early twilight, down towards her fire…She had told herself she'd never think of him and didn't, hadn't, yet here he was dismounting in front of her fire. "Evening, sis." And there once more they lay on the ground together (her blush made her eyes sting, the roots of her hair bristle and heated the breath in her nostrils) till the first light. And he was telling her—while her teeth chattered in the morning chill after the villainous warmth of their unsleeping—about how he would come and seek her out, and how they two would take their mutual endowments and then go find theirself a place to be, and lock the door—She saw him "saving up," as he had said he was going to do for her, in a tangled bed with a haphazard wife, heard his panting orders to be tested, put through the furnace, yea, be cupellated—oh, my God, you vixen—even killed, holding his temptress off, his irascible concupiscible principle, as he had panted in his bishop's voice, insurgent against reason and—look, standing like a pole…Not ten steps now away from Death's countenance, how could she picture anything so vile? And viler still: herself and him together on the ground, her proneness blotting out his stars, and he was as he had been, scaly, goat-shanked, hairy-bellied, smelling of sweat and horses, dried foam on the blubbery lips she fell upon and—Blinking, she came to herself, drew her breath in a convulsive tremor of repugnance. Then it was but five steps. Then two. And the ladies' whispering grew loud. "If everything goes black—" "It ain't going to. Now *look* while you got the chance." "Oh, Brigham, Brigham!" "Look at his apron. That embroidery!" "Will you try not bossing me for once?" "This way, sisters."

Hindle took a step but was not more than at the foot of the bier when a firm spruce usher with an old man and three old women in tow (without heeding, she had heard them making their way up the aisle behind her with loud whispers) said "Excuse me, please," and steered her aside. One of the firm spruce men at the door stepped firmly over. "From Boise," the usher said. "Elder Penrose. He helped—The martyrs—"

"Yep, we brung 'em home," the old man quavered.

"Oh, yes. Well, take your time, sir." The doorkeeper went back to his post. The old man shuffled up to the head of the coffin, bent and spoke as if to someone alive. "Brig, it's Orson—" But what he said then Hindle could not hear above the women's murmuring between themselves. "Don't the man look like a king." "He *was* a king." "He *is* a king." "I just can't think he's dead!" "He ain't. Not really." "How could simple peaches—?" "I just don't believe it." "Peaches from a person's own back yard!"

AND IN A FLASH IT all came back to her. They were heading—where? Oh, yes, Rock Springs. Doctor pointed, off in the distance she could see a few dim lights. And he was in the talkative mood she found he would get in (when she knew him better) as they neared some place that was always, due to the mountain or desert air, the height expressed by angular distance above the horizon or some such thing—he once explained it to her—farther off than it looked. Then he would have a nip of tonic and start to talk as a distraction, and she liked that, for more often than not he rode along in silence. Their first weeks together, the thing he talked about mostly was their leaving Salt Lake. It bothered him, that some people might think he was a coward, his friend at the Tribune, the one he had told his resolve to after he was beaten up, "never to sag with doubt nor shake with fear," or leave the field to his enemies. But as Judge Baskin said, he had no more chance to take over the hot springs and start a spa out there than he had to flatten the Rockies. "Go while the going's good," Baskin said. "He who fights and runs away lives to fight another day."

"He said he told Richardson the same thing," Doctor said. "Told him, 'Listen, son, once they conclude to do you in, why, make your will.' But Richardson just laughed, he had the whole U.S. Government behind him, he said—"

"Who was he? Richardson?" she said without much interest.

"Didn't look the part, I can tell you that, big blue exophthalmic eyes—eyes that bulge out—" He started from the first day to tell her what certain long words meant, and she in her giddiness to forget what he told her, though she would not always. "Peach-blow complexion. Kind of a fat-boy example. But smart and energetic enough for the Secretary of the Interior to send the man out here to make a survey of all the non-metallic resources in the Territory. And he'd have done it, too, whether Brigham took it as a personal insult or not—which naturally he did—if they hadn't killed him. We guessed they had when all of a sudden he didn't show up for supper or anything else and the lies started circulating about his skipping off with someone's wife. 'He's deader than a mackerel *somewhere*,' Baskin said. 'You can bet on that.' But without a corpus delicti, what could we do?" Doctor said. "Nothing. The Tribune wrote up his absence from his old haunts, then it all died down and we will never know, we said. The years went by, but then last spring Baskin was in his office late one night expecting some callers to sneak in by a side entrance. And who these callers were was his friend Sam Gilson and a fugitive by the name of William Hickman, who was badly in need of a good lawyer. If one would be enough! with the U.S. Marshal after him on the one side with a list of crimes as long as your arm, and on the other that bunch of hooligans the Destroying Angels that he used to run with, laying for him for double-crossing them. So he was in a pretty tight corner. Baskin was disgusted that Gilson had brought him along, but Gilson said Hickman knew a lot, which it turned out he did when he started spieling for his life, and one thing he knew was the fate of Richardson."

"I suppose the Mormons murdered him," Hindle said coldly, preparing to stand up for the church not because she was "in religion" herself, but for Papa's sake and for the old neighbors' and the little city of Nauvoo she helped to build out of cardboard in childhood on a Primary table. "And took and threw his body off a cliff."

"Funny you should say that," Doctor said, not enough acquainted with her then to know she was being sardonic. "Because that was it exactly. According to Hickman, they stabbed and shot him. But on their way to—as you say—throw him off a cliff, somebody suggested they go past the Beehive House and give the old man a chance to see the body, as he was the one in town with the biggest grudge. Of course they weren't sure they'd find him at home. He's got places to light till hell won't have 'em. But sometimes he does sleep alone in the Beehive House, to kind of renew his powers, so they say. So the boys hauling Richardson thought they'd take a chance and stop by. And while on some occasions waking his majesty out of a sound sleep in the middle of the night might result in a little Blood Atonement, on *this* occasion he was bonhomie itself. 'Well done, good and faithful servants,' he kept saying after he looked in the wagon, one of his favorite remarks, which Hickman said while he was in the outfit never rubbed him the wrong way. But anyhow, they stood around awhile talking and laughing till it seemed like time to go, which they were starting off when 'Hold up there a minute, boys,' his majesty said, for he had thought of something. And what he had thought of was that no matter how much of a nuisance a man might have been in *life*, why, in *death* he could be redeemed, put into use, turned to account, and serve his fellow men like a son of a gun."

She cast him a withering glance.

"And so, my love, they planted Richardson like a tree. In the back yard of the Beehive House. Head first in the ground, with his fag-end up. To come up trunk and boughs someday and in that fashion counterbalance all his life's misdeeds. Because—in the posterior opening of his alimentary canal—they had stuck a *peach stone*, don't you know."

"Oh! Of all the *lies*," she said indignantly.

But now these many years later, shouldered aside to wait at the foot of the great coffin, she thought suppose it wasn't such a lie? Suppose it really happened? And the peach stone sprouted? And up came the tree that grew the fatal peaches? With their peach-blow complexion and exophthalmic blue eyes—

"This way, sir, and sisters—"

The party ahead, done with their viewing, straggled to the exit, freeing Hindle to skirt him in his flowers. Her gaze was quite experienced, she had seen by then many a symptom of disease. But not a poison case, which would not be easy to tell—would it, by the looks?—unless the poison was a caustic lye or some kind of vitriol. The thing that *did* show plain was the bloat of something wrong with his pancreas, of that she was sure.

Chapter Twenty-one

*

AT ALMOST TWO IN THE MORNING, WITH LUCITIE HAVING TO BE AT WORK AT SIX and Albert scheduled to fix Mrs. O'Naughton's hair at eight, there was no time to talk over her expedition, or tell her sister (not, of course, in front of refined Mr. Alfonce) the story she once heard about the planting of Richardson with a peach stone in the posterior opening of his alimentary canal so long ago. While hurrying home she'd thought how they would visit over coffee, but when she woke up Lucitie, asleep at the table with her head on her arms—who then showed no interest in anything except to tiptoe over and kneel by Mr. Alfonce, as decently disposed upon the floor with his head on a pillow as the corpse had been uptown, and rouse him without shock to his delicate system— Hindle knew their talk would have to wait. As soon as Lucitie had him on his feet, hat on and with his neck enfolded in her scarf against the night air, they departed, and it was just as well. At least Lucitie had no chance to make her usual inquiries as to what Hindle was going to do, or repeat Mrs. Birdwood's observation that years with a good provider could leave certain backbones *very weak*. Of course Mrs. Birdwood was thinking of her own husband's backbone, but there was danger for almost anyone, Lucitie would say, and the time had maybe come for Hindle to at least prove to *herself*—"I don't need to prove anything to myself," Hindle had said somewhat crossly. "And I wish you had told me what you was going to do. Because even if Mrs. Birdwood *had* a job to give me when you asked, I might very well not of took it."

"So what *would* you take, Mrs. Particular?"

Hindle didn't know. She did think, however, that Doctor's being a good provider had hinged more than a little on her own exertions in the background, and that far from being made *weak* by her years with him, she had become, well, perhaps not as strong as the lady lion tamer they saw in Virginia City that time in a wild animal show, in jackboots, pantaloons and with hair wild as the mane of the lion she cowed with her whip, but certainly not *weak*. And next time she saw Lucitie she was going to tell her—

She blew out the lamp and let the shades up, flooding the room with moonlight, undressed and got ready for bed. But not feeling sleepy, she fetched a cup of milk, rummaged for a pasty left over from some she had bought that afternoon from a Welshwoman going door to door with a basket over her arm, and went and sat by the window in Doctor's rocking chair. How could anyone be called weak that, all alone with two young ones, had traveled clear from Prescott, made fires, cooked meals, slept out in the open, a prey to every—?

Thank God she had her wits about her to the extent at least that the awful store-keeper had no name to seek her by. But he had Lucitie's, regrettably, and hadn't she during those first uneasy moments in his store mentioned the Salt Lake House? Maybe not, and perhaps he hadn't listened, his yellow eyes fixed on her moving lips. But just in case, Lucitie must be told that if a man as ugly as an old scurfy buffalo hide ever presented himself and asked for Violet May, she was to say she didn't know anyone by that name and had no sister of any description. He had such gall he might act insinuating, too, as if he had some *right* to try and find her.

What *kind* of right, for heaven's sake? Who *was* the man? Where would he come from? There would be no end to Lucitie's questions, which was why Hindle hated to bring her into it, especially as the man might never appear. But on the off chance that he might, she had to tell her, and she was glad not to have plunged in tonight without some preparation, particularly what to change the subject to when what they were discussing got too unreliable. Something she could throw in all of a sudden. "Oh, yes, by the way, I didn't tell you—" Tell her what? About the neighbor lady in Cloverdale waiting for Jesus on the ridge pole of her house? The Russian Archduke they rode on the same train with, from Great Falls to Philipsburg? (But he was in a private car, so they never saw him.) The gypsy fortune that came true? Or, "Lucitie, guess what. I've got a job!"

That would divert her sister better than anything else. "I know what I'm going to do the rest of my life." It would have to be true, of course. And why shouldn't it be? Why didn't she just sit here all by herself in the middle of the night and figure out the future once and for all? She had put it off long enough. "Begin it, and the work will be completed," as Doctor said a German gentleman with the strange name of Gertie used to say. Begin it by thinking—but nothing came to mind as she ate her pasty, brushed the crumbs off her nightgown, drank her milk and set her empty cup on the windowsill, then settled back to rock, get down to cases and not indulge in wandering fancies.

"Pasty." Short "a," as in "past." That was how the woman pronounced it. Welshwoman, shoe-button black eyes, they have them like that sometimes, Hindle thought of the Welsh miners she had seen and their families. Where would such eyes have come from, back in history? Shoe-button black amidst the sky-gray and blue. She knew what pasties were when she heard the cry, but "Oh! Meat pies!" she said as if in surprise when the tray cloth was lifted. The woman did not take the hint, however, that the more familiar name might attract more customers, and went off down the street crying "Pasties!" as before. Well, with pasties—meat pies—what could she earn in a day?

Or how about the washerwoman on State Street? Fetching and carrying laundry in a child's red wagon. Mrs. Cannon, taking care of children? Mrs. Cannon's sister Edna in a boarding house in Murray? One might trim hats if one had the knack. Open a dame school (outlaw arithmetic). Take in, granted the knowledge (which she didn't have), sewing. Hire on at Auerbach's. Be a cashier—no, arithmetic again. How about—?

If a person could just go out in the moonlight looking for work! Instead of hot old daytime. By the light—"How sweet the moonlight lays upon this bank." And didn't it lay just like that in San Francisco the night they came out of the theater and Doctor spoke that line from the play they had just seen, but making a joke out of it because the *bank* he nodded towards was the California Joint-Stock Bank across the street. How sweet the moonlight really *was*, though, in the city that night, shining so bright the shop windows didn't need to be lighted up to see what was in them. She lallygagged along and window-wished while he walked on ahead, then she'd catch up. Except from in front of the China Palace! He had to turn round, come back and get her. "What do you want with *dishes*?" But next day he let her go back all by herself and buy the set she fancied. And fancied still, what there was left of it. She looked at her empty cup and sighed. Three moves are as good as a fire! the saying goes. She never saw a store like that again, the walls themselves like made out of china, plates standing on end and cups on hooks from floor to ceiling, trembling at every tread like aspen leaves. It was run, perhaps she owned it, by a well-dressed lady.

AND THAT BROUGHT HINDLE TO a thought she'd had before, that some people, when they have to work, think of *getting* a job, while other people think of *making* a job, like for instance opening a store. Why is that? Her own idea was that if you could trace it back, you would find storekeepers here and there along those people's family line, the *memory* in their blood of how to do it. Handed down along the pedigree. Except the trouble with that argument, everything has to start! There had to be a *first* storekeeper, *first* king of England, *first* Shorthorn head of cattle. And that being so, it dawned on her like something wonderful, it follows that every day and hour is a starting point for *somebody* to set out from! with their animal show, smelting-works or—and suddenly she knew. *She* wanted a China Palace! just like the one in San Francisco. To wear black taffeta in, a lace-trimmed apron, and when she climbed the ladder against the porcelain wall her dainty slippers would show, not dusty high-low boots.

Of course there would be things to figure out. How to get chinaware from China without personally knowing the captain of a ship, the Chinese language or who to write to, in it, if one knew. Then tissue paper. Thousands of cup hooks. How to deliver what customers bought, they couldn't walk out of the store with a barrel of china on their back. Right at the outset some might lose heart, not her. She would take it by degrees. "Lucitie, guess what! I'm going to open a store! A china store." "And how are you going to do that?" "Easy." That might not be exactly the truth, but no use saying otherwise. Just do as Gertie said, step forth, begin it. How? Well, first, sell off this outfit of Doctor's.

A PANG SHOT THROUGH HER, the brief, keen spasms of grief she felt each time she thought of letting it all go, because with it would go the old days and journeys. "Physician's

Complete Outfit"—unless she wanted to advertise with his old Latin phrase (he said it was Latin), "Materia Medica." Except she didn't know if that meant physicians' actual gear, such as instruments, or the stuff inside their minds. Inside their minds, that is to say, if it was *in* there in the first place, which sometimes it wasn't! as she had found out much to her surprise when a case would come in—a patient covered with blisters from head to foot when they hadn't even been burned, say, or somebody with two different-sized pupils to their eyes, a club hand, or a discoidal tailbone—and Doctor would be as puzzled as anyone.

Doctors never *say* so. What they do is excuse themselves, go in another room, shut the door, read in their medical books like looking up a receipt in Mrs. Beeton's Cookbook!—and come out acting like this big expert. Hindle even *said* one time that an education with holes in it like that didn't seem like much of an education! "Poor girl," Doctor said, "confounding education with a knowledge of facts, when the best kind is *possession of method*." He always had a smart-sounding answer. But now that she looked back it not only *sounded* smart, it *was* smart, if "possession of method" meant you didn't just carry around a hundred silver dollars locked in a trunk, but owned the *skills* necessary to the conduct of your life's affairs. One skill was to be able to read, another was to keep at hand the right books, law books if you were a lawyer, the Bible if you were a preacher, medical books if you were—a—And she *had* those—the Anatomy, Gynecology, Pharmacopeia and many more—had handled and dusted them, packed and unpacked them, closed and placed them back on the shelf when Doctor was through reading. She had even read a little bit herself and looked at some of the drawings. So what if she set up his office, as she had done so often, did it by herself after she learned how (while he went out to register, buy a license, advertise in the new town's paper and get acquainted), and opened it for business? Business. A practice. To see patients! If you didn't know just what they had or what to do for them, you could go in the other room, read in the books and come out this big expert.

Some things, of course, she already knew. Hadn't she stood at his elbow all those years as he listened to, stared at, smelled, probed, palpated and treated the sick and injured? Wasn't that experience? Maybe, he would say. But experience only tells of what has been, not what must be. Well, if that is so, she found herself saying softly as if to answer him, then that's all the better, because it means all of us *start out even* every day. That notion, added to her former train of thought, took such heady effect that, like an air-ship being pumped full of coal-gas, she could not stay seated but rose and floated about the room. Until then it had been her sitting room. Now it became in the moonlight an indistinct (then quite distinct) survival of where he used to do his work, his office, only it wasn't his now. It was someone else's, and who that someone was it said on the signboard creaking in the wind outside.

DR. HINDLE FAIRBRASS
PHYSICIAN & SURGEON

To see it in her mind's eye was like bumping into a wall. She drew back weak-kneed, felt for her chair, sat down, retreating from the word "Surgeon." "Surgical" means? No, never. Never would she dare undam the terrible blood. She would not need the sharp, thin little blades, surgical scissors or the surgeon's knot she thought she knew how to tie (the thread passed twice through the loop) or febrifuge for surgical fires. "Surgeon," then, paint out. "Physician"? But that, too, laid on trusts hard to answer for. Well—"Practitioner." "General Practitioner"? But wait, a better way to state her purpose—she saw it flying like a mottoed banner:

DR. HINDLE FAIRBRASS
ECLECTIC PRACTITIONER

Nothing new, she'd seen it, people used it. And might as well say quack, Doctor used to say, because that's what it came down to, Jack-of-all-trades, pack rat! stealing from everywheres—hydrotherapy, Galvanism, homeopathy—"But ain't that what *you* do?" she asked him one time. "Don't *you* try different stuff you hear about, to cure up patients? Brunoism, allopathy—?" He said no, he didn't, but she knew he did, and nothing wrong with it either, to be "eclectic," try new things, be open. She liked the word on her sign. And in her office (seen as if from far away, rising from its own reflection) she sat in a swivel chair at a roll-top desk. "Come in," she said when a knock came at the door. A man walked in. "Oh, no," she said, "you mustn't come in here! I don't treat men." "Why don't you?" Because I'm sorry to report their ailments are generally predicated with regard to sex, and Doctor used to have me leave the room (like the gentleman he was to the end of his days) when they brought in their spirochetes, anuria, spasms of the rectum, secret deficiencies and unruly organs. "I just treat women." She pointed out the window, and together they read:

DR. HINDLE FAIRBRASS
ECLECTIC PRACTITIONER
Diseases of Women Only

"What's the spittoon for, then?" She blinked and the spittoon was gone, the man too with all his body parts that through no fault of his own gave such offense to female modesty.

SHE HAD BEEN GOING TO steer clear of Mr. Fogelmarck who lived in the barn-like house out in back. But needing her signboard painted, she went to him. Their transaction went quickly. He did not ask her in, or act surprised that here she had been a doctor since she moved in and no one knew it. But she was sure that when Lennart Palmstedt, her landlord, dropped by and saw what was developing he would be taken aback, while Lucitie's one day a month to come down and see her sister would be entirely taken up with questions! like the Spanish Inquisition. Questions, screams, advice, Hindle, you'll get in trouble, don't do it! But Hindle was committed and full of assurance. Then perhaps not quite so full. But then after she had taken Doctor's diploma out of its frame and bestowed on her own self all the Merits, Dignities, Profound Knowledge and Moral Principles of Physician, Surgeon and Accoucher, was full again and confident in expectation.

Until, that is, she rolled the doctored document up, stuck it under her arm and set out to try to buy a license to practice medicine in Salt Lake City. Then her feeling of being what it said she was vanished, she was a humbug, no clerk living would sell her a license. And think if an applicant had to go before a board of medical examiners! like they did in California. Doctor had helped vote the law in, he and she were residents down there then, he said every state in the Union should have a law like that, it was the only way to keep out charlatans and save the lives of innocent people. Yes, she said at the time, but how about the doctors who *went* before the medical examiners, *passed* the tests, *got* their license and turned out to be *worse* than the charlatans? perforating uteruses, bleeding, blistering, puncturing eardrums, dosing with mercurous chloride, losing their instruments in people's intestines? But doctors were like Freemasons. If they knew the lingo and the handshake, that was all it took.

LICENSES.

With the perturbation of mind characteristic of a bad conscience, she ventured in.

"Yes, ma'am. What can I do for you?" the clerk behind the counter said.

Trying not to tremble, she unrolled the diploma and laid it before him. "I would like to register and—buy a license."

"For what?"

"Why, to—practice medicine." She added quickly, "Just on women," in case he thought her purpose more grandiose than her appearance warranted.

He looked at the diploma, then at her, frowning behind the glasses pinched on his nose. "On who?"

"Women," she said faintly. "Women's ailments."

"Oh." He coughed a little. "I'm usually across the hall in Vital Statistics. This here's your credential? Looks like a diploma."

"That's what it is."

"Physician, Surgeon and—?"

She interrupted. "That part there I've kind of let fall by the wayside."

"What part?"

"Surgeon."

"Oh." He pondered that. Then, "What's this word?" He put his finger on it, turning the diploma around enough for her to see.

"Accoucher?" She pronounced it syllable by syllable, "ac," "couch," "cher."

"What's a word like that supposed to mean?" he said.

What *was* it supposed to mean? Through the years she had asked to have defined all the unimportant words in the world, while the one *important* word—She clung to the counter with wet, cold fingers. "Why," she said, swallowing down a dry throat, "it means just what it sounds like."

"Sounds like 'couch.'"

"Well, you know, that's it, sir. As I was saying, I just treat womenfolk, and you would be surprised how many—get up in the morning, put their clothes on, make a stab at doing their work, but—by afternoon or even before noontime they're *laying on the couch*."

"If that don't beat all," he said. "You got her to a T! Cora, my wife. Bawling, laying down, weaker'n a cat—"

"How long has she been like that?"

"Too blame long. It's getting pretty old. You cure 'em, do you? When they come to you?"

"I do unless—" She fell back on Doctor's old extenuation, that sometimes things do rest in higher hands than ours.

"Because," he lowered his voice, "she was my ewe lamb. But the way it is now, our life—" His voice trailed off as he felt around under the counter, bent down and looked, then sighed, swept up the diploma, turned and walked away.

Eyes wide, chewing the end of her thumb, she watched him disappear through a door in the wall behind him. What was he going to do, show somebody the fabrication she tried to pass? Send for the sheriff?

He came back shaking his head. "—ain't worth nothing," he said, putting down her document and spreading out on the counter the rather crumpled paper he had fetched. He felt for the pen behind his ear.

"Maybe I brought the wrong—" If she could retrieve it, run out—She reached for it, but he brushed her hand away. Would he listen if she tried to explain? That doctors might not have apprentices learning the trade with them like carpenters or blacksmiths, but if a person stands at their elbow year after year and pays attention, don't it stand to reason—? Like take, well, me. There wasn't hardly a time I couldn't of handed Doctor what he needed before he even asked! Not that I done so as a usual thing, they never like you being a jump ahead. She opened her lips to speak.

"Nothing," he repeated. "Our lives. And her and me, I'm telling you, we used to be—the happiest—"

"Oh, I see!" she said, drawing a tremulous breath. "You're talking about—"

"She'd josh a fellow—laugh—" He flipped open the lid of the heavy brass inkwell, dipped in his pen and began to copy from the diploma onto the printed form.

Behind him a man in shirtsleeves stood in the doorway. "Myron," he said, "nobody can reach it, it's too high."

Hindle's clerk nodded but did not turn as he finished and blotted what he had copied out. Then, laying the form on the diploma and rolling up both together, he looked up. "You been at this quite some time?"

"Since—"

"Unless we get Hansen from downstairs," the man went on. "Or a step-ladder."

"Yes," she said.

"That'll be two dollars, four bits," Myron said. "The price has went up, they told me back in there."

"That don't seem too—unreasonable." As steadily as she could, she undid the stiff clasp of her purse, fished out what he had asked and laid it on the counter. "I certainly do thank you," she said, and started to leave.

"Don't you want what you come for?"

Red with embarrassment, she faced about.

He handed her the documents. "Where you fixing to locate?"

She told him and he crooked his finger at her. She leaned forward. "I guess that's what she's needing. An accouch—No one else has done her any good. Including," he whispered, "I'm sorry to say, the Elders. Her name'll be Cora Plume if she comes in."

"I'll remember. Cora Plume," she said.

"Myron!" The man in the doorway sounded exasperated. "Who wants it in the first place, do you know?"

"That laying on the couch gets pretty old."

SHE SAW THE SIGN PROPPED beside the front door and at the same instant the sign painter's coattails disappearing around the house. "Oh, wait, Mr. Fogelmarck!" she called, running after him. "I want to pay you!"

"No hurry," he said as he stopped, turned around and clumsily took off his hat, "no great hurry."

"I haven't had time to see your sign yet like I want," she said, "but the glimpse I caught—it's perfect." She had been opening her purse. Now she reached in and counted out his money.

He pocketed it, and though plainly ill at ease and wanting to go, stayed and said, "I see you been away today."

"Yes, I had to—"

"Where are your children? I see you have some."

"Yes," she said. "They're with the lady I leave them with over on Sixth East when I have to—Like today I had to go uptown and register." She paused. "Being a doctor"—There! She had done it, given herself the office the way that Doctor said Napoleon placed with his own two hands the royal crown of France on his head!—"being a doctor and new in town like I am, I had to buy a license." She braced herself to be struck by lightning.

He nodded. "I was new here once myself. I come from Denmark."

"I know," she said. "Mr. Palmstedt was telling us."

"A long time ago, more than twenty years."

"So you—you must be pretty well acquainted around here by now."

"Yes, if I stayed, but I didn't all the time. First I was called to go to—" He broke off, then suddenly said, "We got a king in Denmark, did you know that?"

"I would just imagine so," she said.

"And today as I was coming home, you know I was thinking what a good thing that really was! For me, I mean."

He spoke with an accent and she wasn't quite sure, but what he seemed to be saying was that it was a good thing Denmark had a king. "What was so good about that?" she asked rather stiffly.

"To remember," he said. "Because to do it *right*, one must have seen the real—lineaments, the position and carriage of the limbs of the actual—and I *did see his majesty*. King Frederick the Seventh stood as close as—this!" He held his hand about a foot from his face to show her.

"That was pretty close," she said. "But you say 'to do it right.' If you don't mind my asking, Mr. Fogelmarck, do *what* right?"

He went on as though she had not spoken. "He gave out the prizes. I won second prize. For painting. Free attendance two years at the Royal Academy of Copenhagen. But I did not go there. My mother died. I was alone. Then I heard—the gospel restored, you know. On the ship, my birthday, eighteen years old. And so I came to Zion."

It was hot on that side of the house. She wanted to take the sign inside and look at it, then fetch the children. But if lingering a minute or two would clear up why on his way home "today" he took time to be glad that Denmark had a king, and why to do something "right" he had to have *seen* that king face to face, she had to linger. "You must of been proud," she said. "And I must say you was brave, coming over here by yourself. But if you don't mind my asking—"

"I painted Mr. Summerlade's sign for him," he said, again seeming to go off on a tack that had no connection with anything said before. "Roscoe Summerlade, Architect." He wrote the letters in the air. "He had a daguerreotype. His wife. She was young when she died. 'Will you paint her?' he said. That was years ago. He liked it so much. So today I seen him again. 'Hello, Mr. Summerlade.' We shook hands, he said to me, 'Fogelmarck, when the time comes, how would you like to paint ten kings of Ireland, each a foot taller than myself, for a rich man's dining room? I am building his house.' 'They will go up through the ceiling!' I said. 'Not this ceiling,' he said, 'for it will be twenty-two feet high.' So, if one has seen a *true king*'s lineaments, that will make it much *easier*."

"Oh, I see," Hindle said, her brow clearing. "Today you heard about this job painting kings, so you're glad you seen a *real* king so when you start painting, you'll remember how a real king looked and match up *your* kings with him!"

"If I matched up my kings to look like King Frederick the Seventh, they would look like policemen," he said sternly.

She laughed.

"It went well for me today," he volunteered.

"For me, too," she said.

"I shall have all I need. The finest pigments, pure gold leaf—"

"Good. That's wonderful."

He did not look happy, though. Or sound that way as he went on to declare that all, no matter what, in this dilapidated world was vanity and vexation of spirit—making great works, building houses, planting vineyards—

"But you won't be doing nothing like that," she said cheerfully. "You'll just be painting your kings, all bright and with that gold—" She broke off when, without another word, he turned on his heel and left to go on out to his barn. Kind of a fanatic, she thought, looking after him. An old religious hermit. And maybe not even so old. Let's see, if he was eighteen when he came over to this country and that was twenty—he said more than twenty—years ago, he'd only be—Well, anyway. She smiled to herself. If ever she saw his kings and they looked or didn't look like an Irish policeman in San Francisco, she would know that Frederick the Seventh was to blame.

THAT EVENING HER LANDLORD DROPPED in and, not without effort, Hindle kept still about her newly acquired license and her plans. Let him wait, and Lucitie too, until her sign went up. She did mention running into Mr. Fogelmarck in the yard and said how they had stood and talked for a little while. Lennart was surprised to hear it.

"I guess he was too happy to be bashful," she said. "That is, he was at first, but later— An architect he painted a sign for one time is going to build a mansion for some rich man. And when it gets to a certain stage, Mr. Fogelmarck's supposed to paint a bunch of Irish kings for the dining room. I didn't know he was an artist, did you? I thought he just painted signs."

"Fogelmarck's quite deep. He worked on ships. He's only just come back here and took up his old trade again after sailing all over the world for about twenty years. Told me he sent in his tithing wherever he was. That should make him a welcome sight. But there's a block teacher in this ward—he's from San Bernardino, where Fogelmarck lived at one time—come up here to go in business with his brother-in-law. In fact there's several new folks from there, and when he seen Fogelmarck at meeting, he just passed him by. I seen that myself, wouldn't shake hands or nothing. And now I hear some of the brethren from down there want him disfellowshipped. They say he's quarrelsome about the doctrine and—just, I don't know, hard to get along with. I just mention it because I thought you'd notice him not going to church and maybe wonder."

"I wouldn't," she said, "not being a member. But if he's so religious—"

"Well, it's a ticklish situation that they say has got to be looked at. But now what's happened, there's been kind of postponement of his case till later on. I guess the bishop sent him a note not to upset the apple cart by going to meeting or nothing till the priesthood has a chance to kind of review—and listen to them members from San Bernardino—"

"Gracious," she said in some alarm. "Did he do something in the nature of—immoral?"

"Oh, no. He'd of been dead if he had," Mr. Palmstedt said matter-of-factly. "This must be—and must of been—some kind of misunderstanding. It'll be settled. The bishop says not to give it a second thought. Me being Fogelmarck's landlord, I naturally inquired. But it's nothing."

"Well, it's nice he's got the Irish kings to take his mind off his troubles."

"Yes, and his sign-painting business is going good, too. I'm sure he never has—but I'm curious," he said. "Has he ever knocked on your door?"

"No, never," she said.

Chapter Twenty-two

＊

But after her sign went up and she opened her office, three long, idle and solitary days after, while she sat at her roll-top desk trying to read a book called *Anatomy* and not give way to panic, Mr. Fogelmarck did knock on her door. He had something in his eye. "Come in," she said, glad her long wait for patient number one was over but at the same time addicted enough to superstition to wonder if the fact of his being the wrong gender might not start her off on the wrong foot. Not that she would have turned him away with a conjunctiva as dreadfully bloodshot and inflamed as she saw at a glance that his was. Did not Hippocrates say a physician must always be ready to do his duty? (She had found out from the books that Hippocrates was the big authority.) "Now, what have we here?"

What they had there was a situation that allowed Hindle to launch her calling with a fine flourish, for he had been filing an iron bracket, he said, when a sharp particle flew in his eye, and when she heard the word *iron* she knew what to do. All she needed was the loadstone! But now the question was, where was it? She found it finally in the bottom of an old canvas bag stamped U.S. ARMY. The rest, once it was positioned, took but a moment, filing and magnet flew together like sweethearts long parted.

"Thank God!" he said, blinking rapidly a few times, then jumping out of the chair.

"Stay there," she said. "We got to wash it out," with eye water she was shaking up with a few drops of laudanum, "and it needs a bandage."

"No bandage!"

"Yes, Mr. Fogelmarck. At least till tonight, your eye's got to rest. You mauled it quite a bit trying to get that speck out."

"I was much afraid."

"Of course you was, but it would have been better to of not tried something like that yourself."

"An artist without his eyes," he said, "what is he? He might as well be dead."

"If the worst had come to worst—which there wasn't no danger of—you would of had one good eye left, remember."

He snorted. "I seen what happened to a good eye once! My father had a friend— his left eye went blind from St. Anthony's fire. That left the right eye that nothing was wrong with. But a few months later *it* went blind, too! Out of sympathy. That's what the doctor said."

"Well, I'm a doctor and I never heard of such a thing," she said, though she had. "Usually the case—The law of—" What had Doctor called it? "Compensation. Whatever a person has *left* gets stronger."

He paid no attention. "Human beings have been born fastened together, when one dies, they both die. Eyes are like that!" he insisted.

"No, they're not."

"You have to admit they're more like that than any *other* pairs of organs in our human tabernacles."

"Well, maybe," she said, tearing a strip of linen in the corner.

Somehow made slack by this abrupt relinquishment on her part, he kept silent a moment, then said, "How kind is God to give us so many things double! Only think now, *two* eyes, *two* ears, *two*—"

"Or *ten*," she put in hastily. "Like fingers! Like the rich man you mentioned that's going to have ten Irish kings when you get through painting them. He must be Irish himself, don't you think?"

He would not be deflected. "But the greatest things are *one*," he said. "*One* brain. *One* heart. *One*—"

"Yes. Now, Mr. Fogelmarck, I really do mean it about this bandage staying on."

"*One* restored gospel of Jesus Christ on earth!" he finished triumphantly. "How else replace us in a state of grace? How else free us from the effects of sin?"

"You sound like you been on a mission," she said, relieved, for the possibility had existed for him to be straying towards the somewhat coarse.

"No," he said. "I don't talk the language good enough."

"Why, you talk *real* good. But if the authorities didn't think so," she placed the strip of linen over his eye, carried it around and tied it at the back of his head, "they could of sent you back to Denmark to preach in Danish." She stood back to survey her work.

"They sent me—not to preach, of course—to San Bernardino. To work. 'Brother Fogelmarck, we need you to help build up the kingdom, in California!'"

"That was right after you got here?"

"Two days I still had coming on my first week's board here in Salt Lake where I landed!"

"I didn't think there *was* a San Bernardino then, to send you to."

"Oh, yes. Not like now, of course. We dug ditches, built roads—" He held up his hands. "Calluses stay, long time. They did not need pictures."

"My sister thinks they do it deliberately. She's got this convert friend that came from England early this year. And the minute he got to Salt Lake—like you, not even getting to use up your first week's board—they counseled him—But first I should say he's a lovely hairdresser, raised in the business, never done heavy work in his life, which you can tell. So what did they want to do but try to send him up into the Uinta mountains to move boulders and I don't know what all. But he was different than you, Mr. Fogelmarck. He just wouldn't do it! So they threw him out. But he don't care, he's started a hairdressing establishment—"

"Tell him, repent of this, his wickedness, and pray God his heart may be forgiven. Meek. Be humble. The church will take him back."

"But he don't *want* them to take him back. He's out of it for good. And I don't blame him!"

"How much you charge me?" he said, getting out of the chair.

"Nothing," she said. "Because you being a gentleman and my practice being limited to ladies, I'm going to pretend you wasn't here." She smiled.

"Well, thank you." But his eye stared coldly, and with his back held stiff as a board he bowed and stalked out.

How touchy he is, Hindle thought. No wonder the ward didn't like him. But a bad disposition was one thing, bad conduct another. What could he have *done* to make some of his fellow church members want to keep him isolated, but that didn't entail punishment or excommunication? There must be *other* touchy people going to meeting. And others running religion into the ground?

AT LEAST HIS MALE INVASION of female territory did not bring bad luck. He was hardly out the door when a proper patient showed up. Later came another, then one more— three that very day. The first was Cora Plume, the wife of the clerk who had sold Hindle her license, a pale young woman dragging shawls and skirts. "My husband sent me," she said, looking ready to burst into tears. She held off, though, until Hindle, after investigating her symptoms and history as she had seen Doctor do countless times, with a few added touches inspired by her own recent medical studies, had her get dressed and come and sit in the chair beside the desk so she could tell her what her trouble was.

So far as she could discover, Mrs. Plume didn't have any, she seemed a fine physical specimen. But Doctor never sent anyone away without what he called a "manubrium" to their disorder, sometimes a real handle to a real ailment (if he could discover what that was), sometimes only put forth as real, and a tonic or pills, sometimes to the purpose, sometimes only not injurious, and Hindle, at the moment of having to deal with what she had diagnosed as the blues and a little nervous weakness, decided to proceed along those same lines. "What we're dealing with here," she said, "and if I may say so, it's no wonder you've been miserable, is an inflamed jejunum."

Mrs. Plume began quietly to weep.

"Don't be alarmed, Mrs. Plume, it's easily took care of, and if you will rub this salve on your lower abdomen and take these boluses, one every morning—" But (as a little more conversation made plain) what the woman was shedding were tears of happiness, because anyone with an *inflamed jejunum* surely had a right to rest, didn't they? Even stay in bed? And shouldn't their husband be a lot more considerate than he had been in the past? Hindle quickly advised against bed-rest, which, because of the warmth of the covers, would inflame the jejunum even more, but said an hour or two a day on the couch—until a cure was effected—would do no harm, and yes, Mr. Plume should be more considerate.

When this first proper patient left with instructions to come back in two weeks, like the Knight who crossed frozen Lake Constance on horseback without knowing it was an inland *sea* and when he found out fell dead of fright, Hindle let herself fall into the fit of trembling she had rigidly repressed during the visit. But she did not tremble again, and by the time two weeks had passed, her position stood sure and had taken good footing. By then her professional connection had expanded to five, not counting the heat stroke (brought on by the hottest September in living memory) she was asked to run out into the street and treat, and she had also developed what would seem to Lucitie, when at last Hindle had a day off and came uptown to see her, nothing less than a swollen head. But that appraisal was wrong. What Lucitie was seeing in her sister was enthusiasm, and the flight-feathered confidence she had taken on when she stumbled upon a powerful secret in a book of Doctor's called *Posology*. That secret was this: that most people while coming to the doctor *do not die*. There is something in the human frame *independent of medicine or medical procedures* that makes them live: life itself, that lives *of its own accord* if it possibly can. So a physician's bets are really hedged! Whoever they are, thanks to the fact of this vantage-ground, doctors can count on "saving" most of their patients. Naturally, therefore, they look as if they know what they're doing and that they are as deserving of trust and reliance from everyone to the highest degree as their diplomas *say* they are. This gives them their air of having what Lucitie called—when she saw it in her sister—a swollen head.

Lennart Palmstedt, Hindle's landlord, called it something else. He called it working a dodge of some kind, he didn't know what, but he'd find out. "That sign outside!" he said accusingly.

"What about it?"

"All these weeks passing yourself off as a widow-woman. Now all of a sudden you're a doctor!"

"A widow-woman can be a doctor!"

"Why didn't you say something?"

"Because I was partners before, with my husband. I wasn't sure if I could handle a practice alone. I thought I might go into something else. But now I know I can." She showed him her license. "You don't get *that* without credentials!" Then she took him into her office to point out the diploma, now returned to Doctor's frame and hanging so that the light from the window reflected off the glass. "What does that look like?"

Lennart gazed at it and then around skeptically at what had been the parlor but now looked and smelled like a doctor's office. "Well—" He shrugged. Was he convinced? He was convinced that a place of business should bring in more revenue than a dwelling. A few days later he raised her rent. And then, as her practice gradually took hold, their acquaintance changed. He would find her engaged or with her nose in one of her books, and even if she was sweeping or mixing bread in the kitchen, some new thing about her, some stamp of professionalization or he didn't know what, put him off balance. The mutual benevolence that had been heading towards a real friendship not only did not advance, it slipped back. And Hindle was just as glad, though she missed his dropping in and the news he would bring. But what could have come of it? Nothing. A man with three wives!

There was, of course, no persuading Lucitie that Hindle was what her sign said, and the only thing *she* marveled at, she said when she staggered in that Sunday afternoon and had to sit down to get over the shock of seeing it, was that her sister was home and not carted off to jail! A *doctor*. Never did she wish so much with all her heart that Mama was alive so she could ask her which side of the family the gall came from, the pure and simple gall!

If she meant her, Hindle said, she wanted to say that first, it wasn't gall, and second, if it was, then where it came from was all those months at Burdick's Institution for the Care of the Sick, chloroforming and doing other things, and ten long years standing at Doctor's side, watching, listening, and when the coast was clear, asking. People *learn* that way.

But not to be doctors!

Of course to be doctors! To be *anything*.

"The upshot will be you'll kill someone. My only sister, the sister I was so glad to see come back to our old home town."

"Aren't you still glad?" Hindle was trying not to say *ain't* anymore.

"With you turned loose like this? Maybe sawing off a human leg?" She ran outside to look at the sign again. "When I think," she said, coming back in, "of such a thing even being possible! Not that I say you're worse of an idiot than the average person. But surely there's a *law*."

"There is in California," Hindle said. "And maybe in some other places. But here in Utah, anyone's a doctor that says they are."

Lucitie gasped. "That's *terrible*." She looked from her sister to the old encrusted skull on top of the cupboard, then back again.

"He died before I come on the scene," Hindle teased.

"Well, I hope so."

"Don't look so worried!" She wanted to tell her the cheerful secret about most people not dying while coming to the doctor, but decided not to. In fact, not to tell anyone. Ever! "I'm reading the books. I've went through four already. Would you believe we got a thing in our body called the 'pouch of Douglas'? If it collects with pus, you know what you do?"

Lucitie shook her head.

"Influence it to bust in the rectum!"

"Don't tell me."

"The names. That's what tickles me," Hindle said. "Dyspareunia. What does that sound like to you?"

"It sounds like you've went crazy."

"It means—" But Hindle, suddenly attentive to the circumstance of her sister's supposed maidenhood, broke off.

"Means what, if you're so smart?" Lucitie said.

"Means—" But so circumspectly did Hindle define intercourse (within marriage, of course) *that hurts* that they might as well have been back to the pouch of Douglas.

After a moment's stunned silence, "I'm sure it comes from Papa's side," Lucitie said as if to herself. "There's only one thing that gives me—and would give Mama if she was here—a little comfort, and that is, that at least you had the due regard to treat women. Because the rampage you're on, it wouldn't surprise me a bit to hear you'd be tackling men."

"Not me," Hindle said. "They're a whole different human race."

"Them's the truest words you ever spoke."

To Hindle's relief, then, Lucitie settled down to do what she had come for in the first place, talk about Albert. Mrs. O'Naughton, she said, with more money than there was stars in the sky, came back to Albert (after he fixed her hair to sit with the Gentile dignitaries at Brigham's funeral) and looked to become a regular customer. Mrs. O'Naughton was Mrs. Birdwood's girlhood chum, married to Mr. O'Naughton of the mining machinery. Mrs. Birdwood had sent *several* ladies to Albert. But one customer Lucitie wished he didn't have was Kate, the girl on the ship with the black hair and blue eyes that Elder—now Apostle—Tennant was sweet on, on the trip from England. The Apostle was still after her! But somebody else was too, an Elder, as well off as he and with one less wife. And neither suitor would be any too happy to hear of her sneaking in after dark for Albert to dress her hair, cut off from the church as he was for disobedience and a proud attitude. It was dangerous for Albert, really, especially as once or twice he had walked Kate home. If Apostle Tennant found out, he might do something mean to him, to say nothing of her other suitor.

Kate was *pretty*. Charlotte saw her, Lucitie said, and said if Albert was anything to *her* she would be worried, him there at night with a customer that looked like that! for two or three hours, door locked, blinds pulled down—

"How *is* Charlotte?" Hindle asked.

Well, sorry as she was to have to say it, Charlotte was as much of a worry as Kate! Lucitie said, or even more so. Not because of Charlotte's looks, by any means, but because thinking she was helping, which she really was—but helping Albert, not her—Charlotte *would* tag along down to Albert's shop after work and pitch in. He was getting used to her. And what *she* was afraid of, Lucitie said, was that before long he wouldn't care *which* girl it was cooking and cleaning house for him, one would be as good as the other! Mrs.

Birdwood said she should just tell Charlotte to withdraw from the field of battle. But how could Lucitie do that? to someone as long at the Salt Lake House as she was herself, and done her many a favor over the years. What *she* was hoping, Lucitie said, was that when winter come on with its ice and snow and that old east wind blowing, Charlotte would give up.

"You don't mean to tell me you'll slip and slide down to Albert's shop *then*!" Hindle said.

"I told you about the crotch?" the other said. "Mrs. Birdwood comes from back east where there's ships, and there's a rig on a ship called a 'crotch' that holds up a thing called a 'boom.' So that's what *I* been to Albert, she says, since the first minute I saw him. And the only way to make him realize is to take away *my* crotch from *his* boom."

"Well, why don't you?"

"Ain't you been listening? Because there's *another* crotch standing by as close as *this* to him. Charlotte! And I don't think he'd even notice the difference."

"Do you think he's in love with Kate?"

"He thinks she's pretty." Lucitie paused. "Well, she *is*. But what worries me most about her is Apostle Tennant! And what he might *do* to Albert if he finds out she's going down there. I seen him on the ship and I seen him on the train, and he does not have a nice disposition!"

"Yes, but didn't you say somebody else was after her too?"

"That's what Kate told Albert."

"So if somebody does something mean to someone, why wouldn't Apostle Tennant do it to this other fellow?"

"Because the both of *them* is high up in the Fourteenth Ward, while Albert's just a Gentile. So he would get the punishment."

"Well, I'll tell you what I'd do if it was me," Hindle said, leaning back in her swivel chair and gazing at the ceiling the way Doctor used to do when he was giving advice. "First I'd tell Charlotte—"

But an older sister does not easily subject herself to inferior conjunction with a younger. "Mostly I'm just talking to hear myself think," Lucitie interrupted. "And like I say, when the snow starts to fall—" She went on, "Maybe I'll just go along like I'm doing for a while. Something might happen."

"Like what?"

"Oh, you know. Fortunate. Like I heard Mrs. Birdwood say once, she come into property and that was the only thing that made Mr. Birdwood propose."

"You'd have a long old wait for property," Hindle, scornful of the dilatory, said sternly. (But a few months later, when something "fortunate" did indeed happen to throw Albert into Lucitie's arms, she had to admit that doing nothing was sometimes the best thing to do.)

That night when Lucitie was taking her leave, she said again that one consolation as respected Hindle's whole doctoring business was the fact that her clientele would at least be decent! *No men.* But the next time she came down, Hindle said that a few days before a man had paid no attention to the sign but walked right into the office!

Lucitie was aghast.

"All it was was my landlord Lennart Palmstedt, though," Hindle said, lowering her effect with this particular only because she had another rise to contrast with it.

"Ain't he in and out of here all the time anyway?"

"Not trying to buy powdered narwhal tusk, I can tell you!"

Momentarily speechless, Lucitie groped around behind for a chair and sat down.

"The whole purpose was to bring up the subject. Anyone could see *that*," Hindle said. "He knew I never had such stuff!"

"But what is it?"

"What would something *be* that a rich man—with a big estate in Sweden that Lennart's father was the gamekeeper of, before he got converted—would try to restore himself with, after squandering himself in Paris like they do, Dukes and Lords, to the point of total," Hindle wasn't quite sure of the word but came out with it anyway, "exossification?"

Lost but not wanting to show it, Lucitie said, "Didn't I warn you? I had a hunch about fine Mr. Landlord! And it's your own fault."

"If that is how you're going to act, that ends it," Hindle said crossly. "I'll never tell you anything again."

Aware then that the comport of unapproachable virtue she had put on for Albert and never taken off might (as at present) work to some degree against her, Lucitie abandoned it. "Oh, come on," she said. "Tell me the rest." But she had to wheedle, and when Hindle finally did tell her was sorry she had, for it wasn't worth the trouble. Just that Lennart said he thought he could use some if she carried it, not very often but once in a while. But what he really came for was to ask her to call on his middle wife, Rosina.

"Call on her? *That* was a funny thing to ask!" Lucitie said.

"What was funny about it?"

"Well—Oh, you mean a *doctor's* call."

"Of course I mean a doctor's call. What did you think?"

"I'm always forgetting you're this big doctor." Quickly Lucitie added, "Was the woman sick?"

Those who had never had a boil on one of the protuberances of their rump might not think so, but Rosina had one and she was. Hindle, under the impression that furuncles went by position in the scale of rank—pimple, boil, big hot vicious carbuncle—pronounced it the latter, and Rosina was much relieved. She *knew* it had to be worse than just a boil! But as Hindle found out when she went home, promising to be back the next day with a cataplasm, and looked up both boil and carbuncle in *Horsley's Medical Milieu*, inflammatory tumors don't go by degree of bigness, hotness or viciousness at all, but differ only in the fact that the boil has a central core while the carbuncle does not! Having plainly seen a hard yellow core in Rosina's anthrax (another name for either boil or carbuncle if you wanted to be fine), she would have to back down a little.

But Doctor would as soon have gouged out one of his eyes as confess to not knowing what he was looking at, and after thinking it over she decided to be like him. Whether, if she had not been at Rosina's re-applying the lard-and-flour poultice she had brought (the lard having melted like grease in a frying pan over a hot fire when she first put it on) when the boil burst and the core shot out and landed with a splat! on a nearby wall, her misdiagnosis would have come out she would, of course, never know. Luckily, she *was* there to swab off and get rid of the evidence, even as the misnamed carbuncle thrust viscid matter up and out through its newly made crater like Vesuvius. A few minutes' fierce erupting, a washing and bandaging, and Rosina could use that part of her bodily frame to sit on once again.

"What *is* that wonderful stuff?"

For the first time understanding Doctor's peculiar saying "Ripeness is all," Hindle said, "We mix it according to the situation."

Rosina stared in admiration. "Oh, you do." Such magic! Like in Odin's hall, she said. Her father from the Old Country used to tell about the heroes killed in battle that would come to life again in Odin's hall and sit there carousing like they had never died. "Like me and you, I hope, is going to do right now with a cup of coffee," she said.

Hindle hesitated. Doctor always kept what he called his "little brief authoritative" distance. "I've got a craniocele coming in," she said. She hadn't, but had come across the condition while looking up carbuncle.

Rosina's face fell. "Please!"

"Well, maybe, Mrs. Palmstedt. But I can't stay long."

"Rosina," the other said. "Call me Rosina." Then, as she bustled about, "I'm not surprised. A real good doctor can't call their soul their own."

With a gesture of modest refusal, Hindle turned this aside.

"No, but I mean it. Look what you done for me! In agony a solid week, and here you come along and in five minutes—"

"Well, where a thing is localized—"

Rosina took the word up later, pouring their second cup. "You saying localized makes me think of something," she said. "And that is, right across the alley there in that house," she pointed through the window, "lays a localized *neighbor*—which I guess I can call the woman after four years, though I've only seen her a few times—in perfect misery."

"What's the matter with her?"

"If you could find *that* out, you'd be doing something. And sometime when you're in

the neighborhood—which you are right now, of course, aren't you? Come to think of it."
Rosina smiled brightly. "Of course, I would have to run over beforehand—"

"Oh, I don't think so—"

"And ask the girls if it's all right."

The "girls" turned out to be one large, gray-haired woman barring the open back door
and two more of the same hovering in the dim hallway behind her. "I just want to get it
straight that we ain't paying," the woman said as she looked Hindle up and down. "If this
doctor wants to collect from Montana for a examination, well and good. If she don't—"

"From Montana?" Hindle said.

"The brother lives up there," Rosina explained in an aside to Hindle. "He pays her
board. You *did* tell me that, didn't you, Myrtle?"

"I did tell you that," the one called Myrtle said. "And I wished we'd of all dropped
dead—"

"Before we ever tied ourself up—" a voice said in the background.

"Hand and foot—" a second voice chimed in.

"The way we done!" Myrtle finished. "If anybody tells me ever again that blood is
thicker than water—" She broke off, then added with a hard look at Hindle, "What's
she supposed to do?"

"Dr. Fairbrass ain't *supposed* to do nothing," Rosina said. "She *does* it! You know my
boil? Well, it wasn't a boil at all. It was a carbuncle! She took one look—and had it busted
and cured before you could say Doctrine and Covenants!"

"Don't need a doctor for a boil. Nor a carbuncle either. But like you say, her being
handy on account of renting your husband Lennart's latest house and probably not
charging nothing—"

"This here is Myrtle Eastman," Rosina said quickly. "Mary back in there's the sister-
in-law. And that's *Mrs.* Eastman. Ninety years old, imagine! Crossed the plains when
she was sixty-five, didn't you, Mrs. Eastman? Hello. You was sleeping when I run over
here a minute ago."

"No, I wasn't," the old woman in the shadows said fiercely.

"Pleased to meet you," Hindle said.

"If you like to meet crazy people," Myrtle said.

"Oh, now, Myrtle," Rosina bantered.

"Well, I mean it. No call whatsoever for what we done. Went miles out of our way
to bring down trouble!" She stepped aside, the others, murmuring, did likewise, and
the callers went in. "Up that stairway there. But I'm telling you, if we had knowed the
hole, the bottomless pit, we was stepping into when we tried to give a shirt-tail relation
a helping hand—!"

"Nobody ever does know," Rosina said soothingly as she went past. "When they do
anything. This old life ain't nothing but surprises!"

Chapter Twenty-three

✱

A BIG SURPRISE WAS WAITING FOR HINDLE IN THE TINY BACK BEDROOM UNDER the eaves. For who should Rosina's neighbor the sick woman on the bed turn out to be but one of Hindle's old employers at Burdick's Institution, Serapta Burdick! though had not the faint strawberry birthmark above her left eyebrow made Hindle search out her features with particular care, she would scarcely have known her! Serapta didn't know Hindle either, and for a moment Hindle was tempted to leave it that way. But a long look at the sufferer, one ineffectual tug at the connecting ties of old friendship, and Hindle was taking a seat on the bed and reaching out to touch the thin, blanketed form. "Serapta!" she said. "Is it really you? What are you doing laying in bed like this?"

"You don't mean to tell me you *know* each other!" Rosina said, as if such a circumstance would pass the known powers of nature.

"I should just guess we do," Hindle said heartily. "Don't we, Serapta?"

"This here's Dr. Fairbrass," Rosina said as Serapta settled deeper into her pillow and half closed her eyes. "Renting from my husband Lennart, her and her little girls, Lennart never even knew that's what she was. A doctor, I mean."

"Oh, Serapta, look at me, won't you? I'm Hindle! Don't you remember?"

But grief, pain and mortifying mischief had turned the once outreaching Serapta in upon herself. Hindle? Yes. Serapta saw her. Yes. Old times. Shadows we are and shadows we pursue. Nodding, she sighed, and lifted and let fall her hand upon the counterpane.

"She ain't in much of a position to be pleased," Rosina said apologetically.

"I guess not," Hindle said. "Laying here prostrate. Her, that used to run—her and her sister, Tot—Burdick's Institution for the Care of the Sick. Why, that hospital—they helped cure all *kinds* of cases."

"And now she's a case herself," Rosina said, always ready to see great things and full of wonder. "Myrtle did say something one time about a hospital—"

"I should think she would! a well-known place like *it* was."

Again the hand was lifted and let fall.

"Mrs. Bearpark said," Hindle said, "she was a neighbor of ours—went with me that first day, Serapta, do you remember? Little did I think—I've often thought I never should of left."

"What did you do there? Like you're doing now?" Rosina said.

"What's she doing now?" Serapta inquired suddenly from her pillow.

"Why, doctoring. That's why I brung her over. What did you imagine?" Rosina said. "She cured up one of the meanest carbuncles you ever laid eyes on in about two minutes. I think it would of killed me."

Serapta was turning her face away when she decided to look around at them again, at Hindle on the edge of the bed and Rosina standing at the foot. "Say," she said, her glance now taking in the shabby old doctor's bag with its rubbed gilt letters on the side spelling out U.S. ARMY that Hindle had placed on her lap when she sat down. "Don't I recognize that? Ain't that," she raised herself up on her elbow, "*Doctor's?*"

"Of course," Rosina said. "What would it be but a doctor's?"

"Yes," Hindle said in a low voice.

"Well, *if* it is, and if I remember *him*," Serapta said, "in all his glory, why, *in* that bag should be some powder and some red stuff in a bottle that would ease a elephant's pain, let alone a human's! And if that is the case, and if you ever had one iota of affection—"

"Are you telling me you're in pain, Serapta?" Hindle put the bag down at her feet and hitched up closer. "What kind of pain? Where?"

"My children got a silly thing they say if someone says something hurts," Rosina said. "'Oh, my head, oh, my thumb, oh, my belly, oh, my bum!' But of course when it's *real*, like this poor thing laying here, and not just somebody trying to get *out* of something—"

"Tell me, Serapta. A pain in your stomach? Or where? Let's put up the shade so I can see you better."

"My heart," Serapta said with a groan.

Hindle reached for her wrist, groped for what proved to be a slow, strong and steady pulse. Her look of concern changing after some moments to one of restored confidence, she was about to speak when the sick woman pulled her arm away and struggled up to sit with her back against the headboard. "You know the place burned down?" she said as Hindle bent forward to help tuck her pillow in under her shoulders.

"I do know," Hindle said gently.

"You know Tot died that very spring?"

"I heard that. And anybody that ever seen you two sisters together—"

"You know that Alice died?"

"Alice?" Hindle said.

"Murdock's wife. Our brother Murdock."

"The English lady. You don't mean to say so!"

"Foot gangrened on her. Went right up her leg. Got to her knee and killed her."

"All them disasters—!" Hindle shook her head.

"Murdock was the one that surprised *me*," Serapta went on weakly, "me and Tot never supposing him and Alice harmonized too good. But I guess you never can tell with married couples. When Alice died, Murdock carried on till finally I just said to him, 'Murdock, *grief* is one thing but *going crazy* is another, and that is what is going to happen to you if you don't watch out! Because it ain't as if you was left *alone*, remember. It ain't as if you had *no one*.'"

"Did they have children?" Rosina said.

"I wasn't talking about children," Serapta said, "which they didn't happen to have. I was talking about his *sisters*, me and Tot. And as I was raising Mavis, who was going on seven by then, why, I was talking about Mavis too!" Hindle was about to speak when Serapta continued, "We went to Murdock's, naturally, after the fire and would have stayed our lifetime. He would have hardly of known Alice was gone. But them that grieves the most—She wasn't hardly cold before this Francis, the one Murdock used to work with at the Land Office, had him writing to *his* sister in Montana—her husband fell off a roof or something, five thousand acres of ranchland—and she was answering in purple ink. And that was the end of Murdock, away he went. Sold the house from under us—but all that wasn't nothing, all that went before, compared to losing—" But she could not go on.

"Tot. I heard about that. Oh, Serapta."

Serapta nodded, weeping.

"And not a year later—Mavis."

"Mavis? Oh, honey!"

"Lisheen come and got her."

Hindle sighed with relief. "Oh, well, then she didn't—I thought you meant—"

"She couldn't be more gone if she was dead!" Serapta said bitterly.

"Lisheen was this actress," Hindle said in an aside to Rosina, who looked quite stunned. "She had this little girl—Honestly, I can't believe my ears! Did Lisheen really come back? And actually take Mavis away from you?"

"'Oh, is this my baby?' was the first thing she said. 'Baby,' I said. 'Yes, she is a baby, but seven years of her life has went by.' 'Come into your mother's arms,' Lisheen said."

"See, Lisheen *gave* Mavis to Serapta when Mavis was hardly born," Hindle said softly. "Went off to some man. But then when Mavis was seven, like Serapta here says, her mother apparently came after her."

"Nothing but an old Indian trader!" Rosina said, enthralled.

"At first I wasn't too scared," Serapta said. "I thought that Lisheen was just passing through, and that maybe a natural curiosity—But then I realized more was to it than that. She'd had to dig to *find* us! Why did she do that? So then she came out bald-faced and said she meant to take her."

"But what possessed the woman after all that time? And how did Mavis feel about going away like that with a perfect stranger?"

"Things had changed a lot for us, you understand," Serapta said sadly. "After Murdock sold the house and left, Mavis and me wasn't living too fancy in that furnished room. I was sewing, machine leaking oil, couldn't see to work on black, nervous, I would raise my voice. Poor little thing, she hadn't no place to play. And we was eating poor in comparison. So in the midst of that comes—Well, imagine. Dressed to kill and loaded down with presents!"

"She had probably got down to where there wasn't no one else left!"

"Oh, she had a husband, so she said. A lovely living. Of course he was gone a lot, he traveled. That could of made a difference, she'd be left alone part of the time. But a seven-room house on a lovely street with sidewalks—!"

"Maybe it wasn't quite as good as it sounded," Hindle said. "*Something* must of been lacking in her life."

"She did mention how it finally dawned on her how nice it looked to see a young mother walking along with her little daughter by the hand, especially if they was dressed alike."

"That sounds just like her," Hindle said. "I hope she's not going to try to pass herself off as a 'young' mother! Wasn't she more than thirty when Mavis was born?"

"Yes, but you'd never of known it to see her, the way she looked."

"But how did she get the child to go? Didn't she just about have to *kidnap* her?"

Serapta blinked back tears. "Maybe there's a instinct, Hindle. Somebody's real mother. Maybe all the changes, I don't know. Maybe there's some—They'll follow anyone, like the children of Hamelin. Or maybe something else, *God* might of had a hand in seeing that she had a home where she'd have care before the Juggernaut rolled over *me*."

"The what?" Rosina, who had not had the advantage of McGuffey's Readers and attending the Salt Lake Theater, said.

"And if so, God was just in time, because that very night of the day they left, why, here it come!"

"You're talking about your health?" Hindle said. "Your health giving way?"

"I'm talking about the muscles of my chest getting the rheumatism and how my lungs filled up with catarrh that very night. Then next thing I know I'm laying there unconscious. Next, a message gets sent to Montana, landlady telegraphs. I can see Murdock, how his mind—We had these second or third cousins here which we never mixed with, but blood is thicker than—"

"She's talking about Mary and Myrtle downstairs," Rosina said.

"And Murdock telegraphed them he'd pay my board, which he has, he never went back on *that*. So up they come to get me like a sack of potatoes."

"I remember the day," Rosina said. "Pearl was just up from having her youngest boy. We watched through the window. The man from the livery stable and Mary was carrying this poor thing between 'em. And Myrtle said, for I run out and asked, you know, if there was something I could do, Myrtle said they was taking in this blood relation. But not for very long, from the way it looked."

"They thought I was on my deathbed," Serapta said.

"And now Pearl's child is four years old!" Rosina said.

"Don't that make you feel better? To hear it's been four years and no matter what it is you *got*, you're still alive?"

"Four years added onto seven," Serapta said as though Hindle had not spoken. "Mavis has turned *eleven* and I—Why, if she was to come walking in here I might not even know her!"

"Oh, you'd know her all right," Hindle said dryly. How many albinos was there in this world? "But Serapta, listen. Right now we got to do some diagnosing. Tell me about the muscles of your chest."

"Nasty. That's all I can say."

"If I ain't clear mistaken," Rosina put in, "it seems to me that at least once or twice since she's been down here—once at least that I know of for a day or two, old Mrs. Eastman was outside scrubbing the back steps and she told me—it seemed like Serapta was on the road to recovery. On her feet and up and dressed. But *then* I heard—"

"Was you, Serapta? On your feet and up and dressed? Because if it happened once it could happen again."

"It was a Thursday. I *was* up, if that's what you want to call it," Serapta said with a look of patient endurance. "I *did* think I was well enough to move around. But by Sunday I was down again."

"That wasn't very long, was it? What happened?"

"Well, I shouldn't of never offered to join 'em in the wild-eyed cleaning that goes on around here of a Saturday. Though that wasn't the only thing—"

"She's right about that," Rosina said. "It *is* wild-eyed. The three women in this house is really fiends when it comes to cleaning."

"Afterwards I knew I was in for something. After helping, I mean," Serapta said. "But little did I expect the pleurisy and irregular dilatations that come on me during the night. I truly thought I would never see the morning! But when morning come and I *was* seeing it, and since the pleurisy had kind of slacked off and the dilatations too, why, I said to myself, 'Serapta, get up, you ain't done for, yet.' So here I was sitting on the edge of the bed putting on my stockings when Myrtle pokes her head through that doorway there. Well, the natural thing to do is say good morning, so I said, 'Good morning, Myrtle.' For a minute she don't say nothing, but then—that side of the family being about as polite as a four-toed stoat—she says, 'My *Lord*, Serapta, but it stinks in here!' Did you ever hear of such a remark in your life?"

"Never," Hindle said.

"And she keeps on. 'Smells like a skunk has got in here,' she says. Imagine. My own mother's second cousin! Then she leaves and in a minute here she comes again with this two-quart fruit jar filled with petals, old dried flower petals and cloves and such as that—"

"Pomander jar," Rosina said. "Me and Pearl have made 'em ourself."

"Takes the lid off and starts to swinging it, up and down and around—You've heard of Pandora?"

"Who?" Rosina said.

Quickly Hindle told her in an aside about the girl who once upon a time had a box that was never supposed to be opened, but one day somebody opened it and out flew all the ills and woes of human life.

"And they are still a-flying," Serapta, who had listened, said. "Which nobody realized better than me that Sunday morning when Myrtle waved her jar around this miserable room. And the *first* clap of doom—"

But at that moment a cuckoo clock downstairs whirred and struck the hour, and Rosina stiffened. "Oh, I got to go," she said. "Tonight's my night for Lennart. Which speaking of smells, don't you think it's nice for menfolks coming home to smell something homey like gingerbread out of the oven or something like that? And to see a lamp lit, even if it ain't clear dark?"

"I do," Hindle said. "And the evenings are closing in, aren't they? Well, the best of friends, Serapta—I got to go too. The lady I leave my girls with was wanting to get out to the country for peaches before it gets dark."

"I didn't know there was any left after the frost," Rosina said.

"Good-bye," Serapta whispered, turning her head away.

"Not good-bye," Hindle said. "Till we meet again. Did you imagine I wasn't coming back *tomorrow*?"

AND BACK SHE WENT THE next day, and twice more, to hear the rest of what Dr. Bywater in his book *Medical Practice* referred to as "our patient's symptomatology." Serapta's was a strange one, so strange that Hindle thought it would beat anything Dr. Bywater could put up against it.

"Remember Gulliver's travels?" Serapta began. "And how them little people tied the man down? Well, that's how I have been tied down here. For four years!"

"Where you broke off yesterday, you was sitting on the edge of the bed putting on your stockings," Hindle said. "And Myrtle had come in and was waving her fruit jar around. Do you think that had anything to do—?"

"Anything to *do*?" Serapta said. "One whiff of them old dried flowers and I was out like a light! And that was only the beginning."

"Of what, Serapta?"

"Of what?" Serapta rolled her eyes heavenward. "Well, for instance—Let me think—" Her sigh was deep. "Oh, I tell you, what I have suffered you would never believe."

"Yes, I would. Tell me."

"My arm."

"What about your arm?"

"Swole up to three times the size, that's all. Then one day about a week later I happened to look down and here it laid alongside me like—Well, you wouldn't remember because you wasn't there at the time, but the first operation we ever done at the Institution was Dr. Morgan operated on a man named Mr. Harland and took his arm off, and Tot buried it in the back yard, and if I had dug *that arm* up out of the grave, it couldn't of looked one bit sicker than my own arm laying alongside me there that day. What a shock! But I got used to it when the same thing happened over and over. Fat, thin, fat, thin—"

"Let me see your arm now, Serapta."

"No use a-looking *now*," Serapta said. Like one counting linen she went on, "I lost my power of speech for a solid year."

"Your power of speech?"

"I couldn't make a sound."

"But it come back?"

"It did. But at what a price! You see that shelf up there?" Serapta said. "It used to have a vase on it till one Saturday morning they come rampaging in, Myrtle and Mary, wild-eyed to clean, grabbed ahold of the bed, shoved it, bumped the wall which caused the shelf to shake which caused the vase to totter and fall down on my hand! And if a lightning bolt had struck me, it couldn't of done me worse. My body started to jerking from head to foot. 'Oh, dear Lord,' I say, 'what's to come next?' I'm talking, see, the shock to my system's done it, which I didn't realize for a minute, but of course they latched right onto it, and laughing like fools said they was going in business making the dumb talk by hitting them on the hand with a vase! And never, of course, a word of apology. They don't know the meaning."

"But didn't it make you happy to get your voice back?"

"Well, naturally it did. Enough so that when my poor body come to rest and they was busy outside scrubbing the leaves and taking the paint off halfway up the house, I thought I'd just slip over to the dresser and try and comb my hair. But no sooner did I raise the comb than I couldn't hold it, my arm went numb and everything went numb and how I ever made it to the bed is a complete mystery, stricken as I was with paralytic spasm and spasmodic asthma!"

"Goodness," Hindle said, trying hard to tally these combinations and derivations. "But now you had your voice back, you could holler."

"Holler, yes, if that was any consolation—which I guess it is when a person's *blind*."

"You don't mean to tell me you went blind!"

Serapta nodded. "Couldn't see a thing. Felt just like a blanket was threw over my head. Later on it lifted, but what come next? Deaf. Turned deaf. Couldn't hear even the loudest thunder for more'n a week. Then my leg started in."

"To do what?"

"Well, remember what I told you about my arm? My leg done just the same, went up and down. And now I was really paining, every inch."

"Tell me what kind of pain."

"Well, that ain't hard to do, because when we was little, Tot and me, a woman hit her husband with a hammer in Nauvoo for skinning an eel alive! So that's how I was paining. Like I was that eel and God was skinning *me* alive—"

"Was you taking medicine?"

"Running out of my ears. Oh, and the Elders come and laid on hands. And Myrtle got the doctor."

"What did the doctor say?"

"Funny thing, he died. Just within days. I wasn't a bit surprised, considering them cheeks of his like they was rouged, and coughing like a drowning person. He got a lovely write-up in the paper because of fighting at Bull Run and everything. And for some unknown reason, after he died I got to feeling better, not because he was dead, of course, but—somehow a kind of surge of strength went through me. I sat up, then I *got* up, walked to the window, took ahold of the shade and started to let it up—"

"And?"

"It flew right out of my hand!" Serapta said, her eyes filling with tears. "Snapped up to the top with such terrible force it jumped off the fixtures and bounced down onto my head! And you can just imagine what *that* did to me! as weakened as my poor frame was to start with. Give me the palsy and struck me dumb again. Then new things started to happen."

"Things like what?"

"My bladder quit me cold. Bladder and kidneys. Took a week almost to behave theirself. Then I could pee if you'll excuse the expression, but what had *that* to be traded for, do you think? Spitting! couldn't *spit* no more, and water wouldn't wet my tongue or throat. And mind you, I was paralyzed and couldn't speak. I had to ring like this!" Leaning over, Serapta showed how she took in her teeth the handle of the bell standing on the table beside her bed and shook it to bring help upstairs.

"I hope it brought them. I hope they didn't neglect you."

"No, to be fair. To give the devil his due. But it's not been *pleasant*. And my brother's paying, don't forget. But anyway, one day a young man knocks at the door downstairs selling electrical shocks and they brought him up. 'I've had enough shocks,' I says. But do you know, there's something to electricity—I believe if he hadn't been run off like the girls said for fighting down in the park and I could of had a few more treatments— Anyway, the palsy loosened and my voice came back. But one worrisome thing, you know at the time of the moon?" Serapta paused, embarrassed, and started over. "When I had my custom, my hand swole entirely up and the skin peeled off like if you would take off a glove. My head done something, too, all by itself, went to arching backwards. And one little ray of sun, one little beam of the lamp hitting my eye, felt like a knife stuck in! Did I mention my tongue, the way it burned? And every bone in my body grating and grinding? And how I'd find myself in a dead faint? Then I vomited for three days and nights. And one Tuesday—I remember it was a Tuesday—I couldn't swallow a thing, not even a drop of water, till midnight Thursday. But to tell you the truth it didn't come back perfect, oh, for months."

"What didn't come back perfect?"

Serapta put her hand up to her throat. "One time it took me a whole entire day to eat two graham crackers, crumb by crumb."

"Well, it has been an ordeal, no doubt of that."

"Ordeal? You know a smokehouse, how the hams and bacon sides is hanging up on hooks? Well, once it seemed to me like things was hanging up inside of *me* that way, heart, liver, gizzard, stomach—hanging. Then all of a sudden they all let go at once! and fell in a heap to the bottom of my trunk."

"The only fallen thing I've ever heard of is a fallen uterus."

"Sometimes I suffocate. And sometimes a iron band—And once in a while—"

The list of symptoms grew, and Hindle, anxiously consulting Abernathy and Hunt's *Symptoma Humanitatem* and other of Doctor's books when she got home, despaired of ever identifying Serapta's disease, as fickle and hard to refer to its proper species as the serpent-tailed, goat-bodied, lion-headed beast of old legend. Prolapsus of the viscera? Recidivous fever? Chronic interstitial atrophy? Late at night after her third visit to the sick woman, while turning the pages of Berkeley's *General Medicine*, she came upon the sentence, "The more signs and symptoms, the more devoid of probable signification is the disease." She read it again, looked up into space. And then, with that sudden insight of the mind that is sometimes better than the eyes of the body, knew very well what Serapta's sickness was. It was *left-in-the-lurchums*, not serious unless you die of it. But there was a cure, and what it was was not the bitter-tasting anthelmintic she brought along the next day, but the promise she gave Serapta that when restored to health she could come and live with her! and if she wanted she could run the house and see to things while Hindle doctored. Small wages to start but better to come, and if Murdock still sent money for board, Serapta could use that for clothes and what she needed. One spoonful before meals with a glass of water.

She rose from her ashes so fast that Hindle had hardly got home before one of Lennart's little boys, either Rosina's or Pearl's, came running to say the sick lady at the Eastmans' was all cured up and waiting to be took away. Hindle rented a buggy, which Serapta said was silly considering how small her valise was, but Hindle thought the occasion called for a little ceremony. There were no tears and the only speechmaker on hand seemed to be Rosina, who ran across the alley as soon as she saw what was doing, to say that if anybody had told her *this* was going to be the end result of her terrible carbuncle, she would have said they were full of balloon juice, but who knows what's building up ahead? One thing she was sure of, that after a miracle as wonderful as this one, which they could all vouch for, if Doubting Thomas Lennart needed any *further* proof that the lady renting Fern's house was a real true doctor, Rosina was not going to mash him any more potatoes!

Chapter Twenty-four

*

WHEN THE DOOR OPENED TO HIS KNOCK, THE SIGN PAINTER NEARLY STEPPED backwards off the step in surprise, for this was not the person he had braced himself to ask a favor of but a strange woman who, skillet in hand, stood in the doorway and asked him what he wanted. For a moment he hardly knew. "Did she move away?" he said. "The one calling herself a doctor? I see the sign I painted for her is still up."

"*Calling* herself a doctor!" Serapta said sharply. "Let me tell you, Mr. Whatever-your-name-is, you wouldn't see *me* standing here today if she wasn't as real as that post you're hanging on to."

"Fogelmarck," he mumbled.

"I know," she said. "We seen you going around the house the other day and Hindle mentioned who you was. She also mentioned taking a iron filing out of your eye! so if *you* don't know what she is, you must be pretty dense."

"I do know," he said, "and you must pardon me. Sometimes an individual misspeaks."

Serapta bore herself indignantly a moment longer, then softened. "I know they do," she said, "especially when they're more of a foreigner, which I understand—Hindle said the landlord here said you told him you was nearly grown before you stepped foot in this country."

Now it was time for him to stiffen, but only for an instant. "I look forward, not back," he said. Then, "Will you be on the premises awhile?"

"I think I very well might," she said with a smile. "Why do you ask?"

"This house looks upon the street while mine don't," he said. "I must go uptown and deliver these sketches. I will be back soon. But in the meantime, a very important visitor might come and might not find the way. Or if he finds the way and I am not at home—"

"Why don't you just tack a note there on the gate and on your door out in back?" she said practically.

"Because the wind—" he said. "A stray animal—children—But also—You see, madam—"

"Serapta," she said. "I should of introduced myself. That wasn't very polite. My name is Serapta Burdick."

"Pleased to make your acquaintance, Mrs. Burdick," he said impatiently.

"Miss, not Mrs."

"So if anyone comes, will you say I will be back shortly? I must go now—"

163

He did come back, as he had said. But in a worse mood than when he left, for the man who was to be shown the sketches, the rich man whose dining room lunettes and panels were to be decorated with the beautiful Irish kings he had worked on till daylight, did not appear. He threw his roll of sketches down on the step, but picked them up again.

"Why, that's awful," Serapta said.

"Mr. Summerlade said—And now I must do these all over."

"But, Mr. Fogelmarck, if your customer didn't appear and didn't *see* your pictures, why do you think you have to do them over?"

"Because Mr. Summerlade—The pictures' eyes must not follow one around the room. This would make the wife nervous. They must not be looking."

"That is crazy," she said.

"No one came about anything?" He stared at her, then suddenly said, "I made an offer to paint the portrait of the new Prophet, Seer and Revelator. No charge."

"Well, my!" she said. "Wouldn't *that* be a feather in your cap! And in his, too. Did the church take you up on it?"

"Not yet."

"Well, nobody's been here. I set right on the porch till it got too breezy. Then I went inside and set by the window. But, say—"

"Thank you."

"Wait right here." She turned and went into the house, leaving the door half open. As she disappeared down the shadowy hallway, a door to the right opened and a man came out. "Thank you," he said, putting on his hat. "I'll tell her you'll come tomorrow. And also what you said." As he came through the doorway and down the steps past Mr. Fogelmarck, he glanced at him and said, "You got female trouble, too?"

"Fool," the sign painter muttered when the man had disappeared around the corner. And then again, angrily, "Fool!"

"What's that?" Serapta said, coming out the door with a saucepan with a lid on it. "Now this is for you, Mr. Fogelmarck, to take home and eat this very minute while it's hot."

"What *is* it?"

"It's beef stew with everything in it that's good for you."

He took it unwillingly, did not smile and did not say thank you again.

"But poor soul, he must of not had no bringing up," Serapta told Hindle at supper. "He's just not friendly."

"Oh, I don't know. Him and me talked real nice today. We really did."

"What about? The millennium?"

"I kept my eye open for him so if anyone came to see him I could steer them out to his barn. Like this rich man he's got to paint the kings for, or a Apostle come to make arrangements for him to paint the new President—"

"An *Apostle*?" Hindle said, laughing. "Paint the President? Mr. Fogelmarck don't want much!"

"He must be a beautiful artist," Serapta said. "Look at your sign. And the sign we seen him carrying around the house the other day for Pope Manufacturing Company Velocipedes."

"A far cry from the head of the church."

"Well, he's a member."

"I know he is, and nearly too carried away by it. But there's kind of a muddle about him some way that has to go before the church court, and in the meantime, on account of some members from San Bernardino, he's not supposed to have anything to do with his ward and the ward's not supposed to have anything to do with him. Lennart was mentioning it, Mr. Palmstedt, our landlord. So I don't imagine he'll get far with painting the new Prophet. Stig Fogelmarck, I mean."

"Imagine naming a child Stig. But I like it," Serapta said.

Several more times she watched for people who might want to see him while he was away, but no one came. She didn't mind, keeping an eye on the yellow leaves blowing in the street, passersby in their garb, a wagon trundling by piled high with pumpkins. And she liked it when Mr. Fogelmarck returned and they talked awhile, her in the doorway, him on the porch leaning against a post, before he would break everything off abruptly and make for the corner of the house. She never could anticipate this sudden flight and would call out for him to wait! She had something for him. Which she did have, and what would it be but soup, a plate of cornbread or a piece of custard pie! and he got so he would smile slightly as he received it.

"Talk about *music* soothing the savage breast," Hindle said, seeing this piece of business through her window.

"You're not mad at me, are you, Hindle?"

"How could I be mad at you, you silly thing? Around this house you can do whatever you want!"

SERAPTA COULD, TOO, FOR SHE had turned out to be valuable indeed. She could cook, that was one thing. And such grace did she dispense towards children that Hindle's two girls were hers almost on sight. Her "cure" also, spread abroad by Rosina and Pearl, their neighbors and kin, before long solicited a patronage for Hindle that left her open-mouthed. Even the Eastman ladies came! Mary with gall bladder trouble, the old lady for dizziness, Myrtle with a wry neck. She knew who was to blame for the neck! Myrtle said, and if ever she tried to do a good deed in her life again she hoped someone would shoot her. "But what I want to know," she said, wincing as Hindle clapped on her cervical vertebrae a cold wet mass which, because of the mustard in it, soon turned hot as fire, "is what Serapta really *had*. For if ever you seen a parade of carryings on! *that woman*—"

"She had," Hindle said, pausing not only to peek at the red neck under the poultice but to test out in her mind, as the circus acrobat tests out his ropes and swings, her new vocabulary, "a bad case of marasmus, complicated by gyrencephalation." And that, the ease with which those names tripped off Hindle's tongue—more than the kitchen prowess, the harmony with children, the "cure" that brought in patients—was Serapta's best contribution. For that ease could only have come from the long, loose stretches of *time* Serapta's presence provided. Not perhaps for study like the dedicated student's of science under a professor, but at least to turn every page of and look at every drawing in Doctor's books, until by diffusion Hindle could bear in mind the ordinances and rehearse the *words* a doctor needed as much as he needed his stethoscope or wet and dry bulb psychrometer.

How many times in their travels had she not packed, unpacked and stood on the shelf those volumes she no more thought of reading than you would sit down and read a shoe or collar box! Now they came down one by one and, as if not seen before (though she *had* mauled them a bit after first seizing upon her new profession), she panned the leaves like a prospector washing his gold-bearing gravel. Even the shabby, yellowed wheat-paper book called *The Sympathetic and Natural Egyptian Secrets of Albertus Magnus*, which Doctor bought off an old woman selling from a pack on the street in San Francisco and read like a joke book, came under her gaze. But he was right, that one was a bunch of nonsense compared to the smartness of today. As Doctor said, in old Albertus's time you had sorcery and charms—Paga! Chaga! Pagula!—while in our modern scientific age there was blood pressure, rubber catheters, iodoform injections, and you could cut a leg off at the hip.

"Couldn't you always?" she had said.

"You could," he said, "but the bugger died."

At first, never intending to do any of it, she left *Practical Observations, Engravings and Principles of Surgery* alone, but when that book too seemed to almost fall off the shelf into her hand, she carried it to her desk and took a good look. And after she had turned all the pages and looked at the engravings, she was still respectful enough, although a thought had crossed her mind that mixed her respect with a little displacency. It *looked* hard, surgery, that "boast and pride" of men. But to follow directions and decipher diagrams with rays going through them connected to a, b and c and do *any* new thing was hard, such as to make point-lace, hermetically seal up plums or build a ship in a bottle. Surgery was just a manual art that any reasonably handy person, if they took pains and went at it step by step, could do, not something like being a grand opera singer where before anything else God had to give you a *voice*. But a surgeon performing an operation never acted like that, like surgery was just a manual art. He acted like he was the opera singer with the one voice in millions singing a song that only the greatest singer could sing. And sometimes what he was doing was the *easy* thing rather than the hardest, cutting something open or off, rather than to grope his way through a case like a cloud of night. A case, for instance, like Cora Plume's.

THE WORD "ACCOUCHER" ON HINDLE'S medical diploma, translated for Myron Plume, the man she had dealt with at the License Bureau, as "to lay on the couch," had not only quickly got her her medical license but brought her his wife Cora (who "laid on the couch" with a vengeance) as patient. After her first visit Cora had got some better, but now she was bad again, and Myron had taken time from work to come himself and ask Hindle to please try again to rouse her up. Hindle told him she would try, paid her a visit, and when she came out of Cora's house found him waiting for her around the corner. "Well, what do you think?" he said.

Hindle didn't know what to think because it seemed like the woman was healthy, but she had been with Doctor too long not to know that to treat the complicated patient (not cheaply) benefited not only the patient but all concerned. So she said it could be several things, thin blood, an irregular dilatation, and there was more than a chance that—

"Did Cora mention the Principle?"

"Why, no," Hindle said in some surprise. "Except to say she's by herself two-thirds of the time, so I just naturally supposed—"

"Say anything about Jen and Bessie?" Before Hindle could answer he went on, "Because *them* two sure ain't had nothing to do with the sap going out of Cora!"

"Can I ask you something, Mr. Plume?" Hindle said with a glance at his flushed face. "Why do *you* think the sap's went out of her?"

"Well, it ain't *them*," he said. "And you know why I know that? Because Jen is my first, Bessie is my second and Cora is my *third* and *last*. Spouse. And if I quote scripture right here and tell you that 'the first shall be last and the last shall be first,' what would I be saying?"

"You would be saying that Cora is your favorite," Hindle said. She had begun walking and he fell into step beside her.

"Putting it like that's a little bald-faced," he said. "But I will say this. She's my ewe lamb. You can see that yourself."

"You mean your concern about her health and everything."

"I mean, ain't she laying in china silk? Ain't she alone there in her own little downy nest while up on Quince Street the other two is sharing the same roof? Jen upstairs with her brood, Bessie downstairs with hers? Did you look at Cora's finger? That's a opal ring! Her cups and saucers is thin as paper. And I'll tell you something else. That girl—anytime and anyplace—can call the tune. So there's where I've fell down, I guess. I been too partial. Been, and am, and getting paid for it."

"Oh, no, Mr. Plume. She's needed you just like you are," Hindle said. "And by the way, today she wasn't so quiet. She mentioned lots more things. Told me what happened."

"Told you what happened *when*?" he said, drawing back.

"Last year," Hindle said. "The baby born dead. But of course I already knew about that from her first visit. And then three years ago, the miscarriage in her third month. When she come out with that, which she never had before, I said to her, 'Mrs. Plume, you've went *through* something, a miscarriage, a baby's death—' And really, Mr. Plume, she has. Some women, a thing like that won't faze. But others—"

"I won't say it didn't *faze* her," he said. "But at the time, her and me was living in paradise. And things don't hit as hard when you're living—"

"This was before she took sick?"

"Paradise," he repeated in a whisper. Then, clearing his throat, "It was out in Murray. I only moved her back to town this last July. But out there—I am telling you, Garden of Eden. Cow. Her chickens. Stuff growing. I had a organ hauled out from Dinwoodey's. And I myself was out there more than I ought to of been, it wasn't easy but I worked it somehow."

"What happened to change all that?"

"Nothing!"

"Well, *something* must have. Losing the baby?"

"Born dead," he said. "Got over it. But then she started laying down. Sap commenced to going completely out."

"And you thought that different surroundings—?"

"All the way along the line I've done my best!"

"I don't doubt that in the least, Mr. Plume." But the stridency in his voice and the mottled way his face looked when she glanced at him made her wonder if he was to *blame* for something. Not deliberately, perhaps, but sometimes a husband's untimely and troublesome demands could be upsetting. The man himself not being likely to agree to grant the asking of such a question, the next time Hindle went to see Cora, she asked *her*. Cora was shocked that anybody would even think of such a thing! Why, Myron Plume was the most considerate husband on the face of this earth! But even if he hadn't been—which he was—that was one of the great advantages of living the Principle. Because there was always another wife to—to—The name of that duty she could not bring over her lips.

"He mentioned you living out in Murray," Hindle ventured after a little silence.

Cora's eyes sparkled for a moment, then dulled. She turned her face away.

"He said you was real happy. So what happened? Did you start to get lonesome out there or what?"

"I got sick."

"You mean, drug out like you are now? Or how?"

Cora turned back, her eyes filling with tears. "I mean it wouldn't surprise me one bit if I died!"

"It would surprise *me*," Hindle said.

And it would, for try as she might with all the examinations Doctor used to give and more too, she could neither see, hear, smell or palpate anything in or about Cora but good health. Still, in the midst of life we are in death, as the Bible said, so she turned the pages of the books again. Malignant growth? A floating kidney? Microzymes too small for the eye to see? A watermelon seed lodged in her blind caecum? The physical possibilities were endless! But Hindle kept going back to how the mind (even a horse's) could perform arithmetical feats without the aid of written figures, *think* a song so you could actually hear it, and if it wanted—Serapta's case was what she kept thinking of, the changes *her* mind had rung upon her self, and Hindle told herself crossly she mustn't get stuck there! To see another case like Serapta's in this short while would be about as likely as to see two cabooses hooked to the same train. No, in contrast to Serapta's cloudy transmutations, Cora's steady weakness was *real*. But—Hindle stopped turning pages, closed the book, got up slowly and put it back on the shelf—what was real? Take air. You couldn't see it, but you would know well enough if it wasn't there. Take feelings. You couldn't see *them*, but they could get hurt like an eye getting black or a nose getting broke in a fight. And a person in the aggregate amounts to more than their blood in a state of constant circulation, their spluttering nerves and splitting cells. In fact the body might, like Haze that time, just be impersonating *someone else*.

LIKE HER STEPFATHER, HAZE, THAT time. Hindle hadn't thought of him—it had been *years*! But in memory here he was again. Here they all were, Lucitie, herself, Mama looking shiny-eyed and young, and him, the man who went his way so long ago and now had come back into Mama's life. It was still Sunday, the sun had nearly set. They had come home from the picnic and were sitting on the porch drinking lemonade, and Mama and Haze were talking about the summer fifteen years before when they crossed the plains, Mama, left a widow two weeks into the trip, Haze, the company hunter hired by the captain of the train. The conversation had got old by then, and she and Lucitie were looking at each other as if to say, how much more could they stand? when Mama, taking account of them, said in her newly frolicsome manner, "You children can't imagine—what a hunter—what kind of a shot this gentleman here *was*."

He shook his head. "All just make-believe," he said.

"Make-*believe*? Why, Haze Blatchford! Who could make believe they could turn their back on a buffalo, shoot over their shoulder and drop it to the ground, will you kindly tell me?"

"Luck of the Irish," he said, acting modest. But from then on till the moon came up and they were sent to bed, big girls of thirteen and eleven, all Lucitie and Hindle heard was brag. And the worst part of it was, he could prove whatever he told! Had the empty place where his finger used to be that he hacked off before a coral snake's poison could rush through his body. Had the scars where a wildcat jumped down off a ledge and nearly clawed his head off. Indian torture. (After they got married, Mama no doubt saw *them* particular scars before she died two months short of their first wedding anniversary.)

Buggers had done their worst, Haze said. And it might of been foolhardiness, but he never give 'em the satisfaction of caving in. Though maybe to say "their worst" was exaggerating. If they'd done *that* he wouldn't be here tonight. And towards the last there, when they come at him screeching and yelling with tomahawks up like this, he thought he'd bought the farm. But instead of that they cut his thongs and helped him to his feet. God knows why! He might of passed a test, or maybe a feather floated down, or a star come out. Ain't no white man really knows the red man. Anyway, it took about a minute to go from tortured prisoner to honored guest. And wasn't they an *outfit* he had stumbled onto! Mandan Indians. Hawk-nosed Indian faces, but with these greenish eyes and grayish hair, even the little children had the hair. And he had seen some customs in his day, but these was—Graveyards without no graves! just big round bunches of brush set round in a circle and trimmed like Christmas trees with Mandan skulls. The men of the tribe never got to step foot in the graveyard till they died, and then not their whole body but just their skull.

"Why was that, Haze?" Mama said.

"Because the graveyards was what you might call the womenfolks' *parlor*. There was a Mandan law against squaws shooting off their mouth around the encampment. If they wanted to talk they had to go to the graveyard to do it."

Mama laughed politely. Then she said, showing she'd heard all this before when she knew him before and they crossed the plains, "Tell what happened when they wanted a new chief."

"Not much to tell. Took the old chief out and made him look into the sun till it burnt his eyes out."

"Imagine. Wasn't that terrible," Mama said.

"Did I ever tell you about the medicine man?"

"I don't believe you did, Haze," Mama said, looking like she expected a revelation.

And in a way, that's what it was! or seemed so now to Hindle as, remembering what he told them, she wondered at the same time if some foolish person might not try to straighten out Mr. Plume's wife, Cora, by a rite of similar magic. If it was magic in the first place and not just a poor demonstration of the force well known in modern times as—they did it on the stage—Mesmerism. And hardly even that if to start with, as Haze said, the patient was put under by a swig of something from an old green bottle tied around the medicine man's waist.

That one evening was the only time Haze put himself out to engage their attention, because a few days later Mama married him and all he did from then on, the less than a year that Mama still had left before she died in childbirth and the baby with her, was take

his hat and go out for fresh air, or grump around the house. There was no more entertainment. But that one night he really put on a show. He made them see it all. Through
the dark stand of trees here came the Mandan doctor in paint and feathers, giving a jump
and rattling his rattles and banging a tin pan, to cure the sick. First the knock-out drops
from the old green bottle, and did whatever it was, work! the sick man was out like a light.
Haze took all the parts. He was the medicine man, old Duck Legs as he called him, and
the unconscious patient. And when old Duck Legs bent over the patient and said "Who
are you?" Haze answered as the *sickness*, too. He was also the interlocutor who explained
to the audience what was going on.

A disease to the Indians, Haze said, was like talking about a claim-jumper or a burglar,
some crook that had got, instead of into your house or property, into your *body*. If you
could see it, it would look like an actual person! No intelligence to speak of. So the
right kind of soft soaping—prettier'n a speckled bird! beat the Dutch! ain't you the
finest!—compliments like that, that the medicine man could reel off to perfection, and
the sickness would start to first peep out, and then—that would be the moment! Grab,
pull, yank—No, you don't, you jobbing dealer! And Haze said he felt foolish to say what
he saw then, but he did see it! as plain as I see you, and it was a fight between old Duck
Legs and something that looked like a man but had no substance, like a blue gauze of
smoke. Powerful, though, it pounded, thumped and shook the medicine man till he was
bleary-eyed and blood run down his face. But Duck Legs hung on and won. Then back
into the forest he dragged whatever the thing was and drowned it in the river. And the
dying patient reared up, *cured*.

His audience sat amazed a little while. Then Lucitie said, "But suppose the sick
person *hadn't* reared up cured? What would of happened to the medicine man?"

Haze didn't know. Nobody died while he was still around the Indian camp. But he
knew a wily beguily when he seen one, and a wily beguily like old Duck Legs can wiggle
out of anything.

WILD, RUDE NATURE! SUCH A contrast to the jets of lighted gas of modern progress!
enlarged pictures, surgical retractors, tinned sock-eye salmon…Hindle wouldn't trade.
But yet, to have the leeway of old Duck Legs! when dealing with a sickness like Cora's.
To believe, as he believed, that you could lure it out of its slumbering host with flattery!
What was in his bottle anyway? The book might mention it, the old green *Pharmacopeia*,
but how would she know she was seeing it if she did? The same with Doctor's labels.
Thorn apple? Belladonna? But who cared what a savage Indian might have up his sleeve
or in his bottle in comparison with the anesthesia of modern civilization? It couldn't
compare! Of that she was sure. Not that she was this big expert, but Doctor did tell her
one time that if ever he had to be operated on, she was the one he would want to put
him under.

So say she does it, Cora lays asleep, the scene's all set. Would any civilized person go ahead then with the rest of that Indian nonsense? Not likely! though it wouldn't take long. And with no one there (awake) but your own self…And don't they say the means justifies the end? Suppose it worked! The ewe lamb restored. An office-bearer in the *License Bureau* grateful for all times to come. The joy, the simple satisfaction. (And the fee.)

Chapter Twenty-five

*

"Mrs. Plume," Hindle said briskly, putting down Doctor's bag and another small satchel. "You remember the last time I was here, when I had doubts about your epiglottic cartilage? but I didn't have the stuff with me to look at it really good? Well, today I have." While Cora looked on wide-eyed, she opened the bag and drew from it an old pair of long speculum-forceps which she held up and laid on the table, then from the satchel took out and did the same with the last purchase Doctor ever made on this earth (it arrived from Chicago the day after he died), a small reflecting telescope with a metallic mirror. "Unfortunately, the only way we can work these down your passage is with you out of the picture to the extent that the fibers, nerves and joints of the—"

"Out of the picture?"

"I mean put slightly under with a—drop of sulfuric ether."

"But I don't want no operation!"

"Of course you don't, Mrs. Plume. This here is what is called a diagnostic procedure, which altogether won't take two minutes."

"Well, I don't know," Cora said.

"Naturally, you don't," Hindle agreed. "I don't either. But two little short minutes and we'll have our positive answer. One way or the other."

And they did. Arrived at, however, after a transaction unsettling enough to Hindle to make her decide never again, while she fulfilled her function, to employ magic. Magic, spiritualism, optical illusion, whatever it was and whatever brought it on …

Was it the hot day, inappropriate to September? Cora's closed-up parlor? Was Hindle breached somehow herself by ether fumes? Whatever made it happen, she was just sitting there (with Cora lightly etherized on the couch) looking around at the walls and pictures when gradually they became outdoors, dim leafy outdoors, deep in drooping fog. And something that was nothing was…someone…taking shape as…the company hunter, painted, befeathered, rattling his rattle, banging his tin pan, his noises noiseless as if under water. She wasn't surprised. Who else but Haze would stick his nose in where it didn't concern him?

And don't care who sees him in that get-up, either. I bet you something. He'll go through the whole blame rigamarole from first to last. Drink up, old socks—the King. Yes, there he goes with, prettier'n a speckled bird—beat the Dutch—ain't you the finest!—And look! He's done it, coaxed out of—whoever this is asleep on this pile of leaves—the outlines and the contour coiling up and winding into the air like smoke from a fire…It *does* come out for him, it *is*…some kind of…sight…to see. He makes a lunge! then, but cloudily strategic, whatever the thing is makes a fool of him and gets away.

And now what, Butter-fingers? Loose in here! and what is to be done, will you kindly tell me, Haze that spoiled our life as surely as if you had shot *Mama* over your shoulder without looking instead of a buffalo? But, trellised by creeping fog, insolvent Haze passes imperceptibly into the wild red medicine man. Old Duck Legs in his turn, painted and laughing, blurs into someone else…and Doctor—*Doctor?*—says, giving a little jump and rattling his rattle, "Didn't I always tell you, my love, *belief cures and belief kills?*" Yes, you did, but now I want to know—He does not speak but, slow as the seven-year itch, vanishes into the spectral wood…

She sat up so quickly the instruments she had brought only for show slid off her lap onto the floor.

"Are you speaking to me?" Cora murmured, her eyes still closed. She opened them and half sat up. "Did you find out?"

Hindle shook her head to clear it. "I hope you don't think we went through all that," she wanted to say *diagnostic procedures* but found it too much trouble, "not to find out!" Light-headedly, she bent to pick up the fallen tools.

"So what is it? Not that whatever it is," Cora said, "will be what caps the climax."

"Caps the climax?"

"What finally kills me. 'Cause that will be myself."

Hindle sat up, spoke sharply. "What are you talking about?"

"Now while I was under—it all just seemed so clear. Like word had come. 'Don't delay no more.' 'Cora, cap the climax by giving up.'"

Never again. Hindle found her handkerchief and wiped her brow.

But one good thing could be said for the exercise, and that was, during the ensuing hour it loosened Cora's tongue! Over glasses of Word of Wisdom cold water and a sack of coffee cake, which Cora said Myron had brought the evening before and she hadn't touched, she became as garrulous as birds talking around the edges of some marsh. And in spite of Hindle's contending with speech and argument against her resolution to cash in her chips, stuck with it stubbornly until at four o'clock (with another call to make) Hindle remembered an old trick of Doctor's. "Well, if you're determined you're determined," she said, tacking to get wind of her. "No use going on with the discussion."

Cora looked startled, as at a tight hold suddenly gone slack.

"But one thing you *could* do before you go," Hindle said, "and that is, lighten your manifest."

There was a silence. Then, "What's that?" Cora said.

"When a ship sails into a port of destination, the first thing they got to show is their manifest. The list of what they're carrying. Their cargo. 'A clean breast and a log that'll bear inspection, and harbor dues won't sink you.' That's what the sailors say. Own right *up* to something and it stops counting, or not to the same extent it done before. Or as the Catholics—"

"Catholics are just terrible, don't you think?" Cora said. But she spoke mildly, wrapped up in abstraction. "The priests and all. Them graven images. Confession."

"Yes, but in a way the *idea*'s not bad. Take in your case, for instance. Before you throw in the sponge—"

"The way I've decided to do," Cora said, as if to herself, "is go out to my sister's and jump in my brother-in-law's tail-race."

"—*you* could go ahead and use the privilege. The Catholics ain't got a patent, after all! 'All your sins efface,' as the old hymn says."

But that night, Hindle added a sin to her own manifest! That is, if the oath of Hippocrates cut any ice as it ought to. From the many times she'd hung up Doctor's framed copy in their wandering years and taken it down again, she almost knew it by heart, and when she hung it up beside her *own* medical license she vowed, only half in play, to do things the way "Apollo the physician ... Aesculapius ... Hygeia ... Panacea and all the gods and goddesses ..." wanted, just in case. On this night, therefore, as she and Serapta sat by the stove in their nightclothes sipping cocoa before they went to bed, and she told Serapta everything Cora had told her, she felt the fault. "Whatever ... I see or hear, in the life of men, which ought not to be spoken of abroad, I will not divulge ..." Of course *abroad* meant out in the world, while all she was doing was just divulging a few particulars *at home*.

Particulars that didn't signify too much. Lots of pregnant women have jumped off high places the way Cora jumped off her kitchen table and then her chicken house roof trying to jar loose what was growing in her. And while in her case three years before this it happened to work, many a poor thing, as Hindle told Serapta she put in quickly when Cora started crying her eyes out at the memory, could jump off the Beehive House and break both legs and their neck and still be tied to deliver right on schedule. Besides— didn't she ever hear that expression "Man thinks, God laughs"? Maybe she miscarried from natural causes!

Cora was positive she hadn't, Hindle said, but stopped crying until later in the conversation when the subject of her *second* pregnancy came up. How happy she had been to find the miracle had come about again. And how she did hope that the little spirit she refused entry to, in life, the first time was the same one that was coming back down from heaven for a second try!

"Flighty," Serapta decided on hearing of this change of mind.

"In a way. But when she went back into her history—You see, Serapta, Cora was a girl right in the middle of a big family. Nobody paid any attention to her till she met Myron.

Then all of a sudden she become a queen. Is she going to want to share that with a baby? Not that first one. But then she gets more reconciled—"

"Is Myron in polygamy?"

"There's two more Mrs. Plumes and a bunch of children."

"So how can he do all this kowtowing to Cora? Though why I ask I don't know, because they do it all the time."

"All the time," Hindle agreed sadly. "But anyway when Christmas come last year, Cora was the wife he spent it with. She was the one got the lion's share of the presents, toilet water, a changeable taffeta petticoat she couldn't get around her, she was so big by then. Well, a blizzard struck, Myron couldn't get back to town, and to make a long story short, *he* delivered the baby. The first one in his life." Hindle waited a little. "Not his first baby, the first he delivered." She paused again. "The so-called stillborn child."

"So-called?" Serapta's eyebrows slowly lifted.

"Cora raised up on her elbow, so she says, and seen it kind of flip and flop and heard it cry."

"Seen it do what?"

"It just about killed her to say so, but the configuration ... seemed like it somehow went down to a *point*."

"What went down to a point?"

"The baby! Almost like a fish. One little foot at the bottom sticking out, maybe two feet, she's not sure of that. But the tapering down she knows she seen! Before he took it away and, so she swears—But cross your heart and promise never to tell—"

"Who would I tell?"

"Well, not Mr. Fogelmarck that you and him have struck up such a friendship."

"Him? I doubt if he could even listen, he's so on edge about his kings and not hearing a word about his offer—But look at how our subject's getting changed. You was telling— What was you saying, Hindle?"

"Something I shouldn't—"

"I'll take it to my grave."

Hindle held back in doubt, then spoke with indecision. "Funny you should use that word," she said, "because a grave figures prominent in this. As I started to say—either the child come early or Cora didn't count right, she was off a couple of weeks but that wouldn't hurt. It was alive and kicking when it got here. She *says*. Then Myron took it in the kitchen and bingo, it's dead. She's positive he killed it!"

"Good Lord."

"Now mind you, she is helpless, laying there shocked to the fundaments and starting in to hemorrhage. He had his work cut out for him. And that wasn't the worst! for then come childbed fever. Cora laid delirious and when she come to herself could hardly tell if what she remembered was a dream, or real. But more and more she thought it was real.

So after that things changed so much between her and Myron they could of been two different people. She couldn't stand to have him come near her. Even to hear him opening up the door would get her heart to pounding. She'd look at his hands and think what they had done. But anyway, when she got well enough he took her out and showed her where the grave was, close to the fence that run alongside the barn. They'd plant a tree or rosebush there, he said. But all she wanted to do was move back to town, it was like something scary was out in back she couldn't stand to think of."

"I can understand that," Serapta said. "Why, me and Tot was bothered by Mr. Harland's *arm* buried in our back yard till we got used to it. The poor man was supposed to send for it if he ever died, but now of course no one could ever find it."

"What preyed on Cora's mind, I think," Hindle said, "was that someday she was going to go out there and do something awful."

"Stab herself on the baby's grave for Myron to find?"

Hindle shook her head. "Go out there, dig the baby up and *see*. Once and for all."

There was a silence. Then Serapta said, "That woman is as crazy as a loon."

"She's not, Serapta. In fact, she's using reason—"

"You call that using reason? To want to do a terrible thing like that?"

"Well, what does a sensible person want to do? Save their life if they possibly can. That's built-in instinct," Hindle said in the tone Doctor used to use when trying to teach her something. "If they got a problem, they want to solve it. If there's doubt, they want to clear it up. If a thing needs settling, they want to settle it. A sensible person uses their faculties."

"So does a addled person. That is just the trouble."

"But can't you see her reasoning? She wants to know! Did the baby go down to a point? If so, it must of been some kind of visitation for what she done three years ago, jumping off the roof that time and all, which to her mind was just as surely her killing that *first* child as Myron doing away with the *second*. So now she's got to pay for everything *herself*. But suppose the baby *wasn't* like she thought, with the fish tail and the little foot? Then Myron *didn't* kill it and she won't need to die. In other words she's trying to save her life even if she doesn't know it. And not only her life but *their* life, the life him and her had together. That's not craziness. It's giving herself a chance."

Serapta considered this without much enlightenment. Finally she said, "Do *you* think any of it's true?"

"Well, I tell you—haven't you never heard of ignorant people living out in the wilderness that think if a baby's born too off the track, like with the brain outside their head or shaped peculiar, it shows its mother has had to do with infernal spirits? Or with some kind of animal running around the yard?"

"But these here are not by no means ignorant people!" Serapta said. "You told me Mr. Plume's a bishop's counselor. He sold you your *license*. Owns *property*. And Murray's surely not in the wilderness! Why, people can walk the distance into town. And town is *Salt Lake City*! the center of everything. Liberty Park. Big stores. Fancy playhouse. Water cart to sprinkle down the dust—"

"Well, all I know—"

"Street lights shining down and lovely sewers. A Temple rising daily."

"Well, all I know is, something happened to Cora. Something *happened* out there to her and him that's threw them so off kilter they got no chance ever to regain theirself, or she even to go on living maybe, if something isn't done."

"Such as what?"

"Such as—well—making some kind of move—"

"The right move. But who knows what that would be?"

"I'm thinking of you and Tot at the Institution," Hindle said after a moment's silence. "Of you always *trying* different things—hot bricks, tonics—Remember the man that time that stepped on a rusty nail and got blood poisoning? Had this blue streak starting up his leg that was going to kill him if it got to his heart? That's what Dr. Bailey said as he was leaving. And Doctor, where *he* was that night none of us knew. But you and Tot took right hold. Remember our brigade of water drippers that kept a-dripping water over that streak until we made it quit and go back downwards till the man was saved? Took almost till morning. My, I was proud. I never had stayed up that late before."

"That was Mr. Clifford," Serapta said tranquilly. "He later worked for the railroad."

"Remember how happy he was he was going to live? And we felt pretty smart too, didn't we? So now here's Cora, she hasn't got what he had, and dripping water's not going to save *her*. But *something* will if a person just knew what."

"Why don't you try—" But her voice trailed off.

"Serapta?"

"Here I am."

"Tomorrow morning we're a-going out there, Cora and me, to Murray, and what we're going to do—" She broke off.

After a moment Serapta said, "Well, what?"

"Something maybe foolish. I *hope* it's not. But I was trying to think—and next thing I know, I'm coming up with this notion. And—*talk* don't mean a person's going to *do* it! But Cora says, 'Yes, that's the only answer.'"

"What is?"

"Well, she'd been going on, you understand, about the way her mind was in a turmoil, and if she just could *know* and everything. So I said, 'Cora, *knowing's* not too hard. Haven't you never heard of a post-mortem?' Of course I never imagined for a minute—"

"There you are," Serapta said, throwing up her hands in dismay.

"'But Cora,' I said, 'if you and me go out there and I find out it *don't* go down to a point, why, things has got to radically change with you.' 'They will, I guarantee,' she said.

'You'll quit combining Myron with destruction?' 'I will,' she said. 'You won't lay down no more except at night?' 'I won't,' she said. 'And no more jumping in the tail-race? And no more treating your poor husband like he had running sores?' 'It'd be easy then,' she said. She give me her word."

"All very well and good," Serapta said, "providing that it *don't* go down to a point. But how about if it *does*? You deliver her to the tail-race coming home? Although she *could* just stand there and die of shock from looking down at what the ground gives up. They say our hair keeps growing in the grave. Our fingernails put forth as shoots. That's what I've heard."

"I got my thinking cap on," Hindle said nervously, "and maybe by tomorrow, I'll think of some other way of approaching this—"

"Or just plain leaving it alone."

"But if I can't, if her and me go out there and we're—there—well, what I'm hoping— a baby is so small and this all happened around about last Christmas and now it's nearly Thanksgiving—it might just be *dust*. Don't the Bible say that dust we are and to dust returneth?"

"Not that fast by any means, I don't believe. Remember the piece in the paper the other day about them digging up that grave in Egypt? Thousands of years old, and when they opened the coffin the corpse almost set up and tipped his hat?"

"That was a mummy, Serapta. Like a wooden Indian. I seen one once myself in a traveling show." She saw it again in her mind's eye, the painted body-shell of whoever it was, and thought how someone clever up against something like what tomorrow had in store (supposing that they knew ahead of time) could have a little angel carved like the ones on children's gravestones—except not *just* the same—to dig up a baby with wings would be as bad as one shaped like a fish!—and that way ease the action being taken. But no time now for sleight of hand like that! and fraught in any case "with great obscurity," as Doctor would say—Ah, well! She sighed and lifted her cup to her lips, but finding it empty set it back on the saucer. "I just think that sometimes giving a jolt to something is only common sense." She hurried on defensively, "Shake up the factors. The parts'll fall back different. Like a kaleidoscope. The same sum total, but a different pattern. And sometimes easier dealt with."

"Maybe harder, too."

"Well, anyway Cora and me are going. It's a airing. I'm thinking of it that way. Also trusting to how life always seems to throw in something. To the common purpose. Like the element of surprise."

"Why don't you surprise yourself and just not do it?"

"Because for Cora's sake—This autumn weather won't keep pretty like it is for long. And sometimes just being *dressed* is enough to help. A person's hair combed decent. Their corset on!"

Serapta's shoulders lifting and contracting disclaimed responsibility of any kind.

"A pair of stays laced on real tight—We had a neighbor in Sutro. She said to me one time, 'You know why they're called stays? Because a ship "in stays" stays upright in any weather. A woman "in stays" does too.' That's what she said. And there's a lot of truth to that remark."

"Cinching ain't a healthy thing to do."

"But don't a corset prop you wonderful? Let you rear back rampant? Give you backbone?"

If CORA'S DID THAT FOR her next morning, it didn't show. She came out of the house so slackened and unbraced, and moved and climbed so feebly into the hired rig that Hindle almost said, let's you and me postpone this. Do not *harm* your patient, Hippocrates said. Perpetrate not mischief. But how could Cora be more harmed than to live laid flat on the couch in there all day in shade and shadow? Or mischief any worse be perpetrated than what her inmost thoughts did to her, running round and round like a wound-up little train on a track? Or havoc be more wreaked than to sit like a stopped clock staring at an outfall with a skein of drowned hair floating on it? Hippocrates, our only hope is *shift*. If you was here yourself, I bet you'd say so too. Go and don't spare the horses, I bet you'd say.

So they did go, started off and went. And Cora's pallor, as the sparkling air filled and sent up her depreciation, streaked with pink and her hands uncurled in her lap, changes for the better that inspired Hindle to try to improve things still more by getting a little discourse under way. But interchange today after her babble of yesterday was too much for Cora, and after a few brief sallies that drew forth hardly a syllable, Hindle fell silent too and used the time, or meant to anyway, for strategical thinking. But rack her brain as she would, they had got to their destination, had gone out and found a shovel leaning against the pigsty and were walking around the barn and out to the grave, and she still hadn't sorted strategy from tactic or parted either from dependency on chance.

Cora pointed. "There," she said. "That sunken-looking little place right there. Myron hasn't put a marker up because he's going to move it when we get our plot in the cemetery in Salt Lake."

"You never mentioned that, Cora. That makes quite a bit of difference."

"What does, Dr. Fairbrass?"

"Why, that there's going to be a—a digging up *anyway* in the near future—a removal and everything! Why not leave looking at the corpus delicti till then? One disinterment instead of the—shock of two?"

"We can't," Cora said sharply. "Because Myron will be doing the moving, and can you imagine the conniption fit he would have at any mention—? I'm sure it's against the church's—Why, if he knew you and me was out here today doing what we're doing—!"

She pushed her hat back off her damp white forehead with a shaky hand. "Just the thought of it makes me—makes me—" She staggered, caught hold of a bush.

"Don't worry, he won't know," Hindle said, taking hold of the shovel and pressing the blade half-heartedly into the ground with her foot.

"I won't have to look except for just a—minute, will I? Because all of a sudden I'm very, very—"

"A minute will be all it takes," Hindle said. "One quick glance—"

"Good, because I'm very, very—"

"Listen, I'll do this, Cora. No need for both of us—You go and lay down on the porch or somewheres in the shade and when I get to the part where *you* got to take part, why, I'll come and get you." She pulled out the blade and began to chop a little as if with a hoe along the edge of the grave. "I'll just bet you something. I bet you come away from home with an empty stomach."

"Can you imagine anyone eating?"

"It's foolish to let our strength run down."

"I just hate this kind of a day, don't you?" Cora said fretfully. "Seems like a person can't breathe. No air or something."

"Go up to the house. I'll come and get you when the—time comes."

"Maybe I'll just sit there on the watering trough."

"All right. Do that."

"Because I'm very, very—sick to my—"

Cora did start for the watering trough, or start somewhere, hands stretched out in front of her as if groping in the dark. She tottered, took a few stumbling steps, then folded and declined with such a strange, slow suspension of motive power that Hindle, watching her, had time to throw the shovel down and run over and catch her before she fell.

"WHAT HAPPENED? WHERE AM I?" Cora said. "Where's my hat?"

"It's there on the step," Hindle said severely. "If you was in as good a shape as *it* is, although I accidentally rolled you onto it when I drug and carried you around here to the house, we wouldn't have no problem. But you aren't and we have. Or we would have if I didn't tell you right now, as your doctor, that you can't go out to that spot anymore."

"We got to finish this!"

"*I'll* do the finishing. *You'll* stay here. Why, girl, when people start to fainting with overtones of a actual syncope—"

"But I got to *be* there. I got to!" Cora said, struggling to sit up.

"Why?" Hindle said, pushing her gently down and tucking her own shawl in under her head and shoulders. "So as not to waste your long years of medical training? Your many experiences as a diagnosti—" she abandoned that word for "somebody scientific, that knows what they're looking at?"

"But if I don't see with my own eyes—how will I know you're telling me the truth?"

"How will you know?" Hindle said like one borne heavily upon. "I'll tell you. You'll know because a doctor that has took the oath of Hippocrates like I have done, and every graduated doctor in the country has done, would not risk going *against* that oath any more than they would go against the oath of the Black Hand Society if they belonged to that. And if I tell you the Black Hand Society is child's play in comparison, that gives you some small idea."

"Of what?"

"Of the power, see. That's as much as I can say. But Cora, I have *took* that oath—one part of which—but I can't tell you—and I have seen the consequences of what happens. And all I can say is, I would no more dare go out in back of your barn there and *not* clear up every confusion you want cleared up to the best of my," what was Doctor's phrase? "*diagnostic ability* than I would dare open up a lion's cage and step inside."

Cora's eyes wavered. "You swear?"

"I swear. I wouldn't dare do otherwise."

"But how can you do it all by yourself?"

"Training and practice, that's how."

"Yes, but to examine—"

"Really, Cora, trust is what you need. My years have not been wasted. So now you lay right here and shut your eyes, and if you take a little nap while I'm gone—and I promise you I won't be long—why, nobody's going to hold it against you."

"Nap?" Cora said. "Why, I'm so wide awake I feel like a goggle-eye on the end of somebody's line."

"Well, you don't look like one. You look real drowsy to me."

"Drowsy!"

"That's nature at work," Hindle said soothingly as she stood up, descended the steps and started down the path towards the barn. "Offsetting the general contrariness of the phagocytes of the blood," she called back without stopping.

Chapter Twenty-six

✳

"DROWSY," CORA THOUGHT TO HERSELF WITH SCORN. "DOES SHE THINK FOR A minute I could lay on this back porch that I used to keep so swept and scrubbed and plant sweetpeas alongside, where I could throw out the dishwater onto them and stand in the doorway when Myron come home, always bringing me some little surprise—and now with all so changed and the poor house empty—*sleep*?" She blinked against a sun ray stabbing like a knife and blinked again…The leaves burned fitfully. She yawned and shivered, stuporous and chilled in spite of the warm sunshine on her legs. *Papa* could sleep…he never had no trouble falling asleep in church or anywhere when he was off the job…sit straight up in a duckblind, dead to the world at the first break of day and head wouldn't even fall forward, so the boys said. Company come, "Papa, keep awake." "I ain't sleeping, just a-resting my eyes."

I ain't…Just a-resting…Heard the clock every hour last night, I swear I did. Tonight I'll…How do you stop a clock unless you bust it? Eight days to run down and stand there quiet so a person can…No rest for the wicked, the righteous don't need any, and in from the clothesline she's brought the wash to dump onto the bed and sort for dampening. Pillowcases embroidered to say *Good Morning* in open morning-glories and *Good Night* in closed, Myron's garments, the baby's bellyband, the baby's shirt—But a dead baby don't need nothing now, and Mama instead of crying and carrying on ought to be glad, he never could of lived, poor little washy delicate thing choking on phlegm and the color of a penny. Ought to be joyful, corruption putting on incorruption, funeral this afternoon, the soul's took wing. She had the yardage saved to make a guimpe, it's spread on the kitchen table ready to cut out. And here's the pattern, brittle tissue pieces, arrange and pin them so as not to waste, for waste makes want and want makes waste, and waste…

So will you kindly tell me where's the scissors? She rummaged in the drawers of the sewing machine, anxious, in agitation, Myron would soon be home, the supper fire not built—in fact, that was him right now! She heard his step—but no, it was Jen. Jen had a picnic basket over her arm and Bessie stood behind her. "We have come," Jen said, "to offer our condolences. We feel real bad about this here that's happened." "Yes, we do," Bessie said. "We've brung a picnic." "What I *need* is my scissors." "I *hope* they're yours," Jen said, "and not the ones you borrowed off of me when you made your baby clothes." "Speaking of scissors," Bessie said, "I ask you honestly, is anything harder to keep track of in a person's house? Where do you think I found mine the other day? Just by chance! I caught this little glint—Outdoors by the coal shed *buried in the ground*!"

AND OUT BEHIND THE BARN Hindle stood looking around. What if Cora hadn't turned green and fainted the minute the grave looked like it was going to be dug up? And what if, after having been dragged and carried to the house and returned to consciousness, she couldn't have been persuaded to stay on the back porch till their hand was played? Nothing for it then but to go ahead! Unless, of course—But no use wasting time thinking of how to get out of a test that Fate had come along and canceled. No, now turn rook and play upon advantage, as Doctor used to say. Pick up the shovel she dropped when Cora was falling, prop it against the barn, take a seat there on the edge of the empty watering trough and then just wait for some time to pass. How much time was the question. How long would it really take to excavate a grave? Six feet deep, as they're supposed to be. Unless for a tiny baby the father of had thought a dead canary's few inches of trough would be deep enough. No use guessing, dig. And then the awful next thing. She had never been in on a post-mortem, but she knew it must be terrible if Doctor in one of his nightmares thought they were going to "post" him and woke up dripping with sweat and crying out that she must never let it happen. After she found out what he was talking about, she promised she never would. "Post" meant *after* and "mortem" meant *death*, and to "post" somebody meant you took them apart after they died to find out what they died of. But even worse would be to be "anatomized," like the paper said the rustler up in Virginia City, Montana, had been that time. HANGED AND ANATOMIZED, the headline said. But Doctor thought that was just an expression to put the fear of God in certain people, though the poor cuss might have been "posted" all right and his pea brain saved for posterity. "Is anatomized worse than posted?" "Smaller pieces," Doctor had said. "Reduces you to atoms." "To dust?" But dust was nothing in comparison, he said. *Atoms*.

"And let me emphasize a point you are no doubt missing," he said in the way he had like the lecturer at a magic lantern show, which always made her want to argue, "and that is that all these billions and trillions of atoms are the exact same thing. No matter what they form theirself into—you, me, Three-Fingered Jake, the rope they hung him with, the hell he's went to, a horse, a tree, that star up there—it's all just atoms, every one like every other one." "Fur?" she said caustically, her eye falling on her muff. "Feathers? Indians? The *sun*?" "Everything," he said. "Everybody." "That is just plain *silly*." "Atoms." He took the paper from her. "Maybe they did at that," he said, putting on his glasses and starting to read. "Who?" she said. "Did what?" "Those guys up there in Montana. Had their craw full, I guess. Anatomized the poor cuss." He chuckled as he read.

SHE DECIDED ON HER TIME span. The shadow of that cottonwood tree touching the pump would be when she could go back up to the house and tell Cora what she had supposedly found in the somewhat shallow (as she imagined it) grave. The coffin had kept snug, that would be her first piece of news. Kept out the wet, kept out the—Better not mention worms. And no hitch whatsoever to the examination. Now, Cora, listen. Your baby was a fine specimen of a child, no sign of anything wrong with it as far as going down to a point with a little foot at the end or any such thing as that. Born dead! for one reason and one only and that was, the cord got accidentally wrapped around its neck while it was in the birth canal and strangled it. Choked. Would choked sound better? Nobody to blame. An accident. *I* couldn't of saved it. My *husband* couldn't (and he was more than just a common doctor). His *teachers* couldn't. The wonder is that as bad off as you was with hemorrhaging and fever and hemmed in by a blizzard, *you* didn't go too. And why you didn't was because of Myron, him a-caring for you like he done. So shouldn't you—now that all this matter has been settled—stop all this and go back to being happy?

But wait. The grave. It ought to look like something had been done to it in case Cora took a notion before they left to come out back here for another look. Hindle got to her feet, went over for the shovel, then betook herself to the fence corner where, as she loosened the dirt and strewed it around, she thought, I know we're not supposed to deceive our patient and all that, Hippocrates, but I wouldn't call this deceiving her, I really wouldn't. The baby under my feet here *could* of been a perfect specimen. It *could* of got strangled in the cord while it was pushing downwards before its father ever laid eyes on it. That's perfectly possible, because in the book called *Obstetrics* it says so. And I am sure that if you yourself was here—if *anybody* was here today with the circumstances such as they are—

But somebody *was* there! and from the look of him about to agitate some desperate design.

"Why, Mr. Plume!" Hindle said, nearly jumping out of her skin. "What are you doing here?"

In a voice shaking with anger he flung her question back at her. Then hurried on to ask where his wife was and say that he knew last night that something was going to take place that shouldn't when he stopped by Cora's place and she come out with this craziness about going on a picnic! A big lie, he could tell. So he made sure to follow and this was what he found. Missus So-called Doctor! So where was Cora? Dead? If he heard she had just been buried and that ground there piled upon her lifeless form, he wouldn't be surprised! What else was the shovel for? *plainly being used.*

"This?" Hindle said, looking at it as at an unknown object as she scraped the dirt a little with the toe of her shoe.

"Yes, that," he said grimly, coming closer.

"Mr. Plume, I am really glad of this chance to talk to you in private, I really am. This *is* a shovel. That, I'll admit. This *is* your baby's grave. But the last thing in this world I'm doing is what it looks like."

"My what?" he said, stopping in his tracks.

"Your baby's grave."

"Oh," he said, irresolution seeming to replace with another plane the edge of his anger. "Oh, yes. So—so don't keep standing there digging and desecrating."

"I'm not doing either one, Mr. Plume. Honestly."

"Honestly I don't accuse you of."

She took a deep breath. "Mr. Plume," she said. "How far are we going to get, bandying remarks back and forth like this from pillar to post? What *we* got to do, if I may say so—and keep our voices down while we're about it or we'll have Cora up off the porch where she's laying getting over her faint and out here wild-eyed—is find a place to sit down and talk like sensible people."

"Fine time to talk about sensible people," he said. "Fainted! I hope you're proud of yourself!"

Hindle went over, stood the shovel against the barn, then sat down again on the edge of the watering trough. As she told Cora earlier, her years had not been wasted. The spectacle of Doctor getting out of tight corners had done for her what example is sometimes able to do, and now she herself could have furnished a precedent in operative expostulation as she began and helped forward a discussion that not only clarified for both participants what was (and had been) going on but ended in their entering in alliance to wait out the time till they could join Cora at the house.

"Though I do think it might of all blew up in your face," he said after a little consideration as he too seated himself, at the other end of the watering trough. "And still might do so. But say, if you don't mind repeating yourself, I wouldn't mind hearing again what you claim you're fixing to *tell* Cora."

"Well," Hindle said, "I'll say I removed the—overlying soil. And so forth. And then I done what we come out here for. The 'posting,' as we doctors call it. And now, Cora, I'll tell her, I want you to brace yourself, for here comes the part about what I found. First and foremost, your baby did not go down to a point."

"It didn't," he said to the cottonwood tree.

"And it was *not* born alive the way you think, moving and making sounds—"

"Oh, no. Oh, God, no. Never!"

"Because while it was in the birth canal the cord got wrapped around its neck and strangled it. I'm not going to put it quite that bald-faced, but that will be the gist of what I say."

He stared at her a moment as if in astonishment, then struck his knee. "If that don't beat a hog a-flying!" he burst out.

It was her turn now to be astonished. "What does?" she said.

"That, sight unseen, a perfect stranger could come along and tell *exactly what happened.*"

"Well, not exactly sight unseen," she said. "Since I've supposedly just examined—"

"I can't get over it!" he said.

"Well," she said, casting him a quick glance, "from a," she searched for and found Doctor's old phrase, "logical standpoint—"

"Logical is right," he said happily. "But did I know it? Did I realize? Being up against something I never was up against before in my life, did I have any idea? Logical! Of course. We'll work from there. Oh, I tell you, missus, last Christmas Eve was a night I wouldn't wish on my worst enemy. Blizzard howling, her a-screaming, blood a-gushing out. And poor old baby—" He dashed a tear from his eye.

"Well, you come through," she said.

"Had to," he said. "When I look back—But what else could I do?" He sat and stared at his hands, then looked up and spoke again. "For Cora's sake I got him put out of sight the minute I seen my chance. Then—There wasn't no grave out here of course," he said. "She could have dug clear to China and wouldn't of found nothing. At first the baby, wrapped in a shawl, was on the porch, where he froze up stiff as a board in about five minutes. Then he was out in the barn in my tool chest which I took everything out of, up on a beam where nothing could get at him. Digging a grave was out of the question, that ground was so hard you'd of had to use dynamite!" Cora laid at death's door for days, he said. Then they moved back to town. Before they left, he took her out here and showed her the so-called grave. And it was then that she started harping on the plot.

"The plot?" Hindle said.

"The burial plot. City Cemetery in Salt Lake," he said. "That big annex they opened up summer before last."

"What about it?"

"Look, here's the situation," he said. "I got the three wives, as you know. Jen, Bessie, and Cora. Between Jen and Bessie nine children. I've been partial, I've showed partiality and now I'm paying the price. Cora wants me to buy a burial plot just for me, her and the baby."

"The baby that's not in the grave out there by the fence," Hindle said.

"That's right. It's all very well to show favoritism in life," he said. "But in death? The Second Coming? The Millennium? I just can't do it. She wants us three to be entirely away *by ourselves*. Like Jen, Bessie and nine young ones didn't exist, like they was nothing to me whatsoever!"

"Well, she's high-strung," Hindle said. "Are you going to humor her?"

"I humored her already," he said, and drew from his pocket a folded paper. "Here it is, the deed to our three plots, hers, mine and the baby's. Just like she wanted, all off to ourselves in the new annex of the City Cemetery."

"Where *is* the baby now, if I may ask?" Hindle said. "In the barn?"

"Notice the date on this—last week," Myron said. "Well, it wasn't no more than signed, sealed and handed to me than me and my son Heber, leaving to go on his mission to the Fiji Islands the next day, drove out here, got the baby, took him up to the cemetery and buried him. I know the sexton, see. Him and me went through the Endowment House the same day. So the grave was ready, Heber give the prayer, then him, the sexton and me sung 'Farewell, All Earthly Pleasures.' Then down he went to his rest. There wasn't nothing slap-dash about it."

"He was still in the tool chest at the time?"

"Oh, yes. Solid oak. Better'n any coffin. But say," he said. "You want to come and have a look?"

"Where?" she said. "At what?"

"The barn, missus."

"I don't see any need of that."

"Well, I just thought—where he was stored—to kind of verify—You know something funny? I told you how I boosted my tool chest with him in it up onto the beam to keep him safe till later? Didn't even wind me. But when me and Heber went to take it down, it fairly staggered us. At certain times where does a person get the strength? But come on—" he said.

"I been sitting still so long, seems like my foot's a-starting to cramp," she said.

"Stand on it, that's the way to do."

She got up and did so reluctantly, resting her weight on her left foot as she worked her toes in her dusty shoe. "Besides, our time's about run out," she said. "Next thing we know Cora'll be out here. Don't you think we better go up to the house?"

He laughed. "What's the matter, you scared of mice? They ain't but little field mice! And the bats ain't swooping, not this time of day. Come on. There's nothing to be afraid of."

"Bᴜᴛ I ᴛᴇʟʟ ʏᴏᴜ, Sᴇʀᴀᴘᴛᴀ, when I followed him up that incline into that dark old barn I felt leery."

"I'm not surprised," Serapta said, pouring the foaming cocoa into the cups and handing Hindle hers as she sat late that night by the stove in her nightgown, feet up on the fender, betraying her Hippocratic oath. "Wild horses couldn't of dragged *me* in there after him. What did the man want?"

"That's the funny part. My *sanction*. That yes, there was a beam up over the harness rack. That yes, the tools was still scattered along the work bench that he pointed out was like he left them when he emptied the tool chest for the baby. Like that was supposed to *prove* something! 'There's the beam,' he says, and it did look away up in the air, 'and there's my tools.'"

Serapta with her own cup of cocoa had sat down in the rocking chair but remained motionless while Hindle was speaking. Now she settled back and began to rock. "So anyway, the baby's buried—in this cemetery plot for the three of them, off to theirself?"

"So it seems," Hindle said. "Cora don't know that, of course. She thinks it's out in Murray. She also thinks their cemetery plots is off to theirself. And so they are. I seen the deed, it's for three graves. But what Cora *don't* know is, Myron's also bought *all the burial spaces around it*. For twenty people 'in case,' as he says, 'Jen and Bessie have more children, and even Cora.'"

"What's that supposed to prove?" Serapta said wryly. "That he loves all his wives and children the same?"

"It's supposed to prove, I think from what he said," Hindle said, "that he's right up there with the best—"

"What do you mean?"

"—that on the Last Day when the trumpets sound and the dead arise, Mr. Plume can stand up in the middle of his flock like a true shepherd and not give God and the angels the impression he's some kind of a bum."

Serapta thought this over. "Has anyone on this earth ever *looked* in that tool chest?"

"I don't know who it would be." At the baby its bleeding mother said flipped and flopped and made a peculiar sound? Hindle sighed. If you thought you saw a mirage on the desert, were you having a hallucination? Or was seeing a mirage some separate—? While a hallucination—? She bent forward to squint at the clock on the bureau. "Gracious sakes," she said. "Look at the time."

"And me with peaches to bottle tomorrow morning." Serapta got to her feet and gathered cups and saucers. "But how did it end?" she said, standing there holding them.

"Well, let's see," Hindle said with a yawn. "We went up to the house. Not together. I went first as I had to do some talking."

"Did Cora listen?"

"It wasn't as if it couldn't really have happened. Yes, she did. And by the time that husband comes up the path, there was such a change you could see he could hardly believe it."

"Just because you said—?"

"Because if it was just a—baby born dead, why, Myron didn't do away with it. And if he didn't, then everything could go back to being like it was. She wouldn't need to lay on the couch, break Myron's heart, jump in her brother-in-law's tail-race or anything."

"So she just brightened up all over?"

"It was more than that. You know what she reminded me of?"

Serapta's spoon fell off the saucer onto the floor and she stooped to retrieve it. "No, what?" she said, straightening up.

"We was in Ramah, Colorado, at the time," Hindle said. "And there was this magic lantern show down the street called 'Travels on the Dark Continent.' So we went to it. And, my. What had happened was, this war party had went away, got lost, been lost for days, and now just when the tribe had given up hope, here they was coming back. Walking corpses! Been through everything, I guess, poison arrows, ant hills with ants in 'em mean enough to kill snakes, wounds, starvation—but their main trouble seemed to be *thirst*. And what did they do, although it's common knowledge that people famishing for water, when they get a chance to drink, should take it very *easy*—"

"That's what *I* always heard," Serapta said.

"But these warriors, pitiful bags of bones as they was, skin sagging, swole-up looking tongues—what did they do but—Guzzle ain't the word. I don't know how you'd even *say* the way they slurped up water. The river nearly went down in its banks! And the strange part, *that water run to every part of their body.* Arms, legs, neck, chest, even their head got it, they filled right up—even their eyes rounded out—fingers, toes—like filling a hot water bottle."

"That must of been a sight," Serapta said.

"And if you'd seen Cora today, she was just like that. Maybe not quite that radical," Hindle said. "But radical enough. Restored, renewed—to every fiber of her being, as the saying goes. She's letting Myron move her back to Murray. They got all kinds of plans to wallpaper—paint—relocate the pump—"

"She thinks the baby's buried out there?"

Hindle nodded. "And no need to move it to town for a while. They got time, she says. Maybe they'll put up a little marker."

"Beneath this stone don't lie a little child," Serapta said.

Through the stove-door's glazed panel Hindle stared at the smoldering ashes of the fire.

The clock ticked louder.

Serapta thought awhile, then said "Well, to be fair, we got to say it ain't really something that goes *on* a lot. Around here, I mean. I don't know about elsewhere."

Hindle knew what she meant, such comings, such goings.

The other carried the cups to the table and turned around. "And what could be gained by making a big fuss?"

"Not very much," Hindle said, yawning. "When like you say, it's not something that happens all the time."

BUT AS SHE SAT BRAIDING her hair after Serapta covered the coals and went off to bed, she recollected the verse penciled in an unknown hand on the fly-leaf of *Surgical Procedures*.

> *By this faith I take my stand,*
> *Knowledge is better than money or land.*
> *When land is lost and money spent*
> *Knowledge is most excellent…*

Educative knowledge that meant, of course, *scholars'* learning, not the acquisition (by making a big fuss) of human answers to dubious human deeds. Tonight though, Hindle thought, wouldn't she like to have a human answer or two to what the day had presented! even if what she ended up with would not go under the heading of "most excellent." Or any heading, sealed book as it was. But…she'd wondered about how close to being the same the word "mirage" was to "hallucination." Maybe *distance* had something to do with what each was. A mirage might be a hallucination far away, while a hallucination might be a mirage close up. But wait a minute—whether far or near, without the *fancy* lodged in the brain—! Sighing, she wished she could seek again the one she used to go to to settle such matters or point out, as he so liked to do, the "knowable relations of unknown things."

Now his books and other paraphernalia had to stand for him in the office set up like his, and as if to find him she went in there, put the lamp on the desk and…just stood, forgetting what she had come for. Then it came back to her, at the same time as she remembered that the dictionary was in the bedroom on the windowsill. But maybe some other book…She went to the shelf and stood looking not very purposefully along it. What she wanted…Here was one called *The Organ of Sight in Man and Vertebrate Animals, an Ocular Treatise on the Faculty of Perception.* She took it down and opened it. Optic angle…axis, square, papillary, the properties and phenomena of light…You would have to read the whole book and then maybe not find out what an image-work oasis in Death Valley (mirage?) and an image-work baby going down to a point (hallucination?)—if that's what Cora's baby was and did—had in common. Slowly she replaced it and selected one called *Medica Sacra.* But that one was all in Latin, and as soon as she had stopped to admire (as always when they moved and she had to pack it) the picture of a hand weighing a pyramid of pills on a pair of scales painted across the top where the leaves squeezed together, she returned it to the shelf. Then here was the volume called *Humanation* with the stitched-in map headed *Anatomical Atlas, Structure and Strata of the Human Form,* which would tumble open if you weren't careful! It did, and she carried the book to the desk to refold the map so it wouldn't bulge. With the usual amount of trouble she had put it neatly back into shape and was about to end her somewhat purposeless act of searching when, as she was slowly closing the book, a passage leaped out at her:

"In isolated instances," it said, "a siren form of foetus will come into being, its lower limbs occurring as a single tapering prolongation of the trunk like the end of a dolphin, at the end of which a foot (or both feet) may or may not be visible…" Startled, as if a medium's spirit-babble had of a sudden become personal, she sat up straight and read the lines again, then closed the book on her finger and looked up.

She knew a dolphin was a fish, having seen one one time in San Francisco in the bay. And that a *siren* was (whether spelled siren or syren) human at the top and fish at the bottom she also knew, because she saw one painted on the side of a circus wagon in

Laramie. At the parade Doctor said "It's not beyond all conjecture," and she said "What ain't?" and he said "What song the sirens sang." "What's that got to do with anything?" she said crossly, for he would sometimes say things out of a clear sky that made people stare. "There's one now," he said, and pointed, and there it was trundling past. But even without the memory of that siren, pink-skinned, yellow-haired, its nether person a forked blue-green tail, she could have supposed it to herself, her imagination being as you might say trained.

It *was* trained. And what had trained it was trying to picture the webs of circumstance Doctor would recite as they journeyed from place to place, the epithetes and bombast of the roughneck tent-towns, the hurdy-gurdy days he knew first-hand. But he would speak from hearsay too, matters of such old repute that when first put together there wasn't even *writing* in existence. Fables, these were called, and if you wanted image-works they certainly filled the bill. People running around half man, half horse! Beasts jumping out from behind bushes with the body of a goat, a lion's head, a serpent's tail! Cockatrices! Eyes that would turn you to stone! A mysterious boy with the wisdom of an old man who was plowed up or who sprang from the ground at a place called—well, something. Elf-fire, fairy money, twilight nymphs! And here's the funny part, when the world was simple and one God could have managed it with one hand tied behind his back, a big *team* of male and female Gods was running the show. But later when things got complicated and an outfit like that would have been just what was needed, the Gods and Goddesses went away and one Clerk of the Works, one God, was all there was, up there jumping sideways (as He's been doing ever since) trying to do the job all by Himself.

But while they were in the ascendancy, as the saying goes, the many Gods thought they were pretty smart and the few human beings wandering around pretty dumb, which they actually were. But one day one of these human beings, a young man, was smart enough to *catch* an uppity Goddess, and was she mad! Buzzing like yellow-jackets, she changed into different things, a crab with silver feet, a bonfire, a slashing osprey, a terrible stink worse than a skunk. The young man could hardly keep track, let alone hang on! but he wrapped himself tight in a gunnysack, put sand on his hands and decided he would rather die than let her beat him. Well, she kept changing. But there's an end to everything, even to what a Goddess can perform, and at last she came to the end of her stock of parts and had no place to go but back to her own self, perfect in beauty and now under his thumb. But did he take advantage? The way he acted was like Ulysses S. Grant at Appomattox when Robert E. Lee surrendered, which was almost like Grant had lost and Lee had won! You wouldn't have known by how she stuck her nose in the air and flung herself off how that Goddess *appreciated* this respect. But she did! and from then on she kept an eye on him, got him out of awkward predicaments, won him the Irish sweepstakes, and when she found out she was not allowed to marry him herself, furnished him with a King's daughter.

Days used to pass replete with such tales because Doctor would say his young wife needed her cares beguiled. And would not a course of that kind eventually have an effect upon the imagination close to what lifting stags and boars had on Hercules' muscles? But if you never *heard* queer tidings or *saw* things of miraculous import, wouldn't the opposite be true? Cora Plume could no more have imagined a siren form than a sheep could imagine a monkey! Hindle told herself flatly. If Cora said she gave birth to a being like in this book here (Hindle opened it and stared at the page again) then that is what she did, no doubt about it. If she said it was moving, it was moving. And if she said it *quit*, it quit because its father made it quit, because its father…

She shut the book, got up, went over and put it back on the shelf. As to what happened then…No one would argue with the winter's cold that froze the ground too hard to dig a hole in. And here is Myron…figuring how the tool chest might serve as a coffin and boosting it to the rafter until spring came. Then here they are, him and his oldest boy, going out to fetch it back to town and up into the graveyard where the sexton waits, a friend of Myron's, to do the thing up brown with prayers and dedication. Yes, but listen, *nobody lifted the lid* to see for sure what went into that grave! And think of this too, magic didn't end when the world got big enough for school. It lingered (lingers still), can set in motion certain forces which, if a syren form (resembling magic in effect itself) concluded to make use of those forces, a tool chest wouldn't hold it for a minute! Its own shape wouldn't either. It could change at will like the Gods could, or like perfect insects, or a cloud-like body of flying birds.

After she went to bed and was falling asleep she saw him quite clearly, a youth perfect in beauty running across a field, jumping a ditch and heading for the woods. Then he was in them, shadowy, a shadow, losing himself amidst the dew-bespangled herbs and trees.

Chapter Twenty-seven

*

THEY DID NOT LACK FOR SUBJECTS, SHE AND SERAPTA, STILL CATCHING UP AFTER the summer together on all that had happened to them in their years apart. They did not wait for the usual hiatuses either, mealtimes or when the coffee pot went on, but would run back and forth, Serapta into Hindle's office when the coast was clear, Hindle tiptoeing across to Serapta's kitchen leaving a patient under a poultice or hooked up to Doctor's cataphoric outfit, to mention something before it slipped her mind.

Serapta wasn't surprised that Hindle had become an Eclectic Physician with a lovely sign, she was always full of enterprise and caught on fast. And she thought nothing of Doctor changing his name from Morgan to Fairbrass. Who wouldn't change their name to throw a bunch of Night Riders off their trail? As to the elopement, well, they eloped, and Serapta said Tot never held that against Hindle. She did blame Doctor till she remembered he got hit over the head with a board and that a fractured skull might cause some funny behavior. That consoled her, that maybe the person that run off in the dead of night that way was not actually *him*. And if pathetic things hadn't happened in the years that followed, such as the fire and not being able to get another toehold, the sisters would have been happy enough. Although Tot did have in her craw some old pining regret such as not getting to go on the stage or ever see Papa again or whatever it was! because the morning of the day she died she made the remark, "My whole blame life's been wasted."

Serapta in the buoyancy of recovered health did not think that of *her* life but acted as if she thought it of great use and just beginning, and Hindle went along with that, although forty-one years of age seemed as old to her as an old tree. Without a lot of confidence she hoped Serapta would live to see the girls raised, not only for selfish reasons but because, old theater-goer as she was, Serapta enjoyed resolutions so much, to see how "it all came right" in the third act. Not that any particular difficulty in the lives of those with whom she now lived awaited unraveling, but one never knew what fate had in store.

"Where has the summer gone to?" Serapta said, rustling the paper. "Would you believe it's Conference time again?"

"Oh, no," Hindle said as if in pain. "It can't be!"

Serapta looked up. "Why should you care? You won't be up there in the Tabernacle voting like they tell you."

"Of course I won't."

"Then what's the difference?"

"Because Conference reminds me of something I got to do!"

"What's that?"

"Go uptown to the Salt Lake House and tell Lucitie that if a terrible man comes asking about me, she's supposed to say—she's to just keep totally mum," Hindle said. With an abstract air she added, "It was the *barest* mention."

"What was?"

"Lucitie's name and where she works."

"To this man, you mean? Who are you talking about?"

"His name is Bishop Dugger, he lives in St. George, he's got a store. And when me and the children was coming north last spring I went in and bought some stuff. Of course people was still riled up down there on account of the—" She couldn't bring the word *execution* over her lips. "And this man—I thought he was some kind of marshal. You know, with a perfect right to ask questions. And I didn't really lie, for Lucitie and me *was* born into the church."

"Like us," Serapta said. "Though after Papa run off with Aunt Ruth—and how glad I have been to get your news of her—Mama didn't apostatize, and she later married into plurality herself, but religion didn't mean a thing to her anymore, and that affects the children, it can't help it."

"Oh, it does," Hindle said. "When Mama give up on Papa it just changed everything. But down in St. George I didn't cast any doubts. So the upshot—this Mr. Dugger may come and try to see me."

"You mean courting?"

"Oh, no, not courting. Just a friendly call, but—he's very *familiar-acting*. So I think I better warn Lucitie."

"Let me do it," Serapta said. "I got to go uptown anyway in a day or two, and I'll stop in and see her."

"No, I don't think so," Hindle said.

"Why not?"

"Well, because Lucitie never lets nothing die a natural death. Mama used to say that herself. She always keeps thinking there's more." Pausing, she cleared her throat. "It'd be different if the whole thing amounted to a hill of beans, but it don't."

It did, though. Amounted to enough to change the course of Hindle's life in such short order she even had to borrow the requisite outfit.

FOR WHO CAN FLY THE feathered fates? Bishop Dugger did come to Conference, hell-bent to do so. He did find her. The place to ask was at the Tithing Office, or as a last resort the Salt Lake House. But on his way downtown from his boarding place the latter came first, so he stepped around to the side, went in and asked Mrs. Birdwood if a young

lady named Lucy worked there. If he meant Lucitie, Mrs. Birdwood said, she did, but
what did he want with her? The man looked decent enough in his Sunday best, but an
employer needed to know what was happening. Nothing to do with *her*, he said, except
inasmuch as this Lucy had a sister he wanted to find. Oh? Mrs. Birdwood said. Find for
what purpose? Because if her sister's name, on the list of lost members of long date of the
joint-stock company he represented, could be verified and the woman be located, he said,
she might get in on some profits. This was by no means a lie. Not if you thought of the
church as a joint-stock company and *heaven's dividends* as its excess of returns! A crafty
speech perhaps, but not a prevarication. Bishop Dugger was not a villain.

Nor did he look like one when Serapta went to see who was at the door and he
swept his cylindrical hat off and pressed it flat against the gold chain looped across his
vest. Later she would say that Hindle had not exaggerated, he *was* familiar-acting. But
all she noticed to start with was that out at the gate, proclaiming the respectabilities of
life, stood a carriage and fine team of grays. And all Serapta thought of was that this
caller with his back against the light must have come on business, to fetch Hindle in
her doctor's capacity home to a wife in childbed or a delirious daughter, and that if ever
well-off patronage was welcome, it was now!

Not five minutes before, through no fault of the landlord, Lennart Palmstedt, who
didn't own the house, it belonged to his third wife Fern, their rent had been almost
tripled, because of its being used not only as a dwelling but a place of business. Lennart
felt terrible about it, he could hardly stand to sit down and have a cup of coffee and a
cruller with Hindle and Serapta. Hindle said, well, that was life, always something. She
told him to tell Fern if she could have two months' leeway to get consolidated before the
new rate went into effect she would appreciate it, but if not then the next step, unfortunately, would be to move.

Move was the word that filled Serapta, who had drunk her coffee quickly and gone
back to her ironing board, with suffering and distress. For if they moved, maybe to
the other end of town, what would happen to the friendly affinity she had so carefully
nurtured between herself and the sign painter and artist out in back? By now she knew
Stig Fogelmarck well enough to know that though she *seemed* to be the only person he
had been able to tolerate in a long time, once she was out of his vicinity he would never
hunt her up. And if she made an obvious effort to see *him*, that might agitate him to
the point of actually hiding from her, and then what would she do? It was during this
conjunction of the planets, with changes imminent for better or worse, that the knock
came at the door and Serapta put her iron on the stove and went to answer it like a
mourner called out from a funeral. The caller's handsome equipage intruding on her
sight, however, her eyes brightened and the corners of her mouth went up. "What is
it you want, sir?" she said. "Nothing for yourself, I hope, because the doctor's patients
is all ladies."

"*Doctor?*" the caller said. "What would I want with a doctor? Never had a sick day in my life! No, who I'm after—Let me see—" He fished in his waistcoat pocket for a scrap of paper, held it at arm's length and read out loud, "Hindle Fairbrass. If you can call that a name. No wonder she tried to change it to Violet May. And may want to change it still further afore she's done." He winked one of his yellow eyes. "Widow-woman. Two tykes." Touching with a spatulate thumb the tip of his chin, where an alive-looking dark blue vein lay coiled like a worm, he added, "Come to about here on me."

"Well, sir, if you want Hindle you also want the doctor, because they're one and the same," Serapta said, beginning to look at him closely. "Her signboard's right there."

"Signboard?" he said.

Leaving the door open behind her, she stepped out to brush aside some ivy tendrils that had blown across it. "See where it says," she pointed, "'Eclectic Practitioner, Diseases of Women Only'?"

He looked and burst out laughing. "Be danged," he said. "Surprised the tarnation out of me *once* in the middle of the night and now by broad daylight she's done it again!"

"Who is it?" Hindle called, putting cup to saucer.

"A gentleman," Serapta called back.

"What does he want?"

"I want to see this so-called Electric Practitioner!" he cried, his eyes still fixed on the signboard.

"That's not what it says!" Serapta snapped, retreating into the house and starting to shut the door, for by now the dread suspicion had formed that this was none other than the man from St. George Hindle didn't want to see. "Can't you read? But it wouldn't make no difference anyway, because like I told you the doctor don't treat menfolks!"

"Oh, she don't, don't she?" he said jocularly, pushing in past her. "Well, if this lady is who I *think* she is, she treated *me* pretty blame good one night last spring! Didn't you, darling?"

Hindle had risen from the table and was looking at him as if some weakness of sight had shaped this monstrous apparition.

"You're the one all right," he said. "Look a lot like your sis uptown. Minute the lady brung her in the hotel parlor I says to myself—"

"Oh, Hindle!" Serapta wailed as she clutched the man by the sleeve. "Here I went and done exactly what you didn't want! We shouldn't of put it off. One or the other of us should have went up and told Lucitie—"

"Don't trouble. I'll handle things."

"No doubt of that," the visitor said with a smirk. "You will indeed. Handle things. Shall I ever forget?" Shrugging out of her grasp, he thrust Serapta away with such force she nearly fell.

"Don't do that!" Hindle said sharply.

"Then tell her not to grab ahold of me again," he said. "I don't like the sex a-grabbing me. Unless of course," he bared his peg-teeth and thick, fiery gums in a smile, "one of 'em's got me cornered to where I can't defend myself. Not mentioning any names."

"Serapta, dear, get the children, will you? And go for a walk?"

"Oh, Hindle, have I brought down plumb disaster?"

"Of course you haven't. Go to the park, why don't you? And you, Mr. Palmstedt," Hindle said, turning to their landlord, who sat like a statue with his cup halfway to his lips. "Tell your missus what I told you. If she'll hold off awhile, why, what she wants is fine with me."

"And what *you* want is fine with *me*!" the newcomer said. "Why else would I be here today, drawed to you like a moth to the flame?"

Hindle ignored this. "Mr. Palmstedt?"

Lennart gave a start that made his coffee slosh over.

"Tell Mrs. Palmstedt—Well, you know. I think I made it clear. And when you leave, be sure and close the screen door."

"How's it acting?" the landlord said.

"The door? Fine," Hindle said. "We'll finish our talk another time. So now if you'll excuse us? I got some business to tend to here." In her office with the door shut, she hurried around behind the desk and, taking up Doctor's muscle slackener, turned to face her visitor. "Bishop Dugger—"

"You ain't forgot my name, I see," he said. "My real right name, while what I got from you was the double shuffle from first to last. But aiming me at your nearest kin made up for it. *That* part of the bargain at least was on the square. And such being the case—and me being as you might say a student of the sex—it didn't take me long to figure out your little enterprise!"

"Enterprise?"

"Set up to gain advantage, honey. Don't I know."

"I don't know what you're talking about."

"Why, your obstacle-race, girlie. That when a man comes out the other end you know he's worth your effort."

"I assure you—"

"Ain't that what you want?" he said frolicsomely. "A man of pure and genuine breed to whittle down to size? To run and ride and lash through the mire?"

"The only thing I want *you* to do is to get out of here!" She pointed to the door that led to the side porch.

"Good thing I understood what God hath wrought," he said with a glance upwards. "Or I would be dumbfounded. For his own purposes he has given a percentage of the creatures orbs that can see around corners! You guessed, didn't you?"

"Guessed?"

"No use trying to pull the wool over *your* eyes. What I went and done was broke my promise. The promise I made the night yours and my two corporalities was clamped together tighter'n a double undertow. Don't tell me you've forgot?"

"I don't know what you're talking about."

"Yes, you do," he said, wagging his finger at her. "I promised you that nothing or nobody could reduce the fullness of my manly force till I was up north for Conference and you and me was laying together upon our nuptial couch! And nothing or nobody *could* of either, for once I set my head to do something I do it. But it just so happened that one night about the middle of July—"

"Bishop Dugger—"

"—I woke up, or didn't wake up, I thought it was a dream, and here's Thirza sliding in under the covers in the expectation—not that I want to brag or nothing—to be sublimed and exalted into pure essence."

"Will you please—!"

"I thought it was a dream."

"I feel sorry for what happened," she said.

"Sorry! I could put ashes on my head and rend my garments. Because the promise I made to you, to save up my engendering powers for our wedding night, that was a hallowed promise. Sacramental. Consecrated. Then what did I go and do but renege on it. I broke it. But on the grave of my mother I swear it was just that once!"

"I'm not referring—I don't care anything about—What I'd like to express my regret for," she said desperately, "is that night on the trail. I don't know what possessed me, I really don't. And I certainly didn't mean for you to take what happened any way except as a trifling—something that happened."

"Trifling! Fume a oak and call it *trifling?*"

"I don't know what gets into a person, I really don't. So won't you please accept my apology and—go?"

"How about *you* accepting *my* apology for Thirza? And you and me going ahead with our plans?"

"We never had no plans. And secondly—"

"I got the store. Cattle. Me and my boys run sheep. I'd build a house, two stories if you wanted."

"Don't you understand? You happen to be someone that the quicker you *leave* this house the better I'll like it."

"I understand all right. Your nose is out of joint, ain't it? Say so! and get it off your chest. But I swear to you by all that's holy that except for that one time with Thirza—oh, yes, and once with Eula which really didn't count and I'll explain how *that* happened a little later—I have not let the volume of my manly force go down one iota! since, let's say, July twentieth. No! Lured, enticed, incited though I might of *been*, I never give an inch. *You* was on my mind. *Fruitage* was on my mind and what the two of us was fixing to do once we took repose upon our place of conjugal longitude." He leered his eye and worked his tongue. "Why, girl, I'm telling you I even thought—and I don't care if the Recording Angel himself is standing in yonder corner writing down every word," but he lowered his voice to a whisper, "I even thought of us taking off our garments, our sacred undersuits! That is to say," he added hastily, "I thought of *you* wanting your willful way and *me* contending helpless as a fly," he was breathing hard, "caught in a spider web."

She spoke with cold aversion. "Bishop Dugger, if you're any kind of a gentleman whatsoever—"

"Stake President Dugger now," he said. "I am rising up. And in the process I am lifting up them that's mine. Terrestrially, celestially and every which way."

"That's nice," she said, and still carrying the muscle slackener went around him to the outside door and threw it open. "But now if you will excuse me—"

"One thing kind of bothers me. You'll never guess. It's the line of work you're in." He glanced around the office.

"That's no concern of yours."

"Oh, but it is. Because when you and me head for St. George—"

"That's not very likely."

"—why, what you're going to do is throw poor Jane off. See, everybody's got their field staked out down there. Catherine bosses the kitchen. Thirza, she's the one keeps the thing a-moving. Eula—Well, anyway. But *Jane*, since the day we took our vows and I brung her home, Jane's been handing out the supplies and whelping the young. She's liable to have a conniption fit when I come driving up with someone in competition!"

"Can't you understand English?"

"They get so mad," he confided to the corner. "And the thing was, I didn't need to tell. My uprightness and integrity compelled me. No false pretenses. Oh, sweetheart," he said, turning to her, "the amount of manly power that I got stored for *you*, you never on your own would of guessed a little siphoning off."

She went out onto the porch and he came after, moving in close. She thought of the neighbors, gave him a push and went indoors again. He followed. Behind the desk she dropped the muscle slackener and took up Doctor's heavy mortar and pestle.

"Listen," he said. "Don't stand there and tell me you never thought of me. Of us that night there? Under them shining stars? Talking? And the way—"

"I didn't. No. And now if you'll kindly—"

"Never thought of Cyrus? pitiful as that old saint I told you was? Tied hand and foot upon his bed of roses while on him fell the dissolutest creatures—?"

"Never."

"The sensuallest?"

"That's quite enough!"

"The fleshliest? After Asmodai, that is to say."

"Look," she said in desperation. "When I was in your store that day I told you a lie. I said I was a member of the church. But I'm not."

"You're not?" he said reproachfully. "There you go with your obstacle-course again! But getting over obstacles is my middle name. I'll have you joined and baptized by immersion quicker'n Enfield converted his rifle to a breech-loader. I will, that is," he went on, "if you're the lady that that night made trial of me till every time I look back on it my tongue starts to curl like a calf's a-licking my hand, and certain bodily openings, if you'll excuse the expression, in my human frame start to twitch till I nearly go loco."

"I'm an agnostic," she said, calling up a favorite word of Doctor's.

He narrowed his eyes.

She said it again, louder.

"All right," he said at last. "Eula's of Laplander descent but people has mistook her for Choctaw and I don't know what all. That don't mean nothing to me. I don't say I'd give house-room to a gal with the mark of *Cain* on her or an extra *tit*, which is a sign of witches. But otherwise—"

"I guess you need a dictionary. Agnostic means—An agnostic don't believe in God."

"I know what they don't believe!" he said fiercely. "But it just so happens that Joseph Smith our Prophet *seen* the living God with his own two eyes! So what more proof do you want?"

"There is no such thing."

"As *God*?"

"As proof." (Doctor had said that to the very end, learned it when he was in Germany and France. Wasn't and never would be. But we mustn't mind, he said. Make do with phenomena, use that instead.)

"You know where talk like that is going to lead you!"

"That execution on the Mountain Meadow," she said, changing the subject. "The man they shot. Didn't you tell me he done more harm to the church in twenty years than the devil could do in a hundred?"

"I said it and I meant it. John D. Lee. Me and my boys went up there for his send-off. When he went past between the soldiers I says to him, 'Burn in hell, you damned old snake in the grass!'"

"Well, I'm his daughter."

"'Burn in hell!' I said while he just looked at me, giving a kind of sneer."

"I'm one of his daughters! He had quite a few, but that don't make the heritage any less. I mean, whether there's one or forty, the *heritage* stays the same."

"Now wait just a minute." He took a backward step.

"My mother always said that anyone that knew him could take one look at me and tell who my father was."

He looked at her hard. "That explains it," he said, passing his hand before his eyes. "I should of known a hag-born devil's demon when I seen one! Brindled and dipped in brimstone! That was it. All the time the trick was being played by the old Serpent, deceiver of the world! 'Simon, watch out!' they warned him. 'Judas, watch out!' Him and his hosts of darkness. But I wasn't took in. Didn't I hold you at bay? incubus as you are, consorting with men asleep, laying there helpless?"

"Oh, yes, very helpless, very sound asleep." She laughed.

"Dear Lord, I done my best. I warded him off, him that like a lion rangeth abroad seeking what virtue and valor he may devour!" Muttering something then about how this world must pass away with all its joys and pleasure because the slimy old Tempter in different shapes and sizes, with different engines, delusions and devices, works six days a week and twice as long on Sundays! he bolted through the door, dashed down the steps, ran to his carriage and was gone forever.

"One more minute," Lennart said, "and I'd of come in there and dusted his jacket!"

"Why haven't you went?" she said accusingly. "You listened to every word!"

"I done no such thing," he said. "But if people raise the pitch of their voice so it comes right through the *wall*—"

"I'm really and truly annoyed at you, Lennart Palmstedt."

"Oh, now, Hindle. *I'm* the one that deserves to be annoyed. When you rented this place off of me, you should of told me a few things!"

"About my noble blood, you mean," she said, biting her lip. "Well, now you know. My father was John D. Lee that last March up on the Mountain Meadow stood before the firing squad and—"

"Don't do that. You don't need to harrow up your feelings."

"Thank you for your kind consideration. And now, to save you the trouble of telling us to move—"

"Who's going to tell you to *move*?" he said. "Why, Hindle, your disposition's worse'n a mink-otter's! The reason I'd liked to of known is because if I *had*, instead of me welcoming you like this," he said, reaching for and giving her unwilling hand a quick shake, "it would of been like *this*!" But she saw what was coming and eluded his embrace.

"Oh?" she said coldly. "And why such friendliness?"

"I'll tell you why," he said. "Because at one time our pas enlisted together in the Illinois Mounted Volunteers. They lightered together on the river. Side by side they helped to shingle the roof of the Nauvoo temple. And when one of 'em headed west the other wasn't far behind. Didn't you never hear your father mention Emil Palmstedt?"

"I never heard him mention no one!" she said. "I only saw him about five times in my life."

"Me the same, according to my ma. And all when I was little, so I don't remember. I wish I did. It was a dirty shame what they done to him," he said. "Why, I wouldn't even been *born* probably if it hadn't been for John D. Lee! He saved my father's life two different times, once a-fighting in the Black Hawk war, once in Independence, Missouri, on election day. I never realized none of that till the notoriety after he was caught and come to trial. That got my mother thinking of the past and she's the one that told me. Not my pa. Pa was dead by then."

"Oh, I'm sorry."

"Maybe I told you. A squall come up on the lake and capsized his boat! They claim you can't drown in the water out there because it's so full of salt your body won't go under, but Pa's, his did, or maybe just his head. Anyway he drowned. Mother took it hard, as hard up to the time she died last spring as twenty years ago when it happened. But what I was going to say—Ma was the history teller of the family, and wasn't she all set! when your pa commenced to getting in the papers. She foretold the upshot too, she really did. 'He'll bear the brunt for the whole blame outfit, you mark my words!' she said. And when it was plain there'd be no leniency, she shed some tears. But one consolation was the thought of my pa being up above in heaven already on the hover to *welcome* John—"

"If he ever got there," she said dryly.

"Oh, he got there all right. They're probably together right this minute. Ma had a gift to see beyond. Why, even before they caught him she come right out and said John would be the sacrificial lamb! 'You wait and see,' she said. 'The sacrificial lamb.' Not that he was anything *like* a lamb, from the way she told it. Or my pa either. Tougher'n shag-bark hickory the both of 'em was, scrappers from the word go. Destroying Angels. Danites. Did you know that?"

"I read somewhere that Papa had been one in the early days."

"A Danite used to be just like a king," he said.

"Funny king," she said. "Jumping through the hoop for other people."

"Not 'other people.' Our *leaders. God.*"

She shrugged.

"You know the caliber our pas was *of*?" he hurried on. "Skirmish, outpost, shoot a hawk-moth's eye out, put away a Gila monster when they had to—eating with the Indians—snake or dog didn't make no difference to them, get caught in a bear trap, hack their foot off, pry a bullet-shell out of their own flesh—" He paused, then said forlornly, "I myself would of never made the grade."

"Of course you would!"

"Although if Pa had lived—But I don't know. A child that's always down with something, their gumption don't develop—"

"Down with what, Mr. Palmstedt?"

"Lennart. Call me Lennart. Oh, the yellow jaundice. Chicken cholera. Quinsy of the throat for five straight winters! Always something. Leaves you measly."

"I wouldn't call you measly."

"Well, take my line of work, for instance. I bet my pa turned over in his grave!"

"I don't see why. There's nothing wrong with tailoring." She glanced at the clock. "But looks like you'll have to excuse me," she said. "I got a patient coming at three o'clock."

"All right, we'll finish talking some other time. But one thing—you probably heard of the petition? That some people was a-scared to sign?"

"For Papa, you mean. The clemency thing."

"I signed it."

"And here was you belittling your gumption!"

He reached across the table for her hand. "Another thing I want to mention. I wouldn't forget what happened if I was you."

"You mean about Papa? That's the first thing I'm going to do!" she said sharply, pulling her hand away. "Who would want to keep thinking of such a thing?"

"Not that! I'm talking about your visitor today."

"Bishop Dugger? Keep remembering *him*?"

"Long enough at least to fix his wagon! Looks to me like you got to go to the authorities and tell them what happened!"

"Such as what?" she said in alarm.

"Didn't the man rampage in here like a wild beast? Didn't he make suggestive remarks? Didn't he come very near to committing the Rape of the *Sabines*? I will gladly stand as witness."

She stared, aghast.

"Don't worry, they'll arrest him."

"But Lennart, I'm just going to act like it never happened. The man's gone. He won't come *back*."

"Maybe he won't, but he'll go somewheres else! It's not just *you* now, Hindle. It's *womanhood*. So if you won't do it, I will—"

"Don't you dare!"

"I got to, for duty's sake."

"For meddling's sake, you mean. Lennart, listen," she said in desperation, "if our fathers was like you say, friends and nearly brothers, maybe I could explain a few things. Because it wasn't *entirely* his fault."

"I don't see no loophole for him whatsoever," he said grimly.

"Well, there is one. If you'll just listen—"

His look of steely resolve began to soften. "Wait a minute," he said, "your coffee's cold." That remedied, "Now, my dear. With our close connection that we have just found out about we can speak our hearts. And mine is saying it don't know whether it's afoot or ahorseback about all this—"

"There's hardly anything to it, as you'll hear," she said. "What *happened*—" She took a deep breath. Then, with a few halts along the way, she told him. Not every little *detail* of her night out in the open with a man whose long suit was his strange passionate feats of denial, but quite a bit. And not everything that afternoon, because Serapta and the children came home, her patient showed up, and Lennart had to be on his way. But that evening (though by rights it belonged from twilight on to his wife Rosina) he returned. And so as not to disturb the others, for it was nearly bedtime, he and Hindle went for a walk. And down on Ninth South, where houses were few and far between, they took seats on a grassy ditch-bank above the water running past with a star caught in it here and there, and Hindle told him the rest. Smoothed out a little but not too far off the mark. And he understood, married man as he was. Yes, the promptings of carnality. They wouldn't understand back *east*, or down in Southern *Baptist* territory or over in the *Old* Country, he said, but here in this kingdom where the special privilege suffered to the fathers of the Old Testament had been suffered once again to God's anointed—

"'Suffered'?" she said mockingly.

"It's not all joy, don't never think."

"You mean the expense? The uproar?" Of polygamy, she meant.

"I'm going to be honest with you, Hindle. I mean the profusion. What I mean to say, living the Principle, with Miss Puss coming at you from every direction, gets a man to where he'll act like that son of a gun today if he's not careful, although I hate to excuse the old rip in any way. But there comes a time—It's like a boar whetting his tusks! for a real slam-bang instead of just the usual dull, tame go. And one thing you got to give the man credit for, he was decent enough to want to marry you and *then* open the flume for overflow!"

Indignant, she disdained to comment.

"You didn't mention—Sometimes a full moon—Moonlight'll act like loco weed sometimes." He took her hand and squeezed it till it hurt, then put it by and moved a little away. "What it comes down to is just old human nature, natural weakness. But that there's got a purpose. Don't it say in the Book of Ether, God 'give unto men weakness that they may be humble'? Humbleness goes over very strong with God. But speaking of human nature, one thing I wish you hadn't done to *me*, Hindle, and that was deceive my mind with the false impression that you belonged to the church."

"I never done so on purpose."

"But worse than that was to hear the denomination you claimed for yourself this afternoon!"

"Denomination? I never even mentioned such a thing."

"Yes, you did. You said you was a," he could hardly bring the dreadful expletive over his lips, "atheist."

"I said *agnostic*."

"What's the difference?"

"A big difference, Lennart. Atheists don't believe there's a God. Agnostics don't believe there's a god that's *knowable*. You can be the smartest inventor, the smartest teacher, a multiplier and divider so smart you're on the vaudeville stage performing before an *audience* but you'll never work the problem out, of God!"

Next should come the part about "making do with phenomena" but she decided not to mention that, for she didn't understand it too well herself, though Doctor had gone on at great length about both prodigies and immediate objects of perception. He would do that as they traveled, call up some matter idly into discussion to pass the time and exercise his reason for later arguments in tap-rooms about different things—provincialism, the Ballot Act, the Trinity, free trade, floating capital and such as that—performances whose rehearsals were all she had any participation in, since ladies never went into tap-rooms. Sometimes she paid attention as he talked, sometimes in an absent-minded state, or straining her eyes to see smoke off in the distance or a flicker of lamplight if darkness had fallen, she didn't. But rather fancying imports and meanings, she was sure she had paid heed enough to this proposition to have got the distinction right. She went over it in her mind. Atheists: no God. Agnostics: no *deciphering* God. Yes, that was it.

"So if that's the way God wants it," she said, "why rack your brain?"

"Why rack your brain?" he said in a shocked tone. "For the simple reason that that is why we *got* a brain in the first place! And how anyone in their senses can say God never can be known when he's *been* known and been *seen* more times than you can shake a stick at! is more than I can grasp. Moses seen him! Was he a liar? Aaron, Nadab, seventy of the elders! Was they insane? Or take our own Prophet, Seer and Revelator—"

"You asked me the difference and I told you," she said, making a move to rise. "I got to go home now, Lennart."

He put a hand out to restrain her. "Not till you tell me. Which one are you?"

"I'm the one that thinks we're just wasting our breath sitting here arguing when God is going to be as much of a mystery at the *end* of the world as he was at the beginning!" The Father incomprehensible, the Son incomprehensible, the Holy Ghost incomprehensible, was what Doctor had said.

"And that's not being an atheist?"

"It is being an agnostic, which I only brought up the subject to Bishop Dugger in the first place to get *rid* of him!" she said impatiently.

"So in other words," he said, "you're still in accordance with God's law and you and me can go ahead?"

"Go ahead with what?"

He swept her into his arms so suddenly she gasped. "Why, with our plans not to leave our feelings in such a wild licentious state that next thing we know we'll wind up in perdition! but bring everything under cultivation by—"

"What feelings?"

"What we feel for one another."

"Lennart, you're silly." She wrenched out of his grasp.

"Am I? Is adultery silly? God don't think so. There's nothing plagues him worse! It gets his goat."

"You and me won't get God's goat, I promise you."

"That I know. Because you and me," he said, reaching for her again but she held aloof, "is going to circumvent the whole situation by getting married!"

"Married!" she repeated, and was in a moment so limp with laughter that he drew her easily into his arms.

"There's not no other way to handle things."

"Oh, yes, there is."

"I don't say today hasn't tipped the scales a little, me finding out who you're descended from and all. But even beforehand, just look back," he said. "Why was I so quick to bring you a screen door? Why did I offer to paint your cupboard? And when Brigham died and it seemed like such a upheaval, why did I run to you? Not Pearl, not Rosina, not Fern. You! The answer is I never knew why at the time. But I do now. Because when earth's foundations was laid and the morning stars sang together—why, you and me—"

Chapter Twenty-eight

∗

"Don't say it," she said.

"Why not? When from the first day of creation we was meant for one another? We was, darling! And there's nothing for it but to set the date. Go through the Endowment House—"

"With your three ladies as my bridesmaids?"

"Just the one," he said, seeming not to hear the scorn and mockery in her voice. "Pearl done the honors when I married Rosina. Then Rosina stood up with me and Fern. So now I guess it's Pearl's turn again."

"Why not Fern?" she said, aware how timid this last wife rendered him, whether because of her age (the oldest of the three), looks (the prettiest), or power (she was the wealthy one).

"Well, Pearl, she likes the ceremony," he said lamely, "and her being my first—"

She decided not to pursue it but cheered herself in the flood of his warmth, a cheer that changed to pensiveness when out of nowhere a door in her memory opened and there in the shadow was Jim Clarendon, perilous, rash, climber of adventurous mountains, rich beyond dreams, attributes that had made him famous, or why would his photogravure have appeared and his opinions been printed in the Salt Lake Tribune? Older and wiser now than the small nursemaid who so dazedly watched his approach that day so long ago, Hindle thought of fame, remembered she had felt it like a whirligig as he came close, a dance that the attention, petitions and desires flying at him had turned the plain air around him into, pulling, inflammatory. To her it felt like love. To someone else somewhere else encountering fame and retrieving as a keepsake its half-smoked Havana cigar (slobbery with Romanoff saliva), it felt like an appropriation to a special purpose. But both ways were leaves sucked into fame's spiral course.

"You understand you got to join," Lennart said. "And we got to get ourself a day in reserve. A month ahead or even longer. You can't just show up at the Endowment House and expect to get in. And I'll have to sit down with Fern—" He said nothing about talking anything over with Pearl and Rosina.

"That would be all very well if I loved you, Lennart, but I don't."

"Maybe not to my degree."

"Maybe not at all."

Where was he now, Jim Clarendon? A lot could have happened in ten years. People lost their money, their handsomeness, it could happen in an hour. An eyetooth gone could make all the difference! A soaking, a draft—Someday she might be sent for, to a deathbed, and when she looked at the face on the pillow—But Jim wouldn't die. One glance would tell her what he had wrong with him: gastroduodenitis! which she had been reading about only last night. How impressed he would open his eyes and be, that she tagged it that fast. Gastroduodenitis, she would go on to say, was an inflammation of the *first* portion of the small intestine immediately below the stomach, terminating in the jejunum. The jejunum was the *second* part of the small intestine between the duodenum and the ileum. And the ileum was the *third* portion of the small intestine succeeding the jejunum and opening into the caecum which was—The book said blind gut but maybe she could say it more politely. Let's see, the narrow passage—By now he would know her true identity, the girl remembered and loved of old at Burdick's Institution for the Care of the Sick had become a *doctor*. If only he'd known! he would say, maybe she could of saved his poor wife's life! Oh, Mr. Clarendon, you don't mean to tell me she is *gone*?

"Hindle!"

She blinked and woke to where she was. "It's late, Lennart. Don't you have to go home somewheres?"

"'Somewheres'?" he said crossly, still smarting from her comment that she might not love him. "Why not just 'Don't you have to go home?' Tacking on the 'somewheres' makes it seem like I'm batting around without no real place to stay at all! What are you trying to do? Wound me?"

"Of course I'm not," she said. "By 'somewheres' I meant—just whichever place you're staying at tonight, that's all. But that reminds me, or something does—You know these magic lantern shows? We went to one one time, 'News and Views of the Ottoman Empire.' Did it happen to come through Salt Lake, I wonder?"

"No, it didn't," he said shortly.

"Well, too bad. Because the same kind of a—a state of affairs—What I mean to say, it's a small world. Over there those Ottomans, they live the Principle just like here! Only *there* all the wives seems to live under one roof so the husband don't have to constantly run around." She decided not to mention the guards for those wives with their privities sheared off.

"How you can even think there's a *comparison*!" he said with exasperation. "What *we* got and *they* got is as different as night from day. Why, they're heathens over there wearing foliage!"

"No, they're not," she said. "They dress up lovely. And where do you think Attar of Roses comes from? They got houses, books, ornamental shrubs, their children goes to school. The lecturer told us but I've forgot. Where is the Ottoman Empire anyway?"

Not knowing made Lennart crosser than ever. "A lot of them shows they shouldn't even *allow*," he said.

"They learn you things," she said. "And oh, Lennart, you'll laugh when I tell you something!"

"No, I won't."

"You will. Because the man, the interlocutor, said—Guess how the Ottomans pick their wives? But four's the limit," she said. "They can't keep on and on unless they divorce somebody or tie them up in a sack and drownd them!"

"So what's so funny?"

"How they pick their wives! They measure how big around their head is and then how big around their waist is, and if their *waist* is bigger around than their *head* they turn them down. Now isn't that funny?"

"No."

"I mean, with rules like that around *here* the Principle wouldn't get far, would it? I mean if you had to compare head measurements to waist measurements around here, how far would you get?"

Deciding to ignore these trifling remarks, "Hindle," he said, "we've come to a cross-roads in our life tonight."

"And that name. Ottoman Empire!" she said. "Like a country calling itself 'footstool'!"

He turned to look at her. "You're doing this for a purpose, ain't you? But whatever the purpose is it's not going to work, and I'll tell you why. Because you and me was born to have each other, and have each other we will. And the way we're going to do it—First, you'll join. Then we'll make our bid to go through the Endowment House. We'll come out married. Then we'll go to your house—"

"Fern's house."

"Yours," he repeated. "All to ourself. We'll lock the door and pull down the blinds. And then—oh, God!" He glanced upwards as if to say please forgive me for taking thy name in vain. "But when I think of what's coming next—!"

"Nothing's coming next," she said. "Nothing. But if something was—which I can tell you there's no chance of whatsoever—but if something *was*, where's the children to be? And what about Serapta? She'd be there! Not that I'm paying you the least attention!" But she was. For if Lennart had been measly as a child it didn't show now on his clear-cut, spirited features or his person trim and tight as the form on a baseball card. She *was* paying attention, and not for the first time either. Wondering, too, as she had wondered before, how it would feel to blow out the lamp and turn in at night—with him.

"They can go to Pearl's," he said. "She loves company. So does Rosina, but especially Pearl. Say for a week or ten days. And let me tell you, sweetheart, that goes to show my feelings."

"What does?"

"Well, that long, you know. A week or ten days. Because ordinarily—"

She laughed and made as if to rise.

But when he reached out, her weariness and the chill of the night air made her tractable enough to let him pull her down into his arms. "We'll come back," he said, his breath hot as a wolf's against her cheek, "and then—my God!" A pause, the old conciliatory upward glance, and he went on, "But when I think of us together—!" His lips came down upon hers, hard, then softened, mixed with hers like honey and wine in one, and she was in a kind of rapture of forgetfulness when, still kissing her, between kisses, he panted, "I won't spend my potency of life on no one else! I'll save it up for you. And if you and me don't set some records I will eat my hat."

So there it was again. That's what they do! she thought wonderingly, men with Miss Puss coming at them from every direction, maybe not all but a good percentage, Ottomans, Bishop Dugger, the Apostles, probably kings! and Lennart. Every once in a while, in the clever way of menfolks, they hold off and preserve their powers for a special occasion such as a honeymoon. They reduce to certainty the point (like finding the highest magnitude of a star) at which their pleasure ceases to increase and begins to slope downwards, then work it out like any other engineering problem, damming the ditches "or the floods restraining…"

"I CAN'T GET OVER IT," Lennart said as, enfeebled and wearied out from exertion, he and Hindle lay abed on their wedding night. "Dugger. Coming down to assail you at your camp the way he slid down that cliff and done that night."

"Of all the people to think of!" she said against his side. "Why would you think of him now? Go to sleep!"

"I can't help it," he said. "Every once in a while it comes back to me. The gall of the man. Because if he would talk to you in *daylight* like I heard with my own ears, I can well imagine the way he would carry on in the *dark* with no one else around."

"Lennart, I told you!" she said. "What he said that night wasn't using nasty expressions or nothing like that! What it was—"

"Well, what?"

"—was more like telling just real things that happened!"

"All right, so tell me."

Sighing with exasperation and half sitting up, she tucked the pillow in behind her shoulders. Did he mean the girl up behind the Indian? The time the wagon train had to get across the Loup?

"What was *that* about?"

Nothing, she said. Someway or other this girl found herself up behind this Pawnee on his horse being took across the river and naturally she had her arms around him, what else could she do? And him not having nothing on, only a breech-clout—

"Yes. And then?"

Nothing. The horse swam the river, she thanked the Indian, got back in the wagon which was on the other side by that time, and the train meandered on.

"There was more to it than that! Didn't kind of a poison get in her blood from being up against his bare—squeezed up so close against his back like that—that later on made her act like a wild hyeenie?"

"I never said that at all."

"What did you say?"

"I just said—" She told him. "Now go to sleep."

But he also had to hear about the saint tied down naked and exposed on the bed of flowers and being tantalized! because if that wasn't something to tell an innocent woman, he didn't know what was!

True, she said. It shouldn't be repeated.

"But just for the sake of realizing all the transgression there is in this world," he said, tunneling into her side, "just tell me again how he put it!"

The girl on the horse? The pitiful saint?

"Start from the beginning."

And from then on, every once in a while, the way the children demanded the story of Goldilocks and the Three Bears without changing a word, Lennart would want an account of what happened on the trail that night with Bishop Dugger. They would be snuggled in bed nearly asleep when all of a sudden he would turn restless. "Honestly. The nerve," he would mutter. "Causing a situation with a innocent woman where he could express foulness and be disgusting and filthy without her having no *recourse*." By then he'd have edged close, gropingly tumbled her over if she was faced the other way and with his lips fastened to shoulder or breast mumble, "How did he put it?"

Sometimes she would pull away, wipe off the wet mark, flounce back the way she was and say, "Oh, Lennart!" But mostly, considering she only had him about one week of the month (though the first year of their marriage it was more), she would hitch close enough to feel his heart with its different hoof beats and whisper, "Well, this fellow with these notions of working himself up—this man come paying a visit to where I happened to be which was entirely out in the wilds, not a soul within miles. And when it got dark— he didn't start telling me these tales of woe in broad daylight—"

"What tales of woe?"

"Well—" Once more the river would be swum, the Pawnee on his horse would salute and ride on, the panting girl get back in the wagon, which the shaking and rattling didn't help matters either, and before long—! That gone through, the bed of flowers would come next, and so on until at last her companion could bear no more but fell upon her like a starving Armenian.

Serapta was aghast, Lucitie was aghast, Mrs. Birdwood, even Hindle's patients. Why would *she* want a husband? "If that's what you can call what Lennart would be," Serapta wailed.

"At least wait long enough to see what your past dividends amount to!" Lucitie said.

"What are you talking about?" Hindle really did not know, not having heard yet how Bishop Dugger had gone about extracting information as to her whereabouts when he came to the Salt Lake House.

"Hasn't he been here?" Lucitie said. "The man that come to the hotel asking after you? 'Past dividends,' he said. Don't that mean money? He said if you was verified—He was representing some company! What *about* all that?" Lucitie seemed to think that that man and nasty Bishop Dugger were two different individuals.

To get to the bottom of that was why Lucitie was at her sister's on this snowy Sunday afternoon instead of at Albert's, where she would rather have been and *needed* to be, to hold at bay her rivals, her friend and fellow worker Charlotte, or Kate, the English girl whose "waterfall" curls arranged by Albert had brought him more than one new customer.

Lucitie did stop by there, it would have been beyond human capability to pass within three blocks and not do so, but only to say she couldn't come in this time, she was sorry. And sorry she was indeed when Albert, saying something about a batch of permanganate wash he was making and how Mrs. O'Naughton's transformation still hadn't come from San Francisco so he might have to telegraph, not only didn't ask her *in* but almost shut the door in her face! She had tottered as far as the street when he opened the door again, stuck his head out and called after her that if she wanted to on her way back from wherever she was going and it wasn't too late, or too early, she could come in and lay the tea.

If she wanted to! Lucitie's surge of joy nearly carried her aloft and also (till she got back to his wondrous presence) so detached her from all else that was happening around her that she was like Sleeping Beauty in her crystal box. As behooved so close a relative, she did utter clamorously against Hindle's forthcoming marriage and did appear brisk when asking about the man from the joint-stock company. But she failed to note the indecisiveness in her sister's voice when she said nobody of that description had ever come down here. And she missed (which she surely would not have done had she not been wondering if Albert had the ingredients for a johnnycake) the nervous glance Hindle cast in Serapta's direction.

"He sure never showed up here!" Serapta said loyally.

"Well, who could the man have *been*?" Lucitie said (debating whether to bake the cake in the ashes or fry it in a pan). "What *reason* could he have had?"

"Maybe none at all," Hindle essayed with some hesitation. "Not if he happened to be a Nephite. I don't mean to say I'm suggesting—"

"That's it, I'll bet anything," Serapta said, sounding relieved.

"A Nephite?" This penetrated Lucitie's abstruseness only to add to it. Because if that was who Hindle's caller had been, then how smoothly and without impediment her and Albert's tea would go! For Lucitie was shy and could not always think of things to say to Albert while the clock ticked and swallowing became noticeable. But with a topic at hand like being visited by a Nephite—! Best of all was the fact that it could (as anyone with a drop of Mormon blood in their body would testify) be true. From the minute Mrs. Birdwood told her to go in the back parlor, a gentleman wished to speak to her about insurance or something to do with her sister, and she went in and he turned from where he stood looking out the window, she knew there was something supernatural, ghostly, mysterious, uncanny, yes, and *odd* about him, Lucitie would tell Albert. Also the way he talked, rattling on about old lists, common funds, substantiation and so forth, which now that she looked back on it she realized made no sense whatsoever but was just an excuse to *materialize* the way a Nephite liked to do. When he left and she ran to the door, the hall was empty, the porch was empty, in the twinkling of an eye he had vanished off the earth! she would say.

Wouldn't *that* hold Albert's attention? Wouldn't he gaze at her with his beautiful eyes and forget to chew his johnnycake as she would go on to tell him the story of the three Nephites "sanctified in the flesh" by Jesus, the time the Savior made a flying trip to America soon after the Resurrection, which a lot of people had no idea? "Sanctified in the flesh," she would explain as in her childhood her Sunday school teacher had done (for she hadn't been to church since), meant that Jesus gave these three men the gift of being immune from dying till the Second Coming! Which sounds wonderful at first, but word that's come down says they're pretty tired of not dying by now and don't know what to do half the time. If they was together that might help, but they fell out long ago and now roam around each in a drove by himself like a snapping turtle. And when you least expect it—! Sometimes a Nephite will *save* something, a cow from a bog or a baby from a steep cliff or a woodchopper's leg from a tree that has fell on it. But sometimes you'll blink and one of them will be standing there for no good reason, just sick of their own company and batting around…(She remembered all this from kindergarten days.)

When that subject was exhausted, Lucitie thought as she floated through the dusk towards her heart's desire, she had another subject for consideration, Hindle's peculiar decision to marry Lennart Palmstedt. Albert had met him. Remember, Albert? Hindle's landlord! though that house she rents is really not his. It belongs to his third wife Fern. Three wives and now Hindle! "You'll be worse off than Mama before you're through!" Lucitie would tell Albert she had said, and how Hindle's reply had shocked her and Serapta. "Oh, I don't know," Hindle had said. "I'll have twenty-five percent of Lennart and if you want to know the truth that's all I got time for, if that." "Then Serapta speaks up, she lives there with Hindle who she thinks the sun rises and sets in, and watches after the children," Lucitie would go on. "'There's many a true word spoken in jest,' Serapta says. 'Oh?' I say, 'and what do you mean by that?' 'I mean you would appreciate what she's saying, Lucitie,' Serapta says, 'if you seen how her doctoring practice keeps her on the jump or the way she's always studying in her books.' 'That's all very fine,' I say, 'but if one-fourth of a husband is all she's got time for, will you answer me this, why any at all?'"

HINDLE'S OWN REJOINDER TO THAT when put to her was pert. And it wasn't the real answer, for the simple reason that she didn't know herself *why* she wanted *any at all*. And alone in her office later that evening didn't seem likely to find out from the book that lay open in front of her, *Quotidian and Tertian Fevers with Semitertian Paroxysms, Their Treatment and Cure*, though she stared deep into its pages as into a crystal ball. Accepting Lennart had been a blind impulse of fatality and fortune, like the time she bought the second-hand chair in Coulterville, California, which turned out to be a prie-dieu, partly a chair to sit on and partly an altar to pray at. Prie-dieu meant *pray God* in French, Doctor said, and the French invented it because the entire nation was Catholic. But what was a prie-dieu doing in Coulterville? He said maybe it belonged to the French girl the Mexican killed and got hung for just after they come to town. "You're trying to make me not like it," she said. "That should only make you like it better," he said, "circumfused with jealous love." And in a way it did, imagining Mademoiselle praying and her caballero sneaking up behind her with a knife…But it wasn't sturdy, someone had nearly worn it out. Unless wedged in a corner, its long sloping back would fall off, and white ants or something had got at the cross-bars to the legs. When they moved to Reseda she left it behind. You could do that when you moved, leave behind whatever hadn't reckoned out, a churn with a stuck paddle, a patent flatiron, a rickety French chair or, if the worst came to worst, twenty-five percent of a husband.

She did rather like Lennart, though. And something about trying to be his favorite excited her interest. Of course he could be less obtuse. One thing her old companion had left her with was a liking for smartness, the book-learning kind but also what he used to call "sabe usted," savvy, a taste as impractical in her present circumstances as a liking for terrapin or Napoleon brandy. But there was a gracious purpose about Lennart that should make the hours spent with him supportable. Especially that part of it, she hated herself for letting the thought creep in but it did, when he was there and everyone but them had turned in and he would look at her and say, Time for bed?

Chapter Twenty-nine

✳

STIG FOGELMARCK, THE ARTIST OUT IN BACK, THOUGHT IT WAS WONDERFUL, Hindle converting and about to marry Lennart. Marriage made women pull in their horns, he told Serapta when she went out to take him a warm loaf of bread and tell him the news. And Hindle could use some of that. "Marriage is a wonderful ordainment!" he said.

"Do you really think so?" Serapta said.

"In its original state, yes," he said, "and even more so as enhanced in degree and enlarged upon for spiritual edification by our Prophet."

"Well, he enlarged upon it all right," she said teasingly. "Especially if you're talking about Brigham. And now Lennart. But why do *you* approve? You that hasn't even got *one* wife, let alone *four*!" It didn't take much to nettle Stig, a hapless glance and he was up in arms. Serapta had scarcely spoken when he pushed the loaf back at her and stalked inside.

Hindle found her replenishing the kitchen fire and at the same time trying to put it out with her tears. "What in the world happened?"

Serapta blamed herself. "Them darts barbed with flame that fly out of him, they're on account of his artistic nature," she said. "And people treat him mean."

"Looks to me like he treats people meaner than they treat him."

"Oh, no, Hindle! They hire and then fire him. Or not exactly fire, but you know that mansion being built up on South Temple that he's supposed to paint the Irish kings for the dining room? Well, now he hears they might want something else. And the people aren't even in town so he can talk it over. And he can't get one word of satisfaction about his offer, either!"

"What offer?"

"To paint President Taylor's portrait for nothing! He wants to contribute that but up in the church office they won't hardly speak to him, let alone let him in. And then that silly postponement or moratorium or whatever it is at the ward house—it just makes him feel awful."

"I know, Serapta. But outside aggravations like that shouldn't make him snippy to *you*."

Serapta agreed they shouldn't and said that from now on, uncourteous pricks and thorns from others would be answered in kind, and no more bread or anything else from *her*! But a few evenings later here she was splashing through the puddles in the back

216

yard to go out there and take him some peach cobbler and coming back in the house like a sunburst from behind a cloud because he deigned to accept it! It took strength on Hindle's part not to say anything, but as friendly association with the painter seemed to work on Serapta the way hard-boiled egg yolk brightened the feathers and clarified the song of a canary, she let the surrender go unremarked.

The friendly association of the two did little to improve Stig. What it did do, however, was, first, give him the idea that Serapta's inner landscape needed spiritualizing and then, coincident in time with Hindle's half-hearted joining of the church in order to marry Lennart, inspire him with the notion that Serapta too should be converted. A job soon done! she wanted so much to please and was so proud that a man like *him* (as bitter as the aloe tree towards women, as if starting with our first mother they were to blame for everything) would take an interest in *her*. But any effort at all to bring Serapta into a fold from which he himself for all his piety appeared to have been turned forth like Adam and Eve from the Garden mystified Hindle, the more so as time went on and the block teachers came to her place (for now that both she and Serapta, and the children, were church members, they were entitled to this periodic solicitation) but never went out back to visit him! Someday Serapta should ask what the cold-shouldering was about, she was the only one who could. She felt it too, that grant of special privilege with regard to him, even taking it into her head that God was behind it with a plan up His sleeve for Stig and her that all in good time would be made visible.

MADE VISIBLE FOR HINDLE WAS a nuptial day so bright with sunshine that flashing off the snow and icicles it nearly put a person's eyes out! "Happy is the bride!" Lennart's first wife Pearl said coyly, pointing at the radiant east. Although about to assist in the division of her husband's magnitude into smaller portions, Pearl seemed to be in fine spirits. And his second wife Rosina, at home frosting the four-layer wedding cake and preparing to enjoy the company of Hindle's two children and Serapta for the week of the honeymoon, was in fine spirits too. For what relieved life's monotony like a wedding? What so cheerful, fresh and full of joy? In this case especially, because by becoming one of the family did not their Eclectic Physician put herself in a position not to charge them and theirs anymore for plasters, physics and potions and restoring and preserving their health? But best of all was the way it would knock the props out from under Fern! wife number three. For more than two years now Fern had gone around acting like because she was rich, pretty and could cook, that Lennart's matrimonial calculations were grinding to a halt with her. Well, fond dream! And how she must be taking it Pearl and Rosina had a pretty good idea from the way that, during the weeks prior to the new marriage, Lennart showed up two or three different times at one of *their* noisy and not very tidy houses!—for the dismal supper a husband deserves if he drops in by surprise—*on one of Fern's nights.*

Of course Pearl was too polite to talk about want of harmony when she came to Hindle's office for another bottle (already gratuitous though the knot had not been tied) of the antimonyl tartrate that was doing her digestion so much good. And when she remarked that she was the wife who was going to stand up (or kneel down) with Lennart and Hindle when they first "went through" and then wed each other in the Endowment House, she could not have been more gracious. Pearl also paid Hindle the compliment of saying that she and Rosina could not believe their *ears* when they heard Lennart had made a capture of *her*, a actual Eclectic Practitioner, as sociable and nice, if Hindle didn't mind her saying so, as she was eclectic. She and Rosina took a liking to her the first minute they saw her, Pearl said, and if ever she should need a helping hand all she had to do was ask!

Not having taken into account the degree of fair fellowship that might arise from the alliance she was about to enter, Hindle found this heartiness a bit unnerving. "Oh," she stammered. "That's very kind of you."

"I mean it, Hindle. It's all right if we call you Hindle? Not the children. *They* start getting familiar, and where's your authority when there's a knee to sew up or nasty medicine to give? But of course as they grow older—Not to change the subject though, is your bundle ready?"

"My bundle?"

"For the Endowment House?"

"Oh! Well, not exactly. I've been meaning—Serapta came home from taking the children for a walk the other day and said she met someone that said machine-stitching was either barred or about to be."

"Barred? Why, I never heard of such a thing!" Pearl said. "*My* outfit's machine-stitched except the stockings and undervest. Rosina's certainly is. Fern's of course—Fern would go *blind* but what every loop of thread of *hers* was put in by hand!" And a lot of good it's done her! Pearl's expression said fleetingly. "But listen. If your stuff isn't quite finished, why not borrow Rosina's? I know for a fact she washed and ironed most of it just last October. And that will give you time. Because you know when you *die*, honey, many long years from now, we hope, you got to have your own Temple outfit to be buried in. But in the meanwhile—"

"Well—"

"All right, it's settled then, I'll tell Rosina you'll borrow hers. And don't you be ashamed to sew on the machine! If machine-stitching wasn't God's idea in the first place, would man's human brain have thought of it? Never. But a person of the caliber of *Fern*—" She paused and when she spoke again abstained from further comment along that line. Later she and her sister might mention to the newcomer what they would bet happened when Lennart told Fern he was fixing to marry Hindle! the swinish squalor she fell into of maniacal rage, how she blasphemed, struck terrible postures and took the Lord's name in vain till, frothing at the mouth, she went into convulsions and sank down into stupor, catalepsy, unconsciousness and oblivion. But on this occasion Pearl's delicate sense of what to say and what not to, kept her silent.

THAT MORNING WHEN LENNART, PEARL and Hindle the bride walked through the huge iron gates into the great walled space that would be Temple Square, and picked their way around the blocks of granite marked for implementation into the Temple that, off to the east, half risen, looked as much like an enchanted castle half fallen down as one going up, and repaired to the grounds' northwest corner, early though they were they found several other suppliants already clustered about the front steps of the Endowment House. And house it looked, some family's common dwelling, with little about it to show it harbored the Divine Presence and provided space (till the Temple could be completed) for the most important rites and rituals of the Mormon church. Porch, cupola, lace-curtained sash windows, chimney sending forth a thin wisp of smoke, nothing about it spoke of templed majesty except the respectful silence and solemn expressions of those who waited to get in, blowing on their fingertips and working their cold toes in their shoes to keep the circulation going. And when the door opened and they shuffled up the steps, filed in and it shut behind them with a soft yet terribly conclusive sound—! But what happened after that must be an inscrutable and entirely mysterious secret kept from the knowledge of the uninitiated throughout the vast forever *on pain of death.*

YOUR FRIEND, HOWEVER? YOUR SISTER? When the honeymoon was over and Lennart had gone, pulled into the cogs of his domestic wheel's new circumference, and Serapta and the children had come back home, something self-willed in Hindle made her want to bring it all out in the open, the ceremonies she had witnessed, the oath to which she had sworn. Negatively commanded, she was like someone ordered to stand in the corner and *not* think of a white bear. Had Serapta shown so much as a hint of curiosity, before she even knew what she was asking a plenitude of incident would have tumbled forth. But then it occurred to Hindle that if she *did* peach to Serapta, and Serapta told Stig she had, and Stig, fanatic that he seemed to be, went running to the authorities—! Not that she believed for a minute revenge-seekers would *really* come and commit all those Bulgarian atrocities. But silliness could travel in any direction, so she said nothing, except for a remark over coffee that while there was probably a lot wrong with the *Catholics*, at least they fixed things up pretty, with different-colored sunlight pouring in, tapers in red glass, nice bouquets—and what was so terrible about statues?—instead of like the inside of an orphan's home. A question then from Serapta—! But Serapta's great interest was in Stig and whether he had missed her, and to give a full account of the good time she and the children had had at Rosina's (who would not, however, win any prizes as a housekeeper). So that moment of temptation passed.

BUT A FEW EVENINGS LATER when a knock came at the door and it was Lucitie come down to stay the night! Hindle was instantly done for, hardly able to wait till Serapta and the children had gone to bed to begin her revelations. But when the moment came and she began, Lucitie sat sideways on her chair, fingered the glassy bumps on the table lamp and started to drum her feet on the carpet. For sisters, like anyone else, "their perplexed ways pursue" (as inclination or sad choice leads them), and Lucitie after a hard day's work had not come down all this way on a cold winter's night to hear about Hindle's finding out the secrets of the Endowment House! (the equivalent of "going through the Temple") when she married her landlord, for that was part of the ritual.

What Lucitie wanted to talk about was Albert. Albert and Kate, the English girl. Albert and Charlotte, who worked alongside her at the hotel. Albert by himself, about to get his block knocked off by Kate's jealous suitors if he wasn't careful. And of course Albert and herself. But she soon saw by the moody and restive compliance accorded her when *she* took the floor that unless she lent her ear to Hindle, Hindle would not with any enthusiasm lend hers to *her*. So Lucitie sat around straight on her chair and said, "All right, you first," adding softly and quickly that it would not be necessary to go into every little detail because she had heard most of it already from Irene, a kitchen helper one time with a brother named Raymond who apostatized and started blabbing. Raymond apostatized from the Masonic Lodge too, and guess what he said? that the *Mormon* endowments was a counterfeit of the *Masonic* ceremonies and the *Masonic* ceremonies a counterfeit of a great big cow-pile! He was a terrible person. "But go ahead, tell me, honey."

"What's the use if you already heard it all?"

"I never said *all*."

"I don't know why I mentioned it in the first place. It doesn't really matter."

But it did matter if Lucitie was going to get what she came down for, attention, sympathy, even a force to act in opposition to, for new perspective. So she asked Hindle to please tell her whatever it was she was going to, and whatever it was she was sure would be a lot more intelligent than what Raymond told Irene. "But," she said with a gracious wave of the hand, "intelligent or not."

Hindle contemplated this, held back in doubt but then began.

SHE BEGAN WITH THE BATH you had to take the minute you got in. Well, not the exact *minute*. But as soon as you piled your coat and hat in the cloakroom, took your shoes off and stood them under a bench and went in and told the man sitting at a center table with a record book open in front of him what your name was, and a lady had ushered everyone into a kind of back parlor with a curtain down the middle to separate the sexes, men here, women there, and a big tin bathtub on either side slowly filling with hot and cold water, why, bath time it was, to get "the blood of this generation" washed off you, as the very thorough-going lady who did the washing said. You stepped out, dried yourself, and while you're standing there shivering along comes another lady and anoints your head with oil.

"Now that sounds all very lovely in the Bible," Hindle said. "*Thou anointest my head with oil*. But trickling down your face and neck while the lady dabbles her fingers in it and touches your eyes, ears, mouth and feet—your feet you hold up to her, she won't stoop over—to hallow them to the Lord—it sounds a lot better than it feels. Next this woman goes along whispering a secret name in our ear. Except that rearing back like she does to keep out of the oil it don't come *out* so secret, and as she goes down the line we hear we're nearly all named Sarah. 'And you remember it,' she says, 'or when you die and go to heaven you'll never get past the Pearly Gates!'"

"Maybe you won't anyway, telling people all this?" Lucitie ventured.

"Since when was my own sister 'people'?" Hindle said with gentle reproof. "Anyway, let's see. We got our secret name. We're washed, anointed—And now to dress in our 'Temple clothes.' I borrowed mine from Rosina, and I hate to say it but that outfit is fit for nothing but haunting a churchyard. No style to it whatsoever. Then we straggle up facing the curtain and when it gets drawed back the menfolks in a line are facing us. And they look as unappetizing as we do—hair wet, eyes all red and smarting from the oil, skin dried out and shiny from the soap! No one knows where to look for a little while and I am wishing I could fall through the floor when all of a sudden—And this here, Lucitie, you might of saw yourself sometime at a theatrical performance. An actor drawing attention in the audience while pretending just to be a human person. But then he goes up on the stage and you see he was an actor all the time. Well, that's the kind of thing happened. A man 'going through' the way we was, or so we thought, all of a sudden stepped forward with a *part* to play, which was to be our guide, or as they say in the minstrel shows our interlocutor. So 'Hark!' he says with his hand cupped around his ear. 'If I am not mistaken I hear conversing.' Well, he's not mistaken, there's murmuring somewhere and we make out two voices that belong to Jehovah and Elohim, as they call each other, old friends that only just have met again after apparently quite a while. 'So how about that world you showed me last time?' Elohim says. 'You mean the one I made in six days and rested on the seventh?' Jehovah says. 'That's the one.' 'Why, it's still a-going strong. You want to take another look at it?' 'I wouldn't mind.' So down at the end of the room a door opens and in come two old men draped in counterpanes—Pearl was saying later she believes Jehovah is the piano tuner on State Street. Well, these two act like visitors to a pleasure garden, promenading around, looking at different things till Jehovah stops and kind of hits his head. 'Something missing here, Elohim,' he says. 'Stolen, you mean, Jehovah?' 'No, I don't mean stolen. I mean *left out*.' 'What can it be?' 'I'll tell you. Someone of higher intellect—'"

Stealing a look at the clock, Lucitie began to take the hairpins out of her hair and lay them in a neat row on the table.

"'—than brute creation, to live here and take charge. But wait, I got a idea.' Jehovah claps his hands and in flaps this big angel. 'Elohim,' Jehovah says, 'this is Michael the Archangel.' 'Pleased to meet you.' 'Michael, how would you like a change of occupation?' Jehovah don't wait for an answer, though, but makes a pass like a magician and Michael's wings fall off. 'Now you're a earthly man,' he says. 'Your name is Adam.'"

Lucitie sighed.

"'And this here beautiful spot, the Garden of Eden, is where you'll live and you are the total boss, beasts of the field, fishes of the sea, fowls of the air, fruits, vegetables, nuts— unless you risk it all by foolishness.' 'Foolishness?' says Adam. He don't even know the word. 'You see that tree there?'—a real tree in the corner trimmed like a Christmas tree with some bunches of raisins. 'That there tree is called the *Tree of Knowledge*, and if you eat of its fruit or even go near it,' says Jehovah, 'you are out on your ear.' 'The cold cruel atmosphere,' Elohim says. 'I'll steer clear, Jehovah.' 'Well, you better.' Jehovah's eyes the whole time they been talking is fixed on Adam like a statue-maker studying a statue to see what more he can do with it. And in about a minute, 'Adam,' he says, 'I want you to shut your eyes and take a snooze.' I'm not telling this just word for word," Hindle said, with an appraising glance at her sister, "because it was very long-drawn-out. I'm just giving the gist. So where was I?"

"'Adam, shut your eyes—'"

"'Shut your eyes…' So Adam's chin drops onto his chest, and we get the high sign we that's watching should do the same. 'And what are you up to now, Jehovah?' Elohim says. 'Performing a operation,' Jehovah says. 'Taking a rib from this here fellow's frame and making him a fellow man to chum around with. Because it is not good for man to be alone!' Elohim starts to argue but he gets hushed, and Jehovah's working fast and pretty soon he says, 'Wake up, Adam! Look what we got here.'"

"And there stands Eve."

"She slipped in unbeknownst, dressed in another union suit like Adam's, which I forgot to tell you was what *he* had on, dyed light pink to represent bare skin. 'This here's Eve.' She goes to Adam's side. And now the warning comes another time about the tree, and Jehovah and Elohim say good-bye. Now Adam and Eve on their own are like a horse let out of the barn on a warm day in March, they frisk around, till Adam's got a errand and away he goes, leaving Eve by herself. But not for very long. The door opens again—"

"And in comes the devil," Lucitie said, trying not to yawn. "Dressed up like a serpent, I imagine."

"Well, if you imagine that you're wrong," Hindle said. "Because he was wearing knee-britches like George Washington! A trig little jacket suit of black sateen. Mustache. Lamp-blacked eyebrows. A regular card! but (you could tell) not for the sake of the proceedings but due to the man that took the part being born that way, swaybacked, and with a peculiar-looking head. But he don't know it and *we* don't give it away by laughing or even smiling when he comes in. So up he walks to Eve on his bandy legs—"

"And he tempted her, she took a bite of the apple, and that's how come we're so miserable today."

Silence fell.

Hindle got up and began to clear away their cups. "A house don't have to fall on me," she said.

"Oh, come on. Sit down. I didn't mean—All I did was make a little remark."

"No, that's the sum and substance."

But Lucitie coaxed and prevailed. Hindle came back to her place, sadly forbearant at first, but then as she went along with her account, replenished again with light-heartedness. "That poor couple," she said. "When the fruit of the Tree of Knowledge got to circulating in their blood. For now they knew what *sinning their mercies* meant. And realized they was *naked*, which of course they wasn't because they both had on these union suits! But they pretended shame and mortification till Eve spied two aprons on a bush, white with green in imitation of fig leaves, and tied one on herself and one on Adam. And we had aprons too, which we had to put on. Then Adam started acting very scared because someone was coming, and Eve still more so, and they run and hid theirself. And in walked Elohim, not Jehovah."

Lucitie looked puzzled.

"Don't ask me why. And when he looks around and don't see Adam and Eve he knows something's wrong. So he calls out the way you'd call a dog, clapping his thigh, 'Devil, you low-down sneak, you get on out here!' and in runs Mr. Knee-pants, fawning and wagging. Which give a peculiar impression of him and Elohim being pardners! And also plants the suspicion that they might have a *sleeping* pardner and that it might be Mr. Piano Tuner Jehovah himself. But anyway that ended the Garden of Eden."

"In other words to take a person's endowments is quite a lot like taking in a stage show, except the show's the Scriptures," Lucitie summed up briskly. "Only twisted around. You mentioning Eve, though, makes me think of *Albert* and something he was telling me the other day. About—before he come to this country to live. He fixed a lady's hair and she just loved it and she said to *name* the style, so he called it 'the *Eve* Coiffure.' Isn't that a coincidence? Piled up in front—"

"'Devil, you low-down sneak,'" Hindle repeated murmuringly.

"—but with the back just falling in natural waves, and sort of a braided crown on top of her head."

"Speaking of heads, you know what I forgot?" Hindle said. "To mention what we had on ours! Kind of a dustcap with a flap behind like the Three Wise Men that when we took the oath we had to reach around for and pull up over our face. We're kneeling in a circle when we get to that, and then comes where we raise our right hand and swear—But this here is the part," her voice got softer, taking note suddenly of their two reflections in the black window pane, "where if you *tell* any of this you get your tongue tore out, your heart ripped loose, your bowels eviscerated by axe and fire—"

"Why, that's terrible. *Please* don't go on!" Lucitie begged piteously with another quick glance at the clock. "Why, if anything like that happened to you—"

"Nothing will," Hindle said with a reassuring smile. "But I do have to say that taking the oath was what you might call fearful. Or not *taking it* so much as *getting ready* to take it. The actual *oath* when it comes along just dwindles down to—"

"—I'd never forgive myself!"

"—to vowing to obey, and not get cocky, keep the world at arm's length and take revenge on the Gentiles. But mostly to look up to the holy priesthood and do whatever they say without no back talk. The Ten Commandments was all right in their day, but now the priesthood's the ones in charge. They even have the word on *words*. 'Adultery', for instance."

Lucitie cleared her throat. "Adultery?"

"What would you say that was?"

"I'd say a boy. Taking advantage of an innocent girl."

"Grown men of every age can do that. Married, single—"

"Yes, I guess." (Lucitie knew it well.)

"That *should* be the meaning. But they've changed it. Adultery now means, they told us, getting married without asking the priesthood or getting married after they have told you you can't."

Lucitie shook her head.

"All right, go argue. That's what they said."

"You know, I'm really proud how Albert stood up to them when they give him orders to *farm*. But now I'm just afraid for his safety's sake he's going too far."

"Too far with who?" Hindle said with a sigh. "He's been out of the church for quite some time. In fact he was hardly ever in it. I'm sure they've lost interest."

"Apostle Tennant surely hasn't. Not when it comes to Kate. But Albert goes right on dressing her hair even though he knows she's being watched and followed."

"He needs her business."

"Her business! Kate don't *pay* him. Albert does it for nothing!"

"Maybe he likes her. It's not beyond the bounds of reason."

"He needs her *hair*. When the Territorial Exposition opens she'll be his model in the hairdressing contest that if he *wins*, his shop will benefit."

"I'd like to see that Kate sometime. To see if she's really that pretty."

"She's pretty, all right. Apostle Tennant is so gone on her he can't see straight. But Albert goes right ahead. At the Exposition he'll be dressing her hair in public, and while I wouldn't say he was vain or conceited, that's all he can talk about. And *she'll* be in her glory too, sitting up there enthroned and being gawked at. That is, if Albert don't get killed in the meanwhile. That's what worries me. Kate told him the Apostle says just terrible things—"

"Can't Albert find somebody else?"

"With hair like Kate's? You can't use rats, you know. He's sure he'll win with her. But like I tell him, 'Albert, if you're *dead* what good is fame and fortune going to do you?'"

"You can't use *rats*?" Hindle said, sounding depressed of spirit with regard to effort. For Lucitie with her dramaturgy had appropriated their interchange so firmly to herself that getting it back would be like returning a butterfly to its original case. "Maybe that's just a good excuse. There might be more going on with the two of them than you think."

But Lucitie didn't think so. She thought (but found no words to say) that yes, Kate was a sight for sore eyes. But so was Albert. So with that we come to a situation like…extension leaves…that if they're not groove to tongue or tongue to groove, they won't fit down together in the dining room table. And that's two people equally matched in looks. They're both either *grooved* extension leaves or *tongued* extension leaves, never *over against each other* enough. No, Lucitie's worry with Kate was Kate's jealous suitor. But her worry with *Charlotte*—"Charlotte and me are on the outs," Lucitie said. "I should of knew better than to of took her down to his shop in the first place."

"Albert again," Hindle said. "Why, he wouldn't *look* at her."

"I know that. He wouldn't, so that's what got my suspicions up."

"What do you mean?"

"I mean we was down there, her and me, paying a call. We still had the same day off at that time and things was fine. So we was sitting there resting after cleaning house and tidying a few odds and ends for Albert. I had laid the tea and we was having it—and all of a sudden I noticed amidst the conversation, it's hard to describe, Albert wasn't looking at Charlotte and she wasn't looking at him! And it was like—You know at a play party when someone goes out of the room and you hide a object, and then they come back and you don't look where it is for fear they will guess that's what it is? Well, that was them. Charlotte was red in the face, Albert was pale, and I just said to myself *she has wiggled in*."

"Maybe you just imagine—"

"I should have realized. So anyway now I'm not speaking to her."

"Don't worry, she'll wear out her welcome."

"By scrubbing his floors and doing up his shirts? Her and I got different days off now, I know she's down there, and now I hear she's writing down receipts from Mrs. Birdwood's cookbook and *making Yorkshire pudding*!"

"We got to put things in their proper order," Hindle said. "Or we'll never—You mentioned being afraid for Albert's safety. Is that your biggest worry? Or is it Charlotte?"

"Both," Lucitie said.

Like one possessed of sudden mental light Hindle gave a gasp and said, "I know! If Albert *married* Charlotte, that would throw the Apostle completely off the trail. Kate could come and get her hair fixed—"

Lucitie started to rise but sat back down. "I don't know why I thought," she said to the lamp, "that I could come down here and get some human understanding."

"But don't you see if Albert—That old Apostle wouldn't have anything to be jealous about!"

"Yes, I see. But saying 'married to Charlotte' is an insult to my intelligence!"

"It's an insult to your intelligence not to take what I said in the spirit in which I meant it," Hindle said. "Why, she could never get him, Lucitie! While *you* can set your course and get him"—she snapped her fingers—"just like that!"

"Oh, of course, and dance on the points of my toes," Lucitie said bitterly. "No, Mrs. Birdwood's right. She thinks it's just not wrote in the stars for me and Albert to make a match of it."

"Well, that just shows her ignorance," Hindle said. "The *stars* was for olden days when people was dumb. Now they're smart, it's modern times, just look how your money zings to the balcony floor in that little cylinder and your change comes back when you buy something at Auerbach's. Look at lightning-conductors. Elevators!"

"Nothing's been patented yet to make somebody love you."

"Don't you be too sure of that. Why, I would bet—" But Hindle's voice trailed off.

"It's not that he don't *like* me. Why wouldn't he? On my afternoons off I go down there—"

"About like Charlotte does, cleaning and cooking?"

"Yes, but I was way ahead of her."

"It seems to me that you'd be *farther* ahead if you would—"

"Just throw in the sponge? I know it, Hindle. But now that he's in danger like he is—"

"Is this your imagination or actual fact?"

"His sign tore down and jumped on seems like pretty actual. And I wish you could of seen the note he got! Kate says he should own a Derringer. And just last week a man come up to him right on Main Street and made some kind of remark about him getting his neck wrung like a chicken! Did your wonderful doctor"—Lucitie always said "your wonderful doctor" in an elusively cutting tone when speaking of Hindle's late husband to her—"imagine it when they kept sending threats to him and then one night come close to *murder*? Fractured his skull, which Mrs. Birdwood said would put a quietus on him for the rest of his life?"

"Well, it *didn't* put a quietus on him for the rest of his life," Hindle said loftily. "But Doctor and Albert—there's no comparison."

"Who says there's not?"

"I do, because there isn't. When he was here in Salt Lake, *Doctor*'s doings and sayings was wrote up in the paper, every little thing he said and did, while Albert is just a violet by a mossy stone. Unknown to fame, as the saying goes. Besides," Hindle added after letting that sink in, "everything is calmer now since Brigham died."

"That don't include Apostle Tennant, I can tell you. And now that he's rose so high he can do about what he wants. One little nod from him—!"

"Oh, I don't know. Apostles don't have the *say* they had in olden days. Is Albert's neck what worries you the most? Because if it was me, I'd think it would be *Kate*."

"Kate? Didn't I just explain? It's Charlotte that's the wooden horse," Lucitie said, not quite sure what the phrase she had heard might mean but thinking it sounded like something heavy about to fall on you.

Chapter Thirty

*

"Then Charlotte comes first," Hindle said. To solve that problem she rummaged through memory's store, but Lucitie had gone on to something else before a duel that once was fought in Sweet Rest, Nevada, came to mind. The duellists were two dance-hall ladies coached by gambler friends (gentlemen from Virginia). So the duel was pure etiquette from start to finish. The ladies landed shots but not to where anyone died, although the one with the splintered crazy-bone later developed a necrosis that cost her her arm to the shoulder. The Sweet Rest Clarion said it was a disgrace, women fighting like that. But the man who let them use his duelling pistols (in a case lined with purple satin) sat down and wrote the editor a letter. "Ladyfolks," he said, "are human like anyone else and sometimes have their *points of honor* too, to put beyond dispute. So let them do it in a way entitled to respect."

To Lucitie, nothing about the story was entitled to respect. She thought it was ridiculous.

"It's not at all. Take now," Hindle said. "If Charlotte has really wiggled in with Albert the way you say, when she knows very well you saw him first, why, *you* got 'a point of honor to put beyond dispute.'" She liked the phrase when she read it in the Sweet Rest paper and now liked the sound of it even better.

"I do believe you expect me to fight a duel!"

"That never entered my mind." (But it had. The minute Lucitie spoke the word, Hindle could see it all happening: daybreak, Liberty Park, the grass all wet with dew, Lucitie and Charlotte cocking their pistols or flashing their sabers bare.)

Lucitie made a derisive sound.

"To get someplace you got to consider all the different *paths*," Hindle said, her eyes beginning to sparkle. "But if you don't want to shoot anyone—Wait, I know what to do! *Pay* Charlotte to stay away from Albert!"

"You mean—money?"

"Cash on the barrel-head," Hindle said splendidly. One of the great principles of Doctor's philosophy was, that there's so many varieties of misery in this life that *can't* be cured by money, if there's one that *can*, why, pay it without thinking twice. Lucitie, of course, with her small wages and still in arrears to the Perpetual Emigration Fund for her passage back from England, was not flush. But perhaps she could arrange a little ... "How does *that* sound?"

"To me personally? Like you have took leave of your senses."

"Well, I haven't. And I still say there's no problem on this earth but what has got a answer!" Before Lucitie could call this specious but nevertheless false reasoning in question, Hindle hurried on, "You mentioned receipts. Well, listen. I know a receipt that if you followed it, you know what would happen? Albert would follow you like Mary's little lamb."

"You mean like a cooking receipt?"

"If it would work on a royal prince, it sure ought to work on him."

"Where would you hear a thing like that?"

"From the son of a English duke, that's where. After he nearly blew his foot off with dynamite trying to run in a mine in Lamotte, Arizona. He was Doctor's patient."

"Listen," Lucitie said dubiously, "I heard about royalty right on the spot, remember I been in *England*. And the son of a duke walking around handing out cooking receipts sounds very peculiar to me."

"I never said *cooking*. What I said was a *receipt*. A receipt for something to *do*," Hindle said. "And paying a visit somewheres don't make people this big authority. It just so happens that in the Old Country—whether you was there or not—there's a custom where the son of a duke that's not born *first* in the family might as well jump in the lake. And the farther down the line you go in the family, the worse off you are. By the time the baby comes along he might just as well be a shoe-clerk. Which I think he sometimes is. So this patient of Doctor's was the youngest of about eleven, and the only worse prospects he could of had as far as land and money was concerned would of been to be a Chinaman. So when he grew up he packed his bag and went away to seek his fortune. And after a while here he was in a land called Ruthenia, working for the royal prince!"

"Doing what?" Lucitie said with unbelief. "You can act like it's nothing if you want to, but I was in England. And I seen enough to know that a person that their father is a duke, no matter *where* they come in the family, has got such a high opinion of theirself they won't hardly even wipe their own behind, let alone *work*!"

"Well, you can take my word for it that Eustace would. That's what this fellow's name was. He went right to the Royal Palace in Ruthenia and got a job. I don't say it was elevating, working around the stables and sleeping in the straw, but it kept body and soul together. Of course it didn't seem to have much future. But we never know, do we? Every day the prince would come out to see his horses, and Eustace would be there and they would say good morning. Then they got to talking, then chewing the fat and laughing, and soon the prince was *chumming around* with Eustace. He gave him some kind of title like 'Master of the Horse,' and Eustace had lovely boots and everything that went clear to the hip and plumes in his hat, and eventually a apartment in the Palace. And everything was lovely till one day the two chums took a notion to climb the Alps and a avalanche come down and killed the prince. So that left Eustace right back where he started. So what must he do but seek his fortune again. And hard the traveling was till at last he come to Lamotte, Arizona, and made a strike that looked like at first it was going to be as good as the Little Emma. But instead of that—"

"He blew his foot off."

"Not clear off," Hindle said. "Doctor saved it for him."

"I don't see where this has any connection whatsoever. With anything."

"But it has. Didn't you say there wasn't no invention to make somebody love you? Well, maybe there is. With Eustace's receipt you might surprise yourself! Wasn't he sleeping in the Ruthenian straw one night and under the Royal Palace roof the next?"

"The prince took a liking to him, that's all. A *receipt* didn't need to enter in."

"Oh, but the prince liked *lots* of people," Hindle said. "But between *liking* and wanting to *chum around with you twenty-four hours a day* there's a big difference."

"And a big difference between *chumming around* and getting somebody to *propose* to you, too."

"Would it hurt to try it?" Hindle said.

"Try what? I haven't heard anything yet. And anyway, why would Eustace tell *you* a thing like that?"

"He didn't, he told Doctor. That foot of his took doctoring for more than a month, and cooped up in that hotel room he got mighty lonesome. Doctor would stop by to dress it. They'd play chess, or whist, but mostly they'd talk. Sometimes Doctor'd come home like he was deaf and dumb. But other times he'd talk, he'd tell me things. So one time, rattling on about this Englishman—Eustace himself didn't use the word 'receipt' and neither did Doctor, but when it come to *my* ears I just said to myself, now there is a *receipt*."

"For what?"

"For how to get in good with a royal prince."

"So what *is* it?" Lucitie said crossly, restless in expectation. "And if it don't work only when you're talking about a duke's son and a Ruthenian prince then save your breath."

"Oh, no, it works with anyone," Hindle said. "But think a minute about princes."

"Think what? Honestly, them years with your wonderful doctor—"

"Well, think how *spoiled* princes are, how much they *got*. People been bowing and scraping and giving them presents since the day they was born. How can you make any headway with a person like that? But Eustace comes into the picture and pretty soon he's a favorite. And when you hear you'll realize. What you do—" But like someone with a gift they have teasingly thrust behind them before they hand it over, she paused.

"Good thing I'm easygoing, or *you'd* be crowned like royalty yourself with that lamp there!" Lucitie said.

Taking pity, Hindle now spoke quickly. "It might sound simple," she said, "but it's like where a twist of the wrist makes all the difference. What you do—" Her revelation came in beams of light. "*Amuse them.*"

Lucitie looked at her with eyes aghast.

"If it would work with a prince in Ruthenia, why wouldn't it with a prince in Salt Lake City?" Hindle said smilingly. "I know that's what you think Albert is! A royal prince."

"*Amuse* them?"

"If you want to get in good, that's the way to do it."

"Amuse *Albert*?"

"A word to the wise—"

Lucitie put her head down on her arms on the table, her shoulders shaking, and said in a choked voice, "Why, that's the deceivingest thing I ever heard. You know very well I couldn't amuse a *flea*!"

DOES IT NOT SEEM LIKE things bunch up together? Obnoxious planets, joys, subjects of grief? One night Hindle had Lucitie's tears to dry and not many days after walked into another downfall, this time from the eyes of Stig Fogelmarck. They had no more than met at the gate, he coming from one direction, loaded down with painting gear, she approaching from the other, and said hello, Hindle throwing in a remark about the weather, than the man seemed to go to pieces. Brushing past her, he blundered through the gate, scraping the posts with his load as he did so, ran up the walk and around to his own dwelling on the alley as fast as he could.

"Now mind you," she told Serapta when she got inside, "this was out of a clear sky. I don't even know what I said! Cold enough for you, freeze the tail off a brass monkey. It could be he was crying already when he come up the street and I just didn't notice till he started rassling with the gate and went flying around the house. What do you think has happened?"

"Happened?" Serapta said. "That's not hard to say. He's been up to the church office again probably and they've hurt his feelings."

"Why would they do that?" Hindle said, taking off her things and going over to the stove. "Oh, I know! The portrait he wants to paint of President Taylor. But the way things are, nobody in Salt Lake's going to do *that* for quite some time. They might in Mexico, but not Salt Lake!"

"Mexico? What makes you say that?"

"Because according to the paper the President's not *in* Salt Lake anymore to govern, rule, be painted or anything else. The deputies and federal officers went in one door and he flew out the other. He's gone to Mexico."

"Well, if that's so," Serapta said indignantly, "why don't they have the decency to *say* so?"

"Because they don't want the word to get out, that's why! Don't you know people around here well enough to know they'd about go crazy without a leader? The Beehive House is well named."

"I'll go tell him," Serapta said, reaching for her shawl. "Although he might just think it's a lie."

"Take this morning's paper. That's where I read about it."

"Oh, I don't know. Stig and the Tribune—" Serapta shook her head. "I been meaning to ask you, though. This—going back in history all of a sudden. I thought it was all settled long ago."

"What was?"

"You know. Utah and the rest of the United States. Not getting along. I mean, a whole *army* marched out here when Tot and me was little. We thought there was going to be a war. But nothing come of it. Wasn't there—like a peace treaty? So now yesterday I see this headline in the paper, 'Hostilities Renewed.' Do you know what I thought? I thought it meant hostilities between the white people and that bunch of wild Comanches up in Wyoming that killed all them soldiers a few years ago."

"Montana, that was."

"But it turns out it's between Utah and the Government, just like in the old days! And what I want to know is, what caused it? What disturbed the peace?"

"Well, first of all it wasn't *really* peace," Hindle said. "Not like between us and England when we quit a-fighting. It was just kind of a hands-off, don't do nothing about nothing till the business interests—railroads, the mining outfits and such as that—I'm remembering what Doctor used to say—gets a toehold. So now they've got it, the *territory* of Utah wants to turn into the *state* of Utah, and Washington, D.C. starts getting leery."

"Why?"

"You know why, Serapta. The *beliefs* around here. The peculiarity. The branched-out husbands." Warming her hands at the stove, Hindle looked somewhat embarrassedly away, she having one of those husbands herself. "They're afraid branching out might get to be the fashion throughout the nation."

"You're talking about polygamy?"

But that was a term Hindle steered clear of, as though by putting the fact of it a different way her tie with Lennart was not (what internal recognition told her it was) a stupid affair of gallantry, but a marriage in good faith such as one might enter into with the commercial traveler who didn't happen to be home a lot of the time.

(And it was going to be even less, Lennart had said that morning when he ran in. At least until the federal spies from Washington thinned out. It made Fern nervous, he said, to have him keep on being so fair to everybody, when sleeping under four different roofs might get him arrested and thrown in jail! So from now on it was either *one* roof—Fern's—or, as far as Fern was concerned, none. She would sell her house, she said, Lennart's chief place of residence since he married her, also Pearl's and Rosina's dwellings, Stig's barn and the cottage Hindle was renting, and move back to upper New York State, and let them all scramble—him, too—if he didn't just live with *her*. As scrambling did not appeal to Lennart, or to do without the cuisine and relative luxury of Fern's abode, he gave in to her.)

"If you want to call it that. It's got several different—The Mormons—"

"You say 'Mormons' like you and me was Gentiles," Serapta said sternly. "Well, we're not. Remember we went back into it of our own free will."

"Why don't you go out and take Stig some of that meatloaf?"

She soon returned, wringing her hands. He wouldn't come to the door. "And what's he doing in there? He could be hanging himself! *Please*, Hindle!"

"If he wouldn't let *you* in, he's sure not going to let me!"

But Serapta kept begging till Hindle took her coat, its wool still cold and stiff-feeling from the sharp east wind that had helped propel her home, put it around her shoulders and hurried out to the alley.

"Mr. Fogelmarck!"

He opened the door and let her in, so quickly and unexpectedly she nearly fell off the step. Later she would wonder if his lack of demur had been because becoming Lennart's wife had destroyed the effect of whatever it was that made their common tangent so uncomfortable when she was single. The extirpation, however (if there was one), had not made him more cordial. "What do you want?" he said.

"To find out if you're all right," Hindle said. "Serapta was just out here and when you wouldn't let her in she got worried. You know—to think of you feeling bad out here all by yourself on such a dark old day—! Don't it get dark early, though? I see you got your lamp lit already! We have too, although it's only—gracious! not even three—"

"That clock is slow."

"—and here it looks like evening! But Mr. Fogelmarck, do you realize—? We had the shortest day already, and from now on the light's going to last longer—and longer—and—spring will come!" She rushed on, "And this *setback* you had today, or whatever it was that hurt your feelings—"

"Setback!" he burst out. "I have been excoriated."

They did not have to talk on long before *excoriated*'s not meaning *excommunicated* would become plain. But as *excommunicated* seemed to fill the bill so well right then, she went ahead as if excommunication had been his news. "From what Lennart tells me, the church *never* appreciated you. And now if the chips are finally down, I'd take it as a blessing in disguise. To a person of your artistic nature? I most certainly would!"

He started coughing.

"What I meant to say"—she spoke quickly—"did you ever see a Ward chapel as pretty as a Catholic church? Now tell the truth, you never did. And *inside*—! We went to the Catholic church in Las Cruces one time, me and my husband. Little bitty church, but it was Easter and I am telling you—! A millionaire's parlor would have to go some to keep up. And you with your artistic nature, Mr. Fogelmarck, wouldn't that be lots more up your alley than—?"

For a moment she thought an effusion of serum to the brain was causing him to choke to death. "Up my alley!" he gasped as she was about to attempt a rescue. "Up my alley if I want to worship idols, calves, the Deities of Egypt and burn in hell!"

"Goodness, I didn't mean—"

"Didn't mean that hell is pretty too? Well, it is! fires, firelight, flames shooting up like fountains!" He had gone over to the cookstove to adjust the damper and now turned to face her, brandishing the lifter. "But I don't guess the *soul* will think so, singed and scorched and caught in the fire's fangs!"

"No, I wouldn't think so," she said nervously. "But what I was trying to say—if people don't treat you nice when all you're trying to do is get in the Beehive House and do President Taylor the favor of painting a picture of him for nothing, then all I can say is they ought to be ashamed. But you know he's not there, don't you? He's gone to Mexico."

"The Lord will unbar the way," he said, his spell of ire diffusing as he fitted the lifter into a stove lid and left it there (to her relief). "But as to Mexico—"

He didn't believe a word of it. First, because the Salt Lake Tribune was the devil's own organ, not even fit for the place of ease out back. And second, because he was sure that this very day, through the window on the left-hand side of the Beehive House's front door, he had glimpsed the great man himself invested with a circle of light! No, he knew what had happened. They had *told* him!

"Told the President? What?"

"What happened."

"When, Mr. Fogelmarck?"

"Twenty years ago. Yet still today—and here, not there—they are as distempered as if *my* harm would infect them all!" Giving her no chance to search into these mystifying remarks, he went on, "As soon as I was able I made my way to San Francisco and signed on the first ship that would take me. As able-bodied seaman." Oddly, he laughed.

"I just never imagined you as a sailor, Mr. Fogelmarck, but I expect it's quite a interesting occupation. They probably had you painting them figureheads in front and all kinds of things."

"I did not get these calluses from painting," he said, feeling the palm of his right with the fingers of his left hand. "Then last year I quit the sea and returned to this center of the world, where Christ will come and the Millennium begin."

"Well, that will be fine if it turns out like that," she said. "With you being right on the spot and everything. But on the other hand, if while you're waiting, your daily life—if people around here is going to act *distempered* to you like you say they do—then it looks like to me that the farther away the better!"

"Emigrants come here," he said as if speaking somewhere else to other ears, "they learn the language. But by the time they learn it, the *language* itself has learned another language. Always flowing by! like the Jordan River, and we left standing."

"Well, *you're* not left standing," Hindle said in total bewilderment, "to judge by all them words you come out with. But what has language got to do with this? Whatever it is we're talking about."

"We are talking about my fort of silence," he said. "Toppled and strewed around." Going across the room, he turned up the flame of the lamp, then sat down heavily beside the high-piled table. "You too, Doctor. Please. Sit down."

The nearest chair was high-piled too, but she pushed back what seemed to be clothing and bunched-up canvases stiff with paint and took a seat on the edge.

"In those times," he went on, "what *I* saw on the sacred page and what was *there*, what *I* heard in the discourses and what was *meant*, were as different as pigment is, from turpentine! I know *now* what I should have done, but *then*—"

"Well," she said, "we've all done things we shouldn't, if that's what you mean. We just have to forget it and go on."

"They won't let me. I'm denied an audience."

"With the President? He's not *there*. He's gone to Mexico. But he'll come back. A treaty or something will be signed with Washington and then—"

"Treaties have nothing to do with it! If they won't let me in the Beehive House now, things will be no different then. Because an old man like the President with his powers failing, surrounded by his Apostles with *their* powers failing—"

"His powers failing?" Hindle said in astonishment. "Why, there's no end to the man's powers! Nothing to look at, can't paint signs and pictures like you can or do anything else much of practical use that *I* know of, up in years—but he can stand up there in Tabernacle and tell practically everybody in Utah to go jump in the lake and they'll do it! What do you call that?"

"His powers as a *man*," he said, "is what I have reference to."

"I don't know what you mean by his powers as a—Was you thinking of painting him sparring with his fists?"

He ignored this to begin without relevance, as it seemed to Hindle, to go over some of his by now familiar life's events. The Royal Danish Art Academy, his conversion to Mormonism on a street in Copenhagen, coming to America, being sent from Salt Lake City to San Bernardino…"I arrived there agued," he said.

This she had not heard before but made no response except to wonder idly if a once ague-inconvenienced spleen might be responsible for his peevishness. Doctor often said…

"But the Elders laid on hands," he said. "I felt the healing power. It drove out the sickness. I could work. I helped to dig a root cellar and roof a house. Then I was sent out into the chaparral to look for strays. But the ague came back, I do not know why."

"Because that's its nature, Mr. Fogelmarck."

"I laid down," he said, "under a tree. A Lamanite came by. He was a convert. He did not help me, for he was on his way home to his people. But he said he would return and bring a curative—"

"My husband always gave potassic arseniate."

"And a few days later he *did* come back. I don't know how he found me. 'We are brothers,' he said. But by that time the Elders had laid on hands again and I had received my Patriarchal Blessing, so I was well and did not need the medicine. But he said it would do many things, not just cure a fever. And since in Europe we hear of the American Indian's *ars*—"

She looked away.

"—*magica*, I purchased it. Then the Lamanite—or devil, as I realize now he was—left, never to be seen again."

"Did you take his medicine?" she said, looking back at him.

"Not for a long time. I forgot about it. But then one night whilst seeking my glass lens, which *also* disappeared never to be seen again, I found this—I can only say it looked like a kind of carnal member of a mummified—" He paused. "What I should have done was burn it! But to my regret and sorrow—"

"You took it?"

"I—" But he jibbed at the leap. A silence, then a turn of mind that brought the inconsequential words "I painted your sign" to his lips.

"Yes." She was not sorry for the change of subject, "carnal member" having somewhat discomposed her. "I been real pleased with my sign from the very first day."

"The physician," he said like one announcing a sermon's text. "Who knows more than he about the lewd, the base, the loathsome rottenness of suffering mankind? Its vile and filthy, turgescent, libidinous—"

"Will you listen to *that*," she interrupted nervously. "And you was the one talking about the English language getting ahead of you! All I can say is if it wants to do *that*, it will have to get up early in the morning!" Though liking much to know and learn, *this* gleaning she decided not to touch.

"'Nothing human is strange to him' was not said of a physician, but it might well have been. The disgusting—"

"True," she said quickly, "nothing is strange to him, a *physician* that's a man. Which is who a *patient* that's also a man should go to if—they got some kind of situation they need to have looked at. Because him being of the same sex—Have you ever happened to see that doctor's sign over on First East? Dr. Beauchamp? From the looks of his yard and everything, I would imagine that if you got a situation *you* need looked at," she smiled determinedly, "he would be the one to go to."

But he kept on about the filthy being filthy and human nature inveterate, and while she wanted to increase their mutual distance, she also remembered the *Anatomy* book saying that the study that repels you is invaluable. For Hippocrates' sake too, she held her ground. Of course when Hippocrates wrote his oath he wasn't thinking of her or any woman practicing medicine, but since that was what she was doing, wasn't it a case of discharge your function or get off the article? Like at the theater, when the call came *Is there a doctor in the house?* How proud she had been when Doctor stood up, went up to where the man lay in the aisle, knelt down and laid his head on the man's glassy shirt-front, then looked up and said "Moribund."

"The only situation *I* need looked at," the painter said, clutching his hair, "is why the vile body—"

Well, stand staunch, she thought. Nastiness was going to get in here in spite of every-thing. And was it any wonder? with a species where their sexuality was hung on them like belling the cat? And what peal had *his* rung? she wondered. Rape and rapine? Bastardy? Deflowering? Getting fresh with a married woman? A innocent sheep? Molesting his own self? What else was there? Wait—let's see—In France—Once on a long journey Doctor got talking about his travels, and about the summer he lived in Paris and stud-ied refraction and peristaltic movement and also the people of Paris till he got where he could read them like a book. Stingiest bunch on earth, he said, had the Scotch beat a mile. Fashion plates but stinky underneath, that's why all the perfume. They can cook. Yes, but what? "Lapin suc de la Viande." In other words, rabbit *that eats its own excrements.* Religious, yes, go to Mass like other people sit down to breakfast, but cheat, backbite, defraud, keep side girls and got more Sodomites per square mile than London, Oxford and Cambridge put together.

Sodomites? she had asked.

Doctor loved to explicate. Men and boys, he said, who used one another the way a man did a wife. Dogs would do the same, but in the case of dogs it was more just jeu d'esprit. (Fopping roosters, too.) And now, he said, you ask me where the word Sodomite comes from.

She hadn't but gave a provisional nod.

It comes from the name of a town! he said. A town called Sodom that ages ago in the land of Judah stood neighbors to another town by the name of Gomorrah. And history wouldn't have paid Sodom and Gomorrah any more attention than it does to St. Paul and Minneapolis had not a fad got started in the two places of fellows falling in love with fellows and pronging fellows to an extent that it even got them noticed by the authors of the *Bible.* Especially when the news got out concerning the two angels sent by God down to Sodom on some kind of heavenly errand—lovely visions, male—a lot of people don't know this but *angels are always male*, like the drones in a hive, there's no such thing as a female angel—and how these actual angels from heaven got accosted, solicited for improper purposes and finally *chased* through the streets like whitetail deer!

Angels, if you please. Had they not had the advantage of wings to unfurl, and had not a family man by the name of Lot shooed them into his own strongly fortified dwelling and drove the buggers away—"buggers" being another verbal expression for Sodomites, and "buggery" the article they deal in—those two pure creatures might have went back to heaven quite bedraggled. When God heard what had happened he said all right, that tears it, and rained down fire and brimstone till Sodom and Gomorrah were totally wiped out. Then he drowned their very *locations* under the Dead Sea!

Well, stand staunch. Could Mr. Fogelmarck be hinting at buggery? How many other offenses in the line of sexual phenomena could man's reproductive structure think up? Did anyone really know?

"The physician's mind has tolerance," he said.

"It does," she said faintly. "Only like I was saying, where it's the case of a man—" But wasn't there a Corporal in the war that fooled everyone till he got wounded and they had to undress him and found out he was a woman? Maybe if the same befell Mr. Fogelmarck—But no, she thought, he would not be sitting there with feet like that or a Adam's apple if he was really a woman. "If you want tolerance and everything, Mr. Fogelmarck, wouldn't your best bet be to go to Dr. Beauchamp?"

"My best bet?"

"Well, you keep talking about going to a doctor."

"No, I'm very healthy."

She clutched at this, hoping it meant that nothing was wrong with him. "Good! Anyway, I always think we can *think* ourself into collapsing by just our mind. Don't you? Just by what we dwell on."

"I dwell on the Millennium," he said.

"Well, fine," she said. "And it wouldn't be a bad idea to dwell on how good you can *paint*, too! so when someone acts mean or rude you can just think 'Well, I'm better than *you* are!'"

"That's easy enough to say," he said. He took a tube of paint off the table beside him and began flattening and smoothing it out. "But something happened which, in all conscience—"

"You mean today? Or twenty years ago in San Bernardino?"

"I mean both," he said. "A life—whether it heaves astern or ahead—is always connected. You see—"

But at that moment a knock came at the door.

"Oh, pshaw," she said (for it did seem as if he might be about to say something at last) and jumped up to answer it. "That must be Serapta come to find out what's keeping me."

But it was not Serapta.

It was someone else.

Chapter Thirty-one

✳

"Mr. Clarendon!" Stig spoke up behind her, elbowing her aside to open the door wider. "Come in, sir! Please come in. I'm glad to see you."

It was none of Hindle's business, she should have gone home. When the caller entered, she should have stepped out. But, weak in the knees and aflutter about the bosom, instead of doing that she edged farther into the room and held on to a chair for support as the clear and distinct concept formed that this epiphany, shining like roses and sparkling with rosy light like a great silver-side salmon, was none other than Jim Clarendon, the rich millionaire for whom she once was stricken with love and who still came to mind every now and then like remembering *Lorna Doone* or a scene of love in a play.

Was it really him? And was this herself so near? inflated with ether and risen in the air. As she came softly down she heard him saying he felt like two cents "—to get you going on the Irish kings and then to have to put the kibosh on 'em. Them three you done already and left up at my steward's office would beat Lardo de Vincent by a mile. But you know women, Fogelmarck."

"Mrs. Clarendon did not like them?"

"She *liked* them all right. But see, we been over there in Europe and we seen these castles. All I *hope* is she's going to be satisfied to live in the house Summerlade's building for us up on Brigham Street, once it gets done, if it ever does! They say spring but I don't know. *She* don't mind, it just gives her more of an excuse to travel and buy more stuff. Well, such is life. We're going over again so I thought I better pull you off the kings, you know, old socks."

"But they would have been most suitable."

"They would! Made the dining room *look* like something. But no, the panels got to be hand-tooled leather. Ladies!"

"I could paint on leather," the painter said.

"Another thing," the visitor went on quickly, "*Irish* kings—You're some kind of foreigner yourself, so maybe you realize. Certain countries—Ireland—Ireland's not too much *looked up to* here in Utah, according to my wife. Not that I believe that for a minute."

"I could have made them Mesopotamian."

"I know you could. But these here panels she's got her neck bowed for, I guess I'd have a better chance to pull the hide off a wild boar with my bare hands than get her to listen to the voice of reason."

There he stood.

AND THERE *HE* STOOD AS well, otherguise Jim, Jim in another case, as on a transparency she held up to memory's light. Younger, emptier, *that* Jim had on rough-cast clothes to prospect in, sleep rough, rough-footed came to the hospital to see his wife, arms swelled out his shirtsleeves till they almost split. He had on an old hat that he took off when he saw the girl coming down the hallway with the baby. Hello, he said, in love with her and she with him, to no avail. But the day will come, she thought his eyes said. The day did come, and here at last he stood weighed down with his millions that meant nothing to her, nothing, she loved him for himself alone, and they would always be true to one another. But then the picture on the glass dimmed and went out.

"I tell you, son, they got us over a barrel."

This Jim (by the fact of being the other) had not removed his opera hat. He pushed it back off his brow. She saw his gray hair, not gray, but getting gray. Had a good chance to study his handsome, disorderly face as he laid the greenbacks on the table, quite a few, a stack, for consolation. But of that gesture the artist was unaware. Stig had gone over to the stove to replenish the fire and try to hide the nervous shambles he was in. To help him, Hindle stepped forward, took a breath and said…

What *did* she say?

She tried to tell Serapta later, but it was as if she had only half heard a stranger talking down the street. Saying…she was there those years ago when they brought in Mrs. Clarendon. Poor soul, broken collarbone, face white as a sheet. Fallen down taking a bath or something. The hotel people brought her, said her husband was in the mountains. But at Burdick's Institution for the Care of the Sick she got along all right, aside from pleurisy caused by the broken bone puncturing her lung. And finally her husband come down and come to see her, looking like he had the world by the tail.

"I did, by damn, have the world by the tail," he said. "That was when—"

"We read it in the paper. About you striking—finding the Galleon mine. But you done that a lot of times. Prospected—found—"

He nodded. "But every time—I'm still *in good*, I say. With whatever rigs the game!" He studied her. "And so you say we met before? I hear that. But I'm one of these—I'll remember a gully, a rock or a beggar's bush but forget *somebody*, faster'n I can see 'em."

She had to set it up again, bring her young self back. She chose the moment of their meeting in the hallway. "You was going to see her, your wife, Mrs. Clarendon," she said. "I was taking the baby to Serapta's room. We stopped, you looked at her. Everyone did that that saw her for the first time. Her being a albino."

"Oh?" he said.

"They're very unusual."

"It wasn't your baby?"

"Oh, no! She belonged to Lisheen. And you know something funny? Lisheen was dark-complected. She didn't no more look like she would have a child like Mavis—!"

"Beats a hog a-flying, don't it? What turns up."

"You know what I honestly think, although it seems far-fetched? I honestly think that you stretched out your hands, Mr. Clarendon, like you was wanting to *hold* her! and that I kind of put her in your arms. You held her careful like she was made of glass. And there was a mirror hanging on the wall. You kind of turned and walked up close to it and looked *in* with the baby. I can kind of see you both … reflected … And she was just as still as could be."

"You got a real good memory, Mrs. Fogelmarck. I'll tell you the truth. I think myself I hoisted a few that day. I wasn't just the soberest, in other words."

"She's not—!" the artist said in a strangled voice.

"I'm not Mrs. Fogelmarck," Hindle said soothingly. "I live in the house in front. The one with the sign on it that says Dr. Fairbrass. Maybe you noticed as you come around out back? I'm—the doctor. And why I'm here, the lady that stays with me—Serapta, her name is—and takes care of my children, she got kind of worried about Mr. Fogelmarck—that he might be coming down with something—so she asked me—"

"A doctor?"

"Yes. I got a—diploma."

"Hydropathic?"

"No, the regular kind."

"Say, that's pretty slick! A person never knows when they might need one."

"Yes, but I don't treat menfolks."

"Very wise."

SERAPTA WAS NOT IMPRESSED BY the personage in whose company Hindle had just been. She knew who Jim Clarendon was all right, that overblown millionaire from several years back. But his wife while she was there at the Institution was lovely, Serapta remembered. Then, "What did you find out?"

"Well," Hindle said eagerly, "Mrs. Clarendon's still going strong and, judging by the errand he was on for her, still pulling him around by the nose. And they're still rich, even richer than before, because you know that mansion being built up on Brigham Street that Stig was supposed to paint the kings for the dining room? Marble from top to bottom and going to have a ballroom? Well, that's *theirs*! They're not in it yet because it's not done and won't be till goodness knows when. But they don't care. To while away the time, they're going back to Europe, where they been already about ten times! and Mr. Clarendon said—"

"You silly girl, what do I care about the Clarendons? It's poor Stig out there suffering that concerns me," Serapta said. "What did *he* say?"

"I wish I knew. He talks and you think over what he's said and it's all just—air. Does it affect you like that? When you go out there with a dish of something and he starts opening up—"

"He don't even offer me a chair," Serapta confessed. "Though before you and me got baptized he *proselytized* a lot. But that's not what I'd call opening up. He looks at me real *kind* though, he really does. Did you tell him that the President's gone to Mexico?"

"*He* thinks the reason they won't let him in at the Beehive House is because they're afraid he'll take away some of the President's power."

"Why would he think a thing like that?"

But Hindle decided not to bewilder Serapta by the strangeness of his remark about old men with their powers failing, their "manly" powers, which a house didn't have to fall on her for her to suspect that he was talking about unmentionable *potency*, or what was still more unmentionable, *impotency*.

"I hear him cough sometimes as he's going around the house," Serapta said. "Maybe he's done that up there. Maybe they think he has galloping consumption!"

"What he's got is galloping *imagination*," Hindle said.

"What was Mr. Clarendon after?"

"To have Stig quit painting on them Irish kings. So there's your lovely Mrs. Clarendon for you. But I must say Mr. Clarendon done it tactful. And from the looks of the stack of greenbacks he laid on the table I'd say he paid real handsome for the work, even though now it's canceled."

"Is he still out there with Stig, the cruel thing?"

"No, he's gone. And he's not cruel, Serapta."

"What did Stig do after he left?"

"Well, he turned around from the stove and I didn't see him actually look at the money, but I'm sure he seen it out of the corner of his eye and it must of consoled him, because when he looked up at the ceiling and said 'Father, clarify thy name!' he didn't sound so blue anymore. Then he opened the door and said we'd talk another time, and I don't have to be hit with a brick so I said good-bye. I was kind of disappointed though, because when Mr. Clarendon arrived I really believe Stig was on the verge of, I don't know, *accounting* for something."

"How do you mean?"

"Well, it's hard to say. But he'd been leading up, telling different—Like he said one time a Lamanite that he thought was really the devil brought him some medicine. That was supposed to fit in *somewhere*, I'm pretty sure. Then other remarks—But the one that really seemed like it was going to count was when he took a deep breath like when you're finally going to jump in and *say* something, and he said 'Something happened in all conscience—' But right that minute the knock come at the door!"

"What do you think it could of been?"

"And why 'in all conscience'?"

What could it be?

Again Hindle thought of buggery. But this being a topic as wry as potency and its opposite, she decided to say nothing of it. Sodom and Gomorrah, the angels' hasty flight and so on would only worry Serapta. And worry her in vain, for the more Hindle thought of it the more she felt sure that Stig's secret was something else, one incidental passage in his early life, one particular occurrence on a particular day, not some settled practice, which sodomy—like the habit of smoking Havana cigars or going to the theater—in all likelihood became, once it got started. (In places other than Salt Lake, of course, where conjunction between the male and female was as popular as the reed-organ and the male impregnating fluid was thought of as kind of a divine Mississippi River down which heavenly souls were laded as cargo to earth.)

"I just think it's his conscientiousness," Serapta said, going to the kitchen window and cupping her hands around her eyes to stare out into the early dusk. Turning back, she added, "When my gingerbread comes out of the oven, don't you think—?"

"No one's going to stop you, honey. Go ahead."

AT FIRST HINDLE HAD BEEN proud that Jim Clarendon in meeting her once more had met someone *risen* in the world. Maybe not "for complete armor fit," as her old companion would say. But not unfit either, a doctor. On considering it further, however, she wondered if meeting a schoolteacher wouldn't have made him sit up and take notice more? Or a singer, a circus rider or just an *heiress*, which if the occasion should then later arise would not be thought of as marrying for money. Still, when she told him about her painted sign, who she had been and who she was, hadn't he said that was pretty slick? And hadn't he, when he left, tipped his opera hat to her?

Thinking about Jim made the fact of Lennart as her husband so petty that not long after, when, braving both U.S. Deputies and Fern's wrath, he came bursting in at the back door, she gave him such a cold welcome he said he'd of done better to have stayed outside in a snowdrift. What had he done? Been cautious, that's all, he said. Not got his self arrested in this time of trouble and confusion. Not lost their homes to the elements. Thought of all concerned. "But after supper," he said, "after I set awhile I says to myself they can do their worst, nab me, shoot me full of holes, Fern can do *her* worst, holler till they hear her clear up to the Tabernacle, but if I don't hold Hindle in my arms tonight I'm not going to make it to morning!"

When Lennart said that, dully insipid though he might be in comparison with Jim, a kindness towards him such as might be felt towards the looking-glass that handed out compliments welled up in Hindle and was not soon dispelled. For not only did he entertain her with trifling rumor and light talk but he had brought presents, a striped sack of horehound drops and a bundle of pinked woolen squares of various hues and hefts, samples of goods from his tailor shop with which to start a patchwork quilt. She could make it as big as she wanted, he said, and until it was finished nobody else, let them complain as they would, could have a single square. "And you and me will be laying under it so close together there won't be room to slide a tintype between us!"

There wasn't room *that* night for sure, and when he sneaked away before daylight to outwit the deputies and stand up like a man to whatever denunciation Fern had ready, Hindle stirred drowsily and missed him enough to put her head in the hollow of his pillow. It did occur to her as she was drifting off again that it might not have been too smart to marry him. But the blessing of polygamy was that, considering no license and one thing and another, it wasn't the most *legal* bond that ever was forged, to get out of.

AT SERAPTA'S URGING HINDLE DID try again—to little purpose—to get Stig to tell her whatever it was he seemed to be about to when Mr. Clarendon appeared. And neither would he confide in Serapta, though she gave him every chance. But his avoidance of speaking freely did not harm him. After some prostration of the faculties he survived his disappointments (the canceled Clarendon commissions, and snubbing by the church), and when Auerbach's department store commissioned him to paint a backdrop for a display of parasols on the main floor, a piece of work which so impressed one of the Mrs. Auerbachs that she hired him to paint a ceiling in her home, blue with gold stars and a sliver of moon (the moon at the full being thought vulgar), he took on quite an air of good fellowship. He also had an order for a sign for Barron's Baby Chicks, and in between whiles, having been paid so much by Mr. Clarendon, he was also painting a *fourth* Irish king, Serapta told Hindle. And when the Clarendons got home from Europe with their trainload of furnishings for the new house, he was going to deliver it to their front door whether Mrs. Clarendon wanted it or not, as a gift!

"Isn't that kind of stubborn?" Hindle said. Then she said, "When are they getting back?"

"Stig said their steward said nobody knows."

THAT WAS WHY A FEW nights later when lantern-light flashed across Hindle's frosted window at nearly one in the morning and a knock came at the door and she lit the lamp, grabbed her wrapper and went and opened it, the last person she expected to see on this earth was Jim Clarendon. For one wild instant with the quick effluvia darting through her brain, she thought it was all coming true. I stayed away as long as I could. I love but you.

Then he spoke. "Poor time to wake somebody up out of a sound sleep, I know, girlie— excuse me—Doctor. But we got a sick woman on our hands that'll cash in her chips if we don't do something quick! So if you could get yourself together and come with me, I'd take it very friendly."

Hurrying to dress, she thought of poor Mrs. Clarendon down, dying, dead, how sad! never harmed a living soul and still so much to live for! him grieving (older though she'd been than him, and plain in her appearance and somewhat snippy), shedding bitter tears, but then recuperating so that by the time a year had passed, or say two years for decency's sake…

Hindle found out in the carriage who the patient was. A friend of his, Jim said, little sap-head took something! tried to do away with herself, poison, probably laudanum. When Hindle heard *that*, how thankful she was (in the midst of the shock to her system) for Professor Ford's *Question Book without Answers*! and for the answers she had over the past months set herself to learn in *Gray's Anatomy, Gunn's Family Physician* and the four stray issues of the *Journal of the Chicago Clinical School* she had inherited. She was prepared. If it was laudanum there was no antidote, so no going through cupboards looking for ammonia, chalk or non-existent limes or sending out for potassium permanganate or magnesium sulphate. No, first see how bad off she was and after that—"Is she bad?" she said.

"Bad?" he said abstractedly.

"Bad off?"

"Oh." He thought this over. "Well, I'll tell you. She sure as hell looked like it to me."

And the girl, the little sap-head, did look like it. But at least she was faintly breathing, so they didn't have to work as on a drowned swimmer trying to make her breathe again. "Do you know for sure what she took?"

Silently the mother, friend or whoever the beringed woman hovering near the bed was, handed Hindle the empty laudanum bottle. Good, she thought, sniffing it. I won't give her ipecacuanha except as a last resort, it's such rambunctious stuff, but I got it if I need it. "The coffee pot had better go on," she told the woman. "Real strong. But first I'll want some salt and some warm water."

"I'll rustle up the fire," Jim said.

The surroundings were nice, possibly a whole house but more likely two or three rented rooms. Hindle could glimpse what seemed like a small parlor through a partly opened door, and the kitchen was in an alcove. The bed was nice, linen sheets, the pillows felt like down. The girl had on a lawn nightgown run through with pink satin ribbon. Pretty curly hair, that must have been what attracted him. He was attracted by *something*, surely, to have branched out from Mrs. Clarendon and cast discredit upon himself with a side girl like this. When the teaspoon gritted against her teeth she started to come weakly to life and tried to pull away, but Hindle drenched the salt water down her, or some of it, the rest slopped over. While this was taking place she stole an oblique glance at Jim in the kitchen putting wood in the stove, a sad sight, full of cloudy import, like it was the last glimpse she would ever have of him on the back of a moving train leaving for the farthest reaches of the world, never to return. Sighing, she put the teaspoon down and began to unfasten her cuffs.

"Should I get some more?" the beringed woman said.

Before Hindle could answer, the girl turned her head and foamy water ran out of the corner of her mouth. Then she was throwing up, Hindle lifted her, Jim came running and reached under the bed for a chamber pot, gold-rimmed with hand-painted roses, and held it up. Her eyelids fluttered and this time some of what was coming up went where it was supposed to. Then they got her out of bed, the woman found some quilted bedroom slippers and they put those on her cold, clammy feet. They started walking her around the room like a rag doll, lifting and dragging her, forcing her to move, Hindle on one side, Jim on the other. Then here came the coffee, strong, black, with a little brandy in it, and Hindle stopped the walking to get as much of it down her as she could.

Her name was Dolores, the woman said. Her own name was Minerva Bohannon. The minute Hindle heard Jim say Minerva she remembered who she was, although her hair was now coal black instead of burnt orange. Otherwise she looked about as she had when she headed up the "Decoy Girls," as the Tribune had called them, a group of young ladies recruited in San Francisco for the purpose of compromising Salt Lake City's Gentile public officials. Arraigned before the bar for well-documented moral turpitude, though, these gentlemen were turned loose while the Mormon policemen who set the snare for them went to prison for two years for entrapment. The "Decoy Girls" left town fast. One of them, Ramona, in Burdick's Institution at the time with feverous peritonitis and in no condition to be moved, was plucked from her bed by Minerva Bohannon and a girl about Ramona's age, scared, looking over their shoulders, and hurried away. "We leave on that train or we leave in the dead wagon," Hindle remembered Minerva saying as they rushed the sick girl out to the waiting carriage. "Pray God we'll never see this town again!" Yet ten years or so after, the same woman was back and apparently living here. Well, we change.

During the watches of the night when Dolores had fallen into childish slumber and the coachman, sent back to await their pleasure after taking Mr. Clarendon home, sat sound asleep in the kitchen alcove, his head on his arms on the table, Hindle ventured to speak of those old days.

"Don't remind me," Minerva said.

"I don't mean to," Hindle said, "only we wondered so often about Ramona and how she got along."

"That day, I'm telling you," Minerva said, "I never thought we'd make it in one piece. But I never been sorry we testified against those g.d. Saints."

"Everybody liked Ramona," Hindle said.

"Yes, we couldn't leave town without her," Minerva said. "And we got her to safety, where she'd be safe. But then—She had an aunt in Sacramento, so I took her there. The aunt wasn't too hospitable. I never went back, and I tell you that's bothered me a lot."

"Well, it shouldn't," Hindle said. (She pronounced absolution whenever she could.) "It's better to be with kinfolk."

"At least I should of wrote, I should of inquired."

"You done your best." To change the subject then, "Remember the doctor that was taking care of Ramona?" Hindle said.

"Do I *remember* him?" Minerva said in such a defamatory tone that Hindle broke in to prevent by anticipation whatever it was she was going to say that might put Doctor out of memory and take from her the efficacy of his grace. "We got married," she said quickly. "We went away together and just kept going. Our two little girls is named Eula and Esther. Then last fall Doctor—I called him that, don't that seem funny, a person's own husband?—why, he died, pitched head first off a wagon. Me and the girls come back here because I was born and raised here and got a sister..."

"I'm sorry for your trouble," Minerva said. "But he was a rare one, wasn't he? And all that difference in your ages! How much difference was there, anyway?"

"A lot," Hindle said, "but we got along."

"I wish I'd had sense enough in my day," Minerva said. "Better an old man's darling than a young man's slave."

"I don't think I was ever too much of his darling."

"Well, he sized you up. But at least he made a doctor out of you, or how did that come about?"

Hindle was beginning a somewhat fanciful tale when Minerva went on to add, "And a good one too, or poor Dolly instead of laying there snug in her bed, warm and breathing, would be laying on a cold slab at the undertaker's with black spots beginning to show and a cloth wrung out of vinegar and salt peter over her cold dead face. And Jim Clarendon's conscience would be hurting like toothache!" Or would it? "You never can tell about men," Minerva said. "He says when he took her away from the club and set her up here he never promised her nothing. And why should he? But he was good to her, and maybe she got to thinking—She'd come up to Commercial Street and bring us stuff, figs or an expensive waist ruined under the arms with sweat, or a nice pair of shoes she bought too small, or gloves with a button off. The girls thought it was a form of bragging. But I think she was lonesome. She'd hold back on the talk though, I could feel it, and the reason was the plans she had, I think. Clear out of reason! To marry Jim. But men with money is spoiled, and before he had the money he had the build and all the rest of it! so women always has been doormats for him to wipe his feet on."

"She should of realized," Minerva went on. "But you know that song 'I Dreamt I Dwelt in Marble Halls'? Dolores really did dream that that was what she would do, dwell with him in that great big barn he's putting up on South Temple that he was foolish enough to show her the plans of! 'Why can't it be me moving in there?' she gets to thinking. 'Riding in his carriage, parading on his arm, going to Europe with my fourteen trunks?' You see them books there on the center table? *Gorham's Gentlewoman's Guide. The Deadly Sins of Social Etiquette. The Code of Style and Title.* What's she reading literature like that for? I'll tell you. To prepare herself! though the actual Mrs. Clarendon wouldn't no more read that bunk than fly to the moon! And then she edged in just a little too close, and everything just flew right out the window. Why didn't she let well enough alone?"

"Because people can't rest," Hindle said. "It's like what Doctor seen on a tombstone one time over in Italy. He was in this graveyard walking around and seen this inscription. Of course it was in their lingo, but he could read it."

"What did it say?"

"It said, *I was well. I would be better. I am here.*"

Minerva looked blank.

"Or in other words *I was doing good, I wanted to do better, but the steps I took to improve my situation, killed me.* See? Like somebody healthy that tries to be healthier, climbs a mountain, falls and breaks their neck. Or a pretty girl that tries to be prettier. She puts white lead on her face, gets poisoned from it and dies. Or a rich person—"

"Now I get it," Minerva said. "*I was well. I would be better. I am a dead duck.* Of course! Dolly's the perfect example. Pressing her luck with Jimbo. Trying for more. She just might of known it wouldn't work."

"Maybe it will," Hindle said. "He might get a divorce and marry her. He certainly acted anxious enough coming here. And anxious after we got here, too—like he really cared."

"He does care. But what he cares about is keeping clear of complications. He told *me* plain enough he's walking out."

"Yes, but the way he bent down and kissed her—"

"What's that noise?" Minerva said.

It sounded like a dog scratching at the door, but when it opened a plump young woman ran in, unbuttoning and throwing off her plush coat before she reached the middle of the room, as if suffocated by the warmth after the cold outside.

"That waist there she's got on," Minerva murmured to Hindle. "That's the one I was mentioning."

"Real lace," the girl said, looking down at it. "It cost forty dollars. Ruined under the arms from sweat, but I managed to fix it. Dolores was always doing the sweetest things! She was so good-hearted." Blinking back tears, she peeped into the bedroom.

"*Is*, not was," Minerva said. "She's still in the land of the living. You and her can go after it hammer and tongs again and pull each other's hair out like you did before."

"Oh, Minerva, what a thing to say. Nobody's gladder than I am if she's going to be all right."

"Well, she is. Thanks to the doctor here."

The girl looked at Hindle in surprise.

"This here's Jewell," Minerva said.

"Pleased to meet you," Hindle said.

"I don't remember telling *you* to come traipsing over," Minerva said.

"You didn't," Jewell said. "Only—Minerva, I don't want to scare you or upset you after the night you've put in, but—"

"But what?" Minerva said, uprearing in her chair.

"Don't get excited now and maybe get apoplexy but—it's Brownie. She started and we thought everything was going to be all right and we'd surprise you when you come home. First I'd look in to see how she was, then Jennie and different ones—but a little while ago—"

"Oh, my God," Minerva said, getting up and running over to the hall tree to grab her fur-lined cape. "You stay here with Dolores till someone takes your place."

"All right," Jewell said, "but things was kind of picking up and—I'm sure Brownie will—"

"*You're* sure? What do you know about anything? Come on, Doctor. Oh, if a one of you had the sense you was born with. Why didn't you come get me?"

"Well, since Jimbo needed you here we thought—"

"*You* thought! Idiots! That's all you are, the whole pack of you. I'd ought to put you out on the street. Come on, Doctor, hurry. Hurry!"

Chapter Thirty-two

✳

BEFORE THEY GOT TO WHERE THEY WERE GOING IN THE CARRIAGE JIM HAD LEFT at their disposal, Hindle found out that her second patient of the evening was to be a little brown dog with a sharp pointed nose and markings that made her look like she had two black eyes. Brownie, her name was, and she was in labor with a litter of offspring that Minerva worried might cause her death, for she was so small and the cur that lay in wait for her at Lagoon when she ran away from them at the Sunday picnic for half the afternoon was feared to be the huge monster they had noticed running around. "You got to save her, Doctor. You got to."

And somehow Hindle did. As she told Serapta the next day, it was really surprising how familiar a book like *Gray's Anatomy* would make you with the galvanic corpus, even a little animal's. But if Brownie hadn't been laying there so pitiful, whimpering but yet her tail trying to wag, and tears in her eyes, and going to go up the flume if something wasn't done—! Minerva was in a state of total collapse. But a girl named Ida stepped forward. Then Brownie starts licking her hand. So Hindle prepared like for a human mother and Ida dropped the chloroform. And what do you think?

"I done a Caesarian section! easy as pie."

"That's all very well, but I *remember* that woman," Serapta said. "And if last night don't show you what respectability is to Mr. Clarendon, I don't know what would!"

"It showed me a lot," Hindle said. "I wish you could of seen where Minerva lives. Everything looks so pretty, colored lamps, crystal drops a-hanging, flowered carpets. Though all *I* seen was going up them long front stairs and through the entry and into Minerva's room. But as we passed a archway with bead curtains, I glanced back and it was like a party going on, people laughing and singing, and here it was nearly daylight! Minerva's got this great big roll-top desk in her room and Brownie was up there in it, on a kind of a folded Indian blanket. I know I was scared because my hand was shaking, but I made it stop. So anyway, now Brownie's got her batch of puppies. The father couldn't of been so big, I don't believe. That Ida's a friendly person! She asked me why it's called a Caesarian section and couldn't hardly believe that thousands of years ago when Julius Caesar was born they had sense enough to cut open his mother's stomach, since he couldn't make it the other way."

"Is she going to live?" Serapta said.

"I don't see why not. I sewed her up just lovely."

"Not the dog, for heaven's sake! The girl that took laudanum! I guess that shows the caliber *he* is, your lovely Mr. Clarendon!"

Yes, Dolores would live. And very well, too, if she didn't spend the money too fast that Jim's lawyer was giving her to go away and leave poor Jim in peace. Minerva was right, he was through with his bit of fluff. His anxiousness had been for himself. (After that night he never saw her again but trundled off to Europe with Mrs. Clarendon, free as a bird. And Dolores the little sap-head moved to Carson City.)

"Would you believe where the white puppy is going when she gets old enough?" Minerva said when Hindle stopped by to see how Brownie was doing. "To the Attorney-General of the Territory's little girl! He showed me her picture, a dear little thing. Believe me, I'd never said yes if it'd been a boy. I wouldn't trust a *boy* as far as the corner!"

THE ANSWER TO ONE QUESTION in Professor Ford's *Question Book without Answers* Hindle certainly knew without having to make a search, and that was, What is the Hippocratic oath? She thought of it the morning after her spirited night as she sat drinking coffee with Serapta. But *try* "not noising abroad sacred secrets" when you have been gone all those hours and people under the same roof want to know where you went and what you did. Noise abroad you must. But sacred secrets would never find a safer receptacle than Serapta. And Lucitie the same.

Lucitie's trustworthiness, however, was more by default. For to her the consecrated pursuits of Dolores, Jim Clarendon and Minerva Bohannon paled to paltry gossip beside what was *really* sacred, Albert and his concerns, his customer Kate, Kate's jealous suitor Apostle Tennant, and Lucitie's own want of assurance with regard to the love of her life. Of *course* she would never repeat what to her hardly seemed worth listening to in the first place. Not that she was so impolite as to say so, but by her vague physical uneasiness Hindle and Serapta guessed that she was only counting the bars till she could come in with her own part-song.

When Lucitie did, it was "loud of love but not of love's delight," and they had heard it often before. Albert didn't know she was alive! And on your afternoon off, how could you keep dressed up and looking nice and your hair curled if all you did was work and perspire? Also, Albert had this enlarged picture of Kate hanging in the shop to show his Lalla Rookh Coiffure that he was looking at how many times a day? Then Kate—if the time ever came when she, instead of just looking at herself and at *Godey's Lady's Book*, looked at *him*—! Don't you know that old saying, Lucitie said. Take a pitcher to the well often enough and it will come home broken?

"How come we haven't heard no mention of Charlotte lately?" Hindle said.

"Yes," Serapta said. "I thought *she* was the fly in the ointment!"

"She was," Lucitie said. "But her mother in West Weber's growth was getting so big she couldn't do her work no more, so her father come and took her home. And when anyone's leaving you know how it is, the good old times comes back, you get to crying and hugging. And Albert never cared for her nor she for him, she claims, which I believe it about Albert but not about her, and a boy she used to like in West Weber is still single. So anyway I give her my ice-wool shawl as a parting gift."

"That was nice," Serapta said, and Hindle nodded.

"I shouldn't of never bothered my head about Charlotte to start with."

"You shouldn't," Hindle said. "Or about Kate either. If she's got the looks and thinks she's as smart as you say she is, she's just waiting for a Archduke to come through here, or John Jacob Astor. She'd never consider a mote in the sunbeam like Albert for one minute!"

Too aghast by this even to speak, Lucitie could only stare at her sister.

"What I mean to say, you shouldn't worry."

"That's right," Serapta agreed. "Most of the things a person worries about never happens."

"It is what you *don't* worry about," Hindle said, "that you got to watch out for!"

"And not falling down in a fit," Serapta said, "when you get too mad."

But no rift occurred between the sisters, and one unusually warm Sunday in late March when the snow had shrunk to a few thin, dirty patches and the crocuses were out, Hindle went up to the Salt Lake House to catch Lucitie before she set off for Albert's. "I know you got your own destination," she said. "But come with me somewheres for a little while. I want to show you something."

"For instance, what?"

For instance, the Clarendon mansion in a muddy expanse of ground piled with building materials. A few days before in passing, Hindle had seen and been stunned by how imposing it was going to be, and because of being *personally acquainted* with its owner felt such a personal connection with its grandeur and distinction that she couldn't rest till someone she knew *saw* it. Will you looky there, she would say. Towers, turrets, fluted roofs, chimneys amongst the clouds. Only just *look*.

Lucitie did look, but coolly, a residue of resentment for Hindle's remark about Albert being but "a mote in the sunbeam" curbing her response. But the next Sunday at Albert's when the work was done (bread baked, floor scrubbed, shirts ironed, new wigs combed out for display), as Lucitie was leaving she asked him as a favor to please go with her to see the most *wonderful* house! It wasn't ready to move into yet and the yard looked awful, but if he didn't almost fall over when he saw it she would eat her hat. Maybe some other time, he said, it's nearly twilight. Oh, no, she said, not nearly, and there'll be a moon, so get your coat. It was so unlike Lucitie to act in opposition to him that out of surprise he agreed to go. But "Oh, my dear," he said after they got there and had gazed awhile at the great pile losing its edges to the dark. "I must tell you that I stand confused."

"What do you mean by that, Albert?"

"I mean, did your stay in England, brief though it might have been, produce nothing?

No standard of true taste? No criterion of excellence? You saw the princely houses," he said reprovingly, his voice filled with pain. "Not only mansions but palaces. And not only palaces but castles. Yet you judge as worth our pilgrimage this—*villa*!"

"Oh, but, Albert!" All pure marble? Six fireplaces? A hundred windows, the plate glass ones in the corners actually *curving* to fit the towers? That thing there on the side? "It's too dark. You can't really see it."

"Alas, I can. The dark doesn't hide its commonness."

"Commonness?" she wailed.

"What do you expect me to say? I did not just *circumvent* those mansions, palaces, and castles I speak of, nor did my father and grandfather before me. We *entered* them. Lord Shelburne's. The Duchess of Portland's—"

"I remember you mentioning her," Lucitie said, anxious to make amends. "The one you said—the Lady in Waiting to the actual *Queen*. The grotto covered with shells! The parrot that had the governess! And once when you was there fastening that diamond crown onto her head so it wouldn't budge, her maid was down on the floor pinning bunches of fresh violets all around the hem of her dress!"

"Fastening her tiara," he corrected her. "Yes, twenty pounds' worth of violets, to fade in an hour."

"A hundred dollars in our money! Think of that."

"Savoir vivre, savoir faire," he said, a little mollified.

"I really do believe, though," she ventured, "that if you could see this place here in the daytime—"

"Lucitie," he said patiently. "I *know* what it is. By night or by day. It's a villa!"

The word was new to her. "Please don't get mad, but why is that so terrible?"

"Because it is middle-class."

The scorn with which he said this made her heart sink. For had she ever thought of it (which she never did), "middle class" to her would have been the quite spiffy division of society that could rent a horse and buggy from the livery stable, go to the dentist to get their teeth filled with gold instead of pulled out by the roots, and have a week's vacation every year. She herself was "laboring" class, of which she became aware by sometimes overhearing Mr. Birdwood (who lived off his wife and so had lots of time to talk about these matters to other gentlemen) on the back veranda. It wasn't what she would have chosen, but nothing to be ashamed of either, not like being a windblown old Indian or tattered hobo. But hearing "middle-class" said so contemptuously about so grand a structure as the Clarendon house made her realize for the first time how very lowly *she* must be, and when Albert turned and walked away and she caught up with him, she wanted to slip her hand through his arm but kept clear and didn't, lowered by now to such a low degree.

But halfway down the block when the three shapes loomed up out of the darkness and plowed into them (changing the direction of motion of both their lives forever), out went her lowly hand to grab and thrust him behind her. But this the hulking figures would not permit. They were there to fight him, and once she had regained her feet after being yanked loose from him and shoved sideways so hard she fell down, fight *her* too, not realizing how the protective instinct, to say nothing of love, in certain individuals can generate the ferocity of a large carnivorous feline quadruped and also that when she fell it was on a stout limb recently blown down. The battle was soon over. Yelping like curs, their assailants fled in the direction of the avenues, and Lucitie, her lowliness forgotten, threw down her thick branch and turned to attend to Albert. He was still on his feet, which showed what a brave hero he had been. She told him so over and over with her arm tight around him to try to stop his shaking as she escorted him home.

What she should have done when they got there was leave him and go home herself to the Salt Lake House if she still wanted a job. Eight o'clock was the deadline, and Mrs. Birdwood watched the time. But when Lucitie lit the lamp, drew the curtains and took a look at Albert, how could she go? He was so pale! And when he peeked in the glass and saw the lump on his temple and the dried blood on his face he staggered back, clutching his heart, and fell into a chair. But the blood had come from where he bit his lip and the abrasion was negligible, as Lucitie found when she came with a basin of water and washrag to wash off his beautiful face. He had defended himself so well, she told him, and her, that they had come away unhurt—hardly a scratch! so he mustn't be frightened— from what could have been a real roughing up. Which it wasn't, she thought as she was making the tea, because not meant to be. What had one of their attackers said? "You with the phyzog like a doll's caboose, lay off!" Choctaw to Albert, but with clear meaning to Lucitie: You with a face like a doll's bum, steer clear or be sorry. In short, another threat from Apostle Tennant, not necessarily marked by urgency. No one need stand guard that night, she was nearly sure. She could leave, the house would not be stormed. With moral courage she could run on home. Moral courage she came up short on.

When she appeared at the hotel at a quarter past five the next morning, it took the best part of an hour to explain things to Mrs. Birdwood. But as everything had turned out like a love story with a happy ending and Mrs. Birdwood's heart was a romantic one, she not only forgave her and dabbed arnica salve on the abrasion Lucitie didn't know she had (and Albert either hadn't noticed or hadn't mentioned) on her cheek but let her go to her tiny cell up under the eaves for an hour's lie-down before starting work. Up there she took off her corset to see if a poked-through stay was what was hurting her side and looked down at a contusion as big as her hand across her hipbone. The sight amazed her, for of course it and the bruise on her face must have come from some kind of physicality during last night's strife, but all she could remember was battering with her branch and nothing hurting *her* anywhere at all!

"Please don't go yet."

"Of course not, Albert. And leave you all alone?"

Long after midnight she made more tea, this time with cheese toasted on bread, and as she set their places saw him touching his bitten lip, fingering the lump on his forehead and gingerly flexing his arms and legs. "Don't worry," she said. "Thanks to you, we're both of us in one piece."

"What was it that one of those ruffians said?" he said.

"Oh, just foolishness," she said. "But the time might of come for you not to be too stubborn about Kate anymore, even if her hair *is* such a walking advertisement for the shop." He sat at the table too tired to chew or lift his cup. "So, all right," she said, "the place for you is bed." He got up and tottered there and lay down heavily. "Not on top of the covers, it's too cold. Get up and get undressed and put your night shirt on." Somnambulant, he obeyed.

But once tucked in, he became animated and so they talked, him half sitting up, her perched on the side of the bed, and he confessed that *he* didn't think he should be too stubborn either, that Kate was indeed the problem and that he must write her a letter. "What a good idea," Lucitie said. "Tell her you've had enough of Apostle Tennant's jealous fears and him camping on your trail, and tonight was the last straw." But that wasn't what Albert had in mind. No, what he would say, he said, was that he couldn't believe anyone could change so much as Kate had in just a few short months! from a nice young lady to a perfect monster of self-centeredness and conceit. And if she wanted to know, he had decided he would as soon have a hedgehog from Madagascar as a customer as her! so if she would make herself scarce from now on he would be ever grateful. Thank you. I remain. Lucitie's eyes widened at this, for she never expected a disquisition against *Kate* (about whom he had never said an unkind word before) when the evil-doer in the case was her suitor! But then it came to her that this must be some kind of manly shift beyond woman's comprehension. So she only said people do change like that sometimes, it's awful.

"I started charging her," he said.

"And that was what brought out the worst?"

"I couldn't believe it."

"Well. I guess it would serve the purpose either way. Her fault—his—so long as the Apostle's drawed off."

Albert nodded even as he sighed, for he would miss so much the lingual sounds of home that Kate had brought him.

"Well, don't you mind. There's all kinds of heads of hair. They'll start a-coming and they'll *love* to pay."

"I don't know about *that*," he said. "But a new lady did come in the other day for a waving and a bottle of Marechal. Very well dressed, diamond earrings. Mrs. Kincaid, she said her name was."

"Why, I know her! With a pug nose?"

"Retroussé," he said.

"Rich! But not a bit stuck-up. Her and Mrs. Birdwood and Mrs. O'Naughton was poor young girls together. They'll sit in the kitchen at the Salt Lake House and talk and laugh. Though I notice Mrs. Birdwood don't go see *them*."

"Charming chapeau. Bird of paradise feathers," Albert said.

"I've saw her *wear* that hat!" Lucitie said with pride. "And you know something? Once *she* gets to coming, the next clatter out of the box will be Mrs. Clarendon, because if I'm not mistaken *they* are old friends, too. And you know who Mrs. Clarendon is? Her and her husband is the ones building that mansion you and me seen tonight. They've got so much money they can't even count it. Oh, excuse me!"

He raised an eyebrow.

"I said 'mansion' instead of 'middle-class villa.'"

"The one word is all that's necessary," he said dryly. "'Villa' by itself contains the attribute." Then Albert did something he had never done before. He reached out and gave her shoulder a gentle pat.

Elated beyond the bounds of sobriety by this, she almost came out with *another* particular about Mrs. Clarendon: that Mr. Clarendon was an unfaithful husband, that he'd kept a bit of fluff and that the bit of fluff had tried to kill herself. But, respectful of Albert's refinement, she held back.

"Yes, Mrs. Kincaid may be a harbinger," he said. "One hopes so. But you know, Lucitie, sometimes I think I'd ought to go back to England."

"Oh, no, you mustn't do that, Albert!"

"But then I think—the shop is taking hold. And what would be there for me now?"

"Nothing! They treated you terrible."

"And when I consider—my ancestors were French."

"Well, there you are. There's no comparison."

"And mountain air is more salubrious than living at sea-level."

"Oh, it is!"

"And you're a good friend, Lucitie, you really are."

"Oh, Albert, I *wish* I was, I truly do!"

"Without friendship, society is but meeting, as the poet says."

"Truer words were never—"

He reached out and for the first time in their acquaintance took her work-worn hand. "Why, you're cold," he said. "You're cold as ice."

"No, I'm not," she said, her teeth chattering.

He threw the bedclothes back and she slipped in just as she was, not even unfastening her neckband and leaving her feet outside in their button shoes at first, but later, not even conscious she was doing so, for they were talking with such seriousness at the time, taking them off and dropping them down beside the bed. Then they were both cozy and warm under the covers, and gradually she worked in the harmless remark that she held it as her opinion and many other people did too that…a wife wasn't an entirely different breed from just your friend that comes in and does your washing and so on, bakes your biscuits, and she could still work for Mrs. Birdwood and contribute. And something that should be faced was, a Gentile *bachelor* coming to Salt Lake City to live was about as popular as a stagecoach robber in a black mask with two revolvers, while if the bachelor got *married*, why, the attitude would totally change.

And I could help in the shop because…

Because her hairdressing talent was what took her to England in the first place, and brought him and her together on the ship coming home, and on the train, and finally here in this bed under one counterpane, she considered mentioning it but didn't, saying aloud instead that she could help in the shop *if he would teach her*.

"With pleasure," he said. "My Lalla Rookh Coiffure, my Lorna Doone, and braiding, crimping, puffing. Waterfalls! Melting soap…and how to make a rinse when summer comes from the yellow powder inside lilies, and rubbing red geraniums into a paste…"

"I'll try my best. And Albert dear, besides—" She then remarked with so much delicacy he hardly knew what she said (but took it to heart) that *she would always keep him safe from harm*.

When Hindle and Serapta heard about the lurking ambuscade up near the Clarendon mansion, and the fight, and Albert (!) putting the three big roughnecks to rout, and how Lucitie and Albert were going to *get married*, they said it sounded to them like the President pinning the medal on the General that won the war. One thing was certain. Till the world was safe for Albert, Lucitie would never close both eyes at once.

Which she didn't for quite some time even though his letter to Kate served its purpose, Kate answered as insultingly as Lucitie thought to herself she was entitled to, then stayed away. Then he too, Apostle Tennant, ceased to exist as a source of mental distress. Actually as a source of anything (including Kate's living), for one Sunday afternoon in Tabernacle he slumped forward and died of compression of the heart, his jealousy and all his other flickering combustibles put out forever. Then stipendless Kate, dressed in black satin, was seen riding around with a gentleman in an open carriage. Then she dropped from sight. So at last Lucitie could close both eyes at once and sleep the sleep of the just. A just galley-man at a bank of oars, for, still employed by Mrs. Birdwood uptown, by Albert at home, under his tutelage in the shop, and also in charge of wig-block combing, when night fell Lucitie tumbled too! asleep before her head could touch the pillow. Unless…But *that* did not happen very often. And just as well, for with so much to do, how could she have breast-fed anyone?

As the shop prospered and Albert became at first used to and then (like many a slave-owner before him) addicted to his creature's arts, employments and labors, he came not to fancy her working out, especially as she didn't earn much. It was a proud day for Lucitie therefore when, ordered to do so by the husband she pretended wanted to give her a life of dainty ease, she came to Mrs. Birdwood and told her she had to quit. Quit! Had Mrs. Birdwood the least idea she was going to perform such an act of treachery just when the couple from New York was driving everyone crazy and her legs was filling up with water, she would never (in this world so full of ingratitude) have lent her her wreath of wax orange blossoms, turned over her parlor for the ceremony or frosted Lucitie's wedding cake with her own hands! She would also have thought twice about the pair of pillow-cases with crocheted lace. And she *had* been going to will her her brooch. What could Lucitie say? She felt like Judas Iscariot all the way home.

WHETHER THEY WERE FRENCH, GERMAN or what they were no one knew, but Mr. and Mrs. Cibaria, the most demanding denizens ever to stay at the Salt Lake House, if they were not—him with his little starched mustache and pearl-buttoned spats, and her in her feathers—aliens from God's mercies, they came very close. Not rich, certainly. Would rich people take on a job that brought them back to the hotel each night as dusty, mussed and harassed with sweaty toil as field hands? Though as time went by and their unheard-of commission—to "decorate" the new Clarendon house with the wagonloads of furnishings, fixtures, fizgigs and accessorial supplementaries the Clarendons had spent years in Europe buying—neared completion, and other helpers moved in, rug layers, drapery hangers and such as that, the two returned at evening about the way they had set off that morning, as clean-handed, soignée and smug as if *they* had money themselves.

Mrs. Cibaria claimed to have been born in New York City, but when she came to Albert for a henna pack (after the age of forty there is no such thing as "natural" red hair, red being the most fragile of all hair colors and the soonest to fade, Albert said) he took a look at the wide gap between her front teeth, her bellying bosom and duodecimo feet, heard her say a few harsh, grating words and—since his grandfather had had an Embassy customer just like her—pronounced her Polish-born. Which she must have been, because when he treated her the way his grandfather said was the only way you could treat a Pole—like dirt under your feet or be eaten alive—she became subordinate at once. Indeed, during the Cibarias' stay in town, chilly Albert was the only person Mrs. Cibaria paid deference to, except of course her employers—and for all anyone at the hotel knew, she might even have been insolent to *them* when they came home to their new house with fires going, fresh flowers in vases, servants moving about, and even hot water for a bath in case anyone wanted one.

Before the site became animated, though, the Cibarias departed and their finished "decorating" was still a still life, Albert alone received an invitation to come with his wife and take a look at what they had accomplished, an honor that left *him* indifferent, as it naturally would, he who had traversed palaces, but sent Lucitie into transports. Wouldn't Hindle nearly die of envy? Hindle did, not letting it show. But what a privilege! Didn't she desperately wish—!

IT IS NOT TRUE, OF course, that say the word "wish" and some sufflation like the breath of the Holy Ghost goes to work to grant it. But sometimes the utterance *does* move some airy element to activity, and one fine day…Wasn't it you who wished for such and such? Well, behold! Hindle would be starting up that grand staircase between the bronze boy and girl statues on the newel posts holding up the branches lit with amber globes, she would be going down that wide upstairs hall to that polished door, turning the silver doorknob and walking into that bedroom all pale blue satin and Brussels lace. She would hear that china cottage clock covered with roses and tiny birds chime once, chime twice, glance up worriedly and see the back of it and her own white face reflected in the mirror over the mantel. Didn't you want to be here? Wasn't that you?

Mrs. Clarendon decided against a bunch of wormy old antiques. The new, the most recherché was for her. The Salt Lake Tribune printed the story of the housewarming on the front page. Twenty-eight rooms, area for a ballroom on the third floor, twenty-two-foot ceilings, corner towers, satinwood, rosewood, two dining rooms, kitchen of solid slate, ten-foot-wide airtight cookstove, built-in safes, one for the family silver made out of a ton of Ophir ore, one for Napoleon brandy and other fine liquors, one for valuables such as the Russian necklace of sapphires and a diamond bracelet that goes around the arm above the elbow five times and has three hundred diamonds running along it, which Mrs. Clarendon will be wearing on the night of the entertainment. If you're going to do something do it right, states Colonel Clarendon. (He has become a Colonel in the meanwhile.) Hot water flows through the towel racks to keep the towels warm. A carriage house, a stable, blooded horses, six house flunkies, two yard men, a stableman, coachman and man of all work. Only one other set of china like it in the world! Peacock-blue satin draperies, four hundred and two and three-fourths yards at three English pounds per yard (fifteen dollars), figure it out for yourself. Drawing room carpet alone cost five thousand dollars. Nothing will wear out. Mrs. Clarendon's gown…Colonel Clarendon…orchestra…roses…champagne corks popping like the Battle of Antietam…

The Tribune said it would like to be able to turn the clock back to twenty or thirty years ago, and see what the bon ton, the elegantly clad company at the party, was doing *then*. Bent over pick, shovel and sluice box some of the haughtiest now, sweat running down their bare backs, or keeping a saloon or working in a boarding house or freighting over the mountains or hammering up a shack. Sleeping at night on a rough board bedstead with poles across for slats and a mattress and pillow stuffed with dried bulrushes; old blankets, bedbugs, lice; a filled-up private place of ease out back; soap made out of soup-fat and clay. Eating pork and beans, greasy steak, spuds, pickles, dried-apple sauce. No swans then of spun sugar and isinglass, no consommé de volaille, galantine of turkey, pheasant, bécasses et bécassines, and twenty-seven kinds of cake and candy.

But such are the opportunities in this great land of ours if people are willing to roll up their sleeves! Or, as Minerva said when she read the account, in some cases roll up their skirts at the right moment. There were ladies up there dancing in their finery of no different caliber, at one time at least, than the demoiselles under her own roof right this minute. Luck, she said. The luck of the Irish. She said it again to Jimbo when he dropped in for a visit, and he laughed like a good sport. But he didn't like it very well. He didn't like the Tribune bringing up the past like that either, and said some of the ginks were saying too bad it wasn't like the old days when you could teach a bunch of sonsabitches, like whoever it was running the paper, a lesson!

THE STORY SPECIFIED PAINTINGS BY Holzapfel, Hurst and Spada, but no mention was made of a local artist named Stig Fogelmarck, for he was not represented. Had he been, as he told the Clarendon steward, that dining chamber would have been a place people would have come miles to see.

"I believe it," the steward said.

"Are they still around here?" Stig said. "My Irish kings? There were three of them—"

"In the back of the cloakroom," the steward said, "where I put 'em the day you brought 'em in."

"What are my chances to get them back?"

"Very good," the steward said, "better than if they had been Mary Queen of Scots, Lighthorse Lee and the Globe-walker! for in that case I would have nabbed 'em myself when Jim went back on his bargain (though remember you was paid), but I never was too fond of the Irish. Don't carry that to Jim."

"Never fear," Stig said. He went in the cloakroom, got the rolled-up canvases and left in haste, for he had a hunch he might sell them to Mrs. Auerbach, whose ceiling he had painted blue with gold stars.

Mrs. Auerbach knew at once they were kings, but that they were (to the detailed description of the Catholic priest hired by Mr. Clarendon to supply his artist with the needed historical particulars) Niall of the Nine Hostages, Loiquire being met, embraced and having his crown knocked off by clumsy St. Patrick when he arrived in Dublin, and Toirdelbach Ua Conchobair in front of the first castle ever to be built in Ireland, she had no notion. And as nothing Hibernian would ever cross her threshold but linen, whiskey, a wolf-hound and an assortment of freckle-faced kitchen mavourneens, she would never find out.

Just as one bit of bad luck can start a run to where a man can break his finger up the posterior opening of his own alimentary canal, so a little *good* luck can do the opposite, and for Stig that sale to Mrs. Auerbach was auspicious. The Baby Chick sign he painted brought him an order for a sign from Eldridge's Wholesale Groceries and Undertaking Supplies. And soon came notice of an inheritance in Denmark! not large, but enough to allow his stopping work to attempt something he had dreamed of for a long time, paint a traveling panorama of the history of the Church of Jesus Christ of Latter-day Saints.

But he had no more than bought his sixty feet of canvas, wooden scaffolding and array of paints and brushes than he took down with what Hindle diagnosed as pneumonia, lay sick for almost two months and might have died but for her stimulants, hot applications, poultices to the head, rubbing of the hands (he would not let her touch or even see his feet), administration of camphor, quinine and carbonate of iron, and Serapta's nursing. During the day, whenever she could leave the children, Serapta would run out to him, and the nights he was the worst she slept on blankets on the floor. He grew childishly dependent, fretted that he could only sleep when she was in the room and would not take nourishment except from her hand.

Then he began calling her my love, my dove, my undefiled (at first in delirium but later in his right senses), saying comfort me with flagons for I love thee and remarks such as that, which changed her so much in every way, form, substance, organ, tissue and nutritious juices that Hindle could hardly believe the fair woman she now saw shooting her vivid ray as she ran in and out (generally out, leaving undone tasks behind) was really Serapta! And when Stig was convalescent and sitting up in a chair and for the first time went so far as to say he had had enough of her leaving him, from now on she had to stay! for the sake of their happiness and so that he could paint a panorama the equal of Bartholomaus Zeitblom's Blaubeuren altarpiece, she became, at least for that one day, a flaming beauty.

But of course she couldn't do that, live with him.

Why not?

Hindle was the one delegated to tell him.

Marriage? In his weakened state he trembled. But then, "All right," he said, "if that's the whack, then that's the whack. We must march out under arms with colors flying and drums beating."

"The whack?" Hindle said.

"Sailor talk," he said. "We'll do it. Take each other for Time and Eternity in the Endowment House."

She hurried to Serapta with the news. And the smelling salts.

Chapter Thirty-three

*

THE ENDOWMENT HOUSE WAS NOT A PLACE WHERE YOU COULD GO AND JUST knock. Only the worthy could enter. But worthy was what Serapta felt she was. She had obtained her Patriarchal Blessing, fasted on Fast Day, handed in her tithing and, although as nervous as a churnful of milk about to become butter, she stood up in meeting one Sunday afternoon and bore her testimony. Without digesting it as yet, she had also got to page eighty-six of the Book of Mormon. But Stig was perfect, his piety could hardly be praised amiss. True, he had not up to now (so far as anyone knew) provided with human habitations any of the spirits crowding around the Pearly Gates like emigrants lined up to get off Ellis Island, but he was only forty-three. And Serapta too, a little younger, could still multiply and replenish the earth. As she made her way to the bishop of the ward's residence, therefore, Stig being as yet too weak for the long walk, to ask about, and maybe even be tendered, the "recommends" they needed to "go through" and marry in the Endowment House, she had no doubt her errand would bode well.

The bishop's door was quickly opened by his own self (a ward member for many years but only lately appointed bishop), and as numerous family members receded through doorways and up a staircase he ushered her into the dining room, brought forward a chair, told her his predecessor's joke about the old woman who said her husband told her to go to the devil "so I came to you, Bishop!" to put her at ease, then asked what brought her out in this blustery weather. When she told him, he rummaged in the drawers of the buffet till he found the form he wanted, plucked a bottle of ink and a pen-holder off a corner shelf and seated himself at the dining table with its stained and askew tablecloth. "Now," he said with a twinkle, "nomenclature of both."

Stig's name was what caused the hitch. Not while the bishop was writing it down but a little later, when he drew his head back and stared in an astonished way as if it had come alive and was starting to crawl off the paper. "Would this be the sign painter over on Fifth East?" he asked.

"Yes, sir," she said. "But he's not only a sign painter, he's a beautiful artist, and guess what? He's going to paint a panorama of the *history of the church* to take around and show in the different wards—"

"Oh?" the bishop said. "And who said he could do *that*?"

"Does he have to have permission?" she said. "He's not going to *charge* or nothing. Though perhaps he *could* charge and give the money to the—poor. People will be lining up to get in, you watch and see," she went on. "Sixty feet *long*? And all hand *painted*? The differentest, most out of the ordinary—"

He held up his hand. "You've nailed it there, madam," he said, laying down his pen and capping the bottle of ink. "Because if this here individual," he tapped the written name on the page before him as one might tap an opponent's chest to emphasize a point, "is the individual that comes to mind at the moment, and I don't know who else it could be, why, out of the ordinary should be his middle name!" While she watched in anxious suspense, he doubled the form over and tore it in two.

"But he's a beautiful artist," she faltered.

"He's an insubordinate, has been from the beginning, and got about as much call for what you're asking as I have to go to Sunday school in my wife's *hat*."

"Oh, sir!" she said, "what are you talking about?"

"Talking about gall," he said. "Go home and speak to him. Ask him, 'Where's the feet you want this pair of shoes for?' See what he says."

"Feet?" she said, baffled. "Shoes?"

"Ask him," he repeated, wadding up the pieces of paper and letting them fall on the table, then brushing them aside.

When she tottered over home's threshold, Hindle sat her down, wrung out a washrag in cold water, handed it to her to press to her tear-stained face and hurried to the cabinet for the tincture of paregoric. "Now," she said, dispensing a large dose. "What happened?"

Serapta hardly knew, the shock to her system had been so great. It might have been her fault too, bringing up Stig's panorama. Why had she ever done such a foolish thing?

"Start from the beginning," Hindle said.

"The beginning went fine," Serapta said, "but all of a sudden—"

When she got through talking, Hindle said she shouldn't blame herself for anything, because once it dawned on the bishop who Stig *was*, why, that put the kibosh on the whole thing.

"What do you mean, who Stig was?" Serapta said.

"Who he was in California," Hindle said, "because that's where it all goes back to, you can depend. Probably back to the time of the Reformation—"

"I bet you something," Serapta said airily, the paregoric by this time having taken effect, "I bet it was just some rambunctious thing like boys will do! that didn't amount to a hill of beans."

BUT VERY FEW BOYS DO anything as rambunctious as to deprive themselves of what constitutes the man. That, however, was what this one had done, though when Brother Lyman found him that morning in the blood-soaked hay he had no idea that that was the situation he was looking at. What happened? Who did this? Striking his chest with a stained hand, the trespasser (for that was what he was, Stig had no barn of his own) seemed to be saying, I did it to myself. Yourself? Are you crazy? Brother Lyman stood there staring down at him like he'd been hit in the head with a rock. And that was how he was standing when Brother Strype came by to borrow an adze. After Brother Strype came Brother Fraser, then Brother Cannon and Brother Roberts, not because the news had spread that something peculiar had taken place in the barn down the road but because Brother Lyman's yard, due to its centrality, was kind of a gathering place for the men in the neighborhood, especially in the off season.

He sensed them like tall trees that came and stood in the empty field he had lain down in, their talk was the wind soughing through the branches. "If he ain't up the flume he's very close," Brother Cannon said. "Very close," Brother Fraser said. But no, he stirred and fetched a sobbing breath. "Conceivably they can survive a situation like this," Brother Roberts said, "though why anyone would *want* to I can't imagine." Brother Strype couldn't imagine why they would either. He thought Brother Lyman should go in the house and get his gun for pure humanity's sake and they would draw straws to see who would administer the—there was a name for it. "I know, I've heard it," Brother Fraser said. Brother Strype was for *everybody* going home and getting their guns and some outside party loading, unbeknownst, live ammunition, blanks, and that way no one would know who was responsible for the—there was a certain name. But Brother Lyman wouldn't hear to it. "Coop de something is what you're trying to say, but that there's no better than murder," Brother Lyman said. "And he's on my property, so I got the say." Brother Fraser agreed. "He's right, he's on Brother Lyman's property so he's got the say." "Does having the say include giving him house-room?" Brother Roberts said. "He's a human being, he can't lay here like a dog!"

But that didn't set too well with Brother Lyman or with any of them, giving him house-room. Impressionable children, nervous wives, plaster not drying, a roof half off, the reasons for disavowal were many, none of them the true one, superstitious alarm—now that the men had time to take in the situation in all its dimensions. For you get cozy with an Aaron divested of his Ephod like this, so to speak, a condition bound to saturate the air with feebleness, and next thing you know you got a case of a fellow with a woman's hash to settle and nothing to settle it with.

"Listen," Brother Cannon said, "I know what we can do. You probably heard of the battle of Culloden. My own great uncle was in it! on the English side. Well, *in* that battle a soldier got the same kind of a swipe took at him by the enemy as the sinner we're looking at right here, a Highlander's claymore sheared him through his thigh-piece and good-bye, Willy." "You don't mean to say so," Brother Roberts said. "What's a claymore?" Brother Strype inquired. "A Highlander's sword that's sharpened along both edges," Brother Cannon said. "But as I was saying—the battle come to an end, the English won, they went around the field stepping over the dead and tending to the wounded except if they had kilts on! which got their skull bashed in. And here laid this soldier, a lot like him," Brother Cannon said, inclining his head towards the stricken man, "and being as he was a Englishman he got tended to. But quite peculiarly, so the story goes." "You mean they tried to sew it back on?" Brother Fraser said. "No," Brother Cannon said with an admonishing frown, "I do not mean that."

"Is *his* around here somewheres?" Brother Roberts said, looking around. "Not that I seen," Brother Lyman said. "But it can't be too far off, I wouldn't think." "So what about this soldier?" Brother Fraser said, turning to Brother Cannon. "Well, they thought they was doing him a favor," Brother Cannon said, "and blamed if it didn't turn out they must of been, though tell this to some of these big-head doctors with the magnifying glasses and they will scream like a eagle! but the fellow come through with flying colors, got old, got rich, my father's uncle knew him till the very end."

"So what was it they *done* for him so fast?" Brother Strype said. "Him with his willy stripped off and the blood a-dripping?" "I'll tell you," Brother Cannon said. "They carried him to a manure pile in back of a cowshed on the edge of the battlefield and stuck him in it feet first up to here, that's what they done—a lot of people don't know this but manure is very healing—and there he stayed till he got over it." "*Over* it," Brother Fraser said. "How could anybody get over a thing like that?" "What I want to know," Brother Roberts said, "is why he had to be *planted* thataway. Why didn't they just plaster the manure on, like a poultice?" "Because you plant something, it keeps out, well, the air," Brother Cannon said. "I personally don't know," Brother Strype said, shaking his head. "I'm from Missouri," Brother Fraser said. "Well, boys, we got the best chance in the world to put it to the test right here and now," Brother Lyman said, "for right out through that doorway there stands as nice a manure pile as you are likely to see, so let's just do what Brother Cannon says and watch what happens." "Don't lay it at *my* door," Brother Cannon said. "All I said was it worked that time at Culloden." "So maybe it will again," Brother Lyman said. "Unless someone has got a better idea?"

A little later, with one accord, they carried Brother Fogelmarck out behind the barn and wimbled him in deep enough so they could waggle him back and forth a little but have him stay fixed at the one end in the manure pile like a fence pole, then left him to live or die as God would see fit. And there ended their kindness to their fellow creature, though not a man among them but what was compassionate, kind, had "laid on hands" while praying for the infectiously sick, even took turns watching through the night and breathing in their noxious exhalations. But a case like the one before them, beclouded, of dark import, hiding who knew what causes of manifest effects on masculinity! was a risk that none felt *he* could assume. Still, they allowed their womenfolk to take turns furnishing the sufferer with food and water and to perform other small favors such as to provide shade when the sun got hot with a sturdy black umbrella anchored in the manure.

The women did these things bemused, for all had had personal experience with men's intractable love of their bodily organ. That he for whom they were caring had pruned and tossed *it* away like you would lop off a twig from a vine they could hardly imagine.

Or think that the men's idea of treatment for him had any chance of success. In a heaving mass like that of stinks and maggots? but they did not argue, accepting the fact that for an injury so wrought and so male in connotation the men might know by natural descent what to do, while women would have no idea.

Sister Lyman scoffed at that. "He will burn to a crisp with fever and be found dead," she said. "I hope not before we get a *hint* at least of why he done it," Sister Fraser said. "Not out of idle curiosity but for the general good." "I hope so too," Sister Cannon said. Once he did murmur something about a horrible vision but would not say what it was or if his self-inflicted mayhem had come about because of it. Sister Lyman mentioned the buttons the Lamanites chewed sometimes. Maybe he got hold of some of whatever *them* were? "Maybe, but the Lamanites didn't go around cutting nothing off," Sister Fraser said, "you can be sure of that." "Well, if he *did* chew on something I'd like to know what it was," Sister Roberts said. "I know who *I* would give it to," Sister Fraser said. "Me too," Sister Cannon said. "My husband. Waving his property about like it was some kind of wonderful rabbit's foot, when truth to tell it would as soon be the death of you nine months up the line as look at you." "Don't I know," Sister Lyman said, "my cousin Belle dying last year of lying-in. Four babes and her not twenty years old." "And that excuse of theirs," Sister Fraser said, "about the heavenly spirits wanting to come down and be earthly! in human shape provided by you-know-what." "Pumped out by the wholesale," Sister Cannon said. "Not to change the subject," Sister Lyman said, "but did you ever see the like of how they're steering clear of the whole situation? Why, since the poor thing's been out there in that manure pile isn't nothing in pants even come *near* the place, and my old man's plumb left for Iron County."

He suffered, dozed and dreamed, came to himself and wondered at the sheen of what he reared up out of like the fleur-de-lis marking the north on a compass. Flies that looked like jewelry buzzed around, green, gold and of a sapphire hue, and the stars were diamonds every night. Not real diamonds, fake, but what they *did* up there was genuine enough, constellating our earthly lives. The fate they handed *him* was noised abroad but paled in comparison with Blood Atonement, a mania just then being rumored throughout the kingdom. Paled because a castrate after all had a chance to *live*, while a man holding still to have his throat cut (so his hot blood's smoke rising to heaven would expiate his sins) would last about two seconds. And death, of course, would get the public notice. But even in Utah's badlands, where the fad started of cutting the throats of sinners to save their souls, such an extinguishment was rare, and in the Mormon outpost of San Bernardino it made no headway at all.

Not that sinners, reprobates and sly offenders didn't live *there* like anywhere else. A headstrong girl turned down a man high up in the church because of his white-filmed eye and the fur on his tongue (and got the licking of her life). One time a calf was stolen, the Roberts lost a shift off their clothesline, pies had vanished cooling on a sill. But of course that could have been thieving Mojaves. The Lord's name was taken in vain, the Ten Commandments went against. Many a wife and house had been coveted. Maid-servants would have been coveted too, oxen and asses also, had any lived around there at the time, which none did. And oddly enough, there in San Bernardino the reading of the Bible betimes was looked upon as if not a crime, at least a misdemeanor. One of which the Danish painter was several times seen to be guilty. Now why would he be doing that? more than one person wondered. With the Book of Mormon at hand, the Doctrine and Covenants and Pearl of Great Price, why would he be rummaging through Scripture? once or twice even at Sunday school, and when he should have been at work. Not to say the Bible didn't *count*. But as Joseph Smith, their own dear Prophet, said, it counted only insofar as it was translated correctly. Which would not have been a problem except that if Joseph was the only man on earth (which he declared himself to be) able to tell which parts were translated correctly and which parts were not, and if a mob came along and *killed* him (which they did) before he had a chance to *tell* anyone, don't that leave things very much up in the air? In a land like ours, however, where Protestant principles long severed from the Roman communion hold sway, to cast off the *Bible* would be like repu- diating soap or the Winchester carbine. So where members of the Church of Jesus Christ of Latter-day Saints dwell the Good Book dwells also, large and with a Concordance, as a parlor embellishment and place to press a flower and keep family records. But as to *reading* it, that, the Saints of the Last Dispensation leave to the Gentiles, while the Saints themselves draw from the clanking Book found hidden like fairy gold in the Hill Cumorah that which, uncreated and eternal, subsists more in the essence of the Deity than all the other evangels in the world put together!

Like his fellow Mormons, Brother Fogelmarck possessed a Bible, but his was small, the size of a deck of cards. Had he kept his distance it would have done no harm. Though what the Bible had to do with his wretched state did not come out until Sister Penrose, on her way down the lane with his supper one evening, impulsively broke off a beautiful stalk of meadow-sweet to take along and stick in the wallow beside him, never thinking to elicit by this small gesture the response she did. But she had no more than presented and tried to anchor it than he said something in a murmur and next thing she knew was holding something out to her that from the looks of it in the dusk could have been a bat or anything (his own dried and blackened appendage, for all she knew!), and she was jumping back with a stifled scream when a last ray of sunshine lit it up and she saw the tiny Testament on his palm. "Oh," she said apologetically, "I'm sorry," and stretched forth her hand. "You wanted me to—?"

No, she was mistaken. He drew it back. But as silence ensued, those low and muttered tones of his she'd heard seemed to leave on the air an answer to what had been answerless. Must have! for, busy as she had been trying to make the meadow-sweet keep from falling over in the dunghill, she had not been listening, yet when she sped off home a text—St. Matthew, nineteen, twelve—echoed in her mind, and why would it do that unless he'd spoken? (Perhaps what hears of us is not always ears.) And was not such speaking an act of intimation? That was how she took it, anyway, whispered it over and over as she ran so as not to forget it and was still saying it when, breathless in her own parlor, she opened the Bible as big as a baby's coffin that hadn't been opened for so long (since Grandma Penrose died) it squeaked like a door on rusty hinges. She hunted until she found the verse she was sure he had named.

And if it did not proclaim—by the way it fit the bill in *regard* to him—eternal fitness to the relations inherent in the nature of things, it certainly came close. "For there are some eunuchs," it said, "which are so born from their mother's womb, and there are some eunuchs, which were made eunuchs of men; and there be eunuchs which have made themselves eunuchs for the kingdom of heaven's sake. He that is able to receive it, let him receive it…" She looked up reflectively, holding the stiff pages open with her flattened hand. It seemed like she had heard he was raised a Lutheran, so the Bible would be famil-iar territory. Did he always know this verse? Or did he just happen onto it one day, like a man wandering the wilderness might happen onto an old abandoned mine-shaft and fall down it? She studied the words again. Well, he wasn't "born so" from his mother's womb, or there'd have been no bloody knife and wound. And he wasn't "made…of men," or the news of *that* would have got around. So all that was left was "for the kingdom of heaven's sake," which she supposed ought to make a person feel uplifted but which for some reason engulfed her with near grief, it was (in their pious setting) so very obvious. Nevertheless, she was sure it was the answer! so, fetching paper and pencil, she copied the verse to take to Relief Society.

But another reason was possible. Do not young men want to succeed? And does not their idea of success depend in large part on what is valued where they live? If spiritual-izing away wickedness is the great pursuit and some straining lad aims a hewing blow at the very *pivot* of transgression, should that come as such a big surprise? The laurel, the laurel. But if success was what Fogelmarck was after when he aimed his blow, he could not have come wider of the mark!

For in Mormondom no obligation is more gladly paid to nature as their creditor by the menfolk than to use their power of increase. Not because of the pleasing excitement of the task, do not think. And not to make up for such *forbidden* pleasures as coffee, tea, whiskey, tobacco, partaking of the cloven-footed roast pig that cheweth not the cud, or sleeping till noon, missing Sunday school and favoring the Democratic Party. No, in those templed towns down the line of the Rockies from Bear Lake in the north to the sunny regions of the Colorado in the south, the constant and close attention given by the master of the house to falling upon the fleshly principalities of his consort has but one purpose: to augment the fruits of his righteousness. For children are like as the arrows in the hand of a giant! (And happy is he who hath his quiver full.) But some people are so blind they can't see the difference between augmenting the fruits of a person's righteousness and a stag going to rut amongst a company of deer. Or between godly communities (like San Bernardino) and supersalient old ancient localities where they used to trundle a big vertical carved and painted statue of the human willy around the streets on festival days. Was it any wonder such places and their dwellers perished in the Wreck of Time? The *worship*, though, of what their statue *stood for*, that did not die with those old nations but communicates power still, even when no acts, rites or ceremonies make it visible. None did in San Bernardino, but there, as elsewhere, the veneration rumbled on. For Fogelmarck to come along, then, querulously *defy* that power and expect no cut-off from society was like a Samson expecting no cut-off from *life* after pulling down a building on top of himself with three thousand Philistines standing on the roof.

Brother Cannon was right about the manure pile, though. As at Culloden Field, it *did* work a miracle. But no miracle could cure the cold shoulder Fogelmarck got wherever he went once he got better. A cold shoulder that would freeze the tail off a brass monkey. So on his birthday he went for a walk, and days and weeks later found himself on the sands of the western ocean. Flat as a plate it looked, sky-blue, a man taking a fit foams more at the mouth than it did that day, and Stig could well see why they called it the Pacific. But as the hulk he signed on in San Francisco as table-steward shaped its course for Van Diemen's Land on ridges high as steeples and plunges deep as hell (cyclones and anti-cyclones being prevalent that year), he thought that nothing could be worse misnamed. Except the dry land he first stepped foot on (vowing never to re-embark), with black-fellows creeping through the dripping myrtles, and irrational beasts and peculiar cries. Far better the sea! he thought, and went back to his ship, the *Marie-Eugene*, with his little gear and the remorse, fear and shame that would hang close over his mind like vultures as long as he lived, he had no doubt.

VISITING HIS NATIVE LAND, HE took up his brush again. But what had been divinely entrusted to him once had now departed. Gingerbread men had their one-dimensional measure and their space, paper-doll ladies opened and extended as a pair of compasses, draperies hung like icicles, trees were cookie-cutters. But it did not matter. Evenness soothed his soul. The accurately coincident put his mind at ease. An alphabetical symbol was beautiful as a face. He did not have to rethink the problem of religion. In orphaned boyhood the church he had chosen was the right one.

Hey the merry, aye the merry
Hey the happy Mormon!
I never knew what joy was
Till I became a Mormon.

And back to America he must go so that when the Last Day came with its rapture, and the dust whirling up out of the rent graves became bones and flesh again (but not flesh and blood, as blood was the principle of corrupt life) and the sky broke open and Jesus the Light of the World poured down like a cataract onto Salt Lake City, he would be at hand to answer "Present." Sometimes along the Chilean coast or sailing to Australia he would start to worry that when it happened he might be too far away. Then he would shake and sweat in a blind panic the way the Eskimos are said to do sometimes in their kayaks when they get out of sight of land. But then his purity would erect his whole self like a member and the fear would pass. At last, before too many years went by for him to risk staying away any longer, he gave up the sea to hurry back to where it would all happen.

And greatly changed he found Salt Lake City from the place he saw first as a young convert! But of course in those long-ago days he had scarcely hung up his hat before someone told him he must leave and go on to an outpost called San Bernardino to "help build up the kingdom." Now, all these years later, here he was again, stunned by what had been accomplished in the meanwhile. Of course there were lots more Saints than there used to be and the Gentiles had been let in, in numbers he could hardly credit. But that was all right. When the Last Day came, the Gentiles would be flattened out like road metal under a steam-roller!

In the meanwhile these doomed ones were better pay than God's elite, and easier to please, too, with shop signs, lettered placards, theatrical backdrops covered with woodland and indoor scenes, and portraits limned from daguerreotypes. One such, its eyes following you around the room, won Stig the Fine Arts contest. Which meant he should get to paint President Taylor, the Prophet, Seer and Revelator who succeeded Brigham Young. Had a Gentile entered the contest (which none did), he would have had about the chance of winning it that an egg would not to fry if cracked on a Salt Lake sidewalk at noon in August. For Saint and heathen were easily told apart. It was *also* known (in Stig's case too late, the prize had already been awarded) who might be in the church's good graces as far as paying tithing was concerned but who had no standing otherwise because of being an *ill-omened embarrassment clotted with singularity.*

His history followed him like a trail of blood, and by the time his first Fast Day in town rolled around he guessed he could expect as much pious sanction in the middle of a blackberry bush as caught here in the brambles of the Eighth Ward congregation. Its blue eyes jabbed like hooks and spines, and by the time he heard it sing "I want no more of you," he knew he wanted no more of it either. What did he need company for? he who all this time had lived the gospel, kept the Commandments and followed the Doctrine and Covenants by himself like an anchorite in the desert? It had not been difficult. The will (apart from any object willed) when unobliged by equity puts armor on, and Stig's had done that. But nothing exists through which there is no path. And if what makes that path happens to be love…

Stig would have paled at the word. And pulled up stakes and moved on had he known that, running in under his life, love's strong, heady stream was washing away the ground! to where his high banks would crumble and fall in. Besides, he was just on his feet again from having had pneumonia. Barely, Serapta helping him into a chair for an hour the first day, then longer as the days went by. She would drape a quilt over the chair beforehand and after he sat down fold it in around him to keep out drafts. It was most kind of her, and one day he said—but never could have told where the words came from (he was as surprised as she was when he heard them coming out)—"Serapta, listen, if you and I would arrange—or how shall I say it? *place*—our lives so they lie side by side like two ropes God can haul on at the same time, I would be *very happy*."

"Oh?" she said, stunned.

It was such an odd remark that even Hindle, when told, hardly knew what to make of it. Some men, talking to a woman alone about anything laying side by side, even two ropes, would sound a little warning bell, but for some reason not when it was him. The purpose, he had said, would be so God could haul them in together… "*I* think he was proposing," Hindle said.

NOW SERAPTA WAS STRETCHED OUT at home recovering as best she might from the Eighth Ward bishop's mysterious snub. She would have to tell Stig, of course. He was waiting… He was also counting the minutes, dreading—For no sooner had she gone off on her errand than he knew it could never be. He would have to tell her *never*, and she would never forgive him. It was hopeless. "Tell me how to let her know," he prayed, and in between whiles thought. About her, this first dear woman ever to be his friend, like the quilt now wrapped around him keeping out the drafts, or carbolized oiled silk laid on a wound, or the cow-catcher on the front of a locomotive. How we need these things, he thought. Especially the cow-catcher clearing the high-dutied line ahead. But it will never be cleared for me. But if I go away, she will never know the truth. Suddenly that was all he wanted in this world, to be strong enough to leave and for her never to know. "Help me, Lord," he prayed. And yet the words *she is my joy and comfort* were so loud in his mind he was sure that was all God could hear.

And there she stood, smiling.

Wanting to slump, wanting to die, he sat up straighter in his chair. "Serapta, listen," he said. "I was such a fool to think for one moment—It is hopeless. You and I can never—"

"Why, how did you find out?"

"Find out what?" he said in bewilderment.

"That he wouldn't give me our recommends! I never saw such a man, no manners whatsoever. I told Hindle—"

"The bishop?"

"I don't think he's right in his mind. You know what he told me to ask you? What a man without feet would want with a pair of shoes! Did you ever hear of anything so—"

"Oh, Serapta," he said, his faculty of vision momentarily lost. She ran to him but he motioned her away. "I have to think," he said.

"I hope you *will* think," she said, watching from a little distance. "About how you've asked for bread and all the way along the line all you have got is just a stone! One look and I should of seen what I had on my hands and walked right out. But we don't care, do we, lovey? One thing I regret, though. I shouldn't of told him about your panorama, that big history of the church you're fixing to paint. And maybe I didn't *really* hear what he said, not like I should. Maybe I—" She studied him anxiously. "I could of got it wrong," she said.

"No, *I'm* the one that got it wrong," he said. "Every single thing from the very beginning." Seeing him sink down then in his chair as in a bog, she took a step towards him, but stopped as he bobbed, so to speak, to the surface again, changing as he did so, becoming strangely different. And suddenly she remembered an odd performance she saw once in her childhood in a traveling show. A man came out on the small rickety stage and—grew. That was his entire act, that was all he did. He grew. While the unchimneyed lanterns flared and the kettledrum rolled he stood there and went from short to tall, say from five feet seven to maybe six feet four. It was his joints or something, eerie, like in a graveyard, a ghost rising jerkily up out of its grave. And she squeezed close to her mother. Now Stig, rearing back, fighting his cover and trying to stand, looked like he was doing that same thing, and it scared her as she'd been scared before, and she cried, "Lovey, what do you think you're doing?"

"I'm going to get dressed," he said, "and go and get our recommends!"

"Oh, no, you're not," she said, hurrying to him and making him sit back down. "What *you're* going to do is bust a blood-vessel!"

And sure enough, though stopped in his tracks and swaddled again in his quilt but unaccountably enlarging still, he *did* bust something. Something snapped and parted. It couldn't be seen from the outside, of course, but when the cinch of ignorant superstition broke in two within him, and its ends fell away, he well knew the moment! and began to lift. Or he felt light enough to do so, to a high-up perch where he could look down and see how the land really lay, and how he had misreckoned, taking his church's contempt (for long-established custom and tradition) for grace abounding, and ebb and shallow for depth, and a gold brick painted to look like gold for a Book of twenty-four carats fine. And once all *that* was clear, he could see as well that the remorse, fear and shame he thought would hang close over his mind like vultures as long as he lived had flapped away. "Why are you crying?" he said, seeing her brush at her eyes with her fingertips.

"I don't know," she said. "There was a man once in a traveling show—And at a young age things sometimes seem scary."

"My love," he said with a reassuring smile, as the noise of life that long ago had stopped began to hum again, "bring that chair and come and sit here beside me. For I have something to tell you."

Chapter Thirty-four

✳

DOCTOR HAD A SAYING WITH A LOT OF TRUTH TO IT, THAT WHAT THE EYE doesn't see and the mind doesn't know, doesn't exist. And when Serapta ran home and, after mulling over till bedtime whether or not to do so, finally told Hindle, she wasn't *laughing*, naturally (as Hindle told Lennart a week later after he crossed his heart and hoped to die), but she wasn't *sad* either. And why should she be?

"Why *should* she be?" Lennart said. "What a silly question."

"No, I mean it, Lennart. Take the Eskimos, they like blubber. To run out of blubber is just a catastrophe for them. But take *you* that's never tasted it and someone makes the remark, 'We're out of blubber!' would you care? You wouldn't care one bit."

"Oh, I don't know," he said. "I might."

"You just want to argue," she said. "But anyway, Serapta's to have a ring. Maybe a ruby."

"For consolation, you mean?" he said. "Seeing as how it's all fell through?"

"Who said it's all fell through?" she said.

"Well, didn't you say the bishop turned thumbs down?"

"So what of it?" she said.

"What *of* it? Without recommends to go through the Endowment House, how can they get married?"

"Easy," she said. "There's all *kinds* of different ways. Couples by the millions all over get married every day!"

"Yes, if you mean Gentiles," he said, looking disgusted. "To God that's just the same as if they was gnats."

"Well, don't say nothing rude like that to Stig and Serapta," she said, "they'd take it personal."

"Why?"

"Because they've quit the church, that's why. They're Gentiles now theirself," she said.

"I'm not surprised," he said, "they're perfect candidates."

"I don't know why you'd say a thing like that."

"Had it in their grasp," he said, "and threw it away. But that's his style, it looks like."

"Oh, now, Lennart."

"First his fleshly principalities, now out goes heaven. Dropped like a dirty shirt."

"Well, don't tell Fern," she said, "she might take a notion to make them move."

"All right, I won't," he said. "But I don't guarantee that she won't hear. Of course that explains the Eighth Ward not being too anxious to welcome him, and the brothers from San Bernardino that knew about his—what he done—having a moratorium declared till the church tribunal could settle—But now they won't have to, so it's probably all for the best."

"The wedding's the twenty-ninth," she said. "You think you'll come? English fruit-cake, three-layered white cake? Oh, and you know what? Stig is drinking coffee now like a perfect fiend, so there'll be coffee, not just lemonade."

Lennart made a hollow guttural sound like a glum pullet pecking in the yard.

So what was the apostate that Stig Fogelmarck had become going to do with sixty feet of sail-cloth? And all that paint and scaffolding? And his plan for a traveling panorama showing how the church had come into being and what it had been up to since? Previous to his bout with pneumonia he had nearly completed Scene One, a woodland setting with a blonde boy in it on his knees before a shaft of light, a roughed-out angel stepping lightly down it. But when he got better and tackled the canvas again, this time to paint out with a broad brush what he'd painted in before, Serapta stood by wringing her hands. "It was so beautiful," she said.

"Yes, but from the wrong point of view," he said, "because now it must be a *Gentile* history of the church."

"Why?" she said, puzzled. "I mean, why any history of the *church* at all, since we've both dropped out? Why not just act like it don't exist and paint some *other* kind of history? John Smith and Pocahontas? Or Rip van Winkle?"

But a history of the church it had to be, she told Hindle. "And the more I think of it the scareder I get. Because it's not going to be what Brigham *Young* would paint, I can assure you! I've saw the plan of it drew on butcher paper, and all I can say is if a Danite ever lays eyes on that panorama, Stig won't never paint a inch of nothing again."

"Forget the Danites," Hindle said. "They're a thing of the past. But you know what makes me wonder? How Stig would even know what a Gentile history of the church might *be*, him being such a good Mormon all these years!"

"Well, I'll tell you," Serapta said. "He knows because of arguing Mormonism, when he was on ships. Hoping to get converts, I suppose. Which I'm sure he never did. But since a argument means *pro* and *con*, the *con* side must of burrowed into his attention deeper than he realized. And just lately he's got books and papers."

"So now he'll paint the *con* side," Hindle said. "Don't men beat all for being odd?"

"They do," Serapta said. "Here's Stig—at one time such a believer he even offers up his manly, well, *ornaments*—you used the expression yourself, Hindle—on the altar of sacrifice! and now he's such a apostate that if the Danites don't offer *him* up his whole *self* on the altar of sacrifice, I'll be surprised. One consolation, though, it won't be right away, not with all them yards to cover and him so slow. The tiny little brushes he uses, and he stands and stares."

"Also he might get tired of it," Hindle said, "like fancy work so fancy it defeats the purpose and ends up rolled up half done in a bottom drawer."

"I'll cross my fingers and hold the thought on that," Serapta said.

AT FIRST IT SEEMED TO Hindle that things might stay the same. Serapta married would be like Serapta single, working for her during the day and going out back to stay with her husband at night. But that husband, dignified now by his new title and rank, and already spoiled like a haggis in the sun by his bride, could no more resume his old semblance than a Pasha of Three Horse Tails corrupted by servants go back to being a humble Turk again. Someone had to take Serapta's place, and the first week in October someone did, a girl by the name of Jean, related to a neighbor of Lennart's first wife Pearl. This neighbor of Pearl's was rich, with a house with a porch around three sides, so Pearl bowed down to her, and when able to do her a favor—such as bringing together with Hindle a relative who was out of work because the lady she worked for had gone crazy during the change of life and had to be sent to Provo—why, Pearl made every effort. Hindle said later, when Pearl brought Jean over you'd have thought she was bringing Aladdin's magic lamp.

Of course the girl fell far short of that, though Hindle did have to admit she knew how to boil potatoes and could stir up a cake. But housework was not her long suit or children either, and a lot of the time that Hindle was in her office or out on calls, her two little girls, instead of being where they belonged, were visiting Serapta in her new home out in back.

"Now, it's no hardship," Serapta said, "having the children. Just the opposite, so don't think you have to say nothing to Jean." But Hindle said she had doubts about her from the very beginning and was going to let her go. Why, to think of Serapta being imposed on like that made her feel awful!

"No imposition to it," Serapta said. "They're the best little girls in the world."

But to think of such taking advantage! Well, Hindle would speak to her and if she didn't do better in future, she would have to go.

"I wouldn't be too hasty," Serapta said. "Hired girls don't grow on trees no more, I understand, due to all the people with smelter money and from the railroads and all. Stig come home the other day and told me he heard that Salt Lake has got *two millionaires* now! can you imagine?"

"Oh, I'll find someone," Hindle said, "they can't *all* be in the mansions. But in the meantime don't let yourself be bothered, and I mean that, Serapta. When the children knock, just say they can't come in."

"Can you imagine me doing such a thing?" Serapta said. "I'd sooner shut my own nose in the door!"

"Well, I wouldn't want you to do *that*," Hindle said. "But remember things is different now. You're married. And brides need 'seclusion from the jarring world.'"

"It can jar all right," Serapta said. "But not on account of your young ones, I promise you. And *she's* not getting jarred, I happen to notice."

"You're speaking of Jean?" Hindle said.

"That's right," Serapta said. "I've never passed that window around to that side of the house yet when I've seen her busy, she's always in the rocking chair rocking away."

"Oh, she's busy all right," Hindle said, "crocheting and embroidering for her hope chest."

"Is that what she's up to? Well, just so long as she's earning her keep," Serapta said with what was meant to be fine sarcasm.

"And speaking of her hope chest," Hindle said, "would you believe it's already been filled up once to where the lid wouldn't shut down? Well, it has, and been emptied, and she's started over. Rosina told me Pearl told her that when she come for her emulsifier the other day. She heard it from her neighbor that's Jean's relation."

"No!" Serapta said. "Filled up once and started over? I never heard of such a thing!"

"Well, you have now," Hindle said. "This happened before she come here. She couldn't close the lid. So she got hold of a trunk, emptied the hope chest in it, stored the trunk in Pearl's neighbor's attic and started all over again."

"If that don't beat all," Serapta said. "Why, that means—the girl could be forty years old!"

"She could be," Hindle said, "but I don't really think so. And by the way, she didn't just store the *trunk* but other things too, a stereopticon and a big cuckoo clock she bought off a peddler that's not supposed to be wound or the cuckoo come out till her wedding day—"

"Well, if she wants one bad enough—a wedding day—she'll have one. Ain't I the living proof that there's a Jack for every Jill?"

"Since you mention your husband," Hindle said, "how is he? And how is *he* taking this onslaught of my young ones?"

"It's not a onslaught and he's taking it fine," Serapta said, beaming to be reminded of him. "If anyone had told me, I'd have never believed—"

"What, Serapta?"

"Why, artists," she said. "They're like they been hit on the head a lot of the time. Did you know that, Hindle? And then when you add the advantage of a *barn*—! Without creatures, of course. Why, you stand between the haylofts and look up, and the roof's so—far away—and the light—comes down—and then the floor, it stretches out like *country*, empty prairie that anyone can have. 'My land is before thee. Dwell where it pleaseth thee.' There's so much room. You noticed the children has brought their stuff out back? You know in that corner by the stove where they always—You seen that Eula's little cupboard and Esther's dishes and their dolls is gone?"

Hindle looked for an instant as if she didn't know what Serapta was talking about.

But she did know and turned red. "When I think!" she said. "I'm drinking my coffee and looking at that empty corner and never even *noticed*! I don't know where my mind is half the time."

"I do," Serapta said staunchly. "It's on your *cases* that maybe you been up all night mulling over. That woman with the streak running up her arm that if it'd reached her arm pit it'd of killed her, and the poor little baby that time that swallowed the hinge, and the poor old soul that cracked her skull in a fall and thought a horse had somehow got in her house—You got good reason."

"No, I haven't. I'm a raven mother."

"A raven mother? Why, you're people's salvation, that's who *you* are, Hindle. I tell you never a day goes by but what I think of you a-saving *me* as surely as if I'd been in the water going down for the third time—in fact I *did* go down, I *had* went down for the third time. But here you come, and just like Jesus saving Lazarus, you brought me back to life!"

"Oh, Serapta, you shouldn't talk that way."

"And you know what? You pulled the same stunt off for your own *self*. Look at your practice and all."

"A lot was thanks to you, Serapta. And good luck."

"Don't talk to *me* about luck," Serapta said. "For I was there, remember, and how many times didn't I see you go out into the dark in wind so strong it nearly wrenched the bag right out of your hand? And then when you come home—Why, my. The *studying* alone! Them books you wrestled with worse'n a grizzly bear. I bet they're hanging in shreds now, but that don't matter. Your little head's a-holding all their knowledge."

"My *little* head? With you around, Serapta?" Hindle laughed. "More like big balloon about to bust!"

"All right, I'll quit if you say we got a bargain."

"What kind of a bargain?"

"Oh, kind of a loose one. The children doing their playing out back with me where I can keep an eye on them like always. Stig don't pay no attention, and they're company. And as far as Jean's concerned—"

"I might just keep on trying her out awhile."

Lennart was pleased to hear that. "I wouldn't want to get into it with Pearl, about Betsy or whatever her name is," he said.

"You have sat at the table enough times," Hindle said crossly, "so you'd at least know her *name*. And why you would have to get 'into it' with Pearl if I fire Jean, I do not know."

"You would if you was me," he said. "Pearl being the one that done her neighbor that she likes to keep in good with, the favor of getting her relation a job here with you. But anyway she'll prove up, I bet, and get some savvy."

"Well, she might. Prove up, I mean," Hindle said. "But for Jean to get some savvy—" She snorted. A missal thrush might take root in the *sky*, as the *Medico-Botanical Guide* on her bookshelf said, but "savvy" needed *ground*, not "a gaping fissure to receive the rain," a phrase she had heard applied more times than once to her own self if she did the least thing wrong, such as giving a drop of chloroform too little or handing Doctor the auscultator instead of a turnbuckle.

When Lucitie heard about Jean, she said she sounded to her like nobody home. And "nobody home" would do, of course. Sometimes somebody like that could be a good worker, maybe really better than someone who was all there.

"But she's *not* a good worker," Hindle said.

"Then if I was you—"

There was something hard to explain, though. Say you didn't get around to taking your supper out of the warming oven and eating it at the kitchen table till almost bedtime, too tired nearly to lift your fork to your mouth. The hired girl you *don't* have to talk to at that moment or form a society with so as not to seem uppity (which you don't if they're gaping fissures) takes on an odd kind of value. Her kitchen in the dust and drouth of life becomes an oasis. Peaceful, restful, like over in the Old Country, where according to Doctor every person is unequal. Hindle thought of trying to put this into words for Lucitie but decided against it. Or speak of something else she had thought of, that once the condition takes hold, of equanimity with regard to hired help whose lack of intellectual strength borders on idiocy, then it's like any other flaw in conduct, putting salt on watermelon or hoisting up your skirts before the fire to warm the back of your legs. And by now Hindle had become accustomed to the intermediate character of her hired girl, the twilight sleep of her mind, to her pervading emptiness like fog.

That emptiness, though, when she told her about the baby coming in March, filled like wind with eddies, Jean stormed around, her stormy looks startled Hindle. But that went by, her essence once again became the absence of anything emphatic. When the child arrived, though, Marie Lucitie, seven and three-fourths pounds, and there was more to do, tasks either not done at all or done with such vehemence that even in her office (to which she fled as soon as she was able) Hindle could hear the commotion, she knew that Jean (as soon as she could be replaced) had to go.

Lennart was really sorry. "I don't know when I've tasted better baked beans," he said. "And her plum duff would stand with anyone's."

"Well, if you like her cooking so well you'll just have to keep track of where she goes to, won't you?" Hindle said sharply. "Though you might not be so welcome there as you been here."

"I wouldn't call myself so welcome here," he said. "Not with the cold shoulder *I* been getting. And never a bit of credit."

"Credit!" she said. "For what?"

"Why, traversing the public streets," he said. "Do you realize how dangerous they are to us men now? They're a regular deadfall. You don't seem to know it, it's all one to you, but Elders is being stalked by Government men. It's terrible. They are standing in back of bushes laying in wait!"

"Oh, now, Lennart, don't pile it on." She studied him, then laughed.

"Pile it on?" he said. "Listen, even the single fellows got to show credentials! If you would read a paper once in a while that print things like they are instead of that lying Tribune, you might find out what's really *happening* in this world. But speaking of single fellows—" He cleared his throat.

"Then he asked me," Hindle told Lucitie later, "what the situation was with regard to Jean. 'What do you mean by that?' I said. 'I just got through telling you. As soon as I can find another girl, Jean is out on her ear.' 'I know, I heard you,' he said. 'But what I'm asking, is anyone *sparking* her?' 'Who wants to know?' I said. 'It's nothing to me,' he said. 'Personally, I mean. But Pearl was mentioning that her neighbor would like to know.' 'Know what?' I said. 'That a head sitting smack dab down onto a person's body like that without no neck between isn't no detriment to finding a husband? Or all that gum showing? And her disposition? A chin sticking out a mile? Unless of course she comes into money.' 'Well, she might,' he said. 'Pearl's neighbor says the woman she worked for that ended up in the asylum died, and while it's not settled yet, she *might* of left Jean quite a little pile. But where you got the notion her head sits on her body without no *neck*—' Lennart says. 'I got it from looking at her,' I said. You know what I think about men, Lucitie? I don't think they see the same things we do at all! It's a case like—Animals don't either, everything's hazy to them, so all they can do is run around and smell."

"Men could well be doing that," Lucitie agreed. "It wouldn't surprise me a bit. Did Lennart go away mad?"

"More like feeling sorry for himself. Pearl—"

"He's always kind of tickled me since you married him," Lucitie said.

"Oh? How so?"

"Oh, I don't know, his ways. Like when the federal agents—That was the funniest thing. Every time I think of it I laugh." Lucitie laughed again and Hindle joined in too, for sociability's sake, but not very heartily.

It *was* funny, though, what happened the year the so-called Utah harems made headlines once more in the Eastern papers, and like a stage magician pulling a tablecloth from under a pile of dishes without breaking any, Congress tried to outlaw the Mormon doctrine's plurality of spouses without doing any harm to religious freedom. This they did, or anyhow claimed they did, with a bill the President signed into law. Then he sent a company of secret service men out west to rout the pluralists. However, hunter and hunted looking enough alike to be brothers, both being of the "common run" of white

American male, it wasn't like an Indian sneaking up behind you, and soon the Salt Lake jail was full of prisoners full of regret. Not regret for breaking a law so new they had hardly even heard of it, but regret for the pretty pass the *country* had come to.

The courts in Utah, for instance. Once high-class tribunals, where Gentiles (few and far between) were barred from jury duty and every Judge stood high up in the Mormon church, had as the years passed plummeted to hell. On the bench and in the jury box now sat formless voids of primordial matter, Democrats, Catholics, wild-haired atheists, Trade Unionists, Masons. A *man* hadn't a chance. "Two years' hard labor, step down"— bang! with the gavel. Chains, the iron ball, convict stripes even on your hat. No appeal either! to anyone, even in a case where the excess "wife" in evidence was not the defendant's wife at all but only the hired *girl* to a wife. So that just goes to show the rottenness.

These events, as they naturally would, shook Lennart to the fundaments. Never would he let himself be railroaded, he said. And he made a vow to tell Rosina, Fern and Hindle good-bye and live only with Pearl, the first wife he ever married. Much as it pained him—for he loved the three he was letting go as much as the one he was retaining—this was what he came round to each and said it looked like he was going to have to do. Fern was the only one to cry. Rosina feared Fern might take it out on them and start in charging rent, but Hindle didn't think she necessarily would. And it wouldn't matter, they were both self-supporting and could afford to pay.

You couldn't prove it by Lennart that Fern would start charging rent, Lennart said, but whatever happened, always remember that "in my Father's house are many mansions, if it were not so I would have told you." His farewell visit to each in turn was quite affecting. Tears gathered in his eyes and his lips trembled as he went through the door, calling back over his shoulder, "Keep sweet in Jesus, dear one, and *forget me not.*"

They'd have had to have been quick to do *that.* For like an inebriate who's taken the pledge in a weak moment only to wake up to an imperative call for *drink*, Lennart waking up to an imperative call for, shall we say? diversification, became a perfect daredevil of a husband, paying calls on one wife or another by night or day, down main streets or up alleys, over fences, in and out of windows, full moon, no moon, it mattered not to him, as reckless as Blondin going over Niagara Falls. And the result was not (by some miracle) prison for unlawful cohabitation, but in due time a baby boy to Rosina and the baby girl already mentioned, to Hindle.

Pretty as a picture, a regular prize, Hindle's baby Marie Lucitie's only drawback was that nothing seemed to agree with her, and Hindle was getting really worried when Rosina sent her a note that said,

> *Dear Hindle, I hear tell your milk don't set too well with your baby Girl sometimes*
> *that happens it happened with me and my second when she was born then not*
> *again and now with this boy I got milk as the saying goes to feed pigs good quality*

too so why don't you bring your baby over to my house and we will see if I can't
nurse her to do some good what do you say?
Your friend
Rosina

Hindle thought that was a very kind offer. But all on edge as she was with worry about the child, and with little rest due to her practice, she took it into her head to fancy a kind of undertone of bragging in the note, as if Rosina was saying, here I am, forty years old, gray hair, and I got it all over *you*. But then she read it over and was ashamed of herself, and didn't even wait to send word but bundled up the baby and went to Rosina's house.

By evening it was pretty plain Rosina's milk was going to do the business. When hours went by without a whimper out of the child, Hindle, who hadn't had a good night's sleep in weeks, was prevailed upon to take a little nap in Rosina's darkened bedroom. Waking up long after nightfall, she found her benefactor in the kitchen with the baby in her arms rocking in the rocking chair by the stove.

"Ain't she the sweetest little thing?" Rosina said, holding her up, then nestling her in her arms and pulling a corner of her shawl up over her face. "Looks like she's mine now, don't it? I *wanted* another little girl and now I got one. Not that I'm not tickled with my boy—" She glanced over at the cradle where he lay asleep. "But you know how you'll take a notion to wish for something and how disappointed you get when you don't get it?"

"Well, *my* wish has come true too," Hindle said, "that *some* kind of milk is finally going to agree with her."

"It is," Rosina said proudly, holding the baby closer. "And now, how shall we do this?"

"I guess I'll have to leave her, I don't know what else," Hindle said. "Unless—" But the two women lived too far apart to go back and forth, and each had too many responsibilities at home to move in with the other. It needn't last, of course. By summer—

"Oh, yes, by summer," Rosina said. "But this spring with me will give her a real good start."

When Hindle staggered to bed that night at past midnight, in spite of her earlier nap she was so tired she was asleep almost before her head touched the pillow. No little wailing, colicky baby to walk the floor with anymore. No more worries on that account. It was like taking paregoric. But at three she woke up crying, great sobs, why would she do that? and all the next day felt strange, weak, emptied out as if by blood-letting, like part of herself was gone, her arms cut off, her side gouged out and open to the elements. She had to get the baby *back*! But Marie Lucitie's only chance—Some things in this world we have to accept and this was one of them. Hindle found a fresh handkerchief, wiped her eyes and blew her nose. What can't be cured must be endured. This start with Rosina needn't be long. By summer, early summer...

Unless Rosina's milk ran out in the meanwhile! which did not seem likely, although for two days *shock* practically stopped her every bodily function but heart and lungs. And that those organs didn't stop too under the circumstances was almost not to be believed, considering it was her that found him in his bassinet—! hadn't been sick, fat, dimpled, not a mark on him, fed, put to bed—At ten past eleven—The hail on the roof must of been what woke her—! Not face down, not accidentally smothered in his pillow, not wiggled over between the mattress and side, laying so sweet it seemed like if you picked him up and kissed him—! But his sweet blue eyes would never open again.

GONE BEFORE
Joseph Lennart
Aged
4 months
6 days

Pearl stayed with her till after the funeral, and Rosina had common sense. The fact that she hadn't died when she found him meant she had to go on living. Her milk came flooding back. How thankful she was to have her darling little Marie! A thousand times she said it. How good God was! He knew, of course, being all-seeing, what was around the bend, and what did He do but fix things so she would have the comfort of an extra babe! Think of that! for grace.

"Though of course I've got *you* to thank too, Hindle," she said, "you're the one that had her. I tell you she's the only thing that's keeping me alive!"

That made Hindle a little mad, not at the poor grieving mother but at God! if He really was behind what had happened. She didn't think He *was*, of course, but what do we know? Going home from Rosina's after a visit she thought, "Rob Peter to pay Paul." *She's* provided, but what about me? God sure didn't take *me* into consideration. How about *my* arms being empty? *My* heart being busted? There was one small advantage, if it could be called so. With the baby gone Jean subsided to "nobody home," and having filled her hope chest by this time to where not even sitting on the lid would close it, she put the overflow in a pillowcase, carried it to Pearl's neighbor to store in the attic and began giving more attention to the house.

The children Eula and Esther took hardly any of Jean's time now that they were back almost entirely in Serapta's care. Hindle paid Serapta (vigorously protesting) in money and also shared with her the flour, sugar, eggs, sides of bacon and other things too numerous to mention that patients sometimes paid her with. "But I still think it's taking advantage," Hindle said with a sigh.

"Trust me, you're wrong," Serapta said. "Why, if I didn't have the worry of the panorama, these days of being a married lady but still having the children like I used to would be my happiest time. But—!"

"How is he coming with it?" Hindle asked.

"Wonderful. But the funny part, you'd never know it to see how he stands and stares, or dabs with his little brushes or grinds his paints. But yet the history's showing up, more every day, and I'm starting to have nightmares. Them Danites will take *one* look—!"

"The Danites don't even *exist* anymore, Serapta. And a canvas as big as you say isn't going to get done tomorrow. Besides—all it is, is pictures strung along! Scenes. Didn't you say so? One after the other?"

"Yes, but against the church like it is? For that's what all the pretty pictures is going to amount to! a great big argument against the church."

"How do you mean?"

"Well, they're *preaching* pictures." Serapta knitted her brow. "To try and make people think—about—Well, let me see. He has drew the entire plan on butcher paper and showed me and explained it so I know, and I'm telling you if he goes around showing it to audiences—!"

"But even sixty-five feet is so *small* in comparison! and the church don't need to worry, it'll be like a fly landing on a—a streetcar. I bet they'll just ignore it."

"Oh, no, they won't. You know how it starts—the history, I mean—with the Prophet Joseph down on his knees in a grove and how these heavenly beings come floating down but their feet don't touch the ground, and they tell him—? And that's how the church gets founded? Well, that's not how it happens on Stig's panorama! In the picture that starts it all off Joseph gets painted, the Prophet Joseph, not like a praying *boy* but like a *author* sitting at a table with pen and ink and paper making up a *religion* like authors make up a book, *Hiawatha* or *Uncle Tom's Cabin*. The Prophet Joseph is *making it all up* from beginning to end! And swiping from the Masons too, the Freemasons' lodge."

"Well, if Stig can paint what you've just said, he'll be doing pretty good," Hindle said.

"Well, he can," Serapta said. "He says he'll make it all unroll—how a book was wrote by a human author with common pen and ink and how it started a church, and how that church become a kingdom and how the king of that kingdom was Joseph who ruled and reigned till he got certain people's goat so bad they couldn't stand it anymore and killed him. But that didn't end it, it was like that old sea-serpent that chop its head off, another head grows to take its place, and the new head in this case was Brigham Young. And he was just another human being like Joseph, but (like Joseph) you couldn't prove it by him because his every breath was took by his congregation for gospel, his every order for direct word from above. Go, stay, camp, march. My folks, your folks, people's folks from everywheres thinking they're religious when all the time all they are being is pulled around by the nose!"

"You know what *I* can't understand?" Hindle said. "How any living person could *paint* what you just said! Will there be printing on his pictures too? to explain what a person's looking at? *You* know what it's all supposed to mean because he tells you, and *I'll* know because you'll tell *me*, picture by picture. But here's these Danites you're so worried about, or just anyone, and how will *they* look at it and know?"

Serapta thought this over. "I'm sure there won't be printing," she said.

"So where will the guideposts come in? What I'm thinking of," Hindle said, "is one time Doctor and me seen a cliff with what looked like pictures but it turned out they was some kind of signs or records. And once an old man showed us what he said was *pictographs* that people *read* like you'd read a newspaper, on a piece of birch bark. He said the Dakotas had what was called a *winter count* where they'd draw the most important thing that happened that particular year, like if their Chief died in battle or if the tribe had smallpox. The Mexicans done that too, Doctor said, he could always come up with something. They'd draw eyes dropping tears, he said, and such as that, and Chinamen paint pictures mixed with words till you can't hardly tell where the pictures end and the words begin or vice versa. But you say Stig isn't going to *use* words!"

"I thought you meant *painted* words," Serapta said quickly. "There'll be words all right, when *he* stands there with a pointer pointing out the different—"

"Oh, you mean he'll be *talking?*"

"Of course he'll be talking—explaining—"

"Well, that's what I mean," Hindle said. "Unless he stands there and *talks*, people could probably look at his panorama till kingdom come and not have the faintest idea what it's all supposed to mean. So you don't need to worry. With that Danish accent and mumbling like he does, I don't mean that as a criticism, but how far is he going to get? Take what you said is going to be the first picture, Joseph at the table writing. How will anyone know he's supposed to be making up the Book of Mormon out of his head?"

"Well, *that* picture, I grant you," Serapta said, sounding uncertain. "But there's others that's as clear as the nose on your face. Like here's the Prophet playing Blind Man's Buff in a meadow with some pretty girls, you just have to give it a glance to see it's carnal. And what does a man think of himself if he's a General all dressed up, up on a big white horse with all his tiny soldiers stretching away to every side far as the eye can see, and all the cannon he needs and cannon balls too? And now he's threw his hat in the ring and wants to be President of the *United States*. And then comes a picture that don't need making clear, of Joseph sitting on somebody's back stoop helping, squeezed up close, the lady of the house shell peas for supper while around the corner stomps the husband and he is breathing fire."

Hindle laughed. "That don't seem too slanderous."

"But see, it tickles you, that's what I'm talking about," Serapta said. "It's all just *human*, the church, the religion. A human made-up thing. But breathe a word of that, the humanness, the funnyness, and the believers want to skin you alive. Though as the scenes go on they're not so funny anymore. What I mean to say, they get scary. The Prophet busts up this printing press with a big sledge hammer, then he's took to jail, the mob busts in and out the window he sails, then here he lays shot in the brisket and dying in the grass. Then Brigham sashays up and *he* takes over. Then here's the Nauvoo Temple being burnt to the ground and a train of white-tops going towards—you can see by the sunset it's due west. Like it had sense to it, like it wasn't all just crazy. And here's the handcart brigade—and whoever's still alive builds the town, Salt Lake City, foursquare to the compass, with the Tithing Office handy to all where they can go and pay their ten percent right next door to Brigham's Lion House. And on the corner stands his Beehive House with him on the front porch with his feet on the railing. The haystack in his barn-lot is a pretty sight because it really is a stack of gold. And real gold leaf is what Stig's going to paint it with so it shines and glitters. And here's a peach tree like they look in spring, and the Restoration—"

"How will he paint *that*?" Hindle said.

"Easy," Serapta said, but looking even more uncertain. "Here's this couple—while the husband was on a mission, the wife deceived him with another man. And now he's home and she's confessed to him. So he will cut her throat to save her soul. She's sitting on his lap, they're both a-crying but he's obliged to do it, there's no other way, he's got his sheath-knife ready."

"It don't seem possible people was ever so mean," Hindle mused, "or so dumb."

Chapter Thirty-five

✶

"WELL, THEY WAS, NO DOUBT OF IT. ESPECIALLY AS REGARDS THE SO-CALLED Restoration. What *that* was, was more like a epidemic," Serapta said. "People kind of caught it from one another. But anyway—in Stig's panorama-to-be, here's Brother Kimball running out of his house like it was on fire to talk to some herd boys going past with their flock of sheep." She explained further. "See, uptown now there's an old man that Stig got acquainted with lately that used to *be* a herd boy in the Nineteenth Ward. In his later life he apostatized. And he was telling Stig the other day that the herd boys used to just dread Brother Kimball seeing 'em, for he'd put 'em on the witness stand with questions they thought they had to answer because of who he was! a General Authority and everything. That was before he died, of course."

"Now wait a minute, Serapta," Hindle said. "Say I'm looking at this picture of out in front of a house, and here's a flock of sheep and some boys and a man. And say it's a hundred years from now. There's no writing or printing anywhere. How will anyone know that what they're seeing is supposed to mean what you just said?"

"They'll know," Serapta said solemnly, "because the boys will be so red in the face from the shame of the *answers* they got to give to these *very inquisitive personal questions* they been asked, that they nearly burn up. Oh, but excuse me, Hindle, for changing the subject, but I just thought of something that might save the day! Why don't I tell *Lennart* about Stig's panorama and ask *him* to talk to Stig about how riled up people will be?"

"Oh, no, don't do that," Hindle said hastily. "Not that I don't trust Lennart, I'm sure he wouldn't go to the Quorum and stir up a hornet's nest. But the doctrine being what it is, and Lennart not being one to find *fault* with it—"

"So in other words you don't think I better?" Serapta said.

"I don't think you better, Serapta."

"All right, I won't. And this here talk we've had out here has really—Like you say, how will people know what they're looking at? Here's Brigham with a locomotive engine sticking out of his pocket, for instance. Stig thinks that'll show he got rich off the railroads, but couldn't it just as well be a toy of one of his children he's picked up off the floor?" Comforting herself, she decided it could. "And who's to know the lady in the furs in the sleigh is the actress he was about ready to throw everything over for? But of course the massacre at the Mountain Meadow—nobody looking at *that* can question what it means! or doubt that we—that is to say the church, with a few Indians threw in for the looks of the thing—ambushed, killed and murdered a wagon train big enough to fill up Temple Square, then left the corpses to be dragged around and gnawed on by the wolves—" She broke off, looked stricken. "But oh, my Lord," she said, "where's my consideration? Talking of this to *you* when your *own father*—Listen, Hindle, there was reason on *their* side too, things that maybe, if they don't exactly *justify*—why, at least *explain*—"

"I don't know what those things would be," Hindle said sadly.

"Well, honey, you won't never hear of this again from me," Serapta said. "That there's a subject will never be broached again."

BUT IT WAS, IN A rather surprising way, a few weeks later when a lady and little girl came to see Hindle. It took her but a moment to recognize under lovely hats and bundled in fine coats Lisheen, the actress, and Mavis, the daughter she thought at the time had been marked by the long white winter she lived through at Burdick's Institution. As Lisheen said at the time, what *else* would have made the child an albino? "Why, Lisheen!" Hindle said after a moment when she opened the door to them. "And little Mavis." She wasn't little anymore but rather tall for her twelve years, though thin as a toothpick.

"Who are *you*?" Lisheen said in astonishment.

Hindle told her, then asked why she had come to *see* her if she didn't know who she was. Lisheen had been sent, it turned out, by Serapta's relatives, three ladies who acted very mad at Serapta for some reason and who said if she wanted to know Serapta's whereabouts she should ask the lady doctor over on Fifth East. When Hindle said *she* was the lady doctor, and that they were acquainted because she had worked at Burdick's when Lisheen was in residence there, Lisheen looked at her long and hard and then said, "The little scullery maid! And you will just about fall over," she went on, "when I tell you that *you* were why I wanted to find Serapta in the first place. In the hopes she had kept track of *you*!"

"Oh?" Hindle said rather coldly, "scullery maid" still ringing in her ears. "And why did you want to find *me*?"

"Why, because—But if you don't mind I'd rather wait awhile and tell you when I've caught my breath a little, for this is just *too wonderful*."

"All right, only—"

At that moment the door that led to the kitchen opened and Hindle's hired girl Jean in bonnet and shawl peeped in. "Say," she said, "I see my uncle's team coming up the street, so I guess I'll run on out and meet him."

"All right, good-bye," Hindle said. "You'll be back on Friday?"

"Unless Aunt Leah takes a notion not to make it," Jean said.

"Well, I hope she won't. Take a notion."

"Who was that?" Lisheen said with a glance out the window at Jean's departing figure.

Hindle debated whether to say *my* scullery maid, for you see I have got one now! but said instead, "I need to have someone in the house to see to things."

"Tell me, are you *really* a—what the sign says?" Lisheen said.

Without speaking, Hindle pointed to the framed diploma on the wall, then took from the shelf where it lay Doctor's old wooden stethoscope as though it had been a distinguishing mark of office.

"How did it happen? You've got to tell me!" Later Lisheen would talk such a blue streak that no one could get a word in edgeways. But at the beginning of her visit, she seemed to listen to every word Hindle and then Serapta had to say. Shepherding Eula and Esther, Serapta did not, when she came in and saw Mavis again (whose loss had laid her so low), stagger back and swoon. No, she stood there quite collected. More than collected, for with those powerful charms her husband's love, the clinging of her charges to her, and Hindle's friendship, she was not the meek dependent she once had been. "For goodness' sake," she said. "Can this be Lisheen and Mavis? Well, will wonders—!" Once she would have wept with emotion, but now she smiled. "Never cease?"

Mother and daughter stayed with Hindle just the one day and night and part of the next day, but that was enough to fix the visit indelibly on Hindle's mind. Serapta, too, would never forget it. She and the children were in and out, Stig begged to be excused from being "dragged into anything" and of course could do what he wanted. Lisheen couldn't get over it, how Serapta had changed, like a shoe, she said, that you put a shoe-tree in. Straightened right up. Became young again. Hindle was like that too, she said, straightened, smoothed, a doctor! it was really wonderful what life could do to people if it took a notion. It had certainly taken a notion with her *own* self, Lisheen said. And after she put Mavis, heavy-eyed and fretful, down for an afternoon nap as though she had been a tiny girl instead of almost a young lady, she enlarged on that. Yes, life seemed to have something up its sleeve continuously where she was concerned. Thank goodness, though, she had the resilient spirit of her roving forebears.

Having heard from Doctor something along the line that *everybody's* forebears were roving to start with, Hindle somewhat stringently made mention of this, for the actress made it sound as if her forebears were the only ones that roved. But Lisheen went on as though she had not spoken. "Only sometimes it can be terrible," she said, "what life's got up its sleeve."

WHAT IT HAD FOR *HER* that she thought she would never survive was the death of her husband Andrew. Andy, everyone called him, the dearest man. She had been married to him four years, never a cross word, he was a drummer. His line of goods was newspaper metal for linotypes, stereotypes and such as that, which he sold to newspapers from Butte to the New Mexico border, where he was—in a town called Artesia—waiting for the stagecoach after doing his business there when a tarantula bit him. That *had* to be what it was—although they found no mark on him—because some other people sitting on the hotel veranda saw him—what he'd done while he was waiting was see this shady spot under a juniper and go and stretch out there—saw him all of a sudden jump up and run in circles and act like he was brushing something off him, then fall down dead! and what would that be but a tarantula? "I have seen them," Lisheen said portentously.

"Me, too," Hindle said.

"And those things," Lisheen hurried on, "when they rear up will stand three inches high, with hair as long as a mouse's. I went down there afterwards, they showed me one, it could have been the very one, someone had caught it, it was in an empty clock case with a glass laid over the top. You could see its mouth, red like a drop of blood with its fangs coming out. A man said we should offer it a poker and hear how the fangs would grate on it, actually *grate*, but we didn't do it. I was down there, as I say, a few weeks later. I saw the shady spot where it happened, saw the parlor where they carried him—The people that owned the hotel said maybe it was his heart, but how could that be? the picture of health and only thirty-eight years old! I could have had the room he slept in the night before it happened, they offered to change the man that was in it to across the hall, but I said no."

"What was you doing down there?" Serapta said, then answered herself, "Putting a person's mind at ease, I imagine."

"It did do that, seeing the actual spot," Lisheen said, "but what I was really there for was on business. For after Andy died—I went to Denver to collect what he had coming—well, I could have written but I went in person, that's usually best, and they treated me lovely, they really did—As I was ready to leave, the Superintendent said to me, 'Listen, Mrs. Fitch, Andy's job is open, why don't *you* take a stab at it? Why, I bet you,' he said, 'in a year's time a beautiful young widow like you making Andy's rounds would nearly have her nest feathered.' So I thought about it and thought, why not? But of course a *year* was being too optimistic, though I'm not doing bad. The *friends* a person makes, that's the important thing. And speaking of friends, do you know, Serapta, I nearly sent for *you* to come to Cheyenne to look after Mavis. And another thought I had was to move down here to Salt Lake so you could live with Mavis and me and take care of things while I was away on trips."

"Well, I don't know if that would of been too good," Serapta said.

"When did all this happen?" Hindle said.

"A year ago last fall."

Resentful of the way Lisheen thought all she had to do was crook her finger and Serapta would come running, Hindle said sharply, "After you come so unexpected that time and took Mavis away after Serapta raising her for seven years, Serapta had a sick spell that she nearly didn't come through. One thing piled on another was just too much. Tot had died and their brother Murdock moved up north. And then to lose her *child*, as you might say. For all of us remember how at the last minute when you got ready to leave that time, you gave Serapta the baby. To *keep*. There was no mention made of any Indian trading."

While Hindle was speaking, Serapta looked nervously away. Lisheen blinked but then, as though Hindle's declamation had been but a sudden gust of wind slamming shut a door, said, "Well, things change. Change for the worse, change for the better, sometimes both at once, did you ever notice? So as it happened I didn't need Serapta after all or have to pull up stakes and move down here. I found this widow lady. But poor little Mavis!" she said, first smiling, then sobering, like day sombering into night. "She missed Andy so! It was just pathetic. Her and him was just like father and daughter, and here he has to go and pass away. Wasn't that cruel? We had a house, I wish you could have seen it. Well, when I tell you—put on the market one day and sold the next, or maybe not the next but very soon afterwards, to a lovely man and lady and three children from Pocatello."

"That was fortunate," Hindle said politely, aware now that further invective would serve no purpose. The last thing Serapta would want under present circumstances would be to have Mavis returned to her. Serapta seemed to realize this as well, as she cleared her throat and said as if to someone just introduced, "That was quick."

"I hated the thought," Lisheen said. "But like I say, I'd taken Andy's job—and I do have to say that selling newspaper metal is a very interesting—I've made lovely friends, newspaper men and editors and such as that. I don't know if you remember or not but I'm an author myself, that is, a poetess."

"I do remember that," Hindle said.

Serapta nodded. "Yes, we had a table put in your room especially for you to write at, me and Tot."

"Nothing came of that," Lisheen said with a little grimace. "That awful winter! even my inspiration froze right up!"

Except in those letters you wrote to whoever the man was, Hindle thought, that sent you the money to buy your ticket and skedaddle.

"And took a long time to thaw, too. Good thing I had other—I went back to the stage for a while. But I did write one poem—it got printed in *Leslie's Magazine*. Actually what happened, I wrote it for a contest put on by Castoria, which it didn't win because those prizes are a foregone conclusion before the contest even starts, so I sent it to *Leslie's*. But when they printed it, they put it on a page that said "American Humor." You never know what to expect from anyone! It wasn't humorous. The way it went—let's see—'Life is restless, days are fleeting,'" she recited, closing her eyes,

> *Children bloom, but die in teething*
> *Warning take, all friends and mothers,*
> *Watch the precious girls and brothers;*

Read the home life of Victoria,
Children nine, all had Castoria,
No sleepless nights, by baby squalling,
Like larks they rise in early morning.

She opened her eyes. "See, for the contest the word *Castoria* had to be in it. But anyway—as I started to say about friends—not necessarily women. I hate to say this, and present company excepted, but women are very much dogs in the manger, don't you think? In their constitution, I'm talking about. So when I say friends, I mean friends like one would meet running a newspaper or maybe traveling around like I've been having to do. Of course those old stages rattling over the roads full of chuckholes, if you could call them roads, crammed in between men with guns strapped on, smoking big cigars—"

They would put them out for a lady, of course, Lisheen said, but she for one always liked the smell of a good cigar, she truly did. Not some of the other terrible smells though, garlic sausage, mince pie—in the heat—cheese and peanut butter—that alkali dust—and then of course spirituous liquors. Trains were a thousand times better, even sitting up all night, but the rails ran out too soon, there was just too much country. Indians…she couldn't tell one from the other but some people could, Pawnees, Cheyennes, Arapahoes…The experts one would meet in different lines was just amazing. And the things that happened. Once the lead team at a full gallop was struck by lightning! and fell down dead. The main thing, though, that happened as far as *she* was concerned, was something that if it *hadn't* happened her whole life would—She probably wouldn't even *be* here, she confided.

"You mean on earth?" Hindle said.

"I mean here in your house, in Salt Lake City, visiting you. Renewing acquaintance with Serapta too, that who would ever think would be a married lady! But that was just—"

"Are you saying you've went out of your way to pay this particular visit?"

That was what she was saying, Lisheen said. Then went on with seeming irrelevance to confide that the editor and publisher of the New Mexico Kicker, one of the papers she made regular calls on, was a true gentleman of the south. Not handsome, not a tall gentleman by any means, some kind of a problem with one of his feet and inclined to drink a little too much, though, as he said, marriage to a good woman would set him right with regard to *that*. His name was Percy Tate, and while Andy would have, and did, lay down you might say his life for her—in that he was working tooth and toenail to keep her and Mavis in the lap of luxury (though he didn't leave any insurance) at the time the tarantula bit him—Percy was a man who recognized *natural ability*.

"And I don't want to seem like I am tooting my own horn or anything like that," Lisheen said, "but to quite a degree I have got it. By which I mean—you take the average individual, they see things and don't pay any attention, while with me they're etched right on my brain. So one time with Percy, we're sitting there drinking apple juice, I mention a few things and the next time I'm down that way he shows me the paper and here on the front page what do I see but one of the very things I was *telling* him! He had wrote it up and printed it with a headline and everything. BEST MAN WINS was the headline. I've got the clipping in my trunk, in fact I've got quite a few clippings by now, some even with my name on them. But that particular story—it was very funny. Would you like to hear it?"

"I wouldn't mind," Hindle said.

"Me either," Serapta said, "though I do have to keep my eye on the clock—"

"Well, I was in Titusville one time, waiting around looking out the window," Lisheen said. "The snow was falling and here come a sleigh. I heard the sleigh bells first, then here it was, an old man driving, a girl wrapped up in furs sitting in back. The Wells Fargo office was just across the street. And that was where they stopped, and you could see she was going to get out while the old man wasn't. But now here's a saloon two men come out of, gentlemen, probably southern by their looks, buttoned up in broadcloth and both been to the barber. They see the girl and make a run to help her, but now she don't want to get out of the sleigh till she looks them over and sees which one she'll give her hand to. So things in other words are at a standstill. Not for more than about a second, though. The men start to pushing each other out of the way. They get to jabbing, one of them knocks the hat off of the other, then that gentleman knocks *his* hat off, and now they're using fists and now I can't believe my eyes, they've pulled out *guns* and they're not fooling either, they are *taking aim.* And here's the flash! this big loud noise, and one of the horses hitched up to the sleigh gets shot in the neck right in an artery, and you wouldn't believe the amount of blood in a horse. All over the gentleman it spurted that's standing closest, and he thinks he's hit! He gives a yell and down the street he staggers and around the corner, while the one that's left picks up his hat but doesn't put it on. He bows and offers his hand, but the girl just sits. She's laughing so hard she can't even move. And the horse keels over."

Hindle and Serapta looked at each other as if to say, she hasn't changed.

"Then last July I was in Fort Sumner," Lisheen went on. "Have you ever been there? Hardly a town at all, one street, the last thing you'd expect to see was a bunch of people."

"We stayed the night there once," Hindle said.

"Then you'll remember the store, the general store with the big show-window?"

"Moffet's?"

"It had a name, but what it was I don't know. There was a crowd standing in front of it and when I get up close I see the window's got a dead man in it—man, I say, but it's really a boy propped up so he's standing-like, looking at you with half-open eyes like a dead kitten's, blue. They've unbuttoned the shirt to show the bullet holes bored in his chest and the dried black blood that's trickled down. He won't be standing long, it's a hundred and five in the shade, so everybody's taking a good look while they still got the chance, laughing and joking. The guns he's got buckled on look big and heavy for a little fellow like that, he looks about sixteen but they're saying he's twenty-one and killed a man for every year of his life, though a man back of me says he only killed nine, and that he's died with his boots on, in boots that look a mile too big. Probably his hat fell off but now it's crammed back on. 'Who is it?' I said. 'The Kid,' they said. 'Billy. The Kid. Where *you* been hiding?' Percy told me later he'd have given his eyeeteeth to be there," Lisheen said.

"So anyway the last time I was down there he had the idea, instead of me just seeing and hearing things by *accident* while I'm traveling around, why don't I go some particular place on *purpose* where something's going on! Like if I had been in Virginia City at the time of the fire in the Yellow Jacket mine, I'd notice things and tell him and he would write them up. But I was somewheres else at the time. And I wasn't there when John D. Lee got what was coming to *him*, standing on the burial place of them he killed in cold blood at the Mountain Meadow."

Hindle gave a start.

Serapta shot Lisheen a quick glance. "That's quite a while ago," she said admonishingly.

"I know," Lisheen said. "I just give that as an example. But I guess I'd better tell you, now's as good a time as any—Hindle," she said, "you remember when we was all at Burdick's you was just a young girl then, I well remember, working there, and little did I think you would marry the old doctor! and be a doctor yourself someday like you have gone and done. Hindle Lee, your name was then. And you told me once—I don't know if you remember but it was in the papers at the time—that this John D. Lee was a fugitive being hunted in the canyonlands. And the subject came up another time and if I'm not mistaken I think you told me he was your—real close kin."

"So what has that got to do with anything?" Serapta said sharply.

"Please don't get your feelings hurt or think I'm overstepping the bounds, Hindle," Lisheen said, "but the reason I come to Salt Lake was *because* of that, because of who you are, to ask you—"

"Why was you so sure I'd be here? I was away from here for ten years! I could of been at the ends of the earth!" Hindle said.

"Of course you could. But I had to try. And I remembered you said you had a sister Lucy—"

"Lucitie."

"That worked at the Salt Lake House. I had to try," Lisheen repeated. "Because you are—I'm positive you said—his own flesh and blood. You and your sister."

"Her and me and about fifty other children."

"Did he really have that many? I tried to find Burdick's Institution," Lisheen hurried on, "and when I saw *that* was gone I asked the neighbors. They told me to go to Paulina's house. *She's* come up in the world, hasn't she? Then down to where Serapta was staying with those ladies. Then up here. Only to find who I was looking for by accident! I think that's a good sign."

"That whole thing with Hindle's father was a long time ago," Serapta said.

"I know. The massacre and all that. And finding and arresting him took years, I guess, didn't it? And then the trials. And the execution long before Andy died, I remember reading about it in the paper. But to get to the point. Percy says a lot of people is still *interested* for some reason in the massacre. Why, I don't know. But they are, he says. In who took part in it and everything. Nothing is changed down there where John D. lived and everything, according to Percy. The houses…A lot of the men that took part has made themselves scarce, but some are still there with their wives and families, and women will talk…Percy says if I go down there to Cedar City and find out a few new things that nobody else has found out, and come back and tell him, why, he will not only write and print it in the paper but *get it published in a book*! and you know Mark Twain writes books and he's a *very wealthy man*. Percy will take half and I will take half, but of course I'll share with anyone that helps me. And Percy also says if I do this and it all turns out, why, *he will marry me*. Not," she added quickly, "that he wouldn't anyway if I was willing—"

"Cedar City?" Hindle said. "I don't believe you realize—"

"Why, a Gentile wouldn't have no more chance in a place like that than a snowball in my oven," Serapta said. "Gentile ladies," she spoke as if they were a separate species, forgetting that she was now back to being a Gentile herself, "is *always* coming through from back east and trying to spy out how the thing is done out here—sleeping arrangements and all that. But it don't do them a bit of good."

"And they're *extra* close-mouthed about some things," Hindle said. "Even if you belonged, there are subjects Mormons is counseled not even to talk to other *Mormons* about. So how do you expect—?"

"First, tell me what *you* know."

"Me?" Hindle said in surprise. "About my father? Not enough to put in your eye. And neither does Lucitie. The last time I saw him I was four years old. In fact I told you that at Burdick's."

"I'll be fair with you, Hindle. If anything comes of this, I'll pay you."

"Pay has nothing to do with it," Hindle said. "I just don't know anything! except that if you think you're going to go down to Cedar City and pretend to be a Mormon—which you couldn't do in the first place, they keep too close tabs on things, records and things like that—why, you're going to be sadly disappointed."

"Oh, I'm not going to do anything like that," Lisheen said. "What I'm going to do—I don't know whether you've heard, but there's a movement Percy found out about—"

"Percy is the one that ought to go down there and get *his* tail feathers singed," Serapta said.

"What kind of a movement?" Hindle said.

"Well, you know how the eastern congregations, Baptists and such as that, Methodists, have their missionary societies?" Lisheen said. "And the missionaries go to heathen Africa and the jungles and places like that? To save the cannibals and redeem all these wild men of Borneo? Well, somebody got the idea—maybe you don't realize how much the papers *print* back east about the polygamy and the different funny customs—got the idea, why not redeem *Utah*? Why not lead some *Americans* out of darkness and ignorance into the light of understanding, rather than cannibals and wild men? Charity begins at home. So this Society or whatever it is sent ministers and mission workers to several different towns like Wellsville and a town in Idaho that's totally Mormon, and a town in Arizona— They start churches, or try to, it's not easy, Sunday schools, Percy heard of one place, they started a home for boarding girls—So what *I'm* supposed to do, I'm to go down there and pretend we're the first contingent, Mavis and I, of Episcopals—"

"You're never in the world going to take that *child* down there," Serapta said.

"Of course I am. I have to. Mother and daughter. It will look so much better."

"And act like you're from some missionary society going to start a *church*?" Hindle said.

"Not a church, a boarding school where—Just a minute." She opened her purse and took out a handful of notes, which she shuffled till she came to the one she wanted. "Listen. 'Where they can be under Christian influence and receive practical instruction in housekeeping.'"

Hindle laughed.

"Laugh if you want. While I'm trying to open this boarding school and everything, why, what I'll *really* be doing is keeping my eyes open and asking questions. And as soon as I find out a few things, Mavis and me will leave. Then Percy will write up the true story of the—" But she let her voice trail off tactfully, without saying "massacre" again to a daughter of the ringleader.

Lisheen and Mavis stayed that night with Hindle, and Lucitie dropped in for a little visit. Mrs. Birdwood told her, Lucitie said, that someone was asking for her in order to find out where Hindle lived, and she wondered who it might be. So it was Lisheen, the actress. She remembered hearing about her from Hindle when she stayed at Burdick's. Didn't she have—? She stopped when Hindle gave her a warning look, but returned one of complacency when the illegitimate child she had been going to ask about appeared in the doorway.

As a full-fledged hairdresser, Lucitie took more than a passing interest in Mavis's snowy hair. It would never grow past her shoulders, Lucitie said, and indeed it never had, but Lisheen said she didn't care, it was naturally curly and when Mavis was older maybe they would tint it. Although a daguerreotyper, or photographist as they preferred to be called, in Cheyenne—She had taken the child to this photographist's studio to have her picture taken and he nearly went wild, didn't charge them or anything, made about a hundred photogravures trying out different ideas he thought of, Mavis in a little night robe with bare feet carrying a candle, hopped up on the bed with her feet tucked under her, with the pillows in behind her like she just woke up and was smelling the morning glories and listening to the birds sing—He was going to sell them to the Moonbeam Fairy Folding Bed Manufacturing Company and give Lisheen and Mavis half. But the strangest thing happened—a few days later some long-horn steers being driven somewhere broke loose and ran down the street and this photographer, Mr. Miller his name was, a lovely man, stepped out to see what the commotion was about and foolishly shooed at one of the steers, it made a lunge, caught him under the chin with a horn, the point come out his mouth and of course he died, Lisheen said.

Lucitie winced and shut her eyes and Hindle gasped. But Mavis, though listening intently, continued to swing her spindly legs from the chair's edge and bit her thumb with a bored look.

"'It was a heavy strong devil,' that is how the man that ran the bakery expressed it," Lisheen went on. "He was there and saw it all and saw the bull drag Mr. Miller two hundred yards before a cowboy shot him. They butchered the meat and gave it away."

"We didn't get any," Mavis said in a drowsy tone.

Lucitie studied her. "It's awfully hot down there in Cedar City, isn't it?" she said. "In summer? A lady once come to our hotel that was married to an Army officer and she said another officer's wife had *died* down around there, of heat stroke. And somebody like your little girl there, with such a fair complexion, those—eyes that color and everything, I'd be afraid to risk it if I was you. Why don't you leave her in Salt Lake?"

"Yes," Hindle said faintly.

"Oh, no. That wouldn't do. It's the effect, you know," Lisheen said. "Mother and daughter."

Chapter Thirty-six

*

LISHEEN SAID SHE WOULD WRITE BUT SHE DIDN'T. HINDLE AND SERAPTA OFTEN spoke of her in the next few weeks and wondered if she was still down there in Cedar City and what she was accomplishing. To find out enough for her editor friend to write a whole *book* about would take a lot of snooping, and Hindle for one felt that was rather risky. Not that anybody would *hurt* a lone woman like that, or a delicate-appearing girl like Mavis. But still, to go down there to the very hotbed of Mormonism and pretend to be trying to start an Episcopal boarding school, and all of a sudden start asking questions about the wagon train from Arkansas and Missouri that years before hadn't made it out of the country alive—

"Do you suppose him and her will really make money like Mark Twain?" Serapta wondered.

"I don't think money's the main attraction with Lisheen," Hindle said. "Do you? I think it's marrying that fellow, whoever he is."

"Will she get him, do you think?"

"Or die in the attempt."

"That poor little child!" Lucitie said when she came down a few weeks later and was told that nothing had been heard from them.

"Mavis got Tot's birthstone ring away from Serapta," Hindle said.

"How did she do that?"

"By whining and saying Tot promised it to her! She was only seven when Tot died, and I don't believe for a minute Tot promised her *anything*. Because Tot was never wrapped up in Mavis like Serapta was. Which she isn't now, thank goodness, since she's got Stig—"

"And got Eula and Esther too, it looks like," Lucitie said. "I never get to see them anymore. Are they ever home? And how's the baby? My namesake? Do you realize I've only seen her *twice*? I might as well not be her aunt! But you were saying about a ring—"

"Oh, just—Serapta had it on, Mavis recognized it and said, 'That's mine.' She said Tot promised it to her. Serapta says she knows she didn't, but she took it off and put it on her finger anyway. And can you imagine, Mavis didn't even say thank you!"

"Albert says the sun can actually *kill* an albino! He was sorry he didn't get to see her. He says they're very rare," Lucitie said.

"Well, they are, with the pink eyes and everything."

"He says they're like jelly fish when it comes to sun. Curl up, sizzle and die."

"Lisheen will watch out for her. When Lisheen gets done with this wild goose chase and marries that editor, why, the next clatter out of the box will be to have Mavis posing for cabinet photogravures like that poor man took that got hooked by that horn. I think he put a bee in her bonnet."

"What if she don't find out anything? Will the newspaper man marry her?"

It was the luckiest thing, Hindle said, that Jean was on her way to spend a few days with a sick relative when Lisheen and Mavis arrived and that they were gone by the time she got back. An inkling of what Lisheen was up to would get to the bishop and be relayed down to Cedar City so fast it would make your head swim, and neither Hindle nor Serapta wanted *that* to happen, for old times' sake and also because love stories ought to end (though Lisheen hadn't said a word about love) happily ever after.

EXCEPT THAT WITH LIFE BEING the way it is, they never do. Not for Cinderella and her prince or anyone. Sometimes they even make it up to the Diamond anniversary, maybe even beyond that if there is such a thing, but eventually the day will dawn—Jim Clarendon and his wife Maybelle made it up to their Silver anniversary, and Minerva Bohannon said if ever there was a case of true love it was there, though he was always stepping out on her. Why would he have stuck otherwise? Maybelle had the money to start with, but then he made so much on his own they both must have lost count, but still he hung around, and why would Jim do that if he didn't love the woman?

Both the Tribune and Deseret News reported the accident on the front page with big headlines, and not just when it was telegraphed to them on the day it happened, but also later. They published reports about her being brought home by train, about the numerous Catholic ceremonies, about the crypt being prepared for her up in the cemetery and the marble statues ordered from Italy. And while it was a terrible thing, and the more so when you thought of all she was leaving, that mansion, the hot water pipes, the servants, all those furnishings that were *still* arriving, somebody was saying, Minerva said, a person couldn't help but be disgusted.

Disgusted?

Because it didn't need to happen, it was Maybelle Clarendon's own fault.

"How do you figure that?" Hindle said, preparing the syringe for the periodic washing out that Minerva had prescribed for her own stomach. "I thought her horse—"

"What was she doing on the horse anyway, a woman fifty-two years old!"

"Well, they invited her—"

"Of course they invited her. But was that any reason for her to go? And if she *did* go—to Hornitos' thirty-second year since gold was discovered celebration—go on account of her and Jim happening to live there one time, was that any reason for her to ride *sidesaddle* in the parade instead of sitting in a carriage? But no, that wasn't showcase enough for her. She had to demonstrate her riding and her diamonds and show off her clothes and that piled-on hair."

"Albert will be sorry," Hindle said. "He's my brother-in-law, you know, Albert Alfonce's Hairdressing. Mrs. Clarendon went to him, or rather he went to her."

"I know, that's what you said," Minerva said. "But he sure wouldn't of knew his customer when the body arrived at O'Brien's Undertaking Parlor. Don't ever mention this but the oldest O'Brien brother, he drops in sometimes, and some of the girls don't like it because of what they do over there and he smells like formaldehyde. But I always tell 'em it's honest work, got to be done and they'll be doing it for you someday. So he was telling Flossie—the condition Jim's poor wife was in—!" Minerva shook her head. "Mr. O'Brien had it from the lady's maid when she come down to bring the clothes. For being the maid, of course, she was *at* the parade. She seen the whole thing, and she said if she lived to be a hundred years old she would never—"

The procession, she said, in passing a narrow place in the road kind of bunched up, and Mrs. Clarendon, trying to fall back and let a float that was crowding up all decorated with flowers pass ahead of her, got her horse to backing. Which she'd been showing off anyway, the maid said, being a good rider and perched up there side-saddle, it was very graceful. She had plumes in her hat and this tight corset. So she backed her horse...right between the heels of the team behind her and this float they were pulling. And the next thing anybody knew she was threw for a loop with full force on the wagon tongue, the horses bolted, the team, her own horse, one of the other riders, people was shoving and screaming. The float was clear down by the canyon before they finally got it stopped, and several minutes before they got Mrs. Clarendon untangled. She was still breathing, but her skull was crushed. They carried her to the nearest house. She never regained consciousness and about a half hour later she died.

"The paths of glory," Hindle said with a faraway look, standing in front of Minerva with the syringe and rubber tube.

"And Jim, that had more women all along the line than you could shake a stick at— would you believe the man is prostrate? Sick with grief! Swore off drinking. Women. Sits with Father Barron all day long. Ain't that human nature? But you watch human nature as the time goes by."

"He'll marry again."

"Of course he'll marry again. And you know to who? Nobody poor, I will bet you that. Some wealthy widow, you mark my words."

But Minerva's next news about him was that the day after the Fourth of July he started off on an expedition.

"An expedition!" Hindle said, thinking of the North Pole. "He won't find many wealthy widows up there!"

"Up where? He's going down through the old mining country. Father Barron was telling me."

"Prospecting?"

"Prospecting nothing. The man's got so much money now he's paving his yard with it. No, stereoscoping. Father Barron give him the idea, he claims, though maybe he did and maybe he didn't—"

"Stereoscoping?"

"You know what a stereopticon is."

Like everyone else, Hindle had one, bought from a hawker who came to the door, a double magic lantern small enough to hold up to the eyes on a handle, with a slot in front in which the stiff cardboard postcard-sized pictures of two identical scenes taken from slightly different points of view could be slipped to show a single image standing forward from the background, so real it looked like you could get in there and walk around.

"And you know what the views is, double?"

Hindle nodded.

"Well, somebody *takes* them views. And that's called stereoscoping, Father Barron was saying. And the man that takes views like that, he's a stereoscopist."

"You don't say," Hindle said. "So now Mr. Clarendon, that's what he is? And he's went away? He must be feeling better."

Minerva shrugged. "But *he* ain't going to do the work," she said. "You want to remember, Jim's been rich now longer than he's been poor. And riches spoils a man in very short order. Once upon a time he'd of done everything himself. Now he's got this stereoscopist hired, cameras obscuras, all that different stuff hauled in a special wagon, while in another wagon is all the camping stuff, and even the butler! to cook and such as that—"

"And take these double pictures—"

"—of the old mining places people's left. Streams…I've seen 'em myself," Minerva said, "where the gold was shining like coins in a net purse. Old abandoned shafts, stakes and markers over graves. Of mostly young men, did you ever think of that? The graves, I mean."

"That won't cheer him up much."

"Oh, I don't know. It's very cheerful to still be alive when other people's dead."

"And it sits there," Hindle said. "The mansion. All Mrs. Clarendon's schemes and hopes, and the Irish kings not good enough for that rich dining room—" She sighed.

"He'll probably sell the place when he comes back. And goodness knows who he'll have in tow!"

But who that would be nobody could ever have imagined! for it was Lisheen's albino child Mavis, more dead than alive to all appearances—cooked, boiled, red as a beet on one of the hottest August days in history. Limp, hanging, dying—The man carrying her in like a baby Hindle didn't recognize, as, bewildered by the teams, wagon and carriage she glimpsed confusedly at the gate, she hurried to make ready a bed. He turned out to be Jim Clarendon's butler, though, or hired man, whatever you wanted to call him. Then there stood Jim himself. "Hello, Doctor," he said. "Kid said to bring her here, we didn't dare leave her anywhere down the line."

"What happened? Where's her mother?"

"The girl says she's dead. Shot to death by someone. This one we found in a canyon out west of Cedar City. Or didn't find exactly. This Indian come and told us where she was hid, see, down by a stream. Plastered with mud. She was nearly burnt to death. That was what saved her, the mud. He kept her in the stream at first, let the water run over her."

"Not burnt in a fire?"

"No, the blamed old sun." He paused, then went on, "We was heading for home here anyways, so brought her with us. Indian said they was after her like her mother, what else could we do? She's got no folks, she says. She mentioned you. We don't know what really happened. Her fever's been high and she's been out of her head. A time or two riders come along asking if we'd saw an albino girl, said one had got lost and they was looking for her. We said no, because this Indian had told us—But I just had a hunch. So anyway she's here now, and if you will take care of her—"

"Of course, that goes without saying."

Several days later when he dropped by to see how she was getting along, in the midst of their conversation Hindle made mention of the fact that he probably didn't remember, but thirteen years ago he had *seen* this very girl as a baby, in fact he had held her in his arms and stepped up and looked in the mirror that was hanging there, at their two reflections. At Burdick's Institution the time Mrs. Clarendon had a broken clavicle and he was off prospecting, then come walking in—

"Why, yes," he said. "I do kind of remember."

"And now you've saved her life! Don't that seem wonderful?"

THEY TOOK ROOMS, MAVIS TOLD Hindle and Serapta when the red started fading away and she was able to sit up and talk, along the main street of Cedar City, to the side of Mrs. Reese's house. Mrs. Reese was a dressmaker that also made hats, but she didn't have any customers, so Mama thought she was just somebody's extra wife and pretended to be in business so the U.S. Deputies wouldn't be after her husband. They never saw him, Mavis said. When they first got down to Cedar City there was quite a few deputies but then they must have got tired of being there and nobody to arrest. So they left. And then there wasn't anybody around but Mormons, so Mama was not quite as at ease as she had been.

But that was all right. She told her not to tell, Mavis said, that she was born in Salt Lake and raised by Serapta till she was seven years old and went to school, and sometimes to Sunday school too, with Mormon children. Because then they might think they was jack Mormons up to no good. She was just to say she was born in Cheyenne and that they lived there till Daddy died. She wasn't supposed to say anything else! about Mama taking over Daddy's territory after he was bit by a tarantula and selling newspaper metal or about the New Mexico newspaper man going to write a book out of what she would find out, and marry her too if she found out enough, or nothing. She was just to keep mum.

The very first day, Mama got ready and paid calls on the bishop and other people like that. She told them she wanted to lay her cards on the table. The Episcopal Missionary Society of New York gave her the job to come to Cedar City to teach the Mormons, just like the missionaries went to Africa and the jungle to teach the savages, she said. She wanted to start a Sunday school and then a school for boarding girls, she said. She had lots of different speeches to say which Percy, the newspaper man, wrote out for her like a part in a play and sometimes she would practice them on her, Mavis said. And she, Mavis, learned a few speeches too. And so they settled down, and Mama made friends with Mrs. Reese, she was of English descent, and several others.

And the Mormons were very nice, Mavis said. They just acted like Mama must be crazy to think she could come and teach them like the cannibals in Africa and start a school for boarding girls but as if they decided to be friendly and humor her along. And Mavis didn't go into the hot sun, she said, she knew better than that. But it got cool and nice after the sun went down. There were play parties and they would be asked to them, and they went to the meeting house and there was a taffy pull and one time a surprise party. They went to that. They danced, there was accordion music and a man played the violin. People would josh Mama and say they bet they would convert *her* and redeem and save *her* soul before she would convert *them*, the spirit was friendly. There was even a man that came and brought Mama a jar of apple butter and said he was throwing his hat in the ring to court her, but he already had no telling how many wives and he wasn't very good-looking, so she refused the apple butter and showed him the door.

Right next to where they lived there was a place, it was called a hotel and probably it was, but it looked just like a medium-sized house where people lived, and a family did live there by the name of Wood, but travelers could stay there too. That is where her and Mama stayed all night the first night, and found the rooms next to Mrs. Reese next day. And there was a lean-to on the side of the hotel, Mormons aren't supposed to drink, but a few would gather there and that is what they would do, drink whiskey or brandy, which was called Valley Tan. It was really a saloon, but that didn't bother Mama and her, though sometimes they could hear singing after they went to bed, old countrified songs. Somebody in the saloon was always sitting so they could look up and down the street and in every direction, and Mama thought that besides a saloon it must be kind of a lookout station. But so that the U.S. Deputies should not surprise anybody, the whole town was watchful. And Mama said she should have realized that Gentiles like them would stand out like a sore thumb and couldn't rent a livery stable wagon and go wherever they wanted. The one time they tried it they were followed, and Mama turned back before they even got close to Pinto, let alone the Mountain Meadow, and nobody believed Mama's story about wanting to look for an opal mine. But she told Mrs. Reese and different ones that she didn't really need to see the place anyway, and that it had been a mistake to try. But saying that didn't help, because from then on everybody was suspicious and watched more than ever and they weren't so friendly, which Mama thought might be because she had been a little too free with her questions, so she decided to ease off on that for a while.

There was an Indian that worked around the hotel and other places chopping wood and such as that, and his face would really scare you at first because of scars from some old battle and his body being pulled over to one side, but he wouldn't hurt you, Nephi said, wouldn't hurt a fly. Nephi was Mrs. Wood's brother's boy, one year older than her, Mavis said. Anyway Mama told Nephi to send the Indian over to help her bring in wash water and gather wood, and what should happen but they knew each other! That is to say, Mama recognized the Indian before he recognized her. They had met at Burdick's Institution before she was born. His name was Loudhawk. Mavis knew all about that stay, how the theatrical company Mama was traveling with had brought her, delirious with typhoid fever, to the hospital, then left town (her father with them, who Mavis thought was married to Mama) to the next engagement, leaving her alone. Then Mavis was born. That was the story Serapta had told her a hundred times. And now here was somebody *from* that story, the Indian that did chores about the place. And while Mama wasn't sure he recognized her, though he pretended he did, when he saw her he said "Papoose," Mavis said. Then, "Snowbird, made of snow." "Snow—and dumplings," Mama said.

Mr. and Mrs. Wood who ran the hotel had several children. Mavis wasn't sure how many because she couldn't play outside in the sunshine but also because the children were always having to do chores, help harvest and things like that. Mrs. Wood's brother also lived with them. Mr. Durphy, *his* name was. You could tell they were related because they both had red hair and looked alike except Mrs. Wood wore a dress. And of course Mr. Durphy's voice was different, it was deep and loud, you could always hear it above the others in the saloon, or outside when he was standing and watching. He was Nephi's father. Nephi didn't have a mother. His birthday was the same day as hers. She found that out at the play party, Mavis said. He might not have danced with her only everybody had to change partners in the middle of a dance and so they found out each other's names and how old they were, and the next two-step he asked her. Then here he was sitting by her during refreshments.

Nephi didn't look a bit like his father or his aunt, his hair was black and something about him made Mama think his mother might have been an Indian lady. But he was very nice and brought her a rock that he said it would be a black opal if polished by someone who knew how. That was what gave Mama the idea in the first place to say they were going out to hunt black opals when really they were going to the Mountain Meadow to see the place, but when they saw men following them they didn't do either one.

Another thing Nephi gave her, Mavis said, was a bunch of blue columbines, but of course they withered almost before you could get them in a cup of water. And another thing that was withered, or rather dead, was a Gila monster, he killed it with a rock because they're poisonous. He brought it to show the pretty colors on its back, like Indian beadwork. The reason Nephi wasn't off harvesting was because he took fits of some kind when his brain got too hot, and anyway his aunt Mrs. Wood said she needed him to help her.

But he would come over to Mrs. Reese's and then he would come in through the back door of *their* little rented house on the side, so nobody in the hotel or saloon could see him, and talk to her and Mama. Mostly to Mama, because she got so lonesome she would put herself out to be entertaining. So she paid attention to Nephi because he paid attention to her for paying attention to him. She told him about when she worked in the Mitigated Mourning Department and when she was on the stage and such as that. But of course she didn't tell him the real reason they were in Cedar City, which was to find out whatever she could about the old massacre at the Mountain Meadow. She did slip in a few questions here and there, but Nephi knew but very little. He had heard of John D. Lee but only that he was in league with the devil and a detriment to the church, that he was shot at sunrise and that any house he ever lived in was haunted.

Nephi said his father said there used to be as many Lees around as prairie dogs but now he didn't know why, but he thought they were all gone. He said the Mountain Meadow was haunted with all kinds of visions such as a complete wagon train wending its way down towards the southern spring, people had seen it. And other things happened. His father and uncle said it was a big waste of time to try to see anything at the execution, shut in on three sides with soldiers lined up in rows and then the snow a-falling. Nephi didn't come to visit very openly, and when he left would go out the back door and around so it would look as if he came from Mrs. Reese's. After Mama and Loudhawk recognized each other, Loudhawk would come around to the back door too, that was where they did most of their talking, usually about Burdick's Institution, as that was their only common topic. He never came inside except with the wood or the wash water. And he wasn't anywhere around when it happened, Mavis said. Or not that she saw.

It was afternoon, so hot the pump handle would feel like a hot poker if you touched it, and sitting on a boulder would raise a blister. She and Mama were taking a nap, she said, there wasn't anything else to do. The blinds were pulled down. The back door was shut. The front door was open, but the screen door tacked with mosquito netting was shut. Flies might have been buzzing around and maybe a wasp and the clock ticking, but otherwise it was so quiet that when all of a sudden they heard voices and a dog barking it was like through an ear-trumpet, it sounded so loud. But of course it *was* loud, Mavis said. It was a big quarrel going on, and when her and Mama got off the bed and went over close to the screen door they could hear, it was about *them*, mostly about Mama being a wolf in sheep's clothing trying to pry into their history and bring the government down on them and also make a match between her and Nephi, but also about her being some kind of a familiar spirit, was what it sounded like. Nephi's father was just wild, they could hear him, swearing, hollering about he wouldn't no more worry putting a bullet through a bilk like that than into a yellow dog and that if somebody didn't watch out! They were drunk, all of them—then all of a sudden there was a rush of footsteps, the screen door flew open, there was a roar, a flash, bang! and Mama fell over dead.

A lot of people ran in then, men, but Mrs. Reese too and Mrs. Wood, there was blood all over. Mrs. Wood was crying, she ran to her brother and said they put him up to it. Then she shook and hit him and they pulled her off. And that night when Mama was all washed and dressed and laid out and some ladies were going to sit up with her, Mrs. Wood took her over to see how peaceful and lovely she looked, Mavis said. Mrs. Wood said they were going to do Temple work for her, be baptized and everything for her so that no matter what her sins might have been, they would be washed away and she would go to heaven. She stayed with them that night, Mavis said, and Mrs. Wood said she could always live with them. She said George was in jail but that what happened wasn't really his fault because he wasn't right in his mind. Then she spoke up and said she wanted to go to Salt Lake, and Mrs. Wood said they would talk to the bishop because he would have to make the decision, and Nephi was there but he acted scared to talk to her. Then they all knelt down and prayed and then they went to bed. And in the night a hand was shaking her and it was Nephi ... getting her outside with no noise ... They were running, and even when they went a long ways he still whispered. They had found Mama's diary and her papers, he said, and said she was a spy, and that she was too, Mavis said, and a witness, and mustn't leave the country alive. Nephi's orders to her was, that she was to go down by the canal, then straight west and at sun-up hide in the ravine, and he would come and find her and they'd wait till dark. There was a bunch of Gentile miners out west of the lake, Nephi said, they would help them get to California. But the night was dark and after Nephi left she wasn't sure of her directions and at sun-up didn't know which ravine, everything looked the same, she was thirsty and kept on going. Then it got so bright and hot it seemed like the sun was as big as a house and only about a mile off in the sky, and she walked and stumbled—and the next thing she knew she felt cold and sick and was going to pull the covers over her, but the covers—But she wasn't in bed but in running water, and a hand was under her. It was Loudhawk, and her head was plastered with mud all over, and then here came this wagon with the leather curtains, and the carriage, Loudhawk had went out and found them, and she was being put in the wagon—in the back—and a man was saying, "Rest easy, you're safe now, little girl."

BUT MAVIS WAS MORE, as it turned out, than safe. She was in the Lord's vest pocket. Or so it seemed at the time. Wouldn't you think so? Adopted by a millionaire? But in this life, don't be too sure. Serapta certainly thought heaven on earth was where Mavis had landed. What better fate was there? And it wasn't as if Mr. Clarendon had been taken in by false pretenses. He saw how spoiled she was (by Serapta for seven years and then apparently Lisheen), her tantrum over the custard being watery, what she did to Eula for sitting on her bed, the way she screamed and carried on when Serapta went home to get supper instead of putting her hair up in rags, he was there.

It was the last thing in the world she ever expected, Hindle told Lucitie. She thought that between them, she and Serapta would have to get the girl raised and married, for there was no one else to do it. The editor who brought about the whole situation had never met Mavis, she was nothing to him. Nothing to the woman in Cheyenne who took care of her when her mother was away, either. But to Hindle and Serapta, they were there when she was born and knew her beforehand, and that obligated a person. Besides, for those first years no child could have belonged more to a mother than Mavis to Serapta. Hindle's involvement had been small, and now it was to see that a home for her needn't jeopardize Serapta's marriage or the arrangement Hindle had with Serapta about her own children's daily care. And when Mavis was older, it was hard to picture her gainfully employed. And whether it was having been so spoiled, or just being born that way, Mavis was not an amiable child. "The wonder is, she's living," Lucitie said. "Albert says for an albino to be out in the hot sun like she supposedly was and not curl up and die is just a miracle."

"Oh, the angels is watching over her, no doubt of that," Hindle said a little sardonically, for by that time Mavis had been adopted.

Those first few days, though, it was touch and go whether she would live. But Hindle read up in the *Family Physician* about burns, for what was the difference who or what did it, sun or fire? and she and Jean kept cloths on her soaked with vinegar water, fed her cooling things Serapta prepared and made her drink water by the quart. Serapta could scarcely bear to leave her home out back, though, and was always looking at the clock and wondering as worriedly about how Stig was getting along as if he had been miles away instead of a hundred or so yards, but she stayed and did what she thought was her duty, more to old though betrayed affection than to the injured girl herself. For it was no easy matter to take care of Mavis. Especially when she started to get better. That she would ever look like her ghostly white self again hardly seemed possible. Hindle even thought she might be scarred, the burning had been so severe, but no, nature is wonderful. Her whiteness came back purer and purer.

Mr. Clarendon, the second time he dropped in, could hardly believe that this gossamer angel sitting propped against her pillows having a dish of blanc mange spooned to her as though, judging by her expression, it had been poison was the skinned-looking, half-dead eel he had had his stereoscopist take into his wagon because it had leather curtains and they could lay her out in muddy wetness on blankets in the wagon bed and bring her back to safety. The way she acted that day of his visit, Hindle said, you could certainly see who her mother was and her father, too. For she might have been little Eva herself on the stage. And after that, every time he came to call…

Lucitie said you had to be fair. The girl didn't *know* he was a millionaire. *She* didn't know about the mansion up on Brigham Street, the servants, carriages and blooded horses. *She* didn't know a child adopted by him would have the world by the tail. Maybe not, Hindle said, but how long would it take even an idiot to find out when every time the man stopped by he was loaded down with presents? a French doll, a little ivory fan carved and inlaid with mica, a white fur muff, a lace parasol no bigger than a dinner plate, that bonnet filled with ruching—She sounded somewhat sharp. Even Serapta sounded that way when she spoke about a girl who didn't know how to say thank you, or hardly anything else polite, falling into such duck soup.

"Maybe it will be the making of both of them," Lucitie said. "Him with a broken heart after losing his life's companion and her a homeless waif—"

"A broken heart!" Hindle said. "Well, maybe. But as for Mavis—"

Child though she was, she must have cast a spell, Serapta said. And probably Mr. Clarendon—Maybe it was always a disappointment to him never to have had any children, especially a daughter.

"Well, he's got one now."

It seemed worthy of being written up somewhere, an orphan girl being adopted by a millionaire. But no, nothing came out in the papers about it at all. A pair of servants, as they must have been, came down and while Hindle and Serapta stood by with looks as though Mavis had won the Irish sweepstakes (though she herself, a delicate white stalk, appeared cool and collected) got her presents and things together and carried her off to the Clarendon mansion. And thus, because some people have all the luck and some people don't have enough to put in your eye, her new life began.

What that would be was easy to picture. Every luxury, comfort and advantage this world had to offer. And first and foremost in Hindle's mind was the fact that Jim Clarendon was the one she was calling Papa and living under the same roof with. Of course he probably wouldn't be single long. Then daughter's snow-white nose would be out of joint, her pink eyes would fill with tears, her silvery mane be tossed in a storm of jealousy. Hindle could just imagine.

Minerva Bohannon, down for her usual stomach bath, had seen Mavis at Hindle's after she got over her near-fatal sunstroke and before the force of ruthless destiny took hold, and she could just imagine too. She was flabbergasted by the adoption, not because in Jim's bereft state he might think he needed the comfort of a child, but that of all he might have opened his life to he would pick a strip tore out of nothing like that one! But in a way Hindle could see how that would come about. After traveling in Europe and even going around the world, and choosing and buying the finest furnishings, clothes, harness, horses and every necessity till you got to be the most critical judge of things imaginable, it seemed to her you would just naturally seek out whatever was different from all others. One painting that there would never be another like it. One Kohinoor diamond that would never be mined again...

"But, my God," Minerva said, "there's albinos—They're not *that* rare."

"No, but maybe because her mother was Lisheen and her father was an actor—that Serapta said you would turn around and look at in the street, the man was so handsome—why, besides being an albino she's got *looks*, where a lot of them look like a baby pig. And who's supposed to have the temperament? The brunette, the Spanish dancer with the rose in her teeth stomping her feet, green-eyed monster wrote all over her, pulling a knife. But here it's this *wraith* but with temperament to burn."

"If he wanted rarity—!" But Minerva gave up. It was just too much for her, the notions people took. With Mrs. Clarendon gone and not having to watch his chance anymore, you'd think the man would stop in and see an old acquaintance once in a while, but not him! And now that he could have a side girl on every block if he wanted, what did he do? Adopt an albino daughter! "How old is she?"

"Thirteen," Hindle said.

Minerva sat thinking. "Well, if she was *developed*," she said. "But skinnier than a yard of pump water—" As she got ready to leave she said she must have a bottle of that medicine.

"For who this time?"

"For Flossie."

Hindle began writing on a slip of paper. "Give it like I say here. If it looks like her blood is rushing too much to her head, or she starts to wheezing—"

"I'll watch," Minerva said. "Don't it seem like God could of done things different?"

"It does to me," Hindle said.

"So the men could of bore the brunt of it once in a while?"

Hindle nodded. "In case it doesn't work, you let me know."

Chapter Thirty-seven

*

IF SHE WAS IN THEIR PLACE, LUCITIE SAID, INSTEAD OF *WONDERING* ABOUT MAVIS she would march up and see the girl. After all, who had a better right? You take someone that raises a baby from birth till the age of seven or eight and if that person can't go to the door like a mother, mansion or no mansion, knock and be let in, then who *should* be able to?

But that was easier said than done, Serapta said. Stig refused to do a thing for himself now, he was too spoiled even to butter his bread. And Eula and Esther—It was hard for Serapta to get away. Besides, as Stig said, if Mavis thought anything of her she would show it, come down, bring some little thing. After a few weeks, much to their surprise, she did. But as Minerva said when she heard about it, if them you've left down below—while you climb up the ladder, up above the world so high like a diamond in the sky—don't know the *details*, then half the fun is lost. So she wasn't a bit surprised that eventually *Miss Mavis Clarendon* came to call with a gift of hothouse grapes.

The details of her life were about like what you would imagine: a governess Mavis didn't like and was going to get rid of, five five-dollar gold pieces a week pocket money, a riding teacher. Papa this and Papa that. Papa wanted her to take piano lessons. She and Papa went up to Mama's grave one day when they were taking a drive. That was not, of course, poor Lisheen's grave, if she had one at all down there in Cedar City and hadn't been thrown off a cliff. Jim's lawyer had said not to try to start an investigation or make any inquiries, the less said the better, especially concerning the murdered woman's daughter disappearing first from the vicinity of Cedar City and then up north into the hush of wealth. Hindle had to laugh at Mavis calling dead-and-gone Mrs. Clarendon Mama. How Mrs. Clarendon would have hated that! But Serapta and Hindle did have to say that in the clothes Mavis had on, coat trimmed with fur, kid-topped shoes, velvet bonnet lined with pink to match her pink eyes, ringlets agleam like silver, she did look more like an unearthly angel than ever.

Stig, who Serapta alerted to look out the window and see her, thought she might possibly *be* an angel, not just the divine soul we all are, inside our earthly tabernacle, but one of the order of actual angels, a ministering spirit or divine messenger. "Why not?" he said. "Nobody knows what they really look like, and heavenly beings *do* come to earth sometimes."

"Maybe so," Hindle said when Serapta told her what Stig had said, but angels are as angels do, and Mavis certainly didn't act like one of *them*. Still, would they in her place do any better? Maybe through the years, with Jim Clarendon to protect her and give her every advantage and finally leave her his money, she would turn out to be one of the great benefactors of orphans and of the human race. If that ever happened, the hired girl Jean coming past with the filled coal bucket muttered, she would eat her hat. Mavis's visit from on high had made Jean almost sick with envy. Eula and Esther said if they had a doll like Mavis's they would let other little girls hold her, and if they had gold pieces in their purse they would open it and offer one, but remarks like that were easy to make.

Stig even reasoned out that a real angel might act disagreeable and selfish and demanding *as a form of disguise.*

Serapta watched her very closely the next time Mavis had the carriage stop and came running in, this time in white almost from head to foot, which she said Papa liked her in the best and which the maid hated because it was so hard to take care of (but she was mean and Papa was going to fire her), and Serapta's honest opinion was: she might *look* like a heavenly being, but she was still just Mavis who had gone off and left *her* without a backward glance and, so far as they could tell, hadn't even shed a tear for her own mother, Lisheen.

Mavis didn't bring anything that time.

The next time, several weeks later, she brought the news that Papa was going to take her across the whole United States to New York City and from there across the ocean to France, Italy and several other countries, and that she was studying Mama's book called *European Travel* with her name, Maybelle Clarendon, signed in front.

Minerva Bohannon caught the few lines in the Tribune in the Society section which Hindle had missed: "Mr. James Clarendon and daughter Miss Mavis Clarendon will sail from New York on April 15th for Le Havre, France, on an extended sightseeing tour throughout the European countries."

Jean said, when she heard about it from Serapta and at the same minute dropped and broke a lamp chimney, that her brother Joseph was going on a mission over there. Because the time, she said quarrelsomely, was coming when the Elders would be commanded to *bind up the law and seal up the testimony.* And then look out! Judgment, hail-storm, thunder, lightning, pestilence, war . . .

FOR SOME UNKNOWN REASON, AFTER her induced miscarriage Flossie, who lived under Minerva's roof and was one of her most popular boarders, took with an affection of the nervous axis of the body, which Hindle, after long study in Dr. Ford's *Question Book* as well as her other standbys, diagnosed as neurarthropathy. That didn't surprise Flossie a bit, considering what an ordeal she had gone through five years before when she had her little boy Frankie. This was in Durango, she told Hindle. She and Buck had only been married six months, and the day after the baby was born a headache started that drove her nearly insane. The midwife was a Thomsonian, and if Buck had known *that* he wouldn't of let her come within a mile of the place. To cure the headache, she gave Flossie warm mustard water to make her vomit, but vomiting threw her into a spasm, and from then on every hour for thirty-six solid hours she had another, while Buck stood by with an iron spoon to keep her from chewing her tongue to pieces. When the spasms finally let up, but not the headache, he rushed out and found another midwife.

That one's remedy was to heat rocks in the stove to put around Flossie's feet and cause perspiration. By that time it seemed like the neighbor ladies was there, and with all the talking and excitement and Buck keeping on stuffing the stove with coal, the rocks got too hot, and that was where the big scar on her leg come from and why the ball was burnt off her right big toe. So while she was screaming and thought she had died and went to hell, Buck rushed out again and this time got a doctor, and he come in and bled her from the ankle to draw the blood out of her head to stop the pain. And that brought on blood poisoning.

"But we're hell for strong, our family," Flossie said, "especially the Beal side. So this whatever-you-said will soon cure up." And in the meantime, rather than work at Minerva's she got to stay home with her little boy Frankie, and Buck went out and took a temporary coal-heaving job, so every cloud had a silver lining.

That was the first time Hindle really realized that some of Minerva's boarders might have husbands, children and homes they went to on their days off. Flossie's was a tiny house on Third Avenue and M Street, close to the City Cemetery. And not long after, Flossie was *in* the City Cemetery, there to abide till the Last Day. To lose a patient was a sad thing, but as Flossie had died by her own hand and not due to Hindle's handling of the case, Hindle was not as bowed down by her sad death as she might otherwise have been. Minerva, however, was very bowed down indeed, and as the winter days went along and she continued to grieve, Hindle mixed her a balsam.

"It was all so unnecessary," Minerva said. "What did it hurt Buck if Frankie still had long curls at the age of five if it gave Flossie pleasure? She *loved* those long golden curls, loved them, and Frankie must have too! to cry and hang back the way he did when Buck took him to the barber! Little boy though he was, *he* knew how bad his mother would feel!" But no, men was nothing but brutes, even the good-looking ones like Buck, so nothing would do but the curls must come off. Did Buck think or realize? Minerva said. A man's own selfish desire is all they know. So off come Frankie's *warm protecting* curls in the dead of winter! And what was the upshot? Minerva could of told him, anyone could. The boy caught cold, it went into double pneumonia and a few days later Frankie was dead. Of *course* Flossie was beside herself. Of *course* she found Myrtle's bottle of belladonna and drank the whole thing. What could you expect? Buck was thinking to bury the cut-off curls with Flossie but then he decided not to, everyone knows hair grows in the grave so Frankie's would have grown in again for the Resurrection, so Buck didn't bury them but kept them for himself, for remembrance.

"But I will bet you something," Minerva said, wiping her eyes. "I bet it won't be no time till he'll be roaming the country hunting another softie, and them golden curls will be scattered to the winds."

HINDLE WASN'T SUCH A BRAGGER as to think (even to herself) that had *she* been called when Frankie took sick she might have saved him. But of course she hadn't been called! When the patient was of the male sex, even small like Frankie, the only doctor good enough to take charge would be a *man*, even if he was shaking with deliriums from drinking, or his septum had been half eaten away by Spirochaeta pallida or the dust of cocaine.

But then *Diseases of Women* was what she had on her sign, allowing Hindle with her two-and-a-half-dollar license to rest easy as to legal capabilities and fitness to function. The treater of females drew no attention, critical or otherwise, from the male medical world. Had she started treating the fecundating race, however, especially in any conspicuous way, and in particular tried to join the Medical Society, she might not have continued so firmly fixed in what had become quite a successful career. From a small newsletter sent from the drug company she traded with in Chicago she found out about the Salt Lake Medical Society, formed since her husband's day, and wished she could join it. From the members' papers on St. Vitus' Dance and other afflictions, and the patients they had shown such as with hard indolent gout, bronchoceles or an unnaturally long neck with an abnormal growth the size of a hen's egg on each side, also jars with seventy-foot tapeworms or gallstones, she was sure she could have learned a great deal. In the years since she started her eclectic practice, she even had a case or two herself worth demonstrating. But she knew there was no more chance of joining the Medical Society than to get to be a Catholic priest or a Mormon Elder.

Had the weather been nice, the sun shining, Minerva would probably not have broken down the way she did over Flossie's death. Over herself too, over her boarder Myrtle's canary that had stopped singing and huddled on the floor of its cage with its feathers puffed out, even over a dying moth batting against the frost-patterned window pane as if trying to escape.

"To what," she said, "poor thing? The snow out there? That wind that would knock *me* over, let alone you?" She took the frayed moth in her fingers and carried it over and put it in the fire, the tears running down her cheeks. Minerva! who had handled the toughest customers, Shagnasty Joe, Al Sponsalier, and in old mining camp days had sat through sporting events like a fight between a bull and a bear, or a bulldog and a wild cat, without turning a hair.

By the butcher's delivery boy, three of her boarders, Big Hattie, Gertie and Blonde Edith, sent for Hindle. Her Carminative Balsam had not worked, they said. She found Minerva fully dressed in her bedroom, face down on her bed, not crying now—she had cried herself out—but with swollen red eyes and puffy lips, hardly drawing breath.

"I just happened to be passing," Hindle said.

"I just happen to be passing too," Minerva said. "Throwing up the game."

"Why, you are doing no such thing."

Hindle left the remedy with Myrtle. Ten drops of the muriated tincture every two hours in a spoonful of camomile infusion.

"You know what life is, Hindle? Bug dust. That's what my old man used to say, and that's the truth." By now Minerva had taken to her bed, her face yellow against the white sham.

"You won't say that when you get better," Hindle said, examining the hard left breast that would not yield to pressure over the sad heart. But Minerva did not get better and finally, during the thaw, she died of poisonous scirrhus of the mammary gland. While Myrtle was giving her the muriated tincture she decided to treat Dickie with it too, her sick canary, and greatly to her delight he revived enough to climb back onto his perch. But then the day Minerva died Dickie did too, so Myrtle, crying till she couldn't see straight, put his little corpse in the coffin with her, under her two hands folded upon the tucked silk that hid the awful crabs' claws her veins had become and the sunk-in nipple out of which water had run so corrosive it would scar a face or blind a person's eyes. Minerva used to stand sometimes and watch Dickie's little swollen and throbbing throat when he was singing and say would you look at that little bugger (though if she had a headache she would throw the night cover over the cage to shut him up).

Hindle wondered if Jim Clarendon had been in town if he would have gone to Minerva's funeral, for Minerva had known him even before Mrs. Clarendon did. In Downieville this was, she once told Hindle, and Jim and she were both as green as grass. But he was traveling in Europe with "Miss Mavis Clarendon," and there was no way to tell him Minerva was dead. Serapta thought that maybe she would get a picture post-card from Mavis, and so she might have done eventually had not things fallen out the way they did, both for Mavis in faraway Italy and for Serapta herself in her vine-covered home. Not entirely covered, part of the vine had died and the south wall showed the bare boards. Serapta told Hindle it would look so nice *painted*, Hindle promised to speak to Lennart about speaking to Fern, who owned both the barn Serapta lived in and Hindle's house, about furnishing the paint, which Stig would gladly put on.

But Hindle didn't see Lennart very often. Because of the watch kept upon polygamists, he was staying permanently with Pearl, his first wife, and abjuring conjugal visits with Rosina, Fern and Hindle. But a man who wants to will go courting. And as Mama's old neighbor Mrs. Bearpark used to say to new brides: "You will be the favorite for a time. But you can depend on it, the man who has the *privilege* of taking another wife will soon use it. He might *say* he won't, but the first thing you know, it's off with the old and on with the new!"

That Jean, Hindle's dull and homely and not young hired girl, should be the "new" astonished everyone. How had she and Lennart got that well acquainted? But they had.

Lennart had even been to Jean's home on her afternoon off, had met her mother, father, brothers and sisters, partaken of roast beef, Yorkshire pudding and fruit trifle. And on one of the evenings Jean went home to stay all night, he had taken her, accompanied by a ribbon-tied box of vanilla chocolate creams with a half a walnut pressed into each, to the theater to see *Trailed to His Doom*. No wonder Jean had just got more impossible by the day, till finally she overstepped the bounds and Hindle had to tell her to pack her things and leave. Which was just what she was going to do anyway, she said, to marry Hindle's husband! So there. Smarty.

"Not only my but Pearl's, Rosina's and Fern's husband!" Hindle said, laughing. She could hardly believe her ears at first. Rosina could hardly either. But for living the new and everlasting Covenant, she said he said, he was starting to inherit some of the thrones, kingdoms, principalities, powers, dominions and heights and depths he so richly deserved.

"*Men*," Pearl said.

What Fern said they did not know, because she was mad at them all.

Pearl, as she had done when Hindle was added to the family, accompanied the happy couple to the Endowment House. However, Jean didn't look happy, although on that day the cuckoo in the cuckoo clock in her first hope box would get to come out, she had an opal in her ring and three tiers to her cake, Pearl later told Rosina who told Hindle. Hindle wasn't surprised. One reason Jean wasn't happy, besides her natural dull contrariness, was because she was going to have to live at home with her parents and brothers and sisters until Fern could be persuaded to loosen the purse-strings and provide a small bower of love for the unprepossessing bride. When that would be, Lennart of course did not know. He hoped soon. Those multitudes of spirits looking forward to honorable bodies in which they could tabernacle in the flesh were always crowded around heaven's gates anxiously waiting to be called down to earth. And what were the majority of men more anxious to do than call them down? Hindle asked Lucitie, who seemed to be made somewhat uncomfortable by this, as Hindle glimpsed out of the corner of her eye. A while later Lucitie said, "Well, if it depended on *Albert*, them spirits will have a long old wait."

"Depended on who?" Hindle said, as if she hadn't heard. So Lucitie went on to say Albert again, and then—considerably more.

Hindle's diagnosis of her brother-in-law's case, especially since Lucitie had to be the one to examine and question Albert without arousing his fear or resentment, and unbeknownst to him report her findings to her sister, was not arrived at in a day. But finally, with the results of Lucitie's judicial inquiry in hand, Hindle could and did give it: "Albert has to be circumcised," she said.

"Circumcised? Are you crazy? A grown man?" Lucitie said nervously. "He would never allow it in a thousand years!" At first she thought Hindle had in mind to do it herself. But of course she didn't. Not that any woman who could dress a chicken without bursting the gall bladder couldn't snip off that little loose fold of integument covering the male cupuled intromittent organ, as Dr. Ford's *Question Book* expressed it, before you could say Brigham Young! But she knew how partial men were to it, Doctor had even given her a little lecture about it on one of their long rides. As boys, he said, it was another boy to them, as men another little man (or big man, as the case might be). It had a head, body, a will of its own. Like the well-formed one-legged bundle Doctor told about, hanging to the lower end of a twenty-eight-year-old Italian two hundred years ago, kind of a tumor with strands of hair and a tooth, that didn't know anything but yet breathed, slept at intervals, moved its body but didn't have to eat, for it was nourished by what the host Italian ate, a man's member was *someone else*. A woman's, on the other hand, was only part of her self like an eyelid or knee. More frivolous on occasion, sometimes more unruly, but never a *being* on its own, a woman's organ was always only *it*. Women would confide about their husbands: "He wants *it* all the time." But a steam engineer brought in injured to Doctor one time, his hands covered with black grease, said when asked to unbutton his pants and show his parts: "He's so clean and I'm so dirty, I hate to touch him." *He. Him.* Mysterious as the coiled rope that performs the rope trick. *More* mysterious! The rope needs its Hindu magician to make it climb, while the penial member has his own ideas, and rises—or refuses—when he will.

Naturally Albert wouldn't want his sister-in-law snipping off his foreskin. And in fact when Lucitie first broached the subject, saying their shop's customer Mrs. Burns had confided to her that her husband had had it done and was enjoying life so much better now and that he said he could kick himself for not having had it done years before (she knew Albert would never ask verification from the lady), Albert resented even the *mention*. But Hindle told Lucitie to tell him that Mrs. Burns's husband's doctor in faraway Illinois, where they were living at the time, told Mr. Burns that not only would he enjoy *life* more but, *as statistics proved*, he would *live* longer by maybe twenty years and that when he *did* die, he would look like a young man. That (or something) persuaded Albert, and he went to Dr. Brierley, physician to many prominent Gentiles, to have it done. But it was much more of an ordeal than anyone anticipated, and after two weeks of taking care of him, besides running the hairdressing shop, and hearing his moans and groans every time he had to make water or when Lucitie made the bed with him in it, Lucitie was so enfeebled she always thought that that was why Nancibel was born, eleven months almost to the day after Albert's circumcision, with sides that didn't quite match, though her face all matched and was sweet and beautiful. Not that Lucitie minded, she was so glad to have a baby daughter. And a few years later she would have a little boy with nothing wrong at all. And all due to Hindle.

BY NOW HINDLE HAD REALLY earned her husband's diploma, no doubt about that. Gradually she took on a physician's best mien, too, the stern and authoritative style that the sick rely on most. The way she found out what was amiss, her clear directions, penalties for non-observance, rigid discipline, sometimes sharp words, and especially the strict professional propriety with which (from memories of ten years with Doctor and her own experience) she had somehow invested herself brought her close to being the genuine article.

If medicine and surgery, though, may be compared to a house of many rooms, and if surgery is the parlor where stand the best and most valuable possessions of the house, *that* grand room (except for a simple lancing or removal of morbid matter from an eye, ear, throat or uterine cavity with a curette) she had never entered. And so she was not proud. Still, she now made her rounds or went on calls in a livery stable buggy, and a new leather satchel with bright new instruments from Chicago had replaced the medical bag marked U.S. ARMY with its forceps for extracting arrowheads, stomach pump to disgorge poisons, wooden stethoscope, turnbuckle device for pulling teeth, and strange implements in their "Army surplus" velvet-lined furled case. She had even bought a fur tippet with toque to match. The "temporary" arrangement, paid off monthly, with Rosina still prevailed, though the baby she had left with her, Marie, was past four, but each time mention was made of bringing the child home it was as if Hindle was suggesting defenestration for both Rosina and Marie, and she would leave things as they were a little longer. The "temporary" agreement she had come to with Serapta with regard to looking after Eula and Esther, even though at nine and eleven they didn't need the care they once had, was also still in place. Of the barn Serapta had made a bower, and of nervous and cranky Stig, busy painter as he was of signs and signboards but mostly at work on his panorama, she had made not only a tender husband but a well-tempered father to her little charges. And Serapta shone with a clear and tranquil light indeed, too happy to mention happiness until the night a note tied around a rock was thrown in through their window, almost striking her. It said,

> *Morphodite Fogelmarck we know all about you and your devils work drawing evil pichurs against the richous of god so if you will consult your own safty and that of others you will make yourself scarce or be burned down.*

How had anyone found out about his panorama? Only twenty feet of it had been completed, and no one had seen *that* fully unrolled, not even Stig himself. The girls had not told their schoolmates, why should they? It was no novelty to them to see him always at work daubing away in "his" area, often listening to their chatter, sometimes tossing a word to them over his shoulder, a laugh or a twinkle, or joining in a song if they felt like singing. They didn't care what he was painting. Close questioning brought out the fact they didn't even know. Serapta knew, of course, and when the note came she told Hindle again that "what I have feared has come upon me!"

It might be modern times, wonderful things might exist in the world like electric elevators, horseless trollies, magneto-galvanic batteries and a thousand other modern inventions, but it was still the same *church*, Serapta said, its law and its testimony were still the same. In the Tabernacle they still got up and preached, said Stig—who for the sake of his panorama continued to read the Deseret News as well as the Tribune—but now knew and cared more about *secular* matters than religion. He did not go around knocking the church, that phase had passed, and now it was live and let live with him, though the pictures he contemplated on his panorama that he told Serapta about still sounded somewhat revengeful. But it wasn't going forward very fast, and as the farther along he got the more particular he became and the more minute his strokes and tinier his brushes, Serapta's mind had been put at ease. It might never be finished, hardly anybody knew about it, so why should she worry?

Hindle certainly hadn't told anyone. Well, perhaps Lucitie, but *she* would never tell. They had kept any mention from Lennart. But wait. Had Jean—? So far as Serapta knew, while she worked for Hindle she had never been out back to their dwelling. All she ever seemed to do was sit in Hindle's kitchen working on her second hope box and (as it now appeared) think of ways to get Lennart. Hindle didn't agree to that, she thought it was the other way around, or six of one and half a dozen of the other. And she was about to read Serapta something from a circular the Chicago Drug Company had tucked into her last order of ergot and quinine (advertising a book called *Psychography*) to the effect that "since all animal instincts are subject to the laws of diminishing return, repetition of the sexual act or its habitual performance deadens the stimuli and increases the need for new instigations ... It follows," it said, "that the natural love life in all its manifestations, and perhaps most of all in man, is based on the principle of infidelity" when she remembered the status of Stig's masculinity, his wife's iconostatic virginity, and tactfully refrained.

No, it couldn't have been Jean. But it was *someone*, and a few mornings later Serapta came outside into the yard to find the word APOSTATE painted with dark red paint, like dried blood, in great sprawling letters across the exposed side of the barn, where the vine had died. Hindle was just starting for the livery stable to get her rig when Serapta ran around the house and nearly bumped into her. "Oh, Hindle," she cried. "They *know*. The church *knows*. They know about the panorama!"

When she saw the scrawl, "That's not a grown-up person," Hindle said, and gave a dozen reasons why she was sure there was nothing to fear. But the more Serapta and Stig talked about it, the more nervously excited they grew, and by the time Hindle came home from her last case that night at a very late hour, it was past two, Serapta was sitting in her office waiting for her. Almost beside herself by then with the thought of all the things that could happen, Serapta burst out that Stig was standing guard and that that very afternoon she had gone uptown to the telegraph office and wired her brother Murdock in Helena, Montana, that they were packing up and arriving Friday.

"But, Serapta, you can't do that!" Almost too tired to speak, Hindle put down her bag and began taking off her hat and coat. "You mean for just a visit? But right now— the girls—and school not being out—" Pale as a ghost from fatigue, she fell into a chair.

"Oh, honey!" As was her way, Serapta put aside her own concerns to say, "What have you been up to, for goodness' sake?"

Hindle had to stop and think, she was so tired.

"Well, the first thing," she said, "this man came and wanted me to come with him to see his daughter! that the way he described what she had it sounded like virulent diphtheria, and when I got there that's what it was. His wife and another daughter had been taking care of her, but a terrible choking spell he heard and saw sent him flying for a doctor. *He* took the notion, it wasn't her. His wife don't believe in doctors. And why me, I guess he's passed my sign and I'm closest, they don't live too far off. Mr. and Mrs. Pratt. Anyway, I thought it was funny Mrs. Pratt didn't stay with me in the room when I was there with the sick daughter. Della, her name is, half grown, I think she's Papa's favorite. The older sister was there, Fanny, real nice, and it was her I give my orders to when I got ready to leave. I did ask where Mrs. Pratt was and went and found her, but—*he'd* gone over her head, which wasn't conducive, she said, and her being a second half-cousin to the Pike that the peak was named after, anything that came up, she could handle. Well, fine, I said. I didn't argue."

"So you didn't go back."

"That was my intention, not to. But as today wore on, enough came up in that house that by the time it got dark, here was Mr. Pratt at my door again—nearly on his knees. I wasn't too anxious, as you may suppose. But then I thought maybe there was something else I could try for Della, so I got my bag. And we rode in his rig," she said, "and went past his married daughter's house, who he had alerted to come with us. So she ran out, eight months pregnant, Maude, and while we was going we heard from Mr. Pratt the situation. Along about mid-morning his wife ran up to the attic for something where their boy slept that was always up and gone before they got up, his job being a bakery job. Only this time he *wasn't* up and gone, he was in bed, dead, and still so warm to touch that Mrs. Pratt wouldn't believe it."

"She shook him and sat him up, tried to make his eyes stay open, it was awful, Mr. Pratt said. But finally she gave in—and then, I guess, well, from the way he told us, you know the expression *floored*—well, she was that in actual fact. Went in the parlor, laid down on the carpet and there she still laid even as we was talking. That kind of behavior, of course, left Fanny the sister to take hold, and I guess she done so as best she could, her and Mr. Pratt. I had told her in the morning when I was there to stay by Della, you know how easy they suffocate—and especially considering I administered laudanum. And I think Fanny did. Which left *him* in charge, as his wife laying on the floor like that, like she wasn't there, was hopeless. Couldn't be shamed or nothing. So he bore the brunt, took a door off its hinges and set it on some chairs in the kitchen, and he and some neighbors laid the dead boy out and put a sheet over him. But then they left and Mr. Pratt was just alone. He peeked in Della's sickroom that Fanny couldn't be spared from, and then in the parlor—and kitchen—and then he said he's walking through the house and up and down and back and forth like an animal in a cage and then he's got to get out, he can't stand it, so he takes his hat and out he goes, for boards to make the coffin with and then uptown to the graveyard to buy a burial plot."

"What happened *then*, I guess," Hindle said, "Fanny got hungry and left her post and went down to the kitchen and made some pancakes. She ate them as fast as she could with butter and sugar, with her back turned so she couldn't see her brother, so she later said."

"Life can be *sad*."

"And about two minutes later she's sicker than a dog, throwing up and going into the parlor, stumbles over her mother who don't even move, and crawls to the sofa, too sick to go back upstairs. The time goes by, Della's laudanum wears off and she wakes up and calls, but no one answers. So she gets up as best she can and goes downstairs, don't know her brother's dead or anything, and into the kitchen, and there she sees this sight. Well, you can imagine. Falls in a heap next to where he's laid out. And that's where Mr. Pratt, when he comes home, finds her and just distracted runs through the house. But now Fanny's sick, his wife's *non compos mentis* or whatever you want to call it on the floor. He puts a pillow under Della's head and comes for me. And we stop by for Maude—"

"Do I just imagine it, or was tonight extra dark?"

"Dark and cold. Like the house when we got there," Hindle said. "But we pitched in, and pretty soon a fire's lit and the lamps is burning. And much to my sorrow I see that Fanny's got the diphtheria like her sister, and like the brother too had to have had, the minute I lifted the sheet I smelled that smell. He was nice-looking, saving to get married—"

"Don't it break a person's heart?"

"It does. But anyway—where she was laying on that slippery horsehair, Fanny could of slid off, but we shored her up. And that Maude was for sure a regular trouper, and what we'd have done without her I don't know. First thing I done for Della when I got there, still in the kitchen down beside her brother, was clear her throat of putrid suppurations. And then—But Maude come running, Fanny couldn't breathe, so I went in and got her breathing again. Then Maude and I, we gathered Della up and got *her* out of the kitchen and into the folks' bed, which was the only bed downstairs. And Mrs. Pratt—Maude said how she'd get mad and maybe not speak to someone for a week, but nobody ever saw her act like she was doing. Laying on the parlor floor flat on her back, full length stretched out like she was Abraham Lincoln. It didn't seem a bit like a natural reaction, but natural reactions are just whoever's the person may be, huh? Then what? Oh, yes, Mr. Pratt. Well, he seemed on the brink for a little while, like fixing for a touch of apoplexy, but he come out of that all right. But Fanny worried me. And then what do I hear but this gasp from Maude—"

"You don't mean to tell me?"

"Yes, I do, she's starting—Where are we going to put her? Not upstairs or downstairs in contaminated beds. Stake out another claim on the parlor floor? But Mr. Pratt somewhere rustled up a military cot, we set it up in the hallway, made our plans—and while the baby could of been a little more—cooperating—instead of trying to come into the world feet first, when he finally got here all was forgiven, for he's as fine a boy as you'll ever see."

"Thank goodness for that!" Serapta said.

"We was plenty relieved. And more relations come and took ahold. And things was under control. Someone said they'd take me home. So I went and got my coat—and then to cap the climax, up gets Mrs. Pratt! and her kin gather round her like she's a hero home from the wars. Which maybe she is, at that. But I bypassed them and tiptoed into the downstairs bedroom to see how Della was doing before I left—and went over to the bed and lifted the cover, it took a while to realize she was dead. Her father's favorite, that was proved for sure. And then of course it's chaos and old night—"

"Well, that vicious virulent disease—" Serapta said in shocked tones after a moment's silence. "Nobody could of saved her. Or the boy."

"Maybe somebody could, but they wasn't there." Hindle sighed. "And Fanny—touch and go with her—"

"Well, they got the baby. That is consolation."

It wasn't to Hindle, though. She just sat. And pretty soon was crying fit to be tied.

SERAPTA MIGHT HAVE DELAYED A few days, but Stig was so worried over the threats that he insisted they go as planned, which really knocked her sideways, Hindle told Lucitie the next time she saw her. Serapta was like more than a person's friend, more like a person's good right *arm*. But go they would. What would she do without her? What would the children do? spoiled by Serapta within an inch of their lives!

"Don't tell me, I know the answer," Lucitie said. "They went along."

And so they had. But school was nearly out. And by the time they came back in the fall she'd have found a new hired girl. And they'd be older, twelve and ten. Serapta said she was going to teach them to cook and keep house. That, Hindle doubted, but it didn't matter. They could come back just like they went away and she'd be happy. And they would get really acquainted and start afresh, and make a real home and read out loud in the evenings. And one thing for sure that she was going to do was go to Rosina and get her baby back. Marie was four now, and Rosina had to be made to realize—And then they'd all be—like a happy family.

But by the end of summer—!

WHEN LENNART AND JEAN MOVED into the empty barn, Hindle suddenly realized in a blinding flash who had thrown the rock in through the window with the threatening note, and painted APOSTATE on the wall and everything. Lennart and Jean, of course. They wanted the barn! She saw him once and asked if he wasn't ashamed, raising such Cain with five innocent people? and he just laughed and said all's fair you know where. So she knew he did it! and wrote and told Serapta—they could come home, there wasn't nothing to fear, and she would find a house for them—but Serapta wrote back and said that Stig said no, that now they had made the move they would stick with it, it was probably all for the best, they liked the surroundings, the girls were learning to ride, the river was close to wade in and all was well.

At first Hindle felt the sadness of left-in-the-lurchums. But plenty to do and lots to think about will nip that ailment in the bud. Also to bear in mind philosophy's little sayings such as *belief kills and belief cures*, and *up the rebels*. Best of all was to learn something, for as the old rhyme said,

> *When house is gone and money spent,*
> *Learning is most excellent.*

Actually you can hardly *avoid* learning, she often thought, usually hard old lessons, but sometimes the enjoyable kind like someone singing you a song in Italian or French, or casting light upon the dumbness on this earth. "There was a man back home that if you got scalded or burnt by fire, he could *talk the fire out of the burn*." "When the skies open and Jesus comes back, it will be a leap year." And two of Hindle's patients, Mrs. Fay Hatch and Mrs. Pearl of Great Price Hatch, said if they had it to do over, they wouldn't (in secret and against the teachings of the church) tip a table to make contact with their husband Douglas and bring him back from the dead. Because now, of his own accord, what had he done but went back to the same schedule he used to hew to when he was alive? Monday Fay, Tuesday Pearl, Wednesday Fay, Thursday Pearl, Friday Fay, Saturday Pearl, Sunday at his mother's house, Monday again with Fay and so on through the week. But *now*, of course, as a spirit or ghost, all he could do was, as you might say, *haunt*, make knocking noises, mischief or a nuisance out of his self. "But that is the blessing of polygamy," Fay said when she told Hindle about it. "Only three days a week."

Chapter Thirty-eight

✳

THE WORD ABOUT MAVIS CAME FROM MRS. O'NAUGHTON, WHO LIVED ACROSS the street from the Clarendon mansion. Mrs. O'Naughton herself was not on visiting terms with her fellow millionaire, having heard somehow of his unfaithfulness to his late wife, but the O'Naughton coachman knew the Clarendon coachman, and the O'Naughton cook did the daily shopping with the Clarendon cook, so a good deal of information was bound to be forthcoming. The Clarendon coachman had been along on the European journey, then was sent home from New York when Mavis went into the hospital there, so what he told the Clarendon cook who told the O'Naughton cook who told Mrs. O'Naughton who told Lucitie when she went to Alfonce's Hairdressing to get her hair dressed, about what had happened over there, was the straight goods. And so unusual did it seem to Lucitie that that very evening, as soon as the supper dishes were done and Albert was sitting at the lamplit center table in the parlor reading the London Illustrated News, she looked at her sweetly sleeping daughter, kissed the top of Albert's head, grabbed her coat, and off she went to tell Hindle.

And how the two sisters did wish Serapta, being the one who had had the raising of Mavis till Lisheen came back and reclaimed her, had been present to hear the news. How startled she would be! For one could think of a lot of things that might happen to a person, but for it to be *that* really did beat all. To Lucitie's great satisfaction, Hindle certainly thought so. She never had heard of such a thing in her life. And neither had Dr. Ford of the *Question Book*, Dr. Gray of *Anatomy* or Dr. Gunn of the *Family Physician*, as Hindle verified after Lucitie had gone home. Or all the great doctors over there in Europe.

In Europe, of course, was where it happened. Italy, Rome, where Mavis came down with an inflammation of the vermiform appendix of the caecum. That part was not strange. Every five minutes, somewhere in the world someone was coming down with *that*. Sometimes it got better by itself. Sometimes it got worse. Sometimes a brilliant surgeon would operate and save the sufferer. Sometimes the person died. In Mavis's case, a brilliant Italian surgeon operated just before her appendix burst and saved her. But after that the strange began, all that went before was common and trite. For Mavis never woke up from the operation! She didn't die, she just never woke up. The ether, the chloroform wore off on schedule. Her incision healed. The stitches came out. No complication there. But the presents from Papa, the dainty doll, the checkers set of ivory and gold, the perfume atomizer, the beautiful flowers that piled up, all these she slept through. A great

322

doctor came from Paris. Every conceivable test was conducted without success. Sleeping Beauty, undiagnosed, her case without precedent, slumbered on. Papa then bundled her off to London. Doctors were engaged that had even treated *crowned heads*. But the white eyelashes still rested on the crystal cheeks, the roseate eyes never opened.

Then Paris again. The same tests over. New ones, never heard of till that time. Then New York, where famous Dr. Reynolds Hundhausen, assisted by famous Dr. Don Augustin Fossati, Surgeon in Chief of the Royal Hospital of St. Ambrosio, Havana, renowned sleeping sickness specialists, attempted to unravel the mystery of Miss Mavis Clarendon's unnatural heavy, prolonged sleep. The piece in the New York Telegraph-Gazette that said all this the Clarendon coachman, before he started for home in Salt Lake City, tore out and sent to the Clarendon cook. She told the O'Naughton cook, who borrowed it to show Mrs. O'Naughton, who borrowed it to show Lucitie when she went to Alfonce's to get her hair dressed and have a hairpiece matched, and Lucitie borrowed it to show Hindle. Of course Lucitie had to take the information back with her when she left, but Hindle kept going over the details anyway, as if she could still see the letters.

For she did wonder. Was it the aftermath of seeing Lisheen shot to death before Mavis's very eyes? but that happened more than a year ago. Also the sunstroke. And being adopted by a millionaire hadn't appeared to faze her. Did their long rich journey so full of wonders put too big a strain on Mavis's maybe delicate brain? How deep did albinism go? It couldn't be some simple thing like her not being watched closely enough in that Italian hospital, getting out of bed, falling and hitting her head? An untried medicine? A particular food? like the wicked stepmother's poisoned apple?

But all those great doctors!

Some days, and nights, Hindle wished she could fall permanently asleep her own self, as Mavis had done. Lie there and be crystalline and a marvel to intellectual minds, burrowed in luxury, dreaming sweet dreams. Forever. But then she would be going on a case, or coming back from one and (if the case was worth it) on her way to see Lucitie or Rosina to tell them about it, and just her own everyday existence would seem as summum-bonum, as Doctor used to say, as inheriting a railroad. Her cases! witch-doctor looney sometimes, but to her, in those years of practicing in that fast-draw vatican that Salt Lake then was, that high plains mecca with its rites and ceremonies as underived as clay and sand from the Garden of Eden, by no means singular. But they often made good telling…

HER CLIENTELE WAS FEMALE, THOUGH once in a great while she would have to ponder on a man's vicissitudes. One such was Brother Joseph Westwood, brought to her attention by the oldest of his three wives, a patient, who was worried because he was old and sick with a hard lump on his stomach, and upstairs in the back bedroom, fended everyone off and was just up there alone, waiting to die. Waiting and being lonesome, Hindle thought by the ease with which she penetrated his fastness. There, from his color and the mid-body protuberance under the bedclothes she was allowed to press lightly, she diagnosed, though not to him, a malignant scirrhus, for which she gave him a bottle of alcoholic tincture of opium, twenty drops in half a glass of water three times a day. This so lulled his pain and distress that he let her come and see him (with more tincture) several more times before he died, which was not long after. He talked freely, too, and soon confided that when it came to pure torment, a lump eating away at a fellow's *stomach* was nothing in comparison with remorsefulness eating away at his *conscience*. The way he spoke in such a low tone, and had to have his bedroom door closed before he began, made Hindle think he might be going to own up to a murder at least. But what came out in the wash really was such a figment she begged pardon of Lucitie before she recounted it to her.

It had to do with "sealing," a Mormon ritual that "seals" brides and grooms, parents and children and whoever else wants it, to each other for all eternity. Joseph Westwood's mother and father met and married in the last days before the Mormon city of Nauvoo fell to the Philistines. The Lord's temple having been finished in a state of siege, and dedicated, and with only a select number of ceremonies gone through, everybody was packing up and going west. When they got there, the backlog would be dealt with. But Joseph's father died a year after arrival in Salt Lake, and his mother the year after that, at age thirty, leaving four children, the oldest Joseph, then fifteen. She had mentioned "sealing" on her deathbed and how troubled her mind was that it hadn't been done, one of the neighbor ladies who had heard her told Joseph, but it didn't go very deep. Until he was thirty-five, had raised his younger brother and two sisters, and married and been sealed on three different occasions in the Endowment House, he seldom thought of his mother.

"Or do anything else except work," he told Hindle. "But that last ceremony, I don't know why, but I got to remembering her a lot. Like her troubled mind on her deathbed about not being sealed to Pa. But as we know, the Prophet, Seer and Revelator worked that all out many long years ago. 'Proxy ceremonies.' Other people can stand up for you and it works as good as if you was doing it yourself. So I arranged—And one of our old neighbors that Ma had liked, and in fact this lady had been with her when she died, she stood proxy for Ma and I stood proxy for Pa. The ceremony that none could put asunder went without a hitch. But Ma stayed in my mind. I was older, you see. Now I could look back and really—For looks she wouldn't of needed to take a back seat to anyone, her hair and—"

He paused, then went on. "Half-sole both shoes with a piece of leather no bigger'n a slice of braunschweiger. But—anyway—that proxy wedding and the sealing, as I went over it in my mind, it wasn't like I'm standing in for Pa, you know, I'm standing in for *myself*. And she's my own bride, and—going to be forever—My sisters, they was glad to hear the sealing was went through with. My brother in California, he—I'm sorry to say—got cut off from the church for mouthiness, so I never told him. And, let's see—it was about this time that I quit at Robinson's and started my own business, and—Well, this here house is the smallest out of three that's mine, and it ain't *small*—"

"It certainly isn't," Hindle said, glancing up at the high ceiling. "You can be proud."

"We're hard workers, even my brother in California, you got to give the devil his due. And also in my days of prime, I had—I was—" He cleared his throat and started over. "Bodily strength. Arms on me, you know. Legs. Back. And this ain't something ought to cross a man's lips, and never till now has crossed mine, but I had—well, considerable rutting energy."

"Oh," she said.

"And with three wives it had plenty of place to go. I never was one to be scared of a headstrong woman, let 'em argue, let 'em try to boss the job, but when bedtime come was when the chips was down, and I could always, I don't want to brag or nothing, but you know, *settle their hash.*"

Hindle nodded in some embarrassment. She waited for him to go on, but he was silent. Finally she said, "Mr. Westwood, a while ago you was mentioning a person's *conscience*—"

"Mine," he said.

"Well, I've been listening but it don't seem to me you've done nothing but what was—just fine. In this life."

He shook his head. "The sealing," he said. "Me standing proxy for my father. I was thirty-five years old—long years had passed—when Ma died she was five years younger than I was then. So in my mind she was this young—There's an old expression, 'prettier'n a speckled bird'—And there the two of us stood, we was a couple, sealed for eternity, not my father and her, but beautiful her and *me*. And one night in the middle of the night I woke up and I was thinking, how would it of been, I was thinking, to of really been—her husband? And that started it. From then on every kiss—everything that happened—it was always *her* before my mind's eye. And wasn't that a deadly sin? A man's own mother! While I settled Miss Bossy's or Miss Smarty's or Missus Contrary's hash," he mumbled so obscurely that Hindle could hardly hear him, "and worked 'em up to go off like a factory whistle every time, why, all the while it was *someone else's* hash—" *Someone else* he was always working up—an image in his imagination, he whispered, but so real he could feel her—smell her—and if that wasn't a sin, he didn't know what was!

He began to cry, old people can't cry to do any good but their shoulders shake, they bite their lips and sob. And he was afraid! he said. Afraid he wouldn't go to heaven where his mother was, afraid that if he *did* go and they met, guilty wretch that he was, how could he look her in the face?

Hindle gave him an extra dose of tincture and patted his back. All his strength was just weak chicken bones by now and scrawniness, and she wished it wasn't so. "Now listen, Mr. Westwood," she said, "you made a confession, and it says in the Bible or the Book of Mormon that *to make confession is to be absolved.* The mere fact you done it absolves you. So that's what you done and that's what you are, absolved. It has all come out in the wash. And peace be upon your soul." She hoped it was when, before the week was out, he went unconscious and died.

Lucitie didn't think it was very nice for him to talk like he had to Hindle, but then of course to his mind she apparently was this doctor that his wife was under the care of, and people say anything to doctors. What did he mean about settling somebody's hash? Did he hit them? What was he talking about?

Oh, just men's talk, Hindle said.

COULD THE CONSCIENCE CAUSE A malignant growth to grow and reproduce itself? Bring on morphew? Yellow jaundice? Rattling along to a call or coming away from one, Hindle often thought along such lines and wondered if subjects like those ever came up at medical meetings. How happy a downright *education* must make a person who had one. Even the chance knowledge she had gained in her years of practice had opened to her view depths and heights she never dreamed of, wild nature supplying all the microscopic unicellular micro-organisms, secret snakes, little tiny black things—so brilliant—and here was human nature, just this—*sap.*

WHY DID SHE TAKE THE case? Why, after they had been back in Salt Lake for weeks, and the foreign doctors had gone back to where they came from, and the pattern fell into the shape it was going to stay in maybe for years to come, and he came to the door at midnight and said *will you come?* did she go with him? Why didn't she just say, "Mr. Clarendon, no. If all of *them* couldn't cure her, what do you expect of me?"

But of course he didn't expect her to cure her.

"Just give me a minute, Mr. Clarendon. I'll get dressed."

In the carriage that smelled of strong drink and cigars, she told him about seeing the piece in the paper. So she knew what the situation was with regard to—And she wanted to say—

"What was your name again? Hannah?"

"Hindle." She wanted to add "Dr. Fairbrass" but let it go. He knew she was a doctor and where to come for her when he needed her, just as he had when Dolores tried to kill herself.

"I don't know why I can't remember that. Hindle, listen—" Whatever he was going to say, though, he changed his mind about.

She waited, then said, "Mr. Clarendon, you did such a wonderful thing, adopting that motherless child, giving her every advantage. If I've heard that said once I've heard it a hundred times. And then in the midst of your lovely trip to Europe to have such a unfortunate—"

"I heard about Minerva," he interrupted.

While talking, she had been thinking about what she had in her bag and what she might try to do as soon as she got there, unaccountably remembering at the same time Doctor once telling her that in ages past, before doctors became scientific and had medical inventions such as the stomach pump and arrowhead extractors and were only barbers, why, a popular remedy was to put a sheep in bed with the sick person because sheep are easily infected and draw the venom to themselves, bringing about recovery—imagine.

"Minerva?" she said.

"Dying and all," he said. "I missed the auction of her stuff. I don't know as I'd have gone. Another loss up there at her place too, wasn't there?"

"Yes. Flossie," she said. "But she died before Minerva."

"Flossie, too?" He fell silent.

Then they were there. The great front door with colored glass. The statues on the newel posts holding up the branches lit with amber electric globes. The softness underfoot, the hush of wealth, ceilings like space too high to see. No butler, maids, footmen passing to and fro due to the lateness of the hour, Hindle supposed. But later he mentioned he just had Charlie out in the stables now, Lap Wing in the kitchen and Mrs. Parrott, the old lady who came in every day to clean. And Mrs. Sharp. She was another old lady in by the day. Mrs. Sharp took care of Mavis. At night they went home, all except the Chinaman. The servants that used to infest the place he let go, a pack of thieves, spies— finally he found them out.

"Nighttimes she just sleeps?"

"Just sleeps," he said. "Daytimes, nighttimes—My room's right next door."

"Well, I certainly do hope I can help her."

But if all those great specialists couldn't, what could *she* do?

In the lamplight Mavis looked the same, except surrounded by so much luxury and in a silk nightdress and with her eyes closed and her crystalline eyelashes resting on her transparent cheeks, she appeared almost—edible, like some kind of ornate article of food, wedding cake with little silver shot sprinkled over, or cream whipped and put through a paper cornucopia—white-mountain icing. Poor Lisheen, the winter had been so long, her windows barred with icicles, her igloo bed, the white dumplings she had to eat in white soup—and always more snow on the way. Hindle opened her satchel, took out her stethoscope purposefully, but when she began making her examination it was as if suddenly she was frightened. Her hand shook, her mouth was dry, she could feel her heart beating in her throat.

"Well, what do you think?" he said.

"Well, I tell you, Mr. Clarendon—"

"Come on into my den, Hannah. We'll have a drink. My wife called it my den. Nothing would do I had to have a den. You remember my wife, don't you?"

"It's—nice," Hindle said as the green-shaded light came on and she saw a dark, filled-up room with filled-up walls. It smelled smoky, dusty, moldy.

"Name your poison, madam."

"Well, actually I don't believe I care—for—Thank you," she said, her hand still shaking. What was it about millions that raw heads and bloody bones couldn't intimidate you worse? And then the fact too that, imagine being friends and calling him by his first name. And just walking down the street to go to a show. And—if God had said to her, back when she was a girl, "Hindle, name your poison," meaning "Who? For you?" she'd have said without even stopping to think: him.

"Well, up the rebels, eh?" He swallowed his drink, set his glass down on what appeared to be a big desk and seemed about to pour himself another but then didn't. "Drink up." He sounded cross so she did, quickly, and choked but was all right by the time they took seats on either side of a fireplace in which many fires had gone out one on top of the other without the ashes being carried out or the hearth swept.

"I feel bad about that girl up there, Hannah."

"I know you do," Hindle said. "I can well imagine. To be wanting to do such a favor for someone, take them to Europe and—give them every opportunity, and then to have them come down with an appendix and have to be operated on—in a foreign land. And then never to wake up. It just must of been—so *discouraging*—"

"It was," he said. "One of the most discouraging things *I* ever come up against."

"I can well imagine. They give her ether, I suppose?"

"Ether and chloroform, they told me, first one, then the other."

"And performed the operation, and she never come to."

"That's about it."

"Was it busted?"

"Hannah," he said, "I didn't bring you up here because I thought you was going to rub on some salve or something and all of a sudden the kid would sit up and take notice." He got up and went over and, leaning his elbow on the mantel, bent his head and studied the dismal dead ashes as though lost in thought before a leaping fire.

"I didn't think I'd rub on any salve," she said nervously. "Unless it was magic, from her fairy godmother—to come help her."

"She hasn't *got* a fairy godmother, poor little bastard," he said. "Nor a guardian angel either."

"Well, if she hasn't, then she sure don't need one," she said. "For she's got someone a whole lot better than either of them, and that's a—father."

"Stow the guff," he said.

She swallowed and looked away.

"Listen, I'd ought to be shot. In fact shooting's too good for me. Took out and strung up would be more like it. Tore into pieces and stomped into the earth. Quién sabe?"

Turning back, she met his angry gaze.

"Yes or no? You're supposed to be a doctor, a doctor's supposed to understand human nature. Minerva Bohannon used to send for you, didn't she?"

"But we was friends, too," she said.

"Well, *we're* friends. Aren't we? 'In need.' 'Indeed.' How smart are you?"

She bit her lip.

"Does a house have to fall on you?"

"No."

"It cannot happen."

"May I make a suggestion? Take her back over to Europe. There must be all kinds of out-of-the-way places—"

"Too late, Hannah. Too much attention's been paid, I'd have to travel with a bunch of people, we'd be watched every step of the way—No, it's now or—" He made as if to put a gun to his head. Then he began to cry.

"Please don't, Mr. Clarendon," she said. "Didn't you never hear the old saying that when things are bad they are hard to mend, but when they get *damn* bad they just cut loose and mend themselves?"

"Oro's no object," he said.

"It's not a question of that."

"It's always a question of that. But also a question of—are *you* going to be the one to avenge and punish? Or leave that to the devil? Don't worry, muchacha. He'll do a better job than you ever could."

"Let me take her—to—" Where? Montana? California? Her voice trailed off.

He knelt in front of her. "La esperanza es la última hez que apuramos en el fondo del cáliz de la amargura," he murmured brokenly.

"I don't understand Spanish."

"You understand human faces with hearts of beasts. Poor dumb beasts that never knew any better, never meant to harm—"

"Get up, I beg you, please. They just cut loose—truly—" she repeated, "and mend themselves—"

He took her hand and kissed it and she felt his tears. And so—

And she thought, wouldn't it be the strangest thing if *that* preparation, the volatile acid in the sclerotium of Claviceps purpurea, and if *those* exertions that had to be resorted to when the first measure didn't work, were to wake her when *all the science* brought to bear on her by the great specialists of the world had no effect? A new discovery, maybe! But not much use, for how many such cases would ever be? Of course they didn't.

If he lived to be a hundred, he said, he would never never forget the favor. He would quit drinking, start going to Mass, found an orphans' home—But twenty-four hours later when the sleeping girl in her fine-spun encasement was found to be in a shivering fit, when she took with fever, when flatulent distention of the intestines blew up her sunk white belly like a balloon, when Hindle, engulfed with terror, felt that small hard wiry pulse and palpated a matrix as fixed and immovable as though imbedded in plaster of Paris, when nothing would help, not fomentations, warm blankets, hot water bottles of the finest gum rubber, a six percent solution of gum acacia in saline, nothing, nothing, and three days later at two in the morning Mavis died of septic endometritis, it didn't seem as if he would live long enough even to need a shave.

For that first dark hour after it happened he was like a man demented, even banging his head against the wall and raking his eyes and cheeks with his nails, and Hindle thought since he wouldn't swallow the tincture she proffered she might have to put him under temporarily some other way, perhaps with a blow to the head to calm him. But when what she was saying at last got through to him, neither recourse proved necessary. She died of sleeping sickness, everyone knew she had it, complete unconsciousness, slow stertorous breathing, such patients just stop, Hindle said. And if that was the cause of death, then no mention of septic endometritis by the physician in charge need be made, that was simply extraneous, and she was the physician in charge, and there was truth to it, the more she thought of it the more convinced she was that it *was* sleeping sickness, an especially strong, violent and hostile kind picked up in a foreign country, which is so much more full of dangers and perils than over here in this country anyhow. And in the old days the departed was never taken from home, she said, for the purposes of preparation, there was no such thing as an undertaking establishment, she and Mrs. Parrott and Mrs. Sharp were perfectly capable, and a casket could be brought, and the drawing room was as beautiful as a church, and the funeral could be held—And Mr. Clarendon could talk to Father Barron, and the family crypt at the cemetery could be made ready—

"I will never forget, Hindle," he said. After almost eight days and nights of seeing her about, he had finally got her name straight. But by then she didn't really care, it is mysterious about feelings toward others. If God said "Name your poison" *now*, why, "Let this be over and done with," was all she would want. "Take it from my mind and memory forever." Mr. O'Donnell the undertaker, one of the first Gentile undertakers to set up business in Salt Lake City, and Irish like Mr. Clarendon, brought the casket, and a beautiful one it was. Leave everything to him, he said, and they could not have been in more capable hands. A young gentleman in a black suit and white gloves was always hovering between the front hall and the library with the shades drawn, where the casket stood banked with hothouse roses brought in an ice-cooled Central Pacific car from California. And he or another one like him kept the family, which was Mr. Clarendon only, from being disturbed by anyone but Father Barron. The Father came at any hour and sat with the bereaved millionaire in the den just as he had when Mrs. Clarendon died, and was not silent on the consolation of immortality.

The funeral services, whatever they might have been, were private. Then the coffin went to the cemetery in a beautiful black hearse with black plumes in the corners and coal-black horses, and Mavis Clarendon was buried beside Mrs. Clarendon. She wasn't just to have a tombstone, either, as came out in the Tribune a few days later. A sepulchre of the most expensive marble was to be erected over the two occupied graves (and one empty, waiting for Jim), with a cupola, beautiful bronze grille work, statues, pillars and so on, Salt Lake City would be proud of it.

Then Colonel James Clarendon, as the paper called him, settled his affairs, closed the house, gave the keys to his lawyers Kelly and Kelly, took the train and went back east. At least that was the train's direction. He could have branched off, could have done anything, no one really knew. Lucitie heard rumors from Mrs. O'Naughton, and Mrs. Kincaid had a friend who thought she saw him on a London wharf. Hindle would have probably been interested, but by that time, due to circumstances, she was far away. Far away and rich. Quite rich.

Between them, Jim and Father Barron had settled the matter of the sins of omission, commission, you name it, and there was another day tomorrow. How brightly the sun shone, how delicious the breakfast was in the dining car, what horizons stretched backwards and forwards and to every side for him. He could have his own private car if he wanted, but why show off? First class was fine with him. All the way through, that was how he'd gone. Demand the best, that was Jim even when young with empty pockets. Boots, bed, food, horse, woman, ask and ye shall receive. He cast a pretty shadow then upon the yellow ground, they turned around and looked at him, he didn't *have* to ask. But who he received the dose from there in Silver City he never really knew. Blonde Kate? Wild Cat Alma? The girl who grabbed the knife away from the tease who cut off her puppy dog's tail, and stabbed him to death so fast he didn't know what hit him? Minerva? young and sweet and not a professional then. It didn't matter, it wasn't too bad a dose. A little hard place cropped up, didn't ulcerate though, kind of a swollen groin on him for a few days, hot and painful, and he laid around the cabin. His partner would come in from their mine singing,

I got the clap
And the blueballs too.
The clap don't hurt,
But the blueballs do!

and he'd throw something at him. But Jaynes' Hydriodate of Potash ointment did the job, Minerva was always up on everything. She said he'd be right as rain in no time, and he was. They could be a comfort, women, to a man, good as beefsteak frying in the twilight. Women grown, that is to say, not a disappeared star of a baby woman that to…force was like piercing her shadow sailing behind and through her self to a steepness like death. Oh, no, muchacho. But as in a mountain mist her strange immaterial power occults like a lighthouse and draws—him—on. Oh, no. No. *Never again.*

Jim Clarendon went to New York, put up at the Waldorf, had breakfast in the suite every morning, had a barber come and shave him, changed shirts three times a day. It's terrible about the poor, their poverty, old worn shoes, their sad starved looks, but as the Bible or somebody said, "Whatever is, is right." Baron Venables of Kinderton said there were even more of the beggars at home than here, a pity they couldn't be transported like criminals, at any rate the ugliest emitters of the worst effluvium …

Chapter Thirty-nine

✳

HE WAS A CARD, THE BARON, A TALL FELLOW, THIN, GREAT YELLOW TEETH beneath a yellow mustache. He and his man, about fourteen trunks and boxes including a gun case, and Jim checked in at the Waldorf at about the same time. The Baron was the one who struck up the acquaintance. He spotted Jim at once as a western "odyssean," he said. In his gold watch chain a gold rod long and thick as his thumb, diamond stickpin, starched linens, tailor-made suit and polished boots. Jim didn't know what an "odyssean" might be but agreed he was from the west. Jolly good, the Baron said, for he was going out there to hunt the buffalo. Jim said he better hurry. *He* remembered, he said, when you'd come upon 'em—the prairie'd be black as far as the eye could see. A stampede would shake the earth for miles. But now—well, he could see the government's point. If cattle was ever going to use the plains in peace, if settlers' cabins was to be made safe, if the redskins was ever going to be put a leash on, the buffalo had to go. So with the government against them as well as everybody else, they had almost *went*.

But of course there was good hunting still. Jim advised the Baron. A breech-loading Sharps rifle, single shot, 45-120 caliber, weight fourteen to sixteen pounds, cost about ninety dollars, was the gun he needed. And if one was good, two was better. Out west buy cayuses, ten to twenty dollars each, about half a ton of gunpowder and bar lead, tools and molds for making your ammunition, one or two dead-ax wagons—beans, flour, bacon, coffee—Look for a small herd. If you can, approach over broken country. The best range is about two hundred yards. "Never had one in your line of sight?"

"No, old son."

"Well, listen then. Your first shot scatters the herd, but it'll hold up for a few seconds and kind of sway like. And then for some unknown reason the whole bunch will wheel right around in the same direction. Then's when you shoot at the ground in front of them—"

"At the *ground?*"

"That turns 'em, see? And you keep shooting at the ground till they're so mixed up that finally they stop in their tracks and just stand there, dumber'n a Dutchman. Then all you got to do is pull the trigger and keep on pulling it. I've saw half a dozen killed that way at once. I've saw eighty. And you know they're big sons-a-guns, weigh maybe two thousand pounds, twenty-five hundred—"

"By Jove!" the Baron said. Then he said, "How about coming with us?"

Jim thought about it. Thought about the summer range, the flowering head of wild bluestem hay, the Montana wind blowing. Then in the fall come back to civilization. If anyone would *want* to come back. Maybe he would just stay out there, turn over the biggest percentage of what he had to Father Barron to do with as he saw fit, and the rest of his life just—Because civilization, with trains going twenty-two miles an hour, the electric telegraph, cable cars rising straight up and so on, was getting to the stage where if everything didn't come a mucker before very long, he would miss his guess. And not only in this country, but everywhere. And not just the modern *inventions*, but the down-right—Jim hadn't thought of his mother's words for a long time—*carnal wickedness*. The carnal wickedness would just floor you. The Baron left one of his London papers in the lobby one evening, the London Illustrated News, and some of what apparently went on over there, if it wasn't just lies, which it probably was, just to sell papers, would curl your hair. But that there wasn't a *law* over there against *printing* such filth surprised Jim, for there certainly was in *this* country.

Even in vile, sorry Bodie you could read the newspaper out loud in church and not a bad word would you have to skip over such as virgin, inveigle, intromittent—and in Panamint, for throwing pictures with his magic lantern on a sheet tacked up on the wall of the human family in the Texas costume at the same time as he played Yankee Doodle on his music box, for which he charged two rials a performance, poor Tony Rico got arrested and sent to jail for two years (though he escaped about a week later). So the west might be rough and tough, but it was *decent*. Things went on, naturally. Jim was in Tessie Wall's one night in San Francisco when this party of gentlemen came walking in. They made no bones about who they were, a legislative committee from Sacramento come down to view first-hand some sporting life before legislating against sin. But no matter what they found out, after a friendly glass of wine, some cigars and a visit with the girls, even if "Little Lost Chicken," to take one example, as everybody called her, had been eleven or twelve instead of twenty-four years, which she was at the time, although only about three and a half feet tall, it certainly wouldn't have been printed in the public *newspapers*. America wasn't that kind of a country. But over in England—!

JIM HAD BEEN THERE, TWICE with his wife shopping and going to see old castles and chopping blocks, the waxworks, pleasure gardens, the theater and such as that, and once on a quick search for sleeping sickness specialists. He had gambled in London, lost considerable money as a matter of fact. And he wasn't born yesterday. He knew the gentlemen in their broadcloth and beaver hats walking so straight they might have swallowed their rolled-up umbrellas, and the bounders too in their billycocks and brown suits, went *somewhere*, did *something*. It stood to reason. But he didn't realize—! He read the piece again under the headline:

THE MAIDEN TRIBUTE OF MODERN BABYLON
BY
W. T. STEAD

which started out quoting from a report from the House of Lords about a law relating to the defense of juveniles. And how young girls in England above the age of eleven had no safeguarding at all, juvenile prostitution was a blight upon the land. The reasons for it were: a vicious demand for young girls, the nastiness that arises when too many people crowd into the same small space, bad fathers and mothers, the sight of older girls who are bad, dressed up and have money, and the bad streets the little girls run about in.

The article went on to say that in ancient Greece the Athenians, who had lost a war with Crete, nearly went crazy because every nine years they had to send a tribute of seven maidens to their conqueror to be devoured by the Minotaur, a frightful monster, half man and half bull. But *every night in London*, year in and year out, not just *seven* maidens but *many times that number* were cast nightly into the jaws of vice! "Can not these young ones be allowed to get a little older? Can not they themselves decide their own fate?"

The Director of Criminal Investigation of Scotland Yard consented to a meeting, the paper said. "You mean to say that the Bureau is *aware* of these things?" "It is not unaware." "And these are actual *rapes* perpetrated on unwilling virgins?" "So it would seem." "And the rapists?" "Rich men who have bought the privilege." "What about the commotion?" "The policeman on the beat has no right to interfere. And the cries soon cease." "But is not rape a felony punishable with penal servitude?" "*Catching before hanging*, as the saying goes."

On Mile-End Road a brothel-keeper agreed to speak. "They're always in demand, you know. And one good way of getting them is to *breed* them, like you'd breed llamas or anything else. Ten or eleven years goes by pretty fast. Then if the girl's a lively one you may get twenty to forty pounds for the first of her, depending on her looks." She herself preferred to scout around, the woman said, sometimes as far afield as a hundred miles, last spring inveigling from Shropshire to London a child for whom "a gentleman paid me thirteen pounds." "Do the children not protest?" "Plied with a mixture of snuff, laudanum and chloroform, they know nothing about it," she said, "sleep as if dead, wake up the next morning sick, dizzy and hardly able to move from pain. Blubbering, of course. But like I tell them, it had to happen sometime. Now it's all over, and you can either live like a cherry-merry lady, or try to get work. But you won't get none, for your character is out the window."

In Hampstead two procuresses acceded to an interview. They dealt only in maidenheads, they said, had no brothel, their place of violation was wherever the customer wanted it to be. A special feature of their business was, the girls never knew where they went or who the man was; they would never see him again. On occasion *no drugging* would be specified, and that sometimes would be like trying to catch a fox-lynx with your bare hands. "We had one wrap herself up in the bed-curtains and scream and carry on till we had to hold her down by main force." "Is the demand for maidenheads still great?" "Very great, though prices have fallen a bit." "Why is that?" "Well, one reason is we're getting larger orders. One customer, for instance, who used to take a virgin a week at ten pounds, now takes three a fortnight at from five to seven pounds each." "Do you mean to tell me you actually supply one gentleman with *seventy* fresh maidens every year?" "Oh, yes. And he would take a hundred if he could get them. But he is so very particular. He will not take a shop girl. And the age must be right."

Imagine a newspaper *printing* such stuff!

In America that W. T. Stead and that editor would be taken out and horse-whipped!

"Are you *sure* you won't want to come hunting with us?" the Baron said again.

"I think not," Jim said. "I've decided on a voyage."

IT WOULD HAVE HAPPENED THE same in Salt Lake City. The seed had been planted long before. The Oracle who said, "Your hopes and pleasing prospects will be blasted in an hour you wot not of, and no arm can save," hit the nail on the head when it came to Jim. For when the rampage started in the gray matter of his brain, no arm *could* save him, it was too late. But he was lucky, fifty years old instead of thirty, he had had those years. And money to burn. And such a prince of a fellow. Even the little screaming girls with blood running down their legs, the sick children vomiting up chloroform-saturated bile after criminal conversation with him, would have loved him had they had a chance to know him. Everybody in London who had a chance to know him, did. Even with his former ideals and standards of living replaced by recklessness. Wearing dirty linen! as over the months he had strangely come to do. Spots on his clothes. Without a bath for days, stubbled like a 'bo on the road. Hallelujah, give us a handout—to revive us—no, don't! He would think of the awful addiction (that only since *her* had he ever had, the habitual use now of the little half-formed women he would once no more have thought of buying, roughly using and throwing away than he would have slurped down an egg with a half-formed chicken in it) and beseech and implore God.

But it wasn't his fault. This was the devil's work. Canst Thou not see, Thou dumb galoot? He had been *set up*. The little sleeper he tiptoed in to cover more securely the night the east wind rose, blowing open the doors to their common balcony—was not—he knew that now for sure—*her* at all but what is called—They have a name, you know it, Lord, descend upon people in their sleep, the dissolutest, fleshliest—You know who I mean. And looking back, it seemed as if he was asleep (like her) and dreaming when it was supposed to have happened. Cross my heart and hope to—beg to—want to—die. But not always.

He said to Father Barron, "Listen, Father, you know in Montana? Some of the Indians are Catholics and I want to tell you something that maybe you don't know. If they want to, the older Indians don't have to make confession in English, or in Crow either, Cheyenne or whatever they talk, all they got to do is use sticks! Lay 'em on the ground—sticks of different lengths and sizes to represent their sins. 'See, Father, this is what I done—'" Then Jim said, "Father, I'd need sticks from here down to the border."

And Father Barron said, "God knoweth our frame. And He is merciful and gracious, slow to anger and plenteous in mercy."

Jim's frame started to shake eventually, his hands and head too, his speech slurred. It by no means follows that because an infecting sore is small, unimportant and quickly healed, the disease of which the sore is the first symptom is going to be mild. In fact, it not infrequently happens that after many years the most terrible afflictions may succeed a sore that looked too trivial even to bother with. Was it Minerva? Make her hellfire hotter. Kate? Wild Cat Alma? His face blotched, his hair fell out, sores covered his now portly body. The world didn't seem to amount to much anymore. Why it ever had he couldn't remember. Couldn't remember how it felt to have a sense of obligation, the stab of conscience, the longing to be forgiven. Hell, he was as good as God.

"Do you know how rich I am?"

Buckingham Palace wasn't so grand. He would build one better, show the sonsabitches how it was done. But not on *this* mucky strand! In Nevada. Montana. In…One day one of the pupils of his eyes was big, the other was a pinpoint. He saw it in the mirror, hell of a note. One day he had a fit, someone took fits…a boy somewheres…Durango? He fell to the ground unconscious, his muscles twitched and jerked, he foamed at the mouth, get a spoon, one of you bastards, he'll chaw through his tongue…the falling sickness…Hell, hell of a note.

And a little girl, or gold, a house, the evening star or nothing…amounts to…*one God damn.*

KELLY AND KELLY HAD HIS body brought home. Mr. O'Donnell did the honors. Thinking a will might turn up leaving what he had to Mother Church, which he certainly talked like was going to happen whilst he was receiving absolution and penance, Father Barron stood guard over such posthumous proceedings as he could get in on.

But human nature is really a bastard.

THERE WAS NOTHING HE COULD do. It is so strange how inheritances always go to those who least deserve them. Take what Clarendon left. None of it went to the Kinnavy family, consisting of wife, husband, three boys and a girl, though Mrs. Kinnavy was definitely related to Maybelle Clarendon, their grandmothers having been half-sisters, which Lois Kinnavy (née Rogers) could prove. Fond of each other too, their grandmothers, by no means not speaking to one another when they died like *some* people, supposed to be so fond.

The Kinnavys were living in Park City when they heard about Colonel Clarendon dying intestate over in London, England, and decided to take up residence in Salt Lake so as to be on hand if Mrs. Kinnavy won title to succeed her half second cousin Maybelle in the enjoyment of the Clarendon wealth. But more and more heirs gathered on the spot or sent in their claims, and by the time the estate was settled Mrs. Kinnavy was so far out of the running she was but a mote in the sunbeam. Because it turned out the deceased had ten brothers and sisters and countless nieces and nephews scattered around the eastern United States. He even had an old *mother*! but she had had a stroke some years before and had no recollection of a son Jim. She thought they were talking about her brother. "Poor Jim! Such a good boy." Could she have cried she would have done so, but her tear ducts had dried up.

"No, Ma. *Jim.* Your *son.*"

But she couldn't remember. He left home when he was only fifteen, his feelings so hurt by *something*, whatever it might have been, that he never wrote, never came back, never had a thing to do with any of them again. They didn't even know he was rich till gradually the news seeped in. But rich he was, and now all the ancestral outfit he wouldn't spit on when he was alive, and of course Kelly and Kelly, would be rich too. Some of the older Clarendons didn't see why the three youngest should fall into such duck soup, they weren't even *born* at the time Jim left, didn't know him from Adam. True, they said, but also they never hurt his feelings either, to the point where he never wanted to see any of them again, bear *that* in mind.

MRS. O'NAUGHTON, WHO LIVED ACROSS the street from the Clarendon mansion and employed Kelly and Kelly, Attorneys at Law, kept Lucitie up to date about the settling of the estate when she came to Alfonce's to have her hair dressed. "Well, at least none of that outfit is going to *live* there," she said. "It's been sold to strangers."

"The house? How sad!" Lucitie said. "Strangers."

"Not sad at all," Mrs. O'Naughton said. She thought the refined couple from the east, with their ladylike little daughter, who bought it—Prentice, their name was—he had something to do with the Park Utah Consolidated up in Park City—would be lovely neighbors. "Inherited wealth." She did not add *always the best kind*, for her husband's and hers didn't come that way, but as she ceased speaking some such sentiment hung in the air.

LUCITIE REALLY MISSED HER SISTER the day the newcomer to Salt Lake Mrs. Prentice took Mrs. O'Naughton's advice and had Albert do her hair. Hindle would be so interested in hearing about the new owners of the Clarendon mansion, Lucitie said, considering she was one of the last acquaintances of the family ever to be *in* it before the end. And also she would be interested in the piece that was in the Tribune about Colonel Clarendon dying unexpectedly over in London two years and seven months after the death of his beloved wife and thirteen months after the untimely demise of Miss Mavis Clarendon. Lucitie cut it out but somehow mislaid it. It said he had a liver complaint, but Mrs. O'Naughton told Lucitie *she* heard from Mr. Kelly the younger that it was just nothing but (she made her listener bend down so she could whisper in her ear) an old *disease* he had caught long ago when he was a young man in the mining camps and which had laid dormant, then flared up in the last months of his life. Not that Lucitie had a lot of *news* about the new people, even if she and Hindle had been in touch. The Prentices were wealthy, well, that went without saying. They'd have to be to buy that place in the first place! with all the furnishings and keep it up, though Mrs. O'Naughton didn't think they were going to be the kind to show off.

ONE THING LUCITIE WAS GOING to say to Hindle when she wrote her was, "I certainly didn't think when you went up there to Helena, Montana, to see the girls and Serapta, that you wasn't going to come *back*. That you was going to knock around up there and get *lost*!" The one letter Hindle wrote right after she got to Helena gave no hint whatsoever. She said she hired a carriage and went out to Serapta's house which Serapta's brother Murdock gave her, located on his ranch of thousands of acres. Once more Murdock had married well-off. His wife wore chaps, if you can imagine such a thing. It was a very nice house, and Serapta, Stig and the children lived there. They were quite grown up by now, had horses, loved school, went five miles for pianoforte lessons, hardly knew their mother, but what could a person expect. From the looks of things, the luckiest night of all their lives was when whoever it was threw that rock and threatening note in through Stig and Serapta's window, and wrote APOSTATE on the wall. The way they were situated now had so many advantages. So we never know, do we? The trip on the train was enjoyable, Hindle wrote. She met a woman she knew so had company. They wanted her to stay with them, Serapta was the same dear thing as always, Stig seemed to be an ideal husband, painting his panorama and doing different things, and the girls had all kinds of irons in the fire. But people had to stay *connected*—all the time. Or it was no use. So she came back to town and put up at the hotel. It just seemed better. And now she was going to find out about Montana's medical laws, and if she could open a practice maybe she would stay. But if not—it was all kind of up in the air. The people were friendly, it was a nice hotel. She would write again.

But she didn't, and Lucitie felt quite put out. She thought Hindle had had on the order of a nervous breakdown, she really did. Because the last time she saw her, she wasn't herself at all. For some unknown reason, Mavis dying shook her so to the fundaments you would almost have thought she killed her. But of course *pride* was always Hindle's weak spot, she probably thought she could go in there and, with her doctoring that she had got into in the first place just from pure willfulness and determination, could do for that strange child what all those famous specialists couldn't do, wake her up. But instead of that—Mavis's time had just come, that's all. Nobody blamed *Hindle*. Mr. Clarendon certainly didn't. Lucitie didn't happen to (casually) find out before Hindle left for Montana what he had *paid* her, but he wasn't a cheapskate, and he surely saw how hard she tried all those days up there to make things come out right. Because that was how Hindle was. Lucitie saw her a few days after Mavis died and she was just to pieces. Though why in particular she didn't know, except—well, really, her ambition. But as Lucitie said to her, "Who do you think you *are*?"

SOMEBODY ALMOST TOO TIRED TO put one foot before the other, Hindle might have answered when she finally slipped out the back door of the Clarendon mansion for the last time after more than a week of endeavor (just before the funeral was to be held that afternoon—it was private) to return to her old life and work. But that was not so easy to do those first few days. Thrown into nervous confusion not only by all that had happened but by a remuneration the size of which sent her reeling, she couldn't sleep at night and went like a piece of mechanism by day, regaining some semblance of confidence only when she sat down in front of Doctor's (and then her) old, worn books and turned their pages. Not that she read, the time for reading seemed to be past, rather she inspected the words, the lists, as one might rows of ornamental round knobs fixed in and projecting from a molding: jalap, crystals of antimony potassium tartrate, mercurous chloride, metallic mercury, nux vomica, atropine, Peruvian bark, digitalis, bitartrate of sodium, carbonate of iron … and gradually re-established herself, to an extent that when a loud knock came at her door one afternoon not long after this she called out in the old careless, absent-minded way, "Come in!"

He came in. A policeman. "Are you the lady that owns the sign outside the house there, ma'am? Dr. Hindle Fairbrass? Or who would *that* be?"

"That would be me," some shadowy someone in back or hovering in the air above her said precisely, preparing addle-headedly to explain why a medical practitioner might have in her bag volatile acid of ergotine to treat certain hemorrhagic occurrences and a small instrument in the form of a small concave—like a spoon—to abrade morbid matter with from the eye, ear, nose or throat, or on *extremely* rare occasions—

But the policeman just wanted to see her license—that must be it on the wall there—and check with her about her certificate of registration.

She sat down suddenly, as if pushed. "I'm sure I have one of those somewhere," she said, opening and shutting a drawer.

"I'd be surprised if you had," he said, "considering the law was passed just a few days ago. But they're easy to get. All you have to do is go to the City and County Building, make arrangements to go before the Medical Board and let them give you a examination that they tell me takes about a day—"

"Oh," she said, "is that all there is to it? I'll do that tomorrow."

So she went to Helena, Montana.

Chapter Forty

✳

HAD SHE NOT MET SOMEONE SHE KNEW, IT WOULD HAVE BEEN A LONG OLD TRIP. But who should be on the train but Mary Thomas, nicknamed Bluegrass, who was boarding with Minerva at the time Minerva died. Mary, from Kentucky, was called Bluegrass because she was blue, usually light blue but sometimes almost violet, according to the play of her emotions, and when she first arrived at Minerva's from Nevada, on the trail of one of her deceivers, a mining engineer who disappeared into the High Uintas, she seemed so imperiled that Minerva brought her down to Hindle's office for a hasty examination. Mary said there was no sense in it. All the Thomases back in Dwarf, Kentucky, up in the hollow and down around Troublesome Creek, were different shades of blue. Old Aunt Sammy, whose face looked like an owl's with a tiny hooked beak in the middle, and who had no sweat glands and had never been to town, was the darkest blue, while Mary herself was the lightest. That's why the family was so mean to her and jealous too, except her cousin Matt, who *his* father didn't think he was his, so he killed Matt's mother. Hindle couldn't find anything wrong.

With her lightened hair and dusky eyes, Mary was quite a novelty for a while, both to her fellow boarders at Minerva's and such company as came to call, though not what might be called popular, the blue jaundice and lividness of her complexion tending more to repel than attract. On the train to Helena she had a veil pinned on so close that Hindle wouldn't have known who it was sitting back there in the last seat, riding backwards with her face to the wall, if she hadn't, when Hindle came out of the dressing room and started up the aisle, put a gloved hand out and stopped him. "Dr. Fairbrass!" They were glad to see each other and sat together for the rest of the journey.

She never had anything hit her harder, Bluegrass said, than when Minerva went up the flume like that. Unless it was Flossie killing herself over Buck getting their little boy's long curls cut off. But how could he know the child would get pneumonia on account of it and die? She felt so bad about Flossie she almost wanted to go right out to the graveyard and be buried with her. With some people it was like that—Minerva was another Mary took to right away. Usually if somebody tells you oh, when you go to Salt Lake you just got to go see so-and-so, you'll love her, it'll be somebody you can't stand. "But not in her case."

"A lot of people will miss Minerva," Hindle said.

"I didn't know *what* to do," Bluegrass said. "But Mr. O'Donnell, a friend of mine that Minerva introduced me to—some people don't care for the smell of formaldehyde, it

342

seems to soak into a person's breath, and of course if I had my choice there are smells I like better—but I do have to say he turned out to be a friend in need. Well, the Irish. When Lily decided we couldn't make it and had to close the place and the girls went different directions, why, I for one was just up a *tree*. But he lent a helping hand."

At the sound of the name O'Donnell, Hindle's heart gave the same sick thud it gave that early morning when from the top of the stairs she saw (and saw herself seeing in remorseful memory) the two Mr. O'Donnells staggering into the darkened drawing room under Mavis's great rosewood coffin.

"Kindness itself," Bluegrass said. "But you can talk till you're blue in the face and they'll never realize, will they? That a favor is lovely, but then what?"

She had never herself been to Helena, Bluegrass said, but she knew people who had, and they said it was the Queen City of the West. There was a lady up there by the name of Blanche Enterline and she owned, didn't rent, mind you, but owned, a place on Last Chance Gulch looking down on Edwards Street which was called the Castle, on account of the style it was built like. The one who told her about Blanche was a very nice blonde girl in Lovelock married to a Portuguese gentleman—they're very jealous, the Portuguese—and she said if a person could get on with Blanche at the Castle, they should really pat themself on the back. It never closed, this girl told Mary, the piano was always playing, gentlemen could come there and sit around and talk business or read the evening paper. It was refined, like a club. And the reason for *that* was, all the Englishmen living in and around Helena that Blanche said were called remittance men.

"They're pretty well known here and there," Hindle said. "My husband that was a doctor too, he *had* a few as patients." Usually with some amatory ailment, she did not say.

"Don't remittance mean money?"

"It does. Their family pays them wages to keep away from home. They're younger sons, you see, and the only one that counts in England is the oldest son."

"I'm glad you told me," Bluegrass said, but did not go on to say why. "But anyway—people can order a beefsteak any time of the day or night, on Christmas Eve they trim a Christmas tree, and as I say the piano's always playing—"

But at noon on Sunday when Hindle had the livery stable man drive them past it from the station so they could drop Bluegrass off before going on out to the Burdick ranch, the place seemed to be closed tighter than a drum. No piano was playing—it did look a little like a castle, though, with a turret and winding stair. But an abandoned one, the window shades all pulled down.

"What's the matter, I wonder?" Bluegrass said worriedly as she helped the man lift her two satchels out of the rig. "Did Blanche die, or what?"

"Blanche hasn't been there for quite some time," he said. "Had a run-in with a Congressman. Mrs. Mover's got it now. No, I expect they're laying low in there on account of the China girl getting her head cut off in the alley last night."

"Her *head* cut off?" Hindle said in horror.

"You mean *cut off*?" Bluegrass said, looking up the steps to the shut front door.

"Unfortunately," the man said, giving a slight start when the wind lifted a corner of Bluegrass's veil and he caught a glimpse of her blue complexion, deepening in hue as anxiety about her future gripped her. "There's a Chinaman runs a opium den on Water Street—we passed it back there a ways," he pointed, "never any sign of life about it and today it looks deader than ever—and he's the one bought the girl off some kind of broker in San Francisco two or three weeks ago. But she either hated or was scared of him or something, because she ran away, went to the Castle, Mrs. Mover took her in, last night she's lured outside, there's hollering and the next thing you know her head's rolling one way and her body another."

"Dear Lord."

"Bluegrass," Hindle said. "Why don't you just get back in the buggy and come on with me out to my—where *I'm* going?"

"All right," the other said. "But first I'll try rousing 'em one more time. Just to be sure."

Hindle and the livery stable man waited. "Have to use dynamite to get in there *today*, looks like," he said, giving Hindle a quick glance. Then, "How are *you* tied up with *her*, if I may ask?"

"She was a patient of mine," Hindle said stiffly. He didn't *talk* like an Easterner, but for a Westerner to ask personal questions was unusual enough for her to look at him out of the corner of her eye. He was about her age, maybe a little older, what some people might call good-looking, didn't look like a livery stable man. But it was Sunday, and in a shirt and tie, shaved, and with polished boots and a hat tipped back it was hard to tell.

"Must of peeked out the window," he said, "seen it wasn't the opium guy—he can't be found, they was saying at breakfast this morning at the hotel—or the Marshal—" He meant, because the door was opening. "Afternoon, Mrs. Mover!" he called, giving a wave. "How are you doing in there? All in one piece?"

"I guess so," the woman called back. Stout, gray-haired, handsomely dressed but with sleeves rolled up above flour-dusted arms and a kitchen apron on over her flounces, "Yes, little dear?" she said then, turning her attention to her caller. "Can you cook?" Hindle and the livery man heard her say to Mary. "Because Cook's gone—he was a Chinaman too, and whether *he* killed her or whether it was Ah Sid and Cook's had *his* head swiped off too I just don't know, but if you want to come in and put an apron on—"

"So I'll try it awhile," Bluegrass said when she ran back down the steps to get her suitcases and say good-bye. "Who knows? The way to a man's heart—"

"So you and her come from Salt Lake?" he said as they drove on.

"Not together. We just happened to be on the same train."

"And you say she was your *patient*?"

At first she was annoyed, but then she thought maybe things were different now than in Doctor's day and that quite smart people, not just those ignorant in the ways of the world, might be inquisitive.

"What kind of a doctor *are* you? I ask because there's so many different kinds, it seems like nowadays, Electro-Magnetic, Water Cure, Contract Surgeon—" She told him and he said, "Well, say," admiringly. Then, turning to look back at her, "It's quite a ways. Why don't you come up in front here where you and me can chew the fat as we go along?"

Before they got there she didn't tell him *everything*, but enough to lighten her heart. And he didn't tell her *everything* either, but because what he did say was sprightly and "inward," it served her heart the same. And maybe lightened his own as well, if that was what his heart needed. Then they got there, and he helped her down and said he sure hoped they would run into each other again someday, for it had been one of the most enjoyable—But it turned out not to be the *Burdick* ranch after all, it was the old *Brossart* place, and that just went to show you where his mind was! So they had to head off in another direction. That made them quite late, but as Mr. Miles said, that was the man's name, Emerson Miles, "If we'd of went to the right place, you'd of been inside eating supper and I'd of been driving along facing the wrong way. We'd of missed the sunset."

"I wouldn't have wanted to do that." And she wouldn't, it was beautiful.

Or the moon coming up, or the stars coming out—

Mr. Miles exulted over the beautiful evening as though he was personally responsible for it.

They stopped and had a drink of water out of a shallow brook. He let the horses drink. And when they got to where he thought they could, he let them crop the grass while he and she walked about a bit. In gentlemanly fashion, he said she might like to wander a little over in back of that clump of brushwood while he kind of explored that brake down there by them boulders, and she said that might be a good idea. Later she asked him if he would like a sandwich because she had some left over from the train, and he said he wouldn't mind, and they would just stop along here and eat them here because this was the lee of the Continental Divide. Then they went on but wished they didn't have to.

There is an old Indian legend that says that in the beginning of the world men had four arms and four feet. They had such a high opinion of themselves they thought they were as good as the Great Spirit. This got the Great Spirit's goat, naturally, so he took a knife and sliced them down the middle. Well, right away the two halves wanted to get together again, and their longing was the first love in the world. They dragged around till one day they met the Spirit of Fire and he asked what was the matter, for he saw they were down in the dumps. "We want you to sear us with flame," they said, "melt us into one, for that is our only desire on earth." So the Spirit of Fire took pity on them and did what they asked. And ever since, all the unconnected halves running around want to be seared with flame and melted together.

Hindle certainly didn't know she was a right or left side of such a being. And neither did Emerson Miles. But all they wanted to do as they rode along was regain their entire magnitude. Respectable people in Sunday clothes, however, they did not even touch each other's hand. But the warmth of the zeal with which they had talked together did project upon their mind's eye when they said good-bye a kind of subtle frame upon the air that needed but a very little searing.

AT LAST THERE WOULD BE no place to go, Hindle said, finding when she made inquiries a few days later that in Montana, as in Utah, a law had been passed. Nobody could just hang out a shingle anymore. To practice medicine you had to have a license, which you could only get by showing a Certificate of Registration, which you could only get by passing an examination by a Board of Physicians, who wouldn't even give it to you unless you had proof you graduated from a medical college. So there you were, dead in the water. Her beautiful framed diploma, the books and all her inner-circle gear, were null and void. In Montana as in Utah, she was exoteric. And while she didn't intend in the foreseeable future to jump off a precipice on account of it, she couldn't imagine ever being happy again, even loved or in love, or with a lot of money (which she now had). Her life was just *over*. She could be a midwife, they told her. But not a doctor. Never again Dr. Hindle Fairbrass, Eclectic Practitioner, Diseases of Women Only. "Oh, Doctor, thank God you've come!" "What's to be done, Doctor?" "Doctor, what do you think—?"

"There's a verse somewhere about 'it's better to have loved and lost than never to have loved at all,' which you probably heard," she said. "I was thinking of that as I came down the courthouse steps today. And confining that to just the one category, it might be so. But when you edge over into a person's *reputation* and *pride*—well, try it that way. 'It's better to of been a king, got run off your throne, and now you're in the mud and nobody will spit on you, than never to of been a king at all.' It don't work, does it? It's—" She looked away. "Talk about pain."

"Don't I know," Emerson Miles said. "Not that I was ever a king. But as I mentioned to you before and now will mention again, I *was* a brakeman, and not so very long ago, on the Arizona Central. And a lot of people don't realize this, but a brakeman is a pretty big Injun. On them smoking old six-wheelers and yellow wood coaches inching across the prairies and twisting up into the high passes with the brakes running hotter'n hellfire on the downgrade, he's the one that counts. Well, he better be a jump ahead. *Fast. Strong. Sure-footed.* Really a better specimen of man in lots of ways—though I don't want to brag—than the *engineer*. The brakeman's respected. He goes out in the world and he's— looked up to. Not like somebody hanging around his cousin's livery stable in the hopes of getting part-time work taking out a carriage now and then. He's—People listen to what he's got to say. You know the expression 'red light district'? Well, there wouldn't even *be* no such name if it wasn't for the brakeman."

"Is that so?" she said.

"How that happened—railroaders in different towns along the line, when they went—calling on the ladies—would hang a brakeman's red lantern outside of where they was, for the dispatcher's call boy. And would you believe, not a one of them lights—whether setting on a curb or hanging on a post, and though the finest money can buy—was ever stolen? Never. People had too much respect. So that's how the red light district got named. And *I* was a brakeman," he said. "And while that's not a *king*—But you're right. The comedown half kills a fellow."

"I feel like I've had a concussion," Hindle said, going over (out of a regard to the respectabilities of life) to push her hotel room door into the hallway back open after the evening breeze had nearly blown it shut.

"Good evening, Dr. Fairbrass," the night clerk, a mustachioed shirt-sleeved man in arm-garters, said from the vicinity of the stairway, stepping down from a chair after lighting one of the hallway lamps.

"Good evening," Hindle said. She came back to her seat by the window to resume watching the sky in the west. Dr. Fairbrass. "Oh, Doctor, thank heaven you've come!" Well, it was nearly over, would never happen again.

"Yes, sir," Emerson said. "Somebody. And now—But of course if I hadn't been driving for Ed that day a week ago, I wouldn't of met *you*. And I wouldn't trade that."

Did you do something the railroad fired you for? she wanted to ask, but Doctor's old precept *no questions west of the Red River* had been learned too well. "Funny how things will come back to a person, isn't it?" she said instead. "But talking of—coming down a notch—my first husband was one of these that made quite a study of history. And one time he told me as we was riding along that when the pilgrims come over to this country, the Puritans and such as them, why, they was all *divided into classes*. Lots of people don't know that. They think they was all just one big outfit, everybody on a level with everyone else, eating turkey on Thanksgiving—but that's not how it was at all. And one of these classes was called 'gentlemen.' And would you believe it, they could be arrested, and tried, and sentenced, but *no bodily harm could come to them* even if they committed murder! But this particular gentleman my husband told about didn't commit murder. What he did was, he stole corn from the Indians. So the Judge found him guilty, made him pay a fine and sentenced his *servant*—who didn't have a thing in the world to do with it—to a whipping. But the gentleman was punished. He was sentenced to drop the *Mister* from in front of his name. Now maybe that don't sound so very terrible, but when you consider that a *Mister* was what set you apart from the common people and that now he wasn't set apart anymore, he was just one of *them*, why, you can see why he ran right down to the ocean as fast as he could and drowned himself!"

"I can see that," Emerson said. "I can indeed. But listen. I just been thinking. How about Canada? There's a place across the border in Calgary called Medicine Hat that maybe you never heard of where I bet we can go and you can take out a license slick as a whistle!"

She turned away from the window and looked at him.

"Medicine Hat," he repeated. "Be right back in business."

"Does the railroad go there?"

"Oh, we won't have no trouble getting there."

Again the door began to swing softly shut, and she hurried to open it wide to the shadowy hallway where two or three other guests were heading for the stairs, this time making sure it would stay open by reaching out with her foot for the room's spittoon and lodging it tight against it. "Medicine Hat," she murmured, and could see herself hanging up her license, her diploma, setting out tools and equipment, how it would all just be beginning. The oath…The way things turned out I'd have looked pretty silly taking it, wouldn't I, Hippocrates, and I never did, but I'm sorry anyway, and I beg forgiveness for when I didn't refrain from wrongdoing and corruption. And I promise, if you will just let me—I will never—in my life again—

"Settle in, in no time," he said, tipping his straight chair back on its back legs against the wall under the wide-framed colored picture of skaters on a clear winter's night, removing and placing in his vest pocket the match he had been chewing on. "You was mentioning pride. We say to people, 'Where's your *pride?*' But pride can be too much of a good thing, too. Take me and my foot."

"What about your foot?" she said.

"What was the name of what you said might be the matter?" he said.

"Well, you haven't took your shoe off—but I said it sounded to me from what you *said* that it might be osteomyelitis—"

"That sounds like what the railroad doctor said," he said. "And you know what caused it?"

"Well, it could be some kind of medullary—"

"What caused it was pride," he said. "Pure, puffed-up, idiotic pride."

"That you was a brakeman?"

"Oh, this was years before that. No. We was living in Cedar City—"

"Utah?" she said, casting him a somewhat startled glance.

"My pa was on the run. Things was at sixes and sevens. He was a polyg, you see."

"Mine was too," she said.

"We never kept on with it after we left. The religion, the church—"

"We didn't neither."

"Time was," he said, "as maybe you know, when a family in that location, down near the border, couldn't pull up stakes and leave so easy. But right at this time there was considerable turmoil, goings and comings, so I said to my ma, 'You been saying you want to leave and go back to Grandpa's'—Ma was a convert originally from Turkey

Creek, Kansas—her folks didn't join—'so now's our chance, let's just pack up and *git*.' Well, much to my surprise, she was all for that, so off we went."

"The railroad had come through by then," he said. "We could of got to a station and went on the cars. But no, Ma had chickens and a cow and calf she loved and wouldn't of no more left than she'd of left one of *us*. And she had come by wagon train to start with, so that way of traveling was familiar to her. But in her day there was wagon *trains*, bunches of wagons rolling along together, while when *we* tried it, we was just all alone out there on that big prairie. We heard that the Apaches and Comanches was none too friendly, but there was still a few buffalo left and maybe they was off hunting 'em, I don't know. Anyway, we didn't see but one party the whole way. Ma give them a crock of apple butter and they give her a ball of something like a great big popcorn ball. It wasn't popcorn, of course, but it tasted pretty good, so we broke off chunks and ate it, though I bet if we'd knew what it was we'd of gagged. I said we felt like all alone, but that was because we was headed *east*. Coming *west* there was still a few big wagon trains, the railroads hadn't got *all* the business."

"I've always been glad I had the experience," he said. "And not just have to sit by when the old-timers get to bragging. *I* been out there too on them old plains, 'cross them rivers and up and down them hills. *I* been under that sun out there at noon. *I* felt the wind rise, no reason, just start to blowing so hard it'd pretty near carry off the baby. And run for cover in rain like the rain that lifted the Ark. Campfire coffee, sunrise bigger'n half the world. But we had it easy in comparison, Ma said, and I guess we did. With only old Bossie and the calf we didn't have to herd no cattle, nothing to stampede, no hostile or hardly any *other* kind of Indians. No buffalo chips to gather 'cause no more buffalo. You know what a government man told me once? Sixty million buffalo just *vanished*. And not a thousandth part of their meat was ever used. One thing Ma appreciated, how quiet our one wagon was compared to thirty or forty white-tops coming along in a line with the uproar the animals, chickens, geese, children, pots, pans, tools and creaking wheels set up from dawn to dusk that give some womenfolks such a headache they'd put a bucket on their head or anything. And speaking of daybreak out there—but I mentioned that, didn't I? And coffee's never tasted that good since. I'm glad I had the experience, the old-timers got nothing on me. But all I wish, I wish I'd had some *brains*."

"Why do you say that?" she said.

"Well," he said, "you take a half-grown boy, the oldest of the family, I was going on fifteen, and his ma says to him, 'Emerson, you're the man of the house from now on.' And then she says, 'Children, *Emerson*'s the boss now, you mind him.' Well, a boy like that—he gets to thinking he's the cock of the walk. Other people can make mistakes, look foolish, have human failings. But not him. So we traveled. There's flatland a-plenty, but there's elevations too, and some of them hills was *steep*. But why I say I wish I'd had some brains—whenever the wagon slid, or wanted to back down, out would go my foot under the wheel, and I'd grab hold and hold 'er, showing off. Out'd go my old foot day after day. Well, siree, we got to Grandma's in Turkey Creek and I am telling *you*, my foot and ankle was so sore and bruised I couldn't even walk! for I don't know how long. Grandpa said in his day he'd saw some crazy stunts, but to stick a fellow's *foot* under the wheel of a sliding wagon time after time just took the prize. We hated one another, me and him. But Ma—you'd think the greatest thing ever to come down the pike was her pa. So when my foot got better, my foot and leg, since her and the kids was satisfied right there and didn't want no place of our own, I lit out. And never went back. In later years Ma died. And my foot," he said, "laid low."

"You never hurt it again?"

"No, never again," he said. "Once was enough, I watched my step. But a bruising like that lasts a lifetime, I guess, deep in the bone, turns to some kind of—what you said. But the funny part, for *years* it—I never limped, never felt no pain. Then's when I worked on the railroad. Worked my way up. Got to be a brakeman."

"And then what happened?"

"Damnedest thing—I went to bed one night free and clear. Woke up about three in the morning thinking my foot was in a bear trap, had to grab onto the bed and bite my lips to keep from yelling. And for two solid months—Now it just comes and goes, the pain. The limp's permanent. A railroad don't want no maimed, halting, limping, lame-duck *brakeman*. Maybe the *President* of the outfit, but not a brakeman."

"You're not that bad off," she said sternly. "Why, if you didn't mention it, a person wouldn't—even notice."

"Calgary's going to change our luck."

"What's this 'we'?"

"Well, us. You and me, pulling up stakes and heading north. It wasn't meant—for me to be one place and you another."

"It's worked out fine so far."

"It's worked out terrible."

"I'm perfectly content." But when she was there out on the Burdick ranch in Serapta's house, Serapta as dear to her as her own sister, and Eula and Esther bouncing around, so happy over their presents—Serapta and Stig happy too, everybody beaming, begging her to stay, and then when she said she'd get a place in town so they could be a family—"Oh, no, Mama! No!" (the girls running to Serapta) and she looked through the window and dwindling off into the moonlit distance was this perfect stranger and all she wanted to do was run after him, "Wait! Wait for me!"

"Why was it when I come driving out the next day you was all ready? *You* never sent for no carriage. I couldn't stay away."

"I was leaving, that's all, somebody would of drove me. I had things to do in town."

"*I* got things to do wherever *you* are—Salt Lake, Helena, Medicine Hat—"

"Such as what?"

"Well, for one thing—Ed thought I was plumb out of my mind to pay what I went and paid at the auction that day for Judge Skipworth's law books. They're way out of date, he says, Judge Skipworth was ninety-four years old when he died. But I didn't care, I bought 'em. I'm reading in 'em—Do enough of *that*, and a fellow can hang out a shingle—"

"Birds of a feather." She saw herself in the lamplight bent over Doctor's old books. But I never was nothing but an upstart, was I, Hippocrates? *But I'll do better—*

"Listen," he said. "You know what we could do tomorrow morning? Get married. Leave for Canada—"

"There's a parcel of things to do before we do *that*."

He hitched his chair up nearer hers. They had already said everything. He knew she was married. Knew all about Lennart Palmstedt, knew in that Wasatch country how hard it was to keep away to windward of the angel Moroni's religion. Even he, jaundiced as he was with regard to an infallible church relying for its evidence and guidance upon revelations made perpetually to its fallible rulers, had taken consecutively to wife two girls he left as better off without him. Her husband was better off without her too, Hindle said, one less connection to rile the government.

They had agreed church marriages weren't worth the paper they were written on, especially as for several years not a scratch of the pen told of any being performed, so they were free. On the surface of their lives, of course, cloud-shadows would trace incoherence and absurdity, each passing into each and back again, and drift over, always, till they died. And so? As no absolutely certain consciousness exists, there might (possibly) be ground of fealty sufficient for practical life. *Their* practical life, that is to say. And so tomorrow morning he was going to come and tap on her door and she would be ready, and they would go and find a magistrate and he would marry them. The way things were turning out, she was glad she had gone up to Auerbach's and bought such nice things before she came away, a skirt, a waist, a coat, a hat. A *beautiful* hat, almost as if she had known what she was going to wear it to. And the last thing she did before she went to bed was try the hat on.

As had been planned, Emerson did tap at her door the next morning, but so early it was still dark. "Who is it?" she said groggily, sitting up in bed and then getting up and going to the door. He said he had to talk to her, so she put her coat on over her nightdress and asked him in, this time and this close to marriage not paying any attention to the impropriety of the door's closing. What did he want to talk to her about? Had they not told each other—? Yes, a lot. But not—He woke up just now, and while he didn't think she would hold it against *him*, he said, still it was only fair—

"One time when I was on the railroad I was going with a girl," he said. "Methodist. And a young fellow will do about anything—Well, you know. Eyes like a dish full of something, ringlets down her back. I went to Sunday school with her. And once I helped her learn some Bible verses so as to get a prize of some kind. *Gather not my soul with sinners, nor my life with bloody men,* was one of the verses. I can still remember it. So anyway, a few minutes ago I woke up, not that I was sleeping real deep or was maybe even asleep at all, *thinking* of that verse, and it come to me that you should have the choice to back out if you want to—"

"Back out?" she said.

"Because my *father* was a 'bloody man,'" he said. "He was John D. Lee. You was traveling around, maybe you never heard of him. But out here—there's no getting away from it, he was a 'bloody man.' Killed people—for whatever reason, there's different versions of that. Lived a hunted criminal, so-called, for twenty years. Then they caught him. And he was stood up and shot. And I'm his son, one of 'em. He had—Well, no matter. The name Miles was my mother's maiden name—"

She looked at him, and as she looked could all of a sudden, as clear as looking at a brightly lighted picture through a stereopticon, see *him.* He was jumping down off the high-piled wagon, throwing the reins up over Chickasaw's neck, and then just standing there smiling, arms outstretched. Papa! They were running to him, her and Lucitie. Mama was in the doorway. It was evening—she could hear his voice:

> *O'Brien? McFadden? Or Bates?*
> *Now what is your name?*
> *And what is your game?*
> *And O what was your name in the States?*

"It's awfully early to talk," she said.

"I thought I should tell you, darlin'."

"Yes."

"So what do you—?"

"It's still night."

She didn't go back to bed after he'd gone. Made her ablutions, dressed, combed her hair. Walked around the room. It got light, but the sky was overcast and the street looked wet. She opened the window and put her hand out, palm up. No, no rain. And at that moment the sun came out so bright she blinked, and when she turned back into the room could hardly see. Her beautiful new hat lay on a chair. She took it up, went to the dresser, bent forward and looked in the glass. "*Something for something,*" *tit for tat, you told me now I'll tell you* she decided to save for her deathbed. Then carefully, just so, she put on her hat and stuck the hatpin in.

Is not the heart deceitful above all else, and desperately wicked?

PART TWO

The Habit of These Groves

Chapter Forty-one

*

Alfonce's Tonsorial and Hairdressing Establishment always sparkled like cut glass just lifted from the dishpan. Lucitie took pride in keeping it that way, especially on Tuesday, when Mrs. Prentice, the new owner of the Clarendon mansion, came in to have her hair shampooed, dried by the gas dryer (which the little Australian girl Wyandra turned by hand like a coffee grinder), curled by Albert with the three-pronged iron, then finally dressed. This Tuesday, however, Lucitie couldn't bear to think what the shop looked like without her early-morning inspection, her swipes with her dampened dustrag and such little embellishments as a nice fresh summer rose in the bud vase on the toilet-table—called "Mrs. Prentice's table"—and triangular papers of fine rice-paper in the paper-curl box, instead of the common unsized kind.

But she didn't dare leave the post she had taken in the dining room near the hall doorway. If Albert seemed about to go into the closed-off parlor, she could quickly head him off. There was no reason for him to go in there, or back upstairs (Wyandra would run up to get anything he wanted, though usually the pleasure was all Lucitie's, even in her present unwieldy condition). She kept her eye peeled nevertheless, and was much relieved when after drinking a third cup of breakfast tea Albert finally betook himself through the long hall to the shop, there to handle without her (for in her modesty she had kept clear of the public for the past four months, ever since she started to show) such business as might come in before the shop's star customer, Mrs. Allen Gerry Prentice, appeared. Before Lucitie could breathe easy, however, the girls must be sent off to school. As soon as they got there, though, and Nancibel (the child Lucitie had after Albert was circumcised) was at her desk, Wyandra's orders were to turn around and nip off back home as fast as her legs could carry her.

While Nancibel at the kitchen table strapped up her books, Lucitie in the dining room whispered these instructions, and the Australian girl's face brightened. Would it be—today?

Almost surely no, Lucitie said. She had at least a week to go, according to Mrs. Bearpark. Though in the practice of assisting women in childbirth only since her eyes began to fail and she could no longer see to dressmake, Mrs. Bearpark was such an expert in figuring such matters that she even foretold the quickening almost to the day and hour, and said Lucitie was carrying too high for the baby to be a girl. With confidence, then, the mother-to-be said it wouldn't be today. No, she needed Wyandra for something else.

Mrs. Prentice? To run down to the post-office and see if the new silk-covered hair-pins had arrived yet, from England?

No, nothing to do with Mrs. Prentice.

"Just come back," Lucitie said, "as fast as your legs will carry you."

"Do I have to ask the teacher—?"

"No time for that. I'll write a note for you to take later."

"Oh, Mrs. Alfonce!" Wyandra said, wild with curiosity at all this. And delight. For she had begged not to have to go to school anymore anyway. At twelve she was the biggest girl in the fifth grade. And didn't even belong *there* as far as numbers went, though she was a fine reader and well grounded in the rudiments of grammar without knowing any of the rules. She didn't *mind* school, even the other children mimicking the funny "down under" way she talked, but it was just better to be home making the beds, sweeping the dining room—and now that she was learning to be a hairdresser—But begging did no good.

Lucitie had her heart set on Wyandra's continued attendance until she graduated from the eighth grade in a white dress, blue sash, white stockings, black patent leather toe slippers, and her hair all in lovely ringlets that Mr. Alfonce would arrange. Wyandra's photograph was also to be taken holding her diploma rolled up and tied with ribbon, and a standing basket of beautiful spring flowers at her feet—and she would always be glad. A good rule in life was when you started something to always finish it, Lucitie said her mother said her father used to say. And she believed that.

But another reason Lucitie wanted Wyandra to keep on going to school was so that Nancibel, her precious only child, would have her hand held crossing streets and not come home pushed in the ditch by roughnecks or run down by a velocipede, delivery wagon, gig, trolley, runaway team or even out of nowhere one of the dozen or so horse-less carriages beginning to infest the city's streets. Lucitie often said so, and Wyandra was as glad to oblige her benefactor now as when she first took Nancibel in tow two years before. Nancibel was six then. Now she was eight and beginning to object to the hand-holding, and often when out of sight of home broke away from her faithful escort to catch up with some little friend or run along by herself. But independence could wait awhile, Lucitie thought, and said that when Wyandra had a little girl of her own some-day she would understand. So as usual, on this Tuesday morning the two children set off hand in hand, but Lucitie had no more than hurried to the tightly closed parlor door when they came running back.

"Mama!"

She jumped as if shot. "Yes, darling, what is it?"

"I forgot my fan!" Nancibel was a proud member of the Fan Drill Team, one of the Yellows, and had to practice opening and shutting her fan with one hand and pivoting with it, and such movements as "Ajax defying the lightning," every night after supper till the Thanksgiving program.

"Well, where is it?"

"I've got it!" Wyandra said, coming through the dining room door. It had been left on the window seat.

"Well, kiss Mama good-bye then."

"I already did." Nancibel grabbed the fan and ran out.

"Mrs. Alfonce, what's the matter?" Wyandra asked worriedly. "You don't look a bit good."

"Nothing, honey. Hurry now, don't let her get too far ahead—"

"But you look like—You're *shaking*."

"No, I'm not. Why would I be shaking? Run now, and catch the little scamp."

Ten minutes later, having seen her charge safely into her schoolroom, Wyandra was back. She looked in the kitchen, the dining room, made a frantic dash across the hall and threw open the door into the parlor.

"Mrs. Alfonce!"

The darkened room, for the green blinds were pulled down behind the starched lace curtain, appeared full of people. But there were only three. Wyandra took a quick look, fell back in astonishment.

"Da'! Agnes!"

"Don't be startled, dear," Lucitie said. "You see who is here."

"But when—?"

Agnes seemed to be in the process of folding up quilts, and there were bed-pillows stacked on the organ stool. As she went over to kiss him, Wyandra thought her father did not look as if he had just *arrived*, but rather as if he had just *got up* after spending the night in the room. "When did you get here?" she said.

"You've grew some more, I see," he said as he took her in his arms. "And what a pickle we are in!" he added.

THEY WERE INDEED. AND LUCITIE too, on account of them. But as she often repeated in conversation with Wyandra in days to come, what else could she do? Wouldn't anybody with a heart do the same? Oh, my, though, she said, when she first heard those peculiar noises out in back and got up to peek out through the kitchen window to see if she could see anything, without waking Albert (he always got a headache if woken unexpectedly), and saw them out there on the back steps! Just dark shapes at first, one thin, one fat and recognized, as was the reason for their being on the premises and afraid to knock.

She started to open the door, then stopped, her heart thickly beating. Did they have it? What if Albert caught it? His beautiful face—his beautiful nose—Nancibel, her lovely child? Wyandra? Herself? The baby under her heart? But they couldn't huddle out there all night, hungry and cold. And what about when daylight came? "Oh, God, keep us safe, I beg you," she prayed as she opened the door.

No one ever touched the Tribune before Albert had a chance to read it, and he therefore was the one who spotted the account first, strangely enough on a back page.

"I say," he said. "Listen to this." Lucitie could have listened and gone on mending, but he liked to glance up from time to time and see her eyes fixed on him as he read aloud. So she put her work in her lap and looked his way, thinking as always that he was simply a picture, sitting there in the lamplight, as handsome as when she married him eleven years before or maybe even handsomer, and how she could ever have been so lucky she didn't know.

"They've got *leprosy*," he said.

"Who has? Where?"

"Listen." He read:

Talk is rife that several inhabitants of the four-year-old town of Josepha have been scourged with the blight of leprosy. The sufferers are members of a group of fifty-three Hawaiian converts to the Church of Jesus Christ of Latter-day Saints who emigrated to this country from Kauai, one of the Hawaiian Islands, under the auspices of the church. Upon arrival they removed to 960 acres of irrigated land some 170 miles south of Salt Lake City, drew lots for their portion and with help from their neighbors set about building the houses, meeting house and school which comprise the settlement of Josepha. There they are said to have done well raising hay and grain, horses, and running sheep.

Whether the loathsome disease, known by the Latin name of Elephantiasis Graecorum, common in ancient days in Europe and Egypt, which slowly eats away the body, and forms shining white scales on the skin, will put an end to the Josepha settlement is not known. Neither can it be ascertained for a certainty how many are tainted with the dread disorder, for the incubation period may be many years. The sufferer whose classic symptoms drew the attention of a Cedar City physician to whom the man applied for treatment for an ailment of the optic nerves, bringing on the investigation which has resulted in the discovery, arrest and imprisonment of not only the original patient but seven other lepers, is said to have been leprous some two or three decades but in a dormant condition.

The detention under safe custody of the rest of the colony while a determination is made as to whether to deport or just what to do with them has not proved satisfactory. Several have escaped the now barred Josepha schoolhouse to roam through the country and spread the infection far and wide should they be imbued with it.

Lt. Col. Leonard Bates, Medical Corps, Fort Douglas, states categorically, however, that his and his colleagues' experiences in the Philippines, the West Indies and elsewhere, have convinced them that the disease is not contagious. Other authorities disagree. When disposition is made both of the infectious cases and those inhabitants not so diagnosed, it is said all buildings in Josepha will be put to the torch and the land itself burned over. Fugitives presently at large if apprehended will be viewed as guilty of grave offense and those aiding them subject to fine and imprisonment.

Too dumbfounded to speak, Lucitie just sat and stared.

The Tribune had printed that piece the previous week, nothing since, and Albert thought the authorities must be trying to soft-pedal it in order to avoid panic. Or do so at least until the fugitives were rounded up and deported, or whatever they were going to do with them. They surely couldn't keep them all in jail! To prevent Wyandra's seeing it, even though the article hadn't mentioned Mr. William Faine of Brisbane, Australia, her father, as one of the eight diagnosed as having the disease, Lucitie cut the piece out of the paper and hid it under her dresser scarf. From the day almost that Wyandra, then a lonesome little Australian girl of nine, boarding at Mrs. Bearpark's in company with her father and wandering timidly about the neighborhood, had stopped to speak to Nancibel in the Alfonces' fenced back yard, Lucitie had been looking out for her.

And she for Nancibel. On that first occasion Nancibel's two little playmates had been called home, there was nothing to do, and not being allowed to leave the yard, she was about to come in and (should her mother not be instantly available) slip through the passageway into her father's shop, where she would stand inside the door behind the curtained-off stove with the boiler on it from which hot water was dipped to mix with the cold that came through the tap, and there exude misery and boredom till someone came and looked behind the curtain. But here was Wyandra peeping through the fence, and Nancibel never needed to do that again.

Wyandra, named after a town in Queensland not because it was her birthplace but due to some connection with her mother, was from Australia. Her mother was dead. The very day she went to work for the Ambrosia Cream Company and Cold Storage, she opened a door she didn't know led to the cellar and fell down the stairs and broke her neck.

The *reason* Mama went to work, Wyandra said, Da' had got hurt well-boring. Some part of the machinery busted loose, flew out and hit him in the head. But the Ambrosia Cream Company and Cold Storage paid damages for Mama's neck. So Da' was thinking of going to Coolangatta and opening a popcorn and peanut stand. Coolangatta was sort of like Lagoon, Wyandra (who by this time had been to the resort) said. Da' didn't go to Lagoon that Sunday but stayed at Mrs. Bearpark's and rested all day, his job—busking lime—being one he said he wouldn't wish on his worst enemy.

The reason the Faines now lived in Salt Lake City, Wyandra explained, was because they had been converted. One day when she was at school and Da' was at home with his injury, thinking, as he told her later, about whether to use the damages from Mama's death to go to Coolangatta, try opal-mining again at Anakie out west of Emerald, try to get a job back he once had had of washer in Sutherland's Cannery, put the damage money in the bank, invest it, or just what to do, sitting there drinking tea—his last cup, as it turned out! tea-drinking being against the Word of Wisdom—and of course feeling sad for Mama—why, he heard a knock, and when he opened the door who should be standing on the doorstep but a Mormon missionary named Elder Wheeler who had come all the way from Utah. Da' asked him in and was converted. Then Wyandra came home from school and in a little while she was converted too. Then the *next* clatter out of the box, they were in Honolulu waiting for the other converts to gather and the other Elders to come, and for the ship to put in that they were sailing on to Zion, the real name of Salt Lake City. There, Da' was going to go through the Temple to be sealed to Mama, and have Wyandra sealed to them so she would always be their daughter for millions of years.

The other converts turned out to be an old couple named Ware whose son had been lost at sea. But when they got to the U.S., instead of going to Salt Lake City, they stayed in Los Angeles, because Mrs. Ware thought Kinau was too friendly to her husband. The reason she thought that was because Kinau, who was one of the Hawaiian girls, let Mr. Ware take her comb and comb her long black hair one day while sitting on the deck in the sun! But besides that Mrs. Ware hated Kanakas, her face was just like a thundercloud when they all crowded around at the dock and the Elders started making introductions. Mrs. Ware said so to Wyandra's father later in back of some bales, that had she known the voyage was to be made with fifty-three black fellows that she was supposed to treat as equals because they were converts too, wild horses couldn't have dragged her from the Kangaroo Hills. But once the die was cast, their place was sold, they'd traveled so far and their trunks were already on board, Mrs. Ware didn't know what else to do only to go, especially as she was the one that made her husband join.

Da' said for Mrs. Ware not to feel bad, Wyandra said. Hawaiians really weren't black fellows, not like the Kanakas they knew that swarmed in and took the jobs away from white men because they worked for next to nothing and paid no attention to the Sabbath. Hawaiians were a different breed entirely, more like white people except for their clothes and actions such as wearing flowers.

But Mrs. Ware was very upset. Why would a big crowd of black fellows like that, she still called them black fellows, want to leave Hawaii anyway, converts or not, unless the pack of them were smugglers or some such thing and the police were after them?

They weren't leaving *Hawaii* exactly, Da', who circulated around amongst everybody, said, because they came off the farthest island of the island chain, Kauai. The old man Kanaka with the long white hair had told him. He was very interesting to talk to. He remembered, mind you, the days of the old religion, and when he was a little boy saw what may have been the last *human sacrifice*. But about leaving Kauai, the reason the tribe did so, them as were left after a sickness in their village killed almost everyone else, was malicious ghosts. And when the priest-doctor of another village (their own priest-doctor had died) said those ghosts couldn't be got rid of for one hundred years and a day, they bid good-bye to the old land and were wandering through the forest hunting a new place of settlement when who should they meet along the trail but two Mormon missionaries, Elder Larson and Elder Jones.

As bad off as the Kanakas were, they were soon converted, especially as the missionaries promised to take them all to Honolulu by packet boat, the old man said. There were two reasons for this. First, the wanderers' need, and second, so they could work on the Temple when that great edifice should start to rise. The missionaries thought that would happen soon. But when they got to Honolulu, where the religion had put down roots since the earliest days, and Mormon meeting houses and even a kind of headquarters dotted the land, those in charge said that as regards the Temple, the missionaries were talking through their hat. None was scheduled to rise for years, and in the meantime, without a Poor House or Orphan Asylum, what were they supposed to do with an influx of fifty-three poor, hungry, half-naked converts? There was little work, and what there was the Japanese, Chinese and Filipinos that the place was alive with latched on to before anyone else had a chance.

Of course the church didn't let these new Latter-day Saints starve, and they got them in under at least *tents*. But the converters were *not* complimented, and Elder Larson, his feelings hurt, sat down and wrote the whole story to the Prophet, Seer and Revelator himself, President Taylor, in Salt Lake City, he being the only man on earth who could ask God what to do and get an answer. So the Prophet did and God did. The fifty-three Kanakas, the President wrote the head of the Hawaiian mission, must have transport to Salt Lake City. Upon arrival they were to go a hundred and seventy miles south to a thousand-acre spread of irrigated church land. There, lots would be drawn to see *who* would live *where*. The tools, nails and lumber to build houses, a meeting house and schoolhouse would be furnished. Dwellers in the vicinity would help. On the land they could raise hay and grain, keep chickens, have cows and horses and run sheep. Their passage to America they could pay back to the Perpetual Emigration Fund little by little. And as long as they followed the path of righteousness and lived their religion, they would be blessed in their baskets and their stores. And their town would be called Josepha, after the Prophet Joseph Smith.

For the first time that old drinkers' expression *as dry as a lime busker's shoe* made sense to Will Faine, he said. Nothing could be dryer, and nothing closer to stoking the fires of hell than lime busking. No offense meant, of course, to his fellow boarder at Mrs. Bearpark's who had wangled him the job. And none taken, the boarder said, for it was perfectly true. He had worked in the lime pit at Langton's himself for six long months one time. Willy stuck it out two weeks. Then Sunday came and there was a freight wagon heading off down towards Josepha. So Willy said he thought he would just go along for the ride and to see how the Hawaiians were doing with their thousand acres, maybe he would help them do a little carpenter work.

Wyandra had an idea who the one was her father had in mind to help. Agnes Puolani, the fat Hawaiian widow lady with the pretty teeth. He was always helping her on the ship. Somehow Wyandra didn't look for him to come back very soon, and he didn't. He stayed down in Josepha, and the next thing they heard at Mrs. Bearpark's was that he had *married* Agnes Puolani. Well, he was a widower, he had a perfect right. And would have had in his new faith even if he hadn't been (a widower). Later on he would send for Wyandra, he said. As behooved a man of honor and also of means, for he still had half of the death damages, which upon arrival in Salt Lake he deposited in the Deseret National Bank (he showed Mrs. Bearpark his bank book), he paid for his daughter's keep. That nice little attic room and three squares a day until further notice, he said, and Mrs. Bearpark agreed. It was an ideal arrangement, especially after Wyandra became so fond of the Alfonces she stayed with them so much of the time that Mrs. Bearpark took her cot out of the attic room and put it in her own bedroom where her long-dead husband's first wife, now nearly ninety and blind, also slept, and rented the attic room out, thus collecting double rent. She gave Wyandra's paid-for place at the table to someone else too.

But the child's home was still there, a plate could always be slapped down for her if necessary, and Mrs. Bearpark went on (or thought she went on) seeing that after her Saturday bath Wyandra still had clean clothes to put on. And Mrs. Bearpark went on cashing Mr. Faine's check every month, until he and his Hawaiian wife had a chance to ride up to Salt Lake for a little visit. When they did so and he discovered how the land lay, he was quite astonished, but not nearly so much so as Mrs. Bearpark, who said she never *dreamed* the child *lived* with the Alfonces now. It had happened so gradually—when she heard that Wyandra had made her home with them for nearly a year, Mrs. Bearpark was too embarrassed for words. Why hadn't someone told her?

Mr. Faine spoke to Mrs. Alfonce alone, as Mr. Alfonce was in his hairdressing shop, but he said he would speak to him too if she thought he should. He didn't want them to think he was a man who didn't take care of his obligations. And in regard to his daughter Wyandra—what would she think would be fair pay for—

"Why, nothing!" Lucitie said. The child was so much help and such sweet company that—She was about to say *they* should pay *him*, but a sudden glitter in his somewhat close-together eyes made her break off. Then she was going to say that she and her husband would think of the expenses as tithing. But for fear that might remind him of *religion* and make him wonder about *their* status in that regard, she did not say that either, but gently brought the conversation around to the new town of Josepha and how they liked it.

About like toothache, he said. Their house was the size of a small chicken coop and that was where people were supposed to live, themselves and the new Mrs. Faine's oldest son, the son's wife and three children. It couldn't hold anybody else, not even a little girl. When Wyandra came home from school and Lucitie sent her over to the Bearparks' where her father and stepmother were staying, she got the same explanation and her feelings weren't a bit hurt. She tore back over to the Alfonces' and into the kitchen, where Lucitie was just finishing up the supper dishes.

"Oh, Mrs. Alfonce!" she said, grabbing a dish towel. "They're not going to take me with them! I don't have to go!"

The following year it was the same story. And the year after *that*. So to all intents and purposes the Alfonces had *two* daughters, Wyandra, aged twelve, and Nancibel, aged eight. But the advent on this particular Tuesday of the pair of hunted fugitives did not bode well. In the dead of night the tale they told Lucitie was chilling. A few of the friends and neighbors the authorities first arrested and put in a dungeon—mind you, a *dungeon* in the St. George County Court House cellar—really had leprosy. But certainly not everybody. The whole town was arrested, though. And the ones that arrested them were so scared and distracted, Mr. Faine said, that after the Sheriff's deputies put the prisoners in the dungeon, they forgot to turn the key in the lock, so nearly all the prisoners got away. There was panic, it was said the soldiers were going to be called out with orders to shoot, and at Josepha the schoolhouse windows had been barred...

In darkness Lucitie had hurried the fugitives in, tiptoed around for blankets, pillows. Could they sleep on the floor? Anywhere, they said, they were so dead tired. Lucitie brought in something to eat, apologized that she didn't dare rustle up a fire and make coffee. They didn't care, they said, because of the Word of Wisdom, although they could tell her this much, they had had about a bellyful of the Church of Jesus Christ of Latter-day Saints. Mr. Faine thought this whole business about the leprosy was just an excuse to get the land back! after the colony damn near killed themselves getting it worked and enough irrigating ditches dug. Agnes thought the Mormon God couldn't hold a candle to the Methodist God, and neither one to the gods of the old religion, who probably wouldn't have done all the mean things they did in the past five years if they hadn't been forsaken. Lucitie tiptoed in and got the newspaper clipping out from under the dresser scarf, but it was hard to decipher by the light of one small candle, so she told them the gist of it, squinting to read under her breath only the sentence which said that escapees presently at large would be viewed as guilty of grave offense, and those aiding them in any way subject to fine and imprisonment.

Back in bed, she tried not to toss and turn. They had a plan. Tomorrow morning she was to go to the Deseret National Bank and cash Mr. William Faine's check for his whole five hundred dollars. The couple would then leave, get a horse and a wagon and start east. They were not suspicious-looking, thanks to what the cruel sun in four years had done to Agnes's complexion and hard work to the rest of her. The once lovely, loose-haired, beflowered Hawaiian lady had become, with her hair in two braids and wrapped in a blanket, to all intents and purposes a Paiute squaw, and Mr. Faine a squawman, the typical border ruffian, not typically shiftless, though, for he meant to get some clock-works and pretend to be a clock peddler as the two made their way east. Western ports would almost surely be watched. But from some eastern port they would take ship—go back to Hawaii—maybe they would even end up in Brisbane! After the dust, sun and stunted sagebrush of Josepha, their so-called Promised Land, the hot wind of summer and icy blasts of winter, the scorpions, snakes and lava outcroppings that cut like knives, Brisbane might look pretty good. And how about Wyandra? Why, she must come with them, of course. She was getting big enough now to be of some help. And who had a better right to that help than her old Da'?

Cautiously, so as not to disturb Albert, Lucitie pulled herself into a sitting position up against the headboard, pushing her pillow into the hollow of her back, the better to think there in the darkness. About all of this, but especially about going to the bank to cash Mr. Faine's check and close out his account. Her! in her condition. But Albert mustn't know. And they certainly couldn't send Wyandra, a child of only twelve. Would the police be there? "Subject to fine and imprisonment," the paper said. Well, whatever was going to happen, by tomorrow night it would all be over! The fugitives would either be gone or they would be in jail. *She* would be in jail, Lucitie thought. Wyandra would either be heading off east with them or she would be…

Suddenly it was a long time ago, Mama had died, the baby had died and been buried with her, their stepfather of less than a year had sold the house, taken the money and gone, Lucitie had the laundress job at the Salt Lake House and Hindle would live and work for her board and room at Burdick's Institution for the Care of the Sick. Their old life was done with. The first Mrs. Bearpark, the one who was now so old and had been Mama's best friend, went with them to their jobs so that that first day they'd feel like they had *somebody*, first to the Salt Lake House to leave Lucitie and then—

"Oh, Hindle!"

"Now don't you girls start blubbering," Mrs. Bearpark said. "You got too much gump-tion for *that*."

But how could they help it? never separated in their lives before. It felt—thinking of this and now of losing Wyandra, Lucitie's eyes filled with tears—like just the emptiest, forlornest—Why, if they took Wyandra, she wouldn't get to see the new baby. Wouldn't get to see how it looked wearing or wrapped in the edges and lazy daisies she helped crochet and embroider whenever she had a spare minute, which wasn't often.

Slowly the warm tears trickled. With so much to do in the house and shop and a newborn to care for, what would she do without Wyandra? Who would watch over Nancibel? But it wasn't just what Wyandra *did*. It was her affection, too, pouring out on all of them all the time, like the water pouring from the nymph's basin to the tier below of the marble fountain in Liberty Park. It was her *interest*. They would be braiding hair for the shop, or shelling peas on the back steps, or with towels around their hair cleaning house on Saturday, putting on the sheets, one on one side of the bed, one on the other, and Wyandra would say, "Oh, Mrs. Alfonce, tell me about when you first went to work at the Salt Lake House—"

"Tell me about Chickasaw."

"Tell me about Lisheen, the actress lady."

"About the ship, when you met Mr. Alfonce—"

"Your sister running away with the doctor—"

"About the people who lived in Mrs. Prentice's house—"

"When Brigham Young died—"

"The place—"

"The time—"

Wyandra gathered it all like a bee gathers honey, propounded it to herself like a set of devotions, a chaplet of good works. It was and would be her *own* history, her *own* myth. Because she cared so much, whatever Lucitie told her became like a book you open and read. *Once upon a time there was no time and it was then that*—

"The Clarendons—"

"Mavis—"

"Oh, tell me! please."

Now there would be no one to sum up to. No one to combine what only *happened to happen* (miscellaneous, no connection with anything else, nothing but a hazard of chance) into a march of logical consequences, like a life of George Washington.

They just can't take her, Lucitie thought, wiping her eyes with a corner of the sheet. But Mr. Faine said they were going to, no matter what. "She should help her old Da' for a change," he said, "and her stepmother here."

"She likes hairdressing," Lucitie said. "My husband says he could make a fine hairdresser out of her someday."

"Won't need much of *that* where we're going."

"She's used to us by now. It's been a long time. And we're used to *her*—"

"We may go back to Brisbane. Just don't know at the present moment—"

"Well, since you don't, why don't you just leave her with *us* till you get settled—?"

"Agnes here don't know, never having seen it, but like I been telling her, it might look pretty good, Brisbane. And due to their guilty conscience, like I was saying, the Ambrosia Cream Company and Cold Storage where her mother broke her neck would probably hire Wyandra like that! She's big enough now."

"Someone around the house for several years," Lucitie said, "running in and out—a person grows very attached."

"The wife here got attached to *an old hen*. Cried like a baby when she had to leave her," he said laughingly.

"Mr. Faine, please—"

"What a pickle we are in!"

While Wyandra stood dumbfounded, her father explained. Leprosy. Policemen. People thrown in dungeons. The town, if town it could be called, to go up in smoke. "But never fear," he said. "By Twelfthtide it will all be a thing of the past. We'll be back where we started like nothing had ever happened. In Hawaii. In Queensland. Wouldn't you like to see old Queensland again?"

"But—Da'!" Wyandra had gone over to stand close to Lucitie.

"She's a very kind lady, ain't she?" he said. "Don't we know. Bedded us down last night. Fed us. Going to the bank this morning to cash my check. Fetch us the money to go our ways."

"How can she do *that*?"

"On her two feet, simpleton."

Wyandra meant, a lady in her condition?

Chapter Forty-two

*

THE THOUGHT OF PARADING OUT ON THE STREET, OF THE CHECK-CASHING ordeal, was making Lucitie feel sick and dizzy. Going down Main Street. Then, the Deseret National—She saw the entrance to the bank as immensely tall, saw what must be going on inside like an eddy of wings in crossing shafts of golden light, saw a starry cage, inside like an eddy of wings herself borne fearfully across the marble floor by whirling winds—

"Sir?" she would say in terror. "This check?"

"*Five hundred dollars?*"

The cageling clutches his throat, turns blue, falls forward so his head sticks through the window—

"Sir?"

Albert took care of all business matters, Lucitie had never in her life even been *in* the bank. But of course she had passed it often, the vast mysterious seat of infallible gold and silver, slag heaps of flowery gems, beds of carefully tended rustling green money. Now she must go there. Her going would lose her their dear treasure Wyandra. But the fugitives must leave and leave today. Otherwise—arrested. Thrown in jail. And her, the wife and mother here, with them. Subject to fine and imprisonment. The rest of your natural life. A jailbird baby. In people's minds the words *leprosy* and *Alfonce's Hairdressing Establishment* ever intertwined. No more customers. The shop—crumbled to dust. Albert, lovely Albert, his beautiful hair that smelled of carnations, his perfect fingernails, his silken complexion, Albert in his broadcloth and linen, crisp cravat and burnished boots, a rosebud in his buttonhole, Albert would have to go and be a—*lime busker*. The thought almost made Lucitie swoon.

"Why can't *I* go?" Wyandra demanded.

"Because imagine a girl of your age walking into a bank with a check for five hundred dollars!" Mr. Faine said. "Why, you'd be grilled to a crisp."

"Well, no use waiting around," Lucitie said, getting up and starting for the hall closet.

"Let me go with you!"

"No, honey, you stay here. You got to watch—maybe someone will come." She didn't say *the police*, but that's what she meant and tried to express in the look she sent to Wyandra. If they *did* come, Wyandra was to think of Albert first and think that today was Mrs. Prentice's Tuesday and not let *anything* happen if she could possibly prevent it—

"You can be getting your stuff together," Mr. Faine told his daughter.

"Da', listen, I don't want to go back to Australia. I want to stay—here!"

"Here?" he said. "For what? Why?"

"Because I love—"

"Get your stuff together," he said sharply.

Wyandra ran to Lucitie.

"Mrs. Alfonce! Please tell him—"

"He's got the say over you, honey. I can't do nothing." Not a spot of her body but what seemed to pain, her heart, her whole insides—If she didn't know better she would have thought it was her *pains* starting. But it couldn't, didn't dare, be.

At the corner of Second West, she knew it *did* dare. Not only the pangs of grief at losing Wyandra, not only stomach-ache brought on by fear, but an actual *pain*. She stopped by, and caught hold of, a gate-post. Should she go back before it was too late? No, time enough. There had to be time. How long had it taken Nancibel to be born once she started? But that was eight years ago, and as Hindle said, there was some kind of merciful... Your memory of how it was was blotted out, you could hardly picture... That's why people went on having children. Well, that wasn't the reason, but...

Gritting her teeth, she started on. She did remember, though, and here it was... the circular saw... Hindle never wrote anymore. She lived in Canada now, a place called Medicine Hat... such a funny name. You didn't have to have a license up there. She had her sign out, Dr. Hindle Fairbrass. When Lucitie wrote back she was going to say, did you get a divorce? but it would have been one of those questions that didn't need an answer. She knew how Hindle's mind would work, that if you were married in the Endowment House and didn't have a scratch of the pen to show for it, why, all you had to say was *I'm divorced* and it was so... But Hindle might write her poor sister once in a while. If only she was here!

Should she turn back? No, they had to have their... Money makes the mare go. Then they would leave. Albert would be safe... He wouldn't even have to know that hunted fugitives had slept in the parlor overnight. He was so sensitive, everybody artistic, which you could tell by their hands, was like that. And then being of French extraction... She hurried on, stopped at the corner... The circular saw, screaming through, it was *the* pain all right, no mistaking it. But she had time. Hindle was there, they had drank coffee, the water on the stove half boiled away, she pumped fresh and poured it in... If only she was here! They just had the pump then, now in the new place they had the faucet, a lovely stream of cold water any time they wanted it. They had everything in the new place. A parlor with double doors... the nice back porch. Nancibel had taken *hours*. This one would be the same. The minute she got home and gave Mr. Faine the money and they left, she would send Wyandra over for Mrs. Bearpark...

But Wyandra would be gone! there would *be* no Wyandra. Never, nevermore, like the raven said in the poem Wyandra had to learn for school. She practiced in the kitchen. It was hard to learn. Lucitie's heart ached, everything ached, the circular saw screamed through again. But she was nearly there. Wyandra…Perhaps if they offered to *pay*. When she got home, she would send Wyandra in to get Albert. Even though the whole thing would come out then. Albert dear, I hated to bother you, but…they are going to take her away! We'll never see her again! So couldn't we make Mr. Faine an…She knew while she was thinking it it was just a pipe dream. You never could come out bold-faced…His nature couldn't stand things to come at him abruptly. Albert dear…? And today was Mrs. Prentice's sacred inviolable Tuesday, this very minute he was turning the handle of the gas dryer…She would write her sister: I thought if we would pay…

Dear Hindle, last Tuesday was one of the worst days I ever…It started the night before, or rather the week before, really, when we heard about the leprosy, for it seems…

Albert dear, now don't get excited, it's all over, but this day was one of the worst days I ever…

She was going through the scary and tall portals, wading seven miles across a marble floor, approaching a starry cage. As through a magnifying glass saw the man inside, the pores of his nose, a tiny glistening flake caught on an eyelash, his collar carved from ivory, his stiff black tie…

"Yes? Good morning, madam?"

"This here check…"

The baby lay as still as death.

The saw…screamed through.

If the police didn't come now from every direction. If…Hindle always said to breathe. To just…slowly breathe. Through your nose and mouth both. In, out. And when you feel like fainting get your head down low as you can, the blood rushing will…Hindle's patient at Lagoon…fainting…they undid her dress…and when one of the men took out his pocket knife and cut her corset string, it sounded like a pistol shot, she was laced so tight…In, out, slowly breathe. The patient was a fleshy girl. A hot hot day…Hindle always said…

"How would you like this, madam?"

"What do you mean?"

Then she had it in a thick sheaf. A tinny voice up near the ceiling said thank you, something pulled the wires to move her legs to a singing-desk in the form of an eagle supported on a column. Wires moved her arms, hands, she opened and put the money in and snapped shut her reticule. Tears…Her sister…Oh, Wyandra, honey, I need you. Then watery fluid cascaded down her legs, what will I do? Where will I go? The saw screamed through a Punch and Judy puppet that the next thing she knew the wires had jerked to another place, an alcove, a recess…

And that was how it was that Herman Alfonce happened to be born in back of a

great pillar on the marble floor of the lobby of the Deseret National Bank. And must
have been the reason his careful nature turned out the way it did.

BUT THANK GOD FOR ONE thing, Mrs. Allen Gerry Prentice's thick hair was still being
dried and her mind was occupied with the new coiffure Mr. Alfonce was going to work
out to go with the cream-colored horsehair hat shaped like pigeon's wings and studded
with hummingbirds' breast feathers that dear Cousin Virginia had handed down. Anyway,
the dressing table known as Mrs. Prentice's stood in the vaulted niche away from the
windows, and in any case she seldom took her eyes off the mirror. And Albert paid no
attention to what was going on in the street.

The Bank President's son's buggy—which happened to have just arrived at the bank
(because a close relation can come to work any time they want to and nobody can fire
them), driven by an old accountant in black sateen half-sleeves with a face as pale as death
because never before at this hour of the day in thirty-seven years had he been plucked
from his stool and ordered out into a public thoroughfare or handled a spirited team,
or indeed *any* team except his mother's one old roan—could roll up around the corner
and Albert would never notice, or his customer either. They would never see the new
mother and child (the baby cut loose by the bank's char, using a pair of great scissors
that never had done a thing in its life before but bank business such as cutting the cords
around dusty sheafs of deeds and bonds) being helped and carried in, the char as happy
as a dead hog in the sunshine, the old accountant near collapse. Before Wyandra ran for
Mrs. Bearpark, Lucitie, temporarily on the dining room couch, said to hurry and get the
bank man a glass of Mr. Alfonce's Christmas brandy, as look! his lips were blue, which
Wyandra did and he gulped it down. Then he and the char went back to the bank, and
Lucitie, when she had time to think about it, hoped he suffered no permanent ill-effects.
Then Mrs. Bearpark came and took over, and there was no way to get out of telling her
about the folks from Josepha. But realizing how serious it was, their danger of arrest
and what could happen to Alfonce's Hairdressing Establishment if the word *leprosy* got
connected with it, she promised her lips would be sealed. She hadn't seen the piece in
the paper about the discovery of the eight lepers but said she wasn't a bit surprised. An
entire boatload of Hiwayans would naturally be carrying *something*.

LUCITIE GAVE WYANDRA THE MONEY to run in and give her father, Mr. Faine. Mrs.
Bearpark first tended to the baby with olive oil, sweet spirits of nitre and wads of cotton,
which took quite some time, as for some reason he had been born spread thickly with a
substance like soft butter—accounting no doubt for his giving no more trouble than he
did but slipping out of his thirty-eight-year-old mother like a greased pig—while Lucitie
rested. Then, the still somewhat slippery baby laid in the little swing-cot waiting for him
in the corner with its silkaleen overhanging dropped to shade his once more tightly shut

little eyes, Mrs. Bearpark turned to the new mother.

"You don't mean to tell me you're *crying*."

But crying Lucitie was, and why? For shame and embarrassment. Because of her dishonor in the bank's estimation, though the cleaning lady said she nor anyone thought no more of Lucitie's untidiness in the alcove than if it was the drip from a soaked umbrella, and anyway, she said, that water was the *water of life*, which the bank should be *happy* and only get richer because of it, and the blood too, which she hoped would remind them of…being human. But Lucitie's tears of course were also for the usual joyous reason, the baby being here, all right and beautiful. And for relief because Wyandra said Mr. Faine went out at the same time Lucitie did to scout around—and now a horse, wagon and stableman to collect the money *waited in the alley*. Wyandra was crying, trying not to but not able to help it because—she would miss everyone so much. And then, to wait so long and when the baby was finally here not to get to help take care of him and sing to him and push him in the buggy. Not to get to go to the Thanksgiving program and see the famous Fan Drill with its red, blue, green and yellow fans. Never to get to set the table with the new dishes they picked out together, her and Lucitie. Never to get the chance someday to dress a lady's hair for a Grand Ball like Mr. Alfonce did the afternoon of last New Year's Eve when he combed down golden bangs on Mrs. O'Naughton's daughter Theresa's high forehead, ringletted her neck and passed a wreath of red roses sideways over her head under a band of gold entwined with one of rose-colored satin. It looked so beautiful! And what about the legends, her relics gathered of a mythical past, her fables of eerie Utah, strange Salt Lake City, the *accounts* of what went unaccountably on—?

"You're a goose, Lucitie," Mrs. Bearpark said. "If Wyandra means so much to you, keep her!"

"But she don't belong to us!"

"Losers weepers. All she's got to do is run over to my place and hide awhile. That blow-hard and his Hiwayan's *got* to make tracks. She's already a-sitting in the wagon out there, and he's…"

Wyandra with a face like the sun was halfway out the door when Lucitie struggled up and called her back. "No, honey, that won't do no good."

"Why not?" Mrs. Bearpark demanded. "He sure ain't going to stop and *look* for her. They *got* to *git*!"

"Please, Mrs. Alfonce. Please!" Wyandra begged.

"Tell me this," Mrs. Bearpark said. "You seen father and daughter together two or three times, if that, in four years. Did you ever hear one loving word out of the man?"

"Well, no, but—"

"Did he ever make one loving move towards the child?"

"Some people just can't help their—cold nature—"

"How about the board money he was going to send so fast?"

"We wouldn't of took it anyway! She's just like our own—"

"Run over to my place!" Mrs. Bearpark ordered.

"Please! Can't I?" The girl's tears fell like rain.

"No, no. Mrs. Bearpark, didn't you see that play at the Salt Lake Theater about the poor old man in the forest with the long white beard? 'How sharper than a serpent's tooth is an ungrateful child'?"

"What's that got to do with anything? This child ain't ungrateful *enough*, and you ain't either, and Mr. Faine ain't got a long white beard!"

"Mr. Faine ain't got what?" that gentleman himself said, coming through the door that led out through the kitchen to the alley.

"A long white beard," Mrs. Bearpark said coldly.

"What kind of a remark is that?" He shot the speaker a look of annoyance. Then, "Get a move on, Wy. We're ready. Mrs. Alfonce, many thanks. And congratulations on that boy there, he's a dandy. That's what a *man* wants. Feels like the bottom of the world's fell out when it's a female."

"Oh, it does, does it?" Mrs. Bearpark said, her hands on her hips.

"Lucitie! Will you be so kind as to tell me *what in the world is going on here*?" In the other doorway, the one leading to the shop, Albert stood, his eyes glazed over as though his frail thoughts dallied with a false surmise. Then, somehow omnipotently taking it all in, olive oil and cotton, Lucitie on the couch, Mrs. Bearpark, the dropped silkaleen curtain, turmoil, mess, no table set, no midday dinner, Wyandra home from school crying bitter tears, a man there—Faine! jail! *leprosy!* gently Albert's knees buckled, and down like warm taffy he flowed in a stylish heap.

Lucitie's scream of alarm woke the settled baby. His wail galvanized Wyandra, who rushed to his bed. But then she turned and rushed back and fell to her knees beside Albert, reaching him just as Lucitie did, who did not kneel but grabbed the edge of the table her dear one had almost hit his head on and stood there swaying.

"Is he—?"

No, he wasn't. Dead, if that's what the anguish on her white face meant.

"Here!" A swish, and half a saucepan of cold water splashed down over face, hair, ears, starched collar, silk cravat. Quick-thinking Mrs. Bearpark had saved the day. But you wouldn't think so to hear the sharply indrawn breaths of the girl on her knees beside or the woman standing over him, their murmurs of dissent, the angry looks they cast on his deliverer as Wyandra with her apron gently blotted his brow, cheeks, sweeping eyelashes. They fluttered.

Mr. Faine took a step towards—

"Don't you dare!" Lucitie turned, stretching her arms protectively out.

"Just thought I'd help the bloke onto his feet."

"Ain't you done enough damage?" Mrs. Bearpark demanded from the wailing baby's bed she gently rocked with one hand while still holding the empty saucepan in the other.

"Come on, Wy. Get a-moving. We're on our way!"

Albert's blue eyes opened, closed.

"Oh, Mr. Alfonce. Wake up, dear, dear Mr. Alfonce," Wyandra pleaded, her little heart with its immense vocabulary crying *what star brings me to thee? To singularly dote and give no reason, to tie me by inseparable link? What trine and sextile aspects? What Lords of our genitures?*

"Leave that fairy man there and if you know what's good for you, come ON!"

THAT WAS A DAY FOR sure, the day that Herman was born. Lucitie and Wyandra often spoke of it. When he was little Wyandra would tell him the whole story, to her as full of wonders as Moses in the bulrushes, Abraham Lincoln being born in a log cabin or the woodland advent of Hiawatha. But Herman wouldn't listen like some children. He wanted to be digging holes or piling up pebbles or not letting anybody play with his express-wagon, a distinguishing sign regarded by both his mother and Wyandra as pressed upon him by being born behind that great marble pillar in the Deseret National Bank.

AFTER THE CLARENDON ESTATE WAS settled, Mr. and Mrs. Allen Gerry Prentice bought the mansion furnished, furniture, rugs, chinaware, varnished oil paintings in foot-wide frames, even old toiletries on glass shelves in the biggest bathroom. Some things may have been stolen, the mansion stood untenanted a long time. Still, perhaps not. A night watchman with a lantern went round and round those blocks where the mansions of the town stood, each on its big lawn with a carriage house behind. And that was the blessing of Salt Lake City, it was full of decent honest religious people.

But its decent honest religious people was not why the Allen Gerry Prentices moved there in the first place. They moved because Mr. Prentice had something to do with the Ontario Mine's main offices. But another great attraction was the city's distance from the source of his and his wife's mutual anguish of mind. For he and she were the poor relations of very rich Elphinstone V. S. Bry on Mr. Prentice's side and of Mrs. William Starr Gerard on Mrs. Prentice's. (That would be *the* Mrs. William Starr Gerard, née Virginia Miller, with her seventy-five-thousand-dollar opera glasses, world-famous ruby necklace belonging to Marie Antoinette and three hundred dollars a month going for chocolates alone.) Poor relations! the Prentices, whose inheritances between them added up to barely a million dollars. Mr. Prentice, however, also drew down a fairly substantial salary from the Homestake Mine, one-eighth of which belonged to Elphinstone, which Mr. Prentice earned by repairing to South Dakota for a few days each spring when the weather was most pleasant.

However, a salary—what was that? Some people are just not *talented* when it comes to money. But as a still *poorer* cousin of hers (with scarcely a hundred thousand to the woman's name) pointed out to Mrs. Prentice one time, it could be so much worse. At least Mr. Prentice didn't try to *manipulate* what they had. Some husbands wouldn't have been satisfied till they *lost* every red cent. At least Mr. Prentice let it lay. And money that lay was not dead like a dead animal. Its living mass imbued with yeasty influence somehow mysteriously, like a batch of dough, rose … So the Prentices when they came to Salt Lake could well afford the Clarendon mansion and furnishings for the price it was offered.

It wasn't a bad place. Mr. Prentice thought it was quite decent, or could be made so with a little attention. The yard was just that, to its new owners, a *yard*, like a—dentist's, not "grounds" or "lands." A gardener, however, might make something of the lawn, and the topiary looked rather nice. One great advantage, the *house* could be run with three or four servants. And as Mrs. Prentice said, out here at the jumping-off place they wouldn't have to do much entertaining! Thank heaven! Because with only eight bedrooms, three bathrooms, no elevator and a drawing room that would scarcely hold a hundred people, it would be *pitoyable*.

As everyone knows, everything arises from, depends on, or is determined by its relation to something else. Especially when it was first built, Salt Lake dwellers (even millionaires such as Mrs. O'Naughton) thought the three-storied crystalline Clarendon mansion, towered, chimneyed, plate-glassed, inlaid, set with bubbles of soft-colored hyaline, brass-bound, carved, completely awninged in summer, its grass automatically sprinkled, was a real genuine palace. The Salt Lake Tribune was at its housewarming. Its account's underlying tone made clear that such extravagance when people were starving in the slums back east was scandalous. Prodigality in expenditure so excessive, the reporter said, might bring from the (even then) arousing masses a good deal more someday than the sovereignty of wealth might bargain for. People going past would turn and stare, some of those on foot would even linger and try to imagine themselves in such a place.

Salt Lakers included it in their visitors' grand tours. The Tabernacle. The Temple (it would soon be finished to stand as long as the Pyramids, the church was pushing to get it done by the Bicentennial Carnival). The Tithing Office there on the corner. The Bishop's Storehouse. Emmeline Free lived right across the street there in that house, she was Brigham's favorite wife till Amelia came along. That showplace on the corner there was Amelia's. And on up here the prestigious Lion House, two dozen odd wives supposedly in under those gables, but that was nonsense. And that house there—the Beehive House, in the back yard of which Brigham was stricken after eating a peach from one of his own trees. The tree might still be growing there. But say, now, look at the streets. Like Rome's, they claim. But Rome's hasn't got pure water running down each side. Millionaires built the mansions, got their money out of the ground, mining. Mormons didn't mine, you know, didn't believe in it, not in the early days thirty or forty years ago. That mansion there to your left—the James Clarendon place. He was a millionaire. Died over in England but buried in Salt Lake. *If* it was his body in the coffin. Nobody was left to take a look-see to see if it was really him.

Sometimes the visitors' guides knew who the Clarendon mansion presently belonged to. Sometimes they didn't. But everyone knew that whoever lived there with those rosy lights twinkling through the rich curtains even in the daylight and the smoke rising from every tall chimney had to be *well-heeled.* All is relative, however. And as the mind, not the place, gives true content, as the mind alone, be your fortune what it will, makes you miserable or happy, rich or poor, Mrs. Prentice's mind, tirelessly at work like a mother bear licking a shapeless mass of morbidity into a recognizable baby bear, had long since licked *her self* into the shape she was to retain for the whole of her life, that of sad, jealous, embarrassed, resentful, unfortunate *poor relation.*

Mr. Prentice's mind by a curious coincidence having done the same thing to *him,* when he and she met on the dim latticed fringes of a Bry-Gerard nuptial celebration, it was as if two Russians all alone in the West Indies had finally run into each other. Their courtship was long, due to one thing and another, but eventually, at ages thirty and twenty-eight respectively, Allen Gerry Prentice and Laura Miller pooled their separate pittances, which together amounted to about a million dollars, and married. A modest wedding at Cousin Virginia's shooting box in Scotland. However, out of the kindness of her heart Cousin Virginia dressed as if for an auspicious occasion, in a white velvet gown with bands of Tunguska sable and old point lace. There was green turtle soup, a crown roast of mountain sheep with marron puree, and the wedding cake of a florid style of late Renaissance architecture stood waist high. Bagpipers strode around the table piping.

Then, like the miserable couple ejected from the Garden, bride and groom were pushed tumbling, stumbling and falling into a confused heap out into the mean gray world. Their expulsion only stood to reason. By unwritten mandate servants around the house, except the butler, chef and possibly the head coachman, were forbidden marriage. Mr. Prentice, related by blood to Elphinstone, was not of course a *servant* in the usual sense of the word, but belonging to the set of flunkies in constant attendance on that very, very rich person, he enjoyed little personal liberty. Mrs. Prentice was not a servant either. For the whole eight years she lived under the Gerards' various roofs, she was treated with the respect due the mistress's own second cousin. And Cousin Virginia didn't *order* her to assist Miss Izard. She just made the tactful suggestion. And assisting Miss Izard wasn't like helping the French maid, the governess or anything like that. Demeaning, you know. In fact it was just the opposite, Miss Izard's aristocratic southern mother having in life belonged to the Society of the Descendants of the Illegitimate Sons and Daughters of the King of England, and Miss Izard's work being of so refined a nature it seemed more befitting a priestess than a common woman.

Still, servants or no, when Mr. Prentice married Mrs. Prentice they had sense enough to cast *themselves* from their charmed surroundings. With all the room in those great households, all those untenanted chambers as big as a tennis court, entire empty wings, whole vast suites never even opened, the word was *o-u-t*. It hardly seemed fair, the poor young pair. Till they got on their feet? But that was rich people for you. *Selfishness personified.* And so Mr. and Mrs. Prentice with their measly million and tiny interest, and the job Elphinstone gave Mr. Prentice with *its* measly salary, tumbled down from the high precipice of untold wealth into the ordinary humdrum of common life. So they thought, though common life would never come much closer to them than a cleaning woman in by the day. But they had each other to traduce their former benefactors to, to their hearts' content, from morning till night if they wanted to, which they did at first after the manner of long-denied brides and grooms in another direction, and *that* satisfaction was almost worth their newly humble condition.

Humble indeed. When their child Birdelle was born, Mrs. Prentice even took care of her herself. Not, of course, to the extent of having her *sleep* interrupted to get up with her in the night, the hired girl did that, as the baby's cot was in her room. And of course Mrs. Prentice didn't wash *diapers*. But she *suckled* the child for three months before her milk curdled and they had to get a wet nurse, on many an occasion she sat and *rocked* the baby, and she picked out the little outfits she was to wear. Cousin Virginia's children saw their mother about an average of seven minutes a day, and not that for years at a time while they were away at school! and how would Birdelle have liked *that*? To be sent away to school? Mrs. Prentice used to ask her daughter when she was big enough to understand, and of course Birdelle said she wouldn't have liked it *at all*.

But what Birdelle meant was (had she been able to put it into words, which she never was), being parted from an effigial mother stiffly encased in a carapax of whalebone, cold silk and sharp-edged jet could easily be borne, while being parted from her *home surroundings* could not. How could anyone go away to school? Endure being uncovered in the pelting, blowing, beaming world? Unscreened? Without, you might say, walls? Open to being shot like President Lincoln, kidnapped like Charlie Ross, beheaded like the Queen of Scotland, robbed like a stagecoach, burnt to blackened cinders like people in Chicago, drowned like Shelley, cooked like Captain Cook, frozen, scalped, buried alive, pushed off a cliff, poisoned, bit by snakes and scorpions, stung by bees, starved to death, choked on a piece of gristle or *made fun of*?

Mrs. Prentice sometimes spoke to her hairdresser Albert about Birdelle, how overwrought and somehow off the mark she was. Not when they first moved to Salt Lake, for Birdelle was only three then. But later, when she got to be six and started school and the hired girl had to go with her, and stay right there in the classroom. Every time she started to leave, Birdelle would lie on the floor and scream and hold her breath till she was black in the face. That wouldn't do, of course. And the thing was, they wanted her to have a common education with common children, for she *was* common, really if you took everything into consideration. *They* were common, Mrs. Prentice opened up her heart after a few years and told Albert as she had never told anyone before (who had sense enough not to agree with her). Or if not exactly *common*, they were certainly not *wealthy* like some people thought because the names of Cousin Virginia, Mrs. William Starr Gerard, and Elphinstone, who was Elphinstone V. S. Bry, were sometimes inadvertently dropped.

"People might also get the idea because of where you live," Albert murmured tactfully above the peaceful whirring of the gas dryer he manipulated. "The Clarendon mansion, as it used to be called. Where you live."

"Mr. Alfonce," Mrs. Prentice confided earnestly, "I want to tell you something. Houses—property—Cousin Virginia and her husband Cousin William own, well, *forty square miles* in Vera Cruz alone. I have heard Cousin William say so with my own ears."

"Forty miles!" Albert repeated in proper awe. "Not acres."

"Square *miles*. In New Mexico. In California. They travel. They have to. And that is my nightmare. That *someday* on their way *to* somewhere or *from* somewhere they will be stopping off in Salt Lake City to see *us*. And I absolutely shudder."

"Why should you do that, Mrs. Prentice?" Albert said.

"Why?" she said. "Have you ever been in our house? Do you know it has only three bathrooms? Do you know there are only two bedrooms with fireplaces? There is no elevator. The drawing room wouldn't hold a hundred people."

"But dear Mrs. Prentice, this is the *west*. Even the Grand Duke of Russia when he came out here, even the Prince of Wales had to rough it, as they say."

"Sometime I must tell you—" Mrs. Prentice said with a pitying glance. And over the months and years after the immemorial custom of ladies with their hairdressers she did so, told Albert all about herself, told him all about Cousin Virginia and Cousin Elphinstone, till finally he had to agree that from a certain standpoint Mrs. Prentice really *had* been meanly and shabbily placed in life, and could be said to be (not to put too fine a point upon it) *poor*.

"Crazy," Lucitie said, "would be more like it. Why, she drives down here in a *carriage*! Look at her *clothes*. And we *know* the Clarendon house is a mansion, we been through it. I know you said it was a villa," she remembered that winter night, the most important of her life, "but most people think it's a *palace*. And does she ever lift a finger? Does she cook or iron? She sure don't hitch up that blooded team *herself*, or tend that yard—"

"It's all *in comparison*," Albert said. "Can't you see?"

Gradually they *could* see, in a way, Lucitie and Wyandra. If one person had a private railroad car and the other had to sleep in a lower berth...If one person had a yacht to get piped over the side of at a cost of five thousand dollars a month just to keep it tied up at the dock, with paintings, Oriental carpets, a French chef, a Viennese pastry maker, a padded stall for a high-bred cow, gold-plated plumbing and a two-story pipe organ, and the other person...If one person's stable on Long Island alone (to say nothing of in the state of Kentucky) had *sixty-eight horses* in it while the other person had a measly *six*...If one person had ninety-seven different sets of china in an entire *room*, a *room* for silverware, a *room* for glassware (champagne glasses with twelve-inch stems) while the other...Yes, they could see. Sometimes with dancing eyes and trying not to smile, Lucitie and Wyandra would tell each other how deeply they felt for Mrs. Prentice in her affliction and terrible distress.

As the years went by, however, Lucitie listened with but half an ear when Albert, after a session with Mrs. Prentice, added some particular to Cousin Virginia's or Cousin Elphinstone's opulence. But Wyandra flew down on these bits and pieces of glittering pageant, pecked them up and carried them off to decorate her mind with forever! like a bowerbird its nest.

After a session with almost any customer, Albert and Lucitie and eventually Wyandra too, who, pronounced by Albert a full-fledged hairdresser at the age of sixteen, now worked in the shop alongside them, had new particulars. For something about a hairdressing establishment, with steam rising that kept the air so sweet and moist from the copper boiler on the stove in back, from the chamomile tea boiling for the blonde-haired, castile soap melting, lavender, bay rum, the acrid smell of singed hair, hot metal, the curtained-off, out-of-the-way corners as secret as a burial chamber in the Catacombs, the devoted ministrant dispensing beauty's holy sacraments, brings a customer on to confessional as surely as the pipe in an opium den brings a smoker on to drowsy dreams.

Of course no one at Alfonce's could set anyone free from guilt or obligation or remit them of sin, though almost any murmured response seemed to act that way. *You* couldn't help it, my dear. What else could anyone do? Don't blame yourself. It wasn't your fault...

It certainly wasn't Mrs. Prentice's fault when a stupid workman helping to put in the bronze elevator, which the Tribune said was the first elevator to be installed in a private house in Salt Lake City, and working down in a hole in the basement, got his coat caught in the hydraulic machinery and was crushed to death! He should have known better! Thank heaven Mrs. Prentice wasn't home at the time. Maggie the parlor maid said she would hear that scream till her dying day.

Don't blame yourself, my dear. It wasn't your fault.

"I only wanted to provide a *few* conveniences in case Cousin Virginia did come visit sometime. Or some acquaintance—on account of President Cleveland proclaiming Utah the forty-fifth state, you know, and visitors coming—"

"That's what happens when a person tries, Mrs. Prentice."

"And Mr. Beale is mad at us, he's the old man that works around the place," she said. "But once you start letting the elevator be used as a *freight* elevator, for trunks and boxes and things going up and down, that silk upholstery—it's an unobtrusive grayish lavender—will just be *ruined*. Let them use the stairways, they've got strong backs, Maggie helps him. That Maggie! so superstitious. She won't step foot on it alone. The elevator, I mean. Imagine! On account of that stupid man. Because he died. She thinks it's haunted.

And another place she thinks is haunted—the bedroom down at the end of the hall, to the left as you come upstairs—"

Mavis's bedroom! Lucitie said she would bet anything when Albert told her and Wyandra about the foolish notion Mrs. Prentice's parlor maid had taken. The bedroom on that back upstairs corner. With the blue satin and lace. Where Mavis's mysterious sleep had turned into a death she probably didn't even know about. On the hottest day, Mrs. Prentice said Maggie said, ignorant Irish girl as she was straight from Ireland, a cold draft seemed to come out of that doorway, and once she said she heard sounds like a puppy kind of whimpering.

Hindle would know if the bedroom in that corner was Mavis's room. She must write and ask, Lucitie said. But Hindle was such a poor correspondent. It had been nearly a year since her last letter came, they got farther and farther apart. Please answer this, hon, as we would really like to know, it's supposed to be haunted! Which room was Mavis really laying asleep in when she died?

All Wyandra had to hear was the name Mavis to be rapt like Elijah alive into heaven. "A legend, sir! It's a legend one requires! A miracle! An advertisement! A stage effect!" Every day and twice on Sunday she could have heard the girl's unfortunate story and never tired. That is to say, such of it as Lucitie knew. But Lucitie never saw Mavis after she went to live in the mansion and Mr. Clarendon took her on that wonderful trip to Europe and she came home asleep (of all the things to happen!) and never woke up again, and later got that fever and Mr. Clarendon went down and got Hindle and she went up and took charge of the case. She was a good doctor (trained by Dr. Morgan, as he was to start with before he changed his name to Fairbrass), did all anyone could do, but Mavis died. That was as much as Lucitie knew.

Of course she knew about the beginning, and she saw the two of them before they went down there on that wild goose chase to Cedar City, Mavis and her mother, Lisheen, that had at one time acted on the stage. Dark-complected, and here Mavis came along and was an albino, the whitest thing *you* ever saw...And Lisheen had her faults, but to be shot down in her tracks like that and killed in cold blood! was terrible. The Mormons thought she was a spy. Which she *was* a spy. But nobody deserves...And if Mr. Clarendon hadn't come along when he did...but of course he wouldn't of found Mavis if it hadn't of been for the Indian. Wasn't *that* strange?

The Indian's name was Loudhawk, he only had one eye and was awfully scarred up from being in some battle. And when Hindle first worked at Burdick's Institution for the Care of the Sick—she wasn't a doctor then, naturally, being only about Nancibel's age at the time, Lucitie said, or a little older—why, this Indian *worked* around the place. So he was at the Institution when this troupe dumped the actress off, this theatrical company she was traveling with, and left her, Lisheen, that is, because she was sick with typhoid fever. She got better but by that time it was winter, so she couldn't leave, and then she had this baby…And what's so strange, all those years later, well, it was about twelve, who should it be but Loudhawk who would find that same baby, Mavis, dying of sunstroke, and lay her in the water, which was very shallow down there and running over rocks, and plaster her with mud—and he was the one went and got Mr. Clarendon that was traveling through those parts…after *Mrs.* Clarendon died, Mr. Clarendon went on a photographic trip to forget his sorrow. And Loudhawk took him down to the river where Mavis was—Lucitie guessed if those Cedar City men had of found her they'd of killed her too, the same that killed her mother. But they didn't. So anyway Mr. Clarendon brought her back up to Salt Lake, to Hindle's, and if ever you seen something the cat drug in, why, it was Mavis. Little did Mr. Clarendon think *then* that he would make her his adopted daughter. But a few months later…

But Hindle was the one who could give you all the details, Lucitie said. And darn her anyway, owing a letter so long. It just seemed like after she married that railroad man up in Montana, which he was supposed to be, but in her last letter she said he was reading for the law, and after they moved up to Canada, it was like the mists had swallowed them up. Not a word about what she thought about Lennart dying, the father of Hindle's little girl Marie, who Rosina turned out to have the raising of, or any of the rest of the Salt Lake news…

Chapter Forty-three

✳

Lennart Palmstedt, Hindle's husband and husband as well to Pearl, Rosina, Fern and Jean, died far away in Colonia Juárez, Mexico, the Mormon polygamist colony he had gone to after serving six months in the Utah state prison for "unlawful cohabitation." None of his wives and children went down there with him. His intention had been to send for them as soon as he got settled. It was a wild goose chase, however, as he had no more than got down there when God put a bug in the then Prophet, Seer and Revelator's ear causing him to write the Manifesto which put an end to polygamy. Putting an end to polygamy put an end to the half a hundred years' war with Washington, D.C. And once peace reigned, the territory of Utah could then become a state, appoint its own officers and do what it wanted. And why God didn't think of such a simple solution before was a mystery to a lot of people.

But before Lennart could get back to Salt Lake, a headache commenced that could not be cured by a week of poultices, hot and cold applications, medicine, prayers, laying on of hands or anything else, and he was buried in the graveyard there in Colonia Juárez.

Lucitie herself had only met one of Hindle's fellow wives, she told Wyandra. Rosina. Apparently Fern was the oldest wife in years, the third in line of descent, the prettiest in looks even in old age, and the best off financially. In fact Fern's money and property was why Lennart could afford the extra responsibilities he took on. Though of course after Hindle hung out her shingle she made her own living…and quite a good one. Hindle's hired girl Jean, with two filled hope boxes and a sulky disposition, was the last of Lennart's wives. And what became of *her* Lucitie didn't know. But she did hear of the others once in a while.

Pearl and Rosina, Lennart's first and second wives, were sisters and as close as sisters could be till Fern died. Then all hell broke loose as far as their relationship was concerned. For Pearl, like a thief in the night, as Rosina told Lucitie when it was all over, moved into Fern's house and just took *command*. She was the oldest sister, sixteen months older than Rosina, and now she was the oldest *wife* as well, or rather widow, for Lennart had passed away by then, and thought she had free rein. Hindle was gone, up in Canada, married to somebody else, Hindle was out of the picture. Jean, who lived in the house that Hindle used to live in and was sitting pretty with the rent from that barn-like building in back that Stig Fogelmarck the artist used to rent, with *deeds* to both places in her possession, such being the insanity of a middle-aged man with quite a young bride in comparison, as Jean was at the time, though ugly as a mud fence covered with toads, Jean could be treated as non-existent.

That left just Pearl and Rosina. And (so as to set the record straight) Pearl *did* offer Rosina Fern's old family album of gutta-percha with fancy metal clasps resembling bow knots. But what was Rosina supposed to do with that, pray tell? And with a gilded easel with a fancy towel of drawn linen work, fringed, draped over one side, while Pearl kept the hand painting that had *stood* on it in the gold frame with the deep blue velvet liner? And a book that said PARADISE LOST in gold letters on a mauve cover that was full of ugly pictures that made you feel terrible? Pray tell. Sadly, Rosina realized that there was a *greed* in Pearl and a *self-centeredness* that she would never have thought possible. Of course there was nothing Rosina could do about it. Pearl was Lennart's only *legal* wife as far as the law was concerned, therefore his only legal heir and heir to the property previously willed to him by Fern. Rosina was nothing. Worst of all, she felt she had no sister anymore. The terrible traits their mother told about in their father's side of the family, these had been in Pearl the whole time without anyone suspecting until (the way a glass fruit jar will turn purple-blue in the hot sun over time) *prosperity brought out* what she really was. Why, she wouldn't even let Rosina *buy* the china shepherdess asleep under a little tree that Marie thought was so beautiful. For *money*, not for helping with the spring housecleaning, which how many times hadn't Rosina done *that* out of the goodness of her heart in years past?

No wonder Rosina's hair came out in handfuls! When she came to Alfonce's with the problem, she first showed Lucitie the almost completely denuded round patches on her scalp, each ringed around by a margin of short broken hairs. Then Albert, finished with Mr. Cutler in the tonsorial part of the establishment, a small room off to one side with one Koch's Patent Barber Chair in it and its own entrance, came in and had a look. Wyandra, having seen her paper curl (Mrs. Parker with the cowlicks) to the door and run out to see if Herman was still playing in the fenced back yard, came and stood near them also. Wyandra knew Rosina quite well, as Rosina sometimes brought Hindle's daughter Marie (who Rosina had taken on the raising of almost from birth) up to see her Aunt Lucitie and was pleased to say hello. But mostly Wyandra wanted to hear what Albert would say, for whatever words dropped from his beautiful lips were to Wyandra pearls, rubies and diamonds, though she knew beforehand what the verdict in regard to Rosina's bald spots would be: fox-mange. And so it was.

It was not fatal, it would grow back. In the meantime, what about a transformation? Of course they were rather expensive, and Rosina would not get the good out of it. The remedy she must rub well into her scalp daily for about fifteen minutes before washing it out with soap spirit would work fast. Perhaps she had just better proceed with the bald spots, which would not be so noticeable if she—Albert was deftly parting, combing and pinning as he spoke—tried a little different coiffure...Since she was a relative of sorts, there was no charge.

What a dear man Albert was, even if everything had to be done the way he said. Everything. The raising and lowering of the blinds. The vase to put the flowers in in case a customer brought a bunch. The pronunciation of a word. Whether the lights should go on. But he just naturally knew a great deal, he *should* have the say, Wyandra was never happier than when taking his orders. If Mrs. Gibson came in and wanted something for the black circles under her eyes, in a few minutes Wyandra had a beauty clay of Fuller's earth and kaolin stirred up with glycerine and witch hazel that she could take home and spread on like frosting, and which would have cured the circles under her eyes as sure as shooting had she lived that long. Being the fourth generation in his family to dress hair and prescribe for beauty, Albert knew almost every beauty remedy in the world.

How wonderful it must be to be the fourth generation in a family! It never occurred to Wyandra that *she* was the fourth generation too, and the thirteenth and even the fourteen hundredth! or no telling how many, for no one knows, of her own line. To her, descendancy belonged only to the legendary, those with stories, and histories handed down by tradition. Her own life, like the goddess Minerva's, seemed to have begun all of a sudden. She was nowhere, then Albert in a brown study fixed his clear gaze on a certain corner of the room, the invisible squiggles of the air all went together to form one mass and there she was, a little plain girl with an Australian accent. Then she was a bigger plain girl, and the Australian accent was more like Albert's pretty English one, and *his* being "of the generations" became *her* wonder, *her* myth.

Would you believe, for instance, that when he was a little boy in London he played with things stored away in the back of his grandfather's hairdressing establishment, Alfonce's Friseurs, that no one ever heard of, such as little rakes to rake loose powder with off big heads of hair stiffened like a statue's, a bellows to blow the powder on in the first place, great tweezers, funny old circular-ended curling tongs. He *played* with those things! like having actual hold of history. Once he found a tiny box of black face patches cut out in the shape of stars, half moons, little coaches of four. And can you imagine? the rakes once raked and the bellows blew and the irons curled and the tweezers plucked wild hairs *from people that would end up with no head*! They lived in France, that is, long ago but not so long ago that there weren't modern improvements, such as a beheading machine. And for Albert's connection to it all, besides numerous *other* reasons, it seemed to Wyandra (and Lucitie too, when Wyandra told her) that Albert should be modeled in wax, dressed in his own clothes and stood in that famous wax museum over in London that he often went to before he emigrated to America, with his name in gold letters: ALBERT ALFONCE.

ONCE ROSINA GOT STARTED RUBBING in daily the eighteen grains sulphur with eighteen grains salicylic acid to one ounce of evaporated petroleum that Wyandra mixed according to Albert's instructions, her scalp condition improved. But as it had been caused, Albert said, by nervousness, if *that* didn't abate, the remedy would cure the *old* bald spots but not prevent *new* ones. Wasn't that clever of him? It turned out as he said. Rosina's nervousness, caused by Pearl turning out to be such a traitor and also by the necessity—since she no longer shared a husband with a wealthy wife (both being dead)— of earning her own living as a chambermaid in the wide carpeted hallways and elegantly appointed high-ceilinged bedrooms of the Knutsford Hotel's fourth floor, did abate as she reconciled herself to both her sister's perfidy and to going from private to public life. The bald spots filled in, no new ones appeared, and sometimes, walking home to fix supper for herself and thirteen-year-old Marie, the only child she still had left at home, Rosina felt so free and easy she would have to remind herself she was a widow and think, poor Lennart! But then she would be happy again with the day's occupation, for really to lose one-fifth of a husband was only twenty percent as sad as to lose a whole one. And the last few years he had hardly even been that. Though scared of the federal deputies as he might have been, he always managed to sneak in a midnight visit to *Jean*, his last and youngest wife, you may imagine why, men being what they are, as a consequence of which Jean had one single child, a baby who died, and two pairs of twins. She also had the deeds to two of Fern's houses. But! let the poor girl enjoy them, homely as she was with her duck feet and hair growing nearly to her eyebrows.

Rosina liked where she and Marie lived, two nice back rooms looking on a neat yard rented from Lucitie's next-door neighbor. The minute Lucitie heard they were for rent she sent Nancibel over to the Knutsford Hotel to ask Rosina if she wanted them, and of course she did. So close to work, and best of all close to Marie's own aunt and two real cousins that she could look in on when she came from school instead of staying alone till Rosina came home. Saturdays and every other Sunday wouldn't be so lonesome for Marie either, she could just go through the fence and around the back door to the Alfonces'. Nancibel was a year younger than Marie, had lovely long curls (as she naturally would have, with so many in the household to put them up on rags at night), Rosina supposed the two cousins would be lovely chums in no time.

And so they might have been had not Bonnie Youngberg come along.

Bonnie was in Marie's room at school, she lived in the same direction. Bonnie's father worked for the J. G. McDonald Candy Company, so there was always a candy dish piled with chocolates that weren't perfect (though they certainly tasted that way). Bonnie's mother made beautiful candy boxes at home on the stretched-out dining room table for the Union Box Company out of gilt paper, paper lace, pictures of beautiful ladies, birds, puppies, kittens and doves, and red, pink, blue and yellow satin ribbon. Between Bonnie and Marie it was love at first sight. And so the blood cousins, Marie and Nancibel, never became closer, even though now living next door to each other, than when one lived on Seventh South and the other uptown.

Marie's new chum Bonnie Youngberg didn't believe in Hairdressing Establishments.

The Tonsorial part was all right, men had to get their hair cut. But curling hair was wrong, frizzing it, putting it up over rats to make it look like you had more, dyeing it black or blonde. All that was *deceitful. Vanity.* Women's hair was supposed to be plain, parted in the middle. Also, women weren't supposed to *girt.* To girt meant to pull your waist in as tight as you could with a corset. Their clothes should be plain, not all trimmed and ruffled. They should sell their expensive jewelry and give to the poor. Bonnie didn't believe in mansions such as the ones up on Brigham Street. The Lion House and Beehive House were all right, Brigham Young built those, so they had a purpose. Somewhat to the consternation of her family (who might really be classed as jack Mormons), Bonnie ran religion into the ground. She was also engaging and persuasive and soon running *that* into the ground too.

To maintain and uphold the Kingdom, best friends Marie and Bonnie went to church, Sunday school, Mutual, and Study Group. They read the Book of Mormon and the Pearl of Great Price, fixing their glazed eyes on one page after another with the determination of a handcarter putting one foot before the other till the plains were crossed. Anything unworthy of angels' pricked ears they put a stop to at once, joking, using expletive words such as darn, laughing in an unladylike manner and silly conversation, such as about boys. However, if boys were discussed from a *religious* standpoint, then that was all right.

If Les Kinnavy's mortal existence as a handsome, cute and stuck-up boy over on Fourth East had not coincided with his being Bonnie's own first cousin, however, his mortal existence would certainly never have been admitted as a subject for discussion. For Les was a Roman Catholic. So was his father, so was his mother, so were his brothers and sisters. He went to All Hallows College, which didn't mean *college* but a private boarding and day school for both little and big boys, where he had military drill under an army officer and played Rugby.

Marie saw Les Kinnavy first at Bonnie's house on New Year's Day. He was a big boy, tall and strong for only fifteen years of age, also handsome, cute and stuck-up. She didn't then know the Kinnavy family was Catholic. That was quite a surprise considering that Les's mother, Mrs. Kinnavy, and Bonnie's mother, Mrs. Youngberg, were stepsisters, both born Protestant. Bonnie at one time had hopes of converting her aunt's whole outfit to the true gospel that Jesus Christ brought to mankind, but as all they did was joke about it, she just left them to their fate. Marie, though, after she met the Kinnavy family, thought they were worth *praying for*, at least, and the more she and Bonnie happened to run into Les skating on the ponds or ditches, coming home from Rugby practice smelling like a horse and with sweat on his brow in spite of the cold, or whatever he had been doing, the harder she prayed. For the spirit life to come was supposed to last throughout eternity, and eternity for her (she came to think) without running into Les would just be ... an eternity. In fact it seemed that way anyway when she and Bonnie didn't run into Les for about a week.

Bonnie knew about Marie's crush and said lucky for her Aunt Lois happened to read in the Park City Gazette about the search for the Clarendon heirs. If Aunt Lois would have missed that day's paper, Uncle Patrick wouldn't have quit his job at the Park City butcher shop, the family wouldn't have moved to Salt Lake and Marie would never have even *met* Les. The reason the Kinnavys moved from Park City was because Aunt Lois thought she was distantly related to Mrs. Maybelle Clarendon and might be an heir, as that was what the lawyers were looking for. And if that was so, no use having to go hunt all over to find her, she would be right at hand.

That is to say, she thought of inheriting until all the close relatives of James Clarendon showed up, which they didn't do until the Kinnavys were settled in Salt Lake and Mr. Kinnavy had a meat-packing job to tide them over and the would-be heirs had the imaginary fun of spending all the money and living in the gorgeous mansion. When the real inheritors showed up in droves, the Kinnavys said they were just as glad. Mrs. Kinnavy (who couldn't imagine a housemaid in apron and cap shaking a dustmop out an upper window, a cook killing chickens in the back yard, a coachman and gardener going about their business) had nightmares about keeping all that plate glass sparkling, all that woodwork cleaned and polished, all those floors scrubbed and waxed, and trying to beat the dust out of a sixty-foot-long carpet on the clothesline. Doing it all *justice*. It would have been the death of her, she told her stepsister, Bonnie's mother. And if you've got your health, who wants a lot of money? She was glad they moved to Salt Lake, though, she had been wanting to get away from Park City for a long time, so it was all worthwhile. And they had the fun of thinking of how it would be to be rich. But even after they let it all go, it wasn't without a backward glance. If any of the Kinnavys went past the Clarendon house, it still seemed like family property, and the new owners, Mr. and Mrs. Prentice and their little girl, like shirt-tail relations. Even Bonnie, whose only connection with the place was her Aunt Lois trying to inherit it, felt that way. When walking past it with Marie, she spoke of it as of a kind of family seat.

All of this seemed like a remarkable coincidence to Marie, who through Wyandra had heard the story of her *own mother* staying in the Prentice mansion years before, actually staying *under that very roof* for several days at the time that Sleeping Beauty took sick and died. Sleeping Beauty? Her own mother? In time Bonnie knew "everything." Marie knew "everything." They were best friends. Eventually Les Kinnavy knew "everything" too, but quite a while after, after the religious stage had passed that his cousin Bonnie and her friend Marie had gone through as strangely and mysteriously as the chrysalis precedes the imago, and they fluttered to earth.

All they cared about *then* was the *opposite* of religious: Running around. Liberty Park. Wandamere. The Salt Palace. Clothes. Minstrel shows. Vaudeville. Buffalo Bill's Wild West Show. Six-day bicycle races. Strawberry ice-cream sodas. Boys. Tall boys, short boys, hanging around, caps on the side of their head, jack Mormons, Catholics, even a boy who *didn't believe in God*, smoking, chewing Sen-Sen. How did it happen?

Too religious one minute to even drink a cup of coffee on a morning so cold the water faucet in the kitchen froze, too religious to waltz on Sunday, curl their hair, let a boy kiss them on the cheek, or take a second look for curiosity's sake at the organ of a dray horse hanging down like a fire hose! and the next minute so lost to all sense of moral obligation that they ate on Fast Day, said their prayers warm in bed, and Bonnie's youngest sister said she saw them *smoke*! On a summer evening when the moths were batting against the street lamp on the corner, she actually saw them take a puff of Les's cigarette. There the two girls stood laughing and *smoking*. The boys were Les Kinnavy and the Robinson boy, or at least that's who it looked like. And another time they hoisted up their skirts and tried to ride some boys' bicycles. The boys had their hand on their waist and ran along holding and pushing them and then they fell off right in the boys' arms, and they didn't let them go very quick either!

By that time Bonnie's sister had come along and was the religious fanatic, and Mrs. Youngberg said privately she didn't know which was harder to live with, sinner or saint.

Rosina blamed herself for some of their new worldly-mindedness, as she was the one who got Marie the job at the Deseret Drapery and Upholstery Company, and one of the girls there was not only *divorced* but told Marie she had once been *drunk*. But when the drapery people came to replace the sun-bleached hangings at the Knutsford Hotel's western window and happened to mention being short-handed on account of the Jubilee, and talked about the mansions they worked in with all the wonderful furnishings, and mentioned their annual picnic out at Saltair that everybody had so much fun at, Rosina thought how Marie would enjoy all that and asked if they could put on a clever and good-hearted girl of fifteen who didn't care for schoolwork, and they said they'd give her a try.

Marie liked the job even if she had to get up earlier than for school, liked seeing inside the president's house of the Oregon Short Line and the owner's of the Telluride Realty Company, and when the annual picnic came along enjoyed that so much that Wyandra, asked to do so the next morning by Rosina on her way to work, could hardly wake Marie up and get her up and headed in the right direction.

But as Lucitie said, "blame" was the wrong word. Marie didn't turn out *bad* or anything like that.

No, Rosina said, but for two years in particular she was a lovely little Mormon girl, went to Sunday school, tried out for and didn't get in the Tabernacle choir, she and Bonnie both, Lennart would have been so proud of her, Hindle too probably. And then!— face powder. Dollar a yard crepe de chine. Three dollars for a cluster of purple grackles. And not only to quit going to Sunday school, but actually to *apostatize*.

"Well, that was *him*," Lucitie said soothingly. "But the main thing is, she got the boy she wanted. She's married, whether she had to join the Catholic church or not. At least she wasn't *ruined*."

"No," Rosina said. "She wasn't ruined. Not in this life, at least."

But Rosina didn't really think the afterlife was going to be full of punishment the way some people supposed. And it was better to marry a nice Catholic boy like Les Kinnavy with almost a college education and a job on the railroad that would take them around the country seeing different sights than maybe get in the hands of a Mormon who wouldn't give up on polygamy though God Himself had wiped the custom out. There were a lot of those stubborn mules around.

Bonnie, even if she didn't get up to go to Sunday school either, and would now drink coffee, and Les Kinnavy was her own first cousin, was very sorry indeed when Marie actually left the church to be a Catholic and said that not for love or anything else would she repudiate the *true gospel* for popery. Especially when you stopped to think that at the Gates of the Beyond if you weren't LDS you would lose the one you sacrificed everything for anyway!

"What would you sacrifice for *me*?" Boyd Cathey said to Bonnie in his cocky way.

"Nothing," Bonnie said. "Not a thing." She spoke without meeting the bold gaze in which he would fix her as in a Cornish hug. But he knew she didn't mean it.

Boyd thought religion was a lot of b.s. If a guy blacks one eye, let him black the other. If he steals your watch, give him your lady friend. Wasn't that stupid? But if Bonnie was a Mormon, if she wanted to be that dumb, well, fine. He'd sooner have them dumb than smart anyway. Once he had a smart girl and the upshot was, he finally had to bust her in the snoot. Boyd *talked* tough like that, but he didn't look tough. He *looked* kind of pale and string-beany, like a boy who grew too fast after a long sick spell. The sad expression in his eyes was like a bedfast watcher's through the window while the other kids go to school, come home, run in and get bread and jam, run out again and play in the streets and he can't join in.

Bonnie's father Mr. Youngberg said in his estimation Boyd was a strip tore out of nothing, and what a beautiful girl like his daughter Bonnie could see in him he didn't know. Men always think their daughters are beautiful, especially if they look like their *own* mother, who in her mother-in-law's case Mrs. Youngberg considered kind of homely. *She* thought Bonnie was lucky to have attracted such a handsome boy. Not sturdily built, true, might come down with lung trouble someday, not a happy-go-lucky disposition, but Mrs. Youngberg pasted pictures on candy boxes every day of young troubadours under balconies, or princes on horseback, not one bit handsomer than Boyd! And that was saying something, for candy-box artists worked with the *ideal*.

When all of a sudden Boyd left for Seattle to work on the Great Northern line, for he was a railroader too, like Les, Mr. Youngberg thought Bonnie should say good riddance to bad rubbish and be thankful, for he was doing her a *favor*. And the girl's lowness of spirits was caused by either a tapeworm or a bilious complaint, he thought, such as his aunt had had at the same age, which would have killed her had she not taken Dr.

D. Jaynes and Son Alterative. But they didn't make it anymore. The drug stores never heard of it, and the Wine of Cardui the druggist talked Mrs. Youngberg into instead was just a dollar thrown away. Bonnie took it but still cried, still lay around, still wouldn't eat, and Mr. Youngberg was about to take the radical step of writing a letter to the drug store in the town where his mother and aunt were raised, if it still existed, or his cousin Hilma, if she was still alive…open *that* can of worms, as Mrs. Youngberg said…when Les and Marie Kinnavy came to town for a few days on their way down to Arizona, where Les was being sent to another Union Pacific division. Marie seemed to bring her old chum right out of it, and when the young couple left they took Bonnie with them for the change of scene that would complete her cure.

BONNIE DIDN'T KNOW ANYTHING. MARIE hadn't either, until she got acquainted with some of the other train-crew wives. They traveled and knew things. Leona Linger, who worked at the Deseret Drapery and Upholstery Company the brief while Marie was there and who was divorced (and would drink), was *supposed* to know a lot, but she really didn't. Not in comparison. A girl named Arlene married to another signal engineer even had a book called *The Fruits of Philosophy*. That certainly laid it on the line! A person doesn't *have* to have a baby. Sometimes a baby was nice, but sometimes, if you just had one room, as you might say, and your husband when on the night shift had to sleep days, why, it would just complicate the situation terribly. Or say you had no settled home. Or wanted to accumulate a few nice things such as a hammock, a deluxe talking machine, a hand-painted lamp…Or if you were a very neat housekeeper and didn't want things getting mussed up all the time. And liked to sit and do fancy work. And go visiting. And see a show. And weren't too well anyway. And some women *died*. Why, you just…didn't have to *have* one.

Dr. Stewart's Female Pills, a Valuable Specific for female troubles such as Delayed Menstruosity and Nerve Difficulties, as it said on the package, were simply wonderful, Arlene said…or you could try and sit in as hot water as you could stand, really your bum would be practically parboiled. Dr. Stewart's Female Pills worked for Bonnie, and as the Delayed Menstruosity cleared up, the Nerve Difficulties did too. So really, scientific progress was wonderful. Not that her low spirits were so high that her eyes wouldn't fill with tears when she and Marie were alone and Boyd's name happened to come into the conversation. But suppose he would have married her? Once he had busted a girl in the snoot, he told that on himself, and a boy who would do such a thing like that *once* would do it again. So Marie said, think what a person's life would—

Think what it would be like. When they and the neighbors in the next car sat outside on the steps, some of them singing "By the Light of the Silvery Moon" and "Dear Old Girl," and the men's cigar smoke wafted and the silvery moon started making everything as bright as day…and down the track at the end of the spur you could see the Chinamen's car and the mysterious dim light behind a little window and heard faintly their funny lingo as they gambled or sweat gold in a long greasy leather sack or whatever Chinamen did at night…and some kind of a bird while the cool wind rustled the sunburned leaves went *whirr* and *whoo* like a ghost, Bonnie *did* think what life would be like with Boyd if he…And she would feel thin and cold, like a peeled wand, and too tired to get up and get her shawl, and the hot tears brimming in her cold glassy eyes ran down cool and hardly salty.

Yonska Locket's heat you could feel a foot away from the man. The red handkerchief from his hip pocket might have been warmed in the oven. "Here," he whispered and handed it to her as he caught the glitter of her tears. For some unknown reason, her tears kept wanting to flow that night. While he and she waited for the fudge to set enough to cut and take over next door where Les and Marie had already gone, why, in spite of how hard Bonnie tried to just carry on a conversation she couldn't keep from crying, and finally Yonska didn't hand her his handkerchief anymore. He just took her in his large warm arms and wiped her eyes himself.

She could go a lot farther and do worse.

Yonska Locket was the genuine article, all wool and a yard wide. That was the consensus of testimony. Drank, ran around with women in his day, but what was a man like him supposed to do?

After their marriage, Bonnie told Marie she didn't believe that *Fruits of Philosophy* stuff and someday Marie and some of the other wives were going to be *very* sorry for the path they had taken, and that she for one was going to have all the children she could have!

"Well, fine," Marie said.

And Arlene said *everybody to suit his own taste*, as the old woman said when she peed in the sea.

But two years later when Marie and Les went one way, to Butte, Montana, sent by the railroad, and Yonska and Bonnie went the other way, Bonnie still hadn't had the first child.

"Yonska must be living the life of Riley, though, getting to try every night," Les said, "without a big argument."

"Oh, pooh!" Marie said, tossing her head.

The last she heard, several Christmas cards later, all the trying had *still* brought no results. (If Yonska *did* try. Mrs. Keeley said the nuns had a saying that "a big man is a promise never kept," which she said was certainly true in her *own* case.) But they were very happy. Bonnie wrote that she didn't know where the past eight years had gone, and she wondered if Marie and Les ever happened to hear from any of the old gang such as the Pollard kids, Swede or Boyd Cathey? Her pen kind of gave a lurch on the B, so Marie knew she still had Boyd in her heart.

Chapter Forty-four

*

AUNT LUCITIE THOUGHT IT WAS LOVELY THAT MARIE AND LES WERE BEING SENT to Helena, Montana, because Marie had two half-sisters up there, Hindle's girls Eula and Esther, or had, the last she heard. And the last she heard Serapta also was still alive, but it seemed to her that Stig was dead. Anyway, Marie would find relatives when she got there. Because nothing was more terrible than not to have any, she knew *that* from first-hand experience in London that time. "Nothing," agreed Wyandra, who didn't have anybody related to her but didn't seem to realize it. "Just terrible."

But Marie said she certainly wasn't going to go out of her way to get acquainted with two half-sisters that hadn't cared enough about her through the years to even send her a birthday card! However, blood is thicker than water "and a good deal nastier," as someone named Oscar Wilde was supposed to have said, and so when Marie and Les got to Helena to start in on the new job, after Marie got their stuff in place and a Turkish corner fixed up (only to be told by the blondined daughter of the landlady that Turkish corners had gone out of style), she did make some inquiries and found her half-sister Eula, the doctor's daughter.

She had a nice five-room house, her husband worked for Anaconda Copper, in the office, with a green eyeshade on and black sateen half-sleeves up over his starched cuffs. They had children who had to wear glasses at an early age and were born with the gift to add, subtract and multiply in their heads. Eula said she had been voted in Secretary and Treasurer of some kind of Presbyterian ladies' club. She offered her half-sister no refreshment but did say that one of these Sundays when things kind of calmed down, Marie and her husband must come for Sunday dinner. Or perhaps they would like to wait until Esther and her husband came through this way and make it a family reunion. Esther's husband worked for Anaconda Copper too, but they traveled. And Eula had a good idea! she would invite *Serapta* out at the same time. Poor Serapta. Alone now ... Stig died the winter so many cattle froze to death, maybe Marie read about it in the paper, it was so cold he couldn't even be buried till nearly May, the ground was too hard to dig a grave in. Serapta was perfectly welcome to live with them, Eula said, as Marie might imagine! her having reared her and Esther from childhood. But old people had their own notions. Nothing would do she must live in this rooming house downtown. But it was nice and clean, they had lowered the ceiling in her room so all the heat wouldn't get trapped above, and she had her own things around her.

Serapta welcomed Marie like a long-lost child.

"I WAS THERE WHEN YOU was born," she said, hugging and kissing her.

Marie thought she was about a hundred, her hair was so white and she was so small and bent, and talked loudly to her as if she had come from Europe and didn't know the language. Marie was ready to adapt herself also to the dementia of old age, but that turned out not to be necessary. Serapta's mind seemed to work perfectly both forward and back, more forward in a way than Marie's herself, for Serapta read the *Enterprise* every day, as well as the young man upstairs' *Work and Win, An Interesting Weekly for Young America*, whenever he lent her a copy, and even a book now and again when one came her way. When the Butte Locomobile Company offered a free ride in the new five-passenger model with the shaft-drive system, Serapta took them up on it. And having a free pass to the nickelodeon, she went to that almost every day until the theater changed hands.

The reason she had a free pass, she said, was because the young man in Number Six down the hall gave it to her for doing his mending. Too bad he didn't still live here, Marie would have enjoyed to meet him. He traveled around selling different theatrical items, Marie must have noticed the announcements such as would flash on the screen, Somebody's Baby is Crying, Is it Yours? When Leaving this Theater Please Turn up the Seats, Don't Spit on the Floor, Remember the Johnstown Flood and such as that? Well, they came in sets, beautiful printing. Oh, the wonders of the modern age! She couldn't get over it, Serapta said. But in a way she was glad Stig never lived to go to the nickelodeon. They had them, the one in Butte was even running when he was still alive, if she wasn't mistaken. But they lived quite far out of town in a house on Murdock's ranch, and Stig was so contented, working at a few little jobs for Murdock, and painting, that he just never wanted to leave. And now that she looked back, she was glad that him and moving pictures had never bumped into each other, for they would have taken the wind out of his sails something terrible.

"Oh?" Marie said.

"Because that was really what his *panorama* was supposed to act like, if he had ever come to the end of it and mounted it up, which he never did. Like moving pictures!" She pointed to the corner of the room, and Marie looked at what appeared to be a big rolled-up rug stood on end and wedged like a pillar between floor and ceiling. "That canvas would unroll and you'd see picture after picture, telling a story."

"Is that a fact? I never heard of such a thing."

"Oh, yes," Serapta said. "Once upon a time an artist, if he was willing to travel to all the little out-of-the-way spots as well as the big towns, could make a good living with one of them things. See, they would unroll to one scene after another while the lecture part was going on, and people paid money for that, just like to see a show. For the unrolling pictures was history, they showed how something took place, the Battle of Waterloo, the

Legend of Niagara where this Indian tribe had to throw one person over the Falls every year and how this chief's daughter—I seen that one when I wasn't no more than about ten. *Stig*'s panorama would of been one of the longest in existence if he had ever finished it, but he was just too slow. By the time he started coming to the end, the nickelodeons was going full blast. And moving pictures was actual living *life*, while the panoramas, even when painted by wonderful painters, was just—more—dead."

"I'd sure like to see it sometime."

"Well, I tell you, honey, it was something I never felt real easy with—his subject matter. And he certainly couldn't of sold many tickets in Utah!"

"Why not?" Marie said, looking with interest at the tall, fat bundle of canvas.

"Because it was a panorama *against* the church, that's why, though it started out to be *for* it. In fact it was to be a *history* of the church. I was born in it, as you may suppose—like you was, sweetheart—and your mother Hindle and Lucitie too—while Stig joined after he'd got his growth, and anytime that's happened, why, there's reasoning connected to it. And the minute you have reasoning—Anyway, after a few years him and the church had a falling-out—"

"What over, Serapta?"

"Oh, just nonsense. But after that his panorama changed. From a history the church would *like*, it become a history of everything they keep *mum* about. Such as, oh, you know, things Joseph done, and the Night Riders, and killing people to save their souls and all such as that. The Mountain Meadows Massacre too, if you'll excuse my mentioning it—" It wasn't very mannerly of her to do so, she said, considering that John D. Lee was Marie's own grandfather, but she for one never did believe he was the ringleader the courts claimed he was.

This grandfather and a *massacre* were all news to Marie.

Les thought he had heard of it once.

"Serapta said it was a public execution. Soldiers lined up and everything. They shot him at sunrise," Marie said. "Imagine. My mother's own father. *Grandpa*. Stood up and shot at sunrise. I can't get over it."

To the best of Serapta's recollection, John D. Lee had had thirteen wives and fifty-two children.

"Fifty-two! And we haven't even got one," Les said. But he sounded cheerful, not like Yonska when *he* talked about him and Bonnie not having children. It wasn't that bad to sleep days when you had to without disturbance, get a shave at the barber's once in a while, smoke ten-cent cigars, button on a Sunday shirt starched and ironed at the laundry like a rich man's. Not that Les wanted to die without the chance to be an ancestor, but he and Marie had only been married nine years...

Yonska didn't want to die without being an ancestor either, or wouldn't have had he ever thought that far ahead, but *his* main grief (his understanding being that the whole germ of the future person was contained in the male generative matter) was like the rose's unable to bud. And why did he not? He tried, tried and tried again. Bonnie tried too, and wondered to herself, for it was not something you talked about even to your best friend, whether somewhat enjoying the trying offended God the way her sin with Boyd Cathey must have done. There was no doubt that she was being made to pay a penalty for *something.*

"They want a baby *so bad.*"

"It looks to me like that would be pretty convenient," Les said. "To have the play without the pay."

"Oh, Les," Marie said. "That's a terrible remark."

"Why is it? Look at all the trouble and aggravation *we* go through for the opposite reason while they have nothing but a high old time."

"A high old time! Don't you realize our advantage? We can change our *minds* if we want to. We got the *choice.* And not to have the *choice* of anything is like slaves. We can say yes, we can say no—"

No was what she said emphatically when she woke up green around the gills on her tenth wedding anniversary and went out in the kitchen to cook breakfast and nothing was ever so sickening, the coffee, the eggs. *No,* when she threw up off the back steps into the bushes. *No,* when she thought, could it be? No!

But did you ever notice how things will change? Calumet Baking Powder used to be so good, then new people took it over and now it was nasty and bitter. Embroidery cotton…Granite iron used to never chip off. And now the latest, Dr. Stewart's Female Pills! for Delayed Menstruosity and Nerve Difficulties. The manufacturers *could not leave well enough alone.*

What a coincidence! Rosina wrote back when Marie rather unhappily wrote her the news. Because her cousin Nancibel was expecting a baby too!

Bonnie didn't even know Nancibel was married.

"Oh, yes," Marie said. "She certainly ought to be, she's twenty-six years old!"

"Well, poor man! if she's as spoiled now as she used to be when we were girls. Who did she marry?"

"Remember the bicycle repair shop on Third East connected to the brick house? Well, *their* son. Uncle Albert and Aunt Lucitie weren't a bit happy about it, I don't know *who* they expected her to get, but it's a nice family, quite well-fixed. And Nancibel has everything lovely, and he waits on her hand and foot."

"That's not everything," Bonnie said, and the way she said it and the way she sighed made Marie think that somewhere in her memory Boyd Cathey was still wandering around.

The Chautauqua speaker when he said *thoughts are things* couldn't have hit the nail on the head better. Thinking *was* a force as powerful as a galvanic current, or electric fluid. Like he said, a galvanic current could turn turbo-dynamos, generators, centrifugal separators and stuff like that, but the *force of thought* could make things happen just as surely. And in the case of Bonnie...well, why else would she and Marie on a shopping trip downtown be walking up the street and go to pass the hotel and who should be coming out the revolving door but Boyd Cathey! if Bonnie's thoughts hadn't brought him? You know? *Him.*

"Oh, come on now, Marie," Les said. "Boyd got *transferred*, that's all."

"Thoughts are things," Marie insisted. "Bonnie wanted to see him so bad she made it happen. She yearned and thought and finally—He's married, by the way, got two children. But his wife's not with him. I've asked him to supper, and so has Bonnie—"

Boyd left a few weeks later. There was nothing in Helena for him, he said.

Marie's baby girl was six months old when Bonnie's baby, also a girl, was born. An exceptionally pretty one, though some of the prettiest babies grow up to be homely. Yonska wanted to name her after his mother, but his mother had such a common name, Mary. The name Bonnie picked was Lavonne, though later, when she had the resurgence of religion the year before she died, when Lavonne was six, Bonnie wished she had chosen a different name, but of course by that time it was too late, the name was as ingrained in the child's sense of herself as the knowledge that her eyes were big and blue and her hair hung down in soft yellow curls.

Marie for some reason, before her baby came, concluded to want a boy. It was the loveliest thing, she thought, to see a mother making her entrance at a family reunion or something like that, her head only up to the shoulder of her tall handsome son, him holding onto her arm like she was the most precious thing that ever walked on two feet. Boys were like that, their mothers were *everything*. While with a girl...

She didn't even have a name ready for a girl.

Les suggested Lois. They always come forward with their mother's name. But it certainly was no favorite of Marie's. Finally she let the little Keeley girl next door name her, which she did after her doll, whose name had been on the box the doll had come in: Rosetta. Wasn't that pretty? They didn't know then about Rosetta's divergent strabismus, as the doctor would call it in later years. It didn't seem to show the first few months. Still, why shouldn't she have a pretty, flowery name? Except for that one cocked eye, she was as cute a little girl as you would ever want to see.

Bonnie's baby Lavonne, however, was beautiful. And while Marie didn't begrudge that to Bonnie, it didn't seem quite fair, taking into consideration *double adultery*, where both people were married to others, Boyd had a wife and two children in Seattle! and Bonnie was married too. But yet they got the prize.

And wouldn't you know that down in Salt Lake City Nancibel, who probably didn't care one way or the other, would get what Marie had wished for, a boy? But that was Nancibel for you, or anybody, that didn't care.

Even when Marie pointed out Rosetta's blemish to Serapta, the old lady refused to see it.

"That?" she scoffed. "That's nothing. Lots of babies' eyes act like that, then straighten up as nice as can be. But what a pity Hindle isn't here. She could rub something on it or galvanize it some way—what a doctor she did become! and all on her own—and there would never be a sign. I don't know when I was ever gladder to see somebody than when she moved to Helena," she went on. "But then she hardly got her trunk up to where she was staying than she traveled right on up into Canada—"

"You know, she never seemed like a mother to me," Marie said. "Rosina's always been my mother."

"I know, honey, but that was because Rosina lost her baby and she felt so bad. And she had milk, see, while your mother's had give out, and you needed that nourishment. Then Lennart come to her and said—And your mother, out of the kindness of her heart—"

"I know, Serapta. You loved her. But she didn't take care of Eula and Esther either."

"Well, who did, then? She sure didn't spend much of her doctoring money on *herself.*"

"You did, and you know it, Serapta. You took care of them, you and your husband. But speaking of Mother, why did she just come to Helena and then go on up to Canada like that? Now I don't even know if she *is* in Canada, no one's heard from her in such a long time, and Aunt Lucitie and I haven't been too good at letter writing. Why didn't she stay *here*?"

"The same problem as down home, I guess. New laws here in Montana the same as in Utah. She couldn't be a doctor no more without proving up that she had went to medical school, while up in Canada—But let me tell you something. If it hadn't been for your mother—! That's why I wonder if I don't owe it to her to tell her something I should of maybe told her years ago when it first happened. But then I didn't *know* it when it first happened!"

"What was that, Serapta?"

"Something mighty important if you believe the gospel! And even if you don't," the old lady said. "Important enough that when I heard what was what, my first thought was to *send a telegram.*"

"To my mother?"

"Yes. To tell her, save her—In my mind's eye I could see the trap door open to hell and down underneath the fires, through the smoke and flame the sinners twisting and turning—!"

"Why, for heaven's sake."

"But then Stig said...And he was right. 'Let them be,' he said. 'If Emerson Miles is her half-brother going under his mother's name, if old John D. Lee was father to the both of them, if the two of them happens to be closer kin than they ought, what of it? The worst that can happen is they might have idiot children, but people has idiot children anyway. Besides, didn't we all come from just one set of folks?' We found that out, you see," Serapta said.

"That we all—?"

"Look, honey," Serapta said. "Stig done a signboard for Ed Miles that run the livery stable—he was still doing a little work like that on the side—and something come up about Ed's cousin Emerson in Canada, conditions up there or something, he had just got a letter. Emerson Miles—opened a law office, his wife was a lady doctor, they was thriving up there. And Ed said, 'Pretty good for a son of John D. Lee, huh?' So Stig came home and mentioned it to *me*. I got to thinking—and as I say, when it dawned on me what the two of 'em was—*brother and sister*—"

"Half," Marie said.

"—why, if I could of called out the militia I'd of done so, I was that worried, to save them from hell. But as Stig said, the damage had been done, they'd been together four or five years by then—they must be happy—why throw a monkey wrench in the works? Of course I never let on to Eula and Esther—they'd have went through the roof!" Serapta added.

MARIE'S FIRST THOUGHT WAS TO rush home and tell Les what she heard. But the least little thing and they throw it up to you. "Who are you to be so high and mighty? with a mother that's married to her *own brother*." "No wonder you broke the gramophone spring." "Burnt the jam." "Had the blanket stole off the line." Marie decided not to give Les the satisfaction. Or Bonnie either, she would set herself up like on a higher plane. She did anyway, as if having a beautiful child like Lavonne that she showed off till it was sickening turned her into something special herself. It was really funny. *Boyd Cathey* furnished the looks, they certainly weren't Bonnie's contribution, as anyone would know who knew the situation (deaf and dumb and blind Yonska had no idea), but Bonnie took all the credit.

"Well, what was she supposed to do?" Les stuck up for his cousin. "Sew an *A* on her dress like the lady in the movie?"

"That wouldn't be such a bad idea," Marie said. By that time they knew about their own child's divergent strabismus, and the pure *unfairness* of it all got Marie's goat.

HAD HE LIVED PAST LAVONNE'S first year, Yonska would no doubt have spoiled the child he thought was his to where she couldn't have been stood by anyone. She got special treatment anyway, from her widowed grandmother Mrs. Youngberg (with whom she and Bonnie went to live after the tragedy) and in fact from whoever was around. "What a beautiful little girl." "Pretty is as pretty does," Mrs. Youngberg or Bonnie would say, pretending to disavow what got courteous regard from even a stray dog running through the yard. But Yonska would have had no disclaimer, he would have been a complete fool

over the child and eventually Lavonne would have just been impossible! like a queen
ruling a country. As it was, princess was as high as she went, and nobody minded that, or
if they did she had only to flash them a sapphire glance and a pearl smile and all would
be forgiven. For Lavonne was a *good* princess, without a spark of that sin by which fell
the angels, ambition, except always to be loved and always to be beautiful. That wasn't
too much to ask, was it?

LES DIED IN THE ACCIDENT that killed Yonska. They were both in the caboose when
the switch engine ran into it. Marie and Bonnie stayed with each other. One night the
two baby girls would be put to bed together at Marie's, one night at Bonnie's. Serapta
tried to go and offer words of comfort the minute she read the news, but had no more
than got to Marie's than her sacroiliac went out and she had to be taken back home where,
gasping and moaning, she insisted on being taken, though she could have stayed with
Marie. But she would rather be miserable at home, Serapta said.

She was still miserable at home when the two young widows, Marie and Bonnie,
left Helena for Salt Lake City. Marie would have taken Serapta with her but Eula, as
behooved a foster daughter, said she would look after her. Not perhaps meaning it but
sounding as if she did, Marie said that *when the railroad settled up*, if Serapta wanted she
would come and get her and take her back down to Utah. By the time that happened,
however, Serapta was dead and buried. Eula wrote Marie about it briefly, and when Marie
answered she said she hoped that next time Eula wrote she would tell her what happened
to the big panorama Stig had painted on, so many years, which stood up in a bundle in
a corner of Serapta's room.

But Eula didn't get around to writing any more letters, and so Marie never knew that
what happened was somewhat in accordance with the way things work in the universe.
Eula's second son showing some artistic talent, Stig's immense landscape of iniquity, devil-
try, death and destruction was gradually cut up into manageable canvases for the boy to
practice on.

ON THE WAY HOME, THE widows thought that when the railroad settled up they might
buy a house and raise their two little girls, who were after all second cousins, together.
Perhaps quite a nice house. Not, of course, a palace like the Clarendon place but with
enough bedrooms, a coal furnace, icebox, screened porch, a big yard … Marie would imagine it as plain as day, herself and Bonnie sitting on the screened porch in wicker chairs
embroidering, with a big pitcher of lemonade with chunks of ice in it on the round wicker
table, and Rosetta and Lavonne running in and out of the flowering bushes. Rosetta's eye
would be cured by then on account of having been operated on, and she would be nearly
as pretty as Lavonne. And at four-thirty they would go in and start to get supper, just the
way Bonnie used to for Yonska and Marie did for Les … And then … Marie had to go on

quickly in her mind when she came to anything about Les or else her throat would ache, her eyes, ears and everything else, just ache, that was the only word for it.

WHEN THE RAILROAD SETTLED UP...

This was what they waited for, Bonnie and her child Lavonne at her widowed mother's, and Marie and her child Rosetta at Rosina's. Mrs. Youngberg no longer made McDonald's candy boxes for the Union Box Company. Elaborate pasteboard boxes were too expensive and had gone out of style. All the bright papers, paste pots, multi-colored ribbons and pretty pictures had vanished. The long dining room table was small and round now under a chenille tablecloth with a bowl of wax fruit in the middle, and Mrs. Youngberg cooked for hire. She made chess pies, lemon tarts and turnovers for the lunches sold at the railroad station and up and down the aisles of the trains. She did this at home so was able to keep an eye on Lavonne while Bonnie worked at the Z.C.M.I. Boot and Shoe Manufactory.

At Rosina's insistence, Marie stayed home and took care of Rosetta while Rosina earned the living. It was no hardship, she said, the work at the Knutsford Hotel was easy, only ten hours a day seven days a week, she had Christmas off and there was talk of giving the girls a Sunday afternoon a month or maybe even two. And what a pleasure to come home to lighted windows and a warm kitchen, supper all ready and everything. Rosina thought she was lucky, and Marie said if she thought *that* was lucky, she should wait until the railroad settled up! because then—! But when that day came more than two years later, the settlement Marie and Bonnie got you could put in your eye. But in any case Rosina wasn't around to enjoy even the new coat Marie thought she would have bought her. Not even that...Hurrying home with a fruit jar of egg-nog left over from a stylish New Year's gathering in one of the Knutsford's second-floor public parlors, Rosina, Marie's beloved foster mother, had slipped and fallen on the icy street, cracked her skull and never regained consciousness before dying a few hours later.

Marie and Rosetta then moved in with Bonnie and her mother Mrs. Youngberg, and Marie tried to get on again at the Deseret Drapery and Upholstery Company. But twelve years is a long time, and there had been many changes. New people owned the business. However, they took her name and promised to let her know if anything opened up. A few months later something did, and Marie left Rosina's old job at the Knutsford Hotel, which had been passed on to her, and went to the Deseret Drapery Company. Leona Linger was still there, with another divorce under her belt, and Mr. Webb still drove the delivery wagon. Only now it wasn't a wagon but a motorized truck he had had to learn to drive. And one thing he seldom delivered was lace curtains, because Nuremberg, Brussels and Battenburg lace was not to be had. Nottingham either, point de Paris and Valenciennes. All those places over there where the lace came from *were at war*.

Chapter Forty-five

＊

THE REASON FOR THE WAR WAS KAISER WILHELM OF GERMANY, WHICH YOU could take a look at his picture and see instantly what the man would be capable of, with his helmet with the spike on top, his bristling mustache and that one little short arm. And his sons were just like him, especially the Crown Prince, n. g. from the word go. In fact all the Germans were terrible, Leona had been quite thick with a German fellow at one time and met his folks, and she said they were the crudest people *she* ever met. Table manners like hogs, grease clear up in their hair, veins standing out on their forehead, red enough in the face to bust, blood pudding, tubs of beer like a dirty wash full of naphtha soapsuds. Ugh, she said. And break wind? *Some* of those bombardments the poor Belgians had to listen to night and day were probably nothing but *that* kind of a situation. And some of the poison gas might be the same!

But the movies showed better than words could express just what kind of an enemy those poor Allies over there had to contend with. It was pitiful, them all alone with their backs against the wall. Why didn't we jump in and help them before it was too late? Too late for us as well as them. For look what the capture of that German spy ring in New York had uncovered. A bomb all set to go off on an American steamship loaded with sacks of sugar for poor France! Factory fires set by Germans. Accidents made to happen by Germans in plants making munitions for the Allies! Strikes stirred up by Germans at Bethlehem Steel! Canadian houseflies trained by insane German scientists to carry germs into the U.S. on their little tiny feet!

What were we waiting for? All the different fellows Marie and Leona and henna-packed Evelyn (who used to work on the same floor with Marie when Marie worked at the Knutsford Hotel but now was at the Hotel Utah) went out with, often together in a jolly crowd of six, wanted to get into it. Wouldn't they make short work of those mutts over there, though! Bonnie had been invited but turned Marie down, and Marie did the same to her when her chance came. The two former chums, though boarding under the same roof (and their two little daughters as thick as thieves), never ran around together now. Their paths seemed to branch off into different directions. Marie had her friends, Bonnie had hers, the few people in the Z.C.M.I. Boot and Shoe Manufactory who believed the way she did, that the Savior was coming to earth again before the next Presidential election. Bonnie hated to think what was going to happen to the Maries, Leonas and Evelyns of this world, with their rouge, lipstick and the tarry black stuff they melted in a tin lid over a candle flame and beaded each eyelash with, on *that* millennial morning. A lot of good their popularity, muffs, puffs and artificial pearls would do them *then*.

Bonnie had one steady beau, not a new one picked up every few days like Marie, Leona and Evelyn. But Mrs. Youngberg said—she couldn't help saying, although she was Bonnie's mother—that Bonnie shouldn't give herself airs, because it wouldn't surprise her one bit if the girls' *chances* with their haphazard drummers and the different acquaintances they struck up with were better than Bonnie's with Rupert. Because for a man of forty-five to still be a bachelor and still be living at home with his folks—! Well, it was better than a peck in the head with a sharp rock, but that was about all. For some reason her mother sided with Marie against her, or so Bonnie thought. But what did it matter? Terrestrial life's ills and woes would soon be over, the Boot and Shoe Manufactory, liverwurst sandwiches, not being appreciated, cold feet, the pineapple stitch, the dull steady pain in a person's side—all these would transform into Eden on that bright new morning!

A lot of people thought that's what had happened when horse-faced President Wilson declared war on Germany. Maybe not all the ten million boys and men who registered for the draft on that scorching hot fifth day of June between seven in the morning and seven at night, but certainly all the fellows Marie, Leona and Evelyn knew. Even Bonnie's friend Rupert said he hoped he would be one of the first ones sent over to France. "Thou shalt not kill" was all very well, but a bunch of overgrown fiends who would tamper with ten-year-old girls, sweep expensive china ornaments off shelves, pee on carpets and put their big dirty boots up on polished inlaid tables the way the Germans did in such movies as *The Beast of Berlin*, which was a true depiction of the way things were, didn't deserve any better. Of course Rupert knew very well he wouldn't be one of the first ones, or even, being over-age, flatfooted and the sole support of his mother, one of the last. But talk was cheap, as Bonnie's mother said.

Talk was different, too, in wartime. Words transmogrified. German measles, hamburger, sauerkraut and dachshunds became liberty measles, liberty steak, liberty cabbage and liberty pups. The word *pretzels*, having no English equivalent, had to be dropped. Songs, too, symphonies, waltzes, band concerts down in the park on Sundays didn't sound the same anymore but like a wop organ grinder's.

Wasn't it the most terrible thing how when men were suffering and dying in the trenches and the poor peasants were eating cats, rats, grass, horses and the limbs of trees or starving to death, in America things only got better? Everybody had a job now. Money to spend. The fellows that didn't have to go to war seemed like better sports than they used to be. Dresses looked prettier. There was more and snappier entertainment. Different dances. New styles: *calisthenics*, which meant gymnastic exercises to develop the figure and make you more graceful (some people said "daily dozen"). "Kiss-proof" lipstick. Beaded purses.

Most wonderful of all, *stars of the moving pictures* that could scarcely be imagined as of human flesh and blood actually *materialized in person* in the four great drives to sell Liberty Bonds, put on by the government in the twenty months between the time America jumped in till the war was over. And the greatest of these were Mary Pickford and Douglas Fairbanks, and unbelievably Charlie Chaplin. The greatest day, the greatest drive, was when these three came to Salt Lake City. The party arrived from California late at night, put up at the Hotel Utah, the Bond Drive was the next day. First the Parade, with the biggest American flag in the world borne along by ants dressed up like Red Cross nurses. Or so they appeared from the high buildings on either side of Main Street, the Utah Savings and Trust building, the Boston block, the Constitution Building and other skyscrapers of five stories or more, to the privileged watching out the windows.

Two of this privileged ilk were Rosetta and Lavonne, gazing down from Alfonce's Hairdressing Establishment, now located (since the old Alfonce's had been sold and torn down) on the fourth floor of the Constitution Building. And they thought, as Lavonne's grandma, Gram, who had brought them uptown for the great occasion, had been telling them for the past week, that they were occupying places that should cost at least a hundred dollars apiece.

Actually, though—except for a rarefied hour like this—the suite on the fourth floor was *not* the best spot in the world. Old Mr. Cutler, who owned the building and whose hair Albert had started cutting back when it was still dark and he had dandruff (look out when the dandruff disappears, Albert often said, the hair soon follows), thought Alfonce's Tonsorial and Hairdressing Establishment, when they had to leave their old location, could go farther and fare worse than rent from him. The Constitution Building was a downtown spot where you could reside as well as run a business in the company of music teachers, china painters, corset makers, custom shirt manufacturers and even people without any business.

Lucitie and Wyandra were all for it. To have a wash basin with hot and cold water in the taps! Two gas burners to cook on. No more dirty old coal and messy old stove polish. Steam heat on cold winter days. No dripping ice deliveries in summer but a cool, shady windowsill for butter, the wire basket of eggs and such as that, and a creamery, greengrocer's, bakery, butcher's and fruit stand much closer and handier than before. A nice flush toilet on every floor. In fact, two. One for Gentlemen, one for Ladies. Lovely garbage cans on every floor also, down by where the toilets were located, so you didn't have to carry your own garbage down to the alley. But even if you had, it wouldn't have been bad, considering that there was a lacy open-work elevator to ride up and down on, run by the janitor or the lady in 506's middle-aged daughter, one or the other. You never had to stand and ring in vain, from seven in the morning till ten at night. Before that, or after that, you had to use the stairs in the great stairwell, open from the ground floor to the roof two hundred feet in the air, where during the day a huge glassed-over opening in the roof admitted light in a five-story plunge vast and glorious enough to be a chute for the Second Coming.

At night it was a different story. Then the stair-pit beyond the surrounding framework of endless balusters was a great, dark, empty space for witches to fly through, spirits out of graves, bats. The halls were scary then, lit hardly more reliably or brighter (for electricity was expensive) than with ten-watt fireflies or the red eyes of beasts in the somber foliage of a wood.

Their old customers would follow them, Lucitie said. And new ones would come, too. But it didn't seem to Albert as if they would, turn in off the street, read the alphabetical board, walk into the elevator and ride up. Still, there being no other place half so advantageously located as half a block from the Hotel Utah and across the street from the Z.C.M.I., and the rent for business and dwelling combined on the low side, Alfonce's Hairdressing Establishment, after more than thirty-five years on the ground, elevated itself to the fourth floor of the Constitution Building. And for quite a while, Albert's fears seemed to be realized. Walk-ins dwindled alarmingly, and even a few old customers fell away.

Mrs. Prentice (still to Alfonce's the rich *Eastern* lady, though she had lived nearly a quarter of a century in Salt Lake City in the mansion that once belonged to the Clarendons) followed them to the new location for Albert's Culpeper herbal shampoo, undetectable tea-colored tint and artful waves. Birdelle, however, the twenty-seven-year-old Prentice daughter, elected to go elsewhere, just to be contrary, Mrs. Prentice confided to Albert in the scented intimacy of the blue-curtained new shop. Birdelle was just going through that stage, she said, when nothing her parents did was right. She and Birdelle had had a *dreadful* scene over the Progressive Tea. But imagine dyeing a beautiful Irish linen cloth, seven yards long and nearly three yards wide, that had been given to her and Mr. Prentice as a wedding present, *pink*. The things that girl had said to her mother that day! that Mrs. Prentice might forgive but never forget. And Birdelle would regret them too, the day would come, but by then it would be too late, her mother would be gone, the best friend a girl ever had.

THE PROGRESSIVE TEA WAS TO take place after the Parade and after the bond-selling program on the temporary stage set up on Second South, an event eagerly awaited. Douglas Fairbanks in a tight, handsome suit of clothes was supposed to knock out the Kaiser with boxing gloves labeled "Victory" and "Liberty Bonds," and Mary would speak through a megaphone. The stars and their entourages would then repair to their half of the Hotel Utah's ninth floor, have lunch, rest a little from their exertions, change into formal afternoon attire and then go to four tea parties, one after the other, at four of Salt Lake's finest dwelling places, where whoever had met the requirement of buying $250 or more worth of Liberty Bonds could drink a cup of tea, eat a cookie and be greeted *as an equal* by Mary Pickford and Douglas Fairbanks.

One of these mansions was the Prentices', and though they played little part in Salt Lake "society," a word that made Mrs. Prentice smile (it had about as much resemblance to the real thing back east, she told Albert, as some lumps of silver ore had to a hand-made set of Baroque silver), she was willing to participate for patriotic reasons, one of her ancestors having come to Jamestown in the very early days and another being a friend of George Washington. The outlay would have been considerable, even with debutante volunteers taking the place of extra hired help (which Mrs. Prentice wouldn't have liked at all, strange "society" girls running upstairs and down poking their noses into every-thing), when you consider hothouse roses as the Committee wanted, baby-breath fern, candles for the candelabras, the electricity, breakage and the rest. And no matter what the world might think, the Prentices were *not* abounding in wealth, and the expense would have been considerable. To say nothing of arctics and umbrellas, wraps with snow melting on them, men standing around outside smoking and expectorating, the cook maybe on a rampage—

Years before, the Chinese cook Sing *had* gone on a rampage, meaning that he chased Axel, the combination coachman and gardener, around the back yard with a cleaver, finally jumping onto him from behind though not splitting his skull, as he was in a good position to do as he rode around waving the cleaver in the air and screeching in Chinese till Axel scraped him off on the side of the porch onto the back walk. Then Axel ran and Sing picked himself up and came back inside. The quarrel had turned out to be Axel's fault, Mr. Prentice spoke to him about it, he answered him back, which made it necessary to fire him, and then was when they hired Carl to drive for them and do the gardening. At the time, although it might not have been quite fair, Mrs. Prentice wanted to make a clean sweep and fire Sing too, but Mr. Prentice said no, Sing wasn't to blame and he could not be a party to injustice. He was also very fond of Sing's roast duck, and so Sing stayed.

But a man who could chase somebody with a cleaver *once* could always flare up and do it again, and having him in the kitchen, quiet though he might be, was to Mrs. Prentice like living on the side of Vesuvius. So that was another problem with the Progressive Tea, in case Sing should erupt. But the argument with Birdelle about dyeing that beautiful table cloth *pink* was the straw that broke the camel's back. Mrs. Prentice decided then and there that the whole thing was just too much. Birdelle got too excited and stirred up, which she always had from childhood. Let her go to a birthday party or have her little friends come to visit and in about two minutes she was wild and hysterical, bang-ing about, laughing till she couldn't catch her breath, then crying, till finally she was sick and there you were.

Mrs. Prentice thought from the beginning that the Progressive Tea was a mistaken idea, but she went along with it. For patriotism's sake, she told Albert. If throwing open her home to a bunch of clodhoppers could help her country in the fight against despotism, she was willing to throw it open, but after her and Birdelle's awful disagreement she realized it was a choice between sanity and insanity, and she chose sanity. Of course Birdelle had a tantrum and Mrs. Prentice's heart acted up, she was not made of iron, and that scared Birdelle. She was really a sweet child. So now the Prentices and their house were out of it as far as the Tea was concerned, and Birdelle was reconciled. However, she insisted she was going to pay $250 from her savings and go progressively around to the other houses (the O'Brien residence was taking the place of theirs), merely on account of that actress Miss Pickford and that acrobat she was supposedly in love with, or whatever he was, Mr. Fairbanks. That a child of *hers* would go out of her way to shake hands with a pair like *them*—! But perhaps Birdelle would wake up with a temperature—

"Oh, dear," Wyandra said, "I do hope Mrs. Prentice won't prevent it. Wouldn't that be awful?" She thought how bad *she* would feel, to think she was going to get to see the two most famous people in the world as close as I see you and then not get to do it! But imagine spending $250 for such a thing! Although it was well worth it.

"How old *is* Birdelle now?" Lucitie said. "Her mother still speaks of her as 'the child.'"

"Going on for thirty, I should think," Wyandra said.

"You'd think she'd leave. She's got no money worries. Mrs. Prentice said herself that that relation she's always bragging about, that's so rich, gave Birdelle a string of pearls the day she was born that's been in the bank ever since. So even if she hadn't nothing else—which you know very well she has—she's got those pearls, which she could sell and have enough to live on. So why doesn't she do it? Strike out on her own?"

"Yes," Wyandra said. "Why doesn't she?" She herself, a good ten years older than the subject of their discussion, since attaching herself to the Alfonces at the age of nine had never thought of striking out. But of course her situation was different. They needed her, Albert in the shop, Lucitie at home. They really did, she thought. When Albert reached for a curling iron, he knew it would be tempered, oiled and ready to heat. He knew Wyandra knew what she was doing, for instance with the bichloride of mercury. Lucitie once mixed it in the proportion of *one to one hundred* instead of *one thousand,* but Albert caught it in time, and from then on Lucitie was never allowed to prepare the sterilizing agent. As the years went on she made other mistakes, for instance *retraced* a bleached coiffure one time that lost the customer half her hair. Once she pricked a woman's finger during a manicure, it got infected and Alfonce's would have been sued had not the woman died soon after in sugar diabetes insensibility.

Now, with business slackening off in the new location and Albert not really needing two assistants, Lucitie was staying home most of the time, and that was as it should be, Albert said. It wasn't a vacation, of course, Nancibel was always wanting her mother for something, either for herself or her little boy Legrand. And Herman, the Alfonces' only son, born when Nancibel was nearly ten and spoiled within an inch of his life, couldn't even knot a four-in-hand without her help, though said to be a virtuoso mechanic. Why he chose that trade, he said, was the Pierce Arrow Mrs. Prentice arrived in for her hairdressing appointment on Tuesdays and what he saw under the bonnet when her driver opened it.

But Lucitie and Wyandra both thought Herman was deliberately trying to offset his father's spotless elegance by getting as dirty and disheveled on his job (as a mechanic at the Columbia Touring Automobiles garage) as he possibly could, coming home sometimes almost like a minstrel man in theatrical lamp black. They thought it an act of defiance rather than a natural aptitude, particularly since after work he took like a duck to water to the starched shirts, brushed suits, shined shoes, glossy pompadours and scented handkerchiefs they provided for his social life. In short—though *they* would never have said so—in his heart he was a dandy, almost an exquisite, wanting to be a roughneck.

When he went to war, swept up by the June fifth draft, not in France yet but leaving New York soon, as driver to a Colonel, Lucitie said she wondered—as she and Wyandra gathered up the artifacts on his dresser and laying carelessly about his room, the pliers, wrenches, screwdrivers, vise, jack, nuts and bolts they felt he wanted to be *seen* as having more than actually *having*, and put them in a box—if he would ever straighten out. And be like his father, Wyandra knew Lucitie meant. But she thought to herself, in situations where people are neither flesh nor fowl nor good red herring, what are they going to do?

WHEN MARIE'S FRIEND EVELYN TOLD Marie and Leona and their escorts that Mary Pickford and Douglas Fairbanks were going to stay all night on *her* floor in the Hotel Utah, they could hardly believe it. Well, why not? Wasn't that where the most luxurious rooms in Salt Lake City were located, including of course the bridal suite? Not that Mary and Doug needed *that*, poor things, for they weren't married, even though so in love that everybody in the world knew it. But Doug's cruel-hearted wife back east wouldn't let *him* go, and Mary's drunken brute of a husband wouldn't divorce *her*. It was so romantic it brought tears to people's eyes, them traveling across the country by train together selling War Bonds, staying in hotels, riding in parades, eating together, sleeping a stone's throw away, chaperoned within an inch of their life, so near and yet so far. Her so beautiful, those golden curls, those dimples, that beautiful girlish shape, him so handsome, that mustache, that strong manly build—!

"Who said they were chaperoned within an inch of their life?"

"I can well imagine," one of the girls' escorts said with a wink.

"The papers said so! *Picture-Play*! that's who."

Evelyn could show them, she said, she wished she had brought the magazine. Why, Doug and Mary would no more pull some underhanded stunt—! They should see the locations of the rooms—*Mary* was going to be clear down overlooking South Temple while *Doug* was way back up north, from where he could see the cemetery! And all the different people in between—the French maid, drivers, helpers, managers, it was the most romantic, pathetic thing—!

Out in Leona's kitchenette fixing baloney sandwiches and the punch their escorts would spike and the girls pretend not to know, Marie asked Evelyn what the chances were to get to sneak up there on her floor in the Hotel Utah on the day of the parade?

"Why, Marie," Evelyn said in something like horror, "you couldn't do a thing like *that*. Besides, they wouldn't even *be* there, they'd be—And anyway those aren't even my and Edna's rooms, they belong to the other two maids, so snotty it would make you sick!"

"Yes, they would, they'd be there. The paper says that after the parade they're going to eat dinner up there in the hotel. Then rest. Then they go around to the Progressive Teas."

"People don't say 'dinner' anymore, Marie, excuse me for reminding you, when they mean 'luncheon.'"

"Well, luncheon. Then they go—And I was just simply thinking—"

"It wouldn't be allowed, that's all."

"Evelyn, listen. I've got to go up to Mrs. Keith's anyway to tell her we can't get her French brocade, she's been like a crazy woman ever since the Committee turned down the offer of her house, I'll be out of the shop right at that time anyway, and I thought—"

"The housekeeper would kill me."

"There'll be dozens of people up there! I could blend right in."

"No. I'd lose my job—we'd both get arrested—"

"Evelyn! you know my blue sunshade that you liked so well last summer that that fellow gave me from Omaha with the terrible breath on account of just getting over having his tonsils out? That you wished you had one like it? Well, listen—"

THERE WERE TWO IRON BARS across that window, so the two little girls couldn't fall out. They were perfectly safe even when Gram and Lucitie got to talking and forgot about the parade, and Albert was staring down from the next window lost in thought, and Wyandra was getting refreshments from their kitchen down the hall. But anyone who happened to stick their head through the bars slantwise, then bring it around straight to look down at the marching parade, then in sudden alarm at having their face hanging out in empty air try to pull it back into the room, why, the fit would be wrong and they would probably just die hanging in the bars. Rosetta screamed, she was the one whose head was caught. Lavonne screamed too, Rosetta had done it this time. But once Albert and Wyandra got her to hold still and let them maneuver her head back slantwise, it slid right through. Just in the nick of time, too! for there came—

"Look, girls, look! America's Sweetheart!"

The big touring car looked from up above about six inches long, and the three little dolls bundled in furs in the back seat in proportion. The top was down, though it had snowed and was going to snow and the wind was blowing, but the tiny creatures didn't care, they smiled, waved and glanced in every direction.

"You notice there's someone in the middle between Doug and Mary. That's because they're not supposed to touch. Isn't that the saddest thing?"

"They smile, but their heart is breaking."

"Do you know how much she makes? Ten thousand dollars a week!"

"That should be some consolation."

"I can't get away to marry you today," Gram sang softly. "My wife won't let me."

"Look, Rosetta! Look, Lavonne!" Squatting down, Wyandra put her head between theirs and her arms around them.

"Mr. Alfonce, I want to ask your honest opinion about something," Gram said.

"Fire away."

"You're an expert. *Is that hair natural?*" Mary's hair glinted like a flash of gold in a canyon stream.

A LOT OF PEOPLE WERE wondering that, yearning girls who had slept on hard lumps of kid-curled tendrils, resentful women with camomiled hair, girls and women in general. *Are those blonde curls the real thing?*

Afterwards Marie used to say her blue sunshade was quite a stiff price to pay to see absolutely nothing, *except*—That used to make new acquaintances who hadn't heard the story before sit up and take notice, the way she would say *except* and then break off.

"Except *what?*"

Up at the Hotel Utah, sneaked in by Evelyn, Marie didn't see Mary Pickford's French maid, *really* French, mind you, that are supposed to be so dainty about their food and not like the Hoi McCoy over in this country that will wolf down anything—she didn't see with her own eyes the woman choke on the piece of somebody else's steak. What apparently *happened*, these plates full of what people didn't eat were sitting on one of the linen-draped portable tables waiting to be taken away—which famous stars are so spoiled, and *Picture-Play* says they eat like birds anyway so as not to get fat—and this French maid as she went past glanced and saw these steaks with just a bite or two took out of them smothered in mushrooms—and something called Béarnaise sauce—and this was in an alcove where nobody could see her—and they really treat them terrible, they really do—remember Alice Roosevelt's maid that went with Alice to Japan, how the poor thing had a nervous breakdown? But anyway Mary's French maid, what *she* did, she cut off a piece of this porterhouse with the Béarnaise sauce and popped it in her mouth—and—They say that's the most ghastly feeling in the world, your wind is cut right off, things whirl around, you stagger, everything turns black—! Someone grabbed her—! But of course if the woman had to choke, she couldn't have picked a better place. A doctor was on the floor, called for someone in the party coming down with a cold—and if you or I tried a stunt like that, *cutting a person's throat* to save their life, we'd end up a murderer. But they know just how to do it! Still, she had to be rushed to Holy Rosary Hospital.

And *that's* the part Marie got in on, on the ninth floor, this stretcher being carried to the elevator—! It was just the luckiest moment, people were rushing around like a chicken with its head cut off, *nobody* noticed. She needn't have traded away her sunshade had she but known, but who could even imagine such a thing? And then's when she heard what happened, then's when Evelyn came up alongside her, grabbed her arm and said, "Too bad your uncle's not here!" and Marie said "My *uncle?*" in a dumbfounded tone, and Evelyn said "Yes, the hairdresser. Without her maid, they don't know what to do about *Mary's hair.*"

Later Marie used to leave Evelyn out of it, not for any malicious reason but because it made it simpler just to say she herself thought of making a dash for the stairway, running down those iron stairs clattering like a pony, across South Temple with all the people and traffic, across Main, then through the crowds to the middle of the block to the Constitution Building. The elevator was on the street floor, the one-armed man had the cage door pushed back—

"Four, four!" she said gasping.

"What's the matter? They after you, to put you in the movies?"

"Mama! We saw Mary Pickford!"

"Douglas Fairbanks!"

"Marie! What are *you* doing here?" Wyandra said.

"Where's Uncle Albert? Quick—quick!"

Uncle Albert was at the far end of the floor in Gentlemen's.

Aunt Lucitie took charge. She knew he would be quite some time, he had taken the morning Tribune to sit and read. And if he hadn't taken it, it still would require half an hour or better for him to change into his broadcloth, comb his hair, still beautiful though he was sixty years old, order what he wanted put into his satchel—and then he would refuse to run and arrive at the hotel red in the face and out of breath.

Wyandra flew off instead, as Gram later told the railroad sutler who came to pick up her tarts and turnovers.

And be blamed if she didn't get in! But that was the English accent for you! that Wyandra could put on whenever she wanted to, and her nice neat looks. Well, the sutler could see her picture when it came out in the brown-tinted rotogravure section which the man from the Tribune that came and talked to her said it was going to do, be in the paper. "'Didn't no one stop you?' 'I walked right in.' 'Did they think the hotel had supplied you?' 'I don't know what they thought.' 'And you dressed Mary Pickford's hair?'"

The Tribune man said the lady readers would want to know two things: Number one, was Mary's hair naturally curly? and number two, was she naturally blonde?

At that, Mr. Albert Alfonce, renowned coiffeur, spoke up for Wyandra, and she was forever grateful. He was the fourth generation of hairdressers in his family, which had originally come from France, he said. And the oath amongst *them* was as strong as the oath amongst *doctors*. His trusted assistant Miss Wyandra Faine would no more betray a secret of that magnitude or even a tiny secret, such as whether Miss Pickford's eyebrows were darkened, than she would betray her country!

"Never," Wyandra said, who had been going to tell the man everything.

Aɴᴅ ᴛʜᴀᴛ ᴡᴀs ᴡʜᴇɴ Aʟꜰᴏɴᴄᴇ's Hairdressing Establishment in the new location started to do even more business *there* than they had in the old. Which it would have been bound to do anyway, Wyandra said, taking no credit. The old customers would all have come back, new ones would have found their way there eventually, Albert's talent was just too great. Her part in it was very small. All she did was hurry to the ninth floor of the Hotel Utah, walk in and dress Mary Pickford's hair. *That's all.*

Like for any customer. She picked up the comb—Mary was sitting in front of this dressing table with its overskirt of lace and yellow satin and all these things on top of it, powder, a swansdown puff, rouge, lipstick, perfume, a thick silver-backed brush, flowers in a vase and little lamps in rose-colored shades that were turned on because of the day being so dark and cold. In fact lights were on *everywhere*, in silk shades, and the heat was expanding the radiators, you could hear it, creak, creak, everything was warm, lit, beautiful. Mary seemed to think the hotel had sent for someone and would put the charge for her services on the bill. Or maybe she didn't even think about it. If your French maid nearly chokes to death on a piece of porterhouse steak and has to be carted away, somebody else that knows how to do your hair will automatically rise up to take her place.

What did Mary talk about?

Nothing. She was talking to two men. They had papers to show her. They were very well dressed, with silk cravats and cuff links. Then a lady came in. She seemed like a friend, they talked about the velvet suit the French maid—Celeste, her name was—hung in one of the bathrooms and turned the hot water on in the bathtub full force and how the room was full of steam and how when they found out where it was, the suit was sopping wet, but it would dry by the radiator before she needed it. And Mary said what time did the train leave? and one of the men said six-ten, and the woman said the doctor said Celeste was more scared than hurt and she should leave with them.

Wyandra misunderstood about her throat being cut. She read in the paper the next day that the doctor just reached down and pulled the steak out. And the way Wyandra herself got in the paper, a young man with a pad and pencil from the Tribune stopped her as she came down the hall with her satchel and said who are you? and she said Wyandra Faine and he said, are you with the party? and she said no, she was from Alfonce's Hairdressing Establishment right down the street in the Constitution Building. She had just been called in to dress Miss Pickford's hair because of the French maid nearly choking to death.

And the funny thing was, it wasn't till two days later that someone recollected that a *local* hairdresser had jumped in and combed the famous hair and wondered what *she* might have to say about the experience.

How thankful Wyandra was that Albert was right there beside her, because *she* didn't know about the oath, she'd have spoiled everything! Certain customers for dyes, bleaches, henna packs, switches and other stratagems might never have come looking for Mr. Alfonce and his staff but for their discretion. And also it helped to have it printed about Mr. Alfonce being a fourth-generation *French* hairdresser.

Chapter Forty-six

✳

THE VOGUE FOR BOBBED HAIR HELPED TOO, OF COURSE. AT FIRST IT SEEMED AS if it wouldn't. Those first bobs, level with the bottom tips of the ears, straight cut the whole way round the head, ends clubbed, when *they* walked out of the shop it seemed like they would never come back. They were hair turned loose, the spirit of hair, hair with wings. And sadly Alfonce's and other shops began to put away the tools with which they had curled, rolled, plastered, twisted and frizzed the stately coiffures, elaborate coronets crimped inside for fullness and lightness, and posticked arrangements of puffs and curls that now lay limp in long, sad locks upon the floor.

But the wings came fluttering back, as delivered over to the beauty shop as the mane had been that they rose from. Departures from the type occurred, skills developed formerly unknown to the barbering trade. The Marcel iron, invented for long hair, with short hair took a new lease on life. And some hairdressing establishments, according to the *Hairdressers' Journal*, made "ondulations" that would withstand water, washing and all atmospheric influences by means of a process called *permanent waving*. But that took ten hours, the overhead machine that did the job with its heavy, dangling electrified and dangerous curlers cost nearly as much as a cottage. Besides, a German invented it, and Albert would no more have bought one for the shop than he'd have ordered an octopus.

He and Wyandra kept busy with bobs, perishable waves and curls and a few old gingerbread coiffures that refused to change. Lucitie helped until common "clubbing" transmogrified into shaping, shingling, singeing, thinning, tapering, feather-edging and other complexities. Then she quit, not of course forever but just until the mysterious tremor went out of her hands and the puffiness out of her legs. Wyandra thought if she rested more that would help, and Lucitie promised to do so, but she was always materializing at the side shop door to see if Albert had time to come to dinner, supper or tea (and Wyandra when he finished). Sometimes she would do some little thing in the shop such as drying under the cool air of the electrified dryer the perspiration on the scalp and hair of a waiting customer, or powdering a steaming neck so that cut hairs wouldn't cling to the moist skin. Some little service like that. But hairdressing wasn't hairdressing anymore, Lucitie said, not like it used to be, even the smells were different, and she wondered if the suffrage movement didn't have something to do with it.

THE FAMILY LOST HERMAN IN the war. Not to an enemy bullet but to a Red Cross nurse he met on the troop ship going over to France, which when news of the signing of the Armistice came over the wireless turned right around in mid-ocean and steamed back to Newport News, where the nurse (Agnes by name) came from anyway. For a while they stayed back there, Herman and one of Agnes's brothers started a garage, but that fizzled out, he got homesick, and back came the wandering boy with a wife in tow who surprised them all.

For one thing, Agnes was a real registered nurse and not just some volunteer in a Red Cross outfit, and she had hardly shaken off the dust of travel till she had a job at the Holy Rosary Hospital. For another, she was not very womanly-appearing. And it was not just her short haircut, either, the way she tapered down from massive shoulders to hips that didn't look like they would hold up a pair of drawers without suspenders, no, she was also of a hirsute condition, kiss her and feel her bristly chin, she had an Adam's apple and her voice had a rumbling tone. Albert and Lucitie didn't know *what* to make of it, especially with Herman acting as if nothing was amiss. And in a way nothing *was* amiss, for through the years Agnes would produce and suckle at astonishingly large mammae three offspring.

Lucitie didn't live to see that day, nor see Herman give up the dirty and disheveled career of automobile mechanic (which had puzzled them so) to stay home and keep house, as a consequence of which he began not only to resemble but almost to *be* his father in looks and actions, which would have pleased his mother. He never asked for his tools and artifacts, either. Well, a few little blades of grass can push up and crack a cement sidewalk, and that's how it is with a tendency sometimes, as Wyandra said.

"Now there's two people," Marie said, "where if they just changed *clothes*—"

"You heard what happened?" Wyandra said quickly.

"Agnes is expecting?"

"Not that. They've been converted! They joined the church."

"What church?"

"What church? In Salt Lake City you ask what church?"

"How did that happen?"

"I don't really know. Some home missionaries or something."

"I'm not surprised."

LUCITIE NEVER HEARD TELL OF that development, that the baby turned out to be a boy, or in fact anything ever again. For one Sunday afternoon in the midst of a nap she died, peacefully, Mr. Larkin the undertaker said he could tell by her face. As easy as falling off a log. Some didn't, they'd come in looking like drug through a knot hole. But she must have had a lovely death, just like a dream. Wyandra wondered if maybe Hindle shouldn't be sent a telegram but found in the buffet drawer three different addresses, and nobody had heard from her in a long time. And the funeral was to be Tuesday, she couldn't get here. Besides, if Lucitie was sixty-nine, Hindle must be about sixty-seven. And she might be dead herself.

Nancibel took it worse than Herman. Who was going to come down and bake bread for her now, hang out a wash in the weather, help with the ironing, run after Legrand while she went to the matinee? Albert said that to all intents and purposes his own life was over, but Marie for one didn't believe it. Uncle Albert was two years younger than Aunt Lucitie, she had been ailing and not herself for quite some time, and it wasn't as if he didn't have Wyandra! She worked beside him in the shop and now cared for him out of it as well, keeping house and cooking as capably as Lucitie used to, and *she* needn't run, as Lucitie always did, to Nancibel's bidding. Marie thought that Uncle Albert would hardly notice any difference.

He might not, his daughter-in-law Agnes said, but the *world* would certainly take note of a widower and an old maid working together, eating together, and sleeping together, you might say, her on the sanitary couch in the parlor and him in the bedroom not ten feet away, and act accordingly.

"But they're like father and daughter!" Marie said. "Wyandra's lived with them more than thirty years. And Uncle Albert—No one would even *think* of such a thing."

"I don't say she shouldn't help him in the shop," Agnes said. "But if Wyandra Faine continues to *live* with him, I will tell you this much, neither his son Herman, nor me, nor this child that is on the way, nor any child of ours, will ever darken his doorstep again."

"Why, Agnes! That's the silliest thing I ever heard of!"

But at least Agnes had the tact not to deliver her ultimatum to Albert and Wyandra *together*, or in earshot of a customer, but came to the shop door on her next afternoon off and beckoned Wyandra outside. "Can we talk in private?"

That scared Wyandra out of seven years' growth, because a bona fide trained nurse, even in ordinary dress, can read the human body like a book, and maybe Wyandra's first thought was that Agnes had read in Albert some life-threatening sentence. At first she was going to take Agnes into the apartment, but remembering the panful of dishes she was going to run in and do as soon as her marcel left, with fluttering heart she led her instead to the built-in seat at the end of the outside hall under the arched window. After hearing with bated breath that all Agnes was worried about in the throes of her spiritual transposition from Baptist sinfulness to Mormon salvation was for her father-in-law and Wyandra to make some changes in their living arrangements, Wyandra leaned back with a sigh of relief.

"Goodness," she said. "I was so afraid you came about Albert!"

"I *did* come about Albert," Agnes said. "And about you. About him sleeping in the bedroom and you on the parlor couch. How does that look? You've got to move!"

Wyandra, her dismay temporarily prostrating her faculties, at first thought Agnes meant *they* had to move, and she was starting to explain that they *had* moved, from Third South to here in the Constitution Building, it had just about killed Albert and she doubted if he could go through such an ordeal very soon again, when Agnes's almost threatening look recalled her to herself. Quickly she said, "Oh, you mean—me?"

"I do mean you," Agnes said sternly. "I do indeed. And if you care one iota for this family that has done so much for you, you will stop disgracing us all as soon as you can!"

When Mrs. Hinchman, carrying (so as not to muss the coiffure Albert had just finished) her violet-massed hat with as much giggling embarrassment as though the hat had been her bloomers, left to ride down on the elevator and hurry to her electric brougham parked in front of the building, and Wyandra's shingle and turn-up had also departed and they were alone, Albert wanted to know what Agnes had wanted.

"What did she have on her mind? 'She,' I say," he said, thinking of her stubble and how indignantly on her last visit she had refused to let him try chemical decomposition by galvanic action, which the salesman of the machine they were making free trial of for thirty days (the time was almost up) said destroyed the roots forever. But of course that wouldn't prevent the trait, if such it was, from being passed on to a granddaughter, which he hoped it wouldn't be.

"It was her afternoon off."

"Did she want anything in particular?"

"She thinks—She's been thinking it over and she imagines—"

"Well, what?"

Finally Wyandra told him. Agnes imagined that people would think that it wasn't nice for them to be living under the same roof together, and she said Agnes said that if— the situation continued—why, she, Herman and the baby when it got here would never darken their doorstep again!

"But that's ridiculous!" Albert said.

At first as they spoke of this, they looked at each other like mates serving together on the same ship, two old friends, forthright, unhesitating, tried by their long voyage and not found wanting. But this directness changed somehow, as they gazed, to the shame-facedness of the Garden. Shamefacedness such as met the Lord God walking there in the cool of the day and said: "I am ashamed...I am naked...I hide myself..."

"That's *ridiculous*."

"That's what I told her. I told her that you're just like my—"

"And you're just like my—"

What were they like? *Who* were they to each other? their eyes asked unhappily.

And there they were, out of their sunny Eden, sprawled in the cold gray mist beyond impregnable Cherubims...

Days went by, and Wyandra could have wept. She *did* weep, for Albert's uncomfortably ceremonious manners, for her own, for what they had had that now was lost. And all on account of meddlesome Agnes! But how to change the existing state of things, that was the question. Wyandra mulled it over, Albert did too, in a shop as charged with self-consciousness as a cloud with voltage until, as it always does, the law of organic life put the case another way.

USUALLY THE PATRON CONFIDES IN the hairdresser, but Margery Hinchman, in the becoming lavender of mitigated mourning, had a warm and friendly smile and a cooing response to remarks anyone addressed to her. And because Wyandra's mind was full of worries, before she knew it she found herself telling the widow of the manager of the Germania Lead Works everything. Mrs. Hinchman was not her customer but Albert's. But whenever possible, Albert got out of the tedium of giving her the dry egg shampoo she wanted before he dressed her long hennaed hair. Wyandra didn't care for the job either. Today, though, the work of applying the mixture of beaten egg, salt and witch hazel with pieces of cotton to Mrs. Hinchman's sympathetic scalp seemed to go fast, and, ascertaining with a quick look in the direction of Albert's booth that his paper curl was still in there with him, Wyandra even slightly slowed her ministrations. Should she go? Stay? Was she really disgracing the family? But who would take care of Albert? He had never been alone, never, he couldn't do the slightest thing for himself, toast a piece of bread, make a cup of tea, nothing.

"Albert is a very refined and wonderful man," Mrs. Hinchman said, after thinking hard about the dilemma. "And *very understanding*."

"Oh, he is," Wyandra said. "But you see, the problem—"

"And who is this Agnes again?"

"She's Herman's wife, Albert's daughter-in-law. Married to his son Herman—" Putting the brush aside to take up a dry towel, she picked up a strand of hair and began to rub it with the towel, then separated and rubbed another.

"And what is it you say she wants?"

"She thinks it doesn't look nice for Albert, who's a widower since Lucitie died, and myself that's not married, and not a blood relation, to be living up here together in the same place. And she says if we don't make other arrangements, why, she and Herman and the baby—it's not here yet but on the way—won't ever darken Albert's doorstep again."

"I've never seen her, have I?"

"I don't think so. But you see, it was bad enough losing Lucitie, but he still had me. But if *I* went—" She finished the dry-towel rubbing, then sprinkled the widow's glowing scalp with rum and bayleaf lotion.

"Men are so helpless. It was the same with my Clarence."

"Of course wherever I went, I'd still come to work in the shop," Wyandra said, peeking through the curtains at the more mirrored and roomy alcove where Albert held forth to discover if his sculpture curl had gone. Seeing the chair empty, she unpinned Mrs. Hinchman's neck-cloth and helped her to her feet. "But what would he do, alone every night?"

Albert turned from the mirror where he had been patting his hair and, smiling in their direction, gave a beckon.

"The answer's simple," Mrs. Hinchman whispered to Wyandra. "*He's got to marry again*."

"Well, young lady!" Albert said heartily, flicking his chair with a towel.

"I got it all out, I guess," Wyandra mumbled, meaning the dried egg, as she handed Mrs. Hinchman over.

"So here we are again. And here's our lovely tresses—"

And here's Wyandra going back to her own recess and pulling the curtains. And here's her blushing face as hot as fire.

BUT OF COURSE MRS. HINCHMAN didn't mean Albert had got to marry *Wyandra*. She meant herself, which became apparent not long afterwards when she invited him to go for a Sunday drive in her tall, narrow electric motorcar with one trembling hothouse rose in it, in a crystal vase. She wanted to discuss something with him, she said. This excursion was followed by an invitation to go and see *Bird of Paradise* at the Salt Lake Theater, Mrs. Hinchman having been sent two complimentary passes, she said, from her husband's old firm. Albert was then asked to dine at the lovely two-story Hinchman house on Fourth East, where he was served the kind of dinner a man with an English accent might relish: Yorkshire pudding, red-running beef, rutabagas, forcemeat and a great many other dishes, including plum pudding with brandy sauce.

At something after midnight, hearing groans from his lonely widower's bed, Wyandra hastened into his room in a great fright to find him green around the gills, too sick even to make it to Gentlemen's before casting up with loathing all he had enjoyed, and missing the basin Wyandra had hurriedly brought. "But don't think a thing of that," she said, "just get rid of all you can." By the time she finished cleaning up he was feeling better, but when she went to turn off the light and got back to her bed on the parlor couch, he said he was starting to feel nauseous again. So she stayed, placing the basin within easy reach. At first she stood but then took a seat on the foot of the bed, at the very edge. He looked pale and uncomfortable, and the way he was shielding his eyes with his hand made her think the light, though not very bright, might be hurting them. "I'll pin a newspaper around the shade," she said, jumping up.

She was nearly out the door when he said, "No, turn it off, the dark feels better."

She did as he asked. "There's enough light from outside if I put the blind up. Do you still feel like you're going to need the basin?"

"If I could just stop *thinking*!" he said.

She stopped uncertainly, then sat back down again on the edge of the bed. "What about, Albert?"

"Why, about the—what we ate," he said. "Rutabagas, forcemeat—that awful, awful—"

"But you said it was lovely!"

He sat up. "Quick!" But he just gagged and didn't need the basin after all, and after a minute or two fell back, closing his eyes again, as she could see in the faint light from the window.

"Thinking of what we ate," he said.

"Well, don't you do that, Albert. Just forget it."

"Courses." He shuddered. "One after the other."

"Put it out of your mind."

The clock ticked, she sat on, but then when it seemed as if he had dozed off and she was starting to get to her feet, he suddenly spoke. "She is not a woman who wants to continue alone, Wyandra."

"Mrs. Hinchman, you mean?"

"She's a woman that's full of affection. Demonstrative. She is very—" He groped for another word but, not finding one, repeated, "Demonstrative. Some people are more—like that." He swallowed and started gently patting the pit of his stomach as one might soothe a fractious child. "While other people—it makes them, I suppose you could express it—*ill*."

"Her house," Wyandra said stiffly to fill the ensuing pause, "is it made out of—brick?"

He nodded. "Hardwood floors. Fifty by a hundred lot. Free and clear." He paused again. The electric motorcar, three hundred and sixty-five dollars a month for as long as she lived, three acres out of town, and she was not a woman who wanted to live alone. Whoever she married, she already had a two-carat diamond, so an engagement ring wouldn't have to be bought. And her husband needn't work, because Clarence worked all the time and look where it got him, Mrs. Hinchman said, when he could have been staying home enjoying himself.

And so Alfonce's Hairdressing Establishment, after more than forty years, was about to— "But of course, Wyandra," he said, struggling up to a sitting position against the headboard, "you can still run the shop if you want and live right in these same rooms and—But that machine the salesman left, there'll never be enough call for that kind of work to justify—I don't think. In fact the only one I can think of right off with that kind of a condition is Agnes."

"Agnes," Wyandra said bitterly. Oh, that awful woman. She was to blame for everything.

"So we could just let the fellow take it back."

"All right, Albert."

"If you thought you'd be too lonesome here by yourself, Mrs. Hinchman's got three bedrooms. Margery, her name is. You could come and live—there."

"I can imagine how she'd like *that*. Oh, no, Albert. I won't be too lonesome. But I was just thinking," she said. "You really belonged to the church at one time, didn't you? Wasn't that how you and Lucitie met in the first place, coming to America on a Mormon boat? Lucitie and Hindle were even *born* in the church. And in the case of Da' and me— he was converted, then me. But of course a child thinks whatever her father does is right. So anyway, then we came to Zion. And then—everybody reneged—"

"What's that got to do with what we're talking about?" he said with some impatience. "Mrs. Hinchman certainly doesn't belong. She's Scotch Presbyterian, I think she said."

"Well, nothing, only—"

"Only what?"

"Well, I was just thinking that if we still *belonged* and *believed* it and everything, and if there was still, you know—" She drew a deep breath. "Why, somebody else besides Mrs. Hinchman—could—" Carefully she smoothed the outing flannel over her knee. "Marry you," she said. "What I mean to say," she hurried on, "is that in lots of ways it wasn't such a bad idea."

"What wasn't?"

"You know."

"Good Lord, Wyandra!"

"I mean, where maybe the—the man wouldn't want the person *by herself* but as a, you know, secondary—"

He looked at her.

She hung her head.

"Why do I have to marry Mrs. Hinchman?" he said suddenly, sitting up. "Why can't I tell Agnes I don't *care* if she never darkens my doorstep again? Or Herman either. Because I don't, you know."

"Or the baby? Oh, no, Albert. The baby will be lovely. And you *would* care. Really."

"As far as that's concerned," he said, "why can't I marry *you*?"

"You mean—" She placed her words without breathing, like on balancing a card on a card castle nearly…almost…finished…"On this earth, Albert?"

"Of course on this earth, you silly goose."

On Thursday morning, he said, because so far as he could remember they only had the one appointment for Mrs. Ridgeway's beauty pack at eleven…And! He lay back against his pillows with a look as satisfied as his who finally, after countless trials, had determined by specific gravity how much of a certain tincture was worthless metal and how much purest gold.

"Albert?"

"What, my dear?"

"Do you think you'll need this basin anymore?"

"I don't think so. My stomach's settled now. You go back to bed and go to sleep."

The day after but one Mrs. Hinchman came in the afternoon to take Albert for a drive down Fifth East and out towards the golf course and past Wandamere. She had it all planned, she said. *He* had something planned too, to tell her he thought she was a lovely woman with hair of remarkable luster and resiliency for a woman her age (whatever that might be), and a real recommendation for the dry egg shampoo, also an example of how you could use henna for years without ill effect but that he couldn't marry her.

"Mrs. Hinchman, I'm sorry to have to tell you—"

"You promised to call me Margery, Albert dear." She turned to cast full upon him an admonishing smile just as from a brake of brushwood a cow chased by a boy with a stick leaped forth onto the road to plow into the tall and teetering box they rode in, made of glass and tin. And crash! The boy was the only witness. He lurched home and got such of the family as was there, his mother, a sister who breathed through her mouth, a brother hopping along with a cut and stone-bruised toe wrapped in a dirty rag. The cow was dead. The lady was dead too. They thought that she was driving, it looked that way. The man was also dead. The crystal vase never got broken, it still had the rose in it but no water. With everything else such a shambles, that caused comment. The boy's mother later wished she had taken the crystal vase when she had a chance, although it had that sharp point on the bottom where it stuck through a loop on the dashboard and wouldn't have stood upright on a table anyway. The boy's father when he got home was of a mind to take the razor-strap to the boy, for if he'd of drove down the cow's stake the way he'd ought to—! But the mother said if God hadn't wanted the accident to happen, *twenty* cows could of run into that motor-vehicle and nothing would of happened. And they had all that lovely beef, she said, and one thing she was going to make was sauerbraten. By that time the war had been over three years, so you could use the German word.

An account of the accident appeared on page one of the Tribune, and farther along in the paper Mrs. Margery Hinchman's death notice, and a page or two beyond that Mr. Albert Alfonce's obituary, proprietor of Alfonce's Hairdressing Establishment at 36 South Main Street. Mrs. Hinchman was seventy-three years old, which nobody would certainly have ever guessed. She still had her own teeth which were yellowed like old lace, but that makes no difference, they're better than false.

Chapter Forty-seven

*

THE MINUTE GRAM HEARD THE NEWS, SHE FINISHED HER BAKING AND WAITED for Rosetta and Lavonne to come home from school so they would know what she wanted them to eat for supper and she could tell them that Rosetta's Great-Uncle Albert had been killed when a cow ran into a lady named Mrs. Hinchman's automobile, and that the lady had been killed too, they had gone out for a ride, and that Gram was going up to stay all night with Wyandra. Then she hurried out and caught the streetcar and went on up to the Constitution Building. The little girls were supposed to tell Marie when she came home and break it to her gently, for there was no "great" between Marie and the dead man, as in Rosetta's case, to cushion the blow, Albert was Marie's real direct uncle by marriage and she would be much affected.

But nothing could compare with the way Wyandra must be feeling, who seemed to worship the ground Albert walked on, Gram thought as she rode uptown. And she wondered what she could say—? But Wyandra was not crying, or at least not hysterically, and she wasn't in a state either, lying prostrate in a darkened room, but was up and around, dressed in a georgette blouse and her serge skirt, her hair was fixed better than usual, and she seemed—Gram never did find the word she was searching for, but it was "triumphant." Nobody who didn't see Wyandra those first few days could imagine the fairness and calmness of her, the way she shone with clear and tranquil light. And why, came out during the evening, after Marie and her friend Leona had come running in, smelling of talcum and perfume, to offer condolences and strain a few careful tears through their beaded lashes, then hurried away to meet their escorts waiting in the street below and catch the last train out to Salt Air (the last of the day and last of the season too), and after Herman and Agnes had put in an appearance, Agnes saying they were taking charge of the funeral arrangements and that she would be up tomorrow to "talk business."

"Business, mind you! and Albert scarcely cold," Gram said. But the reason Wyandra looked like she did and acted like she did, much to the surprise of everyone, was because of the situation that prevailed up until that fatal ride. And that was as follows: Albert's customer, Mrs. Hinchman, had taken it on herself to try to marry him and almost succeeded, but then he backed out because he realized the bluebird of happiness was in his own back yard and the bluebird was Wyandra. And the sole purpose of him *going* for that last ride in the first place was to tell Mrs. Hinchman he couldn't marry her because he was going to marry Wyandra. It was all settled. So even though Wyandra grieved, poor girl, and would grieve as long as there was breath left in her body and would miss him and never get over it, still, the thought of him giving Mrs. Hinchman the air for *her* was such a comfort that the pain just didn't matter. It was like she had earned a beautiful diploma she could hang up and look at forever.

BUSINESS, AND THE MAN NOT even buried! But that was Agnes for you. What she proposed to do was sell Alfonce's Hairdressing Establishment, chairs, tables, new dryers, all that Alfonce's had garnered over the years, the creams, powders and perfumes they now stocked, and most especially Alfonce's *good name*. And she thought she had a buyer, a very nice hairdresser *in the church* who was willing to pay cash.

Nancibel put her oar in there to say, and her husband agreed, that nobody should have Alfonce's Hairdressing but Wyandra, and especially since Papa and she had been going to get married!

"*She* says," Agnes said. "Which is merely her word."

"That's all it has to be," Nancibel said. "Anyone that knows Wyandra—"

But the hairdresser they knew in the church had money in the bank, Herman said. And she was very nice. Maybe she would even give Wyandra a job. And Wyandra could have a room at Nancibel's, maybe. Pay for it, of course. Or stay with them. Or she could start another shop somewhere—

Had Wyandra heard what was said back and forth, Marie told Gram later, at the family confab (which Marie as a first cousin got to sit in on and which settled the matter in favor of Wyandra's keeping the shop by making payments and staying on amongst the old family furnishings, such as they were, nothing to brag about, especially after Agnes but also Nancibel got through taking whatever was pretty or nice!), had Wyandra *heard* the way they tossed from side to side the subject of a person who had worked for and done so much for them all throughout their childhood and growing up, her heart, had it not been broken already over Uncle Albert, would have broken over that. But at least she still had her home and surroundings and way to earn a living, and while she would never dare renege on Agnes and Herman's monthly payments, Nancibel would be more lenient, though she too wanted what she thought she had coming.

Marie had to admire, though, the way Nancibel stood up for Wyandra and held out for her and not the church hairdresser, and how she and her husband won the day. But if the chasm that opened between brother and sister *that* night ever got mended, Marie would be surprised. "Where do kids really come from?" she said. "When they're not like father, not like mother—?"

"Some say a good neighbor," Gram said with a laugh.

Marie laughed too. But what she meant was, what is this mysterious thing of us being *ourselves*?

Mostly when questions would come to Marie like that, the kind with no answers, would be on the dance floor out at the Blue Pavilion, with some nice fellow leaving for Omaha in the morning, after she and her escort would have had such a swell time, and now when the band played "Goodnight, Ladies" and the lights came gradually on they would leave and with Leona and *her* fellow would go get some chop suey or chow mein, then walk home, so handsome, so pretty, under the dark leaves, the cool breeze blowing, then out in the bright white moonlight.

What are we living for?

Why do we die?

Why was Bonnie the one to come down with fatal influenza? though Marie didn't believe it *was* that. She thought if it had been, they'd have all caught it and not just Bonnie.

What is our soul?

Does it slip right out of our body like a magician pulling a silk handkerchief out of his sleeve?

What is love?

Why do we have to suffer?

"A penny for your thoughts, kid."

"Thinking of you."

FOR A LONG TIME WYANDRA didn't use Albert's alcove. It just seemed as if it was still his. He would come back from having breakfast or taking his constitutional around Temple Square or from a nap or Gentlemen's or from Beauty Supply and, shooting his cuffs in the old way, he would call in whoever was waiting for him and pick up his comb … Maybe his customer would already be sitting at the dressing table, put there by Wyandra, looking at herself in the glass with profound interest, or maybe she wouldn't have arrived. Then Albert, even if it was still two or three minutes to the hour, would sigh and look pained.

Wyandra just never thought of using Albert's alcove.

But then one day because Mrs. Hurst got the schedule off kilter by being late, Wyandra was rushed, and when Mrs. Prentice came in and she put her behind Albert's curtains at Albert's table, instead of moving her later to her own alcove, she just did her there. After that she used it all the time and used Albert's combs, curling irons, everything that was his, in preference to her own, and it … made the day so nice. Standing right where he stood, checking as he used to do in the mirror rather than looking directly down at the cocked head, bob or paper curl or whatever was then finished or being done.

Some patrons fell away, they seemed to have imagined Albert was a Paris hairdresser straight from Paris and that "American" hairdressing wouldn't do. At first Wyandra thought Mrs. Prentice, the illustrious owner of the old Clarendon mansion, was going to be one of them. But then she sent her driver up to get an appointment and when she arrived for it said that she had been to California. In Albert's booth with the curtains closed, she confided to Wyandra in the whisper-soft voice of the very refined that her daughter Birdelle had almost been the death of her, of both her and the girl's father, in fact. Did Wyandra have any idea what had *happened*? If Mrs. Prentice was talking about Birdelle picking up with one of the Body Builders, or whatever the man was, traveling in the set of people in attendance upon Douglas Fairbanks the time he and Mary Pickford came to town for the Liberty Bond rally and parade, Wyandra did indeed know, although she acted as if she didn't.

After they struck up an acquaintance at the Progressive Tea that had caused such a rift between Birdelle and her parents, Birdelle *corresponded* with the Body Builder. And of course it wouldn't take a person like that long to find out who she *was* and what she *had*. Or to persuade her to run off and meet him down in Hollywood. But, being an heiress, she wasn't ruined the way a poor girl might have been, tossed aside and abandoned. Douglas Fairbanks's Body Builder *married* Birdelle, fell all over himself to do so, and of course quit Douglas Fairbanks to live off what he thought was going to be the fat of the land.

Wyandra knew all that and considerably more, because Mrs. Prentice had told Albert. But so as not to cast doubts on *his* discretion and the soundness of his moral principles, Wyandra said well, she knew from the paper that Miss Prentice was now happily married to a California gentleman.

"Happily!" Mrs. Prentice said. "Gentleman! California!" She shook her head, clamped her lips tight shut and said no more.

But gradually it all came out, and oh, Wyandra missed Albert then. Nancibel came every week to get her hair done. But she was nobody to tell anything to, as far as the comfort of *that* was concerned. Her mind was always wandering to her mildewed ironing, the ineptitude of her scrub lady, her husband's heartless neglect (he was always in his shop trying to invent something), and how to get her only child Legrand to play outside more in the fresh air, his bowels to move, his cowlick to lay down or his ears to lay back. Some people are just too full of their own concerns to *join in*, and Nancibel, as she had been since childhood, was of that kind. But Marie was different. She *joined in*, none better, and the day of the week she came after hours to get her hair done was as good as a feast.

Marie never saw Mrs. Prentice or even her Cord limousine go by, that she knew of, and had glimpsed Birdelle only as a narrow shape in a large, cloudy hat shadowing a blurred face in the Sunday paper's brown rotogravure. But the Prentices owned the old Clarendon mansion, Marie's own mother in supernatural times had actually gone in and out of the front *door* of that house, Mavis—that relic of a mythical past—had died in one of the bedrooms there—and Marie and her husband Les wouldn't probably even have *met* if the Kinnavys hadn't moved to town from Park City to try to *inherit* from the Clarendon estate, which they had no more chance than a snowball in hell. And there wouldn't be any Rosetta. So while Marie always *joined in*, no matter what the subject, when the Prentices were mentioned, with all these ramifications dangling like a long tail to a kite, she paid the kind of attention Wyandra could only show her appreciation of by putting down her scissors or comb or sticking the Marcel iron back in its heater and do nothing for a little while but talk.

TONY AUDETTE WAS THE NAME of the Douglas Fairbanks Body Builder the Prentice daughter Birdelle ran off with and married down in California. Brown and muscular on the outside, a *whited sepulchre within*, an expression Mrs. Prentice used when she came to Alfonce's and was so worried about the turn events had taken. Of course he was after her money. But the funny part of it was, he didn't get any. Birdelle was the paymaster. She paid their apartment rent for the almost three years she was with him, thirty-two fifty a month, paid for groceries and incidentals, but if Mr. Audette thought he married Aladdin's magic lamp, he was very much mistaken. Birdelle *did* take her string of pearls out of the bank that the rich woman Mrs. Prentice was related to gave her when she was born, and as her mother had feared, she *did* dispose of them. But in a careful, cautious manner and to great advantage (the pearls were not of the finest water), though Mrs. Prentice's mind was not to be put at ease on that score, or as to just what Birdelle *did* with the money, until Mr. Audette left the poor girl for another woman.

Left her, thank goodness, Mrs. Prentice said, in a civilized *country*, at least, not like poor Ella Haggin, whose fortune-hunting bridegroom the Count De Toina took her on a trip among cannibals and went off and left her to be *devoured*. And Birdelle came home and lived happily ever after.

"Because from then on everything was free?" Marie said.

"Because she came home to a mother and father who, when they heard what she had done and how she conducted herself while she was away, never disapproved of or crossed her in any way again!" Wyandra said.

"How was that?" Marie said.

"Because every step she took, except of course to marry the Body Builder in the first place, showed that the example her folks had set and the principles they had tried to imbue her with through the years had *not been in vain*," Wyandra said.

"But *I* think it's born in them," she went on. "When anybody comes from a line that's got people in it as rich as Mrs. Prentice's second cousin, and Mr. Prentice's relatives that's rich like that too, why, the business ability *somebody* must have had back in time was so strong that it's bound to keep on as a family trait through the generations, like *one* black Welshman with shoe-button eyes can put his mark on generations of light-complexioned descendants. *Money sense* gets passed on like that, I do believe, and Birdelle Prentice turned out to have it. One little part of the brain. But of course," she said, "your surroundings have a lot to do with it too, and if you have been brought up preached to every day of your life about how healthy it is to make a profit, and how smart to save, and how money makes the world go round, why, you just naturally believe it. I was reading someplace that the Catholic church says 'Give me a child until he's five years old and then you can have him, *because he's mine forever.*' Preach something and keep on preaching it and it will sink in."

"Well, what did Birdelle *do* with the money she got from selling the pearl necklace that made the Prentices so proud and happy?" Marie said.

"She *saved* it, that's what! She didn't throw it around. She spent just what she had to for their bare living, pretending to get a check every month from her father, which they didn't send, as they wanted to make her give up on the Body Builder and come home."

"What's so wonderful about that?" Marie said with some impatience. "Anyone can save. It looks to me like somebody with real *money* talent, the fellows we girls go out with talk about making money in the stock market on Wall Street, *doing* something, making the money earn money, buying 'on margin' and things like that—"

"Well, I don't know," Wyandra said. "You see, Birdelle had never had a chance before to show what she would do, and her mother had been so upset about the valuable tablecloth that she wanted to dye pink for the Progressive Tea, she didn't trust her to the corner. But what does she do? She goes out into the world with thousands of dollars in her pearl necklace to dispose of however she pleases and ends up *saving* most of it, putting it in the *bank*. So the Prentices are so happy they don't know what to do."

Marie snorted.

"But I've been thinking. She'll like the praise and approval, which I don't think she's ever had before from her folks, so much that she'll probably try to repeat it. You know— just keep on *saving*."

"And that will be her big accomplishment in life!" Marie agreed eagerly. "The Body Builder was poor, of course? Wouldn't you like to have been a little bird and heard the different ways he tried to talk Birdelle into divvying up a little? Thinking every morning when he woke up, maybe *today*?"

WHATEVER WYANDRA HEARD ABOUT THE Prentices she passed on, for she knew Marie, even if she had never laid eyes on them, viewed them almost as family connections and the mansion as ancestral. So when Mrs. Prentice told her about the cook backing the laundress (who came one day every two weeks to wash and iron the linens too fine to go to the laundry) into the butler's pantry and attempting to *lay hands upon her*, and she a nursing mother although her baby was nearly two years old, and getting fired as a consequence, Wyandra could hardly wait to tell Marie. This cook happened to be another Chinaman like Sing, the one who chased the gardener with the meat cleaver. Sing had saved up and gone back to China several months before.

Mr. Prentice was always the one who hired their cook, Mrs. Prentice said. For no reason in particular except they started out that way as young marrieds and Mr. Prentice thought he had a special knack for it. This last cook he found someplace on one of his business trips. But just because a person is a Chinaman with a pigtail down their back doesn't mean they can cook. Li Po had been a disappointment from the beginning, his sponges fell, his codfish cakes didn't taste right, he couldn't seem to bake a pot of Boston baked beans, all you could taste in his mayonnaise was oil, and now, after all their patience and forbearance, to try to lay hands on the laundress! Inez, the hired girl, had taken his place temporarily, but to put a simple meal on the table seemed to prostrate her, she let the rest of her work go by the board or very near it, burned out the back chimney, but worst of all even told Mr. Loomis like it was a great joke that Li Po had *tried to lay hands on her too* at one time and she had pushed him off the back steps. Which she never said a word about at the time, making Mrs. Prentice fear for the character of anyone like that, although they were going to keep her on, she was a good worker when she wasn't trying to cook.

Now Mr. Prentice was really looking. On the train at St. Louis, where he went on business, an omelette greatly attracted him, and a cream puff, but when he ran down their creator and offered him a position, the man, who was of negro extraction, said that on the advice of a passenger he had invested in the stock market and now was rich enough to quit and open a restaurant in Wilmington! So people were very presumptuous and disrespectful nowadays. And Chinamen like everyone else, those of the newer generation. One that Mr. Prentice attempted to hire wanted every Sunday off, and another said he must have help for parties. Not that they *had* any parties! They couldn't afford it, Mrs. Prentice said, the *real* kind, such as at a dinner one time, for instance—one hundred guests when they unfolded their napkin found a hundred-dollar bill. Or the napkins when each lady guest opening hers found a solid gold bracelet with her monogram. When cigarettes rolled in hundred-dollar bills were passed around after coffee. She once saw a black pearl in every oyster! And a friend of Cousin Virginia's borrowed sixty extra housemen, besides six butlers at double wages, from her neighbors for a birthday dinner. Why, the gorgeousness of assemblies she had seen from the sidelines, cotillions, massive evening receptions—! The freesias, roses, jasmine, anemone, tulips…fifty thousand dollars' worth of flowers was nothing. The perfumed candles burning like the Milky Way! She knew of a costume ball that cost four hundred thousand dollars. One man wore a suit of armor that cost ten thousand dollars. Red carpet on the sidewalk, linking the front door with the limousine—or the carriage, as of course it was in those days. Three hundred a month just for chocolates.

So Mrs. Prentice had first-hand knowledge of what a party should *be*, and because she was a person who if she was going to do something was going to do it right and they couldn't afford it! she just didn't have any parties. Or associate either with people who called themselves "society" but never saw a footman in livery in their lives, a collapsible black silk gibus, an opera from a box through a pair of gold and diamond opera glasses, or a string of polo ponies or anything else that amounted to anything. Besides, the mining people were nearly all ignorant Irish Catholics. And all the money in the world couldn't make silk purses out of the sow's-ear Mormons. So the Prentices, parents and daughter, lived in their Salt Lake City house like aloof conquistadors in a stone fortress above a plain teeming with pinheaded Nahuatlan tribesmen. Exiled, a million to their name and that was it, but happier so than to be galled each day by the sight of fortune's darlings back east (the ones who really counted) going their glittering rounds.

MR. PRENTICE'S SEARCH FOR A cook continued. And then one day on his way to California, a man came through the cars selling chess pies so delectable that Mr. Prentice almost risked life and limb hunting him from car to car to find out who had made them. When he got back to Salt Lake the first thing he did was look up Mrs. Youngberg down on Seventh South, and sure enough there were the very pies cooling on the kitchen table in an aroma so alluring that had he not been tied to the mast of his importance, he would surely have been swept away. But as the poet says (the banker too, and man of business), "Never seek to tell thy love, love that's never told must be" if you want to strike a good bargain. So Mr. Prentice did not seek to tell *his* love, even when Mrs. Youngberg insisted he help himself and he bit into a pie even more delicious than the one on the train. He merely said he wondered if she had other strings to her bow or if these pies were the only things she could make. If he meant, she said, could she put a decent meal on the table, she should certainly hope so by this time, being almost sixty years of age and no complaints yet. But why did he ask?

Because he was Mr. Prentice residing up on South Temple street, they needed a cook and if she wanted the position she could have it. He would pay such and such, not a cent more, free board and room, and she could start tomorrow.

Whoa up, Gram said. She was quite well situated as she was, rent not too high, a nice young widow lady boarding with her by the name of Marie Kinnavy who had been a chum of her daughter Bonnie who died in the influenza epidemic and left a little girl, now eight years old, Lavonne, that she took care of. She also took care of another little girl named Rosetta, age nine, seven months older than Lavonne. And she didn't know what the young ones would do if they had to get out and find another place. Also it would be mean to separate the little girls, who were practically like sisters. And if she *did* take the job, she would have to have Lavonne with her.

"Have her, bring her," Mr. Prentice said, as transformed temporarily by the warm chess pie as an Ithacan sailor by Circe's famous cup.

All of a sudden it dawned on Gram who Mr. Prentice *was*.

"Why, you folks live in the Clarendon mansion!" she said. She did not add, which her own stepsister Lois and family had almost inherited! She said she would think it over and let Mr. Prentice know.

Marie knew Wyandra would want to hear of *that* development and so hurried to the shop. But also she wanted to talk over Gram's attitude and the oddity of the whole thing. Apparently Mr. Prentice had tasted one of her chess pies on the train and that was the way to his heart. But the way Gram took his finding out who she was and coming to the house to offer her a job was like she was Cinderella and the Prince, after looking everywhere, had finally found her. It was ridiculous. When she was so needed at home.

"Is she going to take it?"

"She says not, but it's hard to tell. And like I told her, don't it strike you as peculiar that Mr. Prentice would do a thing like that in the first place? 'Like what?' she said. 'Listen,' I said, 'your chess pies don't go through the *drawing-room cars* or the *private cars* that a rich man like him ought to be traveling in to California!' 'So what?' she said. 'So he must of been traveling *common coach*,' I said. 'Well, what of it?' she said, quite huffy. She has no understanding of when things don't jibe. And she acts so independent. So I've been thinking—"

Wyandra waited, thinking how she could add to her mythology if Gram really went to live in the Clarendon mansion.

"So independent," Marie repeated. "She's changed, Wyandra. A little thing like this chess pie business and she's a different person. So I've been—I believe the time has come for Rosetta and me to move—"

"But what if she doesn't take the job? and you have went ahead and mentioned moving? Wouldn't her feelings be hurt? Which you can't blame—It's been lovely for Rosetta—"

"I know," Marie said. "But she's big enough now. I think it's time her and I branched out on our own. Maybe come up here."

"Up here in this building?"

"Well—if I was late coming home from work or invited out of an evening or something, she could entertain herself. Go to bed. And *you* wouldn't have to be bothered about her, but at the same time you'd be on the premises."

Later Gram said she hadn't really been going to take the job, but with Marie acting so snippy, jumping at the least little excuse to tear the two little chums Rosetta and Lavonne, that had been together almost since they were born, apart, and flounce off on her own (if you could call it going off on her own to plant herself and Rosetta right under Wyandra's nose)—she thought she might just as well. At least go up there and see if the offer was still open.

It was, Mrs. Prentice passed favorably on Gram's pleasant manner and the clean appearance she thought was Scandinavian but which was Pennsylvania Dutch. Then Gram and Lavonne moved into two rooms in the Clarendon mansion with an entrance on the back alleyway, and the old domestic establishment on Seventh South, like any field mouse's when the plow tumbles it over, passed into history. There was a moment when all might have been saved, when Mrs. Prentice reviewed the situation and almost decided against Mrs. Youngberg on account of her *embonpoint*, as Mrs. Prentice told Wyandra. But then she didn't. She didn't mention it to Mrs. Youngberg, she said. And Wyandra didn't mention her own acquaintance with the new cook. In a beauty shop, everything has to go into compartments. She did drop a word to Marie about Mrs. Prentice's momentary indecision with regard to hiring a *fleshy* cook.

"Did she think she'd eat too much or what?" Marie said. "The one I'm worried about is Lavonne."

"What do you mean?" Wyandra said.

"Well, you know how pretty she is, and always has been since the day she was born? What if she inherited—I was reading that in the movies if you want to look like you weigh a hundred pounds, you've got to weigh eighty."

"Oh, Marie, that's just silly."

"So what if Lavonne turns out to—put on fat? I mean, her beauty would get her in the movies, but if she's on the heavy side—"

"Maybe she won't be that good-looking, either," Wyandra said, glad that Rosetta was upstairs in bed in the small apartment that Marie had rented on the fifth floor, for she had seen her bite her lips and look away when Lavonne's beauty was mentioned. She went on, "The Gates girl was supposed to be so beautiful, but when people don't *know* straight up, that does something to the general effect. Or a mean disposition."

"Well, Lavonne's *smart*," Marie said. "And I wish Rosetta had half her disposition. I mean, for pleasantness. Always smiling, always affectionate. And don't that seem funny? Bonnie could be a real scowler, and Boyd Cathey with that chip on his shoulder, that cruel streak, kind of a sneer—"

"He was who you think was Lavonne's real father?"

"He was the one I *know* was her real father. I *know* that. And you would too, if you'd ever saw Yonska. But as I was saying—Boyd so mean, Bonnie crying half the time, and I personally never thought her much on looks, but here they come along and get this beautiful, sweet, smiling *doll*—"

"Maybe 'doll' is right," Wyandra said. If Rosetta had been sitting there listening, Wyandra's remarks couldn't have been more delivered for her reassurance. "And she's got a few years to go."

"Oh, she'll be a beauty," Marie said, "you mark my words. If size don't stand in the way."

"Not to change the subject," Wyandra said. "But can you believe that *rats* would be strong enough to lift the lids off the garbage cans down by Ladies? I saw old Dr. Farr, the chiropractor, out in the hall this morning and she swears that's what they do, she says the shirt lady saw them!"

"Rats?" Marie said in horror.

"But whoever heard of such a thing? Dr. Farr said she heard a noise and looked out, the shirt lady *saw* them just as they nosed the lid up and tumbled it off. Not during the daytime, they're only out in the open at night, when everybody's in bed and just those little dim hall lights are burning. During the day they hide somewhere, I guess. But at night they gather around the garbage cans—" There were two of these to a floor, both down at the end by the toilets.

"Oh, my God," Marie said.

After that she had a good (not poor and feeble, as before) excuse for her escort to bring her clear upstairs rather than saying goodnight in the foyer by the locked elevator cage. Had they met anybody on the long, dark flights of stairs covered with old brown linoleum and edged with strips of metal, she would have laughingly explained that her escort was going to protect her from the rats. They never saw either, though, people *or* rats, at one or two in the morning, sometimes even later. But of course their shoes made a clatter, Marie's high heels especially, try as you would you couldn't come up those steep steps softly unless you took your shoes off, and she wouldn't do a gypsy thing like that, so the rats were warned. People too, if any lurked about, could shrink back into the darkness.

If her escort had never escorted her before (which was generally the case), Marie would mention the fact of the rats standing on each other's shoulders so as to push off the garbage can lids—galvanized iron, mind you—and the men would make various remarks. "Quit your kidding." "Come on now." "I wouldn't put it past 'em." "I'm from Missouri." Even if she didn't mention it, in the back of her mind, all the way upstairs, she would think of *them* squeaking and chattering, their dark long shapes, as she put the key in the lock and turned it and tiptoed in, groping for the center where the bare bulb hung down from the high ceiling. Breath stopped, rising neck hairs, hot-flash panic, styptic chill... But the light would come on... old chairs, oilcloth-covered table... no rat in the sugar bowl, tail and all... no sprung rat-trap by the washstand.

"Come on in," she would say. "But just for a little while. I'll put the coffee on."

Maybe the escort would still be standing out in the hall, out by the railing, gripping onto it, staring from the tier where he was across empty space to the dimly lit tall, balconied floors stacked opposite, one above the other. "Golly gee—" Some people can't stand looking way down from a high-up place. "How far to the bottom?"

Through measureless depths of darkness.

"This here's the top floor—"

"I hope you don't walk in your sleep?"

Chapter Forty-eight

✳

Rosetta would be perfectly safe at the time, sleeping at Wyandra's. That wasn't what Marie had in mind, she never *thought* of such a thing when she moved in, she often told Wyandra so, and Wyandra believed her, but really if it wasn't too big of a bother—? Rosetta could run home in the morning and fix her own bowl of cornflakes.

Oh, for goodness' sake, Wyandra said. No bother, a dear little girl asleep on the parlor couch while she read under the floor lamp. It was nice. Company. She didn't mind in the least, and what was breakfast to get? Nothing. A piece of toast, a cup of cocoa, maybe an egg, an orange. What was combing the child's hair, seeing she washed her face? No bother at all. And after school—she might as well wait in the shop for Marie to come home from work, or wait in the Alfonces' apartment (it would always be that to Wyandra, though she lived there alone), not wait in those closed-in rooms upstairs all by herself.

And if Marie was going to be late, Rosetta might as well eat a bite of supper. Why not? And on Friday night or Saturday, when Marie was *sure* to be late and Rosetta didn't have to go to school the next day and Wyandra would probably go anyway, what bother was it to take her along to see *The Sorrows of Satan* or *Why Girls Leave Home*, buying a few chocolate creams to eat in the show along the way? None whatsoever! Walk around and look in the store windows beforehand, breathe the fresh air? What she was doing was *herself* a favor, Wyandra said.

And so Rosetta was hardly ever "home." She was with Wyandra. Marie came and went. Any escort that had acted fresh during the evening, she said, she never let accompany her to her own door. Them she left abruptly downstairs at the entrance and ran upstairs by herself, so out of breath and scared when she got up to 525 that she could hardly get the key in the lock. That was her policy. But if they acted like gentlemen, they got treated like gentlemen. Especially in winter when the radiators were turned off but in comparison with the freezing weather outside, the place would feel cozy and warm. Then, wasn't it homelike! The gas ring burning blue, the coffee pot boiling, the memory of snow coming down outside. Just the memory, for the only windows in both rooms opened on the hallway, and anyway didn't open because they were painted shut, and anyway couldn't have been seen *out* of, they were opaque pebbled glass. Would it had been always winter!

Homelikeness in summer was detrimental. Then, stay out late, forever if possible. Hot-blast hot-press streets cool down, cold water ripples, fresh evening breezes eddy down. Sometimes they lock the massive gates on the South Temple side of the Temple wall, sometimes not. If not, it's a good place to invite company, except the grass stays damp from daily watering and juicy from constant cutting and will stain white shoes, and can't be sat or lain down on. But there are places to sit, the rim around the basin with the spout of water in the middle, the cool flight of steps leading up to the front door of the Temple. Sometimes a guest will act leery, like they will ask about human sacrifices and if young girls haven't been dragged gagged and bound into this very building and done violence to by prominent old men wanting to renew their vitality, and if there aren't babies buried under the roses and flower beds…All that makes a good topic of conversation if there's not much else of interest.

"WYANDRA, PLEASE BELIEVE ME. I would no more have moved up here with the thought in mind of having you watch after Rosetta than fly to the moon!"

"I know that, Marie. But don't worry about it, she's no trouble at all."

"TELL ME THE TRUTH NOW, Mrs. Youngberg. Are you sorry you took the job?"

"Well, I'll tell you, Wyandra. I am and I'm not." She certainly had everything to *do* with there, she said, every pot and pan under the sun, pure copper, and Mrs. Prentice wasn't even mean about wanting to keep it polished. Wash it, dry it, hang it up on the big hooks overhead, let it get dark if it wanted, Mrs. Prentice paid no attention. The same with blacking the stove the size of a small locomotive, two ovens, eight lids, nickel trimming, never seemed to look at it. The sink the same. The big table with the stained marble top could still be stacked with the dirty breakfast dishes at nine o'clock when she came down to give her orders, it wouldn't matter. But run out of a pound of lard too fast, a pint of cream, bananas or a piece of kippered salmon and the woman's hackles would rise. A glass of marmalade. A package of cocoanut. She couldn't stand waste, she said. Waste not, want not. And just because Mr. Loomis kept the bin full of coal and basket full of kindling didn't mean the fire had to blaze continuously like the fires of hell.

Mrs. Prentice ordered the groceries. She bought the potatoes, the onions, the apples, peaches, pears and walnuts off the man from Bountiful and his little son. She stood right there tabulating while the grocery boy, the butcher boy, the watercress lady put their stuff on the table. Anything in the line of food, drink or staple goods she added up to the penny. Stood by while it was stored, unlocked the one end of the pantry where luxuries went such as tinned asparagus, the thick cream-colored spears, slabs of Swiss chocolate, Mr. Prentice's plum cordial, canned green turtle soup, marron puree, pineapple, tiny oysters and such as that, then locked it up again. Anything wanted from there, call Mrs. Prentice, she would come open it, she was always home, or nearly always. The daughter Birdelle the same, hanging around the house. They had no life as far as Gram could see. Clothes to wear, a limousine to ride in anywhere they wanted to go, money in the bank, able-bodied, hear, see anything in the world! But all they wanted to do was lay around home.

What did they do all day? Saved and conserved. When the cleaner came around, Mrs. Prentice seldom sent anything: "Cleaners wear things out." She saved old letters to write on. She bought a second-hand law library so as not to have to consult their lawyer a bit more than necessary. She read books from the library. She did the tedious work of picking apart the old dresses the dressmaker would make over when she came and stayed during the month of October. She forbade Inez using the new electrical vacuum apparatus on the carpets more than once a week, the suction would wear them out. She pulled down shades where the sun shone in, it would fade the carpet. The tea tray Mrs. Youngberg took up to her big shadowy bedroom had graham crackers on the cake plate, the chess pies Mr. Prentice loved so well contained too many expensive ingredients to be baked very often. Graham crackers, mind you. Birdelle was usually at the door to take the tray. Mrs. Prentice often had a headache and would be resting on the bedroom lounge.

"Thank you, Cook."

Gram didn't know if she cared for being called "Cook." But it wasn't a hard place to work, Inez didn't think so either. Keep out of sight so seeing you wouldn't remind them of something they wanted you to do to better earn your wages, make the soap last and the cake of Bon Ami, hang onto the scrub rags, don't move anything an inch from the exact spot it had dug its casters down into, protect the table from water stains, use the vase with the chipped rim or the one with the handle off, don't turn on an electric light if you can grope your way in darkness, be saving of hot water and everything will be perfect. You didn't have a bad job at all. They wouldn't give you a word of praise for fear you might get conceited and slack off or want more money, and they found fault for the same reason, but they didn't mean it, you could tell that. They weren't mean, just stingy, and not like some people, stingy to others but generous to themselves (there were people like that). No, the stinginess went all the way, *they* went without too. Mr. Prentice was said to have taken up golf at one time but only went three rounds. You could drive too many balls into the rough, it was too hard to find them, they were too expensive.

Mrs. Prentice and Birdelle would sit upstairs in Mrs. Prentice's bedroom, in the alcove hung with curtains more than a quarter century old, like all the rest of the curtains in the house, and drink the tea, nibble on the graham crackers and chat. Mrs. Prentice told Wyandra that since Birdelle left that awful Body Builder husband of hers and came home from California and filed for a divorce, she was just a different person. So cooperative, so much more what a daughter should be, she realized the best place on earth was Home Sweet Home. Be it ever so humble. And that her best friend was her mother. Now Mrs. Prentice could really converse with her, and oh, how nice that was. She really took an interest, not like she used to be, so Mrs. Prentice told her about Miss Izard and the old days with Cousin Virginia. Of course she had told her all that before, but now she really *listened*. And at last she sympathized with what her mother had gone through, enduring the painful condition of being a poor young relation with only the quarterly pittance from a few hundred thousands in municipal bonds to spend on herself, in a household where...

"AND I CAN SEE HER point," Wyandra said. "Because from what she says, that Cousin Virginia must have been *so rich*—well, I guess she had a man just to go with her and handle money, like a *walking purse*! Any money transaction, such as buying an ice cream cone, a diamond broach or bunch of violets, this man would handle. Mrs. Prentice said he wore a derby, those riding pants that bulge out at the sides, and canvas leggings. And then there was Miss Izard. But you heard all that!"

"Tell me again," Rosetta begged, crawling around on the floor of the beauty shop picking up hairpins with a magnet while Wyandra stuffed towels in the laundry bag when the day was done.

"There's nothing much to tell except that all rich people have servants. That's the test. Not jewelry. Not big houses. Not an automobile. No *thing* at all that doesn't live and breathe. Nothing counts but human people you can boss around, take up their time and interfere with, wind up and set to running like a clock. Like J. P. Morgan's servants over in London. The paper says he hasn't been to his house over there in years, but yet every night they turn his bed down, lay out reading matter, set a glass of warm milk on his bedside table, just like he was coming home from a party down the street instead of being five thousand miles away in New York, or wherever he is, with his big red ugly nose. But whether," she said, "whether he's got anything to equal what Mrs. Prentice's Cousin Virginia had, a *paymaster* and a *personal artist*, I just don't know."

"Miss Izard and Mr. Thomas," Rosetta said eagerly.

"That's right. Mr. Thomas in the derby and those riding pants that bulge out at the sides and canvas leggings—"

"Paying for what Cousin Virginia bought. An ice cream cone—"

"A diamond ring—"

"A puppy—"

"Laying out the greenbacks. Counting the change."

They both laughed with delight.

"Tell what Miss Izard did," Rosetta begged.

"Nothing! only paint and draw Cousin Virginia, every day, in whatever she thought she might want to wear that night so she shouldn't have to try the different outfits on and get all tired out before the evening started. Miss Izard would show how the colors went together. And whether the different jewelry would look good, which of course she knew by heart, drawing it every day like she did, the finger rings, the pearls and stomacher, the diamond dog collar—"

"—so Cousin Virginia could judge how she would look. But she really couldn't, could she? Because Miss Izard always drew her prettier than she was. But yet she thought she looked like that!"

"And Mrs. Prentice, that was still a girl then, a poor relation with only her measly hundred thousands, not millions, an orphan girl living in the place, she was told to help Miss Izard, to lay out these ensembles (the two French maids were busy with other jobs), and then she had to put them on and stand still so Miss Izard could draw the folds right and everything. And stand and stand and stand—"

"And she just *hated* that!"

"She felt *demeaned*."

"She will never get over it as long as she lives!"

"The hurt, the humiliation—"

"She had to do other things, too. Keep records with Miss Izard. Show where people sat at dinners and luncheon parties, what they ate and what the dishes was, and the flowers in the vases—and about the wine—"

"And *she* wasn't even invited."

"That was the worst. Only for family parties."

"Was it any wonder that she was scarred for life? even though she didn't have to peel potatoes, scrub, do the washing or polish floors! Living with millionaire relations and being treated like a dog?"

Wyandra and Rosetta would pretend to be very serious about all this, Mrs. Prentice's terrible experiences of having to stand and pose for Cousin Virginia's fashion secretary in a beautiful dress with a big ruby necklace on that used to belong to Marie Antoinette, or square-cut emeralds, the lightest of which weighed twenty carats, with a long sable coat lined with white satin brocade and lace frills over her arm. Or having to dip an ostrich-feather pen in a gold inkwell and write on vellum catalogues and lists of utmost luxuries! Was it really any wonder? And Mr. Prentice the same where *he* was, a poor young relation amongst the rich. When they got married with barely a million dollars between them, and only his measly job paying whatever measly thousands it paid per year plus expenses, was it any wonder they moved as far away as they could from those awful *reminders*? the scenes of their misery and degradation, and that they would never return? That they haggled, quibbled, saved and conserved? Lived like beggars with only a cook, housemaid and combination gardener and chauffeur in a Salt Lake City (*Salt Lake City*) house on a corner lot only a quarter of a city block in size, with only one elevator, three marble bathrooms and no ballroom? So that never again, never *never* again, would they find themselves in the terrible position of having to accept charity!

After allowing the echoes as from some operatic extravaganza to die away, Rosetta still said, always as if for the first time, "But why did they hang around like that? They had lots of money!"

"Yes," Wyandra said, "in comparison with *us*. But not in comparison with this Cousin Virginia, with too much money even to *estimate*. It's all how you look at things." She pushed the chair in under the table in what was still and would always be Albert's alcove, with a quick look around to see that everything was tidy for tomorrow, and turned out the lights. "You see, honey," she added as they walked down the dim hallway to the apartment, "everything in this life is really just *in comparison*."

"Like we're *rich* in comparison with the Little Match Girl and beggars and hoboes!" Rosetta had not actually encountered any of these on the clean, wide streets of Salt Lake City, but she knew they existed, like the beggars at the palace gate in *Kismet* with the flies crawling in the corners of their eyes, the hobo in rags who stole the apple pie cooling on Aunt Marilla's windowsill in *Anne of Green Gables*, the terrible-looking bunch of tattered scarecrows in *Orphans of the Storm*. "But we're poor," she went on, "in comparison with Mrs. Prentice. So what I want to know, why doesn't she use *us* in comparison instead of Cousin Virginia?"

"It'd be easier," Wyandra said, turning up and then lowering the gas flame under the hash in the old cast-iron frying pan that had nestled in the coals of buffalo-chip fires long ago on the plains (it had belonged to Lucitie's mother) and starting to set the table. "But I guess it's just human nature to compare yourself with them *above* rather than them *below*."

"But how can anyone living in the best place in town imagine—? Lavonne says Gram says their *piano* alone cost six thousand dollars! How can they be *poor*?"

"The mind," Wyandra said gently. She tapped her forehead. "Everything's right there to make or break you. But you were saying—about Lavonne—Why doesn't she come home with you sometimes? Since you're not supposed to go up to the Prentices' and play?"

Rosetta looked away and swallowed. "Lavonne don't like me anymore," she said.

"The mind, the mind—" Wyandra said.

"She don't! She's got a new friend now named Florence. They walk to school. Sometimes they run ahead or sometimes walk real slow in back of me. They tell secrets. But I don't care!" Rosetta added fiercely.

"I TELL YOU IT'S PATHETIC," Wyandra said, "the way those two little girls that have been together since they were babies all of a sudden got this rift. I'm sure it's because of you and Gram. Your quarrel and everything."

"What quarrel?" Marie said.

"Well, what do you want to call it? You haven't seen each other since she took that job. Rosetta's not supposed to go there, Mrs. Prentice doesn't want strange children running through the yard. Poor little thing *did* wait on the corner and they walked to school together, but now—Lavonne's got a new chum—"

"Is that my fault? It's only natural. A new neighborhood—"

"If Lavonne could just come down and stay all night, like on a Friday or Saturday when we go to the show! But Gram's pride is hurt and she won't let her—"

"This ought to be a lesson to Rosetta not to put all her eggs in one basket," Marie said. "I'm going to talk to her. *She* needs a new chum, too!"

"Maybe you could go and see Gram—"

"Maybe she could come and see *me*," Marie said.

"You know she only has a day off every second week. She's been up here to the shop, but you're always at work—I just don't see how two old friends can break up like that."

"Not such a friend. She used to say things that would cut me to the quick. About my acquaintances, my escorts. Little cheap remarks. About where we went, what time I got in—"

"I'm sure she didn't mean any harm by it. And she was awfully good to Rosetta."

"I know she was, but I was good to *her*. I paid her plenty! Not that I begrudge— Rosetta's got to get a new chum herself," Marie said firmly.

"That's the worst of getting in a building where the policy is *no children*—"

Marie laughed. "I flirted with old Mr. Cutler," she said. "No, I didn't. What I did was make him feel sorry and gave him my word that if he let us move in, nobody would even know a child lived here."

"It's like the Pied Piper of Hamelin," Wyandra said. "When all that was left in the town was one little crippled boy that couldn't keep up with the others—"

But Wyandra was mistaken. There *was* another child living in the building. Up on five, around the corner and down the hall from Marie's apartment, in 527-8, where the opaque glass panel in the entrance (and only) door had painted on it: *New York Custom Shirt Manufacturing, Ltd.* A young child, younger than Rosetta, lived in there with her father and mother, or would again when she and her mother returned from a trip back east. The family had moved in two years before, quite openly, Mr. Cutler nor no one else would think a body five feet eight or nine inches tall and weighing a hundred and sixty-eight pounds might just be the wrapping for a tiny little girl.

BUT SUCH WAS THE CASE. Her name was Ivy Rudart. She and her mother came back the week after the fire that burnt Rosetta's school down to the ground. The fire would not have been of much significance to the Rudarts anyway, Ivy having been taken out of a school a long ways away and a long time since when cursive, and roguish arithmetic, stopped her in her tracks.

Even to Rosetta, the school fire's main importance at first (besides winding time on a different warp beam) seemed to be to demonstrate that a big pile of brick, stone and cement near to four stories high *could* burn down. The hardest, coldest things could burn, slatey blackboards, wrought-iron desk-frames bolted to the floor, vitreous door-knobs, toilets, radiators, somebody's lunch bucket, Frances E. Willard, clocks with frozen hands…Burn right up! Burn down.

Rosetta remembered the book only as she and Wyandra stood near the site the next evening. *Leatherstocking Tales.* "Teacher was reading us this book about—" She had been so happy! Ashamed of being, but happy, because the school had burned down and she could stay with Wyandra all day. But now as she gazed at the ruins piled upon Natty Bumppo, who was brave and true, and Chingachgook, his friend, and the Huron warriors…not a book, but *they* were under the ruins.

"WHAT HAVE YOU BEEN DOING with yourself all day?" Marie said, getting ready for an escort to come and pick her up and take her to the show.

"Oh, playing."

"Pretty soft, huh? No more school!"

Rosetta's heart leaped up. "Ever!"

"Of course not 'ever.' Just till the school board decides what to do with all you kids. But that won't take them long, I don't imagine. Playing what?" Marie said, looking searchingly in the glass. She pursed her lips, lifted a strand of hair.

"Oh, jacks. And I helped Wyandra."

"Well. Be careful of the banisters. Don't lean!"

"Mama—"

But this was no time to tell her about Ivy. Because even when she wasn't rushing around till the last second and had a minute to sit in her coat and hat, as now, Marie would be thinking of something else. Her eyes would be on you, "Yes," her lips would say, "yes, go on, I'm listening," but she really wasn't, there were ways to test her, and Rosetta had.

Ivy was her new best friend. When Rosetta first saw her waiting for the elevator, she thought she was a grown-up woman, and as it turned out she actually was. That is to say, in body. But in her mind a child, as Wyandra said after Rosetta brought her down to the beauty shop to meet her. "Grown up outside. In her mind a child."

But to another child, what could be better? not to be all alone in the Constitution Building anymore but to find first a footprint and then, in front of the elevator, going down to Skaggs's store for a can of milk, frisky, sociable Friday. Mrs. Rudart had wrapped the money in a piece of paper folded into a square and Ivy was clutching it and ringing for the elevator. Rosetta was attending to some business too, fetching her mother's alarm clock that didn't go off for Wyandra to look at. If she could bang it or jar it in some way, it might not have to go to Clock Repair.

They said hello. Rosetta paused at the head of the stairs.

"I always ride down," Ivy confided in a friendly tone.

"I'm just going down to the beauty shop. That's only on the next floor down."

"The *beauty shop*? What for?"

"Because Wyandra, she runs it, and she may be able to fix Mama's clock. It didn't go off this morning."

"Oh," Ivy said.

"I bet you think I'm late for school!"

Smilingly Ivy blinked her eyes as she pressed the button again, then rattled the elevator cage a little, as though to waken a sleeping beast. But Mr. Williams was no doubt out in front of the building talking to some passerby.

"But I'm not," Rosetta said. "I don't have to go on account of the fire. I guess you heard about the fire. It burned the schoolhouse down. Lafayette School."

"No," Ivy said. "Mama and me was gone to Akron. See, my grandpa died and Grandma had to move. And then my uncle—That took quite a while! But Mama finally got her rightful share."

"That's good," Rosetta said.

"How old are you?" Ivy said.

"I'm nine. How old are you?"

"Eighteen."

Far below they heard the elevator gate slam to, the mechanism whine, the cables make their slipping sound.

"Who do you doohix?" Ivy asked. "Like, a movie actor."

Rosetta thought hard, then said, "I doohix Kenneth Harlan."

Ivy gave a sigh of relief such as might be sighed by him who, playing the bravado game, has put a revolver with one bullet in the chamber to his temple, pulled the trigger and still lives.

"I doohix *Rudolph Valentino*," she said.

What *she* thought, Wyandra told Marie, was that the girl was feebleminded, and Marie wondered what kind of an element that was for Rosetta to get so thick with. But of course she would soon be back in school, if the school board ever made up its mind. Had Marie known it, even as she spoke, its mind was made up, the complicated answer to its problems was in the hands of the Tribune and the Deseret News, charts, tables and a map were about to be printed. Then they *were* printed, indeed the very next day. But you couldn't have proved it by her, Wyandra or even Rosetta, who had taken to reading Uncle Albert's newspaper (it was still called his) quite carefully since a chorus girl named Dot King was strangled in New York with her own silk stocking and the police were after the man who did it. But not carefully enough to run across the news about where the homeless population of Lafayette School were to fetch up on the following Monday to continue the education that had been so rudely interrupted. It took Mr. Williams, with nothing better to do than run the elevator, gab and go through the paper with a fine-tooth comb, to do that. And had Rosetta known then about the ancient custom of certain old kings to kill the messenger who brought them bad news, she would not have thought it a bad thing at all.

Some grades went here, some there. Mr. Williams doubled the paper back and showed Wyandra. Charts, tables, a map...He had it all figured out. Grade four, *everybody from A through K*, Whitney Hall, basement room C, one p.m. to six p.m., Monday through Friday.

Rosetta Kinnavy. *K*.

Grade four, *everybody from L to Z*, Whitney Hall, basement room C, eight a.m. to one p.m., Tuesday through Saturday.

Lavonne Locket. *L*.

It might be even better, Wyandra said, taking Rosetta up to Whitney Hall on the avenues that nobody had ever heard of until then and whose reason for existing except to accommodate the burned-down school's rudderless fourth grade nobody ever found out. Wyandra took Rosetta past it the Sunday before so she would know where to go. But imagine! school! one in the afternoon till six.

ROSETTA KNEW LAVONNE WOULD BE in the morning class, not in hers, but yet not to see her familiar blonde curls that Gram always either put up on rags the night before or curled with the curling iron in the morning, somewhere in the room, was like looking up at the Temple and not seeing the Angel Moroni. But then the teacher, a new teacher never seen on earth before, Miss Littley with a cameo pin pinned on and gaps between her teeth, began to call out every person's name that ought to be there, and Rosetta when she answered hung on to her little desk with both hands as if it were hurtling through space. Which it was not, but *she* was in a way, deviated by the strange parameters of the schoolday into absolute time.

"There is surely," the poet said, "no greater wisdom than well to mark the Beginnings and Onsets of things." And that year of going to school in a basement room with no light coming in from outside because of the bushes crowded around the windows and the ceiling light always on, the hours strange and out of joint, was a Beginning, an Onset, of an epoch so wrested into magic for Rosetta that even getting back to regular school hours again after only one little year, in a real school, and that for a long period, and graduating and going to high school and being friends again with Lavonne, none of that at all brought round old champing, snorting *time* at less than a right angle until...

Chapter Forty-nine

*

"You were the one wanted me to go visit Gram," Marie said. "Well, it's not a choice, we have to go. She phoned in an order!"

"Who did?" Wyandra said.

"Mrs. Prentice. Because the Zion Cleaning and Dye Works took down her draperies in that big front room and took them away and cleaned them and the solvent ruined all the ones that hung in that round bay. That's what Mrs. Prentice says. They say not. They were ready to fall to pieces anyway. But rather than have her sue them, they're going to pay. So our outfit got the job to make new drapes, if we can ever suit the woman with material."

"So when are you going up there? You can sneak in the kitchen and surprise Gram," Wyandra said.

"That I don't know," Marie said. "If nothing suits Mrs. Prentice that we got *here*, and we got to send *back east*...And of course Zion's Cleaning has got to agree as to price. There's more conferences going on about a little thing like that than France and Germany combined after the war."

They *did* have to send back east, and then Mrs. Prentice's daughter Birdelle wanted a different gathering arrangement to the folds (at no extra cost), new trimming had to be picked out, the old no longer being manufactured, and a battle fought over who was to keep the old draperies (Mrs. Prentice won). Many weeks therefore passed before Marie stepped foot in the old mansion up on Brigham Street that she almost—almost—especially according to Wyandra, family mythologist—came to own herself! Of course that was an exaggeration. As she told the others at Deseret Upholstery while they worked on the sixteen-foot panels, at one time her husband's family stood to inherit that very place—"and you'd be making these for *me*!"

"So who's the easy-to-please-in-a-pig's-eye lady we're making these for, your cousin?" the hemstitcher said.

"No. Mrs. Prentice. They're no relation to the original owners. They just bought the house from the heirs."

Three from Deseret Upholstery went to make the delivery, Marie, Leona and Mr. Fagergren. He drove the truck and also had to climb the stepladder with the heavy drapes. They really should have taken two men and one woman or even no women, it was a bigger job than they bargained for. And Leona should never have mentioned the finial missing from the end of one of the ornate brass curtain poles. What did it matter? But to show off in front of Mr. Prentice, who had let them in (Mr. Fagergren didn't know what *else* would be the purpose), Leona approached the open doorway into the library where, nervously perched on the arm of a chair, the master of the house was keeping an eye on the proceedings, and asked him where the knob could be. It seemed to startle him greatly to be asked such a question. He got up quickly and came out into the drawing room and stood at the foot of the rickety stepladder.

"See, like that one up there," Leona said at his shoulder, pointing. "Maybe Mrs. Prentice would know where it was."

"Well, she is resting," Mr. Prentice said. "And so is my daughter."

"The place where it should go won't really show much," Marie said, tipping back her head to look at herself in the large mirror over the fireplace as she steadied the tall, rickety ladder with Mr. Fagergren on the second step from the top.

"Won't show at *all* once this goods gets squeezed up in there," Mr. Fagergren said, casting down a dirty look over his shoulder at Leona.

"Oh, we want it properly done," Mr. Prentice said. "Mrs. Prentice wouldn't be a bit satisfied if it wasn't properly *done*."

"Maybe someone *else* would know," Leona said.

"I daresay one might try the box room," Mr. Prentice said.

"That's a new one on me," Leona said, using on the speaker, whom she thought a person of immense wealth because he lived here surrounded by every luxury, including a tea wagon which she glimpsed in the dining room, the dulcet tones generally reserved for gentlemen she thought might be "serious."

"This—this knob or whatever it is—is missing?" Mr. Prentice said uneasily, peering up at Mr. Fagergren's worn heels on the ladder rung.

"Oh, yes, it's missing, no doubt about that," Leona said.

"Not changing the subject," Marie said, hoping to do that very thing, "but your *cook* was my husband's *aunt* on his mother's side."

Mr. Prentice turned his nervous gaze upon her like a deaf person intending to ask for something in writing.

"And after he—he worked for the railroad and—passed away in an accident—why, I and my little girl boarded with her. Mrs. Youngberg. So I was thinking when we get through here, if you don't mind, I'd like to step in the kitchen and say hello?" There, the die was cast, she was going to make the first move to make up with Gram, even if the rift wasn't her fault. Wyandra would be pleased, and now that she had done it Marie was too.

"What is this box room?" Leona asked.

"It's the—Up on the third floor. I'll get Inez." He started purposefully for the door, then stopped. "No, she's having her teeth pulled today and that's why I—why Mrs.

Prentice—" Plainer than any words, his look as he lingered by the door said that his orders had been not to leave the upholstery people alone on the premises to pick up something and walk off with it that they might not even miss for weeks, or handle things, the statues, the music box, the velvet-lined work basket too handsome to use—

"Why can't *I* go, to try and find it?" Leona said.

"Why don't we just forget it?" Mr. Fagergren said, turning his head to send her an angry look. "The thing will never be seen!"

"Oh, Mrs. Prentice wouldn't like it if it wasn't properly *done*," Mr. Prentice said nervously.

"Where did you say this box room was?" Leona said.

"On the third floor," Mr. Prentice said. "There's an elevator, but sometimes the door doesn't open. And Mrs. Prentice doesn't like people to—Anyway. It's for private use. So perhaps this lady had better take the stairs. They're down at the end of the hall."

"I know, I noticed as we come in. Be back in a jiffy," Leona said gaily, but was just starting out the wide doorway when Mr. Fagergren called to her to stop where she was.

"Come back here!" he said. "Let Marie go."

"Why?"

"Because you're the biggest, that's why. And I need somebody *solid* down there holding this damn ladder!"

Leona turned around, ready with a somewhat sharp rejoinder, when she noticed how white his face looked up near the ornate ceiling and hurried back, pushed Marie aside and took hold of his perch. "If you're dizzy or anything, you come down, no job's worth a broken neck," she said.

"No, I'm fine," he said. "I just don't want no nonsense." Then, "Marie, let loose and run on up to that storage room or whatever it is and let Mrs. Buttinsky here hold the ladder."

"Third floor," Mr. Prentice said. "Door farthest from the head of the stairs. You can't miss it. Window—Light switch by the door—"

And thus it was that Marie scampered up the stairs of wealth, past the newel posts with the bronze figures in blowing garments welded to them and garlands of bronze thrown over their heads like a jump rope punctuated with flame-shaped electric light bulbs, the stair treads wide and thick with carpeting, all the richness of half the inside of the house laid out before and beneath her when she turned on the landing and glanced back. And the doors along the wide hall, millionaires' doors with millionaires' things behind them, things never seen in real life, a chaise longue, a pier glass, curtains around the bed, skirts around the dresser, a tea wagon, a real fireplace. And once upon a time there was no time and it was then that...

I SAW MAVIS, I REMEMBER her, they call them albinos, that is what the white worms must be under a rock, but yet she was as beautiful as pure white flowers of any description, or snow coming down. White eyelashes resting on her cheeks as she slept *under this very roof*, in one of these bedrooms…that one, maybe…

Like ladies taking their nap that mustn't be disturbed. Only Mavis's wasn't a nap, it was like Sleeping Beauty, they brought her home from Italy? asleep. Everyone spoiled her…

And Mr. Clarendon, didn't he buy her everything? A muff, dolls with beautiful eyes that shut and opened, but Mavis's eyes never opened, and then…*Did* I see her? *Do* I remember? Or did Wyandra telling her stories make me think I—? All these paintings, so many they hung on walls where they couldn't even be seen. And statues—where nobody but the family would ever—Mr. Prentice said at the end of the hall, and here was a door. Then up to the third floor, carpets on these steps too, they wouldn't want to hear the hooves of servants clattering up and down. But ugly carpet, brown carpet, whatever was for servants was ugly, their bedrooms small, low, cots hard and narrow, single, for the inconvenience of breeding in them, and matting on the floor, white plastered walls without wallpaper or even a coat of kalsomine, a washstand, bowl and pitcher, slop jar. One of these cells must be where Inez slept, the hired girl who wasn't there to answer the door today because she was having a lovely day off having every tooth in her head pulled out—! And oh, wasn't life the meanest thing anybody could have wished on them? But I wouldn't of missed a minute of it—And this must be the storage room, "box room," millionaires apparently called them. With the light switch—here.

Only it wouldn't click on. Marie flicked it again. No, maybe it had been turned off at the bulb hanging on a chain in the center of the room. She tiptoed there. But that wouldn't turn on either. No matter, her eyes were enough adjusted to the cold north light coming in through the small fan-shaped window that came clear down to the floor. And oh, would you look at all this…stuff. Around the walls were cabinets with doors, locked doors locked up with padlocks. Somebody would have to carry a key ring with eight pounds of keys on it to open the trunks too, huge trunks, some stood on end, with stickers, Paris, London, H.M.S. Berengaria, boxes, not everything was locked up, bundles of stuff, baskets, and there indeed stood a sheaf of old curtain rods, brass but not like the ones downstairs, and no ornaments on their ends that Marie could see. Old hats, hat boxes, chests, tables, and oh, if Rosetta and Lavonne was ever turned loose here, wouldn't they have a time, for there was a doll buggy with a little umbrella hanging over it, and a real little iron stove and a sewing machine—look at that—probably really sewed. The kids would go out of their minds! But there was a wooden chest with the lid half off. Dust, moth balls, crammed with—Maybe down amongst the—rusty silk—Where would anyone look for a finial like the end of a spear in a performance at the Salt Lake Theater? A knob with a point on it—brass—She lifted off a rotting lampshade, set it aside, and then randomly, for she had no hope of finding it, poked down into a bundle of scraps—oh, the doll clothes they could make!—old velvet, fur, what funny names they used to have for things, pelisse, mantles, all this lovely—But as she dabbled in it, from the downy depths something came alive, turned lithe and living, had a beady eye, whatever it was and she knew what it was, leaped out, caught, clamped onto and pierced her finger to the bone—

"My God, a rat!" Running, she tried to shake it loose. It hung twisting in the air, teeth like a vise of sharp nails, jaws clamped shut—"Leave go, leave go!" It wouldn't, she ran on, shaking it, down the attic steps, out into the wide second-floor hall, gibbering, yipping—"Jesus! Help! Leona!" It felt like a cat hanging onto her, big as a cat or dog dangling from her finger, twisting and threshing in the air. Doors opened—a woman at one door—another in lavender silk—

"What is the meaning of this?"

They ran to the central hall, Mr. Prentice, Leona...Running, Marie held her hand out, the rat a-dangle, the weight, the live, curling, moving weight—

"Hit it against the railing!"

"Bang it! Hit it! Hit it! Bash its head!"

She gibbered something, stopped halfway to hit, bang and swat it against the balustrade, its hard bullet head, its curling body with a whiplash tail, till it let loose and tumbled, fell, leaped up, a living devil, gone so fast, even with a fractured skull they know up from down, it knew, streaked up, or like the demons do they just disappear?

The thing that I have feared has come upon me.

You would suppose the finger lacerated, but no, two wounds hardly bigger than would be caused by a darning needle run in one side and out the other. And hardly any blood, though you would have thought the finger would drip like a faucet. Thank heaven it didn't! those beautiful carpets.

Mrs. Prentice was very much annoyed and got to the bottom of what was going on, Mr. Prentice had no business sending the drapery woman upstairs. The finial was off the end of the curtain pole because it had always been off since they moved in the house and was never noticed, and after this she would take it very kindly for him not to take things upon himself that he had no business—Not that she thought it was a rat at all.

But they saw it, they all saw it, and Marie would certainly know if she had a rat jump up and bite her! Look at the marks, just look at the *marks*. A sharp nail could have done it, the hook on a curtain stretcher—

But they *saw* it!

If someone comes screaming a rat! a rat! you can imagine anything. *They* didn't see it.

"Did you see it, a rat hanging onto this woman's finger?"

Birdelle didn't. Of course it's terrible to be woken up out of a sound sleep.

Mrs. Prentice didn't know what the world was coming to. People wandering around the house.

Gram didn't hear anything. She was out on the back porch sitting where the spring breeze came in through the screen, cracking black walnuts. That was a terrible job Lavonne promised to do, but she wasn't home from school yet and might stop at Florence's.

Just those two little wounds and only a drop or two of blood on the handkerchief Marie wrapped around it. She had to laugh, she told Wyandra. Here she was so scared of the rats that ran around the halls of the Constitution Building at night, strong enough to lift the lids right off the garbage cans. And never thinking that in a *millionaire's* house, in broad daylight—!

Whap! Swat! It took some force to make the thing let go. And then it was gone.

Bit by a millionaire rat. She laughed. She woke up screaming that night, could see it as plain as anything—big thing, brownish-gray color, short tail and ears, hard tapering skull you could hardly crush with a hammer, fierce, cunning…She sat up shaking, covered with sweat, breathing in gasps, "God, oh, God."

But it was funny in the daytime.

After being so scared of *poor* rats…poverty-stricken rats…scurrying…scrabbling… lifting off lids…

No blood, a drop or two. Its teeth were so sharp, it writhed so heavy, you'd have thought it would have bit the end of her finger off. No damage, two little marks. But they felt hot as fire, like nipped by a devil. They itched. The end of her finger itched till she could have clawed the skin off. At work she would put her finger in her mouth to try to scratch it with her teeth.

The weather was warm. Wasn't it very warm for the end of April? Wasn't it hot? She was hot. She felt like she was burning up. Oh, wouldn't it be nice when Saltair opened up, the open-air ballroom, riding out there with a lovely escort in the open-air cars…

She would have to feel more like herself before *that* happened, though. The way she felt now she couldn't dance even a waltz clear through. Tired. Out of breath. Hot. She never seemed to cool off. Shiver, out at night with an escort, walking to the Chinese restaurant over on State Street, teeth would chatter. But burning in the marrow of her bones.

The well-marked rash her friend Evelyn diagnosed as some kind of chicken pox. But chicken pox, his foot, Mr. Fagergren said, that there was poison ivy. Leona thought it could be flea bites from a dog, but Marie hadn't been petting any dogs. Wyandra didn't like the looks of it. She didn't like Marie looking like she did either, sunken eyes, a red spot in each cheek, or turning down the chance for a little recreation at the vaudeville or anywhere. She didn't even want to see *Smilin' Through*. And she wasn't eating. So Wyandra made her stay all night with her and Rosetta one night. And then not go to work one day, or possibly two or three till her strength was built up. Just lie there and rest, sleep in the daytime for once, nothing to disturb her except her dream about the rat.

Sometimes it wasn't a dream, she would be awake but with her eyes shut, that was the scariest, when she knew she was awake and would look down and there would be the rat at the foot of the bed, and make a spring for her, her face, come lunging at her…She would swat and hit at it…try to scream but not be able to like she was gagged, and wake with a terrible start and pounding heart. For she had been asleep, it *was* a dream, though it seemed so real. The tiny wounds had healed over blackish, like dried blood under them, but that was days ago, two weeks, three. Now you could hardly see a thing.

But the fever was wasting her away. Not steady now, sometimes lit and burning, roaring through her chimneys, sometimes out, the cinders, ashes, dead. And then she would wish she was warm again. And when she was hot, wish to be cool. "Always wanting what is not," as is the lot of man. And then Herman's wife Agnes, the registered nurse who worked at Holy Rosary Hospital, came to collect the monthly payment for Alfonce's Beauty Shop, equipment and good will, and for once Wyandra was glad. Agnes was just the person she wanted to see, because she had poor Marie sick in bed in the apartment.

Agnes found the swelling in Marie's armpit, the left side, and the one along her neck under her ear, and the thin red lines like tracks leading from her hand towards the nearest group of lymphatic glands, which she didn't like the looks of at all and said Marie ought to have a doctor. One came that evening and put her in Agnes's hospital, where three days later she died of lymphangitis.

Millionaire Rat-Bite Fever!

FOR QUITE A WHILE WYANDRA was afraid someone would come to claim Rosetta, some of the Kinnavys over from the state of Washington or wherever they lived, or one of the Palmstedts, or Marie's half-sisters up in Montana, even her grandmother Hindle in Canada. It had been hard to get addresses, Wyandra was only able to send out a few notifications, but of course the news would get around and some relative would feel duty-bound…

But the summer came on and none did. Nancibel said *she* ought to take Rosetta, after all she and poor Marie were first cousins, but just having Legrand…It would be different if she had a girl, then the two little girls could play together and be companions, but with a boy and a girl, they couldn't undress in front of each other or sleep together or anything.

Wyandra didn't want to act like she wanted Rosetta. Then someone would surely come and take her away. Agnes thought of it. *They'd* take her to raise, she said, she could help with the children, except that Herman was taking charge at home. But maybe later, if they needed her. They didn't right now. But it did seem to her it was the child's *father's* people that had the obligation…

Wyandra packed up such things as were Marie's, and Mr. Cutler rented Marie's two inside rooms to Mrs. Louise Hyland, the poetess, who was said to have had a poem published in the Deseret News several years previously. Mr. Cutler wondered what was to become of the little girl, and Wyandra said she was taking her to raise. Which Mr. Cutler said was quite an obligation to take on a person's self, but Wyandra said it really wasn't, she knew the mother when she was just a little girl herself and the whole family so well, and Rosetta had been sleeping in to her place anyway for quite some time and having…a few meals, so it really wouldn't be too much of a change for either of them. And Mr. Cutler said the little girl was very fortunate and he hoped she would look back and be grateful and appreciative. Because too often, as he had reason to know, they would take and take your very *life's blood* if it came to that, and not even say thank you in return.

It was too bad about her eye, wasn't it? Cocked like that, spoiled a girl's looks, wouldn't be so bad for a boy. But perhaps it would straighten itself out someday, that sometimes happened. Cute little thing though otherwise, seen and not heard, like her mother promised she would be when they moved in. And to think, now hardly a year later that mother was dead and gone. Of what, did Wyandra say? Of getting blood poisoning from some kind of bite, Wyandra said with the tact habitual to her, not wanting to upset the old man with talk of rats, people were always complaining to him anyway, and that would just remind him. Well, it was a shame, he said. Why couldn't it have been him, that had lived his life, you might say, instead of a young woman in her prime?

AND UNDER THE RUINS OF Lafayette School lay Natty Bumppo and Chingachgook and the Huron warriors. In Whitney Hall the new school started at one p.m. *Started*, mind you. You could sleep till eleven if you wanted to, noon if you wanted, and still get there on time. Stay up till midnight if you wanted, one, two in the morning if you wanted. Not that Rosetta and Wyandra ever did. But now they didn't have to wait till Friday or Saturday night to go to the movies, they could go any night of the week, or could when it wasn't the week Agnes came to get the beauty shop payment, or when Wyandra happened to run short. And when you are a little girl and come out of school and it's dark, as it was in winter, and lights are on along Main Street, electric signs running around in patterns against the clear evening sky, you feel very grown up, like Tillie the Toiler coming down out of working in a *business office*. Time seemed to do it, cast the spell, time wound on a different warp beam as it was, the late hours of evening folding out to time that had never been seen before, unclosing like a hand. And serious morning arborized, a sparrow cheeping at noon was an entirely different proposition from cold-feathered twittering by first light.

But however it happened, one day Salt Lake was just Salt Lake, and all about was the true and actual state of things, the schoolhouse stood, Mama dressed up and waited…a day later—irised interference to the natural world! Magic bounded the vaporous air. By herself Rosetta would not have known. Wyandra supplied (having read in her youth a book called *Old St. Paul's* and another, *Balsamo the Magician*, and others too that happened at one time to fall to her hand) the facts, that there was an old church in

England called Old St. Paul's with tunnels, tombs and dungeons under it, and dark and scary cells and crypts, and vaulted spaces and a shaft of light that the Constitution Building was a *whole lot like.*

It was also like a place over in Spain, Wyandra said, the Alhambra, the name of it was, all winding stairs and passageways and central clearings where gypsies could camp and criminals hide, or for that matter anybody, or just be honest people such as Wyandra and Rosetta were, or say the Rudarts, or Dr. Farr, and keep a beauty shop or the Swedish Vice Consulate, or make violins or hair tonic or paint china, simmer stew with onions in it, or burn the toast...working people, business people, or just be old and not do anything, or write poems and fry a beefsteak or a few strips of bacon and a potato...just so long as it wasn't cabbage. Or rutabaga.

Wyandra just happened to mention those other places one night at past eleven when they came home from seeing Fatty Arbuckle, and the elevator not running after ten, they had to walk up. They usually did have to walk up (staying to see the show over), up the many flights of dark stairs with all the banisters and a newel post on each landing that if you slid down (forbidden) would catch you against a great knob. And all the railings on every floor railed the great plunge of emptiness in the middle, dark nothingness five stories tall when you started from the bottom, five stories deep when you got to the top and looked down, and protected you against it. Rosetta could have run all the way up the stairs, but it would be quite scary to get up on three or on four all by yourself in the dim dark hallways, the tiniest light bulbs burning (a red one in each toilet) while Wyandra, toiling up, looked tiny as a doll below...

Until Wyandra mentioned about the Alhambra one time, and Old St. Paul's one night when they came in and the light was out in the foyer, Rosetta never thought of the Constitution Building being *like* any other place, she hadn't even thought about *it* any more than a Christmas doll thinks about the pasteboard box it lies in, but now, helped by evening when she came from school, the building would have tunnels, tombs and secret crypts where undertakers played cribbage on a coffin lid waiting for people to die of the Black Plague, and Mr. Williams, an old soldier from terrible old wars, took you in a cage up the dark vaultage.

"Romantic" was a word Wyandra used often that seemed to mean...If put to it, Rosetta could not have said exactly. Except perhaps: not real. Or rather: better than real, such as in *Smilin' Through*, where the ghosts of the sweethearts come smilin' through this beautiful orchard all in blossom after they have died.

IVY WAS GLAD TO HEAR their building constituted far different surroundings than she ever dreamed, it made her almost imagine they were in a *movie.* She wrote a letter to Rudolph Valentino on ruled tablet paper, her mother let her have the stamp for the envelope, and she and Rosetta went down to the post-office and mailed it. They then lost track of the days but finally an answer came back, it was his picture in a brown envelope, his name written on it in cursive: Rudolph Valentino. Now if he would go that far, doesn't it seem possible that he would go farther? Rosetta had heard from Wyandra that there existed a secret ink that you could write with and the words would be invisible until you passed a candle flame before it. The heat would make the words stand out and you could read them plain. And wouldn't it be wonderful, Rosetta said, if on the back, written in invisible ink so that no one else would know a thing about it, wouldn't it be wonderful if—? Not that there probably *was* a secret message. But *maybe*. Ivy got anxious to know. And that was how it happened that Rudolph Valentino's picture went up in flames and nearly caught the cretonne tacked around the sink. Mrs. Rudart was so upset she ran down to the beauty shop and said she had a good mind to tell Mr. Cutler! It was her daughter's picture all right, but Rosetta who had put her up to trying to read a secret message with a lighted candle! That was the only time Wyandra was ever severe with Rosetta. Did she realize what could have happened? That ruffle Mrs. Rudart was talking about, yes, but a dishtowel, the Tribune, *anything* could have caught fire! and them as well! the whole building a raging furnace. It shamed her to think of it, Wyandra said. That a smart, bright, intelligent girl of almost *ten years*—! Playing with matches! like a baby. But they *weren't*, playing, Rosetta blubbered, hiccuped and explained.

And because it really *would* have been so romantic if the flame had exposed a secret message, Wyandra hugged, kissed, comforted and forgave the wrongdoer. Not only that, she put the blame on herself for telling Rosetta about invisible ink in the first place. Then Mrs. Rudart forgave them both, she was quite a nice woman, who had once been pinned to her power machine by the needle running through the end of her finger, nail, bone, right through to the wood casing. But she wouldn't let Ivy mail a second letter to Mr. Valentino. And so that love affair was broken off. And the picture that went up in smoke said on the back forever: *My love, I love you, at every moment of my life I am waiting for you…*

Chapter Fifty

*

SUMMER CAME, NO SCHOOL, YET TIME STAYED WOUND ON THE DIFFERENT WARP beam. And Wyandra did not need an optical instrument to throw a magnified image on the blank walls of the beauty shop or even the Temple walls as they went walking by it. No, she beamed them there just by her tidings, her news of wonders, of old days, of actions and affairs she knew for a fact were true history. But how can there be a true history when no living being on this earth can give truly a systematic account of even last week? No matter about last week, Wyandra tackled last year and the year before that and clear on back when there was no time, to where Rosetta's great-grandmother Louiza stopped her covered wagon down in Pioneer Park and her great-grandfather John D. Lee came along and tried to trade Louiza fresh eggs for a paisley shawl. Wyandra had tangible evidences of history: for instance, the frying pan their potatoes were frying in right this minute. That frying pan had crossed the plains! But Rosetta needed no proof.

Being young, she was not expected to contribute anything historical to their conversations, but a time or two she did, reminded by something of her and Mama's old days down on Seventh South when they lived with Gram and Lavonne. One noted event was the fist fight that was supposed to take place between Mrs. Sharon, the rowdy mother of the five rowdy Sharon kids, and Maggie Allen, who ran a punch in a factory and lived with her mother. The two women couldn't have their fist fight on a weekday because of Maggie working. But they had to go through with it *sometime* because Maggie called Mrs. Sharon a thief. So Saturday was the day they picked. Quite a few housewives and children (men still worked six days a week) gathered in the empty lot in back of Ware's Main Street Grocery. Mrs. Sharon arrived, with her round cavities between her teeth like portholes. Then here came Maggie Allen, who had big dark circles under her eyes. They faced each other in the middle of the lot. But before a blow could be struck, Maggie's knees buckled and she fainted. So the fight was called off. Some who had waited all week acted very disappointed, as if it was Dempsey going to fight Firpo and they had paid ten dollars a ticket. The children played the two combatants for weeks. ("Look! I'm Maggie Allen!" and down they would go.) But another match was never mentioned, so the two ladies must have made up.

Mrs. Sharon really did steal something, a baby buggy. But only to replace a go-cart somebody had stolen from *her* from out in front of Woolworth's. And where the *moral* came in—for that was what the fight would have been about—her go-cart wasn't worth anything, while the *buggy* she stole was beautiful cream-colored wicker lined with pink corduroy and with little round plate-glass windows on the sides and big wire wheels with rubber tires. She brought it home and painted it brown.

It depends on what you think is history.

Wyandra must have thought the fight that never came off belonged there, for she mentioned it a time or two and even spoke of someone keeling over "like Maggie Allen." And after she heard about the Indian women taking a bath at Gram's, although there was hardly anything to that—they came over to the back door from the Wild West show in the Ball Park and asked Gram if they could take a bath in the kitchen and she said yes, so they did (while Gram and Rosetta and Lavonne sat outside on the back steps), in the round galvanized-iron tub, in only one teakettle of hot water but plenty of cold from the tap, and when they got through left the kitchen so clean Gram said she wished they took a bath every day, and looked so clean themselves they looked like washed and dried brown glazed earthenware and their wet hair like black satin, parted in the middle and done in two braids—Wyandra didn't forget it but a long time afterwards said, "They must have used the bath water to scrub the floor that time…"

Chronicles are soon told, however, by the young. Soon told and seldom "bounding with magic the vaporous air." But what *Wyandra* made of history, and made of movies and old stage shows gone to before Rosetta was even born, and books she did not read so much as fatten on like honeycomb, did do that. As did time awry. And common day being overmastered by the two, Rosetta's little fancy skipped like rams.

As a consequence, what the Salt Lake Temple and the Tabernacle behind their twenty-foot-high stone walls were to their little neighbor across the intersection and half a block down Main Street would have surprised the odd, dull and monumental former and the turtle-backed latter. They were towers and ramparts, pavilions overhung the roses, flickering oranges and myrtaceous trees, the palace of a king. Absent, which was why the Temple looked uninhabited and forbidding, blinds pulled all down and its great doors shut and bolted. No one knew where the king was or when he would be coming back. But boy, if he ever did! Rosetta could just imagine.

He had probably left orders for everything to be kept up, like Little Boy Blue in the poem where he said, "And don't you go till I come" to his toys, "and don't you make any noise"—and so the palace grounds were kept picked up pretty, the statues clean of seagull droppings, citizens were let in during the daylight hours through the big gates to wander through the landscaped grounds and even provided (so they'd not rise up and be belligerent) with entertainment in the form of organ concerts, an acoustic demonstration which included dropping onto the Tabernacle floor amid a solemn hush *a common straight pin*, and a Historical Museum to go through free of charge.

This, of course, contained countless objects, such as a pair of pillowcases the Prophet Joseph Smith's head had rested upon with the words *Good Morning* embroidered on one and *Good Night* on the other; guns, swords, and things men need to equip and outfit themselves with, ugly and made out of wood and iron, but practical for daily life; also a dog-hair cloak, bells and enlargements. When Rosetta realized that the old dried skeletal bones covered with shriveled hide and still with teeth and dirty, horsehair-looking wispy hair in the glass case was a *real person*, dead, buried in the ground, dug up out of a *grave*, it gave her a scare such as if a skeleton's hand suddenly reached out of darkness and touched her on the shoulder. She left in a hurry, only to come back another day out of fearful fascination, first standing some distance away, then closer, then familiarity almost bred contempt of the dead and mummified Mound Builder circa 8000 B.C., as the placard on the end of the case said he was.

Across the street from the King's Palace stood the most famous hotel in the then known world, the Hotel Utah. Of pure white marble, its steep walls of French doors, balconies and awnings soared up twelve or fifteen stories to a roof-garden with latticed pergolas, bunches of flowers, a jazz band in tuxedos...Now say for the sake of argument that you resided half a block from a place like that, as well as nearly next door to the royal palace. The impact on you by whatever Paris, London or New York would have to offer, if in later life you ever went to any of those world centers, would really be minimal. You would be exhausted by grandeur before you ever got started, almost disgusted with it.

Almost disgusted with History too, so plentiful and hardly a block away: the house of the twenty gables, a homemade lion over the portico, the dwelling called the Beehive House, with the small adobe office of Brigham Young nestling between. *Brigham Young* being along the lines of George Washington for fame, or Edison, or Herod, or Eli Whitney, if ever in later life you got to see any of the landmarks connected with those individuals, would your eyes bug out and your mouth hang open? Hardly!

IN THAT SMALL OFFICE NESTLED between the two big houses, Wyandra said, she would bet that many a time Rosetta's own great-grandfather John D. Lee had sat talking as big as life with Brigham Young. She said that Lucitie had said that at one time Hindle's and her father John D. Lee was as prominent as any man in the valley. A man of means, too, and then through no fault of his own to be so disgraced! and finally stood up and executed. Wyandra told Rosetta about all this so she wouldn't hear it somewhere else sometime and feel bad for being related to someone such a thing had happened to. She told her about the Mountain Meadows massacre and the whole thing, but it was a little hard to keep the details fixed in mind. Except that it was awful, her great-grandfather was roped in by his religion, and those were the days that try men's souls. But as Wyandra said, a great-grandfather hardly seemed related at all really, the blood was so diluted, and especially when there were thirteen great-grandmothers in the picture, so Rosetta shouldn't feel cast shame upon in any way because he was shot at sunrise.

His prominence, though…She *did* descend from a prominent man, and *that* she should remember, that part, Wyandra said, when he was well-to-do and came to Conference and went to the Social Hall, another place of eminence around the corner, where one of the dances they danced was, a man would sashay *two* partners around the floor instead of one so everybody would get their turn, both "new" wives and "old."

And at the Salt Lake Theater…everything was in perfect condition, lamps burnished and filled with coal oil, wicks trimmed; gold-leaf edges on the painted panels; curtain a still wet-looking masterpiece. That was in those times. *Now* as Rosetta approached, she saw papers blowing across the outside steps, a peeled and marauded old building, old tattered show-bills flapping on the outside walls and beside the wide double doorway open only a crack, and a sign that said *Free Admission*. At least on that one cold, gray winter afternoon for the lecture on Diseases of the Human Organism that Rosetta went to, happening to pass by at the opportune moment, there was no charge. She groped her way up to a box and in through the draped doorway, took a seat in a dusty armchair covered with worn old velvet, and leaned forward and rested her arms on the box's rubbed velvet rim. The other dozen or so persons of the audience could have sat as grandly as she was sitting had they wanted, instead of here and there on the main floor. The lecturer with a table nearby full of brown bottles of medicine stood in the middle of the stage against a backdrop like a dim and foggy dream of fences, houses, a lamppost on the corner…

Wyandra hoped Rosetta didn't hurt the lecturer's feelings, leaving from a box like that after a few minutes because of the darkness and coldness, but that was the chance performers had to take, whether free or paid. When the old showhouse was at the peak of its glory, only the highest of the high, she said, ever *sat* in the boxes, and if *they* got up and walked out in the middle of a performance, it would be like letting a rock fall down onto a railroad track in the path of an oncoming train. It might not wreck the show but would give the passengers a nasty jolt. Was it the box closest to the stage on the right-hand side? That was supposedly *his*. And the one who usually sat in it with him was his favorite of all his wives.

AMELIA. ROSETTA KNEW THAT WELL enough. The Beauty. Number One. Blonde hair, blue eyes, white teeth, pink cheeks. (Like Lavonne.) She could just see her, her clothes and jewels. Wyandra said once when she and Rosetta were taking a walk and went past the house Amelia lived in when she was alive, very expensive naturally, that if she wasn't mistaken there was a big enlarged *picture* of Amelia in the Historical Museum. And sure enough, there was! her name was under it, so there could be no mistake. Otherwise Rosetta would no more have accepted it with a consenting mind than have said yes, a mud fence covered with toads was Mary Miles Minter. There wasn't one pretty thing about her! Yet this was The Beauty. Which only went to prove that *history* was no more dependable than *Ivanhoe* or *The Heiress of Redstone Hall*, and hardly as dependable as that.

True, history lit its own self up like phosphorescence, no shining in the dark where it was not, no ghosts without it, no such thing as a landmark. But take the old covered wagon and an automobile. Was there any comparison? And it was the same with recent times and modern improvements. They were wonderful, there was no getting around that fact. Take for instance fancy garters! which could be seen sometimes below young ladies' bare knees as they stepped onto the streetcar. Or take the taffy-pulling machine in Spears' Candy Store window, bright, silver, pulling away at a thick belt of satiny taffy. Or Kodak pictures. Or soap in the shape of a kewpie, a hat or a roadster. But the modern accomplishment above all others was the *glass staircase* in the foyer of the American Moving Picture Theater, steps, banisters, the whole thing of pure thick greenish glass with *actual water* colored in rainbow colors from imbedded lights *running down underneath*.

History is just *silly* in comparison (it really is) with modern times!

But yet Rosetta would have been sorry not to have got acquainted with the Mound Builder with the dusty strands of horsehair stuck to his dried old skull, his human teeth and dried-up, long old bones in shriveled hide with shreds of brown old gunnysack cling-ing here and there like wisps of old dried moss. For he it was who made her try to think back thousands and thousands of years…as sickening a sensation as to lie on your back on the ground and stare up in the sky and try to see…continuous and unlimited exten-sion in every direction. Back…back…It made the senses reel.

It's fun, though, Ivy. Just to try to imagine how it was.

But Ivy wouldn't try it, never. She hated old times, providing there *was* such a thing to begin with. Until Rosetta led her through the museum and made her look at bones dug up out of the ground and other second-hand stuff like that, she never even thought of such a thing. That is to say, she knew her mother and father had been born in a remote age without Fig Newtons, Victrolas or moving pictures, but that past lives and bygone days might stretch back to sunless centuries where even *apartments* might not have existed, or even *bread and butter*, was a thought that if your object was to go crazy you were on the right track. She was glad to get out of the museum and back outside where things were new: the sunshine, the cool breezes, the shade under the trees.

THE SHADIEST SHADE ROSETTA FOUND to be in the vicinity of a tiny graveyard she happened upon by accident one day keeping her bankers' hours and wandering around alone when Wyandra was busy and Ivy's mother had put Ivy to work at picking out bast-ing, which she could do if nobody distracted her. The graveyard was through the Eagle Gate, up the hill and along the avenues a ways, a kind of leveled-off plateau about as big as a little dance floor with a retaining wall around rising up a couple of feet above it, with a sharp-pointed iron railing mortised in along the top, making a high fence with a gate opening on the street side. Only the gate didn't open, it was locked tight. Because this was a private graveyard. And that must have been what made the shade so shady and all within so cool, pretty and handy-looking: because of not being able to get in. It was like a mirage of beauty. Nice flat slabs of marble you could use for a table and chairs, grass in strips and squares like green rugs, flowers in bunches... One grave, not satisfied with the fence around the whole property, had a fence of its own around it, bristling with spears. That made the tombstone within it hard to read, but it would have been anyway, lying flat the way it did and some distance from outside the locked fence. Still, his name and age could be made out, BRIGHAM YOUNG, AGE 76, and Rosetta was quite staggered. Wyandra thought that what he had in mind was to be buried here at the back of his down-town property with just his favorite wives, say five or six, with Amelia nearest him. But the way it turned out, Amelia's body wasn't within miles of his! and the wives' who were, those three graves along there, he hardly even *spoke to* for weeks at a time, or so Wyandra said she heard from an old dressmaker who used to sew for one of the Mrs. Heber C. Kimballs, who knew all about everything. And the children, those little graves there in under those bushes with the white flowers on them, were from different mothers, Brigham hardly would have known they even *belonged* to him if he met them on the street! and anyway he wouldn't to save his soul live under the same roof with children. So here he was, probably not as he'd have liked at all, kind of a joke on someone whose will was law. Although the fence, he'd want that, privacy, around his grave, around the whole place here, and for the gate to be always locked. Maybe he even knew people would be more drawn... and want to get in... and that way he would get more attention, even in death.

Ivy didn't like graves. When Rosetta took her up there to look in through the iron fence rails, she said she wouldn't go in even if the gate was open. She hated dead people. Ugh. But look how cool it looks in there, what a nice place to play house... in the daytime, of course. Nobody would want to come in here at *night* except to be scared out of seven years' growth, would they! Rosetta spoke in fast-gathering twilight and they hurried away before the dark could fall, to finish their post-prandial walk along Main Street. At Keith O'Brien's store they were looking in the window when two young men stopped and greeted them.

"Good evening," they said, tipping their straw hats politely.

It would happen from time to time that Ivy, going her somewhat awkward way, would be spoken to by some stranger. She never answered, though. Her mother had warned her. Men and boys always wanted to take advantage of young girls, and especially when they looked easy. Ivy explained this to Rosetta one time when they were going down to Schramm-Johnson's for strawberry ice cream cones and a passing gentleman said, "Hello, girlie." Ivy didn't explain the part about "looking easy" but what "taking advantage" meant. It meant trying to stick old Fiddle Bow into Jack Nasty-Face (Mrs. Rudart's Welsh names for these terrible human attributes), which men and boys would rather do than anything else in the world. Why, Ivy did not know. The only Fiddle Bow she ever saw was her little cousin Petey's back in Omaha, and that was just this little snail-looking thing laying against a soft little pink tobacco pouch growing between his legs. That matched what Rosetta and Lavonne saw the time Bobby next door ran outside without his diaper when Mrs. Sheldon was looking for a clean one, and got clear into the street (in fact he nearly got run over) before they caught him. A little soft thimble kind of thing attached to this little—The trouble was, they didn't stay that way. As the boy grew, this grew. And then, watch out.

"Wyandra, what does it mean when somebody looks easy?"

"It means they look dumb."

But forewarned is forearmed, and so when spoken to by strangers, Ivy did not answer. She knew what they wanted to do, stick old Fiddle Bow into Jack Nasty-Face and ruin her life. But these two young men, newly arrived from Pocatello, Idaho (they said), merely wanted to ask the whereabouts of Larkin's Funeral Establishment, where the shorter, fatter one's grandfather was lying in state, not take advantage. They didn't *say* so in so many words, but anyone could tell that by their sad, long faces. The shorter, fatter one's name was Will, the taller one Davis. Rosetta agreed with Ivy they should show them the way, Ivy walking ahead with Will, Rosetta with Davis. Davis didn't feel bad, because it was not *his* grandfather, and didn't appear to mind that his companion was a child of ten, he was only a friend of the family, he said. Still, dying was no laughing matter, and especially from drinking canned heat.

Rosetta had never heard of such a thing. It was on account of Prohibition, Davis explained. Will's grandfather couldn't cure his cold with the genuine article, so he tried this stuff which was called "canned heat," which was denatured alcohol, which could kill a person. And in this case, had. It turned his tongue black, his hands black, oh, Davis said, they heard the sight of him was something terrible. So that was why they couldn't invite Ivy and Rosetta in to view him. Ivy squealed at that, they were in front of Larkin's. She wouldn't go in if she could, she said, they couldn't make her.

On the way home she told Rosetta that since Will and Davis were so nice and had to go back to Pocatello on Thursday, and since it was so sad about Will's grandfather, she had promised to sneak out and meet Will tomorrow night, to go for a walk and try to cheer him up a little. Rosetta would have to go too, she said, so it would look the same as always. But what if Wyandra wanted to go to a show? What if she said she wanted to go for a walk too? Leave that to her, Ivy said. As luck would have it, neither show nor walk was mentioned. Wyandra had to clean the shop and wash her own hair, so she said to go and enjoy the fresh air. But be back by nine. Whatever would have come up, though, Ivy would have fixed, she said confidently, as they waited for the elevator. She wouldn't say how, but in later years when Rosetta knew what a womb was, and many more things as well, she looked back on that evening and thought that a womb might have an intelligence of its own, and might really, if up to it, have had the capability of removing any hindrance to its getting out into the summer night…

And so they went, Ivy with a scent-dabbed handkerchief and powdered nose that for some unknown reason affected the grudging old elevator man, Mr. Williams, to where he bowed and scraped to *them* for once as if to Mr. Cutler, the owner of the building, or the Swedish Vice-Consul. He held the door way back and even took hold of Ivy to help her down the inch to the floor.

"Why, where's your muscle?" he said, giving her arm a squeeze.

Ivy just hated him, she said when they got out on the sidewalk. Old men were so silly!

BUT IF OLD MEN WERE silly, young men were mean. Or why weren't Will and Davis in front of Keith O'Brien's the way they promised? Did they go back to Pocatello today instead of tomorrow? Ivy pouted gloomily. She did so want to go for a walk with Will and cheer him up about his grandfather. Rosetta looked disappointedly up and down the street too, having hoped for more light to be thrown upon the subject of canned heat.

"Well, we don't care," Ivy said finally. "Shall we doohix something in the window before we go? Me first," she added with a deep sigh.

"All right, you first." To distract her from the coral organdie Rosetta really meant to choose, she gazed desirously at the ugly blue dress with puffs on the sides, and so didn't see the boys, nor did Ivy, until their reflections shadowed the display window. They had got there first, they said, and walked around the block…

How was the funeral? Sad, very sad.

Ivy and Will started up ahead, not up Main Street, as Mr. Williams when he wasn't running the elevator hung around outside the doorway, or someone else was always going in or out, maybe even Ivy's *father* to buy a cigar. Instead they went west a block and on up to Brigham Street, Rosetta and Davis following, the first two like a courting couple, the second like relatives, or like that when Rosetta put her hand in her companion's.

"I bet people will think you're my big brother," she said proudly.

He gave her a kind of exasperated look. "How come she lets *you* tag along?" he said.

Rosetta pulled her hand away. "*She* tags along with *me*," she said, tossing her head.

"Oh," he said. "You don't say. Well, I didn't know. So don't get mad." He reached out and took her hand again. "Where are they headed?"

"I guess into the palace grounds," Rosetta said.

But the great gates were shut and wouldn't open.

"The what grounds? The last I heard, this here's the Mormon Temple. And that there's the Tabernacle."

"Well, you heard wrong," she said, and told him as they talked on about the king who had been gone away a long time, and lots else besides.

They went past the great hotel, up past the mansions. Amelia's house, although she had been dead for about fifty years, had lights in it, in a bedroom upstairs and one light downstairs showing through colored glass. There is probably no actual difference between a *millionaire*'s lindens and elm trees and anyone else's, but walking under their branches and past their hale trunks by moonlight, it really does appear so, as if even clear out past the curb, into the public domain, their roots had access to richness that other trees don't. By now, ahead in the leafy shadows, Ivy could be seen cheering up Will, their sides pressed close together and their slow steps matching.

"Hey, you slow pokes!"

"You go on ahead, we'll follow," Will said over his shoulder in a soft but hoarse tone.

"We got to be home by nine, remember, Ivy," Rosetta said as she and Davis went around them.

"Oooh. Don't let's stop *here*," Ivy said when she and Will finally strolled hand in hand up to Davis and Rosetta, standing and looking through the fence of the tiny graveyard.

"Guess who's buried here?" Davis said with an air of good-fellowship, turning to look at Will.

"Dead people!" Ivy said, pretending to shiver.

"Brigham Young! Him and some of his wives."

"And some of his children too," Rosetta, who had led them all here, said with pride, pleased to have excited their curiosity.

"That grave there with the fence around it, that there is his," Davis said, pointing.

"*Is* it!" Will said, pulling Ivy in closer to him as he studied the scene.

"They keep the gate locked. Nobody can get in," Rosetta said.

"*Can't* they!" Will said. "What do you think of that, honeybunch? What do you say we give it a try?"

"Give what a try?"

"Getting in!"

"*In there?*" Ivy squealed but didn't draw away as he pulled her over to the gate and commenced rattling and pushing against it. "Why, I wouldn't go in there for a million dollars!"

Will let go of her, causing her to subside against the fence in some surprise and fall abruptly silent.

"Look," he said, placing a foot on the stone ledge, then climbing up and, after getting a footing between the sharp spear-ends of the fence supports, jumping down into the enclosure.

"There's nothing to it! Honeybunch, come here. Davis, lend a hand."

"Of course you get the general idea by now," he said, "of why the *grave* is fenced."

Davis laughed.

Will laughed too, walked over and took hold of that sharp-pointed barrier around the sacred spot.

"Now that is a *fence*," Davis said. "Shear a leg off a fellow. Or something else—"

"Oh, I don't know," Will said meditatively.

"We might haul her up over this one, but *that* one—" Davis shook his head.

Ivy waited, like an astonished sheep.

"Oh, I don't know."

"And what would be the object? It's right out in the moonlight!"

Will considered, staring down through the enclosure at the rectangle of marble about the size of a three-quarter bed with the rows of carved letters across it. Then he dropped his hands and turned and went back to the cemetery gate. "Honeybunch," he said, jumping up on the ledge and reaching over, "Catch a hold here, darlin'. Davis is going to boost you."

"Don't you do that, Ivy," Rosetta said worriedly. "There's people coming. And we got to go. Besides, think how scared you are of dead people! And your mother—"

But the boy on one side of the fence and the boy on the other managed to push, haul, lift and boost resisting but at the same time reconcilable soft and sagging Ivy up and over into Will's waiting body—which fell and staggered back and went down under her.

"Cheese it!" Davis said. "Hey, cheese it, will you? Hide, someone's coming—"

The two on the grass crawled and rolled, entwined, Ivy giggling and gasping, in under some bushes…

Davis took Rosetta quickly by the hand.

"Come on," he said, starting down the hill.

There were indeed people approaching, a couple so deep in low-voiced conversation that though they absent-mindedly went single file for a few steps, the youngish woman stepping ahead of the oldish man to let Rosetta and Davis pass, they paid them no attention and Davis need not have said, "You'll catch it when we get home, Mom's really mad!"

Stopping a few paces farther on, "We got to go back and get her!" Rosetta said.

"What for? I'm taking you down to the corner and then you run on home!"

She broke from him and ran.

"You don't want to go *back* there—"

"I do too! I got to get her!"

But at the cemetery when Rosetta called softly through the fence, nobody answered. Only the rustle of the wind, the faint gurgle of water running somewhere.

"Ivy! Come out! What are you hiding for?" She took hold of the fence, put a foot tentatively on the ledge it was anchored in. Had they climbed back over and gone someplace? She looked around and Davis had disappeared too, she couldn't see him anywhere, and all of a sudden the terrors of night, death, spirits and graves assailed her, she jumped down, and under whispering leaves and the ghostly moon ran home as fast as her legs would carry her.

WHEN THEY GOT UP THERE, which they did as soon as they could, Wyandra and Mrs. Rudart, not Ivy's father who was in bed asleep and wouldn't need to be woken up to his misery (whatever Mrs. Rudart may have meant by that), and of course Rosetta, they found the lost one crying inside the gate by the fence. She couldn't climb over by herself and the boys were gone. She was very mussed up, her hair shaken down on one side, one stocking hanging down with a broken garter in it, her dress torn. She had tried to get out, she said, had fallen and skinned her leg and her foot turned under her—!

"You idiot, you perfect idiot." That was all Mrs. Rudart could find to say while they tried to think how to get her over the fence.

"Look, it's all swole up," Ivy blubbered, sitting down on the ground and bending forward to touch her foot.

"You *idiot*." Her mother glared.

"No use in *saying* anything," Wyandra said. "What we've got to do is get the poor girl out. I'm sure there's a No Trespassing sign somewhere. And when there's one of *them*, they put people in jail!"

"I'm scared," Ivy sobbed.

"This gate's got to be unlocked," Wyandra said. "That's the first thing on the agenda—"

"By who? At ten o'clock at night?" Mrs. Rudart said. "You just said they put people in jail!"

"Well, maybe under the circumstances—"

"What circumstances? That I have an idiot while my sister has children that go through business college? That when her father hears about this I'll probably end up a widow? Ivy Rudart," she said, "you get up off that ground. And stand here. And not a word, not a *peep* out of you."

Something in her mother's voice made the girl do as she was told. She got to her feet and then, no one knew how it was done exactly or who did what, with longer and stronger arms than any of them *had*, they all clutched, pulled, hauled and dragged, Mrs. Rudart in her reckless desperation almost over the fence herself for part of the time, pendulous Ivy up and over the railing's pointed heads sharp enough to pierce or transfix a boar and down in a heap like a sack of sobbing potatoes on the other side. Wounded in the fray she was, scraped, torn and raveled out, bleeding (her thigh) but safe and sound. Her mother kissed her then and brushed her hair back off her inch-high forehead and said to stop crying, they would soon be home, and pray to God nobody would be wandering about to see them …

Chapter Fifty-one

✳

AS LUCK WOULD HAVE IT NO ONE WAS, A STRAGGLER OR TWO, SOME PEOPLE coming out of the restaurant down the block but nobody they knew, so they got into the building undetected, and upstairs too. And no great harm done, as Mrs. Rudart told Wyandra the next day when she ran up between customers to see how Ivy was. Black and blue from the fence, her dress was ruined, she had a bandage on her leg, but her father knew nothing about it and would not be told. The boy had apparently been a nice boy, no funny stuff, Ivy would confide in her mother, Mrs. Rudart said she felt sure. Wild was all, at that age, full of the old Nick. See a place where trespassers will be prosecuted and over the fence they go. She didn't seem to realize there had been *two* boys, and Wyandra, after thinking about it a little, decided not to tell her.

Not long after that Mr. Rudart went out for a cigar and never came back. But Mrs. Rudart did not go to the police station about it. He did the same thing once before, she said, and they found him seventeen months later in a place called Midland, Michigan. So she wasn't worried. Just before Labor Day she closed the New York Custom Shirt Manufacturing Company and took Ivy and returned to wherever they came from. Rosetta minded quite a bit, enough to cry while the van was loading. But as Wyandra pointed out, school would soon be starting (the same strange, diffracted school of last spring with hours on into six till winter term, when all would square with a norm again in a brand-new schoolhouse), she would have new books and everything.

And Mrs. Rudart had kind of come between the friends since the night Ivy marooned herself in Brigham's private burial ground. She wouldn't let Ivy out for walks anymore, they couldn't go down for ice cream cones, and palling around in the building was cut to a minimum. Still, the two did get to talk a few times undisturbed in the window alcove at the end of the hall, and that was when Rosetta heard that it really did happen. Old Fiddle Bow...

"Remember what I told you Mama said? Well, Will—It was when you left Davis and run back down here to get Mama and Wyandra. You shouldn't have done that, Rosetta. Because then Davis, *he* climbed over the fence too! and got down in under the bushes where Will and me are laying. And Will says—And Davis says—And me, I'm sitting up, or trying to, and saying 'Listen here, what are you doing?' And they, they're pushing me back and laughing kind of—and then he had it out—"

"Who had it out?"

"Davis! And then, well, *he did it too!* It don't take very long. About a minute."

Rosetta said uncertainly, "Is that all?" Then, "It's like your mother said."

"What about?"

"About boys…wanting to…take advantage…"

"Oh, they do," Ivy agreed. "They most certainly do. But the reason for *that* is—"

Rosetta waited.

"Well, look. Here's old Fiddle Bow *here*—" Ivy put out her pudgy right hand, palm up, "—and here's Jack Nasty-Face *here*—" She put out her pudgy left hand, palm up.

"So then what?" Rosetta said with great interest.

"So then, well—" Somewhat helplessly Ivy clapped her two hands together.

After a moment, "Another thing I was going to mention," Rosetta said, little the wiser, "are you sure those names you said are right? *Jack* Nasty-Face? Because Jack's a boy's name. And what you're talking about is a girl's—Shouldn't it be *Sally* Nasty-Face or *Betty* Nasty-Face rather than—"

Ivy withdrew her rapt gaze from the streetcar she had been watching take on passengers in the street far below. "I suppose you know better than my mother."

"No, but I just wondered—"

"It's *Jack* Nasty-Face," Ivy said coldly. "That is what they call it…*in the Bible.*"

THE RUDARTS LEFT SOON AFTER this, promising to write. But they never did, and so Rosetta never found out if Ivy was "ruined" by her experience with Will and Davis in Brigham's private graveyard or not. Rosetta used to pass it sometimes and thought she could about imagine which bushes…and Ivy too, on the ground in under the shadows right next to those graves. But not a peep out of her! that was supposed to be so afraid of ghosts and dead people. The term "Jack Nasty-Face" didn't seem to be in the Bible. It was also not in the largest Webster's Dictionary in the world, on the dictionary stand in the eighth-grade room of the new Lafayette School. "Fiddle bow" was, but it had no connection with boys.

IN HIGH SCHOOL ROSETTA BEGAN to write down new words she ran across. Quaquaversal. Labyrinthine. But Lavonne didn't think the kids *liked* kids that used big words like that, it made them seem—Well, they wouldn't get invited to anything. After what her chum Florence did to her, it seemed as if a veil dropped from Lavonne's eyes and she realized you had to pay attention to every little detail. Not that paying attention would have *helped* in the case of Florence—she was just a snob, that was all. Started to high school and made a clean sweep. Lavonne was good enough in grade school, Gram was good enough even if she *was* the Prentice family's cook. Where she and Gram lived was good enough, too—two rooms in a basement, but a basement in a mansion people drove past slow to look at because it looked so expensive! A *basement* better than Florence's family's whole entire *house*, their whole front *yard*. And didn't she and Gram have a radio? an Atwater Kent too, while Florence's was just any old kind. But just because Florence's father worked in an office! Just because they had a new Dodge sedan! Just because—

Gram said it was very simple. Florence stopped being friends because she was jealous. At West High School here she is walking down the hallway with Lavonne, and who gets the attention? Who cuts the swathe? The girl that looks like nothing, or the girl who looks like somebody just ready to be discovered and put in the movies? Of *course* Florence broke off the friendship. It didn't surprise Gram one bit! and couldn't suit her better. For now Lavonne and Rosetta, that had been babies together and playmates and schoolmates and were also related, were chums once again!

Wyandra was glad about it too. Rosetta had grieved over Lavonne. There weren't any other children in the building. But Rosetta was a great one for entertaining herself, and Wyandra didn't mind having a little girl tag after her. The ladies liked her too, in the shop, they petted her. But of course that wasn't just the best policy either. Through the years, you know, she should have had a—*party* like other children, with paper hats and favors and where you pin the tail on the donkey…little deviled-ham sandwiches with the crusts cut off, hard-boiled eggs, a nice frosted cake…And Wyandra felt she shouldn't always be taking her to the show or talking or reading her a story. But—she was sweet company.

"Her mother was the same," Gram said. "Otherwise, would I have put up with what I did? Marie. Sweetest company in the world. And Les the same, she comes by it honestly. Isn't it just a shame about that eye? Spoils her looks entirely."

Wyandra didn't think so. It was such a small part of the whole. The last time Nancibel was up here visiting—she brought Legrand, usually he's got something else to do, he's fifteen now—"You know they're second cousins—"

"Who are second cousins?"

"Rosetta and Legrand. Through her *mother's* side, the same way she and Lavonne are second cousins through her *father's*—"

"I know all that."

"I know, but I was just going to say—Legrand is such a nice boy. And so artistic. I wish Serapta's husband Stig could have seen some of—That boy can copy *Bringing Up Father* till you couldn't tell the difference, and while Nancibel and I were talking—I was giving her a water wave, might as well keep my hands busy as sit idle—And how about you, Gram? Marcels today free gratis!"

"Well, maybe a crimp or two—"

"So anyway, as I was saying—" Wyandra went on a few minutes later as she twirled a hot iron with her left hand while lifting a lock of gray-streaked blonde hair off her visitor's scalp with a comb in her right and began marcelling, "while we were talking and Rosetta was trying to entertain Legrand by showing him the old dryer we used to have in the old place, it's back of the curtain there, I suggested it but he couldn't get interested, you never know what will interest them, why, all of a sudden he said, 'Here, I'll draw you.'"

"What did he mean by that?" Gram asked absent-mindedly. It always made her sleepy to have her head touched.

"Why, that he would draw Rosetta's picture. And he did. He had a pad and pencil with him. He drew her profile."

"And what's that supposed to prove?"

"Why, nothing, except that he must have thought her profile was nice, and it *is* nice, and in fact if it wasn't for her eye—"

"Do you want to know what worries *me*?" Gram said.

"What?" Wyandra said.

"Lavonne's bust. It's the only thing that's liable to put the kibosh on everything, getting in the movies, getting a rich husband—not that I believe in a person marrying for money unless there's love as well—but just everything a pretty, beautiful girl would set her heart on."

"Lavonne's *bust*?"

"By that I mean—I mention her bust," Gram said, gazing at Wyandra desperately in the mirror, "but *what if she gets fat?* She's fat now!"

"Oh, now, I wouldn't say that," Wyandra said soothingly. "She's just—I haven't noticed her being so fat—"

"Of course she could outgrow it," Gram said. "She's only fourteen. But the question is, *where is it coming from?*"

"You're just too good a cook. All those lovely—"

"No, I mean—which side of the family is the tendency coming from?" As though if she knew *that*, she could shut off the supply by closing the border and posting guards.

"I wouldn't worry," Wyandra said. "With that pretty face—"

"She cried her eyes out over that snippy Florence. Wouldn't walk to school with her anymore. Started with these new friends—and for just nothing but jealousy!"

ROSETTA HAD TO WRITE A theme. It was for Civics class. It had to be about some other country, some way they did things *there* in comparison with how we handle things over *here*. Wyandra always thought it was very interesting about India, which would come to a person's attention now and then. The Untouchables. How if even their *shadow* falls across a Brahmin, they can be arrested and fined. And other things along that line too numerous to mention. She thought it would make an entertaining theme, show the contrast between a backward country like India and America.

Rosetta thought so too, and in the library nervously found out enough for her paper, which was called "The Class System in India." The classes were the Brahmins, the Nobles, the Clans and then the lower classes shading off down to the lowest of all, the

Untouchables. They had it terrible. They were Hindus but not allowed to go to church. They could buy or rent only in certain terrible locations, out by the tannery, down by the salt works, over by the garbage dump. "Uncleanly" work was the only kind they could do, gather up dead dogs and cats off the street, trap the kind of animals who live in holes, weave baskets, lay bloody hides in stinking ooze, heave coal, work down in sewers, spread manure on fields, dig graves, hammer and pound, be a barber…

When Rosetta read *that* in the back number of the *National Geographic* that one of the librarians helped her find and where she got most of her information, she was astounded, as she always thought a barber, in nice starched shirts, ties and suits such as Uncle Albert used to wear and looked so nice in with his glossy hair and buffed fingernails, was quite high up on the social scale. And especially when they did hairdressing. But no, "barber" was on the "uncleanly work" list. Rosetta left it off though, not only so as not to hurt Wyandra's feelings when she read it but because she didn't want to think of it herself.

The Untouchables needn't have stayed untouchable. If all the forty million of them had banded together and said they wouldn't stand it anymore, they could have rolled over the land like a Juggernaut and flattened everybody out flatter than a pancake. But *they* believed they were untouchable *themselves. They* helped enforce the system *their own self* more than policemen with clubs could do. "That 'never the twain shall meet' expression," Wyandra said when she read Rosetta's theme. "I always think it means never shall some complete foreigner with a dark skin and those bloodshot-looking eyes marry somebody— English, you know, or Scotch. Or take a Swede. But these low Untouchables and high Brahmins, they're all cut from the same bolt of goods, they're all *Indians*. Going just by looks, you probably couldn't tell one from the other!"

Lavonne hated the very idea. She thought it was the meanest and most unfair thing she ever heard of. To squash down a person at birth so they never had a chance! How about if an Untouchable was *beautiful*? That part about their very *shadow* contaminating things! *She* would get out of a country like that so fast it would make your head swim!

"In *this* country—Thank goodness," she said.

"Born equal."

"Except certain kids—"

"Run everything."

"Their folks are rich."

"Well, be nice. Be friendly," Wyandra advised.

"We *are* nice."

"We *are* friendly."

"Remember when we first started? We went to some of the Freshman activities, didn't we, Lavonne?"

"I was in the Klatwa and the Philomatheans, but they acted like I wasn't there."

"We just gave up."

"If we go to the, say for instance, the annual dance between Thanksgiving and Christmas—"

"It's not fun—"

"They dance among themselves—"

"If we go to the games it's the same way. They—"

"Who's 'they'?" Wyandra said.

Rosetta suddenly laughed. "Why, the Brahmins. Who else? Because where did we ever get the idea there wasn't a class system over *here*?"

"Well, you just wait till you graduate from *Normal School*," Wyandra said when Lavonne had gone and she and Rosetta were sitting down to supper. "And get to be a *teacher*. Do you know what I've been thinking?"

"No, what?" Rosetta said.

"June will be here before you know it. Graduation. Then fall will come along. And the way to solve the problem of Normal School—Your Uncle Albert was against it in his day, I grant you that, but I don't believe if he was here today that he'd have any objections whatsoever!"

"Against *what*, Wyandra?"

"You know that salesman I told you was here the other day? for the New Improved Mondeville Overhead Spiral Permanent Waving Machine? Well, *he* said business would double, and I believe it. So start getting ready to be a beautiful teacher—"

WYANDRA BORROWED THE MONEY FROM Agnes, and now she would be right back paying her again, that high interest, as she told Gram. It seemed like she would never get the shop paid off, the good will and everything, but finally she did, and now to start in over again! But she didn't mind, a Mondeville Overhead could be a gold mine. The trouble was, she should have got it months ago so as not to have to skimp on graduation.

"That yearbook they got to have, imagine," Gram said. "Five dollars."

"Rosetta didn't want one for some reason."

"Did you see Lavonne's picture? Nobody could have a prettier face! I just can't understand it. She's heavy, I grant you that, but by no means a *tub*, and—" She thought of something and broke off.

"Rosetta's turned out nice, too."

"Don't it seem selfish to you how they hang on to everything like their life depended on it? All those beautiful old dresses and coats and furs? Hinting don't do no good, I just gave up. Deaf ear. And all through high school I could of made over and dressed her so beautiful."

"Mrs. Prentice and Birdelle, you mean. Their stuff."

"Not that I didn't see she always had a nice dress and a nice coat—and with them looks, for anyone must grant that that's what she was blessed with, I never had no doubts the boys would *flock*. *Nice* boys, *rich* boys. But—Mr. Loomis's grandson that helped with the yard, cap on the side of his head, cigarette dangling out the corner of his mouth, he had a case on her. And the soda fountain boy at Schramm-Johnson's with the pimply complexion. Don't it worry you when you see that, that it's a disease?"

"But she's going steady now, isn't she? Rosetta said she was."

Gram nodded. "We've known that kid ever since we went to the Prentices'. His dad raises the fresh stuff Mrs. Prentice buys, they've got a farm out in Bountiful. That first year he was still using a horse and buggy, and this kid would be along. But now of course they've got the truck and the boy drives. He comes by himself lots of times—"

"Well, that's *lovely*."

"But don't it seem funny to you? All the rich boys that there are in this town—"

"Farmers can be rich."

"I mean, *society* boys. Because Lavonne is so—You admit it, Wyandra. You know she is."

"I know she is," Wyandra said.

"Hasn't she got a beautiful face?"

"She has," Wyandra said. "I've always said so. Everyone does. Beautiful."

"And she's not a *tub*. She has a shape on her."

"She most assuredly does have. And she's awfully sweet. But to get back to what I was saying, I could kick myself."

"For what?"

"For not borrowing the money from Agnes and ordering this permanent waving machine that I'm getting months ago. Rosetta could have had her yearbook, her baccalaureate dress, her formal, instead of going without everything but just her new dress for the class picnic out at Saltair."

"When are you getting it? The new machine?"

"They say, next Monday."

"Will you know how to work the thing?"

"Oh, sure. They show you how, exactly. The company."

They did show Wyandra how, and she had so much natural talent that in five minutes she could have demonstrated the machine herself. But just to be sure, she permanented Dr. Farr's stiff gray locks for nothing, and the soft, limp Swedish hair of the lady from down on three who painted china, and spent from the time they got up from supper till two the next morning doing Rosetta's shoulder-length locks. It was a very tedious process, blocking off, winding the rods, wrapping, and twice, at least, Rosetta fell asleep hanging in the machine from forty or more points, like a creature caught in some terrible web.

"Wake up, little dear!" Wyandra chucked her under the chin, fanned the heavy heated curlers with Lucitie's old fan, spooned in coffee, tried to entertain her with the old family stories she had told so often, encouraged her to talk, sympathized, cajoled—and finally pronounced the steaming done, the cooling done—then everything done! at last. But it was *too curly*. That pained Rosetta worse than the pull-blister on the crown of her head, not bad but enough to know she had one. Wyandra said that taught her a lesson, the blocking must not have been *even* there. She was sorry if Rosetta didn't like that tight a curl because she herself thought it was becoming, she really did, but maybe tomorrow a tar-gel shampoo, an egg shampoo, a vinegar and lemon rinse—or perhaps—By the day of the Senior Picnic, though, she was *sure*.

But the day dawned, and in spite of all Wyandra's attempts at counteracting the evil, Rosetta's hair (to her mind) still frizzed. Her pull-blister too, raw from the many remedial operations and burning like fire from combing, didn't burn as fiercely as her anguish when, alone in their living quarters down the hall from the shop, she combed her fleecy mop back, parted it in the middle, parted it on the side, put it behind her ears, slicked it down and tried to get ready for the picnic.

Lavonne found her in tears.

"It just looks *awful!*"

"No, it don't," Lavonne said. "And if we go in bathing, I bet you'll be so glad you won't know what to do, that it won't go straight on you."

"Why did I ever let Wyandra do it?"

"Well, she had to practice."

"I wish I was *dead*." Against the door frame Rosetta hid her head in the crook of her arm.

"You don't wish any such thing. Now you come on." Lavonne leaned toward the small looking glass on the wall to flick an imaginary speck of powder off a long eyelash stiff with black mascara. Gently then she poked a finger under her water-waved hair, inspecting as she did so the color on her rather thin but prettily curved lips. She narrowed her eyes, then opened them wide, appreciating the burst of clear sky blue under the line of her fleshy, curly-fringed eyelids.

"You just go and meet them by yourself," Rosetta said in a choked voice, meaning Anita, a girl they knew from typing class, and Anita's friend Frances, with whom they were going to ride out to the Saltair Pavilion, site of the Senior Class Picnic.

"But your hair looks *nice*," Lavonne said without a second glance in Rosetta's direction. "Your dress too. Come on, honey. Say, I told you, didn't I? Darrel's coming out to meet me, but not till about six-thirty, so that won't spoil *our* day. You can go to the dance with us or whatever we do."

"It doesn't make any difference to me, because I won't be going." Rosetta ran into her bedroom and shut the door. It used to be Wyandra's, and before that Uncle Albert and Aunt Lucitie's, but when Rosetta started to high school Wyandra said she should have it, to have a place to study like the girl in *Daddy Long Legs* when her benefactor sent her away to college. And it was really better for her own self, Wyandra said, to go back to sleeping on the couch, first because she was used to it and second because she stayed up later. As it turned out, she was so tired by the time bedtime came from all she did from morning till night (her last chore on the night before the picnic was to put the water-wave combs in Rosetta's hair, secure them with hairpins and rubber bands and swathe her head with net) that she almost fell asleep before she could get her bedding out of the old clothes-press and make up her bed, and Rosetta was the one who stayed up late.

The nights they went to a movie Wyandra did better, but only if they stopped at Schramm-Johnson's for a dish of ice cream or a chocolate soda for Rosetta and a cup of coffee for her. After the coffee, she said she could run up the three flights of stairs like a deer, but of course she couldn't. Rosetta usually dawdled along with her, still talking about the show or discussing something momentous, such as how when she became a teacher she was always going to wear silk stockings and beautiful collar and cuff sets like Miss Corcoran, and how by that time the great surgeons of the world would know how to operate on her eye and she would have the operation, and how she and Wyandra would go to Yellowstone Park someday, and Hollywood and Paris.

But if the coffee didn't take effect and Wyandra climbed the stairs like a sleepwalker, yawning and forgetting what they were talking about, then Rosetta, as she had done when she was a little girl and first came to the Constitution Building to live, would run on ahead, up, up the dark stairways by herself, and at the top lean over the railing and look down at Wyandra toiling upward far below, hardly bigger than a doll. Now, of course, the dark empty center of the immense stairwell did not seem as deep as the deepest mountain cleft worn by some vast torrent, its steep tiered sides not fifty stories high, as they once had been, but only five.

And now it was hard to remember the Alhambra and Old St. Paul's, the tunnels, tombs and dungeons that once existed. Tenants still cooked stews with onions, simmered split pea soup, fried bacon and burnt toast, but they were never gypsies. And no more hooded monks, unhanged pirates with scarred faces, undertakers playing cribbage on a coffin lid in a dark crypt lit by the light of a single candle while the Black Death roamed outside. Childhood was a funny time. It was like that poem Miss Corcoran read in English class about the poet comparing the willow tree to a "flock of tall birds," "thin-fingered women are underneath that hair" and other romantic comparisons like that until the time came when, as she said, the *thing itself* was enough, the poet didn't *need* comparisons anymore because

The actual willow, the fact of a tree
Seems fanciful and beautiful enough for me.

And that was the way it was with the Constitution Building. The place *itself* was dark enough and peculiar enough, with all its railings and flights of stairs, stair-heads and narrow and day-blind hallways, and the slits of red light where the toilet doors at the end of the hall stood partly open, and the garbage cans that the rats were said to lift the lids off of bodily in the middle of the night, and scary enough for those that couldn't stand to look down from a height as great as the empty center space, without comparing it with any place else. The fact of it just standing there "seems fanciful and beautiful enough for me." But no, it wasn't. Not beautiful at all, ugly. Haunted too, or so Ada said who ran the elevator for part of her and her old English mother's rent, haunted not by Mr. Williams, who had died a natural death in Agnes's hospital, but Mr. Cutler, who owned the building and who had blown his brains out in the garage of his fine home the summer after Rosetta's junior year, no one knew why.

"And Richard Cory, one calm summer night, went home and put a bullet through his head," Miss Corcoran had read that poem to them too. But of course Mr. Cutler wasn't young and handsome like Richard Cory, but eighty-two years old. Rich, though, "richer than a king." Nobody in the building guessed that, he always looked kind of poor and shabby going to or coming from his office on the second floor, or if you went into it to pay the rent, the way he'd be sitting there in his swivel chair before his big desk with everything so dusty and dirty and piled everywhere, and old frayed ledgers and account books, or if you would see him waiting for the elevator on one of the floors. The paper said he had been *Governor* at one time, imagine. And he owned banks and insurance companies and the Utah-Idaho Sugar Company and all kinds of property. Dr. Farr said she would bet he was worth up in the millions. But yet one fine summer's day he went home and put a bullet through his head. So old, that was what Wyandra couldn't get over, that a man eighty-two years old would do away with himself. But whatever it was he couldn't stand anymore, his spirit was still troubled, and bound to earth because of it. Or so said Ada, who *saw* him with her own two eyes up on the fifth floor and then on the second, his own floor, looking the way he always did except that you could partially see through him, the very day after he died, while his body was still at the undertaking establishment and not even buried. She just caught this glimpse, his worried white face and open eyes like a ghostly sleepwalker, still definitely hanging around the building.

"You go on without me," Rosetta said in a muffled voice, face down on the bed.

But Lavonne had gone to the shop to fetch Wyandra.

"Why, darling, what's the matter?"

"I'm just not going to go, that's all."

"But, Rosetta. You didn't go to the party. You didn't go to the dance. This picnic was the one thing you said you would do, that you had your heart set on. You got your new dress—" Wyandra sat down beside the weeping girl and put a gentle hand on her shoulder. Her hand was stained with henna, for she had been giving a henna pack, and her eyes nervously caught Marie's old alarm clock ticking (five minutes fast) on the scarred old bureau, so as not to leave the dye on too long.

"I hate it!" Rosetta sobbed.

"Her hair," Lavonne said sadly. "She can't make it look like she wants it to."

"Honey, listen, please don't cry. Let me comb it for you. I wanted to, before I opened the shop this morning, but you wouldn't let me. It's beautiful. Your hair is beautiful. Isn't her hair beautiful, Lavonne?"

"Sure it is," Lavonne said, turning her head as far around to the back as she could, to glance down and, lifting first one plump leg and then the other, see if her seams were straight.

"Let me see how you've got it fixed now," Wyandra said. "I can't see, with your face down in the pillow like that."

"I just don't want to go, that's all! Can't you leave me *alone*?"

Wyandra looked at the clock again, then cast a stricken glance in Lavonne's direction. It was not returned, for Lavonne had taken her compact from her white patent leather purse, clicked it open and was peering into the tiny round mirror.

"Here's—a little more money," Wyandra said, taking a silver dollar out of her apron pocket and sliding it under Rosetta's clenched hand. "You girls—are going to have—the most fun."

"Rosetta! You quit it now. Acting like that. You look *wonderful*," Lavonne said.

Reluctantly Wyandra got to her feet, her anxious eyes still on the girl on the bed. "I've got to go back in there. It's Mrs. Beck's henna pack, and she's so hard to please! But as soon as I get her washed out and set—"

By the time this task was done, however, the girls had gone. Somehow Lavonne had presented motive and inducement enough in her rather aggrieved way to prevail upon Rosetta to get up off the bed, splash her eyes with cold water, comb her hair and go with her. It looked *wonderful*. Really it did. Rosetta on her way out was going to look in the shop and kiss Wyandra and tell her she was sorry for saying leave her alone, but Ada had the elevator door open, someone on another floor was ringing, Lavonne was pulling on her arm and saying to hurry, they might even miss the *train*! and so she didn't. She wanted to, she never went anywhere without telling Wyandra good-bye, it bothered her a little, the pale tired face she had glimpsed through her hair when Wyandra stood up and told Lavonne she had to get back to the shop because of the henna pack. Oh, well, tonight she would tell her…

All the afternoon, Rosetta kept thinking how glad she was going to be to get home and put Wyandra's mind at ease about the permanent. It really wasn't terrible at all. Frances even liked it and said she wanted the same kind. And so much depended on the machine, making enough money to pay Agnes back with interest, for Normal School, even just keeping things the way they were. Since Mr. Cutler died and his heirs took over, the rent had been raised. Wyandra said supplies cost lots more too, the light bill, everything. I'm going to get a job! Rosetta thought suddenly. I'll go to the Hotel Utah, maybe I can be an elevator girl, or a chambermaid like Mama's friend Evelyn. I could be something like that. I'll ask at the…overall factory. Put my name in Woolworth's…I shouldn't have cried and been snippy. I hurt her feelings. And it wasn't even the permanent! I'll tell her. It was just…Lavonne came in, and she's not thin but she looked so beautiful, she always does, her blue dress, I like my dress too, it's the one I wanted and you let me buy it, but Lavonne…It's my *eye*. Why can't they operate on it? They can do everything else…It was that, Wyandra, it was Lavonne and my eye and everything, not my permanent, I should have told you…*I love you so much.*

Chapter Fifty-two

*

"You know who's going to get a permanent today?" Rosetta said as they waited for Anita and Frances to come back from the restroom.

"No, who?" Lavonne said, stepping back out of the wind and smoothing her hair, the while she cast about the cold looks of a young beauty at such fellow seniors as were still disporting themselves in the open-air annex where all of them, even the rich kids, had eaten a catered lunch of chipped beef or cheese sandwiches, sweet pickles, Oreo cookies and Coca-Cola or orange or strawberry pop.

"Mrs. Prentice. She was coming at eleven. But you probably know it already," Rosetta said.

"How should I know it?"

"Well, you *live* at their house, don't you? Your own grandmother cooks for them."

"So what's that got to do with me?"

"Well, I just thought maybe she mentioned—"

"They're upstairs there like the Queen of England, *I* never see them," Lavonne said. "And they never see me. Oh, once in a while. I'll come in through the side basement entrance and go in our place to leave my books and stuff before I run up to the kitchen and they'll be bowling across on the other side."

"Who'll be bowling?"

"Oh, Birdelle and Mr. Prentice. Then I'll just lay low, not turn the radio on or anything, till I get a chance to run up to the kitchen, Gram says it's best not to remind them."

"Of what?"

"Of me! Of me living there with Gram and eating and everything. Especially since I'm not a little kid anymore like I was when we first went there. So I've always laid low."

"I know," Rosetta said. "But I just thought Mrs. Prentice might have mentioned to Gram that she was going to get a permanent today."

"Well, if she did, Gram didn't tell me."

Wyandra had not persuaded Mrs. Prentice to take the momentous step, it was the other way around. Her hair had thinned out, her mother's did the same, Mrs. Prentice said, and if her daughter Birdelle lived to be sixty-three, *her* hair would probably thin out too. Mrs. Prentice was tired of trying to make a little look like a lot, she said, those odious kid curlers every night, the lumps and bumps to sleep on. She had been reading about

475

permanent ondulations, the *Delineator* said in an article that they not only furnished and filled the hair out but that the galvanic rays were beneficial to the whole system. And what was the sense of living in the twentieth century if one didn't make use of some of its innovations? Wyandra told her it took six hours, maybe even seven, and it was awfully tedious. No matter. She had brought *Lorna Doone*, an apple, a pear, some gingersnaps, but she would prevail upon Wyandra for a cup of tea later on.

"Oh, by all means," Wyandra said. "Anytime. Just say the word."

"The process isn't painful?"

"Oh, heavens, no. Some of the rods might feel a little tight—"

"And there's no real danger?" She knew there wasn't, the *Delineator* article had said so, and Wyandra too had explained about the connection of a conductor with the earth and how nothing could happen, but she didn't mean that. What she was talking about was any further loss of hair. Because she would take *that* most unkindly, Mrs. Prentice said.

No, just the opposite, Wyandra said, and started to explain again that what a permanent wave did was to change the…internal structure…

But Mrs. Prentice didn't really care about the details. She just wanted Wyandra to be careful, and if she could make it look like Sarah Bernhardt's in *La Reine*, that would be sufficient.

Wyandra never saw Sarah Bernhardt in person, she said, even though she had played the Salt Lake Theater, but remember when she died? How the papers were full of pictures of her, and one especially? The one she had taken in that coffin she carried around with her, that she used to sleep in, the very one they finally buried her in!

She remembered the picture, Mrs. Prentice said, the lilies in her hand. The woman was a dreadful eccentric. Still, her coiffure in *La Reine* was charming, as why wouldn't it be? Created by Monsieur Lavallière, the best in Paris. Cousin Virginia used to go to him, or rather he came to her, though the women he would leave his salon for, and actually go to their *house*, you could count on the fingers of one hand, and that included a Royal Princess.

"You must have gone to Paris with your cousin about every year, didn't you?" Wyandra said as, with particular care and attention, she began to block off the now sparse but somehow strangely patrician hair.

"Halcyon days," the old woman said with a sigh, forgetting for the moment the stifling or ice-cold rooms shared with Miss Izard up under the eaves of the grand hotels, and all the other indignities she had had to endure as a poor relation with only a few hundred thousands to her name in the midst of wealth beyond the dreams of avarice.

"The skies of Paris," she said. "The trees. The river."

"The stores too, I imagine, isn't that right? Jewelry stores." Wyandra had heard it all a hundred times, but what matter?

"Perfumeries. Over there they have these rows of exquisite little shops only selling one thing. Lace, for instance. Parasols. A marzipan shop on the Boulevard Poissonnière where all the little things were made out of marzipan, sculpted by real artists."

"Imagine," Wyandra said, beginning to sweat. "And then people would come along and eat them." Her chapped hands, still stained with henna though she had scrubbed them hard, shook a little as she tried to work fast.

"And did I ever happen to mention the time—? This was before I met my husband."

"I don't believe you did, Mrs. Prentice. No, please don't move your head just yet. What time was that?"

But Mrs. Prentice had forgotten what she was going to say. Instead, "Oh, this *desert*," she said bitterly. "To be surrounded—ignorance—poverty of soul—" She paused. "'Savoir faire'! The French *never* say 'savoir faire.'"

"Don't they, Mrs. Prentice?"

"'Présence' is the word, of course. 'Présence.' They *never* say 'faux pas' either. And it is *not* 'pièce de résistance.'"

"Is that a fact? It must be lovely over there, hearing the French language. You know Albert's grandfather's *father* came from Paris originally," Wyandra said, not daring to pause long enough in her work to wipe the drops off her forehead.

"'Gaffe,'" Mrs. Prentice said. "'Tour de force' or '*plat* de résistance.'"

"I'll bet you speak it like a native, don't you?"

"These canaille. Well, I might be forced to *live* in this wilderness, but I can honestly say I have never—" She paused, then said, "Little does one know!"

"How very, very true."

A little later she roused herself from the brown study she had fallen into to say, "I hope, Wyandra, that you aren't pulling my hair out by the roots."

"Oh, no, Mrs. Prentice. What I'm doing now, you can see there in the glass, is what is called *winding*."

"I hope I may be able to endure it."

"Oh, you'll be able—Aristocrats can always—Well, let's see. You'll be out of here by—" Wyandra's heart sank as she looked at the clock and realized how very far they still had to go.

"Would you be so kind as to hand me my book? And I shall need my glasses."

"Well, if you don't mind, Mrs. Prentice, I think—I don't believe that right this minute would be the time—"

"This is all very inconvenient."

"I know it is. But it will soon be over."

"This is dreadful, Wyandra," Mrs. Prentice said when the operation had progressed to the stage where the heavy heated curlers that dangled from the long, twisted electrical cords had been hooked on and the steaming had started. She began to move restively in the web.

"No, Mrs. Prentice, you mustn't touch," Wyandra said, catching and holding the hands that fluttered upward.

"Don't do that! Don't hold onto my hands! I can't stand it."

"But you'll burn yourself if you touch."

"I'm smothering. You must unhook these dreadful—I've got to go!"

"Now, Mrs. Prentice, please—please!"

She tried to get up. Wyandra pushed her back. She tried again, kicking, flailing about, hitting out with her fists.

"I'm dying! Smothering!"

"No, you're not. No, really—"

But her face was white with little red spots, her eyes bulged, her breath came in little gasps, there was a blue line around her mouth, she sagged in the wires.

"You can't faint! Oh, you mustn't faint!" Wyandra looked around wildly, saw the pitcher of water on Albert's dressing table, ran over, grabbed it, ran back and threw the water in the ghastly face.

A sputter, a flash, a cracking sound.

"Now, Mrs. Prentice, I'll hurry and we'll have you—out of there—in no—And then some other time when you feel more—When the weather—On a cooler day—Mrs. Prentice?"

Shaking, Wyandra reached out and picked up the limp hand, dropped it. Then she reached out and took it again, this time feeling for the pulse in the bony wrist. There was none. She sought for it, it wasn't there. She dropped the hand, gathered up the still form hooked to the wires so as to place her own head against the wet taffeta chest with the row of little buttons—and listen—and try to hear. And not hear—

"Mrs. Prentice! Please, I beg you! *Please*—"

The head heavy with the curlers lolled forward, the eyes—white within the open lids, rolled back, no color showing.

Carefully Wyandra placed her back in the chair, tilted the slack chin, adjusted the cords to distribute the weight more evenly, even looked at the clock to see how much longer the steaming…As though the process was still going on. As if the expensive machine, instead of having with some terrible logic of its own passed a current of electricity through Mrs. Prentice's body sufficient to cause her death, was going to finish its appointed task and merely send her forth curly-haired and not dissatisfied, to the old Pierce Arrow sedan parked down on Main Street with Mr. Loomis leaning against the side of it, waiting…She had said when she arrived that she sent him back home, six hours was rather a long time to wait, although when she thought of Cousin Virginia's coachmen and chauffeurs and the waits *they* had had to endure in zero and every other kind of weather! it made her realize how the world had deteriorated in the meanwhile…She would call Birdelle to dispatch him when her hair was done.

AND IN THIS DREAM I had her all hooked up...

Wyandra stood there looking at her and it wasn't true. She put her hand out, drew it back, no, the time wasn't up, it still had to...steam...But she was dead. Mrs. Prentice was sitting there hooked up getting a beautiful spiral permanent wave, without dry burns, without steam burns such as the demonstrator had warned her against, without an accidental pull-blister like the one on poor little Rosetta's scalp, Wyandra was absolutely positive, she was getting better at this all the time, Albert always said she had a natural knack, he always encouraged her so much, and the wave was going to be just perfect. Wind, wrap, steam, cool...The only problem, *Mrs. Prentice was dead.*

Wyandra took a faltering step backwards. The...machine generated a current at a pressure of...How many volts did the man from the company say? High voltage, low, then high again...Be careful about water. But Mrs. Prentice...all of a sudden to get in such a panic, going to jump out from the chair, pull all the cords loose...starting to faint. What was a person supposed to do. It crackled, flashed, the most terrible sound, like lightning had struck, like a bolt of lightning, cracked like a whip...A woman got struck with lightning on the streets of Salt Lake one time, in one split second her blood stopped circulating, so the paper said, she never drew another breath, consciousness was blotted out instantly, the permanent derangement of the vital functions beyond recovery...Lightning and electricity were the same thing, as Benjamin Franklin was the first to—

Sick to death, Wyandra slumped down to the floor by the pretty shoes on the motionless feet. Old shoes...You could tell that by the style, the cut steel buckles, not because they looked the least bit old or worn. That was because...rich people always bought the best, and the best of course lasted a long time and looked beautiful...And they had beautiful feet, too, from not having to stand on them all day till they were flat and spread out, old ruggeds. And they had...shoe trees. Beautiful closets. And she had...

What am I going to do? Call Dr. Farr, she is only a chiropractor, but they know about the human body, where everything is located. Wyandra put a hand on the dressing table and pulled herself up, shuddering with nausea. No, can't ask her, wait, I have to think, call a doctor. But she's dead, struck by lightning, it zigzagged and cut through her...Notify the...But no, I can't, they'll come and arrest...I have killed her, I put her in the chair here, and what I should have done...And nobody will come to Albert's shop anymore. It took so long to pay for it and the good will, but the funny part was, I already *had* good will, a connection of customers already, because do you realize, Agnes, I have been with Albert and Lucitie Alfonce since I was nine years old, since Da' and me left Queensland and came over here with those Hawaiians...What a long time ago that was! I have *worked* in the shop. Oh, I wish you could have seen Albert in those days, how he looked, and when he was sixty he was still...

This is a very good permanent waving machine. Agnes was very kind. I will soon have her paid back and then Rosetta can go to Normal School and be a teacher. But if nobody comes to the shop anymore for fear they will be electrocuted? If I can't pay what I owe?

Sick, sick, she stood and swayed.

And the worst of it is, a license. They never thought of such a thing in the old days when Albert...when Lucite...I was ten years old when I started in the shop, and the first thing I did was braid hair! They used to wear so many coils, braids, switches, waterfalls and false pieces of every description in those times it was funny, transformations, really you would laugh, everyone had to look like the Sutherland sisters in the advertisements, with their long rippling hair, eighty inches long or whatever it was, dragging on the floor. And then I used to...shave up the soap for the shampoos, and stand and stir...And I learned how to make the different...Camomile tea for blonde hair...Capsicum. Oil of lavender and lemon. In those days Albert took red geraniums and rubbed them to a paste, the yellow inside of lilies...No one ever dressed hair so beautiful as Albert. And first I just brushed, and learned to massage the scalp, and parted off the sections. And then I learned...paper curling, round curling...And I could tell by the smell of the iron...And marcel waving. Nobody had a license in those days, but now with the beauty schools that have opened up...But, you see, Alfonce's Beauty Shop *has* a license, it's made out to me, I know the people in the office, Albert knew them, they understand how things used to be long ago, Albert's grandfather belonged to a *guild*, they called them guilds, that was all the license he needed. And he taught Albert and Albert taught me. But now they won't live forever down there in the bureau, and the new people will come in and you have to take a *state examination*, and I am fifty-one years old...and what good will a license do anyway if I have destroyed Albert's shop? If nobody will come anymore because a woman died here getting a permanent? And my dear child Rosetta...How will we live? What will we do? And if they put me in prison?

What about the good will then?

I must call...I must notify...

I have to go...

ADA SAID AFTERWARDS SHE THOUGHT Wyandra seemed somewhat strange when she went down on the elevator, but she had her hat on and she said something about getting something she had run out of, and Ada had said, well, don't take a sunstroke while you're at it, walk on the shady side, though it will soon be evening, and Wyandra said she would, that was her intention, and then she was gone. Ada *knew* Mrs. Prentice hadn't gone down in the elevator but she thought perhaps at about five, when she left it untended to go in and have a cup of tea with her mother, that perhaps Mrs. Prentice had *walked* down, but now that she thought of it she realized that could never have happened. The minute she saw the operator wasn't there, she'd have summoned Wyandra to go and find her. Ada knew her, Mrs. Prentice was an old customer of Alfonce's. And she'd have looked vexed and been vexed, she didn't appear like a woman to stand annoyance …The girls was out to Saltair at the Senior Picnic? Ada said. And Wyandra said yes. Then Ada said, the happiest days of their lives! and Wyandra nodded and that was all that was said.

A crowd gathered down by the entranceway when the policemen came sweating in their brass-buttoned blue serge and helmets, with their sticks in their hands as though at the commencement of destructive action, and word went round that someone had been murdered some way in the beauty parlor upstairs, a woman, stabbed, electrocuted or something, though somebody said the elevator girl had said …That was Ada, she was the source of information, about how the chauffeur and the daughter came, and rang, and rode up to Alfonce's on four, as by that time it was past suppertime, and the door was unlocked, so they went in—And of course it was an accident, what else could it be? There the mother was! hooked up to the permanent waving machine, dead. The doctor came, two doctors in fact, an ambulance …But the ambulance was sent away, and then came the police pushing their way in through the crowd, plainclothes detectives too, you can be sure of that.

Ada said the Prentice daughter wasn't crying, she looked more like somebody had hit her on the head. Mrs. Prentice's husband apparently was still at home. Their car was that limousine which the end stuck way out into Main Street, none of the family drove it, just the chauffeur. Ada couldn't *imagine* what became of Wyandra. About there, Ada kind of came to the end of pertinent facts and fell back on a few serious admonitions such as, In the midst of life we are in death. Rich, poor, we all have to go. If life was something money could buy, the rich would live and the poor would die, and so on.

Then the police went upstairs, and some plainclothesmen, and police barred the entrance and wouldn't let anyone in, only just the tenants coming home from work, the ones that worked. That was as an accommodation to Mr. Cutler's son, heir to the building, who didn't live or even have an office there as his father had had, but who didn't want the place full of curiosity seekers. One policeman was posted at the door and there was one up in the beauty parlor waiting for the proprietor to come home. What had ever possessed Wyandra to *leave* like that? just *bolt*, with the woman in the chair, dead, electrocuted by the permanent waving machine, although one of the doctors was saying it could have been a stroke, or her heart, they wouldn't know until they did the—examination. And if those clumsy men up there didn't have a time getting her loose from all those rods! There's a certain way to undo them. Ada was in and out of the shop watching, the elevator standing empty with the door open. Let them ring. This was an emergency. She took the cage down and brought it up when *she* wanted, and ran in and out of the room of death.

Some of the men even wanted to just take a scissors and whack the rods off up where they joined the cords, wound so tightly with Mrs. Prentice's hair. "You just do that," Ada said, "if you want a lawsuit on your hands." But then, as luck would have it, the china painter peeked in and at first nearly had a conniption fit, because she herself had been hooked up that same way to that same machine not a week before! and the dead woman might have been herself! It prostrated Dr. Farr, the first person to undergo the operation, when she heard. But the china painter was a sensible woman and soon got control of herself, a miss is as good as a mile, she said. She even went in, offered to help and soon extricated Mrs. Prentice from the octopus that took her life as surely as if she had fallen into the clutches of a monster of the deep.

They carried her down in the elevator wrapped in a blanket and put her in the hearse and it drove away. By that time dusk was falling, plum-blue the way it is in June and the western sky a rosy orange. The lights coming on looked white and pale. The crowd drifted off in different directions. A man came from the Tribune, and another man. Ada was the source of information. But where was Wyandra? "The poor thing will *have* to come home," Ada said. "She can't walk the streets all night!" Or do anything else, by night or by day, for Wyandra was dead, though no one realized that then. She had gone to the Bamberger Railway Station at some time after seven, for what purpose no one knew till it dawned on Rosetta later that she must have gone there to meet *her* coming home from Saltair on the six forty-five excursion cars. But they had been so crowded they waited for the eight forty-five—and when Wyandra couldn't see Rosetta anywhere in the throng coming home, she couldn't think or anything and must have wandered across the tracks hardly knowing where she was going, and got in the path of another train.

In the station the stragglers heard talk about some woman getting killed on the tracks earlier, no one knew who she was, but not until Rosetta got home did she realize—!

And for weeks, months, years, if she thought of Wyandra that last morning, her pale, anxious face, the henna stains on her hands and slipping her the dollar, her eyes would fill with tears, she would feel like she had a big goiter pressing on her windpipe.

Agnes and even Nancibel wondered if Wyandra, in the state she was in, had stepped in front of the train *on purpose*, but Rosetta said no, oh, no.

No.

After Darrel got to the picnic and found Lavonne, and he and she went down by the lake and wandered around waiting for the dance to start, and Anita and Frances started talking to two boys who didn't even *go* to West High so had no business being there, Rosetta found an inconspicuous place to sit and just look at whatever there was to see until time to catch the train back to Salt Lake. The day had been long and she was glad it was nearly over. Oh, when she got home, how *good* she was going to be to Wyandra, and tell her—her hair turned out *fine*, she got *compliments*, her dress was pretty, she loved it, and remember her theme? The Brahmins, the Untouchables? Well, the caste system was going strong at Saltair for sure. But where it was different in America than in India—she and Wyandra would really discuss this—Nancibel's son Legrand, for instance. Because to look at him you would think *he* was a Brahmin. That nice white shirt, nice tie, tweed pants, jacket and nice haircut. But he wasn't. His father repaired bicycles in a shop made out of part of their garage, they lived in a common house without even a nice porch, just a small stoop in front. But his every action somehow was of somebody *privileged*.

Legrand was nice, though. Before Darrel got out to Saltair and Rosetta and Lavonne were walking around together, they encountered Legrand several times with his friend Palmer and said hello. Then Anita and Frances, temporarily at loose ends, joined Lavonne and Rosetta in their stroll and all four passed him and Palmer, and Frances said she thought Legrand was awfully cute. Anita didn't agree. She said she thought he looked like a sissy and was quite embarrassed when Lavonne said he was Rosetta's cousin! Only her second cousin, Rosetta said hurriedly, so Anita wouldn't be embarrassed.

Sometimes Legrand and Palmer said hello, sometimes they and the cluster of four girls just smiled at each other as they passed and repassed, wandering around, sometimes they even pretended not to see each other, though not in a snubbing way. Legrand had had a picture he drew of the football field printed in the yearbook and also a piece called "This School of Ours." In Lavonne's copy he signed both, as well as his photo over in the section entitled "Seniors." Then he asked her to sign her picture in his book, that was the custom. When any signing was going on at school, Rosetta, who didn't have a yearbook, always pretended to be deep in study or just on her way to the cloakroom or Domestic Science, so she hadn't been in on this exchange. She rejoined Lavonne that day just as Legrand and Palmer were going down the hall. Palmer was Legrand's best friend, so *he* signed Lavonne's book too, but didn't have the manners to ask Lavonne to sign *his* book. She just couldn't *stand* him, Lavonne said.

All of a sudden Rosetta, sitting in her vantage point on a corner of the stairs with her arms around her knees, watching the passersby, thought she could see the difference between the caste system in India and the caste system in America (no mention of which, that America *had* a caste system, had she made in her theme), and that was, as she knew from *National Geographic* and a book called *Mother India*—in India there was *no social intercourse with those of another caste whatsoever*! while in America there was. But social intercourse didn't mean spit, and that was why people in America were so wild and nervous and up in the air, because they didn't know *really* where they stood. The social intercourse part just confused the whole issue, while over in India—

"Hello. What are *you* doing, sitting here all alone?"

She looked up, startled. Legrand stood there in his shirtsleeves, his jacket over his shoulder.

"Oh, nothing," she said. "Waiting to go catch the train and go home."

"What happened to Lavonne?"

"She's with Darrel. They're coming to the dance. Where's Palmer?"

"I don't know. Talking to some kids." He took a seat beside her.

"It seems kind of funny to see you by yourself."

"It seems kind of funny to see *you* by yourself."

"Well, you know who Lavonne's boyfriend is, Darrel. He just got here a little while ago. He's a Future Farmer and I don't know if you saw it or not, but his picture was in the paper. Raising the biggest cantaloupe?"

"I didn't see it," Legrand said.

"But speaking of pictures. That was certainly a wonderful picture you drew of…the football field. And that piece you wrote too, 'This School of Ours.' I'll bet you something, you could write a book if you wanted to. Or be an artist. I mean, you really could."

"Boy, that Miss Miller," he said, not acknowledging the praise. "That chin."

She smiled weakly. "But I liked English Four," she said. "In fact it was the favorite subject I ever took."

"Well, if I think about it…mine too," he said.

"You and Palmer always like to sit way in back," she said.

"We get out faster," he said. "Palmer hates poetry, *Isaac and Archibald* and all that stuff. Say. Remember *Captain Carpenter*?" Legrand laughed.

She laughed, too. "Wasn't that the dumbest poem?"

"A person could hardly make head nor tails of it," he said.

"John Crowe Ransom," she said. Her voice held a loving tone.

"Why, if *I* tried to perpetrate something like that…"

"I took it home and read it to Wyandra. 'Captain Carpenter rose up in his prime…'"

"Did she laugh?"

"Kind of. But she thought it was sad, too."

"First he had his nose cut off."

"Then somebody broke his legs."

"Then his arms…"

"His arms got bit off at the elbow," she amended.

"Oh, yes. Then 'another plucked out his sweet blue eyes—'"

"That's right. Then what?"

"Well, at the end he's fighting there, blind and with no arms, holding his sword between his teeth…"

"His 'rotten teeth alack'—"

"And whoever he's fighting with *that* time knocks him flat on his back on the ground…"

"He's old by then."

"Real old. Sixty or more."

"But he still keeps fighting. And then he gets it. And his enemy digs out his heart on the sharp point of his blade." Conveying this sentiment into pantomime, Legrand pointed his trophy heavenward, then shook it contemptuously off the end of his imaginary sword.

"'His round red heart,'" Rosetta said as though gazing on that very relic pitiful in the dust. She really felt sorry for Captain Carpenter, who had tried to right the world's harms. But when Legrand laughed again, she laughed too.

"'The curse of hell upon the sleek upstart,'" he recited softly, pretending to make a slashing cut,

That got the Captain finally on his back
And took the red red vitals of his heart
And made the kites to whet their beaks clack clack.

She turned to look at him. "Why, you *know* it," she said.

"It's just so comical," he said shyly.

"Well, it is, but at the same time..."

"Say, that reminds me," he said. "Palmer heard a joke at the Pantages along the same line. This guy tells this girl he loves her so much he would cut off his arm for her, so she says to go ahead, so he does. Then he cuts off his other arm and then his legs, and you know what the girl said? She said, 'Take your trunk and get out of here.'"

She laughed. "I'll bet Palmer could go on the stage if he wanted to himself. He's so witty, and his looks."

"He's going away," he said abruptly.

"Palmer is?"

"To Circleville."

"Gee, you'll miss him, you guys are so thick. Just for the summer?"

"Probably to stay. He's not going to go to college."

"You are, though, aren't you?"

"Mom wants me to. How about you?"

"Wyandra wants me to go to Normal School. Lavonne...she's going to get married, I guess. If Darrel's folks will let him."

"I guess I'll take art and...stuff like that."

"Gee," she said. "That's awful—about Palmer. You're such a—a team."

"That's when you get tired of people."

But later when they saw Palmer walk past deep in conversation with Orval Gowdy, who won the Steno Club's prize for the fastest typist, Rosetta with a quick sidelong glance saw Legrand's Adam's apple go up and down and his lips tighten.

"Orval's folks bought him a car for graduation," he said. "Second-hand. An Essex."

"I don't see where that's so wonderful."

"Palmer's going to help work on it and then Orval's going to drive him to Circleville, because it's Orval's uncle down there that might give Palmer a job."

"What doing?"

"Working on a ranch the uncle owns."

"Well, he'll come back. Palmer, I mean. I bet he'll get so lonesome for Salt Lake he just can't stand it."

"It certainly doesn't make any difference to *me*."

But she knew it did and cast about for something to say to fill the sad silence.

"Would you look at that sky," she finally said.

"Looks like it's burning up, doesn't it? And there's the moon."

"This early, you can see right through it."

"I like the night better than the daytime."

"Me too."

"It seems like you can think better."

"I think so too."

But she wasn't thinking very well that night, though it wasn't really night, just twilight, when she and Legrand started to walk down to the beaches, following a sign that said *Sunset, Silver Sands*. They never did get there, because all of a sudden they heard the train whistle and turned and ran back, but by that time it was too late, there it went, puffing out smoke and with a few lights shining, and every once in a while a toot on the whistle.

"Gee, it'll be almost *ten* before I get home," she said. "Wyandra will think I drowned or something."

"Mom the same, always worrying."

"There's nothing to do but wait, I guess." Because he was her blood kin, she could speak to him as she couldn't to just a boy who was no relation. "Now, Legrand, please don't feel like you have—to stay with me and talk or anything. I mean…because it's almost dark and everything…and having to wait for the next train…"

"I want to," he said. "I'd just as soon talk to you as anybody…"

Chapter Fifty-three

✳

AND SO THEY DID TALK, AT FIRST ON THE STEPS WHERE THEY HAD BEEN SITTING before, and then walking around. Legrand was out of money by then because of the roller coaster and trying to win a kewpie doll with an ostrich-feather skirt for his mother at the Cane Rack or Wheel of Fortune, and because of buying a package of Lucky Strikes. It turned out he smoked, but Rosetta didn't think that was sinful. She thought it was sinful for a girl but not a boy. Or not really *sinful*, she just didn't think it looked nice. For a girl it looked tough.

She still had the silver dollar Wyandra slid in under her hand when she lay on the bed crying, her conscience had pained her so that she was going to give the dollar back and tell her how sorry she was...But maybe if she just...Wyandra would want her to treat Legrand, Rosetta was sure of that, and so she dropped the dollar in his pocket and said for him to buy them a hot dog and some root beer, and at first he said he certainly wouldn't do any such thing! but finally he consented and did.

And they walked around some more and then she suggested they have an ice cream cone, so Legrand bought two, vanilla, and they sat on a railing outside the pavilion licking them and listened to the band playing "Sweet Sue," "What Is This Thing Called Love?," "Diane" and a lot of other songs...As Palmer and Orval didn't go past anymore or seem to be anyplace, the cousins thought they must be on their way back to town. Probably couldn't wait to get started on Orval's dumb old car!

THE MINUTE DARREL APPEARED LAVONNE forgot everything, and when she and he ran past Rosetta and Legrand after the dance was over and the last train was ready to start back and Rosetta called out to her, Lavonne flashed her a lovely warm smile, but her eyes didn't look as if she knew her from Adam, which she really didn't seem to do at that moment, all wrapped up in Darrel as she was. And the funny thing was, she wasn't *really* crazy about Darrel, she said so, even though he had been elected National President of the Future Farmers and had his picture taken in Washington, D.C. with the President of the United States. There were about four hundred other delegates in the picture, but still, Darrel was the one that was standing next to the President on his right, while a Japanese boy stood on his left. There were lots of boys Lavonne would rather have had than Darrel, she admitted it, but yet when they were together, the whole rest of the world just faded away.

487

Anita and Frances had two boys in tow when seen climbing aboard the open-air car at the end of the train, so Rosetta and Legrand stayed where they were and sat together for the ride back to Salt Lake. Then from the terminal they walked the long blocks down South Temple to Main Street, and because Legrand was going to telephone his mother from the beauty shop to say he had missed the earlier train and would be home soon, he walked with her to the Constitution Building. The police had gone by then, the doorway looked the same as always, but when they got inside the foyer the elevator, instead of being dark and locked up, was brightly lit, and Ada stood there holding the door open. A man about Ada's own age was with her, a relative of the Hair Tonic Manufacturers on three who had recently come to live and work with them. He had been riding with her since this afternoon, Ada said in a strange voice, keeping her company. She didn't know what she would have done otherwise, gone all to pieces probably. And the funny thing was, when it first happened . . . that is to say, when the daughter and that chauffeur arrived and found out . . . everything . . . she was as cool as a cucumber, while a little later . . .

"Started shaking like a leaf," the man said. "Cried and shook . . . "

"But of course I got ahold of myself, a person has to," Ada said, stopping the car exactly on a level with the floor and sliding the door open.

"People have to, Rosetta," Ada said firmly. "And you will have to, too."

NANCIBEL'S MOTHER-IN-LAW COULDN'T SEE ANY reason why someone as distant as a second or third cousin should live with them and add to John's burdens. Rosetta was eighteen, a high school graduate, of course it was very sad about Wyandra, but it would be different if the girl was a small orphan. Let her take care of her own self! Get a job doing housework. Besides, she's got aunts and uncles, hasn't she? Not whole, Nancibel said, and as for a job doing housework, why didn't it occur to anyone to think that she herself might be in the market for a hired girl? Because she most certainly was! with all the *extra work* around here. She said this pointedly, her mother-in-law, called Mother Hollis, having moved in the previous Thanksgiving. But Mother Hollis paid no attention, it was just ridiculous, taking the responsibility. And how about throwing a boy just at the most crucial age together with a girl day and night, her bloomers hanging out on the line, her silk stockings blowing in the wind, tucking in her collar when she washed her hair, things like that? Except for the saving grace of the poor girl's *eye* and Legrand being so set on beauty, tacking up pictures of movie actresses and drawing them too, and—"For that matter," Mother Hollis said, "why can't she go and stay with Herman, your brother, and his wife Agnes? *They're* as related to her as you are!"

"Because they don't need her, that's why," Nancibel said, "and we do. And besides . . . she can walk to beauty school from here."

"Beauty school! And who is paying for *that*, if I may ask?"

"We are, if you want to know. She's got to have a trade, and she was practically raised in the beauty shop business. It's only going to take a year. And she'll be helping me after school and Saturdays and Sundays. She'll pay it all back."

"I can well imagine!"

"She signed a note. Interest and everything."

"Have you taken a look at your husband's *color*?"

"What's that got to do with it?"

"Has he told you about that stitch?"

"What stitch?"

"The stitch in his side when he goes to lift something? Did he tell you about his *father*? I'd be watching my husband *pretty* close if I was you," Mother Hollis said.

GOING TO BEAUTY SCHOOL WAS Nancibel's idea. And she even went on to say that when Rosetta got out and worked awhile for somebody, and paid back what she owed and started saving, why, she could come along someday and open another one of Alfonce's Beauty Parlors! kind of a memorial to Nancibel's own father and mother, Albert and Lucitie Alfonce. Besides, it seemed so sad that something that had gone on so long, in one unbroken line, you might say, clear back to *France*, would finally die out.

"Are you crazy?" Agnes said. "Who would go to a place called Alfonce's now? After all the stuff in the paper about the permanent waving machine electrocuting the woman and Wyandra throwing herself under the train!"

"She didn't throw herself under the train. It was an accident."

"She just threw in the sponge."

Nancibel didn't argue. As Agnes owned everything Wyandra had, she having put it all up as collateral to get the permanent waving machine, Agnes disposed of it as she pleased, selling most of it but storing some of the old beauty shop equipment in their basement, and even acted like she alone should have the say of the circumstances of Wyandra's last hours.

Mrs. Prentice's picture had been prominently displayed on the front page, under the headline SOCIALITE DIES IN BEAUTY PARLOR ACCIDENT. A small picture of Wyandra also appeared on the inside (the one taken during the war, when she was interviewed by the Tribune about dressing Mary Pickford's hair after Mary's French maid choked on a piece of steak), beside the story of her death on the Bamberger train-tracks. And because of the connection with Mary Pickford, the piece ran on at some length. She operated Alfonce's Beauty Parlor in the Constitution Building, 36 South Main Street, where she also resided with a foster daughter, Rosetta, it said, and went on to say that the Constitution Building was the first commercial building in Utah, built two stories high in 1850, then forty or so years later having the three top floors added by John C. Cutler, owner, "who also died of self-destruction last July 30 at his residence at 925 South West Temple." Why *his* name should have been brought into the tragic affair of a permanent waving machine electrocuting a beauty parlor customer, his family certainly did not know. It made it look as if there was some tie or something between his demise and the suicide of the hairdresser Wyandra Faine, which there certainly was not! and they threatened to sue the Tribune. Whether they did or not is lost in history's shadows.

THE PRENTICES, MR. PRENTICE AND his daughter Birdelle, were none too pleased either with the sensational way Mrs. Prentice's death was reported, or *her* obituary. She was sixty-three, not sixty-five, and she was *not* a recluse. Would a recluse be up at Alfonce's Beauty Parlor having a permanent? She had not played a role in Salt Lake society, true, but that was because *her* definition of the word "society" and a grubby *reporter*'s definition of the word were two different things. Also, her relationship to the Gerards of New York City and Bar Harbor was through the maternal, not paternal, line, and to speak of *wealth* in an individual's death notice was not only vulgar but inappropriate. She was *not* a "millionairess."

Wasn't it just sickening? Birdelle said, down in the kitchen telling Gram what to fix for dinner. It was, Gram agreed. In fact the whole thing was just so terrible that sometimes she wondered if the Mormon church wasn't right and if the Last Days weren't really nearly upon us. When she thought that never again would Mrs. Prentice come in through that doorway! She could see her in her mind's eye as she spoke, always with her corset on, always like she just stepped out of a bandbox even though laying around most of the time. And always with those cold hands, which would sometimes, in the midst of pointing out an economical recipe, handing over a list or getting help to turn the key in the storage-room lock, would touch Gram's hands, half-dried and steaming hot from the dishpan or from peeling hot potatoes or something, always warm, while hers were like ice even in summer...

"*Our* consolation," Birdelle said for about the fifth time, "is that she need never become a chronic invalid in a wheelchair. Or suffer the pain of losing her loved ones!"

One of Mrs. Prentice's loved ones, her husband Mr. Prentice, suffered a good deal of pain for a few days in his stomach, and his head hurt too. Birdelle had to see to everything, the funeral, speak to the newspapers, and have long consultations with Mr. Swan of the law firm of Swithin and Swan. Always running here or there, she could hardly call her soul her own anymore, Birdelle said. But she was glad her father had let her take the responsibility, it was good for her and good for him too, to just follow Dr. Beauchamp's advice and go right to bed till he started to feel better. Just lie there and read the Sherlock Holmes stories, eat nourishing meals, nap and doze and, as the song said, "let the rest of the world go by." With a daughter of Birdelle's ability (hadn't she hung onto, as you might say, her birthright during that test by fire, her unfortunate marriage to that Hollywood Body Builder?), her father could rest easy, turning decision-making over to her...

Mrs. Prentice had not believed in dealing on the New York Stock Exchange, the market situation meant nothing to her, in that she was ignorant, we all have our blind spots. Birdelle herself did not realize the scope of what was possible and her own natural talents along that line until Mr. Swithin happened to speak of his own fortuitous investments and she ventured an investment or two herself, and then a few more. It was like Alma Gluck not knowing she could sing till she was a grown woman and one fine day opened her mouth and out came a beautiful, well-placed and diamond-clear "L'Heure Exquise." American Cyanide B, Radio, Cities Service, Commercial Solvents, American Railway Express… "You just rest here, Father. Let me handle everything…"

Gram had no objections to carrying up the trays, then fetching them back down, an easier job than Mrs. Smith's by far, who did the cleaning and washing. Mrs. Prentice had had Mrs. Smith come in two days a week, but after Birdelle took charge and her father took to his bed with a contentment that amazed her, for she always thought he *liked* bustling about, Birdelle engaged her to come in every day of the week but Sunday.

"We can afford it," she said. And told her father what she had been doing in the Great Bull Market, the greatest the world had ever seen, that would go on and on, thanks to the man who had fed Europe and finally now had triumphed over poverty. And thanks also to far-seeing Calvin Coolidge, who really started it all years before when he was President, and to a Secretary of the Treasury who knew if you want prosperity, you have got to reduce income-tax. So said Mr. Swan, whom Birdelle was happy to quote on any and all occasions, for he was a very wise and distinguished-looking man.

Mr. Prentice nodded, settled more firmly back against his pillows and went on reading *The White Company*. He had a complete set of Sir Arthur Conan Doyle and was going to read every volume, even the ones he had already read, even *The War in South Africa; Its Cause and Conduct*, whether boring or not. Gram didn't mind the tray business. He never wanted much on it, a bowl of Campbell's soup, a piece of toast, and he had taken to drinking coffee since his wife died. It was a terrible thing to say, but he seemed much more contented as a widower confined to his bed, reading except for an hour or two a day when he shaved, tidied himself up and strolled bare-shanked about the halls in nightshirt and bathrobe and Mrs. Smith made his bed and dusted and swept his room, than as a husband in high starched collars and English woolens as heavy as a suit of armor, running about (it appeared now) at Mrs. Prentice's bidding, not his own. The same with Birdelle, her eyes shone, her cheeks were pink, she had bought herself a roadster, she had things to do outside the house, at the lawyer's, a brokerage firm by the name of Fite and Lethaby that kept the phone ringing for her to run and answer when she was home. Or *she* called *them*, or other people. She took another newspaper besides the Tribune, pored over the columns in its back pages. Or she kept her father company. "How about a game of bowls?"

"Not today, Birdelle."

She didn't care. Sometimes while "loose in the halls" (as Gram called Mr. Prentice's time out of bed) he took the elevator and came down to the kitchen to tell Gram to bake some of those chess pies, or how about a good old-fashioned lemon meringue pie or walnut layer cake with caramel frosting? But all he would eat was one piece. Then it would be left to her and Lavonne to finish it, maybe with Darrel's assistance if he was calling at the time. But Gram was not so cordial to Darrel as she once had been. What was he waiting for? Lavonne was through high school now, she had taken Commerce and Domestic Science, and look at the girl! if she couldn't be Miss America, Gram would miss her guess. She could easily get in the movies. All she needed was to cut down on her intake a little. But did Darrel appreciate her? No! Because of having his picture taken with the President of the United States, he acted like he was doing Lavonne a favor to still be going with her. Of course the Cartmills were nice people, a nice family, they had all that land out there in Bountiful, and Darrel *had* talked about getting married and his father building them a home. Now, though, he was mum on the subject, Gram hadn't heard it mentioned for a long time.

"What are you going to do, Lavonne? You are at the height of your beauty. If Darrel isn't going to step forth like a man and declare himself, then you have got to find someone who will. And let me say what I wish someone had said to *me* when I was your age, for I didn't always look like I do now, I can assure you, and that is this, that it's as easy to fall in love with someone rich as poor."

"His folks are giving Darrel land, they're going to build us a house."

"That's what *you* say, Lavonne. But *when*?"

Lavonne didn't know. She went downtown, occasionally during the noon hour she dropped in at the beauty college on the eighth floor of the Kimball Building to see Rosetta, not to let anybody practice on her. They would sit in a windowsill, Rosetta would make her eat part of her lunch and then they would walk around the block. Sometimes Lavonne went to a movie. Sometimes she went to the library, though she hadn't time to read much. At home she did her nails, her hair, Gram said to her you will wear it out (but of course you couldn't wear out *hair*), she painted her face as artists paint pictures, getting better at it all the time. The only mirror in their two basement rooms was the one suspended over the dresser that you could tip back and forth. It was only about a foot and a half square, so she couldn't see her whole self. She did see her whole self on occasion, of course, caught glimpses in the stores, in theater foyers, but she was so used to just concentrating on head and shoulders that the rest she more or less let go, as some painters let part of the picture go with a few broad strokes.

When the date for their wedding was set, then she was going to get down to a size 32 because you look bigger in white satin, or even start before that. A very good mirror was in the entrance hall, and there was no reason why she couldn't run in there from the kitchen whenever she wanted now that Mrs. Prentice was dead, poor lady, and Mr.

Prentice was in bed most of the time. But the daughter Birdelle was in and out as she never used to be, and Gram thought the best policy was for Lavonne to lay low and not remind anyone that the little dependent that Cook had been permitted to bring with her nine years before (providing the child was no trouble) was now a resplendent young lady with a fiancé! But the day came when Lavonne *had* to come out of their obscurity, and that was the day the carbuncle on the side of Gram's nose that she couldn't put a bandage on looked so fierce that she couldn't let Mr. Prentice see it, Mrs. Smith was ironing the starched pieces on the back porch and there was no one to send upstairs but Lavonne.

Mr. Prentice was glad to see her, Lavonne said.

She only had to carry up his tray a few more times, not because Gram's carbuncle got better but because Birdelle *fired* Gram. She fired her because of something that took place hundreds of miles away in New York City called the Panic, which caused Birdelle to lose all her money and become a pauper. That was what she *said*, wringing her hands, crying and carrying on in a way she certainly never did over the death of her mother. But it's a funny way to lose all your money (Lavonne was to remark this in later years) and become a pauper when you and your father keep right on living in a beautiful mansion! When you never have to do a tap of work in your life that anybody knows of! When you hang right on to your mink coat, your diamond rings, you've still got all your mother's jewels in the safe and there's no big auction sale, you've got a big car, plenty of gas, oh, no, indeed. The only difference was, Birdelle fired Gram.

She would cook for her father herself! she said, and began ordering Campbell's soup of different varieties by the case. She fired Mr. Loomis too, and hired a boy to cut the lawn when it needed to be cut, the rest of the gardening could go. And she fired Mrs. Smith, the cleaning lady. How dirty could two people get in twenty-two rooms when they only lived in about three of them? The washing could go to the Troy Laundry. Years hence the roadster, a Hudson, would fall apart and Birdelle would not replace it. Where was she going anyway? To the grocery store for half a pound of hamburger. To Auerbach's August Clearance Sale. For a walk. Up to the cemetery to her parents' graves. Or (still farther up ahead along the path of time) up the street to the twin-towered Cathedral of the Madeleine.

But it was a funny way to lose your money.

The Panic, my foot, Gram said. Birdelle ran upstairs and into her father's room and saw Lavonne sitting on the edge of his bed *talking* to him! that was all that ailed *her*. He politely invited Lavonne to sit there while he crumbled his toast up in his soup and ate it off his tray, and she politely did so. There *was* a so-called Panic, Gram would grant you that, the Tribune said so, the radio did too, big bankers and financiers were throwing themselves off skyscrapers, that could well be possible, but *Birdelle's* panic was caused by one thing and one thing only: green-eyed jealousy.

Lavonne was talking on the telephone long distance to Darrel in Bountiful when the thought dawned on Gram. What Birdelle was afraid of was that Lavonne was going to *attract* Mr. Prentice!

"Oh, *Gram*," Lavonne said when she had hung up and come back upstairs to the little room they had rented from Mrs. Smith temporarily till they knew what they were going to do, and Gram expressed this wild idea. "He's an old *man*."

But of course he wasn't, only sixty-four and probably as full of ideas as anybody. *That* was what ailed Birdelle, said Gram. She saw her father was enjoying a beautiful young girl's company and she couldn't bear it. And as Gram went on with her train of thought, to herself (for Lavonne wouldn't settle down to be sociable and help eat the box of chocolates they bought to celebrate this new phase of their lives but only selected one now and then as she wandered about absent-mindedly doing her beauty chores), Gram realized that if she had had the sense she was born with, Lavonne could probably have *married* Mr. Prentice and had the world by the tail. There they were on top of a gold mine and never even realized. Fortune had been within their grasp ... Here is the widower laying around in his nightshirt in bed, lolling around in the daytime, blinds half pulled down, and here comes this beautiful young girl in with his tray, well-developed, dimpled elbows, big blue eyes ... Gram reached for another chocolate and could have wept. It was a friend of her father's who was a tailor and could have traded a suit of clothes for half a block on Main Street and Third South and turned it down! And what was that property worth today!

Gram selected a chocolate-covered oblong of nougat, and a few tears did trickle down her cheeks. What was she supposed to do, seventy-two next April, and those squiggles before her eyes that used to just come and go but now squiggled all the time, and with a bladder constantly on the pour?

"So what did Darrel have to say? What does *he* think of the situation?"

Future Farmer. What kind of a farmer was that? *Future* supporter of Lavonne. Maybe, but maybe not. Gram wiped her eyes with the back of her hand, sniffed and bent forward over the chocolate box again. No one could say she was a big eater, but she did love a chocolate now and then, especially in the midst of a crisis.

"We might have a date next Saturday night," Lavonne said.

Gram drew an anguished sigh. "You have heard the expression 'young man's slave.' And that other one: 'old man's darling.' When I think what *you*, in the situation we was in, might have accomplished. And still might! If we could figure out some way."

But by that time Lavonne, popping a caramel into her mouth and on her way down to the kitchen (to ask Mrs. Smith for a little bit bigger and better looking-glass if she had one, the one in their room was all wavy), was out of earshot and Gram was talking to herself.

"Sitting on a gold mine and never had sense enough to know it!"

Gram did not have long to repine. At three the next morning the pain butted her in the stomach like a goat and must have lasted, for she moaned and groaned, but yet her eyes stayed shut, the lids working as if she was trying to open them but couldn't. By daylight the lids were motionless, the sheet over her chest scarcely lifted. When he came the doctor tried to force a solution of baking soda stirred up in milk down her, but it dribbled out the corner of her mouth. Next he tried unsuccessfully to administer a hot toddy with sugar in it and called for more blankets, though it would be ninety in the shade before eight a.m. Lavonne began to get scared, Mrs. Smith said she had smelled that sickly sweet smell before, when a neighbor lady died of sugar diabetes.

"Gram! Gram!" How was Lavonne supposed to get along without Gram? She didn't even know when she was going to get married!

The smell was in the sweat, Mrs. Smith said.

The doctor said one great danger of the comatose condition was for the lungs to gangrenate, the first stage of mortification, but tomorrow morning when he looked in he would—

Gram had taken sick at three a.m. without ever gaining consciousness and died the following three a.m., when human vitality is the lowest, and the doctor looked in in vain.

He sent his bill in vain, too.

Mrs. Smith wrote on the envelope which was addressed to Executor, Mrs. Youngberg's Collective Assets: *none here by that name.* The nerve of some people! Anyway, Lavonne wasn't there. She had gone to stay with some people named Hollis and, the last Mrs. Smith heard, was going to beauty school.

Nancibel told Mother Hollis she was getting twenty a month for Lavonne's room and board, but she wasn't. The poor girl's grandmother had insurance enough to bury her, she left Lavonne a legacy of two hundred dollars, enough to send her through business college if she wanted to go, but how in the meanwhile was she going to pay room rent and feed herself? Rosetta was the one who said if Nancibel would let Lavonne come and share her room, Lavonne would pay her something every week till she was paid, and Rosetta would help her. Also the two girls would help around the house, wash windows, iron, do whatever Nancibel wanted.

But of course this was an exaggeration, and Nancibel wasn't mean or demanding. After school and Saturdays and Sundays they behaved like typical girls. So said Mother Hollis in caustic tones as though speaking of a mingled horde of typical Mongols and Turks. But in one way it was better to have Lavonne in the house than not have her. Because there is safety in numbers, and Mother Hollis had been getting quite leery of all the laughing and talking going on in the kitchen and elsewhere between Rosetta and Legrand, them listening to the radio down in the dining room together till all hours, and the way Rosetta was giving Legrand hot oil shampoos and all that. Of course she had given them *all* a hot oil shampoo the way the school taught her, but in the case of young men…the very touch of a girl's hand…And a pair of *second* cousins could find themselves with a village idiot on their hands just as easy as *first* cousins, don't think they couldn't. To say nothing of…So Mother Hollis was glad to see *two* girls in the house, rather than one, both chums and both going to the same beauty school, which threw Legrand back on himself and his university studies.

But then Nancibel couldn't let her son be lonesome, with his friend Palmer gone down to southern Utah and no new friend to take his place, so what did *she* do but keep him company as much as she could herself, and *that* wasn't as it should be either. Why didn't she devote a little of that attention to her husband, out in the shop from morning till night inventing things, making the living and trying not to go under now that times were so bad? At least they soon would be! so said the paper. And that John was worried was plain to be seen. Had he had any idea of what Lavonne was tucking in under her belt those first weeks after the girl moved in, he would probably have had a nervous breakdown, but Mother Hollis wasn't going to bring one on by telling him. Not at present, anyway. But she did speak to Nancibel about it, and Nancibel said she had noticed but expected it to wear off when this crisis the poor girl had been going through smoothed down more to common daily life. What crisis? Well, leaving the place where she and Mrs. Youngberg had lived so long. Then Mrs. Youngberg, who had taken care of her for most of her life and waited on her hand and foot, dying like that, alive one day, dead the next. Then her boyfriend keeping her on tenterhooks, not giving her a diamond, not setting the date. And having to come and stay with *them* and be dependent, asked to work and having no choice anymore. Enrolling in beauty school…No wonder Lavonne ate!

BUT IT WAS NOTHING ANYONE said at Nancibel's house that hurled Lavonne as from a catapult into the reducing diet that would change her life. No, she overheard a remark at the dance out at the Old Mill that she and Darrel went to after she hadn't seen hide nor hair of him for two weeks. Then when she did see him he didn't say a word about her hair, which had been slightly bleached by her friend Colleen Gutke at the beauty school and arranged by Rosetta in a beautiful new way, or how beautiful her fingernails looked or how her eyes reflected the color of her dress. Not a *word*. All he wanted to do was talk about the section of his father's farm that he was farming, and how far behind the times his father was, and the stunt he, Darrel, was going to pull off in the Young Republican Club! and unimportant matters like that.

But *he* was not the one who made the fatal remark. What happened was, Darrel had left her temporarily on the edge of the dance floor full of romantic waltzers while he hurried around to the other side of the hall to have a word with a Future Farmer he thought he saw over there. Whether that was really who he saw or what words they exchanged, Lavonne never knew. Darrel explained when he came back, he must have, his lips moved, he was smiling, even laughing, but she (though her eyes were on him and she smiled too, as she always did like when your own reflection smiled at you in the glass) heard never a word. She stood pierced through, fixed, fastened, by sharp-pointed agony. Two handsome young men had hovered near, she felt their stares, felt as always her own transilluminate beauty as the great ball gemmed with cut and polished bits of looking-glass went around in the ceiling and its rays streamed past the radiant point she herself was in the soft star-shower, and "Diane" was playing, but yet the two were close enough so she could hear—and they said—one said, "They call them barns where I come from," and the other said, "Yeah."

Chapter Fifty-four

*

COLLEEN WENT ON THE DIET WITH HER. BUT IT WASN'T A DIET, IT WAS UTTER starvation such as the starving Armenians died of that caused their very name to be a by-word of *dying of hunger*. A cup of coffee, a lettuce leaf. Go to beauty school all day and then come home and eat a few canned string beans. Even Mother Hollis was worried, no human frame could take that, the first thing you know she was going to break down and then Nancibel would have her to take care of, an invalid, the child's stomach maybe dropped down onto her intestines, her kidneys floating…Mother Hollis spoke to her. "I speak to you like I would do if you was my own flesh and blood." Deaf ears, Lavonne starved on. Nancibel spoke to her. "Lavonne, honey, I don't know what you hope to accomplish…" Part of a carrot, a slice of the hard-boiled egg decorating the top of the bowl of potato salad. Legrand said to leave her alone, she knew what she was doing.

Rosetta had told him in confidence what Lavonne told her the boy at the dance had said that made her cry half the night and start dieting, and Legrand said maybe the remark was a blessing in disguise, because all she needed to be a real knockout was to lose weight. That was the first thing they did to you when you went to Hollywood, because *thinness* was one of the main reasons why actresses were so beautiful. And wouldn't it be a joke on those guys if one of these Saturday nights she went out there to that same Old Mill looking like a movie star and they fell for her like a ton of bricks! but she wouldn't give them the time of day. Nancibel asked Legrand not to encourage Lavonne. Going to the university like he did, taking art and things like that, would naturally give him authority with a young impressionable girl, and what he *should* be saying, if he had any human feeling, was that she would be *homely* if she didn't quit starving herself to death.

Finally, for her sake, he did say without conviction that a starving Armenian wouldn't win a beauty contest, but Lavonne didn't seem to pay any attention one way or the other. Her eyes hardly blinked by then, they were large, dazzlingly lovely, her set smile was like a doll's painted on. She stayed on course. That a girl would literally waste away and starve completely to death in *her* house, Nancibel said, she certainly never thought would ever happen. Her husband John stepped in. "Lavonne, I speak to you like a father…" "And men don't even *like* a woman that's nothing but a rack of bones."

That seemed to be true with regard to Darrel. Of course it was still his year as National President of the Future Farmers. They paid his way here and there, even to Hawaii for five days, he had to go, make speeches, write letters. He sent Lavonne several picture postcards saying he wished she was wherever he was at the time. But Nancibel told Rosetta that if Lavonne wasn't careful, she was just going to *lose* that wonderful beau of hers! but Lavonne paid no attention.

The strangest thing was that she didn't collapse. But something kept her going, a kind of dementia, it began to seem like to Rosetta, a species of insanity. But yet knowing Lavonne so well, she could understand. To hear a word disparaging her *looks* was exactly like rich Birdelle Prentice getting word that she had lost the family money on the stock market. *They call them barns where I come from* and *Your fortune has vanished* were one and the same remark. There never had been a time Lavonne wasn't pretty. "Oh, what a pretty child!" "Isn't she beautiful!" On the blackboard the list would say, "Christmas fairy: Lavonne." "Queen of the May: Lavonne." "I choose Lavonne." Of course in high school it was different, but that was because the kids who ran things were like the Brahmins over in India (Rosetta considered herself an expert on *them*). Anybody that wasn't in their category they dispersonated, turned into vapor, ugly or pretty was neither here nor there.

But Lavonne in high school didn't even seem to notice, maybe *didn't* notice, perfectly free from risk as to the continued possession of the blue eyes, golden hair and everything else beautiful and lovely that she had always had and always *would* have. She did have a large bust, yes, it gave her a somewhat matronly look that the most Brahminical high schooler could hardly have got by with, but she didn't concentrate on that. And anyway she started to go with Darrel in her sophomore year, Darrel who had a case on her from the first minute he ever laid eyes on her, the day he and his father stopped at the Prentice mansion with their fresh produce and Gram said she and her granddaughter had just come there to live. He was a little barefooted boy then, would come running up to the back door with his bundle of rhubarb or bucket of tomatoes, too shy to look straight at Lavonne, too tongue-tied to hardly speak.

She was the one on top of the world then, the subduer. Who would have ever thought that Darrel would be *famous*? Raise the biggest cantaloupe, the best lamb in the state? Get his picture in the paper for his yield of wheat? Become and do all the things he had? Make *speeches*. Travel to *Hawaii*. But for all the heights he had reached, he still went with Lavonne, still kept—when he had time for them—the same self-righting thoughts of her. To him the remark at the dance would have been about some object marking a boundary line in history, a leaning tower. The tower's precariousness was not, however, why Lavonne didn't tell him what the boys had said. She couldn't for the shame of it, her life's first defamation, and Darrel attributed the tears that soaked and saturated her on the way back to town, and when they parked up on the North Bench, to his neglect of her. He *had* neglected her but told her "Dear, I love you," kissed her again and again and lolled like a pasha on her downy billows.

Dear, I love you. Well, she thought he did, even though it might look like he was wrapped up in nothing but himself and had forgotten marriage and a home altogether.

Was he wrapped up in nothing but himself? *Had* he forgotten? No matter. Something other than Darrel had influenced Lavonne's volition to starve herself to death almost, and that, Rosetta came to the conclusion, was not the young men at the dance either. They had been of only minor importance. The trouble was...it was hard to think about the backsliding, falling away and apostasy of the very *world*, but so it must have seemed to poor Lavonne.

At first she talked about her diet, but that was no novelty at the beauty school. Nearly everyone, fat or thin, was dieting or going to, or coasting down the happy hill of self-indulgence after losing weight. Colleen Gutke had been going to diet ever since she enrolled at the school the day before Lavonne, and now decided to join her. But long before Lavonne finally gave up due to having hit solid bone and anabolized and katabolized to the point where she could have died without losing another ounce, Colleen was eating her boyfriend Balsha Filipu's chocolates, her mother's scalloped potatoes and everything else within reach.

But fat was never so much Colleen's problem as a curious shapelessness, which, however, when she went through her astounding metamorphosis, hardened into a powerful corset's definite form. But her substance was always loose, not dense. Some people are like that, porous, not compact. Their feet, everything, interstitial. Their nose, everything. But Colleen did go through an amazing transformation while at the beauty college. Some girls are mean, they wouldn't give a compliment if it killed them, even to a customer. And in those days there were only two boys taking the beauty course, and one should by rights have been a girl, the other a painter. The teachers complimented the operator: "That's a very nice wave, Rosetta." Never the one *with* the hairdo. But what happened to Colleen's appearance was noted, or at least afterwards.

The day Colleen Gutke started to beauty school she should have had a *Before* picture taken, she really should. Her supercilia grew clear across the bridge of her nose. Well, eyebrows can be plucked and shaped. It wasn't long till Lavonne, who had the station next to Colleen's, plucked and shaped them for her. "Nicely done, Lavonne." Colleen's skin was bad. Pale, gray, big pores. Lela Winegar tackled that, the pupils practiced on one another. A paste of beauty clay and kaolin, with glycerine and witch hazel, soften the adamant Salt Lake water with borax and soda, splash on. The facials made a big difference. Miss Keeney lectured on "You Are What You Eat." Not that Colleen's mother, Mrs. Gutke, with what she earned at the Salt Lake Knitting Mill, could afford to start feeding Colleen and Colleen's thirteen-year-old brother Duane broiled steaks and fresh pineapple and strawberries and soft-shell crabs (it was enough that she gave Colleen this chance to make something of herself by going to beauty school). But after the lecture, Colleen did start eating the carrots and onions in the stew better and more of the canned applesauce, and laid off the fudge Duane stirred up when he was home alone. And that, too, made a big difference.

The hairs of the head are called capilli. Hair color is handed down from one generation to another, especially muddy brown. Hair grows from three-eighths to three-fourths of an inch a month. One hair can live from four to seven years, longer than you do at the last! but that it will grow down over and around a body moldering in the grave is probably not true. Rosetta bleached Colleen's muddy brown capilli. White henna, seventeen-volume peroxide of hydrogen, hold back the action in back, hurry it in front, egg shampoo, hand dry. From the beginning, Rosetta showed talent with bleaches and tints.

You take one of these big, bare, bald foreheads. Some people say they are a sign of intelligence, even genius, but idiots frequently have foreheads like that also. The thing to do if *you* are a high-foreheaded girl, even a debutante with money, is wear the hair banged low over it. Think of the forehead as a high stone wall, think of the improvement when the wall is draped with leafy vines. Bangs made all the difference with Colleen. The wild civility of those pale blonde tendrils. "You did a very nice job on that, Rosetta."

Then makeup. Lavonne helped Colleen with that, but of course eventually it's like the soul's salvation, up to the person's own self with the pale eyelashes, freckles, crowded teeth and short chin, the *person*'s knowledge of creams, softening and astringent lotions, powder, paint and waxy black mascara, her own true eye and steady hand, not another beautician's, not the sinusoidal current in red, white and blue carbon filament bulbs, nor mercury-vapor lamps shooting out purest ultraviolet rays serene, Colleen! it's like the spider or whoever it was that said that time: Try, try again.

Now look! Here's the *after*, but nobody took a picture *before*, though someone should have, shouldn't they? Someone was saying that afterwards. But of course when the only *before* was in the memories of the few kids in Colleen's class that paid any attention to *how* a plain, common girl like her looked the day she started, an *after* wouldn't signify a lot. Lavonne would remember, so would Lela. Richard, who kept taking the *World History of Art* out of the library, said in retrospect that Colleen had started out as a "Flemish sow," Rosetta remembered. She did more than remember, she *thought* about it, even years from that time. Because it was amazing, the metamorphosis. And the terrible price … When she told Gene, he was nagged by a certain line of poetry he couldn't recollect exactly that went "Beauty," then a verb, then "me till I die." Goads? Pains? He left it at "Beauty *bugs* me till I die."

When Rosetta thought of the girls that had it (beauty) on a silver platter! Lavonne, for instance. She did have to diet, at least divine preordination didn't make her a size six without effort, but the rest of her beauty, you might say, was free, whereas Colleen … Sometimes Colleen felt sorry for herself, she shouldn't have, but she couldn't help it. Not just for how hard she had to work to look the way she now did, the hours she had to spend, but the discomfort, the actual, pernicious misery. Bleached hair won't take a permanent so has to be put up every night, the Inquisitional dogs and devildoms of Spain invented aluminum curlers. They invented the female shape of iron from breast-bone to below the backside too, and the high French heel that curves an unshapely leg.

Colleen's girdle cost fifteen dollars. Mrs. Gutke used her savings. When she saw the miracle they wrought at the beauty college, technological science and everything, Mrs. Gutke's heart leaped up, Colleen had the chance not only to make something of herself *professionally*, but as a girl, a pretty girl, which somehow her mother just hadn't expected. She just hadn't taken that into her calculations, a mother has to face reality, and while Colleen had always been a *sweet* person—But one that's pretty! a whole different ballgame, for you know what that can mean! First and foremost a *good provider*. Say a lineman for the light company, say a fellow on the police force, maybe own his own business, a storekeeper or something, you just can't foretell with a beauty. Mrs. Gutke dug down for the high-heeled shoes, a dress cut on the bias, nothing can beat plain black satinback crepe.

THE MAN COLLEEN CAME HOME with from the park that Sunday afternoon when she walked down to find her brother Duane skating on the lake was certainly not the man Mrs. Gutke would have *chosen*. But it had been several weeks, and for all Colleen's new bloom, suitors for her hand were not lined up around the block. He was decent-looking, wore a dark suit, clean shirt, tie, hat, he carefully scraped his shoe soles before he stepped in. Of course you take a man of forty-two who has never been married, you really have grounds for suspicion right there. With his dark curly hair though, to give the devil his due, he didn't look that old. And it is strange how a foreigner will have better teeth than we have, white and even. What *kind* of foreigner he was, although he told her in not too broken English, Mrs. Gutke never did get clear. A Tosk, is what it sounded like, from a country called Leskovik, if there was such a place. And what was he doing in Utah? Search her. But he was steadily employed as a fry cook at Mulroney's Restaurant over on State Street, open till midnight every night but Sunday, so he said. Not the most elevating job in the world, but better than odd jobs or marching with that Bonus Army, even if Mamie next to her at Salt Lake Knitting shook her head when she heard about it and made a clucking sound (as if Mamie's own husband was anything but a drunk now, whether he once taught Manual Training, as she claimed, or not!). Mrs. Gutke was sorry she ever mentioned him, and she kept mum about the Greek Orthodox church.

But a mother can't help being proud if it's nothing but presents, presents. A bottle of perfume called Christmas Night, that was what Balsha said the French name meant. Balsha Filipu, his name was, which could easily be changed to Bob Phillips later on at no great expense if a person so desired. A lovely Fabrikoid case lined with pink satin containing a brush, comb, hand mirror and several other toilet articles of ivory-colored celluloid. A Brownie camera. Silk stockings. Constantly a box of chocolates. Roses from the florist's on Colleen's twentieth birthday. A table-model Zenith for her to have in her room if she wanted to hear Kate Smith while Mrs. Gutke and Duane tuned in another station in the front room. Usually it was vice versa, Mrs. Gutke and Duane in the one bedroom in the house listening to the table model on the dresser and lounging on the bed, and Colleen and Balsha in the front room sitting on the couch listening to the console Philco.

He must be a man with a bank account, their line of work and low pay didn't necessarily mean they lived from hand to mouth. A poor starved Chinaman bowed down under a bundle of dirty laundry bigger than he was turned out to own half of Chinatown. That actually happened! down in San Francisco. It was in the paper. But money wasn't everything, love and devotion were all that really mattered. Though even love and devotion could be run in the ground if you had a jealous nature on your hands. No one had ever been jealous of Colleen before, and at first she liked it. It made her feel like a natural blonde with long dark eyelashes and as pretty a shape *without* her powerful boned combination girdle and brassiere as *with* it. It made her feel her face would not wash off and that her lips were really full like that and rosy-red. Her feet looked dainty and her legs were nice, as if she even smelled like Christmas Night her natural self. Yes, jealous love will make you out a beauty, and Colleen did not mind that at all. It even provided something in perpetuity to talk to Balsha about and cry and kiss about.

They were going to get married after Balsha straightened out some matter with the Greek Orthodox church and also got something he had coming to him from his native land of Leskovik, also he had the promise of half a house out over Jordan as soon as the present renters left for California, more suitable to take a beautiful bride home to than his tiny furnished room. Also Colleen would be through beauty college by then, and while he would never allow his wife to *work* for any length of time, still, if she could get a job till the furniture they would buy was paid for…Colleen's engagement ring was a ruby, and right then when Mrs. Gutke saw it glistening like a bright red drop of blood and the strange feeling swept over her, she should have taken it for what it was, a terrible warning, and put a stop to everything! right then. But we don't, we let things drift, we take the path of least resistance.

Colleen would have liked to take that path! at least part of the time. The beauty unexpectedly bestowed by her fellow students, her own hand's cunning and Balsha's pain was a heavier lot than she bargained for, a burden of Babylon, really. Sometimes she wished it could be given back and not expected of her anymore. Wished that no one admired her, no fiery-eyed man with a heart that thundered like a plunging horse. No lover, waiting. That the deep red marks from the cruel girdle could fade away *forever*, not just those few hours from night till morning. That when the girdle lay by, the metal curlers didn't have to take over, and the smothery cream from the suffocating paint. Barefooted, barefaced and loose-haired again for Jimmie Lunceford and his Band, eating fudge with Gang Busters. Comfort and rest. And yet…

Once you have had some luxury, it's hard to do without it, say a bathroom or a car. Poor people who thrive and prosper, then get poor again have a lot rougher hustle than those that stay poor. And the born rich when *they* get poor will generally go insane, and the reason is not so much losing the money as losing *the power to boss people around without ever being bossed yourself.* Beauty acts a lot like that. Do this, do that. You are so beautiful, oh! Your slightest wish…And still, Balsha almost broke her wrist one time. Another time he fitted his hands around her throat and squeezed, but he didn't mean to hurt her. Afterwards he got down on the floor and kissed her shoe, and she could have planted it on his head had she wanted, his tears wet her strapped and stockinged instep. Sometimes he got quite fresh, out for an evening walk, at the movies, dancing to radio music, but he would stop as if what bastioned her within an inch of her life was not something that could be bought at Auerbach's in the corset department but her own maidenly virtue. He would respect that. And when her feet were killing her in her high heels, to him her hobbled gait meant her refinement.

"What Is This Thing Called Love?" Colleen always paid attention to the words of a song and after she started going with Balsha made him do likewise. Shhhh! now listen. And he would listen as though to a will being read leaving everything to him, but then look blank at her when she asked him to tell her what it meant. Rosetta thought Colleen might not really be in love with him, from her various remarks when their customers from the general public were under the noisy dryers, or they were in the restroom having a smoke or eating their lunches in the hot little cloakroom cross-coursed with big steam pipes, when they talked as they gazed through the dirty windows at the falling snow.

He gave her a Longines wristwatch for Christmas, seventeen jewel, they were not cheap. If she wasn't exactly crazy about him now, she would be after they got married, her mother knew of several such cases where it turned out the wives cared more as the years went on than vice versa. The same thing happened in the movies. Or they realized it after the husband died. Sometimes while conversing, Rosetta would lean over to re-arrange a lock of Colleen's hair or pull a wisp out over her cheek, as a little girl will do with her doll. Lavonne would do the same, she would be talking or listening and suddenly tip her head back to study Colleen's eyebrow curve or take her finger and smudge her cheek along the line of rouge. Lela would break into any discussion she was having with Colleen to inspect her pores. They held her like property, in a way, in private ownership. And that was why (after it happened) Mrs. Gutke got in touch with Rosetta and asked her to please ask the others if they would be so kind…

When Mrs. Bryant down at the corner saw what was happening, she told Colleen, "He's married, don't forget that, and they've got two kids." She was talking about her younger brother Raymond, at her house because of driving a load of furniture from Lodi through to Cleveland for Silver Wheel Trucking & Transportation. By then it was spring, after Easter, too warm for a coat one day, blossoms bloomed out, leaves unrolling, the next day snow a foot deep. How glad Raymond was the snow didn't catch him on some of those passes, that he had to lay over on account of a mix-up with a shipment, sometimes it seemed like those things are all planned out ahead of time. Our lives.

And it did seem like that. Why else would Colleen just suddenly, after supper, decide to run over and tell Mrs. Bryant she had decided to take her up on that offer to subscribe to *Pictorial Review* for half price? even though her name and address were about to change and it might be better to wait. Something just made her do that. Mrs. Bryant's kids were cute little things, but walk in there at bedtime and they were like wild hyenas, they ran all over their poor mother, and their father was gone to Union meeting.

"Colleen, I want you to meet … This here's my brother Raymond." He was in the front room listening to the radio. Maybe he wasn't listening, he could have just been sprawled there in his brother-in-law's big Fabrikoid chair half asleep, but the broadcast coming over was from KSL, the marathon dance at Wandamere, and the song wasn't new, it was "Shaking the Blues Away" …

The human body, as every beauty college scholar has to know in case the question comes up in the written part of the state examination, is composed of sixteen principal elements, which are as follows: carbon, hydrogen, oxygen, nitrogen, sulphur, phosphorous, chlorine, sodium, potassium, calcium, magnesium, iron, silicon, fluorine, iodine and manganese. That is absolutely all a human body is composed of, but if you had tried to tell Raymond that, holding Colleen in a slow foxtrot while his sister was out in the kitchen making another pot of coffee to keep awake on at least till Mr. Bryant came home from Union meeting, well, Raymond wouldn't even have heard you. Colleen knew the list, she could have taken the State Board right then, and passed, but that it should apply to *him*! above the firmament. For that matter she herself, in the circle of his strong warm arms, her cheek against his whiskery one (for which he apologized, he wanted to go shave but she wouldn't let him—at eleven o'clock at night?), felt higher than above the heavens her own self.

At nine, when Mrs. Gutke sent Duane to see if she had got run over, Duane mentioned that it was starting to snow, but Colleen and the others didn't believe him. "Come on and see!" The snow made the proceedings like a festival of some kind. Or like when everything stops because boys in the streets are crying *Extra! Extra!* and a war has started somewhere or a king has died or even Miss America. Nothing stays! The twinkling of an eye! So live, come on, what are we waiting for?

Mr. Bryant coming home at twelve-thirty ended the party, Mrs. Bryant woke with a start in her husband's chair and told Raymond and Colleen, still on their feet locked in an embrace so close a postcard wouldn't have slid between them and moving dreamily over the linoleum to the dim crackle of dance music from Chicago, not to go outside without putting something on, Raymond was sweating, they could catch their death of cold. She made Colleen put an old sweater over her shoulders, but Raymond said the cold night air would feel good and went out in his shirtsleeves. Colleen only lived down at the corner, she could run home by herself, she said, but of course he wouldn't let her.

SHE GOT POSTCARDS FROM CHEYENNE and Omaha, then he had to go to Tulsa. Then Amarillo, then Prescott. When she came home at night, the only thing she wanted to do was be in his sister Mrs. Bryant's company and make a fuss over the Bryant children. After they were in bed, all she wanted to do was talk about Raymond. Mrs. Bryant told her exactly how things stood, he was a married man with one little boy and one little girl, his wife Mae was a very nice individual, they lived in this house they rented in Lodi. But Mrs. Bryant did have to admit it wasn't like him to go overboard for somebody the way he had for Colleen. Then he wrote a letter, *all I can think about is you*, and said he was coming back, driving for Silver Wheel if they had a shipment up that way, but if they didn't then by himself and on his own … And Mrs. Bryant said well, the fat was in the fire.

And all of a sudden Colleen couldn't stand the sight of Balsha, he made her sick at her stomach, she couldn't bear to have him near her. He knew there was something wrong, but not at first that there was another man. All she wanted to do was run over to the neighbor's. The reason for that was Mrs. Bryant was sewing for her, Colleen said. She would run over there and leave Balsha sitting in the front room for her mother to entertain. Mrs. Gutke wasn't pleased at the turn of events, she hadn't even *met* this Raymond, when he got here he might not even have a job! And if he could do what he was doing to his wife Mae, why couldn't he do the same thing to Colleen after he married her and saddled her with the responsibility of a family? *If*—a great big if!—he married her in the first place. Balsha was steady, never laid off work, he looked to the future, didn't drink, was kind, generous …

When Colleen ran over to the Bryants' she was dressed in her best, had combed and fixed her hair, put new makeup on, dabbed on her Christmas Night. Raymond's letter was tucked down in the front of her dress. He could be there already, or ten miles down the road. Or make it in by Thursday … or maybe Sunday … Some people, when they are nervous and on edge waiting for something to happen, their appetite will abandon them, it will be all they can do to choke down enough to keep body and soul together, while with others it will be the opposite. Colleen was one of these latter, she could almost have gnawed on a stick of kindling, but of course she tried not to eat and cause her girdle to hurt worse than ever holding her in, in the bias-cut dress she might not even be able to get into! if she wasn't careful. She did try and did succeed, except that the red marks around her stomach and hips and rear end were deeper than ever when she got ready for bed. As she lay there and thought and dreamed of Raymond (and a piece of Duane's fudge, if there was any left on the buttered plate on the drainboard), she would gently smooth the ridges, as slaves must in the dark the marks of the chain and the cruel whip. She had another letter saying *it won't be long now, all I can think of is when I get there.* It was under her pillowed head gnarly with aluminum curlers, *I love you.* She couldn't write to him, he didn't dare try to receive a letter, but she had told him about Balsha the night they met. There is this fellow…He saw the ring, it's not really an engagement ring, *I'll* buy you a diamond, give it back, give the damn radio back and everything.

She tried to, but Balsha wouldn't take it, the ring, nothing. He acted like he didn't believe her. He thought he had made her mad. What did I do? What did I do? You didn't do anything. Mrs. Gutke, what did I do? You didn't do anything, Balsha. It's just that circumstances have apparently changed, they will do that, you know that yourself. Had he acted like a reasonable individual, Colleen would have told him then that there might be somebody else, and they could have parted friends and everything would have been all right. But he was not reasonable. Colleen got a Post Toasties carton from Skaggs and put everything in it, thinking Duane could help Balsha carry it to his rooming house. And what did he do? Kicked it off the porch, busted the carton, he didn't have a radio, he would have *enjoyed* the Zenith table model very much. But no, cut off his nose to spite his face. The ruby ring he threw furiously onto the bushes alongside the house, it could have been lost forever. The Longines wristwatch he stomped and jumped on like a crazy man. Weren't Mrs. Gutke and Colleen glad then that they had found out about Balsha's terrible disposition before it was too late!

Finally Mrs. Gutke's patience was worn out. They had tried every way to be friendly and fair and part in a nice manner, but if he was going to act the way he was acting, then there was only one thing she could do, and that was call the police. He straightened up when he saw she meant it. If that was what Colleen wanted then he would go, don't worry, they would never see him again. But the next morning he followed Colleen to beauty school, unless she was mistaken, which she might have been. That night they kept the blinds all pulled down. Colleen didn't intend to go over to the Bryants' after dark for a while, but when the clock in the City and County Building struck eight, she just couldn't help it, it seemed like seeing Raymond's sister was her only consolation. And maybe she had news. Maybe Raymond…The first thing he would do when he got to the Bryants' was shave…And then…

Mrs. Gutke made Duane run over there with Colleen, and at quarter to ten she sent him back to bring his sister home. Colleen would have stayed longer otherwise, she was already helping Mrs. Bryant like a sister-in-law, to dry dishes, fold sheets, she went out into the back yard with her to take the laundry off the line, there was moonlight. Soon the moon would be full, and as far as her mind ever went was when he would come back. That was all, that moment, when she would walk into the Bryants' front room the way she did that night…Or a knock would come at her own door…His arms around her once again, his lips on hers, that was as far as her mind would ever go. At beauty school, working on some lady, yes, combed back and parted on the right, she would think that far and stop, his arms around her … think that far and stop. Today … tonight …

Chapter Fifty-five

✳

IT WOULD HAVE BEEN TOO GOOD TO BE TRUE THAT BALSHA WOULD JUST DROP out of the picture, go south or north. Mrs. Gutke came home from work and here was his letter in the mailbox, hand-delivered, no stamp on it, he must have used up half a ruled tablet writing crazy insane things about his love for Colleen and how nobody else could have her, and the worst news was, he had quit his job! So anytime and anywhere, he could pop up…Coming out of beauty school Colleen said good-bye to Rosetta and Lavonne, they went on up the street and she turned the corner…and out of nowhere, as if up through a trapdoor out of hell, he stood in front of her.

But all he wanted to do was talk things over, because now he knew for sure that whatever happened had been his fault. But he could change, he *would* change, would do anything…She must have been taking fast, long steps, for it seemed to her that he was running along beside her like a child.

"Please, please," he said, "I can no more! I can no more!"

"Balsha, listen, you've got to understand."

"I do! I do! I'll *change*!"

"Changing won't help. I just don't love you anymore!"

"Oh, God, my sun." He used to call her that, it sounded silly. "Sun" like it was *s-o-n*, at first she thought that's what he said, but it was *s-u-n*, like "you are my sunshine."

Mrs. Gutke was home when they got there, Colleen as white as a sheet. She ran right in the bedroom and shut the door.

"Now, Balsha, we have got to settle this like sensible human beings."

"All right, Mrs. Gutke." His handkerchief looked terrible, like a bachelor's will that does his own washing. He dried his eyes, blew his nose and stuffed it in his back pants pocket.

"You know that you can't force someone to love you that doesn't love you."

"I know that, Mrs. Gutke, but she *does* love me, she let me…She made me feel so good…Would she…be so kind…if she didn't love me?"

"Believe me, Balsha, she doesn't. And nothing you can do will change that." Then she told him there was someone else, came right out and told him, it was the only thing to do, Mrs. Bryant's younger brother from Lodi, California, who drove for Silver Wheel Trucking & Transportation.

He took it like a little man, she said, said he would leave and not bother them anymore, he was sick of Salt Lake anyway, he had a cousin in Michigan. All he asked was to see Colleen one more time. Mrs. Gutke went in the bedroom, but Colleen was out of her girdle, had her old bathrobe on and was lying on the bed, the shock had been shocking. He just seemed to materialize out of thin air, she said, and he talked so crazy, had she realized he was crazy…He wasn't, Mrs. Gutke said, or anyway not now, he had calmed right down even though she told him about…that Colleen had this brother of their neighbor on the string…but he just wanted to see her one more time. Well, not now, Colleen said, she was still shaking and sick to her stomach, and anyway they had nothing to say to each other.

"How about tomorrow?" The next day was Sunday.

"But Raymond might be coming in…"

"How about in the morning? He only wants to see you one more time."

"But he'll just start in again!"

"He won't, he promised, he's got it through his head now. Then he'll leave and go to Michigan."

COLLEEN DRESSED AFTER HE LEFT and ran over to Mrs. Bryant's to find out if she had heard from Raymond, but the house was dark, they had taken the kids and gone out to her sister's, Colleen remembered they were going to go, it was someone's birthday. Had Mrs. Bryant had word, she'd have sent a note over with the oldest girl, but Raymond wouldn't necessarily let her know, he would just drive up. But just in case, Colleen stayed dressed till ten p.m. and with her makeup on, fresh lipstick and everything. But then if she was going to look like anything for him tomorrow in case he arrived, she had to take the makeup all off and put her hair up. She pulled the blinds all down before she did that so that if Raymond did come and looked over their way, he would think they had gone to bed. Then she did her beauty chores.

She hadn't eaten much supper, so now she started in and made up for what she had missed, and considerably extra, and Duane had stirred up a batch of fudge, and there were some good programs coming on, one of them was a murder mystery called "Castle of Hate," and then they would get the ballrooms and the bands…Her mind was lulled to rest, but then Mrs. Gutke started worrying, she and Duane had been going to go to eleven o'clock Mass tomorrow, but maybe…Balsha acted all right when he left, but he did have kind of a peculiar look, and a foreigner like that, especially when they went so crazy over a girl…Maybe they shouldn't go to Mass. Go, Colleen said, as sure as could be all of a sudden that Raymond was nearly there, and after Balsha left (she would get rid of him as quick as she could)…Raymond could come over, and that way their first meeting would be when they were alone. She would put the coffee on, try to find something on the radio besides religious stuff or classical music…and…

Balsha would really thank her someday. He hoboed his way across the country when he was only nineteen, he had told her, and he could do it again, maybe some nice girl when he went up to their back door to ask if he could split some wood for supper would take a liking to him…and he to her…Colleen took another piece of fudge and bit luxuriously into it because everything was going to work out, she felt, she and Raymond, Balsha and some girl with a nice disposition in Iowa or someplace like that…She put her feet in slipshod old felt slippers up on the footstool, her dingy white stockings hung in rolls around her somewhat swollen ankles.

"Balsha ought to come in right now," Duane said, looking at her. "That would cure him!"

"And what do you mean by a remark like that, Mister Smart Aleck?" Mrs. Gutke said.

"I mean he's supposed to be so crazy about her, and jealous, and not going to let nobody else have her, but if he could see her at night when she gets ready to go to bed, or in the morning before she gets fixed up, why, he'd be cured so fast it would make his head swim!"

"Duane Gutke, you stop those mean remarks."

"They're not mean, they're true. All he ever sees is her *fixed up*! But if he seen her like *we* see her! And how about this other guy? Him the same! Wait, just wait, if she gets married. Is somebody in for a surprise! Like buying an auto and driving it home and—!" He made a noise like machinery falling to pieces and air escaping from a tire.

"Duane Gutke, you shut up this very minute."

But out of the mouths of babes, as the saying goes. The next morning Mrs. Gutke gently broached the subject to Colleen, who was sitting at the table having more pancakes and another cup of coffee, the subject of her just staying *like she was* till after Balsha had come and gone. *Then* she could fix all up for Raymond, take the curlers out, that ugly bathrobe off, put on her girdle, get her war paint on…Even high-heeled slippers made such a difference!

Colleen just stared at her, inflamed at once with anger and disdain.

But think what a relief! Balsha then would realize…He would start for Michigan, no more spying, crying, crazy letters, popping up in front of her, no more threats! Did it ever enter her mind, Mrs. Gutke said, if things went on as they were going that Balsha *might even lay for Raymond*? But besides that, just out of human kindness, didn't she want to send the poor thing away not longing, or anyway not so much, and not grieving? Cured, you might say.

"Cured by what?"

"By how, you know, you really—"

"You mean I'm ugly."

"Of course I don't mean that!"

Colleen began to cry. She pushed her plate away and laid her head down on her arms…The whole last two weeks, since she went over to the Bryants' house and met that Raymond over there and tried to get rid of Balsha, Mrs. Gutke said, patting her tenderly on the back, fondling her curlers and noting that her hair was showing black at the roots, the whole time had just been one long nightmare to all concerned, her nerves were all on edge. But now it was nearly over, and if she would just…*stay right like she was*…Why, she would bet, Mrs. Gutke said, that if you walked in right this very minute on some beautiful…so-called beautiful…*actress* that didn't know you were coming, why, she would look just as bad or even worse!

"All right," Colleen said. And she promised.

BUT WHEN MRS. GUTKE AND Duane, after happening to walk with a lady after Mass and being invited by her to come in and see her gesso work, got home and found Colleen, she *hadn't* stayed like she was at the breakfast table. She was all fixed up. Not one bit of her beauty, to the last brushful of mascara, was missing. And she died for it, you might say. *Died for it.*

AT THE UNDERTAKER'S, THOUGH, THEY start from scratch, take it all off, then consult with the nearest of kin as to whether the hair was parted right or left and what the natural color…But Mrs. Gutke wanted Colleen's fellow scholars from the beauty college to come and do the makeup. Lela happened to be sick with tonsillitis that day, but Lavonne and Rosetta obliged as well as they could after school. It was the scariest thing, it shouldn't have been, it was just Colleen, after all, like she was asleep. You couldn't see the stab wounds or anything. Elva said in the lunch room, when they were having a cigarette and talking about what they had to do, that you couldn't hire her to go near the place, she just had this terrible fear of dead bodies. And especially somebody that was *murdered*, Billie said, the very thought sent cold chills down her back. Nadine said she knew somebody that said the only way to keep a murdered person from being a ghost that had to walk the earth forever and never rest was to tie their feet together.

JUST QUIETNESS IS A VERY scary thing, semi-darkness after the bright sunshine, the smell of wilting carnations, everything so carpeted, doors half open, a casket seems to come into view in an exaggerated and indefinite form. They don't feel cold to the touch in warm May weather, and after some original stiffness they soften again, the fingers bend…Rosetta put Colleen's nail polish on, Lavonne her mascara. That is tricky when the eyes are shut. The lids could probably have been lifted, but neither she nor Rosetta had nerve enough to do that, let Colleen's dead eyes look up at them. Rosetta fixed her hair. Another week and it would have been time for a bleach, Colleen had wanted one right after she met her new guy but Rosetta said to wait on account of the scalp, the way it shed its skin like a snake if there wasn't enough time between. She combed it so the black roots hardly showed except if you stood at the head of the coffin and looked down, and fluffed out the bangs. Mrs. Gutke came just as they were getting through, and she was so glad, it gave her a chance to say thank you. And doesn't she look a perfect picture! Rosetta thought about saying something about what Nadine had said about tying Colleen's feet together, but she didn't, it seemed too terrible even to suggest that she could turn into a ghost and wander around and scare people.

It wasn't far out of their way, and so because she was so sad, they accompanied Mrs. Gutke home. She hadn't intended to stay at the undertaker's this time anyway, she said, she just wanted to see if Colleen was ready to lie in state, as the neighbors were asking could they go and see her. Duane had come with her, but when he saw two girls there at the door of the slumber room and especially Lavonne...he said quickly that this was a good chance for him to go and get that tube. Sunday when they came home from Mass, Mrs. Gutke said, the radio was on...Not that they paid attention, with the terrible sight that then met their eyes and everything. What Colleen had done, apparently, was run into the kitchen heading for the back door, and he—! But the radio was on when she and Duane stepped in, they both remembered that. Then, click! it was off! like a hand had shut it off. But Mr. Logan next door said it was the tube that by a coincidence just happened at that very minute to burn out. If Colleen had screamed, but it seemed like she had been more racing to get away than screaming. He wouldn't get far, the officers said, they'd get him, but Mrs. Bryant said oh, yes, she bet they would, in a pig's eye. She was just *sick* about it. Raymond arrived before Colleen was hardly cold, but what could he do? It was all over, he turned around and went back where he came from, the Gutkes' house was full of neighbors, Mrs. Bryant persuaded him to vamoose for his children's sake, because to hang around and maybe get murdered too by that crazy lunatic would serve no purpose whatsoever. And this way he could always remember Colleen like she was that night...

They say you can't scrub human blood off of bare wood, it sinks in and you would have to gouge it out with a knife, but the Gutkes had a Congoleum rug in the kitchen, so where she was laying there between the table and the back door when her mother and brother came home and found her could be cleaned up without a trace.

Rosetta and Lavonne didn't stay long at the Gutkes'. With a goose-pimply feeling, they sat in the front room. Mrs. Gutke wanted to get them some coffee or maybe a glass of blackberry juice, but they said no, thank you, and she didn't insist. Mr. Logan was the one who pulled the console radio out from the corner like that to get at the tubes, she said. It didn't look very good, but no use to push it back till the new tube was put in. She told them about Duane being with her up until he saw them, and then how quick he made the excuse that he would go and get the tube and come on home...especially Lavonne. He was getting to the age...He didn't even stop for his mother to give him some money. But then he had his own, enough to buy the tube at least. He helped at Holloway's Grocery on Saturdays. If Colleen had only listened to Duane! He was the first to say, let Balsha see her like she really was. He was very good at his lessons, always had been, that was why

Mrs. Gutke wanted him to go to high school and make something of himself. But it just seemed like Colleen had got to believing she really looked that way...

"What way?" Rosetta said.

And Mrs. Gutke said, "Beautiful. Like it belonged to her." And then with tears that she dabbed at with a handkerchief taken out of her purse down beside her chair, as if she was also a guest instead of just at home, she told them about how Mother and Duane had tried to *tell* Colleen. But she turned a deaf ear. And laid down her life for the sake of beauty.

They talked about that going home. Rosetta said she felt the most to blame for making Colleen a blonde, and for the curly bangs, and for how she complimented her. But then a lot of the girls had done that. Wow, they said of the improvements. Wowie. Remarks like that. She looked so different. Of course makeup was probably even more important than hair, and Lavonne was responsible for that. Well, *she* for one wasn't going to feel guilty, Lavonne said in a crosser tone than she would have used had chronic hunger not provoked her, because *beauty* didn't kill Colleen, a crazy man did.

"You're almost doing it yourself," Rosetta said. "Really, you are, Lavonne. Dying."

"Dying?"

"Of starvation! Just because of what those two boys said at the Old Mill dance. And *you* were *born* beautiful. So imagine poor Colleen! that never in her whole life dreamed...And all of a sudden she goes to beauty school and we do stuff to her and here she's beautiful. She's got this magic wand at last! And finally at the end—it turns out to be worth—her *life*."

"Oh, pooh," Lavonne said with a toss of her head. But she didn't argue. She only hoped she'd never meet a nut like Balsha.

BUT THEY DIDN'T HAVE TO be a nut to be impossible. While Lavonne was at Nancibel's finishing her course, Legrand was always drawing her picture or telling her what she should wear, paying attention to every little thing about her, each little detail. But when she broke off with Darrel and showed her friendly feelings towards Legrand, that is to say the friendly feelings she could feel under the right circumstances, why, he turned her down cold, snubbed her, the way he acted wasn't a bit nice. But every term up at the university made some people more conceited, and Lavonne said she probably wouldn't have wanted to go out with him if he had asked her.

But talking about conceit! Darrel was the one who would take the cake. He was so conceited because of being elected National President of the Future Farmers of America, which was after all only for one year, it wasn't like being born Prince of Wales, with bowing and scraping guaranteed *forever*. Then to top it all off he had the nerve to come and tell her he was taking another girl to the Harvest Home banquet, the bishop's daughter, not because he liked her but because it was one of those situations where *she* asked *him* and he couldn't get out of it. To that Lavonne just said good-bye, Darrel, and ran in the house and shut the door. Had she not been staying at Nancibel's she would have slammed it.

AFTER THAT, ALL SHE WOULD have had to do to get somebody *else* was crook her little finger. But temporarily her ambition didn't run that direction. The diet as it continued seemed to chill the blood in her veins, she could stand over the furnace vent with the hot air belling out her skirts and her thin flanks and buttocks would stay cold as ice. Her hands were cold, her hollow beautiful face, her very eyeballs. It is always warm weather when one's in bed, and so she went to bed early, slept as late as she could, and wrapped her troubles in dreams. Such troubles, for instance, as still, for all her thinness, having a *bust*, a jutting and hanging bust, not girlish as it ought to be, and also a tiny decay spot starting between her eyetooth and the one next to it in front, and the supervisor's bossiness. Do not chew gum. Do not use slang phrases. Idle conversation is weakness. While serving a patron, remember that the health and beauty of *her* hair, not yours, and the contour of *her* fingernails, not yours, are the most important subject in the world to her...Do not place hairpins in the mouth.

Lavonne wouldn't even have had to crook her finger. The salesman that brought in the college's beauty supplies fell for her like a ton of bricks, but he was short and dumb. She had other chances, a young clerk in Auerbach's shoe department, different girls' brothers, a boy in the next block whose father used to work for the Utah Power & Light Company till he got laid off, a young man pasting up a new advertisement on the billboard where she and Rosetta waited for the streetcar. Lavonne was almost out of the habit of eating by now, but oddly enough almost out of the habit of playing at courtship too, at practicing coquetry...

Nancibel said if they didn't go in and find the girl dead in bed some morning, she would be surprised. But Lavonne outlasted her diet, lived to pass the State Board, written exam and oral both, with demonstrations, and beat Rosetta getting a job. Where she got on was at the Chic Salon of Beauty, and when Rosetta got on there too, the two girls found a small apartment and moved. Then something strange began to happen to Lavonne. When she stopped dieting because she was thin enough (and so beautiful that her smiles had to constantly turn in every direction like a searchlight, in order to either acknowledge the gratified contemplation of her admirers or disarm whoever might be resentful and jealous of her), she did what people who have nearly starved to death generally do when food is plentiful again: she ate. And then she ate some more. And ate, and of course eventually gained, to the great delight of Mrs. Daybell, who owned the Chic Salon sweatshop, and Penny and Mildred, the other two beauticians. Rosetta tried to stop her, but nothing but putting her in a prison cell would have done that. But then a button flipped off the middle of her uniform and plopped right into the coffee cup of a thin young usherette whose hair Lavonne was waving for her wedding, and even though the girl was only marrying (in street clothes and no veil) a mechanic without a steady job and they were going to live with her folks, the girl's laughter about the button flipping off into her coffee cup was the critical point. Lavonne turned and changed direction, and while she never again went down to skin and bones, she also never allowed herself to get fat again. It was when she settled on the middle degree between the two extremes that the strange began. The terrible, exceptional, anomalous, unheard-of contingency that before very long would sell her into bondage to the world.

Iꜰ ɪᴛ ʜᴀᴅ ᴛᴏ ʜᴀᴘᴘᴇɴ, she would always rather have had it happen where it did than on her face, like John Pierpont Morgan's nose, which the Sunday supplement said all his millions could never remedy. You couldn't even call it a nose, the reporter said. It was a huge, blue, brown and mauve mass of granulation-cells which showed pus in some places. But why did it have to happen anywhere? John Pierpont Morgan's nose acting like that? Or Lavonne's mammary equipendency? The doctors did not know. Nancibel's doctor treating Nancibel's kidney trouble, the internist at the medical school whom Nancibel's doctor recommended, who in turn recommended the endocrinologist, who called in the surgeon who finally took Lavonne's case and did what he could for her, free and at the county hospital, none of *them* had any idea. They never saw anything to equal it. That was why Dr. Cogan had pictures taken, to publish (a white strip blotting out the upper half of Lavonne's face) with his paper on the case in the *Mountain States Medical Journal*.

In later years when Lavonne would tell about it to a select few, her eyes would fill with tears as though what she was talking about was the surgical removal in times past of what she had *now*, a beautiful bust line. She could never seem to say or remember what had *really* been taken away, mammae exuberant to begin with but which in her nineteenth year, after her bout with starvation, began a wild spurt of growth (without inflammation) that finally got scary like the speed-up one reads about in the paper that ends as a morbid commensal the surgeon removing it can't even lift onto the *scales* without help.

"The rapid increase of tissue in this patient, however," Dr. Cogan told his students as they watched him lift with his left hand the large protrusion like the primal stuff from which bosoms may have been fashioned in the first place, and make a swift incision with the scalpel in his right, "being exterior rather than interior, may have ceased." But there being no way to *prove* that it had except to sit back and wait, and waiting in a case of protoplasmic fluxionary of this magnitude carrying with it no little danger, he had decided to operate, he said—as they in their turn as surgeons would also, he was sure, were they ever confronted by a pathology of this nature, which he very much doubted they would be, for he had been in practice since before they were born and never saw anything remotely like it before. If he was wrong to relieve or free this beautiful girl of only nineteen years of age from what should be her chiefest ornament, to save her life! he prayed God would forgive him.

Lavonne, soundly sleeping, knew nothing of either lecture or prayer, nor of the weighing of the amorphous quantity of material removed from her thorax to the quiet astonishment of the audience, nor the test for malignancy, which, proving negative, made what had happened to her more baffling than ever. All she knew as she whirled away into glittering blackness was that at last it was coming to an end, her painful ordeal. How could anybody's breasts start growing again at nineteen after they had stopped five or six years before? and the more they grew, the more agonizing they became.

When she first started to get really alarmed, she was in the bathroom taking a bath. "Rosetta," she called, "come in here, I want to show you something."

With open mouth Rosetta caught her breath. "Why, honey, what in the *world*—?"

Lavonne was sobbing. Imagine if Clara Bow or Jeanette MacDonald or Jean Arthur had had to contend with such a catastrophe? "What if they grow and grow and never stop?"

"Oh, they'll stop," Rosetta said, trying not to show her alarm.

But they didn't seem to, and finally one morning Lavonne just gave up and stayed home from work crying. "I can't go on!"

Rosetta having to do that for her, she called Nancibel for the name of her kidney doctor. That started the ball rolling, first him, then the medical school internist, then the endocrinologist, and finally the surgeon who performed the surgery. And Lavonne came out of the anaesthetic to find herself in the same eighth square where those whose sight has been restored or who have been made to walk again find themselves after inspired intercession—and wasn't it the purest joy to discover she was the person she knew she had been all along, a perfect size six, wearing A cups, and with a figure *at last* to match her lovely face.

Her figure had never done that since pubescence shaped the stolid matronliness that even dieting down to a skeleton did not efface. Now *that* was gone in a prodigious sacrifice, and Lavonne became the wood nymph she was born to be. But young as she was, and innocent, she did not know then with what devotion a great many members of the opposite sex view the full orbs of womankind. Becoming informed put her, in a way, in the category of Eve finding out what *naked* was and sewing herself a fig-leaf apron. She looked in the glass and loathed herself because of what was gone. But she loved herself too, and between these disorders became two different representations at the same time: haughty princess and abashed scullery maid, imperious but at the same time crawling, dichotomized like the moon with half her disk afire.

Her chin was in the air when she and Darrel met again by accident that next autumn up on Main Street. He was coming out of the bank where he had both a checking and savings account, and when he saw her he acted as if he'd been struck by lightning.

"Let's have coffee."

"I can't, I'm running an errand."

"You look *gorgeous*. How about a movie tomorrow night?" The bishop's daughter meant absolutely nothing to him, he said. Was Lavonne going with anyone? A month later he asked her to be engaged again and this time to name the wedding date. By then she had told him about the operation. He would be the first lover she ever told. And also the easiest, for he was as young as she was, and as innocent, and with even less awareness that there was more to things than met the eye. Of the busts, bubbies, udders, knockers, branched and flowering tits that were a part of the female of whatever species, he as a farm boy had been well aware from an early age, but except for clutching social handfuls of bosom from time to time, much as a nursing baby does, after he grew big enough to take girls out, or using them for a pillow on a picnic, he tried to steer as clear of *them* as of the abominable connection with domestic animals (especially the licentious she-goat) that could send an innocent boy to hell. Somehow synonymized in his rural mind were *beasts* and *breasts*, and so Lavonne's disclosure by no means dismayed Darrel. Just so long as she *looked* like a million dollars, that was all that mattered.

But after Darrel, every revelation got harder. As the years went by, each confession seemed to mean a hostile encounter between opposing forces, the so-called soldier's battle, the one decided by the courage and energy of the soldier, which sometimes she would win and sometimes lose. It was just *crazy* how the men cared, some of them, most of them, for what? Mere protoplasm! (as she read in *Popular Mechanics*, which someone had left in the shop)—oxygen, hydrogen, carbon, nitrogen and a few other elements in an extremely complex and unstable combination, manifesting "vital properties" and not worth five cents in actual money.

What Lavonne gradually came to believe after the operation, Rosetta thought in future years, was that what she had lost belonged—as she herself belonged—not to herself but to whoever would (especially by marrying her) substantiate her inconclusive beauty. She was like the lady in the French story who borrowed the diamond necklace to wear to a ball and lost it, replaced it and had to slave to pay for it the rest of her life! only to find out when the debt was paid that the *lost* diamonds weren't even real. Only Lavonne would never find that out and never stop paying...

She did want a white dress and veil and a round white bride's bouquet with different-length ribbons hanging down, knotted here and there with tiny flowers. And a three-tiered wedding cake decorated with roses and sprinkles of silver-shot candy. And have a photographer there with a tripod camera. But the Cartmills had got very stuck-up because of Darrel's achievements and Mrs. Cartmill buying into the cannery, and also their new piece of land. They wanted him to marry somebody more suitable, the bishop's daughter for instance, even though the Cartmills weren't Mormons themselves but Congregationalists. So they might not have come to the wedding even if Lavonne could have paid for it, the way Dorothy Dix in the paper said the bride was supposed to do, which of course Lavonne couldn't. Or come out in a wedding outfit. She did get together "something old," her orchid-colored dress, "something new," a new pair of pumps, "something borrowed," five dollars from Rosetta, of which she still had one eighty-five in her purse at the time of the ceremony, and "something blue," her eyeshadow.

Rosetta was her attendant. Of course she looked beautiful, both the Justice of the Peace and the lady in his office who acted as the other witness congratulated Darrel and said he had most assuredly picked a peach in the garden of love. Sometimes a blonde will be a terrible disappointment, promising so much from the back, but when you walk up past her and give a sidelong glance! The eyes are too close together or there is something wrong with the chin, but Lavonne's front was even better than her back. For their honeymoon they drove in a northerly direction for a few days, then headed back to Bountiful, Lavonne returning in the chains that would never be struck off again in life, although they did not show, in requital for the deprivation in this case to Darrel, which he knew about beforehand so wasn't deceived but yet, young and inexperienced as he was, did not convert into reality until, amorously sportive in the night and tugging the mounds and sheltered hollows of his bride's tight-fitting underbodice, he whimpered for divestiture. "You must, you must!" But "No," she said, "Darrel, you must never ask me that."

Chapter Fifty-six

✳

THEY LIVED IN BOUNTIFUL OR DOWN THE ROAD A PIECE ON THE OLD CARTMILL place to start with, then on the new land. Lavonne, sending her smiles everywhere like a searchlight, soon won the Cartmills over, won the neighbors over, especially the wives who were prepared to dislike her, won over dogs, cats, chickens. And then lived by bond-service rendered to them all because of what they didn't know about her. But more than that, because if an eye doesn't see something and a mind doesn't know something, then it doesn't exist. And that goes double for beauty.

Lavonne couldn't have found a refuge and haven out of the rough hustle at a better time than she did. Which is not to say that business, jobs and stock-market values were not in the same sorry shape out in Bountiful as in Salt Lake and everywhere else, still falling or at rock bottom, but out there the low level of activity in the sleepy countryside didn't show the way it did in town. And anyway, Darrel was one of these who always improved the shining hour. That was why as a Future Farmer of America he had been so written up. And now he was getting rich as well, while everyone else was going under, which of course always happens. Lavonne became a perfect farmer's wife except that she did no work outside the house in the dirt and hot sun, Darrel wouldn't have wanted her to start looking like some kind of run-over gypsy. She learned canning from her mother-in-law, sewed with her sisters-in-law, drove various makes of cars, caused slips from house plants to grow amazingly, had a fine baby boy, quilted at the Grange, managed to be the prettiest wife at the Young Republican Club annual dance without alienating the other women or inciting the other Young Republicans to too much lust. In short, with Darrel she patterned an obedience worthy of the holy angels. From then on, honeyed, concurring, inducing, sanctioning, covenanting, crediting and yielding, she played one role and one role only: *to give each man she faced whatever he needed or wanted at whatever the cost.*

THOSE FIRST YEARS ROSETTA ENVIED her, her baby boy in yellow rompers with a duck embroidered on the bib, the renowned husband, the house with new Venetian blinds at every window, the freezer, the dusty Buick she drove to town, the five-dollar kid gloves. Legrand thought she was foolish not to have taken a chance and gone to Hollywood, he was an authority, she could well have made it. That is, after her operation. He knew about that. Everyone did at the time, Mrs. Daybell, Penny and Mildred at the Chic Salon sweatshop of beauty, Nancibel, Agnes. Penny thought it was the most terrible tragedy she ever heard of, a girl of only nineteen having something like that happen. Without what *she* had, she certainly couldn't have got Jake, her husband, Penny said. That much she knew. She could have been the most beautiful thing on this earth, but without that added incentive Jake would have said *so long, farewell* so fast it would make your head swim. Some men are just like that.

Legrand was sure she'd have been photogenic, that doors would have opened. But didn't the fact that she didn't even *try* mean that maybe a person's subconscious knows just how far the person can go?

One of Legrand's courses up at the university was philosophy. And when he learned how, he tried to deal with the general causes and principles of things, and ultimate reality, as often as he could. Other courses were literature, art and sociology. After Lavonne married Darrel and Rosetta lived alone in her tiny apartment, Legrand used to drop in and see her every once in a while. When his short story entitled "Cherry-merry" appeared in the university literary magazine, he came and showed it to her that same evening. She thought it was wonderful. He could be a writer if he wanted, she said. Or paint pictures. Design dresses. He was very artistic. Well, he knew he was, and that was why it was so hard for him to decide on an occupation. He could probably have sang. Danced. Acted. He played the part of Pisanio in *Cymbeline*. Had he studied the piano, he would probably have shown a great gift for piano-playing.

That was the trouble. Legrand had too many talents. His father John Hollis only had *one*, and he was glad of it. One good shot (concentrated), he often said, of the *power of invention* was worth all the other niminy-piminy so-called artistic talents put together. He was talking about the invention of useful objects that had made America the great land it was, such as the flashlight, the retractable clothesline, cider press, electric toaster, to name but a few of thousands. John had invented many useful objects himself, a new kind of screwdriver, an ice cream freezer, a letter holder and shoe-stretcher. Most of these inventions were patented, some he had manufactured small lots of himself, then gave up on, none as yet had made any money. But his latest invention was something that *could not fail*, and as soon as his son Legrand got through college and settled into something and John Hollis discharged the last of his debt to his mother (for the times had affected his Bicycle and Repair Shop to the point where to keep the mortgage from being foreclosed over their heads he had to tap even his mother for the few hundreds in her savings account, as well as having her borrow on her five-hundred-dollar life insurance policy), he was going to start manufacture. Sometimes Legrand was a disappointment to John, the way the boy was proceeding. What was he going to do? The possibilities were unlimited, Nancibel said. Yes, John said, the possibilities for being a bum.

Rather than discuss the subject again and again with his father sitting in judgment, especially in the evening after supper, Legrand would drop in and see his second cousin. The only two people in the world, it seemed to him, who understood him were his mother and Rosetta. And the latter even more than the former, because of his and her being the same age and understanding modern life better. So he would drop in, they would drink black coffee and smoke the cheapest brand of cigarettes, called Wings. Penny at the Chic Salon bought a cigarette-making machine which would turn out cigarettes at a third of the cost (she said) of even those cheap things. But those she made were fragile, lumpy and the ends never full, so the other girls didn't follow suit and Penny herself soon went back to the tailor-made. Legrand asked his father why *he* didn't invent something useful like that, that would really work?

Nancibel said she could see how a father with four or five sons might differ with one or two of them from time to time, have a quarrel or argument. But when he only had one! She felt that father and son being constantly dead set against each other was undermining her health, and she did look bad, dark circles under her eyes and her nose pinched. The day Legrand graduated from the university in cap and gown, John wouldn't go to the ceremonies! At home afterwards, fixing cake and punch in the kitchen to take into the front room, Nancibel cried in Rosetta's arms, it was such a tragedy. To refuse to go up to the university to see Legrand graduate! And one would surely think his grandmother, Mother Hollis, would have made an effort to leave her daughter Madge's place in Jasper, Minnesota, where she was making a visit, in time to attend the ceremonies too. But no. Why didn't Mother Hollis move *in* with Madge if she liked it there so well?

The upshot of the graduation rift, for rift it became between husband and wife, and serious too, was that John decided to drive by himself to his sister Madge's place, visit awhile, try to get his brother-in-law to invest in the Thief Repulse Auto Lock, the one thing he ever invented that would make millions for everybody concerned, then bring his mother back with him to Salt Lake City. Nancibel and Legrand didn't find out for nearly the whole summer that a hundred miles west of Madge's, as John and Mother Hollis were driving along heading for Utah, two opposite charges of electricity from clouds and earth formed a funnel-shaped whirl which, roaring like a locomotive and sweeping a path fifty feet wide across only seven miles of country, sucked John, his poor mother, the old '31 Dodge, Thief Repulse Auto Lock, patents, correspondence and everything else up into it. Madge didn't start to worry for several weeks, but then sent a postcard. Did John get home all right? Nancibel replied, she thought they were still there with Madge. Mother Hollis's body was never found. John's couldn't have consisted of much by that time, but it came home in a normal-sized coffin. The family dentist Dr. Mitchell (who drank) identified John's two gold crowns and partial plate, he would know them anywhere. Had John borrowed money from Madge's husband, Nancibel and Legrand would have heard of it. Nancibel talked of sending Legrand back there to the vicinity where the tornado passed, but the Thief Repulse Auto Lock probably never could have been found. The Dodge must have been almost pulverized, nothing was heard of it again. Which only went to show that you should never part with your loved ones in anger, for you may never see them again. Nancibel cried her eyes out, it was such a tragedy. A newspaper clipping Madge sent said that the destructive power was not in the straight wind but in the counter-clockwise rotating mass moving in a north-easterly direction, and that the barometric pressure just beforehand had taken a terrible drop.

LEGRAND DID HIS BEST TO make head or tails of what was in his father's shop, drawers and strongbox. How glad Nancibel was to have her big grown-up son, a college graduate at that, to depend on. He had always been important to her, but now, the man of the house, the sun rose and set in him. At first she was going to ask Rosetta to move in again and pay board and room, but kept putting it off. It was so nice just to have her son all to herself for a change. Cooking supper at night, she felt like a bride, setting the table especially nice, picking a few nasturtiums, Michaelmas daisies or last roses of summer for the blue satin-glass vase, using the best china and silver. The only trouble was, Legrand wasn't punctual like John used to be.

But that, of course, was because he was out every day, or almost every day, looking for a job as writer on the paper, window decorator, announcer or singer on the radio, florist's assistant, buyer for a gown shop like Makoff's, movie projectionist, floorwalker, or he would even take a position like desk clerk at the Hotel Utah, interior decorator or Cadillac salesman. But jobs were very scarce, even those you would think of only to keep from starving, bus boy, garbage man, street sweeper. It even got so a job advertised in the paper for a *dishwasher* in Kresge's coffee shop had applicants standing in line clear around the block!

But then Legrand did get on somewhere, and that was as a writer and researcher. What he worked on was called a "project." He happened to run into one of his school friends doing office work there and he said Legrand ought to try to get on, so he did. It used to be called the Public Works Administration, Bert told him. PWA. Now it was called the Works Progress Administration. WPA. Nancibel wanted to know the difference, and Legrand wasn't sure. His friend in the office, Bert, who still at age twenty-two didn't have to shave because he didn't have any whiskers as yet, wasn't sure either. But then the middle-aged supervisor told Bert, and Bert explained to Legrand: The PWA just used to *finance* projects. The WPA not only *financed* them but also *hired, fired* and *did the work.* The PWA used to try to give you a job doing anything (building a water supply, flood-control system, port, road, bridge, hospital, city hall, courthouse or sewage-disposal plant), no matter what your profession was. The WPA tried to give you a job *in your own line*: a writer would earn his money writing, a painter painting, a dancer dancing, actors acting, a sculptor sculpting, a composer composing, and one musical anthropologist on the Salt Lake City WPA fanned out to record folk songs, as others of his profession were doing all over the country. "Well, did you ever hear the like," Nancibel said. She had noticed all that stuff mentioned in the papers over the past few years since the Democrats got in, but just didn't realize what it meant. But who was paying for it? Well, the government. And last but not least, who *wanted* all that stuff?

"What stuff?"

What she meant, weren't there an awfully lot of statues in the world already? hand-painted pictures, musical compositions and such as that? And the library was full of books...

"Oh, Mother!"

"Well, really, Legrand dear."

But Nancibel was all for it. Although now that she was aware of what was going on, she did hear the meanest things over the radio. The President of the church, President Grant, said terribly mean things. No *Saint* was ever going to work on WPA or take welfare, he said. The Mormon church was pure Republican and against everything.

Nevertheless, Legrand met Mormons on the Project.

Its purpose was not very clear at first. Different "writers" did different things, had different home rooms or offices in an old building. Important "writers" or supervisors had desks and swivel chairs, other people had tables and chairs. There were filing cabinets, typewriters clacking, stenographers of all ages, not just young and pretty, as they would have been had businessmen picked them out. Mountains of supplies came in and went out, yellow, pink, blue and white paper, scratch pads, yellow pencils (thousands of yellow pencils), quarts of ink, typewriter ribbons, erasers, library paste in pound jars, rubber bands and paper clips, pasteboard folders. Ashtrays abounded. The air was always blue with smoke.

The Mormon workers didn't like it, such of them as didn't smoke. Another thing the Mormon workers didn't like was to be assigned to trying to get information from some official connected with the church, the Salt Lake City Relic Hall, Brigham Young Museum, the Church Office Building, the Bureau of Information and Museum in the Temple grounds, the Church Historian's Office and Library. The reception they would get would freeze the tail off a brass monkey. Of course they didn't flaunt belonging to the church. Even the public library, where Gentiles worked as well as Mormons, the university library, looked on the "writers" as lonesome mouse-turd strangers running some kind of a scam. Of course they were always going out for coffee, or to the restrooms for a smoke, leaving old newspaper files spread all over the tables, big reference books scattered with bits of paper marking certain pages, their belongings too, old coats and jackets with snow melting on them, briefcases, a sandwich in a paper bag, and always asking for help to find this and that. And what business was it of theirs? All the things that had happened in the ninety years since one hundred and forty-three Mormon men, three Mormon women, two Mormon children, seventy Mormon wagons, one Mormon boat, one Mormon cannon, ninety-three Mormon horses, fifty-two Mormon mules, sixty-six Mormon oxen and nineteen Mormon cows, and three Mormon "colored" servants by the names of Green Flake, Hark Lay and Oscar Crosby entered the Salt Lake Valley and founded Utah? That stuff was private property.

It was old history that people either knew already, didn't want to know or would just as soon forget. Let the dead past bury its dead. The PWA guys leaning on their shovels were bad enough, but these WPA busybodies prying into what didn't concern them were even worse. Their own history ought to belong to *them*, said the high church authorities, and be written up by them, highlighting what the church wanted to highlight, casting into shadow what they didn't, not be waded into wholesale by a bunch of Gentile atheists, Communists, radical Democrats, I.W.W. and Free Love Socialists, Jews and a few jack Mormons who ought to hang their heads in shame, not a one of them who knew Theogamy from their behind.

Gradually the "writers" both great and small, photographers, mapmakers, even the typists and mail and supply people, began to realize that they (like their counterparts in the other forty-seven states) were compiling a book of facts about their state's places, resources and people *for the use of automobile travelers on hard roads*. "Solid information intertwined with various fascinating true stories" was what the supervisor in Legrand's home room said was wanted. The book was to be called *Utah: A Guide to the State*. One historian with his own book inside his head will know just what to latch on to, like a bird building a nest will know just what twigs, grass, string and bits of fluff caught on the wire fences he's going to need. Thirty or forty "writers" turned loose on one book will have to guess.

And so at the end of a day, Legrand and the others too would turn in to the typists an omnium gatherum from old newspapers, documents and worm-eaten books that no one could classify. Often Legrand copied out a sentence or paragraph for himself alone, or his mother, or Rosetta. "I been in every kind of fight there is in the world." "Hot... We'd drink water, you know, and it just run off us." "We never knowed what was going on in the rest of the country; heck, no." "The robbers wouldn't never bother nothing but only a bank or a train." "There is more rascality to be seen in Utah in thirteen days than thirteen years even in rough and tough California. It would seem familiar to old Leo Africanus, like the City of Murderers in Biledulgerid." "The coals of three night fires lay behind." "Back then a lot of people were on their guard. They'd be... bearded guys with six-shooters buckled on. And they'd kill you, too, if you messed with 'em. You didn't have to mess with them *much*, either, just ask 'em a little question..." "The Ute worshipped a bisexual deity, the He-She, represented by the sun." "If the past were suddenly opened up to our inspection, we would be overwhelmed not only by the sheer mass of material, but by the brutality, horror, and tragedy of the centuries that lie behind us. It is one thing to read about massacres, battles, plagues, inquisitions, or to see them enacted in the movies. But what man could bear to look upon the immutable evil of the past, knowing that what he saw was real and beyond all remedy?"

Through Wyandra's penchant for history Rosetta had developed a taste for it too, but Legrand did his daily delving with about the interest he would have felt collecting a stack of old Kleenex. Such enthusiasm as he did muster seemed to go to *tearing down* the past, the *obliteration* of memory, *rejection* rather than organic growth. The new, the zippy, as behooved a young man, an artist, as he thought himself to be. Art was supposed to be in the forefront. But from a practical standpoint, how many automobile travelers on the hard roads of Utah were going to care that the first Utahn to plant a garden was named Goodyear? That two teams of hunters in competition in the year 1849 killed 14,367 ravens, hawks, owls, eagles, minks, pole cats, wolves, foxes, catamounts, bear and panthers? Or that where the state Capitol now stood an arsenal used to be located, which when accidentally blown up by two boys practicing with a rifle broke every window in the city? Boys who would be eighty-two years old today if they had survived that blast and other of the world's harms! Or that the Temple walls were twenty feet high when Brigham Young died? However, Legrand dutifully turned pages and copied out excerpts with the yellow pencils on the pink paper, turned them in, and the typists typed … and one day he stood face to face with his old progenitor, his mother's mother's father, John Doyle Lee, and history took on living semblance, the noise of life began for him in the quietened past.

Half musical, half literary, the musical anthropologist on the Project, Roman Gibson, might as well have hung out with the WPA Orchestra, instrumentalists and singers in the Utah Art Center as with the "writers." But his home room, like Legrand's, was 407-B, his table stood next to Legrand's and it was he, therefore, who (on the occasion of the birthday party his girl gave for him in the attic bower they shared on Fifth West) sang to the guitar a ballad entitled "The Mountain Meadows Massacre." It didn't have much of a tune, but it sounded pretty to him, Roman said, it was such a hard bugger to get ahold of. An old guy that didn't know all the words put him onto it. The Mormons would have liked to make it disappear off the face of the earth, but a few old-timers would still give it a sing after looking carefully around beforehand, like a sober guy about to oblige with a dirty song. A few weeks later Roman brought his guitar, but not his girl, to Legrand's party. Well, it wasn't really a party, Nancibel just said she thought it would be nice if Legrand asked some of his new friends over for the evening, the ones who had asked him, Bert, Roman, Robert … maybe the one who sold the story to a magazine and bought his mother a Mixmaster. He sounded like a lovely boy. She would bake a nice big chocolate cake. But Legrand turned thumbs down on the cake. Just some chipped beef sandwiches, beer and stuff like that, dill pickles. The idea of beer rather shocked Nancibel, John never having drank, or her hairdresser father either although of French descent, and they are supposed to be very fond of wine. But this was Legrand's home that he was the head of now, and they wouldn't get drunk or anything like that, would they? Nancibel thought maybe some girls would be nice, but of course then the menu would be different and they'd have to play games … No, no girls. Especially not from the

Project. One had boy-cut hair, two were old, in their forties at least, Elizabeth Driggs, the poetess, was pretty and probably not thirty yet, but once she tried to jump out of a Newhouse Hotel window and another time cut her wrists, and someone said she was going with a married man.

"Well, I'll fix everything and get out of the way," Nancibel said.

Legrand hooked up the radio in the bedroom for her.

"Well, nighty-night," she came in from the kitchen and told the boys when they all seemed to be there. "Enjoy yourself, have a good time, I'm very glad to have met you, help yourself, make yourself at home." Then she withdrew, shutting the door firmly, but she didn't get undressed. At midnight she sneaked out in the kitchen to see how the food was holding out and if anything was wanted. And it was then that, lurking near the kitchen door trying through the dining room archway to discover and signal Legrand in the dimly lighted front room hazy with smoke, she heard Roman sing the ballad he was so proud of having found. She didn't know anything about that, or that he was the one named Roman, the musical anthropologist. It was hard to keep them straight, but his voice took hold of you, every word stood out plain, and did Legrand realize what a slap in the face that song was to *them*? she asked him the next day. To accept their hospitality, then sing that awful song about her mother's own father! "Your *great-grandfather*," she told Legrand.

But of course Roman had no idea.

Legrand said *he* knew, Wyandra had talked about John Doyle Lee, remember how she was always telling stories about the family and here she wasn't even related. But even before *that* he seemed to have heard…something about a massacre down in southern Utah, a firing squad, some close relation getting in trouble…

"Naturally we never went around bragging about it," Nancibel said. "But I'll tell you this, I certainly never knew there was a *song*. Did somebody write it since the Project started?"

"Oh, no, it's as old almost as—what happened. That's why Roman likes to sing it. And because it was just touch and go whether it would ever, you know, survive."

"Well, all I can say is it hurt *my* feelings. And your Grandma Lucitie would have felt terrible. At a social gathering like that!"

"I've just been thinking—Great-Grandpa could have heard the song himself. Roman says it was made up by some soldiers—dragoons, he said—that rode through the country down there about a year after the massacre. There were still bones scattered around the meadow at that time and they gathered them up and buried them where a lot of other bones were buried, and piled up a bunch of boulders as a marker. *That* soon disappeared, Roman says, but the song can be a monument forever. And since Great-Grandpa didn't die till about twenty years after *that*, he could very well have heard it."

"Whatever could have possessed the man to have got himself into a *situation* like that?" Nancibel said with a sigh. "I suppose it's true? You didn't say anything to Roman?"

"No, I was going to, but something held me back."

"Well, I certainly wouldn't."

But one day when he found himself alone with the musical naturalist in their home room, he did happen to mention it. "Hey, Roman," he said. "You know your song? Well, I'm related to that guy."

"Which song? Which guy?"

"John D. Lee. The Mountain Meadows Massacre. I'm his great-grandson."

Roman's eyes gleamed like a man's whose shovel has just struck a buried chest of pirate gold. But the chest proved to be empty, for Legrand didn't really know anything, or his mother either, and they had no writings or relics. But what did Roman expect? All that fifty-seven children, dozens of grandchildren, and hundreds, maybe thousands of great-grandchildren are going to get out of their founding father's leavings will be a few chromosomal units of heredity and that will be *it*. But Roman acted half mad at Legrand from then on, as though he hadn't paid back something he owed him or reneged on a promise.

But Legrand didn't strike up any great friendships with any of his fellow workers. He was often at Rosetta's, she gave him the key Lavonne used to have so if she was at work he could let himself in and make a cup of coffee, her apartment was closer to the Project offices than home. Sometimes he would be asleep on the couch when she let herself in. Nancibel didn't like him being at Rosetta's so much, or wherever he loitered, rather than coming home. Sometimes she cried softly and said why was it, when she tried to do everything in her power to have everything nice for him, when sick as she was with her kidneys, head, back, stomach, calves of her legs and all the rest of it she cooked, cleaned— and took care of the lawn too, he shouldn't forget *that*—and how much longer she was going to be able to do it she just didn't know—why was it that instead of *appreciating* his surroundings, *appreciating* the lovely food she tried to put on the table, he always wanted to be somewhere else? He told her he didn't, he just had to go around gathering stuff, they were all *compiling a book*, remember, it wasn't like Papa keeping his shop open regular hours, or Rosetta working from eight to five.

"I don't want to nag or anything like that," Nancibel said, "but why don't you keep looking for a *real* job? You ought to listen to the radio sometimes, what President Heber J. Grant says about—that Works Project Administration. He thinks it's just—"

"What do *you* care what a Mormon president says? You're not a Mormon! And by the way," he said, "how come we're *not*?" Not that he wanted to be one. But old family as they were in rampant Salt Lake City or Zion, why weren't they? He had never thought to ask before.

He compared his mother's version of why with what Rosetta had heard from Wyandra, who seemed to have been a walking history of old times. Mostly Nancibel had let life go by without paying much attention to the myth of their days and all the interstratifying that had gone into the past. But Legrand remembered as a little boy Wyandra's bard-like celebrations of little things that had happened, the names she made illustrious: Albert, Lucitie, and back beyond them Mavis, Hindle, Colonel Clarendon, and how she made the town loom up like a great-historied land. But even when older, he couldn't have told you what she really *said*, her Celtic system droned like bees to him. And young men look forward, they back the *future*, whose business it is to be dangerous ...

But then he heard Roman's ballad, and old lineage twanged like a plucked string. No longer did he chip away in ex libris libraries and museums for dead corallum to scatter on a typist's desk at the end of a day. Now he dug the way trapped Floyd Collins's would-be rescuers dug for Floyd, to free a living, breathing man from what he was buried under. For Roman had acted as if that old, terrible massacre was a matter of import, and that John D. Lee, the so-called "ringleader," was too. And since a "matter of import" to Roman could only mean something to be turned into words or music, or to do with the theater or movies, why couldn't *he* make something himself out of his great-grandfather's villainy? Legrand wondered. A scenario, a play? It wasn't as if he would be betraying some family icon. His mother said his grandmother never even *saw* her father again after the age of six.

Rosetta thought it was a wonderful idea, she was sure if he wrote a scenario and sent it to a movie studio, they would snap it right up. After that most of his research, though on WPA time, was for himself, and every little scrap of information he got hold of he would go running with to her. He never found much, though. Juanita Brooks's true, authentic history entitled *The Mountain Meadows Massacre* was years from being written then. She had not yet devotedly put together three decades of John D. Lee's own diaries in *A Mormon Chronicle*, nor composed the true, authentic biography *John Doyle Lee: Zealot, Pioneer Builder, Scapegoat*. Had her two thousand or more pages been available, they would have helped Legrand like an army with banners. Or maybe not. Maybe nothing can help the "writer" who wants the name without the game.

Rosetta encouraged him as much as she could. She could just see his movie, ending somewhat like *A Tale of Two Cities*, John D. Lee standing up to be shot and saying with an English accent "It is a far, far better thing I do than I have ever done before ..." Not those actual words, because that would be plagiarism, and couldn't they put you in jail for that? but along that line. She would get gooseflesh on her arms, tears would spring to her eyes, just thinking about it.

Added touches for him to put in would come to mind sometimes while she was at work, swirling in a head full of pincurls, twisting up a spiral or waiting for a bleach to take. Not that there was a lot of time to stand and stare in the low-ceilinged little cut-rate Chic Salon of Beauty's noisy turmoil. But sometimes in the blue smoke, during that mysterious moment of silence which settles on every company, no matter how animated, every seven minutes due to the angels passing overhead (as Wyandra believed), or if her customer's relentless secrets required no answer, Rosetta's mind would form first this scene and then that, hazily, smokily…

Everyone smoked. A cigarette's nightshade alkaloid was not harmful then. You could smoke for eighty-two years and not die. Women did it to keep thin and also for the reason of not being able to stop. Some who tried to stop did not do so for their health's sake but because five or more dollars a month during the Depression was a lot of money to send up in smoke. Think what you could buy for that in six months or a year! The whole Elizabeth Arden line…a Five Foot Shelf of books that in fifteen minutes a day would educate you to where no one could tell you from a Harvard graduate. Dentistry for the whole family…a round-trip ticket and week's stay in Burbank…a second-hand Dodge…But mostly after a day or two the smoke would seem better than the substance, and back the smoker would go to the old habit.

"Empty the ashtrays." Mrs. Daybell was always after them. "How many times do I have to tell you? Keep your ashtrays clean!"

That was how Penny lost her job. Because she emptied an ashtray with a still smoldering butt in it in the trash box in the storeroom and started a fire that would have cost the owner two or three hundred dollars had she not been insured. Rosetta and Mildred lost three days' work and they were lucky it wasn't more, Mrs. Daybell said. She gave Penny her walking papers. If the girl had apologized! but no, impudence itself. And that talk of hers about beauticians organizing themselves into a union! But that was that husband of Penny's, with his Western Federation and marching with the Bonus Army and all that, a Bolshevik if there ever was one. And *why* was there no work? *Why* were conditions in the mines so bad? For one simple reason: trouble-makers like Penny Bonkowski's husband! Later Penny got on at the beauty shop in the basement of the Newhouse Hotel, and when she called Rosetta, said she wondered how she had stood Mrs. Daybell as long as she did. "If there's ever another opening down here," she said, "I'll let you know."

Rosetta said thanks, if she was still in town. Legrand and her mother's cousin Nancibel were talking about moving to Hollywood, and maybe she'd go too. It all depended. She didn't say on what, but what that was was Legrand's scenario, which now had the title of "All on the Meadow Green." Legrand wanted it to be based on something solid, on more than just an *idea*. But details were hard to come by, not only because of his ineptitude as a researcher but because his efforts had attracted attention. Some librarian or curator's assistant must have told someone about the books and papers he asked for, that person had gone to the Project's director, he in turn to the supervisor, and she now, a large, angry woman by the name of Mrs. Horsely, confronted Legrand. "What in the hell do you think you are doing digging in that Mountain Meadows stuff? *We* don't need it. And we're having a hard enough time as it is. Who put you onto it?"

"No one. I just happened to see it mentioned a time or two, and I thought it seemed interesting."

"Well, it's not," she said. "To us. And it shouldn't be to you, either. Leave it alone."

Chapter Fifty-seven

✳

THE SECOND-HAND BOOKSTORES HAD A FEW OLD WESTERN BOOKS THAT LEGRAND thought he might have got some good out of, but the prices floored him! Even with spines loose, covers off and scribbled in by demonic children, they were collector's items, he was told. And...as he could see when he thumbed through the pages...awfully full of crap he didn't want. Because what *he* was after was—well, how do you do it? "High deeds in Hungary that pass all men's believing?" Of course he didn't *say* that, even to Rosetta, but she surmised it. How *does* a poor young man get rich and famous? Mae West, when interviewed on the radio, said, "The first thing to learn is to use what's lyin' around the house." And as that in his case was his great-grandfather and a massacre, Legrand must go on, they were bound to lead somewhere. Rosetta encouraged him. "It will be wonderful," she would say. "The best movie of the year. In fact, maybe you could even write a book! Like *Riders of the Purple Sage.*" But no, he had his mind set on a scenario. It was faster...and more modern and...results were quicker. And maybe he was thinking of June Mathis, too, Rosetta said, who wrote *The Four Horsemen of the Apocalypse* for Rudolph Valentino and had such a fuss made over her because she was born in Salt Lake City. Her father had the cigar stand in the Felt Building, and as a little girl June used to jump rope outside the building. No, Legrand said, he certainly wasn't thinking of June Mathis!

"Well, she's dead anyway," Rosetta said soothingly, guessing that he might be jealous. "And her scenario...the paper said she took it from a book already written by some Spaniard named Blasco Ibáñez. So that's not so wonderful. While with you, you're making the whole thing up *yourself*! which is twice as hard. Especially when all you've got to go on is just...a bunch of stuff that happened. Like first, this wagon train from Arkansas or wherever gets ambushed down in southern Utah by—"

"Mormons and Indians—"

"Wasn't that kind of unusual?" she said. "For white people and Indians to be fighting *on the same side*? Didn't white people in those days usually stick together no matter *where* they came from or *what* church they belonged to? Wasn't it always just Indians against whites? Never *Indians and whites* against whites?"

"Well, the times—"

"And Great-Grandpa John D. Lee," she said (for he was *her* forebear too, which she sometimes forgot, as though he was a piece of property belonging only to Legrand). "Did they *elect* him? To be the ringleader? And why was it twenty years after it all happened

531

before he was executed? And why just him?"

"I haven't got it all worked out," he said, as though it wasn't history but a plot he could do anything he wanted with.

"What June Mathis did was *nothing*," Rosetta repeated. "She merely took a book that was already written—"

And wasn't that a smart thing to do! Legrand thought, fretting and fuming at Rosetta's kitchen table as he lit one cigarette off another and tried to…begin at the beginning…go on to the end…and…He didn't want to tear up the earth. A simple little thing like *write*! Simple, easy…On your mark! But there it was again, that empty void, that rudderless feeling, that conscious want of some great touchstone for the trial of motives and actions…He would sit and think. Of Hollywood, and that damn June Mathis and the *Four Horsemen of the Apocalypse*.

"Why don't you go down there and *see* the place?" Rosetta said.

"What place?"

"Why, where it all happened. The Mountain Meadow. That is, if it really exists and there hasn't been a town built over it or something."

"Oh, it really exists. At least I think so."

"Well, maybe if you saw it, walked over the ground and everything, you'd have…like a vision. It would all come clear in your mind. And doesn't Palmer live somewhere close around there?"

"Not real close." He had looked at a map.

"But you could stop in and see him and what's her name? His wife."

"Betty."

He wanted Rosetta to come with him, but she couldn't. Mrs. Daybell would have a fit. She still hadn't replaced Penny, though she booked *appointments* as if she had. But human events—it seems like they're predestined. The first night Legrand was gone away was when Nancibel took her bad spell. She called her brother Herman's wife Agnes, called the doctor, then called Rosetta. And it was Rosetta who went down and stayed with her till the time came she had to be taken to the hospital. Rosetta didn't go to work those days she was at Nancibel's, let Mrs. Daybell fume her head off. She certainly owed Nancibel that. But then she got too bad to keep at home…Lucky for Rosetta, Mrs. Daybell said. Another day and that would have been *it*. Young people had no sense of responsibility anymore, go their own sweet way, no concern for anything but their own selfish interests! But, Mrs. Daybell…"Save your breath," said Mildred. "The main thing is, you still got your job."

By a miracle Legrand had *his*, too, when he got back. (After burying his grandmother, he told the supervisor, and finding a handicapped relative a place to live.)

"And so you viewed the very spot," Rosetta said. "Imagine. Did it inspire you?"

Strangely enough, it had. Or *something* had. He and Palmer drank a lot of beer while he was down there, maybe it was that, they ran around…Talk about scenery! Ugly, beautiful…But nobody knew a thing and Palmer said not to ask, the massacre was a touchy subject. But of course Legrand talked to *him*, and Palmer said he didn't see why it wouldn't make as good a scenario as any, if somebody didn't put the kibosh on him beforehand. A couple of years after he got down there, Palmer said, the National Park Bureau or somebody like that took it on themselves to put the monument up, and that made a lot of people mad. "That damn Rosenfeld," they said. They wished *he'd* got it in the neck that time instead of Cermak. They didn't *want* the Mountain Meadow designated a national landmark, that big plaque put up and everything, attracting curiosity-seekers. Palmer said *he* heard that at the time the massacre happened, seventy or eighty years before or whenever it was, the main road to California, the Old Spanish Trail as it was called, ran right along *past* the place, but after the killings and the mass grave, the people eradicated it and built the new road off to the east, the one that's U.S. 91, the highway to Las Vegas, so no one would go by there anymore, they wanted the place to be forgotten…and now here this bunch of Socialists and no-goods living off the Government comes in and would open up the whole can of worms again if they could.

But the actual locale was on private land. That was done deliberately, Legrand said. Sightseers had to ask permission at the ranch house to visit it, and open and shut gates. He and Palmer the day they went there sure got some dirty looks. But of course…two guys…not working…in the middle of the afternoon…loafing around…The Mormons are great on work.

"THE MONUMENT," HE SAID, "is not what I'd call a monument at all. It's a wall about four feet high made out of boulders set in cement going around…this space, maybe thirty by forty feet, where most of the people are buried. It's got these steps going up and over at one end, the western end, I guess, you climb over and there you are, down in their defense pit where they fought from Monday till Friday. It's kind of eerie, even in the sunshine. Not a sound except the wind, and a hundred and thirty murdered people down underneath…So anyway," he said, "that night, because of all the beer, Palmer was out like a light and she got him to bed, Betty, that is, and went to bed herself and I stayed up by myself to have another smoke, and she said if I burnt the house down around their ears it would be all right with her."

"Why would she say a thing like that?"

"Well, the foreclosure coming up and one thing and another. They lost *her* farm, but that wasn't Palmer's fault, he did the best he could, though *she* doesn't think so. This place where they live now belonged to somebody else, her uncle, I think. A terrible old shack. But anyway, I sat down at the table and was going to write—kerosene lamp, imagine, a little tiny one, flickering—a note to myself about the monument. But all of a sudden…it was the strangest thing…The movie…I was *in* it, *seeing* it and *writing* it all at the same time. No! The strange thing was ... it *wasn't a movie.*"

"Well," Rosetta said gently after a silence while she waited for him to go on, "it soon will be, I'll bet." She reached over to touch lightly the pages he'd been reading from.

"No, really, what I mean to say—it happens. *It's always happening.*"

"I think I know." She didn't, though.

On an old Underwood borrowed from the girl in the basement, she typed it for him and thought it plain to see that he was drunk that night at Palmer's, the great slashing, unfamiliar cursive wasn't his usual small half-printing, and it was kind of crazy. Still, as she typed, it did cloudily, mysteriously, unfold like a real play, and she said she was sure someone would take it down in Hollywood.

He wasn't going to send it, though (they don't even open the package), but take it down in person and find someone with some kind of pull.

The California climate would be a lot better for his mother. He wanted Rosetta's honest opinion. Was his mother really sick? Or, as he remembered reading about in General Psychology, was she using her health as a weapon to control *him*?

"Oh, no, she's really sick," Rosetta said. "Agnes said the doctor told her that her two kidneys have fused into one horse-shoe kidney. And that's pretty—serious."

Legrand felt so sorry he didn't know what to do. Oh, how good he was going to be from now on. He would never go against his mother's wishes in his life again, never leave her alone, he would tell her how much she meant to him, try to get another job, stop drinking beer and staying up half the night, start appreciating all she did for him, his nice ironed shirts, his pressed pants, the dumplings, the oatmeal cookies he said he was tired of. He rushed to her during afternoon visiting hours, rushed to her in the evening. Rosetta went too, Herman was sometimes there, Agnes also if she wasn't on duty. Nancibel lived nine days after she was put in the hospital. She died during evening visiting hours. No one was there. They were all just on their way.

The house was heavily mortgaged. What little Legrand got out of it went to pay on doctor and hospital bills. A sale of the contents paid for the funeral. Agnes wanted Nancibel's plain white Haviland with the gold rim but didn't want to pay for it, and Legrand didn't think they owed her that, so Agnes and Herman got on their high horse. Agnes had been going to tell Legrand he could stay with them until his affairs got settled, she told Rosetta, but now she was glad she hadn't asked him. And he was the loser. His cousins, her and Herman's children that he never acted like he wanted to have anything to do with, had he got acquainted with them, might have changed his life. They were active in the church, paid tithing, loved all the various activities. They kept their bodies healthy. The oldest boy's hobby was to trap. And it was the cutest thing at Thanksgiving. He called them all to the window to look out on the lawn and see what he had laid out there, a whole row of little dead animals laying on their backs with their eyes closed and their paws kind of crossed over their chests like little people. Rock chucks and prairie dogs, squirrels and things like that. A little fox that looked like a little collie. Wasn't that cute? and showed how the boy took after Agnes and was always trying to accomplish something, not lay around. So Legrand was the loser. It was no skin off his uncle's family's nose...

Legrand moved in with Rosetta and cried for days, wished he had died instead of the beloved mother that, now that he looked back, he realized he was so cruel to and neglectful of, wished he could live his life over, wished he had another chance. He drew Nancibel's picture from her photograph, tried to write about her. But really, not very much had happened to her in the life he decided she had sacrificed for him. Her father running into a cow in a lady friend's electric brougham. Her mother-in-law being blown completely away in a tornado. Her grandfather being shot to death by United States soldiers for participation in a massacre. Her own life, except that she had given birth to *him*, was not too eventful. He gave up trying to write it. Gave up teetotalism too, the malt in beer was very good for you. Rosetta didn't care for beer, but she agreed about the malt.

They went up to the cemetery. Legrand knelt down by the grave marked with just the little temporary stake with Nancibel's name on it in framed glassine that would stay there until Rosetta would in days to come replace it with a gravestone, then, weeping, threw himself face down along the mound. If only he had been better, kinder! She comforted him as best she could, he was good, he was kind, a child wasn't supposed to hang onto his mother like a little first-grader. They walked home instead of taking the streetcar so they could see the buds coming out, the leaves. He told her about De Quincey when Wordsworth's little daughter died. De Quincey would go to the churchyard and lie on the child's grave the whole night long. Sometime *he* was going to do that, lie up there and just think and remember...A few times he stayed out late, once till five in the morning, but Rosetta didn't imagine he was up at the cemetery lying on his mother's grave. She didn't ask. If he wanted her to know where he was, he could tell her. He slept on the couch, went to work long after she did in the morning.

Gradually his grief subsided. He even went back to wondering if maybe some of his mother's ailments *hadn't* been psychological. It was so peculiar about the mind. He drank beer, kept tinkering with his scenario, adding things here and there. Rosetta typed it again. They started to save to go to Hollywood. Bus fare was cheap. If they could both quit smoking...But just at the present time that seemed rather hard to do. However...And then one day a knock came at the door. It was the new manager. And she was not just the manager but the officious middle-aged daughter of the man who, unbeknownst to the tenants (for how would they find out a thing like that?), had inherited the apartment building. When Rosetta said the young man sitting at the kitchen table was her second cousin, the manager took a long look out into the kitchen at him in his shirtsleeves with papers spread out in front of him, a bottle of beer at his elbow and smoke eddying around, and said yes, well, but there was a city ordinance, and that kind of thing was what they were going to put a stop to.

"No, but he really is," Rosetta said, flushing with embarrassment, and she had proof of it. "His mother and my mother were first cousins!"

The manager waved her hand as though to shoo away a fly. "Listen," she said, "I once knew of *twins* that had theirself a baby! So what kind of ice is 'second cousins' supposed to cut? Human nature is human nature. Either he leaves or you do, settle it betwixt yourselves."

They decided to get married. That would solve the problem once and for all. They got their license, picked out a platinum band, Rosetta paid for it. At first they were going to have a civil ceremony, but every day on her way to work Rosetta passed an ivy-covered Baptist church, and she wondered if it wouldn't be nice to have the minister of that church marry them. It would seem more real somehow. The minister was glad to, in the church parlor. Rosetta called Lavonne the night before, and she came in from Bountiful and stood up with them. She looked so beautiful in a summer dress, lacy summer hat and white high-heeled pumps that the minister acted quite shaken and developed a frog in his throat. The other witness, a plain woman of about forty with very pointed eyeteeth that were yellower than her other teeth, who appeared to be the minister's secretary or something like that, looked down her nose at them all, and when Lavonne talked and laughed after the ceremony, the secretary stood looking at her, frowning, as if she were a sphere-born harmonious siren of some kind strayed off an ocean rock. Lavonne's figure was perfect. You would never know she had a child. He was being taken care of that day by her mother-in-law.

Nothing could have made her happier than this wedding, she said. Rosetta looked darling. She loved that black dress, it made her look like about a size six. Lavonne was a six, she said, seemed to be stuck with that, though she usually had to have the waists taken in. She loved Rosetta's hair, loved it. Privately she said she hoped Rosetta had got over worrying about her eye, her eyes were a pretty color and no one was going to pay any attention to that slight—It didn't amount to a thing! And if she could get *Legrand* to fall in love with her and marry her! an artist like he was, so critical and particular, and the way he used to collect pictures of all the beautiful starlets and movie actresses and noticing every little detail, if Rosetta could get *him*, why, she could be *pretty proud*.

Rosetta really wasn't, because it was just an arrangement so they could share an apartment, but she didn't say so.

The last thing Lavonne said after they had lunch at the Golden Pheasant and she was getting into her Buick was that there was a couple out in Bountiful and her mother-in-law told her they were *full cousins*—well, they had to drive up to Wyoming to get their license and get married, and they had *beautiful children*. Perfectly smart and normal in every way.

That night Legrand said Lavonne could really have probably made it in Hollywood had she had the ambition. What was all that about an operation a couple of years ago? Somehow Rosetta supposed he knew, but of course Nancibel wouldn't talk about things like that in front of him, or his grandmother Mother Hollis, either. He remembered it seemed mysterious, all the whispering. Rosetta told him and he thought that, speaking from an artistic standpoint, it was the best thing that ever happened, the difference between night and day.

That first night after Rosetta went to bed, Legrand brought his beer in, the first time he had ever done so, and, settling a pillow under his shoulders at the foot of the bed, lay on top of the covers and talked awhile about the scenario and going to Hollywood and how he was sure she could get a job down there, maybe in some studio's makeup department. She was sure she could, too. Then they talked of other things, remembered high school, Miss Sessions, remembered Captain Carpenter in the poem too, rising up in his prime to go out into the world and little by little be lopped and chopped up to pieces. Legrand could still recite the poem all through. He went out in the kitchen and got more beer and came in reciting. Rosetta had to hush him a little, as the window was open.

The next night Rosetta was wondering whether to put the potatoes in the oven or wait a little in case Legrand should be late when a knock came at the door. Outside stood Palmer with a suitcase down beside him. He had left Betty. The whole thing had just got…impossible. Betty claimed he lost her ranch which her father gave her, and maybe he *was* responsible in a way, but God knows he worked, and she made no allowances for the economic—that the times were bad or anything like that. No, everything was *his* fault. So no use to stay down there and fight, the God-forsakenest country in the world anyway. So Orval was going to overhaul the old car. Palmer had called him and Orval said he would, or help him figure if he'd better trade it, and then Palmer was going to head either for Oregon or California.

Rosetta had him make himself at home, and as she switched on the oven said dinner would be ready in about an hour. But if he wanted a little snack beforehand? Sometimes a person would be driving and forget to eat. While the coffee was heating, she made him a baloney sandwich and then another. She told him about Nancibel dying…but Legrand had had a key to this apartment for a long time anyway, Rosetta gave him Lavonne's key after she left, it was closer than home…which Legrand didn't have now anymore in any case. And his Uncle Herman's wife, Agnes—Legrand couldn't stand her, and she was mad at *him* on account of Nancibel's…set of china. And this building—they had a new manager. And *she* said…So yesterday…

He thought she was kidding at first. But no, really…See, here was her ring. Well, no reason why not, he said. Two can live as cheaply…as the saying goes. He wished them all the best. Many long years of happy wedded life. If he'd have known, he'd have brought a present, but it wasn't too late. And he sure didn't mean to barge in on their *honeymoon*.

But every place he used to have, to hang his hat—Pop was laid off two or three years ago and he and Mom went up to Boise.

"You're welcome to stay here," she said.

"Well, that seems like kind of an imposition."

"I don't see why. You can sleep—Let's see. If Legrand doesn't keep you up all night talking! He's a terrible night-owl..."

One year Nancibel invited the family for Christmas, including Gram and Lavonne, though they weren't really relatives except to Rosetta. She and Lavonne were little then, maybe second-graders, and Legrand was too. And the first thing Rosetta noticed when they got to Nancibel's house was that Legrand was acting mad and banging his new toys around as if it wasn't Christmas at all. And the reason for that was, he didn't get what he wanted, which was stilts. A boy in the next block had some and *let him learn to walk on them*, which if Nancibel had known she would have had a fit, because one time down on Fourth West there was a boy who fell off a pair and broke his leg and got gangrene and died!

Legrand wrote Santa Claus and everything, not once but twice. But no stilts. Legrand was just like he'd been kicked in the stomach. But all of a sudden after they got there and Nancibel had explained that Santa never brought stilts, they were too dangerous! why, what should happen but John, Legrand's father, surprised the company by holding his hand up for silence. "Legrand," he said. "If I'm not very much mistaken, I think old Santa *made an exception in your case* and there's something for you *down behind the buffet* in the dining room! Why don't you go see?" John picked a time when he thought Nancibel wouldn't fight with him in front of guests, which she didn't, though she glared in his direction. And Legrand went rushing and careening into the next room, and everyone followed. And sure enough, down behind the buffet—! Rosetta didn't know then that there was a word to describe his face when he tore off the wrapping to his present, but there was. It was *rapture*.

And the same word would apply again, she saw, when he walked in and there sits Palmer.

IT DIDN'T TAKE LONG FOR Orval to overhaul Palmer's car. By Sunday morning the boys were packed and ready to go, down U.S. 91 to Las Vegas, then across to Reno and down...

"Be sure and write," Legrand said.

"I will. You too," Rosetta said.

"As soon as this scenario business gets settled..." He leaned over and patted Marie and Les's old leather suitcase as though it had been a horse. In it was the manuscript Rosetta had typed again, the third time being the charm.

"They'll take it, don't you fear," she said. "I have no doubts."

"Me either," Palmer said. "It'd sure be better than a lot of the junk you see!"

"I'll phone. And then you come on down. But you don't have to wait for that."

"I know," she said. "I'll come. A little later when we're more caught up."

While Palmer was in the house getting the bottle opener and then when he came back out and was checking the load, she said to Legrand, "Remember the stilts that Christmas? Did you ever get the good out of them?"

"I can hardly remember," he said. "Let's see. No, not really. I think I fell one time. And Mother—What made you think of *them*?"

"BOY, OH, BOY, I'D SEE me letting *my* handsome young bridegroom go down to Hollywood without me!" Mildred said at the Chic Salon of Beauty the next morning.

"Well, the rent was paid for the month—and see, he quit his job," Rosetta said, "because of having this chance—And both of us wouldn't dare. To quit at the same time, I mean."

IT WAS LONESOME WITHOUT HIM. Instead of bigger, the place seemed smaller, as if his personal consequence was like the gas in a balloon that pushed the sides out, but when he was gone they shrank together. Lavonne said she thought it was a good idea for him to go when he had the chance. She came up to the apartment unexpectedly one evening to get a touch-up. Darrel dropped her off and said he would be back to get her about ten-thirty. He was going to a meeting of the Young Republican club. She brought the baby, a diaper bag, bottles of milk to heat up. He was sleeping. They laid him on the bed. Rosetta looked at how perfect they are, their hair, eyelashes, lips and everything, their perfect little fingernails...

"Look," Lavonne said, and held her foot up. Alligator pumps. "And look at this!" An alligator bag. "And guess what Darrel came home with the other day!"

"A tiara?"

"No, a mangle." They were having the house painted, and next summer they were going to have the whole back part of the yard paved. That was one thing she had to give Darrel credit for, his business ability. Everything he touched...His own father said so. "Darrel never lets a chance slip by..."

"But boys are awfully spoiled, aren't they?" Lavonne waited till her hair was rinsed and Rosetta turned off the kitchen taps and wrapped her head in a bath towel before she added, "But Legrand's disposition is nothing to brag about either, is it? As we well know from when we stayed there. He's good-looking, though. He really is. I was thinking that the other day."

"Shall we pincurl this? Or what do you want?" Rosetta said when she had sat Lavonne down by the kitchen table and taken the small mirror down off the wall and given it to her.

She studied her reflection for a moment. "Kind of a lift at the back. More than I had to start with."

"Okay, I know what you mean."

Lavonne didn't think she could stand it anymore to work at the Chic Salon, she said, and Rosetta didn't think she could either, two operators were now doing the work of three, and Mrs. Daybell was getting meaner by the day. But of course Lavonne would never have to work like that again.

"Don't think I have an easy life, though," Lavonne said. And as she talked about her days, Rosetta could see that she really didn't. She had to be beautiful, kind, loved and approved of every minute of every day. Not by Rosetta, any more than a plant would, attached to another plant in a symbiosis of old times, or by Gram, or her own reflection. But by everyone else. To Rosetta she could come running to get her hair touched up, shampooed and curled at night without thinking that after a ten-hour day at the Chic Salon she might be tired. The sharing and sharing alike through babyhood and right on up the line meant time and energy too, why not? Moral support…

Not then or for many years did Rosetta have the range of language to draw from Lavonne's curious mixture of reigning queen and manacled slave any kind of conclusion. Nor did she need such a range, for at that time Lavonne was nobody very interesting, just someone she had always known, more sister than chum. Lavonne had made a good marriage, her husband was going to get rich, there was no need for Rosetta (for her own mental satisfaction) to sort out how it should have come about that Lavonne had an ego but no *self*, utter self-absorption but no *will*, force but no *essence*. Later Rosetta would want to be able to specify, to herself, for her own satisfaction, more. As a botanist might the meaning of the alternate leaves, elliptical or obtusely serrated, on the *Thea sinensis*. But for tonight she just wanted to get Lavonne's hair put up, and sit down and put her feet up and smoke a cigarette and talk till Darrel came and rang the bell.

The baby cried, but not until the pincurls were all in. Rosetta held him while Lavonne warmed his bottle in a saucepan half full of water on the gas ring. He stopped crying the minute Rosetta picked him up and seemed to know that what was going forward was for him. "Look, Lavonne, his eyes—how they follow you. Isn't that darling? He knows his mother." She squeezed him a little, not tight, felt how a young warm baby conforms to the curve of your front and the hollow of your neck like a piece of a jigsaw puzzle that exactly fits.

Lavonne squirted a drop or two of milk on the inside of her wrist, then put the bottle back for a bit more warming. She was looking at them, but her look went through and past them as if what she was thinking of was far away, not there. Her voice had something in it when she spoke, of someone's who has tallied up a sum and now reports the answer.

"I guess he proves," she said, "that I'm a real woman."

"Oh, Lavonne! what a thing to say. Of *course* you're a real woman, who could ever doubt it? The realest, the prettiest—"

"Rosetta, he's so mean! The things he says—" Her tears before they fell shimmered sapphire-blue, the baby watched in wonder.

Rosetta in the Chic Salon by now more or less said the same thing to every misery, that time heals everything, that this too shall pass, that it's always darkest before the dawn, that every cloud has…and other ponderosities. Life is just a bowl of cherries. The baby smiled like a fairy fish as the oozing rubber nipple approached. "Just don't let it bother you. Just tell yourself—"

Lavonne's got everything, Rosetta thought in the little while after her head touched the pillow before she fell asleep. Heaped-up blessings…Didn't have to get up while it was still dark and walk to work in the rain. She had a house. A husband. A little boy and a baby. A Buick. A mangle. Alligator pumps…and…All paved…And clothes. And beautiful…Even with her hair plastered down and her mascara running, she was beautiful. And loved. And beautiful. And yes, she'd had that operation, but as it *took away* it gave. Gave or helped to give her the life she had now, and would have, and admiration and compliments till hell wouldn't have them. But now Darrel was mean. All right, who's to say he might not have been mean in any case? But Lavonne was starting to grieve, not for what she *really* lost—which she despised and deplored—but what she imagined she lost. "Who's got my silver leg?" It was like the ghost in the story that must always wring its hands and haunt and moan because its leg had been stolen from the coffin. "Who's got my silver bosom?"

Chapter Fifty-eight

✳

AGNES CALLED WHEN SHE SAW LEGRAND AND ROSETTA'S NAMES IN THE MARRIAGE license column. Was it really true? She wanted to congratulate them both and offer the wish that inborn selfishness and sissifiedness such as Legrand seemed to show at times would never mar their happiness. She and Herman were talking about it just now, how a boy like Legrand could just as easy have went his whole lifetime without even thinking of … and probably *would have*, had Nancibel lived … And if Rosetta would just put him on the line, his Aunt Agnes wanted to tell him that she had no hard feelings about the Haviland china, all the world loves a lover, and also she had a joke to tell him about a newly married couple that she heard at the hospital. He would get a kick out of it. Jokes didn't have to be dirty to be funny … And also she wanted to ask him …

"He's not here, Agnes. He had this chance to go to California with this friend of his—"

"To *California*? A boy on his *honeymoon*?"

They talked another ten minutes, Rosetta sweating blood, and then Agnes said well, when he came back—Or whatever. Give his Uncle Herman a call and they would have them over for Sunday dinner. And one more thing she wanted to say, this time in her capacity as a nurse, and that was that their chances of having normal children were as good as anybody else's. So when he came back—Or whatever.

PENNY BONKOWSKI DIDN'T SEE THE notice. She called to tell Rosetta there was going to be an opening at the Newhouse Hotel beauty shop. The other girl was leaving to go back east, no sense whatsoever, throw up a good job, of course there was a man in the picture. But anyway a good time to see Mr. Lund, the owner, was in the morning. He ran the barbershop next door too, a nice family man, two children. Decent, not always pinching a person's behind and making remarks. Wages wouldn't be anything to brag about, but the shop was a lot bigger than the Chic Salon. That meant more running, of course, but being in the basement, and tiled, it was cool in summer, and the relief of not having those eagle eyes watching your every move from morning till night made up for a lot. The tips might not come up to anyone's expectations. Hotel customers, you know—henna rinse, eyebrows plucked, manicure—sometimes they really *are* somebody, but most of the time they're not. And the ones with the money—well, Rosetta knew all that. Penny was tickled to hear about the wedding. She ought to have a shower for Rosetta, a nice kitchen shower, ask Mildred, even Mrs. Daybell, she'd probably bring a five-cent dishrag!

Several times after Rosetta started working at the Newhouse Hotel shop, Penny spoke of it, wanting to do that, have a shower, but Rosetta always said please don't, if she ever moved it would just be more things to pack. But that was later, at first she didn't even *hint* she might not be there long.

But she was. A long time.

Because we never know.

"DO YOU HAVE ANY IDEA," Penny asked one night as they were cleaning up the shop and getting ready to go home, "what that war over there in *Spain* is all about? Are they fighting an *enemy*, or each *other*, or what?"

"I really don't know," Rosetta said. "But you can't turn on the radio without hearing *something* about it. Or read the paper—"

"I know," Penny said. "Jake says, where have I been? But working down here, and keeping house, or trying to, without a speck of help from him, not even to get the supper started at night—"

"So what do you want to know for, Penny?"

"Well, because after the meeting they're coming to *our* house, there's Jake for you again, never a word to me, just hands out invitations. Some of them, I mean, are coming, I hope not the whole audience, and I'm supposed to serve refreshments. Jake is the chairman. See?"

"So what's that got to do with the war in Spain?"

"Because the *speakers* at the Union meeting have *been* there," Penny said. "*Fighting* over there. Even *wounded*. The ones on the program tomorrow night. They belong to something called the Abraham Lincoln Brigade. Jake's going to meet them at the bus depot tomorrow afternoon, him and some of the others. One of the guys will probably *stay* with us. They're real hard up. Why don't you come? You can walk to the Hall from your place, then ride home with me. Please," Penny said. "I'd appreciate it *so much*. Helping me, I mean, with the refreshments…"

THE THREE SHABBY YOUNG SPANISH War veterans, said to be brothers, who stood up after the meeting got started and sang in sweet Irish voices to the tune of "Red River Valley" "There's a valley in Spain called Jarama" didn't go on to the Bonkowskis' afterwards. They had a relative in town they were going to stay with, somebody said, a priest. And wasn't *that* a joke, considering what they had been trying to do to the priests over in Spain! But the other three Abraham Lincoln Brigaders showed up, and so did enough of a percentage of the somewhat small audience they had spoken to, to scare Penny when she glanced in through the crack of the kitchen door and saw there weren't going to be chairs enough and maybe not enough of anything… But some of the other wives coming in with their husbands through the open front door without knocking and straight on through the house to the kitchen brought wax-paper-wrapped sandwiches in shoeboxes or brown paper sacks, which Rosetta was deputized to receive at the kitchen door and thank the donors for, Penny having temporarily disappeared into the depths of the pantry for a stiff jolt to relieve a nervousness similar to stage fright which had suddenly assailed her.

"If you want some," she said when she reappeared, "it's up alongside the bin. Some guy delivered it from the Union last Christmas when Jake wasn't home and I didn't tell him, I thought I'd wait till he mentioned it, but he never did. So they never got thanked for it…Oh, Rosetta!"

"Don't be nervous, honey. Everything's just perfect. And wasn't the meeting interesting? I didn't realize one of them was *blind*. And they did explain what the war's about and everything. Didn't you think?"

But Penny had retreated to the pantry again, to put lead enough in her pencil, as she said, for the rest of the evening.

It was a nice party, beer, coffee, the men standing around, the majority of them bunched in the front room cloudy with smoke, the women clustering here and there in the dining room and out in the narrow hall at the foot of the staircase, plain young and middle-aged housewives or working women, several in clean starched percale house dresses. One, however, a straight-backed, high-busted woman of about forty-five, stood out for the reason of her elegance. This was Margaret Woods, Penny's best customer. Being head housekeeper of the Newhouse Hotel and right on the hotel's premises, where she occupied two rooms on the fifth floor, the office from which she ran things and a corner bedroom, she was handy enough to the beauty shop in the basement to look or stop in almost every day. No society queen had hair more assiduously dyed, washed, coiffed and combed than Margaret's, a face more smoothed and maquillaged, or more manicured fingernails. Penny would have done her toenails too, but like the peacock, Margaret had ugly feet and never showed them to anyone, so she said. A widow twice over, she must have been very capable at her housekeeping job, for once Penny saw her in conversation on the edge of the vast hotel lobby with an unremarkable couple Margaret said later were the *owners* of the hotel, and Margaret looked and acted a lot more like people who ought to own it than they did! Very nose-up-in-the-air. You can't always tell by that, though. She did take up with the salesmen, and started *something* so serious with one of the common painters named Slim, sent by a painting contractor to help paint the upper floors, that six months later when on another job Slim fell off a scaffold and broke his neck, she acted like a widow for the third time.

The man was not worthy of her, Penny made so bold as to say, drunk half the time like all painters, and what did he ever do for her? Nothing. But after office hours Margaret cried for days, and said she would never forget him. The chambermaids had a good deal to say about it. Juanita, one evening while having a permanent, said another girl told *her* that Slim said his wife would never divorce him and he was glad of it, as he didn't want to marry an *old woman* like that anyway! Wasn't that a fine thing to say about someone who bought you a suit of clothes, shirt, tie, shoes, and goodness knows what else?

His body was shipped to Idaho Falls, or Margaret would probably have paid for his funeral too, and put up a tombstone. The tragedy had occurred on an unseasonable and peculiarly sleety day in early May. Now August was nearly over, and no new love had come into Margaret's life. Dinner with a salesman once in a while, a movie with Mr. Helfrich (who resided in the hotel and who with a urine bag strapped to his leg happened to be heading in the theater's direction one sultry evening when she was walking along looking in store windows, not knowing what she saw, she was so blue), but nothing of any promise. Perhaps, she told Penny, her life was really over. What a remark! All she had to do was look in the glass, Penny said. Why, she hardly looked thirty years old. Her life nearly over? With *her* class? "Don't make me laugh," Penny said.

The reason she invited Margaret to the meeting and then the party afterwards was, first, because she was her star customer and she wanted to show her that Jake was a pretty important man in the Union even if his wife had to work and he had hardly earned enough since New Year's Day to keep the car in gas, and second, because he had a friend in the Union whose wife had recently been taken to Provo to the insane asylum, his name was Art, and maybe Art and Margaret could get together, they were about of an age. Penny didn't expect Margaret to get much out of the *meeting*, but the *party* afterwards would be a nice change for her.

Because she was too groomed and dressed up, in dark blue silk and with clocked stockings and suede high heels and an onyx dinner ring with a diamond in it, to feel comfortable with the members' wives, she stayed close to Penny and activities in the kitchen, which made Penny so nervous that every little while she would make a quick trip through the smoke-filled rooms to see if she could see Art, the man with the insane wife. She had only met him once or twice, however, and thought she might be looking straight at him and not know. But she finally found Jake and got him off to one side and asked him to point Art out, and he said the bugger hadn't shown up. And did he have a bone to pick with *him*.

Penny was afraid Margaret would go home disappointed if she told her Art wasn't coming, but finally she did tell her, and Margaret said well, that could happen. She took her coffee that someone goosed into a Cafe Royale, wandered into the men's domain and struck up a conversation with one of the Spanish War veterans, who, pale and needing a shave, was standing a little off to himself, looking tired after his long bus ride and the meeting held earlier. "Can I get you some coffee?" Penny heard Margaret say as she went by. The crowd mixed better after that but didn't stay long. By quarter to eleven, almost everyone had gone. One of the veterans went with the couple he was going to stay with till the next afternoon, when he and the two Brigaders sleeping over at Penny and Jake's would be picked up, taken to the Greyhound bus depot and put on the bus for California, the last stop of their tour.

In the kitchen Penny could have cried, she told Rosetta, this time bringing the hidden bottle out of the pantry and openly pouring herself a drink in a used glass she hoped was hers. All that work and effort, washing the woodwork, putting up clean curtains, scrubbing the porches, and the whole thing a complete failure! Why, how could she say such a thing! Rosetta said. And when she had dragged Penny into the front room, by now cooling off and only one small bulb burning in the floor lamp, and the radio playing low in the corner, Margaret said so too. It was wonderful, a big success, everybody said so. And it wasn't over yet, heck, no. The two veterans, and Jake and a Union organizer by the name of Bill, had taken their coats and ties off, unbuttoned their collars and looked comfortable where they were, Jake a-straddle a dining room chair turned back to front. Each had a glass in his hand. What it had in it Penny didn't know, and in the depths of Jake's easy chair didn't care…

Rosetta had been going to leave earlier, but Penny begged her not to right then. Bill and Viola went right past her place and she could ride with them. "Isn't that right, Viola?" "Be tickled," Viola said. Now Rosetta, on the footstool near Penny that belonged to Jake's big chair but had been pushed into the corner for the evening, was yawning. "Well," she said, "it's been quite an evening."

"I don't dare say so," Penny said, lowering her voice to almost a whisper, "but I *still* don't understand that crazy war. I mean, Americans over there in Spain! And just to think, that poor Jewish boy losing his *eyes* for the sake of whatever it was…" She looked towards the shadowy corner where on the couch the Brigader she had reference to spoke earnestly to Margaret, who seemed to listen as earnestly as he spoke, her head bent towards his. Viola's glance followed Penny's. And Rosetta looked that way, too.

"He must have been quite a nice-looking boy," Viola said softly. "When he could see and everything, I mean. What was his name again?"

"Gene something," Penny said.

"Abeloff," Rosetta whispered. "I noticed on that sign in the entrance as we went in. And that's what the man said when he introduced him to give his speech. Gene Abeloff."

"And what's the other one's name? That's going to stay all night with you folks?" Viola said.

"Frank Tracy, I *think*," Penny said.

"Either Irish or Jewish, all of them, doesn't that seem funny? Over there fighting in Spain," Viola said.

"Say, that lady there talking to the—Jewish one," Penny said, fixing her sleepy gaze on the two across the room. "She's my best customer."

"I've been *wondering* who she was," Viola said. "That dress cost a hundred dollars if it cost a cent."

"I don't know what I'd do without *her*, I can tell you."

"Which one's her husband?" Viola looked over towards the little group of men, among which were Jake and Bill with their heads together.

"She's a widow," Penny said. "You know the organizer whose wife went crazy not long ago and they took her to Provo? Well, I was going to introduce Margaret to him tonight. But he didn't show up."

"Lady of leisure, is she?"

"Oh, no. She's the head housekeeper at the Newhouse Hotel. I don't know if you realize how important a job like that *is*, or how much they get *paid*."

"Or how many chambermaids run around in fear and trembling because of them," Rosetta said.

"But she acts lovely with me," Penny said. "Asked me to call her Margaret and everything. Of course that wouldn't last long if everything didn't turn out just to suit her."

"She must have been a real looker in her day," Viola said. "About how old is she? and how old would you think the blind boy was?"

"Forty something—Twenty something—" Penny said.

"Well, she's nearly got him on her lap."

Feeling their eyes on her, Margaret looked across at their little group and smiled. They smiled back, and Penny flirted her fingers in a little wave.

"We better get off of *that* subject," Penny whispered as her best customer turned back to the young Brigader in dark glasses on the couch beside her, "and talk about the speeches or something. Rosetta, you listened. What did they really say?"

Rosetta cleared her throat, but before she could answer, Viola said that speaking of Spain, that was one place she always wanted to take a trip to. Not of course *now*, in the messed-up situation it was at the present time in, but—"Say," she said, "those three brothers should of sang 'In a Little Spanish Town' while they was at it." Softly, over the tuned-down dance music coming over the console radio that Penny was still paying on in the corner, Viola began it herself.

In a little Spanish town
'Twas on a night like this...

Taking care not to dislodge the framed family photograph above her, Rosetta rested her head on the wall and looked at the young man on the couch. She would have liked to have gone over and sat on the other side of him and had a conversation too, but shyness held her back. Besides, he and Margaret seemed to be hitting it off really well. Now he was holding her soft hand, or not so much that as, where it rested on his left wrist, feeling with his right hand the almond shape of each carefully tended glassy fingernail, much as one might finger a string of beads. Margaret must really make quite a lot, and then no rent or anything to pay except maybe her meals—that made a big difference. A beautiful fur coat—Rosetta hadn't been in the shop long enough to have seen it, but Penny said she had one. Fox. And always in rustling silk. Always wearing that lemony perfume. Now his hand had come to rest upon hers. His brave hand...

It came to Rosetta how brave and heroic fellows had to be to go to war like that, and of their own accord, not because somebody made them. She glanced across at the other side of the room, where the Brigader named Frank Tracy was flicking the end off a kitchen match with a thumbnail and lighting a cigarette, shaking his head as he did so. "No," she heard him say as he blew out the match and took a deep drag. "The sons of bitches are lining up with the cheapest crooks in Europe." He looked tired, red-eyed, rubbed his bristly chin as he spoke.

And imagine caring that much about a *belief*, Rosetta thought. That was what they had gone over there and fought about, fellows from all over, French, English, Irish, Scottish, Canadian, Swiss, South American and of course Americans. A *belief*. That was what the Union man that introduced them told the audience, that they went over there and joined the International Brigade—the Americans had their separate bunch called the Abraham Lincoln Brigade—and took sides and fought in the Spanish Civil War because with all their hearts they *believed* that the...

Her mind had wandered, though. It was hot in the small, shabby auditorium. Once she read that in a crowd like that, every person gives off heat equivalent to turning on a hundred-watt light bulb. There were noises, shiftings on the rickety folding chairs, feet scraping, coughs, the rustle of folded paper as a sweaty woman here and there fanned herself. And the speakers... At the back of the room you could hardly... But up there on the stage, something set apart the soldiers, the volunteers, from the other men sitting in the half circle. Gene Abeloff stood out at once, of course, the way the shoes on his wounded, hobbling feet looked like wooden blocks, like the base for a toy, and him being the only one not bareheaded but wearing a beret, and with dark glasses on that covered up two blue glass Orphan Annie eyes that flashed once like gem-fire or like the first letter of a signaled message when he took his glasses off to rub the bridge of his nose. The other Brigaders, though in cheap civilian clothes like everybody else, not conspicuous with wounds and looking related to Jake and Bill and the other Union men, *they* stood out too. Because... when somebody is convinced enough of something to die for it, it condensed them somehow, like different rays concentrated by a lens, it made them... gave them...

"What gets *my* goat," Frank Tracy said, "is that son of a bitch of an England. International law! Don't make me laugh. It's the same old shit. Anytime it's a question of the *people* against the guys in the castles and the Rolls-Royces and the gold crowns, you know who England's coming out for. They don't like Fascism, but they like Spain as a Democratic Republic a whole lot less! So if the Germans want to goose-step in, roll in their new weapons to try them out, if Mussolini wants to send in troops and fly in planes, well, what of it? But you mark my words—this is just the beginning—"

And now, Rosetta thought, her eyes straying back to the soldier in the dark glasses, he'll be blind for as long as he—Twenty-six or twenty-seven? Live to be an old man, and never see another thing on this earth again!

"What I thought was," Penny said, exhaustion making her sound like a conspirator, "that I'd put the *other one* on the couch and *him* out on the back porch on the cot out there. Poor things, all they got was just a ticket home and a handshake, that's what Jake said. On this tour they stay with people—line it up ahead, but sometimes just land somewhere and take a chance—Like they were saying about Los Angeles—"

"Haven't they got a place to stay down there?" Rosetta asked with concern.

"A *woman* wouldn't get mixed up with stuff like that, but that's men for you," Viola said. "Not that I don't think whichever side they fought on over there wasn't right."

"I guess they haven't," Penny said. "But they'll find something—"

"I told you about Legrand, didn't I?" Rosetta said to Penny.

"Who's Legrand?" Viola asked, with a more elaborate yawn than before.

"Her husband," Penny said. "He's down in California." She turned back to Rosetta. "What about him?"

"Well, he and Palmer—that's our friend, you know—I guess Palmer was the one who answered the ad—Palmer got this job of caretaker of this big—house while an estate is being settled or something. So, why don't I—? Tomorrow morning—?"

"Do what?"

"*Call* Legrand?" Rosetta said. "And ask him to ask Palmer. And let these two boys stay with them for however long they'll be down there?"

"How would you like *that*?" Penny called out suddenly to the young man on the couch, startling and discomfiting Rosetta but not catching his or Margaret's attention. Rosetta's hand went out in a restraining gesture, but Penny tried again: "Rosetta here is going to call her husband down in Hollywood because maybe he and a friend of his—that the friend is taking care of a house down there—can let you and Frank over there, or whatever his name is, *stay* with them as long as you need to be down there!"

Now Margaret realized that the loud and carefully articulated words, as though Gene had been deaf instead of blind, were directed at her companion on the couch.

Penny then repeated the proposition, and Gene said it sounded like music to his ears.

Rosetta whispered to Penny that as soon as she found out in the morning she would call, Penny relayed that, and Gene said great.

Just then the light in the floor lamp gave a kind of pop! and went out.

"Well, I guess we can take a hint," Viola said, getting to her feet with a laugh. "Come on, Bill. Come on, Rosie, if you're going to ride with us. And how about what's her name? Your star customer there."

"Hold your horses," Jake said.

"Simmer down," Bill said, as though his wife were raising a row.

"I guess they're not done talking," Viola said, sighing as she sat back down and the men resumed their discussion. "Say, look at that moonlight out there on the porch and coming in through the windows! You don't notice it when the light's on. Don't it look pretty! Must be a full moon. I never look at it anymore, but I'm telling you, when I was getting my growth…"

"It's almost as light in here as when the light was on," Rosetta said.

"Well, it's still on in the kitchen," Penny said, "and that shines in the dining room, and the reflection."

"'How sweet the moonlight sleeps upon this bank…'" the blind boy said, taking a package of cigarettes out of his pocket, fumbling for one and sticking it in his mouth.

"Here, let me help you," Margaret said.

BUT DURING THE NIGHT SHE couldn't help him, she was too sick herself. Nobody could help anybody!

"We have been the sickest mortals *you* ever seen," Penny said in a weak, trembling voice when at nine o'clock the next morning Rosetta called to report on her long-distance call to Los Angeles, the first she had ever had occasion to make.

"Sick!" Rosetta said. "Why, what are you talking about?"

"Me, Jake, Margaret, the soldiers. Margaret's still here. I thought for a while there we was—Boy, oh, boy—"

"But what in the world *happened*?"

"Just a minute," Penny said. "I got to pull a chair up, the sweat's running down my ribs, things go kind of black—But there, that's better. I hope I've quit a-heaving, that's the worst, when nothing's left to heave but bitter bile—"

She *had* quit, though. When Rosetta, as soon as she could get down there, ran through the disordered house and found Penny sitting on the back steps, she said that nothing more came up, which wasn't to say, however, that the other end—! But poor Margaret. And the poor blind kid—

The liverwurst sandwiches *could* have caused symptoms like that, the doctor said, acute toxic poisoning. Liverwurst was cooked, and cooking would kill the bacilli, but if what they were talking about, and they might well be, was a diseased animal, cooking wouldn't alter the toxins to which such bacilli *dead or alive* would give rise.

"Well, dead was the kind of diseased animal I thought *I* was going to be," Penny said, "and here poor Jake was, *crawling* out through the kitchen to vomit in the yard—"

The doctor left medicine, said to stay in bed and keep warm (as if they could keep anything else but warm with the thermometer standing at ninety-seven before noon), and in forty-eight hours they would be as good as new.

"I blame Margaret," Penny confided to Rosetta from the cot on the screened back porch as the latter moved about cleaning up and setting things to rights. "If she'd gone home when she was supposed to, Jake and me and the boys would of went to bed. But when you kids left, you and Bill and Viola, what does she do but say she thinks Gene is hungry! He's been passed by, she says, so her and I went out in the kitchen and I put the coffee on and there was still two or three bottles of beer bobbing around in the washtub, though the ice was melted. And all the sandwiches was gone! So I'm worried because I'll have breakfast to get, and if I use up the bread—And what am I going to put *in* them? But right that minute, here I find this big shoebox on the drainboard in under the cupboard, somebody brought it and we hadn't used them. So I take the lid off, and here are these liverwurst sandwiches on rye bread all wrapped in wax paper as lovely as you please. Well, we drag things back and forth and fix up this picnic out on the porch in the moonlight—and Margaret—So I say, as long as she's stayed this long, why don't she just stay all night? Then I think, where will I put everybody? Though covers won't be called for, not to any extent. Now, Rosetta, you know Margaret, you've seen her in the shop, and tell me if I'm not right when I say she would no more have stayed in this house all night to wake up here in the morning than fly to the moon if that poor boy *hadn't been blind*. And get up and let him see her looking a sight? But if he can't *see*—Well, anyway, me and Jake goes to bed upstairs, Frank the Irish one says he'll sleep in the porch swing, Gene the blind one is on the couch, and I fixed Margaret a bed out here on the back porch on this cot. We all settle down. And then—all hell breaks loose!"

THE THREE BROTHERS, THE ONES who had sung together at the meeting, and the other Brigaders left on the 4:30 p.m. bus, leaving Frank and Gene to recover from their food poisoning at Penny and Jake's. They could then come on to California, they were told, but it wouldn't be much use. By that time the others would have given their speeches and be ready to turn around and come back, their tour over. So why not just wait in Salt Lake and be picked up towards the end of the week? The two agreed with that, got better, regained their strength and waited. But when the time came, only Frank Tracy boarded the bus to go back to New York City with the others. Gene Abeloff stayed, and not very long after that he and Margaret Woods were married.

AND YOU COULDN'T SAY THE luck of the Irish, Penny said, because Gene was a Jewish boy. Though in Salt Lake, of course, he was a Gentile! But it sure enough was luck. To fall into a nest like that, to find, as you might say, a mother waiting to spoil you to death! Of course Margaret didn't think of herself in that capacity, she thought of herself as Romeo and Juliet, not Romeo, of course, but Juliet, because if Romeo couldn't *see*, well, Juliet was who Margaret could be to her heart's content!

Can't a man *feel*, though, if the woman he's in bed with is twenty years older than he is?

Maybe not. Had she told him she was that much older in so many words? Probably not. And as Penny said, he sure as shooting couldn't read their application to wed. She and Rosetta talked about it for quite a while, fate and all that. It made you wonder. Margaret kept on with her job. Nobody seemed to have any objections to a husband in her bedroom and in the office she did over so that it could become their living room after office hours. Within a month she bought Gene the magazine stand in the Felt Building, it came up for sale, put on the market by somebody related to June Mathis who wrote *The Four Horsemen* and whose father had started the stand forty years before. Gene went there every day. So everything fell out about like everyone wanted. The world is a shabby fellow and uses us ill, but not all the time.

In the midst of her happiness Margaret changed as no one would expect, at least not Penny, her beautician, or Rosetta. But still—there was logic to it in a way. Margaret grew old. That is to say, she stopped having Penny color her hair. Why bother? Gene couldn't see it. She still had it nicely coiffed, but simply, much simpler than before. She left off a lot of her makeup. She still looked structured, high-busted, svelte as she went about her work, but she told Penny something: "If I had known what I know now!"

"What's that, Margaret?"

"There's just one kind of man to marry in this world. Blind," she said. "The peace that passeth understanding."

But of course Margaret definitely would not have felt like that about an *old* blind man, a *weak* old blind man, or as Rosetta said a *dumb* weak old blind man. Or as Penny continued the thought, a *drinking* dumb weak old blind man. Or a *mean* drinking dumb weak old blind man. Had Gene Abeloff not been all the other things he was *besides* blind, young, healthy, handsome, educated and nice, Margaret might not have been so pleased with her bargain. But Penny said she knew what Margaret was talking about. After office hours, she could *let down* as she probably never had before been able to do with a man. She could *let down* the way you can when you're alone, quit holding her stomach in, leave her bra off (though that of course depended), let makeup and hair go, and in Margaret's case with her ugly feet, kick off her shoes and if she wanted to, wear sloppy old slippers and even go barefoot. Or in other words, Rosetta said, have the pleasures of solitude while enjoying a man's company.

But nothing is perfect, and as the months went by, Margaret found a good deal to complain of. Gene had insisted on having some kind of job, and when she heard about the old Mathis newsstand and smoke shop being for sale, he had agreed that that might do for the time being. But she didn't expect him to be at *work* so much of the time, or that he would turn out so *independent*, eventually even hiring an assistant. And he was always doing something at home, instead of just relaxing and listening to the radio. If he did listen to the radio, it had to be the news, or a program of classical music, not just *Charlie McCarthy* or *One Man's Family*. Margaret could listen, he had no objection to that. He would go in the other room and learn Braille or, after he learned it, read it, or just sit and think, which he liked to do the way some people like to work out puzzles. But the fun to Margaret was for them to listen *together*. To do things *together*. Then, the kind of records he would buy for the phonograph he also gave her for her birthday! Opera. The screechiest, awfullest stuff you ever heard in your life, though she let him play them. Or music like in a funeral parlor that dragged on and on.

He had the idea of their reading books, her reading to him in the evenings in the living room, or cozy together in bed. She wanted to do things together, didn't she? But these books... Probably she should get glasses, she had to hold the book so far off, her arms and neck would get tired, but they were also a pain *elsewhere*, the books he would pick out. *The Discourses of John Selden. Owen Felltham's Resolves*. A whole book of just nothing but poetry. And not telling a story either, like *A Girl of the Limberlost*, but just... stuff. The big *words*... "Such and such." "Margaret, that can't be right. Spell it." So then she would spell it and he'd say "Oh, *such* and such." One time he did let her read him *The Trail of the Lonesome Pine*, which her first husband had brought to their marriage from a lumber camp in Oregon, and said it was all right, but she could tell he wanted the big words and the complications for the mind, the "parajaraffes," as Amos and Andy on the radio would say, that you could take the meaning of three ways or maybe even nine or ten. She never was much for reading anyway, and as she told Penny and Rosetta when she was getting her hair fixed, she didn't want to brag, but she didn't think if she *had* been she would be in the position she was today!

So nothing was ideal. Still, Gene was a very good husband. And one thing in his favor (besides being blind), he didn't have an army of relatives. The family had come from a place that he said was called Georgia, just like the Georgia in this country only *this* Georgia was over in Europe. But they died, all the ones close to him but one older brother, supposedly a lawyer. And what should this brother be *on* but something in Washington or somewhere called the—Margaret couldn't remember the name, but it was some kind of a government board or a bureau where they were *after* the Abraham Lincoln Brigaders. In other words, the two brothers were on opposite sides, the brother— Sidney, his name was—saying don't interfere over there in Spain, let the Spanish people work it out, and Gene saying if something's not done about the Fascists now in *Spain*, there's going to be a war that will involve the *whole world*. Sidney said if Gene went over there and fought on the side of the Communists, which is what he said they were, which Gene said was begging the question and had nothing to do with the real issues, why, he was no brother to *him* anymore. Fine, Gene said. Just like your Civil War, Rosetta said when Penny repeated all this. Brother against brother. The Blue and the Gray. Like in *Birth of a Nation*.

And somebody else who went back on Gene was a girl named Clare. Margaret kept at him about her until she found out. Well, she knew he had to have had *somebody*, and so she kept on and it was Clare. He said she was a blonde, but he didn't have a picture of her. He lost his wallet when the hand grenade blew up, or later in the field hospital. But he couldn't have looked at it anyway while he was all those weeks at a big castle over there in Spain that had been turned into an American hospital. He couldn't see where he was, of course, as he got better and started edging his way along the slabby cold stone floor and touching the stone walls with tapestries hanging on them, but the other guys filled him in. A castle in Spain! Just like in the songs, the guys said. It belonged to a Royal Princess, but she was gone, waiting somewhere for the Germans and Italians to get it back for her. But the Princess left two big, terrible, wild, ferocious dogs to guard the place! but all the poor beasts wanted was company, so when the Americans moved in the dogs were licking their hands and jumping up to lick their faces in about five minutes. The Americans called them Franco and Bruno. "Here, Franco!" "Here, Bruno!" And they'd come lunging and plunging up, ready to knock you down with joy.

What a man could see in a girl like Clare! Margaret talked to Penny about what she had found out. One of these smart-ass *college students*, if you please, that is to say, going to night school nights and working in a bookstore days, knew all about Spain, talked to the customers. When Gene told her he was going to join the Brigade and go over there to fight, did she try to stop him? No, she encouraged him, and she was at the dock to bid him good-bye. One of these girls, Margaret told Penny and Penny told Rosetta, with their hair parted in the middle and done in a knot in back. But it was a different story when Gene came home five months later with both eyes blown out of his head! And wounds in his feet. Of course Clare said his blindness wasn't the reason. That wouldn't have made a particle of difference to *her*, she said, had she not fallen in love in the meanwhile with another man. And Gene's *brother*, instead of standing by him—Well, he would have, Sidney claimed, if Gene would just admit he was wrong! but of course he would die first.

So what with this and that, when the guys said come on, we're going to go across the country giving speeches about the war in Spain and who's fighting who and what it's all about, and why if the Republicans lose—over in Spain the Republicans are the Democrats, which just goes to show you how crazy the country is—the world's going to combust, why, Gene said why not? and went along. Better make tracks than rot in New York. But he couldn't have traveled forever, and after California the tour would have been over, and then what? No girl, no brother … at the end of nowhere, at his rope's end anyway, so what did it matter where he hung his hat? Salt Lake City or Timbuctoo was all the same to him.

Chapter Fifty-nine

*

But Gene Abeloff *had* fallen into duck soup, no doubt about that, Penny said and Rosetta agreed. In a way, though, Margaret had too, she could *have* a young husband without the *perils* of a young husband, and *grow old gracefully* in his blind eyes. Whereas in her own case, Penny said, there was this constant criticism. And why? For the simple reason that Jake could *see*. He was running out of steam, too, more every year, while Margaret supposedly—Of course she could be bragging. But it might be true. After all, didn't the kings in olden times over in the Old Country have their canaries' eyes put out so they would sing better? So they would concentrate all their energy into just *singing*? Rosetta said she read that too, it was in "Ripley's Believe It or Not."

"But speaking of husbands"—sooner or later the question would be asked—"when is *your* wandering husband coming home?"

The Sunday morning Rosetta put in the first long-distance call of her life, to Hollywood, after the operator gave her the number, she debated whether to call "person to person" or just whoever answered. She called whoever answered, and it wasn't Legrand. It was a girl. The girl called Palmer to the phone. "Didn't Legrand tell you?" he said.

"Tell me what?" Rosetta said.

"Tell you I met this girl?" Palmer said. "From Oklahoma? Phyllis? That's who you were talking to, she moved in, we're going to get married. But the way Legrand took it, you'd have thought I stabbed him in the back! But of course he's been feeling pretty bum about his scenario. The studios are mean down here," he said. "This guy Legrand's rented an apartment with—he's been down here since the Crash, and *he* says he plays Indian parts, although he's not an Indian—"

"Palmer, listen. Are you telling me Legrand's not there with you?"

"That's right, Rosetta. He moved out. He's with this guy that takes Indian parts. He's an extra. And I suppose Legrand thinks he can get him a job or something. I'm surprised he hasn't written. But you'll hear—"

Rosetta did, soon after. Legrand's nice long letter ended with a request for a small loan, if that wouldn't put her out too much. It wouldn't, times were starting to improve a little, you'd get a fifty-cent tip now instead of a quarter. They wrote each other affectionately, Rosetta always apologizing because she had so little news. Things happened, though. Legrand was quite taken with the head housekeeper of the Newhouse Hotel in her forties marrying the Abraham Lincoln Brigader in his late twenties who had had both his eyes destroyed by a hand grenade in the Spanish Civil War, and how she said…And Legrand said *that* would make a good scenario. The title could be "The Peace That Passeth Understanding." He was on the Brigader's same side himself, he said, and the Spanish Republic, and so was this actor that was paying half the rent, Jerry. So tell this guy Gene *bravo*, although what they did might have been an exercise in futility, a sacrifice made in vain. It sure was starting to look like it in the papers.

Rosetta had no occasion to do that, tell Penny's best customer Margaret's blind young husband *bravo* or anything else, until, after the war started, he took over the Cigar and Newsstand in the Newhouse Hotel and let the one across the street go. Then she sometimes skirted the lobby and went over there to buy a paper or package of cigarettes for a customer. He knew her voice. "Hello, Rosetta." "Hello, Gene." Because of both being at Penny and Jake Bonkowski's that night and in on what the mystic mysterious hand of fate had decided to accomplish with a shoebox full of liverwurst sandwiches, it seemed as though they had more knowledge of each other than mere recognition. But they really didn't. Sometimes when there wasn't much to do in the shop and Penny was on the phone to Viola or her mother, Rosetta would go over and buy a paper and cigarettes for herself.

He was usually talking to somebody, some traveler, an Army officer passing through or someone, more important people because of the war than used to stop and talk. For the Second World War, twice as big as the first one, *had* happened, just like the Abraham Lincoln Brigaders said it would that night at Union Hall. But once in a while he would just be standing back of the counter smoking and his blue glass eyes staring out, and then Rosetta would make some shy remark about the headlines or some such thing, the weather, and they would interchange a few remarks before she had to run back. Mr. Lund was much nicer to work for than Mrs. Daybell but kept close watch over the beauty-parlor activity from his nearby barbershop (in spite of being busy enough since the war started to have to add another chair and barber), and neither Rosetta nor Penny dared stay away long.

"He must be fun to really sit and talk to," Rosetta said, speaking of Gene. She thought Legrand would think so and always wished she had more to say about Gene in her letters than she ever did have. He would be in her mind, and she would think about him when she sat at the kitchen table trying to type a letter to Legrand. Gene's mind and everything. Margaret told her and Penny that an overhead pipe had started dripping in their bathroom, and they were in there and Margaret was looking up and talking, but Gene held up his hand for her to be still because he was counting how many seconds would elapse between one drop and the next one, so that when the hotel plumber came he could tell him right where to go in the maze of pipes to find the trouble! Imagine that.

Margaret was relieved, Rosetta wrote, that not many Lincoln Brigaders came through Salt Lake anymore. A lot of them were in the Army now, since the war they predicted had started. But they weren't doing much traveling, because Gene said—Rosetta heard he said—that in Washington, D.C. the American volunteers were called "premature anti-Fascists" and didn't get combat duty. Instead they had to unload supplies and stuff like that, sort stuff, work at desks and lay low. Wasn't that something? Margaret was glad they didn't come through the way they had in the past, she told Penny. Because the veterans were kind of disruptive in a way. They sang that song about Jarama and another one about "Mamita Mia," and when they said good-bye they hugged each other and said "No pasarán" and things like that, and Gene couldn't cry tears like a normal person, so that wasn't really fair. So the less often the Brigaders got together the better, Margaret thought. Gene had a new life now...

"No Pasarán" would make a very good title, Legrand wrote. When the war was over and he got out of the Army, he might take a stab at—That was the burden of his letters now, getting out of the Army. He might come home and write a book about this blind guy! More would have happened by then, it would all have shaped up better. He knew definitely he was going to write. No more scenarios, though. When the war was over, he might come home and turn the Mountain Meadow Massacre into a novel. Then when *that* got published, it could be turned into a scenario again. What *he* had done was put the cart before the horse. But a person catches on.

His roommate, Jerry, was in, Legrand said, meaning the Army. He was a terrible liar, claimed to have been in several pictures, know everybody, said he sat up all night with Barbara La Marr's body. All lies. And not dependable with regard to finances, not trustworthy, moved out taking shirts, ties, would probably have taken Legrand's suit had he not been wearing it for a job interview at the time, which he didn't get. And which was just as well, considering he got drafted the next week. Lou was a much higher type, worked for Western Union, read *The Atlantic*, too bad he just got moved in when Legrand's draft notice came...but Lou could find somebody else to share expenses. He wouldn't be drafted, on account of having asthma. Palmer was in. Legrand hadn't seen him, but somebody said so. A completely changed individual. Shallow, no depths to him, that Okie had him wrapped around her little finger. Eighteen years old, the dumbest bunny you ever laid eyes on, laughs, plays like a little child, bites her fingernails, yodels. Phyllis! Oh, well. When the war was over...

But life was over for Legrand before the war was. The rather old man who brought the telegram asked Rosetta if she was alone and she said she was, so he said he had better come in and kind of hang around while she read it. That made her shake terribly, for she knew Legrand must be dead, and he was, not from enemy bullets but from ours. He was with an armored transport section in Fort Dix and the way the accident happened, as she heard later, they had halted and his sergeant told him and another soldier to correct the movement of a machine gun, which they were trying to do when a jolt from the truck starting up set it in action. Legrand, in the line of fire, was so badly wounded he died forty-five minutes later. The other soldier was wounded too, but had a chance to survive…Legrand's captain wrote that later, and said Legrand would have been a good soldier on the battlefield. The telegram just regretted to inform her…that he was dead. The rather old man stood with his hat in his hand and said he was very sorry, and he looked sorry, like a sad old bloodhound who has done some heinous act.

Tʜᴇ ᴛᴇɴ-ᴛʜᴏᴜsᴀɴᴅ-ᴅᴏʟʟᴀʀ Aʀᴍʏ ɪɴsᴜʀᴀɴᴄᴇ ᴘᴏʟɪᴄʏ Legrand had taken out and, much to Rosetta's surprise, made over to her she chose to receive not stipendiated over the rest of her life but in a lump sum. And Penny said when she dropped in to see her that a few months ago, she would have said that was a very foolish thing to do. But now, since her operation, when they just opened her and without doing a thing sewed her right back up, she thought different, Penny said. Now her motto was, live and enjoy yourself, for we pass this way but once. And as soon as she got her strength back, that was just what she was going to do. Quit kowtowing to Jake, who was bossier than ever since he got that job with Utah Copper. Tell a few people off, Viola for one, always calling up for Jake to come and fix something because her husband Bill was now a warrant officer in the Navy and stationed somewhere back east. Buy a whole new outfit, hat, shoes, purse, a fox fur, come up to the shop and let Rosetta give her the works…That was what Penny was going to do.

"I'll come down to your house," Rosetta said. "Bring the stuff…or you could come up here to the apartment. But of course I want you to see the shop, too…"

But no, Penny said, she wanted to get her strength back a little more, gain about ten pounds. If somebody had ever told her the day would come when she would step on the scales and *pray* the needle would point *up*, she'd have said they were crazy. But a man didn't want you *that* thin, with nothing here anymore, she plucked at her bosom, or here, she slapped at her behind, they just don't like it. And here's Viola…

"Sometimes she'll call and say she's got these ration stamps for coffee. Well, I'm glad of that myself. Or she's queued up and bought cigarettes for Jake and me, she don't smoke herself. And I ought to quit, the doctor says so. But what pleasure have I got? And Jake'll go running up there. But you wait till I get my strength back. No more taking *anything* off *anybody*, coffee, stamps, cigarettes, guff or nothing else. Buy a new dining room set, new drapes, paint the kitchen pink. Jake don't like pink! but he can lump it. Oh, I tell *you*," Penny said. "Charge the stuff and send the bill to him."

When she thought of all the times she wished she didn't have to get up and go to work in the morning! Now she had her wish. But why is it God never grants anything when or the way we want it? It's always *his* version, like you tell a guy over and over just what you want for your birthday, then you open the package and it's…not it. Jake had his good job, she finally had a chance to stay home and enjoy her new stove and icebox and see the sun shining in through the dining room curtains at ten in the morning and catch up with her ironing and make stuffed cabbage, and…her strength was gone. But as soon as she got better…

"How's the girl working out," Penny asked, "that Mr. Lund hired to take my place?"

"Not bad," Rosetta said. "Her name's Jewel. Not experienced like us, just out of beauty college, eighteen, but looks older. Quite willing—"

"I'd hate to put her out of a job," Penny said, "but Mr. Lund said when I get my health back—"

"Oh, yes, of course!" Rosetta said. "We're looking forward—Mr. Lund will probably get down on his knees and beg!"

BUT IT WAS ROSETTA a few months later who begged Penny to come back, or at least asked her before she asked anyone else, in order not to hurt her feelings, though she was almost sure from how much worse she looked that she wasn't up to it. Penny said if it just depended on her, she would jump at the chance. Thanks to Divine Metaphysics, the Principle of All Harmonious Mind-action and to the fact that as a practicing Christian Scientist, she was now as well as she had ever been in her life, and in fact better.

But Jake didn't want her to work anymore. Twelve years was enough, he said. But if it depended on her…

She congratulated Rosetta on having bought the Newhouse Hotel beauty shop with her insurance money. The equipment should probably start being replaced, Mr. Lund never put a dime more into the place than he could help, and some of the clientele…well, remember the traveling companion of the Air Force captain who came down and got a wave and set before she called the police to say she killed the man the night before? That he was upstairs dead in bed in Room 506? There were other beauty shops, or with ten thousand dollars Rosetta could buy a location and start a shop from scratch herself, but when Mr. Lund went out of his mind over Jewel and Mrs. Lund found out about it, he and the girl ran off and Mrs. Lund put the barbershop and beauty shop up for sale, why, Penny thought Rosetta had been very smart not even to stop and think but just bought it.

But what did Jewel *have* to cause a decent, respectable barber like Mr. Lund to go berserk like that?

"Well, not looks," Rosetta said. "Plain. Dumpy. Upper lip too short to come down over her teeth. Eyes slanting down at the corners. Brown hair."

"Don't it make you"—Penny was about to say *sick* when she recollected that the non-spiritual elements in the so-called human mind do not contribute to harmony and health, and substituted the word *wonder* instead—"wonder what gets into them?"

"I do have to say I liked the girl," Rosetta said. "She could tell things very cute with that hillbilly accent."

"I can imagine," Penny said. "But that still doesn't *explain*. It's like Viola. Jake doesn't make complimentary remarks to me about her *now*, he knows better, but he used to. And I ask you truly: is Viola so much?"

"She is nothing," Rosetta said loyally. "Nothing at all."

"Too bad Lavonne isn't around here anymore," Penny said. "She's a real good operator. But of course by this time she might of lost her touch. Not working for so long and living in the lap of luxury—"

"Oh, I don't think so," Rosetta said. "If she was here I'd ask her, I'd have to, we being related. But besides, I'd want to, because, as you say, she's a good operator."

"Wouldn't it be terrible to have to pull in your horns like she had to? Though of course if you go someplace where nobody knows you—Where did you say they finally lit?" Penny said.

"Carson City, her card said. But I haven't heard since."

"And I thought her husband was supposed to be so wonderful!"

"He *was* wonderful."

"So rich and everything. Farms, machinery."

"He *was* rich."

"So what happened?"

Rosetta shook her head. "It's beyond *me*. You never saw her lynx coat, did you? And forty-two dollars for a John-Fredericks hat. Then the next thing I know, here she's on the phone at eleven o'clock at night crying and saying they've pulled the rug out from under Darrel."

"Who has?" Penny said.

"The banks or someone, I just don't know, and they're all packed up and leaving and going to drive all night…"

"It scares *me*, I know that," Penny said.

"What does?"

"Prosperity. Everything going good, it's like classical music, let it go along soft and calm for a little while, then bam! Take Jake and me," she said meditatively. "We're doing real good now as far as his *job* is concerned, but look at my health."

"I know what you mean," Rosetta said. "It scares me, too. Sometimes when I come down in the morning and open up *my own shop* …"

"Legrand getting killed, you mean. You being the one to profit."

Rosetta nodded. "And it wasn't even *like* him. But anyway, when I come down here and think—"

"Don't think. Look at it like this," Penny said. "If it wasn't supposed to of happened, it wouldn't of happened. These things are all arranged. I was just reading that the other day. 'Today was on the calendars a thousand million years before calendars were printed.'"

Today was? When Rosetta turned on the lights and looked around and the pretty shop images threw back their beams… Wednesday was? when she saw exactly the tiny-waisted, round-shouldered, round-hipped dress she wanted in Makoff's window and had the money to walk right in and buy...Sunday? when she cleaned up the apartment and perched for a minute on the arm of her new green velvet chair and just...sat there while the breeze rippled the gauzy curtains inward and the clock ticked...The day she bought the Pontiac? from the girl upstairs when the girl joined the WAVES and was sent to Brooklyn. Perhaps. A thousand million years ago. But when she thought...how she abounded now in wealth, it somehow seemed a confusion of goods, palmed off, reproachable. And if, as sometimes happened, she found more money in her purse than she thought she had, say an extra twenty-dollar bill, she would feel kind of a faintness of heart, a peculiar *loss* of something, moral resolution or she didn't know what.

ALL HIS POSSESSIONS CAME TO her, his haversack, toilet kit and footlocker, the scenario she had typed three times, shabby and blurred from handling, titles on the first page all crossed out but one: "All on the Meadow Green." A cautious diary. Poems he wrote, not dedicated to Palmer, Jerry or Lou, but you could see them pictured there like boys reflected in the running water or the light of the moon cast back from frozen snow. Drawings. He drew well, quickly, trying to catch some look that might not come again on someone's face, and catching it? He had not caught Palmer's wry-nosed half smile, she knew Palmer but not the others. Maybe they did look like that and nothing was wrong with the mouth. A corner of some room had looked like that too, no doubt, some windowsill with weedy flowers in a jelly glass...But stars had never...these of his, five-pointed, childish, going up the wall like pawprints, over and across.

Legrand could always draw and cut with scissors, and recite better than nearly anyone in his grade. He was the best Sir Walter Raleigh throwing down his cloak, the clearest-voiced Mikado, might have been a dancer had he tried. And if his father hadn't swept Legrand's stuff up off the window seat that winter day and into the fire, doll, goods, trimming, needle, thread, he might have become a great designer. He looked like one, artistic. That was what he was. Talented. But talented like a river that's all little streams and runs. Like, say, for Christmas you get nothing but little stuff. Not one big whopping present, like a diamond or Cadillac. What it ought to be, talent, was concentrated, collected. At a center, like those throbbing black stars one teaspoonful of which would weigh one hundred million tons. The purest...all the different rays...the burning glass that sets the Burning Bush on fire. Maybe, if Legrand had lived, some intentional lens—? But maybe not. And that was one thing you could say for early death. It put off for the failer of full performance a date of grief forever.

She turned over a page or two of the scenario, then put it back in the footlocker and the rest of the stuff with it, letters (some that she had written), snapshots...One snapshot was of Legrand and Palmer taken by Betty, Palmer's Mormon wife, the time Legrand drove down there to visit them and see the Meadow. It showed them lounging on the broken steps of the couple's old shack, both boys smoking. Betty hated that, especially in the house. But Legrand said that the night he sat up all night to write at the kitchen table, about two in the morning Betty came to the door and said not to worry about smoking, or if he knocked the lamp over or anything, because if the house burned down and *all three of them along with it*, she wouldn't mind. He said there was such fierceness in the way she said it that he shivered.

JEWEL, THE BEAUTICIAN WITH THE hillbilly accent, would certainly have shivered if she could have seen Mrs. Lund when she heard the news about the elopement and stormed up to the hotel and into the beauty shop (the barbershop being locked) with a gun in her purse and said she was going to kill everybody. Of course Mr. Lund and Jewel were well on their way to Seattle by then, or wherever they went, and anyway Mrs. Lund had children (the oldest girl a year older than Jewel), she couldn't go after the lovers. Besides, she collapsed after that first wild flare-up, her mother had to come down from Provo and take over, and one of her brothers had to handle her business affairs. For a while nobody knew just *what* was going to happen. Mr. Lund could always get tired of Jewel or she of him, he *might* show up and Mrs. Lund would take him back. Margaret Abeloff, the head housekeeper, thought so, Rosetta thought so. The barber from California that Mr. Wintler, the manager of the hotel, put in to run the barbershop temporarily, when he heard what had happened before he came on the scene, thought so too. But weeks passed and no Mr. Lund, they must have made it all right together, Jewel without a pretty feature except youth and being an Okie and him a middle-aged businessman that had hired dozens of beauty operators in his day and never got mixed up with one before. Well, maybe not dozens, and perhaps he had, who knew?

The Californian couldn't afford to take over the barbershop on his own, buy the lease, equipment and good will, and he was just as glad, he said, because Salt Lake was going to be one dead town! when the war was over. Through her brother, Mrs. Lund sold the barbershop to a local man with prematurely white hair who was going to work it alone, and sold the beauty shop to Rosetta. All through the transaction Rosetta looked sad because of feeling so happy and proud, and the higher her spirits rose, the lower down she felt she *ought* to feel, because all this had come about through another's misfortune. And then she did feel that way, because, well, here she was, her check would go right through, every advantage, move things around in the shop, fix it up—"nothing but love in view" (as the old song said). And so, on general principles, her being fell, gathered and fell again, into layers of guilt and uneasiness.

She mentioned conscience, stopping at Gene Abeloff's stand to buy an evening paper and some cigarettes on her way home. If no one was about except a bellboy over by the elevators and a few people lost in the deep, plush armchairs between rubber plants and lamps with fringed shades, and she didn't have to hurry, Gene and she would talk awhile.

About the war, the weather…Usually they brought in mention of the Bonkowskis too, not because of being much in contact with them anymore (Penny slowly dying and Jake holding down two jobs) but because they had met at their house seven years before, and so somehow the name must needs be furnished, like the watchword to some dim old lodge, before their meeting could be called to order and the different items of business brought before it, such as on this occasion: conscience.

"Gee, I don't know," Rosetta said. "It's just been bothering me an awfully lot. Other people dying, other people having their life wrecked and their stuff scattered and me right there ready to rush in and reap the benefits. Like a vulture. Did you ever—? probably not, probably you already know, but I have wondered lots of times, just what it really is—"

"What what really is?" Gene inquired.

"Conscience," she said, laying her hand on the pit of her stomach. "We know where it's *located*. And it's got its own pain. Like a tooth has a *toothache* and no other ache. And a corn has the ache of a *corn*, and a burn feels like a *burn*—"

He did not try to reassure her personally, the way she would do in the shop with some customer grieving over something she had done or hadn't done. Nor did he ever express objectively the relation of anything to *her*. Instead, standing there behind the glass-topped counter lined with open cigar boxes, he would fix his mind on whatever subject might be on the agenda, like a visitor to a museum looking at an object. One that stood all by itself on a pedestal, inapplicable to calamitous life. Plato must have been like that, Rosetta thought, who heard a discussion on the radio one time about him while she ironed her uniforms. The Groves of Academe (this was in ancient Greece), and Plato…Gene would reflect: According to Kant…the Stoics…Thomas Hobbes…

"I just got to wondering," she said this day. "We say 'my conscience' like we'd say 'my nose' or 'my hand.' And we feel its pain, and its pain, like I say, is *its* pain, not like any other. But then we don't know what we're talking about."

"King David's *heart* hurts him when he's been crooked," Gene said after a little thought. "Job's *heart* tells him, 'You did nothing wrong.' But old Thomas Aquinas had it figured this way, *conscience* is really a telephone line. Telephones hadn't been invented then, of course, but that's how he described it, man and God hooked up like…What he really meant…a *hot* line. Lift the receiver, 'Man?' 'Yeah.' 'God.'"

For some unknown reason, when they had talked awhile and she went on her way, she felt brisker, instructed, also smug, like someone who knows where a treasure lies. Which she really did, his store of what was to her immense knowledge, where, for instance in the desperate situation of having to know a certain magic precept or your brothers would turn into swans, your castle sink beneath the waves and you yourself be locked up in an oak tree, you could run and ask, and the answer would be forthcoming. "Tell me, oh!" "Why, soitainly," he'd say in his New York melting-pot, Pantages-vaudeville, gone-to-college voice. "It's merely…" Then you'd *know*, and all be saved.

PART THREE

All on the Meadow Green

Chapter Sixty

*

Of course she called Penny about the beauty shop deal going through, Penny being the one who got her the job there in the first place.

"And now just think, you *own* the crummy joint!" Penny said. "Well, it's all in the draw, as Grandpa used to say." Sometimes she sounded cold and almost mean. Or her voice would break and she would start to cry. Or else, her Christian Science working again and faith reactivated that there was no cancer, death or worms that eat dead bodies in the grave and God is Love and Love is Everywhere, she would sound drunk. And sometimes she *would* be drunk.

"Gee, though," she said, "I don't mean to say crummy. The best years of my life...Isn't it funny? We don't know at the time...Walk to work in the snow, pitch dark, wind like ice. Noon, cold coffee, sandwich, four o'clock, backache, feet, flowing a stream...And no rest for the wicked, wash to do and iron tomorrow night, and Sunday scrub the kitchen. But what wouldn't I give to do it all over again. Bra a thirty-eight C, high heels all day long, remember my hair? Fellows would whistle...Had my own damn money, never had to beg on bended knees for a measly sack of caramels or *Photoplay*...But don't mind me. Congratulations, honey."

There's the hirer, the hired, the boss, the bossed, and for quite some time after she bought the shop, Rosetta found it as hard to exchange one role for the other as for the earth to flip and reverse its magnetic fields. Or that was the comparison Gene supplied when she sought for one, and she thought it must be apt, him being so smart. The problem was, she said a few days later as she stood at the stand buying a Hershey bar (for a permanent wave in the shop who was trying to quit smoking), not to be overbearing and not even realize...Because in Sunday school she learned a verse one time that said: "Whoever exalts himself will be humbled, and whoever humbles himself will be exalted."

He laughed. "That's too easy. No," he said, "life's style is more...disruptive accidents. Darling, a storm of casualty, believe me."

"Well..." she said uncertainly. She smiled and he smiled back, directly, purposefully, as if he could see her, not the unfocused baby-smiling of those who are born blind. When he turned his head the blue articulations, as she once heard him call his glass eyes, glinted between his eyelids (he only wore dark glasses on the street), not awful, somehow by his heroism excepted from the scope of that sad proposition, become a rich adornment like diamonds. And "darling" sounded different when he said it.

567

PENNY WAS AGHAST. "ALL I can say is, how can anybody call themself a beauty operator and not be able to *marcel*?" She was talking about Sharon.

"Because they just don't teach marcelling anymore," Rosetta said. "It's not part of the course. Nobody wants it. The state exams ignore it like it didn't exist."

"Remember when we took ours? Marcelling was the most important part of the whole test!"

"Well, it's a lost art now. But speaking of Sharon, she's quite good otherwise," Rosetta said. "Patience for manicures and a knack for timing. I think she's going to stay, too, even when the war's over and Robert comes back, her boyfriend, and they get married."

"I sure wouldn't count on it."

"I count on how the kids *want* so much nowadays," Rosetta said. "You ought to see her list! and mind you, a beauty operator. And Robert only clerked at Skaggs, that's how they met. But here she writes down crystal chandeliers, Spode china, and she wants a bar. They see these things in the movies and magazines. You'd have laughed the other day. I got this invitation to a wedding. So I said to Sharon, she's about the same age as the bride, I said I'd have to buy a wedding present for my second cousin and she suggested a sterling silver tea set."

"On a tray, of course."

"Oh, yes, a tray. But she did say some of the *plated* silver looked even prettier than the sterling, for some unknown reason—"

"I don't imagine I know the bride, do I?" Penny said.

"Did I ever mention my mother's Aunt Lucitie? Married to Uncle Albert? In the Constitution Building?"

"Alfonce's Hairdressing Establishment."

"That's right. Well, Aunt Lucitie and Uncle Albert had two children. Nancibel and Herman. Nancibel was my husband Legrand's mother, so she was my mother-in-law. And Herman—"

"Or in other words, 'I'm my own grandma.'"

Long familiar with the restlessness of Penny's expectation, Rosetta hurried on. "So anyway, Herman, he's the father of the bride."

"WHAT'S THIS HERE NAME 'NORMAL'?" Sharon said, in an idle moment subjecting to close scrutiny the wedding invitation Rosetta had left lying on one of the dressing tables. "Mr. and Mrs. Herman Alfonce request the pleasure of your company at the marriage of their daughter Agnes Lucitie to Sergeant Normal Lloyd Sleigh on Saturday, June twentieth—' *Normal?* What kind of a name is that?"

"A misprint, I imagine," Rosetta said, looking at it over Sharon's shoulder. "It's probably Norman."

"Well, I wouldn't of accepted them from the printer if it was me!"

But it wasn't a misprint. "Normal" was really the bridegroom's name.

A WEDDING BEING ONE OF the most interesting topics in the world to Sharon at this time, she waited eagerly for the following Monday to hear the details. But Rosetta hadn't been asked to the actual ceremony, which, being performed in the Mormon temple, could only be witnessed by members of the church in high standing. Along with many others, all she was qualified for was the two p.m. reception, where punch was served with slices of orange, a few grapes and even some thin discs of unpeeled cucumber floating around in it, several plates of one kind of cookie, and of course the wedding cake. There was a profusion of flowers, presents glittered on the net-enswathed dining room table under electrified candles, and the bride had on a white-satin dress with points coming down over her hands, lace appliqués and a veil that stood out all around. The groom had on his Army uniform.

It was Sharon's idea that the groom probably hitched a plane ride from Fort Bragg and left again the day after the ceremony. One night of love, torn from each other's arms, sent to New Guinea, who knows where or when? they'd ever meet again. Sharon wanted the romantic account, her tears hung lonely in remembrance.

But this was one of those fortunate situations where the bridegroom was stationed about forty miles south of Salt Lake at Topaz, guarding the Japs, the American Japs locked up out there in the barracks for the common good, Normal was an M.P., military police. And another thing Agnes was very thrilled about (this was Agnes the mother, whom the bride was named after, though *called* Dotty after Dotty Dimple), as she told Rosetta, who had stood and talked to her awhile, was that Normal was a Latter-day Saint. "Because you take a soldier walking into an office," Agnes said, "to deliver some forms. Dotty works for the War Relocation Authority, they're the ones that move the Japs around, she's a typist, and coming from the South the way Normal does, he could have been *anything*, Catholic, Holy Roller, and love is blind. But he's a *Mormon*, it's almost like a *miracle*, and his bishop sent his Temple 'recommend' from North Carolina *so fast*."

What Rosetta thought was kind of a miracle, considering that opposites are supposed to attract, was how much the bride and bridegroom looked alike. And not only did they look alike—blonde, blue-eyed, same strong chins—but, broad-shouldered and long-legged as both were, Dotty could have worn Normal's clothes and Normal hers, and they'd have been a perfect fit, and they could even have exchanged *shoes*!

Sharon refused to sanction this. She wore a seven-B, Robert elevens, she came up to here on him, her eyes were green, his were brown, and *that was the way it was supposed to be.*

Rosetta didn't go on to say then that the two big blondes standing shoulder to shoulder cutting the wedding cake together were quite striking and that she heard several remarks about what beautiful children they would no doubt have. One guest said that if those two had a daughter and she didn't become Miss America someday, or at least Miss Salt Lake City, she would eat her hat.

For a start the couple had a son, and he did indeed turn out to be beautiful. One morning on her way down to open the shop, Rosetta met Dotty struggling up Main Street against the sharp frost-wind with the child in tow. During the little while they talked, for it was starting to snow again, Dotty said she was parked around the corner, this was her firstborn, Normal the Third, he was three years old, they had an appointment with the doctor and he was going to be c-i-r-c-u-m-c-i-s-e-d. Otherwise Rosetta would have thought he was about six, he was so large, but of course he was bundled in a bulky snow-suit and had on boots and a tasselled cap. "Oh, my!" she said. "You don't say!" She gave him a friendly smile that might also have been a little rueful, for who could help but be sympathetic? Whether Normal the Third couldn't stand the complexity of that, made more complex to him by the cast in her eye, whether goaded by his mother's spelled-out word, or if all strangers were liable in any case to his censure Rosetta did not know, but suddenly he made a rush and struck at her, the blow landing in the vicinity of her handbag.

"Why, Normal Sleigh, what do you think you're doing!" Dotty jerked him by the hand, then cuffed and shook him.

"Please!" Rosetta said, twisting her hands together in distress. "I'm sure he didn't mean—"

He did not cry but glared balefully, with eyes so undilutedly blue from all his lines of descent that they blued his orbits and cast blue shadows across his rosy cheeks.

"Oh, yes, he did," Dotty said. "But maybe this o-p-e-r—" She broke off, then went on, sounding on the instant as affectionate as she had been harsh before, and with an expression of benignity replacing her angry look: "Tell Rosetta what we're going to have! When we get through up at the nice doctor's office?" She answered herself: "We're going to have *a banana split*. And what else, Normal? Tell Cousin Rosetta."

Another baleful glare. Again Dotty answered: "A pistol! In a holster."

"Goodness sakes," Rosetta said as heartily as she could.

"And all we have to do is just be nice!"

Several times during the day, Rosetta thought of the fierce little boy and wondered if he had made himself competent for the treat and the pistol. It couldn't have been easy with that nature, provoked to rage by every trifle. Not, of course, that what he had to *face* was a trifle. Sharon couldn't understand why they waited till he was a big kid like that. She thought they did it right away, like her girlfriend's baby. Without even asking! the minute he was born, and put it on the bill, it was common procedure, all the doctors did it, the nurses said so. Her girlfriend's husband was not a bit pleased. He said it could take away some of his pleasure (when the baby grew up) and that it was just a racket.

But that's what they do, snip, snip, and also put drops in their eyes and charge for *that*.

Well, Margaret said, hurrying in just then for a shampoo, she wished Mr. Wintler could have drops put in *his* eyes, magic drops that would show him just how roughshod and impossible he was getting to be. No one could please him, or at least no one in the housekeeping department. Maybe that new little guttersnipe of a bookkeeper, or whatever she was, in his office in the tight red sweater could, but otherwise it was nothing but find fault from morning till night! And how could anyone change that much! from a sweet, reasonable hotel manager to a monster that over a *dust rag* being left on a stairway, and only a back stairway at that up on six, which it *never* happened before, could turn purple in the face and fly into little pieces?

Sharon said that she, for one, had never *seen* the man that he didn't look upset.

Rosetta hadn't seen him for quite some time. He never paid attention to the beauty shop, she said.

"Oh, no?" Margaret said. "Listen, my dear. He's manipulating right this minute to get the rents raised."

"Mine, you mean?"

"Yours, Gene's newsstand, the barbershop, the florist's, the gift shop. And I mean *raised*. In fact, you'll be lucky if you don't get moved!"

"Moved?" Rosetta said, almost dropping the shampoo bottle.

"Over above the furnace room. He wants to put a specialty store in your spot here, beaded sweaters, alligator purses, earrings. *You* know."

But it didn't happen.

Something else did. "Things happen," as Gene said was carved above the west portal of the Abbey of St. Molaisse on the Island of the Oxen. And amongst these possibilities, *one* thing always happened, to look back on (thrown into true perspective years later) and say, *there was where the pathway branched …*

Mr. Wintler's death occurred at 1:45 in the afternoon.

He had just stepped out of the coffee shop after eating the halibut, mashed potatoes, peas and carrots, green salad, roll and butter, cherry pie à la mode and coffee and was lighting a cigar when all of a sudden someone noticed he was down on the floor. Then he was being carted out on a stretcher to an ambulance, then in the hospital, then he was no more. Heart case, stroke or some such thing, the doctors like to open them up to see for sure. But Mrs. Wintler in Minnesota wouldn't allow an autopsy. Also, she didn't come out from Minneapolis to get the body but sent a family friend. No funeral in Salt Lake City, burial and attendant observances were to be in Minneapolis.

Margaret thought that was typical of a wife and children who would let husband and father come to the Newhouse Hotel *alone* in the first place and toil here for *them* for twelve long years! It was pitiful to even think of. That was why Margaret Abeloff, head housekeeper, was not only going to forget the hatefulness of his last months, which no one can blame a man with a brain tumor or whatever he might have had, and remember only his earlier sweetness, but as the train with the baggage car carrying his coffin pulled out of the depot, she was going to be there and stand and wave as it went past and say *Good-bye, Mr. Wintler.* In memory of their long association, that was the least she could do.

Greatly touched, Rosetta offered to take her down to the depot in the car and stand there on the platform, or wherever, with her. When she got back, Rosetta said as she was leaving the shop, Sharon (who because of the snow had had nothing to do since morning but manicure her nails, thumb through magazines and look at the clock) could go home. Sharon looked at the clock again, this time brightly smiling. Before, she was just going to open a can of pork and beans. But getting home that early, she would give Robert a big surprise: pigs-in-blankets, fried potatoes, gingerbread served warm with whipped cream. Then she was going to ask him to help her move the living room couch to the only place she hadn't tried it yet, and the chair where the couch had been, and the radio where the chair…Of course he would probably argue, they always did.

THE STREETS WERE AWFUL EVEN with chains, and lit up like nighttime, though it was only a little past two. Rosetta parked, wishing they could see the train without getting out. But of course they couldn't, so stepped out into a snowbank—that is to say, Rosetta did—then floundered to the entrance, went in and across the station and out the other side. A man in a conductor's cap by the turnstile pointed out the 2:47 for Cheyenne and all points east and Margaret said thank you, they would just walk down that way and kind of along it, because a friend of theirs was in the baggage car, his remains, being shipped to Minneapolis, which was where he originally came from, and as there had been no funeral…Go ahead, the man said, but don't cross the tracks. Both said they wouldn't, and started down the snow-covered space between the depot and the tracks, slipping and sliding in frozen wheel-ruts and footprints. They clung to each other as they went, blinking and snuffling against the bitter wind.

"I realize this is kind of foolish," Margaret panted. "'Cause what does he care now? But I do feel—considering what a different person in every way the man was when he first came to Salt Lake—" This was, of course, before Gene came into her life and even before she met the painter who fell off the scaffold. Also there *had* been a certain fellow, but he didn't count…She took a lot of pride in how she looked in those days, she said, more than she ought to, maybe. And Mr. Wintler when he first arrived acted bowled over, or at least to a certain degree, whipping out his lighter for her and all such stuff. Of course they had to have these conferences, him just starting on the job and her because of her position knowing a lot of what he would need to know. So sometimes it might be midnight! and they would still be talking. And she might as well say it, something might have come of such a situation had nothing interfered. But something *did* interfere, and it was *most peculiar*…

A roar and rumble drowned her out, steam shot away, a headlight big as the moon bore down on them, the blast of a powerful whistle buried itself like a hatchet in their skulls...Margaret lurched, her foot slipped, in a frozen rut her ankle bent, and she went down on it sideways and pulled Rosetta down on top of her. Rosetta, on the instant scrambling halfway up, tugged her out of what seemed like the path of sure destruction but was only din and darkness. They were safe! and had been. The train clipped by, and there, finally, was the baggage car with all that was left of Mr. Wintler in it clicking past, and they'd forgotten him, Margaret crying on the ground, Rosetta bending over her.

"Are you hurt?"

Men came running up from the baggage room, a redcap came, a man knelt...Ankle broken? No. A leg, an arm? Her spine? Well, here, let's see. On her feet, Margaret took a cautious step. Maybe her shoulder...? No. Here, on her side? No, nothing there to break. She was *very lucky*. Back at the hotel she resumed her duties, and when she met Mr. Wilson, the temporary manager, coming down the hall, said nothing about a fall. For the very *mention* when they're young like that—he was twenty-six—means you've took out a patent on old age.

THAT'S HOW IT WAS WITH the doctor she called at one in the morning when the pain in her side got unendurable. Well, she didn't call *him* but here he came, bright-eyed, bushy-tailed, new bag, new stethoscope, new strip to wrap around her arm and pump up tight. The old doctor's new young partner. Everything changes. It's very discouraging. They've got no bedside manner. Think they have! of course. Glasses, kind of a frown like the wheels are turning. And here comes out this *stupid, dumb* remark. "It's no joke when an old person falls down!"

"Did you ever hear of such a thing!" Rosetta said the next morning with zeal and indignation, taking a seat at the foot of the bed.

"But in a way I'm glad it happened. I've been laying here thinking and *I'm glad it happened*," Margaret said.

"Glad you fell down?"

"Glad the boy said it. I guess you heard the saying 'When the policemen start looking young, watch out!' and it's the same with doctors. But anyway I'm glad, for the simple reason that sometimes it takes a stupid, dumb remark to make a person make their mind up!"

"About what?"

"Listen, *you* know the way I used to look. And the way I've been coasting along these past years."

"That's your privilege."

"And why? For the simple reason—a husband that can't see and judge and criticize—you feel so free and easy. I've mentioned that. I've let myself go, you know that. And maybe a little more than I ever meant to. But it's never too late to mend, as the saying goes. So as soon as I get better…in fact, tomorrow…"

"What did the doctor think?"

"I had this awful—Of course I wrenched my—It could be a bruise. You can get black and blue inside, your bowels and all, just like on the outside. That is what the doctor claims. He left these pills and they help a little. What they seem to do is kind of disconnect the pain. It's *there*, but now I'm not the one that's feeling it. Or yes, I am, but in a dream, more like. It's funny…I'm supposed to stay in bed, today at least."

"So you be sure and do that. Knowing you."

"I mean it about an appointment."

"What do you want?"

"The works. Just like when Penny used to do me."

"Henna pack?"

"The works! Manicure, facial. A house doesn't have to fall on me."

"Okay. Can I get you anything before I leave?"

"How are things downstairs?"

"You mean in the lobby? Practically deserted. The weather's awful. You're lucky here in bed. Oh, say, Margaret—"

But her eyes had closed. Rosetta would ask another time, she thought, getting up and walking softly to the door, *what* was "most peculiar" that Margaret was talking about before she fell, that "interfered" between her and Mr. Wintler, or in other words kept them from having a love affair, which of course she wouldn't say in so many words. When he first came to town? Or no, better let her bring the subject up again herself if she wanted to.

"Rosetta!"

"Yes?" She turned. Margaret was still lying back against her pillows, her eyes still closed.

"Pull that blind down, will you?"

"Which one?"

"The Main Street one."

"Okay." Five stories down, the street looked as empty and sad as Sunday. A bird huddled on the ledge. "And we shall have snow," Rosetta was remembering, "and what will the robin do then, poor thing?" when suddenly a cry came from the bed.

"Oh, God!"

She whirled. The shade, let go of, flipped to the window top.

"I'm dying! I'm sick, deathly—help me—going to throw up—" Margaret pushed the covers off, tried to sit up, Rosetta tried to help her. Sweat poured down, her face was white. "My lungs, they're pushing up through my head! My arms—the pain, oh, God. My lungs are pushing up—"

Rosetta ran out, called to a man down by the elevators, "Hurry! Oh, please! She's having a heart attack!"

He turned and loped towards her.

AT THE HOSPITAL, AFTER A day of ineffectual search and inquiry, an intern finally thought of sticking a needle in Margaret's abdomen. Blood spurted all the way to the ceiling. Rosetta wouldn't have heard anything about that, of course, if she hadn't run into Agnes, Cousin Herman's wife. And that was really strange. She would say as much to Sharon later on. Not strange because Herman's wife Agnes was at the hospital, she was a registered nurse and had worked there more than twenty years, but because she was on night shift, which she said she hadn't been, oh, for ages (but the weather and all, she couldn't get out of it). However, the real coincidence that Rosetta was talking about was to run into Agnes's *daughter* one day taking her little boy to the doctor and a few days later, here's Agnes herself! After all this time. Let's see, well, since Dotty's wedding. Nearly five years.

"Rosetta! What are you doing here?" Agnes said.

"I'm here with a man that they brought his wife up here in the ambulance this morning. He's blind. He runs the newsstand at the hotel."

"Oh."

"You know my beauty shop is there, at the hotel."

"That's right, I remember. After Legrand—His G.I. insurance."

"So anyway tonight as I was leaving, I stopped at the newsstand to see if he had heard any more, and just then the phone was ringing and it was the hospital! So—"

But this was of small interest to Agnes. "Isn't this weather something!" she said, looking toward a row of black window panes.

"Awful," Rosetta said, somewhat discomfited. "Winter was really starting the other day when I ran into Dotty with her poor little boy. Thursday, I guess it was. She was taking him to be circumcised. I hope he got along all right."

Agnes gave a snort of disgust. "That whole thing," she said, "was ridiculous. From beginning to end."

"How do you mean?"

She shrugged, and as though she owned the franchise to do so, changed the subject: "Where are you going?" she said.

"You mean right now? They said the cafeteria was down this way."

"Come on, I'll go with you, I'm a little early." Agnes chose a dish of grayish-orange Jell-O cut into cubes, and Rosetta took coffee and a roll. No cashier was on duty, but Agnes said to leave eighty-five cents in the cigar box by the cash register and thanked Rosetta for the Jell-O. As they came in, the lights on one side of the room were being turned off, and nearly all the tables were empty. No more service after eight p.m. They sat down on the dark side by a drafty window overlooking the arc-lighted parking lot.

"So why is it you're here?"

Rosetta told her again, this time in more detail.

"I know who you mean now," Agnes said. "She's up in surgery now. Maude was telling me. The new intern stuck a needle in her stomach and blood spurted all the way to the ceiling!"

"What in the world—?" Rosetta said in horror.

"Sounds like her spleen ruptured, that's what Maude thinks. That would fill the cavity with blood, and when the needle punctured—they'd realize then and rush to operate. She'll probably make it all right, Dr. Galley is the one *I'd* want, even if he is a Catholic."

"Well, I certainly hope she does. Her husband's blind, it would just be terrible. They've been married ten years, and they're a very—devoted—By the way, right now when I left him, he was talking to—When we got to the desk, the girl there called this doctor and when he came, who should it be but—the two of them went to *college* together, at Columbia!"

"What are you talking about?"

"The man I brought up here to the hospital tonight, Mr. Abeloff, and the doctor! that came out to talk to him about Margaret. Mrs. Abeloff. It turned out they knew each other!"

"I know who that doctor is," Agnes said with cold disapproval. "He was stationed out here at the air base during the war, and that's just the trouble with the Army, Gentiles come in and get attracted. The climate, the canyons…first thing you know, they've moved here."

"Well, they seemed—happy to see each other. I say 'see' although Gene, Mr. Abeloff, is blind, as I was saying. So that will be a comfort, their doctor being a personal acquaintance. He took Gene, Mr. Abeloff, by the arm and it looked like they were going into a little office, so I just said I'd go and get some coffee. The least I can do is wait and drive him home." Rosetta took a sip, it was weak and lukewarm, and Agnes watched her swallow.

"Isn't it funny?" she said, her eyes following the cup as Rosetta rather nervously set it back down in the saucer. "Here your ancestors were some of the early Latter-day Saints, your own grandparents lived the Doctrine. Or so I understand. Isn't that right? Your mother was baptized. The work was *done* already. *Handed* to you, really, on a silver platter. Yet here you are—! *Coffee.* As if the Prophet Joseph never existed! And I see you smoke also—"

"Well, yes, I do," Rosetta said.

"—while *I* was a grown-up woman when I came here," the other went on. "That is to say, I was still only a young girl, but married, a bride—"

"And also a registered nurse," Rosetta said, taking another sip. "I was about five when you married Cousin Herman, and I remember them talking about it. Him bringing home a bride."

"Religion was the least of my worries," Agnes said as though bearing her testimony in meeting. "I was a Baptist, born one, everything was fine. But all I had to do was hear the Word and something said as plain as I'm talking to you now: *Agnes*. And who converted Herman? Me, a stranger, and him born in the church or should by rights have been, and ought to have been an Elder by that time! But I'm happy to say my *children* are making up for all that unfortunately went before!"

"Speaking of children," Rosetta put in quickly. "That little boy of Dotty's could be in the movies, he's so cute. How did he get along?"

"What are you talking about?" Agnes often interjected this in conversations, like someone prosecuting in a court of justice.

"He was going to be circumcised."

Agnes gave a sigh of exasperation. "She had the baby in the night, they didn't even call me. I didn't know it till I came to work. Naturally I thought it had been done, they always do it, till come to find out one testicle hadn't descended. But what difference did that make? None whatever. But the doctor says to wait and let it descend. Like he's got some kind of guarantee that it will. But the worst of all is Dotty's husband's *father*. *He* got in the act. That's his specialty. So his advice was, leave that kind of business to the Jews and also the Mohammedans, which *I* personally had no knowledge of. About them, I mean. You know they all moved up here?"

"Who?" Rosetta said.

"Normal's folks, the whole entire outfit. *We* thought the kids were going south after the war. But no, they stayed through the Japs being turned loose and everything and Normal getting on with the government—he helped with that—and the next thing we know, Normal's whole entire family's here, right in our ward!"

"Well, that's a compliment to Utah. And how lovely you didn't have to part with Dotty."

Agnes gave her a disgusted look. "I can tell you one thing. I wouldn't mind parting with *him*," she said. "Mr. Sleigh, the father-in-law. Takes right over. You know how *cancer* performs, well, the next thing he'll be *bishop*. And the mother's no shrinking violet. But anyway, when little Normal was born I tried to tell them. One undescended testicle don't make one particle of difference! But who did they listen to! Me, a professional? Or Mr. Loud Mouth? It's supposed to descend, the doctors say. But what's that got to do with it? It's like cutting off a puppy's tail. Do it before they get their eyes open. They had to give in eventually, why wait till he was three? The child's *still* raising Cain, you'd think they chopped his leg off. But of course both Normal and Dotty clamp down on him. They're very hard-boiled. I don't know where she got that, Dotty. Maybe from some ancestor. Say, my gosh! Look at the time! I got to run—"

"Agnes, just one more question about my friend Margaret. Is that very *serious*, a ruptured spleen?"

"Well, it's no laughing matter, I can tell you that."

Rᴏsᴇᴛᴛᴀ sᴀᴛ ᴀ ʟɪᴛᴛʟᴇ ʟᴏɴɢᴇʀ after Agnes left, thinking of old times and how Wyandra and she used to hate to see her coming, the one who always caused the trouble. She looked the same. Older, but still like she had to shave, still with that large bust and small and shrunken-looking rear. A few more lights went out, and Rosetta stood up and cinched her coat belt tighter. Thinking of Agnes made her think of other people. Gram. Legrand. Uncle Albert combing out a lady's hair. How long it was, the lovely way it rippled down her back. Mama. Next year I'll start being older than Mama. Imagine that. But one that I won't think of... She can't be dead, she's got to be alive. Wyandra! I've got to tell her—No, no. *I will not think of that*. Of that night. Her. Of how I loved— how sorry—But some things you just never do get over.

Chapter Sixty-one

*

A HOSPITAL IS A SAD PLACE, MAYBE A CATHOLIC HOSPITAL MORE THAN OTHERS. The nuns start them when a town's just young, labor's cheap, materials, people donate. The building is big and rambling, too commodious to tear down in later years. They convert the gas lights to electricity, put in partitions half the height of high-ceilinged rooms, leave the woodwork brown (men vote for that), leave movable wooden screens inside tall, narrow windows so the rooms stay dark even in bright weather. The pictures are sad, if you could make them out high up on the walls. Plaster saints stand lost in thought in hollows, Jesus pierced and bleeding sags in lilies, at the dim hallways' end candles flickering in red glass look as alive as corpuscles in blood. Yes, sad. Or maybe it's the winter night ... Not sad for the new mother with the hearty baby, the divorcée with the face lift, the skier with the cast on his foot, his bare toes sticking out, who's flying back to Harvard Saturday. Not for certain people. But there, through half-open doors, in greenish shadows ... I am sick, I must die, Lord, have mercy on me ...

At the nurses' station they said Mrs. Abeloff was still in surgery. Rosetta went and took a seat along the wall. Gene was nowhere in sight. As soon as he appeared ... should she stay and keep him company while he waited? Or maybe just go? He and their doctor knew each other, it wouldn't be like leaving him alone. In fact, it might look rather silly to stay. They weren't intimate friends, after all, never had become so. People where you work *aren't*. Lots of times it's better that way, a kind of unspoken agreement. We know each other there but not here, it's better. In the ten years of their acquaintance, tonight was the first time she ever walked along the street with Gene, to where the car was parked, not far, half a block, her hand on his arm. He hardly faltered, it was amazing. And then in the car. When she switched the ignition on, the radio came on ... "It Had to Be You." She turned it off quickly. They talked about Margaret's fall in the railroad yard, Rosetta went into detail about that. Mr. Wintler dying and the connection of things. About the cold. And how if winter comes, can spring...? and then they were at the hospital.

She got up and went to the desk. The nurse, bent over a ledger writing, did not look up, her work securing her somehow, as though by religious sanction, from encroachment. Rosetta did not even clear her throat. She waited. A large alarm clock ticked. Then came a clatter from the direction of the open stairway by the elevator and Rosetta glanced that way at a platinum blonde descending there, you might almost think an actress, in a tight black dress, broad silver fox jacket swinging open, pearl beads. Her perfume was My Sin, it preceded her like an invisible handmaiden.

"High heels!" she greeted the nurse but also included Rosetta. "When you work in *flat* heels all day." She was apologizing for the noise on the linoleum-covered stairs.

"I never wear 'em," the nurse said, glancing up only briefly from what Rosetta now saw was a personal letter she was writing on pale blue stationery laid flat on the record book. "What are *you* doing here this time of night?"

"Damn woman didn't show up."

As the platinum blonde seemed to be speaking to her, Rosetta responded as best she might, with a look that was supposed to say, well, that's the way it goes sometimes.

The blonde smiled. "Don't you hate people like that? Promise faithfully to come and then…"

"Well, maybe the weather…"

"No, I don't think she could swing it, that's all. But why would a person come and *look* if they haven't got the money?"

"You can't prove it by me," the nurse said.

"Say, don't I know you?"

Rosetta gave a little start of surprise.

"Aren't you…Lavonne? No, Lavonne was your girlfriend! You're—*Now* I remember. You kids were the ones that went and fixed Colleen's hair and put her makeup on that time. At the undertaker's. This guy had murdered her."

The nurse's eyes were fixed now on the speaker's painted lips. "What's all this?" she said.

"We went to beauty school together!" the blonde said. "Her and me and this Lavonne I mentioned." She turned to Rosetta. "Don't you remember? I'm Rilla Johnson."

"Oh, yes…" Rosetta said with the let-down feeling she always had when she thought someone remembered her on account of her eye. Now that she was reminded, she did remember Rilla Johnson, whose distinctive feature as a fellow student was, her fingernails wouldn't grow. Miss Grey said they would, with proper care and three packets of Knox's gelatin per day, anybody's would, but hers didn't, except one thumbnail that grew thicker and thicker. They *still* hadn't, one hand rested on the counter, the fingers tapping. The nails were so short you'd think they were bitten, and without polish, the only feature that spoiled the picture otherwise of beautiful glamour.

"Gee," Rosetta said, "you've changed, you look like a movie star."

"Oh, I don't either."

"Yes, you do."

"No, I don't," Rilla said. "My hands are terrible." Quickly she hid them in the pockets of her coat. "The one that looked like a *movie star* was your friend Lavonne. Does she still live around here?"

"No, they moved. She lives in California now, she and her husband and two little boys."

"And she didn't go in the movies? Well, no, I guess she didn't have the figure—"

"Oh, she had it later!" Rosetta said.

"What did she do, diet? You should of seen her," Rilla added to the nurse, who had gone back to her letter. "Her face, this Lavonne we're talking about. She could of been a model."

Rosetta nodded.

"Say!" Rilla said, turning to her. "*You* didn't come about the shop, did you? It just dawned on me!"

"What shop?"

"My ad? In the paper? I just advertised once, I thought I'd take my time. My shop here in the hospital! Listen, come see—" She grabbed Rosetta's hand.

"Wait…" Rosetta turned back. "Miss?" she said.

"That's Dora," Rilla said of the nurse.

Dora looked up.

"If a man comes here and asks…he's blind…would you please tell him…"

"Tell him she's gone with me to the beauty shop!"

"Hey, wait a minute. What was that about some girl getting murdered?" Dora said.

"Tell you later," Rilla called back.

It was a beautiful shop, or at least appeared so when its proprietor turned on a pink-shaded lamp. Good equipment. New chair, press this thing right here with your foot and it would raise or lower. A hospital clientele…Bet she was going to miss it, Rilla said. The patients, relatives hanging around waiting, they would get their hair done, people working here, nurses, the clerical staff—new mothers always wanted manicures. It did real well. A captive audience. Widows…sometimes they came down right from the deathbed for a shampoo-set, their husband wasn't cold yet. Of course Las Vegas would be interesting. She waved Rosetta into a chair, offered her a cigarette and took one herself. Each lighted her own. Rilla perched in the hydraulic seat, inspected her extremely high heels, holding up one foot and then the other, then crossed her legs.

"Shoes make such a difference," she said. "Down in Las Vegas I'll probably be seeing him every day, he'll come in the shop, I hate to have him see me looking short and dumpy. But I certainly couldn't go around in *these* from morning till night."

"Me either," Rosetta said. "I've got a shop too, in the Newhouse Hotel."

"Is that a fact! Well, why don't you get rid of it and take over this one? You'd love it, I'm telling you. Stuff happens here you never would believe!"

"Stuff happens where I am, too," Rosetta said. "You'd ought to come and see my shop sometime."

"I'd love to have you have this one," Rilla said. "I really would. Someone I know instead of a stranger."

"How come you're letting it go?"

"Love," Rilla said, turning so she could look in the mirror and fluffing up her hair. "That's another big advantage. You meet guys. Are you married?"

"I was. My husband was killed in the war."

"Gee, tough," the other said, swinging around to face her. "I was too. We got a divorce. No kids, thank goodness. Our generation!" Rilla shrugged. "But anyway, as I was saying, this guy that's getting me this shop in Las Vegas ... You have to have pull down there, you know. It's in the Sands. Actually it won't be mine, but I'll be running it. That is, during the evening hours, if everything goes through. I'm telling you, it's the chance of a lifetime, and where do you think I met him? Right here in this hospital! So that's why I say like Brigham, *this is the place*. The nurse called down," she went on. "This guy with the broken neck wants his hair washed and cut and a manicure."

"Broken *neck*?" Rosetta said.

"I'm supposed to go up there. Sometimes I do. Go to the rooms. But mostly they don't want anything done till they feel good enough to come down to the shop here under their own power, or be brought down. Oh, my, yes, a broken neck. That's nothing nowadays. They cure them all the time. Haven't you seen people walking down the street with this big collar on? He wrecked his Cadillac out here on the baseline road, driving down from Canada. An older man. I think he had this gal with him. He says not, but from what some of the girls say ... But what care I? as the song says. So anyway, I went up there and it was love at first sight ... "

"That's wonderful," Rosetta said.

"How about you? What's all this about a blind guy?"

"Oh, he's just the husband of a customer of mine. He runs the newsstand at the hotel. His wife was brought to the hospital here this morning ... "

"Well, you just wait until you get up *here*."

"I'm really pretty well satisfied ... where I am."

BUT THAT WAS SUPPOSING THINGS were fixed in amber. Of course, they never are. The temporary manager left and the permanent one came in, as frowning and preoccupied from his first day as Mr. Wintler had been on his last. Shop rents went up. And the new man must have found Mr. Wintler's master plan tucked away somewhere, for sure enough, the notice came that the beauty shop was supposed to move to the spot above the furnace room and a specialty store come in where the shop had been. The new head housekeeper had graduated in Hotel, Motel, and Restaurant Operations, she did her own hair, no one dared call her by her first name. Gene moved into a room at the back, on the floor above his and Margaret's old rooms. He told the maintenance men who moved him (and one of them told a maid, who told Sharon, who told Rosetta) that he didn't know just what he was going to do.

Sharon said that for quite some time she thought Margaret was Gene's *mother*. She was so old…

"She wasn't really so old," Rosetta said. "The paper said fifty-five." But of course that would seem old to a girl of twenty-two.

"How old is *he*?"

"My age," Rosetta said. "Thirty-five. Or thereabouts."

"So he was twenty-five when they—You said ten years. How long had he been blind?"

"Not very long. It happened in that war in Spain."

"I know, you told me. But what was he *doing* there? I mean, that's a foreign country."

"Lots of people went there, from different places…Canada, South America…They volunteered. See, Germany had a dictator, Italy had a dictator, so Spain was trying to get one too. Worse than a king…So all these guys jumped in to try to help the ones that were against—Gee, if they'd won!"

"What then?" Sharon said.

"Well, that might have stopped everything. There might never have been a war."

"*Our* war, you're talking about?" Sharon said with eyes aghast. "World War *Two*? Why, golly. Robert and I would of never met!"

AT MARGARET'S FUNERAL, PENNY SAID privately to Rosetta that she was going to take it on herself to call Gene's brother long distance in New York and tell him what had happened. Why, it was like a child's mother dying, the most pitiful thing, and especially being blind.

It was a large funeral. The coffee shop gang were almost all there, it was past the lunch hour, the maids, girls from the business office, Lefty and Fred from maintenance. Mr. Wilson, the temporary manager, wasn't, but he hardly knew Margaret. The white-haired barber closed his shop and came. That was nice, considering how he kept to himself. When her head was bowed in prayer, Rosetta happened to look along the row at his hand hanging at his side, the thumb and finger in a kind of pill-rolling tremble. The start of creeping paralysis, she thought sadly, and so that will end too, the little routine of saying good morning and good night, not much else, the barber wasn't a friendly person.

Jake and Penny came, Viola was with them, they sat in the mourner's room with Gene. The doctor Gene used to know at college sat in there also with his young wife, who Penny said later was taking her nurse's training when she and the doctor met, which she never finished, and his first wife divorced him on account of her. Viola, single now, looked younger than she had ten years before when Rosetta first met her, slimmed down, artificial leopard coat, a charm bracelet, spun-sugar hair, polychromed face of rosy yellowish gray, blue kid eyelids. At first she had hold of one of Penny's arms while Penny clung to Jake's thick overcoats with her other hand, but a look went between them, Penny's like one engaged in hostilities, Viola's all innocence, and a little later they were walking on either side of Jake, Viola determinedly sending sweet smiles round. Penny looked like a figure in an old medieval woodcut, her clothes were intact but yet for some reason she gave the impression of being in tatters, that strips and scraps fluttered about her bones in the icy wind.

Margaret's was the first corpse Sharon had ever seen, she said it was scary, her heart beat fast as she walked up towards the coffin. And just think, Gene standing there at the last all by himself saying good-bye, never saw Margaret to start with and couldn't see her at the end! He couldn't cry, of course, no eyes. But Sharon wondered if his tears trickled down inside.

IT DOES SEEM FOOLISH WHEN somebody with coal-black hair takes a notion they want to be blonde. It's very expensive, and if Mrs.—?

"Smith," the woman said agreeably.

If Mrs. Smith really wanted her hair bleached really light, she should plan on staying at least eight hours in the shop. And if she wanted it cut and styled, too...

"Price is no object."

And she didn't look as if it was, either, in her dressmaker suit, georgette blouse, lizard shoes with matching purse and thick, encrusted costume jewelry.

But the problem was, working an eight-hour job like that into the schedule the Saturday before Easter. It couldn't be done, that's all. And Mrs. Smith said she was leaving Monday. How about *tomorrow*? she said. Or in other words, Easter Sunday. "I'll make it worth your while."

Rosetta shook her head.

"How about...?" Mrs. Smith drew a deep sigh.

Rosetta studied her appointment book.

"No, you can see...we'll be busy right up until...Sharon's last appointment is at five. I promised to do her comb-out so she can leave as soon as...She's having her first big family dinner tomorrow. And my last appointment...that's at six-fifteen. So it would be at least seven-thirty before..."

"I don't suppose...You couldn't take me then?"

"If it was just a shampoo-set. But..." Tiredly she looked up at the blue-black waves flowing from under the hat of organza flowers. "Why, we'd be here till three or four in the morning! It'd be all right with me *ordinarily*, maybe, but the day before Easter like this...I opened at seven this morning! And just in the home stretch to face..." Again she shook her head. "I say it for your sake. I might dye it green!"

"Well, that has happened to me too in my lifetime, and it didn't kill me," Mrs. Smith said. "But you won't dye it green. They tell me you're one of the best in the business."

"Why don't you just get it done the next place you stop?"

"Because we're not going to stop anyplace till we get where we're going. And I just found out that someone will be there that I never thought I'd see again in a million years, and if I'm not blonde when I see *him*, like I was when we said good-bye, well, whether I live or die…I mean it, honey. I'm asking for my *life*."

Of course she wasn't, but her big brown eyes diffused a trembling shimmer like a deer's, and so Rosetta looked at her book again and said well, let's see, if Mrs. Lamar came at six-fifteen and she took Mrs. Smith…

But Mrs. Lamar was late. She couldn't help it, poor thing, it had been a madhouse there at the Royal Bakery. And as Mrs. Smith was early anyway, she had more than half an hour's wait. But she didn't mind, she might as well be here, she said, as up in their room staring at the four walls. *He* had gone to the movies, so that would keep him busy. They had an early supper…Mrs. Smith slipped out and, as Mrs. Lamar was going in under the dryer, came back with a tray from the coffee shop…a plate of stew, apple pie and cheese and coffee. "Come on now, eat, before you start on me."

"That won't guarantee it won't be green," Rosetta said.

"That's my lookout."

The food did infuse her with new energy, though for a few minutes Rosetta's cigarette almost slipped from her grasp in a fit of post-prandial drowsiness. But that was because she took the comfortable chair. Once she jumped up and began, she was all right.

But by one in the morning she was moving like a zombie, and cold enough to put her sweater on, though generally she'd be perspiring in the midst of a job like that. About two was when she started to talk with more sound than sense…when her human vitality was at the lowest. Or why would she do a thing like that? It was the *customer* who usually did the blabbing and confessing and sometimes shed the tears, never the operator. The operator just listened, went on with her work and murmured the comforting words. Don't blame yourself. You couldn't help it. You did the best you could.

Mrs. Smith murmured, "I don't wonder you don't know what to do. It's a very tough predicament. I mean, it would be for me…"

"It makes me so *ashamed*," Rosetta said, something her pride would never have let her say, she was sure of that, if she hadn't been obfuscated with tiredness. Why else would she say all the things she burbled out that night to a perfect stranger? Well, that was why, of course. Because Mrs. Smith *was* a stranger. Rosetta would never see her again. It was like a hearse passing. Did you know a funeral parade passing is your chance to get rid of whatever's weighing heavy on your mind? Mrs. Smith told her that. All you have to do as the hearse goes by is say "Take it! Take it! Take it!" and think of whatever your trouble is, being carried to the graveyard and buried. And that will be the end of it. A lot of people don't know that, hearses go by all the time and they miss the opportunity.

That was it, Mrs. Smith was a stranger, the fatigue of her long day had got to Rosetta by then. *National Geographic* said that Indians dancing the Bear Dance eventually got so exhausted they didn't know whether they were Indians or bears, and she always thought afterwards it must have been like that with her.

"I'm so ashamed. And the reason is because I love him. I want to be with him all the time. I want to put my arms around him and hold him. I want to kiss him. I never want to stop. He's so smart, he went to Columbia, he listens to opera. If you ask him what *sine qua non* means, he'll tell you. He'll pronounce it. Anything, he'll tell you. *Quid pro quo.* He reads Braille. Margaret wasn't his type at all. Not in the slightest. But then a person's own *mother* might not be their type. Did you ever think of that? My own mother wasn't. She wasn't my type at all! But yet I loved her. And listen, just imagine…he had just got back from Spain. His girl had another guy, he really loved her, beautiful, well, he told Margaret he knew what was coming, he felt it, he was ready…but yet it knocked him for a loop. And he and his brother, it was like in the Civil War, brother against brother. Though after Margaret died, Penny took it on her self to get in touch with Sidney and tell him about Margaret dying and Gene being—left—"

"Does he love you?"

"Well, you see, that's just the point. How would I ever know? Look at the way my eye looks. If he could *see* me, would he even—like me?"

"Of course he would. All your eye is, is cocked a little. Actually, it's kind of cute. You're cute yourself. People would think so if you'd only let them. But you won't let them."

"Besides," Rosetta babbled on, "I'm just in the category of Margaret. No education. Of course I'm younger, he and I are the same age, while she—But if he hadn't lost his sight, could *she* have got him? Never. And that's how I feel about myself…"

"What I'd like to get straight is, are you and he *going* together?"

"Oh, no! Margaret only just died two months ago."

"So the problem hasn't really come up yet?"

"No, but I took him up to the hospital that night she died. And that's another thing that makes me feel awful. I was there with him in the waiting room…it was about eleven then, but he said he thought he'd stay till she was out of the recovery room, and I was just saying 'Well, then, Gene, if you don't mind I think I'll go on home.' Because I knew he could get a taxi back to the hotel. And he said 'Okay, Rosetta, and thanks again a million…' Earlier, while I was waiting, I ran into this girl that Lavonne and I went to beauty school with. Rilla Johnson. She runs the beauty shop up there at Holy Rosary. But she's going to sell it—probably already *has*—because she met this man in the hospital, broken neck, and now she is—or was—moving to Las Vegas. An older man. Gee, she looked different…hair like yours is going to be…"

She rubbed a strand of hair clean of the bubbly white paste and bent close to inspect the color. No, miles to go yet, miles to go before I sleep…She did not say: he knows poetry. She did not say: I love him for the dangers he has passed…

"So then what happened?"

"I said I thought I'd leave, and he said—And then was when the nurse came and told him Margaret was dead. It was so strange. I mean, I saw the *beginning* of their life together, the very minute they met and everything, and now I saw the *end*. And he couldn't cry, not having any eyes, and I thought, oh, God, not to be able to cry, and my arms went out to him and around him, and his around me, and all I could think of was, oh, my darling, and...I wanted to kiss him, not on the cheek like a friend, a trusted friend, but...truly! And I was so ashamed."

"But if you *love* him—?"

"But don't you see? It was the hour of his wife's *death*. And not only that, I knew then I had always loved him and wished he was mine. And maybe in my heart that morning when I ran back into her room with that man, when it looked like she was having a heart attack but it was really a ruptured spleen—did you ever hear of such a thing?—and she looked like she was dying, why, maybe, they say in our subconscious...I wished she would...I don't *remember* wishing...but I very well might have. In order that I...And another thing, you know Margaret and I were down at the Union depot when it happened in the first place..."

"When *what* happened?"

On Rosetta babbled, above the hair growing ever lighter with each application of white henna and seventeen-volume peroxide. That is the stuff that does the business. It is tedious. It hardens in a hard-to-wash-out cake all over your head. And with black hair like Mrs. Smith's, the paste must be applied with a toothbrush to every strand *pushing against the grain*, then allowed to work out its strength, then washed off and a new batch applied, not once, but maybe five times, and each time dried beforehand. It was a wonder the poor woman could stand it, and indeed sometimes her scalp burned so that tears came into her eyes and she bit her lip, but it had to be done. For reasons of her own *it had to be done*, and so she bore it bravely, as women do. And Rosetta babbled on, her face white with weariness. "You see, why we were down there—The manager was named Mr. Wintler..."

And now she would never know what the "most peculiar" thing was that had kept him and Margaret when he first started on the job from having a love affair, because the only one who knew *that* was Margaret. And she was dead...It seemed like such a sad thing, not to know. Not for curiosity's sake, but just when people's *secrets* vanish, too. Their little secrets. Death's so *sad*. And here *she* herself was, Rosetta said, worse than Viola any day—!

"Viola?"

A vulture if there ever was one, flying and circling around. Waiting for Penny to drop in her tracks so she could have Jake. She saw them at Margaret's funeral. It was just disgusting. Viola, watching and waiting. That's why she hated herself, Rosetta said. And another thing, maybe *she* ruptured Margaret's spleen in the first place when she fell on her down at the station, though if she did she couldn't help it. They got so scared when the train suddenly—! And here was Gene...

"You know what you're doing? Deliberately putting obstacles in your path."

"We still... talk. But it's not the same. And here I wanted—I'll be working along and all of a sudden I'm thinking how it would be if I invited him to dinner, I'm thinking what to serve. Shrimp cocktail, steak, I'm cutting it up for him..."

"Like the song. Come on-a my house, I'll give you peaches, pears..."

"I'll see us, I'm feeding him, like that picture in our reader, I don't know if you had that one in your school, 'Feeding Her Birds.' My heart feels so—But yet he asked me to have dinner with him here in the coffee shop one night, and I said I couldn't, I was going to a friend's house. And then another time he asked me. And I said no."

"Why did you do that?"

"Because my heart—And poor Margaret! that might not even be *dead* if it wasn't for me. Maybe if I hadn't said I'd drive her down to the depot so she could say good-bye to the baggage car with Mr. Wintler in it when it went past—! Viola circling and cawing—"

Mrs. Smith clicked her tongue and started to shake her head. But Rosetta was working on a stiff strand of hair, and the tug on her scalp hurt so much she stopped, biting her lip. Tears sprang to her eyes, only to be winked away when, looking in the mirror, she realized that the lock was light, light blonde, and that at ten to three in the morning their long ordeal was almost over.

"That's no answer," Mrs. Smith said, revitalized. "But I'll tell you what *I* think."

"About what?" Rosetta said, straightening her tired back.

"About going to a psychiatrist. Some people think it's foolish, but I know someone— would you believe she was going to *kill* herself? And now she's outside painting the house! And your basic trouble—You think that because of your eye—But don't you know by now? We *all* think we're ugly in some way. With you it's your eye, with me it's my bowlegs, and also this fellow with this yen for blondes. With somebody else it's something else. I mean, why would you *want* him otherwise? A man that can't distinguish light from dark? Ask yourself. Because he can't see what you think is *wrong*! that's why. And that's his virtue. But is that worth the sacrifice? Would *that* be worth taking on such a burden?"

"Well, you see—he was awfully brave in the Spanish war." (The glory of princes is in their pride and in undertaking great peril.)

"I grant you that. But even so—"

"He's awfully smart. It'd be like, you know—well, imagine getting to live around Einstein. And he said one time that Aristotle said, 'All men by nature desire to know.'"

"Well, they probably do. And before life is over we *will* know, maybe things we might damn well wish we didn't have to know. Hard old lessons."

"Yes, but what I mean—Oh, you know. The thirteen varieties of power they mentioned on *Information Please*. Stuff about—well, England. Important knowledge.

'Though what is that?' he said one time. 'Important information can be *anything*!' Then, it was strange—to say the least—"

"What was?"

"That night. He had never been in the car before. So we got in, I turned the switch and the radio came on, and what song were they playing? "It Had to Be You"! and he said something like, or it sounded like, although it doesn't make sense, 'So what peeps from the unhewn dolmen arch?' I know that's silly, to take that as a sign—"

"It *is* silly. If you'll pardon my saying so after you've done such a beautiful job on my hair and everything, which I know it will be when you get done, and I certainly wouldn't want to come along and hurt your *feelings*. Because by this time you and I are friends, or least I hope so, I certainly feel so, and that is why I'm going to say I think you should— Well, look at it this way. Why not take advantage?"

"Advantage?" Rosetta rubbed her tired eyes with the back of her hand.

"Of our times. The age we live in. After all, a hundred years ago such a thing didn't even exist. As a psychiatrist. And once you get it clear in your mind—that the one and only reason you *want* this man is because he can't *see* you, why, the whole thing—will just fall into place—"

Chapter Sixty-two

＊

DR. GOLDENBERG WASN'T A PSYCHIATRIST BUT A PSYCHOLOGIST, BUT THAT WAS just as good, his receptionist said, or even better. They cured you much quicker and for a lot less. Rosetta went to him because one day on her way to the furrier's up in the Jackson Building to have her fur jacket remade into a collar and cuffs for her tweed coat, and a toque, and accidentally getting off on the wrong floor, she saw his name on the pebbled glass door. So later she remembered. And Dr. Goldenberg thought Mrs. Smith was right and that what had attracted Rosetta to Gene was the fact that he couldn't *see* her and find fault. Another reason might be, he thought, that a blind man wouldn't *leave* her, and thirdly, if there was a particular person in her environment that she always thought of as a rival, well, as most people wouldn't necessarily want to go out of their way to marry a sightless individual, there would be no danger from *that* quarter. Unless of course he was a millionaire? Also, Rosetta might be confusing her enjoyment of Gene's *conversation* with enjoyment of a man's plain physical *company* (which, if he was the type who would go and fight in Spain in the first place, might be considerable) and his *masculine viewpoint*, which she could get from other males too, remember! But of course if she didn't *know* any other men? Or get out and mix?

Had she continued to go to Dr. Goldenberg, he would certainly have got to the seat of *something*, for he did seem judicious and had a whole row of framed documents on the wall behind his desk. But all of a sudden, out of a clear sky, here was Rilla Johnson on the phone telling her the other arrangement fell through and that if Rosetta wanted to take over the Holy Rosary Hospital beauty shop, she would make her the best deal she ever heard of in her life, because Pete had finally got her the Sands job! She was in like Flynn, Rilla said. So Rosetta made a quick decision and said she would take over Rilla's shop rather than stay at the Newhouse Hotel. Where Gene was, she did not say to herself. She had been there long enough, people got in a rut.

Moving up to the hospital made her miss two appointments with Dr. Goldenberg. Then, in getting into the swing of things in the hospital environment, she missed another. Then she heard that Gene had left town. So in a way the problem had solved itself, you might say, and she never went back for more treatments.

She said good-bye to Gene when she closed the hotel beauty shop. She went around saying good-bye to everybody else, so naturally he was included. They shook hands and wished each other well. But days before that, the in-beaming had gone off between them.

She always felt him seeing her even when she knew such a thing wasn't possible, felt him knowing if her glance strayed to a headline or cover picture on the rack, or casually around the lobby, as he and she stood talking. A mariner with a fix on a star couldn't see that star plainer than she felt he could see her! But then either her doubts about herself, or her feelings for him and guilty feelings about Margaret, rose up like fog and blotted her out for him, or he had his own reasons. Whatever happened, all of a sudden one day she felt that for him, her diagram and lineaments were gone. His wondrous power had been cut off as absolutely as you turn off a light. The two stood in Stygian darkness, their voices calling to each other until too far apart to hear. It was that way on the last day when Rosetta went around saying good-bye.

When Gene left for New York, he called Penny. She thought it was absolutely the thing to do, make up with his brother the way he now had (family quarrels were terrible), get acquainted with his new sister-in-law, go back there and take that dispatcher job they offered him in the new in-law's inherited moving and storage business, make a new life for himself. When Penny phoned Rosetta and told her Gene had gone back to New York, she said she was glad. A remark he had made one time came back to her, about the sorrows of banishment being infinite. Had he meant banished from New York, or banished to the world of darkness? She had kept silent then, when maybe she shouldn't. But what could she have said to the grief in his voice that day? when he spoke of his sorrows, "the city and lands of Carthage being all destroyed and circuited in exile ..." He only spoke like that the one time. She should have said ... Things happen for the best? That it's all planned out?

THE CATHOLIC SISTERS SHE GOT acquainted with after she bought Rilla's Holy Rosary beauty shop said that often. Planned out, they said. Everything! from time's beginning to somewhere down the line when *nuns personally* could wear nail polish and have a permanent wave! The concern of the majority of them for their hair surprised Rosetta, in the first place because she did not know they had any hair. Somewhere she had picked up the irrational and unfounded Protestant notion that on the day that nuns took their final vows, their yards of rippling hair came off, snip, snip, and then the awful razor, like in Paris after the war the French girls had their heads shaved who had slept with Germans. But of course that wasn't so at all, under their hoods they merely had short haircuts. And the day was coming, Sister St. Joan told Rosetta, when they could wear their hair any way they wanted! Within reason, of course. Zoopies, pageboys, bangs. Even change the *color*. Sister Faustina heard that too, the same rumor of the wind among the garden trees. Then, not based on definite knowledge, no clear evidence as to its truth, the talk began circulating that even the *habits* were to go, the old massive enclosed vestiture, and other ancient usages, so that the spoiled girls of postwar America in its profusion would come and be nuns in the usual numbers and the calling not die out.

Sister Perpetua heard that things would proceed so far that instead of refectory meals and tiny cells along a gallery like for catacombed monsters of an extinct race in a worked-out stone quarry, they could live in apartments! buy their own groceries! Sister Mary Martha heard they could even invite a man to supper! Other hearsay was they could wear nylons, pretty shoes, makeup, have *braces* put on their teeth, warts taken off and even have their ears pierced if they wanted. Well, not that, perhaps. But the old ways were on the way out. Five years from now, ten years, maybe even *next* year, the old customs would be deader than the first Abbess of Remiremont. If that was so, Holy Rosary's oldest nun, Sister Bridget, said (who took her final vows the day O'Donoghue of the Glens died in County Kerry) then she was going to write her sister's oldest boy for a ticket back to Ireland, take up residence in Nanny's Cave and never step forth again. But of course it would never happen. Wait and see, said Sister Mary Martha.

Rosetta heard this talk circulating in the nuns' community because hardly a day passed but that one or another of the Order didn't come in for something. They lived on the premises, on the top floor under the eaves, worshipped in the chapel and worked about the hospital, some as trained nurses, some in the office or linen room, and Rilla before she left said this was one of the beauty shop's few disadvantages. Because the nuns would come in and you had to do them free. But Rosetta didn't think that was so bad. It was fun, in fact, to have one of them in her black surplice swishing along the floor, her sash-like cingulum, rosary, crucifix and gabled headdress, softened along the edge by a fold of white stuff, peep around the door towards evening, when they thought Rosetta was about ready to go home, and ask for a haircut or quick shampoo. Like entertaining a ghost-bird or a capriciously irregular living curiosity. "Come in, of course, I'll be right with you," Rosetta would say. For some reason they avoided Sharon, perhaps because her time didn't coincide with theirs, and Sharon was just as glad, she said, not because the work was free gratis and no tips, but because they made her feel odd, like they weren't normal. Or at least they did at the beginning. Later she got used to them, seeing them in the cafeteria and around the hospital, the sisters were just like you and me really, homely, not so homely, Sister Genevieve who worked in surgery was even beautiful.

Because if you look good without a speck of makeup or a spear of hair showing, wearing white that yellows your skin and teeth, and black that squashes you down like a heavy weight, why, you are *it*, the real McCoy. A woman lived in Greece like that one time by the name of Phryne. When Rosetta made her acquaintance long years after this in the pages of Galen, the weird old doctor who lived in the second century A.D., she thought of Sister Genevieve, because she was one person who could do what Phryne did at a party one time, lead off a game of Follow the Leader by washing her face in a bowl of water and coming up shining like a rose, a stunt not popular, of course, with the other hetaerae, whose painted faces after they were washed disgraced them. It's the features.

SHARON OPENED THE SHOP AT eight in the morning and left at four. Rosetta came around noon and stayed—before she got married—till eight in the evening or even nine or ten. After the dinner hour was when a sister would first peep in, then venture in. Never, however, if one of the two priests in residence was at the shampoo tray or in the chair, there seemed to be kind of an unwritten law about nuns and a priest being in a beauty shop together. Rilla made no mention of the priests' patronage, but Rosetta had not been in possession long when "smoky and drinky old Father Lane," as Sister Faustina called him, edged in while looking in another direction and wondered about a quick trim. Then the other priest, young and opalescent Father Boniface, said he wondered if just this once—? after which cutting Father Lane's coarse gray hair and Father Boniface's baby-fine reddish curls became a part of the assistance Rosetta seemed bound to render, like knight-service, as a condition of holding her lands. But she didn't mind. The priests were interesting customers who wouldn't have ventured upon the former owner Rilla's stiff, sprayed theatricality in a thousand years.

But Rosetta couldn't help thinking her reception into their grace was due mainly to the cast in her eye. It was really funny about a defect like that. Babies and little children would start out keeping their distance while they deliberated. But those past that period in life when everything peculiar or individual excites dislike and is in itself an offense seemed to find her imperfection calming. The lost and strayed would ask where you caught the Highland Drive streetcar. The ones without their watch would want the time. Beggars (not many on Salt Lake's clear and spacious streets) singled her out with the confidence of siblings. Those in liquor approached like long-lost kin. Not that she felt *hurt* by this. She found it touching. Still…

BUT SCIENCE IS WONDERFUL, AND men of science never stop discovering. They demonstrate astounding truths from morn till night. That is why nobody with cancer or a tiny petrified brother sitting on his hip, the wobbling, the flapping, the snouted like an ant-eater or anyone unhappy should ever despair. Tomorrow will be better, it really will. Rosetta's mother took her to an eye doctor before she could walk, Wyandra took her, she went herself in later years. Now? Not yet. The word was always the same: *inoperable.* But they keep on, the seekers after truth. Rest assured of that, my dear. While you sleep they continue like your heartbeat, your soft breathing, the dreams deep under your mind. They do not take their ease, they toil, fall back, then toilsomely advance again.

So one morning old Dr. Reynolds, who was on the staff, stopped Rosetta in the corridor. She now cut the doctor's hair, as well as the resident priests'. He became a customer when his regular barber, Fred, across the street from the parking lot, was felled with a coronary and, happening to pass the beauty shop's open doorway one evening, he saw Father Lane in the chair. "If you can cut this old so-and-so's hair, why can't you cut mine?" His patronage encouraged another doctor or two to slip in, as timidly at first as if stepping into an Indian Mussulman's forbidden zenana. The old doctors, also custom-ers of unfortunate Fred, who by this time had died, none of the young ones, and Rosetta felt quite honored.

Almost at once Dr. Reynolds brought up the subject of her divergent strabismus, a doctor wouldn't ignore something like that out of politeness, and said he bet the eye man could do something about it. But Dr. Brophy, when he brought him in one noontime on their way to the doctors' dining room, after he took a look at Rosetta's eye with about the same personal reference as a vet with a horse or dog, said no, this was just the kind of case he was talking about. Surgery couldn't be done because … As they took their leave he was dropping Latin words right and left, and Dr. Reynolds, not above prescribing sulphur and molasses in springtime and mustard plasters in winter, was looking entangled and confused. Looking after them and also for Sharon to come back from the cafeteria so she could go to lunch herself and get a package of Luckies from the machine, Rosetta drew a sigh.

But never a day, all should remember who are fretted, or corrupt, corroded and consumed in secret, but what *somewhere* in the world the most astounding truths like opals in a mine are being found. And so one morning Dr. Reynolds, meeting Rosetta in the hallway, stopped and asked her if she saw the piece in the paper about the eye men's convention up at the Hotel Utah! Because according to the write-up …Dr. Brophy claimed the guy was a bag of wind, but that was just the green-eyed monster. The *A.M.A. Journal* certainly didn't think so. Dr. Fremoth's was the cover story, and he was the one of the whole eye convention with his picture in the Tribune.

Or in other words, never give up, because today, tomorrow …

And "Yes," Dr. Fremoth said. Rosetta's condition *did* lend itself to certain of the new techniques. Not one hundred percent successful, but in her case worth a try. So when he got back to San Francisco—he and his wife were flying to Hawaii for a little vacation—why, if she wanted to call for an appointment …

It took a while to see the results, however, as that side of her face was blackened clear up into her temple and down across her cheekbone. Lumpy with swelling too, she looked, said Sharon when she got back, like she'd been sorting wild cats. But the swell-ing went down, the black changed to purple, then to blue, pale green, yellow, then faded away. And then …

Have you not heard the saying, "Place a man of feeling in a Hussar's uniform and he will move like a Hussar"? The uniform makes civilian recruits act like soldiers! Place a girl of feeling into Beauty's golden line of mail, and she—! Though perhaps thirty-five is a little old to set up as a beauty. The thing that gave Rosetta pause, how could putting right so tiny a part of the whole anatomy as an *eye* suddenly give you a nice figure, nice features, nice hair and a nice complexion? Even sharpen your ears! and make more hear-able compliments for all these things you never knew you had? At first …oh, you mean *me*? She felt as fraudulent as the African orchid that gets attention for a special type of wasp not by offering nectar but by fooling the male wasp into thinking its flower is a female of his own species! Look, you just imagine—!

Paul most certainly did. He thought she looked just like the girl in the commercial, the one where…Paul was a contractor and builder, he built the four-plex Sharon and Robert lived in, and Rosetta met him at a surprise party she felt she had to attend because Sharon worked for her. Another beau she suddenly found herself possessed of was Stuart, related in some manner to the owners of the beauty supply company she bought her supplies from. He thought she resembled the girl on the Clairol bottle, or at least quite a bit.

Even Lavonne said, "Gee, Rosetta, you look nice and I don't just mean your eye, you must have a new girdle on or you've been dieting or something, and I love that color lipstick, what color is it? And that's a good permanent, too, the cut's what's important." Inferior conjunction with the sun, however, lasting too many years, can make it hard indeed to "move like a Hussar," and it didn't help to have Lavonne back in town looking as beautiful as ever.

BUT POOR LAVONNE, AFTER ALL! two little boys, Gary and Bobby, to raise, a husband vanished off the face of the earth with seventy-seven thousand dollars belonging to the company he worked for, no property except their five-year-old Buick, a few clothes (not so few), her diamond engagement ring…

When she got to Salt Lake she took the boys out to her in-laws in Bountiful, living on a farm would do wonders for them till she found a place to live and got on her feet. How she was going to do that, she didn't know. *She* certainly didn't have any of the seventy-seven thousand! though when it came out that Darrel didn't just take it in a lump sum but had gotten away with it over the previous few years, his mother blamed Lavonne's extravagance. It was so unfair, she didn't even have a fur coat! But of course Mrs. Cartmill had to blame somebody besides her son. His folks were just destroyed by Darrel. To climb so high as to have your picture taken with the President of the United States and then to fall so low as to steal, abscond and disappear without a word, it just shattered them. Lavonne was not shattered. As long as people still thought she should go in the movies, her strength was as the strength of ten.

And she was *so* happy to see that Rosetta was finally branching out a little instead of spending her evenings reading library books, the Book of the Month and magazines, even if she was jumping out of the frying pan into the fire with that Great Books course. How people could sit around for two or three solid hours talking about the difference between tragedy and comedy when anybody knew that one was sad and one was funny was a mystery to her. Far better for you physically, your mental health and every other way, to do what she herself was doing, take a course at Arthur Murray's. In a way, though, the money was wasted, in that any step that had come in style since she and Darrel used to go dancing Lavonne had down pat in about a minute. But the main reason was that Paul didn't dance! He was this big outdoorsman, hunting and fishing.

Paul wasn't what you might call Rosetta's boyfriend, she was just going out with him once in a while at the time of Lavonne's advent home, she didn't really love him or anything, did she? and anyway she had Stuart, it wasn't as if she was being stranded with no one. And Stuart was the best-looking of the two. His car was also newer. Of course Paul had a Cadillac, but it was an ugly color. Rosetta by the window, idly watching him park it out in front of the apartment house (a process that took about five minutes, as it was parallel parking) one time when he came to call for Lavonne soon after the two of them met, said that she had read that in France before the Revolution, that color was called "Caca Dauphin"—"caca" meaning what you might suppose, and "Dauphin" meaning the Crown Prince. Rosetta even thought Paul's *hair* and *eyes* were that color! so that showed her heart wasn't broken or anything. You don't imply that somebody's automobile, hair and eyes are the color of a cow-pile if you're very fond of them. So that put Lavonne's mind at ease. It wasn't her fault if he fell for her like a ton of bricks. And just at the psychological moment he would have married her, too, but a divorce is more complicated when your husband disappears, and so that moment passed.

But by that time Lavonne knew Paul was no great bargain anyway, even if he did build and own the four-plex Sharon and Robert lived in, several small prefabricated houses and the three-story apartment house he let her have an apartment in rent-free. One of his crummy little apartments with one closet not even as deep as a clothes hanger, cupboard doors that wouldn't shut, a shower, no bathtub, no place to plug anything in and walls the color of…well, talk about "Caca Dauphin." But all right, say it was nice not to have to pay rent. There was more to life than just rent, my dear. There was sympathy and understanding that would make a man realize that to have to get out and *work* at age thirty-five, after fifteen years of a person's own free time, was by no means pleasant. And what disgusted Lavonne was the man pretending to be so generous. The way he would come staggering in with these big sacks from the grocery store, and what would they be? Toilet paper, paper napkins, paper towels, facial tissues!—on sale. And forty-watt light bulbs, since he took care of utilities.

One thing she knew: she was *not* setting the alarm and getting up at daylight to go to the best job in the world, for it said in this article in *Photoplay* that a famous French actress had said that rule number one for preserving beauty was to wake up when you would naturally wake up and not by an alarm clock harshly going off or a servant rudely parting the curtains. As luck would have it, she could continue to wake up when she woke up. Because just at this trying juncture, Sharon told Rosetta she was pregnant and going to quit and not work anymore, because Robert had got another raise and she didn't have to. That left her job open and Lavonne could go to work for Rosetta, which eased the transition back into the laboring force a lot, especially since Rosetta was even willing to trade shifts and work from eight a.m. to four p.m., while Lavonne came on at twelve noon and quit at eight. This arbitrary pushing around of other people's lives and calculating and wresting far-reaching events for her benefit by her guardian angel seeming no more out of the common to her in her beauty's splendor than to royalty the factotum who goes ahead and takes charge and smooths the way, her thanks were low-keyed. Still, it was rather nice, how things worked out.

Aren't men brutes, though! really. Rosetta should be glad that Stuart was the one she got to keep. Paul was nothing in so many ways! guns, fishing rods, tents, boats, boots up to the hip, never a murmur about how much all these cost, but scream like an eagle over a light left burning! And *no* social life, cocktail dresses just hanging in that miserable closet, formals pinned in a sheet…while Rosetta was having all the fun.

Well, it *was* fun, glamorous, driving miles in practically a convertible to eat steak and a baked potato wrapped in aluminum foil and green salad in a roadhouse, and pick out songs on the jukebox and dance—maybe there would even be a little orchestra! and look down a great sweep of mountainside at Salt Lake City spread out like a swathe of stars trembling in their light. Then driving home again along the canyon roads. Glamorous, romantic, the radio on, the winds of evening blowing. Stuart was quite a romantic type himself in that he knew a lot of the words to songs and would sing and whistle them absorbedly, like a singer listening to a recording of himself. He didn't like to be interrupted with remarks about this and that, not when singing or actually any time, for the reason that he said he heard nothing but yakking all day long. So much so that although the gals in the shops around town were a lot of laughs, and delivering beauty supplies got you out in the fresh air, he sometimes thought he would take advantage of the G.I. Bill before it ran out and go to business college and become a Certified Public Accountant. A man who wants to do that is not a complete idiot. Other proofs of his intelligence that Rosetta named over to herself after he asked her to marry him and she was trying to decide if she should were his ability to fix his car himself, operate a ham radio and remember almost any telephone number he had ever called. This is not someone who is retarded.

As Gene Abeloff expressed it one time—She couldn't remember exactly. Something about the "ancient alphabets of jealous nature," and how—She often thought of Gene saying things just in the lobby there, both of them standing. How nice it would have been to have sat down with him just once and really talked.

After he left, Gene didn't have anyone write to anybody for him, but Penny, when she called Rosetta, would still bring his name up once in a while. Poor Gene, he must be happy? reunited with his brother, some real home life for a change, made to feel useful working the phone in his brother's in-laws' moving and storage business? Rosetta would say she hoped so, some offhand remark like that, a little too offhand for Penny not to mention him again. Like the hermit in his cell who reinvented on his own the already invented typewriter, Penny had discovered in the isolation of her long sickness that part of the mental field whose processes take place beyond attention's range. What she said, she said to hear the words come back that *weren't* said, the undertow. Rosetta trying to make it seem that Gene was nothing to her! Her husband Jake pretending what *he* pretended, that he would grieve when she was gone. Her so-called friend Viola. Human pretense! Penny saw through it now as through the window of a bathysphere. It was her hobby-horse. Her pleasure in it was why she didn't tell Viola, the woman waiting in the wings for Jake, to go sit on a tack. The study of Viola's crummy little subconscious was worth the outrage of the woman's friendship. It was like putting up with a pinochle partner you despise rather than not play. Naturally Penny invited Viola to her and Jake's eighteenth wedding anniversary party. She wouldn't miss seeing her fraudulence in action, the trickery Viola would practice at a time like that, for the world.

THE EIGHTEENTH IS MOTHER OF pearl. What saddened Rosetta when she shopped for a suitable gift, finally finding a vase with pieces of nacre glued all over it quite prettily, was how it looked like it would last for hundreds of years, while human life went quicker than a bunch of flowers. Stuart didn't like remarks about life being brief or being anything, better run through the multiplication tables or think of telephone numbers. He was invited to Penny's party too, but couldn't make it on account of his lodge having installation of officers that night. However, if it wasn't too late, maybe he would drop by the apartment and have a cup of Sanka. But don't look for him, he said, installation night, some of the officers were off hunting and other guys had to pinch-hit, those that knew the work—which they were getting fewer by the day—so that guess who would probably bear the brunt! and it was all by heart, too, no looking in the book.

Penny called Lavonne up and invited *her* to come to her anniversary party too, and at first she said gee, she was sorry, but she and Paul had something on that night. But when the date turned out to be the night before the opening of male deer season and he and some friends left town before daylight, she told Rosetta she really could go if it wasn't that she had to give herself a cream pack oil treatment, pumice her feet, use a callus neutralizer and try out that new cream fortified with human placenta. "How long will Paul be gone?" "A week." "Well, do it the next night then," Rosetta said, so Lavonne said okay.

ROSETTA PICKED HER UP AT seven-thirty, it was still light. Lavonne came running out looking like a million dollars, in white with pearls. When in doubt, wear white. And so they went to the anniversary celebration—if you could call it that with weakly clamorous Penny in the jaws of death, her face a death mask—found the porch light on batted by moths, found lights in every window, the last time Penny would light her bungalow up like a Christmas tree. The door was open. They went up the steps...

"And you remember Frank?" Jake said. "Frank Tracy? Married now and four kids! The Spanish Civil *War*?"

Lavonne had never met him, so Jake said Frank was one of the Lincoln Brigaders who came through here on their tour—how many years ago was it now?—on their way to California—

"And here we are again," Frank said, "and here *you* are, and who is *this* beautiful creature?"

"Lavonne," Rosetta said, looking around and beyond him into the living room and wondering if—But wouldn't Penny have said something? Wouldn't she have *told* her? Her heart began to beat fast.

"Lavonne?" Frank said with satisfaction, looking her up and down. "Well, hi ya, Lavonne."

"And this here's…You remember Rosetta," Jake said. "She's the one…Remember that night, Rosetta? First time this bugger's been back here since that crazy night!"

"When was that?" Lavonne said, politely pulling her hand away from both of Frank's.

"You should of been here," Jake said. He turned to Rosetta. "Remember next morning when Penny called you and you hot-footed it down and found us all nearly ready for the morgue?"

Before Rosetta could answer, Lavonne said, "The *morgue*?" as though she hadn't heard the whole story long ago.

"Well, that's not what I'm ready for *now*," Frank leaned over to murmur into Lavonne's ear.

"You know, Lavonne," Rosetta said. "This woman brought some sandwiches to Penny and Jake's party and they developed ptomaine or something—"

"I never been able to look liverwurst in the face since!" Jake said.

"That was the night Gene Abeloff met Margaret—and later they got married—" Penny said from the doorway. "Gene and Frank spent the night with us here and it was one to remember, I'm telling you. They were still sick enough the next day not to go on with the other Brigaders to California, and by the time their tour was over and they doubled back here on their way back to New York, why, Gene—"

"So we're doing it again, my old buddy and me," Frank said. "On tour—" This time not as Paul Reveres, however, just back from Spain, criss-crossing, warning the country the bums are coming! from Germany, Italy, watch out. This time it was a pleasure trip. The Lincoln Brigaders…a reunion. "Down in L.A."

"And this here's…"

"You don't have to introduce Rosetta to *Gene*, you dumb bunny," Penny said. "They saw each other practically every day for—Oh, excuse me, Gene!"

"What for?"

"For saying you 'saw.'"

"I did," Gene said quietly, putting out his hand. "I'd know her anywhere. Hello, Rosetta."

Due to confession, a *Catholic* married man with four children feels more free than, say, a Methodist, but the way the Spanish War veteran Frank Tracy fell for Lavonne like a ton of bricks that night, he would no doubt have worked around to where when the party broke up he would take her for a moonlit drive in their rented car and then home even if he had been a Methodist. And if it had been two in the morning instead of just a little past eleven. That left Gene with no way to get back up to the Newhouse Hotel, where he and Frank were staying, had not Rosetta said he could ride with her. This was decided on the street under the street light in the littering leaves, the two cars parked on the same side of the street with only somebody's driveway between. Wasn't that a coincidence?

"Well, don't do anything I wouldn't do!"

"Don't you either."

"See you tomorrow, Lavonne."

"Bye, Rosetta!"

"Good night, sweet repose, sleep on your back and not on your nose!"

"That guy!"

GENE DIDN'T GET OUT AT the hotel, where Rosetta parked in the taxi zone, because he was mentioning the … pockets of feudal and even Stone Age mentality to be found about the land. And how … and then … And she was telling him … the shop … the nuns …

"Coffee? A drink? The times I asked, you wouldn't eat with me. Was that because—"

"Gene, listen."

"Come up and talk, Rosetta."

"Oh, I can't, Gene, really." A deep breath and then, "*You* come up and talk."

"SIT HERE, WHY DON'T YOU?"

And so in her apartment he sat in the green armchair for the first time and she made coffee.

HE CALLED HER FROM CALIFORNIA.

Lavonne couldn't believe her *ears*, that somebody with a chance to marry a wonderful person like Stuart, with a good job, whose relatives owned the beauty-supply company, nice-looking, high up in the Masonic Lodge, lovely car, and then to turn around and tie herself down with a *blind* man. "Why, you won't even exist!" she said.

"How do you figure that?"

"Why, because…" Lavonne didn't know how to say it, but never an absolute, always a contingent being, *she* wouldn't exist without the instructions in admiring eyes. Unless they *looked* at her, the human doll she had carefully made of herself lay on a dark shelf, consumed away like a brindled moth.

"Oh, I'll exist, I'm not afraid of *that*," Rosetta said.

"But after all your trouble and expense! And it turned out so *well*, your operation. To see you now, you'd never know how your eye used to look. But if it's all going to turn out like *this*, you might just as well not have bothered. I mean, who cares about something that spoils a person's appearance if they're just going to marry a blind man anyway!"

Rosetta decided not to say that *Stuart* was the blind man, and Gene was the one who could see.

"Why, you could be the most beautiful bride in the world," Lavonne said to the mirror like an actress practicing for a later, more formal appearance, then turning to give Rosetta a pitying look, "and your bridegroom wouldn't even know!"

But he knew, all right. And in fact *because he knew* was how it happened that Rosetta actually was!

Chapter Sixty-three

✳

OF COURSE THE BLAZE OF BEAUTY DIDN'T LAST, IT WAS JUST THAT ONE BLINDING flash, you might say, at her highest meridional altitude, then sinking away to just her usual flicker. At least as far as Lavonne was concerned. Otherwise, working in the shop with Rosetta every day from noon, when Lavonne came on, till four, when Rosetta went home, she would have been quite put out of concert. And what about the shop's mirrors thrown into confusion crying "You! you!" to *two* lollapaloozas?

The rest, the beauty that then commenced building inside Rosetta and piled up during the next years like laminae, didn't matter. Or wouldn't have even if Lavonne had known of the deposition going on. She didn't, of course. All *she* knew was, Rosetta gradually changed to the point where . . . In her opinion, it was just too bad. With her eye *fixed* and everything, she could have done so much better, branched out, went places and did things, met people on tours, kept up with the dances, had a real fun *life*. But instead of that, what did she do? Took on the burden of a man stark staring blind, not even *eyes*. Married him! Read more books than ever! Changed . . . stayed the same . . . did nothing! So what good was the operation she waited for all her life? Believe her, if the time ever came that *her* operation was possible, Lavonne thought, the one restoring her to what she had been—or thought she had been—*she* would certainly know how not to waste the time!

Because men were so mean, so hateful. You would think cleavage was part of the rights and privileges of their being born. And they were so contrary that even if down in their hearts they really didn't *care* one way or the other, or even if they looked on and really hated (as some men did) bosoms as morbid growths instead of formed of the normal tissue of the chest, they would pout, and act like heirs that had been only left one dollar.

When Rosetta ran across the medical journal again (on the top shelf where she put it to return to the lady intern who left it after her shampoo-set and then was sent to another hospital, so she never got it back) with the article in it about some of the surviving Bataan Death Marchers who, after they were rescued, *grew pendulous, female-looking breasts that had to be removed surgically* in that military hospital down in San Francisco, she thought Lavonne would be fascinated, because it perhaps kind of explained the spurt of mysterious growth to *her* breasts years after they had attained their normal (somewhat large) size. Of course the starvation the Bataan Death Marchers went through that reduced them to skeletons was the fault of their Japanese captors, while what happened to Lavonne was something she did to herself. But, voluntary or involuntary, the *results* were the same. Due to the stress of starvation, both marchers and Lavonne had had their hormonal systems thrown so completely out of gear that when they started to eat again (and gorge), their breast tissue somehow began to activate pathologically. Not all the Death Marchers, of course, but those of a certain *glandular vulnerability*. Like, apparently, Lavonne.

She was *not* fascinated. Rosetta had little to do, she thought, to point the article out to her. "As you can see, they were *men*. There's no comparison whatsoever!"

"But, Lavonne. See here where it says…the whole hormonal system…starvation can cause…It doesn't matter whether it's a man or a woman. In a certain percentage of cases, breast tissue will suddenly take this spurt and…"

"Are you trying to say *I caused it myself*?"

"Well, no, only—whether the *Japanese* starve somebody or a person starves their own *self*—"

"So *I'm* to blame!"

"I didn't say that."

"You did. You're blaming *me*." She burst into tears. "For falling into the hands of a quack?" No one will take the blame if they can help it. Not willingly will they blink the mote from their eye and see that it was *this* characteristic in me that brought the tragedy about in the first place—*this* vanity, *this* greed, *this* whatever. *This* brought the house down around my ears. It wasn't my fault, we say, victim, bystander as I was, standing there minding my own business, without one thought of harm or wrong.

Then Rosetta realized the story Lavonne must tell and have told each time, like the knight-at-arms entering the lists—Captain Carpenter! over and over sidling out to clash with the world's harms, *that* harm of all harms: rejection. "No, I love you not." She would say…

They gathered the flowers of the oak tree, of broom and of meadowsweet, which with their mumbo-jumbo they used to fashion the most beautiful and most perfect maiden in the world…who then…incensed with the love of finding love went forth…only to meet with jealousy and malediction. Or no, fever, a sudden fever. Or no, this strange…poisonous substance. But all a bewitchment. Magic to cast it off she would have found, or the spell's potency would have worn off by itself had not she fallen on an evil day into the hands of…Scientists, doctors, we respect them so, but they are sometimes stark staring crazy. The white coats, the rubber gloves, we think they are so sterilized and clean, but sometimes their wearers are stained old abortionists with dirty fingernails, they drink, smoke big black cigars, take dope, they're rotten with disease, their hand trembles, they hate women, a woman betrayed them once and they will have revenge, they rent this terrible old office above a plumbing shop, filthy, old green blinds, tattered old *Life* magazines, you go up a side stairway…Come in, my dear. Will you walk into my parlor. And! Many a young and innocent girl has been crippled for life by such a man! by falling into the hands…

But I myself had nothing to do with it.

"Hamartia," Gene said when Rosetta told him about Lavonne. The tragic flaw that makes the tragedy that makes the tragedian. H-a-m-a-r-t-i-a. A Greek word. Lady Macbeth. Oscar Wilde. Fatty Arbuckle.

"For that matter, this girl we knew at beauty school that her boyfriend killed her," Rosetta said. "Colleen, her name was." Sometimes she would enlarge on such a subject and Gene, the whales of his intelligence exulting under him, would listen with interest.

"You're right," he said when she came to the sad end. "Poor Colleen brought it on herself. Did they ever find Balsha?"

"Not that I ever heard of."

"Hamartia," he said. "But present company, shall we say? excepted?"

Present company in the Groves. She told him that when she first heard the expression, she was ironing her uniforms in Nancibel's breakfast nook while she listened to *Information Please* on the radio. The Groves of Academe. Where you went to school in the cool shade of the trees...

In Athens, Gene said. About a mile from the center of town. A fellow by the name of Academus owned this house out there surrounded by this viridarium (though that word is Latin, not Greek). It means: a pleasure garden. It had trees and grass. Whether Hipparchus, when he bought it after Academus died, landscaped it any more extensively we don't know, but he put a wall around it. The next owner was a very rich man named Cimon. He put in walks, groves and fountains. Money was no object. When he died he left the property to the city as a little park, probably thinking it would be called Cimon's Park. But people still said, "Let's stroll out to Academus's grove." Shall we? To the Groves of Academe, the first university in the world.

And that is what it became, Gene said, when Plato, who lived a few blocks away, sauntered there to hold classes in the open air. And Plato's scholars didn't come with him to sit on the grass and learn about wheels and axles, to operate the potter's lathe, make brick or how to be a caulker. Their object was the cultivation and promotion of literature, to demonstrate truths, observe the mysteries of the natural world, then to try to bind these things together. It was a tough curriculum, and all for nothing. That is to say, no diploma at the end, no high honors, no job waiting at General Electric, nothing but the cover full of foxes, the gallop at full cry...

One of these scholars was Aristotle, Gene said. When Plato died, Aristotle took his place. Then came Speusippus and Xenocrates, Arcesilaus, Polemon, the scholars ever disposed about the grass... And the olive groves of Academe lasted a thousand years.

GENE'S LASTED BUT TWENTY. AND the only scholar in his *universitas magistrorum* was Rosetta. Within 2-A at the back, in a bigger apartment than the one she was living in upstairs when they got married, were their walks, fountains and shade. Well, they did have their own little hedged-in back yard, but it served more as the pure space beyond their back door and windows that indulges that instinct for expanse also known as love of liberty than got them out into the open air. An old man cut the grass and trimmed the hedge, and the climbing roses grew by themselves.

At first Gene was going to take over another newsstand, but none were available right then, and to start a new one somewhere took considerable looking into. He had plenty of time for that, Rosetta said, after he rested up and when he got tired of the study corner she fixed for him in a corner of the big living room. His easy chair and footstool stood there, the phonograph at his right hand. The dining room table opened clear out, and with its leaves put in held his Braille books and embossed-print papers, and the device he could use to put a line of words on the page, mostly for Rosetta to read when she came home, for them to ponder together. Of course she kept on working, that was the ridiculous part, Lavonne said, when she could have married Stuart and been taken care of.

But she liked working, Rosetta said, and she really did. And even Lavonne had to admit that if you had to work, a hospital beauty shop was as good as a never-ending movie. Lavonne also liked the idea of doctors running around loose. Of course they thought they were God's gift to the world, even the interns, even old has-beens like Dr. Reynolds, even homely as a mud fence with patchy crew cuts, even poor (as two or three of them were said to be) in thick-soled, run-over wingtips, driving a car you'd be ashamed to be seen in. Of course they were susceptible, especially the little short, dark individuals from some other part of the country. They would show *interest* in the halls and on the elevators making their rounds, coming from surgery. But doctors were worse than society women, or the Gray Ladies, for toeing the line and caring what each other thought. They were *snobs*, their smiles and remarks didn't mean a thing, they would buy you a cup of coffee and be all buddy-buddy and then act like they never saw you before in their life. So after a while Lavonne gave up as far as *that* element was concerned.

But it did burn her up when Miss what's her name who looked like a bag of meal tied up ugly in the pale green Arab's garment they all wore in surgery and the cap down around her ears, with those little black shoe-button eyes of hers and *long* nose and *big* nurse's shoes walked off with Dr. Tengbaum and they flew to Acapulco for their honeymoon and then she became a lady of leisure. In the case of Sister Genevieve, that was a little different, she really was beautiful, there was some excuse for that, thick creamy skin like a gardenia and those long black eyelashes, a person could understand, Dr. Lloyd falling for her and working on her resistance till she left the Order and married him when he finished his residency and went back to wherever it was. However, Lavonne said that she herself wouldn't have a doctor on a silver platter.

There were lots of other men, the orderlies, technicians, though a big percentage of them seemed to be of the type of male beauticians, in maintenance, the kitchen and cafeteria, ambulance drivers and out around the grounds. But there again you had so many mere *boys*, pimply, greasy hair…impressionable, yes, easy to bowl over, but that was just the problem, a Gray Lady forty-nine years old with a good figure, a seventeen-year-old nurse's aide in a size twenty and a half, a gold-toothed girl from Housekeeping, one of the stenographers with her only attribute long hair which wasn't even a pretty color, or yourself, it was all the same to them. Other men one might meet were the visitors to the hospital, but in time *they* fell into categories, too. The young father with the new baby. The fifty-year-old bachelor who never left home and now his widowed mother had had a stroke and was dying and what was Sonny going to do? The husband with the wife with the hysterectomy. The visiting lodge brother. The old man smelling of moth balls and brown-specked damp old books. Sometimes men were patients. Rilla Johnson's friend who got her in at the Sands Hotel in Las Vegas had been a patient with a broken neck. No one knows what fate has in store.

One kind of male patient you certainly wouldn't want to have anything to do with was…It was just so *disgusting*. Of course they were very rare, though Loretta from up on three said she had seen and heard of several such cases in her twenty-four years of nursing. The one who opened Rosetta's and Lavonne's eyes to the fact of there being individuals with that kind of a proclivity was the man brought in and laughingly scheduled by the nurse on duty for a turnipectomy, though the foreign body recovered by the surgeon from the posterior opening of his alimentary canal turned out to be a Hot 'n Sassy Summer Sausage, as it was said to have said on the label. And some years later a case would be brought in of a Certified Public Accountant with a wire coat hanger straightened out and run up through his membranous ureteral tube. That was from the front, but that happened too. And men were not the only ones in heat, temptation and concupiscence. One stormy Sunday afternoon the ambulance picked up a forty-one-year-old lady in a bathrobe wearing bedroom slippers like two dustmops and her hair in curlers. Inside her genital theca was a hundred-watt light globe; in the toil of her body and shaking of her bed, it had got away from her. Vulvae can be vulpine, very ferocious, gobble up everything in sight, broom handles, bananas, candles…The drivers carried her in like a time bomb, the globe could have shattered and she been dead. And wouldn't you think she'd have wanted to be? caught in such a predicament. The devil wipes his tail with a poor man's pride. She wasn't poor, though. Just homely and slovenly on a Sunday afternoon, and…incited to voluptuous lust. By something in the strewn Sunday paper? By Brantôme's *Lives of Fair and Gallant Ladies*? By a crotch-cutting nylon undergarment generating enough static electricity to put a computer out of order?

Gene said that David Hume once wrote to a friend that a certain book "contains no bawdy at all, though if it did, I see not that it would be a whit the worse." He personally, Hume said, and many reverend gentleman acquaintances of his were not aware of a "more agreeable subject both for books and conversation." The woman with the light globe made Gene wonder about the built-in "love mechanism" that animals appear to have that triggers off intricate courtship patterns, and whether the curious behavior of the human being corrupting himself might not also be the product of an inherited sex pattern? And in the light of a study made by an otolaryngologist of all the thimbles, spools, pipes, dried peas, safety pins, shells, jewelry, beans, coins and Cracker Jack prizes recovered from people's windpipes, nostrils, lungs and esophagi, wouldn't a comparable list of all that has gone up the *other end* throughout the ages, causing death no doubt in many instances (think of cave men days and being fixed upon a saber-toothed tiger's femur), be even more interesting?

Thomas Aquinas said true reformation ought to begin "here" and tapped his head, Gene said. But Dr. Johnson's opinion was that as the lower end was most corrupt, amendment ought logically to start there. Boswell said it all depended on whose lower end it was, thinking of the tendency in some persons to be emotionally affected and the different capacities for receiving mental and moral impressions. That human testes might vary from ten to forty-five grams in weight (a eunuchoid individual's one-half to one gram, as in the case of Paul Bern, Jean Harlow's bridegroom, who committed suicide) or that *all the problems of sex* revolve around heat, cold and two types of hormones Boswell did not know, of course. But he did know that testis tissue in mammals requires a lower-than-body temperature for superior functioning, and that the cool breezes blowing up under his kilt was why Bonnie Prince Charlie almost won back England.

AT FIRST ROSETTA WORRIED ABOUT Gene being alone all day and wondered if when he said he ought to look into getting another stand she oughtn't to encourage him to do so. But then she began to realize how important it was for him just to be in a safe, comfortable place "out of the swing of the sea," all by himself with nobody to disturb him, and just do his putterings and *think*. He thought almost for thought's sake. It was for him a metaphysical necessity. With Stendhal he said, "If I am not clear, my whole universe crumbles into nothingness." Gene thought about living, and the hours flew. He enjoyed, analyzed, and enjoyed *through* analysis whatever experience he happened to be experiencing, even being blue. He thought about things Rosetta came home and talked about at dinner or over a post-prandial cup of coffee, hospital and beauty shop happenings, the reality of other people's lives. But mostly he offered to his mind not the ease of the familiar, but the resistance of the never heard of such a thing! and would mull over subjects like solid unyielding actuality, the human need to create elites, how barbarians are a kind of solution, that most things are foreign to most people, that there is no such thing as the last word. He had a faith in knowledge, thought the world would be saved by it, though as Rosetta ventured to think to herself in later years, here we've got all these libraries groaning with books and the world isn't saved yet! *I'm* not saved. But you're more saved if you've got the foundation on which to erect an intellectual structure (within the limits of your abilities) than if you haven't. But what was "saved"? Gene liked to be asked such questions.

Well, "saved" might be to learn to bear what happens to you. Because how you bear it is more important than what it is. To line up the unchangeable amid constant change. To protect your freedom with a certain amount of discipline, the way a rancher fences in his grazing lands. To mark your pivots through the abyss, and (order being heaven's first law) run a course of action through the formless void. But because the biggest part of the entire universe of space and time can never be apprehended by direct, first-hand experience, you've got to get at it in other ways, he said. By such as the mechanism of Wyandra's perception and her memory, and by books. But books that give rise to something, like a steam engine produces steam.

Sometimes in spite of herself, Gene taught her her true interests, how valuable or valueless those interests were, how to feel at home in the world, how to locate herself in time and space and never be lost, what her capacities were, where she was limited, what America signified, what large general movements of history had produced *her*, and how to climb the stairs of particular instances to abstract conclusions. And that, just as you might develop a taste for raw tuna or Salvador Dali, you could develop a taste for enlarging your horizon, that obligation more important than any other.

As if Mount Rushmore carved with tremendous visages went clear around the circle of the earth, he made her acquainted with the great ones, the ones who hadn't got lost in the shuffle. Not that many. As Emerson said, "When we look at the world of past men, we say, what a host of heroes; but when we come to particularize, it is like counting the stars which we thought innumerable, but which prove few and rare…" She got so she could speak of them quite easily, pronounce their names.

The books she read aloud to him of evenings (they could be anything, *A Biographical Dictionary of Scottish Graduates to A.D. 1410*, Wilkins's *Coptic Gospels*, *Westward Ho!*, *Across the River and into the Trees*, *The Viga-Glums Saga*, they read anything, as a goat eats tin cans, apples or underwear off the line) taught her to say words properly. Not the books, of course, but him. It's Gae*d*elian, darling. Multi*tu*dinous. *Vol*scian.

And just as somebody who learns French begins dropping French words and phrases around, there was a fallout in Rosetta's shop from her education. At first Lavonne said Rosetta was getting *so boring*, but when it became apparent that certain customers whose pictures would be snapped at an Art Museum tea or Republican banquets costing five hundred dollars per plate, or their husbands led the symphony or built the Kennecott Building, or they handed you a full-length sable coat to hang up, that these women did not act with the same condescension towards Rosetta as Lavonne thought they did to her, she began to tune into *Sunrise Semester* and pay attention to programs on the public radio station, and read, and soon she too could allude to the way the royal princesses' heads in Ptolemaic Egypt were trained to go to a point, Genêt's "Letters from Paris,"

Wittgenstein's nervous breakdown, Palladian architecture or Ovid's wrinkle remover. The trouble was, though, there weren't enough customers that it *mattered* if they did or didn't condescend, and you certainly couldn't talk that way in cocktail lounges or at dances or the movies with a date. "Books!" Sarah, Duchess of Marlborough, was said to have said, "prithee, don't talk to me about books. The only books I know are men and cards!" Still, knowing things of no use to anyone, Lavonne found, was rather nice once you got used to it, like listening to opera.

In any case, Rosetta could not have helped the fallout, for her husband, while he did not teach anything quantitatively measurable, like all great teachers performed certain actions and said certain things which, quite without intent, created another teacher! the one hidden inside *herself*. His mind jumped into answers, he sparred with and cuffed problems around, pausing for a sally now and then, or to quote poetry, which he said was the most economical way to make certain difficult statements.

"Speaking of which," she said, "the poem called *Captain Carpenter* by John Crowe Ransom, that sounded so dumb to me and Legrand when we were in high school—" (and which she and Legrand had talked about at Saltair at the Senior Picnic, she somehow did not say) "well, later, it—said, well, a lot." Gene knew the poem, Rosetta first mentioned it to him in the course of one of their conversations, to make the point of how experience, as you go along, will make you change your opinion about things. But she had no more than cited and begun to read it aloud than she wished she hadn't. For of course within the poem were those sad lines about Captain Carpenter's "sweet blue eyes" *being plucked out* on one of his venturings out into the cruel world. But Gene's jawline only tightened a little when she came to that part. When she got to the end, she said hastily that a few days before, she had thought of *Lavonne* in connection with the poem. She hadn't, she only said that so Gene wouldn't think she connected it with him fighting in the Spanish war, but as she went on, she could see that in a way, Lavonne *had* rushed forth in the prime of her beauty against sundry harms, exactly the way brave Captain Carpenter had done. And the first terrible "stroke and counter" shore her of...her bosom.

"But really, she didn't seem to *mind* at first," Rosetta said meditatively. "She acted *glad*, she really did, because that was the thing that was spoiling her looks, and when it was gone and she had this perfect figure, why, she—And in *Vogue* or somewhere that same month, there was this piece about Agnes Sorel, the mistress of some king—"

"Charles the Seventh," Gene said.

"—and it said her breast was just the size and shape of a lovely teacup, and I could tell by the satisfaction in Lavonne's voice when she showed me the article that she was thinking of herself and because now with her A cups she had perfect proportions, while before—We were just girls, remember, not even twenty. She didn't realize then how men—"

"Could you be exaggerating her beauty?"

"I don't think so," Rosetta said after a little thought.

"Because Shaw says somewhere that his aunt said," Gene said, "that usually the 'beauty' of any given family was just the daughter who was the *least plain*."

"Well, that's not the case with her. I see the impression she makes on—In the shop, in the cafeteria, on the street. Some people, of course, would have their head chopped off before they'd give a compliment, but even *they* look at her out of the corner of their eyes. And others come up to her and say 'You're beautiful, you ought to be in the movies.' She's always heard that and still does today, even though she's thirty-seven—"

"I'm surprised she *didn't* go to Hollywood."

"Well, the times and everything. And she had Darrel."

"Read me *Captain Carpenter* again," he said. "I haven't thought of him for years."

"I think of him every once in a while," she said, and began:

Captain Carpenter rose up in his prime
Put on his pistols and went riding out
But had got wellnigh nowhere at that time
Till he fell in with ladies in a rout.

It was a pretty lady and all her train
That played with him so sweetly but before
An hour she'd taken a sword with all her main
And twined him of his nose for evermore.

Captain Carpenter mounted up one day
And rode straightway into a stranger rogue
That looked unchristian but be that as may
The Captain did not wait upon prologue.

But drew upon him out of his great heart
The other swung against him with a club
And cracked his two legs at the shinny part
And let him roll and stick like any tub.

Captain Carpenter rode many a time
From male and female took he sundry harms
He met the wife of Satan crying "I'm
The she-wolf bids you shall bear no more arms."

Their strokes and counters whistled in the wind
I wish he had delivered half his blows
But where she should have made off like a hind
The bitch bit off his arms at the elbows.

And Captain Carpenter parted with his ears
To a black devil that used him in this wise
O Jesus ere his threescore and ten years
Another had plucked out his sweet blue eyes.

Captain Carpenter got up on his roan
And sallied from the gate in hell's despite
I heard him asking in the grimmest tone
If any enemy yet there was to fight?

"To any adversary it is fame
If he risk to be wounded by my tongue
Or burnt in two beneath my red heart's flame
Such are the perils he is cast among.

"But if he can he has a pretty choice
From an anatomy with little to lose
Whether he cut my tongue and take my voice
Or whether it be my round red heart he choose."

It was the neatest knave that ever was seen
Stepping in perfume from his lady's bower
Who at this word put in his merry mien
And fell on Captain Carpenter like a tower.

I would not knock old fellows in the dust
But there lay Captain Carpenter on his back
His weapons were the old heart in his bust
And a blade shook between rotten teeth alack.

The rogue in scarlet and grey soon knew his mind
He wished to get his trophy and depart
With gentle apology and touch refined
He pierced him and produced the Captain's heart.

God's mercy rest on Captain Carpenter now
I thought him Sirs an honest gentleman
Citizen husband soldier and scholar enow
Let jangling kites eat of him if they can.

But God's deep curses follow after those
That shore him of his goodly nose and ears
His legs and strong arms at the two elbows
And eyes that had not watered seventy years.

The curse of hell upon the sleek upstart
That got the Captain finally on his back
And took the red red vitals of his heart
And made the kites to whet their beaks clack clack.

When she came to the end she said, "The kids in class thought it was the craziest poem. How could anyone get something like that published? But yet all on his own, Legrand memorized it. And now twenty years later I see we're *all* Captain Carpenters." And Lavonne, because of what had happened to her already, losing an actual part of her living self and maybe of her nature, had more connection with Captain Carpenter than anyone. For she *would* now with curly bangs and porcelain caps, false eyelashes, a merry widow and Christmas Night, sally from the gate in hell's despite…

PAUL HAD IN LAVONNE'S LIFE long been replaced by Stuart (to whom Rosetta had been briefly engaged and who Lavonne thought it would have been a shame to waste), and Stuart by George and George by Vaude and Vaude by Dave. To each of these she geared her days and nights, adapting, as she always had, her own to their needs, and let existence replace essence. In constant cosmetic metamorphosis, what she needed but did not have was the bedrock sense of self that would have helped her transcend not only her biological fate but the way love always came to some bad end. Sometimes it was the fellow who left, accusing her of giving the impression she was looking in the looking-glass even if she wasn't, of doing her beauty chores with the piety of the Kildare virgins tending St. Bridget's sacred flame, listening to him like a cephalophorous saint at Mass with her decapitated head—not exactly in those words, of course—under her arm. Or she would be the one to dump *him*. This one, because what was she getting out of the relationship after all? Nothing! That one, because he was always talking about himself. The other, because of his so-called roving eye. Another because she had someone new waiting in the wings. Another for masculine indolence and insupportable selfishness. Another for dumbness. Phoniness. Not calling next day. Well, she wouldn't either, under the circumstances. But there were always more fish in the sea than had ever been caught.

She had moved, once to the Belvedere, once to the upper half of a duplex on Sixth East. She would have brought the boys to live with her there, but kids are so loyal to their school, hers certainly were out there in Bountiful, and in a way Darrel's folks had turned them against her. She felt it (that they had) in a subtle little way. And in the Covey Apartments, where she moved to next, she really wouldn't have had room for them. But maybe if she married Palmer . . .

Chapter Sixty-four

✳

ROSETTA SAW HIM FIRST, SITTING ALONE IN THE CAFETERIA. "AREN'T YOU—?" And he was. Legrand's old buddy from high school days, the one he went to stay with down in southern Utah, the one he drove to California with … Palmer Clive. He looked older but a lot like his old self. He thought Rosetta looked like her old self, too. She didn't (she didn't think) now that her eye was fixed, but that just went to show, people don't pay half the attention to every little thing about us that we think they do. Although with some people maybe they do. The sight of Lavonne, when Palmer walked Rosetta back upstairs to the beauty shop through the maze of corridors, knocked him out. He thought she looked like a million dollars. "What have you done to yourself?" She looked even better than she had at old West High!

"Look who's talking." He looked pretty great himself, she said. And to have that dog of a wife! she didn't say.

Phyllis, in Holy Rosary for abdominal surgery, was not a dog. Rosetta thought she was quite an attractive girl, or would be as soon as she got back on her feet. She was the movie extra Palmer had let move into the Bel-Air house he and Legrand were taking care of while the owners were away, the girl who caused the rift between the two old friends Legrand and Palmer, for when Phyllis moved in, Legrand moved out, and he and Palmer never did make up. But Rosetta could see that Phyllis must have been very appealing in her young years and why Palmer, on the rebound from his first, unhappy marriage to Betty, would fall in love. She was an Okie, though, and had gone through terrible hardships like the family in *The Grapes of Wrath*, and it's the nutrition or lack of going to the dentist or something, they age more quickly than they ought to, sag in the middle, their cheeks fall in.

Rosetta got quite well acquainted with Phyllis while she was in the hospital. She thought it was only right to run in and say hello when coming back from the cafeteria or during a lull in the shop, considering how much the boys had thought of each other all through high school and later on, too. Phyllis said she certainly hadn't meant to break up their friendship, and Rosetta said she knew that, Legrand was just very sensitive, really the artist type born to clash with their environment and feel pain at every turn. Well, he had certainly been a very nice *looking* boy, Phyllis said, though she saw him just a few times, she remembered him like it was yesterday. And she bet if he hadn't rushed off in a huff like that and they had got acquainted, they'd have hit it off real well.

But life took these twistings and turnings. "Palmer only married me," Phyllis said, "to keep out of the draft."

"Oh, no, I'm sure not."

"Oh, yes. But we got along all right. Except—he wanted children. They'll say things just to be contrary." If she hadn't had her tubes tied but shelled out a kid every other year, he'd have probably been complaining about *that*, she said, all those mouths to feed. Talk was cheap, and just because she couldn't have any, all he wanted was a family, which she was sure he didn't mean at all, he just wanted to sound like this deprived father, it really made her mad. Because he certainly didn't object, to start with, that she and her two girl-friends that she hitchhiked out to Hollywood with had talked it over and had it done, to be ready in time of need. They certainly didn't want to bring a lot of helpless young ones into the world like their mothers had, with sometimes not even enough cornmeal mush to feed them—*mush*, mind you—let alone buy shoes and notebook paper for school. So nuts to that. And Palmer was *glad*, no big worries every month, no operations to have to pay for, footloose and fancy-free. But now to hear him, he's this deprived *father*. It made her sick. Still, they got along as good as anybody, and he made a living. That was one thing she could say, and she was thankful, because if it had depended on *her*...

Well, girls—! when they develop, and get to putting on makeup and using Blondex or Golden Glint and wear four-inch heels and the men start whistling, and not only men in general but the husbands in the family...So your sister gets mad at you, your cousin gets mad. But you can't help it, can you? Is it your fault if you've got "it"? So then you get to thinking you'll go in the movies. But it's not that easy. Although she was in the stadium scene in *College Capers* (1938) and in the hallway of this tenement crowding around while the police were trying to get the girl on the roof not to jump, maybe Rosetta saw that picture, *Midnight Town*? Her girlfriends, well, three's a crowd, as the saying goes, and anyway Pat married this guy in the coffee shop and moved to Salinas, and Billie's mother claimed to be dying with heart trouble, so Billie went home on the bus (and her mother was still going strong). So anyway, then *she* met Palmer...and now, as soon as she got better...

It didn't take long, considering the terrible incision, tubes going in and out in every direction and all those stitches, but long enough for Palmer to fall like a ton of bricks for Lavonne and tell Phyllis, when she got well enough to stand the shock, that it was all over between them. Well, Palmer had supposedly always been crazy about Lavonne, even at West High. Or so Lavonne said he *said*. Rosetta didn't remember anything about that and told Gene, when they sat around talking about it after supper, that Lavonne had always had this beautiful face but in high school, because of being quite heavy and skirts being long, the kids just disregarded everything. And besides, she started going steady with Darrel when she was a sophomore. And all *Palmer* seemed to care about at the time was cars. But anyway, the story *now* was that he was always carrying this torch for Lavonne!

And poor Phyllis... "But you don't want to hear dumb stuff like that."

"Oh, yes, I do," he said. "As Goethe said to Eckermann, 'Every truly excellent endeavor turns from *within* toward the world.'"

Palmer drove down to Las Vegas, resided there six weeks and got a divorce. Then Lavonne packed up and left and went down and they got married, twenty years almost to the day after high school graduation. Rosetta said for her to stop in at the beauty salon at the Sands Hotel and ask for Rilla Johnson and give her her regards. Maybe Lavonne would need a job there someday. But Lavonne wrote that they didn't stay in Las Vegas but soon after they got married went on down the line to Albuquerque, where Palmer's cousin Lester had a Buick agency, but anyway Palmer wouldn't let her work.

Two Christmases after that, Lavonne wrote on her card that Rosetta should brace herself—! And six weeks later sent a birth announcement: Judy Carmen, weight seven and three-quarter pounds. The following August Lavonne turned forty. So that was quite an undertaking, to start in at that late date and raise a daughter. But the Cartmills must nearly have Gary and Bobby raised by now. And back home in Oklahoma, Phyllis would never really have to hear about it, get that one more twist to the knife. She and Rosetta wrote a few times, then stopped, there really was nothing more to say. So the last Rosetta heard, Phyllis was living at home, her younger sister was also there with her three children, their father had Parkinson's, he sat in a chair all day, their mother had a gall bladder, Phyllis worked in a dress shop in alterations.

"Well," Gene said, "as Péguy said, 'One cannot always be thinking of Babylonian revolutions, one has honestly to live one's daily life; it is drab, and woven of coarse common thread...'" He loved to quote, the way other people like to show their coin or stamp collections. Rosetta smiled across at him and he smiled back, as though he saw her smile. Life wasn't woven of coarse common thread for *them*. Their study was unsystematic, for Gene's scholarship was slipshod (even if he hadn't been blind, it might have been), and although he possessed high energy, his organizing abilities were limited. As the years went by, Rosetta realized that. But she wouldn't have realized had not this same slipshodness and ill-organization but nevertheless *passion* set them both on the course that stretched her mind to where she *could* realize. And she loved him for that stretching, unfixed as he was, made of the only stardust upon earth that could turn around and contemplate itself. He was her alma mater, her Groves of Academe, without realizing it she had been freshman and pretentious, immature and superficial sophomore...and had run (by means of books and her husband's patient capacity for general discourse) a streak of order through chaos, marked a direction through space, fenced parts of her freedom with discipline, in manifold variety found the unvaried (or knew it was there). And then she was in her juniority, then of the body of seniors...

And Bran was an old-time Celtic hero to whom one day a marvelous woman appeared. She gave him an apple-tree branch and invited him to come and regraft it at a beautiful, remote island called Emain. "What do you say?" Bran said to his companions, and they said, "Let's go!" So off they traveled, over the sea.

He met a horseman riding on the surf who introduced himself as "the waves" and guided him to Emain. There Bran and his fellows lived an enchanted life among the women, and when one day in a fit of homesickness they returned to Ireland, they realized that not years but centuries had passed. One of the sailors leapt ashore and instantly turned into ashes. Bran and the rest put back to sea without landing...

Had mild Cordelia and her father King Lear been able to do what his poor old majesty so pitifully wanted, gone off together to a prison cell and took "upon us the mystery of things, as if we were God's spies," twenty years would have gone by for *them* as they did for Gene and Rosetta. In the twinkling of an eye. At Gene's funeral, after a fall that caused an intracranial complication made worse by an abscess and terminating in a cerebral meningitis with wild delirium for three days and nights that burnt up as in a big fire all his quotations and the wonderful things he knew, Rosetta thought how that was what he and she had really done, taken on themselves to sort out—But poor spies they were, and now it was all gone. The fine words. The fine phrases. The solutions they came across. The solutions he found for himself and told her when she came home. The years, the love, wiped out, the tears he could not shed because he gave his eyes away like you give money to the poor.

IT TOOK SOME WHILE TO realize she had not leapt ashore and instantly turned to ashes, that somehow when he, the hero of her story, put back to sea without landing, she was left (one of the mysteries of things) still living and breathing and in her own land. Had it been a dream? The grove, the shade of gnarled and eccentric pine, of cedar, balsam, quaking aspen spangled with silver, the mulberry bushes giving shade against the mud-brick walls, currant bushes, vines of ancient Athens, laurels with their incantatory leaves, the Etesian wind puffing and eddying through all this had vanished, the grass where they would sit was gone, the grounds, there had been willows too, the sound of water, these were gone, the thrushes, doves of ancient Greece, the teacher (How did the universe begin? What is human destiny on this earth? Is sense-evidence an illusion? Is change or permanence more real?)—all gone. Departed, where? east or west from their given meridian, computed by dead reckoning, dead, dead...And only the apartment left, 2-A, where the groves had stood and given shade by day and been the pillared nighttime. ("Our court shall be a little Academe.") An ordinary, perfectly ordinary apartment. "Ah, no; the years, the years! And the rotten rose," as Thomas Hardy said, "is ript from the wall."

LAVONNE SAID OF COURSE IF Rosetta *wanted* gray hair, why, more power to her, but in her opinion it was so *unnecessary*. A sign of giving up was what it was, which she would never do if she lived to be a thousand. No matter *what* happened, no matter *how* many times you were left holding the …Never! Nevertheless, she said, she would admit it could be most discouraging. One's trust in men. They lied. If nothing else they died. Or take for instance Palmer. Had she imagined even for one minute how he was going to act…An absolute *fool* from the day the child was born! Of course she was his spitting image, his and his mother's, all they ever *really* love is their mother, except the exception that proved the rule was her own case and her own sons, Gary and Bobby. But that was the Cartmills and par for the course.

But anyway, one little whimper and Palmer was up and rocking her or walking the floor. And don't think a baby doesn't know! She was spoiled so rotten. Already at *that* time! when Lavonne had it up to here and left, so just imagine what Judy Carmen must be like *now* at age eighteen. With a father so *determined* to grant your slightest wish that at forty years old he all of a sudden not only gets on his *feet* but even becomes well-to-do! when never before did Palmer Clive amount to a hill of beans. And all just for Judy. But even had Lavonne known, she wouldn't have stayed, or not unless the situation radically changed. She could have taken Judy, of course. The mother gets custody. Any judge…But she couldn't be that vindictive. Let him have her if a daughter meant that much to him. He named her, Judy Carmen, probably for someone. But who cared who? By that time, Lavonne could see as plain as the nose on your face how things were going to end. But at least he kept his promise through the years as to support, so that was something.

Sons were never the comfort. Hardly a day passed in the shop but what you heard that lament. When they grew up they had lives, wives, children, and Gary and Bobby, fortunately for them, their *security* after the Cartmills died and left them the farm out in Bountiful that Darrel had been raised on. Gone up so in value that it was just ridiculous, it really was, the price they sold it for! And they had their jobs, Gary with the State Farm Bureau, Bobby selling insurance and real estate. Their wives made a point of *Grandma* almost to the point of, well, annoyance. Homely girls both of them, kind of a defiance on the boys' part, Lavonne didn't know what else to call it. But they did pay a visit every few weeks, turning a deaf ear to *let me know beforehand.* "Say hello to Grandma," "Go give your grandma a kiss." Homely, petite, brown-eyed wives. A form of defiance.

In other words, give it an inch, life will take a mile whenever it can. It couldn't very often with Lavonne. She wouldn't let it, knuckle under, frown, get wrinkles. At night she pasted small wings on her forehead and up along her cheeks to pull the lines out. Everybody said, in various ways, "Lavonne, you look beautiful." She replied in the way the movie stars probably do. "Thank you." "So kind." "Isn't that sweet of you." "Bless you." But only one appraiser counted—the looking glass. And *it* said that even at her age, even with a hysterectomy (that really doesn't make any difference if you take hormone pills), she was the fairest, she need have no fear. And she had none. Her hair was golden. Her eyelashes looked so real nobody could tell the difference. Nobody could tell about her porcelain caps. Her lips turned up sweetly like Mona Lisa's with a cold. Old ladies especially, in the hospital, patient, sturdy old mothers visiting middle-aged daughters dying of carcinoma, old grandmothers with smashed-up family issue, would tell her what a sight she was for sore eyes. "Like sunshine." "Like an angel." Well, say a thing three times and it will be true. Say it a thousand times…it *was* true. Lavonne was sunshiny and like an angel and did her fellowmen kind deeds, brought in the evening paper, gave a neck rub, said this too will pass, massaged a scalp, dried tears, solaced the sad as the smaller birds solace the woods. And (this did not happen in her young days but as the years wore on) the old ladies became an element of her constituency almost as prominent as her men friends. They were generally not charity cases. A few were unusually kind. Some were quite rich. But rich people don't want to make things too easy, they want you to show initiative and hold up your end like a true American.

And they seldom leave you something in their will. That's the strangest characteristic. Here they may adore you, and not have spoken to some relative for thirty years, may actually detest this person, what have they ever done for them? nothing—but then their will be read and one-third or half or even *all* their estate will go to this very nephew or cousin or whoever it was they couldn't stand. Of course it was love of their own self and *their* blood running in this person's veins, the worst relation was better than the best outsider not in on the family ordinances, it was really sad. Old Mrs. Hunter, in Holy Rosary for three months with a broken pelvis, told Lavonne she was going to leave her her dinner ring with the rose diamonds around it, she had been so dear and kind, but—although Lavonne had been to visit her twice in her home just out of the kindness of her heart, and took her a box of candied fruit one time and on another occasion a lovely scarf, besides doing her hair free of charge—when she did pass away a year or two later, not a word was ever heard about the ring.

"You wouldn't even have wanted it," Rosetta said to comfort her when Lavonne made mention of it. "You said it wasn't very pretty."

"I know, but it would have been…" Like getting something back, she didn't say, that had been lost. She was always trying to get things *back*.

A good deal had been lost by now, her matrix in a hysterectomy while she was in San Diego married to Dale. Several times Lavonne had left Salt Lake to start anew in another town, and with Dale, gutter and downspout man, Rosetta thought she was really going to make it, but then something would go wrong and Lavonne would return to Salt Lake. Gene called those times of being gone Lavonne's "sabbaticals," times of absence from duty for the purposes of study and travel. She always came back to the shop. Rosetta ran it alone in the meanwhile, that was the beauty of self-ownership, you could do as much or as little as you pleased.

But even had she been in Salt Lake at the time, Lavonne said, she wouldn't have had her hysterectomy at Holy Rosary Hospital for a million dollars. And be stripped bare of every secret? Her operation she had had so long ago? Her toenails being treated for that fungosity she picked up on that lovely trip down to Mexico? It was the stubbornest thing, the chiropodist said if he could save them she'd be lucky. They didn't allow a hair-piece (just a simple fall) in surgery, wasn't that vindictive, hair could be sterilized just like anything else. And a person's teeth, a partial to be removed in case the patient would aspirate it during surgery, that was deliberately cruel. Eyelashes, everything, leave them behind when you go to surgery. So no thanks, Lavonne said she would die first. Whereas in San Diego the doctors and nurses were strangers, and no nuns. Because don't think nuns don't like to find things out and gossip just like anyone else!

Rosetta thought the nuns were too busy, now that the so-called reform in the church was going full blast, finding things out about *themselves*—what kind of legs they had, whether their foreheads were too low to wear bangs, their right shade of lipstick and a thousand and one other secular details like that—to care about anyone else. But of course it was human nature to be curious. Lavonne was more than curious herself. Not about most people going their ordinary little rounds, doing their tedious little things, but if a patient having her hair done happened to be getting over a nose or eye job or a complete face lift, then she asked questions, but this was never resented, due to her tact. One plastic surgery case, recovering and down in the beauty shop to get a permanent, she conferred with with bated breath, the woman's operation having been to restore a lost breast.

Yes, *restore* it! as absolutely as these cases where a boy accidentally gets his foot cut off by a freight train, the bystanders pick it up and rush it to the hospital with him and the brilliant surgeon sews it back on! before the foot has a chance to die. It knits and functions and is as good as ever. Well, not *exactly* like that, Lavonne told Rosetta the minute they were alone in the shop together (she had bided her time, nearly bursting). The woman's breast was taken off, oh, when Eisenhower was president, and she never dreamed the day would come—! But with the new methods, and *water* sealed in this new development of plastic—they don't use silicone anymore—and the way they treat scar tissue—But the thing that makes it like an *invention*—Lavonne's words tumbled over each other. They peel these strips of muscle off your back. And how do you think they make the nipples? and the different-colored rings around them, the areolas, as they're called? They use some earlobe gristle for the nipple! and the areola, that, they make from the skin inside a person's—their *vagina*. It's just the right shade. Of course while it heals it's agonizing to go to the bathroom, the woman said, and while your back heals it's agonizing, you feel like scalped by Indians, raw and bleeding where the strips were peeled off. But is it worth it!

"Listen, it's the most real thing you ever laid eyes on in your life, and she said if she had to choose—it, or be Shirley MacLaine or even the Queen of England—she wouldn't even stop to think. She was only thirty-one when they discovered she had carcinoma. On the operating table. Just for a biopsy. And the next thing she knew..."

"I know, I've heard that before," Rosetta said, shaking her head sadly.

"She said her husband was just *awful*. Men are so cruel. But later on he died. Died some way at work—kind of a punishment. But now she's met this darling fellow—"

Such a one Lavonne, too, as soon as she went through the same trial, the equivalent, so it seemed to Rosetta from the description, of plunging the hand in boiling water, carrying molten iron and walking barefoot and blindfold through red-hot plowshares so some old Cimbri god could judge if she was innocent or guilty. Lavonne could think of nothing but this operation she was going to undergo. It was as if his two forearms bit off at the elbows would be made to connect and grow again to Captain Carpenter's upper arms by modern surgery.

But Lavonne certainly wouldn't have it done here at Holy Rosary, where nothing would give a lot of people more satisfaction, especially that bleached blonde in the recovery room, than to find out…everything. Dr. Cannon on the staff wasn't the only one who could do it. He *acted* as if he was, the only one on God's green earth with the skill and talent. But there were lots of plastic surgeons. Lavonne began slipping into the doctors' meeting room when no one was around and borrowing the slick-papered medical journals on the shelves and scattered about with articles in them about noses, chins, silicone augmentations, fingers and…here was the *Intermountain Plastic Surgery Quarterly*, where the whole issue was about nothing but that! And it was *unbelievable*, what they could do. Then one day, sure enough, here was this article about the *very operation* Lavonne's customer had had, with the strips of muscle taken off the back to use in front, the skin taken off the inside of the vagina (here it was called the *vulva*) to make the areola, the part about the earlobes to make the nipples—it was all right here, and Lavonne was so excited she could hardly breathe.

This doctor's practice was in Tucson, not far by plane. Why didn't old Mrs. Horton name her in her will? As kind as Lavonne had been to her, the trouble she had gone to! It was really sad. However, she could sell the car, she didn't really need it, she was within walking distance now of Holy Rosary and walking was the best exercise, and Rosetta would go on her note at the bank. If this operation did for her what she *thought* it was going to do, she would pay the note off before she could turn around, and replace the car too. She got a little mad talking to the surgeon, though, him going into the matter of her age and probing into why a person nearly in their sixth decade, and after more than forty years since her original operation, would want such a thing *done*. He also said, he was a very glib talker with kind of an English accent, that even the most beautiful mammae by that time of life would be beginning to droop and shrivel anyway, and once-lovely nipples be but mammiform excrescences! which Lavonne could hardly *hear*, let alone understand, and she almost hung up and looked for someone else. But she didn't.

Another thing he said was—but that was in Tucson, after she checked in—that he wouldn't go along with the *Playboy* photographer who said in an interview that the female breast really has but *one perfect moment*, when the girl is about sixteen, like a rose in a rose show! and that you can actually see that moment come and go in one photographic session! But he did want to remind her that no matter how successful a restoration of the type she wanted would be, she was *still* a woman of a certain age and that all the agony and effort and expense wouldn't change *that*. She was, if not old, on the threshold of old age, and wouldn't it be better…? You have to beg and plead, give them a big sales talk like they were a *judge* or something, when all the time they know very well they're going to do it, take the money. They just want to show their power and torture you.

But when he said agony, he wasn't kidding. They take these strips of muscle, oh, my God, and the skin off the inside of your…Can you imagine…Using the bedpan, it burns like fire, *worse* than fire. And this weight on your chest, they weigh, they hurt, they're heavy—you dream you're buried under—a wall's caved in. You wake up trying to scream. He wasn't kidding.

"But oh, Rosetta, look. Will you look at this."

Finally. At last. It's simply perfect, couldn't be more so, really.

"Feel them, do they feel natural? Soft and—?"

"Very soft and natural."

"Nipples! Look—"

"I see. They're beautiful."

And real?

Cleavage and everything.

Even *he* had to admit…

It seemed as though it would make a difference, Lavonne and men. And at first it seemed to. She didn't have to do any explaining anymore, bow to the ground, try to make amends. The prison doors had swung wide and she was free.

She acted like a queen at first, Catherine the Great who had had living men stripped naked and stood outside to freeze to death in the Winter Palace courtyard at forty below zero weather. Ice-coated human statues. The wicked queen, off with their heads. But! how use doth breed a habit…With each new man it was the same. She would start out as absolute as any monarch in India, and then, as though following to the letter the action inserted in a play, would change her character to passive and dependent, obedient and loyal. This strange stage direction acting on the man like the ethereal fluid from a star, he would become in *his* turn Ivan the Terrible, though maybe before that he had bossed not even a rabbit. Again and again this stagery would play, Lavonne the principal female, the male lead changing; a delivery man, assistant cafeteria manager, laundromat operator, patient, visitor, convenience installer at the airport, electrician who came to fix the dryers…

Had Lavonne been able, Rosetta once thought, to stand in space upon a great gleaming half shell and show the whole entire world at one time as it revolved on heaven's great axle that Aphrodite *lives*! with all her graces, pleasures and elegances (the undulant store-bought strands floating on the Primavera breeze need only to be firmly anchored to the scalp to have grown there, eyelashes are one's own if they don't fall off, the teeth in your mouth certainly do not belong to anyone *else*, and what are even a centerfold's rosy protrusions at the height of their glory but 98 percent water?), why, maybe she could have found repose and rest. But of course this was not possible, and so her natural forces toiled on, first subduing, then being subdued by her successive boyfriends and the rich old ladies who might have given back so much but never did.

But all luck turns at last! a most true saying. And so one day a patient by the name of Birdelle Prentice entered Holy Rosary Hospital to have her adhesions operated on. "Can you imagine! I was up in the surgical wing to comb out Mrs. Fox and who should I meet wandering down the hall in just her hospital gown with the whole back end out and fur-lined boots on but this old woman who I find out is *Birdelle*."

Emily, one of the nurses, looked up from the *Photoplay* she was turning the pages of without much interest (for who knew who the stars were anymore?) at Rosetta parting off and winding her nice hair in a permanent, then at Lavonne. "Miss Prentice. She's one of mine," she said.

"Did she know you?" Rosetta said.

"The condition she's in, she wouldn't know her own mother," Lavonne said.

"What happened? A stroke?"

"Chemical psychosis, from what I could make out. And one of the nurses was saying."

"They do that all the time," Emily said. "The doctors. Prescribe. Give out free samples. To shut them up, I guess. Sleeping pills. Pills for high blood pressure. Pills for headache. For being blue. For feeling nervous—and they all mix together and next thing you know, you've got a dope fiend on your hands."

"Chemical psychosis. Jan says they've got three in the hospital right now. But I think I made her know who I was." To Emily, "We used to *live* in their house," Lavonne added. "Gram and me. My grandmother was their cook."

"Whose house?" Emily asked, wincing as a curler clicked shut against her scalp.

"You know the one. Marble, with the towers on the corners, up on South Temple. Rounded windows?"

"I thought that was a *club*," Emily said. "Somebody was saying—"

"No, it's a residence. This lady I'm talking about lives there. They were millionaires."

"Maybe Birdelle doesn't own it now," Rosetta said. "Maybe she's sold it and lives in the Hotel Utah. She must be about as old as an old tree."

Birdelle Prentice *was* that old, but she hadn't sold the house and hadn't moved. How long it would be, however, before that fatal day arrived, she told Lavonne, she just didn't know. The taxes were—The slightest help cost—Mabel on Thursday wasn't worth her salt, one seventy-five an hour and help herself to soup and sandwich. And then the temptation, not that she'd succumb, but Jim said—Jim Benedict, her lawyer—*he* said she could get a pretty price if ever she wanted to sell, people were eyeing it for the Governor's mansion—

"I'm not a bit surprised," Lavonne said. By this time Birdelle was not so spaced out anymore, she vaguely knew her faithful visitor was some relation to Cook and kind of a kindred soul, because she remembered things nobody else in the world—Dr. Wallace, Jim Benedict, Monsignor Tate and Father Peacock of the Cathedral, Mabel on Thursdays— would know anything about. The conservatory at the back of the house when it was full of flowers. The gray Pierce Arrow. Hampers still came then from Cousin Virginia, or did they? Papa. Mama. The dress with chinchilla around the bottom. The time…The day… In this day and age, to be able to do that (remember with someone) was simply wonderful.

"What was your name again?" she said.

"Lavonne."

"When I get home, you must come and see me."

"I'll *take* you home, if you'd like, when you get to go."

They don't appreciate anything, though, the rich, all the extra services, they take them for granted. After Birdelle was maneuvered into inviting her to move in with her, and Lavonne accepted the invitation, the shampoo-sets, manicures and pedicures and hot oil treatments, washed and ironed wrappers and the running with trays and to cut a pill in half down in the kitchen and being a companion were to Birdelle like water off a duck's back.

"Only the obligation of fidelity on the part of a feudal vassal," Rosetta said.

Lavonne didn't know about *that*, but it was something, it really was, their attitude.

Chapter Sixty-five

*

ROSETTA DIDN'T THINK THE ARRANGEMENT WOULD LAST A MONTH.

Lavonne spoke from her heart. Birdelle was all alone, she said, no natural heir, and while she acted worried about money, they did that, it was natural to the species, the house alone, that property, must be worth an awfully lot. Of course the priests from the Cathedral, they hung around wanting the church to inherit it. Monsignor Tate was just impossible. Father Peacock, though. He was nice, not tall but broad shoulders, one of those sloping necks, looked like he could box. In fact he did use to box back in Ireland when he was a boy, was what he said. He'd talk to you and laugh, throw back his head, quite a lot of dental work, but they don't have to pay for it personally, the church pays everything. He was a chaplain in the Army, World War Two. More of the human type, you could talk to him. So Lavonne was thinking of *joining* the church, taking instruction, it's not like the Protestants, you can't just say "I join." Then on a Sunday morning, when she escorted Birdelle up the street to the Cathedral, she would take more of a personal interest. That would please Birdelle, and making the sign of the cross, kneeling and all, was kind of romantic, like *The White Sister*. But why couldn't they have gone to Mass at eleven instead of staggering up there when it was hardly light? Lavonne asked Rosetta, and answered herself: *Because* they're thinking only of themselves.

About giving up the apartment and moving in with the old lady, Lavonne's boyfriend Foster said: if that's what she thought she wanted. The decision was hers. Her own responsibility. All the things men say when they themselves don't want to take any. Not that Foster was happy about the rug being pulled out from under him as regards a cozy apartment…beer in the icebox, sandwiches, somebody sweet to watch television with. Because once she was up there, it wouldn't be the same, it wasn't the same. He couldn't come upstairs to Lavonne's bedroom to watch a program when it was just across the hall from the old lady's. Though why not he didn't see. After she was in bed asleep? But Birdelle kept her door open, she could look right across, old people in their eighties are always switching on their light to see what time it is and going to the bathroom. And really (give them an inch and they took a mile), Birdelle had no qualms whatsoever about barging across, turning on Lavonne's light and waking her up to close a window she wasn't strong enough to close or go down to the kitchen and fetch a cup of hot milk.

Rosetta didn't think the arrangement would last a month.

Foster didn't care for it at all. But then why didn't he speak up, say don't do it, you like this location, I like it too, why don't we get married? For the simple reason that everything's supposed to fall into their lap without any effort on their part, they are selfish to the core. In fact Lavonne had about had it with Foster anyway, another dead-end street. And when she would *not* let him sneak upstairs and maybe ruin everything with Birdelle, or go to his mobile home, which was just horrible, dirty old shag carpeting even on the walls and that cold, trapped tobacco-smoke smell, and he said okay, if that's the way you feel about it and didn't call up anymore, why, she just let him go. There was something wrong with him anyway, a man staying single *seven years*, batching for himself. It's different if they've never been married. But it was discouraging, really. Where *were* all the men? "Where are they?"

"There aren't any in our age bracket," Rosetta said.

But age doesn't have to even exist, said a paperback somebody left in the shop, *The Magic of Believing*, and Lavonne believed that. It really doesn't. And any dream can come true if you wish it strong enough and have the energy to choose your own fate. The dream Lavonne decided on, after giving it considerable thought, was when Birdelle died to inherit her house and all her money. She would be charitable, give some of it to the church, send the clothes and various odds and ends to the Salvation Army, sell the house and contents except certain pieces she would take with her to her place in the Ambassador Apartments, made by knocking down the wall between two apartments on the top floor. She would then stop for a face lift...trade the Chevrolet in on a...really expensive car of some kind, though rather small, not a great big sedan but more like a convertible. And buy a...probably mink coat. And...go for a long leisurely trip around the world with lovely matched luggage. Jewelry...in a bank vault, she had never seen it, diamonds, emeralds. Birdelle told Lavonne about the string of pearls Cousin Virginia gave her when she was born (but left her nothing when she died) worth fifty thousand dollars, which she sold during her brief unfortunate marriage to a Body Builder of Douglas Fairbanks. But her husband *didn't get away with the money*, Birdelle conserved and invested it, and though she didn't realize it at the time, she told Lavonne, *that* was the crucial test. After that she was her mother's and father's equal, they trusted and accepted her, she was their golden child.

BIRDELLE DIDN'T *HIRE* LAVONNE, SHE had enough expenses as it was, she said, but Lavonne was welcome to come and stay for a while. She allowed her two shelves in the icebox, the huge old icebox Lavonne remembered so well, to keep her provisions in. Part of the pantry, too, her own supplies. Birdelle couldn't afford to keep anybody, she could hardly keep herself, she said, and wondered if her money would last her till she died or if she would have to go to the poorhouse. It frightened her terribly to hear there was no such thing as a poorhouse anymore, or none that Lavonne had ever heard of. No real roof at all for over a pauper's head, she would be exposed to the hail, the snow, the cold whistling wind.

Jim Benedict, her lawyer, told her she would never want, and she knew herself that she was a rich woman, but that was *presently*. In the world she saw on television (the way Elaine the Lily Maid of Astolat saw but counterparts or images pass by in her looking glass) you could be broke tomorrow, a loaf of bread could cost a thousand dollars, anarchists could take over the government, banks and financial houses be steam-rollered into rubble. Each day Birdelle's worries grew, till Dr. Wallace had to start prescribing green, orange and pink pills again, capsules with a red strip around them, yellow pellets. Monsignor Tate prescribed religious zeal and rendering unto God the things that are God's. Father Peacock, who paid the house calls, injected humor into his visits. He told little jokes about Irishmen in an Irish brogue and took his leave with a quick, warm hug. If Lavonne was there she got one too, warm, close, parochial. Priests were human, they must have quite a struggle overcoming their natural inclinations. Lavonne was glad she joined the church, it made it so much better now that she lived with Birdelle, her being such a Catholic. And with all the pretty statues and candles and the beautiful altar, it did seem as if it might be true.

BIRDELLE'S WORRIES INTENSIFIED AFTER THE evening news. She would turn the television off then, and Lavonne would have to talk to her or try to learn Mah Jong or double solitaire. Lavonne hadn't had a date, been to a dance or gone to a show for two months. Her sequinned and other dresses just hung in the closet, her Shalimar slowly evaporated. Worst of all, she had to change her hours, get up and go to work early so as not to be dragging home at eight-thirty or nine at night, when Birdelle was starting to think about bed. How else get in any companionship? Rosetta didn't mind, it didn't matter to her what hours Lavonne kept the shop, now that no one was at home waiting for her. It mattered to Lavonne, an alarm clock going off in your ear at six-thirty in the morning every weekday could only be harmful. It aged one. Also it aged one not to have human contact except with people who came and went at the hospital, the personnel, customers, Rosetta and of course Birdelle, who seemed to get more dependent by the day. But not so dependent that she wanted Lavonne to quit the beauty shop and be a full-time paid companion.

She couldn't afford that! she said, and little of anything else, right next door to the poorhouse as she was—and no poorhouse! But her mansion alone, Lavonne would say to try to reassure her, her piece of property only three blocks from Temple Square *alone*, to say nothing of all the furniture and—Oriental carpets are very valuable now—statues, paintings, dishes, all that sterling silver…her jewelry she was mentioning in the bank, why, a big auction sale, she could live like a king the rest of her life. "You're in your eighties, after all," she was too tactful to add, "how many hundred years do you think you're going to be around?"

"*Sell?*" The word struck terror to Birdelle's soul.

"Well, then, why don't you rent some of it out, Miss Prentice, if you're so concerned about finances? Look how big this place is. If you rented out some of the rooms, you could pay all your taxes and expenses—"

"How do you mean?"

"Well, people do it all the time nowadays, right up the street, too. That house with the stained glass—whatever it is, on the side—"

"That's their conservatory. The Caldwell family."

"That's a *boarding house.*"

"No!"

"It is. I'll show you on our way to Mass. The world's a lot different now than it used to be."

It is said that many great inventions and works of art are thought of in a flash like the universe, they spring full-blown from their creator's head. When Lavonne said "rent," everything else came together in a concept as brilliant as the pop-up toaster. The diverse parts…herself in her position, trapped. Birdelle in hers, imagining her poverty. Rosetta, whose grocer on the corner told her he heard her apartment house was going to be sold and torn down and a parking structure put up on the spot. Rosetta could rent the room Lavonne was unhappily occupying opposite Birdelle's, it was so lovely and big and had a fireplace, while Lavonne would move downstairs to the den. The den had a door out onto the side porch. That way Lavonne could come and go at night as she wanted. To a dance, a show. Unbeknownst to Birdelle, a friend could come in for a little social chat. And Rosetta would have a place to live, much better than in that apartment house that was going to be torn down, Birdelle would have a person to keep an eye on her who wouldn't mind an eye being kept on *her,* or mind if the doors were open to their two bedrooms, or somebody coming arbitrarily in and turning on the light. Lavonne would be free again! but yet on the premises. All their problems solved at a single stroke.

"Oh, Lavonne, I don't know about that," Rosetta said.

"Well, come and look at the place, that's all I ask. You *know* it's a mansion."

She could take her books with her, Gene's easy chair, his desk, the rest of the stuff didn't mean much by now anyway. (And the shady grove was going to be cut down.)

To Birdelle, Lavonne explained that it would be lots better to have someone familiar with the place *downstairs* so that if something should happen during the night, she would be right there. And at the same time, Birdelle would have help across the hall upstairs and be collecting rent at the same time. Maybe they could even find another nice roomer!

THINGS THAT ARE GOOD TO start with, the finest materials, the best workmanship, where cost is no object, can stand around neglected for hundreds of years and be hardly any the worse. Under the ivy climbing in like burglars at every window, under the dust, the fuzz-balls, the dead moths and flies deep as moss in Sleeping Beauty's castle, the stuff must have stayed almost as good as Sleeping Beauty herself in her immortal finery. Rosetta thought of that when first she came up the back steps onto the big latticed back porch and into the great kitchen, with its stove big enough to roast an ox, its huge table, the sink that ninety or more years ago to Sing or Pon Look or whatever the Clarendon's Chinese cook was called must have seemed, with its two faucets (one for hot water), like some great scientific accomplishment. All the cutting and chopping, washing and peeling, roasting and boiling, dragging in and out that had gone on for nearly a century hardly showed, on tile, iron, the hardest polished wood and slick gray marble. The same in the other rooms of contradictory and fabulous properties.

Nobody was at home the day Rosetta moved in. (The shop at the hospital was closed too, Lavonne was taking Birdelle to the dentist and also to her lawyer's.) Through the back way, which Lavonne had left open, she came into the hush of wealth. It looked the same as when, their two families having separated, Rosetta and her mother went to live in the Constitution Building and Gram and Lavonne moved here, Gram to be the Prentice cook. There were hard feelings, but the place had to be viewed, and so at an opportune moment it was, when no one was at home but Gram in the kitchen and a lady ironing on the back porch. "You can show Rosetta around," Gram told Lavonne, "but don't touch anything." They didn't, Rosetta remembered, except the tall pink silver-footed atomizer on the lace-covered dressing table. She touched that, it was irresistible, squeezed the silk net-covered rubber bulb once and smelled the spray of fine perfume.

And all this while later, there it stood! She saw it as she went past the half-open door, the same atomizer, same dresser, same slant of sunlight … as if no time had passed at all, although a lifetime had. Or nearly. Or more than a lifetime, when oh, dearest and sweetest, thou diest and my dear love is sped like a dream. But the best materials, the best workmanship, where money is no object, things simply do not wear out or show much change.

"Wouldn't Wyandra think this was something, though. After all these years!"

"Who wouldn't," Lavonne said.

"Yes, but Wyandra—Don't you remember? This house to her was like 'The Fall of the House of Usher,' Rochester's manor, where his crazy wife … Kenilworth or something. What I mean, to *her* it was … like … the setting of … Where stuff … like *legends*, don't you know. She used to tell me about Mavis, the girl the Clarendons adopted—well, *Mrs.* Clarendon didn't adopt her, she was dead at the time, it was him—and then … You know they built this place, the Clarendons, with money from their silver mines."

"Weren't we related to them in some way?"

"You mean blood relationship? Someone was, very slightly. But I don't know who."

"So we should inherit it, shouldn't we?"

Rosetta smiled. "Wyandra used to tell—Kids don't listen, though. She'd be talking away…"

But something must have listened, the same thing (whatever it is) that stays awake when you're asleep and hears the tape under the pillow reiterating what the Guelphs and Ghibellines did to each other in what century so that when you see the question in the finals the next day, the answer's there to pluck from the thin air. The same that's unsusceptible to chloroform so that when the surgeon comes into the room to tell the rousing patient what he found, the patient already knows. That makes the inattentive babe able to lisp all through Hail Mary, full of grace…

And this (whatever it is) *had* listened. So when Rosetta moved up to the Prentice residence that had been built by the Clarendons, why, inattentive though she had often been to Wyandra's recitals of events that took place there, she yet had stored them up enough so that when she walked in, it was like Mark Twain going aboard his old steamboat, fraught with such imaginative appeal that her scalp crawled and gooseflesh stood along her arms. Before the house was even finished, Aunt Lucitie and Uncle Albert walked up here and were set upon by… goons of some kind. Why was that? Oh, yes, because some old Mormon Elder was jealous of Uncle Albert. And Lucitie fought the avengers off, which showed Uncle Albert what a brave and useful partner he could have for life if he but grasped the opportunity. And he did grasp it. He was so handsome then. Part French…

And the Clarendons, rich beyond the dreams of avarice, childless. And very vain *she* was, always dressed in beautiful clothes and her hair just so. Vanity was what killed her in the end, riding side-saddle in a big parade in some mining town in California. Jim Clarendon had had lady acquaintances on the side all along (in fact one had tried to commit suicide), but nevertheless when his wife died, though she was older, he grieved as if she was all he ever cared for. Then to try to get over his grief, he went on this expedition with photographic equipment—a millionaire can buy and do anything that strikes their fancy—and with a professional to take the pictures of old places throughout the mining country. His valet went with him, too. All the comforts of home. And who should they stumble onto down in southern Utah but…

She was almost dead by then. And only a little over a year later…

And Loudhawk was an Indian, wounded, scarred, crippled from old battle wounds… from… oh, of course, the Mountain Meadow Massacre, which was going to make Legrand a well-known scenario writer like… June Mathis, the Salt Lake girl who got famous writing *The Four Horsemen* starring Rudolph Valentino.

It was the biggest wonder Mavis didn't die down there after they killed her mother for coming in to spy on that community in… Cedar City. Being an albino in that pitiless sun. Wyandra said pitiless. But Loudhawk saved Mavis by digging kind of a grave under the willows and then, when darkness fell, carrying her down to the river and laying her in the shallows where the water could ripple around her. And right in the nick of time, here came Jim Clarendon with his expedition. He didn't bring Mavis to the mansion at first, never thought of such a thing, but took her to Hindle's, from where Mavis and her mother had started out in the first place. The sign on the front of the house said *Dr. Hindle Fairbrass, Eclectic Practitioner, Diseases of Women Only*. That was her own grandmother, Hindle, who at fourteen years old ran away with a forty-five-year-old ex–railroad physician, who she then assisted till he died, and then she was a doctor herself. She came back to Salt Lake and set up practice. Why not? She was as experienced as anybody, cured people for years. But then they made a law that physicians had to take examinations, and show proof of going through medical school, belonging to the Medical Society and such as that. So Hindle went up to Montana and … just … disappeared.

Hindle's sister was Aunt Lucitie. The two girls' father was named John D. Lee. Their mother was his sixth or eighth wife. Altogether he had twelve or thirteen wives, and fifty or sixty boys and girls. Think of the relatives running around! And John D. Lee didn't *mean* to take part in wiping out an entire wagon train on its way to California (this is what Wyandra always said she was sure of when she told about it), but because he was a good Latter-day Saint and did what he was told and happened to be in the vicinity at the time. The deed was called the Mountain Meadow Massacre. And about twenty years after that, trying to find out more about it, was why Mavis's actress mother was shot down in cold blood in Cedar City. John D. Lee was shot too, but many years before *that*. And not just shot, but *executed* by the U.S. Government. For being the ringleader. And the place of execution was that very Meadow, on the spot where, under the ground beneath his feet, the bones of the slain lay all jumbled together. In an Army supply wagon, his executioners poked their rifles through the canvas curtains at the back and fired anonymously, due to the presence of several revengeful-looking Lee boys standing around waiting to take their father's body to Panguitch for burial. In Legrand's scenario, John D. Lee stood on his coffin beforehand and gave kind of an explanation. It was March, a sleety snow was blowing. All that was sad for a little girl to hear about, but interesting too.

What Rosetta liked best of anything was after Mavis was rescued more dead than alive, brought back to Salt Lake, nursed back to health, turned out beautiful (but very spoiled), and Jim Clarendon adopted her, how that child had everything in the *world*. Dolls, toys, books, a white fur coat and cap and muff, pink silk dresses, genuine small diamonds, beautiful shoes, stockings, anything she wanted in the line of food, pineapples, chocolates, reindeer milk if she wanted, a maid to brush her hair and wash her back, the cutest cats and dogs that when full grown would weigh about a pound. Books, skates of solid silver like Hans Brinker's, a horse and buggy …

Wasn't it strange, Mavis was *really* an albino in those times, when nowadays the so-called Gothic novelists of the southern states and other places will put an albino in their stories for decoration. But she was real, of cotton candy, snow and crystal, with blinking, peering, winking eyes of pink chalcedony. They blinked, that is, and peered and winked until in Italy she fell asleep and stayed asleep back home in Salt Lake City, in this *very mansion* where she was carried to, until she died at age fourteen, as she was at the time, and was buried up in the graveyard beside Mrs. Clarendon. And Jim put up this...more than a monument to both of them, mother and daughter who had never met, a kind of little noble *edifice* of pure Carrara marble. And then he went to England, where he also died.

Wyandra used to say the house must surely be haunted.

Mavis's room was the one at the end of the hall, to the left as you come upstairs. That was where she slept for, what was it? two months, six months? after Jim brought her home from Italy, France and England, where the finest doctors couldn't wake her up, and where she died like a snow princess attended by Hindle, who stayed right in the house and tried to save her after she started burning up with the fever that no cold, shallow river but only death, this time, could cool.

The Prentices bought the house from the Clarendon heirs, who had almost torn each other limb from limb. They were people from back east. Rich, but they didn't think so, because as Wyandra used to say, all is relative, and both Mr. Prentice's and Mrs. Prentice's kinfolks were *incalculably* rich. So he and she felt poor and somewhat disgraced in comparison, as they had only about a million to their names and his good job, and were glad to live where civilization had hardly penetrated and nobody (who was anybody) ever came to see in what humble circumstances they had to live. They had one daughter, Birdelle. It wasn't at all peculiar that *she* felt poor, she always had, because she was raised that way.

And...out of this house, out through these great front portals or the noble entrance under the porte cochere, Mrs. Prentice stepped on that fatal day of June fifth, descended to the car, the chauffeur held the door open, she got in, he shut it, went around and got in behind the wheel, they drove away. She had an appointment at Uncle Albert's Hairdressing Establishment. Wyandra was going to give her a spiral permanent. Then Mrs. Prentice was coming home to have a well-earned dinner...and listen to the radio...and be...But instead of that she came back dead, electrocuted in the permanent waving machine, to lie in state in the drawing room with electric fans turned on and discreetly blowing and the window shades pulled down nearly to the bottom...

And that June night was when Wyandra...

But Rosetta blotted *that* from her mind.

MAMA WHEN SHE DIED WASN'T brought home to lie in state. Nobody ever was who lived in the Constitution Building. Especially in the inside apartments, with no outside exposure and their inside windows painted over, small as they were and smelling like that first whiff of gas before the match set the ring on fire, and the Campbell's soup boiled over, and coffee and chamber pots, even emptied and swished out, and dirty clothes in a closet, they didn't just have the tone for classy, snooty death. This great mansion, this was the very house where the big brown rat... What Wyandra said was—let's see, a crew of three came up here, Mama was one of the crew. Whoever would suppose! in a millionaire's attic. What was she doing up there? to get... bitten like she did... and run screaming down this great central staircase with the rat's teeth clamped through the end of her finger to the bone... the thing whipping and thrashing like a fish on the end of a line till she banged its hard skull on the handrail and it... let go, tumbled, fell, lit scrabbling and running. And all you could see were two little tiny punctures. "A *rat*. Don't be preposterous. *Here?*" It could have been a European rat, accidentally trapped and sent in an antique... cupboard or a hamper from a... French dressmaker or from Cousin Virginia's house...

In any case, this stairway. And Mama died... but not right away.

I will not dwell on that. I'll think... other thoughts... such as... Lavonne was right, my room is really beautiful. One room as big as Gene's and my whole apartment, nearly. They like big rooms, high ceilings, hardwood, plate glass, the best of everything. It pays, too. Look at these carpets. Look at these window blinds, seventy or eighty years old maybe, but roll up, pull down, better than new ones today.

That room there down at the end of the hall was where Mavis slept and dreamed her life away. My grandmother stayed here that last week, Wyandra said, taking care of her, probably sleeping in the same room... yes, on that faded sofa there, maybe, still strewn with pillows, a paper pinned around the light. Didn't the Prentices when they bought the house buy all the furnishings, too? Or was it empty at the time? Wyandra would have known. Everything Wyandra could, she exempted from oblivion. Are you listening? Then put your book down, darling, you really will want to hear this (when I'm gone, who will remember?). *Once upon a time there was no time and it was then that...*

EMILY, THE NURSE FROM INTENSIVE care, having her weekly shampoo-set, said her kid would have a fit when she heard where Lavonne and Rosetta had moved to, June was crazy about those big old mansions up on Brigham Street. When Rosetta went in to see her, she should tell her. About the chandeliers, high ceilings and everything, all the fireplaces. June would *flip*!

"How is she this morning?"

"She'll be going home Tuesday or Wednesday, Dr. Bender says."

"That was a close call."

"You're telling me. It had bursted, you know, by the time we got her here. But of course now that there's penicillin—"

"Even so."

"And of course Dr. Bender's the best. If he wanted to cut my *head* off I'd let him, wouldn't you?"

Emily's daughter June had company when Rosetta looked in on her on her way home, a blonde-haired, blue-eyed young man who even in a business suit gave the appearance of someone about to ski down a slope. June introduced him, and when Rosetta heard the name, she said well, for heaven's sake, then said that he and she were related, and without much interest he said how come?

"Yes, how come?" June said, and had the bed wound up so she could sit up straight to pursue the fascinating subject of the bloodline she herself hoped someday to have descendants branching out from.

Small world! For June's visitor was Normal Sleigh, the little boy Rosetta had met coming up Main Street with his mother Dotty (Herman and Agnes's daughter) on that snowy morning twenty years or more before, on his way to be—it all came back to her— circumcised. (And wasn't he the child…it was ridiculous what one remembered…who had one undescended testicle? But his grandmother Agnes insisted at the time it would come down.)

June, now bolt upright in her clean white hospital gown with cream-colored polish on her rosy nails and cream-colored lipstick on her rosy lips, shook back long dark hair, blinked her lovely matching eyes and said, as though this were incredibly wonderful, "Well, come on. Related. Are you his *aunt*?"

Normal stifled a yawn, glanced down at his Rolex wristwatch, pushing the Montagnard bracelet he was wearing above it up his arm an inch or so with one finger, then moved to the window to look down to the parking lot to see his MG shining in the sun. But the parking lot was around to the other side, there was only lawn and trees and flowers to look at below, so he turned back.

Between June and Rosetta they were unraveling the connection. If Rosetta's mother's Aunt Lucitie was Normal's great-grandmother, why, then, Rosetta and Normal…June clasped her head in her hands, the better to think it all out, and the sapphire ring on her right middle finger sparkled. Rosetta knew who the ring belonged to, for June had made a point of telling her on an earlier visit, and taking it off and even insisting that Rosetta try it on, she was so proud of it. It was Normal's. Originally, however, it was Ed's ring, Normal's best friend. They went on a mission for the church together, then when they got back to Salt Lake they joined the Army together and got to be Green Berets. And one time when they were on leave together in Bangkok, they bought themselves each a sapphire ring. They were just alike except Ed's was a little more, June explained, *bluish*, while Normal's…But Rosetta could see for herself. This ring was Ed's. Normal took it off Ed's finger when he died at Phu Bai of a case of U.R.I. turning into terminal pneumonia and replaced it with his own ring. Then *Normal* wore *Ed's* ring, and *Normal's* ring went home to Idaho to be buried with *Ed*, unless somebody stole it along the way.

And really, June said, she took that as more of a sign that Normal really loved her, to let her wear it, than if he had given her a diamond engagement ring. A boy like Normal who would make a gesture like that, when Ed meant so much to him, was asking her to marry him just as surely as if he had got down on his knees and proposed in so many words. At least June took it like that, she said. Of course it was just a temporary loan. He and she had come home from a movie and everybody was in bed, but Mom said she could make some cocoa in the kitchen for Normal if they would be real quiet, so she was doing that, but she was still in awful pain, which she thought was from the pizza they ate before they went to the show. And the pain got worse till finally she just staggered out and started upstairs and collapsed and called out for her mom, and then the whole family got up, and Mom called Dr. Bender, he didn't come, of course, but said for them to get an ambulance…And then the intern…But before the ambulance came, everybody was getting dressed and Normal came over close to her and that was when he took the ring off his finger and put it on hers, just to wear for luck through the appendectomy and until she got home. Wasn't that sweet? Although knowing it had come off the finger of a dead boy kind of scared her too, that it might not be too lucky and *she* might die her own self on the operating table and never come to, but of course she didn't say a word. And the ring did bring her through, and Normal's love also, for what else was it but love if a person would do that?

Rosetta congratulated Emily on her daughter, June's looks and actions, and Emily said yes, she and Bill were pretty lucky, their oldest girl Debbie worked at Zion's National Bank, the boy next after June was an Eagle Scout, the youngest boy had a paper route, and June did have many wonderful qualities, especially in this day and age of a lot of people's kids acting so senseless. And if Normal was really serious, it might be all right. But to go overboard for him like June had if he *wasn't*—! And Bill wasn't too satisfied, Normal was out of the service, but he didn't seem to be trying to *do* anything in particular. But of course after Viet Nam they needed time to get their head together, as the saying went. June said that was what he was doing. She said what he wanted to do was go down into the wilds of southern Utah to train mountain lion dogs and take hunters into lion country. Wasn't that crazy, with his folks as well off as they were? They owned the Deseret Motel up by the university. That was how June met Normal in the first place. Her university scholarship wasn't enough to do any good, so she had this one job at the library and another in the motel coffee shop. And when Normal came home, he went in there for a cup of Postum and there she was. But if she wouldn't throw up her schooling and both jobs to go traipsing off with him if he *did* go down to southern Utah, Emily would miss her guess. That ring didn't mean a thing. On her right hand! But Rosetta thought it might.

"Do you really think so? A mother worries in this day and age. But what can I do? Nothing, only to try to keep Bill from scaring the boy off before they even get to first base. Did you tell June? About you and Lavonne living in that mansion?"

"No," Rosetta said. "I never thought of it."

"Well, tell her. She goes right past it on the bus, and she'll be thrilled. The kids have got this notion about old houses, how they're better built and everything, and I've been past it with her and she points it out."

"She could even *live* there if she wanted."

"How do you mean?"

"Well, see, the owner imagines—She thinks she's poor. *I* rent from her, the room's just beautiful, there's kitchen privileges—"

"So who all lives there?"

"Just us. Miss Prentice, she's the owner, and Lavonne and me."

Emily thought deeply a moment, then spoke. "Listen, this might sound peculiar, a mother wanting her daughter to move away from home to the extent that she would even use some of her hard-earned wages to pay the daughter's *room rent*—but I tell you, Rosetta, this boy may be a lovely chance, and home isn't just the place—Bill's outspoken, and if he starts talking about Normal's intentions and everything—Bill smokes, too, and *will* have a beer, and Normal's very—almost fanatical. And June and her sister Debbie don't get along a bit. They will later, me and my sister were the same, fought like cats and dogs when we were their age, though now we're—We call each other. In *our* case, though, Grandma lived right next door, so whoever was maddest could run over there, but *my* kids—no place to run! So what I mean, if I could rent a room for June in that mansion where you and Lavonne are, she'd be in safe company and things could maybe work themselves out, while with her father around to maybe scare Normal away—and Debbie looking daggers—and June would be closer to school and to her jobs…"

Chapter Sixty-six

JUNE HAD MAVIS'S ROOM, AND TWO OR THREE TIMES ROSETTA, THINKING IT might amuse her, was on the verge of telling her about the girl of long ago. But then she decided not to. It might make her feel a little leery, waking up in the night and thinking of somebody dying in there, and that maybe her ghost…

June's father and younger brother helped her move in one rainy February evening at nearly nine p.m. It was a good thing Birdelle had taken one of the new prescription capsules guaranteed not to space anybody out in a chemical psychosis (unless taken to excess) and was sound asleep in her bed. Otherwise she'd have had a fit—the side door wide open to the wind and rain, curtains billowing, muddy feet traipsing in. And nothing would do but June had to show her dad and little brother the drawing room, dining room, Turkish side parlor and everything—the whole downstairs was blazing with lights.

And of course they traipsed up the wide central staircase bringing her stuff up to her room, clothes on hangers, grocery cartons full of books and stuffed animals, her radio and a bulging suitcase. Speaking softly, though, not yelling at one another, showing respect and awe. Mark did connect up her radio, but when "Baby Don't You Tear My Clothes" came blasting out, he quickly turned it down without being told. Wealth does make known its presence. June's father let off a little steam to Rosetta. As she was the one who, without meaning to, had instigated the move, and Birdelle was in bed, she was the welcoming committee, and so he said to her that it really made you sick to see money spent like water the way it had been around here, as anyone could see! when people were starving. Well, Rosetta said, it was spent a long time ago when the situation was different, not like now. And being the last of her line, Miss Prentice would probably leave the place to the city for a museum or…an old people's home. Of course the bathroom situation, there was only the one on the second floor, but it was really nice. And there was an *elevator*—supposedly the first one in a private house in Salt Lake—

"*Now* she tells us!" June's brother Mark said, wiping the sweat from his brow.

"Well, it's not in very good—running order, and Miss Prentice doesn't like anyone to use it."

Downstairs again, nothing would do but Mark must see where the elevator was located. Then he opened the door and stepped in. "Where does it go to?"

June's father got on, too. "Look at this filigree work," he said as if offended. "This padded silk stuff…"

"Oh, come on, Rosetta," June said, "can't we just take them upstairs once, and then down again? What would that hurt?"

"I guess it wouldn't," Rosetta said.

"Come on, you come too—"

They all crowded in and stood expectantly. What are we waiting for? Oh. June's father, making room by moving his shoulders, felt the edge of the door, then carefully slid it shut. Now. Then everyone seemed to think of finding and punching the mother-of-pearl button at the same moment. Mark's jab started their slow ascent. Wasn't this something? How they used to build...Suddenly it shuddered and stopped. June's father tried to open the door, it wouldn't open. The reason it wouldn't, the cage was somehow stuck about four feet above the second floor on its way to the attic.

Lavonne had gone, slipped out the side door on a date, nobody else was on the premises but the slumbering owner, whom she would not dare try to rouse, Rosetta was thinking in a cold, claustrophobic sweat. What to do! But June's father, punching the button and rocking the cage, somehow managed to make it inch on down to about a foot from the second floor, where the door did finally open and they stepped out. He wanted to know where the cellar was, because one of these days this thing would stall and trap somebody. Maybe down there he could see what caused the hitch. Lead the way. He would not be deflected, and so Rosetta nervously led the way down into the basement. He stooped down and, squinting through the cage, recognized the safety buffers and pointed out to Mark that, see, that there's the piston, and the way this works, it's different from the kind that—

"It was the first elevator ever installed in a private house in Salt Lake," Rosetta repeated.

"And people cold and hungry at the time," June's father said, standing up and brushing his hands together as though just finishing a job of work. Of course he had done nothing, what did he know about elevators? but with an air of accomplishment he went on, "Well, up and down, up and down!"

The lift? The fortunes of mankind? Before he left, he took Rosetta aside and said he was trusting his little girl to her to watch out for just as if June was her own. Don't let her drink Cokes, they're fuller of caffeine than coffee, make her get to bed, not start washing her hair at one in the morning, and as for that Green Beret...In back of her father, June was frantically signaling *say okay*...Her room's to sleep in, not to entertain. Right? Right, don't worry, she will be just fine.

ROSETTA HOPED SHE WOULD BE. But June did drink Cokes, she did wash her hair at one in the morning, and her beau must have been in her room with her about half the time, though once those thick hardwood doors closed, you couldn't hear a sound. Rosetta's own door stood open (had it not, Birdelle would have opened it on her way to the bathroom, leaving her own that way as well throughout the night), but whether Normal came up by the staircase or even went in and out by climbing the trellis and swinging up over the balcony, Rosetta didn't know. He was there, though, she knew which car was his, big wide tires, pipe-things sticking out in back, cover buttoned down tight as a drum over the seat and steering wheel. He parked it down the block a little way. And? The world was changed, so different a place that on the radio they talked about allowing the mentally deficient to run loose and have meaningful relationships, and letting old men and women in nursing and retirement homes sleep without benefit of clergy in each other's arms.

They talked about all *kinds* of things on the radio now that they never used to. Heber Merrill's local talk show would curl your hair. He interviewed celebrities as they came through town or fell back on local people, which was more often than not the ones in some kind of a mess, it seemed like, rather than those to hold up as an example, he would ask them their opinion of various issues. Not at all nice issues, either. And if he could see that his guests would be shocking enough on their own, without any encouragement from him, he would let them. "Feel free," he would say.

"LIKE TAKE FOR INSTANCE THAT Jerry something, that New York composer or whoever he was that Heber Merrill had on his program last Thursday night, teaching up at the university—our innocent children!" Rosetta's ten o'clock perm said in an aggrieved tone.

Rosetta laughed. "I heard that program, Mrs. Prather," she said, beginning to block off her hair. "That was Jeppe Casement."

"Well, who is responsible for such a thing?"

"I don't know. Some committee up there at the university, I guess. I thought he was kind of cute. The way he wiggled out of that remark of his to *Time* magazine—"

But Mrs. Prather's attention had wandered to how the color of her eyes and the plastic curlers Rosetta was beginning to use matched, and how pretty that blue was, and wasn't that a coincidence?

"—about how glad he was to be coming to Utah because it was such a boring state."

Alice blue. "Beg pardon?" Mrs. Prather said.

"Boring. The state. Utah."

"Utah is *boring*?"

"*I* didn't say so. That was Jeppe Casement in that radio interview you're talking about."

"Who?"

"The composer from New York who said—"

"What is he *doing* here, anyway?"

"They call it a seminar."

JEPPE CASEMENT CALLED IT DYING and going to hell. Had he really only been in this wild waste since last December twenty-seventh and not the Valentinian thirty Gods and Aeons?

HE WAS WALKING UP PARK Avenue. Trudge, body... towards the office of an alienist so without the milk of human kindness that his motto was put up or shut up. Old patient, old friend though you might be... aging, gaining, hair starting to fall out, misled, seduced, deceived... ride up to the top of the Empire State Building and... when who should grab him by the arm and swing him around but—

"Howdy, partner!" said Ariel Luebke with his Hungarian accent.

"Howdy yourself." Also go fuck yourself. Why did some people—? Luck. Go out to guest conduct the Symphony in Utah while Werner Janssen and Ann Harding vacationed in the Bahamas... and end up married to a branch of... Kennecott Copper! Betty, whose influence and subsidia...

"You bring it with you?" Jeppe asked coldly.

"What?"

"Your Salt Lake City Symphonette? Your Pops?"

Ariel said no, he left it home, said it like it was his Mercedes or cabin cruiser. He was in New York, he said, to attend the International Conference of Symphony and Opera Musicians. "Come on, have a drink, I want to tell you—! Say, I saw what what's his name had to say about your opera. I hope you didn't let it—get to you."

"Get to *me*?" But later, having a martini, Jeppe wept, about that of course, he having worked on it the whole time he was in Paris, but mostly about Paco. "'I have lived long enough,'" he quoted with pathos, "'having seen one thing, that love hath an end...'"

Ariel's teasing smile made him start to get up and leave in indignation. "Come on now, Jeppe. I'm sorry! Sit down, come on. But knowing you—" Gently, he asked what happened.

What happened was that fatal interview between him and Paco. At the Hamptons. "And all that did ensue..." Would Ariel believe there had hardly been a day since Paco bought the loft and they moved in that he, Jeppe, hadn't been put to labor worse than a galley slave? Except when he played a concert or gave a lecture. Not that he *minded* at the time. They were in this for keeps, body and soul, this was for their lifetime, this was Paco's home and his home as long as they both should live. All right, he wasn't too much of a practical help, Paco had the money, his father was in this piece *Fortune* magazine did on South American real estate, but had the situation been reversed, he, Jeppe, would have spent as freely. Which instead he gave his life's blood. Ruined—ruined—look at his hands. He helped expose the brick walls, install the kitchen, build the elevated seating nook, or anyway he kept the coffee going, ran back and forth to the delicatessen and liquor store, went to the laundromat, he had been a slave, a *slave*. Stripped the paint from the old original columns, helped with the pass-through. And who took care of the rabbit? will you kindly tell me. A darling thing, Easter present, grew. And Edgard, the watch dog, a Rottweiler, you should see him! Watered the plants—and they had six Norfolk pines. Oh, God, the hopes and dreams.

"Well, I came home—tonsils and hemorrhoids torn from my adult body, aged ten years—and what do I find? Andrew there, making a quiche. At first I think—But no, the boy's ensconced, an odious creature. Next thing, Paco and I—" A sob broke from his lips. "Oh, yes, indeed I have lived long enough…"

"So then what?"

"It's Paco's loft, he's the one with the money. All his promises—My work! My fame! Not that I accomplished—For his sake, in fact, I totally *sacrificed* a year and seven months. Only to be cast off like a dirty shirt."

"Where are you staying?"

"That is a very good question."

"Jeppe, listen. For old times' sake, old Curtis days, when the Benny Goodman Trio came to Philadelphia, remember?—your fight with Zimbalist about Ravel—"

"Betrayed—betrayed—"

"Listen, I've just been thinking—how would you like to come out to Salt Lake and conduct a seminar? An opera workshop—something of the kind? I could arrange it. Maybe—"

With his wife Betty's pull, Ariel did arrange it. Eighteen thousand dollars for six hours a week, spring term, vacation, then back again for fall term, long enough for Jeppe at least to catch his breath and start to think about the future. "You start January fifth."

Flying out there, Jeppe didn't watch the movie. His own movie was playing in his mind, filling him with such ecstasy he almost floated free of the seat. He would become a new person, diet, lose twenty pounds. No more chocolate ice cream, lemon pie glistening with meringue, devil's-food cake, cream puffs, Brie, orange tarts, cherry clafoutis…His skin would clarify, his hair get thick. People could reverse the aging process. Work out mornings. Hike. Go skiing. Up with the larks. Live celibate. Oh, yes. Not smoke. Quit biting his fingernails. Read. Practice ten to twelve. Purcell, Satie, Hindemith and Berg. At the piano. Sit there. Get the Pindarian Hymn out of the way, the piece for flute, the Votive Mass for unison chorus and organ, finish once and for all the damn sonata. But first on the agenda…like they always say, when you get thrown off a horse, get right back on, conquer the fear. He should have, when it failed, got right back on, written another opera. But Paco…And anyway he never did accept…What do they know? *The Necessary Outrage of the Death* was as good an opera…The stinking Ford Foundation and crummy New York City Opera never would commission in their crummy lives a better one, nor would the critics get to hear anything even remotely…"Jeppe Casement should be seen and not heard." "He only does it to annoy, because he knows it teases." "The worst composer in America."

Damn it, he would show them, find a great libretto, write *the* opera…but "aye, there's the rub." Pick the libretto right and you took the track home. Pick it wrong—! *This* time, though…no *Velvet Guards and Sunday Citizens*. No *Necessary Outrage*.

Something like—Some people thought the Mormon stuff had kind of a blood-stained grandeur, and since that was where he was going…But Talley Gibson stubbed his toe on that one. *Brigham Young and His Wives*…Poor Talley! Lyric drama, televised one Sunday…Slunk to Crete or to the Hebrides. Because, of all the boring subjects on this earth! Polygamy. Those wives with a face like a knife in the back, those Calvinists in codpieces, the vapor of bad taste hovering over those snow-capped peaks, the sunsets…

But Ariel said the kids out there without a doubt were beautiful. Even his own offspring, due to the minerals in the water, the air or something, bypassed his and Betty's shortness and darkness and sprang forth Greek divinities. Like they just stepped out of a Maxfield Parrish painting. Well, look at Miss America! It was the sun, the altitude…But of course the students at the university came from everywhere. "Would you believe," Ariel said, "that the *biggest Mohammedan population* in America lives in *Utah*?"

"No."

"Well, it does. And the reason is the Mormons. Their kids go out on missions, and in the Middle East they feel right at home because the land's a lot *like* Utah, mountains, desert, ice and snow, or hot and the wind blowing, here and there an oasis. Their beliefs too, Islam and Mormonism, they're a lot alike. Purify and pray, keep the women humble, don't drink, fast on certain days…They emigrate. That's why you can get pilav out in Salt Lake City, and shish-kebab and…"

"Arabs I can do without. Listen, if I told you what happened to me in Marrakesh…"

"Jeppe, listen. There's a *lot* of things you'll have to do without in Zion, as they call the place. Because it's not long since—I don't suppose they'd slit a man's throat today for, shall we say, immorality, or take him out and—But underneath that corporate image, as I guess you'd call the prosperous well-being, teeth, short haircuts, attaché cases, double-knits and all the sporting goods—these people are *primitive*."

"The Mormons? That's fine with me."

"Well, fine. But you be careful."

Jeppe knew what he meant. That personal boast that sex was, that mystique and ideology, *o-u-t*. No more libidinous promenades, Hylas with his gorgeous genitals, Dion, Abderus, Clinias and Bathyllus. "Are you the opposite sex or am I?" In fact Ariel said so in so many words, "Don't do that to us," meaning him and Betty, "it's another world." "You don't seem to understand," Jeppe had said, "I'm absolutely through with all that coy, mean, destructive…plowing the sands…the ripping, shrieking, ferociously passive…"

"It's only for two terms," Ariel said.

"My lifetime," Jeppe said in a stern voice.

"Well, while you're out there," Ariel said, "stay away from Larr Farr Park, those blocks around the Newhouse Hotel and Hotel Belvedere, a place called the Radio City Lounge…"

Jeppe would, he intended to. Study. Work out. Lose weight. Save money. Quit smoking. He lit another cigarette, the better to think about the change…Tailor-made suits with buttonholes, Italian shoes, French ties…Quit drinking. His hair, his skin…Paco would flip. But too late, Paco. A little too much on the agenda nowadays to slave for *you*, to sit around in the dark with *you* eating chocolate, drinking Cokes (ugh) and watching TV, to waste time with those cretins you call friends, because the New York City Opera is doing my opera, the one I wrote while I was out in Utah—!

"How do you do, sir. Regent of the—?"

"I see you've got a lot of scenery and so on, but with my friend Don DeLillo, who wrote *Great Jones Street*, I regard nature as a 'hideous screeching bitch of a thing.' And as I understand your metropolis here ain't hitting on nothing either, *work* is going to be my watchword!"

"Oh, yes, very glad to be here. I expect to get a lot done," he told the young girl interviewer at the Salt Lake Airport, "because of no distractions, I guess, as far as the eye can see."

That lit up the switchboard. Who the hell is *he*? Who hired him? Who does a morphodite like him think he *is*? Is *my* tax money paying that bastard? coming out here and insulting *us*? Mr. Castrate, or whatever his name is, is no gentleman.

"The name is Jeppe Casement," Ariel said before he interviewed Jeppe on KSL two days after he settled in at the Alfonce Deseret Motel. "He is a gifted, versatile and important composer. His work is a demonstration of how music can still express beautiful and noble sentiments. His sense of shape, dimension and dramatic logic…The University was most fortunate…However, at the airport Monday it seemed Mr. Casement had inadvertently put his foot…" He gave the high sign, and Jeppe delivered the apology Ariel said he would either deliver *or else*.

"Of course I did not mean what I said like it *sounded*," he said. "Utah is wonderful, the greatest thing since egg cartons. In the words of that great poet Edgar Guest, 'God won't ask if you were clever, for I think He'll little care; when your toil is done forever, He may question: *Were you square?*' And the answer that will rise up around here will be a resounding *yes*!"

No, no, no, signaled Ariel.

"This is a place for work," Jeppe went on. "A place to dream. Jung—who once hallucinated a golden turd unloosed by God—would have loved it. As my friend Carlos Castañeda said, all paths in life lead to the same place—nowhere. And this is the ultimate. So let's go get—not stoned, but with an attitude toward circumstances of detachment, ataraxia, and holy indifference. And see what we shall see."

Jeppe was not assassinated, so they put him on again, to himself interview such celebrities as came to town—Arthur Fiedler, Henry Mancini, young and British-sounding Nigerian Ambassador Alhaji Mahammadu…But that was as far as he got, because Ariel Luebke's wife Betty put a stop to it. He and she were responsible, she said, for that monster being here in the first place, and if she ever let Ariel talk her into anything again so utterly fraught with ... They had *reputations*. Betty had helped found the Salt Lake chapter of the Junior League, was on the board of trustees at the Episcopal Academy, chairman of ... one of the two women directors on ... They had *children*. Of course their home was out of bounds to the man. Other people's too, the ones who counted, and the *Mormon* establishment certainly wouldn't touch with a ten-foot pole a corrupter of Casement's magnitude.

"What in God's name did he say?" Ariel asked. He had been in San Francisco when Jeppe was on. "What did he *say*?"

Of course they bleeped ... He said ... Let's see ... "I'll read you from the transcript." He said the President of the church seemed to be, although he didn't know him personally, but just judging from his photographs, callipygous. That the only kind of wealth worth having is the kind you do not earn, the kind unassociated with the mean and slavish virtue of thrift. That the advantage of the emotions is that they lead us astray. That you should never get in a peeing match with a skunk. That like his friend Melvin Van Peebles there were three things in life which because he liked them so much he had to avoid: smorgasbord, libraries and beaches, the first because he wanted to *eat* everything in sight, the second because he wanted to *read* all the books, and on the beach he wanted to *bang* everybody he saw. That one time his friend *Frank Sullivan* invited him out for the weekend but said he would have to take *pot* luck because he only had one bathroom. That nothing improves a person's diction like marrying money. That the Aztecs called avocados *ahuacatl*, the testicles of the tree. That according to old legend the first time Adam and Eve went to bed together she bit him. That in Paris the woman of fifty-six was no longer considered to be among the living. That maturity was a hideous word and only a coward would use it. That the essence of Chanel No. 5 is a secretion from the anal gland of the Abyssinian civet. That he was reading in *Science* magazine that the life forms on Jupiter may be big gas bags floating through the atmosphere absorbing organic matter just like whales swallowing tons of plankton as they swim through our seas, so if they want to land a spaceship where they would feel at home, they should try Brigham Young University. That his friend the playwright David Edgar had touchingly written:

Greater love hath none in time of strife
Than laying down his friends to save his life!

And last but not least, he said that according to his friend Dr. F. Avery Jones, pathological fermentation in the stomach may generate enough methane gas to cause a pretty big explosion if a person should belch while lighting a cigarette. As a comparable microbic effect in the lower intestine generates inflammable and explosive hydrogen sulphide and plain hydrogen, if God had not in his mercy arranged for evolution to place the anus quite far away from the mouth, smoking would never have become popular. And what of insouciance then? "And so since the whole of life is a folly and the best we can do is commit it, I say to you, baby, *nunc aut nunquam*. For degrading practices, play Ravel. Do not put on a Bach fugue. And God forbid the Tabernacle choir."

He was now, of course, *persona non grata*. Well, what did he expect? Thank heaven it was late at night, a local program nobody really watched, an hour when De Servientibus— the kind that tarred and feathered and rode offenders out of town on a rail and lynched and eunuchated people—slept the sleep of the just.

"I merely said..."

At the university it was decided that since Jeppe promised not to make any more public appearances during his sojourn but to confine himself to teaching, and since it was only a composition class in a basement room in the Music Hall, not the important nuclear physics department...and for Betty Luebke's sake, through whose good offices Kennecott Copper had been *most gracious* to the institution...they would let Jeppe stay and give his seminar.

He didn't mind pariahdom. Not in Utah. There, it only worked to his advantage. The artist who is going to do something spins out of his own mind a cocoon, he goes mentally into it, he seals it up and never comes out till the job is done. He wouldn't go if they asked him to their silly parties, cold and timid souls as they were who knew neither victory nor defeat. He would roll up his sleeves...The credit would be his, actually in the arena, his face marred by dust, sweat and blood...striving...knowing the great devotions, the triumph of high achievement...

All right. Make a schedule. Get the show on the...The north and east winds blew. It snowed. Gray hours blurred and merged, and snow piled higher. Knowing that nothing would come of it but their memories, he taught his students conscientiously. Practiced in the studio the officials gave him, tried to compose, but dreadful things could happen in the building known as the Music Hall. One night in the empty auditorium, eight large, middle-aged women under the tutelage of a ninth, performing unison exercises on their contrabass tubas, so shook him to the fundaments that he almost tried to find some place to buy a bottle. But he pulled himself together. He did not smoke for nearly three weeks. Bought a calorie counter, let's see now, six feet, ideal weight depending on build...He dieted. His new clothes would have to be two sizes smaller. Saved money for them and for the apartment he was going to lease when he got back to New York. Two-story living room, terrace, little garden out in back, a wood-burning fireplace... *Tried* to save, that is. Where did the money go? Even out here it dribbled through his fingers. But the motel was quite luxurious, handy to the campus, its coffee shop was said to be run by the same people as ran the posh Rafters, an apartment wouldn't provide room service. The French Hand Laundry—imagine there even *being* such a thing out here at the end of nowhere— was sinfully expensive, but what was he supposed to do? All right, and he should keep out of the Antiquarian Book Store. But these were trivial matters. He was composing! Twenty-seven minutes' worth of music in the first three weeks. And he might well (at last!) have the libretto that would take the track home. He began to work on it.

And so the balls were all in the air at once, the juggled plates, the drinking glass on the end of the nose—he was writing, teaching, exercising, dieting, teetotaling, saving money (not very much, that's true), taking a bath every day, reading, letting his nails grow, keeping up his journal, avoiding the odd fandangos of sex.

Ariel was proud of him. Were Jeppe in touch with them, which he wasn't, his relatives would be proud. He was proud of *himself*. He would do this forever, keep all these wonderful virtues circulating at once, all the rest of his life. My God, what a man could accomplish. But it's really funny how a talent is called a *gift*. Gifts should be free, shouldn't they, while his gift had to be paid for like you pay back a loan to a loan shark, doubled, tripled, with interest, and under pain of death the whole damn time.

The libretto he fixed on was the kidnapping of Charley Ross, a nineteenth-century concept within a twentieth-century medium. Clothed with his music, it would have everything, the harmonium, piano, celesta, two harpsichords, three clavichords, four contrafagottos in unison, an oboe's blues, a bass singing high, a tenor singing low, an aria to erect an audience like an unruly organ, or a moonshot poised to go, a drinking song on cruelty, perhaps within the context of tonality, a homesick aria, blood, candles, women dressed as men, and love, a ghost, a picnic, a dream sequence, colored streamers...

One moment he was sitting on the radiator writing almost in mittens, a watch cap pulled down over his ears, going to bed by snowlight in a sweater, piling covers over himself and over his songs, drama and orchestral music, and the next it was *spring*, hot, crocuses, forsythia, cherry trees like pink popcorn balls, flowering quince, he was sitting orchestrating, naked, at his window. Nearly sainted by now, due to the exceptional holiness of his life. At least an angel. Not a drink, a chocolate, love's transports, a slugabed hour, a wasted moment. And then one day...

Oh! Why hadn't he *waited* to take the esquisse of *Charley Ross* back to Aline of the New York City Opera and Richard of the Ford Foundation *himself*? when he could have defended and explained...And the last person in God's world he should have *breathed* the project to was Aaron Copland, but he came through this wild waste, and the sight of his familiar, jealous lineaments...And Gary Graffman, whom he wouldn't give the time of day to back home, but here he laid himself wide open...And all their jealous judgments came at once: nix, nein, drop it, worse than Wagner. Aline, Richard, Aaron, Gary: No, darling. Even Ariel! supposed to be his friend! moody, groaning, very uncompelling, as static as an opera can get without freezing in its tracks...It also rained. He also had a toothache. His face broke out. That bitter rejoinder also of his mortality rolled around, his birthday, a memento mori...And if all these weeks his magnum opus had been barking up the wrong book!

Chapter Sixty-seven

*

RAIN BEFORE SEVEN, FINE BEFORE ELEVEN. BUT AT ELEVEN JEPPE DIDN'T SEE HOW fine it was, how bright the moonlight shone, he was inside, had had it, defiantly he sat in the Radio City Lounge on State Street. It was dark and smoky, "California Blues" swirled round, and "Hogtied," "California Dreamin'" ... He was present and accounted for, had two drinks, had another and looked around. Ariel had said don't go there, that was one of the places *not* to go in town. Because he might *enjoy* himself! and approbation and reprobation of the same instrument was out of the question! and Jeppe Casement (bringer of fire to mankind) was supposed to be *miserable* and *suffer*.

Not be happy. Not have this guy as he edges by take hold of his arm, and gently squeeze his fingers, or that one in the mirror darkly drink to him, kissing the glass before he drinks. Nor anybody lovely coming up and putting their arms around him. And the guy on his way to the john stopping in *his* tracks to stare into his eyes ... Avaunt, be gone! And your opinion of rock? Very simple. Rock is cock. A boy came over and asked to dance, or didn't ask, he swept him up, they danced!

His name was Steve, his game was splitting wood, running six miles before breakfast, lifting weights and slogging fifteen miles on three-foot skis with roller-skate wheels at the U.S. Ski Association's training facilities up in Park City.

I believe you, baby.

Then here's a guy that's making signs, a black about seven feet tall, looks like a Watusi dancer and that's what he *is*. Or anyway a dancer. He is with Alvin Beam's Chicago Dance Company, they will give a matinee and one more performance tomorrow night, then mosey on.

Dreamin' ...

It doesn't take just two people to be sweethearts, sometimes it takes ... three, entwined and walking arm in arm under the trees in Liberty Park, over the grass, down by the weedy water ... Sometimes the graces are (in the shadows) are (on the ground) are (beneath the branches) Steve and Jeppe and Ailey all intertwined, entangled and enwoven ...

All you need is love.

And the world well lost! as they will say when it plunges into the bottomless pit of electromagnetic space ...

The east was pink as Steve and Ailey drove Jeppe up to Alfonce's Deseret Motel, in

Steve's car, or someone's car, Steve was driving, and going to drop Ailey off next at the Union Pacific porter's home where he was staying out on Eighth West and Fourth North. Then it was light and all the tenderer for the liquid looks that passed between the three. They kissed, parting is such sweet sorrow. Ailey got out, all seven feet of him in his black gorgeousness, to let Jeppe out, then he got back in. They drove away, waving and looking back. And Jeppe waved, blew kisses, he was drunk, quite drunk.

Oh, no, on *dope* would be more like it! Herman Alfonce said when he ran in and told his wife, Agnes, hardly able to contain himself till she was awake at eight or thereabouts. Dope! Out there as usual, up with the chickens as he always was, working in those beds along the walk there where it curves around, he sees this car drive up and out steps this big kind of overgrown ... "I am telling you, as black as inside of a cow, and what am I saying, overgrown? this fellow's *head* was almost to the eaves! He helps out this guy in 17-A. They're bringing him home, they're kissing, loving, how 17-A even knew where he *lived* is the biggest mystery to me. He staggered up the steps ..." Oh, it was dope, no doubt of that.

The dope in the picture, Agnes said, was her husband Herman Alfonce, not to walk right up when he had the chance and make a *citizen's arrest* ... Also the coward! not to at least have ordered the man to check out instead of standing there letting him go right in and go to bed without a word! Why didn't he get Normal out there? *He'd* have made short work ...

"Normal?"

"Your *grandson*, dummy! Have you forgot we've got a Vietnam *hero* living in this motel now? A Green Beret!"

But in her heart Agnes was glad Herman hadn't caused a ruckus. She talked it over with her daughter Dotty when she got up and Dotty agreed that nothing would have been gained, only maybe some unwanted publicity. But wasn't it terrible what wolves in sheep's clothing so much of the public was? Who would ever have thought that Mr. Casement, a *teacher* and a *musician*, so nice-appearing and quiet (he practiced his instrument, whatever that might be, at the college) and polite, no noisy friends, the maids hadn't found any bottles, but of course if the man was on *dope* ... They decided to let him get his sleep out. If aroused too soon ... one never knew. In fact Dotty wondered if maybe they shouldn't ... taking into consideration the fact that he was going to be leaving anyway in two weeks, when school was out ... But Agnes said no. If it had been just a drunken party, that would have been different. Even a lady friend holed up in there with him wouldn't have been—People were human. But when you were dealing with *dope*, opium dens or God knows what, cocaine, bought off of underworld gangsters, and when nigras came into the picture, and last but not least when you had a perversion of the *laws of nature* on your hands ... No, Mr. Casement must be told to leave.

Dotty was going to be the one to do it. She and her husband, Normal Senior, managed her parents' motel, but Normal Senior was up at Brighton with his sister's husband for the last tobogganing, like some kind of a ridiculous teenager, instead of being where he was wanted, so Dotty was the one the onus fell on, of everything. Of course her son Normal Junior was home now, safely delivered from shot and shell and still the same wonderful boy he was when he left. How many mothers of Vietnam veterans could make that statement? No bad words, no nasty diseases, no bad habits, car paid for, Rolex paid for, money in the bank, still true to his religion. All the making him toe the line through the years, act decent and amount to something—holler and yell though he might, like his father was killing the child—had paid off. And if the day didn't come someday when at a Conference meeting he didn't come walking in through the sacrosanct door beside the great organ pipes and down the carpeted stairs to the armchairs on the Tabernacle platform behind the speaker's rostrum with the *rest of the General Authorities*, or be sent to Congress in Washington, D.C., Dotty would be very much surprised. Karate, kung, whatever that was, jumping out of airplanes—! Normal could handle 17-A. But no use putting innocence up against…He probably didn't even know such things existed as…*Oscar Wilde*. Written up in a copy of *True* that had been left by a guest one time.

Dotty knocked, tried his door, it opened. Mr. Casement? Missing. She found him in the nearly empty coffee shop sitting up at the counter, smoking and idly looking at the hours-old morning paper. "May I speak to you?" "Certainly, madam."

WHEN JUNE CAME BACK FROM the kitchen with his bacon and eggs and more coffee, Jeppe murmured that he should have his domestic officer *in charge of tasting* here. Mr. Casement wasn't much for fraternizing with the help and June had no idea what he was talking about, but she nodded and half laughed. In case this stuff was poisoned, he said. But no, they wouldn't want a dead body left on their hands, would they? A dead *body*? she said. Although they might have one on their hands in spite of themselves. Why, Mr. Casement! what could he possibly mean. Sometimes, he said he meant, it just was all too silly—life was just too silly—to bother about anymore.

He tipped her five dollars, which he never had done in the four, or was it five? months since he arrived from New York, though as he usually sat in her station she thought maybe he liked to have her wait on him. Now to be left five dollars! and him so woebegone. When June got off work a few minutes later, the lobby was empty and nobody seemed to be in the halls, so she hurried to Mr. Casement's room, on tiptoe for extra caution, though the way was softly carpeted. But Normal might be back from working on his and Roger's cars, or their guns, over at Roger's house, though often he stayed till she didn't know whether to give up and go to bed, wash her hair, go down and fix a snack or just what to do. And his mother Dotty or that awful grandmother, called Agnes (Herman, his grandfather, was cute), if they saw her tapping on Mr. Casement's door—! "Mr. Casement, it's June. Are you all right?"

HE WASN'T ALL RIGHT. He had called Ariel, Ariel said to just move out, it wasn't the end of the world. But Ariel had warned him, some of these people's influence around here reached farther than he supposed, and if he was going to get that federal grant—and taking into consideration what certain fanatics around here were capable of—! But he was all right money-wise, wasn't he? Are you kidding? Bills paid—the dentist, the psychiatrist he was going to have to go back to *if he lived*—the room, meals out, taxis, French Hand Laundry, a few stinking books, a first edition *Histoires Tragiques*, Belleforest's translation—he sure wasn't going back to New York *rich*! *If he lived.*

"Mais, bon Dieu! quelles énormes et étranges drames!" Ariel said ironically, quoting from something. "It's not the end of the world. So you went down there where I told you not to go, you met some guys, you didn't get robbed or beat up, *Betty* didn't see you, President *Fletcher* didn't see you, you got home all right. *Someone* saw you, okay, drunk, okay. Mormons—so they've asked you to move. Go to a hotel! is that so shattering? You know I can't ask you here. Betty—But wait a minute. You could call Mrs. Bachauer, *she'd* take you in."

"You want to kill me." Mrs. Bachauer conducted in Salt Lake City what passed as a salon. She had given a cocktail party for him when he first arrived, before anyone realized he had insulted Utah and would go even farther over the air, till he was stopped. She had clasped him to her, powdered his tie with her wrinkled cleavage's obscenity, her mascaraed clumps of lashes raked his cheek like hog bristles, she had fed him a shrimp with her pincers of polished horn. She told him and several other people standing around that his art songs vibrated through her body as if she was one of the instruments, that she felt herself becoming a full percussion orchestra, becoming green, blue, orange. The waves of the sounds ran through her hair like a caress. The music ran down her back and came out her fingertips. She was a cascade, she said. Later she talked even more insanely.

Like a tank smashing through San Quentin, she alone would have smashed through the pariahdom that soon befell him. He had to be uncivil and impolite, she went on a trip around the world, starting from Fort Lauderdale. Now she was home, Ariel saw her at a dinner party. She was a forgiving woman. Call her.

"You want to kill me."

"All right! Okay. Sorry. Go to a hotel. Why should you go to *pieces* like this? Over nothing, Jeppe."

"Nothing!" He had eaten, drank, done the wild thing, the floodgates were down, everything was washed, would wash, away! all his schemes and plans to go back to New York thin, fit, rich and handsome, the best opera ever written in America (at least its esquisse to back abundantly) in his new attaché case…Paco on his knees there, begging, pleading.

"But nothing has *happened*, Jeppe."

Oh, no? Nothing but the Johnstown flood, that's all, the death of P. P. Bliss.

Ariel called back. "Jeppe, there's a *convention* at the Newhouse Hotel. If you can believe it. Tops, the Take Off Pounds Sensibly Society of America. They're all booked up. Listen, though, I'll call a motel over on West Temple—"

"Don't bother, Ariel. I've got my thing—more on the straightaway now—"

"Well—you take it easy and—"

"I know. Keep in touch. Balls to the wall."

When June knocked at the door, he was crying like a child in the armchair, his face hidden in his hands. Mr. Casement! so sophisticated. Before she shut the door she looked up and down the hall, and once inside ran over for a quick peek out the window to see if Normal was anywhere in sight.

"Mr. Casement! What did Mrs. Sleigh *say* to you? Or did somebody die, or what's the matter?"

ONE TIME, THE TIME HE was up at the New York City Opera's headquarters at the end of his rope before he got the commission, crying and carrying on, and told Aline he was mortally ashamed that she should see his disarray, it was after hours, they were having a sherry in her office, Aline said to think nothing of it. The way he poured everything out, the way he showed how he felt, his tears, these were most important in a creator, a composer. They were *as* important as his virtuosity, his knowledge, she said in her voice of an old midget. Aline used to be sweet in those days, not reduced to a vulture's nose which smells a carrion in every rose-bed. She *understood*. People used to *understand*. But now! The beautiful days of Aranjuez…His shoulders shook.

"MY GOODNESS, MR. CASEMENT, PLEASE—"

The nubile maiden is Joan of Arc bringing up reinforcements to relieve the besieged place, succor with her puissance him that's fallen…She is nervous, what if Dotty—Mrs. Sleigh—happens to come in? Or her boyfriend Normal comes home? But pity flows like milk in her nubile breast, someone has to help this man, who she knows is a great composer because once he came in the university library and Maureen who was also working at the check-out desk at the time and who played the violin and was taking his opera workshop, said he was. She said he was wonderful, well-known clear across the country, and June knew herself from waiting on him in the coffee shop that he was a very nice man, usually reading the paper or a book, and on a diet, and smoking like a fiend.

Maureen also said that back in New York he was gay. But who cared? everybody should be allowed to be themself. June's boyfriend Normal didn't have that tolerant attitude. The one thing he didn't understand about God, he said, was why with the Power and Glory at His command He would *allow* what He did! Gooks, the niggers, redskins, freaks, yuppies, dope-takers, fat people, people who wouldn't exercise, smokers, liberals, gun-controllers, bums on relief, spendthrifts, Jews, drunkards, Russians, the Yellow

Peril...Had Normal been God, powie, one big blinding flash and it would all have been over. And don't forget perverts. He and Ed despised them, he and Roger too (his buddy after Ed died), just abhorred them, they were lower down than a snake's belly.

But Normal was handsome and cute. If you were his girlfriend, wow, how does *she* rate. He had this neat MG, this secure future, this lifetime government pension for hurting his knee when he jumped out of an airplane over Thakhek which didn't bother him, his education would be paid for if he wanted to go ahead and get to be a tax expert, he could work for the FBI or CIA, the IRS, Standard Oil, all a former Green Beret like him had to do was fill out the application. When he got older he would be bishop of his ward. Then right on up to the top. Another good thing was he didn't like to talk much, so you didn't have to disagree with him *too* much of the time—inside, that is, doing violence to your feelings because of holding in what you really thought. Because it would have been sheer insanity at that particular stage to have come out and disagreed, considering that he thought women were really "poor protoplasm poorly put together" *anyway*. And that being the case (that Normal believed that), it was most peculiar that the desire of his heart, like some kind of a mysterious...genetic...should be what he claimed it was. June did feel free to scoff a little, her woman's intuition telling her he would enjoy an argument about *that*. And between long silences when they'd just be lying holding each other or kissing, sometimes almost to the point of cannibalism, discussing the matter (about the only one that could actually engage him to any extent) made kind of a pleasant pause. Because Normal in his secret heart was a Fundamentalist, and being a Fundamentalist meant...

For one thing, that if he happened to come home and see her helping poor, banished Mr. Casement get his shit together and, while he went out and settled his bill, packing his things, then helping to carry them out to her little VW parked around by the back entrance, Normal would scourge them both off the premises like perpendicular Jesus the money-changers from the Temple. But June went ahead and did her duty as she saw it. Her very marriageableness, the conformity of her little womb to righteous deeds, the ancient requirements of divine law, made her brave. Mr. Casement was going to the Stadium Hotel, a place too far from the campus to be practical, also from the practice room at the Music Hall, which—*if he lived*, he said, he would need these next two weeks as never before. But perhaps he could rent—? June didn't think they would *ever* allow a piano at the Stadium Hotel. But wait! Maybe he could come and practice at the house where *she* lived.

June lived in the most wonderful old Salt Lake *mansion*, she said. She rented a room there, the landlady was a rich old lady who thought she was so poor she had to take in roomers. There was the most wonderful *piano* in the drawing room. Not a living room, mind you, a real true *drawing room*. The piano...Nobody ever went in there, it was to the left as you came in the front door...The owner was Miss Prentice. Two other ladies lived there. They were old, too. Not as old as Miss Prentice, who was in her eighties, but old. Lavonne was still beautiful like sometimes you hear of old movie actresses being, dressed up all the time, had dates, talked about dating, she was really neat. Funny, but neat. Rosetta was the other one. They ran the beauty shop at Holy Rosary Hospital. Listen! Mr. Casement could rent a room at Miss Prentice's, *too*. Why not? No one would bother him! He could *practice*, make a cup of coffee whenever he wanted, he would *love* it.

Normal, Normal, the name flashed like a warning light in her brain as she was telling Mr. Casement about this haven. But Normal would never see him. Or he Normal, for Normal didn't use the door but came up over the balcony, a foot on the wistaria's thick, bent trunk, up the trellis, grab the drainpipe, up and over the railing, down in reverse order, a Green Beret could jump about ten feet to the ground without harm, even with a lifetime disability pension. Nobody ever saw Normal in the household, he never saw them. Mr. Casement could rent a room, practice on the piano in the drawing room, come and go, and Normal wouldn't even know it!

"No, no," Jeppe said.

"Come on," June said, "we'll just drive past…"

When Birdelle, in the kitchen letting water run into the cracked cup from which she had just drunk some lukewarm beef tea, met Jeppe, she knew he was a young man decent and trustworthy enough so that women alone need have no fear of his sleeping next door or sharing the bathroom upstairs at the end of the hall. Everything about him bespoke the gentleman. And of *course* he could practice on the piano in the drawing room, she said. June could take him in and show him…On second thought, Birdelle would take him in there herself. June said, wasn't this cool? and he said it was. As he was only bald on top, which Birdelle was too short to see, she got the idea he was a music student at the Conservatory preparing for a concert career; that is to say, young. Forty-five or twenty was the same to her.

And because he had bowed slightly at the waist when they met, she also believed that, like herself, he came from a once wealthy but now impoverished family whose seat, which was falling to pieces like her own (a drawer knob had felt wobbly that morning), was located far away…This family once had traveled extensively when he was small, no doubt, as her folks had done with their rich relatives before they were married, dressed him like a little prince, he drove a pony cart brought round by a groom, these things show, can't be eradicated. Birdelle wished, she truly wished, she didn't have to charge him rent for the southwest bedroom, but of course she had to if she wanted to survive, and she even charged him a dollar extra for electricity, besides a dollar, or let's say one twenty-five, per day for the privilege of coming in and practicing on the drawing-room piano, the wear and tear on the…strings.

Delighted, he said.

BIRDELLE WAS PLEASED WITH THE little girl, whatever her name was, who lived in the northeast bedroom for finding this serious pupil from the Conservatory preparing for a concert career, it was a pleasure to help in such a case. She knew they would all be proud of him someday…

"Miss Prentice," June said. "Would you mind if we went upstairs on the—elevator?" She turned to Jeppe. "Miss Prentice doesn't usually like us to use it, although it runs and everything, and *she* uses it—"

"Because of the state of my health," Birdelle said, also because she owned the house and had to have a *few* honorable distinctions beyond the common advantages of others under its roof.

"But she'd rather we used the—" June pointed to the great central staircase. "There's where I'd like to come down when I—" She saw a wedding dress step down, dragging its train, a cloud of veiling. "But this here's the elevator, just look, Mr. Casement! Victorian."

"Get in," Birdelle said suddenly.

"Oh, goody," June said. "She's going to take you up herself. You'll love this, Mr. Casement. I'll run on up and meet you upstairs."

"No, you can ride too," Birdelle said graciously. June got on and made herself as small as she could in the right-hand back corner, Jeppe stood back till Birdelle entered, then he got on, Birdelle slid the inside door across and pressed the pearl button. "This was the first elevator ever to be installed in a private dwelling in Salt Lake City."

"Is that a fact," Jeppe said rather nervously, his eyes on the old lady at the controls.

She pressed the button again, the cage shuddered. "It was manufactured in—Solid brass, the thing down underneath. This damask—Paris. My mother had the idea that anything from Paris—She was so often there as a girl. She lived—We are related—You have no doubt heard of Allen Gerry Prentice? And Elphinstone V. S. Bry? Well, Cousin Virginia…"

"Really, Miss Prentice, I don't mind climbing stairs at all! In fact, I prefer it."

"It's been fixed," June said reassuringly. "The man fixed it. It'll work."

And sure enough, another press of the button and the golden cage did start upwards. Started, gave a lurch, went up…

"And my mother—It was not a normal girlhood. She said herself in later years—" Talking along, Birdelle did not notice their conveyance had stopped again till June ventured to interrupt with, "Miss Prentice?"

Jeppe took his handkerchief out of his pocket and touched it to his brow and upper lip. They were trapped between floors.

Thank heaven Lavonne was home! It took several minutes, however, before they could make her hear. A few weeks before, while waiting in the Wooden Chicken Flight One Eighty for Foster to come back from talking to the boy in the control room, in order not to block the way of a newly arrived party of Country and Western dancers, she had slid politely into a seat under the largest of the earthquake sound system's amps, and ever since had felt like her ears were stuffed with cotton. The deafness hadn't worn off, either, to any degree, and she had taken to reading lips. But luckily she had had to go out into the hallway to look out the stained-glass window for Foster's car and so did hear their faint mewling.

She called the elevator man, she had called him the other time so knew his number, and he soon arrived to rescue the trapped occupants. It was only later, however, that Lavonne met the roomer June had introduced to the household, as just when the service truck drove up Foster arrived too, so she had no more than time to let the elevator man in before she had to fly to the car in her fluttering spring draperies. When she finally met the newcomer for a moment in the kitchen as she was going out and he was coming in, she quickly calculated, as she always did if the man was a bit taller, what kind of looking couple they would make entering a dark, cool nightclub. But a glance revealing to her long experience his tendency to lack the elements to form her kind of compound, she let him sail by like a ghost ship it would be no use to speak to. For his part, for just an instant he thought he was seeing Marion Davies in all her theatrical irrelevance, only to realize, no. Still, it was rather like that, age clothed across as youth in violation of old custom...

Later he inquired of Rosetta who the woman was who lived downstairs, and she said Lavonne. Sick in bed with the flu, he had asked as one might ask for reading matter to pass the time. But as Lavonne hadn't been on the stage or in the movies, he soon lost interest and asked Rosetta, whose name he didn't know at the time—she was just "the other one"—if she or someone in the place had a little transistor he could borrow, and she quickly brought one in and hooked it up on his bedside table. But he had turned it on and it was terrible, so he turned it off and was trying to sleep when she came back in with a tray.

He was very hot and miserable by then with twenty-four-hour flu, diagnosed as such by Rosetta, but it lasted till Tuesday. By that time, as the building going on at Holy Rosary had temporarily closed the beauty shop and Rosetta was at home and had nursed him very capably, they were on the way to being friends. He had told her, why not? his troubles, how cruel everyone had been, Aline of the New York City Opera, Richard of the Ford Foundation, the absolute demons who wrote about his opera *Velvet Guards and Sunday Citizens*—and Paco! He had made himself cry speaking the words *I have lived long enough having seen one thing, that love hath an end*, told about Ariel's fair-weather sponsorship and how his awful wife Betty (somehow related to Kennecott Copper) *could* have stretched out her hand but *had not*, how he had tried to diet and not drink, and work, and go back to New York after his six months' sojourn here with an opera, *the* opera. Then he idiotically sent a synopsis of the plot and as much of the score as was finished, which he never should have done, to people who did nothing but kill it just as surely as if you drown a sackful of puppies, and then how he went...He might have caught this flu from Ailey or Steve, though since, he had fraternized with others. What hadn't he done to ruin everything! ate, drank, spent, neglected...and it would soon be time to go back, and where was he? Worse off than when he started!

"Don't you say that," Rosetta said. "But as Swinburne said one time, 'We are at the mercy of a God, whom 'twere gross flattery to call a Marquis.'" So if he sometimes felt intense flip-out feelings about all the changes he had been, and was being, put through, it was no wonder.

Her reply made Jeppe look at her. When she left to go down and see who was ringing the front doorbell, he asked, indeed commanded her like a spoiled child, to come back at once to keep him company. The caller was Father Peacock, whom she ushered into the family dining room where Birdelle was sitting at the end of the long oval table crumbling a cracker into a bowl of tomato soup and scattering crumbs around her high-backed chair. Still higher-backed chairs stood in the state dining room (beyond the big double doors, where Cousin Virginia would have dined had she ever come west to visit her poor relations, which she never did, and where the Prentices' part of the Progressive Tea would have been laid in Mary Pickford and Douglas Fairbanks's honor if Birdelle and her mother had not quarreled about dyeing a tablecloth pink), which had never been used for state dining in human memory.

Father Peacock asked after Lavonne, who usually let him in, and Rosetta said she was on a few days' trip down to Tucson to a trade show or something of the kind. Holy Rosary Hospital was torn up again, this time the wing where the beauty shop was, plumbing pulled out, plaster down, walls splintered like a bomb had dropped, so she and Lavonne had canceled their appointments...

"Oh," Father Peacock said somewhat disappointedly.

"And Lavonne went with these friends of hers to this trade show in Tucson. Lights and sound effects. They flew down..." Rosetta said friends instead of friend (and particularly not boyfriend) because Father Peacock was the one who had given Lavonne instructions before her confirmation.

The bond between them was also strengthened by Lavonne's cutting the priest's majestic Irish hair and because he and she had to do most of the contending with Birdelle, he assigned to the job by Monsignor Tate, who wanted the church to come into Birdelle's property, and Lavonne wanting the same for herself. Rosetta did not know, but might have divined from her own long years of beauty shop experience, that Lavonne also heard the priest acknowledge his true state, whatever that might have been, and heard him repent and desire *absolution*, and that she even—as beauty operators do, and bartenders, and taxi drivers—shrove him and pronounced their kind of penance, which was to think of *himself* for a change and not always of others and think that *he* deserved a little of life's pleasures too once in a while, and to stand up to his overbearing superior. Lavonne also didn't believe it hurt him to smoke cigars, saved an article for him out of *Esquire* magazine about the benefits of drinking Bourbon, said he should at least *eat*—how else was a man constantly on the go like he was to keep his strength up?—and from time to time assured him that he *was not fat*. So, looking forward to some of this gentle cajolery, when Rosetta told him that Lavonne was out of town, Father Peacock's disappointment was plain to see. "But she'll soon be home. They weren't to be there long."

"Oh. Well. Of course it doesn't matter," he said, fanning himself with his hat, for he had walked fast from the church, then run up the front steps, and the weather was more like August than May. He was still catching his breath when Rosetta left him with Birdelle.

Chapter Sixty-eight

✳

JEPPE TOOK THE HEAT AS KIND OF A PERSONAL INSULT, COMING ON THE HEELS OF a deep freeze as it had, and being sick and feverish he felt it worse than he might have otherwise. When Rosetta helped him to the bathroom, giving off waves of heat like a bald eagle, they met Birdelle coming up the stairs, being assisted to her room to watch her afternoon shows by Father Peacock.

"Where is the elevator man?" Birdelle demanded.

Rosetta looked surprised.

"Didn't you *phone*? Because Father Peacock here has just been down in the basement and found stuff strewn all over!" That was the expert nowadays, tear something apart, then walk away and leave it. Birdelle was angry. "What did he say?"

"You mean the elevator man? Lavonne was the one who let him in," Rosetta said. "She did mention that when he left he said he had to send away for something and would be back when it came."

"That is no way to conduct—" But wait! who was this? Birdelle caught her breath in terror when she suddenly noticed the hairy-legged man in a bathrobe at Rosetta's side. If Father Peacock hadn't caught her when she stepped back, she could have fallen downstairs. "Who *is* this drunken—How did this man get into my *house*?"

"He got into your house because you rented him a room, Miss Prentice. This is Mr. Casement, the composer."

"Oh, yes. The student. Music. Yes." A kind of patroness look crossed Birdelle's face. "But why—?"

"He's got the flu, Miss Prentice."

"Oh, I see."

"I'm helping him to the bathroom."

"Yes, that's nice. We must always try to help our fellow—"

The *flu*?

Jeppe staggered on, Rosetta went too, glancing back over her shoulder.

"Well! that just goes to show what happens when you try to do a good deed!"

"Oh, now, Miss Prentice." The priest and she were in her room now, she was very upset.

"And also that there's no safe place—"

"The everlasting arms," he said gently.

"The arms, my foot." Birdelle shook with anger.

Father Peacock had to leave soon after that, but out in the hall he called softly to Rosetta and she stuck her head out of one of the bedroom doors. "She's in quite a state," he said.

"Right." Rosetta went in and reassured her, then went down with her bedroom pitcher and got water from the kitchen, as Birdelle didn't want to drink water that came from the bathroom tap. When she got back, Birdelle had her pills laid out and took them and two or three teaspoons of something from a sticky bottle, asking as she did so where Lavonne had got to. Lavonne had told her before she left, but Birdelle said she didn't remember. All *she* knew was, that's the way people acted nowadays. Disappeared. Just when they were wanted. Tucson indeed. And where was the elevator man?

"I called him and he said to tell you he'll be here Tuesday."

"I need my elevator."

"He'll fix it Tuesday. The parts will come—or whatever is the matter—"

"Everything is the matter!" With life, with the world, when into the innermost stronghold anyone could devise, germs could sneak, disease could come and murder you as surely as any homicidal maniac. "Poverty!" she wailed as the pills took effect. Parents should not bring children into the *world* unless they can take care of them. Had she not been destitute, she would not have had to…open her home to…lodgers, influenza, trouble, molestation…

Whether she really caught something or whether her agitation caused it, Birdelle *did* get sick, but only for one day and part of the next. Rosetta called Dr. Wallace and he came and gave her a shot, also a little bottle of pills to take, one every four hours. "It's been going around," he said. "She has a mild case, temperature only just above normal, lungs clear—" He would like to have that heart and that blood pressure, live to be a hundred. "Drink fruit juices." He also looked in on Jeppe, having no idea this was an Eastern composer lying there famous enough to have been asked questions by the Tribune and *Time* magazine and his answers printed. But he did seem to remember vaguely something about two radio broadcasts that nearly got somebody horsewhipped, possibly him? Rosetta in his mind being an old family retainer, his conduct towards her was kindly and propitious. All would be well.

AND ALL *WAS* WELL. BIRDELLE must not, however, have had what Jeppe did, for by Tuesday morning she was up and dressed while he still lolled against his pillows, pale and unshaven, heavy-eyed. Prolonging his state on purpose, Rosetta feared, so as to be waited on, which he seemed to need as desperately as starving persons need food. Wasn't that strange? Babying. She tried to remember what celebrity it was who said in a magazine interview that he once wrote a play in which there was a brothel where you could go every night and they'd give you a bath and powder you and dab a little Vaseline where it itched and dress you in pajamas with feet in them and put you to bed and tuck the covers in and kiss you and turn off the light and tiptoe out, leaving the soft, staticky murmur of the little turned-on radio with the lighted dial, which you wouldn't even hear because you'd be fast asleep. And in the morning a sweet and loving voice would call you up with morning face and morning heart—"Wake up, sleepyhead, time to get up!" For that, this celebrity—oh, yes, it was Lenny Bruce—said he personally would be glad to pay a thousand dollars a night.

Rosetta really hadn't done much for Jeppe. Brought him things to eat, coffee, helped him down the hall to the bathroom that first day and night when he was dizzy and nauseated, changed his hot, tumbled bed, opened and closed his windows, kept him company. It surprised her that he would want her to, but reading made his head ache, what came over the air he couldn't stand, the Tabernacle choir, the Symphony, nothing. "Sit down there, talk to me."

AND SO SHE DID SIT down, and he, steeped in self-pity, the most enervating state of mind imaginable, talked with his eyes closed, or open, fixed on the ceiling, reiterating his complaints and griefs. Nobody better to talk to than a beauty operator forty years in the business. In old Russia the Countess Saltikov did not keep her favorite hairdresser in a cage only to prevent his fixing anybody else's *hair* but for the comfort of his counsel, so it was said. He wasn't brilliant. Yes, but there are few concepts so difficult that they do not yield to the repeated attack of the ordinary mind, and after dealing with all the basics over and over, love, death, money and simple bits of local confusion, the hairdresser can tell you as well as any menticultured abstractionist that an inch is enough to keep us from drowning, that solutions are always partial and always subject to expiration, either short-term or long-term, and that...oh, yes, you could go farther and fare worse.

And so Jeppe began to feel better, the conversation then became more two-way. Rosetta told her legends, told Wyandra's, about the town, old times, this very house, the orphan girl who fell asleep and never woke up. He liked that, Mavis, and to hear about the millionaire Jim Clarendon, sat bolt upright, but then slumped down again. No, no. It wouldn't do. What wouldn't? For what? To base an opera on. Too *Ballad of Baby Doe*-ish. Too...An idea! he said, knocking on his forehead as on a door. If he just had *that* to take back to New York it would all make sense, this whole hieroglyphic, dumb, unaware trip out here to the jumping-off place of the world! But...tell me that again, he said. Why did this Mavis and her mother go *down* there to southern Utah in the first place? Because people in those days were still interested in the massacre and stuff connected with it, she said. And where was it they went? he said. To Cedar City. And the mother, what was it again she was trying to *do*?

"Lisheen, her name was. She went down there pretending she was going to start some kind of Protestant day school for girls. But really what she was going to try to do was spy

out what she could about the massacre. This was twenty-odd years after it happened, you
see, and several years after John D. Lee had been stood up and shot as the main instigator.
It had been, and still was at that time, a kind of *cause célèbre*, stuff had been published
about it for years across the country, yet because the Mormons are *like* they are, the whole
thing was still quite a mystery."

"Did the Indians fight alongside the white men?" he said. "How many fought how
many? Did Brigham Young give the orders?"

"No one knew that," she said, "or knows to this day. So Lisheen had this wild idea
that she could go down there and find out what really happened. She had a good reason.
Her gentleman friend put out this paper in some little town, and he said if she really got
something new on the massacre, he would—oh, lots of things. She was a widow. So she
took her child and went down there—"

"No," Jeppe said. "No."

"What do you mean, no?"

"I mean, it won't do."

"You're talking about your libretto."

"How many people were killed?"

"In the massacre? Well, let's see—I once read a piece in the Sunday paper that said
there were really *two* wagon trains that had teamed up, so there were quite a few—way
over a hundred."

He had sat up again, slumped back down. "And what's that today when thousands…millions…The Jews! My Lai. And—"

"Well—"

He shook his head. "It wouldn't seem like *anything*!"

"Now wait," she said. "It seems like something, doesn't it? when they scare poor
Falstaff in the woods? When Madame Butterfly kills herself? When the stone man, the
man of white marble, comes clomping into Don Giovanni's dining room, bump bump
bump? That's what *art* is for, isn't it? to take something measly—measly in comparison
with the universe—and make it *count for something*?"

He sat up again, hooked his arms around his knees.

"Besides, I'm related to John D. Lee," she said, "supposed to be the ringleader. Me
and about six thousand other people. He had thirteen wives."

When Jeppe didn't want to take a nap and wouldn't let her go, she asked him if he
would like to see the scenario her cousin who had died in World War Two had written
about the massacre. Because when she was moving over here to Birdelle's and her stuff
was all stirred up, it had bobbed to the surface. Legrand was on what was called the
Writers' Project, this was Depression days when Roosevelt—So he combed through all
this historical stuff, she said. "And John D. Lee seemed to be the—Bamboo Chief, as
they used to say in those days. And we know we're kinfolk. So Legrand went down to

southern Utah—like doing research, but it didn't do much good. And then after we got married, he went to Hollywood with the thought in mind to—"

"You mean you married your cousin?"

"Well, second cousin."

"You know something?" Jeppe said. "The only girl *I* could ever have married would have been my sister."

"Like a Pharian king," she said. "Robert Burton said the same."

"Can I see it? Legrand's scenario?" he said.

She ran and got it, left him alone to read it, found him later galvanized, up, dressed, pacing the room. "*It just might do.*"

"Well, use it with my blessing. With Legrand's blessing. He would be *so* pleased. After all these years. In fact, just wait a minute!"

She ran out again, this time brought back Legrand's picture. That had bobbed to the surface too. Legrand and Jeppe *looked* alike, didn't Jeppe think so? Graduation picture, class of…

"I can't use this word for word, you understand," he said, touching the scenario, "because an opera—"

"Use it however you want."

"The title, though—I might use that. *All on the Meadow Green*. Is the meadow still there? The actual place?"

"Oh, I think so," she said.

"I mean, it's not a town or a shopping mall or ski resort, is it?"

"I think it's some kind of historical—There's a monument—"

"Listen," he said, but stopped.

THEN! YOU WOULD NEVER HAVE known that he had ever been sick, humiliatingly ejected, meanly dispossessed, cruelly deprived of what both corporeally and incorporeally he deserved. He rushed off to give his lecture, called Ariel, met him for a drink.

Ariel saw Jeppe had things so covered he thought for a minute he was drunk.

"But no, listen, I've got it, my libretto! the *last* for which the whole dumb, unaware *first* was made."

"So what are you talking about?"

"I'm talking about—" Jeppe told him.

"I'm sorry," Ariel said, "but you have hit on the *one* subject you absolutely *cannot* use. And especially not during a presidential campaign year when the Republican candidate this time may be a Mormon. The church wants that to happen, for a lot of reasons. And you come up with a theme like that, you're dead meat."

"Why? They wined and dined Talley when he was out here getting material for *Brigham Young and His Wives*."

"That was the polygamy stuff. That's just quaint and ditsy. They don't care about that. But this stuff *you've* got onto—forget it, Jeppe."

Ariel sat looking worriedly at him. He wasn't Verdi, that was one consolation. What had that critic said? "Composer Jeppe Casement, indulging his proclivity for eclecticism to the utmost, and parodying one style after another, has produced a harsh onslaught of ornamental coloratura writing without sufficient melody or legato line to sustain it…" One performance maybe. But on the other hand, addicted to tonality as he was, what if he really wrote operatically for the human voice for a change? Gave it songs and melodies, cut out the grotesquerie, mannerisms and technical complexities—and—hit the jackpot? The media would revive the old scandal. People would want to know. Did that massacre really *happen*? Did the Mormons *really* team up with Indians to murder and mangle their fellow Americans like that? Could nice, decent, conservative Republican non-smokers like them ever have been that crummy and cruddy? *So how about this Mormon running for President?* Fanaticism doesn't change. "Please don't do it," Ariel begged. "Read *The Fan Man*. Use that for your libretto. Use—"

"But Betty's not a Mormon! What's it to *you*?" Jeppe said.

"No, but Kennecott Copper—her dad—It's Mecca, see. Her whole *life*. She paints. And she's mad enough at me anyway for bringing you out here in the first place, having her stick her neck out to get you the opera workshop, only to have you arrive and say you're glad you're here because Utah is so boring you'll get a lot of work done. And what you said on the radio. Thank God she doesn't know you're running around loose now till you leave for New York. Listen, Jeppe, how about this? You go back and don't write what you've just told me at this particular time and I'll tell you what I'll do, I'll *help* you. I know somebody in New York, you can stay in their apartment. And didn't I hear you say once you liked Yaddo, but you're on their shit list? I'll get you *off* it. Yes. I'll call Aline, I'll talk to—There are people I can call. But for God's *sake*—"

Jeppe promised, as King Alan of Ireland swore upon the reliquiae of St. Germanus knowing that, as the bones actually belonged to St. Celestine, the vow need not be kept. He and Ariel shook on it. But when they parted, not to meet again in Salt Lake, as Ariel was leaving to run the Summer Conservatory in Claremont, California, Jeppe went straight to Sam Weller's book shop for books about the Mountain Meadow Massacre, to get himself a feel for the time and place. And that night he went on the town, sort of a laughable expression considering that at ten p.m. in the whole downtown area you might encounter one pedestrian. But the Radio City Lounge was open.

He brought a boy home. Rosetta, opening her door a crack and about to tiptoe to the bathroom, saw Jeppe usher him into his room, a tall boy in track shoes, and saw the door close. She knew that Normal was in June's room…and as Lavonne had come home from Tucson, Rosetta had heard the car drive up and voices, she supposed Foster would spend some time with her. Wouldn't Birdelle be surprised if she knew what was going on under her roof? Truth was, Rosetta would have been surprised herself. For *nothing* supersalient was going on at all! Instead, in Lavonne's room Lavonne and Foster were sitting fully dressed, he eating a last dish of the hand-packed butter-pecan ice cream she kept stocked for him, and she weeping quietly into her diet Fresca. They were parting. He explained why. It was a long story. And while he was talking, she examined with despair the large hole through his head like that sculptor over in England that makes the statues with the big holes gouged out. When was it going away? Ever since getting to Tucson, the hole had showed up in everything, wherever she fixed her eyes, like if you took a big cookie cutter and cut out a circle from a face, the back of a chair, a waiter's chest, a pair of dancers, and threw the circle away, leaving empty air, let's see, since, well, let's see... The pilot said they were making the approach... and that down to the right was one of the only four high-energy laser experimental sites in the United States... beam-weapon research... and said they were to look... or did he say *not* to look? It was the University of Arizona's Catalina Observatory... and charged-particle beams such as for beam-weapon research... Foster repeated in her ear what the pilot had said, as since she had sat under the giant amp that time she could hardly hear. She turned her head and looked down at a huge flash. Don't! He grabbed her, clapped his hand over her eyes, she thought he said to look! and she was *so mad*, her eyelashes tore loose, some of the bristles... At first she thought *they* had scratched her eyeball. But it must have been... the beam. Of course she didn't act mad at Foster, but it was the most annoying thing, having a big hole in your vision. There it was, the minute she opened her eyes in the morning. A round part of the whole world simply gone, whatever she focused on, her lips while putting on lipstick, her cheek for rouging, her nose, eyebrow... or her hair! At any given moment, the one part she needed to see was cut out by this cookie cutter and thrown away!

So anyway, he was saying—no hard feelings? He didn't lead her to expect? Without a mouth and nose, which she had cut out with the cookie cutter when she looked at him with blue, tear-filled eyes, he recited to her muffled ears the words to "Taps," which he had framed in his office. Perhaps he sang them.

Fades the light,
And afar
Goeth day, cometh night,
And a star
Leadeth all,
Speedeth all
To their rest!

"Lots of people don't know that thing's got words," he said.

In June's room, Normal was lying on her bed with all his clothes on but his coat and shoes, and his arms under his head, gazing at the ceiling. June had jumped up in her short little nightgown like a tutu pulled up under her arms and gone over to plump down in the armchair and throw one bare leg over the arm. "A fine polygamist you'll be!" she said. "A person who doesn't even want *one* girl, what will they do with three!"

"Will you or won't you?"

"I've told you I will."

"No, you didn't. You didn't say you'd drop everything and—"

"But it's all so silly!" she said. "Polygamy in this day and age. Why, Mom would flip! And Daddy—But I said I would. I said I'd leave with you. And I will. But listen, I've got finals, everybody's got finals, they need me at the library. Your *mother* needs me at the motel, people checking in for Commencement, parents—! Gee, Normal, those two jobs—if I didn't have *them*—You don't seem to realize. My scholarship wouldn't begin to pay for—"

"*You* don't seem to realize how close the world is to the end."

"But school will be *out* in a few more days."

"School," he said and laughed.

"Well, you can laugh, but if I go now I'll lose everything I've worked for. And some-day you might be pretty glad to have a wife that earns a nice—"

"Now," he said. "Tomorrow. I've had all I can take around here."

"You know what I think? I think the whole thing from beginning to end is just—battle fatigue. Most of the guys come home—they're shooting up and into things, it's in the paper all the time—but *you* come home, and do you want my honest opinion? You're just as gone to seed as they are, only *your* crystals is this Fundamentalism. It's the absolute flakiest—You could be an *executive*. You could go to *school*. But no, you want to live back in the mountains with a bunch of nutty Washed in the Blood of the Lamb charismatics, or whatever they call themselves. You could have *me*. Right now. A psychi-atrist would be very interested in you, Normal, wanting to wait till you get married! Oh, but that's moral and nice, you know? But wait till you tell him what you're waiting for! *Three* brides—*one* ceremony—*one* bed—*one* wedding night! for cripe's sake—"

"Blah—blah—blah," he said, sitting up and starting to put his shoes on.

She looked at him like she hated him. But as she didn't, and thought as he bent over there he looked handsomer than any movie star, and as a lock of hair fell forward over his eye and he had this deep voice, she waited a minute, sighing. Then she said, "Where do you think you're going?"

Where, was to his friend Roger's, where he had been staying ever since he had the big fight with his father over Fundamentalism. His father had said that Mormonism right like it stood was fundamental enough for anybody in their right mind, and Normal had said probably *too* fundamental for a hypocrite like him! and finally Grandma Agnes had

had to come between father and son, and then Normal flung himself off the premises. His shoes on, he reached for his jacket draped around the chair back and was going to get up when June came running over and knocked him back on the bed, falling on top of him and pressing her lips to his. But Normal didn't like a girl to come on too strong, so he pushed her off and struggled up and left in spite of her pleadings. That made her lie in the darkness and think how handsome he was and such a great skier and everything and how all that really mattered was not jobs, a scholarship or a profession, but just pure and simple love. And after all, when he was in college he had got A's in differential and integral calculus, and they didn't take morons in the Green Berets, if he believed in the world ending, Jesus coming back to earth, the Millennium, a bunch of brides and all that, why, maybe some of it might not be...that dumb.

Roger didn't have a phone, so June spent most of the next day figuring out how to get in touch with Normal without going to Roger's house, Normal wouldn't like that, he hated people on his trail, as he called it. He wouldn't read a letter, and anyway by the time the mail carrier delivered it...And a telegram would embarrass him in front of Roger. On her way home the next night she drove past Roger's house, but Normal's car was nowhere in sight and neither was Roger's. It looked as if no one was home. What if he had really left town? If she never saw him in her life again? She got so weak, so sick with despair that when she got back to Miss Prentice's she could hardly get out of her car. Had Rosetta or Lavonne been about, she could scarcely have said hello. Miss Prentice's door was shut, so was Mr. Casement's. She tottered to her room, lay fully dressed on her stomach across her unmade bed, her face pressed into the pillow where his head had lain.

THE BOY IN JEPPE'S ROOM wasn't really his type. When he got undressed he proved to be pear-shaped, narrow shoulders, wide intercolumniation, he never seemed to stop yakking, mostly about politics. He said he was on Senator Arble's team even *though* he himself was a Methodist. The Mormons were wonderful people. Senator Arble would bring prayer back into the schools, give the Pentagon a chance to *protect* this country, loosen the reins on business, throw out Social Security, quit gouging the middle class, choke off relief and bring back differentiation. The new word for non-integration, the boy said in a stage whisper. When he smiled his tongue somehow showed, and he carried a little bottle of Listerine to swish around full-strength in his mouth from time to time, and if spitting it out was not convenient he would swallow it. He said this was good for people. Had Jeppe really brought this monotreme home? How hath the mighty fallen. He had been so happy, carefree, had his libretto now, was going home next week, start fresh again, Ariel would fix everything. He had practically *floated* down to the Radio City Lounge for a little celebration.

By midnight, wipeout, down amongst the dead, this unspeakable companion sitting over there naked swallowing Listerine! "Listen," the young man said, glancing at himself in the mirror over the dresser, "as Senator Arble says, don't worry about what you *can't* do, make the most of what you *can* do." He added that American technology—for instance, now there was this new invention, they inserted a plastic tube *here* and when an old guy was having a little problem, all he had to do was squeeze the bulb and the, you know, would stand right up—was wonderful.

Jeppe said he had a terrible headache and contributed twenty dollars to the Mormon Senator's presidential campaign. Alone, he went to bed as though the power had been off and there was nothing else to do, not because he was sleepy. And he lay there in the cold darkness, not counting sheep but counting Franz Josef Haydn's achievements from 1742 till…one hundred and four symphonies, seventy-six quartets, twenty-four operas, three oratorios, sixty-eight trios…thirty-one divertimentos…fifty canons and…lay there crying like a baby.

But things always look better by daylight. Unless they look worse. They didn't look too much worse to Lavonne, except for that hole in the middle of existence. That wasn't nice! a person's nose gone, their eye. Thank goodness, though! not really. By shifting focus, you could bring them back. Yes, there it was, her nose, her beautiful eye, her beautiful…and honestly to goodness, Foster wasn't that great, he truly wasn't. And the way he thought people were looking at *him* on the dance floor, every kick, every whirl, you could tell he did, the bend of his back, the tilt of his head, that sort of…unfocused baby smile. The skin-tight pants that flattened his privates, such as they were—it was really surprising how little was really needed to produce a family—up against his stomach, his piercingly white shoes. So practiced was she in the comforting word after all the hairdressing years that she even comforted herself, and Rosetta, sitting and drinking coffee with her in the kitchen, hardly had to contribute anything except that the object in life was hard to keep in mind, and that the thing that always cheered *her* up most, this was rather off the subject, but—Lavonne looked to *her* like she had lost weight! not that it showed in her face, which of course she wouldn't want. She *had* lost, Lavonne said, tying her sash a little tighter. So at least she had *that* going for her to show for all the wasted time. But as Father Peacock said…

Wasn't it a shame about priests? Not being able to date or anything. Because Father Peacock was the sort of man, he'd be lovely, really. Masculine, everything about him. And that look in his eyes. And the way he always seemed to be keeping such a tight rein on all this…strength.

But Lavonne had more to worry about than men. Because it was very annoying. They were just coming into Tucson, she told Rosetta, and the pilot was saying…And ever since she sat down under that great huge *amp*, her ears were just like filled with cotton. Rosetta knew about that mischance. Now came the news that Lavonne had accidentally looked at *what*? Some kind of beam. Foster was telling her, only four places like it in the whole United States, and she thought he said to look but what he said was *don't look*, and ever since, this...like a hole, the middle part was missing. Of everything! About as big as a saucer. Gone. "Oh, no, Lavonne," Rosetta said.

(*Captain Carpenter rose up in his prime...*)

Lavonne's bosom, she didn't cry or realize at the time, being young, what the loss would mean, she was only happy to be shunt of it. Because it kept her from being beautiful, and she didn't know men set store by it, some men. And it had been restored.

(*They twined him of his nose for evermore.*)

Her fleshly principalities, as Robert Herrick called his sweetheart's private parts, still remaining, who would miss the organs of gestation, womb, ovaries, inside, when you can't see them and can take hormones the rest of your life and never get uterine cancer or wrinkles?

(*They cracked his two legs at the shinny part.*)

And science and technology nowadays, they can make the realest-looking partials and pale, transparent—Of course they're very expensive, you have to get the *very best* and no one will know, I guarantee it. No one!

Human hair will wear out. A lot of people don't realize that, but it's true. You can just torture it so long, bleach, tint and twist it up in pincurls and let it blow in the evening wind in convertibles and sit under burning hot dryers to speed up the drying, and soap and suds and manipulate it, and all of a sudden one morning you've only got enough left for about four pincurls. But science and technology, oh, the twentieth century, soft bases, mono-filament, beautiful, silky, synthetic, natural colors... With a fall or two, you need never feel deprived, but just the opposite.

And in Lavonne's case, where she picked up this fungus that caused her toenails... Sometimes she thought the podiatrist himself was responsible.

And one thing she almost sued about was to have this stuff advertised so highly as such a scientific breakthrough for problem fingernails, lovely glue-ons an inch long and hard as a rock and looked absolutely beautiful, but in the night you woke up with your hands on fire and in pain and the false nails are on there *like iron*, like bolts riveted on. But of course they can be soaked off, there is a scientific breakthrough to do that, only your own nails fall off in the process. Not all (the thumb and middle finger of both hands, for some unknown reason). But they will grow back normally, eventually, and just be problem nails again.

(*The bitch bit off his arms at the elbow.*)

That amp business was really a big mistake, she had been running around with Foster long enough by then to these different places where Gribble Company put in the lights and sound effects to know an amp like that (in fact it was clustered there, plural) could practically tear your head off, but these couples were coming through this narrow space and some girls gave an attractive...older woman the most hostile...Sometimes they seemed so *resentful*...and so she just slid inconspicuously into this seat where there shouldn't even have *been* seats, it was like being up in a church steeple with bells, they would rupture your eardrums and crack your skull and kill you, and ever since…her hearing…totally muffled.

(*Captain Carpenter parted with his ears.*)

And now this hole in everything!

(*They took his sweet eyes.*)

But you could look at Lavonne and not a thing seemed to be missing. What stood there was her will, her determination, the fifth essence, distinct from the four elements of ancient and medieval philosophy that the stars and everything were supposed to be made of, her specific difference, her conceptual—not real—substance.

(*They pierced him and produced his heart.*)

She still had her heart. And if there was such a thing, she still had her soul. No one can lose *that*. Some churches think so, the Catholic church especially. *They* think you can lose your soul forever.

(*Making the demons of hell to whet their beaks clack clack.*)

But no, Lavonne still had her soul.

Chapter Sixty-nine

*

JEPPE WOKE UP IN SURPRISINGLY GOOD SPIRITS, CONSIDERING HIS SADNESS WHEN he went to sleep. He knew what he had to do now, concentrate more, conquer his human failings, address himself totally to the problems of artistic creativity. At quarter to eleven he was at the piano in the drawing room trying to express, in a chorus for the homesteaders of Iron County, the dissonances of everyday life. He imagined his awful guest of last night over and over, that was the kind, the mentality, he was glad he had met him. The time wasn't wasted after all. The young man epitomized perfectly the *ignorance in action* Jeppe must express if he wanted to set his scene.

"HE'D BE LOVELY, REALLY—isn't it a shame?"

It was a shame, Rosetta agreed, but since Father Peacock was just totally out of the question—

"The young priests today," Lavonne said, "I heard this commentator—it's entirely different. Every year about ten thousand drop out, they want to date, they want to get married. But you take a case like—" Not that she was even thinking of such a thing! Only there he was, and had the circumstances been a little bit different...

"Speaking of young ones," Rosetta said, going to the window to peek out through the curtain, "who might that be out there in the yard?"

"Don't you hate those beards and that awful hair?" Lavonne had come over to look, too.

They had no more than decided to confront him—Birdelle would fall in a fit if she saw a sight like that in her yard—than a knock came at the back door. It was the Premier Elevator Company man come to finish the elevator repair. *If* the part would fit! That was the trouble with the handmade stuff, the tenons, the scarf-joints, every cog filed out by hand. They asked him in, pointed the way to the cellar. Just a minute, though. "Damon?" He ran back out onto the porch. "Where's that dang kid got to?"

"Oh, he's with *you*, that boy out in the yard?"

Yes, the cave man was with him.

Damon's eyes shone starry as he hurried up the steps. "Oh, my gosh, Mr. Stewart, this *house*! That oriel window. I was just around to the side there looking at it. But gosh almighty!" In the marble and brass kitchen now, he looked around with wonder.

"He's not from around here," Mr. Stewart said. "He's—what's the connection again,

Damon?"

"No particular connection. I just stopped to see Gary, that's all. He's in my fraternity…"

"He's the boss's son," the elevator man explained. "Gary is. And this guy here is Damon, Gary's—They belong to the same scout troop or something."

Rather shyly, Damon said that he was on his *wanderjahr*, and Mr. Stewart, for Lavonne's benefit, he had kept eyeing her, said he had one once but the wheels came off.

Rosetta smiled and Lavonne laughed a little, her hand going to her tangle of curls.

"Damon here's going to be an architect," Mr. Stewart added. "Well, come on." He started for the basement door, but the boy lingered. "Come *on*." He paused at the head of the stairs and looked back. "I thought you wanted to see this old elevator down here so fast?"

"I want to see *everything*. Oh, could I, do you think?"

Rosetta and Lavonne exchanged glances. "I don't see why not," Lavonne said. "The lady that owns the place is watching some of her programs."

"At least you could see the downstairs," Rosetta said.

Damon went to the butler's pantry, stood looking through to the so-called family dining room. "Holy Toledo."

"Listen, I'll go on down," Mr. Stewart said. "I may need a hand, though—Well, hell." They heard him going down the stairs to the basement.

Lavonne excused herself, too. That left Rosetta to take Damon around, but really it was he who pointed out things to her, she said later, about the different woods, the pseudo-Jacobean construction and everything. What students knew today was really amazing. Jeppe thought so, too. He was in the drawing room at the piano, papers scattered around, and Rosetta wasn't going in there with the visitor and disturb him, but he saw them at the door and said to come on in. It turned out that Damon knew who Jeppe was when Rosetta introduced them. His best friend played cello, and this chamber group, they often played—what was it?—a trio of Mr. Casement's for flute, cello and piano—really super. He loved it.

Later that day Jeppe, speaking of Damon, was to tell Rosetta that he liked people according to their vulnerability, how easily they could be hurt, their lack of self-confidence—all the things she suddenly saw in Jeppe himself when she brought the bearded boy in and introduced him. Jeppe stood—she didn't expect him to—and, turning his head to the side and looking down like a girl, with long eyelashes, he extended his hand as a girl does, palm down, making it hard to shake rather than kiss, but Damon shook it manfully, awkwardly.

There wasn't much to see after the drawing room. The library…Jeppe stopped composing to go with them. After that Damon said maybe he had better go down and see how Mr. Stewart was getting along, and Rosetta was saying she would show him where the basement was again when Jeppe said, wasn't she going to show Damon the upstairs? Because if she wasn't, he'd be glad to. The boy was already starting up the stairs by then, Rosetta noticed he had cowboy boots on, she noticed the heels, and she really didn't have the jurisdiction to stop anybody. "Just don't run into Miss Prentice if you can help it," she said.

But of course that was the first thing they did! and the worst of it was that Jeppe had gone into his room thinking Damon was at his heels when instead the boy had turned back and gone down the hall, the better to see the stained glass on the landing. So when Miss Prentice, coming out of the bathroom, collided with him standing there gawking, the boy was alone. She screamed, Rosetta came running, Jeppe flew from his room. Damon had reached out, took hold, she had tottered, he said, he was afraid she was going to fall. That made her suppose a murderer had grabbed her, the beard, the long hair. Lavonne didn't hear her screaming, but Mr. Stewart thought *he* did, clear down in the basement. They had a terrible time calming her down, and back in her room on her bed with two pillows under her head, Rosetta, fanning her with a folded newspaper, saw that she had broken out in red blotches, her face and down her neck, and was probably spotted over her whole body. The shock could really have been dangerous.

When Mr. Stewart left, he told Rosetta to tell Miss Prentice the part didn't fit the way it should, so it would be another couple of weeks before her elevator would be running and to be sure and not fool with the doors, because the safety device on the one side—"Now where has that dang kid got to?" Damon was in the drawing room. Jeppe was playing for him and he was standing beside the piano looking rapt. Both were smoking, and no ashtray. "The elevator repair man's leaving," Rosetta said from the doorway.

"Oh, thanks," the boy said without turning his head. "I'll be right there."

AT EIGHT THAT EVENING HE was back. Rosetta answered his ring. "Why, Damon!" she said.

"Is Mr. Casement around? We're going to dinner—"

"Here we are," Jeppe said, materializing behind her.

"Who was that?" Lavonne said when Rosetta rejoined her at the kitchen table.

"That same boy with the beard that scared Birdelle out of seven years' growth this morning. He and Jeppe are going out to dinner."

"He won't invite him in when they come home, will he?"

But of course they couldn't do anything about it if he did.

"When is Jeppe leaving for back east, anyway?" Lavonne said.

"Next week sometime, I don't know which day."

Lavonne sighed.

"You don't mean to tell me you'll be sorry?" Rosetta said.

"I was sighing because when the doorbell rang I thought it might be—" Rosetta thought she was going to say Foster but she said, "Father Peacock at the door. He's really so nice to talk to. You know what he told me last week? He said when he was a boy in Ireland—his folks left there when he was only about in the third grade, so that's why he doesn't have more of a brogue—why, he remembered the old priests lashing the girls with their riding whips. 'They lashed them round,' was the way he expressed it, when they didn't go to confession. Imagine such a thing!"

"Imagine," Rosetta said. "But the girls over there must be pretty ferocious their own selves. Not necessarily in Ireland, but—remember what he told us one time in the shop when you were cutting his hair? About the girls somewhere in France filing past the statue of this saint with a fork in their hands and saying if they didn't get a sweetheart or a husband within one year they would jab out his eyes? And somewhere else where they would stick pins in another saint's nose if they didn't get their wish?"

"And throwing rocks. Yes, I remember."

"And the way they set fire to a laurel tree, that's the tree that's sacred to Apollo, to make their sweetheart burst into flames and be consumed with love?"

"I love to hear the man *talk*," Lavonne said with a sigh.

By nine she was in bed with her light out. Rosetta's burned till eleven. She heard footsteps on the stairs and muffled voices, so Jeppe must have brought the boy home with him. Birdelle had nearly died of fright, she really had. That was because the papers...were so full of horror stories. And the television...

Rosetta didn't think she was asleep but she must have been, because she was dreaming—something about a dim, tall figure coming out of the closet wearing long dark clothes and a high silk hat and moving over and at her bedside bowing from the waist, and it seemed as though hat and head both toppled onto her, and she screamed, or tried to, woke in a sweat to hear someone *else* screaming—she sat up, her heart pounding—wasn't that—? It came again. Not a scream, a terrible noise, more of a...She got up, you can't just lie there, ran to the door, peeked out—saw him run, saw the figure running down the stairs and followed him as if walking in her sleep, it seemed as if she had to see him leave, but she didn't see him, only the open back door when she got dreamlike down to the kitchen, the cold night air blew in on her cold feet on the cold marble floor. She closed it, threw the bolt, then in terrible fright whirled...to empty darkness, just the street light shining in.

Lavonne, of course, hadn't heard a thing. Rosetta shook her awake, they went upstairs. Birdelle was all right, curled up like a baby in crystalline insensibility. The one in trouble was Jeppe, he had nearly been choked to death, if he hadn't somehow got hold of the poker and with his last strength...Oh, my God. He vomited. He thought his larynx was broken, he was nearly strangled. They wanted to call the police, the doctor, but he said no, no! and it was understandable why. They got him to bed. Who was it? It surely wasn't that nice boy Damon? He shivered and shook, gagged, Rosetta had to take him

to the bathroom, he made her stand outside the door. Was he gone? They got him to
bed, Rosetta promised to sit by him. Lavonne sneaked in and got some Nembutal tablets
out of the drawer in Birdelle's bedside table. He cried out with pain when he swallowed,
clutched his throat.

You're all right, you're alive, they kept telling him, and of course he was, a miss is
as good as a mile, and gradually he settled down. But the light had to stay on. And after
Lavonne went back downstairs to bed, Jeppe murmured that he had had it, that was it,
three more lectures or not, he was leaving tomorrow. Would Rosetta take him to the
airport? Yes, she said, be glad to, now go to sleep. Holding tight to her hand, he gradually drifted off…

She sat amazed, a lovely, starry-eyed fraternity boy like Damon, so interested in
architecture and music and everything—and on his *wanderjahr*!—turning out to be
a homicidal maniac! Jeppe could be dead, look at his face, so bruised and swollen, his
arms too, the livid marks of cruel fingers on his throat. "Let something happen to us!"
the poet Rilke heard some young girls implore the Blessed Virgin. Anything, sometimes,
even death, was better than nothing.

JEPPE WAS SUPPOSED TO BE leaving the next day, but morning came and he didn't stir.
It got to be ten, eleven. At noon Rosetta looked into his darkened room, and he was just
waking up. She brought him some toast and coffee and word from Sam Weller's bookstore that the books he ordered had arrived, they had just phoned. Good, he said in a
hoarse whisper, and asked for a couple of aspirin, which he then could hardly swallow for
the pain. But he got the coffee down and the toast and said in almost his normal voice
that he was going to dress and go out, go to the bookstore, drop in at the Hotel Utah
and get his reservation…Shaved and dressed, he came looking for Rosetta. She was in
the kitchen making out a grocery list. Does this show very much? He was talking about
the bruise along the side of his jaw. When she got back with the jar of stuff to cover it, he
was sitting at the table smoking a cigarette and drinking the coffee he had poured himself
out of the lukewarm percolator.

"Listen," he said, turning and lifting his head so she could pat and smooth on the
cream for him, "I've just been thinking. Instead of taking the plane from here, I think
I'll go down to Las Vegas and leave from there. And you know you said you'd take me to
the airport? Well, listen, Rosetta—"

He wanted her to come with him, drive him to Las Vegas. They could stop at the
Mountain Meadow on the way! He had been looking at the map and it was right on the
highway, or not very far off it, and he wanted to see it so that when he was at Yaddo he
could shut his eyes and remember. *All on the Meadow Green*…

"Well, I don't know," she said. "My car…It's quite a way down there to the Meadow,
and from there to Las Vegas, and I'm not that much of a—Why don't you just rent

yourself a car? Then you could drive along and think—"

"I don't drive." He sounded cross and *was* cross, because, like Paul, the good he would do he did not: but the bad, that, he felt, he did, and was often wretched.

"It's way down the line."

"Don't you want to see it again?"

Again? She never saw it even once, she said, and didn't want to, that sad, terrible spot.

"Oh, come on," he said, "it's part of your inheritance." By court-impudence he thought he persuaded her. But the real reason she said she'd do it was because she couldn't drive Mozart to Las Vegas, or Sir Arthur Sullivan, and it came to her that had she had the chance, she might not have taken it, left to her own judgment alone wouldn't realize who *they* were in *their* time either, because with the out-of-the-ordinary, how did the ordinary know? A man just standing in front of you in *your* time, no great flapping wings…you'd let the opportunity slip by.

"When did you want to leave?" she said.

"Tomorrow."

Tomorrow was Saturday, and good weather like this, the traffic would be awful… Why not wait till Monday?

"Tomorrow," he said. "'Wake me early, Mother darling…'"

"Crack of dawn," she said.

"Oh, no!"

"Most certainly. If you want to see the Meadow while it's still light…"

"Mother darling." He spoke the words again, as if to himself, but as he went out the door said to her over his shoulder that he wished it was true.

I wish it was true too, Jeppe. If Legrand and I…he'd be about your age and likely as big a headache, and maybe crazy because of the cousin-with-cousin relationship. But I wish it was true.

It was so annoying, that hole in everything that Foster had left her to remember him by. When she looked at the blouses at Auerbach's, the costume jewelry at the Z.C.M.I., the dresses at Makoff's. And his lack of tact still hurt. But the May day was too warm and pretty for distress, and doctors were so clever! or it might be that the hole would fill in by itself. At least her hearing didn't seem quite so bad as it had been. And at a new little shop called Desiree's she saw just the dress she was looking for in the window. Of course *no* one was small enough for that, but as luck would have it, they had it in stock in a ten and it ran large, so it fit her, and it wasn't *exorbitant* and she already had shoes to match. Now all she had to do was meet somebody really nice, which in itself was no problem. The problem was to get where a man might be, such as a nightclub bar, resort or some place like that *without having a man already*! to take you there. Because a more…mature…woman all by her lonesome in a place like that, it was a problem. And everybody where one might have access was getting so young, the maintenance men, ambulance drivers, the man in the parking lot at the hospital, they spoke a different language. And the funny part was how ugly the girls were they picked out. Mud-colored hair, straight as a string, parted in the middle, no makeup, terrible skin, sometimes they had a nice figure, but they could also look like a bag of meal tied up ugly. And their outfits. But yet these fellows would be crazy about them. And the girls would be crazy about *them*. It was like how a squirrel knows it's supposed to mate with another squirrel and not a cat, they were like a species.

The one who would be just perfect in age, looks and every other way was Father Peacock, but no use thinking about him. A pity, though. Lots of things were a pity, but she wasn't blue, not the way she thought last night she would be. There was the sight of herself cast back from windows and the mirrored shops, everybody should look like that, and with her chances! to inherit, have and buy, and to be shopping as she might be right this minute for a trip to Europe, where short dark millionaires abounded. And a person who could stay a size ten in the better dresses (cheap sizes didn't count) ought certainly to be able to have a piece of pineapple cheesecake with their coffee! She also stopped in at Martha Washington's and bought some chocolates, coconut, vanilla-nut, butter-creams and mocha, two or three of each.

When she got home, she went looking for Rosetta to offer her some and also show her the new dress, but she wasn't in her room or anywhere else in the house. Nobody else was, either, except Birdelle, who was watching television in her darkened room. Lavonne just peeked in and saw her, then tiptoed back downstairs, if Birdelle knew she was back she would start wanting to be waited on.

She hung up her new dress and thought she would take a bath and "get ready." But there was nobody to get ready for and maybe never would be again, so she lay down and took a nap. An hour later she woke with a start to find Birdelle at her bedside. "Come quick!" she cried. "I called the police. Burglars out on the sidewalk are looking at the house figuring out how to get in!"

By the time Lavonne had got up, looked quickly in the glass and ran up and down a time or two peering out of windows, they had arrived, two very young policemen both seemingly growing a mustache, ready for whatever would befall. Nothing did, they went through the house, peeped into closets. "Nobody here!" In the entrance hall as they were leaving, the shorter one noticed the beautiful elevator cage, walked over and opened the door. "Say," he said, "this is dangerous. Look down there. This door shouldn't open, somebody could kill themself!"

"It's out of order," Lavonne said. "They had to send for a part, the man's coming Tuesday."

"Well, put a chair or something in front of it."

"Nobody's going to use it."

After they left, the young policemen having put Birdelle's mind at ease by their praise of her locks and bolts, and saying they would like to have a dollar for every private watchman in her neighborhood, Lavonne made her some milk toast, before and after which Birdelle took the pills of different sizes and shapes she said she was supposed to take, and helped her back upstairs to her room to watch her programs. She settled first in her chair, but a few minutes later when Lavonne went past her door, she saw she had decided to move to her bed.

Jeppe was thinking as he walked along that he should have taken a taxi, a Salt Lake City block was like three anyplace else, the day was really warm and he feared the shopping bag he was carrying was going to tear, the books in it were so heavy, and shifting, when a car stopped and someone called, "Need a lift?" It was June, she had just been past Roger's place again and no Normal, the house looked deserted, had he and Roger taken off together to go and find the brides? As soon as she got home, she was going to write him. But where?

Jeppe put his shopping bag in first, just as it tore, a string handle pulled loose and the books tumbled out on the seat. He pushed them aside to make room to sit down and got in.

June glanced at them. "What's all this?" she said. "*A History of Utah. The Mountain Meadow—The Definitive Years of*—Don't tell me you've taken up *genealogy*!" Just as she said this she put her foot on the gas, flooded it, and they had to sit a few minutes. "Have you seen the big vault system dug out under Cotton Canyon? Solid granite, last for millions of years."

"No," he said, putting his hand up to his neck to hide the bruise. "I figure I'm the highest branch, who cares about the tree?"

"Me too." Idly she picked up the book nearest her, looked at the title, then at him. "What is this Mountain Meadow Massacre?"

"An opera," he said. "My opera."

"Really? I'm just starting to dig opera a little," she said, putting it down. "The only one I've heard all through is *La Bohème*. It's beautiful."

Now he took up the book she had put down and began turning the pages.

"Is that really an opera?" she said.

"It will be."

She stepped on the starter, put her foot on the gas pedal and this time the engine took hold. "Well," she said as they drew away, "a massacre—won't that be quite gloomy?"

"Everyone will die," he said.

"Why, that's terrible."

"Where have *you* been?" Lavonne asked Rosetta when she came in at six. "We've had some excitement here!"

"Excitement?"

"Well, as you know Birdelle takes those different pills, I think the doctor should take everything away from her again like they did in the hospital, make her start over again with just aspirin—"

"What happened?"

"She called the police and two of them came and looked all through the house. It's that medication—"

"Well, she had a legitimate reason to be scared of that boy she got into such a fright about yesterday that later on last night almost choked Jeppe to death," Rosetta said. "But of course she didn't know *that*. And we sure didn't. Would *you* have guessed? A boy like that so interested in architecture and old stuff, and such nice manners?"

"How is he by now? Your fine Mr. Casement?"

"All right, I guess. He's leaving tomorrow."

"Tomorrow? I thought—"

"I'm going to drive him to Las Vegas."

Lavonne stared. "*You* are?"

"What's so strange about that?"

"Well, everything. Remember when I wanted us to go to Yellowstone National Park? You acted like it was to go to the moon!"

"I just thought as the shop was closed and he's this composer and how quick I'd drive George Gershwin if I had the chance—and who am I to know? So I've been getting the car checked and the tank filled and everything. And I bought a dress."

"Great minds," Lavonne said. "I did, too."

They showed them to each other, Rosetta's gray shantung, Lavonne's pretty flowered silk, exchanged compliments about them, as they never would have exchanged the dresses, then Lavonne said, "I can't get over you actually driving to Las Vegas. It's so odd."

"It *is* odd," Rosetta said. "But I was just thinking it's kind of in memory of Legrand, too."

"How do you figure that?"

"Well, you know he was on that government—writers'—historical project and found some stuff—and then he wrote that scenario—"

"I do kind of remember something about a scenario. But what does that have to do with Las Vegas?"

"Nothing," Rosetta said. "Except that on the way down there, just before you get over into Nevada, there's this high mountain plateau called the Mountain Meadow, and that's where something *happened*, an old historical massacre of a big wagon train heading for California. That was what Legrand's scenario was about." She decided not to say that Jeppe was going to use it too, as a base for his opera. "So I thought that as long as I was going to be down that way, why not stop and see it? Kind of in memory of Legrand. You know he went down and visited Palmer and they went there for a whole afternoon just wandering around—"

Lavonne had been holding her dress up to her, it was pretty and going to be becoming, and now she laid it across the bed and took a cigarette and lit it. "So you'll sightsee along the way," she said, perching on the arm of the chair. "But what's Jeppe going for? To Las Vegas, I mean."

"He thinks he'll like that flight to New York better than to go from here."

"Well, don't tell Birdelle. She likes all of us on the premises—kind of like soldiers— guarding—What time are you leaving?"

"Oh, early."

WHEN JUNE DROVE INTO THE driveway, she saw Normal sitting on the steps of the carriage entrance. "Well, hello, stranger!" Then she said, "Where's your car?" For that he would be anywhere other than *in* it as he waited for her she could not imagine.

"I'll tell you later," he said.

She ran to him. "Oh, honey, where have you been? It's been three *days.*"

"What're you doing with *this* guy?" Stiffening, he pushed her to one side, took a step towards Jeppe.

She tried to take his arm, but he brushed her off. "He lives here," she said. "You know I told you? Teaches that seminar. It's over next week, but he's leaving even sooner—tomorrow, in fact. Mr. Casement? This is Normal Sleigh, he's a Green Beret, or at least he was before he got out of the service—"

Jeppe, getting his books off the car seat and trying to keep them together in his arms as he slammed the car door, nodded. "Hello," he said. One book slid, and then they were all sliding and on the ground. "Shit," he said, and began picking them up.

June ran to help him, Normal at her heels. "Go back," he said angrily. He picked up a book, looked at it. *The Mountain Meadows Massacre*, by Juanita Brooks. He glared.

"He's going to write an opera about Utah," June said quickly.

"Who gave you permission to do that?" Normal said.

God, Jeppe was going to say but decided not to. Hurriedly he gathered up such books as he could carry and started for the steps. June could bring the others or he would send Rosetta out.

But in an instant, Normal was upon him and running him up against the wall. "Listen," he said, twisting and lifting a handful of his tie and shirt front, "you gook! which you're no better than, I can tell you that! If as good. I was on a mission, see, and one thing we learned was how to answer malicious questions. And one thing we could of answered…but no one asked it. And why didn't they? Because *finally*, after more than a hundred years, it was being forgotten, it was laid to rest. Now *you* come along and stir it all up again." Viciously he kicked the book at his feet.

"Why, Normal Sleigh!" June said. "Kicking a library book like that. He'll have to pay a fine!"

"He *should* pay. There used to be such a thing as Blood Atonement, 'when upon Zion, that perfection of beauty, God hath shined.' But if it keeps on the way it's going now, it shall be a habitation of dragons and a court for owls, a possession of the bittern—"

June ran over and wrested his hand loose. "You go inside, Mr. Casement. Don't bother about your books. I'll bring them."

Normal did release Jeppe, who stood trembling a moment, touching his already bruised throat and pulling the knot of his tie back where it belonged, then took a faltering step. One only before the other pinned him again.

"Normal! You stop that!"

"Answer me one question," he said, shoving Jeppe down onto the steps, hard, on his tailbone, so that he winced. "And that is, why now?"

"What are you talking about?" June said.

"I'll tell you why," Normal answered his own question. "Because a Mormon is about to run for President, that's why! The Millennium is almost here, a Mormon whose heart is pure, who does not cast abroad the fitches, and scatter the cummin, and cast in the appointed barley, and if you and the other slimy crawling creatures can stir up an ancient old stink so that it permeates the atmosphere from coast to coast, if you can blacken and defame, if you can prevent…if you can hand this country over to the—"

Rosetta was in the kitchen warming up a TV dinner when June ran in. Now they came running, got between the two, Jeppe on the steps, Normal standing over him, June tugging at Normal, Rosetta helping Jeppe up. "What in the world—?"

"But you can't wreak this havoc, not you, not your friends, not Russia, not *Eisenhower*—not Satan, not witches that peep and mutter, not familiar spirits—"

"Normal, you quit that," June said sternly. "The next thing you know you'll be going crazy. Mr. Casement is a famous composer. He doesn't want to do anything—"

"Except drag this country to hell," Normal said.

A quick look at his pale face and glittering eyes told Rosetta it was useless to argue, and she hurried Jeppe into the house. "Go upstairs, Jeppe, I'll get your books and bring you some supper. Do you still want to go to Las Vegas?"

"Guess," he said. "My God. And that nice little girl macking around with a nut like that!"

Outside, Rosetta found June trying to put her arms around Normal, and him fending her off. As Rosetta went to pick up a book, Normal broke out of June's grasp and kicked it away. Rosetta stood and looked at him, then deliberately went and retrieved it and gathered up the other books as well.

"You're one of 'em too, huh?" Normal said.

"If you mean one of your shirt-tail relations," Rosetta said, making herself smile, "why, yes."

"Hi, everybody!" Lavonne said from the doorway. "Isn't the weather beautiful?" Then she said, "Rosetta, where's the colander? I've been looking all over."

"That boy has gone *out* of his mind," Rosetta muttered as she went past her and out into the kitchen and dropped the books on the table.

"You mean Normal?"

"Did you see his face?"

Chapter Seventy

*

He looked the way he did, June found out by degrees as first they sat together on the steps and then went together to dinner at the Pagoda (she paid), because he hadn't had one mouthful of food for three days! or very much sleep, either. He and Roger had gone to Centerville—

"Centerville? Of all places in the world? Why?"

"Roger heard the renters were moved out and it's going to be torn down, so we had to get there—! to fast and pray and try to receive the sign while there was still time!"

"What was going to be torn down?"

"The house," he said, gobbling chow yuk, sweet and sour pork and shrimp fried rice.

"What house?"

"Where *they* appeared—Jesus, God the Father, the Prophet Joseph and Hyrum—to President John Taylor when he stayed there and hid under the floorboards—when they were trying to catch him."

"Who was?"

"The officers, dummy! for being a polygamist. So he hid in this old abandoned house on the edge of Centerville, and during the night, it was pitch dark, all of a sudden the room lit up as bright as day! and there *they* stood. And God said—So anyway, Roger heard they were going to tear it down and we decided before it was too late—"

"I was so *worried*," June said. "I drove past Roger's—" She signaled to the wrinkled old waiter with the body of a slight young boy and when he approached told him in a whisper to bring more of everything except the duck. "I thought you'd gone down to that town or settlement or whatever it is back in the mountains and…married the brides…and not only wasn't I *first*, I wasn't even *amongst* them…And oh, Normal!"

"I sold my car," he said.

"Sold your *car*? But honey, you were so *crazy* about your car."

"I won't say I had an actual vision—Roger says *he* did, but he was sleeping, he says he wasn't but I could tell by his breathing, and what he had was a dream. No bright light or anything, just this guy comes in and says something like he's got this delivery and where should they unload it, and Roger says he don't know anything about any delivery—what kind of a vision is that? Nothing! A dream. And maybe mine wasn't an actual *vision*—but I did have this funny peculiar feeling, and a voice did say—all of a sudden I heard it as clear and plain as could be, right there in that empty, dirty room with the rats running between the walls and under the floor and the windows rattling—it said, *Sell your car.* So this guy that's been pestering me anyway to buy it, when we got back to town I called him—"

"But why? Why would a voice tell you to do something like that? When you were so crazy about it?"

"You don't question heaven's will," he said. "We'll go tonight."

JEPPE SAID THE CHEMICALS IN foods and even in the water could be one reason why twice in twenty-four hours he had been choked by madmen. The chemicals affected their brain.

"Or television. There's been quite a bit in the papers lately about it being television," Rosetta said. "The constant—But of course they also learned how to hurt people in the armed forces, and Normal was a Green Beret. In the Army, they were a branch of the Army, weren't they?"

"Well, I'll tell you what I'm going to do," Jeppe said as if to himself, as he threw things into the open suitcase on his bed, "I am going back to New York, and I'm going tonight, and wild horses couldn't—"

"You mean from the Salt Lake airport? That you *don't* want to drive down to Las Vegas tomorrow? You know, Jeppe, I'm kind of relieved—"

"Of course I don't mean that! I'm *counting* on it, and especially on seeing the Mountain Meadow. In fact I feel like I've already met a couple of the perpetrators," he said, grasping his throat and swallowing, "regular, standard, simple-minded, plain old assassins from those times."

"Maybe you have in a way, considering—Let's see, John D. Lee—"

"Ringleader," he said. He snapped his suitcase shut, went over to the table by his bed, picked up the Nembutal tablet left over from what Lavonne had brought in the night before, put it in his mouth and, with a swallow of water from the glass beside it, painfully got it down.

"Good," Rosetta said. "You go to bed and get a good night's sleep. And tomorrow—"

"An hour or two's shut-eye is all I need," he said, stretching out on the bed. "Let's leave about four—as early as we can—"

"All right," she said, feeling giddy and excited as though about to depart for Nephelococcygia, the city Aristophanes tells us is suspended between heaven and earth and ruled by the birds.

"Don't go—sit down for a minute—talk to me." His eyes were shut. "You were saying—?"

"Nothing, really," she said, perching on an arm of a chair. "Except that Normal really is related to—"

"My protagonist? My heroic baritone? Old John himself? How?"

"Well, let's see. By his seventh or eighth wife Louisa? John had two girls, Lucitie and Hindle. Hindle was *my* grandmother—"

"Hindle?"

"—while Normal descends from Lucitie. Lucitie's son Herman is Normal's grand-father. So that would make Normal your heroic baritone's great-great-grandson—"

"Imagine," Jeppe said drowsily. "A beauty like that! and does not have both oars in the water—"

"Well, he was in Vietnam."

"And the funny thing is, they *look* so great. Maxfield Parrish would have flipped. But regular," he took a deep breath, "Savonarolas." Slowly his chin sank forward, he saw Florence and the burning of the vanities, saw…the hell of the Cinquecento…and the boy had golden hair and was wearing jeans.

LAVONNE SAID SHE WISHED *she* could take off and go someplace wonderful, but of course she had to stay with Birdelle. Birdelle acted so helpless now, while only a few months ago, before Lavonne moved in, she lived here and did everything for herself! They got spoiled and dependent so fast! But of course she wasn't doing anything else in partic-ular at the moment, she might as well be here as anywhere till she decided to…make different arrangements. That depended on a man, Rosetta knew she meant. Whoever he might be. After her nap Lavonne had got dressed up, freshly starched eyelashes, fresh makeup, flowered silk, high heels, nice perfume, and when she went out on the side porch and asked Rosetta about the colander, could have been on her way to a gala. To the *scene* she stepped into, Normal threatening Jeppe, June trying to intercept, Rosetta defiant with the books in her arms, Lavonne had hardly paid any attention. Foster wouldn't come, it was over and she knew it, and it hadn't been that much of a shock, but yet she looked up and down the street and touched her hair and felt her flounces blowing around her legs, and after all…people have changed their minds.

But he hadn't, it seemed, changed his, so after the ten o'clock news, which she didn't listen to because it was the same old stuff, she went upstairs to check on Birdelle, and she was in bed asleep with her ill-adjusted television flickering and crackling, so Lavonne turned it off and tiptoed out. A light shone under Jeppe's door, wasn't it terrible about one in ten supposedly being like that when there was such a shortage? And the thing was, they were so often nice-looking, and sweet too, just what a girl would love. Rosetta's room was still and dark. June's door was open, she was out somewhere. But when Lavonne got back downstairs, she met June in the back hall.

"Where's Rosetta?" June said.

"She's in bed asleep."

"Oh, gee."

"She's got her alarm set for two-thirty, she's going to take Mr. Casement to Las Vegas.

He's going to New York—"

"I'm glad for *that*, I can tell you," June said, heaving a sigh. "But gee."

"Maybe I can help you." Because of the ability of the human mind to make anything that was put on, stuck on, fastened into, in contact with, incorporated into, or applied to her surface a part of her body, and also because ladies grow handsome by looking in the glass, Lavonne always felt beautiful like the White Queen of an African tribe and, early or late, in a kindly frame of mind.

"It was just—I thought maybe Rosetta—We're going to elope," June said. "Normal just took the car—my car, he went completely crazy and sold his—down to the Standard station, and I'm going upstairs to pack, so if he comes back before then, maybe you could just—"

"Of course," Lavonne said. "I know exactly what you mean."

A few minutes later she hurried upstairs with a pair of blue earrings that used to go with a pair of pumps that wore out ("something blue") and one of the new fifty-cent pieces ("something borrowed"). When in love, Lavonne's role had always been to give each man whatever he needed or wanted, life's-blood cost no object, but her advice to June was not to let Normal get away with anything, they could be unbearable if you let them.

After the couple went out the back door, keeping their voices down, she wished she had thrown a handful of rice after them, but it was slippery, tomorrow Birdelle might go outside and her feet fly out from under her. Besides, there wasn't any rice in the cupboard. In the morning she was supposed to call Emily at the hospital and tell her her little girl June had run away to marry her beau Normal. Such a handsome couple. But it never looked right to Lavonne for the man to be the best-looking. Wasn't it funny how these homely girls…? Or not so much homely as medium-sized, medium build, brown hair, medium—what was called a "real person." Not what Lavonne would call pretty at all.

A cold night breeze was blowing and it was a quarter after twelve when, with the blinds down and the door shut, Lavonne began undressing as solemnly as the cephalophoric saints in Christian epic who, decapitated, take their heads under their arms and continue their Masses, glad it was this late, for Foster would never come at this hour. She cold-creamed her face, then dabbed on ointment made of turtle oil and the precious pollen of the orchid and went to bed. But she had no more than got to sleep when she was wakened by a cold, bony hand trying to grasp her slippery face. She screamed, shot up, tumbled out and saw it was Birdelle. "Did you want—?" Birdelle's eyes were open, which was why Lavonne hesitated about putting on the light, but now she realized from the strange, stiff way the woman moved that she was asleep, walking in her sleep but in a fright too, and headed—They say if you wake them suddenly it's dangerous, and so when Lavonne, nearly at Birdelle's heels in the dark hallway, saw she was headed for the elevator, she hesitated a split second, thinking to catch—but Birdelle was so quick!—before she screamed "Wait! Wait! Birdelle, it doesn't work, remember! The man said not to—Don't open that door!" But she had, opened the elevator door and ran in, and Lavonne right behind her, reaching out to—ran into emptiness and fell and plunged, going too fast to stop! and landed in the bottom of the shaft on—"Oh, my God!"

Rosetta, wakened by Lavonne's first yell and armed with a bronze bud vase, was half-way down the stairs when she heard the muffled screaming. Had the strangler got back in? "Jeppe! Jeppe!" she called back over her shoulder as she ran. "Call the police! Call the—" Downstairs, she started flipping on lights. "Lavonne!" She saw it then, the open door to the elevator. At first she thought it was just Lavonne down there screaming something about somebody being—It was pitch-black, she couldn't see a thing, ran back to the foot of the stairs. "Jeppe! Jeppe!" He didn't answer, wouldn't have heard a fire engine roaring through the house. She ran back. "Hold on—I'll call—I'll get—"

"Birdelle—she's dead—she must be dead!"

"You mean to say *Birdelle's* down there?"

"She's underneath me!"

"Oh, poor thing—my God—" On that machinery down there in that pitch-black hole. "She must be—"

But by a miracle she wasn't. Bent and broken, out like a light, but not dead. And only unconscious till they were sliding her onto the operating table at Holy Rosary, when she opened her eyes and said she had changed her mind…about selling…Then they started the anaesthetic. She was badly injured, both legs broken in several places, two ribs broken, awful contusions, tongue bitten through, maybe internal injuries. Somebody called Father Peacock, or perhaps he was on the hospital premises. "Now, my dear, for Christ and Kathleen ni Houlihan." He gave Birdelle extreme unction and recited the prayers for the dying.

But she did not die at that time, although in her eighties and grievously hurt, and Dr. Coates said he didn't think she would (die), he thought she would pull through. Father Peacock stayed around, though, for a while, repeating the Holy Names, the Acts of Contrition and so forth, Faith, Hope and Charity. It was very sweet of him. Lavonne stayed nearby, too. By an absolute miracle and because of landing on top of Birdelle, all she suffered was a few bruises and a muscle pulled in her leg. What hurt a thousand times worse than these was how terrible she thought she must look without makeup! and in a frumpy old nightgown. "Rosetta, please—" Rosetta knew what she meant, so while the ambulance was on its way, she bundled up what she thought Lavonne would think she had to have and took it along, and shielded her and helped her with making such amends as they could between them while Lavonne still lay in Emergency not knowing if or how badly she was injured.

Father Peacock came by on his way to try to see Birdelle and squeezed Lavonne's hand, he was ready to do whatever was necessary for both women, they could lean on him.

He looked as if he had been abruptly wakened too, dark-jowled, hair dragged through by a coarse, wet comb, his cowlick awry and staring. He didn't stay long but would be back, he said. After checking her over, the doctor said there was no reason to keep Lavonne, it was one of those cases where providence … Rosetta had driven to the hospital as soon as the ambulance pulled out, she brought Lavonne back to the house. They talked awhile, too stunned to say much. There was no reason for Rosetta to stay with her, though, Lavonne said, and of *course* she should go ahead and drive Jeppe down to Las Vegas as planned. In fact the sooner the better, it seemed like all the bad luck appeared after he showed up.

"There *are* people that are bad luck, you know," she said. "Remember that movie where the sailors on this ship thought their ship almost capsized in a storm because there was a preacher on board? and first they were going to throw him overboard, but then they left him on this island and their luck got better right away? Sometimes there's a lot of truth to those old superstitions. Not that Jeppe is a preacher," she said. "Just the opposite." Then, "Say, that reminds me! June and Normal eloped tonight!"

"Well, *that's* good news. No more confrontations."

Tomorrow Lavonne was supposed to call June's mother and break the news.

"She'll be pleased. To me Normal seems to be slipping off the edge of the planet, but maybe once he's married and settled down he'll be all right." Rosetta remembered again the angry little boy scuffing through the snow with his mother on his way to be circumcised. And thought, well, that was more than twenty years ago, while poor Moses—She knew she wasn't educated, but those years in the Groves of Academe had furnished her mind with bits she could marshal up and put together with other bits, and why that should give anyone joy like a boy taking a piece of a Tinkertoy and putting it together with another piece she did not know, but it did. So in her thoughts, happily, she put the two circumcisions together, furious little Normal's so long ago and Moses', who wasn't a Jew but one of the Pharaoh Akhenaten's exiled captains—although he became a Jew and was circumcised on the night before his wedding night.

"Well, he's sure good enough *looking.*"

"You turn your light out now, honey. Jeppe and I will be leaving about four, and I won't disturb you. I may have to stay in Las Vegas one night, so don't look for me, but I'll be back day after tomorrow. Will you be all right? If you need something, Emily would come—"

"Or I could call Father Peacock. Or maybe he'll drop by. I didn't realize until tonight how much of a comfort a priest can be. I'm sure Birdelle got along a lot better to wake up and see him there than if he wasn't. I just can't imagine how she survived!"

"You either," Rosetta said. "You fell down that shaft, too."

They suddenly embraced, and Rosetta pressed her cheek against Lavonne's. Their sisterly friendship had been formed so long before that it was like a physical something they had been born with, almost the way that Chang, the old-time Siamese twin, was

part of Eng, and Eng of Chang, even when those two never spoke their hearts to one
another, and indeed once Eng tried to throw Chang off a wagon. "I'm *awfully* glad you're
all right," she said.

"Me too."

"You could have been killed."

"Don't I know it."

But there are many ways to die, as the poet has said. And one death mimics life
"while its soul in hell…burns in the fire in which it dwells…"

LET'S SEE, ROSETTA THOUGHT LYING fully dressed on the bed in the dark, for she
wouldn't need to wake Jeppe for half an hour, she would get a map at a service station
and…It really seemed funny in this day and age for a boy, or rather man, not to be able
to drive a car, and…Now she remembered what Agnes had said that night in the cafeteria about one of poor little Normal's testicles not descending. Had she said it might
later? It really didn't make any difference as far as fathering children was concerned,
although once the subject came up abstractly and one of the nurses said wherever you
saw a family of all boys or all girls, that meant the father had only one testicle. People
made these wild statements. Let's see, now…plenty of identification and…maybe she
would gamble just a little bit before she turned around and came home. Once they got
to Las Vegas she would just drop Jeppe off and say good-bye, and…If June *did* turn out
to have all girls or all boys, why, then it would prove…Birdelle of course was done for
in a way, because old as she was…the house…things would be bound to change…with
the shop too…a superannuated beauty operator (as Uncle Albert never lived to find out,
or Wyandra either) was like a too-old Greyhound bus driver, not safe to be trusted with
people's lives, because some people's looks *are* their very life, and…The alarm went off.
It wasn't light yet, the stars twittered up above the trees, the birds twinkled standing on
their twigs. Then it was light.

NORMAL DROVE, HE CERTAINLY WOULDN'T let June, but so casually and fast around
curves down the empty black highway, with dark walls and trees running in the opposite
direction, that she wondered if they would really make it to—wherever it was. Where
are we going? South. He didn't say to the fastnesses, the brides, where the flying saucers
play, where the Millennium will set down its adhesive foot and Christ will make a landing with his gold propellers whirling like a sun, his diamond guns strapped on, people
seem to imagine He's some kind of milquetoast, but have *they* got a surprise coming…

"I know we're going south, but *where* south?"

Silence.

"Normal? I'm awfully sorry you sold your car."

"What makes women yak all the time? Have to stop at coffee shops all the time? Go to restrooms all the time?"

"They also have to sleep."

"So sleep, nobody's stopping you."

"Why can't we stop at one of these…motels? You're sleepy, you're as sleepy as I am, sleepier, I saw you doze off and the car swerve."

"Why don't you quit yakking for a change?"

"Sweetheart, why don't we just go in like two sensible…people and just get a motel room with one bed and just…*sleep*. Or even two beds, I don't care. I know we got to wait for the other brides, but it looks like you could at least *sleep* with me!"

"You're hopeless," he said.

"But I'll be the first," she said.

"That all depends," he said.

"On what?"

"On age, it will go by age," he said. She looked at him, he was looking straight ahead, he always did when he drove, at him being so desperately gorgeous, the kind that at a dance if he will come over and say to you *if you wanna dance, this next one is for shaking it up*, why, you can die happy, because they are the living end of evolution. But maybe he had (and maybe it wasn't just battle fatigue, either) a loose pulley somewhere in his brain.

But women *do* always have to stop at coffee shops. Just as the street lights were going out along the deserted streets of—what town was this? Beaver—and robust day was taking over, they drove into the nearly empty parking lot next to the Wishing Well Restaurant, went in and had a handsomely pictured breakfast. June boldly ordered coffee with hers, much to Normal's disgust—he said she was going to have to cut *that* out for sure and she said she would, as soon as they got where they were going. "Come on now, pretty please, tell me where."

But he wouldn't tell her. Why did women yammer so much? Sitting across from her, he noticed his sapphire ring on her engagement finger. "Hey!" he said. "I didn't put that *there*."

"No," she said. "You put it on this finger," she showed him, "the night I had my appendix out. But I changed it to this one. But cripes, if we aren't engaged, running away together and everything, I don't know who is!"

"Don't say cripes. Give it here."

"No!"

He reached across and she had to give it to him or make a big scene. He put it on his little finger, looked at it.

"You sure liked him, didn't you?" she said.

No answer, he blinked and yawned, still with his eyes fixed on the ring.

"A penny for your thoughts." They were about Ed, of course, them being such buddies, going in to—whatever town it was that day, buying their sapphire rings and then later him going into the morgue, or whatever they called it out in the field, and seeing Ed and exchanging—and saying—what? I love you? "But gee," she said, rubbing the smooth, empty place on her finger.

Back out in the car, she offered to drive and let him sleep awhile, but he said, "Sleep? With a woman driving?"

"You could hardly keep your eyes open in there," she said. They got in the car, warm already, though the sun was hardly up over the mountains and he had parked under a shady box-elder tree.

"Listen," he said, "if you could quit yakking for five minutes..."

She watched him sleep awhile, collapsed against his bent arm in the corner, her heart as soft as a rotten persimmon. No matter what, he was the handsomest thing ever to walk on two legs.

But he stirred, there's some kind of ancient watchfulness which seems to know...so she turned her gaze elsewhere, at how the traffic on the highway had picked up, the big trucks rolling by, the cars...He wouldn't deviate anyplace to drive around and see the sights, like in Provo the insane asylum, where it just so happened June knew a lady that used to live on the corner before she flipped out. Was he in touch with this place they were going to? Did he already know the brides? Maybe they had dresses and wedding veils all ready, knew the day, had been to the beauty shop, while she...She looked at her pants, her dusty loafers, fingered her cotton shirt, out of the corner of her eye looked at him and then away again.

What he went through over there in...must be the reason...napalm and everything, some of it must have seeped into our boys' systems...But as Sigrid was saying—she worked in Periodicals and was a psychology major, and June had to confide in *someone*— this Fundamentalist craziness, see, sex combined with religious fanaticism, is just a real live drug rush, really, St. Augustine knew it, the old Puritans knew it, to certain people it's just space city. And another thing, we don't know who we are, do we, you know? just running around. But get into an ancient old pattern like pastoral polygamy and you're *defined*, it's like getting a part in a play, all you have to do is learn the lines! you don't have to *make it up*. It's all been done for you, laid out, it's easier. And maybe the whole guy isn't really that rocking a good time *all* the time—so you and the other girls can gang up and divide him, don't you know, the work and effort, cooking, ring around the collar. Have the protected feeling without *oh, God, I need some air*. That *total* emotional thing just won't be required. It might be like—well, take the father figure and how the daughters of the family love...him, and how if they could marry *him* they'd rather live in his own family—well, this takes the place, kind of. And anyway liberty corrupts, and absolute liberty corrupts worse than...the free enterprise system and...some girls have this *fear* of...being so shuckin' independent and so equal. To boss a person's *self* takes...terrific effort, talent, it takes picking up on the...weird universe. And some girls, a guy they can rely on in kind of a karma way, who staves off entropy and, you know, weird forces, why, he makes up for—his protection—you just being one of maybe three wives instead of the only one and maybe low *low* man on the totem pole as well. But at least there's *structure* down there, there is *meaning*. So Sigrid figured things out, and it might be true.

Chapter Seventy-one

*

IT GOT WARMER, BEES BUZZED IN THE BUSHES ALONGSIDE, WHATEVER THEY WERE. June rolled the window down farther. Normal slept on, as beautiful as one of Raphael's big seraphs. In kind of a karma way, she *could* really rely... She put her head back, then closed her eyes just for a little minute... And then it was—! She fell over on him to lift his sleeping wrist and see his Rolex—

"Normal Sleigh! do you know how long we've been asleep in this parking lot?"

"What?" he murmured, his arms coming around her and his warm lips finding hers as in a dream, his eyes still shut, he strained her against him...

"Sweetheart, it's one o'clock! In the afternoon! Why don't we just—this is a nice little town—go and get a motel room and just—?" She melted against him like frosting on a warm cake, her lips sweet and soft.

He pushed her away, sat up and rubbed his eyes, looked at his watch himself. "Holy Toledo! we got to get going."

A man goes to the john, he's out again in half a minute. A woman... what takes them so long? What are they doing in there? Rather than go back inside the Wishing Well Restaurant and use its facilities the way June wanted to do before they went on, and also order another meal off them (at those prices!), Normal said heck no, there was a Standard station with restrooms across the street there. So they ran across catty corner, needed to fill the tank up also but would do that down the line, he certainly wasn't going to buy gas off that... Did June have any idea what the Rockefeller Foundation *really* stood for? Because if people really knew, there'd be some bombs set, that's for sure!

He was back beside the car in half a minute, you had to be quick in this day and age or find nothing but a stripped chassis. Boy, oh, boy. But all the crime, the sin and devilishness, it all went to prove that the time was nearly here... Normal saw Rosetta the instant she saw him, saw her companion too, that s.o.b., the two of them coming out of the Wishing Well. She said something to the man, urgently, quickly. He stopped dead still and looked at where Normal seemed to be swelling up like a puffer-fish. "Go!" She gave him a little push. Jeppe went. Their car must be parked along the street somewhere. The lot by now was full. Normal could hardly speak for his disgust, an old woman like this Rosetta, who was supposed to be some kind of a shirt-tail relation, two hundred miles from home with a skunk like him!

"Hi!" Rosetta called. "Lavonne was telling me—" She approached him smiling.

"Where's the bride? Though the thing to do right here is probably just to act like we didn't see you and go our way, seeing as how you're—Young Lochinvar—today." She waited.

Normal glared.

"That's what we'll just do," she said gaily, her smile beginning to fade.

"What you'll just do is burn," he said between gritted teeth. "And it shall come to pass that instead of a sweet smell there shall be stink; and instead of a girdle a rent; and instead of well set hair baldness; and instead of a stomacher a girding of sackcloth. And burning instead of beauty. And you being desolate shall sit upon the—"

"Rosetta!"

Nervously she looked around Normal to see June, back from the service-station restroom, jump over the low curb into the lot, run between two parked cars and come up close.

"What are *you* doing here?" June said, setting down her overnight bag and cordializing as only she can do whose hair has just been combed, face made up, teeth brushed and a clean blouse put on. "You're the last person in this *world* I ever expected to see!"

"Listen, I know what you kids are up to," Rosetta said. "Lavonne told me—"

A terrible thought struck June. Had Rosetta been sent after them by her mother? "Is Daddy—*all right?*"

"Your father?" Rosetta said. "Nobody sent me. When we left, nobody even knew you were gone except Lavonne. No, this is just—one of those coincidences. I'm driving Mr. Casement down to Las Vegas."

"Are you *blind?*" Normal said. "Can't you see what's going on?"

June looked bewildered, then gave a happy laugh. "Rosetta!" she said. "How wonderful! I never *dreamed.* Imagine! You and him, of all people. Why, honestly—" Here was an old woman with really nothing except ballsiness and a kind of gradually running down inorganic life principle, and yet she fights like a tiger and goes on demanding and fighting for happiness, it was the most magnificent...Do not go gentle...Had it been Lavonne, she would not have been surprised. But Rosetta! And the fact that Mr. Casement was so much younger, and also...

"Sorry to disappoint you," Rosetta said. "But I'm just driving him down to Las Vegas, where he's going to catch his plane for New York. He doesn't drive."

"Where *is* he?" June said. "And where's your car?"

"He's in it, we're kind of in a hurry, it's around in front. You heard about Birdelle, I guess?"

"No, what?"

Rosetta told her quickly. "They think she'll live, but things will certainly change for us on account of it, we're sure of that. The house and everything. Are you coming back to finish school? Or was all this so sudden you just don't know?" She started backing away. "Well, dears, congratulations, happiness—be happy—you're a beautiful bride. You really are—" She turned and ran.

"Find out where they're going!" Normal hissed, grabbing June's arm.

"She told us. To Las Vegas. Mr. Casement can't drive, that's why she's driving him. And there's certainly nothing going on like *you* suggested."

"Listen," he said, "when I said 'Can't you see what's going on?' I meant the *plotting*—the evil—"

"Oh, come on," she said. "I've just been noticing how pretty it is around here. What's our big hurry? Why don't we just stay here till tomorrow? We could go for a walk. They've got—We could see *Midnight Cowboy*—"

"We're following them."

"Oh, honey. That's just *silly*."

"Is it?" He went around to the back of the car. "Give me the keys."

"What are you asking *me* for? They're in the dashboard."

"No, they're not. They're here!" He took them from his pocket, gave her a severe look. "You don't leave keys in any *dashboard*. Not and leave the door unlocked." He fitted the key in, lifted the door to the trunk.

She stared. "Normal! My God!" It was her car. Where had all the *guns* come from? He must have, when he took the car last night to fill up the tank, stopped at Roger's or somewhere and loaded it up with this *arsenal*.

"Thou shalt not take the name of the Lord thy God in vain," he said, "for the Lord will not hold him guiltless that taketh His name in vain."

"Normal, we can't be traveling with all these guns."

"We can't? Watch us." He bent over and selected what June thought was a long and ugly-looking pistol, but all guns to her were ugly. He loaded it, looked to all sides and behind him quickly, then went around and opened the door on her side and thrust it in the back, down on the floorboard.

She had followed nervously. "Normal—please—"

"Get in."

"We don't need that gun back there! What if we hit a bump and it went off? And all those in the trunk—"

"Get *in*."

She stood there looking at him, her eyes wide, her heart for the first time failing. Could it be that he was…*really* out of it? Should she just turn back? Tell him go on without her, and go and catch the next bus through here back to Salt Lake?

Suddenly he smiled a most boyish and sunny smile. "What do you think I'm going to do? We're getting down here now where it's he-man country, going to shoot me a few prairie dogs—"

"Oh, no, don't do that! They're—not doing any harm—"

"All right. Shoot me a jackrabbit, then."

"Not that either—" Little things that run and quail ...

Suddenly he took her in his arms and laid his cheek against her soft washed hair. "All right. Get in." Doubts vanished, love came rushing back. He smiled again, a tender, luminous smile.

But she didn't like it when he speeded up and passed a big hack-rack loaded with cars and dodged in and around several other cars till Rosetta's car came in view, then hung behind it. Rosetta was going at a fast enough clip so Normal didn't get more than usually impatient, though resenting it when others passed.

"Why are we doing this?"

"Doing what?"

"You know well enough what. Following Rosetta."

"We're not following anybody." He gave her his sweet smile.

"I don't know what you're doing, then. Listen, Normal, why don't you tell me? Where we're going and everything. What will it hurt? Or don't you really know?"

"I know all right, baby." He never called her baby, and she cast him a quick glance. "Not Glen Canyon City, I can tell you that." He waved towards the pine forests growing on the sides of the mountains to the east with humps and bumps between as if to say it would be hard to get to them. "And not down thataway," he pointed straight ahead, "down to Short Creek in Arizona. They're a bunch of punks down there. Roger has checked out both places, and he knows. Old guys. Want the say. The pick of the gals, too. Not that they're much to pick from, Roger says."

She found this oddly comforting. "So where—?" Maybe just to a mountain cabin by themselves, no other brides. Maybe *that* was to be his wedding present, his big surprise, that she was the only one, that he'd just been hyping her all along ... She wouldn't put it past him, all these weeks putting her on. "So tell me." She snuggled over close. "And give me back my ring."

"Wait till we stop somewhere." Both of them looked at it, sparkling on the little finger of his left hand.

But when they stopped at Bud and Lucy's Cafe in Parowan, she had forgotten about the ring. He hadn't let her drive and she didn't remind him, happy that nothing living— she thought she saw a coyote once in among the rabbit bushes and greasewood anchored in the red, rocky ground—had been shot at, wounded or killed. A nice soft program was coming over the car radio, and ... night must fall, and they would be somewhere ... She forgot the ugly-looking gun. The guns.

Rosetta's car was parked in front of a restaurant called The Old Barn, a restaurant so new that plants ranged along the windows with ribbon pompons from the Chamber of Commerce and other business firms still bloomed in their papered pots, though brown around the edges and starting to rot with too much water hopefully poured on. Normal turned corners till he located the car but didn't stop there. Instead, he drove quickly back to the highway and to Bud and Lucy's Cafe.

"Why you would want to follow them I do not know," June said as they waited for their hamburgers and milkshakes.

"Can't a guy be curious?" During the drive from Beaver to Parowan, with the soft program playing instead of what he usually twirled the dial for, he and she had definitely been more on the good side of the vibe scale than usual. He talked more, she didn't let it rattle her cage so much, no sense worrying about what he said, just rock on through, people didn't always believe tomorrow what they sound off about today. And it was kind of marvelous, the hieroglyphs he had picked up on. The reason for sexual desire, for instance. Well, to hype a man into delivering the seed the woman will then cultivate, everyone knows that. But the *real* reason...

"God is pure intelligence," Normal said, "and it's all planned out. Why does that *peak* that feels so cool some people would die for it, why does it only last for those few seconds? I'll tell you. Because if it *lasted*, no one would care for God or anything else. So what that peak is, is a *foretaste* of what's to go on for eternity if we want it to, in *Paradise*. See, to make a promise of a rush we don't know anything *about* would be poor strategy. But give us a *sample*—wow, is this for real? It becomes a *powerful motivation*! to love God, to keep the Commandments, work, pay tithing, do what you're supposed to so you can go to Heaven and you know? *do the wild thing forever*! Tactics, is what God uses. So is it any wonder," he said, "that sexuality is a religious matter? That divine laws...Don't take this personally, but woman is a destructive element. To put it in the simplest terms: Man *screws*. Woman *screws things up*. She's a destructive element. So that's the reason..."

June watched the cars ahead, and the cars and trucks that sometimes passed when he lifted his foot off the gas pedal just enough to keep the distance uniform between them and the blob of blue they chased like an ape would chase a butterfly. That senselessly. She looked at license plates—Quebec, what do you know? Montana—stared off into the sagebrush flats, the dry old hills, trying not to squint in the afternoon glare. She had mislaid her dark glasses and must get another pair, even young girls could get wrinkles around their eyes, and if she was going to stay a jump ahead of two other wives...And why stop at two? But no, he didn't really mean it, he was trying her, testing her...Hey! those Indians by that store and service station. Bundled up like that, wouldn't you think they'd melt? She didn't make the remark, didn't interrupt, listened as to the language of the Murzuqs, dead these thousand years...The soft program was still on too, like the top off a bottle of ether, she breathed it in and listened to the tuneless sentences he would not modulate and felt suspended somewhere between heaven and earth where birds, the silly birds...

"—three positive vital functions," he was saying. "One, it allows men to perpetuate themselves on earth, which has to be if the social order is to keep on existing. Two, it's a foretaste of what's waiting above if we don't do anything to blow it. Three, it's necessary to intellectual effort. Because a lot of people don't know this, but civilization is the end result of satisfied sexual energy—"

"So why don't we satisfy it, then?" she said.

He went on as though she had not spoken. "So that shows how far the Prophet was ahead of his time. Polygamy entitles a man to satisfy his sexuality to the saturation necessary to do the world's work while at the same time not getting sick and tired of always the same old—And because—"

"You *know* they're just going to Las Vegas," she interrupted. "Where else can they go? There's just this one highway."

He cast a pitying glance her way. "I don't say Rosetta's in on it, she's not that smart. Although we don't know. The thing you've got to learn—we don't know about *anybody*. But *he* definitely has been sent out here from headquarters to keep Senator Arble out of the White House. They don't *want* a Mormon president, they want the country to go under. So he's got orders—but it just so happens that *I've* got some orders, too."

Suddenly frightened, she inspected her nails. "Normal, you know what? Let's go back. Why do we have to go so far away to—to do all this?"

"All what?"

"The brides and everything. I know some girls right at school who would just *love* to marry you. And you'd love them. I don't know why I didn't think of it before!" He was crazy, she had to get away from him, go back. Off to their right, as the day tarnished the lofty piles rearing up out of the gray cliffs, were steep towers hung with banners streaming rose and orange. The sun still glared, but now its white had yellowed like linen, had a lilac tinge. The heat was as hot yet as a kitchen after canning, but as if a back door had opened onto a cold, narrow breeze.

She tried again. "I sure didn't think we'd end up in *Las Vegas*. Which we are naturally going to do if we keep on—"

A sign flashed by: Summit.

"—following *them*. And what is that going to prove? Please, honey."

He watched the blue blob, kept it just as far ahead as he wanted, with a foot that seemed to have its own intelligence.

Cedar City Motor Inn, the billboard said, thirteen miles, Water Beds Sauna Color TV Jacuzzi Heated Pool Restaurant and Lounge Major Credit Cards.

"I'm not kidding, Normal. I want to go back. I think you're very tired. Your mind and everything. I really do. I've come to the conclusion."

"I think you're very tired." In a forced voice a register above the natural, he mimicked her and barked falsetto laughter.

At the Cedar City Motor Inn restaurant, where they stopped for coffee (but Jeppe changed his mind and ordered a Scotch instead), Rosetta spread the service-station map out. "See, we bear right, we go to Enterprise—this place here, Enterprise—and from there, off to the west, should be the—"

"Where are you folks heading?" the large, corsetted woman in a dark crepe dress that made her look like the well-coiffed owner of a dress shop said, putting the drink before Jeppe and the coffee at Rosetta's elbow.

"Why—uh—St. George."

"You're on the right road, then. I heard you say Enterprise. You don't need to go *there* to get to St. George. That's *way* off your track."

"Well, we thought—" Rosetta began.

"We want to see a place called Mountain Meadow," Jeppe said, taking a sip of his drink.

"*Oh?*" The woman looked hard at him and then at Rosetta. "That'll be about as exciting as watching paint dry. To go there."

"How come? You mean there's nothing to see?" Jeppe said. "No monument?"

"Nothing worth a person's trouble."

"Well—tourists—" Rosetta said with a little shrug, folding up the map and pushing it aside. "It's farther than we bargained for anyway." She drew her cup and saucer close and reached for her spoon.

"You won't be missing a thing," the woman said, writing out the slip. "A bunch of rocks." She tore it off and laid it down. "I kid you not, as they say."

Rosetta smiled. The woman did not smile back. But when two new customers, obviously business men from nearby in crew cuts, shirts and ties, came in and took stools at the counter, her handsome dentures gleamed like the columns of Capua. The men ordered Frescas, and when she brought them joshed with her. They asked her if, when the Senator made it, she and old Charlie were going to go back there and drive Granddaddy's covered wagon down Pennsylvania Avenue in the inaugural parade.

"You better believe it," she said.

"Think he'll cut the mustard?"

"I don't think it, I know it. He *better*. It's about our last chance."

They laughed at that as at a piece of wit.

Jeppe raised a finger.

The woman called over, sober-faced, "Yes?" Her voice was cold.

"I'll have another."

When she came back to their table she said, "It's private property. A ranch. Gates to open and shut. You got to ask up at the house. Nothing to see."

"Oh, we've decided—It was just a thought. We'll stay on ninety-one," Rosetta said.

As they went out through the door, she looked around to see the woman had gone back behind the counter in front of the men. No one was talking now, they only watched, and one man swirled his Fresca as in a dream.

"MAYBE SHE WAS RIGHT," ROSETTA said as they pulled out of the parking lot. "This country down around here is all—Thirty *miles* from here is the same as right here. And I was reading once that Robert Graves, you know, the authority on Greece and Rome? never went to either place in his life. All he had to do was take a little trip to see what he was writing about, but he wouldn't do it. He'd rather see them in his mind, he said."

Jeppe pointed. "There's a sign," he said. "Panguitch. St. George. Kanab—"

"Why don't we just forget the Meadow?" They still had sunshine, but the shadows now were stretching out. "It's really quite a ways. I didn't realize."

"Enterprise," he said. "Look. We almost missed it! We go that way." He was sitting on the edge of the seat. She turned right. He settled back and lit a cigarette. When he put it out in the full ashtray he said, "It's not the same."

"What's not the same?" She looked in the rear view mirror. Yes, there it was again, the small brown Volkswagen—but why would they be following?

"The country. Like you said. All the same. But it really won't be. Because when something with—you know, motive force—that human thought and human concentration are going to think about and concentrate on, *happens* at a certain spot on the map, even when it all goes back to being just like it was before whatever it was happened there that drew the attention in the first place—why, it never really *does* go back. Human attention has changed it forever, changed the positively charged mass of, you know? the atoms. X marks the spot, and from then on something *transmits*, you know, like radio—or radium—sets it to going, ticking, starts it *sending*. It never is the same again. Nor people either, kings, celebrities. 'They're just like you and me.' Don't you wish they were! They're *not*, of course, because if nothing else, people concentrating their thoughts on them—hundreds, thousands, maybe millions—has changed the fundamental arrangement of the—" He broke off.

"That's why," she said, "Queen Anne could touch for scrofula. And why Ford's Theatre—and the mountain pass between whatever it's called and the Gulf of Lamia—"

"Rosetta," he said in a fretful tone, "come to New York. Live with me, take care of me, be my famulus. Make random remarks. Keep my hair from falling out. Make me work."

She laughed.

"My mother...What I need...Listen," he said, and took out a cigarette. She felt he made it up on the spur of the moment, what he told her then about who his mother really was, but yet it sounded true. She listened—lies tell truths that are astonishing sometimes—as they drove along the narrow graveled road in the strange landscape, stranger than before, the ground in places black and vitreous, black obsidian rock in hardened streams that boiled and bubbled once in bowl-shaped hollows and bubbled over, flowed. The fixing frost...

"In nineteen twenty-two—that was the year," Jeppe said, "that the last Sultan of Turkey, Mehmet the Sixth, sailed away in a British warship, and Turkey became a republic.

Mehmet's harem was disbanded. The harem ladies were told to write their folks, relatives or old friends, sweethearts maybe, men they might in childhood have had an understanding with, to come and get them. But back home in Karassi or Samarkand or Venice, Albania or Gallipoli, where these ladies had been recruited from in the first place, things had changed. Especially if they were old by then. There might not be anyone left who knew them anymore, kinfolk and lovers would be dead. Or feelings would be different. And sisters and cousins, wives, they wouldn't want some kind of a beauty from the royal harem, as spoiled as a mackerel three hours in the sun, back amongst them. Uncool, they'd say. What letter? They never received one.

"So anyway, on the last day, when the palace was going to be closed forever—or not forever, later on it would become a museum—and the girls nobody had come for," he said, "*had* to finally leave the palace harem and find other accommodations, on that last day when they were hanging around there with their luggage or looking out the windows or towards the entrance, maybe hoping against hope, why, a couple of young Americans, nacre buyers from New York, who wanted to see what the Sultan's palace looked like inside—you could go inside it then, where before the Janissaries would put you through some changes—went there and went in. And someone explained to them who the ladies *were* sitting around there and what they were waiting for …

"Mihri," Jeppe said, "was sixteen when her Circassian father sold her to a Turkish merchant who sold her to an agent who booked her into the Sultan's harem. Twenty years afterwards, she was still good-looking—though fat and with bad teeth from too much nougat and Turkish delight—but with her heart frozen stiff—she not only didn't write her father that she was now free, she didn't write anyone, and in fact hoped that they were all dead! Her intention was to stay in Constantinople. Old Pertevale, one of the other harem ladies, the only one Mihri could stand—and she didn't like her very well—had been talking about opening a brothel and charm school for girls, they supposedly being experts, and Mihri thought she might go in with her. But then a man from Pertevale's old home town came to get her, Pertevale forgot everything, and off she went with him. So Mihri was just sitting there, trying to figure out what to do before she had to leave the palace and fend for herself, when these two guys from New York showed up.

"So anyway they got married, Mihri and the younger of the nacre buyers," Jeppe said, "which you know is mother of pearl. He was thirty-one and she was thirty-seven. And went to New York, where Mihri became Maisie and had a baby boy. And that was me." And when he was five, he said, his father died on a nacre-buying trip to Marseille. But that didn't matter, he hardly knew him. Or any of his connections either, because when his father came home with a Turkish harem-lady bride, the family went through the ceremony for the dead. But Mihri or Maisie and them wouldn't have liked each other anyway. She never learned the language, couldn't cook, couldn't keep house, a child to her was like an unbroken house pet to someone who doesn't like animals. The neighbors down the hall—their name was Casement, he was a doctor—were the ones who really raised him. Then he showed this talent for music—Maisie didn't like music, it made her head ache. After she died they thought she must have had a tumor on the brain, Mrs. Casement thought she acted like it—and Dr. Casement got Jeppe in at the Curtis Institute, which was where he met Ariel Luebke. He was eight years old at the time, the Casements adopted him, changed his name to Jeppe after the doctor's youngest brother, who had been lost at sea in World War One. His actual name was—Maisie had called him Nedjed. Which he found out later wasn't a person's name at all but a place, a beautiful desert kingdom.

Rosetta sent him a sidelong glance. Could any of this be *true*? "Now *there* you've got an opera," she said. "Royal harem broken up, royal beauty sitting on her suitcase, handsome young traveling man, Maisie in New York..."

"I hated her," Jeppe said. "Cold, cruel. Sitting there drinking coffee, ashtrays full, dirty old housecoat, hair hanging down...See, they had servants to do everything, Nubian slaves, eunuchs—she hardly even knew how to take a bath."

She glanced at him again, dreamily looking out the open window at the grim scenery, dreamily smoking, a peaceful expression on his face. It wasn't true. Or was it? "It would be great," she said. "Lots better"—much as she'd like to see Legrand's scenario come to life—"than this old—Mountain Meadow thing."

"*All on the Meadow Green*," he said, listening to how that sounded.

"Because really it's kind of stereotyped, a wagon train and all that same old—" For some reason now, she wanted to discourage him. She didn't want to see the place, it would soon be evening, and suppose they got stuck out here? No houses, no place to buy gas. Legrand said the Mormons tried to get the bloody bodies under the ground as quick as they could. But they didn't dig very deep, and after they left...there were wolves...and the terrible halitosis of grizzlies...mountain lions...Right today there are descendants walking the earth of the most heartless murderers and they wouldn't hurt a flea, in fact they might sacrifice their life for somebody, she thought, and a...great-grandfather, maybe you wouldn't inherit one murderous gene from him. How could he have done it? But yet Wyandra said John D. Lee wasn't really a bad man. She said Aunt Lucitie *loved* her father, Hindle did too, he'd catch them in his arms and hug and love them, two of his twenty-five or thirty daughters, take them out to pet the horse named Chickasaw, tell them stories.

Legrand said once that Hemingway would be proud of the way John D. Lee had died. Grace under pressure. As John's great-grandson, *he* was proud, Legrand said. They brought him out here, it must have been along this very road, in a wagon. There were soldiers. The Indians have a name for every moon. Crow Moon was March, when the crows starved and flew in the cold gray skies or lit on snowy branches. John's last moon of his life was that one, Crow Moon. In his movie Legrand wasn't going to have him sit on his coffin to be shot, as supposedly he did. He was going to have him stand against the gradually growing light sky in the icy wind in his shirtsleeves on the order of someone really together, head up, half smiling, looking straight at the guns. "Aim for the heart, boys. Don't mangle my body." He wanted to look nice for the Resurrection. But *their* bodies, the murdered ones, when the wolves got through scrabbling and tugging, and the bears, and all the little sharp-toothed creatures, there wouldn't be enough left to put in your eye.

"You say it was nineteen twenty-two when Turkey became a republic? Your sets and costumes would be wonderful." She very much wanted him suddenly *not* to use the massacre.

"The cat's pajamas," he said, proud of knowing the antique expression.

"Right." A moment later, "Let's just drive on by. The place, I mean. Not stop. Or let's turn back and get back on the highway. It's still a long ways to Las Vegas."

"You are *so silly*." He was seven, she was Nanny, naughty. "Here we have come all this way"—he took out his handkerchief and wiped his brow—"and just when we're nearly *there*—"

They *were* nearly there. The sign said *Enterprise Pop. 327*. He looked at the map. "We don't go through the town. If you can call it that. Turn left—" He broke off. "There!" he said. "The crossroads...See, the sign says Veyo."

She was looking in the rear view mirror. "That's the oddest thing. That car back there. But now I don't see it—that's the car they're in, I'm sure of it. That crazy boy is driving. But what I wonder about, why would they be following *us*?"

"Look! Good thing I saw it." He pointed to the sign.

Site of the Mountain Meadows Massacre.

Chapter Seventy-two

*

PRIVATE PROPERTY, IT SAID IN SMALLER LETTERS DOWN IN THE RIGHT-HAND corner. *Ask at Ranch*. An arrow pointed. They turned at the first access road, drove along a range of dry hills, turned and saw the windbreak of poplars, the house nestled under a cottonwood tree, a barn, an empty machine shed, farm machinery, chicken coops. A visitor would fetch up in the back yard before a long, screened back porch, a pump to his right, clotheslines. There didn't seem to be any front entrance, but after Rosetta had knocked to no avail at the back screen door, she waded through white silverweeds around a corner of the house and then another corner, and there it was, a tiny ginger-breaded front stoop. But nobody answered the front door either, with cobwebs on it and a drift of last year's autumn leaves along the bottom. She waited, then peered through a lace-curtained, green-blinded, dusty lavender window at a dark, high-ceilinged parlor, then went back. "Nobody home."

Jeppe stood by the car looking about him at the pump, an arbor grown over with budding grape vines, a big old wagon wheel laid flat on the barren ground and planted with dry-looking plants. "Would this—I wonder—have been standing then? The house, I mean, and everything. No, this is later..."

"Maybe we'd better not go to wherever it is," Rosetta said. "The site, I mean, since there's nobody here to get permission from."

But there *was* somebody. Even as she spoke, he sidled towards them from the vicinity of the barn, an old man of obviously weak intellect. He mumbled a greeting, and when told what they had come about took off his greasy old cap and scratched his head, the better to think out his reply. "The folks has went into town. They always go a Sattidy. Buying. She's a spender. Me, I got to do the milking."

Jeppe spoke loudly, enunciated carefully, as to the deaf. "We'd like to see the site," he said.

"The sights?" the man said. "No sights around here. Temple's in St. George, the County Court House. Them there's your sights. I should know. Born there."

"No, where the massacre...took place..."

"My sister—Way I come here, my sister's reading the ads. I used to work for Kraxberger's Fruit and Garden? But they went bust, so she's looking in the paper. It ain't too bad, grub's good, nowhere like Ma's, but better'n the slumgullion my sister slaps down onto the table since Ma's gone. And one thing—"

"We want to see the monument," Jeppe said. "Where it happened."

"It's around here someplace," Rosetta said with an encouraging smile.

"—out here, you got no place to blow your cash. I'm saving up—"

Rosetta went to the car, reached in through the open window and opened the purse she had left lying on the seat. She came back.

"Want me a TV," the man was saying. "I'm out back. They let me watch but then they claim they're going to bed, but I sneak back and listen by the window, and it's still on!" He put his hand out, Rosetta handed him a folded bill. "Let's see now, a massacre? Guess you must be talking about—down there." He pointed off to the west, putting the bill in his shirt pocket. "Looks like where a house had fell down, but of course there never was no house there. Indians scalped—now I remember—yes—a bunch of folks from the east—"

IT DID LOOK LIKE THAT a little, as though a house of grand proportions had once stood, then fallen here and sunk away and left only its foundation built of cobblestones. A house of fierce, savage murder, red in the evening light, made of slanting rays of the evening sun and a few shadows. They had driven around the barn and down the way the old man pointed, following a road, or kind of road, that wound through fields dry-looking even now, though summer had just started, they rustled with a parched-cattail sound, quail clicked dry as gourds or the clicking dice of the false loco-weed.

"Down there a piece," the man had said. A piece indeed, they must have come two miles. They circled a boss of rock and the road ended. No, it still went on, tire tracks there, faint. Ranch buildings, trees... When Jeppe got out to open a pair of gates, Rosetta stuck her head out the window and looked back, but there seemed to be nothing back there. She drove through, stopped ahead a few yards. Jeppe ran up and opened the car door. "No, you have to close it, too. The gate," she said.

"I'll close it when we come back."

"That's not the way the code works. Of the hills. The west," she said.

"The Western Approaches." He laughed and ran back and did as he was bid. "That would be a good title." He reflected on this as she drove into a sunset vast as half the sky, squinting through her windshield that mirrored it to see the tire tracks.

"When we come back!" She repeated his words. "I only hope we do come back," she said. "It's like going through a stargate into another...magnitude. We should have crumbs to scatter."

At the top of the deep gully overgrown with willows and tules, they parked the car and walked the rest of the way. The land stretched out. Once upon a time there was no time and it was then that...autumn stood, blue haze along the horizon, the dusty smell of dry grass and wheat stubble in the air. And they came, fixed, perpetuated in unchanging form, sometimes at night, sometimes by broad daylight. It happens like that in the vicinity of churchyards, marshes, great buildings, solitary places, or places notorious because of some murder or where a very dreadful crime has been committed. *Ambulones*, they move about at midnight on great heaths and desert places.

The trail boss, he comes first, heading the procession of carts, white-tops, horse-men…silent as clouds. God, they have banged along. Drive a man crazy, gritty wheels, the iron clank of traces, neck yokes, clumped hooves, clump clump clump, buckets, rattling pans, a crying child, laughter, moos and bleats, yells and barking dogs and squeaking brakes, men taking the name of the Lord in vain, the long whip's crack when deadhead oxen drop back and let their mates do all the pulling. This causes, God damn 'em, the doubletrees to scrape the wheel and the ox doing the pulling gets nervous…and then…

But all is noiseless as the still moon now, as pinnacles of aged snow, they plod behind thick glass, walk like treading water through soft sand with feet like leaden weights, stum-ble on rocks, climb and run downhill, bodies with their measure and their space but instantaneous pictures on the air, shadowgraphed like life there, eerily…

"Moving people," the Paiutes called the white men.

This wagon train was different, really two trains, one a bunch of prosperous home-folks riding along in more than a dozen white-tops and a few riding carriages, the other party of mostly young single fellows on horseback traveling west to the gold fields. The two outfits had thrown in together out on the plains, as much together, that is to say, as was convenient for their horses and cattle to graze, and for the purposes of camp at night. The families from Arkansas in the wagons and rigs had a preacher along who led them in prayer night and morning. The Missouri Wildcats, as the wild young fellows called themselves, had a fiddle, plenty of tangle-leg to drink, and at night over by their campfire sang, swore, and leaped like aborigines and shot off guns.

Together, when the two outfits trundled and rode into Salt Lake, they looked to the mistrustful Mormons (a-bristle with word of war impending between themselves and the rest of the country) like a dangerous circus parade. The riders, even with their guns slung across their saddles—pump the lever and it'd shoot ten or fifteen bullets in a string—were really soldiers, spies, what else could they be? And more of the same in the wagons, in under those canvas covers! Right? You couldn't fool the Mormons. The travelers camped down by the Jordan, tried to buy supplies. Damn near out of everything, barter or buy—No dice, the word was out. Don't sell so much as a crumb! So they went on, down the Old Spanish Trail. A cabbage, a dipper of milk for a child with fever, one egg—look, a carrot, sir? (Sir, I'm calling you sir.) The land's possessors didn't say I'm sorry, just *no*. An axle tree, a horseshoe? Fresh feed, flour? Castor oil? A horse! my horse died on me. *You are the enemy.* Look who's talking enemy! We wasn't, sports, but now we damn well are, I'm telling you. Fifteen settlements and not a one would give us even a goddamn drink of water if they could of helped it. What we ought to do is come back through here someday with an army and teach you some manners. *Look who's talking manners! thieves and spies.*

Unique and beautiful, peculiar in the sky, the Meadow lay like Eden. Seven miles long, hemmed in by hills, a mile wide here and three miles there, it had a prominence running down through the middle lengthwise called "the rim" or "the rim of the basin" that sloped what waters trickled there off east to the lakes or west to the ocean. An old western traveler once wrote that he had journeyed over "much of this extensive Territory, and the Mountain Meadow valley is the most extraordinary formation west of the Rocky Mountains, probably in a higher altitude than any other valley small or large, on the continent; yet a continuous and handsome meadow furnishing grass for much stock, but in too high an altitude for agriculture of any kind." Too short of water too, he thought, with only one spring at either end.

IF THE PAST WERE SUDDENLY opened up to our inspection, we would be bowled over not only on account of all the stuff that went on back then, but by the hideousness and dreadfulness of it all. Or anyway a lot of it, a big percent. It is one thing to read about awful tragedy, Massacres of the Innocents, bloody Culloden, heretics on pyres, the guillotine, My Lai, the German ovens, dancing on the air at country crossroads, or see these things on television. But what man could bear to look upon the immutable evil of the past, knowing that what he saw was real and beyond all remedy? Tamerlane will *do* it, go ahead with it. Bluebeard will do it. John Wilkes Booth do it. Cortes's men. Lizzie Borden. Nothing can stop them. Nothing can stop what *will be*, therefore was—and *is*—as long as time shall last.

And so the riders ride. They set up camp (too far from the spring at the southern end of the meadow). Today the bronze tablet reads:

MOUNTAIN MEADOWS

A FAVORITE RECRUITING PLACE ON
THE OLD SPANISH TRAIL

IN THIS VICINITY, SEPTEMBER 7-11, 1857 OCCURRED ONE
OF THE MOST LAMENTABLE TRAGEDIES IN THE ANNALS
OF THE WEST. A COMPANY OF ABOUT 140 ARKANSAS AND
MISSOURI EMIGRANTS LED BY CAPTAIN CHARLES FANCHER,
ENROUTE TO CALIFORNIA, WAS ATTACKED BY WHITE MEN AND
INDIANS. ALL BUT 17, BEING SMALL CHILDREN, WERE KILLED.
JOHN D. LEE, WHO CONFESSED PARTICIPATION AS LEADER,
WAS LEGALLY EXECUTED HERE MARCH 23, 1877. MOST OF
THE EMIGRANTS WERE BURIED IN THEIR OWN DEFENSE PITS.

THIS MONUMENT WAS REVERENTLY DEDICATED SEPTEMBER 10, 1932
BY THE UTAH PIONEER TRAILS AND LANDMARKS ASSOCIATION
AND THE PEOPLE OF SOUTHERN UTAH.

The monument is a wall four feet high and about a foot and a half thick, thicker in some places, made out of cobblestones. It is thirty feet wide and runs longways, north and south to the compass, thirty-four feet. An arrangement of rock steps on the west side allows passage over the wall into the area inside, with a handrail to hold by, if anyone wants to go in and stand there. Children could scramble over in a second. It could be the start of a fort or a fine clubhouse, lay boards across the top…It's a big huge grave, what is called a mass grave. All the bones where they fell and where the beasts of night-time worried and dragged them were gathered up in armfuls like kindling and brought here and thrown in, skulls tossed in, dirt shoveled over, rocks. If it was ever lush, green meadow—! that time is long past. Some little old brown grass, an old gnarled tree, some dry old brush, rough, rocky and barren ground as far as the eye…What happened? Denudation, the land was overgrazed. Washaways, the rain instead of soaking through the grassy ground formed streamlets, ran and gullied out arroyos, the nice topsoil washed down…till finally…

The land's a-cursed, blasted and blighted by what happened here, the deed of blood. Consigned to evil by divine wrath. Oh, come on, if you believe that, you are dumber than I thought. *Erosion* was to blame. Deed of jetting blood indeed. Blood at a trickle, more like, thick and dark, the people were dehydrated. Got there on a Sunday. Made camp. Monday afore daylight came the first attack. Indians. Didn't they wish then, in spite of the spring having washed out a deep rut and ground adjacent being wet and marshy, didn't they wish *then* they had camped around it! It wouldn't have made any difference in the end. But thirst on top of everything else…They died a Friday, that's a long old time to be under siege, close onto a week. Still, they got a good big drink of water before they died. From the hour the villainous negotiators rolled in in their buck-board with their white flag waving till these were back with the so-called guard, which one on one was going to escort the travelers back to Cedar City, they could have run to the spring and drunk their fill. And let me tell you, a shriveled, famished, dried-up body can gulp down enough water in minutes to swell up under your eyes to what it was—the water seems to run down and fill up legs, arms, the shriveled head and everything—like wrinkled old wineskins filling up with wine. It's not too good for you, they say. But what did it matter? By five that afternoon they'd all be dead anyway, except for a few babies and a handful of toddlers too little to blab.

They melted down with one accord
Like wax before the flame,
Men and women, old and young,
O Utah, blush for shame…

So maybe the blood that ran from them wasn't thick and dark, a slow dehydrated trickle, but fountained out in bright red sparkling plumes. Water turned to wine, a wine-dark salty sea that soaked the ground, consigned it to evil, fraught it with malediction…Well, it sure looks desolate, I will say that for it. But superficial denudation…An erosionist would say…And take into consideration: if God was going to make every spot on this earth where evil was done a curse to all the nations, commencing back at time's beginning when huge beasts…why, you wouldn't have enough good ground left anywhere to raise a mess of turnips. No, it doesn't seem that much of a thing to signify. A mere one hundred and twenty people! When at Waterloo alone…Or consider the place where the tower stood that the great Lord Timur Beg commanded to be built out of the chopped-off heads of one hundred and twenty thousand prisoners of war with every face turned outward…Or when six million…

(Real, and beyond all remedy.)

Smoking a cigarette, Jeppe walked around inside the enclosure. Rosetta stood leaning against the wall outside awhile, then sat on the next to the bottom of the steps that went up over it. Her eyes on the bonfired air, she too smoked, rather forlornly. It's forlorn there. Dark hills at evening in the west…That couldn't have been June and Normal following them, it was no one, someone going home, she thought. Starlight, star bright…Why do we keep coming back to this awful place? Are *we* the ghosts? We could be and not even know it. Ghosts probably think they're people. Think they're just going about their business like anyone, when all the while they're *haunting* some other dimension and don't even guess.

Jeppe paced over the killing ground like a Le Corbusier asked to look over a particular situation with a view to putting up a building. He frowned, squinted, tapped his teeth, stepped back a few paces, tipped his head…Because with new sonorities, new intervals and forms, excerpts from court records spoken and sung, journals, letters, and the lintel posts of major chords to discharge the superincumbent weight, and his passion and tonality, a building was what he *was* going to put up, fluid, ethereal, the transparent double of an eyried castle.

Rosetta stood up and stretched, looked over the wall at him down at the far end of the enclosure. It was time to go, the stars would soon be coming out, in fact they were out now, the evening star and a few others. Not that she was scared, but she would just as soon not be here when it got dark. Jeppe wasn't moving, just standing sort of like a cataleptic. That she had seen in the hospital, catalepsy, cases brought in, one woman had sat on a ditch and sat all day from morning till night under a black umbrella without moving a muscle. The drivers carried her in by the elbows in a folded position, like bringing in a sitting Hindu god.

She had never been as associated as this with a creative artist before. What zeal, what fury hath inspired…

His sudden movement, turning his head and sending her a smile, was as surprising as though done by a manikin in a show window. "Well, I've made up my mind," he said. "Five hundred dollars is my gambling limit. When we get to Las Vegas." He didn't come toward her but retreated the few steps to the far north wall, turned and leaned against it facing her. It was really evening now, the sky's fire out almost, he was more a shadow.

"I think that's very wise," she said. "So shall we—move on?"

They still had miles to go. Back the way they had come to the ranch house, down the access road to the county road, then right? or left? to get back onto the highway.

"Does it seem like they're here?" He raised his voice as though the dusk itself were distance. He meant the corpses, bones, the slain. "If only—! Like under the Basilica of St. Sebastian on the Appian Way near Rome. Lying there in niches in these galleries. Grinning. And with the hollow sockets of their eyes…"

"No," she said, "it doesn't seem like that. But *someone's* here—or will be pretty soon— There! See them? Coming down the way we came." She couldn't see the car, just its headlights' beams, but something told her it was they, Normal and June. Normal was a weird person. And what he didn't want was Jeppe here gathering impressions at just this landmark. Or want him anywhere. At all. And they did awful things. To the enemy. (They learned how in the war.) And it was just imperative—"Jeppe, come on!"—not to hang around. "It's them, it's June—"

"Okay. But wait, I thought something dropped—"

"Because *she* can't do anything. With him, I mean."

"Maybe not, but it sounded—" He was feeling in his pockets.

"Hurry. Really. Please!"

BUT SHE WAS MISTAKEN. THE newcomers were two Indian girls with an Indian and a white boy. They were surprised. At least their spokesman was, the Indian boy. "Hey, you're not kids, man."

"No," Rosetta said, "we're just—"

"What ja do, get lost?"

"Let's *split*," the thinner and prettier of the two Indian girls said. "Who wants to eat or nothing in a *graveyard*?"

"This ain't no graveyard," the other girl said. "It's a *monument*."

"Don't look like a monument to *me*," the white boy said.

"Don't look like a *graveyard*." The fatter and homelier girl, Pona Mae, would be truly fat someday, and homely, and so while she was not (or only fat in comparison with people, she often thought, who were thin because they smoked Viceroys continuously and had osteomyelitis in their blood and thought they were *movie stars* because of being an extra in one movie in Kanab and one in the Cedar Breaks—neither of which had even come out yet, although they were made two summers ago, or maybe they came out under different titles and no one knew—and only homely in comparison with Avon ladies who piled the product on their own face inches deep and backcombed and sprayed their hair till it was like mattress stuffing), Pona Mae used the time to be agreeable, have a nice personality and not just concentrate on looks, so that (as Mrs. Weazel Tail advised) when Mr. Right came along she wouldn't have to wear herself out fixing up all the time for fear she'd lose him, he would love her for her *soul* and *personality* and not just what was on the surface. "Curley Jim knows what he's doing," Pona Mae said. "This is a *neat* place. Otherwise he wouldn't of brought us up here." Agreeably, with her nice personality, she defended her date. Not that Curley Jim was her actual *date*. He was more like a brother.

Pona Mae's *date*, could she have had her choice, would have been the other boy. The minute Curley Jim and Steve came driving onto the reservation in Curley Jim's boss's old pickup, Pona Mae wanted Steve. But his blind date—which Curley Jim had arranged beforehand—was movie star and Avon lady Rita. And of course the minute the boy's blue eyes lit on Rita, in a cloud of dust running over from the commissary on her stork legs, with her five-inch heels and dirndl skirt and white ruffled Mexican blouse pushed down over her skinny shoulders, her tumbleweed hair and the big gold rings in her ears and the whole cosmetic line she represented plastered on with a trowel, and smelled her Matchabelli perfume (which wasn't an Avon product), Steve was a dead duck.

Rita was a dead duck too, even though the white boy she met traveling with the movie company in Kanab had done her such dirt she swore *never again*. So technically those two, Rita and Steve, were the ones on the Saturday night *date*. Curley Jim and Pona Mae were just together, Pona Mae having been—on that afternoon, after a bath and in her best outfit—at the right time in the right place, Mrs. Weazel Tail's ramshackle front steps—when here came the pickup with the kids in it. So all four of them could be up in front, the boys made room for Pona Mae on the seat between Curley Jim and Steve. Mrs. Weazel Tail hollered that she would send her little boy James Dean over to Pona Mae's house to tell her aunt she wouldn't be home for supper, and they should have a nice time, enjoy themselves, you're only young once.

Rita sat on Steve's lap. He said she was so light he wished she would press heavier so he would know she wasn't a feather. Curley Jim started asking Pona Mae about this or that old acquaintance as they turned around and headed off the reservation in a cloud of dust and onto the main road. Curley Jim didn't live on the reservation anymore but in Veyo, where he worked for Mr. Bryant in Bryant's Store and Service Station and saved up for a second year at the Branch Agricultural College in Cedar City. So what was new? Not much, Pona Mae said. Frank Corndropper accidentally shot part of his thumb off. Jody Crow tried to start an Alcoholics Anonymous. Mrs. Crappo finally got her claim against the government settled. Pinkie was the main suspect as to who was telling the new agent everything that was going on. Wixom got another letter from that white girl, the one he met at the Bear Dance, and paid old Eask to do the magic with the rocks and the coyote's heart, so now he was waiting…And Mrs. Weazel Tail…

Rita said if Steve knew how much she weighed, he wouldn't say she was a feather. She was a big heavy girl. Oh, yes, very heavy, he wondered how he could bear up under such a big heavy girl. Her shoulder bag was heavier than she was. It was down on the floorboard between his cowboy-booted feet, and her Viceroys and matches were in it, she had to twist in different shapes to try to reach down and open it—for what?—for her Viceroys. He squeezed her waist, held her arm, *he* had cigarettes, for Chrissake, L&Ms! the only way to go, better'n her old Viceroys. But neither was nothing in comparison with—Him and Curley Jim had a bag full of real organic—man, it was really beautiful stuff, wasn't it, Curley Jim?

"What you talking about?"

"What you and me got us for tonight."

"What's he talkin' about, I hope not dope," Pona Mae said agreeably with her nice personality, "because you know what could happen if the cops…And it affects your unborn children."

"Oh, Pona Mae," Rita said with an exasperated sigh and sidelong glance before she lit her L&M at the cupped flame in Steve's calloused hand.

"Man, I don't *care*. We get us where we're going, I'm going to stay blasted till Monday," Steve said.

"The question is, where we going?" Rita said, twisting on Steve's lap to look flirtatiously out of the corner of her eyes at Curley Jim.

"Don't know," Curley Jim said, "but we're on our way." On their way fast in the old truck, stuff bouncing around in back, tire chains from last winter, a pick and shovel (Mr. Bryant was always looking for uranium), the paint for his lady friend's kitchen, and stuck in under a bundled-up dropcloth, Mr. Bryant's old gun. That was one of his inalienable rights, to bear arms. He often said so. And so he bore them—behind the counter of his store, in back of the cash register of his service station (just in case), concealed in his and his wife's clothes closet and even in under his lady friend's bed. However, whether it should be one of the inalienable rights of *Indians* and people like that was something else again.

But in the case of a good worker like Curley Jim, who unknowingly had passed various tests for honesty and integrity set up along his pathway by Mr. Bryant when he first came to work for him, was saving for college and would stay around nights if asked and not expect overtime, Curley Jim, Indian or not, could grab a gun and let some robber punk have it between the eyes anytime he might need to (because these hippie no-goods, you could give them all the leeway and they'd still kill you as soon as look at you, that came over the TV every day). Shoot first and ask questions later, was Mr. Bryant's motto. But Curley Jim couldn't shoot for sour apples. And him supposed to be this pure Shoshone. So shoot, *practice*, Mr. Bryant urged, not out where there's cows or sheep or nothing, empty countryside for gosh sakes. Holy Toledo, a man's got to be able to *shoot*. Practice!

Curley Jim did, of course, know where they were going with the bag full under the seat of real organic—beautiful stuff that Steve had happened just by lucky chance to stumble onto that a guy he met—mescaline, the real McCoy. Steve was cold in hand, so Curley Jim had had to pay for it, but Steve was going halfers next month when his mother's alimony check arrived.

"Cedar City. I'll bet that's where we're going. To the drive-in!" Rita said. "Maybe my picture's playing there. You didn't know I was a movie star, did you, hon?"

"And also an Avon lady," Pona Mae said agreeably with her nice personality.

"Curley here told me," Steve said, hugging Rita up tighter with his left arm while he rolled the window down farther with his right hand, plucked his lighted cigarette from his lips, tossed it out and pushed his nose in under the thicket of her perfumed hair. "But what would surprise me would be if you *wasn't* a movie star. 'Cause you're a very—very ballsy chick—"

Where they were going was where it was nice and quiet, where Curley Jim himself used to go after he discovered the place when he worked at the ranch the summer after graduation. At first he thought a house had gradually fallen down there, just leaving the foundation. Or it might have been a church. The big tablet of metal inserted at the end close to the steps had words enough written on it, for sure. The letters stood up high enough so that had it been pitch dark he could have read them with his fingers, like Blind Wingo: *On this spot*…But the night he read it first, it was bright moonlight. And it was never truly dark out there, the stars were always shining. It was a neat place. And not having tombstones around, it didn't seem like a cemetery. Even knowing about all the dead men and dead women and dead children buried underneath didn't make it horrible somehow, but more like a historical spot, like Plymouth Rock, or the log cabin where…or something like…Still, they *were* there, and up over the wall and inside the enclosure, to sit down on the ground and have a smoke, might *start out* very cool—like hey, man, dig me in my own—but then the snaky cold starts slithering up, a draft sweeps kind of in, and it's like whispers, and a pebble, you can hear it dislodge under a foot that's nowhere. And getting scared, well, what a rush, you know? So that whole summer Curley Jim was dreaming about bringing Carol Simmons up here, her dad was Indian Agent, with her blonde hair and shorts and beautiful legs, and she acted sweet. But in what, you know? a wheelbarrow? and she was shooting up, and what could he…I can't give you anything but love, baby, as the song said on Mrs. Weazel Tail's old 78—that's the only thing I've plenty of, baby…And he was so damn tired when night came anyway, and workin' all day Saturday. And then Sunday…Then he heard she had blown her mind with nitrous oxide, and later on she married a guy with the geological survey…So that's the way it does go down sometimes.

But that feeling, good and bad at the same time, cold chills but also the rush, the beano...like a Saturday night, old antique movies like *Isle of the Dead* on TV after midnight with your girl in your arms and her folks gone to bed...only better, because up here under the stars with the coyotes howlin'...And on campus Marilyn Reimer was sweet to him and everything, in class, but what could he do? Hittin' on nothin'. Walkin'. Cold in hand, as Steve would say. Not even enough left over to buy the Branch Agricultural College annual with her picture in it, Queen of the Freshman Prom, Secretary and Treasurer of the Thespian Society. But next fall, if she was still on campus, even though she would be a senior while he was a sophomore, since he had to miss...But he was a lot more together, with a lot more of the attitude that since all everything meant anyway was a big flying fuck, et cetera, why, he'd pick up on her again and this time they'd like make it. And one place he was going to bring her was out here...

If it still existed. Because when he was out here that summer he worked on the ranch, *he'd* been dreamin', sometimes it seemed like the *place* had been a dream too. What he'd find would be that somebody had backed up a pickup and carted off the stones to build a patio or something. And nothing to tell about it anymore, what place it was, what had happened there, the skeletons...Because that was the whole point, to have it be so neat up here above the ground, the stars and all...and underneath of where they were sitting death and horror, and hell. Marilyn would scream like girls do when he told her, and try to scramble up and get away, but he would pull her back down, draw her close and say don't be afraid. And say...and lay her down like, darlin'...

Chapter Seventy-three

*

So he was always going to check it out. And this was as good a time ... When they turned off to go up the access road to the ranch, he said this was where he had worked the summer after graduation, him and another guy, Glen. And Saturdays the folks would go to town, so he knew they wouldn't be there. And it didn't look like they were when they got up to the house. Curley Jim stopped the pickup out by the machine shed and honked a time or two, Glen would be around here somewheres, somebody had to do the milking ... But the old guy coming out of the bunkhouse wasn't Glen, he looked to be some kind of a nut. Rita started laughing the minute she saw him, and Steve had to squeeze and hug and try to make her shut up by pressing her face in the hollow of his neck. Glen didn't work there anymore, the old guy said. And yes, the folks ... might not be back till late on account of the—whatever the doings was in town. Young Missus had said—

Young Missus? The missus Curley Jim remembered was an old bag about sixty-five or seventy.

"Ain't nobody here like that," the old man said, "this un ain't old. Pants and hair a-hanging, runs around, skinnier'n a yard of pump water ..."

Changes, changes. "We're going down to the monument. I used to work here."

"What's all's happenin' down there anyway? Powwow? Gold been found down there or what?"

"What you talking about?"

"Folks down there already."

"Folks?" But it didn't really matter. When Curley Jim checked it out he'd take the kids somewhere else, and in fact he would just as soon anyway. Leave the meadow for another time, the moonlit night with Marilyn Reimer, just him and her alone, not waste it on Pona Mae ...

"Who wants to go to a dumb old *monument*?" Rita said as they drove in gathering darkness down the winding dirt road through the fields.

"I do," Pona Mae said agreeably.

"Well, there's bodies there too," Curley Jim said. "A whole bunch of people got killed there one time. It tells on the marker. They're buried there. So see, it's kind of like—"

"You got to be kidding!" Rita said.

"No, there's bodies."

"—to think you could get *me* down there."

714

But Steve held her tighter and said the dead never hurt no one, it was the living you had to look out for, and this here was gonna be a real sweet something night.

Pona Mae said she would gladly get out and open and close the gate, but being in the middle…Steve would have to get out anyway, and she couldn't get past Rita. Curley Jim had to keep the gas feeding in. So Steve had to pluck, as best as he could bear to do, Rita off him like a perfumed suctorian covered with sucking disks off a reef, disengage her long slim arms and legs and everything else about her that stuck and adhered, and get out and run over and open the damn gate and close it, and then another. And the way he got in, sliding in under Rita's sucking disks and pasting her to him again, it was like somebody in an oxygen tent where the power went off but now it's on again, the air's swooshing in and everything's cool.

"Hey, man!"

"The old guy was right. Somebody's beat us to it." The Pontiac sedan parked along the road above the monument *looked* like tired old folks, but it would be kids down there.

"Let's split." Rita was all the more anxious when she found out that they had to park along the road too and walk down there, up over a little hill, down and across a gully overgrown with willows and tule. "It don't even *look* like nothing down there to me," she said, still pasted to Steve though now they were out and down on the ground standing alongside the pickup.

The car would be somebody's family car, the kids would have got to use it and wouldn't you know! come here to have their kegger, do their amyl nitrite and PBD, party or whatever the action was on the agenda. Curley Jim was going to check it out, however. Steve said they could soon clear the place if they really wanted. He was from Berwyn (wherever that might be), just like Chicago (heavier than Cicero nowadays), they could soon clear the place. But no use to start something. Curley Jim knew lots of other places. However, it wasn't kids. It seemed to be this guy and his mother…

They met amongst the willows and tule, the two coming up, the four going down.

"What ja do, get lost?"

No, they had just been to see the monument, now they were driving on.

"To where? Salt Lake?"

"Las Vegas."

"Why would anyone put a monument way out here?" Rita said, hanging on to Steve with one hand while, hopping on one foot, she tried to pull a heel strap up into its next perforation.

"Because way out here was where it happened," Pona Mae said agreeably.

"Where *what* happened? I don't even know!" Rita said, giving up the heel strap to cling with both hands to her companion.

"Lovely evening," Rosetta said. "You've still got some pretty sky." A streak of red still floated like a banner over night's hemisphere.

"Excuse me," Curley Jim said, "but you guys—there's nobody else down there, is there?"

"No," Jeppe said. "Just us. We were the only—"

"Right. Okay."

"Have a nice evening," Pona Mae, enlightened and refined by television, said agreeably over her shoulder as she and the others went by.

"Thank you, you the same," Rosetta called back.

"Indian kids," Jeppe said as he and she moved to the car.

"That one boy was white."

"Yes."

"Well, now you've seen your—where it happened," Rosetta said as they got in and closed the doors and she turned the key and put her foot on the starter.

"Where it happens," Jeppe said as if far away. "*Happens.*"

"It's not much of a meadow." She waggled the key, pressed her foot down again.

"They're too far from the spring," he said. "Tomorrow they will circle in closer."

"Jeppe, I hate to say this," she said. "But the car—it won't—"

He was leaning out, gazing at and then over the sweep of low hills and gullies to the west, God-forsaken, dim in the gathering dark.

The monument could not be seen from the road, or its four new visitors. They soon scrambled down to it. Rita hadn't understood it was an actual *graveyard*. Squealing when she did finally grasp the fact, she shrank against Steve. Of all the places to try to rock on a Saturday night…

But nothing could really start without the refreshments. Curley Jim hurried back to fetch the plastic bag hid under the seat, lurking near the top of the little hill behind some willows until he should hear the strangers' car pull away. Maybe they could use Mr. Bryant's paintcloth as sort of a blanket. Pona Mae had called that out as he started back to the road, for him to bring that bundle of canvas too, or whatever it was that she noticed in the back of the pickup as she was getting out. The way she set about making the domestic arrangements the minute she went up over the stile and into the enclosure, they might be settling into a house instead of just onto a patch of bare ground. With her hands resting on her hips, she looked down it—and across—as though deciding where furniture and gear should go in bedroom, living room, dining room and so on. She tugged at a boulder—well, let it stay—then flicked it lightly with her handkerchief as though it had been a cupboard.

Steve helped Rita up over the stile, leaving her to totter on the top step in her five-inch heels from Frederick's of Hollywood while he jumped down inside the wall and turned back to reach for and catch her as she squealed and fell forward into his arms. Oh, baby—baby—

As soon as they pulled away…

BUT WHAT WAS HOLDING THEM UP? Curley Jim hurried on up the little hill to the road and stared over at the Pontiac. The mother and son were both inside and leaving, the mother had her foot on the—Quickly Curley Jim got the stuff out from under the seat, thrust the plastic bag inside his shirt, ran around and gathered up the dropcloth—hide the gun—Mr. Bryant's Remington Army .44—shells—he let the canvas fall back down.

What had she done? Flooded the—? No, it sounded more like—Women!

Curley Jim walked over to them.

"Need some help?"

The look he cast at the son (really an old guy about forty-five), who sat on the passenger side smoking and seeming to pay no attention whatever, was withering. Why wasn't *he* taking care of this the way a man should?

"It won't seem to start," Rosetta said.

"Let's take a look."

"I just don't know what could have happened. It was running fine."

"Maybe you're out of gas."

"Oh, I don't think so. And I didn't leave my lights on." She switched them on.

"Could be the starter—or the points." Curley Jim made a quick check, got in the car and tried to start it, got out. "Well, shit." He stood there with arms akimbo. He could drive them up to the house in the pickup, he said, the old crazy up there, whoever he was, would probably let them go in that side door to the dining room and use the phone, though the *old* old lady (his boss's first wife) would have had a fit at strangers coming in when nobody was home. Or he could go himself and phone for help.

"Curley Jim! Come on! Where are you?" The girls' voices sounded faint and far away.

He looked under the hood again, shook his head. Shit. If they did get up there and used the phone, or *he* went up and phoned and somebody *did* come—but who? on a Saturday night? from Enterprise? from Veyo? in a tow truck, the night wasn't just happening for him anymore, the place wasn't that groovy, maybe the best thing to do was just go down and get the bunch and leave. But where could they go to that would be as much off the beaten track as this place was and at the same time *manitou*, pervaded with the awesome? Wait—he knew—if he could find where it was. On the road to Modena. Glen told him about it one time. They were always going to go sometime and see if it was true or shit, but they never did. It was this rocky gorge close to where Utah ended and Nevada began. It was haunted. A scary trick would be played on you there by some old guys called in the Book of Mormon the Gadianton Robbers, cursed to live forever. What they would do, according to freighters hauling supplies to the Nevada mining camps in the old days, was to cause the canyon walls to close in on you till you thought they'd squeeze you flat. Then suddenly, just when you were the most scared, the walls would start pulling back like machinery and let you out. On the road to Modena. Glen said that was an actual fact.

Curley Jim looked down towards the monument, then back at Rosetta. "Them others and me, we're out of here. So maybe you better—I mean, you got to get somebody out here and, uh, wait and everything. You want to ride up to the house with us? The old guy up there, he'll maybe call—or let you folks use the phone—"

"Well, let's see." Rosetta was out of the car now. So was Jeppe, brisk, rubbing his hands.

They heard the maidens calling in the early dark, like sirens in the sea.

"Hey, man. Hey, look. Somebody's coming." Curley Jim was right. Headlights. Then here was the Volkswagen, and here were June and Normal.

"Are *we* glad to see you!"

June was out of the car almost before it stopped. "Listen." She ran to Rosetta. "Normal thinks that Mr. Casement—he thinks he's down here to find out something or do something to keep Senator Arble from getting the nomination! Can you imagine anything so *dumb*? He thinks he's a spy!"

Thought arrested by utter bewilderment, her eyes straining through the dusk at June's pale face, Rosetta glimpsed Normal behind her only as a blur. But Curley Jim took a good look at them both, the dark-haired girl and, moseying on up beside her, the blonde-haired dude, and stiffened. Uh-oh. He edged around the pickup slowly and casually, gathered the bundled dropcloth and loaded handgun in one sweep, then, pressing this armful to himself, he took an easy step.

"Hold it! Who's the Lamanite?"

Now Rosetta saw that Normal was carrying a gun before him with both hands, like an archbishop his episcopal staff.

"He's been trying to start my car," she said. "They're kids. They came in that—" She gestured toward the pickup, saw the boy standing there with an armful of something. "Visiting the—" She broke off, did not say *monument*. Because that, of course, was why Normal was so upset. They had actually come here, she and Jeppe, would be what he was thinking, she thought. What gall. Something had to be done.

"You," Normal said to Jeppe.

Her quick sidelong glance took in her companion, petrified. To shield him more, she stepped a little forward, tried to sound as if she had it all covered, started to explain about the trouble with the starter—

Normal threw one hand out in a chopping gesture. She stopped.

"Come on," he said. "Mr. Whatever you are and whoever you are! Where is this so-called monument? Let's go see it, you and me, huh? take a little walk—"

"Normal!" June ran to him, tried to take him by the arm. He shook her off. "Please let me take—this—" she said, tugging at the gun. "You know you don't want to do anything foolish. Why, honey, have you forgotten? We're late already—going to the brides—"

Curley Jim had been motionless, watching this encounter. Now he stirred.

"What do you think *you're* doing?" Normal barked.

"We got to get out of here," Curley Jim said. "We're heading for—We gotta be someplace."

"I bet you do," Normal said. "I just bet you do."

"This boy is a perfect stranger," Rosetta said. "He has nothing to do with anything. They're kids from around here—"

"And who'd suspect a kid?"

"You know perfectly well—" June began.

"They're all in it," he said. "You too, for all I know."

"In *what*?"

"It's all been planned. Everything. This meeting. Do you think I don't know? Do you think *we* don't know what they'll try to do? Come on, get going. *Show* me this so-called monument." With his gun he shepherded them, Rosetta, Jeppe, Curley Jim, June running along beside. "You lead," he said.

They heard the girls calling.

June tried to take his arm. "Get up ahead," he said.

"But, Normal—"

"Move it."

She did and they did too, Curley Jim hugging his armful of canvas against the old Remington Army .44. They went up over the little hill. No moon, or none as yet, but all the stars were out. They could see their way, see the watchers leaning on the wall—

"Wha's up, Doc?"

"Bring your own shit, can't do ours—"

"Who dat?"

Steve saw the gun, they were getting busted, he thought, nobody was going to stay blasted till Monday, no one was going to get laid…To pick up a rock and hurl it was not brilliant, but that is what he did. Rita close beside him stood on her stork legs, her high high heels, this was…how they did it in Kanab, over in the Cedar Breaks, the good guys, the bad guys, this was the way the movies…All these extras milling around…

"All right, you guys, *reach*. Hands up high. Get over by that wall."

"Normal, you stop this—" June touched his arm, which felt like cement, he shrugged her off. "For God's sake."

"Don't take the Lord's name in vain. How many times have I told you?"

"Listen," she said, "this is just *Rosetta*, your own *cousin*, and Mr. Casement who's in Who's Who, I know because Maureen said so, he's a *composer*. Composers don't want to do anything to anybody! *No* one does, except you."

But someone did, and it was Pona Mae. She too had picked up a rock, and now she threw it. It bounced off the side of Normal's head. He sank to his knees, his gun went off, the shot went wild, all in one superimposition the armful of dropcloth fell away, Curley Jim had his gun clicking and up, June ran to him, grabbed his arm, "No, no, you mustn't hurt him!"

"Get away—"

"No, no! He's sick—he rainbows—he's been—"

Somebody broke and ran, Jeppe, clambered up over the wall, fell down inside, knocking Rita onto her seat an angry moment before she scrabbled up totteringly onto her stilts again, Rosetta grabbed June, dragged her, June still hanging on to Curley Jim's arm.

"No!"

"Now, while we got a chance—"

Normal wobbled on the ground.

"No!"

Steve threw another rock, Curley Jim's head turned, June grabbed his gun.

"You crazy chick," he said. "What d'you think you're—"

She threw it into the pit and it went off. Bang! In one motion, Curley Jim's hands were on the wall and he had vaulted over, no one hurt, then outside Normal was on his feet running backward to a big rock sticking up out of the ground. He had the gun trained on the monument, Rosetta and June had stumbled up over the stile, everybody inside the enclosure was down on the ground, Curley Jim on one knee, ready to shoot as soon as his head got high enough…except…

"Is it the cops or what? What's going down?" Rita on her rickety legs still stood, movie star–like. Steve, crouched low, was reaching for her skirt when Normal fired again. Rita went down like a crane, her leg bent under her, she sank beneath her ruffles, gaped, said nothing, saw the sky and died.

"You *bastard*." Curley Jim fired and hit the rock as Normal dodged behind it. Silence. Rosetta crawled on her hands and knees to the dead girl, felt for a pulse, laid her ear to the chest.

"What're you *doing*?" Steve yelled into the dark.

Rosetta called out, "Normal, listen. This girl is dead. She's *dead*."

No answer.

"Quit it now, you stop it!"

"Oh, Rosetta, is she really—?" June crawled close. "What shall we do? Oh, God, poor thing—"

"Rita!" Pona Mae was there then too, squatting. "We wasn't doing *nothing*," she told the others.

"He's a crazy man."

"I *guess*!" the Indian girl said, dumbfounded. "Anybody who would kill Rita will just climb over that wall there and kill anyone!"

"No, he knows there's guns—a gun—He doesn't know but what that boy there—can fight back."

"Curley Jim, he's the one with Mr. Bryant's gun. But he's not that great of a shot."

"The ranchers up there, they'll come home from town," Rosetta said, "and then—" Her lights had been left on, maybe they'd see them from the ranch house, come down and investigate. "We've got to wait, is all. Keep down and wait."

"Something just freaked him out, he just—flipped out," June said. "I felt like he was going to, I wanted for us to turn back—"

"What's going down, that's all I want to know," Steve said. "Who *is* that asshole? In fact, who's everyone?"

By the time the moon swung up they knew, they all knew more or less who they were. Only Normal, still behind his rock, didn't know who was trying to get him, didn't know they weren't trying hard, because first of all to shoot, you had to stick your head up above the wall, and second because the only bullets they had were in the gun and when daylight dawned, if help didn't come before then, they would be sitting ducks. And of course—Rosetta had taken off her new gray and white scarf and put it over the dead girl's face. But before that, Jeppe had come close. "Why, she's an—Indian—"

"A Shoshone girl," Pona Mae said. "She had the agency."

"The agency?"

"For Avon. She was the Avon lady on the reservation. And she was in the movies, too. One time in Kanab and one time—" They smelled her perfume, Matchabelli. Pona Mae crawled over to where Steve sprawled in shadow, his back against the wall, to offer him her condolences, for after all Rita had been his date, and it was terrible. And he consoled her. She also consoled herself. Life wasn't going to stop in its *tracks* without Rita, but some people thought she was the glamour girl, she subscribed to *Cosmopolitan* magazine, had met all kinds of…One time when she was in the hospital with her tuberculosis of the bone or whatever kept her so skinny (and that she was such a smart-ass about, as if it was some kind of weight control she invented herself), she started in with one of the young doctors and really thought for a while she was going to get him, but of course she didn't. Two or three times like that, though, she came close. And now to be laying dead for no good reason whatsoever, in her washed and ironed blouse, her new shoes—they were new, she tottered over in the dust in them and in her great ball of fluffed and painted hair to show Pona Mae and Mrs. Weazel Tail just yesterday morning—"Oh, Steve, isn't it terrible?" It was, but he postponed being consoled to crawl over to Curley Jim crouched down on the ready with Mr. Bryant's gun, sit back on his heels and reach inside Curley Jim's shirt for the plastic bag. "Help yourself," he said.

It was beautiful stuff. Curley Jim took some, Steve pressed more upon him, put the sack in under his own shirt and, whispering loudly that he would be back to take over guard duty and shoot the son of a bitch, he crawled over in Pona Mae's direction, stopping to get a better look…and it was true, his ballsy chick, his Saturday night date before he had to get on that goddamn Trailways bus, had been blown away. It would just give you cholesterol, the whole scene. And this guy over there…who're *you*? Sort of an old guy about forty-five, and the lady was *old*, if somebody's Saturday night date had to be blown away, why couldn't it be someone like that? Though Steve had a feeling Rita was about twenty-five or twenty-six her own self, but nevertheless it wasn't no *hype*, Curley Jim said if she was there and not already out with somebody else when they got out to the reservation, why, Steve would really pick up on her, and he had…and they might have made it very good.

"Have you—I do hope you have a gun too!" the dude about forty-five years old said.

"Who, me? Hell, no. I don't even know what's going down, man. Do you?"

The guy kind of gibbered something then and wiped his forehead with his handkerchief, though the night was getting chill, and Steve took pity and fumbled the plastic pouch open and said to have some, go ahead, go right ahead, the altitude's completely informal, and took some more himself just to be sociable. And it was beautiful stuff, better than they deserved down there in San Antonio. Then Steve crawled back to Curley Jim for him to follow the yellow brick road and said have no fear, Magoo is here, then he crawled back and it was beautiful…

And then here was this other chick, the fat one, with her round, flat, chocolate chip cookie face and "Oh, Steve, isn't it terrible?" which it most certainly and assuredly was. And she shifted closer and put her arms around him and held him against her soft warm woolliness somewhat like a fat-tailed sheep, to console him because Rita was dead, who he hardly knew. But because this chick felt sorry and her breath was warm and smelt of new-mown hay, he felt bereft, terrible, like his uncle when his aunt died. And Pona Mae wrapped him closer still, his ragged sadness.

June edged up close to Curley Jim. "If you want to know what this is all about—"

Chapter Seventy-four

✻

HE COULD SEE HOW THEY WOULD FREAK OUT ALL RIGHT, OVER THERE, CHEMICAL warfare…and then home and all the changes, but just the same, to shoot an innocent bystander down like that, like she was nothin', when all she was trying to do was rock on through like anybody else. Rita Owl Woman Starley never did harm to any living soul. "Steve!" Curley Jim broke off to call out suddenly. He had thought of some diversionary tactics.

"Shh—" June said.

"He knows we're all down here, where would we be otherwise?"

"I know, but if you draw his attention—But my hope is, he really got hit with that rock and lapsed into…that he's out of it."

"You think he might be?"

"I'm *hoping* so. Oh, no!" she added. "Don't do that, come back!" But Curley Jim had jumped up and was going over the wall when…Bang! Normal's shot just missed taking the top of his head off. Whoee. Hunkering back down, he nearly fell on June. "Well, he ain't lapsed into nothin'."

"No."

"Get Steve over here. Hey, man! Or can you ease on over and get it?"

"Get what?"

"What do you think? The prize—the beano—"

She eased on over and got the plastic bag and Curley Jim said go ahead, but June said no, thanks. She didn't do dope, because at a Mormon university they march to a different drummer. It is subliminal and also liminal. But the circumstances—maybe this was the end of the world, and June wanted Curley Jim's arms to go around her, and if it was, what did anything matter anyway? So she said maybe she would change her mind and did, and Curley Jim partook and then she crawled back over to give Steve the plastic bag, and then she crawled back and it seemed like everybody was pretending…Here they were, out here in the wilderness and look at the stars, which when she looked up at them for some reason made her insides clutch together like when you come plunging down in a high-rise elevator—and there's the moon—and—Later, hayseed as he came on, June was surprised to hear that Curley Jim had been to college and was going back, but then nobody sounded educated anymore except…Normal did. Curley Jim said he couldn't analyze it, it wasn't his shot, he wasn't smart enough…For Christ's

723

sake tell him, though, what a chick like her was doing with an asshole like that? They had time to talk.

Waiting there, they all had time.

Except Rita Owl Woman Starley. All *she* had was cold, and the heaped-up dark.

Night, I love you and salute you and glorify you,
and you are my big daughter and my creature.
O lovely night, night of the great cloak,
my daughter with the starry cloak…

They had no tags sometimes, the sweet furnishings of Rosetta's mind, but then she remembered how the book looked (and her dear love) and it came back to her who the poet was, Péguy. Jeppe wasn't trembling so much but mellowing out when she made her way to him on hands and knees. He made a place for her beside him. "Can you think of all this?" He gestured.

"How do you mean?" she said.

"Because I can't," he said.

"The fact of how it's happening?"

"Tha's right," he said.

"On the spot of where—the other—? The massacre?"

"Tha's right. Listen, Rosetta—" He beckoned as though she were far away instead of right next to him. "C'mere, c'mere." She bent her head. He whispered.

"What?" she said.

"Nostalgia de la Bone." He thought of something. "You know how they say the murderer always returns to the scene of the crime. Well, maybe the *crime* returns to the scene of itself. Maybe it does. Who knows if tha's right or not? No one!"

She looked around. This one dark spot on earth, moved by the winds of savage hate…

"Hey, man! Wanna follow—" Steve spoke in a loud stage whisper.

"What?" Jeppe looked toward him.

"The yellow brick…Huh? Private enterprise…Why shouldn't…just like anyone else!"

"Right," Jeppe said, looking blank.

"I think he means he wants to *sell* us some of that—whatever it is," Rosetta said.

"Mescaline," Jeppe said. "At least that's what I think it—I personally—my generation—I personally—I'm a drunk."

"No, you're not," Rosetta said.

"Right, man?" Steve's loud whisper came again.

Jeppe nodded grandly, and Steve gave Pona Mae a little slap and push, and she, as though she were his burro, and well-trained, head down, traversed the space to them. "He said to say that it's the real organic shit, you know?" she said.

"So, great."

"Private enterprise."

"Okay." Jeppe took a bill out of his billfold and gave it to the girl, who then proffered the plastic bag not only to him but, when he had helped himself, to Rosetta as well.

"Oh, I think I'll pass. I'm tired old folks."

"No, you ain't. He says it's the best—it won't hurt you. Vitamins and everything."

"Modern time, mon," Steve called out in his stage whisper cheerfully.

And that it was. (Because it always is.)

SO THEY WERE THERE BESIEGED, that was the place. In the case of the dead Indians, the ones killed in that first attack running down the slope there in the dawn light shooting and yelling, that the men of the wagon train shot, they were carried home and buried beneath fresh branches of desert juniper and pinyon pine with funeral rites in cold rock crevices or holes, and the women then who had to do it all wailed the loud wail of anguish. The men did not go to funerals, their job was to destroy the property of their dead comrades, Red Shirt, George, Red Cloud, Saddio, Kicking Bear and Elk Hollering in the Water (that first morning). Then get new orders from the Mormonees, the giant children, some retarded, some looking and sounding bright but being mad as the winds.

NORMAL BEHIND THE BOULDER, WHILE he watched ready to shoot at anything that moved, began to preach to the sinners within the monument's wall, to the stars and also in case some angel might be listening. It would all go into his service jacket. If blood has to flood the world to the height of a convertible, so be it. This here's the doctrine of the Millennium. Christ is coming, reign for a thousand years. And you, you scum.

> *You common cry of curs! whose breath I hate*
> *As reek o' the rotten fens, whose loves I prize*
> *As the dead carcasses of unburied men*
> *That do corrupt my air, I banish you.*

Mystery is coming, majesty and death, heaven and hell! So vote for Senator Arble for Grand Old Party President and it shall come to pass in that day that the Lord shall hiss for the fly that is in the uttermost part of the rivers of Egypt, and for the bee that is in the land of Assyria. And gather my saints together unto me, those that have made a covenant by sacrifice…They will strive to their uttermost to stop him, but the die is cast, a fire shall eat before them and be tempestuous…And in the same day shall the Lord shave with a razor that is hired, namely, by them beyond the river, by the King of Assyria, the head, and the hair of the feet, and it shall also consume the beard. So I say unto you, who *sayeth* that God rescinded? Not the Seer and not the Revelator! God did not rescind, my friends, the *politician* rescinded, the *banker* rescinded, the *railroad man* rescinded.

The Brides...the Way...Since saturation of the sexual impulse for a real...*man*...requires one thing and one thing only—the Way—and since it is vital to a man's protection against *sheer chaos*, why—But be warned, the law laid down says keep to a set rotation schedule, give each her day. Don't let the Great Bear...He will restore city, state and nation, and if blood must pour...

At first they listened. Listen! What did he say? What's he saying? But as he rambled on, they stopped paying attention and went about their business of enduring, keeping down, waiting for help to come, the rancher, the cops, the guys with the butterfly net. Normal! Oh, boy. Another time Curley Jim had in mind to rush him, but he no more than started to edge up over the wall than, bang! Curley Jim fell back, not hurt, took a chance, could catch a glimpse...fired and missed, goddamn it. Normal then, angry, furious, fired a barrage, anger made his voice break when again he stormed at all his enemies and God's and the first Mormon president's of our great land.

June stayed close to Curley Jim. Once, after midnight, she attempted to patch things up with their besieger enough at least to treat with him. "Normal, it's me! It's June! Let me come over and let's us talk this over, you and me. Let's leave, let's go, you don't want to act like this." Bang! "You know you don't. The brides, sweetheart. Normal, listen! They're *beautiful*—they're *waiting*—they are—" Bang!

"Run that past me again," Curley Jim said softly, smoothing the ground for her close by his side.

"Well, you see, Normal..." She told him about the brides Normal thought were waiting somewhere.

They talked of love.

Oh, it was so sad about Rita. All dressed up for Saturday night. And then. To die. What *she* least expected, or anyone. Never to see those movies she was in, if she *was* in them back in the background somewheres. Somebody else going to be the Avon lady on the reservation. Her *Photoplay* magazine coming and everybody else reading it except her. Pona Mae thought she had a snapshot with Rita in it someplace that she was going to try and find and give to Steve. His head was upon her cleavage when she told him. He and she were some little distance away from the others, along the wall in shadow. He said he would appreciate a snapshot. Wow. He really would. Oh, baby—baby—

"You know what it is, Rosetta?" Jeppe said. "Personal menace. One's science of ideas. About it! Sex, you know? The way it's a mystique." He couldn't make it plain enough to suit himself, gave up and spoke of other matters, Paco, betrayal, a woman Paco hired to come and clean one time by the name of Fairy Sidesinger, said he might go to Paris and work and buy orange tarts at Vaudron's.

Rosetta nodded. Here they stood the siege and here was where the crime...returned to the scene of the...And *he* returned, Great-Grandfather, to the scene. In a suit, an overcoat, a hat, a shirt and tie, his shoes shined, shave and haircut...Not the most willing, not the most resigned. But still, thy will be done. Thou up there! whom 'twere gross flattery to call a Marquis!

Now here we are, and there must be some force or influence in the universe that wants things tidy, interbedded, parts of the new pattern, parts of the old as well, linked in happening and very tidy, dead folk here and crazy people there, volleys and piety and terror, wounds, the pattern on top like the pattern underneath, deep-seated, chronic, laid down and genetical, where what came up once might *again* bob to the surface for consideration, tidy like that. Even Indians! their recurrence here. And of all the insane people in the world, it had to be one of Great-Grandfather's hundreds or maybe thousands of great-great-grandsons crouched in back of that mass of bouldery with a rifle. Bang!

"I DO NOT GIVE A damn," Jeppe said grandly. But he was, of course, what held the two parts of the conductor of all this in contact there under the same old stars. The strange force needed him. When it inflicts—like the Dutch housewife on the Dutch Cleanser can—tidiness upon old mare's-nest life. That's for him alone to see, the artist. He half sat, half lay, and tried to think of getting to Las Vegas. Flying on...and then...and after that...Not about these dumb and unaware...hieroglyphics in a discredited place. Ah, but it has to all unfold. The way *hers* has to, the destiny of the little girl tossing flowers in the lake (though someone in the audience tries to save her). It has to, in his artist's mind, take place. He lets it, like seduction.

And they come in from the north, down the Old Spanish Trail upon the reverberations of his overture. Through sagebrush and brush oak and mountain mahogany to the green meadow. Maybe you're not aware, but opera is a bastard. To write and produce. This one is called *All on the Meadow Green*. Or *The Western Approaches*? Or maybe simply *The Brides*, because to have and keep them is one reason why the torchy old polygamists...But also, it must be said, the riches of the passing emigrants provide temptation. All is fair in greed and...two ideologies scrapping in blood all day. Masons, Odd Fellows, Baptists or be you who you will, Friends of Humanity! When this you see remember...how we're out here on a real hard path, Indians has attacked siege been on without no interruption ever since Monday sunup looks to us like white men is with the Indians all are well supplied with powder and weapons Help us in God's name we are 40 wagons, mules and horses, milk cows, beef cattle near a thousand head oxen family people young men going...

It's theatrical, not vocal, opera's challenge. He loathes the human voice that needs words as much for their acoustics as their meaning (only one word in three is heard, in any case) and *operative* writing. But here one needs an aria to prick the audience up, like a man's sex in full invigoration. Behind the circled white-tops with their wheels sunk in the ground, the besieged lie in the pit they have dug not knowing it is their grave. They sit or kneel. Some of the men are dead, one has pennies on his eyes, somebody put a rock on his bloating belly. Living men this morning... The aria begins and oh, my God, batting back and forth across these moonlit canyonlands it is unspeakably... He almost had forgot how good he was. And only because... It had not been easy to be this regular, standard, plain old simple-minded... composer who stuck to the principles of tonality when all about... were losing theirs and blaming it on you. "Not that I would mind some new sonorities," he said to Rosetta, stoned out of his mind while the soprano's tessitura soared into the starlight and the edifice formed out of the sounds of harpsichords, an organ... arose, then fell like a riddled rainbow, rose again. "Not that I'd mind new intervals, either. Or really new forms, actually I would *welcome*..."

"I would too," she said, and lit a cigarette, her eyes on the little blur that Rita was, across there in the darkness on the ground like a garment stepped out of and left. The point about... But that's the point, of course, to entertain the notion even for a minute that things might *have* a point. Or that, you know? they're relevant in any way.

Sᴏ ʜᴇʀᴇ ɪꜱ Lᴀᴠᴏɴɴᴇ ɪɴ her mansion room rosy with sunset, doing her face again, pinning on a fall, changing, and with her high heels on, which she will probably regret, but they make your legs look so much prettier. (And she can take a taxi home.) She's going to the hospital to see Birdelle and also see how near they are to being done with repairs to the shop. What's she supposed to do, stay home in that big old barn and finish the candy and watch TV and think about Foster walking away like that and feel sorry for herself? There's just as good fish in the sea as ever was... And take the night she met him, did she think she was going to meet someone like Foster? Never. So fate, or your astrological... If it happened *once*...

Bɪʀᴅᴇʟʟᴇ ʜᴀᴅ ᴀ ʀᴏᴏᴍ ʙʏ herself, one of the old rich Holy Rosary rooms that hadn't been remodeled through the years of change and expansion because the sisters thought that once in a while a room like that, with fifteen-foot ceilings and stained glass halfway down the long windows, would fetch a handsome price from those who wanted the best, and it often did. It would from the heiress of the Prentice fortune. Last night when it happened, when the responsibility fell on her, the extent of Lavonne's injuries then not being known (and she had to think, where would *I* go if I was a millionairess fallen down the first elevator shaft ever installed in a private mansion in Salt Lake?), Rosetta engaged one of those rooms, of course. Birdelle's eating habits were like an old miser's and that is what she was, a miser, but she was used to gorgeous old rooms, so when she came down from Recovery and opened her eyes it would seem homelike.

For quite a while she thought it *was* home, and that her legs were somehow caught between the balusters on the upper landing and that her mother and father were to blame. But then everything came round the way it ought to, and she wasn't mad about the *cost* of the rich old room because her lawyer left word that she wasn't to be told. But what she *was* mad about was Lavonne not only not *preventing* her from falling down the shaft, but *falling in on top of her*! Her private nurse, at the midway point of her shift (but pale-faced and tired-enough looking to have already put in her eight hours and then some) when Lavonne tiptoed in, after her greeting whispered that if that would be all right with her, she'd just go down to the cafeteria for a little snack and be right back.

"Excuse me, what did you say?" Lavonne said.

The nurse said it louder and then louder still, and had to come quite close.

"Oh, yes." Not as if she hadn't heard, but as if she'd been deep in thought. "Certainly, go right ahead." A nice girl, new, or new to Lavonne, she didn't know her, and the nurse didn't know that Lavonne was one of the operators of the Holy Rosary beauty shop (closed for remodeling). She thought maybe she was the rich elderly daughter of her rich old patient (said by the night nurse to be in the millionaire class). Lavonne *looked* rich, the somewhat innocent nurse thought, all made up and costume-jewelried and with what looked like a merry widow on underneath her pale blue georgette dress, like pictures of retired ladies in *Town & Country* magazine in Florida.

Birdelle was sleeping, she had been in pain and she had had a shot. No sense in letting them suffer. And besides, the nurses often discussed it in the shop, some old people, about five minutes and you wanted to crown them, while others weren't that bad. Well, poor Birdelle. There was a lovely dresser over by the window, and Lavonne went to it and looked in the glass. And there was that round hole in her reflected hairdo! and now when she shifted her gaze it punched out part of her nose and mouth, leaving empty air like the middle of a doughnut. She poked a stiff curl, pulled a strand forward on her cheek—ah, there it was! her nose, and her mouth. Would she recover her whole sight? Probably, gradually. Surely! just glimpsing that silly death ray or whatever it was sticking up there in the sky as they flew over it on their way to Tucson wouldn't cut holes in everything you saw *forever*. She was sure her hearing was better too, it hadn't been permanently damaged by sitting under that… Without a doubt, those decibels… There was simply no *sense* to that kind of a volume, she nearly told Foster at the time, but they don't like a person always putting in her two cents' worth, that is why she was popular. Her hearing had been muffled ever since, her head like it was up inside a feather pillow. But who could imagine a hole in everything? You could learn to manage it, though, like the man in the nightclub managing the baby spot on different performers. There! her mouth. She wanted to see if she needed more lipstick and she didn't.

"Good evening," a voice boomed out from the doorway. "May I come in?"

"Father Peacock! Of course you may come in!" In a swirl of georgette, Lavonne ran over to shake hands and usher him into the shadowy room. Smelling of aftershave lotion, he was scraped and softly pink, had fresh red lips. Impulsively she reached up to brush a tiny white flake off his glossy dark eyebrows. It fell to his black broadcloth shoulder and she brushed it off there, too.

He said, "Thank you, my dear."

"Don't people have their nerve? to do that," she said softly.

"Well, but in your case—you have a proprietary interest," he said, meaning because she regularly cut his hair.

"The shop'll be open again Tuesday, or maybe sooner!" she said. "Then you won't need to feel so—although I personally *like* hair a little longer—neglected."

They smiled at one another.

"How *is* our patient tonight?"

"Having a little nap." She walked over and pulled up the cover an inch or two, then smoothed it back down where it had been.

Lavonne was feeling a little annoyed with the nurse because she had stayed away so long. But she didn't say anything, it was better to be sweet, men wanted you sweet, they didn't want an old battle-axe, and sweetness paid off in less wrinkles too, unless you ran it into the ground and were so persistently sweet your face froze that way. *That* could happen too, she had seen it many a time, laugh corrugations, smile fissures, dimples worn to chasms. The line was fine that beauty had to tread.

With the Viaticum to administer (whatever that might mean), Sister Fiona to see in her office, and "rounds" to make, Father Peacock's visit to Birdelle had to be brief, but he said he might get back to pray beside her later on.

While Lavonne held the fort, walked around, smoked, looked out the windows at the lit-up downtown evening view with that maddening hole gouged out in it, she kept hoping he would. Not that she thought a *priest* was going to fall for her, necessarily, but that look in his eyes of being *affected*, of *undergoing* something when he was near a desirable feminine person, helped one's morale, it really did. Birdelle just lay there knocked out, not a peep out of her, which was a good thing in one way, but in another she wouldn't realize how *concerned* Lavonne was about her, the way she walked clear up here to the hospital and everything. However, she'd be awake tomorrow…and thank goodness the fall hadn't hurt her *mind*, her capability to…handle her affairs…*choose* who was going to eventually get the house and so on. Not that Lavonne's devotion hinged on *that*.

Had Father Peacock come back and the nurse come back so Lavonne could leave, and had she and the priest left Birdelle's room together, he was walking too and they went in the same direction, why, they could have had a nice visit as far as to the parish house. But he didn't come back and the nurse didn't, and then finally she did and Lavonne was quite annoyed at the way they take advantage, but she smiled and soon after left. And who should she meet down in the main lobby just coming out of Sister Fiona's office but him. Both said *What a coincidence!* and laughed heartily, as if it was sort of a practical joke. Then Father Peacock held the revolving doors while she went in one section, he stepped in the one behind, both pushed forward and were expelled rather breathlessly out into the summer night. She hadn't counted on walking home, but in his company the blocks didn't seem long, her feet in their high-heeled sandals hardly hurt at all. The breeze was a little cool, though, smelling of watered grass and wet sidewalks.

She should have brought her pale blue sweater beaded with little pearls and pink and blue bugle beads to drape across her shoulders. But he thought it was a warm night, almost like August. They dress so warm, priests, that tight collar, all that heavy clothing. But men do, in general, it's not good for them. He didn't turn at the Cathedral corner but went on the extra blocks, escorting her home. And when they got there he went in with her to look around the dark mansion (lit only by the purple grapes held high by the bronze boy and girl on the newel posts) to see that everything was in order. She appreciated that, having someone go with her into every room, turn on the lights…As from the concealment of a jewel-box lid or painted stage curtain, the great chambers one after another sprang into view dancing and vibrating with shabby richness, like the air with dust particles and worthy of note. But she who might inherit the whole thing and had it all planned out what she was going to do with it, take the money and run, didn't say "Isn't this something?" or "They don't build them like this anymore, do they?" and he who knew Monsignor Tate's plans for the place when the church came into *its* possession also appeared to ignore everything but burglars.

And now! if anybody ever deserved a nice libation for being so kind, it was Father Peacock. He didn't know whether he should, but Lavonne prevailed upon him. And she had one too! although she didn't usually drink, she wouldn't be that impolite, and he sat in the armchair and she sat on the great tufted divan in the sitting room with the French doors standing open now to the overgrown side garden and a breeze coming in. They talked and smoked. She fixed him another and freshened hers, and what they were talking about was just different things at the hospital, the new administration and Sister Marie Adora giving up her vows. First it was the changed habit, then her hair, she came in the shop, wanting streaks in it—streaks, mind you—and to let it hang down, then psychiatric counseling, then her own apartment. And now! but really it was to be expected, giving up her vows.

The trouble was the way everybody today thinks they have to be so *happy*, Father Peacock said, and have whatever they want, and Lavonne agreed. He was still warm, he dabbed at his upper lip and forehead with his handkerchief, so Lavonne opened a window too, as well as the doors. Then here were two big moths fluttering about the one bulb in the lamp with the pleated silk lampshade, so she went over and turned the light off. With the window blinds flipped clear to the top and the doors wide open onto the side lawn, it was light enough. "There must be a moon tonight," she said, and he said there must be and went on remarking how lax the rules for conduct were today. All the young wanted their own way, didn't want to have to pay for things the way we all have to…pay for life on earth. "Isn't that the truth." Denial, discipline, they didn't know what the words *meant*.

Would she mind if he just slipped his jacket off?

"Why, no, Father Peacock, not a bit. Men dress far too warm."

When he got started he was an interesting man to listen to, very well read, born in Ireland, left there as a child but he well remembered Father Alcuin whipping the big Kelly girl with his riding whip one time when she didn't go to confession, lashing her round. For her good. Sometimes he wished somebody cared as much for *him* and *his* soul's salvation as that. Father Alcuin really *cared*, his flail like Great Gideon's whistled as it lashed down.

"You're such a good person, Father, you certainly don't need any lashing round."

But he shook his head and said, "And that servant, which knew his lord's will and prepared not himself, neither did according to his will, shall be beaten with many stripes..." While she was trying to think how to change the subject and talk about something more cheerful, he said one of his besetting sins was *reading*, and she said, "Oh, that's not so bad. There's lots worse things in this life than reading. Why, Rosetta—"

Did she ever hear of Dr. Samuel Johnson? he said, and she said yes, in high school, she believed so. Wasn't he the one who when he ate dinner the veins stood out on his temples and the perspiration ran down and he gobbled like a starving Armenian? Funny how a certain little detail will stick in your mind.

The Mighty Doctor to the life, he said. And what *other* little details stuck to her—?

"Well, let's see." But try as she would, that was all she could remember. After a moment he helped out. "Dr. Johnson was a great English author, a great man at the time he lived, a wit, a talker, he compiled the first English dictionary," he said.

"Oh, yes," she said, it was kind of coming back to her now. And this was a little bit off the main trend of what they were saying, but my, Johnson was a common name, wasn't it. Two of the day nurses were Miss Johnson, the new manager of the hospital cafeteria was going to be Mr. Johnson (but don't quote her on that), and in the apartment house where she used to live before she moved to Birdelle's there was a man with no legs and a wheelchair with a motor in it just like a car, and *he* happened to be named Johnson too.

"Lavonne, I beg you to talk about this with me," Father Peacock's deep voice interrupted solemnly through the darkness.

"Why, of course, Father!" She didn't know what "this" was, though, her attention having flitted in the meanwhile. She moved closer and there was a movement from his direction too, his chair being hitched closer to her.

"Because this is important—"

Had she missed some crucial remark? She wriggled along the few inches of space to the end of the sofa to be nearer and hear better, and waited.

"I have thought—this is not the first time I have thought it—that you might *understand*," he said. "But to go back—this wonderful genius—he was large and heavy and could hardly see, they say."

"Oh?" she said, unobtrusively cupping her hand around her deafness.

"He had a friend. And this is very important."

She waited and then ventured, "Father, I guess—If you don't mind—who are you talking about?"

"We are talking about Dr. Samuel Johnson and about his friend Mrs. Thrale," the priest said. Suddenly he got up and came over and sat down at her side.

"Their friendship—" he began and paused, moving closer.

She felt heat discharging, from his warmed broadcloth and wilted linen, his warm woolly socks, even his large moonlit shoes. "Friendship," she said. "I don't see any reason why a man and a woman can't be *lovely* friends if they want, just like two women can be friends or two men, why not?"

"To get back to discipline—" He told her then how she could be a friend to *him* as Mrs. Thrale had been to the Mighty Doctor. That was what his peers called him, the Mighty Doctor, Father Peacock said. People feared him, his sharp tongue and high I.Q. that nobody knows *how* high it was because in those days there was no means of measuring it. But it was very high and he was very—And it *had* happened. Of that there was historical proof.

"What?" she asked with the dreamy languor of the tiger's catch inches from the beast's flaring acetylene eyes.

Madness had at one time overthrown Dr. Johnson's reason, he said. He feared it would overthrow it again, lived in fear of that. "And in the eighteenth century the countermeasures he wanted to adopt would naturally be what people believed efficacious in those days," he went on. "That you treated madness by restraint and discipline. So Dr. Johnson's friend Mrs. Thrale—her house was out in the country and stood off by itself. There were many rooms. Servants and children could be deployed. Her husband often stayed late in town. He begged her! To save his reason. And she, like the very angels in ancient days with their bulrushes and whips with knotted lashes, was a very obliging—" He broke off. "Mrs. Thrale was a smart, wonderful, obliging person like yourself."

"Oh, no, I'm really not," she said within the claws, under the tainted breath.

"You see, Johnson, Lavonne—"

"Johnson?"

"Samuel Johnson, the one we're talking about—he would have these—terrible—melancholy—Then he would just hole up and stay by himself. And by one's self, holed up—well, Saint Sebastian—he would have these—He was a genius, but yet the human mind—sometimes he would think thoughts," he paused, "*like the lowest scum*. He would imagine—pictures would come in his mind … because this melancholia that always weighed him down, it seemed like it brought out in his … bodily nature—I hope you don't mind the mention, but you are a mature woman with … a knowledge of the world. And in these days—"

"Isn't it terrible?" she said. "From all sides. Just at Holy Rosary alone—the *language*— the things that go on. Well, we all know."

"Yes, we certainly do," he said, and drew a sigh, laying his scalded-feeling hand upon her knee like a large plaster that stuck. "So anyway it brought out this strain—in Latin it's expressed *de pedicis et manicis insana cogitatio—*"

"Imagine, to know *Latin—*" Weakly she sank against his bulk, her hair breaking like spun sugar against his ear.

"—of—this form—where abuse and cruelty—She locked him in, she *beat* him. Mrs. Thrale, I mean. I'm talking about Samuel Johnson."

"Well, of course, in high school we wouldn't have heard about anything like *that.*"

He pushed her away. And from the upright he slid down onto the floor and groveled at her feet.

She had heard of husbands getting drunk and beating their wives and getting pleasure of a certain kind out of it, it was awful. And nowadays you couldn't avoid reading… Topics would be discussed. *Cosmopolitan* magazine… even the Salt Lake Tribune! Things that would curl your hair. About sex and so forth. Everything was so modern. Consenting adults. She never minded consenting, that was part of the bargain, but what you consented to was letting a man take advantage. In Utah and in her day, that was really all there was to consent to, anything else (unnatural activities) happened far away. In Paris or somewhere like that. But now, due to the leisure or something, and movies, and now the television, and more time to experiment, and girls menstruating at ten or eleven, and the boys… and with sex education in the schools, charts, diagrams… Of course Dr. Johnson lived way back at the time of the Revolutionary War. And after she was exposed to those amps… What did *he* have to do with anything anyway? Lavonne couldn't figure. Perhaps Father Peacock's meaning was, that because he wanted to make love to her, and because he was a priest and making love was forbidden, that he should be—that God should strike him *down* or something like that.

Chapter Seventy-five

*

BUT THAT WASN'T IT AT ALL. FATHER PEACOCK KNEW WHAT HE WANTED. HE trembled as he begged, his voice hoarse, his face (to her cold hand) feeling like it was on fire. For a minute she didn't know what to think. But caught short by everything, especially getting older, and by men, to whom her life was geared, all of a sudden getting even more undependable than usual (and so odd), she had to suddenly develop in ways that you no more could imagine than fly to the moon. Make me beautiful so the world will fall at my feet, she had once prayed. And men had, and even now—rather down in the dumps though she had been over Foster, last night's accident and not at her best from the charm standpoint—a most *unexpected* man had fallen at her feet. But as he groveled and begged for severity, for the first time she felt her looks had nothing to do with anything, any more than the angel's looks had that wrestled with Jacob. "Despise not thou the chastening," he gibbered, "nor faint when … rebuked. For whom the Lord loveth he chasteneth and scourgeth … Now no chastening for the present seemeth to be joyous, but grievous; *nevertheless afterward it yieldeth the peaceable quiet of righteousness* … Wherefore lift up the hands which hang down, and the feeble knees …"

"Is that from somewhere in the Bible?" she said nervously.

"It is from somewhere in my agony—"

"Well, I don't know, Father." But did she not always play a role to give each man whatever he needed or wanted?

When foreordained by some eternal purpose to a specified fate, can anyone—? And so she proceeded. And it meant so much to his soul's salvation that his eyes rolled back till just the whites showed in the moonlight, and his unclothed body was ghostly white with dry, mossy hair growing everywhere, even down his back, so that he felt like a real barnyard creature when she whipped him, slashed, lashed and rode him whinnying with satisfaction and licking the dust through the carpet, digging her heels in his sagging flanks. He couldn't get enough, it was ecclesiastical penance, he bit his tongue, gabbled, drooled. By penitence the Eternal's wrath is appeased. Oh, you are my good angel, you are the instrument of divine chastisement, a bull's pizzle would be better than a belt, but we shall have to make do, shall we not, my heavenly scourge, my torment.

It grew late, it wasn't really woman's work, it might be different if he was small and thin, but a large man like him, if he wanted all that severity, needed a large man with muscles to give it to him, like the bare-bicepped executioner bulging in his leather jerkin in old movies. Do not…fail to continue, but she had to, to rest and for a cigarette. Her hand trembled as she lit it, and her arm kept trembling. Bull's pizzle? Was that what he said? He lay supine as she smoked, under her feet. He had placed himself there to be her footstool. But now she must begin again. From annoyance and fatigue she was very severe, the time dragged on, and then he gave a cry beyond the cries and groans and strange exclamations, grabbed her arm and fell over on his back, beneath his heaving belly in the light of the moon she saw his sex subside while he cried "Oh, Holy Mary, Mother of God, I'm dying—dying—"

Dying? His hands like chunks of ice, his feet the same, his face like a scary mask, his mouth a black hole…She stared in horror. No, no. But maybe—No, it *couldn't* be. "You're not, of course you're not, Father. You just got too stirred up, but you just lie here and take deep breaths and I'll get you some—" She ran for the whiskey, but whatever spell this was, it was too bad for whiskey. Quickly she ran over and pulled the blinds down, shut the French doors, turned the lights on, ran back and looked at him again. Panting and gasping, he seemed to be trying to vomit, his heart down under his chest plunging and rearing. "Are you—feeling a little—" But of course he wasn't. She hurried to the telephone out in the back hallway. Emergency! And started to dial when she remembered who was on the hospital switchboard tonight—she had noticed her alopecia and rhinestoned harlequins as she and Father walked out through the lobby—Deanie, one of the worst gossips that ever lived—and hung up. What was the man *doing* here without anything on, dying of a heart attack or a stroke or whatever it was and needing an ambulance at three in the morning? The first thing—get him dressed.

She gathered up his clothes, started the heavy task, he was semi-comatose now, his eyes vacant, sagging, but she talked to him about how as soon as he was all nice and dressed, the ambulance would come and they would rush him to the hospital and everything would be…but then the words trailed off. Because what good was dressing him going to be if when they got him there and undressed him they found the—They'd think she was some kind of a pervert, when really all she wanted to do was…be sociable, hold up her end of the, you know, bargain. But the talk would never end. They would see the strokes, the stripes, the welts as hot as fire, the ridges in the flesh. And what if the man was *dead* at the time? Could she be held responsible? She kept on struggling with the heavy priestly underpants, the trousers, over the weighty, chilled, damp feet tugged on the socks…

But if he were himself, he would realize *too* that until the marks died away—no matter what his purpose had been, for the glory of God, ecclesiastical penance or whatever—until those marks died away, nobody must be called. Nobody! For her own sake, yes, to a certain degree—to a certain degree was the way she would explain it to him—but mostly for *his* sake, to be found in such a compromising…Really, Father! Why, think what Monsignor Tate…

When he was dressed, a kind of rattle began like the horrible turning of a crank, and she tried to pull and boost and hoist him up onto the sofa, but he was too bulky, and so she left him where he was on the floor and put one of the old damask pillows trimmed with tarnished gold lace under his head. He opened his eyes, moved his lips, she knelt beside him.

"Call—get—"

"Father Peacock, listen, you don't want to go to the hospital right now, people don't understand about…psychological…and *they* wouldn't realize when they saw the— marks that this was all…on the religious…The conclusions *they* would jump to—people have such suspicious minds…So you just lie here and relax—and they'll fade away pretty soon—clear away—and then we'll get the ambulance here and the…Because you know I've been at Holy Rosary hospital a long time, and I know what's dangerous. I've seen strokes come in. Heart attacks. And I tell you, I can *tell*. You're going to be *all right*. This is just a little *spell*. It isn't dangerous. Why, probably by the time—we're ready—why, you could just—walk out of here on your own power. And you'll be very, very happy that I didn't—panic."

The crank turned, rattle, rattle, his head moved back and forth, the black hole opened, shut and opened again. She bent her head.

"…sacraments."

Sacraments?

"Last…the Holy…Acts…" He looked up at her with his eyes of Irish-tenor blue. "Call Monsignor—"

"Tate, Father, do you mean? Monsignor *Tate*? But don't you understand that would be as bad as the *hospital*—even worse! I should think—for a, you know, priest's career. Why, your career might just be *ruined*. And all for not wanting to wait—a little while—"

The priest lifted his hand, dropped it, tried to shrug as though to say, what does all that matter *now*? One duty remains, the sacraments administered in preparation for death. "Call—" Somewhere he found strength to lift his hand again, brush it across his ice-cold face, trying to demonstrate extreme unction, prayers for the dying, the formal act of humble recognition of the will of God, absolution—"Please. I beg—"

She took his hand and patted it. "You'll be *all right*."

He said something she couldn't make out, but she heard the rattle like the horrible turning of a crank. The marks would soon fade. Nobody would know. And it wasn't *her* fault, *he* was the one who wanted to be treated like that. How long would the stripes— the terrible strokes—? Could they be some kind of…allegorical…Could he be taped up like an athlete and then when they pulled the tape off it would look like the strips of adhesive…?

"Please—beg—" He tried to tell her then that if she *would* prevent (why? why? because he had tried to discover the *open door into the closed castle of the king*, of which the alchemists wrote?) Monsignor's coming to attend him at this most desperate moment, then later, listen, he could administer conditional absolution. That meant, oh, for Jesus Christ's sake, listen! the last rites even if he was *dead*. Monsignor would do that, the Holy Church had always made allowances, she knew that the moment of death is hard to define with exactness...

"Father, just relax, it's getting light now, see? I've put up the blinds and turned out the light. Pretty soon you'll either be walking out of here or you'll be...in the hospital and everything will just be—perfect—"

Gradually a change came over him, the face altered. Foam and blood oozed from the black hole, she wiped them away. His breathing changed, his pulse began to flutter. He heaved a deep sigh, the limbs seemed to stretch and stretch. What were the rites he said for Monsignor Tate to administer in case it was too late and he was already dead? She tried to remember. But (quite a bit later) Monsignor would know...

Dead how long, however? Was there a point of no return where if the Holy Names were left unsaid, the Acts of Contrition...and unctions ceremonious not done, was there a point where, well, forget it? Hell would admit of no escape? And she who might have saved his soul and didn't, must her soul then too burn eternally?

Because *that* kind of an outcome would be no laughing matter.

The Cardinal said on the Catholic Hour one time, before the dial could twirl, that the Pope's Syllabus Errorum was...central and inalienable doctrine and that the bounds of his infallibility must be set wider and wider and that...*he* saw no objection or difficulty in the doctrine of hell and everlasting punishment. And another station *It had to be you* and then his voice roared back and he...saw nothing to doubt in it, no cause for squeamish modern-day revulsion, *I wandered around, finally found* O be not tempted to doubt the doctrine of hell.

(Worse than jangling kites are its fires' demons.)

But through Lavonne's inner emptiness, as streams in rarefied air, flowed the azure ethereal fluid said to run in the veins of the gods and which flows too in that elite of the earth, those who *never give up*. And so she said well, it was all just superstition anyway. What did a Monsignor, or for that matter a Cardinal or a Thomas Edison or anybody else, know about death, judgment, heaven and hell more than you or I?

Or about the soul. Ears exist, one can be twined of them. A lustrous bosom may be sliced like cake, and out of the blue-eyed world a hole be gouged, the smile strewn, tresses caught on thorns, nails fall off like dahlia petals, and the red vitals of the heart...Even the breath invisible will suspend on a cold morning, engined like a plume, and ghosts diversify with patches of undefined outline. But a thing as absent of place as a *soul*? Not to worry, honey, I am telling you...

(Though worse than kites whet worse than beaks, in hell.)

AND MEANWHILE, BACK AT a stargate of a different dimension and a green meadow, they wait for certain death. Is not everything man does, when recollected, especially over the music of harpsichords, an organ, a celesta, three clavichords and four bass flutes in unison, a marvelous legend? It was too late in the season to go by the northern route. There's a war on too, an action of the U.S. government against Zion's army of giant children, some retarded, some not. The lonely mouse-turd travelers don't know *that* till they're in the war. Look through the glass here at the sons of bitches, all them single scoundrels manufactured in hell, soldiers and spies, what else could they be? That ain't no usual wagon train, my word on that, brothers.

But it is. The dust is usual too, it blisters lips and peppers eyes, gives the horses glanders, makes the children cry for water to Mama, who can't hear because she's walking up far ahead to keep from hearing. Through soft sand walking, tuckered out. Epidemic erysipelas, Asiatic cholera, see 'em every day, a throbbing head under the blazing sun, shallow graves marked by a wagon chain or piece of tailboard wood along the trail. And the monotonous…drive you crazy…gritty…clinking…clump, clump…squeaking, rattling…goddamn banging…That's right, swear! swear your damn head off. If there was shade! If it would just cool off! If Fancher's goddamn dog…if the cows, the chicks…and that squalling goddamn Dunlap kid…Ah, but wait—here is stillness, here's a darkening sky, here's…the most terrific explosion of electricity down the hemisphere anyone ever…Thunder! peal upon peal rolling around the sky, burning bolts leaping from cloud to cloud…cyclone winds, rain in torrents, hail as big as…Well, we done 'er, weathered everything. Made it through! This far, huh? Long ways yet. But this green meadow, ain't it paradise? As night falls? As the stars come out?

They lie along the eastern hills and watch, giant children, Indian friends, all with rifles, and more artillery in wagons rattling up the trails, and when the day begins to break…

AS FROM A BED OF down, Steve slid off Pona Mae and half sat up to light a cigarette. Downily she still clung, her chocolate chip cookie face pressed against his shoulder.

"I just can't believe it about Rita," she said.

"What?"

"Why, that that is *her* laying over there, dead like she is. When she was so successful. Thin. Her picture was in the Avon magazine, of course she was in the back row and you could hardly see her, but it was her all right, in her cowl sweater. And in Kanab, she even went with a *cameraman* one time."

Without answering, he pushed her away and partly crawled over to where Curley Jim half lay against the wall, Mr. Bryant's pistol in hand, hammer in a cocked position.

"Let's go over and get the bastard, shall we?" But not exactly meaning that, Steve slid in beside him, saying "Hi" to June as he did so.

"Hi," she said. She and Curley Jim had been sitting close together, but as Steve crept up she moved a little away.

"Well, how we doing?"

Curley Jim shrugged.

"Well, who wants to be a pipe insulator, tool and cutter grinder anyway?" Steve said, proffering the plastic bag he had once more pulled out from under his shirt. "Space city, huh, man?"

"Listen," Curley Jim said, "when this is all over, before we split—"

"Who says it'll be over? Who says we'll split? Me? You?" He looked towards the dead girl in the starlight.

"Now *she* has what I would call *split*," Curley Jim said, and stretched out a sociable hand.

And though that wasn't really where she was at, June did the same.

"Want me to stand guard or whatever the hell we're doing?" Steve said.

"No, I'll let you know."

"That's very kind of you," June said.

"Don't mention it. Say, the freaked-out guy behind the rock or wherever he is, wasn't you with him?"

"Yes, but—"

"He's her old man," Curley Jim said.

"What the fuck happened?"

"Well, you see—" She tried to tell him, but it was rather complicated, and when he thrust the plastic bag in under his shirt again and crawled back to Pona Mae's arms and the friendship of her thighs, all he could tell her was that the guy that it *looked* like for the time being had them by the balls was a vet and a religious weirdo of some kind. And when it got light, well, shit, him with a high-powered rifle and them with nothing but that fucking Sears & Roebuck handgun and about two bullets...

"And Curley Jim's not too great of a shot," Pona Mae said. "He come out to in back of Mrs. Weazel Tail's and practiced one time." She added quickly, "Maybe he's better now." But there wasn't only just this moment anyway, like when a song you love better than anything in the world comes over the radio and you drop everything and run to it, run to it as into someone's arms. It wouldn't get light not for ages, the way Juliet thought. And Steve when he got back from his Trailways trip, he'd come out to the reservation again, it would be Saturday night, she'd lose a lot of weight, have a permanent, be all ready...if they didn't get killed, but if they *did* happen to, like this in each other's...holding each other, kissing...why...it would just be dying happy.

June glanced out of the corner of her eye every once in a while at the dim outlines of Steve doing the wild thing with the Indian girl in the darkness and it was kind of disgusting, especially as Curley Jim said they hardly knew each other and Steve had started out the evening as the dead girl's date. If you were going steady that was different, you knew each other, like when Normal used to climb up over the balcony...though technically he wasn't really her old man, she said aloud, because technically somebody that you go steady with that won't make love to *you* until he can make love to two other brides at the same time, well, technically that is...

"That is shuckin'," Curley Jim said. "Don't ever give *me* the chance."

"Why not?"

"Because I wouldn't wait for *nobody* else."

She looked into his eyes, then down.

"This'll end," he said. "Someday. Maybe Normal out there, maybe he'll be dead like Rita over there, that is not entirely beyond the bounds of possibility, and what I'm asking you, are you gonna cry?"

"What a question to ask somebody."

"That's a good enough answer." He paused. "Steve. His mother answered an ad and married some old guy in Veyo, but he hates it out here. He come in the store. So anyway this afternoon—Mr. Bryant said I could take the truck, so I said to Steve, let's go out to the reservation and I'll introduce you to Rita if she hasn't got a date—and here was Pona Mae, we was raised together, so when she come along it was like a guy's sister—The ones with the *date* was Steve and Rita. And now"—he looked over in their direction—"it's them. I just mention it because—once I heard a guy say on public television that when God doesn't want to sign his real name, he signs *Chance*."

She too looked over at the blur the two made together in the darkness and said, wouldn't it be funny if they really turned out to *like* each other? And got married. And had a baby! And the baby turned out to be—like a scientist that would benefit the world. And all because of the way things happened *tonight*. "We'd all be responsible—Normal, you, me, Rita—her death wouldn't be in vain—in kind of a karma way, I mean."

"It'd also be funny if it was *us*," he said. "If *we* had the smart kid that changed the world. On account of tonight, man. He'd be part Shoshone, part—But wait, I got Hawaiian in me, too."

"Hawaiian?" she said.

"Because I had a grandma way back, she was a Mormon! Converted in Hawaii. They brought a shipload of 'em over here, gave 'em a *town*. Josepha, it was called. Grandpa used to tell—But old people when they just repeat the same old stuff over and over, nobody pays attention. So I don't know...But a grandfather way back there named Loudhawk married a girl, one of these Hawaiians. She was on the lam someway, I forget just why. The town burnt down. Most of the people went back to the islands. But she—"

"Gee," she said. "All these different chances we got to take. To *get* here. To be *born*, I mean."

"The strangers that had to meet."

"The turnings they had to take."

"Yeah," he said. "And another thing that's funny. I was thinking of it just a while ago. What Glen said once. He was the guy that was working on the ranch here the same time I was. He knew all about the monument and everything. And once he said to me that one thing that maybe drew me to it was because he said that relatives of mine could very well have *been* there."

"At the massacre?"

"They could of been," he said. "None of us has drifted far. But why I was thinking of it now is because *I'm* here. I mean, with Mr. Bryant's gun. I'm waitin', see. Watchin'. We're under *siege*. And back behind that rock there, there's a Mormon again, just like there must of been all that while ago trying to pick us off. Ain't it kind of—? I mean really. Like a rerun! This could of been built *up* around here. There could of been a *house* here. A garage. A chicken yard. Something shaking. But instead it's still a meadow. Not like it used to be, but empty, wild. And here we go again! A fucking *siege*."

"Yes," she said, "but this time you're the good guys."

"We were the good guys *then*, helping the Mormons. They thought so, anyway, though Glen said they wouldn't have much to do with us afterwards. They were ashamed to have teamed up with Indians, he said, to kill white people."

"You mean to say this is the very *spot*?" It suddenly seemed to dawn on her. She looked around. "The sign said there's a *monument*."

"What do you think this is?"

"Well—some kind of a wall."

"Around what? Around *them*. The place where they fought and everything. They're buried right there!" He pointed toward the center.

"You mean to say—?" She shrank against him.

"And Rita over there's our token dead. Where *you* been?" Gently he pulled enough away from her to be able to move if he had to.

"Well, when we got here tonight—the hassle and everything—I didn't really realize—" she said.

"Say. Listen. Shithead quit preaching quite a while ago. Wonder how come?"

"Maybe he's gone to sleep. He sure is tired enough."

Curley Jim looked disgusted.

"No, but really," she said. "From going to Centerville and all that." She decided to tell him. "See, there's this old house there that they're going to tear down. But it's a landmark. It's where one of the presidents of the church hid out for a while during polygamy days and where one of the presidents had a vision of God and Jesus, Joseph Smith and I don't know who all. So anyway Normal, see, and Roger—he's Normal's buddy—not like Ed was, but they pal around—Roger's a Fundamentalist too—and they work on their cars—but anyway they heard about this house in Centerville going to be torn down.

And because during the vision the president had that time God told him he didn't want polygamy *repealed*—and because the Fundamentalists' big number is polygamy—this house is considered a *shrine*. So when Normal and Roger heard it was being torn down they rushed up there, and it was empty, so they went in and stayed there Wednesday, Thursday—well, three days and nights—not sleeping, not eating—all they did was pray. Trying to have a vision—"

"And the guys came and tore the house down and Normal got hit on the head with a falling beam."

"Oh, Curley Jim, don't make fun. He can't help it, really. He's *disabled* in a way. His nerves—His pension is for his *knee*, but…he was in the Special Forces. So anyone like that should *never* fast and keep awake, because what happens, they will just…flip out." Her eyes begged pardon in the starlight.

"Man, would it solve our problem if he was asleep." But Curley Jim had barely raised his eyes above the wall when, bang! Normal was still there standing sentry.

Back down on the ground, Curley Jim said he felt the bullet whistle past his ear. June slid closer, touched the shaking hand he held up to it. "Jeez," he said, letting out his breath.

"He didn't want to hit you, really," June said. "Or else he could have, he's had lots of practice. The one he's mad at is *him*—"

"You mean the old guy? Why?" He looked down towards Jeppe and Rosetta huddled in the nearest corner.

"Because he's a composer."

Curley Jim laughed.

"And Normal found out he's going to write an *opera* about the massacre."

"You mean *this* massacre?"

June nodded.

"So what?"

"Well, Senator Arble is a Mormon."

"And—?"

"And maybe he'll get to be the Republican candidate for president."

"I see, said the blind man."

"And Normal thinks this is part of the plot to try to keep him from it."

"Because of an *opera* that guy might write? Come on."

"Well, just that if it got on television or in the movies, the plot would remind people that the Mormons used to be pretty uncool. They really were. In those days…Normal wouldn't have stood out a little bit, he'd just have been the normal rube citizen of, you know, the place. They hard-timed people. Of course they had a reason, but even so…it's better not to bring the subject up."

"But in an *opera*? Especially the parts where they sing the talk between the songs. That is torture."

"He's a real composer. They play his stuff on the Boston Pops and everything."

JEPPE WEPT SOFTLY. THE TENOR in wool shirt open at the neck, rough pants, boots, sings his elaborate melody of being brave, of offering to slip out before the rising of the moon with the letter they all have signed, begging deliverance from their foes. But if he gets through the barricade, where then? Emptiness and silence. Canyonlands…down below, a trackless desert. He does get through, but then they track and kill him, so that solves that, kill him by the Virgin River getting a drink. And Jeppe wept for the braveries of this world, the young man's beauty and his own talent that knocked him out, it was absolutely, I mean stupendous. And he heard combinations of sounds beyond the whole electronic movement, unimaginable instruments of the centuries to come figured in the dim shades of moonlit night the deaths of wayfarers, which we all are, every one. And underneath, far far below, where Henry Mancini and Aaron Copland and a lot of others waited, clapping commenced like a light drumming rain and swept in every direction, because, you see, it had to happen sometime, and we'll take the track home.

"Don't cry, Jeppe. It won't be long. Our car lights are on, out there on the road. Someone will come. They'll find us. Help will come."

"What people don't understand," he said, letting his tears fall, "the *layers*." The unimaginable instruments told about them. "Like in the Holy Land. The Princess…we were on her yacht. Somebody said let's do that, so we did, we went to Tell el Hesy. They'd cut away the side of this…hill, you know, and I couldn't see it exactly, but they said it was so and I believe it, there were *eleven cities* piled up one on top of the other. Two thousand years, maybe five thousand years. Piled up there one on top of the other. But you take out here, there's the *crustaceans*—" He brushed his wet cheeks.

"And behemoths," she said. "Once upon a time there was no time and it was then that…"

"But eventually," he said, "no matter what, *that wagon train came down through that gap!*"

"It did," she said. "And eventually, no matter what, my mother's grandfather must have sat on his coffin right about over there," she pointed, "to be shot at sunrise. And Legrand was going to sell the bones to Hollywood—not just his, but everyone's—like the sacks of blood-soaked ground of Waterloo with its nice rich calcium that came by ship to England to be used as fertilizer. Did you know that?"

"My God," he said, and the music took it up, the marketing of blood and bones, and slipped it in, a new sonority.

"So according to the ancient and wonderful rites of this kind of Kabuki—"

"Stop it," he said like a fretful child. "Don't say that. Don't say anything."

"I thought you wanted to talk."

"I want…want the *truth*," he said. The music wanted it too, like a strayed songbird where no birds sing wants the functional incremental hardware of birdsong.

"About what?"

"All I ask you is to *tell* me. Am I a butterfly dreaming I am a man?"

"Oh, dear," she said with a rueful smile. "*That* old hieroglyph."

"Or Madam Butterfly dreaming I am a composer?"

"You are a composer," she said, "dreaming of making it through tonight, and getting to Las Vegas, and then home, and writing your opera…"

"You come, too." The music whispered he was now great people, rich, the Hollywood science-fiction standard of rich, had a town house, had a Bentley and driver, had a coat for winter with a fur lining, had a summer place and acolytes and…wine and rubies. Therefore he spoke firmly to this woman as to hours, time off, vacation time, wages. He had lived for many years with Princess Avity de Coeur Koreska. Her housekeeper was Mrs. Ravenstein. Later they would go to Paris and Rosetta would meet Mrs. Ravenstein. Then she would learn…precisely…

"What?"

"What to say if Paco calls…I do not wish to talk to him. He is *never* to be shown in."

"Okay."

"And the Ford Foundation—I want you to say: when I want you in my pond, you assholes, I will let you know."

"Right."

Now the musical ideas dissolving into one another were so heavy he could lean on them, and he leaned and said, "*She* shall have an aria. Her, I mean—"

"Rita Owl Woman, the Avon lady of the reservation…"

"That is fiction, you are making that up," he said crossly. "I have decided. Nothing must be made up. Nothing!"

"Nothing is, my dear. Her Matchabelli. Her day's disasters. Her Shoshone appointment to lie there tonight. Don't you know the difference? What was the sense of her dying? None. That's how you can tell the difference between fiction and real life. The trouble with fiction, it's too reasonable. Real life isn't reasonable at all. Or anyway not to us…"

Huge pillars reared for him of dissonant atonal sound, and he knew he was there at last.

"Maybe to God looking down the way—those ant colonies you can buy in a frame between two panes of glass—maybe *he* can see some point to all the action. But to us it's just one damn thing after another…a dog run over in the street, an eclipse, a baby with the hiccups, gravediggers down in a grave throwing up the dirt…"

"We shall go to Paris," he said, assured now of everything. "I must *concentrate* more. Conquer my human failings." Filled with the terrible responsibility of tearing down the musical architecture that had risen round him and then putting it up again in another place—like a Crusader's castle torn down in Mitanni, shipped (every stone numbered) and rebuilt on Long Island—he fastened his hand upon his heart. "Got to address myself *totally* to the problems of artistic creativity…"

"If you ever come to where you don't know which is dream and which is reality," she went on softly, "I am old and I can tell you. Check for nuttiness. Is there no…conformity…to logical principles whatsoever? That's reality."

Which made it perfectly possible that in this fantastically terrifying and violent cosmos, what Normal behind his escarpment had been clamoring to the stars about might well befall. The polar caps *could* melt. The oceans *could* turn to ice. The ozone layer *might* just someday hang in tatters. Gamma-raying war was possible. Astronauts could bring back from space something meaner than cat shit on a pump handle. Yes! and snow might fall till everyone was dead. The earth's magnetic fields reverse! A meteor, WHAM. All the volcanoes, BOOM. Tsunamis coming sweeping in. No more Japan. No more dreamin' about California. And up on Mt. Timpanogos, none other than John the Baptist: "Well, old socks, you wouldn't listen, would you?"

AT ONE THIRTY-FIVE THE RANCHER came home with his young wife. There were packages in the car till hell wouldn't have them. But so long as she was happy! After buying out the town, they went and had dinner at the Blue Horizon. Then she has to walk and window-wish. Then they went to a movie, which it was unbelievable the things they showed in a movie marked P.G., meaning young people could attend, which the place was full of, and the *language*, but it held your attention. Then nothing would do but they had to go to the Chinese restaurant and get chow mein. She drove home. She said, "Oh, please! let me drive," and drove with the window down and the chill night rushing in and her long hair blowing. Then they were there and going up the access road and around to the back. All the packages went in the spare room, plumped on the bed, she was too tired to open them tonight, tired like a child, loving like a child. You go to bed. He took a quick turn around the place, habit, the stars to glimpse, the hiding moon, and stand and have a grand seignorial pee. Then was when he noticed, down through the fields to the west in the direction of the gully down there, a pair of headlights shining!

THE STATE POLICE WERE FINE fellows. One of them was at one time employed by Howard Hughes. They made short work of the stand-off, brought lights, knelt and examined the dead girl, took capable charge.

But what happened to Normal?

When the officers rushed it, nobody was behind his escarpment. He must have wandered on over the rim into the high surrounding hills. That was June's deposition. Seeking the brides and other distances.

In the bright light of the police station in St. George, June saw that Curley Jim was even cuter than she thought. She was afraid she looked terrible, but he said she looked great, like a girl at school he used to sit by. Pona Mae's and Steve's eyes did not meet. Rosetta explained everything as best she could. Jeppe, expecting to be taken back out to the Mountain Meadow and shot, stayed close to Rosetta, he was her child, forty-five years old. The officers had never heard any of his music, but one of them remembered a piece in *Newsweek* magazine or somewhere about a composer who was hired to teach or something in Salt Lake City who thought Utah was an ugly state.

"Oh, no, not ugly," Jeppe said. "Boring."

Rosetta explained why he and she were where they were, they had taken a wrong turn and when they saw the sign thought they would just take a look. And as the others were following, they came too. And then the four young people showed up, apparently just riding around on a Saturday night. Normal seemed perfectly all right but then something came up about Senator Arble maybe being the Republican candidate for president, and how he would be the first Mormon, and in the meantime Mr. Casement had been reading the plaque on the monument and he said that might be a great libretto for his new opera, and Normal got very agitated, he gets that way, he's what used to be called in the old days shell-shocked, he gets a pension from the government and everything.

The officers almost acted shell-shocked themselves when she mentioned Senator Arble and nearly in the same breath an opera based on what the monument to the Mountain Meadow Massacre said on it. Won't people never let anything rest? they said.

"Mr. Casement will," she said. "Because then he said that a wagon train was just too much of a cliché."

"I said it was as much of a cliché as Christmas," Jeppe said, standing close to her.

Everybody got to go then. Rosetta couldn't believe it, the pupils of their eyes, the dreamy lingo, all of them were as full of stuff as a fat goose, but they could go, the quicker the better, down they rolled and tumbled from the magic mountain meadow.

Both the Cedar City Herald and the St. George Clarion reported the accidental death by gunshot wound of Miss Rita Owl Woman Starley of the Shoshone tribe, who resided on the Shivwits Reservation, during a "kegger" at a field north of Veyo on Saturday night, whoever was responsible not yet apprehended. Not a word came out about it in the Salt Lake papers.

AND ALL THE WAY TO Las Vegas Jeppe heard the unimaginable instruments of the centuries to come playing the overture to *All on the Meadow Green*, but on the plane to New York it faded and never came back.

CPSIA information can be obtained at www.ICGtesting.com
Printed in the USA
BVOW09s0423091214

377506BV00009B/12/P